Marna

A NOVEL IN SEVEN WASPS
BY M.A. HENDERSON

Marna
By M.A. Henderson

This is a work of fiction. Characters, character names, institutions, businesses and organizations portrayed in this novel are fictional. Any semblance to real persons, living or dead, is coincidental and unintentional. Specific references to actual places and historical events were made purely for fictional purposes.

Published by Killer Bs, Richland, WA, 99352.

www.ninefruitbooks.com

Library of Congress Catalog Number 2019916262
ISBN: 978-0-9987195-4-2 (trade paperback)
eBook ISBN: 978-0-9987195-5-9

Cover photographs obtained from Thinkstock (www.thinkstock.com)

Cover design © Spark Design & Communication (www.sparkdescom.com)

Chapter artwork layout © Spark Design & Communication (www.sparkdescom.com)

Printed in the United States of America

Bond – fly high, Too Tall

WASP 1

A REMINDER OF DEATH

CHAPTER

1

STUNG

No matter how many times they said it was the thing to be, patience never made much sense to her. If what she needed was already hers, then why not have it?! But all those adults kept telling her to wait, proving that none of them really cared. To them, she was nothing more than another small child among many. So... instead of looking to the grownups, she learned what she could from the kids. Most were like her – sad and afraid. Not one would ever become a real friend, that much was sure.

Everything she once cared about in this world was gone... and the little that remained could easily be fit within the small Samsonite that Uncle Amos gave her on the night they came to take her away. Said it was the best he could do for her. She felt grateful... even though one of its clasps was broken and the inside seemed stained with ink. She had that suitcase open on the bed and started tossing in the few bits of clothing she owned.

It was so unfair! Without so much as a word of warning, Mrs. Jaworski had taken hold of her wrist and dragged her upstairs to pack. The woman even stood by with crossed arms and a crossed look on her face to make sure the job got done. Though she right off insisted to know why... the old lady only grunted out that it should be obvious to any child with half a brain. Mrs. Jaworski was not a particularly kind person... something she pointed out to the woman not three days after being moved in.

"I don't get paid for being nice."

"Well, you could try anyway!"

"Watch that lip of yours, little girl, or I'll turn it fat in a flash! You think you're the only one with troubles?! You have no idea of the hardships I faced when I was your age! The Great War left half of my homeland fatherless!"

Mrs. Jaworski did so much talking about that Great War… almost as if it was one of her own making. But whether it happened to be that terrible one her parents told her about… or the one the radio reported on in that strange place called 'Co-re-uh'… she considered all such adult talk as simply a way of getting kids to obey. She had a mind of her own to know what was best.

Glancing up from her suitcase, she noticed that tight-jawed expression on Mrs. Jaworski's face – the one that warned of her being on the verge of swatting someone – so she sped up the packing. Thinking back, she realized that the old woman really had been annoying lately. Maybe she should have known that something was about to happen… but being a foster child still felt so wrong to her. The only thing Mrs. Jaworski would say about the move from the upper bedroom was that space had to be made for the arrival of a new child. She knew this to be a lie. Though adults kept telling her that a six year old was practically a baby, she thought herself plenty smart at seeing through their tricks. Even Uncle Amos's silliness about the suitcase was plain enough. It was rubbish as a gift… but that was hardly the point. He had tried his best to cheer her up… even though he too was sad. But what made her really mad was that her parents had owned plenty of suitcases. After all, they had travelled together on so many weekend trips. She even had a bag of her own… a soft, plaid-covered one. It had a combination lock that only she knew how to open, and lots of little compartments inside for hiding her special treasures.

So where is it… and where're my other things?!

She repeatedly asked Mrs. Jaworski such questions… and always got back the same answer.

"Just do as you're told."

Perhaps it made no difference what suitcase she used, for she had very little to pack. The few things she was taking out of the dresser were 'granted' to her by 'the State'… something that Mrs. Jaworski made a point of reminding her nearly every day. What she had once called her own… her clothes, toys and stuffed animals… all of it had been locked away in some strange place the man at the courthouse called 'ar-bee-tray-shun.' That word made no sense to her… though it was probably just one of those that adults enjoyed hearing themselves say. Besides, nobody needed to tell her to shun bees. She was absolutely terrified of those bugs!

The packing job was scarcely done when the old hag snatched up the suitcase and shuffled her downstairs toward the back of the house, all the while complaining about how much work it would take to get the upstairs ready for the next foster child. She also knew this to be a lie. One of the older kids had told her that the state of Michigan paid Mrs. Jaworski whether their rooms were cleaned or not.

Whatever she had done to deserve being moved, it was serious. Her new room was the one every child whispered about – that dingy little pantry-like space just off the kitchen. Kids got put in there as punishment for doing bad stuff… or whenever Mrs. Jaworski got tired of dealing with an attitude. She had never been sent there herself… until now.

The door closed behind her without a word from Mrs. Jaworski as to how long she would be there. She clearly heard the key turn, but checked the knob anyway.

Locked.

This room was super smelly… sort of like wet socks… and really dinky. There was only one window up high… and it was boarded over, making it impossible to know night from day. The only furniture was a wicker-bottomed chair with so many pokey parts to its worn-out seat that she doubted anyone could sit comfortably in it. The rest of the floor was taken up by a bare mattress, much older and thinner than the one she had slept on upstairs. No matter which way she flipped the disgusting thing, it was impossible to avoid its many overlapping rings of pee stain. Still… it would be better than sleeping on the floor.

She was not allowed to leave this nasty backroom all day. To use the bathroom, she had to call out until Mrs. Jaworski could find the time to take her. Even her dinner was served there on a lap tray rather than in the dining room with the other foster children. One of those kids… that pimply-faced teenager named Rudy… came round just to taunt her. He started out stupid by murmuring her name through the key hole, while also laughing his head off, before finally getting around to his real reason for being there. With his I-know-so-much-more-than-you-do voice, he informed her that because Mrs. Jaworski had been unable to find anyone willing to buy her, she was to be hauled away with tomorrow's trash. Not for one moment did she believe him. He had once claimed to be the secret son of President Roosevelt, and therefore the rightful heir to the throne of America. She called him a liar… just like before… to which point he pounded on the door before finally leaving her be.

Nothing Rudy said had made her afraid. She was already scared out of her mind. Whispered words from Carla did not help.

"Marna… are you okay?"

"Go away."

"I'm sorry… it's… it's not fair what she's doing to you."

"I said go away!"

"You need to know… they're coming for you tomorrow. I heard her say it on the phone. She's worried that you might try to run away. It's happened before. She doesn't get paid unless you're here when they show up."

Carla went quiet after that… which was fine with her. Nothing more needed to be said about who 'they' were in order for her to know that she did not want to know.

Truth be told… up until that point… staying in Mrs. Jaworski's house had not been all bad. Carla was a nice enough girl to share a room with… even if she cried in her sleep. Mrs. Jaworski sometimes allowed them into the front room during her radio programs… as long as everyone stayed quiet… and by keeping the house rules, no one ever got denied food. Oatmeal was ladled out from a large pot every morning, then there was peanut butter on bread for lunch, with boiled potatoes, cabbage and a bit of hash for dinner. Having the same thing day after day did not much bother her, as she had little appetite for food. Leastwise not for anything other than what Mother once cooked. Besides… food was just one of those things that got a foster child into trouble, either from complaining about how little there was or whenever something got swiped from the kitchen. Mrs. Jaworski was immensely concerned about children eating too much, but never gave a thought to those who ate little.

That night, she lay uneasy atop the sheet and blanket Mrs. Jaworski gave her, waking whenever those things got tangled up beneath her. Once, she spent a long while staring up into that bulb hanging from the cracked plaster above. To her, it looked very much like a great big glob of yellow glue… or maybe a huge teardrop about to fall from a really wrinkly face. Rolling onto her side, she tried to think about something else… something other than who might be coming for her in the morning. She really should be getting herself ready for that. So many words had been said in that courtroom about her future as a foster child… but that day seemed so long ago.

Father always said… he said a person should think their way out of a problem before the problem occurs. He said…

She closed her eyes tightly against the memory… and then thought better of herself. Being sad could not prepare her for the morning. She must be brave… and do as Father would have her do. So… if something got forgotten… something really important… then she should go back in time and let the smallest of things rebuild the memory. By bringing to mind those little things, he promised that she would eventually remember the big ones.

But going back hurts too much. Thinking ahead... it's... safer. So how far back do I have to go?

The whole week following the accident was still too horrible for her. Trying to discover what had become of her parents was the worst part. She had begged them over and over, but those ambulance men refused to tell her anything. Then the needle they stuck in her arm ached terribly... and its liquid made her head real dizzy. The whole ride was so bumpy... going around so many turns... and she was already tired. She remembered falling asleep because the stretcher they put her in was real soft.

She woke up in the hospital... and not one person there would say a word about her parents. The nurses kept insisting that she rest... yet would not stop fiddling with her or pressing her to eat. Actually... she had been genuinely hungry, but nothing they gave her tasted like food. It was while sipping on a cup of broth that she first realized a piece of her back tooth had somehow been broken off. She had no idea how that might have happened. From then on, she could not keep her tongue away from that small gap... while the rest of her sought after the more important things missing from her life.

No matter how frustrated she became, no one would answer her questions. Not until that policeman showed up. He made her so mad. He was far too young to be acting as grandfatherly as he did... with too much sympathy mixed in with too much calm. It was not her fault. He got her so worked up that she was screaming like crazy for Father and Mother. But only nurses came running. Not until Uncle Amos visited later that night did she finally believe what the policemen had said.

A woman and a different policeman came the next morning. They said Uncle Amos would be taking care of her from now on... but first they had questions. The woman right off called herself a social worker... which made no sense. Mother said that socials were parties for really fancy ladies... but this woman was definitely not dressed for a party. The woman did most of the talking as the policeman stood by. Every time she glanced over at him, he smiled back as if he wanted to be her friend, but a sternness about him felt differently. She was sure that he stood there for only one reason – to decide whether she should be taken off to jail for killing her parents.

Try as she might, she could not remember a single thing about the accident. After a long time of pressing her, they finally gave up and called Uncle Amos into the room. He then took her out of the hospital and drove her all the way back to his apartment, the whole time working hard to distract her from thinking about the accident. He said he had been over to her house for clothes and some of her stuffed animals, but was unable to get in. She remembered sleeping on his couch that night in one of his beat-up t-shirts, having nothing to hold.

She was only at his place for a week before a different social worker lady and another policeman showed up one night with papers. There was a whole lot of shouting, and Uncle Amos said things he ought not to have said because the policeman got angry and shoved his face into a wall. They took her away that night, saying only that the courts would decide what was to become of her. They drove her to a strange building with bars on its windows and a tall wire fence all around. A lady there said it was a dormitory for children with no place to go. That made no sense since Uncle Amos had promised to care for her. His apartment was nothing fancy, but it clearly was a place.

They made her change in a tiled bathroom very much like the one in her elementary school… except this one had lockers. Because it was late, she was led into a darkened room with many lined-up cots. Most were already occupied. The woman put her in one and told her not to leave it until morning. She tried, but could not sleep because the mattress sagged terribly and the feather-filled pillow kept poking at her face. Still… what stood out most in memory was the echoed coughs of the other children all about her in the dark.

After a day and another night… neither of which she could remember much of… another lady came to take her away.

"Today's the day that a judge hears your case. Whichever way he decides, you won't be staying here any longer."

She demanded to know what 'whichever way' meant, but the lady said it was for the judge to decide. That woman drove her to a large building with a clock tower on top. She said it was the Ingham County courthouse… something that was pretty obvious from the lettering written way up high over the front. They walked down hallways packed with people, none of whom looked in the least bit happy to be there. Stopping before a set of heavy-looking wooden doors, the social worker lady took hold of her shoulders and began lecturing her about proper courtroom manners. This judge, she said, would not tolerate children acting up in his courtroom. So it was most important that she be on her best behavior and not give him cause to discipline her. She remembered the feel of the woman gripping her hand tightly while pulling her through those doors into a large room filled with many pews. Each one faced toward a place much like where the priest at her Episcopal church stood.

The man up there even had robes on… though he seemed to be doing more listening than sermonizing. The social worker put a finger to her lips and then pulled her into a pew.

It was obvious that the man sitting up high was the judge, as those at two tables… one to the right and one to the left… spoke very properly to him, saying things like 'your honor'… and 'with all due respect'… and 'may it please the court.' All that seemed so odd… especially since she could tell that every word lacked true feeling. In return, the judge never spoke for long, but when he did, everyone obeyed him immediately… sometimes with smiles and sometimes with frowns.

Just as she was beginning to pick up on what was happening, the judge brought his hammer down and everyone up front rose to leave. When the tables were cleared out, another man… this one in a uniform… shouted out some names, and then a bunch of people moved up through the little swinging gates. These did as the other groups, arguing between each other and the judge. The whole thing only lasted a few minutes before the hammer came down once more. Over and over, this strange parade went on before her, and each time she asked the social worker what was going on. Each time she received the same answer.

"Never you mind. Your turn'll be here soon enough."

She could not help it… all those boring adult voices soon put her to sleep. But she woke suddenly when the social worker lady took hold of her hand and yanked her forward. She found herself being seated at one of those tables… and remembered barely being able to make out the top of the judge's head. He gave a wave to the uniformed man… who turned about through a rear door. He was soon back with a thick cushion for her to sit on. She said 'thank you,' as she knew she should, and so did the social worker, except the woman called him 'bay-lift.' That really struck her as funny since 'bay' was the color of his uniform and the cushion was obviously a lift. She was quickly reseated after a bit of rearranging… which unfortunately included a rather loud chair-on-floor screech that made the judge clear his throat in that way adults do to show their displeasure. At least the new arrangement brought her eyes up enough to see all of the judge's face… though not far enough for her to get her elbows up on the table. With the cushion, her feet now dangled even farther off the floor than before. She did her best to hold them still… and not because the social worker had ordered her not to wiggle. Mother once said that some grownups had a difficult time thinking straight with a child nearby. So she purposed to sit still… even though she never had trouble thinking with adults around.

Somehow, being up higher made her feel more grown up... and ready to hear whatever the judge would decide. She waited for him to speak, but he just sat up there silently fiddling with his hammer. So she looked to the uniformed man, but he only stared at his watch. She was about to ask the social worker lady what was going on when a very thick man came huffing through the doors and down the aisle, all the while apologizing to the judge for being late. Through the swinging gates he came and sat at the other table. She had been so distracted by the size of this man that she did not right-off notice Uncle Amos coming in behind. Instantly throwing her hand up in a wave, she was ready to shout out a hello when the social worker rudely yanked her arm back down.

"He's not allowed to speak to you, and you're not to speak to him... his lawyer either. As a matter of fact, you're not to speak at all until spoken to by the judge. Understand me?"

"No, I don't! He's my..."

"You're to obey regardless."

She remembered giving the woman a scowl... even though Mother would not have approved. No one had told her that Uncle Amos would be there... and surely it was to demand that she should be returned to him. Any moment now, he would stand up and tell the judge just that... except it was the social worker lady who rose first. Very irritated, she looked over at the fat man, still lumbering up beside Uncle Amos. He was struggling to button his suit coat over his belly. Uncle Amos's team had lost the chance to go first... all because that man was so fat. But the social worker hardly got a sentence out before the fat man butted right in. Soon, the two were arguing so much that the judge had to call them forward. The three then went at it in their private hisses, completely ignoring everyone else in the courtroom. That was fine with her, as she was more interested in Uncle Amos. He mouthed out a question to her about how she was doing, and she nodded back her answer. Though he smiled, it was not at all in a happy way. It struck her as the same sort of droopy-eyed look of worry that Mother gave off to her whenever she felt sick.

The meeting in front broke up with the judge telling the courtroom that the state of Michigan was prepared to hear arguments in the custody case of 'Marna Constance Forde.' Hearing him say that felt so odd, seeing as no one but her parents ever used her middle name. The social worker lady spoke next... and what came out of her mouth was nothing but meanness toward Uncle Amos. The woman said his character was questionable and that many of his 'associations' were 'fill-loan-he-us'... which sounded like a good thing for Uncle Amos to do for his friends. But something about that strange word made the fat man pop right up and shout 'objection.' She knew that word. Father sometimes said he wanted none of it out of her. But both sides… the fat man and the social worker… were doing so much objecting at the same time, both throwing out such big sounding words at each other. She looked up to the judge, expecting him to be upset. He just seemed bored.

None of this was making any sense. This was supposed to be about her, but everyone was talking about her uncle. The social worker was saying that he owed money – lots of money – to some really bad men with books, and that made him unfit to be a 'trusted he.' Sure… Uncle Amos was a bit peculiar in his ways… staying out all night and sleeping all day in his clothes. But he was the only family she had left.

And he's always been good to me... even if his place smells like cigarette butts, burnt fish, and spilt beer.

All she wanted was to be back home in her room with her special things… or at least some place where nobody kept reminding her of all the sadness. Yet in looking over at Uncle Amos, him with his face buried in his hands, he seemed the saddest of all.

Though people had been coming and going quietly all morning without anyone taking note, everything in the courtroom suddenly stopped when the big wooden doors burst open and a man came rushing in. He was shouting for the judge's attention about his 'junction'… or at least that was what the word sounded like to her… though he did have a really funny way of speaking. This man, with short gray hair and a wrinkly sort of sunburned face, was obviously old… but that was not the strangest thing about him. He was waving a piece of paper about in the air with one hand, while the other held both a briefcase and a cowboy hat. She had seen cowboy hats plenty of times in movies, but never in real life.

The judge just nodded the man up to the front as if he had been expecting a cowboy at any minute. This man was obviously there about her… as his eyes went to her on passing. So she was especially curious about which team he would be on. It was only then that the obvious hit her – she and Uncle Amos were at different tables, which meant different sides.

As the cowboy went up to the judge, the social worker and the tubby lawyer fell in behind. She heard her name being sent back-and-forth between the four of them, yet no one bothered speaking directly to her. Although she had finished the first grade and knew a great many things about the world, the rules to this game of law were a complete mystery. It was most obvious that children were not allowed to play. Odd… this game of theirs did remind her of the one she had learned at school – four square – except there was no bouncy ball.

Or maybe that's me...

In the moment, she could not really say what had made her do it. Perhaps she was still worn out from the hospital... or being taken from Uncle Amos in the middle of the night... or having to sleep in that creepy dormitory. Or maybe it was simply the obvious – that her parents were dead. Still... she had no inkling of it coming on, but suddenly could not contain herself. Without regard to the rules of the court, she burst out crying.

Uncle Amos was immediately at her side with comforting words, but the social worker got there just as quick. With one hand clamped down on her wrist and the other fending off Uncle Amos, the woman... so clearly annoyed at being made to leave the four square game... pulled her through the swinging gates and out of the courtroom. She was plopped down on a hallway bench and ordered to stay put. And to make sure of it, the lady asked a nearby policeman to keep watch. Without offering a word of comfort, the social worker lady turned her back and re-entered the courtroom. Sitting there fighting off tears, she realized that she had gotten her wish. She was alone.

After hours of lying awake in the backroom of Mrs. Jaworski's house, she suddenly remembered what she needed to know before 'they' showed up in the morning. It was the very thing that had made her cry in that courtroom. Putting Father's trick into action had actually worked. Uncle Amos's fat lawyer said it during the arguing... and not at all in a nice way.

"Judge, you simply must reconsider. My client clearly has the girl's best interests at heart. He's here subjecting himself to all this unwarranted abuse, whereas that woman's not even bothered to show up. She just sends her lawyer. That's got to tell you something."

"I've made my decision, counselor."

"Your Honor – please! You must hear me out! I flew down there to personally speak with that woman. I know what she's like. I can guarantee you that the crafty ol' bitch is only interested in the money, whereas my..."

The cowboy-hatted lawyer immediately got real mad... as did the social worker lady... the judge's hammer came down hard... and she fell apart crying.

In her shock, she had taken the fat lawyer's cruel words to be about her, but in the relative quiet of the courthouse hallway came to realize that he must have been speaking about someone else... someone old. A mean woman somewhere supposedly wanted her as badly as Uncle Amos did... but had not troubled to show up.

She never heard anything else about what happened in the courtroom that day, as the social worker came out when it was all over and took her down the hall to a small waiting area. After a long time, another woman showed up with her suitcase. She was then driven to Mrs. Jaworski's house… and there she stayed for the rest of the summer. Her last sight of Uncle Amos was while being hustled out of the courtroom. She had not even been given the chance to say goodbye.

She only made it through the months of being a foster child in Mrs. Jaworski's house by pretending that she was not actually alone after all. Each day, she tried hard in imagining the pride Father would have on coming home from work to learn how courageous his daughter had been. He would say that there was nothing in this world too difficult for her. Then, each night, she would pretend that Mother came to her bed, and there they would talk for hours about all the horrible things she had endured. Over and over, Mother would do that little tickle thing with a fingertip under her chin… and each time, the memory of it made her tears well up. Her mother was the only one capable of making her laugh such tears away. In her imagination, they would both then kiss her in their special way… a double kiss with a parent at each cheek… say their goodnights… and be gone forever.

It really did not matter what was to become of her when she would never again have that which truly mattered. She was alone… and tomorrow they were coming to take her away. At least now she knew. She could now bravely face the morning with the memory of Father's encouragement and Mother's tenderness. Lying on the thin mattress in Mrs. Jaworski's backroom, she decided that the answer to the question on her mind was actually not such a big problem. Still… she wanted to know… maybe even needed to know. She should be prepared.

What's a crafty old bitch?

She had heard Uncle Amos say plenty of swear words… especially while on the phone… but never that one. Of course, it was not the first time she had heard the word. An older kid at school said it to a teacher on the playground… and got swatted real hard on his rear as a result. From that, she was pretty sure it was a terrible thing to say… and a terrible thing for a woman to be called. During those first few days as a foster child, she had been convinced that Uncle Amos's lawyer was referring to Mrs. Jaworski, but it was not too long under the woman's roof before she considered it as very unlikely. Mrs. Jaworski was old, but far from crafty.

Lazy's more like it.

She tried to put the question out of her mind in order to sleep, but the memory of herself crying in that courtroom because of that word kept her awake.

The tomorrow of Carla's warning came… and true to her promise, Mrs. Jaworski was there first thing in the morning to unlock the door. After being shuffled in and out of the bathroom, she was given a cup of water and a biscuit… then ordered to hurry along in the eating of it. Of course, her foster guardian insisted on standing by as she changed. The old woman then snatched up the suitcase and pushed her along to the front parlor. There, she discovered that the 'they' was actually just one person – a social worker. In fact, it was the same lady who had taken her to the courthouse months before. The sight of her was an instant reminder to once again ask about her things.

"Not to worry, dear. Everything's already been boxed up and sent ahead of you."

Then, the heavy-set foster caretaker who had cooked and sheltered her for the summer said goodbye to the social worker lady, but not to her. She was led out the door to a waiting car, yet absolutely refused to go down the row house's front steps without knowing where in the world 'ahead' was.

"Weren't you paying attention in court? You're going to live with your aunt in Texas."

CHAPTER

2

WEST TEXAS

"But I don't have an aunt!"

That much, she was sure of. Mother had only a brother (*...no way Uncle Amos ever got married...*), and Father said he had no family left. This strange aunt... it must be a lie... or maybe there was something so terribly wrong with her that her parents acted like she never existed. The bad word spoken in the courthouse came back to her again.

Well... at least she knew something about Texas. It was big... and hot... and a place where real cowboys once lived. Of course, the talk on those radio programs about gunfights... and cattle thieves... and face-painted Indians... she knew all that stuff was from long ago. None of it was interesting to her. Sitting in the social worker's car as it pulled away from Mrs. Jaworski's curb, she tried to picture the shape and location of that state on that map hanging in her first grade classroom. Nothing clear came to mind other than that it was somewhere in the middle... and sort of at the bottom.

"Of course you do."

"What's her name?"

"Gwendolyn Forde, your father's older sister. I believe she goes by the name Gwen. That's easy enough for you to remember."

"I've never heard of her... and I don't know her. Why can't I stay with Uncle Amos? I know him. He's nice. You could drop me off there and pretend..."

"It's not up to me. The judge has decided. Your uncle had his chance in court. Besides, I know for a fact that his appeal was denied."

"What's that mean?"

"It means everybody agrees that you being sent to your aunt in Texas is the best thing."

"Well I don't agree!"

With a jerk of her head, the woman shot over one of those adult looks of irritation at her… just like she was a little baby making a mess.

"It's final… so there's no sense fussing about it. She's now the executor of your parents' estate. So everything's…"

"We don't have a state!"

"It simply means your house and everything that's in it. Now enough of this. I've only got so much time today for dealing with you… and three more cases requiring my attention. We should talk about what it's going to take to get you to Texas. You've got a long bus trip ahead of you."

"I've… never been on a bus."

"Nothing to worry about. Children do it all the time…"

As with most adults, this social worker lady was completely incapable of knowing the difference between those things that were and were not important to a kid. The whole way to the bus station, the lady jabbered on with 'don't you worry about that' and 'everything'll be just fine,' yet refused to speak plainly about who this mystery aunt was… no matter how persistent her questions became.

On reaching the station and getting to the ticket line, the woman went silent… and so did she. Not that she had run out of questions, but more so from finally facing the fact of being sent away. They stood there for what seemed like forever, then twice as long at the window as the social worker filled out forms while speaking with the man behind the glass. Sometimes the two of them would stop what they were doing to stare down at her, and then picked back up as if she had not been there at all. She hated when adults did things like that… treat her more like a thing than a person. Sure… she was small… and afraid… and very much alone in this world, but she would show them. She would ride that bus all the way to Texas and think nothing of it.

Then what?

Her question to herself went unanswered. The social worker suddenly had a hold of her wrist, wheeling her about to a nearby bench. She now sensed a growing urgency in the woman's voice unrelated to the time, as the man behind the counter clearly said that the bus left in an hour. It was something different. The social worker was nearly free of her. The lady was even talking more rapidly now, smiling all the while as her fingers fumbled about in pinning something to her collar.

"It's all arranged. You're to wait here until a man comes out to escort you to your bus." The woman nodded back toward the ticket booth. "Not to worry – they won't forget you. As there's no direct route from here to where you're going, you'll be making several transfers. Have no fear… the bus company knows exactly what to do. They've called ahead and arranged everything. All you need to concern yourself with is keeping track of your things… and not removing this tag from your dress. That's very important."

The woman leaned back to take in a view of how the tag appeared, giving her a chance to look down at it too. Its large print lettering was clear enough to read ('*My name is Marna Forde. If lost, please call…*'), but she was not so good with upside-down numbers as she was with letters… and there were lots of them. Many more than was needed for a phone call.

"What's all this mean?"

"Don't fiddle with the tag. That's only your transit number… nothing for you to worry about. You just make sure that you don't remove it from your dress."

"It makes me look like I'm already lost."

The social worker lady ignored her, instead holding up a small knapsack – light pink with the emblem of the bus company on its front. Her voice got sweeter, which meant that the woman expected to be gone soon.

"Look what they've given you! Isn't this special?! I'm told there are *surprises* inside! Isn't that exciting?! There's a box lunch, and… that reminds me… they're providing you with meals along the way… so you needn't worry about food. Now see this pouch…" She pointed to a zipper on the knapsack just below the bus emblem. "All your papers are in here. There'll be a representative at each station to meet you. You'll know them by the card they're holding with your name on it. Don't talk to anyone else. They'll take a ticket from this pouch and then escort you to the next bus. Easy enough… as long as you follow instructions. Well… I guess this is goodbye."

The woman rose and moved away, but had only gone a few steps before turning back.

"Almost forgot…"

She searched in her purse and took out a photograph not much bigger than a matchbox.

"This is a picture of your aunt. Her lawyer gave it to me for you to have… so you could recognize her at the other end."

She accepted the photo without looking at it... at least not until the social worker was gone. The face in the picture staring back did not smile, but neither did it bear any quality she might imagine from a crafty old bitch. No sinister eyes. No sharp pointy teeth. No horns atop her head. The woman... her aunt... did not seem old at all. Maybe the nose and chin were like Father's, but she could see no other similarities. She flipped it over... there was nothing on the back. Without giving the photograph another thought, she slid it into the knapsack's pouch with the other papers.

Suddenly, she felt very alone... though not entirely due to the long trip ahead of her. It was something... sadder. In the months since the accident, no one had bothered to give her a photograph of her parents. In fact, she had nothing of theirs to hold on to... nothing at all to make this big change in her life seem easier. After a deep breath and a fingertip's worth of rubbing to each eye, she bore her teeth against themselves and leaned back on the bench's wooden slats to wait, very much afraid that she was losing the memory of her parents.

The social worker lady had pinned the nametag too high on her dress collar. One of its sharp plastic corners kept poking her chin. So she had to hold her head up. She watched the people hurrying through the station. Some glanced her way, giving her an uncomfortable feeling. She was just a thing with a label that told the bus company where to send this little package of a girl. From time to time, she looked instead to the large clock up high above the ticket windows. Just as the big hand had moved about in a full circle, a man came out from behind the counter and made for her. As with all of the busline employees she noticed while waiting, this man had on a solid blue uniform, its only other color being from the red and white patch sown over his breast pocket. He said for her to follow him. Taking up her suitcase, he led her through the station to where several buses were idling. They passed by two before stopping at the open door of one with a 'Detroit' sign in its window. He then spun her about. She could hear the zipper on the knapsack being slid open and papers being taken out. The man handed one to the driver... who looked at the ticket, at her, back at the ticket, and then motioned her on board. She climbed the first step awkwardly in making sure that the other man was storing her suitcase beneath the bus.

The driver instructed her to take the seat directly behind the door, as this was the spot for 'unaccompanied minors.' She knew what that meant – children who had no parents. She sat quietly, ignoring the other passengers as they climbed the steps and sought seats in the rear. As the bus finally pulled from the station, she came up a bit straighter in her seat. Out there was something that might serve as her last memory of the place where she was born. Somewhere was their street leading off the main road into her neighborhood. Somewhere was her school… and that park with its benches about a duck pond. Perhaps she might catch a glimpse of the grocery where Mother liked to shop, or that office where Father designed buildings. Or maybe the church yard… with its cemetery… the place where they were buried. She recalled it had rained that day. Standing under Uncle Amos's umbrella, she remembered holding his hand tightly as the caskets went into the ground. Afterward, strangers kept saying to her over and over how sorry they were for her… and how special her parents had been… and that one day she would look back fondly on the memory of them. Man or woman, it did not matter. Their words meant nothing to her. Every single one came from an empty face and died as an echo in her ears.

She suddenly realized that she had been staring down at the dirty floor beneath her feet. Looking up, she discovered that the bus was travelling down a busy highway, cars and trucks streaming by her window. A big city skyline was dead ahead… and Lansing was gone.

The transfer in Detroit went by in a flash. A man… another busline employee… was there holding a small sign with her name on it. He spoke briefly to the driver… something about a tight turn-around… and then she and he were dashing through the crowd to another bus, this one having a destination of Nashville. Its driver quickly stowed the bag and then hustled her onboard… right back into the same seat as before.

"Sorry for the rush, missy, but gotta keep schedule. Bathroom break in an hour and a half. Can you hold it until then?"

"I don't have to go."

He nodded and turned his attention to the task of steering his bus out of the station. She watched through the windows for a long while, sometimes catching sight of water off to the left… Lake Erie, according to the driver. Not until she overheard passengers behind her speaking of their route to Florida did it occur to her that she should learn something about how she was getting to Texas. The social worker lady in Lansing said for her not to touch the papers in the zippered pouch, but that woman was far behind.

She scooped up the knapsack from the floor and pulled out a small pile of folded papers, each of which she would be careful to return into the pouch once done. They were mostly carbon-copies of the forms she had watched the social worker fill out while standing at the ticket window. One had the words 'Unaccompanied Underage Traveler' across the top. At the bottom, in blanks filled in by someone's hand, was her route. Lansing to Detroit was already done, with her on the next leg – Detroit to Nashville. From there, she would make more stops at Memphis, Texarkana (*…that's a funny name…*) and Dallas, before reaching a final destination of Lubbock. Dallas, she had heard of, but knew nothing of Lubbock. She folded the form back the way it had been and returned it to the pouch along with the remaining tickets.

The last item was a very wordy set of pages paper-clipped together at the top. These had something to do with her personally… with her future. She found her name all over the first page, but could not make sense of it… especially that she had been named the 'ward of the state of Michigan.' She skipped to the next page. In line after line, she found the signatures of people she did not know, nor would she have been able to read had not their names also been typewritten. The last line had very clean and clear cursive of the aunt she had not yet met – Gwendolyn Ann Forde. They obviously shared the same last name, yet the woman was a complete stranger.

She sought for the small photo given to her by the social worker, but was alarmed not to find it in the papers she had pulled out of the pouch. In a panic, she searched about her lap, in her seat, and then down on the bus floor. She eventually found it tucked into a corner of the pouch. After settling herself back into place, she stared for a long time between the signature and the photo, trying to make something out of the person behind the two.

Why's it that I've never been told about this aunt? Is there something… bad about her?

The fat lawyer's verdict came back to her. She could almost feel again everything about that courtroom – the cushion beneath her, the armrests to either side, and her strong sense of helplessness.

A crafty old… bitch.

Is that why this Aunt Gwen didn't come for me herself? Is that why I'm sitting all alone on a bus?

She looked down to the photo once more, then inserted it back into the pouch with the papers, zipping it closed with a determination to prove herself strong and capable. This aunt might be her guardian for the rest of her life, but she would be her own person. Grim of face, she would be more than a survivor. She would be the daughter her parents would have been proud of.

The bus stopped briefly in Toledo… a place she knew Father had once gone to on a business trip. In her opinion, the city looked terribly worn out and dirty… and not the kind of place where she would have wanted him to work… had he still been alive. She used the station bathroom and was back on the same bus long before the ten minute stopover was completed. During the break, she opened the knapsack for the first time. Within was a small white cardboard container, slightly mushed on one side… probably from when she had stepped on the bag by accident while getting a better look at Lake Erie. Not much was inside – a tiny box of raisins, a small can of juice, a packet of crackers, and a thin piece of cheese wrapped in plastic. She set these items on the seat beside her, content to nibble away whenever the urge came. The only other things inside the knapsack were a coloring book and a box of crayons, eight in all. *A Bus Trip Across America* was clearly more suited for a preschooler than someone as old as her… but it would do. For the next eight hours, she wore those crayons down to nubs filling in pictures on the twenty or so pages. Most were of places and things she knew to be famous… the Capital, the Statue of Liberty, Niagara Falls, the Golden Gate Bridge, and the Grand Canyon… though she had never seen any of them in real life. Not one gave her new insight into Texas.

There were more stops for bathroom breaks, along with exchanges of passengers. She snacked, colored, and gazed out the bus window whenever the view changed to something more interesting than fields. She left that bus in Nashville to switch to a different one. The woman who met her there stood by with her as her suitcase was being taken off the bus, saying that there was time for a quick dinner in the station's diner before boarding for Memphis. That woman was really nice. She got the waitress to quickly bring a bowl of beef stew, a slice of white bread and a piece of cherry pie… and then left her to eat in peace… but was back in plenty of time for another bathroom break. Just after handing her a small blanket of coarse wool at the door to her next bus, the woman unexpectedly kissed her on the top of the head before 'God blessing' her inside. Mother often said bedtime prayers with her… though Father never did. So many things that had once seemed of no account now become so very precious to her in the losing.

The next driver… a man named Maurice… was very talkative, speaking in what she knew to be a Southern accent. Addressing no one in particular and never looking back to see if anyone was paying attention, he went on and on about a 'unity of nations' making lots of young men die in foreign lands… about how the government would allow him to drive a bus but not sit in its front seats… and about all the things a clever person could do with shoe polish. She felt sorry for him, though not because he was colored… a thing he kept telling anyone listening even though it was obvious. It was that he had to drive mostly into the setting sun, and she could tell by the way he grimaced that it was hard work. From time to time, she would ask him a question about where they were and what he knew of Texas, seeing as he said he had once been there. He never asked her anything… which she very much liked about him.

Though this seemed a shorter bus ride, it was dark by the time they reached Memphis. Maurice was replaced there by an older man with very thick glasses. He made everyone get off for the bathroom, then told them as they got back onboard not to complain that he was going to be playing the radio, something the bus company allowed for night driving. The music he chose was a twangy sort of thing he called 'country.' By the time the bus crossed over to the other side of a wide, dark water, the sad rhythms had put her to sleep.

She was aware that they had stopped once in the night, but was not truly awake until the man with the thick glasses shook her out of sleep. Still dark out, he said the morning was soon upon them and it was time for her to change buses. Unlike in every other place she had been, there was no one to meet her in the predawn dim of Texarkana. She had to lug her suitcase into the station and all the way to the ladies' bathroom. While in there, a curly-haired woman burst in, calling out her name in a panic. The woman then scolded her for not waiting by the bus. There was no use arguing with this lady, who took hold of her suitcase in one hand and her wrist in the other before pulling her out of the bathroom. She was told that there should be enough time for a quick breakfast, one which was ordered for her by the curly-haired lady. In that, she was served something called 'grits.' The white glob beside her scrambled eggs sort of looked like the cream of wheat Mother had often prepared… though tasted nothing like it. The waitress behind the counter told her it was good with crumpled up bacon, but she was not willing to risk the best part of breakfast on this runny goo.

The journey, to that point, had been connected in her mind more with its starting point than with its destination. In fact, if asked how long it might take to get back to Michigan had her next bus just turned right around, she would have expected it to be no time at all. But when her new driver, a balding man with multicolored suspenders, announced that they had entered into the other version of Texarkana… the Texas one… the place of her birth suddenly seemed so far away. She had been on an adventure of sorts… a vacation from thinking and feeling like an orphaned child. There had been plenty of sights along the way, though none that might be described as 'marvelous'… her mother's favorite word for things of beauty. But now that she was in Texas, a different sort of thing took hold. Part of it was her unease about the future, but also the feeling of a sad ending… of being convinced for the first time that things would never go back to the way they had been before. Any moment now, the bus would come to a stop and an aunt-of-a-stranger would be standing there holding a card with 'Marna Forde' written on it. All of a sudden, it was terribly important that she find out how much time remained before that happened.

"Excuse me, Mr. Bus Driver…"

The man first looked up in his mirror, and then briefly turned his head about.

"Yes… what is it, young lady?"

"Can you tell me how much longer it is to… ahh… hold it a second." She pulled the knapsack into her lap and quickly rummaged through its pouch. The name of the place had been on her mind not minutes before, but now the only word she could think of was 'Texas.' She found the page and flipped to the end of the list of stops.

"It's called Lubbock. That's where I'm going – Lubbock…"

She caught herself before adding something about being forced to move there to live with an aunt she did not know.

"That's a long, long way… twelve hours at least. Texas is a huge state. I expect you'll be switching buses in Dallas as this one here'll be heading back to Texarkana."

Now, she had to pay attention to everything along the route. The highway was like those in Michigan, having the same kinds of cars and trucks riding on the same kind of surface… but the landscape was completely different. From what she saw out her window, it seemed that a Texas August was very unkind to green things. There were trees, but not many. None were like those she was familiar with. These were scraggly, with needles rather than leaves.

The next stop – a town called Sulphur Springs – made it so very clear to her how different this state was from Michigan. As she stepped off the bus, a wave of heat hit her unlike anything she had experienced on the hottest of summer days back home. The feel of it completely took her breath away… just like that time when she stuck her face into the oven to check on the progress of their Thanksgiving Day turkey. Even before she could get to the station door, every inch of her was prickly with sweat.

Back on the bus, the driver helped her slide open her window. The gap was too narrow for her to get her head out, but the breeze was more than welcome. The day got hotter as it got older, and soon the heat made her lose all interest in watching what was passing by. It did not matter anyway, as there was little of interest to see. The farther the bus went into Texas, the smaller the trees got, while everything left over opened up into an exposed countryside of brown.

A short while before Dallas, the bus passed a thing that did get her perked up, becoming for her the first interesting thing about Texas.

Cows!

Not that she had never seen a cow before. Every kid knew a cow by sight. It was their number that shocked her. The fields along the highway were jam-packed with them. Thousands upon thousands of cows, each with huge horns sticking out from the sides of their heads. How they kept from poking each other in the eye was beyond her.

The driver pulled her attention away from the cows to point out the skyline of Dallas. Though not as tall as that of Detroit, somehow the openness of Texas made the cluster of buildings ahead of her seem… almost like an island. Soon, the bus was in that island of buildings, and Dallas became like any other city she had ever been in, with busy roads filled with busy people.

At the station, she stayed in her seat until her bag had been taken off the bus simply to avoid waiting in the heat. The man greeting her there was dressed in the same blue as the other busline employees, except for his shiny belt buckle and a white cowboy hat on his head. He right off gave her a 'howdy' and a handshake. He then would not stop telling her how nice she looked, how brave she must be for traveling across the country all alone, and how very welcome she was to be in Texas. It made her feel special… sort of like a princess… if such a thing was possible for an orphan.

During lunch, she accidently spilled some sauce down the front of her dress. One minute, she was enjoying some strips of meat covered in that sauce… and in the next, the man in the cowboy hat was apologizing like it had been his fault. No matter how he dabbed at the spot with a damp napkin, the red stain would not come out. It was worth it. The meat was unlike anything she had ever tasted before – both tender and tangy. After a quick trip to the bathroom, which included her own attempt to wipe away the stain, she was on the final part of the bus trip… the one taking her to Lubbock.

The person behind the wheel of this new bus seemed more like a teenager than a grown-up man. He might do the kinds of things expected from an experienced driver… like cursing at the traffic or yelling back at anyone who stuck a leg out into the aisle… but she suspected it was all for show. He was probably as new to being an adult as she was to Texas. She kept her face turned away from him as much as possible because of his disgusting habit of spitting a nasty stream of brown liquid into a cup.

After passing through a city called Fort Worth… or so a sign said… the bus moved into barren countryside. Leaning against her window, she had it in her mind how the Dallas bus station escort told her that he had been raised in this part of Texas and considered it to be the most beautiful place on earth. She kept looking for the beauty, but the farther along the bus went, the flatter the landscape became. What trees there were, from the highway to the horizon, were shrunken to the size of bushes.

The bus stopped briefly in the mid-afternoon at a place called Abilene. There, the driver made everyone get off and then closed the bus door until his break was over. The August heat was present here too, but to her surprise, it seemed not as bad as in Dallas. With a gentle breeze and the shade of the bus station's overhang, she easily endured the wait outside until the driver allowed everyone back on.

From there, her attention was fully on the things outside her window, believing that what she saw might somehow prepare her for the person to whom she would soon be entrusted. If she had thought the Texas leading up to this point to be bleak, it was nothing compared to the feel of what lay beyond Abilene. The land was so naked that she struggled with the discomfort almost as if it were her own. There was absolutely nowhere to hide from the sky. Scattered farmhouses put up some effort at it, but the small clusters of trees that marked their whereabouts just seemed to increase the loneliness. As she marveled that anyone could live in such emptiness, a sudden fear hit her that Aunt Gwen's place might be exactly like one of these.

The stretch of highway they were going along also had cows in the fields, but unlike the herds on the other side of Dallas, these clung to the fence line. Perhaps it was nothing… or maybe they were bored and found the highway to be interesting… yet she could not help but imagine that they were begging to get through. All of West Texas spread out behind them in wide-open space, and here these cows had collected themselves at the only place offering freedom. The thought made her sad for them… and for herself.

While cows were the only living creatures to be seen, they were not the only things in the fields lining the highway. Sometimes she saw crops not much higher off the ground than her waist. The color of them was mostly green, though mixed in were small dots of white. As row upon row flipped by like in an old-time movie, she ran through a list of growing things that a person might eat. She knew her vegetables well enough from school books and from Mother's backyard garden. Nothing came to mind resembling those white blotches. These fields, she concluded, did not grow food.

Maybe Texans mostly eat meat…

She was in the process of working herself up at the thought of an entire state of people living off of cows… and how terribly frustrating it would be not to have the kinds of fruits and vegetables she had come to enjoy in Michigan… when an object passed by unlike anything she had ever seen. So stark was it that she instantly came up on her knees in the bus seat to follow the thing out of sight to the rear. But then there was another… and another. Some in close to the road and some far off in the distance. Each one was an ugly blackened creature-like thing… sort of like dinosaurs that she had once read about in a school book. They faced in all different directions… a few toward the highway, but most out toward the nothingness of Texas. They were not alive, that much she was sure of, as it was easy to tell that they were made of metal. But they moved.

Well… not like cows do.

To even imagine that one of these hideous things might be capable of getting out onto the road was terribly disturbing. But they all stayed put. Instead, something like a head kept bobbing up and down as a bird might in pecking the earth… yet to the bidding of a wheel-like thing in the rear. It was all so strange looking – the back end going around in circles while the front end… it just kept pushing a pole down into the ground and pulling it back up again. Over and over, the same thing. Some carried on merrily in their task, while others labored along very slowly, as if each cycle might be their last. And then there were those that sat frozen in place, not moving an inch.

They're probably just resting… or maybe they're… dead.

Even for something so hideous, she could not easily imagine such a thing. Instead, a different thought came to her… one that made her much more sad than if those still machines had somehow lost their mechanical lives. Many of these metal monsters were planted in fields, with the farmers having plowed around where they sat. Others were in pastures where cows roamed about them without fear. Those metal things were of no danger to anyone. They were bound to one spot and forced into never-ending motion… up and down to a taskmaster's wheel.

They're prisoners.

Unlike before, she now wished very much to see one break away, jump the fence line, and canter like a horse along the highway. It would be so much more than fun. It would be relieving to see even such a nasty-looking thing be made free. Of course, she knew it was silly to consider. They were just things. Still… given a chance… she knew she would never risk getting near one. Not because it might snatch her up and pound her into the earth, but because they were all so very ugly. Just like Texas.

The August sun was now setting through the front window with such brightness that it made looking straight ahead nearly impossible. The driver had to keep flipping his visor about whenever the bending of the road shifted the glare into his eyes… and each time he cursed out loud. Unlike with the driver named Maurice, she did not feel so sorry for this young man. Sparing her own eyes from the sun's fire was all she cared about.

That driver was soon counting off the time before the arrival into Lubbock.

With thirty minutes left, the sun had crept close to the horizon, turning its fiery yellow into a duller orange version of the same. But she no longer had an interest in seeing anything out the window. It was all the same – flat and barren. Her eyes were on her hands, once again studying the photo of Aunt Gwen.

Her first real impression of Lubbock came about not by way of sight, but through her nose. All of a sudden, she was hit by a heavy sort of earthy smell… not a particularly nice one… not fresh and sweet like the forest after a spring rain. The air was full of it, sort of in the same way that could be said about how East Texas had its heat. But this West Texas smell had an uncomfortable tingle to it… sort of like Father's lawn fertilizer. She lifted her head to find that the bus was still in farmland, but up ahead was a city. With a tremor of fear, she heard the driver announce the approach into Lubbock. The sun's last light, now just off the horizon out the left side of the bus, lit up the city limit sign well enough for her to see that the population started with the number eight. Math had always been challenging, so it took a few moments for her to go through the names of the number places that her father had taught her.

Let's see… hundreds has three… thousands four… ten thousands five… so Lubbock has… eighty thousand something people in it.

Whether that was a lot or a little, she could not say, as the bus had just left the highway and entered the city. It would soon be time. She looked down once more to the picture… and began to tremble.

This is happening too fast.

The wheels bumped as the bus turned onto a cobblestone road.

Aren't those supposed to be for old-timey cities?

She found this bumpy street of Lubbock to be terribly wide. Her parent's house could easily fit within the width, and still have plenty of space left over for side yards much bigger than hers. Though dusk was upon her, she could still make out a tallish building off in the distance. But most structures were small, and just flowed by her.

Now the bus was beginning to slow, making her far too nervous for looking out her window. Without warning, they swung off the street into a large lot. A small gathering of people already there creeped along with the bus until it finally came to a stop.

It's time.

Strangely, her shaking suddenly ceased.

CHAPTER

3

GWENDOLYN FORDE

It was not too many weeks after moving to Lubbock that she came to accept how most men dressed in West Texas. Jeans, boots, big belt buckles, and cowboy hats were often worn by both men and boys because that was who they were. But for a woman to dress like a cowboy... that, in her mind, would always be a different matter. The only boots she recalled Mother having ever worn were those for walking in the snow.

Though only familiar with her aunt from the shoulders up in the small photo she held, she easily recognized the real life version in the crowd of waiting people. The cream-colored cowboy hat on her head was tipped back far enough to make out both her face and the clustered strands of short, blondish hair poking out about the sides. The rest of this Aunt Gwen was covered in a plaid shirt of mixed purples, pale blue dungarees, and rather dirty brown cowboy boots. The face seemed to recognize her too, but gave off no sign of having done so. No smile. No wave. No tip of the head. But her aunt's eyes were definitely looking directly through the window at her.

The other passengers were getting off as quickly as they could after the long trip, but she took her time gathering up her things. She glanced out once more... Aunt Gwen was there as before, staring back without welcome. Maybe there was still a way to avoid those eyes. Maybe she could just stay put on the bus and pretend to be anyone other than a little orphaned girl. Maybe the bus driver would pull away, and she could go on to whatever lay beyond Lubbock. Anything had to be better than those eyes.

But really… she should put this silliness out of her mind. The best way to do that was to raise her hand in a wave and smile. To her relief, Aunt Gwen smiled back. That made it easier for her to stand up, move down the stairs, and greet for the first time the woman she expected to spend the rest of her life with. Stepping to the pavement, she put out her hand bravely and waited. Aunt Gwen took hold… and then pulled her in for a big hug. With her face pressed against the woman's shirt, she picked up on the smell of flowers… maybe roses… and something else that she could not quite figure out.

Something of the earth… sort of like the Lubbock air.

"Welcome, Marna. I expect you've managed your trip well enough… because here you be. Now let me have a better look at you."

Without being told, she took a step back. With that step came an awareness of the stain on her dress. She looked down, unintentionally calling attention to it.

"I see you've been properly introduced to Texas BBQ. What'd you make of it?"

"It was… really good! Kind of tangy." She looked down at the stain again. "I'm sorry… I wasn't being careful when I…"

"Think nothing of it. Is that dress special to you?"

"Not really. It was given to me by… some people."

She was not quite sure how to explain that nothing of what she had with her was actually from her own things. That thought brought back the memory of that social worker's promise – that her possessions had been sent ahead. She was just about to ask if anything had arrived from Michigan when her aunt spoke next.

"You've practically outgrown that thing anyway. What's say we continue to treat it as the napkin it's become. How about some dinner?"

They left the station with her trailing slightly off the side of Aunt Gwen. Whether it was that the sun had set or that a bout of nerves had hit her, she found herself shivering. Her sweater, folded up in the knapsack, had seemed unneeded in the heat of the day. But instead of stopping to take it out, she fell back a step in order to rub goose bumps off her arms.

"You chilled?"

Her first thought was to say no… but this woman with eyes in the back of her cowboy hat might know better. After a couple of quick skips, she made up the distance between them before answering.

"A bit. I was really hot before… on the bus… but now…"

She allowed the explanation to dangle there.

"You'll get used to that. Hot days and cool nights. We can get all four seasons in the space of a day. I suppose there're more things you'll be getting used to. For example… when a child responds to an adult, it's always with ma'am or sir. Not to worry… I'll be helping you remember that."

They came up on the back of a really large car. She watched as Gwen… not bothering to look at what she was doing… somehow smoothly inserted her key into the trunk's lock, popped the lid open, and dropped the suitcase and knapsack inside… all while staring at her.

"Yes, ma'am."

"Good. Now hop in, and we'll see about that dinner I promised you."

She could not take much notice of the inside to the car or of what was passing by out the windows, as she had to be more careful about what she said. Questions from Aunt Gwen were all about the bus trip, and as yet nothing was being made of the bigger matters in life – the death of her parents and her coming to live here. Entering a drugstore, Aunt Gwen led her to the counter… but did not offer to help her up onto the stool. When the time came to order, Aunt Gwen had her speak directly to the waitress herself, saying that it was a mark of 'the confident woman.' She ordered a cheeseburger and fries, while her aunt requested only a salad. With the ordering done, Aunt Gwen went into their first serious subject… and not at all what she had expected.

"So, Niece… let's discuss your health. I've done a little reading on my own, as well as had a consultation with my personal physician. By the way, I've made an appointment for you to have a check-up. From now on, my doctor'll be your doctor. In the meantime… I understand from the medical records my lawyer obtained that you're severely allergic to bee stings."

"Wasps too. Wasps are much worse for me than bees."

"Remember to say 'ma'am'… if you can."

Which she understood to mean that she must.

"Yes, ma'am."

"And why're wasps worse?"

"Because bee's only sting once, ma'am… and then they're dead… ma'am. But not wasps… ma'am. They can sting over and over… until I'm the one that's dead… ma'am."

"You need not say it in every sentence. Just when it's appropriate. Well, Niece… we're going to do our best to keep that from happening."

She turned to face straight ahead over the drugstore counter toward the shelves loaded down with jars of candies. At a different time, she might have been taken in with the many shapes and colors inside those glass containers, but at that moment, they were just something to stare at... something that an adult might expect a child to be fascinated with... something that gave her an excuse for not looking at Aunt Gwen. The conversation had turned very uncomfortable.

"I'm sure you realize that I'm now responsible for you... for your safety and well-being. I know you understand this, but I want it said between us to start off right. So... it's my job to raise you, and I intend to do that to the best of my ability. In return, I'll expect you to show me the kind of respect that responsibility merits. Are you following me?"

"Yes, ma'am."

"Good. I'm your aunt... your father's sister..."

She doesn't really look much like Father. He had a kind face.

"...and I have my own ways of doing things. And you're my niece, with your own way of being. I'm not out to change any of that. Truth be told, I'm brokenhearted for you. Having both of your parents taken from you at such a young age... it's terribly unfair. But fair or not, the fact of the matter is... I'm not your mother, so you shouldn't expect me to act as if I am. Similarly, I won't be placing a burden on you to be a daughter. I won't treat you as some adults do their children... with silly expressions and references to 'we' when I actually mean 'you.' I'll shoot straight with you, and expect you to do likewise with me. Who knows... maybe one day we'll end up being more than just aunt and niece. Maybe one day we'll become best of friends. Until then, I purpose to care for you as would an aunt, and expect you to attend to me as would a niece. Does that sound reasonable to you?"

She delayed in responding more so to make sure of how it was done. In truth, she felt as if a huge weight had just been lifted off her shoulders, and her hesitation was from the unexpected surprise of it. Whether living with this Aunt Gwen ended up being easy or difficult... whether she could ever be made to like this barren place... at least knowing that she could still be the daughter of William and Betsy Forde... though they were no longer with her... somehow made being alone so much less so than she had expected.

"Yes, ma'am. That makes sense."

Their food arrived, so both sat quietly eating. Despite not having had anything since Dallas, her appetite was lessened by the conversation. She managed a few nibbles on the burger, and then went about sucking on the end of a fry until it turned into a pasty mess on her tongue. The next one she took more seriously on remembering how Mother often reminded her about all those starving children in China. That memory worked for a few more fries, but before long, she found herself using them to carve little trenches in the glob of ketchup on her plate. She dragged fry after fry through that red stuff, sometimes in neat, even lines and sometimes in a crisscross pattern... but not another was eaten. As one went limp or broke up in the slush, she set aside what remained and picked up a fresh one. Still... she managed to spy a bit on her aunt between fries... just to see how a cowboy-hatted woman ate. She carried on just as lady-like as Mother.

But... I wonder if she's going to call me 'Niece' all the time?

All of a sudden, she felt very tired. She tossed aside the fry in her hand, it worn down to a nub, and leaned her chin upon the countertop.

"I understand that you were once stung quite severely, and that you almost died had it not been for immediate medical attention."

"Yes... ma'am. But I don't remember it... I was only four. It was yellow jackets. I got stung... a couple of times. It's not happened since, but Mother always says... said..."

She turned away, as an urge to cry must be fought off. But after only a few seconds, she was determined to be brave for Mother and Father. So she sat up straight and came back to her aunt.

"The doctor said it would be far worse for me to be stung again, even just once."

"And do you know why that is?"

She grabbed another fry as an excuse for not answering right off, but still found herself wagging her head about. Truthfully... she had no idea why her body was so weak. She knew of nobody in her class or neighborhood that was as deathly allergic as she was. There was that one boy who could not eat chocolate, but all it did was make him run to the bathroom. It would not kill him.

"No... ma'am. I don't understand it. All I know is that I mustn't ever be stung again. I'm supposed to stay away from all those places where wasps and bees like to be... I mean, where they're found."

"I understood what you meant. Please continue. Do you have a list of those places in your head?"

"Yes, ma'am. They're... mostly outdoors." She was trying to think, but all she wanted to do was sleep. Her head drooped... and then snapped back up so abruptly that she startled even herself. "Ahh... wood piles, old sheds, garbage cans, flowers... Mother especially said for me to stay away from flowers because they're dangerous."

"Nonsense. Flowers are a gift of Nature. They're..."

"My mother said they're dangerous for me, and she wouldn't lie."

"Don't interrupt. I'm not contradicting what your mother once said. I'm simply pointing out an inaccuracy in your statement. Flowers, of themselves, are not dangerous. They're special… I hope you can come to appreciate that. It's just some of the insects that habit them."

She turned away again, concentrating on the nearby customers or the waitress behind the counter… anything other than Aunt Gwen. A feeling inside her was ready to burst out into tears.

"Marna… I don't mean to upset you. I knew your mother. Not well… but I knew her. She was a special woman."

She sensed Aunt Gwen coming off her stool, but still kept her face turned away.

"You're tired. Best get you to bed. Tomorrow's another busy day. I'm afraid we won't have a chance to discuss these things again until the weekend."

She slumped off her stool and followed Aunt Gwen out of the drugstore. Stepping out together, she trembled at a breeze that had picked up since before. It was a cold one, biting at the exposed parts of her arms and legs. Somehow, she felt even more miserable than when she had been so hot earlier in the day. Nothing mattered anyway… not the heat or the cold. All she wanted was to be back home, in her own bed, with her parents kissing her goodnight. She wanted her stuffed animals gathered about and her favorite blanket pulled up to her chin. Most of all, she wanted not to remember anything from the last few months.

The engine's roar startled her to the fact that she had somehow gotten herself seated into Aunt Gwen's car. She set her head against the passenger door, and the hum of travel soon took over. She was asleep before she knew what had happened.

She awoke unaware of anything other than being under sheet and blanket, with her head resting on a pillow… and that she needed to go… real bad. Rolling over, she was drawn to the yellow glow of a nearby lamp, using its light to survey the room she was in… and most importantly, the way out. Quickly tiptoeing across a wood floor and through the door, she paused within a short hallway. Finding that a bathroom was across from her, she made for its toilet. In still being groggy-headed, she did not notice what she was wearing until turning about to sit down. In pinkish stripes running the length of her, she had on matching pajama pants and shirt. The fit was perfect. She sat down, trying to remember when Aunt Gwen had dressed her… or had she done it herself? Either way, Aunt Gwen had bought her something new even before she had arrived to this place.

When finished, she hesitated to flush… and was relieved when the rush of water was quiet. She rinsed her hands and turned out the light. To her left and right down the hallway was darkness… and it occurred to her for the first time that this must be the house where she would be living. Resisting an urge to explore, she crossed back into the room that evidently was hers and went to the source of light – a small lamp on the desk beside her bed. From a very young age, she had always slept in a darkened room. It was one of those things she could be proud of – that she had outgrown a fear of the dark. Looking this lamp over, she was surprised that its glow did not come from under its shade, but from many holes in its base. The bulb was in there. Fumbling about the shade, she found two small pull cords, one to the left and one to the right. Deciding to pull on the left, she did not expect the blast of light from the main part of the lamp to hit her square in the eyes. This lamp actually had two bulbs. Quickly yanking on both cords at the same time, she threw the room into darkness. Feeling her way along the desk edge, she found the bed and climbed back in. Rolling over to face the wall, it was no time before she fell back asleep.

She awoke again, this time in the pale of early morning with Aunt Gwen hanging over her.

"Marna… Marna… time to get up. I'm sorry to do this to you, first day here and all, but I need to get going… which means you need to get going too."

"Whaa… Uhh… What?"

"I'll have breakfast waiting for you, so hurry it up."

She managed to sit up on the edge of the bed, coming to grips with having been awoken too soon. One thing was obvious – she needed clothes. That meant that she needed her suitcase. As it was nowhere to be seen, she guessed that her aunt might have already emptied it into that dresser standing against the far wall. To her surprise, the drawers were full of socks, underwear, and pajamas that she at first believed were her things from Michigan… yet none of it was familiar. She went to the closet and flipped through hangars of shirts, jumpers, dresses, skirts and pants that were all brand new.

"Hurry it up, Marna. Your breakfast is getting cold."

Her aunt stood in the doorway dressed much as she had been the night before.

"Aunt Gwen… I don't understand… where'd all this come from? It's… really nice."

"Glad you think so. To be honest… I've never shopped for anyone other than myself, so I guess I got a bit carried away. Most of the things in the closet still have their price tags… so they can be returned if you'd rather pick out things on your own. Only thing I didn't get for you was shoes. We'll see to that on the weekend… if you don't mind sticking with what you have for the time being."

"No, ma'am. Thanks a lot! So... what're we doing? I mean... how should I dress?"

To her great surprise, Aunt Gwen gave off a giggle before clearing her throat... and then spun about like a ballerina.

"Just like me. Oh... best wear something with long sleeves. It's cold in the shop."

Aunt Gwen disappeared down the hall before she could ask what was meant by 'the shop.'

She went through the hangers again... but not as slowly as she would have liked. She so longed to try on everything, but since Aunt Gwen said to hurry, she slipped on a pair of crisp blue dungarees with wide cuffs. The fit was perfect. She put on a checkered shirt to match. With no mirror in her room, she was unable to get a good look at herself, but felt that the combination might look enough like Texas... which should please her aunt.

Fully dressed, she stepped out of her new bedroom. Looking both ways, she turned left down the short hall toward a combined living and dining area. It was still dark out, and without lights in those spaces, she had to follow her nose through another left turn into Aunt Gwen's kitchen. The place was nothing special, having the same kinds of things as in her mother's kitchen – cabinets, counters, ice box and stove, with a small breakfast table by a backdoor. What did interest her was the plate of fried eggs, bacon and toast, with a glass of milk, set before a seat that would soon become her place at the table. She gave her aunt a genuine 'thank you' before diving in. It was her first real breakfast in months.

Aunt Gwen soon sat at the table with her.

"There's no way for you to have known, but I'm a business owner. I have a floral shop just north of the downtown area. 'Forde's Flowers'... kind of catchy, if I do say so myself. But here's the hard news for you – you're now the niece of... well, you've always been my niece... you're just now the live-in niece of the owner of a flower shop. That probably doesn't mean much to you at the moment, but you'll soon come to see it for its value... and for the hard work it requires."

The way Aunt Gwen's eyes flashed – she was definitely sending a message. But the breakfast was a stronger one at the moment, so she left her aunt's grayish eyes to spread blackberry preserves over her toast. Her aunt was of a similar mind, picking up a piece and doing her own share of spreading.

"What it means for you, Niece, is a bit difficult to say... but there's really no way to dance around the subject because you'll understand soon enough.

The store's my life. The buying, arranging and selling of flowers is what you might call my passion. I'm not expecting it to be yours… least not while you're still a child… but you should understand from the get-go that the store'll have a lot to do in setting your day-to-day schedule. For example… seeing as I work most days, and seeing as I can't leave you here alone, you'll be coming with me."

"I'll be going with you to your shop? That sounds neat!"

"Glad to hear you say that, cause you'll be working there too."

So many unpleasant thoughts suddenly poured into her mind.

I'm not going to be living here for free! I'll have to work for it! What if I don't do a good job? Will she send me away? Or lock me in a pantry like Mrs. Jaworski does? Maybe she's going to turn me into a slave… like in olden times.

She brought a fork of food to her mouth… and the taste of perfectly cooked eggs argued against her fears.

Slaves don't eat well… but she's feeding me real good food.

The feel of her flannel shirt sleeve was a reminder of a closet full of new clothes.

Slaves only wear rags.

Aunt Gwen had provided her with a very nice bedroom in this house of hers… not some dark closet with a locked door and no window.

Maybe being her niece won't be as bad as being a foster child.

She looked up to find Aunt Gwen staring at her with those intense gray eyes of hers.

"Take heart, Marna… I won't be working you beyond what you're capable of doing. You're just a child… hardly suited for the things required of an adult. But hopefully… in time… you'll come to appreciate the shop as much as I do."

"Yes, ma'am… I'll do my best. You know… you're not like they said you'd be."

She put the words out there hoping them to be a compliment… and perhaps a small test of this person with whom she would be living. But the frown coming to her aunt's face warned that she might have gone too far.

"What do you mean?"

She shrugged her shoulders just to give the impression that it was no big deal… even though the memory still bothered her.

"In the courtroom… a man called you a… a bad thing."

"What'd he say?"

"I don't want to repeat it. It wasn't nice… and it made me mad."

That was not the half of it, but seeing as she was growing worried by that look of sternness on Aunt Gwen's face, something had to be said to soften the words to come. Either 'mad' or 'sad' would have done the job.

"I've got pretty thick skin. Go on. I certainly won't hold against you what someone else has said."

She looked again into the unblinking stare of her aunt's eyes, trying to make out if that was a promise she could count on.

"Yes, ma'am. He… ahh… said that you were a… a crafty old… bitch."

She put that last word out with a whisper so Aunt Gwen would know for sure how embarrassed she felt. But her aunt just sat there absolutely still. Now she was in big trouble. She had definitely crossed a line. But then her aunt burst out laughing, long enough and loud enough that she felt comfortable to smile back.

"Now that's the truest thing I've heard all week!"

"But what's it mean?"

"Well… as a matter of fact… it's just a female dog. But as you say… it's not a particularly nice thing to be called. Still… there's an element of toughness to it… and independence. I do fancy myself as being crafty… every successful businesswoman should. So all in all, I guess you could say his words accurately describe me… except the part about being old. No woman, regardless of her age, should ever take kindly to that."

"So… how old are you?"

To her surprise, there was the faintest return to that stone face from before, so she quickly did a thing to show that she meant no harm in asking.

"I mean, I'm six."

What she thought to be hardness immediately turned into something different. Aunt Gwen, if possible, had the makings of tears in her eyes.

"Marna… dear… you're seven. Been so for well over a week now. Didn't you know you had a birthday… or has life been that hard on you?"

"I… yes, ma'am… I mean, no, ma'am… I mean… I just don't know what day it is. They… they never tell you those kinds of things in there."

"They… in there?"

She did not want to explain what 'they' or 'there' meant, nor did she care what day it was, or whether she was six or seven. She wanted not to be looked at, not to be thought of as that child she had become. She wanted to be home.

"It's nothing."

"I see… Well… just so you know… I'm thirty six… which is not so very old after all."

"Seems old to me."

"Yes… I suppose it would. And in the opinion of some men, it's just about the time when a young woman starts becoming a crafty old bitch."

A smile slowly crept over her aunt's face, finishing into a wide grin just as she reached along the table to pat her forearm.

"But what's say we keep that between us two? After all, we're both Forde women, and we should stick together."

That conclusion remained in her mind throughout her first day in Lubbock. Though its full meaning was unclear at that moment, she somehow felt that it would end up being carried along with her throughout her life with Aunt Gwen.

CHAPTER

4

RELIEF AND THE ART OF
FLORAL DESIGN

"August is always a slow month in the shop. No holidays or graduations… and not many brides are daring enough to set their wedding date for the hottest time of the year. Lots of folks… the kind with money for buying flowers… are off on vacation. So… being the crafty businesswoman that I am, I came up with my own special occasion for flowers."

She was doing her best in paying attention to her aunt, but her mind kept straying elsewhere. She was thinking about something she suspected that an adult might consider as unimportant… something very small. She could not remember having come into Aunt Gwen's house on the previous night, and was completely unprepared for the first thing she saw on stepping out the front door. The yard was a big disappointment. Her first impression of the grass was that of little sticks, dull brown and all flattened out as if each and every one had been beaten down. Making her way to Aunt Gwen's car parked in the driveway, she stooped down to run a hand over this grass. It felt nothing like the delicately thin blades of her old yard… so soft to the touch, spongy to walk on, and full of that warm, rich smell whenever cut. She had absolutely no interest in testing out this lawn by sitting in the stuff… much less walking across it barefoot. Looking about at the other yards in the neighborhood, she was surprised that they were as Aunt Gwen's. None of them were bright green. Just a dull olive… one of her least favorite crayons in the box. Few houses had much in the way of flower beds worthy of her old street. Worst of all, the trees were so terribly small. Not a one towered above a house.

Now in the car and traveling along the street in the early morning dim, she glanced back toward Aunt Gwen's house, comparing it with those they were passing. All of them, hers included, were rather small. Like the trees, they seemed really lacking. Almost as if… by being denied of whatever a house's vitamins and minerals were… they had not grown up as they were meant to be. The only things that stood tall in this neighborhood were the telephone poles. Yards without big trees… or no trees at all… made those poles feel all the more barren to her. Like they had once been planted with hope, but somehow had never formed leaves when they grew. Someone had tried to cover up their nakedness by stringing wires along them. Only in late Autumn when all of the leaves had fallen did she ever feel the same sad way in her old neighborhood. But that was only for a short time, as winter soon brought its white wonder to decorate every limb.

Aunt Gwen, looking back and forth at her while driving, was speaking excitedly… so she really should be listening.

"The technical college here in town… it's about to start up for the fall. There's a thousand young women arriving on campus. Young women who adore flowers! So… I got this idea a couple of summers ago. I petitioned the college to establish a new program… a kind of 'welcome back to school' thing for the ladies. Gift baskets. With a little bit of persuasion… I got the school to give me the budget for pulling it off… which unfortunately also meant that I had to partner with other florists in town… something that sorely went against my better judgment. You see… they're my competition. I've still made it work out for my benefit. I won't bore you with the details… just wanted you to know that the next few days… Saturday included… are going to be especially hectic at the shop. It's time to start putting those baskets together. I won't be in much today… got to coordinate things at the college… but I'll show you around first… introduce you to my floral designer… and hopefully pop back in around lunch. In the meantime… I'll give you some simple things to try your hand on."

In focusing on Aunt Gwen, she had not noticed where the car was heading. Looking out the window when the feel of road gave way to gravel, she saw that the sun was rising on a wide-open horizon. Nothing much was around except for a small farmhouse and a barn-like structure of glass.

"Aunt Gwen… is this your flower shop?"

"Heavens no! We won't be getting there for a while. This is the first of the greenhouses I visit daily. Early bird gets the best bud."

Aunt Gwen smiled big and broad as if this was a special saying… though she could not see what birds had to do with buds. The old man that came out to greet them seemed to know already that a niece from 'up north' was coming to live with Aunt Gwen. He said hello to her… but that was it, as Aunt Gwen was already asking him all sorts of flower questions. Without forewarning, her aunt and he moved toward the glass building, so she hurried to keep up. The inside was surprisingly muggy… and smelly too. Kind of like the basement of her old house. There were lots of plants up on tables… most too high for her to get a good look at. She saw well only those things underneath – empty pots, bags of dirt, tools, coils of rubber hose, and lots of spider webs… which made her want to go sit back in the car. Her aunt sometimes took a moment to explain what she was after and what made for a good deal, but mostly she talked to the man. They made three more stops, all just the same. When they were finally ready to make for the shop, the car's trunk was packed with buckets of flowers that Aunt Gwen had bought at the four 'greenhouses'… which was such a weird name since none of them were green.

On the drive back into town, she gave up struggling with what her aunt's daily schedule might mean for her, and instead turned to face out her window. With the fingers of both hands gripping the sill of her car door, she pulled herself up a bit so as to get a better look at Lubbock. In everything they passed, she was searching for little scraps of beauty… anything that might compare favorably with where she had grown up. Michigan won every time.

Aunt Gwen said her shop was on 4th Street, which meant nothing to her other than that there must be three streets before it and probably others after. In finally pulling before the shop, Aunt Gwen made a point of saying that she always parked in back, but would give her a peek at the front first. The building was painted in a light blue… lilac, according to her aunt. The shop's name was lettered all the way across the front, with a large display window to either side of the door. Windows with really big pieces of glass had always fascinated her. They continued around to a side street… and then into an alley behind the store. The alley was nothing special – the back of the shop on one side, a wooden fence on the other, and lots of gravel in between. There was also a large Dempster-dumpster. Though pretty scuffed up, it was actually the only green thing in sight. Her aunt parked beneath a little roof sticking out above a big metal door. This, her aunt said, was the backside to Forde's Flowers, her normal way inside. The front entrance was only for customers.

In helping her aunt tote buckets of flowers through the backdoor and down a short hall, her first glimpse inside was of the cutting room – what Aunt Gwen called the heart of the flower shop. In the center was a large table where she was told to put the first bucket. She was about to take a look around when Aunt Gwen steered her back outside. On the second trip in, she noticed large metal sinks with countertops sloped in to drain water from drying racks above. Scanning along the wall of shelves, she saw vases, baskets, pots and cans of so many shapes, sizes and styles… but Aunt Gwen wanted her back out for another load. The next time, she took a moment to look at the huge glass-covered cabinets full of flowers and leafy things in other buckets. A constant hum from a hidden motor told her that these were refrigerators… and likely the reason why this room was so cold. On the next trip, she studied the wall full of wooden prongs, each bent upward to hold things – spools of ribbon, clusters of bows, rolls of paper, rags, aprons, and cutting tools. She had no idea why any of those things were important in selling flowers.

Before her fifth trip in, a van with the lettering of the shop's name on its side pulled up next to her aunt's car. Out popped a woman somewhat younger-looking than her aunt. With a shriek, this plumpish lady was all over her before she knew what was happening. Pinning her arms to her side, the woman wrapped her about in a bear hug that lifted her off her feet.

"Ohhhh… you must be Marna! I knew who you was the moment I laid eyes on you! I could just hug you to bits! So beautiful… just like your aunt! I can't tell you how excited I am to have you here! Now let me look at all of you…" The woman dropped her and pushed her away at the same time. "So grown up… and so brave! Takin' a bus 'cross America on your own! And what with all you've been through!"

Thankfully, the woman was interrupted by Aunt Gwen coming out of the shop.

"Where's Clem?"

"Why, isn't she just precious?!"

"Patsy… where's Clem?"

"Oh, I don't know! Delivering fertilizer I 'spect. Told me as much last night. Said I'd be makin' the Amarillo run by myself. But would you just look at her, Gwen! Sweetest thing I ever did see! I could just gobbler her up!"

This Patsy turned her about in a circle, and the feeling of being a thing poked up in her again.

"I tell you what… I certainly see a resemblance in the mouth… chin too… and a bit in the eyes. Same nose but not the same hair. You know, Gwen… I do think this young lady might just grow up to be a real beauty! Can't you see the graceful curves comin' in all over her face?!"

"Patsy, you're smothering the girl. Set her loose and show me what you've got for me in the back."

"Certainly… It wasn't at all easy, but I managed to pick up some fine deals."

In a flash, she went from being the object of Patsy's admiration to being completely ignored… all without a proper introduction. Of course, she knew right off that this must be Aunt Gwen's floral designer… whatever that was supposed to mean.

Don't flowers sort of… design themselves?!

But the other person that Aunt Gwen referred to was a mystery.

"Who's Clem?"

"You're interrupting an adult, Marna. But if you must know, he's Patsy's husband. Does deliveries for me."

The two ladies, standing within the open rear doors of the van, were exchanging the names of flowers she had never heard of. Without warning, her aunt shoved a bucket into her arms and flicked her head toward the shop's backdoor. Sloshing around in water were blooms of a pinkish sort, all of them clustered along stalks.

Del-fee something-or-other…

Both women were already discussing the next bucket. Without putting up a fuss about it, she carted that one inside, fully expecting them to be coming in behind with buckets of their own. When she turned about, no one was there. In many trips until there were no buckets left, she single-handedly unloaded the van. In the end, all she got was a thank-you from Aunt Gwen and a pat on the cheek from Patsy.

The two women went about making plans for the new things brought in that morning – what to store away in the coolers, what to put out on display in the showroom (…*which no one's bothered showing me yet…*), and what might be used to fill orders. She stood by quietly through all of this, but on noticing Aunt Gwen preparing to leave, she moved with her in the direction of the car, but only got as far as the two hallway doors she had passed by several times – 'Office' and 'Employees Only' – before being sent back.

"Marna… I'm sorry to run out on you, but like I said… I've got important meetings today. It's about that special project I mentioned earlier. Won't be back for a while. Patsy… nothing too difficult for her. Maybe start her out with trimming foliage and cleaning buckets. Marna, do as you're told. I'll try to get back in time for a nice lunch."

Without another word, Aunt Gwen was out the rear door and gone.

In that first hour at Forde's Flowers, her hurt feelings were not so much from being abandoned by her aunt as from having to endure the irritating oversight of Patsy. The woman would not stop talking, and none of it was about things a kid cared to hear. How so-in-so did such-in-such… and how Patsy thought it was so funny… or rude… or 'scan-dull-lust.' And the woman just had to stand directly over her as she struggled with cutters made for adult-sized hands. She had the real fear of clipping off a finger to deal with. At least this work was easier than mopping floors for Mrs. Jaworski. Her summer as a foster child had taken fun right out of her thinking. She had not played with a friend in months.

Not since before… you know what.

But now she had a new home… so maybe things would change for the better. She reminded herself again to ask Aunt Gwen about the boxes shipped from Michigan. Within one of those was her stuffed animals. As Patsy kept up the instructions on how to clip a stem so the flower could still suck up water, she did the job while pretending that she was actually setting out a tea party for an afternoon of fun with Teddy, Minney, Rapscallion, Angler, and Humphrey, 'the bravest elephant of them all.' She always called him that because she thought him too shy. Her stuffed animals were her only friends left in this world.

From time to time, the bell dangling over the front door rang to announce the arrival of a customer. Patsy would then dash out of the cutting room to greet the person coming into the shop. She stayed in the back each time, having no desire for people… no matter how many times Patsy swore they would love meeting the niece of the store owner. She knew that the woman was trying to be patient with her slow progress at the clippers. Looking at Mother's garden had always been fun… but getting into the dirt with her was never something she enjoyed doing. Mother had always been understanding… but not this Patsy. At least the woman gave her a bit of a break for a tour of the showroom… but soon had her right back at the frustrating job of cutting stems.

And then she made her first big mistake at Forde's Flowers. It really had not been her fault. Patsy gave her such confusing instructions while rushing out of the cutting room… returning from the front to say that she had lopped off far too much stem from the leatherleaf. The whole bucket of them was ruined.

"Your aunt'll be most displeased."

Without thinking much of where she was going, she immediately fled in a fit of angry tears. Dashing through the curtain that separated off the cutting room from the checkout counter, all she wanted to do was get far away from Patsy. But finding that the showroom was no place to hide, she took to that narrow little nook beneath the cash register. She would stay there until she could calm down enough to endure Patsy's presence again.

Because I'm not doing any more work until she says she's sorry!

Crammed into that tight space, she was dreading having to face the person who had not yet been her guardian for a full day. For now… she would go on fuming in silence… but then the bell rang again. She had completely forgotten that this was a shop with customers. So this was actually a pretty stupid place to hide seeing as Patsy would be coming up front any second now. The office would have been better… though she had not yet set foot in there… or maybe the bathroom… though Patsy would probably chase her out to use it herself.

Her next thought… a dreadful one… was that her aunt was here to discover what she had done to the leatherleaf. But then she relaxed on remembering that Aunt Gwen said she only used the back door. It had to be a customer. Drawing her knees up to her chin, she tucked herself even further out of sight. She then heard voices. More than one person had come in.

"Roy, keep your hands to yourself. You understand me?"

"Yes, ma'am."

She sucked in a deep breath and held it, craning her head forward a bit in order to better listen. The adult was definitely a woman, whereas the other was a child… a boy… maybe about her age by the sound of him.

Just then, Patsy came through the curtain and shot her a nasty frown before looking up with a smile toward the customer.

"Mornin' Mrs. Meitner. You've come at the perfect time… just finishin' up your arrangement. Hold it a sec while I get it."

"Take your time."

Patsy reversed direction and disappeared into the back. She became aware of something being placed on the counter above her… perhaps the woman's purse. She strained to hear whatever else might be going on in the showroom… anything to reveal the whereabouts of the boy. Nothing of him came to her before Patsy's return.

"Here we are… a dozen of the purtiest yellow roses you ever did see… all cradled up nicely in baby's breath. Wanted to use leatherleaf, but it's… *gone bad*." She could only see Patsy from the waist down, but was pretty sure that those last two words had been directed at her. "So, what's the special occasion? We've some lovely greetin' cards over there by the winda."

Patsy went up on her toes, likely in leaning across the counter to point out the display cases.

"Already have a card. These are for George. He's crazy about yellow roses. I get him an arrangement every year on his birthday. Kind of a family tradition."

"How nice. My family always gives…"

"Patsy, dear… I don't much like this ribbon. How about a piece of that satin back there?"

An arm suddenly shot over the countertop, pointing at the rolls of ribbon along the back wall. The sight of that arm froze her in place. With a view from the woman's elbow down, she followed as a bracelet of white stones slid about the wrist.

Mother really liked pearls...

Patsy reached back to pull away a length of white ribbon from one of the many spools mounted on the wall behind the counter. It was a small reason for why she had ended up in this hiding place. Somehow, she had hoped that the jam-packed rack of colors might sooth her. If she could concentrate on them hard enough and long enough, perhaps they would do something special for her. They might blend themselves into a rainbow... or sparkle as if magic was about to happen... or at least dance about a bit once she had calmed down enough to blow on their many dangling ends. The whole lot of them might ripple and flutter about just for her. She could whisper to them... and they would understand.

"No... I don't much care for that one either. How about that silky one?" She followed Patsy's finger as it moved from ribbon to ribbon. "No, not that one. The one beside it."

The woman's face suddenly came into view over the counter top. She could not help herself in letting out a sudden gasp, frightful in sound to even her own ears. The woman's eyes immediately darted down to her.

"Oh... hello there."

"Never mind her. That's just Gwen's niece, Marna, come to live with her." Patsy lowered her voice to whisper out words that were not spoken nearly softly enough. "She's the one I was tellin' you 'bout last month... you know... from *up north.*"

Patsy then cleared her throat in exactly the way a grownup does when delivering to a child a message that was meant more for the impressing of a nearby adult.

"Where's your manners, Marna?! Say hello to Mrs. Meitner."

"Hello."

In looking from the woman to Patsy and then back again, her eyes were suddenly drawn to something very different. Down the length of the counter to its corner, she made out a slight movement. A head covered in a child-size cowboy hat poked into view... and then withdrew just as fast.

"Marna, be a dear and go sit in your aunt's office. She won't mind."

Without giving either woman another look, she slid herself from under the elbow-bend in the counter and made for the fabric barrier that separated off the cutting room. But on reaching the end of the counter, she took the opportunity to turn toward where the boy was crouched. She had ready for him the best scowl a girl could give to a snoop. There he was, hunched down at the edge and not expecting her. She might have been discovered in her hiding place, but she had not looked so stupid in falling over backward as he did at that moment. That, at least, gave her some bitter delight.

On pushing through the curtain into the cutting room, she paused to consider how that boy was dressed. Funny-looking leather things were wrapped around his legs, and on his feet were boots much too fancy for a child. That dull brown vest did not at all match his red checkered shirt... or that bandanna about his neck. And his cowboy hat – *Ugh!* – it was so cheap looking. But most silly to her was his belt holstered with toy guns. How could anyone his age dress himself up like a pretend cowboy?! That was for little kids! Not something that she, a soon-to-be second grader, would ever stoop to do!

The pleasure to her scorn suddenly disappeared. Before her on the cutting room table was the bucket of mangled leatherleaf... exactly as she had left it. Patsy was surely keeping it there to show Aunt Gwen the evidence of her mistake. Not a full morning at Forde's Flowers and she had already messed up. Now, the silly boy in his silly outfit did not seem so silly to her. She wanted to be him. To have the worst thing in life be the ridiculous way in which a child might dress up.

She was just about to step away from the curtain and head to the office when a voice from the showroom made her pause. Someone had spoken her name. Shifting to the side, she brought her back up against the wall beside the cloth barrier and waited. After a short silence, the voice picked up again... with every muscle in her tensing up. It was Patsy... and though she clearly heard words coated with sympathy, the rushed pace was definitely that of a gossiper.

"Poor thing... orphaned when her parents were killed in a car crash."

"How horrible! You never told me that."

"I'm sure I did."

"Where'd it happen?"

"Up north somewhere. But you ain't heard the worst of it..."

It was getting difficult to make out Patsy's whispered words, so she inched closer, placing her ear right up against the curtain so as not to miss whatever came next.

"...that little girl was in the car when it happened!"

There was a gasp... much louder than the whispers... and then she heard a hummed out assurance from Patsy. Right now, running to Aunt Gwen's office would be the sensible thing to do, but a much bigger part of her wanted to hear what she could not remember.

"It's a miracle, I tell you! That child survived the accident without a scratch. Gwen said the troopers said the car went clear off an embankment and down into a ravine. Must have been goin' sixty at least. Gwen's brother and his wife were killed instantly."

"How tragic!"

"And that ain't the half of it…" Again, Patsy lowered her voice to a whisper. "It was near on two days before anyone came across the wreck."

"No!"

"As sure as I'm standin' here, that's what Gwen said. Truck driver happened on it when he pulled over to do his business. Spotted the tire tracks headin' over the side. Might never have found her alive otherwise. When the police finally pried open the car, there was little Marna passed out on the back floorboards not feet away from her dead parents. Poor thing was barely alive herself."

Without realizing it, she found that she had slid a finger about the curtain's edge, creating a gap wide enough to peer through… even though both of her eyes were clamped tight. Memory after memory was pouring in. The unbearable shock of the images coming to her suddenly forced her eyes wide open. Through the narrow slit, she saw the boy, crouched down as before… except now with his cowboy hat off. The blood had so drained from his face that his crew-cut scalp gave her the impression of a cue ball… like one of those dirty-looking ones that Uncle Amos did tricks with at his pool hall. But this cue ball had bulging eyes and a mouth gaped open so wide that she could see into his throat.

This would not do. Though deeply disturbed by her memories, she sensed that a greater embarrassment was only moments away. The boy was about to do something really stupid. Unable to bear the thought of Patsy knowing that she was listening, she slowly pulled the curtain open a bit further so the boy could better see her face. With one hand holding the fabric, she laid a finger over her lips. The boy closed his mouth and nodded eagerly… almost as if he had just been forgiven for having made a mess.

Patsy was now relating about how clever Aunt Gwen had been in sending that lawyer up to Michigan to fight for custody, even though it had taken months to work the whole thing out. She already knew all of this. Becoming aware of an unpleasant feeling growing in her stomach, she turned away without another look toward the boy. Crossing through the cutting room, she made directly for the back of the shop and entered Aunt Gwen's office. Without bothering to look for the light switch, she closed the door and felt her way to the wooden desk she had seen on entering. Moving its chair away, she crawled underneath and drew the chair back in as close as she could. But the office door opened just then, flooding her dark with unwanted light.

"Marna? Are you in here?"

"Go away."

"Are you okay?"

"I said go away!"

The door closed without another word… but she knew the tricks of adults. Quietly, she shifted about to peer from beneath the desk. With her face close to the floor, she looked to the thin line of light coming from under the door. There were no feet waiting on the other side. Patsy had indeed left. She was finally alone.

With that knowledge came an unexpected change in her. Maybe it was only the cold air flowing in from under the door, bathing her with an unwanted reminder. Being crammed under Aunt Gwen's desk did not help… nor did the darkened room or seeing that thin sliver of light. She suddenly found herself shaking uncontrollably, and absolutely must close her eyes as so many terrible images were popping into her mind again. The raging, roaring reality of them curled her over into a ball, as she fought the nearly overwhelming urge to throw up.

She remembered it all.

Well… not the accident itself. That was still as clouded in her memory as when all those adults at the hospital kept pressing her. She had told them the truth back then. The last thing she could recall was sitting in the backseat of her parent's car on the way to vacation. Next thing she knew, she was lying in an ambulance with a man leaning over her. All summer, she had remained completely unaware as to what had happened in between. And to be fair… if she had known then what she knew now… then she definitely would have pretended not to know.

She awoke in a daze, unable to focus on anything other than that it was impossible to move. She was in a very tight space, with something above pinning her against the hard surface below. After struggling about for several seconds, her head finally cleared enough to recognize where she was – on the floor in the back of the family car. So she immediately called out for help… to her parents and then to anybody who might hear. A wave of fear shook her fully awake when no one answered. She started thrashing about wildly, kicking her legs because they were the only part of her that was free.

In wiggling about, she finally managed to get an arm out from underneath her. She wore herself out doing more screaming for help, rested a bit, and then wore herself out all over again trying to get out.

During one of those periods of quiet panic, with the side of her face flat against the floor, she noticed there was a gap beneath the front seat that enabled her to see straight through into the driver's foot space. In a thin slit of light, she just made out one of his feet, bent sideways in a way that did not seem natural. She called to him again and again, begging him to wake up and save her… but that foot never moved.

All about his foot was movement of a kind. In a multitude of little twinkles, a beam of sunlight piercing in from somewhere above lit up the floor with a great many sparkles. She watched those for a long time, following in some of them a change of colors from blue to green to yellow and red. Eventually, they all faded to a pale nothing. It was then that she recognized them for what they were. Just worthless shards of broken glass.

By twisting herself, she was finally able to flip over onto her back, and came to realize that she was being trapped by how the front seat had collapsed over her. With both arms free, she pushed up with all her strength, but just could not budge her father's seat. She spent more time calling out and more time listening. When she had quieted herself enough, she could make out the sound of cars somewhere nearby. They had that passing-on-a-highway feel – a rising rush as of thunder coming from far away, followed by a sudden 'swoosh'… and then disappointment. Like how a campfire slowly sizzled into silence after water was poured onto it. Not one car ever stopped. Those drivers could not possibly hear her… a trapped little girl… but still she yelled until her throat gave out. And then she just cried while beating her fists against the front seat until there was nothing left in her.

She woke in faded light, very much convinced that it was all just a bad dream. The terrible feel of confinement told her otherwise. How long she had been asleep was unclear, but something new had happened in the meantime. She now smelled gasoline. Not just a gentle whiff as when her father filled the tank. It was strong and nearly overpowering… yet somehow opened her mind for clearer thinking. She had to get herself out.

After working at it for a long time, she finally managed to get an arm up to the door handle. But try as she might, it could not be moved. Her rage came on again, and she fought against the car so intensely that in clinching her jaw a small piece of a tooth broke off. She spit it out as if it were nothing.

The sun set before she knew what was happening. Somewhere in the back of her mind, she had been sure that someone would soon rescue her. It had never occurred to her that the darkness would find her first. That night of being trapped was so very cold... colder than anything she had ever experienced... and much more terrifying. Unlike in the day, she lay quietly now, listening with all her might. The traffic on the highway became an annoyance... a temptation to scream out with no hope of being heard. Even the wrecked car kept tinkling all over as it cooled. But those sounds were not so important. It was the gentle rustling of leaves, the hush of wind in the trees, and every other forest noise that foretold of foxes, badgers and mice coming out to nibble at parts of her. She tried to stay awake all night, but still fell in and out of shallow sleep. The worst moment came not from fright but from embarrassment, for she awoke with a jolt at the feeling of having wet herself.

Morning brought no relief. She was so very cold and hungry, and in greater need of something to drink. As the first rays of sunlight hit the wreck, she began to notice that the smells of gas and melted rubber were not the only ones in the air. Faint odors of something else were growing in strength. The thought that it was only herself... the result of her accident in the night... soon gave way as these new smells proved very different... something closer to rotting vegetables and poop.

As the minutes crept on... and the sun's rays broke through the shattered windows of the car... the morning brought its curse. The heat and the new smells attracted them – the flying things. At first, it was just a few black flies, their buzz adding an annoyance to her desperation. As their numbers grew with the smells, many went for her, biting at her legs and arms. Soon there were so many flies, crawling about on her face and tormenting her with their presence. She pitched about insanely, screaming at them to leave her be. But like the passing motorists, none heard her.

The crows arrived next... and their nonstop cawing nearly drove her mad. At least they were easy to scare away... at first... by screaming and banging against the seat. But they eventually grew braver as she grew more weary. She was dreadfully afraid to know what they were doing in the front seat... and more so ashamed that she no longer had the strength for fighting them off.

But it was the noise of a different sort of flying thing that caused her the greatest terror. Their sound was softer... and their touch more gentle... but they were death to her.

Wasps!

She lay still from then on, allowing the mosquitoes and flies to have their way. It did not matter. She was going to die soon. Right there beside her parents. She closed her eyes and waited for the sting that would kill her.

She woke once briefly in the night, but soon passed out altogether. The next thing she knew, she was in the arms of a man in a rough canvas overcoat. There were people all around her whispering words no more understandable than the buzzing of insects. They soon had her strapped into some kind of a bed and were moving her up head-first. She made out sky through tree limbs above and heard the sounds of scraping below. Only when the stretcher had been dragged to the top of the hill, with sunlight hitting her full in the face, did it occur to her that she had been saved.

The memory was out to hang there as a blot upon her thoughts... one that would never go away. Lying under Aunt Gwen's desk, face flat against the floor much as when she had awoken in that wreck, she opened her eyes wide. The gap beneath the office door was there as before, so she concentrated on it with all her might, hoping that its brightness could somehow push the whole experience from her mind. One side of that thin line... the one to the right in her vision... was sharp in its difference between light and dark, whereas the other side faded gradually as it stretched out across the floor toward where she lay. Within its grayness were many small sparkles where the light seemed to be reflecting off of something in the concrete floor.

All of a sudden, she could not stay there for another second. She needed brighter light... and space... lots of wide open space. She banged her head on the underside of the desk in her rush to get out... and nearly tripped over the chair... but did not stop. She had to see sky above her and have openness all about. Bursting from the office, she turned right and threw herself in frustration against the back door when it would not immediately open for her. Out into the blinding light of a West Texas afternoon, she was not satisfied with having gained the alleyway behind the flower shop. It was wide, but not nearly wide enough. She ran to the left, for that way was the sun and a sliver's worth of horizon. Only after having reached a street did she stop. Standing there on the sidewalk, panting in an awareness of the August heat, all connection to cold and darkness slowly faded away. She shivered one last time, and let that feeling express itself fully into a joyous shaking out of her hair. Then, raising her arms upward toward a perfectly clear blue sky, she cried out for no other reason than from the pure pleasure of finding herself alive.

For the next few days, she worked at the flower shop from morning's first light until well after dark, coming back to the house far too exhausted for anything other than sleep. They managed to reach Aunt Gwen's goal of fifty welcome baskets. Riding along with her aunt during the delivery to the technical college gave her an opportunity to see more of Lubbock. To her, everything seemed so spread out, enhancing a confused feeling in her. Already, she was growing to appreciate the sky, from horizon to horizon, but at the same time could not help but resent the absence of trees and green things. She put all such thoughts away when the wind unexpectedly picked up and covered the city in a shroud of dust. Oddly, nobody else moving about Lubbock… Aunt Gwen included… seemed to find this in the least bit disturbing. But her scratchy eyes and throat told her that it could not be good to have so much of the earth end up floating about in the sky where it did not belong.

On her first Saturday night in Lubbock, she naturally asked about church in the morning, as her family had always gone. Aunt Gwen gave off a little laugh and said that she should not bother with such things… which did not seem right to her. Her parents said it was important. She was about to point this out to her aunt when a stern look on the woman's face warned her against trying. So she went to bed with even more unanswered questions about her aunt.

On Sunday morning, she awoke mindful of Aunt Gwen's instructions from the previous night. She was to tend to her own breakfast and then do as she pleased… as long as everything was done quietly. This was the only opportunity her aunt had for sleeping in. So… dressed in pajamas and with a bowl of cereal in hand, she left the kitchen with nothing particular on her mind other than to roam about the sitting room while eating. Once done, she would dress and go outside to explore the yard… and perhaps seek out some neighborhood children.

She spent a good long time standing in front of Aunt Gwen's china cabinet staring at the dishes on display there, eating a spoonful of corn flakes for each item behind the glass before moving on to the next. Most things had some kind of flower on them. Seeing these reminded her of her mother's china cabinet, especially those crystalline figurines of animals. She really loved looking at those… but what had become of them was a mystery.

They're not here in this china cabinet… so maybe Uncle Amos got ahold of them.

Without having a reason for believing it as so, her mind suddenly jumped to an obvious conclusion. Placing her bowl down on the dining room table, she went to sit on Aunt Gwen's couch to think it through. After only a short time, she became absolutely sure of it. As with most serious arguments she had ever been involved in, either at school, in the neighborhood, or at the foster home, an adult had to step in and settle it for the children. She thought back to the courtroom with all the lawyers shouting at each other. She had always thought that they had been fighting over her, but not now. Clearly, the judge had chosen the winner. Uncle Amos must of won… and gotten all of her family's special things, whereas Aunt Gwen had lost… and been stuck with her. That was why it had taken so long for her aunt to claim her. The little girl was not the prize after all. Maybe Aunt Gwen was actually planning to make a slave out of her. Kids were supposed to get the summer for fun… but not her. She worked without play.

She fell back against the couch on the verge of tears… when a wonderfully new thing came into her sight. Hanging there on the opposite wall was a very unusual picture… rectangular in shape and twice as wide as it was tall. At first glance, she took it to be the sort of thing that only an adult might be interested in. Something very old and very fancy. But in dipping her head slightly, she came to see that it was not at all a flat thing. The picture had texture and depth. Rising from the couch to take a closer look, she came to recognize this as something cut from a big slab of white stone.

Hey – it's a sculptor! Wait… that's not right. It's a… sculp-chur. The other's the guy that did it.

She knew that the thing was clearly heavy. Aunt Gwen had to use such big brackets to hold it on the wall. The greater part of its picture was a band of delicately carved characters crammed in together between the right and left borders of the stone. These were clearly of people, yet none were shown in a way that seemed natural. Their arms and legs were all bent about at funny angles, and their faces were so ugly… some in angry ways and some with great sadness. The whole thing was like freeze tag… except this was no game. This was real life. All of them were clothed in simple robes, but they were not all the same. Half were mean-looking in wielding clubs and swords over timid neighbors who were begging for mercy beneath the blows. Some had fallen and were being trampled upon… and some looked dead. Studying it from side to side, she felt both pity and horror at these stone prisoners. Old or young, man or woman, the whole lot of them showed the worst sort of misery. Not one of them had any hope of ever breaking free.

Though her eyes had been held by the faces, she eventually looked up past to a thin stone barrier at the top. What she had at first thought to be the upper border, she now saw as a narrow margin of perfectly smooth stone that had two small figures carved into it. She quickly dragged over a dining room chair and climbed up so that her eyes were at the same level. The sculptor had included two birds in the rock above. Each had a swift-like quality to it – split tail and angled-back wings. With wings tucked in, one bird was diving while the other was clearly heading back up. The sight of them instantly spoke to her of motion… and speed… and the freedom to go wherever she wanted to. These birds, with a feel of air to them, were happy. They reminded her of play… of the first time she rode a bicycle… and of going dizzyingly fast on a merry-go-round. Looking back down at the bottom, she was left in confusion over how any sculptor could combine these two things in one – all that human suffering with the joy of flight.

She sat before that sculpture all morning until Aunt Gwen happened to wake. She then asked about it as casually as could be. Aunt Gwen told her it was called a relief. She like that name very much… and felt that this stone thing was exactly what she needed in her life.

Over the coming weeks, she would return often to study this relief, but only when Aunt Gwen was not around to notice. She was not sure why, but having it known how much she liked it… and hated it at the same time… felt too difficult to explain. She wanted terribly to know all about it – where it had come from, how old it was, and what the artist was trying to say. But to ask such questions might reveal more about herself than she felt comfortable having this stranger of an aunt know. Sometimes, she even found herself talking to this relief, telling it about her sad life. It seemed to listen and understand. She could always find a face there to match how she felt, whether it be anger, sadness or fear. And the birds… they reminded her of how she wanted to be – free.

This relief, with all its cold mystery, became her first genuine friend in Texas.

CHAPTER

5

THE SECOND DAY OF
SECOND GRADE

Finding the right words for describing adults was not something she considered herself very good at. She knew their tricks, but not what made them tick. Aunt Gwen sold flowers for a living, but Aunt Gwen was not at all flowery… not in the soft and sweet ways she expected from someone owning a flower shop. But after only two weeks in Lubbock, she easily came to understand that West Texas had three things in common with her aunt – the heat, the barren feel of the place, and how everyone she met was so very proud to be called Texan.

The heat was the most obvious likeness between her aunt and Texas. Aunt Gwen could make her sweat, both in how she worked her and sometimes made her feel. Her aunt had this way of staring eye-to-eye for several seconds before speaking her mind over something done wrong. Those eyes could turn her face hot with fear, even in the cold of the cutting room.

The dreary feel to Texas was also very plain to her, though the likeness in Aunt Gwen took her awhile to figure out. Part of that was from how difficult it sometimes felt in cracking through her aunt's hard outside. The only time she ever really saw Aunt Gwen's softness was that very first morning on discovering a closet full of new clothes. From then on, Aunt Gwen was all about getting things done. Her life was arranging flowers… and turning out a hardworking and respectful niece. Aunt Gwen was never quick to give out compliments… not like her mother had been… and when she did praise a job well done, it often came across as stern owing to the way she held her chin up while speaking. As adults go, Aunt Gwen was careful with the things she said, never gossiped… something Patsy was real good at… and seldom used bad words. Yet her aunt hardly ever spoke about herself… what she was feeling or things from her past… which somehow kept a separation between them.

Something about Aunt Gwen was very sad… and distant. Like not enough rain had fallen in her life, so the tender parts from when she was young and green had all gone brown. Yet she seemed not to need anyone in her life… which was so odd, because the woman knew just about everyone in Lubbock… especially their birthdays and anniversaries. Aunt Gwen was real friendly with every customer coming into the shop, but none of them seemed close enough to be called a friend. Her aunt obviously never married, which fit with her having no room in her life for a man. As far as she could tell, her aunt worked all day, six days a week. Even on Sunday, Aunt Gwen mostly spent her time alone in her home office sitting at a small roll-top desk writing letters. Come Monday morning, she got handed a fist full of envelopes to be run into the post office before starting in on work. She asked only once about who those letters were to… and was told to mind her own business… which did not keep her from peeking at the addresses before dropping the pile into the box. Always, they were to women all over the country.

As to Texas, there was not that much left for her to understand. Texans thought that their state was the best place in the world, and Lubbock was the very heart of it. If someone were to ask her, she would tell them that she considered herself fortunate to have been born in a place like Michigan. She knew her friends and neighbors there felt the same way. Yet nobody in Michigan went on and on about it as if that part of America was so much better than any other. No one back home made a big deal out of what they were called like Texans did.

What's someone from Michigan anyway? A Michiganer? Michiganian? Michiganite? They all sound dumb.

Aunt Gwen was sort of like that side of Texas too. Not so much in considering herself Texan (…*since Patsy says she can't be because she wasn't born here…*), but in acting as if her flower shop happened to be all that there was in life.

Texans were so full of themselves… but also really nice… which just confused her. Everybody always smiling, being helpful and kind. They w ere such a 'con-tra-dic-shun.' That was a word her father had taught her… when something was one way and the opposite at the same time. She never thought much about that word before moving to Lubbock. Aunt Gwen was a big 'con-tra-dic-shun.' Making sense out of her was harder than putting a puzzle together with the picture-side facing down. Sure... the pieces could eventually be made to link up well enough, but without a picture, she had no idea of what was being formed. Everything was just blank cardboard. That was Aunt Gwen... both hard and friendly at the same time. The two things connected, but made no sense when put together. There was also something about her aunt that had her thinking the woman had seen and done more than anyone else in Lubbock... but refused to speak about any of it. That was sort of like having the picture part of the puzzle to her life hidden, with only cardboard blankness showing.

Aunt Gwen was quick to offer help, but just as fast to deal with disrespect. Like that time when she took her first walk about the yard. She thought the whole thing to be so ugly, from the front curb around to the broken-down fence in back. No lawn, no trees, no flower beds, and no garden. So... on reentering the house, she told her aunt very nicely that no one could possibly know that a florist lived here based on the state of the yard. Somehow, that earned her a reminder as to the 'scare-city' of water in West Texas... and a lecture as to the proper way of speaking to an adult. It was so unfair that she was made to pull weeds all that Sunday... just for saying the obvious. But when she finally finished the job, Aunt Gwen surprised her by filling a huge wash basin with water and plopping her down in it... right before handing over a lime-flavored popsicle. To go from being so hot to that liquid coolness was about the best thing she had ever felt. All in all, she liked the cool side of Aunt Gwen... but it always came connected with the hot.

As to pride, there was no missing the way Aunt Gwen carried herself. Her aunt was unlike any woman she had known from before when her 'sir-come-stand-zis' were different. Like the bicycle her aunt gave her for a late birthday present. It was deep blue and had a bar from the handle to the seat... obvious signs that it was for a boy. Since it had to be a mistake, she asked to have it exchanged for a girl's. Aunt Gwen just said that she should do her best not to give in to such things... and that was that. It made no sense to her, especially since she liked everything about being a girl. Just because Aunt Gwen said over and over that there was nothing a man could do that a woman could not do also, that was no reason for a woman to dress like a man! But Aunt Gwen took real pride in clothing herself like a man... and in speaking her mind just like she was the man in charge.

Her aunt could be as impressive as the wide open West Texas sky. Powerfully thunderous when riled up, she could get right up into the face of a 'vendor'… that was her word for those greenhouse farmers… if a deal went bad. Aunt Gwen was especially good at giving the shop's suppliers the what-for whenever they dared to provide her with the 'little lady' treatment. More than once in the last two weeks, she watched her aunt bellow harder than the wind at one of those men for promising one thing and then bringing another. Yet just like the Texas rain, her aunt's anger would come down hard for a short time and then dry up without a sign… especially once she got to working on a flower arrangement. Then, Aunt Gwen was as bright as a cloudless summer afternoon. The woman could stand from sunup to sundown at the cutting room table humming away to herself while doing the simplest of tasks… as long as flowers were before her.

But the place where West Texas had her aunt beat was at night. The one, weary from a day's work, would collapse in an armchair and say no more, while the other would show anew all of its twinkled bands of wonder. The starry skies over Lubbock were like nothing she had ever seen in life. Big, bold and clear as crystal. In time, she began to see the daytime skies in the same way. Whether it was watching a storm sweep across or just following tiny puffs of white crawling along, being able to see movement in the sky… from horizon to horizon… was the only thing capable of softening her dislike for Texas. For what the land lacked, the sky made up for. Aunt Gwen said that having so much of Lubbock's dirt in the air was the cause for those spectacularly colorful sunrises and sunsets. That might be true… but she preferred that the dust not get in the way of the midday blues and whites. Seeing those was like splashing about in Heaven's pool and billowing out a milky froth. It made her want to be up there… if only to escape this prison of flatness below.

Perhaps the one difference between Aunt Gwen and most Texans was that her aunt never flew the flag. The man next door told her that her aunt was touchy on the subject, and then chuckled in saying that it had something to do with 'con-grass'… whatever that meant!

Aunt Gwen might sometimes act like a man, but she loved flowers like only a woman could. She considered her job to be more than making a living. It was noble work… even for a child. That was made clear on a morning a week into her life in Lubbock when she overheard Aunt Gwen and Patsy talking about her. Patsy was tip-toeing around the subject of children working… and Aunt Gwen cut her right off.

"Don't you think… seein' as her parents were recently kilt… that you should…"

"People die all the time, Patsy. Nothing at all unusual about it."

"Yes… I understand, Gwen… but she's just a child. She should be out playin' and makin' friends instead of…"

"Tell you what, you mind your own affairs… which at the moment involve getting these corsages ready for the Firemen's Ball… and I'll worry about Marna."

She absolutely hated being made to work all the time, but that was not the thing most frustrating about her aunt. It was the unconcerned way her aunt responded every time she brought up the subject of her things from Michigan. Though she knew little about how the mail worked, she definitely heard the social worker lady say that everything had already been shipped ahead. So if it only took a little girl a couple of days to get to Lubbock all the way from Michigan, then surely a whole post office full of grown-ups could find a way to get some boxes here in a few weeks. At first, Aunt Gwen said to give it time. Then one day, she was told that everything had been lost in the mail… and that was the end of it. She cried for days after… but Aunt Gwen seemed not to care.

She finally gave up thinking about the lost boxes to concentrate on what it meant to be a second grader in Texas. With only two days left before the start of school, she needed to stop thinking about what was behind, and start worrying about what was ahead. Of course, she had thought that she would be going to the elementary school a few blocks down the street from their house, but learned that Aunt Gwen had instead enrolled her in one near to the flower shop. Each school day would begin and end with a walk between Forde's Flowers and that school because Aunt Gwen was too busy for 'show-fur-ring'… a word that somehow meant being driven in a car. She was to work at the shop before and after school… which right off she knew meant no time for making friends in the neighborhood.

Aunt Gwen drove her to school on the first day of second grade for the purpose of getting things 'sorted out.' They arrived before the start, but went to the main office rather than her classroom. From there, they were taken to the school nurse, who seemed to be expecting them. Seated on a stool with wheels, this woman scooted right up to her before speaking with a kindly sort of softness in her voice… the tone she knew that an adult used so as not to frighten a little child.

"Have a seat here, dear. This should only take a minute. I understand that you have an allergy to bee stings."

She caught a flick of the woman's eyes upward to where she knew Aunt Gwen was standing behind her. That meant the two ladies had already talked about her.

"Yes, ma'am. I almost died when I was four."

"That must have been terrifying."

"I don't remember it."

"Well, we certainly don't want that to happen again, do we?" The nurse went on, not waiting for her to answer. "We want you to be safe while you're at school. To do that, we have some special medicine for you in case you're stung. I keep it here in this office. It's called epinephrine. Do you know what that is?"

She knew about that stuff. Her father told her that it had saved her life. Again, the nurse's eyes shot up to somewhere over her shoulder, and Aunt Gwen answered for her.

"It keeps her heart from stopping if she gets stung. It also keeps her air ways open."

"That's correct. Now... the thing is... by Texas State law, this drug can only be administered to children by a certified professional." The nurse's eyes were back down at her level. "Here's the situation, dear, I'm the only person at this school approved by the State. Do you understand what that means?"

"Yes, ma'am. If I get stung, I need to come to you."

"Correct... but there's more to it than that. You see, I have many other students to look after. As much as I'd like to, I can't be with you every minute of the day, so you'll need to be extra special careful to steer clear of situations where there may be wasps or bees." The woman paused again, looking up to Aunt Gwen before continuing. "I've talked this over with our principal... and he's confirmed it with the school district... as long as she's in our care, then she'll need to..."

The noise of many children scurrying about had been growing as the nurse spoke, but at that very moment, a loud ring filled the air.

"Pay that no mind, dear. It's just the first bell... the five minute one. You have plenty of time before the next bell rings. Now where was I? Oh, yes... I have what you need if you're stung, so you should stay near to me. What that means, Marna... I'm sorry, this is just the way it has to be... you'll not be allowed to ride a school bus... or go on field trips... or be on school grounds if I'm not here also. You understand what I'm saying, don't you? There'll be restrictions put in place for your safety."

She heard the woman... understood that she should respond... but her mind was on the voices out in the hall. Some were nearby... perhaps just outside the door. Would any of those voices understand why she had to be in here... or would they make fun of her for it?

"Marna, she's waiting."

"Yes, ma'am. I understand."

The woman nodded before turning back to Aunt Gwen. Her tone was again as one adult to another.

"Once she leaves the school grounds at the end of the day... or before the start... that's completely up to you. Have you decided on how..."

"She'll be walking to and from my flower shop. It's a short way, and she's a smart girl. She'll know how to avoid trouble."

"Good. Now, Marna... there's one other thing we need to discuss. Because your allergic response to stings is so severe, we need to take advantage of every precaution to keep you safe."

The sounds outside were already dying down. Any minute now, the second bell would ring... and she would be late for her first day of school.

"Yes, ma'am. I do that anyway. May I go now?"

The nurse smiled at her, refusing to understand how desperate she was not to be the last student into the classroom. The lady just went on speaking with Aunt Gwen about playground policies... and fire drills... and all kinds of situations where she might find herself outdoors. They kept jabbering away, ignoring that she still had no idea where her classroom was, or the name of her teacher, or how to find any of the things important for starting out well as a second grader.

"...and she should certainly continue to do that, but I'll check with the front office just to make sure." Not expecting it, the nurse patted her on the knee. "Dear... don't be concerned. You're not in this alone. I've alerted the school staff as to your condition so they know to rush you to this office without delay if you've been stung. Everyone from the principal to the school janitors wants to help. They're all so concerned for you. That should make you feel better, don't you think? You do want people to be able to help you if you're in need, don't you?"

"Yes, ma'am."

"I'm glad you see it that way, because I've instructed each teacher to inform their class that there's a student enrolled this year who is highly allergic to bee stings. You'll especially want your classmates... those in second grade... to be extra vigilant while they're on the playground with you, don't you?"

A tremor of fear ran through her nearly as bad as if a hive of bees had suddenly burst into the room. Even before anyone had met her, she would already be labeled as 'that girl who's allergic.' Nothing could have started out her new life here worse than this. She nodded... because she could no longer speak.

"I'm glad to see you agree again. I've arranged for Mrs. Taylor to speak directly to your class."

She shuttered again at the thought of everyone hearing about her weakness. She felt a hand to her shoulder, and took comfort in knowing that Aunt Gwen understood. But her aunt only wanted to wish her a 'fine first day of class'… and then she was gone.

Whenever it was that the final bell had rung, she completely missed it. The nurse led her out of the main office through empty halls. They passed many closed off doors, each with a teacher's name and a class grade. Some were quiet and others had much commotion going on within. The nurse came to a sudden stop outside a door labeled 'Second Grade,' it being terribly loud inside.

"You'll like Mrs. Taylor. She's an excellent teacher."

Without time to prepare herself, the nurse opened the door and nudged her inside. The activity of the class came to a stop, starting with the desks nearest her and then sweeping through the whole room. By the time the nurse had moved in behind her, the entire class was graveyard quiet. Twenty or so faces had turned her way with all the cheer of tombstones. Not one smiled. Not one waved. Not one could possibly understand how embarrassing their blank stares were to her. A good many of them were Mexican… a thing Aunt Gwen once said simply meant that they were Americans 'from down below'… but most were like her. None of that mattered. They were all looking at her as if she was a foreigner.

It seemed like forever before the teacher – Mrs. Taylor – made her way from the back corner to the front of the room. As the wave of silence reached the back, it bounced toward the front in whispers as the teacher passed through. She could see them all – girls leaning across aisles to whisper to other girls, and boys tapping a pal on the shoulder. It was so very obvious that they already knew all about her. Mrs. Taylor first spoke privately to the nurse. The nurse nodded once, smiled at her, and then was out the door. Everything in the class was totally still in waiting for the teacher to speak.

"Class, this is Marna Forde. She's recently moved here to live with her aunt. Please extend to her your best Texas welcome."

As unbearable as that introduction was, what followed seemed just as bad. The entire class gave her a 'Welcome, Marna' all at once… and then, it was finally over. Every kid went back to whatever they had been doing.

"Come, Marna… I have you up by me… that way I can help you get familiar with how we do things here. A complete set of your learners should be in the desk there. I see you have a knapsack with your school supplies?"

"Yes, ma'am. My aunt bought me everything I need."

Mrs. Taylor smiled and then moved to the front of the classroom. She tensed in dread, expecting more to be said about her… but the lady got right to the job of teaching without any mention of her. She could finally breathe out a sigh at being just another student with tasks to do.

Through the first hours as the classroom activity permitted, she was greeted by the kids sitting nearest her. They asked where she was from and why she had moved to Lubbock. To these questions, she had prepared the simple answer that she was from Michigan and that her parents had died in a car crash. This was received in much the way that all such news is taken in by kids – with coolness. They quickly shared their own stories of tragic deaths… a grandfather, a neighbor, and a parakeet… all now in Heaven.

Her first real opportunity for making friends came at morning recess. As instructed, the class began to line out into the hallway to where a different teacher was waiting at the head of another line of students. But she never made it out, being pulled aside at the door by Mrs. Taylor.

"Marna… one moment please."

Mrs. Taylor waited until the last child was gone.

"I need to hold you back from recess today. One of the janitors spotted a wasp's nest up under an eave this morning, but hasn't had a chance to get at it yet. He's going to check over the rest of the grounds after school. For now, I think it best if I keep you in. I'm not on playground duty this morning, so it'll be just us two."

Her teacher smiled in a way meant as a special treat, but she felt the opposite. She had been singled out because of her allergy.

"I'll be careful – I promise! I'll stay far from…"

"I'm sorry. It's just the way it has to be. The nurse informed me about your condition, and it's my responsibility to protect you. Chin up… you're not the only child in the class with health considerations."

But I'm the only one being held out of recess.

She watched the clock closely over the next twenty minutes, taking time out only to draw little pictures of bees with their eyes X'd out. She was far too angry to look at her teacher, who seemed very satisfied with the quiet. But the moment came that she had been dreading. In the reverse of that morning, she sat silently as the class filed back into the room. Face after face turned her way before making for their desks. For the remainder of that day, including lunch time taken in their classroom, no one spoke to her. She might as well have had cooties… or worse.

When the final bell rang, the madhouse of every child escaping the school left her as just one small second grader in a throng of older children. What she really longed for was someone to walk with… someone who could be a friend. Instead, in moving down busy halls and out of the building, what she got was being alone.

The walk to the flower shop was not so difficult. Aunt Gwen had put a map of Lubbock in her knapsack with the path to the shop highlighted... but she did not need it. In fact, she had her own route in mind... one that took her over the greatest number of railroad tracks. In short time, she had forgotten about the cares of being a stranger in a strange land, and was in wonder at watching a huge locomotive move a line of box cars along.

The second day of second grade started out much better than the first. Having done the early morning greenhouse circuit with Aunt Gwen, she walked from the shop to the school with plenty of time to spare. Entering her classroom, her worries from the previous day were gone. She was treated like any other second grader. Everything was perfect right up to recess. After a nervous glance toward Mrs. Taylor... and getting a smiling nod back... she happily marched down the corridor with all the other wiggling second graders anxious to reach the playground.

She knew... as most children do... that recess had rules that could not be taught. They had to be learned. As a newcomer to Texas, she did not dash out onto the playground to claim space on the swings or monkey bars. Instead, she fell back to watch. From the great number of kids out there, at least two other classes had to be sharing this recess time. With only a few minutes of hunting, she finally spotted what she was hoping to find – some girls from her own class. They were seated in the grass watching a larger group of boys playing a game of their own. Crossing over to these girls, she asked if she could sit with them, and was relieved when they said yes. What she had been attracted to was not so much the girls themselves, but the way they sat with their skirts spread out about them. That... and something that none of them would dare admit. They were playmates engaged in the game of watching boys play. Somehow, she found all that running-around that boys did to be interesting... but knew enough not to show it.

Texan boys were no more capable of noticing girls than those she had known in Michigan. The ones on the other side of this fence went about their game without knowing that they were being watched. Actually, they had not yet started playing because they were taking so long to choose up sides. In her opinion, the boys were putting more effort into arguing than in actually kicking their kickball. It made her and the girls snicker so.

Their game eventually got started... and she found that one boy in particular caught her interest. It was not his ability or cuteness... a word she was not yet ready to use out loud... but that he seemed very familiar to her. She watched him as he kicked the ball and ran the bases... and then as his team moved out onto the field. He was not in her class… that much she was certain of… but she had definitely seen him somewhere.

"That's Roy Meitner."

She had completely forgotten about the other three girls… who were now giggling at her.

"What?"

"The boy you keep staring at. That's Roy Meitner. He's in third grade."

"I wasn't staring at him. I was just…"

Whatever she was going to say never came out, as she and the other three girls were suddenly startled by the kickball crashing into the chain link fence right before them. Having jerked her head over, she saw that particular boy running to the fence. Though he scooped up the ball, his eyes were on her.

"Hi, Marna. Remember me?"

How he knew her name was something third in line behind why he was so familiar and what must the other girls be thinking. Of course, they were giggling again… while the boys on the field were shouting for this Roy to hurry it up. He just spun about and punted the ball onto the field… then turned back to her. Looking past him, she saw several boys scurry after the ball, whereas the greater number were yelling their irritation at this Roy. He just ignored them all.

"Bye, Marna…"

Again, she had forgotten about her classmates… who were up and making their way to the swings.

"Wait… I'll come too."

"Let 'em go. Who needs 'em anyway?!"

As if his question was answered in the asking, he started fidgeting about on the fence while still smiling at her. With fingers in the chain link, he leaned into it and pulled it back… over and over until she could stand it no more.

"What're you doing?"

"Nuttin."

He finally gave up that ridiculous activity… except to instead seek toeholds in the links for the purpose of climbing up to the cross bar… and then made a silly show out of flopping right back down.

Why doesn't he just go back to his game?!

"So… you like flowers?"

"Who doesn't?"

"Just askin'… 'cause your aunt sells really swell ones. Mom says so all the time. She goes there whenever…"

"You're the boy from the flower shop. The one in the cowboy suit…"

She was immediately lost in thought. She could hear him respond ("It's not a suit. Those things have ties. Cowboys don't wear ties."), but could not say a thing in return. Embarrassment had a hard grip on her, for she knew that he had heard her story. What she saw now was not a third grade boy standing behind a fence, but that comical cowboy face transfixed with horror at what she had been through. He had not seen into her memories… those things were still hers… but he had seen her face. Soon, every kid on this playground would know what he knew.

She was just about to decide to hate this boy when something making a buzzing sound bounced off her cheek, sending her falling backward in a panic to swat it away. As if from a long way off, she heard the chain link fence rattle… and then in a blur, a set of blue jeans bounded over her. Next thing she knew, this Roy was swinging his arms all about madly in a fight with some flying insect. She saw him make contact with the bug, and watched it spiral to the ground. He then quickly set about stomping on the thing as it skipped across the grass. After several failed attempts, he finally came to a stop. Slowly lifting one foot, he placed all of his weight on the heel of the other.

"Got him!" He then stooped over to inspect the site. "Not a bee. Probably just a stink bug."

"What do you think you're doing?! You nearly knocked me over!"

"I… I did? Sorry… I just…"

He turned away from her to twist his foot one last time into the spot before coming to face her.

"Sorry. My teacher said you're…"

She could not make out the rest due to his mumbling.

"She said what?!"

"That you're deathly 'lergic to… I mean… that you don't like bees."

"I don't see how that's any of her business… or yours for that matter. I can take care of myself."

"I know. Mom says you're probably the bravest girl she's ever heard tell of. Leastwise that's what I heard her say." He peered over his shoulder once more at the dead bug, and then came to sit down beside her. "I didn't mean to clobber you. Does it hurt?"

"No… it's okay. And… thanks for killing the bee. It's true… I don't like them."

He muttered again… something about a stink bug… when the playground suddenly filled with the sound of a loud horn blast. Her first thought – that recess was over – proved wrong owing to the odd direction in which kids began to run.

"Come quick, Marna!"

Without another word, Roy joined the herd hurrying to the back of the playground. There, a locomotive with its line of boxcars was pulling past the fence, not much more than a stone's throw beyond the schoolyard. She was not surprised at all to see what the boys had run there to do – that thing with the up and down motion of a clinched fist and bent arm, all meant to get a horn's blast from the engineer. Sure enough, a second blare much longer than the first sent the fence line crazy.

What happened next seemed odd to her. After the second blast ceased and the kids finished jumping about in cheering, most everyone returned to the playground… even though the greater part of the train was still passing by. Out of the corner of her eye, she could see the kickball game starting back up and kids dashing to claim spots on the swings. But she kept watching the train until the red caboose was well out of sight. Seeing that train move by so near was exciting… yet it also left her feeling sad and empty. It was just a bunch of beat-up box cars being pulled along by an oily-looking engine, but it was going someplace. Where to, she could not possibly say, only that it was moving… and she was not.

The end-of-recess bell rang. She, having not done this part before, waited until the other children had begun to form lines near the back entrance to the school. Being nearly the last child to leave the grounds, she passed by a set of swings still moving back and forth, each to its own pattern from when the kids had catapulted themselves out. Standing there for a moment, she watched in sadness as each swing, held in place with nowhere to go, slowly wore itself down to stillness. She then passed through to take up her place at the rear of the line.

At the end of her second day of second grade, something happened that changed her outlook on walking to Forde's Flowers after school. She left the front of the building, expecting to make the trip alone as on the previous day, but was greeted there by Roy Meitner.

"Can I walk with you?"

"Do you live that way…" She pointed off in the general direction she had gone the day before.

"I don't live anywhere near here. Dad put me in this school 'cause it's walkin' distance to his store downtown. I go there after to help out… and do my homework. Then he takes me home after work. He sells TVs. You got a TV?"

"No. My aunt doesn't like them."

"That's too bad 'cause my dad says they're 'Merica's future… or somethin' like that."

They walked on in an uncomfortable sort of quiet until she realized that this was a golden opportunity, and she should make the most of it.

"I'm heading to my aunt's flower shop."

"I know. I saw you walk there yesterday."

"You were following me?"

"No. I… ahh… just saw you."

She stared at him for long enough to conclude that he was okay after all, and then changed the subject to the thing she wanted to talk about.

"Does your father make you work after school… because my aunt makes me work. I don't mean just helping out. These aren't chores. She makes me do real work! Like the kind an adult's supposed to do. I don't think that's fair, do you? I mean… I'm just a second grader. Second graders are still kids, you know. Second graders shouldn't have to work. And second graders shouldn't have to go through terrible, horrible things like… work. And what do I know about flowers anyway? There just things growing in the ground. They don't even last that long after they've been cut."

"What if…"

"And I never get to play! Back home I had all kinds of neat toys and stuffed animals and fun books. I don't have any of that now. All of it's lost in the mail. That's what Aunt Gwen says. 'Lost in the mail.' She's not even bothering to look for my things because it's not important to her. Well… it's important to me!"

"Maybe if you could…"

"And she's always correcting me. *'Cut it this way, Marna, not that way.' 'Don't put that there – put this there.'* How am I supposed to know all that kind of stuff?! Ever been in the back of her shop? I can tell you it's no fun! She's got these… these… huge ice box things for keeping her flowers from wilting fast. They make the whole place feel like winter. I can barely stand being… Hey… do you get snow here?"

"Sometimes. Once it covered…"

"We got gobs and gobs of it in Michigan. Big flakes the size of a nickel. Or sometimes the teeny-tiny ones where you can see all the little parts as small as hairs. That's where I'm from… Michigan. It's way up north. Last winter, we had snow on the ground from Thanksgiving all the way into spring. We'd sled, and build snow forts, and make snowmen all the time. Me and my father once…"

She stopped at the memory of how her father would drop whatever he was doing to come outside with her into the new fallen snow.

"What?"

"Nothing. I don't want to talk about snow anymore."

All of a sudden, she was upset with herself. She was being foolish in talking so much. None of it was really about her aunt... or being made to work... or anything to do with second grade. She simply missed her parents and wanted someone to know that. She wanted someone to understand her loneliness, the guilt she had for being the one who survived, and how bad her memories made her feel all of the time. She had such terrible anger for everyone and everything because it was so unfair that her parents had died. She wanted someone to tell her that it was not wrong for her to feel those things... and that she was normal... and not sick in the head. Most of all, she just wanted to have someone who understood how terribly homesick she was, and that no place... not even a place supposedly as great as Texas... could ever make her feel any better. She was alone, and would probably be that way for the rest of her life. But being open enough to share such things with him was a price too high to pay... especially since he already knew far more about her than she cared for anyone to know.

"Come on, Marna... let's go this way. I wanna show you something really neat."

Aunt Gwen told her that the distance from her elementary school to Forde's Flowers was a little over a half mile if she walked along a direct pathway down Avenue P, across the tracks, and then west on 4th Street. That day, as with many to come, she followed Roy as he turned east toward the railyards. She went along gladly, not in the least bit nervous about where he was leading her or how late it would make her in getting to the shop.

In the days to come, it became their habit to sit there along the tracks... perhaps for fifteen minutes or so... until a train might pass by. They would then guess what it might be carrying and where it might be going. The whole time, they talked about those things only kids knew how to say to other kids. In this first visit, she was surprised to discover that he seemed to know exactly what she needed – to see something in motion progressing with great speed and power straight out of Lubbock.

That whole school year, Roy Meitner was her friend. Though not quite a best friend, he was, in her mind, nearly as important to her as that piece of stonework hanging on Aunt Gwen's living room wall.

CHAPTER

6

CESSNA 172

Perhaps more so than most of her classmates, she considered fifth grade to be a move from childhood toward something more significant in life. Part of this belief came from all the time she spent working rather than playing. Work simply made her more serious than the average kid. Having turned ten prior to the start of the school year, she also felt that her age being in double digits was proof of a change. To be sure, she was already beginning to view herself in terms of those things that she suspected might define a teenager's self-worth – looks, popularity, abilities, and friendships. In actuality, she understood that three things made her out to be a different sort of ten year old.

The first, and most obvious, was that she would never be a Texan. Even though everything she had once loved about Michigan – the four seasons, the forests, the sense of living in an interesting place – was slowly vanishing from memory, Texas could never fill up the holes. She did not speak as other children, nor did she think much like them. Her classmates through second to fourth grade had all accepted her. She still sometimes wondered if they secretly thought of her as a Yankee in great need of Texan sympathy… a foreigner unclaimed by Texas or anyone else who could possibly love her as their own. Anyway… three years of living in Texas had not changed her opinion. Lubbock was nothing but a flat and dusty city landlocked by cotton fields that went on for as far as she could see. The place would never be her home.

Second, she was cared for by an aunt and not by a mother or father. The boxes sent from Michigan had contained the only things from her past life, but since those were lost, she had eventually given up on the concept of family. She still openly referred to her aunt as 'Aunt Gwen,' but no longer used that title in her thinking. Perhaps that was a disrespectful attitude for a child, but she did not think such a restriction should apply to her private world of thought. Gwen was her guardian, and nothing more. Still… she was very thankful to Gwen for so many things. She had a room of her own to fix up as she saw fit. Gwen fed her well, let her pick out her own clothes for school, and was not cruel in speech or discipline. In all the time since coming to Lubbock, Gwen had cared for her every need. But in making her work at the flower shop, her aunt had also defined her in an unexpected way. She had come to believe that she was more involved in Gwen's life than Gwen was in hers. That unfortunately led to a separation between them… a gap that could not be bridged by something so simple as having the same last name. Maybe that feeling was to be expected. After all, Gwen had a life of her own before she was called upon to share it. The woman could never be a mother to her.

She's called 'aunt' for a reason.

Still… it did odd things to her thinking in being regularly faced with the fact that she was the only child she knew of without parents. She simply could not help but believe that she did not belong to anyone or anything.

Not being Texan and not being daughter together contributed to a third way of thinking about herself. At ten, she could not express it in words, but definitely felt an ache within her to become something grand… as only something grand could possibly remove the aches of not knowing who she was and what she was to become. Her longing to be someone special had formed into a 'forward' way of thinking… which went well with her reluctance to dwell on the past. The present day existed only as a hopeful foundation upon which to build her future. The relief was a strong influence in this thinking, for she was determined not to end up like one of those faces stuck in stone. She would make herself look upward to the open sky above… where the birds flew.

Whatever she grew up to become, it would definitely not be a florist. She had absolutely no interest in arranging flowers… much less in dilly-dallying with bows or ribbons. She was no good at it anyway. Unless Gwen or Patsy stood by giving her instructions, she could not help herself – she was the flower's worst enemy. About the only work in the shop she seemed suited for was sweeping floors, scrubbing out the endless number of dirty buckets and vases, and cleaning glass. Twice a week, she would take squeegee and sponge to the film of West Texas dust that had collected on the outside of the shop's two huge storefront windows. For all such work before and after school… and on Saturdays… Gwen paid her five dollars a week. Most of that went into a savings account Gwen set up for her. Being paid to work at Forde's Flowers… and putting the money away… secured in her a feeling that the future belong to her… and she would be ready for it.

The future that became fifth grade was not altogether as pleasant as she had expected when the school year began. The sister that Roy had occasionally spoken of last year as being 'kept at home' for first grade… which was code that meant something weird about the kid… entered second grade that year. Sybil Meitner was a wiry little girl whose hair always seemed to be tangled-up in dark wads. Not at all as well kept up as her mother. From the very first day of school, she found this girl's presence to be annoying on several counts… the most obvious being that she no longer had Roy to herself after school. As the younger sister, Sybil clung to her big brother throughout the walks, most often clutching a hand on the same side of Roy in which she was standing. It never failed – if she switched sides, then so did Sybil. That would have been bearable had the girl any personality at all. Unlike her mother, who was a well-turned out woman… or Roy, who was tolerable as a boy… this little girl was so annoying. No amount of coaxing could ever get a nice word out of Sybil. Roy was no help.

"She's just shy. That's why Mom and Dad had her out of school last year. Don't worry, she'll come out of her shell. You'll see."

He might live with her… but Roy had no clue about his sister. Sybil was nothing but a bratty little girl that made the walks after school so miserable. She absolutely refused to go anywhere near railroad tracks… even made Roy carry her over them. Sybil complained like crazy all the time… especially if they changed the route in even the smallest of ways. And she was so terribly slow! Worse, she was such a scaredy-cat about everything… cars, dogs and even the wind. Sybil's whining got really bad on those winter days when it was cold and stormy… so much so that she just left the two of them behind and made her own way to the flower shop.

Fortunately, Sybil was not always there after school. Mrs. Meitner often picked the girl up directly, which meant that she had Roy to herself, just like before. On those days, they got to do the kinds of things that they enjoyed… walking to the railyard, visiting Yellow House Canyon after a rain, or just talking together without interruption. Being with him was always fun.

Of course, Gwen still worked her every day after school. That would never change. Even during summer breaks when other kids were goofing off, she still had to sweep floors at the flower shop. Her aunt just had this way of making her way be 'the' way. Her aunt dragged her out on all kinds of trips to places like Amarillo, Midland, Wichita Falls, and a whole bunch of smaller towns that she could not keep track of. Driving in West Texas was so boring. She did get to go to Fort Worth a couple times. That was neat. And once they went all the way to Austin for a floral conference. But she could never persuade Gwen to leave her home alone.

That's because she wants me along to do things for her... and turn me into a florist!

She was careful to keep her feelings to herself and do whatever Gwen said. It was always smart to stay on her aunt's good side. By doing that, she found that things were improving now that she was in fifth grade. Gwen finally gave her some time to hang out with her friends. Friday afternoons were hers as long as nothing like high school homecoming, a big wedding or some other special event got in the way. For the most part, she had Friday afternoons free, and started those by walking with Roy from school directly to his father's store. To her surprise, she discovered that he also had worked at the family business… sweeping floors, just like her. She also came to know his father a bit better. The man actually had two businesses – selling TVs and what Roy called being the 'master of cable.'

Whatever that's supposed to mean...

Mr. Meitner tried explaining it to her once. Towers… and wires… and getting invisible signals from one place to the next… it all sounded so terribly confusing. The only thing that really interested her about TV was the funny way in which a whole wall of them in the appliance store could be made to show the same program at the same time.

On an afternoon toward the end of April, with her homework done and a broom in her hands, she was thinking about the summer to come when Gwen called to her from the front of the shop.

"Marna… you've got a visitor."

Pushing through the curtain, she found Gwen staring over the counter at Roy's mother.

"Mrs. Meitner has something for you."

"Hello, Marna. Roy couldn't be here to deliver this himself… I'm afraid he's a bit behind on his chores. But as I was coming by to see your aunt anyway…"

She followed Mrs. Meitner's eyes over to her aunt. Maybe it was just Gwen's mood, but there was something not right between the two women… a sort of chill her aunt seldom showed toward a loyal customer.

"By the way, Gwen… any of those tulips left?"

"All out."

"That's a pity. Well… here it is, dear."

Mrs. Meitner handed an envelope across the counter. After a quick look to her aunt that was not returned, she accepted the envelope without wanting to open it in front of the two women. Printed big and bold across the front was her name, each letter with a different colored crayon.

"What do you say to Mrs. Meitner?"

"Oh… sorry. Thank you, ma'am."

"Well… go on and open it so Mrs. Meitner can see you at it."

She caught a little smile on Mrs. Meitner's face… one sort of like the kind Gwen sometimes gave when she thought someone's uncomfortable situation was funny, but had the polite sense for keeping it to herself.

Sticking a finger into a corner gap, she ripped open the flap and pulled out an index card. Roy had drawn small bits of artwork along its edges – some balloons, a cake with candles, a couple of footballs, and a stick-figured man hanging from a parachute. Across the top was a plane pulling a banner on which something was written, but she could not make out the words. In the middle of the card was neat cursive… probably his mother's… giving a date, a time and an address.

"It's for Roy's birthday party!"

The thrill she felt instantly melted away on seeing the sour look coming to Gwen's face.

"Can I go?"

Gwen just stood there staring stone-faced back at Mrs. Meitner. This made no sense. These two women had always been on the best of terms as customer and store owner. Something unspoken was definitely hanging there between them.

"Gwen… it's only natural. They see each other nearly every day at school. They're friends. Besides… it's just a birthday party. Surely you wouldn't allow the past to…"

"Fine! She'll be there. I'd never deny my niece such a thing anyway."

Both women said their goodbyes and turned away… Gwen to the backroom and Mrs. Meitner to the shop door… but she remained at the counter staring down at her invitation. Maybe Gwen disapproved of Roy. Maybe it was because he was a boy… and a year older than her. Or maybe Gwen simply did not want to spare her from work.

She returned to the cutting room. Gwen was not there. The office door was closed… which meant that her aunt wanted to be left alone. She knocked anyway… because she needed to know… and entered only after being told she could.

"Excuse me, ma'am… sorry to bother you. I'm starting in on work now… but I was just wondering… is… umm… something wrong between you and Mrs. Meitner?"

"It's nothing. Don't trouble yourself."

"Maybe I shouldn't go to the party if it's…"

"Of course you can go… as long as I've got you all day Sunday. Mother's Day is coming up… as well as commencement at Tech. Lots to get ready for."

She already knew all of this. The week had been circled on the shop calendar long ago.

"Yes, ma'am. Definitely. And thanks for letting me go…"

"Tell you what… let's close up early, get something at that burger joint you're always going on about, and then we'll head over to Woolworth's for a present… and maybe a new party dress."

That was so much more than what she had expected. She thanked her aunt again and quickly left for the cutting room. With broom in hand, her thoughts somehow skipped over anticipation of the party to that odd expression on Gwen's face when she first entered the office. Her aunt seemed… embarrassed… with something else added on. Something distant… and maybe a bit sad.

The next day at school, she was waiting for Roy in the hall outside his sixth grade class before the first bell rang in order to thank him for the invitation.

"Keep it quiet, will ya! Dad's only allowed me to invite five kids, and I don't want it to get around to anyone else." After quickly looking about, he leaned in close with a sneaky little smile on his face. "Boy, have I got a surprise for you. Can't tell you anything now… so don't bother askin'… but this is gonna be the best birthday party you've ever been to. I guarantee it!"

Come Saturday morning, she was pacing about the flower shop, itching to get to Roy's party… even though it was still several hours off. She could not possibly help it – her new outfit was simply too cute. So it was impossible not to admire how good she looked in it… nor keep herself from fiddling with things in order to look even better. Patsy liked the outfit too… though Gwen just kept rolling her eyes.

Finally, it was time to leave. She got out to the car first… and sat there forever fighting the urge to honk the horn so Gwen would hurry it up. With Roy's present in her lap, they drove from the flower shop without her much paying attention to where they were heading. Naturally assuming that Roy's house was in a neighborhood like hers, she busied herself instead with asking Gwen questions about what went on at birthday parties. But as the last of the grain silos gave way to wide-open farmland, she got an uneasy feeling that maybe Gwen did not know where she was going. They passed farmhouse after farmhouse... none of which looked like the kind of place where the owner of an appliance store might live. Now convinced that they were lost, she was surprised when Gwen pulled into a gravel drive just past a metal-framed tower... one of those so tall that it required many wires to hold it up. She had seen plenty of such structures before. They had something to do with radio signals... or maybe TV... but she was not really sure which. Pulling her eyes from the tower, she noticed that they had entered a long driveway lined on both sides with newly planted trees. They all had those sticks and ropes to support them against the wind. Far ahead was a house that looked sort of like...

"Damn fool."

Being startled, she quickly turned to Gwen... whose eyes were on the side mirror. So she twisted about for another look at the tower, trying to figure out what she had missed.

"Where's the fool?"

"Never you mind. That's their house up ahead."

Even from a distance down the long driveway, she could see that the Meitner house was unlike any other she had come across in Lubbock. Painted in a bright white with a bluish-gray roof, the house was really huge. With two stories she could see, the front corners rose up even higher... just like steeples on a church. The whole thing seemed boosted off the ground... sort of like a castle on a hill... except she knew that everything in West Texas was as flat as a board. But as they got closer, she recognized a set of steps leading up to the front and realized that the house was, in fact, lifted up off the ground. Its porch seemed to wrap around on both sides toward the back. Between the porch pillars was very complicated woodworking... sort of like those things that vines grow all over in a fancy garden. More of the same was above each window.

As interesting as this house was to look at, she was struck with a funny feeling that it was doing its own share of looking... right down the long driveway at her. Not so much that the front had the appearance of a make-believe face, but that the barren farmland all about made this house seem lonely... and maybe it was looking for a friend. That was fine with her... because this house was one of the most beautiful things she had ever seen.

The driveway ended in a big circle with a flagpole in its center. As Gwen pulled the car halfway around, stopping right in front of the porch steps, she noticed another building off to the side. If the house was beautiful, then this gigantic thing was a monster. If it had ever been painted, its color had somehow become a blotchy mess of bare metal and worn-out wood framing.

The oddest thing about it was that its roof was not flat. It curved down to the ground on both sides… sort of like the whole thing was a big tube that had been buried on its side halfway into the dirt. Actually… the strangest thing about the building was not its roof, but its front door… if it could be called as such. It was absolutely humongous! Big enough for Gwen's whole house to fit through. Off to one side within was a normal door… though in comparison it seemed more suitable for a mouse rather than a person. Of course, she knew what this huge building was for… but could not understand what it was doing here.

"Aunt Gwen… do the Meitner's own an airplane?"

Her aunt, studying this structure too, unexpectedly broke into a laugh… and not at all a funny one.

"Damn fool doesn't even know how to fly."

"Who doesn't know how to fly?"

"Never you mind. Let me have a look at you. Straighten your hat a bit… Good. Now you be on your best behavior. Make sure it's sir and ma'am all the time, you understand me?"

"Yes, ma'am."

"And don't get your dress soiled or stained with cake."

"Yes, ma'am. But who's the… darn fool?"

"Like I said – never you mind. Now go on… get going."

"Aren't you coming to the door with me?"

Gwen's eyes shot up past her to the front porch.

"I expect you can handle that on your own."

She left the car confused, but climbed the porch steps anyway and rang the doorbell. She was greeted by Mr. Meitner. On finding her alone, he frowned over the top of her toward Gwen's car as it was heading down the driveway… and then came back down with a warm smile.

"Marna… so good to see you. Come in."

"Yes, sir."

She had grown to like Roy's father a lot. He had a much more kinder manner than his wife, who always had a way of getting exactly what she wanted out of Patsy.

Maybe not so much out of Gwen… They're so alike.

He moved off down the hall to give room at the door for Roy's mother.

"Marna! What a beautiful sailor dress… and with bonnet and gloves to match. Don't you look lovely! Did you pick this out just for Roy's party?"

"Yes, ma'am… I thought it sort of went with my eyes."

"That it does! Now don't just stand there, dear… come in!"

Her first impression of the inside of the Meitner house was not as favorable as that of the outside. She stepped into a narrow hallway with paneled doors to her left and right, both closed off.

It's so dark in here… and kind of… woody.

What hit her next was a faint smell… like dust getting burned on a radiator when it was turned on for the first time in winter. The feel of it tickled at her nose… and somehow gave a tingly sort of taste to her mouth… almost like she had licked a rusty nail.

"Let's put that sweater of yours in the closet here… I don't think you'll be needing it. Should be quite warm all day."

She handed over her sweater and her hat… as Mrs. Meitner opened a hallway door. She caught a glimpse of the usual things within – coats, boots and what looked like the underside of some stairs. Looking down the hall, she noted the beginning of a staircase running up to the second floor. But at that moment, Roy burst through a door at the very end… with three boys following behind. All of them were familiar to her from school, though none were in her grade.

"Maaar-naaaa! You came!"

Running full out at her, he jumped the last bit, landing on both feet right in front of her. His delight was a bit overwhelming… especially in front of his mother. Those boys clearly did not share his enthusiasm. The worst was Roy's best friend, Christopher Pritchett… or 'CP,' as most nearly everyone at school called him. Bucktoothed and highly freckled, this boy was nothing more than a playground bully.

"Shee-it, Roy! Why'd you have to go an' invite a girl?!"

"CP! A civil tongue in your mouth… or I shall certainly call 'round to your mother."

CP bowed his head and moved behind Mrs. Meitner… but then immediately lifted his face in a scowl.

"Marna is more than welcome at Roy's party."

Roy had been staring at her the whole time… completely unaware of his friend's crummy attitude.

"Come on, Marna!" To her shock, he took hold of her hand… and then dropped it just as quick. "We're in back."

Without another word, he snatched the birthday present from her other hand and ran down the hall, the boys trailing behind. But she remained in the same spot, suddenly unsure that coming was such a good idea.

"Mrs. Meitner… am I the only girl?"

"Yes, dear… it would seem so. We're still waiting on another boy."

"Where's Sybil?"

"Oh… I expect you won't be seeing her today." The woman looked to the stairs for a second before continuing. "She's up in her room and won't come down until the party's over… not even for cake. Dear… please don't worry about being the only girl. One of us is worth a half dozen of them. Funny… they never seem to figure that out, do they? Well… we'll just have to go on humoring them then, won't we?"

Mrs. Meitner gave her a wink and then motioned to the door at the end of the hall where the boys had disappeared. Beyond was the kitchen. Before she could take a step in that direction, out again came Roy on a run.

"Quick, Marna – we're playing hide-and-go-seek. CP's it. Outside's out-of-bounds."

He tore past her and through one of the paneled doors near the front, slamming it shut behind him. There was only one place she had seen thus far in this house, and it seemed good enough.

"Mrs. Meitner… can I hide in that closet?"

"By all means, dear… and may the best woman win."

Another wink, and Mrs. Meitner left for the kitchen.

On closing the closet door behind her, she immediately had second thoughts about this as a hiding place. The inside was terribly cramped and smelled like moth balls. Worse… it was really hot. She had just decided to find a new spot when the door suddenly opened.

"Ha! Got you!"

CP then slammed it back on her… which was really rude! But being caught was not so bad. It meant that she could get out of this stuffy closet. Turning the knob, she was surprised when the door did not move. The reason soon became obvious.

"Very funny, CP."

"Hellooo? Anybody in there?"

"Stop it, CP!"

"I caaaan't heeeeear youuuuuuu…"

She pushed on the door and turned the knob with all her strength… only to have it come off in her hand. Full of anger… and a sudden fear that Roy's parents would be mad at her for breaking their door… she screamed with all her might.

"OPEN THIS DOOR!"

She was trying to put the knob back on… but her panic in the dark was making it impossible. CP's voice came back in a sing-song tease.

"Oh, help me, help me, please. I can't get out. I'm gonna cry."

"I'm telling your mother!"

"You'll have to get out first, Crybaby! But I 'spect you'll be done in from fix-e-ation before then. Ain't nobody coming for you. They're all hidin'. You'll probably be dead a whole week before anybody finds your corpse."

"I'm going to scream again!"

"Oh, I wouldn't do that if I were you. Fastest way to use up ox'gen. And you don't got much left."

"You're a liar! I can see light coming in under the door. I know air's getting in that way."

Suddenly, it got real quiet.

"CP?! You come back right this second and open the door!"

She listened, but heard nothing.

"Hello, anybody?! Help… I'm stuck in…"

All at once, the light under the door went completely out… and she heard again that annoying snigger of his.

"Thanks, Marna. Got that covered up now with a floor mat. Just relax… You prob'ly only got… two minutes left. What you want on your tombstone? How about 'Here lies Marna Forde. She died in a closet.' That's perfect."

With all she had, she screamed her lungs out while also pounding on the door. But all that effort was making her head spin. Any second now, she was going to pass out from...

The door suddenly opened, and out she fell onto Roy.

"What's going on?"

"WHAT'S GOING ON?!"

She thrust the door knob into his stomach.

"I hate your friends! And I hate this house! I want to go home – now!"

Without caring to hear anything from him, she pushed past out the front door.

Maybe it was the fresh air or the bright sunshine of that afternoon in May… but something made her stop on the porch steps. She was beside herself in crying, and more so angry, but somehow knew that leaving the party early was impossible. Someone would have to phone Gwen… and she would want to know how it was that a boy had gotten the better of her niece. That thought immediately calmed her down. She would not go back into the house… no matter what… but was just as determined to stick it out at the party. So she wiped her eyes and fell into a porch chair.

In a matter of minutes, both Mr. and Mrs. Meitner were there to comfort her. Even with their encouragement… and a scolding that made CP apologize…

she still refused to go back inside. Despite the disappointment on Roy's face, she was determined to wait there until whenever Gwen showed up. CP was reason enough. The boy was far too sneaky, giving off a teary-eyed acting job in his apology… and then smirking at her once the adults had turned their backs.

To her surprise, the Meitners moved the party to the front porch. She told herself that this was only done for Roy's sake, but the kind looks on their faces said otherwise. So she ate cake with Mr. Meitner sitting close by as the five boys played pin-the-tail-on-the-donkey on the other side of the porch. Roy glanced over at her from time to time. His cheerful smile slowly took her anger and turned it into shame for having allowed an idiot like CP to bug her. More than anything, it was Roy's delight over her gift of a yoyo that changed everything for her. He was her friend, and she was his too.

"Okay, Gang, cake eaten and presents unwrapped – it's now time for the big surprise! Everyone pile into the truck. The faster we get going, the faster we get there."

This was the first she had heard that part of the party would be held somewhere else. The boys all bolted down the porch steps, screaming for dibs on spots in the truck bed. No way would she sit back there… CP or no CP. So she inched up to Mr. Meitner and whispered so only he could hear.

"Sir… can I ride up front with you?"

"Of course. I was going to suggest it."

"Thank you. So… where're we going?"

"To the Lubbock airport. We've planned quite a treat, Marna. Ever been up in an airplane?"

"No, sir. You mean me… flying?!"

"There's nothing to be worried about. Folks do it all the time."

She was not afraid… nor did she think it such a crazy thing for some machine to carry people into the sky. She just never gave thought to her being one of those people.

"Yes, sir… I think I'd like that."

Which hardly at all expressed how eager she had suddenly become. To be up in a plane… that would be super neat! He smiled at her… almost as if he knew what she was thinking.

The five boys were already carrying on in the back of the truck. A couple of them were hanging over the side as if they were in a sinking raft. Mr. Meitner walked her to the passenger door and opened it for her. As she was climbing in, she heard Roy call her name. Through the rear window, she found him kneeling beside one of the wheel wells as if he had been saving that place for her. Their eyes met and she turned away with a smile… for he had just shoved CP to the truck bed for trying to pounce on the spot. She chanced one more look back as Mr. Meitner came around… and CP stuck his tongue out at her. His nasty gesture, along with the seating arrangement, made things so uncomfortably clear to her. They were boys and she was a girl… and maybe this flying thing was meant more for them.

As he drove out, Mr. Meitner began telling her about the planes he had seen during the war. His were not the kind of stories that she knew boys preferred – ones about dog fights, dropping bombs, and machine-gunning the enemy. Instead, he spoke about watching pilots gliding their planes around clouds… about the noises that engines made… about his experiences riding in different kinds of planes… and the thrill of chasing the horizon's setting sun. From his voice, she sensed that there must be something special about flying… maybe something far greater than a feeling… something that the bird's in the relief knew all about.

"Marna, there's nothing in this world like being up there. You'll see. You'll love it. After all… it's in your blood."

She had no idea what he meant by that, though grown-ups usually said all sorts of weird things expecting kids to know exactly what they were talking about. Perhaps it was one of those Texas things, since everything was supposedly bigger and better in this state.

But I'm not Texan.

They were near the airport when he started pointing out its features – the tower, the runways, parked planes… and a whole bunch of buildings he called 'hangers.'

"You don't mean those things in a closet for hanging up clothes, do you?!"

"Sounds the same… but this has two 'a's in it… h-a-n-g-a-r."

She was just about to ask him why he had a 'hangar' at his house… when they came to a stop before one such building. She felt the truck pitch about as the boys in back threw themselves over the sides, whooping it up as only boys could do. The spell was suddenly broken. Once again, she was aware of being the only girl. Out her window, she saw them goofing off in a tangle of arms and legs. She got out cautiously, hoping to go unnoticed. But Roy immediately broke away, running to her with his arms stretched out as if he was flying.

"Marna! We're going up in an airplane!"

His smile made her smile, for he seemed as excited for her as he was for himself. This did not go unnoticed by the boys.

"Ha! Not her! She'll wet her panties!"

CP, in an imitation of a crying baby, began wagging about like one of those 'metro-no-me' things that her teacher had shown the class during music lessons. He soon had the others piping in with their own girly screams, each boy coming so near to deliver their insults. But only one hurtful taunt actually put her on the verge of tears.

"Watch – she'll get up there and start crying for her mommy… if she had one!"

"Knock it off, CP, or I'll knock your block off!"

Roy stepped in front… which only made her situation worse. The boys immediately started chanting that stupid 'Roy and Marna sitting in a tree' thing… which thankfully never got very far because Mr. Meitner was calling everybody over. He was standing just inside the hangar with another man. As one, the four boys dashed away, with Roy staying long enough to throw her a 'don't pay attention to those idiots' frown before following. No longer feeling part of the party, she walked over slowly, stopping far enough behind the group of boys so as not to be their target again.

"Gang… this is Mr. Butch Carlyle. He's an old Marine buddy of mine from way back." With the word 'Marine,' the boys oddly straightened up into a line before the two men. "He'll be taking you up for a short flight, but first… he's going to cover some safety information. I'll tell you plainly – no one will be going up if he's not convinced that you've taken him seriously."

She nodded her obedience along with everyone else as Mr. Carlyle went through his rules. No horseplay… no undoing the harnesses… no messing with the plane's controls… no causing trouble of any kind… and always following his instructions. These were all things that she would be very good at… and the boys would not. So maybe flying was actually for girls after all. But she did not miss that the man's eyes moved back and forth along the line of boys without including her.

"Okay… we'll be going up in a Cessna 172." He pointed a thumb back over his shoulder toward a white-colored plane with a red stripe running along its side. "It's nicknamed the Skyhawk. This plane's brand new. Just released this year…"

As each boy craned about for a better look at the plane, Mr. Carlyle lifted his chin ever so slightly to wink her way. She was not forgotten.

Everyone then moved around the plane as Mr. Carlyle named off its parts and answered questions. She had her share, but did not ask any. It was stupid, but she still felt out of place. One of the boys wanted to know what kept a plane from falling out of the sky… which started an argument over engines and rockets.

"You boys aren't quite getting there. You're missing something. Any ideas?"

Before she knew what she was doing, she blurted out the first thing coming to her mind.

"Air pressure under the wings."

Each boy turned her way, some with mouth wide open and some with clinched jaw. But Mr. Carlyle had a great big smile on his face.

"That's absolutely correct, missy. What's your name?"

"Marna."

"Well, Marna, how would you say that works?"

"It's sort of like a bird's. The wings..."

"Jeez, Marna.... even a baby knows that a plane don't flap its wings."

She tried to ignore CP, but felt less sure of herself in continuing.

"I was thinking... it's because... of how they're shaped. Sort of like a bird's. Air kind of... moves around them in... and... umm..."

The feeling suddenly came over her of being called on in class and finding that her answer was falling short of what was expected. Though she had watched the wings of many a bird as it glided upon the wind, she was having a hard time finding the words to describe it. Each boy... Roy included... was staring at her. So... she held up a hand, slightly cupped with palm down, and tried to think of it as a bird's wing. With a finger, she pointed up under her model.

"Air does this... this thing... as it moves around the wing. It kind of... pushes up."

"That's exactly right! In aerodynamics, we call that 'lift.' Along with 'thrust,' 'drag' and 'weight,' it's one of the four fundamental forces acting upon a plane."

The warmth of knowing something unique completely filled her. This was more than the simple pleasure of being correct. Her terrible feeling from before... of being weak... was gone. For the first time that afternoon, she felt like a person rather than a girl. But the special moment was short-lived. As Mr. Carlyle opened the plane's cabin door to explain its controls, the boys... being more aggressive and benefited by number... pushed their way to the front, forcing her to the rear. Fortunately, it was soon time to move the plane out of the hangar. But to her disappointment, Mr. Carlyle pulled a folding chair up outside the hangar door and asked her to sit there. So she watched in envy as the five boys and the two men used their muscles to push the plane outside. Looking down at her hands folded over the skirt of her dress, she had thought hours before that this outfit was so cute. Now, she felt cursed by it... and something else vaguely beyond her control.

Being the birthday boy, Roy would go up first and be given the second seat beside the pilot while two others sat behind. To her surprise, he chose her as one of those to be with him on his flight... but Mr. Carlyle said it might be best if she stayed on the ground for now. Let her see what the plane did first, and then decide if it was something that she actually wanted to do. Every boy except Roy thought this such a smart plan. Girls, they said, should not be so quick to do things meant for a boy. So she went back to her chair, not wanting to take part in Mr. Carlyle walking about the plane with the five boys following him like a litter of puppies. She had that terrible sense again of being considered as worthless… and not even more of Mr. Meitner's encouragement made her feel any better. She could only watch as CP and another boy climbed into the plane with Roy. The two boys not on this flight came over, and Mr. Meitner began talking with them. She was left alone to stew in her misery.

But then something truly wonderful happened. The plane's engine came on with a sputter, wound up and down in pitch, and then settled into a beautifully sounding rumble. It was the most put-together sound she had ever heard in all her life. Sort of like… laughing, sighing, humming, and breathing deeply all combined into one. The propeller was spinning so fast that it became like a glass plate hanging out there on the front of the plane. As it crept out toward the runway, she could almost sense the plane's desire for getting up there. It sat in place for a time… and then finally it headed out onto the runway. She had no idea how a plane's wings actually worked, but as it picked up speed, she imagined that many little fingers of air were poking up from underneath… lifting it from off the ground. She followed as it rose, veered away, and faded into the distance.

The whole time it was gone, she sat quietly as Mr. Meitner and the two other boys talked. Unlike them, she was scanning the skies for the plane… but also doing a lot of thinking. Gwen would certainly be disappointed if she heard that her niece had allowed a bunch of silly boys to get in the way of such an opportunity. No sailor outfit would have held her aunt back. So she would do it!

She was the first to spot the plane returning and jumped to her feet in pointing out that tiny dot above the horizon. The boys did not believe her at first… but eventually they saw it too. Mr. Meitner said she must have 'fighter pilot eyes'… which really made the boys jealous!

When it finally landed and rolled up to them, the three boys inside came out howling it up… but also a bit wobbly in her opinion. They clearly had enjoyed themselves. So… she would not hang back by the hangar waiting to be called. She would get right up there at wingtip with the other two boys. As she was heading to the plane, she felt a gentle nudge at her back and looked up to see Mr. Meitner smiling.

"Your turn. Let's go."

For reasons she did not stop to understand, it just felt natural to hold his hand as they walked out to the plane together. There, the other two of her group were already arguing over who would get to sit by the pilot.

"Boys. Boys. Where're your manners? Don't you think the young lady should get second seat?"

They obviously did not… and neither did CP or the other boy. All four insisted that a girl's place was in the back of the plane. Roy settled the issue.

"It's my birthday, so I get to decide. Marna gets the front seat." He then leaned in close so only she could hear. "You're gonna love it – you'll see."

He was the one to help her inside after the other two boys had squeezed in behind. Suddenly feeling very small, she found herself sinking into the plane's seat, yet wanting so much instead to sit up tall like an adult. She also had an awkward moment of needing to tuck her skirt under her… and then one of the boys in back tugged on a lock of her hair. Fortunately, their harnesses went on, keeping that from happening again.

From the moment she was strapped in with a headset in place, she felt like a different person. Every dial and every indicator before her was a fascination. Mr. Carlyle finally started the plane. She knew the engine was up front… just like in a car… but the power shook her as if it was coming from everywhere. Everything she could touch vibrated with excitement. A voice in her ears made her aware of the headphones again. It was Mr. Carlyle, speaking over what he called the plane's 'com system.' His words sort of quivered in the same way that the plane did… but she payed close attention as he read through a checklist out loud, focusing on every word with longing to know what it all meant.

The plane was finally out onto the runway, and she waited with anticipation for it to tear into the sky. She could see very little over the instrument panel, so she kept her eyes to the clouds, concentrating on the feel of going faster than she had ever been before. Remarkably, she sensed the very moment that the wheels came off the ground, and looked out her window to see the runway shrinking away. Gradually, the plane rose into the sky. For the first time in life, she was above the horizon. She was flying free like one of the birds.

It was not too long after they were up that the boys in back began to dominate the headsets with their 'pilot to bombardier' nonsense. She glanced over at Mr. Carlyle – he seemed content that they should wear themselves out first. Sure enough, both boys soon rejected 'pilot' for 'bombardier' and began making all kinds of annoying explosion sounds in their microphones. After telling them that he would not fly over their school so they could blow it up, Mr. Carlyle started explaining the four things that all planes could do – glide, soar, bank and dive. He called these 'man-new-vers.' She had heard that word before, and knew that it had nothing to do with being a man. Listening intently to everything he said, she was also becoming frustrated with how the boys kept shouting out landmarks below. So Mr. Carlyle turned the plane to the left and right, giving them what they wanted most – a better view of the ground.

Soon enough, the boys became occupied with finding their houses. She finally had the pilot all to herself… and wanted to know everything. In rapid fire, she began pointing out gauges and asking him to explain how each worked. She was not really understanding much of what he was saying, but the simple fact that he knew what each one was… knew its purpose and importance for being there… that somehow put her in a special little world of her own.

When they finished with the last gauge, Mr. Carlyle surprised her by telling her to take hold of the 'yoke'… that thing before her looking very much like the steering wheel to a race car.

"There's no cause for worry, Marna. I'm right here. So… what I want you to do is bank the plane… you choose the direction. Just go slow and do your best to keep the nose on the horizon."

He gestured ahead out the front window, so she came up a bit in her seat. The sun's brightness made her eyes blink… and she noticed in the propeller a bit of that weird thing a bicycle's wheel sometimes did. That thing where the hazy outline of its spokes seem to stand still or even rotate backwards at a creep. She made herself squint past this oddity to the distant horizon.

"Yes, sir… but why do that?"

"It's the pilot's reference point. That's how you know the turn's going well. If the nose drops below the horizon, then just pull back a little on the yoke… and if it climbs above, push forward a bit. Got it?"

"Yes, sir."

She turned the yoke ever so slightly to the left, guessing that it would make seeing the horizon somewhat easier. Out of the corner of each eye, she sensed the left wing drop and the right wing lift as the plane banked. But what with everything bopping about, she found it difficult to keep the nose right on that hazy line. With slight adjustments to the yoke, she did manage to correct her worst errors. Briefly glancing to the console, she found the thing that he had called the 'turn coordinator,' but had no idea what it told about how well she was doing.

The pilot gave her a thumbs-up on taking over the controls. Half relieved and half disappointed, she shot quick looks down both wings to those things at the end.

A-la-something-or-others…

She might not remember their name, but she was pleased to see that they were bent in opposite directions – his side up and her side down – just as he had said they would be. She was trying to picture in her mind how the air might be hitting those pieces of metal differently, but gave it up when he pointed out the rod-like thing called a 'throttle.' This, he said, was the control that made the plane go up or down.

"Okay, kids… I'm going to show you an interesting maneuver. Hang on… this might get a little scary… but don't worry. You're perfectly safe."

Without explaining what he was doing, he messed with that throttle thing… and the engine suddenly went quiet. She could feel the plane shutter as a little alarm sound went off. For just a second, she seemed to be floating in the air… and then the plane tipped forward and fell like a rock. Out the front window, she saw much more of the ground than before, throwing her into a terror that was echoed by screams from the backseat. Then he did something with the throttle, and the engine came alive… got louder… and the nose of the plane lifted back into normal flight. Instantly, she was begging him to do it again. This time, she concentrated on the feel of the plane rather than the feel of herself. She could almost sense that exact moment when the wings gave up the air and the plane tipped downward. It was like nothing she had ever experienced before.

"We're going to do it one more time… but I want y'all to watch these two gauges if you can. That's the altimeter… and that's the airspeed indicator. Try following them together."

To her, both seemed as nothing more than odd clock faces… but as he did the throttle thing again, she noticed that both changed in the same way. Without taking her eyes from off the gauges, she gave him a thumbs-up… all the while repeating the names in her head.

Al-ti-meter…

Airspeed indicator…

Mr. Carlyle fell silent as he headed the plane back to the airport, acting very much like Gwen does at the end of a long work day. She still had so many questions… and plenty of energy for more… but kept all that to herself. He offered no explanations for how a landing was to be done, so she concentrated herself on recognizing that exact moment when the wheels touched down. There was a bump… a skidding sound… and then her first-ever experience in flight was over.

She was still lost in wonder… even after the plane had come to a stop and the pilot signaled it was safe to climb out. The two boys rushed off to be with the others, yet she hung back simply to stay near to the plane for as long as she could. But as Mr. Meitner was calling her over, she put a hand to the side of the plane and silently thanked it for taking her into the sky. Walking back to the hangar, she was surprised on reaching the waiting Mr. Meitner when the pilot suddenly placed his hands on her shoulders.

"George… the girl's a natural. You know… with most kids… it's all about looking out the windows or wanting to fiddle with the controls. Most show no genuine interest in how flight actually works. But not her. She thinks like she's part of the plane."

Mr. Carlyle then gently turned her about to face him.

"Marna… when you're a bit older, I'd like you to consider taking lessons. I think you'd make a pretty good pilot. I'd be happy to speak with your parents about getting you into a…"

Like a sudden downpour of cold rain, everything changed.

"I don't have any parents."

She slid from under his hands and stalked away from the hangar, barely aware that Roy had taken up step beside her. She kept quiet the whole way to the Meitner house, completely lost in the sadness of not having anyone close with whom she could share this wonderful experience. Once back, she waited for the boys to dash into the house before getting out on her own. She made for the same rocking chair as before… but Mr. Meitner stepped in the way before she got there.

"Marna, what's say we go round back and find the Mrs., then you can tell her all about your flight?"

He held out a hand to her, and because of the kind look on his face, she accepted it. Somehow, she knew that he understood how she was feeling. He led her around the porch to a backdoor. Together with Mrs. Meitner, the three of them sat at the kitchen table taking nibbles from what remained of the birthday cake as she excitedly related to them all of the wonders of her first flight. From time to time, one of them left whenever a parent arrived for a boy, but always they came back to her. These two adults might be strangers to her, but having them there to hear about her adventure in the Cessna was the closest thing she had experienced in a long time to having a family.

That feeling instantly disappeared on hearing Gwen's 'shave-and-a-haircut' honking rhythm. By habit, she knocked out the 'two-bits' on the Meitner's kitchen table.

"That's Aunt Gwen… I gotta go. Thank you so much, Mr. and Mrs. Meitner. Thank you for the party… and the cake… and for… everything… but especially for the flight. It was perfect!"

Mrs. Meitner walked her to the front, calling for Roy to see her off. She was soon out the door with the only thing on her mind being an eagerness to tell her aunt about flying. She bounded down the porch steps and burst into the passenger side all a titter about this having been the best birthday party of all time. Even though she was the only girl, she had been better at it than any of the boys.

"Better at what?"

"At flying in a plane. Mr. Meitner took us to the airport and…"

Even though the car was barely at a creep about the circle, the suddenness with which Gwen slammed on the breaks sent her crashing into the front dash.

"He did what?!"

"Took us flying."

"You stay right here."

Gwen shut down the engine and was out of the car before she could say 'yes, ma'am.' She knew the look. Her aunt was furious… although the reason was far from obvious. Gwen climbed the porch stairs on a run and burst right into the house without knocking.

She sat there for what seemed like hours, looking between the door and her lap… trying to figure out what she had done wrong. The first sign of movement was not from the front door, but from Roy coming around the porch. He was making for her, but doing so with an eye kept on the house. She rolled down the window as fast as she could, yet did not wait for it to go all the way down before asking.

"What's happening?"

"It's your aunt. She's… she's in there blowing her stack. Mom and Dad are trying to calm her down, but she's… she's gone nuts. I couldn't stay in there another second."

With her window down, she could now make out the sounds of someone yelling inside. She was just about to ask Roy for details when Gwen came storming through the front door, slamming it behind her. Her aunt bounded down the stairs in making for the driver's side, but on seeing Roy, left-turned it at the front bumper and came to within arm's reach of him. The intensity in her face made him take a step back.

"Young man, you listen to me. It's regrettable that this has come about on your day, but it couldn't be helped. I'm not saying it's your doing, but right now… that doesn't matter one bit. From here on, you steer clear of my Marna, you understand?!"

Before he could answer, she came up in her seat to object… but Gwen stuck a stop sign gesture right into her face. So… she turned a wordless appeal toward him, shaking her head so he would know how to answer. He flicked his eyes toward her… and then straightened his shoulders.

"Yes, ma'am."

She fell back completely embarrassed, slouching down all the way so he could not possibly see her. And she stayed that way until Gwen had gotten into the car.

"But why?!"

"Not now, Marna! Roll up your window!"

"Yes… ma'am."

Gwen had nothing else to say until they had cleared the Meitner property. Some distance down the county road, she pulled onto the shoulder and shut down the engine.

"First of all, Marna… you've done nothing wrong. Understand me?"

"Yes, ma'am."

"Second… and here's where you're going to have to trust me… nothing good comes of flying. It's just not the sort of thing a young woman should get herself tangled up in."

"But you said a woman could do anything that a man could do?! So why can't I…"

"It's got nothing to do with that. It's… it's all together a different matter. Flying… it's a thing that'll rip your heart right out of you. It'll lift you up to the clouds, and then drop you right back down to earth just as quick. Besides… it's dangerous… and expensive. Marna, you're a bright girl. You can do almost anything you set your mind to. The world's out there waiting for you… just… don't waste life getting caught up in… in something like that."

The soft sincerity in her aunt's voice was as alarming as the previous anger. Perhaps Gwen recognized this oddity, for her voice immediately got stern.

"Another thing… you're not to associate with that Meitner boy anymore. I'm absolutely serious about this. It was a mistake letting you go to that party in the first place."

"I don't understand. He's my friend. There's nothing wrong with him."

"It's the principle of the thing. He went behind my back in doing the very thing that he knew would make me the maddest."

"Roy did that?!"

"Not the boy. But it doesn't matter anyway. The whole family can't be trusted."

"But I really like…"

Her aunt did the one thing that always put an end to any argument. She stuck an index finger directly into her face. That little gesture bore the full intensity of her aunt's anger… and she knew from experience to respect it.

Gwen restarted the car and pulled back out onto the road. The way her aunt was gripping the steering wheel… the knuckles on both hands going white… told her it was best to give up on the subject of Roy… for now.

CHAPTER

7

UNTIMELY

Nothing more was spoken between her and Gwen that weekend regarding Roy's birthday party. She was first taken home to change out of her party dress, and then the two of them spent the rest of Saturday at the shop trimming rose stems. She worked silently, bringing to mind every detail she could from her flight in the Cessna. Patsy was making that so difficult, taking every free minute to poke her with questions about the party. She kept her answers short and never said anything about flying, particularly seeing as Gwen was staring at her across the cutting room table.

At seven o'clock, Patsy closed up the shop and left, but Gwen kept her there late working on roses. Not until her aunt stepped out for boxed meals from the diner across the street could she act on the plan that had been forming in her mind all afternoon. Quick as could be, she darted into the alley and rummaged through the pile of discarded cardboard. Picking out a good sized piece, she hid it beneath a blanket in the backseat of Gwen's car, hoping it would go unnoticed until she could retrieve it once home.

Long after Gwen had gone to bed that night, she worked by flashlight to recreate from memory the details of the Cessna's cockpit controls. Starting first with a pencil and moving on to a black marker, she laid out what she could recall of the instrument panel's many gauges. Though she could almost see each in her mind, she had to fudge many of the details. With a small tray of paints and a cup of water, she then decorated the gauges in different colors. She so wanted each to look like the real thing… but also to be nice and pretty… exactly like in her memory. She used her most fine-tipped brush and took her time in getting everything just right. As the paint dried, she quietly snuck into the kitchen for some paper plates from a cabinet. In each, she cut out the same pattern of a yoke and then carefully pasted the stack together. In a final step, she formed a throttle out of a big button thumb-tacked to the eraser end of a pencil.

Late that night… as on many to follow… she sat cross-legged on her bed with this special instrument panel propped up against the headboard. The very first time, she closed her eyes and allowed the springs in her mattress to recreate the feel of a plane bouncing about beneath her, and had the hum of crickets outside the window to be the purr of her engine. She then opened her eyes to act out the maneuvers that Mr. Carlyle had performed… sliding the pencil throttle in and out of a hole in the cardboard… turning the paper plate yoke about in her hands… and always keeping the nose of her plane perfectly positioned on the headboard's horizon.

With summer approaching, her nighttime thoughts were more often being turned back toward the anticipation of finishing the fifth grade. She gradually lost interest in the cardboard instrument panel, as the stone relief… overlooked in her fantasies of flight… once more became as important to her as when she had first laid eyes on it. Her anxiousness to break free into something more significant in life could never be satisfied with play. So she less frequently dragged out her model of a Cessna's cockpit, until one day she put it away behind her dresser for good.

As for her friendship with Roy… that would never change. For the most part, she considered herself to be an obedient child, doing as told simply because that was the right thing to do. But in those times when she sensed that Gwen's judgment had gone wrong, she would not hesitate to do what she thought was best. Perhaps such an attitude was common to an orphan's mind, though she had little interest in trying to figure out why she did what she did. Roy was her friend. It did not matter that he was a Meitner… as if that was something so terribly bad. Even as the words forbidding her from being with him were leaving Gwen's mouth, she had made up her mind to disobey. Whatever had gone wrong between her aunt and Roy's parents was their business… but if it affected the only real friendship she had in Lubbock, then it was her business too.

She and Roy left school together on the Monday following the party… fortunately without Sybil around. This was the first chance she had for talking with him about what had happened afterward... though she had tried during recess.

"Not here! Remember... my friends' parents are my parents' friends... and probably your aunt's customers too."

Coming to the tracks cutting across Avenue P, they turned on their usual path toward the train yard. Finally alone, Roy gave her his best guess.

"Maybe it's politics..."

"That's stupid. It can't be politics."

"Why not?"

"Because my aunt doesn't care about such things. She's only interested in flowers. Besides... it's got something to do with flying. That's why she was so upset."

Roy did not seem impressed with her reasoning. In fact, he was not even paying attention to her anymore. He was concentrating instead on tight-roping a rail... something he often did during their walks together. At such times, she would move out of the center of the tracks so as not to get clobbered by him whenever he fell off. But now... watching him holding out his arms for balance... his books in his left hand and hers in his right... it reminded her of flight. And that just brought back all of her irritation with Gwen. Him goofing off in such a happy way was not very nice. So she shoved him off the rail just to show how frustrated she was at not getting answers. She thought that should get him serious... but he instead picked up a piece of railroad rock and began tossing it about... sometimes high enough and far enough that he ran beneath to make a one-handed catch at the last second.

Why do boys always have to be so... boyish?!

She put up with this stone throwing nonsense for a while before insisting that he stop showing off and pay attention.

"I suppose you're right... Dad hates politics too. He says the Publicans are..."

"Republicans."

"Yeah... those guys. He says they're only good for hunting down Commies..."

"Communists."

"...and padding their pockets with dough. And he says the Damn-it-craps are..."

"It's *Dem-o-crats*! If you're going to say a thing, then say it right!"

"Geez, Marna... you gonna correct everything coming outta my mouth?!"

Roy spun away, moving several railroad ties ahead of her. Of course she was aware of needing to apologize, but the subject of her aunt was a good enough excuse for being rude. Without warning, he took the rock that he still had in his hand and hurled it into the side of a small metal switch box set off from the tracks. It hit with a loud clunk and bounced right back in her direction. She could not help but scream as it whizzed past her head.

"Sorry!"

"Will you stop horsing around?! I'm trying to be serious! And I don't correct everything coming out of your mouth!" He had come to her side with such a look of concern. It made her feel bad for having been so short with him. "It's okay. I'm just… upset at my aunt. So… what's he say about the… Damn-it-craps?"

They were both standing within the rails of the same track as Roy placed a hand lightly upon her shoulder. It felt nice… and weird at the same time.

"He says they cause double the problems they solve. It's really funny, Marna… when he's watching the news. His face gets super red and he starts arguing with the TV. You know… he doesn't really like any kind of… *pol-i-ti-shun.*"

She did not miss the extra effort he put into saying the word properly.

They walked on in silence from there, each fixing their steps to the spacing of the railway ties. For her, the distance was greater than that of her normal walk… but less so for Roy. Every third or fourth tie, he paused until she could catch up. After a while, they left the railyard by turning toward 4th Street.

"Marna, I don't think my parents hate your aunt. Mom's always buying flowers at her shop. She could go other places… but she likes your aunt. You know… it's kind of weird… Mom won't talk about your aunt no matter how many times I ask her. She just says I'm too young to understand."

That was exactly how she felt – frustrated that adults thought she was too young to understand.

About a block from the flower shop, Roy handed over her books and then crossed to the other side, waving one last time before heading downtown to his father's appliance store. Sometimes she would stand there and watch him until he disappeared from view, and other times… especially when Sybil was with them… she would continue on without a second look.

In the weeks following the birthday party, she began picking up on a strange feeling about Roy. Each Friday afternoon, he made a point of saying that he wanted to hang out with just her rather than joining his friends somewhere downtown. Though odd, she did not so much care, as it was easier at times being with him than with some of her girlfriends. For one, he never bombarded her with silly gossip about crushes. He just liked talking about whatever was on her mind… and having fun. But ever since Gwen had forbidden them from hanging out together, she was noticing him get antsy whenever the subject of summer break came up. He was not at all excited about it, and kept asking her all sorts of weird questions about what she would be doing during her free time… even though he knew full well that Gwen made her work every day. But the thing that really puzzled her was his relationship with Sybil. He had always been so understanding with his sister's annoying ways. But as if overnight, he began forbidding Sybil from following them after school. He even went so far as to demand that the girl leave them alone. And if that failed, he would simply turn down the nearest railroad track, leaving his sister to fend for herself.

She really appreciated not having Sybil around… but this change in Roy left an itchy sort of impression in her thoughts. Not something that she could ask him about… or put into words for her friends. She just had a foggy notion that something was on his mind… and having a little sister around got in his way of figuring it out. But since boys were weird in the first place… always tackling each other… shouting when a normal voice would do… or wiggling about when it was important to sit still… then she decided that this 'new Roy' was just one of those strange things that happened when a boy got another year older.

On the very last day of class, it being a Friday, they had plans to meet up with some friends at a downtown drugstore to celebrate the end of school. As usual, they stopped first at his father's place. Without much saying what he was up to… if anything at all… he led her into the store's office. For some reason, he just plopped himself down in his father's desk chair and began spinning about. They were supposed to be heading down the street, but here he was going round and round… over and over.

"What're you doing?"

"Playing a keen game. Watch this."

He planted the balls of his sneakers on the floor and twisted off of them, sending the chair into another spin.

"Gets your head real goofy fast."

He spun again, but this time with his eyes closed. She was getting really annoyed… but also a bit amused… especially by how he kept flinging his arms and legs out as if he was caught up in a dust devil. When he finally came to a stop with his eyes still closed, his face went into a tight-lipped strain… sort of like he was trying to figure out a really hard math problem.

"I think I'm… facing the desk… right?"

"Yeah… sort of. So what? Let's get going."

He opened his eyes with a bit of confusion in not finding himself where expected. Without paying attention to her, he set off on another spin… and she waited with growing irritation.

"I'm facing the door."

One of his eyes opened.

"Got it right. You really have to listen carefully cause dizziness messes up your ears real bad. Let's see you spin me… fast as you can… except do it in the other way."

At least this sounded like some fun. She would spin him so hard that he fell out on the floor… and then they could finally get going. Grabbing the back of the chair, she used three false starts in building speed, saying out loud the expected 'one for the money, two for the show, three to get ready…' before heaving the chair around on the count of four. She just barely jumped back before getting clipped by his flung-out trainers. Roy's head immediately tipped to one side… but right off she thought that the spin was not that good. When the chair came to a stop, he was quick to point straight ahead.

"The filing cabinets."

"Good guess… but that was a lousy spin. I can do better."

She was more satisfied with her next effort, as it almost sent him flying out of the chair. When he stopped, he sat for a longer time before pointing directly at her.

"It's you."

"You were peeking."

"Was not. I'm just good at this. Now you try."

They switched places, and he spun her in what she thought to be an easy one. In circle after circle, she picked up on how the sounds around her changed as she spun by. But she had not been ready for that giddy feeling coming to her head and opened her eyes to see if she was still moving. The door was straight ahead.

"Hey! That's cheating."

"Sorry… I couldn't help it. Let me try again."

With eyes tightly closed this time, she concentrated on the sounds rather than the feel of the spin, allowing her ears to speak to her. A squeak to the chair as it went about was an obvious sign of motion. So she knew she had come to a stop when that sound went away. A mishmash of voices was now louder in one ear… likely from the showroom's many TVs. On her other side, she picked up on the faint whoosh of cars passing on the road outside the office window… and somewhere behind her came the ticking of a wall clock. The last sound was of Roy moving about… likely in his silly way of confusing her.

She was just about to guess which direction she was facing when several things happened, nearly all at once. The first was a bit odd… just a little puff of air to her face… and then came something pressing against her lips. With a jolt, she opened her eyes to find Roy kissing her! So she let out a scream and shoved him away with all her might… which nearly toppled her over backward in the chair. Having to regain her balance cut short her scream… but another picked up where hers had left off. There was Mrs. Meitner standing in the doorway with her arms in the air. As surprised as she was over Roy's kiss, his mother's outrage was even more alarming. The woman went right for her son's ears, and though he threw up his arms in defense, she gave both such an extra-strong tug that he was now the one screaming. In a flash, his mother dragged him out into the hall.

"HOW DARE YOU…" Whack. "…TAKE ADVANTAGE…" Whack. "…OF A YOUNG LADY…" Whack. "…LIKE THAT!"

The whacking did not stop even when Roy's many apologies gave way to the obvious sound of him crying. Her embarrassment, Roy's punishment, and his mother's anger was all together sickening her to tears. She wanted it all to stop, but could not produce a breath worth of speech.

Mrs. Meitner's head suddenly came into view, her leaning backward into the doorway.

"Marna, dear… I'm terribly sorry. Please… stay right where you're at… until I can get back from delivering this… *thing*… to his father."

So she sat very still waiting for her shock to stop while listening to Roy's whimpers diminish in the same way that the chair's squeaks had faded. No sounds could be heard after that. Not the showroom's TVs nor the hum of traffic outside. Her head was all abuzz with embarrassment, and her heart was pounding away in her chest. But oddly… she could still hear that clock on the wall… ticking away to torment her. Soon, Mrs. Meitner would be back… and maybe with Mr. Meitner too. Soon, she would receive her share of their displeasure. Roy had kissed her, but maybe they would think it was her fault. Maybe his parents would decide that she had wanted him to kiss her in the very same way that she had once heard Patsy talking about that game called 'spin the bottle.'

Spin the Marna.

As horrible as that sounded, she knew they would believe it. And soon it would get much worse, for there was Gwen to answer to.

Mrs. Meitner came back unexpectedly, but with many more apologies than her son had left behind. The woman took her by the hand, wrapping an arm about her shoulder, and asked only one question – where she should be taken, her home or her aunt's shop. The answer was obvious… but difficult to provide.

The short drive was done in complete silence. She could not bear to look at Mrs. Meitner, nor could she bring herself to stare out the window. Her shame kept her eyes down on her lap. Coming into Forde's Flowers through the front door… one of the few times she ever had… added to her embarrassment. Thankfully, it was not Gwen behind the counter, but Patsy. The young woman's cheerful greeting to Mrs. Meitner was quickly replaced by surprise on finding her there too. Somehow, Patsy knew that something was wrong, for she shouted back into the cutting room… which immediately produced Gwen. Unlike the concerned look on Patsy, her aunt's face was unreadable.

"Gwen, your niece has had a bit of a fright."

Then, from the reason for her being at their appliance store to what had happened in the office, Mrs. Meitner put into words what she could not possibly have understood… even with years of having known Roy.

"Being sweet on a girl's no excuse for poor judgment. Just want you to know, Gwen, we're taking this seriously. Roy'll be disciplined at home… but I'd also like to bring him 'round your place so he can apologize in person. Would Sunday afternoon suit you?"

The word 'sweet' stuck sourly in her mind.

Her aunt said little through it all, and not much more after Mrs. Meitner had left.

"We'll wait for the boy's apology on Sunday, then you and I will have a private talk about what happened… including how you disobeyed me. Now get to the cutting room. Might as well use the rest of your Friday off in working. Go sweep the floor."

Work that afternoon and the next day was so different than most times she spent at the flower shop. Patsy steered clear of her… which was something that only happened whenever she and Gwen got into a tussle. But Gwen avoided her too. At least she found that having her hands occupied was a good thing. It gave her something to do while struggling through that humiliating and confusing experience. She replayed the spinning game over and over in her mind, searching for what she had done to make him act the way he had. Was the kiss something that just happened… or had he been planning it all along? Maybe he had always been thinking about kissing her every time they were together. Maybe all those walks along the tracks were his way of building up to it. Searching through her feelings toward him… and toward every boy she knew… made her all the more confused.

I know what he did was wrong… but… isn't that sort of what I've always liked about him… that he liked me more than other girls at school? So… shouldn't I be glad… and not mad… that he kissed me?

She liked boys… the nice ones… but could not see how liking boys should be reason for her liking what he had done. Even if this apology of his on Sunday ended up being really sincere, she could never be alone with him like before. Worrying about what might be on his mind… that was enough for her to decide that she never wanted to see him again. Roy Meitner used to be nice, but now she knew him for what he really was – a liar pretending to be her friend, just to get a kiss.

Without needing to be told, she understood exactly what it meant when the phone rang on Sunday afternoon. Gwen was only on the line for a minute, telling the caller that it was a fine time to come over. She automatically went to wait by the front window. Every car passing by put a jolt of fear into her… but she stayed there, wanting to know of his arrival long before he reached the front door. What she expected to happen at that moment had not yet been worked out in her mind when a car pulled up to the curb. Inside, she made out Mrs. Meitner at the wheel and the top of Roy's head as he slumped down in the front seat.

"Aunt Gwen… they're here. Please… I don't want him coming inside. Can you have them stay on the front porch… and then make them go away after?"

"As you wish. This is for you… not me."

Turning back to the window, she was startled to find that the two of them were already halfway up the walk. She quickly backed out of sight from the window. In the corner of her eye, she realized that her aunt was already at the front door. The bell rang, Gwen opened the door, and she heard the familiar voice.

"Hello, Mrs. Forde. I'd like to…"

"I'm not married. Just call me ma'am."

There was a pause before she heard Roy again.

"Uhh… yes, ma'am. I'd… like to speak with Marna please… but before you get her… I want to say how sorry I am for… disobeying what you asked."

"You mean when I told you to steer clear of Marna?"

"Yes, ma'am."

"Apology accepted, but the statement still holds. Excuse me while I get my niece."

With the door left open, Gwen gave one look toward where she stood hiding by the front window… and then Gwen left for the rear of the house. It took a few seconds to realize that Gwen was leaving this mess for her to sort out on her own. Taking a deep breath, she moved around the corner to the door. With a screen separating them, Roy somehow seemed smaller… and farther away than she had expected. She looked up to where his mother stood, backed off a bit on the porch… but fortunately not so far that she felt a burden in being left alone with him. She came back to Roy, but not to look at him fully. She focused instead on the screen between them, which put him into a meshed-out haze in her sight.

"Marna, I'm… sorry for what I did. It was rude and… insensitive." She could tell right off that this was a prepared speech by the way his head went to the side a few times… as if being mindful of his mother somehow helped him recall the words to say. "I had no right to… presume… on your affections. It won't happen again."

"That's for sure, Roy. Goodbye."

Not allowing him to say another word, she closed the door with care so as not to give him the impression it was being slammed. She went directly to her room, shut her door… and had just enough time to bury her face in a pillow before breaking down into tears.

The afternoon's glare through her bedroom window had faded to a yellowy gray when she was awoken by Gwen.

"You've not had anything to eat since breakfast, and if you continue in napping you won't be able to sleep tonight. You need to get up anyway… it's time for our talk. Why don't you head outside. I've got ice tea and sandwiches waiting."

They ate quietly on the section of porch that extended from the front around to the rear, as it was fully in shade and the most comfortable place to sit. She had little in the way of an appetite, but nibbled anyway as an excuse for not looking at her aunt. Gwen was in no hurry, which was probably all part of the punishment.

"So… let's start with the subject of you not obeying me when I said sometime back for you to stay away from that boy."

Gwen paused to take a sip of tea, which she knew to be more of the same… making her wait in dread.

"I suppose I could say I told you so… and then come down hard on you… but I'm not going to do either. My reasons didn't have anything to do with the boy. I've got nothing against him personally. He's just a boy. I'm sure he's got his winning ways… just like his mother and his un…"

Gwen stopped mid-sentence… awkwardly taking another sip of tea. When the glass came away from her mouth, her lips seemed unusually tight… sort of like she did not find the taste to be as expected, but must swallow it anyway.

"Like his un-what?"

"Never mind. I just wanted you to know something about the situation… that way you'll understand a bit of my feelings regarding that family. In a nutshell, the father owes me an apology for some terribly painful things he's done to me, and the mother… she should have backed me up, but chose to side with her husband instead. In time, I came to understand the predicament a married woman can find herself in regarding such things… but it still took me years to get to the point where I could stand the sight of her."

She waited… but nothing more came. Her aunt, facing out over the handrail into the side yard, showed no sign of wanting to go on. Sitting very still, Gwen seemed stuck in some sad thought. This time, her aunt's silence seemed not to do with punishment… at least not any directed toward her.

"Aunt Gwen?"

Gwen flinched so suddenly that she could not help but do the same.

"Sorry… Is everything okay?"

"Yes. Absolutely. So… Marna… what I initially wanted to talk about was the birds and the bees… but there's something different that we should discuss first."

For several minutes, Gwen went into a long speech about the things women faced because they were women. Not being taken seriously… Treated as second class citizens… Made to be objects rather than recognized as people… She said again that thing about a woman doing anything a man could do… even though they might be physically weaker. Men just wanted women to follow their rules… like dressing in ways that pleased them. Women were always told what to think… or made to believe they had no ability to think at all. It was so unfair that women were denied the same chances in life… all because men were so proud. Women were made to believe that they were not smart enough for this… or not strong enough for that… or too emotional to be depended upon. It was all wrong, she said, the way men dominated the world. After all, it was them who started the wars and them who fought in them. Why was it so difficult for them to see that?! Something made them blind to their own weaknesses. Over and over, she said how wrong it was that women got stuck managing the household while their men went out to work… and society was near-criminal for keeping it that way. From time to time, Gwen would come back to the subject of women being made to have babies, and what that did to their plans… their goals… their dreams.

She was really trying hard to follow all of this, but her thoughts kept going back to what birds and bees had to do with anything. She was nearly eleven after all. That was clearly old enough to pick up on many adult ways of thinking. But Gwen's words had her mind all gummed up with the birds in the relief… it hanging inside the house just behind where her head was leaning… and those terrible flying things responsible for her allergy.

At last, Gwen wrapped it all up by swinging the chair around to face her.

"You see, Marna… it's all because of their urges. Those start out small… when a boy's just showing off… and in no time they turn… *sexual.* But that's not the half of it. They also develop a will to dominate. You need to realize that's something far worse than just wanting their way. They will certainly bring you down if you let them. So… are you… understanding anything of what I'm trying to say?"

"Sort of…"

Sure, she could see how boys and girls behaved differently in class and on the playground. And she obviously knew that a girl's body was made differently than a boy's… for the purpose of having babies. That was something she was not yet comfortable discussing with Gwen. But whatever her aunt was talking about now… that was totally crazy! Like aliens from outer space!

"Let me ask you a question… how did it feel in that split second when you discovered the boy kissing you?"

She did not need to think long. The memory of it had been stuck in her mind ever since.

"It felt like… something wasn't right. Like I had no say in the matter, and… like he tricked me."

"So you felt taken advantage of?"

"Yeah… that's right."

To her, this was more of an admission than an answer to her aunt's question. Because of that, she knew that Gwen did not fault her for neglecting to say ma'am.

The memory again of his touch made her close her eyes. It was not the kiss itself… which amounted to nothing more than a peck on her lips. It was the shock of finding him so near. Before she had been spun, he was simply Roy, her friend… but after… whatever she might call him… it was something completely different. Somehow, the look on his face made her feel even worse. Almost as if it had all been her fault. Like she was the one responsible for the change in him. None of that made any sense. Not then and not now. All she really knew was that she would never be able to be with him as before. He had forever ruined their friendship.

CHAPTER

8

THE GIANT ICHNEUMON, CLOTHED AS FOR DEATH

I'm going from the top of the heap to the bottom of the pile... but that's fine by me. The pile's so much bigger than the heap.

Senior high was the real deal, and she was more than ready for it. More freedom, more independence, and finally some respect. Senior high kids got taken seriously. They got to make their own choices on things… like what classes to take, what clubs to be in, and which activities they liked best. They drove cars, went to parties and dances, and had real dates. Not those idiotic chaperoned things. A bunch of girls hanging out with a bunch of boys. So boring! Junior high was mickey mouse. Completely forgettable. She was more than ready for senior high, for she could not wait to become an adult!

The only thing that really bugged her about growing up was how frequently people were saying that she resembled Gwen.

Such nonsense!

They were totally different in every way! Different hair color and different shaped eyes! And Gwen had absolutely no fashion sense!

Well… okay… maybe there were some small similarities to their faces… but not that much. And so what anyway! No excuse for that old lady in the shop last month making such a big deal about how her mouth was just like Gwen's. Bottom lip straight across and top curved up so as to show a hint of white. Lots of people held their lips that way! That woman got her head

108

so mixed up that she needed an hour in front of the mirror that night to sort out her smile.

Patsy kept insisting that the resemblance was more in the eye brows... thin, with what she said was an air of elegance.

What's Patsy know about elegance anyway?!

Whereas one of her girlfriends had told her it was all in the nose... a bit upturned, with a look of 'sophistication.'

Right! That's just West Texas code for being stuck up!

Sure... they were similar in other ways than in the face... like any aunt and niece might be. Both stood lean and long-legged... but was that so unusual?! Except... she was among the tallest of girls in her grade... taller than even a good many of the boys. It was not her fault that she had to look down on her classmates. Sort of like how Gwen looked down on her. Somehow, the more frequently people made a point of comparing her to Gwen, the more she was fearing that Gwen's stern bearing might one day become hers too.

But really, she had much more important things to worry about than being compared to Gwen! The beginning of senior high was only days away. Everything depended on her starting out right. One embarrassing moment... one bad scene... one tiny mess up... and she might get a label that followed her throughout senior high. The kid who goofed up on the first day.

So be cool... not lumpy. Stay smart and funny... not a goof or a spaz. Nobody likes a pooper. So stand out... in a good way... and then you'll absolutely kill it!

But why now of all times?! Why in the world should I be made to wear a stupid medical alert bracelet?!

That idiot school nurse at orientation... it was all her fault! She just had to make such a fuss over her allergy! The lady suggested the bracelet... and Gwen jumped on it!

It's so unfair! What a royal shaft!

Now she had to wear this hideous thing all the time! So humiliating! Its dreadfully plain-looking steel chain clashed with everything she wore! From now on, it would go wherever she went and be with her in whatever she did. When she used a fork... when she wrote with a pencil... when she waved to a friend... and when she went out on dates. Anything she did with her right hand, there was that annoying bracelet. A constant reminder for everyone to see! She hated the thing! Nothing but a loop of shame! Its so-called 'Caduceus emblem' was supposed to be something special, but it was just a nasty-looking set of bird wings outstretched over a rod of intertwined snakes.

Of all things – snakes! Might as well make it wasp wings!

This bracelet was nothing more than a daily sting to her pride.

Okay... sure... if she was *actually* stung, then the writing on the small metal plate could alert others to her condition. It might one day save her life... but would surely embarrass her to death in the process. She had managed her allergy without much fuss up until now. She was plenty careful... and not a kid anymore! So why should she still be treated as one?! Just like Gwen to make her wear it! Always keeping her down!

She entered her first day of senior high with a brand-new school bag, as did many of her classmates. Unlike them, she clutched hers to her chest with her right hand stuck inside just past the wrist. She crept into her homeroom class, Biology, just before the bell rang, and took a spot in the back of the room. She spent that first hour of senior high trying to go unnoticed. The rest of the day, she clumsily found ways of concealing the embarrassment from others. But one by one, her friends eventually picked up on the bracelet such that the cat was finally out of its bag. To her surprise, nobody made a big deal about it.

After an entire week, her friends no longer seemed to care about the bracelet... so she stopped trying so hard to conceal it. From time to time, she could even pretend that it was a piece of jewelry... as long as she did not have to look at it. With another week, she was beginning to tolerate how it slid around on her wrist, and found a few matter-of-fact ways of speaking about it whenever asked. After a full month in senior high, she finally came to accept its presence in her life. She wore it because she had to... but was equally determined that it would never actually become a part of her.

She was sure that senior high would be the beginning of great things for her. Opportunities for learning new stuff, making serious friends, and getting into clubs and student government. All of that foretold of something greater on the horizon. Soon, she would have a driver's license... which meant having to make deliveries for Forde's Flowers. That was fine with her. Sweeping floors had been her childhood. Getting out into the streets of Lubbock would be the first step in her journey toward becoming an adult... and breaking free.

After a month of lectures in six classes, she concluded that senior high was not so difficult. Just a step on the stairs or rung on the ladder for moving her up. Sitting and listening was fine enough, but going and doing was far better. She could handle three years of this... and then finally be out on her own. As to her classes, she had no particular favorites, though Biology was definitely at the bottom. This subject was the least likely to open up the future for her. That was especially true with what the class was set to study for its first big project of the year. They spent weeks being lectured on the 'amazing world within a world'… which was nothing more than Mr. Davies' way of having entomology sound less disgusting to the girls in the class. No matter how hard he tried to make his lectures exciting, she had absolutely zero interest in the taxonomy, anatomy, habits, or life stages of bugs. Neither did any of her girlfriends. But what Mr. Davies did not realize was that he could say whatever he liked about whatever he liked, as nearly every girl in the class was in love with him. Well… not exactly with him, but definitely with his dreamy James Bond double-O-seven accent. She hated biology as a subject… but absolutely loved his class!

"Everyone, if you please… let's begin. Now… each of you shall be given an insect specimen of your own to… Yes, yes… they're all quite dead. On your lab tables you'll find paper, cardboard, pins, and magnifying glasses… and in a moment I'll be round passing out vials of… No, you may not choose your own. What I distribute is what you shall work with. Now, the assignment is quite simple. Delicately lay out your specimen on the cardboard and then pin the little blighter down. Each pertinent section must be properly labeled for… No, Miss Jenkins… no working in pairs. Use your textbook to identify the anatomy, and then the order, family and genus. This will surely require library time. Bonus credit for anyone accurately determining the species."

Her teacher then went about with a tray distributing a vial to each student. As the tables up front received their specimens, the boys began displaying theirs to those nearby, while the girls showed much less enthusiasm about theirs. Throughout the classroom, she heard 'moth,' 'beetle,' 'horsefly,' and 'grasshopper,' along with kids making offers to trade.

"No exchanges, class. Oh, and another thing… be careful not to inhale the formaldehyde. Nasty stuff. Best take out your specimen and then close up the vial right off. Now have at it."

Mr. Davies reached her table in the back and handed her a vial packed with a black mass. She immediately placed the vial on the table top to study it from a safe distance. Slowly, she rotated it about, noticing that the balled-up thing inside had a mesh of wings and legs.

Some kind of flying thing…

Following the teacher's instructions, she unscrewed the lid and spooned the insect out onto her cardboard, aware that others at her table were doing likewise. Carefully, she went about splaying out the insect using her tweezers, concentrating first on straightening out the wings and legs. The thing's body was black with a bright sheen to it, whereas its antennae, face and legs were yellow. The combination was altogether creepy.

It was with this observation that she finally realized what this thing was. Other students about her were already working on pinning down their specimens, but she could go no further. She just stared at hers. On the cardboard before her was the preserved form of a huge wasp.

A shrill scream one table over suddenly overwhelmed the chatter in the room. Apparently, a boy had stuck his bug in a girl's face. She had no mind for the ensuing uproar of laughter, as her eyes were still fixed on the wasp. With the magnifying glass in her left hand, she extended the tweezers in her right, vaguely aware of how her medical alert bracelet was dangling about her wrist. Very carefully, she touched the wasp's rear section with the tip of the tweezers. A part of it was still curled up under the rest of the body. Using the tweezers, she slowly began to extract a thin, stinger-like appendage out from under the wasp. She kept drawing on it… and it kept coming… eventually extending out to a length greater than that of the rest of the body, antennae included.

I've… seen this thing before.

"Ahh, Miss Forde! You know what you have there, don't you?! That's Darwin's wasp! More precisely, a distant cousin of it. Nevertheless… a very prominent member of the Ichneumonidae family. The very ones that led that famous biologist to express his… umm… skepticism… in a benevolent God. Oh, my – the uproar the Church of England made over that! Such rubbish. But… ahh… what say we not repeat that to anyone? Texans are quite touchy on the subject of religion. Well… carry on. Enjoy your wasp."

She was not really paying attention to Mr. Davies. Had not even bothered to look up while he spoke. As in a dream, she slowly rotated the cardboard about so as to look directly upon the wasp. Hesitating for a second, she lowered her eye to the lens for a closer look at that yellow face. What she saw was far more than what could be seen. She was instantly drawn back in time… and the memory stole her breath away.

––––––––

The giant ichneumon is one of the most intimidating looking wasps in North America. Though its body is nearly 40 millimeters in length, it is the twice-as-long ovipositor that most terrifies the observer. Add to this the metallic black color of body and wing from which its name was derived – 'brokenhearted, clothed as for death' – with bright yellow colorings to its face, legs and antennae, the *megarhyssa atrata* is truly a disturbing wasp to behold.

In all actuality, she is a remarkably docile creature, posing absolutely no threat to humans. She can not even sting, unlike most wasps of the Hymenoptera order. She is a solitary sort, spending her time strictly as a huntress. Using her ovipositor as a probe, she ceaselessly searches for grubs hidden within the crevices to tree bark. On finding one, she injects it with a single egg. The thing she has planted within will remain hidden there for a while, unbeknownst to its host. But then, just as a seed of terror brought forth in a hideous awakening, it bursts asunder with grotesque awareness to slowly traumatize its host into insanity. That which hatches then grows large and strong by gnawing away at its victim until only an empty husk remains.

The magnifying glass spilled from her hand, bounced off the benchtop, and disappeared over the edge. As if from a great distance away, she heard metal clash and glass shatter, with everything going from bright white to solid black… just as her head made contact with the floor.

She awoke in dull lighting, aware only of a gray ceiling above and an intense throbbing in her head. Initially, she tried blinking herself awake, but the result was just more confusion. Closing her eyes, she instead flexed her fingertips over the coarseness of the surface she lay upon. It was then that she made out the murmur of low voices nearby.

"She's coming around. I guess you can get back to your class now, Reginald. And what say you open a few windows?"

"Of course. Let me know how she's doing."

She sensed movement and turned her eyes toward the doorway. Her Biology teacher was leaving.

"How are you feeling, dear?"

"Where am I?"

"In my office. You've had quite a spill. Classmates said you fainted, but I checked you over for stings anyway. Nothing but that welt you've got there on your forehead. Must have hit your head on going down. Might have a mild concussion, so you best…"

The face before her was going in and out of focus such that the overall effect was rather nauseating. For a moment, she lost track of what this strange woman was saying… but then recognized her as being the school nurse.

"…probably caused by all those fumes. Just gave Mr. Davies a piece of my mind. I've told him and the other science teachers to be more careful, but do they listen?! Seems to happen to one of you poor dears every year. Men just don't understand what we women go through. Here… put this ice pack on your head."

It was all coming back to her now… and she wanted nothing more than to leave for some quiet place where she could be alone to face the memory. In shifting weight to her forearms, another wave of dizziness arose, causing her to fall back where she lay. She brought a hand up and easily found the huge lump.

"Woe there! Take it easy. You've hit your head something awful. Best just stay put until your aunt gets here."

"You called my aunt?!"

"Yes, of course."

That was the last person she wanted to see.

"I feel fine. Can I… get up?"

Shifting to her elbows once more, she managed to push herself into a sitting position on the small cot… despite the resistance being applied to her shoulders by the nurse.

"I'm serious, Sugar! You've had a terrible experience. You need to…"

The woman was interrupted by a sharp two-beat knock on the doorframe. Even without looking over, she knew who it was from the sound. There stood Gwen appraising her with an all-too-familiar look – arms crossed tightly over her chest with that inscrutable expression on her face. She knew that an opinion had already been reached, and the delay in relating it was simply Gwen's way of getting her full attention.

"So… what happened to you?"

"I, uhh…"

The dizziness returned as she strained to craft a persuasive answer.

"She had a bit of a tumble in Biology. Inhaled too many fumes."

"Someone on the phone said something about her being sick. She looks fine enough to me. Marna… you okay with getting back to class on your own?"

"Yes… ma'am."

"But she can't! She's had a huge blow to the head! She could have a concussion. She needs to be taken home and put to bed."

"Can't do that just yet. Marna… I can't spare the time to take you home. Stay here if you don't feel up to moving. I'll be back later if I'm actually needed."

Without another word, Gwen was gone… back to her flower shop or wherever it was in Lubbock that required her attention.

"Well, I never!"

"It's okay. She means well… just not good at showing it. Mind if I stay here for a while?"

"That would be wise." The nurse glanced down to her watch. "I've got to attend to another matter… shouldn't take more than thirty minutes… then I'll be back to check up on you."

She waited long enough for the sound of the nurse to fade down the hall before getting up from the cot. Though her head was still light, the pain to it was not the worst thing she was feeling. She peeked in both directions along the hall, then scurried from the administration wing along what she thought would be the best route for avoiding people. Her intention was simple – to leave school as soon as possible and find a quiet spot where she could remember alone. She got as far as the northern end of the building when the wooziness returned. Seating herself on a small bench just opposite a stairwell, she lowered her head to her knees as she knew she should, and waited for her mind to clear.

She was her teenage self… but oddly also a little girl, not yet seven years of age. Sitting in the backseat of the family car, the humidity was doing its sticky trick of bunching up her dress in the back. She ignored it, as she had everything she ever wanted in life sitting in the front seat. Being sweaty was such a small price to pay for this perfect summertime with her parents. School was out, and this trip was a reward for her having finished first grade. Her parents knew the whole year had been fun for her, yet were still doing their best to pretend that she had endured some great hardship in being on her own for six hours a day. She loved them for doing little things like that for her.

This June holiday was into the forests of the Upper Peninsula. Father had rented a cabin for the weekend, promising her fascinating trees the likes of which she had never seen before, with so many secrets just waiting for her to discover. She found that hard to believe, seeing as their neighborhood had the best trees in all of Michigan.

On the way, they stopped briefly at a place with gas pumps out front, though not because the car needed fuel. Mother said that this was the nearest country store to where they were heading, and would be the perfect place for picking up supplies for the weekend. They shopped and planned… laughing their way through the store. After completing their purchases, she climbed into the backseat in a mild huff at being denied a bag of roasted peanuts that instead went into the trunk along with all the other groceries. That was okay… soon they would be cooking out on an open fire… and singing songs… and listening to Father's silly ghost stories. The warmth of the sun was all over her face and neck. Everything was perfect!

They drove out of the parking lot after a mild disagreement had been settled between her parents. They rarely fought… and not at all in the way some of her friends' parents did. It was just a discussion over whether the car windows should be up or down. Father was hot, but Mother was worried about insects. They settled on a compromise – the driver's side would be partly opened for him.

She was not thinking about anything in particular, just enjoying the passing forest now that the car was up to speed on the highway, when a faint hum came into her left ear… and then a little tickle to that side of her face. She thought nothing of it. Just the way the gentle breeze from the front was making her hair dance about. But as the feeling persisted, she finally turned that way to deal with the distraction.

In a flash of recognition, she let out a scream and began swatting wildly in the air all about her. She could tell that Mother had turned around in the front seat, and so had Father's head… but they were up there and it was back here with her. Without really knowing what she was doing, she slid to the floor behind her mother's seat, perhaps hoping that to be down there was to be hidden from the creature. She could hear Mother ordering Father to pull over. A hand made contact with her head, and she somehow knew it to be from him, as he must be craning over the backseat to pull her up from the floor.

Her eyes, however, were on that awful thing, suspended in the very center of the car mere inches from her nose. It just floated there before her, staring back with its eyes of black set within an eerily yellow, triangular-shaped face. The way its quivering antenna searched out the air froze her in horror.

Then something terribly weird happened. As if in slow motion, the wasp began to backflip before her… or perhaps it was she who was spinning about it. Either way, she somehow felt tethered to it, and made to pan in a circle about its grotesquely hovering form. At first, a strange backward pull came upon her as the wasp's underside rotated into view. There, its yellow legs twitched about in a folded position beneath its body, sending another shiver throughout her. As she continued to swing under it, she was strangely aware that the insect did not seem to feel any of the forces acting upon her. It just hung there in space, adjusting itself against a pull of gravity that had her being dragged toward her feet within that twisting can of air. Around she went to the rear of the creature, feeling herself go upside down and shift toward the roof of the car. She was so near to where the thing most dangerous for her would be. And there it dangled, exaggerated in length by her terror. For a split second, the end brushed the tip of her nose as she passed by. Now coming around over its top, she felt herself falling down toward the creature's back. Those black wings were moving so fast as they paddled about in the air… clearer than ever before. Between those wings was that iridescently dark body. Her eyes were made to pan its length, section after section from tail all the way back to its yellow head… just as she completed the full rotation about it.

At that precise moment in which the car completed its mid-air, twisted spin from off the highway embankment, she got pitched forward over the car's driveshaft hump and into the footwell behind her father's seat. Her face hit the floor hard, and something came down on her back with crushing force just as the car made a horrifying impact at the bottom of a ravine. Instantly, everything went dark within the sounds of shattered glass and a crippled metal screech.

She was shaking beyond control on the bench, replaying that horrible memory over and over, when a gentle touch came to her shoulder.

"Marna? Are you okay?"

She lifted her head from between her knees to behold a face she had not seen in over four years. Though stretched out a bit and more full in its near grown-up form, enough of the boy was still there for her to immediately recognize its owner.

"Roy...?"

"You're shivering... but you can't be cold. What's the matter? Are you ill? Let me..."

"I'm fine. I just..."

"Marna... you have a huge bump on your forehead! Did you fall? Did someone hit you?!"

She noticed his hands ball up into fists as he looked up and down the empty hallway.

"No. I... I only fainted. I'll be fine. I just need to sit here for a few minutes until my head clears."

"I'm not leaving you until it does... and then I'm taking you to the nurse's office. You should call your aunt. I can do that for..."

"Stop! Like I said – I'm going to be fine!"

For a reason obvious to only her, she felt better in being able to express an irritation at something other than herself. Roy Meitner had shown up just when she needed him most... though he probably did not deserve to be treated so brusquely. Yet anything was better than thinking about what she knew would soon come back into her mind. She looked away from him, seeking for something else to be the surrogate for her disgust with herself. Before her was just the thing.

"I absolutely hate the underside of stairwells! They're so... dirty and ugly! You can't tell me that the school couldn't figure out a better use for that space other than allowing it to sit there collecting dust." She watched him look that way, knowing by the perplexity on his face that he had no idea what was going on with her thoughts. "It's like that stupid closet in your house. You know... the one under your stairs. I mean… why close the thing off like that, making it all dark and dusty just because people can't figure out a better place to hang their coats?! If I had my way, I'd open it up and turn it into a cozy little nook. A private place where a person could go and no one would come round to pester them."

She had him looking in confusion between her and the stairs.

Good! Let's keep it that way.

"Uhh… maybe I should go get the nurse…"

"No… don't! I'm… just carrying on. Please stay. I appreciate the company while my head clears. You know… I'd forgotten that you were going to school here. You're a junior, right?"

"Yep. And you're a sophomore. I saw you on the first day of class… from a distance… but couldn't… you know, get over to say hi. We haven't seen each other since… well, not since… you know."

"Roy… that was a long time ago. Ancient history."

They sat silently for several minutes before he insisted that she be walked to the nurse's office. Roy parted from her there to go about whatever had accounted for him having a hall pass. Alone again, she faced once more the memory, saw the wasp, and finally understood.

It's all my fault. I'm responsible for my parent's death. All because I was afraid.

Without realizing it, her left hand took ahold of her right wrist, compressing the alert bracelet's metal against her skin. The resulting sting of pain was minor and barely noticeable… hardly significant enough to displace the thing piercing her heart. She now fully bore the horrible weight of her past… and nothing about the future would ever seem light again.

END OF WASP 1

WASP 2

DISCARDED DAUGHTERS

CHAPTER

9

CHASING TRAINS

She kept to the nurse's cot for the remainder of that school day, ignoring the appearances of other students with injuries and illnesses of their own. Pulled inward, she had a mind only for her memory. Each tick to the wall clock set a rhythm in which she replayed the accident over and over. The outcome never changed.

Gwen returned prior to the final bell and drove her to their physician's office. There, she was instructed to stay off her feet, keep ice on the bump, and take aspirin if her head continued to ache. She was then deposited at home alone. Lying in her bed with the lights out, she had no mind for pondering on running into Roy Meitner for the first time in over four years. Even the oddity of having gone for so long with the memory buried in her head did not really register. To her, the accident had happened that very morning. So she swept all other thoughts into a far corner in order to concentrate on the memory itself. For hours, she poked at its edges, only reluctantly delving into the heart of it – the wasp and the consequences of her fear. As dusk came to darken her room, she found herself drawn exclusively to those last fleeting impressions of her parents just prior to the crash. The way her mother screamed and her father shouted… their voices both bore her name on their lips.

For weeks afterward, she dwelt in a lackadaisical state, going about life without vigor or resistance. She gave no thought for how she dressed, what she ate, or what she did with herself. Each school day was simply a matter of going from bed to shop to class to shop to bed… all without awareness of time. She knew that her chores were being shoddily attended to… as were her studies… but she did not care. Her biology project received a failing grade because she turned it in with a single pin stuck through the wasp's head. Weeks turned into months, with her friendships being put on hold. Every previous aspiration of hers for dating, learning to drive, or taking part in student body government seemed to have never crossed her mind. She thought only of her parents. The memory of the accident became intertwined into her mind… just as that metal bracelet was wrapped about her wrist. She was living as an orphan in the heat, dust and wind of this West Texas outland all because she had given in to her fear… and that fear had senselessly led to her parents' death.

She never told anyone about what she had remembered, least of all Gwen whose brother she had killed and whose burden she had become. Not that Gwen was unaware of a change in her, particularly when her first set of high school marks came out at midterm in underwhelming fashion. Gwen's reprimands and restrictions were hardly as disturbing as knowing that she was responsible for the death of her parents. The only incident that even remotely registered with her during that time was when Patsy, elbow-deep in preparation of Christmas poinsettias, proclaimed confidently what could only appear as obvious to that ditsy woman.

"Gosh, Gwen… it's written plain-as-day all over her face. Been sayin' it for months – Marna's in love."

The two women, as if debating the best means of fixing an off-center arrangement, stood before the cutting room table nipping at the topic with no regard for her feelings.

"Can't be love, Patsy. Maybe unrequited infatuation. That's about the best you could expect from a teenager. That you, Marna… unrequited? That why you've been so terribly dull of late?"

"It's none of your business."

She noticed Gwen's eyebrows shoot up at being addressed in such a curt manner, but did not care. All she wanted was to be left alone.

"Woo-hoo! I think you've hit on it, Gwen! Sure as rain, she's got secret feelin's for someone! Marna, dear… who's this mysterious fella of yours? Come on, you can tell us. It'll do you good to get it out. Is it Francis Polk? Or maybe that Xavier boy?"

"Hell no! My niece's got more sense than to be attracted to that hunchback."

"Gwen – that's so cruel! I think he's cute. Well then… what about that undertaker's son? His folks have gotten filthy rich!"

"Pritchett? That's an excellent family. Is that your would-be beau, Marna? What's his first name?"

"If you two are determined to be rude... and nosey... then I'm leaving. I've got... homework to do."

She passed them by without another word, making for the shop's office where she could find some relief from idiotic questions about idiotic boys. But she only got as far as the hallway before Patsy threw out her next guess.

"Good gravy, I know who it is! It's Ruby Meitner's boy!"

She shot a quick glance at Gwen. The glare back was enough for her to know fully what her aunt thought of Patsy's latest suggestion. She ignored it and entered the office, closing the door behind her. Seating herself at Gwen's desk, she did not bother to move aside either the ledger or the stacks of invoices piled there, for she had no intention whatsoever of studying. Leaning forward onto the desk and closing her eyes, the images of her father and mother came back to her once more... as did the wasp.

I've gotta get this out of my head!

Fortunately, the approach of Christmas offered her some distractions. Nothing of the accident was forgotten. She simply covered everything over with the false gaiety of the season. With many smiles, she buried the images of the accident into a shallow grave of her thinking, with a weak resolution not to dig them up and expose them to this land of the living until after the holidays. New Year's Eve, however, brought a new worry... although minor in comparison to her memories. That fall, Gwen had set her sights on making Forde's Flowers the preferred floral supplier of Lubbock's funeral parlors... a goal that included targeting one of the county's largest – the Pritchett Family Mortuaries. This was nothing more than the typical wheeling-and-dealing that Gwen was adept at, albeit with a new twist – socializing with Harold and Madeline Pritchett. Though not really appreciating it as so, she found that her first moment of true relief from her memories came on the day Gwen informed her that they would be attending the Pritchett's New Year's Eve party... to be held at one of their establishments. As morbidly unappealing as that sounded, she felt more disgusted with the possibility of having to cozy up to their son, CP. The thought of being around that boy was almost as bad as the sad memory of her parents.

She had only occasionally crossed paths with CP at school owing to the fortunate fact that she was a year younger than him. In junior high, he had been widely known for his demeaning sense of humor... as well as his tendency for teasing any kid with a weakness. She, being an orphan with a life-threatening allergy, sometimes found herself as his target. It was mostly juvenile stuff...

hallway antics and the like… but hurtful enough that she did her best to avoid being anywhere near him. Others had it far worse. She still shuttered over the time that he highjacked the school's PA system to do a mocking rendition of a fellow eighth grader's speech impediment… simply because that boy had beaten him at a track meet.

At least in high school, CP's complexion had cleared and the rest of his face had caught up with those buck teeth. So… out of courtesy to the host family, she ended up dancing with him a few times during the party. She was surprised not to find a hint of the derisive child in the teen. Throughout the evening, he was respectful and considerate, placing her at center stage in their conversations. Her best explanation was that he had finally gotten serious about life… and maybe that was why he had become one of the best basketball players on the varsity squad.

Into January, she found that her depression was lifted enough for her to start thinking about her school work again. She also began socializing more, going out with girlfriends and attending school dances. She did not go so far as to date… though she was beginning to look kindly on receiving offers. That is, until they started coming from CP. In graciously declining, she could not possibly explain to him that the memory of the boy he had once been still lingered in her opinion of him. Truth be told, she was also creeped out by the thought of hanging around with the son of an undertaker. So she was not at all happy to find out that CP had gone behind her back to Gwen… and Gwen had accepted the invitation on her behalf.

"Stop your whining! He's a fine young man from a fine Lubbock family. Besides, you'll be double-dating with that Atkins boy and his girl. Christopher's promised to have you back from the theater by ten, so what's the worst thing that could happen?! You'll eat stale popcorn and make fun of a corny B-movie."

The other couple, both juniors, were friends of CP's. Though she did not know them well, she knew of them well enough to feel comfortable around them. What she had not expected on being picked up by CP was discovering that this date involved a trip to the passion pit.

"CP… you never said anything about a drive-in! And you brought a truck?! How're we all supposed to fit in that?! I certainly hope you're not expecting me to sit in the back… not wearing this!"

Actually, she was in one of her least favorite dresses – the pale green one with so many pleats that made it an absolute nightmare to iron. She did not care much about the dress, but she did care a whole lot about being too near to CP at a drive-in movie.

"No problem… Stiles got his old man's Eldorado. We'll put the top down and sit up on the back."

"Then why didn't he drive here with you to pick me up?"

"Oh… we're meeting them there."

When they arrived at the drive-in, she was surprised that CP pulled his truck directly into the line for the pay stall.

"Shouldn't we wait out here for them… that way we only have to pay for one car?"

"I forgot to mention… Becky's gotta get home before the feature's over. That's why we're meeting up inside."

Though there were plenty of spaces up front, CP chose a spot in the back corner of the lot… a great distance from the screen and the concession area. She pointed this out to him, but he said he wanted to find Stiles first before settling on something closer. He left the truck, and she waited there, searching through the arriving vehicles for the other couple. When CP returned, he was still alone.

"Did you find them?"

"Nope. Let's stay put until they show. Got popcorn and coke."

Something in the way he said it… not the words themselves… but a perk to his voice gave her a shudder's worth of flashback to the sneaky CP of junior high. She brushed the thought aside with the start-up of the short. CP was being a gentleman in offering her the popcorn first. When he rolled down the driver's side window, she assumed it was to pull the speaker in. Instead, he poured out a good portion of the coke, and then began groping about beneath his seat. Stooped over with the side of his head up against the steering wheel, he sent her the strangest look. Something halfway between the tongue-protruded concentration of a kid and the unnerving leer of an adult.

"Why'd you pour that out?"

"Makin' room for this…"

His expression turned into a wicked smile… and she immediately knew that she was in trouble as he pulled out a bottle. As if so very proud of himself, he sloshed the dark contents in her face before unscrewing the cap. The smell of it instantly filled the truck's cab – a burnt sort of sweetness, unmistakably alcoholic in form. He brought the cup's level back up to where it had been and took a sip. With disgust, she watched him appraise the mixture's quality before topping it off once more. He then took a much longer draw on the cup.

"Ahh… pure magic! Now you drink up, Marna. You're gonna love it."

"I'm not touching that stuff!"

"Suit yourself... but I can tell you, it sure makes going to a drive-in loads more fun."

Everything she had told herself not to hold against CP came rushing back, and whatever she had laid to his credit was gone. She turned to the screen and fought through her options. She could leave his truck and hunt for someone at the concession booth to go home with... which was unlikely, seeing as the main feature had already begun. Maybe she should call Gwen?

No. She'd never believe me. She'd say I was making much ado about nothing.

She went round and round before finally deciding to stick it out in the hope that he would not drink himself into trouble. She would stay on her side of the truck and ignore him. And if it got real bad... then she would just leave. But already it was becoming so annoying with how he was slurping on his drink and munching away at the popcorn. He was making those noises on purpose... just to irritate her! It was then that she realized that another sound was missing.

"CP, you forgot to put the speaker in the..."

Turning his way, she was startled to find that he was not facing the screen. With a knee drawn up on the seat between them, he was turned in her direction. He was watching her! For the first time since entering the drive-in, she was genuinely concerned.

"We don't need a speaker."

Before she could respond, he dropped the coke and the popcorn to the floor of the truck, lunging across the seat at her. The impact pitched her into the passenger side door, jarring her shoulder and stealing a good bit of the volume to her scream. Before she knew what was happening, he had his arms about her waist and was yanking her down onto the seat. She went to scream again, but his hand came across her mouth to stifle her gulp of air. So she swatted that hand away, but the other replaced it just as fast.

"Gert owf meee!"

In complete terror, her anger was still red-hot enough to put up a fierce battle of slapping and clawing at his face... at the same time trying to knee him where it would hurt most. She kept up the screams and curses... until he knocked the wind out of her by dropping his full weight down on top of her.

"Stop fighting, Marna! You know you want this!"

He had her shoulders pinned to the seat with his forearms and was forcing his bourbon-laced lips upon hers. She tried desperately to pitch him off, thrashing about with all her strength. But he had such a strong grip on her arms – it was impossible to fight him off with strength alone. Finally managing to slip her forearm underneath his chin, she pushed up into his throat, making his head jerk back. She then took advantage of his surprise to search out with her other hand for something soft. Finding an ear, she sank her nails in and twisted.

"Ouwwwchhh! You bitch! Let go!"

This was the moment she had been hoping for. She put everything she had into her loudest and longest scream, praying that someone would hear. But in horrifying slow motion, she watched him draw back a clinched fist… and just knew that she was about to be struck in the face. Instinctively, she turned her head to brace herself… but the blow never came. Instead, the truck's dome light came on… and then CP's body inexplicably slid down hers and out through the driver's side door. She caught just a glimpse of the shock on his face as he failed in a frantic effort to lay hold onto her legs. As he disappeared over the far edge of the seat, she heard a rather loud thud… and recognized it as his forehead colliding with the truck's runner board on the way out. Terribly shaken, she still managed to pick up on the sounds of a struggle going on outside the truck. Curses and yelps of pain were flying everywhere. She quickly scootched across and out of the open door to find two bodies going at it in the darkness. Someone was astride CP, and with horrific force was pounding away at his face with many fist blows. Over and over, the sound of the punches overwhelmed her with their violence.

"Stop! You're killing him!"

In that terrifying moment, freakishly lit by the flickering light from the drive-in movie screen, she beheld the fullness of fury in Roy's face. Lurching forward, she wrapped both arms about him and pulled back with what remained of her strength. She finally got him to topple backward off of CP… which unfortunately also brought her to the ground. Just like that, Roy had changed. He was immediately on his feet helping her up and apologizing for knocking her over. Below them, gurgling out weak threats, CP rolled onto his side and began to cry.

"Get your things – I'm taking you home."

"I only have a purse… But what about him?! We can't just leave him here like this!"

"Oh yes we can! He can count himself lucky to be alive!"

Without another word, Roy retrieved her purse and then came back to wrap an arm about her shoulders, steering her away from CP. Moving toward the front of the drive-in, he led her along rows and columns of parked cars. Though she knew that their occupants were only expressing a mild displeasure at them for the distraction they were posing, she nevertheless felt that their voices of objection were because of something different. The danger was behind her, but not the horrible shame threatening to overwhelm her. Somehow, Roy's whispered reassurances gave her the strength to keep going. So she rested into his side, trusting in him to prevent her from collapsing. She soon found herself beside another truck. With the passenger door open, Roy was helping her inside… but also arguing with someone already within.

"I said move over."

"Where's the popcorn and… Hey, what's she doing here?!"

"I didn't get any… and it doesn't matter anyway. We're leaving. Now move over."

"Roy Meitner… if you think I'm sharing this seat with another girl, then you're…"

"Give it a rest, Judy!"

Before finally shifting in the seat, Judy Kingman threw out a nasty glare at her. For however long it took, she remained silent as Roy drove out of the drive-in and through the streets of Lubbock. The whole time, she did not once lift her face from her lap, being far too overwhelmed with the shock of what had just happened to her. When the engine suddenly shut down, she looked up to find that they were parked outside her house. Purposing not to say a word to either Roy or Judy, she sought to get out as quickly as possible… but ended up clumsily fumbling with the door handle owing to her distress. The humiliation of CP was still on her… and soon she would be confronted by Gwen. But Roy had already come around to help her out. As before, she was touched by his gentle care… by how he wrapped an arm about her and slowly walked her to the porch steps… even offering to accompany her inside and explain what had happened.

"No, Roy. That would *not* be a good idea. I can manage it from here on my own. Thank you for the ride and… for what you did for me. I… umm… hope you won't… think badly of me for… going out with him."

She looked up to find Roy silently shaking his head.

"You don't have to say a thing, Marna. I'd never think ill of you. Besides… he had it coming."

"Do you think he'll… you know… get you in trouble?"

"Nah. If there's one thing I know about CP, he'd rather die a thousand deaths than admit to being beaten. He'll probably stay home for a week claiming to be sick or something."

Just then the horn on Roy's truck sounded. Looking that way, she made out the faint outline of Judy Kingman staring straight out the windshield as if nothing unusual had happened.

"I'd better get going, Marna. Good night."

He stuck out a hand to her... and in reaching down to accept it, she instantly flinched at the sight.

"Roy! Your knuckles... they're all beat up! Oh lord, you're bleeding! Let's get you inside so I can wrap them... "

"They're okay, Marna. Absolutely fine. As a matter of fact, they've never felt better."

He turned away with a grin.

She watched him all the way down the walk, around his truck, and up beside the stone-faced Judy. Only after he had driven off did she take a moment to straighten out her hair and make herself look as unflustered as possible. Then, with a deep breath and an artificial smile, she stepped inside as casually as she imagined any unmolested teenage girl might do.

"I heard that horn – you're home early. Something gone wrong with your date?"

"CP's not feeling well... probably too much popcorn. I had one of the kids take me home. Anything happening around here?"

Gwen looked up from her easy chair with a flash of appraisal, so she deepened her smile in response... at the same time leaning against the wall in her best depiction of lethargy.

"Nope. Just the usual. Going through these floral magazines. Interested in a game or two of cribbage before bed?"

"Mind if I pass? I feel a bit queasy myself. I think I'd rather shower and get this greasy smell off me... then turn in. We working tomorrow?"

Gwen nodded before returning to what she had been doing.

"I don't think I'm going to go out with CP again."

She knew Gwen would look up at this, so she was prepared. Fluffing out her hair with both hands, she made a show of annoyance out of having discovered a ragged spot on one nail. Picking at it while conveying a look of mild dissatisfaction, she breathed out just loud enough to give Gwen the impression that it was such a bother to explain.

"He's just not my type. Way too consumed with himself."

She left only after being convinced that Gwen had grown bored with her presence.

Having scrubbed every inch of herself with a hand cloth, she lingered under the shower even longer in hopes that the dirty feeling on the inside might also be washed away. The water was hot, but she still shivered at the thought of what had happened tonight. Cloaking herself in towels, she left one sanctuary for another. She dressed in her cleanest and crispest set of pajamas and climbed into bed. Only after turning out the lamp did a different sort of feeling come over her. Someone had risked it all in coming to her rescue, for Roy had been there when she needed him most.

Come Monday morning, she set about meandering down corridors largely unfamiliar to her, the whole time telling herself that it was nothing more than a whim… a change of pace in expanding her horizons. That is, until she found what she was looking for all along – Roy alone at his locker. Now that they were together, she took care not to express how she was truly feeling. She was especially careful in what she said, not wanting to come off too strong. After all, it was more important to show appreciation for what he had done for her. She returned at the next break in order to check-up on the condition of his hands, as she had forgotten to ask about that on her previous visit. Then after lunch, she just so happened to be passing through that part of campus again. Roy smiled and chatted pleasantly with her… just like he had done on the other two times she had come by. Most of all, she took silent pleasure in seeing that he only parted from her when the bell required it.

At the end of the school day, it was he who sought her out at her locker.

"So, Marna… wanna go out with me sometime?"

"I'd like that, Roy… very much."

So began 'the romance of Marna Forde and Roy Meitner'… as she frequently would refer to their relationship in her daydreams over the next few weeks. From day one, having Roy as her boyfriend made her feel more secure and protected than she ever had in her whole life. Not like she was some dainty damsel in need of a prince charming… or a fragile porcelain figurine kept safe in a glass cabinet. Hanging off his arm… she simply felt special. Sort of like a beautiful flower on display in its vase. But to many of her classmates, she knew that they were just another new couple amidst a student body's sea of other such ships passing in the school year. She did not much care what any of them thought. She was happy. Of course, they received the same kinds of attention worthy of the 'going steady' news they eventually conveyed. Many of the ensuing rumors about them got distributed hotly when all was fresh, with a few predicting an impending break-up within a month or so. Those grew less common as their relationship moved beyond the 'item' stage. Spring became summer, and they were still together into the new school year. The presence of Roy holding her hand became as common to her classmates as cotton in the fields. For some, the outlook for them together went far, whereas the greater number of her friends no longer gave them much thought at all. So it was for her and Roy dating – they had become accepted as a couple. This opinion was universally held… with the exception of two individuals.

Gwen, for one, did not take kindly to the news… nor did she refrain from doing something to put an end to the relationship at the beginning. When she informed her aunt on the weekend following the disastrous date with CP that she was going out with Roy Meitner, Gwen jumped past her normal stare of intimidation right into immediate outrage.

"No way I'm allowing that!"

"Really?! And what do you plan to do to stop it? Can't exactly follow me around…"

"I absolutely forbid you from dating that boy! If you do… you're grounded! For every weekend from here 'til hell freezes over, you understand me?! You're not to…"

"It's none of your business who I date!"

"Like hell it isn't!"

Their fights were frequent and intense, usually degrading into shouting matches that involved a whole lot of door slamming on her part. No way would she back down to Gwen on this one… because Roy was worth it. Her initial 'dates' with him ended up being restricted to those times that Gwen had no ability to control – between classes, lunch time, and their walks to and from school each day… just as in their youth. Gradually, her defiance wore away at her aunt's will for reprisals… especially since dating Roy produced in her nothing but good in terms of the tangibles that Gwen cared most about – good grades and an excellent work ethic at the shop. Gwen was at a loss for using any more punishments, and instead resorted to a tactic not well practiced in the years of raising her – earnest appeals.

"But why date him, Marna?! Of all the boys in Lubbock, why date the son of that horrid man?! My nerves can't take it! I know you're doing this to get back at me for… for making you work!"

"Aunt Gwen, it's got nothing at all to do with you… and it's definitely got nothing to do with his father. I like Roy. He's nice… and he's kind."

"There's a world of nice boys out there…"

"Nobody like Roy."

"You don't realize how difficult this is on me seeing you with him."

"Then don't look."

In contrast to the blatant resistance shown by her aunt… manageable by experience… nothing prepared her for dealing with the subtle, yet pervasive displeasure of Roy's sister. The cunning of that thirteen year old was unlike anything she had encountered from even the most seasoned of high schoolers. It did not matter that Roy's parents approved of their relationship. From day one, she knew that Sybil was against it. On the very first instance of her return to the Meitner house… it being a family dinner arranged for her by Mrs. Meitner… Sybil went about undermining her confidence with trivial little comments delivered with unusual precision by a girl better known for her morose outlook on life.

"We usually only eat in the dining room on special occasions."

"Roy, what's the name of your other girlfriend? You know… the one you were necking with on the front porch the other day?"

"Hey, Dad… you're always going on and on about Marna's aunt being crazy. What's crazy look like?"

"Mom, take me to the flower shop next time you go. I want to see where Marna sweeps floors."

"You two thinking about getting married soon?"

Somehow, the embarrassment of the other three Meitners every time Sybil opened her mouth made things much worse. It would have been better had everyone just ignored her.

Over the months to follow, Sybil's tactics shifted from pert comments to outright criticisms of her brother anytime she was around… though the girl was obviously being purposeful in veiling everything within the guise of helpful suggestions. On one instance near the end of the school year as she was waiting for Roy in the showroom of the Meitner Appliance Store, she was startled to find Sybil standing at her side.

"You know my brother's going to be taking over management of this store once he graduates next month. Heard it from Dad himself."

"That's fantastic. I bet he does well with…"

"You think so? I guess that's sort of Roy's speed… So easily satisfied with being simple. He doesn't have an ounce of ambition in him."

"Sybil, you shouldn't… "

"He'll never get up the courage to leave Lubbock. Likes it here way too much! How do you deal with that, Marna… knowing that you and your boyfriend are so very different?"

"What're you talking about?! We're not that different."

"You're like me. I can't wait to get the hell out of this shithole."

"Wow, Sybil… quite a tongue you've got hidden in there."

"Don't act like you don't feel the same way. I see it in your eyes every time you're over at our house. You detest this place."

"No I don't! There're plenty of nice things about…"

"Have you told my brother how much you hate it here… because I'm pretty sure he thinks otherwise. Pretty sure he thinks you just *love* Texas. I could have a talk with him. You know… break the ice about your true feelings. Can't see how those won't one day cause trouble for your relationship."

"Sybil, don't you think you're a bit too young to make out like you know what's best in relationships? Roy and I… were just dating… that's all."

"That's not how he thinks… leastwise not how it seems to me… and I've known him all my life. All he can talk about is you… and this crummy store. Pretty sure he's thinking about one thing and one thing only – marriage."

"That's none of your business!"

"But like you said… I'm just a little girl. I'm not as smart as you. I'm sure you've got it all figured out. Well… so long, Marna. Enjoy dating Roy… while it lasts."

These kinds of verbal assaults by Sybil constantly pricked at her sense of well-being. She had finally reached a point in her life where the past was the past and the future looked bright… and here was a person of no consequence repeatedly picking away at her satisfaction of the moment. Still… the substance of Sybil's subterfuge could not be ignored. Roy was sweet, affectionate and very attentive, but he seemed totally disinterested in anything beyond Lubbock. In time, she would have to move him along… or move along without him. It would be difficult to be parted from him… but some were driven and some stayed put. Now that she was finishing up her junior year, she was beginning to set her sights on something of what the greater world had to offer an ambitious young woman such as herself. So maybe it was best that she not bother planting notions in Roy's mind, for when the time came for her to leave, she would make him understand… especially once she actually did have it all figured out.

Being a year older, Roy graduated ahead of her as expected… and just as his sister predicted, the reigns to the Meitner Appliance Store were handed over to him. She was more than happy for him… he had talked of nothing else during the last few days of school. That summer, she witnessed for herself how he rose to take on the new responsibilities… dressing in a tie every day, throwing himself into a deeper study of the store's inventory and sales, and trying so very hard to be an adult. She felt that the summer of them dating should have been no different from that of the previous year, yet she still sensed something changing between them. He spoke more often of a future of them together in Lubbock… and she thought more secretly of her own future outside of Texas. She was now spending many private moments imagining what it might be like to go to college in some far off state. Oddly, Roy never seemed to play much of a role in these daydreams. He might come with her… and she could easily see them make a go of it together… but the possibility that he would stay behind never seemed that disturbing to her. She was quite certain of one thing though. In a year's time, she would no longer be calling Lubbock home.

Roy's expectations for their future as a couple were not really a thing on her mind… not compared to her concern over Gwen's lack of engagement on the subject of college. Whenever she brought the topic up, her aunt responded with a noncommittal 'let me think about that.' As she had only been able to save up four hundred dollars from working at Forde's Flowers, the cold reality was painfully clear – even with a scholarship, she was going to need Gwen's financial assistance to cover the full cost of college. So, for the months of September and October, she put on an advertising blitz toward her aunt, talking up everything from private schools up north that she had read about to the technical college right there in Lubbock. Nothing seemed to nudge Gwen beyond her indifference.

In early November, when applications for colleges and placement tests were coming due, she began to fear that there was a hidden side to her aunt's caginess. The shop, she was told, had not been doing so well. Gwen was quick to blame the downturn on the poor local economy… and something vague to do with 'that man.' But all of Gwen's sour talk about Mr. Meitner and the waning Texas oil industry really meant nothing to her. In all her years of living with Gwen, there had never been anything but upbeat feelings about the shop's success. Even as recently as that past summer, Gwen had been encouraging her to consider a future as a florist. Her aunt said that the prospects were good, and if she worked hard, full management of the shop might one day go to her. So it all made no sense!

She went on looking for subtle ways of talking to Gwen about money without provoking an outright fight. Meanwhile, she also began seeking the advice of anyone who would listen – girlfriends, teachers, the school counselor, and even Patsy. Most everyone could not understand her hunger for getting out of Texas. She was becoming desperate… so much so that she did what seemed to be the only thing left to do – speak with Mr. Meitner. After all, he was both ambitious in life and sympathetic to her situation. He had seen the world while in the military… or so said Roy… and even though he came right back to Lubbock, it was only to start his dream business.

On a Sunday evening in mid-November… while Roy and his mother were cleaning up after dinner… she asked for a moment alone with Mr. Meitner. He led her to their family room just off the main hallway. She was not particularly fond of this dark and rustic space… but it was plenty good enough for a talk.

"Mr. Meitner… I've… got a problem… and I suppose I really shouldn't be asking you... you know, seeing as... well... you know... you and my aunt don't exactly see eye-to-eye. But I'm desperate... and could sure use your advice. The thing is... I think she wants me to stay on at the shop after high school... seeing as business isn't so good... but I'd rather... do something else."

"I see. And would this something else involve... say... getting as far away from Lubbock as possible? Maybe going to college out of state?"

"How'd you know that?! I mean... I haven't even discussed it with Roy!"

"I won't comment other than to say that it's pretty obvious, Marna. But you do realize that you're putting me in a doubly difficult position – coming between you and your aunt, yet also between you and my boy. So let me just say..."

The family room door suddenly opened, with Sybil sticking her head in. The cautious manner in which the girl did this struck her as odd, especially seeing as it suggested that she might be snooping.

"Excuse me... Mom says to come... pie's ready."

Before leaving, Sybil's eyes shot over from her father and remained on her longer than was necessary. But Mr. Meitner gave no mind to his daughter, starting up again once the door had closed.

"Basically... I think you have an age-old problem on your hands. Your responsibility to family versus your personal aspirations. Both are on your heart... and both deserve your respect. I'm not telling you how to choose simply because I don't believe it's an issue of one versus the other. It probably looks that way to young eyes... I know, I've been there. All I can say is that you need to find a way to be faithful to both – your dreams and your obligations – because it's the only way to have balance in life. I don't know what to tell you other than that. But don't worry, Marna... it'll all work out. Now... what's say we go see about that pie?"

She spent the remainder of that evening and into the following week reflecting on Mr. Meitner's advice of 'both' rather than 'either.' Intuitively, it made sense to be true to oneself and true to one's commitments... but that advice did not come close to solving her problem. In her case, there was absolutely no compatibility in 'both' if it meant staying in Lubbock to work in Gwen's puny flower shop. Her desperation constantly gnawed at her. Nobody was like her – so very anxious to make a mark on this world. Everyone she knew seemed so very happy to go about life just the way things were. She really had to get away from that attitude. But the issue of money, like a cold Canadian air mass flowing in over the plains, kept shriveling the hope right out of her. There was no way around it – she needed Gwen's support.

After wrestling all week with her urgency, she swore to herself that today would be the day. They were in Gwen's car completing a Friday morning circuit of Lubbock greenhouses. Fall weather was well at hand, and most places had already begun to winterize. While her aunt was out fraternizing with some old crotchety grower, she remained in the car trying to figure out the best way to broach the subject of money. After tinkering around with various approaches, she concluded that the only way was straight through. She would simply ask for the funds needed to enroll in the cheapest option available – the technical college right there in town. At least this way she could dangle out a promise of working at the shop while also getting a college degree. She could endure four more years of Lubbock if it meant…

The driver's side door suddenly opened, and Gwen popped right in. Her look – silent self-assurance with a strange hint of dissatisfaction mixed in – brought an instant hiccup of sorts to her rehearsed speech.

"Is everything okay?"

"Don't know why you'd think otherwise."

"Are we done for the morning?"

"I expect so. You got somewhere to be before school starts?"

"No, ma'am. I was just hoping to talk with you about… you know… money for college and…"

"Funny you should bring up that subject, because I had an interesting visitor in the shop the other day. Care to guess who?"

Her immediate fear was that someone she had spoken with had blundered in to lecture Gwen about taking better care of her niece's future.

"Ahh… no idea. Who?"

"Sybil Meitner. She came by after school all in a rush to pick up one of our cornucopia arrangements for her mother. Care to guess what we chatted about in the process?"

Oh crap… this is not good!

"Umm… the weather?"

"Close. But more like whether or not my niece has the common courtesy to hold her aunt's affairs in confidence."

Shit! That little weasel!

"I'm not sure what you mean."

"Stop playing games with me, Marna. You've never been very good at it anyway. You told George Meitner that my shop's come on hard times. Don't even bother denying it."

"I only said…"

"I'm not interested in what you 'only said.' I'm interested in what that girl told me, seeing as that reflects what she happens to know. Really,

Niece, I thought better of you than this. You need a stern lesson in loyalty and respect."

"That's not fair. I've been more than…"

"Enough! We'll talk about this later… after I've had time to better think it through. But let me leave you with a clear message – I'm not paying for your college education. Aside from the fact that there's no money available anyway… what with the store and house tied up in mortgages… and all my other debts. So if you want to go to college, then work your tail off like the rest of the world has to. Stop whining about your dreams and your big plans for the future. You want to be independent?! Well then, earn it!"

Not another word was exchanged between them on the drive to the flower shop. To make sure of this, she turned her face fully away from Gwen and toward her own side window. Through a thin layer of glass, she watched the pre-dawn of Lubbock's streets flow by. Sidewalks and buildings sped past in purple hazes, none of which came into focus as she was not really looking at anything. Her mind was completely engaged in bitter thoughts. For Gwen not to have the decency to hear her side of things…

…or the smarts to know that Sybil Meitner is a little backstabbing bitch! Well, it cuts both ways! She owes me some loyalty and respect too. She's made so many promises she hasn't kept. All her talk about women pursuing their own ambitions – what a load of cow turds! She's only ever cared about her shop and her stupid flowers. She'll try to keep me here right up until the day she croaks. I'm tired of being her slave! Tired of her not respecting that I'm my own person with my own dreams… and the right to make my own choices. Well fine! She'll make me work at her stupid little shop, but that's it! First chance and I'm outta here! No questions asked and no looking back. I'm gone forever!

But a familiarity to the many silent blocks they were passing brought a sudden and sad conclusion to her rant.

Who am I kidding? I'm going nowhere. I'll never escape this place.

This unspoken verdict brought a sour twist to her feelings of resentment. This would not do. Above all, she must keep her anger fresh and perfectly focused on Gwen's betrayal.

She shot a quick glance toward her aunt as they made a turn onto 4th Street. Here, at least, was something she could latch onto. They happened to be moving along the streets of Lubbock in Gwen's 'little blue baby' – a 63 Skylark convertible… a thing she purchased that summer on a whim. At the time, it had been such a neat little joke between them… a Skylark picked up on a lark… but now it spoke volumes about her aunt's hypocrisy.

'Broke' my ass! She must think I'm an idiot! She bragged on and on for weeks about being able to pay for this thing with cash. Here I clean buckets and floors so she can buy herself a brand new car!

Gwen pulled over the shallow curb into the alley behind the shop. As the suspension beneath her gave a sudden lurch, she was reminded of another aspect of her anger at Gwen because of this new car. Not two months previous… when Gwen put the top down for the car's maiden voyage… she had thought this convertible to be so fine. But now, she detested it. Then, she had lifted both arms above her head and whooped it up at the feel of rushing air. Now, with arms tightly crossed upon her chest, she felt tricked into that false pleasure.

"You getting out… or are you planning on sitting in there all day feeling sorry for yourself?"

She had not registered that the car was at a stop, or that Gwen was already outside.

"I'm coming…"

With a touch of rebelliousness, she delayed until Gwen had reached the shop's backdoor, and then slunk out as slow as could be done.

"Hurry it up, Niece. We've got the finishing touches to put on those bridesmaid bouquets before tomorrow… not to mention the dozen or so boutonnieres. You've barely got enough time before class to get…"

"You know what… do it yourself! I'm taking the rest of the morning off."

Turning away, she took savage delight in the shock that had appeared on Gwen's face. Continuing down the alley, she did not stop until she reached the side street that would normally take her across 4th in the direction of her high school. With a brief look back, she noted with satisfaction that Gwen was no longer there. She instead turned northward away from school, purposing to cut classes for the first time in her life. Putting a city block worth of separation between herself and the flower shop, she doubled back eastward along 3rd street, making for the rail lines where she and Roy had once walked together. Coming across a set of tracks, she allowed gravel, steel and creosol-soaked ties to be her guide, leading her back into a purer time of life. As the morning air was cool… somewhere in the forties by the feel of it… she buttoned up her jacket and ignored the cruel breeze nipping at her exposed calves. The sun would be up soon enough.

Thirty minutes of meandering along tracks brought her into the heart of the railyard… just about the time she imagined her homeroom teacher was registering her absence. Hanging out counting box cars go by was obviously not something that a respectable young lady should be doing on a school day, but she chose this diversion for a reason. Making for the very switch box that once had been the place where she and Roy sat together, she plopped down on its cool metal surface and began watching the activity in the yard. Not really watching. She was simply aware of having once done so with a childlike longing. For a moment, she wished he was here with her, listening to her struggles and doing the kinds of silly things that always took her mind off of her grade school problems. But Roy was not in school anymore… and would not even be aware of her having skipped out. He was in a completely different world.

All about her were two kinds of reality – box cars in motion and box cars staying put. The fortunate ones, in being linked up to an engine, were moving on, whereas the others lay abandoned on one of the many lonely spurs common to any railyard. That was her – feeble and forsaken. Orphaned to a side track in life. She was completely incapable of moving. In truth, she had no idea what college was supposed to be like… or what options it might open up for her. Money was not even the real issue either. This, she now knew for certain. It was something far worse. Out of fear or simply to exert control… she knew not which… but it was so abundantly clear that Gwen never intended to set her free.

After mourning over her situation for what seemed like hours, she noticed an engine creep from the switching station and begin the tedious process of maneuvering backward into one of the sidetracks. A man then got out to finalize the connection with a long line of idle cars. In short time, he climbed back in, and she watched as the engine did that strange thing in preparation for leaving. Pushing backward, it began to compress the line of boxcars in order to remove the slack in each coupling.

Instantly, the memory came to her of her father showing her how this worked. He was explaining in that quick sort of way he did whenever he got excited about something. She could see in her mind how his hands straightened out a length of chain on his workbench, positioning one link so it dangled over the edge. She had not been surprised in the least to see the whole thing just sit there. One isolated link hanging over the side was hardly sufficient for pulling the entire chain along. Then… as if the chain was right before her eyes… she could see him bunch the whole thing up. Now, the first link hanging over the side could pull on the second without the burden of having to move the entire chain at once. From there, the first and second worked together, inching the third off the edge… which next pulled the fourth along. In wonder, she watched as the process accelerated until the entire length of chain had slithered to the floor.

That memory, having brought a smile to her face, suddenly turned to sadness. She could remember fully this demonstration of the chain... see the dents and dust on his workbench, smell again their garage's subtle scent of motor oil, and even hear the metal links as they jangled and clanked to the floor... but not one detail came to her of the person's face who had shown her the effect. One memory, so very clear, had failed to pull along on another.

The clatter of the train moving forward brought her back to the here and now. In a matter of moments, its engine would come abreast of where she sat, and then she would sadly watch the entire chain move past and out of Lubbock... leaving her behind.

In a flash of angry despair, she brought forth a most reckless idea. Delaying only long enough to take note of the engine's number and the general direction in which it was heading, she pitched herself up from off the switch box into a full-out run back to the flower shop. Owing to the irregular spacing of the ties relative to her stride and the fact that she was not all that good of a runner, her sprint soon degraded into a jog. Though less than a mile in distance, she wasted fifteen precious minutes in getting back. Turning into the alley, she was relieved to find the Skylark parked exactly where it had been left. It would be as it always was – unlocked with the keys in the ignition. Gwen was not a particularly trusting sort, but rarely was a car stolen in that part of Lubbock.

Until now!

With an impish sort of pleasure, she threw incorrigible intent into dangerous action. Gingerly opening the driver's side door, she eased herself in without fully latching it behind her. Once seated, she closed her eyes and considered one last time what she was doing, then quickly turned the engine over. She was halfway down the alley before daring to look in the rearview mirror. No Gwen. Though relieved, she also felt a touch of disappointment in not being able to see her aunt come bolting out of the flower shop on realizing that her niece was not so niece-ish after all. It mattered not. Now or later, she knew there would eventually be a reckoning.

She went half a block along the side street before pulling over. First things first – the Skylark's top had to come down, no matter how cool it was outside. If she was going to pay the price for joyriding in Gwen's blue baby, then the absolute most must be made of the 'lark'... short-lived though it might be.

With the top down, it was now a simple matter of guesswork – a fifty-fifty chance.

Go west or north?

She chose the latter for no other reason than because that particular track, running from Lubbock to Amarillo, was the very one that happened to pass by her old grade school. She flicked the car radio on and turned its tuner about until she found a rock-and-roll station. With the volume cranked all the way up, she began a rabid search of the horizon for any sign of the train she had witnessed pulling out of the Lubbock railyard. On the outskirts of the city, she caught sight of a line of boxcars lumbering along parallel to the main highway, yet still a good ways ahead. She finally managed to close the distance near the town of New Deal, but nearly lost the train once again as it unexpectedly took a spur off the main line. Backtracking to navigate through that town's narrow patchwork of streets, she caught sight of the train again as it was traveling eastward along a line that paralleled a lonely county road. Because the stretch ran flat and straight beside the track, she opened the engine up, using speed to displace her despair.

Faster. Just a bit faster...

Finally gaining the locomotive, she confirmed that it was the same one she had seen leaving the Lubbock yard, then decreased her speed to match its. With radio blaring and her hair flapping in the convertible's slack stream, she travelled along beside the train within a pure joy of motion. It was just her, the Skylark and the train… and nothing else mattered in this world.

Fortunately, she came to know of her danger just in time, largely owing to a sustained blast from the engineer warning her of what was ahead. Screeching to a halt just shy of the weather-worn crossing signs where the tracks bent over the road, she threw the gearshift into neutral and remained idling there as the full length of the train passed before her heading northward… to where, she did not know. Turning the radio down, she let the rhythm of wheel upon rail speak to her through all of its click, clatter and squeal. But its message was not a welcoming one. In a language of power and speed, the train echoed a command at her not to continue on, for where it was heading she could not follow.

The last car eventually passed and the train's sound faded, though she continued to watch for as long as the West Texas flatness permitted… until the train's profile became but a mere speck off in the distance. Ahead and in her mirrors, the road was empty. From horizon to horizon, she was completely alone. The possibility never occurred to her that she could simply throw the Skylark's transmission back into gear and floor it onward into the east. To her, those tracks crossing the road were an impenetrable barrier preventing her from moving on. This wild pursuit of significance through speed had ended, leaving her with a heavy realization. She was in serious trouble.

Not yet though.

She could delay the inevitable a bit longer. Shutting down the Skylark's engine, she turned the radio back up… though not blaringly as before. She adjusted the volume low so the music was there with less of the static. Bobby Vinton's *Blue Velvet* had just begun. So she tilted the driver's seat back as far as it would go and stared up into a sky of the same color. In just half a verse, the song's melancholy became hers, for it spoke to her of something so beautiful lost forever… with only memory remaining. The melody and the words blended together within their slow tempo as she followed an isolated cloud creeping across her sight. Northward, it went, in the same general direction as the train… yet not in the same determined way in which those boxcars had left her behind. This cloud, in billowy folds, spoke softly a whispered invitation for her to come travel along. 'Up' was the way for her to leave… for only in 'up' would she be free. Up there with that cloud… and with the birds carved into a stone relief… she could finally break away and find…

We interrupt this program with an urgent news bulletin. Multiple reports are coming in from Dallas indicating that little over fifteen minutes ago President Kennedy's motorcade came under gunfire while traveling through Dealey Plaza. Sources in Dallas and within the White House have confirmed that the President is among those wounded, though the extent of his injuries has not yet been made public. The assailant remains at large. Please stay tuned as we bring additional updates on the situation in Dallas. Once again – President John F. Kennedy has been shot.

CHAPTER
10

A POLE'S FLAG

She sat stunned for several minutes as the music resumed, but then finally recovered enough to know that she should close the car top in order to better hear the radio reports. Even though she had become good at this... mostly because Gwen always made her do it... she still fought through the rushed frustration of having to get out of the car, haul up the top, and then lock it in place... all while keeping an ear out for the next report. Back into the car feeling tense, she spun the dial until she found a station that was more serious about the news. Its reports gradually went from bad... to terrible... to far worse. Only after the broadcast moved to the live press conference in which the nation was officially informed of the President's assassination did she turn off the radio and begin to cry.

How long she remained at that railroad crossing, she could not say. She knew only that school was already out based on the dashboard clock... but really did not care. Eventually, she calmed herself enough to drive back to the flower shop. Parking the Skylark in more-or-less the same spot she had taken it from, she went inside to find Gwen and Patsy standing about the cutting room table listening to the radio. Both women were bleary-eyed and sniffling. For the remainder of that afternoon, no one said anything other than to express their sorrow or outrage. In her own grief, she spoke less than did the other two, for Kennedy had always been something more than president to her. He was a youthful hope. A sign of better times to come.

She spent the weekend fully consumed with her sadness. She and Gwen listened together to the evolving news of what had happened in Dallas, along with the details of Vice President Johnson being sworn in, the accounts of sympathy coming from dignitaries both at home and abroad, the capture of the assassin and his own unexpected murder, and the endless media speculation as to motives. The tragedy behind all of these happenings allowed her to overlook her own offenses... which was made all the more forgettable since Gwen seemed unaware that her car had ever been moved from the alleyway.

Returning to school on Monday morning, the talk up and down the halls was all about Kennedy's assassination. Yet on entering her homeroom class, she got handed a note requiring her immediate presence in the principal's office. She had little doubt as to the reason, and used the slow walk to the administration wing for strategizing on her best form of an apology. As to punishment, just about anything would be acceptable so long as Gwen was not involved.

Arriving at the principal's office, she ventured a weak knock on the door and was called in. He was not alone. On recognizing the square shoulders and short blond hair of the person seated before him, she immediately felt the blood drain from her face. Gwen spoke without the slightest shift of her eyes from Principal Adams.

"Marna... have a seat."

"Aunt Gwen... I didn't expect..."

"Of course you didn't. Now hurry up and sit down. Your principal and I are busy grown-ups. He has things to say to you... then you and I'll talk later."

She took a seat beside Gwen, with her growing panic pushing her to get in a word on her defense. But the principal spoke before she could.

"Miss Forde... let me ask you something... did you happen to see the flag this morning on your way into school?"

"Ahh... yes, sir. It was... halfway up the pole... on account of... what happened on Friday."

"And where were you on Friday... because it most certainly was not here at school? The attendance record has you down as absent."

"I cut classes."

She noted him briefly glance toward Gwen before continuing.

"As you probably know, it's the responsibility of the homeroom teacher to administer discipline for such infractions, but I rather think this is a different matter... as I'm sure you realize. You were not present at the Friday morning assembly. According to Mrs. Patterson, it was your responsibility to lead the school in the Pledge of Allegiance."

Oh no! I completely forgot about that. Mrs. Patterson's going to kill me!

"Miss Forde… you ran for the position of Senior Class Representative to the student body government and was elected by your classmates…"

She ventured a quick look toward Gwen. The same expression resided there as before, though one eye brow momentarily twitched upward.

She's enjoying this.

"…and to have you shirk your duty on the very day of our President's death. It pains me to speak of it. Miss Forde, you should have been in attendance caring for your responsibilities and being available as a leader to your classmates. I can tell you that Mrs. Patterson was beside herself. You know the work she puts into being the faculty mentor for student government."

"I… I don't know what to say…"

Suddenly, the thrill of chasing a train seemed so juvenile. If she could only burst into tears, then maybe that might go some way toward convincing these two adults how much she now regretted her choice. But there was not the slightest hint of such feelings in her… only emptiness… and a terrible awakening to her capacity for making foolish decisions. Above all, she purposed not to look over at Gwen again, for to do so would only increase her shame.

"…I have no excuse."

"And now your aunt tells me that you spent the day joyriding about in her car… which you took without permission."

"You knew?"

"Of course. You think I don't keep track of my own things?! I gave you the weekend to fess up to it, but you didn't. Says a lot about who you think…"

"It wasn't anything like that."

"Don't interrupt. Now you listen to what Principal Adams has to say, and you accept the punishment he has for you. We both know you deserve far worse."

"So… Miss Forde… I've briefly spoken with your homeroom teacher, as well as with Mrs. Patterson and Mr. Ruckerson…"

Ruckerson?! What's he got to do with this?

"…and they're all in agreement. As of right now, you're suspended from all extracurricular activities and your high school record will be amended to show your removal from student government…"

"But you can't…"

"There's more, Miss Forde. As further punishment, I have decided…"

His emphasis suddenly gave her the sickening feeling that her aunt had personally recommended some aspects of this punishment. Quickly turning that way, she caught a corner of Gwen's mouth creep up a notch.

"…that you will serve your detention on flag patrol while the nation is in mourning over the President's death. It so happens that one of the boys on that duty broke his arm this past week, so you'll be taking his place. You're to see Mr. Ruckerson during lunch period today for instructions."

She sat there slack-jawed, completely unable to speak.

Flag duty?! No… anything but that!

"Marna, your principal's waiting."

"Yes, sir."

"You may return to your homeroom now."

Without another look toward Gwen, she left the office completely lost in her own misery. Being a student government representative was something she was proud of… something she was sure would lend her high school transcripts the sort of prestige needed for getting into a good college… though the possibility of college had already slipped away. Far worse was the embarrassment she would have to endure as everyone learned about her punishment. Being put on flag duty would make sure of that. Flag duty was for squares. It was a place where socially inept boys hung out. She knew not one of those who served on it. Had never even spoken a word to them. They were all just ROTC wannabes. Having to associate with them would be beyond humiliating, for everyone knew that flag patrol members strutted about school wearing a ridiculous badge and belt get-up. No matter what work came with raising and lowering the flag, being forced to wear something as hideous as that during school would be far worse punishment than she deserved.

As instructed, she skipped lunch and made for the office of Mr. Ruckerson, the school's automotive repair instructor. He, like the other shop teachers, was located in that part of campus most girls would never visit during their three years of senior high… though all knew the way to. She went through the gymnasium, out its back past the boy's locker room, and around behind the visitor's side of the football stadium. Beyond its parking lot were the metal framed huts dedicated to vocational classes. A roll-up garage door on one was open. Stepping within, she paused… not so much to take in what an automotive shop looked like as to prepare herself for an uncomfortable situation. There was no one here… other than the half dozen or so cars being worked on. To her, the way they sat there… with hoods up, parts dangling out, and tool cabinets on wheels all about… it gave off the odd feel of an operating room where the doctors and nurses had abandoned their patients in favor of lunch. She shook off the thought… and an awareness of the nasty smell of grease… on noticing a small glass-enclosed office in the back corner. She could just make out the sounds of murmured voices coming from there. Hopscotching her way over oily spots on the floor and taking a wide berth around the last vehicle, she came to see that a gathering of boys was responsible for the chatter. One was standing at the door... almost as if on lookout. On seeing her, he turned his head back into the office.

"She's here."

Normally, a female in her situation would be repulsed by the décor of a shop teacher's office. She did not deny having such feelings on seeing a desk overflowing with oil-stained engine schematics... or wall-mounted shelves jam-packed with grimy auto parts... or posters of bathing-suited beauties lounging across the hoods of hot rods. She noted all those things, and just as quickly disregarded them in favor of concentrating on the six stern faces appraising her... five being of the teenage boy variety. Three of these wore the shoulder-and-belt garb of the school's flag patrol.

The teacher seated behind the messy desk gave a flick of the wrist, and a boy immediately closed the door behind her.

"Mr. Ruckerson, I'm Marna Forde. Principal Adams said I was to meet with you now about my... umm..." She quickly panned the faces again, doubting that any of them would be sympathetic to her situation. "...with placement on the flag committee."

She had not really meant to use that word. It just sort of came out. Eyes rolled, tongues clicked, and heads wagged.

"Yes... I received a call from him regarding your situation. The boys and I were just discussing your placement on the... flag committee. Please have a seat."

In wiping off the metal chair before her, she knew that she was sending another message of feminine quality... but did not care.

Better a dirty hand than a dirty skirt.

"You should know that as the faculty advisor for the flag patrol, I have latitude in accepting or declining participants. Principal Adams is aware of this. In your case, Miss Forde, I've not yet decided one way or the other because I'd like to hear your views first. By the way, I thought it important to have the other members present. So... the first thing I'd like to ask you is simply put – will you faithfully accomplish this duty both morning and afternoon of every school day for the time specified by Mr. Adams?"

Her first inclination was to decline as graciously as possible... or at least to accept with such a show of hesitancy that his hand would be forced toward rejection of the principal's request. Any other punishment had to be better than flag duty. But the sound of whispering from behind instantly changed her mind. As his eyes darted disapprovingly over to one of the boys, it suddenly occurred to her that this was not really between her and him, or her and the principal. Even those five boys standing about were nothing more than observers to her greater struggle. It was her aunt who had cruelly sprung on her the verdict of no college, and it was also because of her aunt that she had skipped school and taken the Skylark. Backing out of this discipline would be giving in to Gwen, and therefore taking it on and conquering it would be to show Gwen as wrong. This was between her and Gwen.

"Yes, sir, I will. You have my promise."

"Then can I also expect you to carefully observe the instructions of your flag detail commander?"

This was a title she had not expected, but seeing as it was likely just one of the boys behind her, she once more agreed.

"Miss Forde, the task of raising and lowering the flags each day is reserved only for those who can undertake the responsibility with the utmost respect. That person represents this school to a public who sees those flags flying every class day. To bring shame on either our nation's flag or our state's is to bring shame upon this school."

He went silent, but she knew it was not in waiting for her response. She could tell that he was studying her. Maybe it was to assess the extent of her understanding... or just to see if she might crack. Even with the five boys breathing down from behind, she felt that Mr. Ruckerson's stare was nothing compared to that of Gwen's.

"Okay, we'll give this a try."

Groans and moans filled the office, but just as when Mr. Ruckerson had waved for the door to be shut, they immediately ceased at his command.

"Gentleman – enough! You may go now... except you, Higgins."

She resisted the urge to turn around for a look at who was leaving and who was staying, once more imagining that this was Gwen sitting across from her. She would not turn away until it was absolutely necessary.

"Miss Forde, your detail will start next Monday and run through the remainder of December. Higgins here will be your detail commander."

She hazarded a quick glance at the one standing beside her. He was just a typical West Texas boy – white t-shirt tucked into blue jeans with a head topped off by a crew cut.

"There're two details of three taking monthly turns at it. Normally, selections are made at the beginning of the school year... though from time to time, I've had a slot open up unexpectedly. Those are usually filled from a waiting list.

But… this is the first time I've been asked to take on a student as part of a detention. I should also tell you, Miss Forde, that in the nearly seventeen years I've been the detail's faculty advisor, you're the first female to serve. So you see, there'll be a double heaping of scrutiny placed on you. You'll need to take this very seriously. I'm going to give you one more chance to back out…"

She could almost hear her aunt's challenge. *Show me you're ready to succeed in a man's world by first taking on a boy's.*

"No, sir, I'll do the job… and just as well as anyone else."

She waited for some kind of an objection from the boy named Higgins, but he just stood by quietly.

"Fine. You'll be needing this." He rummaged about in a desk drawer and produced a belt. "Higgins'll show you how to put it on. And Miss Forde… you're expected to wear it the entire school day while you're on duty, you understand me?!"

"Yes, sir. Each school day for the entire month of December.

"Good. Now you've got about fifteen minutes left in the lunch period, so I suggest you both make the most of it. Scat – I've got grading to do."

Neither she nor Higgins spoke until they were nearly to the football field.

"Are we going somewhere?"

"Ahh… yeah. Sorry… I'm supposed to show you the ropes."

Up until that moment, she had not considered this Higgins as possessing any noteworthy trait. He looked like all of the other boys she did not know. Yet in acknowledging his pun with a smile, she was surprised to see him get red-faced and quicken his pace. He seemed even more embarrassed when she hurried alongside him.

"Hey – what's your first name?"

"Cletus."

"What grade are you in?"

"Same as you – a senior."

"How's it that we've never been in a class together?"

His weak smile instantly vanished, being replaced by a wounded scowl.

"We're in the same homeroom, Marna. We also have the same sixth period government class. And we've had loads of others together in the past…"

"Oh… sorry. Must be because I always sit in the front row."

Which she knew not to be true. Her feeble lie would hardly go the distance in soothing an unintended implication – that she had never noticed him before.

"So… you're going to show me how to put this thing on?"

She stopped outside the rear entrance to the gym, supposing it to be a good place not to be noticed while trying on the belt for the first time. Her request was also a suitable distraction from having just hurt the boy's feelings.

Cletus took the belt from her, looked her over once, and then loosened the slide bar on the shoulder strap to match her height.

"Just slip your arm in and then connect up the belt. Pretty simple."

She nonetheless found herself struggling with the thing.

"This shoulder strap… it doesn't feel right. It's got way too much slack in it. I think it needs to be tightened…"

"It's got to be that way so the belt rides on your hips."

"Cletus… you do realize that a girl's body is made differently than a boy's?!"

She tried to say this in a playful manner, but could tell by how he looked down that she had embarrassed him again.

Just get the stupid thing adjusted and be done with it.

Now with the belt on, the angle at which she was working away at the sliding mechanism was making it difficult to manipulate.

"I can't get this thing to… move! Is there a trick to it?"

In glancing up, she found Cletus stuck in a most peculiar pose. Having stepped away from her, his outstretched arms were held close together… almost as if handcuffed at the wrists… with his fingers working away at the air. Most odd was the extreme look of discomfort on his face. It was then, from the angle of his eyes, that she came to realize he was looking directly at her chest… to where the sliding mechanism sat smack-dab between her breasts.

"I… I think… I think it looks fine. Maybe you should… umm… fix it later… when you're alone at home."

He turned about into the gym, leaving her with the awkward task of pulling off the belt while trying to catch up with how very fast he was walking.

"You don't want me being on the… team… or whatever you call it, do you?"

"The fellas don't think any girl should be on the squad, especially one who's… who's…"

"Who's what?!"

"Who's accused of swiping her aunt's car and skipping class on the day that the President was shot. They say it shows a lack of respect for…"

"You don't know what you're talking about!"

"I didn't say it. The fellas did."

"Well… they don't know what they're talking about. What I did… it had nothing to do with the President! Besides, who says a girl can't do this job just as well as a boy?!"

"Not me… I'm just tellin' ya what the fellas said."

"How about telling me what 'Cletus Higgins' says?!"

He did not respond, but instead quickened his pace such that they were practically jogging down the corridor toward the front of the school. But he stopped suddenly at the entrance to the administration office as the fifth period bell rang.

"I was gonna show you were the flags are kept, but we don't have time. I've got to get all the way back across campus for woodshop. Just meet Owen and me here thirty minutes before the first bell on Monday, okay?"

"Sure… I'll be here. But Cletus… you didn't answer my question. You also feel that I shouldn't be on flag detail?"

He blushed and turned his face away.

"Yeah… but for a different reason. I just think… you're… too… too pretty for it."

He quickly moved into the throng of students before she could say anything else.

The Thanksgiving break with Gwen was one of the oddest times in memory. Each of them purposefully carried on as expected on a holiday, attending to the same traditions established over a decade of living together. Yet strained feelings lurked just beneath the surface for her… as she suspected they probably also did for Gwen. Their talk was pleasant, though superficial, and not once did the conversation veer toward the Skylark… or college… or the oddity of flag duty as detention. Even her own sadness over Kennedy's assassination was bottled up out of spite. Gwen must be busting for some piece of news regarding her punishment… any slip of the lip… but she was determined to remain quiet.

On Monday morning, she left the flower shop with plenty of time for reaching the administration office. There, one of the boys she had seen in Mr. Ruckerson's office was waiting, him also wearing a belt-and-strap get-up.

"You're late."

"Cletus said to be here thirty minutes before the first bell, so I'm right on time."

"On-time is considered late in the Corps."

"Well, *chum*… I'm not in the Corps! And in case you haven't noticed, this is senior high!"

She crossed her arms over her shoulder strap, determined to stare down this up-start sophomore until Cletus arrived… which, in the periphery of her vision, happened at that very moment.

"I see you two have met. Owen, this is Marna. Marna, Owen."

"Owen says you're late."

"I did not. I only said…"

"Can it, you two. We've got flags to raise."

Owen gave her a sneer before falling in behind Cletus. She followed the two around the front office's main counter to a cabinet behind where one of the school secretaries sat. Purposing to stand a bit away from them, she watched as Cletus first transferred the American flag over to Owen, and then turned to her with the Texas one.

"Always carry the flag in front of you like this."

Cletus held the Texas flag against his chest with both arms crossed over it in such a way that his hands were clutching at the ninety degree corner-fold as it pointed up toward his chin. She modeled the same grip after being given the flag, though it felt terribly awkward to her.

"What difference does it make how its carried?"

"You see, Cletus… already with the jackass questions. It's no wonder she got booted from student government."

"Owen – enough! I'm detail commander, so it's my responsibility to teach the… ahh… new recruit everything she needs to know… which also means answering her questions."

Owen gave her another sneer, and then headed out of the office with the American flag pressed especially tight against his chest.

"Marna, we hold it that way so you're less likely to drop it or have it unfold on you. Doing things exactly the same way every time is also a sign of respect for the flag. It means that you're being… attentive to it… rather than to other things. So… you need a three man… I mean, 'person'… detail for two flags… two to raise one flag and a third to hold the other. That's you today. American flag goes up first… then Texas."

They followed Owen out of the school's front doors to where the flagpoles were located. She watched as the two boys carefully unfurled and connected up the American flag. The care with which they went about this, attending to the wind and in no way being hurried by how cold it was outside… it oddly impressed her. Owen, hand over hand on the rope, rapidly raised the American flag all the way up the pole, then switched directions and drew it back down slowly to about the midway point… which she recognized as the half-staff position signifying a nation in mourning.

"Flags always go up fast and down slow. Not sure how that came to be, but it's symbolic of the start of the day and its ending. When you do half-staff, you always need to go all the way up and then retreat from the truk on top. We'll do Texas next, but don't pass it until asked for… and always use two hands in the giving and receiving… that way there's less chance of it being mishandled."

The two boys repeated the same process, then tied off both sets of ropes. Owen left for the front door, with her turning in behind him.

"Hold it, Marna. I wanna teach you the parts of the pole so you're not confused when we mention them. Like I said, that ball on top's called the truk. We attach the flag with clips on the halyard. Please don't call it 'rope' or Owen'll flip out. It runs through a pulley up there by the truk. Whatever you do, don't yank on it if it gets stuck. There're ways to get it unstuck. Now this thing here's called the cleat. There's a proper way to tie down the excess halyard to its prongs… I'll teach you how to do that this afternoon. Let's see… what else? Umm… oh, the long side of the flag is called the hoist and the shorter side's the fly. When we fold it up, we'll go from hoist to hoist… not fly to fly. After that, we form it into a triangle going from the stripes to the union – that's the star field on the American flag. Most important thing is to go slow and be careful, 'cause if you mess up and the flag touches the ground… then it has to be destroyed. Burned… actually."

"Really?! Whatever for?"

"It's a respect thing."

"I understand that… but it still seems like a waste of a perfectly good flag. I mean… who'd know?"

She was surprised by his look, as if she had said something terribly offensive.

"Marna… I would know… and so would you."

All morning, she endured a constant stream of ribbing from her friends for having to wear the belt and shoulder strap. Most of it was good-natured teasing – just as she would have doled out as generously if one of her girlfriends had been subjected to the same punishment. But the most humiliating part of the day was lunch. She, with sack and milk carton in hand, was heading to her usual spot with friends when Cletus stepped in front.

"Marna, flag detail always eats together. It's part of the job."

With glum resignation, she turned about with him to a corner table where the other four boys… along with the broken-armed Timothy Willows… were already at their lunch. Not one of them greeted her with anything better than a sinister look. Everyone in the cafeteria was probably staring at her, enjoying her discomfort, and thinking up new ways of ribbing her later. She ate hurriedly, fleeing as soon as Cletus gave her leave to do so.

No sooner was the afternoon duty accomplished than she had the belt off and hidden away in her locker. Her irritated attitude did not lessen as the week went on, partly owing to the frustration that Cletus had not yet allowed her to do anything beyond holding the Texas flag while he and Owen did all the raising and lowering. At least that changed in week two, as Cletus made a point of saying he was mildly convinced that she could do the job without goofing it up.

Perhaps the thing that most surprised her regarding the detention was that Gwen had not once said a word about it. Maybe Gwen was satisfied, or maybe she was afraid of finding out that her niece was actually beginning to enjoy the job. Actually… there was one thing about flag detail that Gwen had not expected… though she could tell that her aunt was trying hard not to show the annoyance of it. In order to attend to her daily duties, she had to leave the shop earlier than usual in the morning, and did not get back after school until much later than was her habit. It cost her aunt at least an hour a day of labor. That, she privately found to be very pleasing.

Still… a more significant change was occurring in her attitude as a result of flag duty… and not at all what she had expected on starting out. Fortunately, her embarrassment only lasted through the first week. In enduring the lunchtime nonsense of the boys… who constantly demonstrated their complete ignorance at how to behave around a girl… she surprisingly came to appreciate their focus and dedication to the flags. She too was gaining a measure of that respect, particularly as the boys related to her their various aspirations for military service. But respect was not the main thing she felt each day as the flags went up and then came back down. She kept her true feelings to herself, not even sharing them with Roy.

She pitied the flag.

The flag had become a symbol of her own state of mind. When the wind tore at it, thrashing it about on the halyard, she felt its pain and heard in its rippling an earnest plea to be set free. She would imagine all the places where it might glide if it were allowed to ride upon the air currents rather than being buffeted by them. On those days it hung limp in the cold rain, she felt its surrender and knew well the frustration that its useless striving had wrought. The flag was a prisoner, bound cruelly each day to the pole. Not able to express itself, it was helplessly made to parade about for the metal's pleasure. That soft cloth might pull vigorously against its chains… and that pole might give it just enough leash to tempt at a hope of release… but always the hooks gripped tightly.

To her, the pole was ugly and the pole was hard. It symbolized all that was inflexible and unwavering. It held there rigidly insensitive to the sincere desire of its flag to fly free. And there it stood each morning, waiting in stern expectation of holding captive for yet another day its thing of red, white and blue beauty. She hated the pole for the service it made the flag perform. Hated how it stood so tall and straight, with so much pride to its shiny smooth surface. It never gave in, and it never softened. Nothing phased that pole. It commanded both ground where it had bolted itself down, and sky where its intrusion could not be avoided. Not even the thwacking sound of the halyard, so alike that of a whip's crack, could produce sympathy in that pole.

She felt the flag's pain and sorrow, though she herself was conscripted to administer it. Daily, she was forced in league with that pole, binding the helpless flag to it, then was compelled to watch as the wind tortured the poor thing. She would come round again later to compress it into tight folds and lock it away in the dark. Each day, she sensed its delicate form cry out for release, and each day she ignored its plea to break away and fly free. She could sense it all because she was that flag.

The pole knew this too, and held on all the more tightly because of it.

CHAPTER

11

SERVITUDE AND A FALSENESS TO LIBERATION

In the new year, with her detention completed and Timothy's arm healed, she retired to civilian life with an unspoken sadness carried along. She told her friends… Roy included… how very glad she was to be done with the belt and shoulder strap. But in her heart, the opposite was the case. She had somehow developed a powerful affinity for flag duty. As ridiculous as it might seem, she missed the flag. She missed touching it… seeing the wind tug at its fringes as she released it on the halyard… and the pleasure of watching it flap about from just below as she hoisted it all the way up to the truk. Through the weeks of January, she frequently found herself going out the school's front doors during breaks simply to check on how well everything had been tied down. Whole class periods were spent absentmindedly staring out the window at those emblems on their poles rather than listening to her teachers' lectures.

She repeatedly told herself that the flags were not really hers. So dwelling on them was silly… and foolish. Yet she could not resist this urge to look back rather than forward. With only half of her senior year remaining, she found herself putting much more thought into those three weeks of flag duty than into anything that might lay beyond graduation. The future, whether high school was finished well or not, seemed lost within the certainty of servitude to Gwen. At her worst times of depression, it was 'think about the flag,' or be stuck thinking about where she always feared to be stuck – standing at the cutting room table. She had never considered herself to be a fearful person, yet the possibility that she might one day soon come to accept life in Lubbock was more terrifying than the dread of being stung.

Graduation came and went uneventfully, though it triggered something unanticipated in her. She was nearly eighteen years old, with the entirety of her adult life ahead, yet somehow began to feel that a different sort of currency to time was now being spent. Before, in childhood, life went by in nickel and dime quantities, with spare change always to be had by searching through the day's hidden places. But now, an anxiousness for getting on to something greater in life grew within her such that living required a more substantial form of payment from her. Too often, she felt as if her days were wasted dollars.

Most of her girlfriends went off to college, got engaged, or chose employment in town, all of which accentuated her urgency to find something greater for herself in life. Perhaps this feeling had something to do with being made a fulltime employee at Forde's Flowers… as if she had willingly conscripted herself to it. Or maybe it was only Gwen's insistence that she start paying a room-and-board fee now that she had graduated. This, she was told, would build an appreciation for adult responsibilities. Yet just like the song *Sixteen Tons*, she could not help but feel that the more she earned, the more she ended up owing to the Forde company store.

Perhaps her dread was nothing more than a side effect of her restlessness to be out on her own. Gwen was paying her nearly double per hour what she had received as a high schooler… and she was determined that every available penny of it should go into savings. She would live frugally. She would live desperately. Knowing the exact balance in her account became a weekly obsession. Every payday trip to the bank was undertaken with relish. If she ended up putting in less than she weekly planned, then she became her own personal loan shark. For every dollar held back to be spent on some pleasure required that double the amount be kicked in on the following week to pay off the debt.

With her working fulltime came also a surprising attentiveness to the art of floral design. Not that she had changed in her regard for the craft… or for working under her aunt. Her private little war of resentment never went away. Her new dedication resulted primarily from an unexpected event – Patsy's departure, as her husband found better work in the Houston area. She then became Forde's Flowers resident floral designer. She threw herself into this new role because it meant slightly more pay, and because she had managed… after ten years… to finally pick up a thing or two on how to do the job properly. On her feet nearly all of the time, she worked twelve hours a day from summer to fall, ten in the winter, and sometimes all night when there was a big event or holiday to get ready for.

Irrespective of the hard work, she knew beyond a doubt that flowers would never be a true interest of hers. She loathed nearly everything about the job… especially cajoling customers into making decisions and dealing with the idiotic things they would say.

"I demand a refund! The flowers you sold me have died!"

"Can you add a bit more scent to these?"

"Do you have anything that says 'I love you, but I'm not in love with you'?"

"I don't like this color much… can you change it?"

"I'm sort of looking for a bloom that glows in the dark."

By far, the worst part was working with the bride-to-be and her mother. She could never seem to satisfy those women's fairyland imaginings of the wedding day. But in truth, her disdain for preparing wedding arrangements was really no different than for any other occasion requiring flowers. She simply could not see herself investing a lifetime into someone else's special moments… particularly when such labor involved a token that only lasted for a couple of days on somebody's coffee table. Gwen repeatedly said that it was the people who made being a florist so special, but she never bought into that. Whatever meager meaning might be derive from her efforts, she only ever saw fleeting glimpses of it within the shop itself. Customers would come, put considerable thought and emotion into their orders, and then take the joy right out the door with them, leaving not a petal's worth behind for her. No… being a florist would never satisfy her. The wide world was out there waiting to be conquered, and she was determined to seek out the greater things in it to accomplish.

She still was proud of herself for doing a job well that she secretly hated. In the process, she was regaining Gwen's trust. This was evident from the amount of time that her aunt was now spending outside the shop in her floral society activities. With the exception of doing the books… which was something for an accountant to handle… she had mastered nearly every aspect of running the shop, including finding her own ways of streamlining operations and coming up with advertisements for the paper, radio and TV.

Truth be told, Roy was about the only thing keeping her from falling into despair. He listened to her go on and on about her frustrations with Gwen… or her hatred for flowers… or her dreams about how much better life would be if she could but break away. She treasured how he would whisk her off for something special… like a day trip into New Mexico so she could lay eyes on the Sandia Mountains… or the time he built a huge bonfire for her under the stars… or when he took her to a rock concert in Dallas. So it came as no surprise to her when he said he was taking her out for a 'secret date' on the Thursday she turned twenty. Leaving his truck in the parking lot of their old grade school, he led her along the same route they had taken so many times as children, walking hand-in-hand along the rails as they reminisced about those times and how far they had come together. Without really realizing it, she soon found herself standing in the very spot where they had spent time together watching trains go by.

"Okay… I want you to sit there on that switch box… just like when we were kids."

She hesitated for a moment about the possibility of getting her skirt dirty before deciding to sit herself down. After all, this was where he had specifically chosen to reveal her birthday surprise.

"Am I to face any particular direction?"

"No, you're fine just like that. Are you comfortable?"

"I suppose so."

"Okay… here goes. Marna… I love you. I think I've loved you since… well… ever since when we used to come here as kids."

His eyes were fixed on her, but she noticed that his hand had begun rustling about in a pocket. Just as he seemed to get a grip on whatever was in there, he dropped to a knee in the gravel about the switch box. Everything within her tensed, for out came a small black box bearing a ring.

"Marna Forde, I, Roy Meitner, make you three promises that will last your entire lifetime. I will never leave you… I will always love you… and I will always be true. Will you marry me?"

She was in complete shock, for this was not at all what she had been expecting.

"Oh, Roy… this is so… sweet."

"Not exactly the word I was hoping for…"

"Sorry. I'm just… surprised. I had no idea you felt quite this way for me. I mean, I know you've talked about one day getting married… like your parents… but I thought… you know… that it was… for the future."

"Well… we don't have to get married today. It can be in the future."

"I know that. It's just… Roy… I have so much else on my mind right now. I'm not at all ready for making this kind of a decision. Not yet. I mean… there's so much out there in the world to explore… and I want to be part of it. Don't you? Don't you want to see the world?"

"Marna… you are my world."

"That's so..."

"Don't say sweet. As a matter of fact, if you're not yet ready to say yes, then don't say anything at all. Just tell me that you'll think on it."

"You... umm... don't mind if I... you know...?"

"Have some time? Of course not. Marna... you can have whatever you need."

"Thanks... but what about your parents? Oh my god – what's Gwen going to say?! She'll never approve of this!"

"Well... Mom and Dad are tickled pink. You know how they feel about you. But I guess Gwen's a different matter. Funny thing about that... Come on, let's head back to the truck and I'll tell you all about it."

Helping her up, he gently turned her about with the obvious purpose of leading her back to the grade school parking lot. But before that, she thought it necessary that he understand she had no intention of hurting him in declining his offer. Slipping around in front, she wrapped her arms about his neck and kissed him in the sort of way she knew he would appreciate – soft and slow. They then walked back to the truck as before... hand-in-hand... while he went about describing his attempts at finding a private moment in which to ask for Gwen's blessing. He tried waiting in the alley behind the shop or driving along their street in hopes of catching Gwen outside alone. He even enlisted his mother's aid by sending her into the shop to see if Gwen was there. Such efforts went on for several weeks before he figured out that the best way to get one-on-one with her would be at one of the greenhouses she frequented in the morning.

"So... there I was sitting on my truck hood outside Emerson's nursery at sunrise when Gwen drives up next to me. I barely get out a word of greeting before she interrupts. 'Young man, if you're here to ask for my niece's hand in marriage, then all I'll say is that's between you and her. But if you're here seeking my blessing, then you can just get right back into that truck of yours and head on out of here.' "

"Damn... How'd she know?"

"No idea."

"Well... what'd you say to her?"

"What could I say?! I just smiled, dipped my head in acknowledgement... and then got back into my truck... just like she said. Tell you what... she certainly knows how to steal words right out of a person's mouth."

"Yeah... I know! Still... I'm impressed. You, Roy Meitner, have guts."

"Maybe makes you want to marry the guy?"

"Admire you? Most definitely! Marry you? Well... we'll see."

In the days to follow, she would occasionally ponder over Roy's proposal

without a hint of second guessing her decision to decline. She was touched...
and very flattered... but not at all tempted. Roy was her best friend, a great
kisser, terribly handsome, and sweet too. She giggled to herself at how he had
responded to that conclusion. She loved him... but not to the extent that could
be defined as the marrying kind of love. To seriously consider marrying him...
or anyone else... had not crossed her mind in all the span of her short life. She
had ambitions to pursue first. So she decided to go about her normal day-to-
day affairs with the greater plan still intact – to save up her money and get the
hell out of Lubbock as soon as possible.

She was a bit nervous on their subsequent dates, but also pleased that he
seemed not to harbor any ill will toward her. He was just as cheerful and attentive
as always. Maybe he had finally come to understand her heart, because he never
repeated his proposal or even discussed the subject of marriage again. Their
relationship was back to normal. Still... she had a sneaky suspicion that grew in
the months to follow. Maybe Roy was under the impression that she had said yes.
So try as she might, a little bit of fear came to her whenever they were together.

Years into the future, she would sometimes look back on Roy's proposal
in the Lubbock railyard and come to a sad conclusion. It was probably then
that she first began to outgrow her fascination with trains.

In the spring of her twentieth, having completed nearly three years
of working fulltime at Forde's Flowers, she witnessed the balance on her
savings account cross above a thousand dollars for the first time. It
had been such a good weekend, what with her depositing the latest
paycheck and Gwen departing for a five-day floral conference in Dallas.
She had the house and the shop entirely to herself. From Monday through
to Thursday, she went about her responsibilities with an unusual air of
cheerfulness. It might only take another year... two at most... before
she had enough saved up to finally feel comfortable about venturing out
on her own.

In the months leading up to this point, she had privately begun exploring
the idea of finding a job in radio. Somehow, seeing that transmission tower on
the Meitner property every time she visited kept the prospect on her mind.
The notion of her words spreading out in air waves across the sky intrigued
her. So whenever Gwen was on travel, she would close the shop at lunch in
order to visit stations in Lubbock... most often just to see what kind of
experience was required for getting started. She was pleased to discover that
many entry level positions required only a high school education. The

idea of quitting the flower shop no longer seemed to be such a far off thing after all.

Returning from one such visit, she made her way through the shop to unlock the front door and flip the opened/closed sign… only to find an older gentleman standing outside.

"Hello, sir. I hope you've not been waiting long."

"No, quite alright. You're back when your sign said you'd be. You must be Gwendolyn's niece – Margie, right?"

"Marna. Please come in, sir."

"Thank you. You know, I do see the resemblance. Both of you are very attractive women."

Feeling a bit uneasy at receiving such a compliment from a stranger, she waited until she had rounded the front counter before responding.

"Thank you, sir. Now what can I do for you?"

"Allow me to introduce myself… I'm Murray Abramowitz, of Abramowitz and Associates… your aunt's accountant. Odd that we've not met before… but perhaps you've seen my office on Broadway near the old Nightstar theater?"

"Ahh… no, sir. Sorry. Leastwise not that I can recall. Gwen's out of town at present. Is there something I can help you with?"

"Oh, no. Just popped by after a quick lunch to drop off her return in person… seeing as tomorrow's the filing deadline. Can't stay long." He lifted his briefcase to the counter and began fiddling with its latches while talking. "I understand from what she told me last week that she won't be back until tonight…" He pulled out a folder, waved it briefly in the air for her to see, and then placed it on the counter between them. "I need her to sign the form in there and mail it in tomorrow. Oh… if she asks, please tell her that I've not had a chance to get at that comprehensive assessment of her finances… what with it being tax season and all. Should be able to in the coming month. There's a cursory overview in there, just so she has a feel for how things are going in the new year."

"It… can't be that bad. I mean… I've been working here fulltime since high school… and things seem to be doing well… but I know Gwen's got lots of debt to deal with. Right?"

The man suddenly went stiff, staring back at her as if she had requested something terribly inappropriate from him.

"I'm sorry, sir… I didn't mean to pry. I was just… curious. You don't have to get into the numbers or anything like that."

"No… it's fine. I was just confused for a second there. I do so many returns… it's easy to lose track of who's who. But to answer your question… your aunt's shop has turned a nice sized profit for the last… oh, I don't know… ten years running."

"Really?! I mean… the thing is… Gwen's always going on about being on the verge of bankruptcy."

"What?! You must be misunderstanding her. She certainly can be a penny pincher… but *bankruptcy*?! Poo! Far from it. Rest assured, young lady, your aunt and Forde's Flowers are as solid as a rock… what with her properties paid off and her making excellent progress toward gathering the capital needed for those expansion plans."

"I had no idea… I mean… about the progress."

"I assume you know that's why she's in Fort Worth? Scouting out real estate. You're aunt's something special. You must be very proud of her… and excited about the future."

"Yeah… really excited. So… umm… you'd go so far as saying that Gwen's… well off?"

"Quite well off. Of course, as her niece, you'd already…"

And then it hit him. She did not miss how his satisfied smile at being part of a client's success slowly gave way to a frown. His eyes flickered to the back curtain… almost as if expecting Gwen to suddenly walk through.

"Well… I really should be going. Like I said… tomorrow's the filing deadline…"

She noticed him glance down to the folder, as his hand seemed to twitch with an impulse to pick it back up. Instead, with a thumb and index finger along the edge nearest him, he slowly pushed it across the countertop toward her.

"You know… you should really think about having a conversation with your aunt about the finances. Best that such things be kept within one's family, don't you think? Good day, Miss Forde."

She sensed him turn away… clearly heard the bell over the shop's door signal his departure… but could not pull her eyes from off the folder. Having already tumbled downward through confusion, denial and hurt, she was rapidly plunging into outrage. It would be such a simple matter to pick this folder up, break its seal, and extract from within the truth about all that was Gwen and Forde's Flowers. For her many deceptions, Gwen certainly deserved to be found out.

She reached out for the folder… but stopped inches short. Gwen would surely use this small transgression to divert the issue away from her own lies.

No… I'm going to do this right. That way Gwen won't have any excuse.

Shifting her hand slightly, she placed a thumb and forefinger on the folder's edge… just as the accountant had done… and pushed it along the countertop away from her. For the remainder of that work day, the folder sat there as customers came and went. To them, it was as innocuous as the surface on which it lay… but for her, the reoccurring sight of it brought new insult each time. Though tempted, she dare not touch it, for to do so risked the release of a good part of the fury she was storing up for Gwen's return.

She closed the shop at seven, drove home in the delivery sedan, ate a meager dinner of canned soup and crackers, and then positioned herself on the sitting room couch with a pile of magazines. Near on eleven, the sound of Gwen's car pulling into the driveway awoke her from a shallow doze. She straightened herself up, aligning in her mind the things that needed to be said, delaying only as long as it took for Gwen to get her suitcase through the front door.

"We need to talk."

"Well hello to you too. Something gone wrong at the shop?"

"Not really. Quite the opposite, actually. Your accountant came by today. He told me some very interesting things. Apparently… according to him… everything's been just fantastic business-wise at the shop for years on end."

She waited and watched, knowing that these first few seconds would reveal which way her aunt chose to go. Disappointed, yet not surprised, she saw a spark of understanding flicker in Gwen's eyes just prior to her looking away.

"That's fantastic news. Listen, I've had a long drive, so I'm turning in."

"Or are you just turning away?"

"I don't much care for that tone. Whatever notion's gotten into your head, you best rethink…"

"I've thought quite a bit, Aunt. You said that your business was near-on broke. You said both the house and shop were mortgaged to the hilt. You said you were buried in debt. Your accountant seems to think otherwise. He seems to think that everything's been paid off for years and that your personal finances are… what were his words… as solid as a rock. In fact, he says you're thinking about opening up a new shop in Fort Worth. So… which is the true story, Aunt… the one he says or the one you've been telling me for years?"

"What I do with my own things is…"

"I believe I'm paid up room-and-board wise through the end of the month. I'll stay through May while I look for somewhere else to live, and then I'll be moving out. Oh… and this is my final notice. I'll be leaving Forde's Flowers at the end of next month, so you should start looking for a new floral designer and shop manager. Shouldn't be too much trouble for you to find someone more qualified than me. Guess that about sums it up. Goodnight, Aunt."

She rose, thrust the accountant's folder into Gwen's hands, and then quickly sidestepped past on the way to her own bedroom.

"Marna… can we please talk about this? I don't want you making foolish decisions without all the information. You need to realize…"

"What I realize is that I've never had all the information, Gwen. Your life has always been closed off to me. All I know about you is that you love flowers more than you love me."

"That's not fair…"

She got her door closed behind her before another word could be registered. Her immediate impulse was to do what she had always done in similar frustrating situations with Gwen throughout her life – throw herself down, beat her fists against a pillow, and then eventually cry her eyes out. Instead, she went to the desk and sat there to dwell upon the finality of her decision, waiting patiently until all was quiet in the house. Only then would she ready herself for bed. She had spent so many wide-awake nights wondering what was going on in Gwen's head, but on this night, she thought only of fear. All her life she had wanted nothing more than to break free… and now she had. She was a liberated woman with absolutely nowhere to go.

For the coming weeks, she coexisted with her aunt, both at home and in the shop, without conversation or much eye contact. She revisited every radio station in town for work, but without success. Daily, she combed the want-ad section of the *Lubbock Avalanche* for anything resembling a fulltime job for someone with absolutely no experience other than sweeping floors and clipping stems. The opportunities of substance were always beyond her skills. As the end of April drew near, she had only made progress toward identifying a part-time waitressing job. At least she had enough money saved up to get a place of her own… though the thought of signing a lease that had her stuck in Lubbock terrified her even more than being out of work.

Into May, its days just ticked off without the slightest regard for her need. The pressure on her to do something grew to an unbearable level… almost to the point where she was considering the possibility of begging Gwen to take her back. On the second-to-the-last day of the month, with nowhere to go and no job from which to support herself. She, in a grave state of desperation, made the craziest decision of her life. She agreed to marry Roy Meitner.

In her mind, the choice made perfect sense… almost as if it was meant to be and not at all like something she had been cornered into doing. To his credit, on first hearing about Gwen's deception, he had not reminded her about his marriage proposal. For near on six weeks, he had patiently listened to her unburden herself about all the pain Gwen had caused… from denying her the opportunity of college to how hard she could be to live with. She let it all out like she had never done before, putting into words resentments she was barely aware of ever having. How Gwen never let her use the front door to the shop… How Gwen was stern with every little infraction of hers… How Gwen had no pictures at all of her parents… And how Gwen kept saying that a woman could do anything, but repeatedly denied her the opportunity of trying. Then, the ultimate of hurts was conjured, just so she ensured that Roy was fully on her side – how Gwen had forbidden the two of them from being together. This, of all things, came to the forefront of her thoughts, growing in proportion until the measure of it overwhelmed all other offenses.

Desperate minds bend themselves toward desperate actions, especially when deprived of truer ambitions. So… she unceremoniously took Roy up on his offer of marriage on two conditions – that they immediately elope, and that they move into his house together until such time as they were able to find a place of their own… preferably out of Lubbock. The first was so eagerly accepted by Roy that he turned his truck about to make for the county courthouse. He pulled off the road just as quickly on hearing the second.

"But Roy… you don't understand! I need you to promise me that we'll move away from here as soon as possible. I simply can't stay in the same town as Gwen! Listen… I have over a thousand dollars saved up! We can go anywhere with that… just the two of us. We can get jobs in…"

"Marna… I've got responsibilities here. Dad's depending on me to run the store. He's under tremendous pressure with his cable business. You don't realize it, but people are threatening to sue him! It's really bad."

"What about Sybil? Why can't she help out?"

"Come on, Marna… you know her. She's got no mind for the cares of others… and she's certainly not the type anybody can depend upon. Besides, she's graduating in a week and going out west for school. Pretty sure I already told you that."

She slumped back in the truck seat and looked out toward the cotton field they happened to have pulled alongside. The furrowed rows ran away at a slight angle relative to the road. Stuck with the feeling of being stuck… she found herself concentrating on that one row perfectly aligned with her, sighting all the way down the full length of it. Whatever compass direction it pointed to made no difference to her, for all that mattered was that it ran in a straight line toward the horizon… and away from Lubbock. For a moment, she imagined getting out of the truck and following that row to wherever it might lead, not once looking back.

"You do love me, don't you, Marna? That's why you want to get married, right?"

She pulled herself away from the window in order to find the proper frame of mind for answering in the way she knew she should… exactly the way she expected herself to feel. As a person filled with a richer sort of devotion worthy of making a commitment to another.

"Of course I do… you know that! I've loved you for… well… forever. You're my best friend. It's just that… I'm scared."

"Then maybe we shouldn't be rushing into this."

"I'm not afraid of getting married. I'm as ready for it as a person can be. It's just… I don't want to end up being here for the rest of my life… and never getting out there." She nodded back toward the field, instantly realizing that he would not understand.

"Then how about this? We'll get married tomorrow… have a honeymoon… and then move into my parents' house… I'm sure they won't mind. We'll only stay there for as long as it takes Dad to work through these lawsuits and find someone else to manage the store. That shouldn't take more than a couple months… half year tops. In the meantime, you and I can start planning our future together. I'm sure we'll be able to find jobs somewhere out of Lubbock… maybe in Dallas or Austin… I don't care where, as long as we're together. Does that plan seem… acceptable to you?"

"Yes, Roy… that would be more than fine with me. I'll follow you wherever you go, if you but take me away from this place."

What she was saying may not perfectly have aligned with her preferred pathway into the future… but such an inconsistency was irrelevant to her present circumstances. The way forward was to marry Roy. That, she saw as clear as day.

But do I actually love him enough?

She asked herself this question only once… just as he was restarting his truck… before deciding to fully commit herself to him. For an answer had come back in exactly the same way she had weekly contemplated her savings account. Driven, as she was, by the well-defined objective of getting out of Lubbock, the balance toward love and marriage had clearly been exceeded not by an increase in her affections toward him, but in her great need for him. Of course, she would never admit to such a thing. The thought that he was nothing more than a means to an end felt too barbaric to consider. Yet to stand still and do nothing was far worse. She was being reckless, she knew, but sitting around waiting for something to change only guaranteed that nothing would. Besides… being married to Roy would be fun… and she desperately needed a distraction like fun.

After secretly getting a license that afternoon and then purchasing wedding bands at a downtown jeweler, they made an appointment for noon to be married on the next day in the Lubbock County Courthouse. Throughout the rest of the day, she avoided Gwen like the plague, fearing that the woman's sixth sense might pick up on some vibe from her regarding the elopement. So she went to bed early all a jitter, wishing very much that she could shut down her brain so as not to think about what she was purposing. She finally was able to ease into sleep by boiling down everything to one simple fact of anticipation – she would be sleeping with Roy tomorrow night!

In the morning, she waited in her bedroom until Gwen had left the house and then called Roy over. They quickly went about packing into his truck everything she could call her own. In her final trip out of the house, she paused at the front door to look back into the sitting room where she had spent a good portion of her childhood. For a moment, she contemplated writing Gwen a note telling her the obvious – that she had moved out – but decided against it. Gwen did not deserve such thoughtfulness.

Just as she was stepping out, her eyes fell upon the relief. She had not considered it once in her haste to pack up. This sight of it would be her last. From now on, she would be forever separated from the very thing that had meant so much to her orphaned heart. From elementary school through junior high and into her three years of senior high, this relief had been there for her through all of life's ups and downs. Her secret ambition would always be to break free like those birds, but now that longing would have to find itself in memory alone. In truth, a part of her would never really be free of Gwen because she would never be able to forget this relief. With bitter resolve, she left Gwen's house to join Roy in the cab of his truck.

The trick now would be to quietly deal with her belongings through a quick stop at the Meitner house. There, Roy would gather up whatever he needed for the trip… as well as retrieve the engagement ring that she had not yet worn. Fortunately… or unfortunately, as the case may be… Sybil was the only one home. In that clever girl's quick way of sizing things up, she took one look at the effort they were exerting in moving her possessions into Roy's room… and then burst out laughing.

"You two are eloping! Now I've seen everything! Oh, don't worry – I won't say a word to anyone. It's going to be so much more fun watching everyone discover it on their own. You two are hopelessly pathetic."

Even after Sybil retreated back into her own room, she could still hear the girl laughing hysterically within. Now in an even greater haste to get started on their elopement, she threw clothes into the same suitcase as Roy's without putting much thought into what she was selecting. They both were out the door heading to the courthouse within fifteen minutes.

The ceremony went by in a flash. They said their 'I dos' before a judge, kissed a bunch, signed some papers, and then were out the door. Of course, she was so giddy with excitement that she just had to have Roy pull over several times so she could make out with him in a way that she had never done before. But since they had a long drive ahead of them, they eventually got going in earnest… even though all the miles needing to be travelled were driving her absolutely crazy. They spent their wedding night in an Austin motel after getting wildly tipsy at a nearby bar. The sex came on so fast, completely overwhelming her with its rush of intensity. She hardly slept at all through the night from constantly revisiting the wonder of how he was made. Come morning, the thrill of the previous night was replaced by a headache and a ravenous appetite for more. As per plan, they drove from there to Freeport so she could have her wish of honeymooning at the beach – her first time seeing the ocean. They spent another night in a motor inn and then rented a small bungalow one block off the Gulf. For the next four days, she satiated herself with as much sun, surf, sand, shrimp and sex as she could take, with only sporadic sleep thrown in. If only all of life could go on like this! Her honeymoon days with him were such a blur of fun!

But on the morning of the seventh day, they packed up and headed back to Lubbock, each of them noticeably sunburned. Those ten hours of driving through Texas were some of the most somber she had ever experienced. Though she actively engaged him in their optimistic prospects of life together, she knew that much depended upon the reception they would soon receive from Roy's parents.

It was early evening when they pulled into the circle before the Meitner house, near to the time Roy had indicated in the note he left behind for them. There, sitting in rocking chairs, were both Meitners, patiently waiting for their return. After many reassuring hugs and well-wishes of newlywed bliss, she was unnerved when George took hold of Roy's shoulder and led him alone into the house.

"Sit here with me for a few minutes, Marna, while we talk woman-to-woman."

Ruby patted the seat her husband had vacated, so she moved quickly to accept the invitation, fully expecting to receive some form of reprimand… which she was eager to get out ahead of.

"Mrs. Meitner, I know what you're thinking – that we've acted rashly by not seeking your blessing. I just want you to know that I…"

Her new mother-in-law held up a palm in the same manner Gwen did when taking control of a conversation… except there was also a soft smile of sympathy on her face.

"First off… it's 'Mom' or 'Ruby'… you choose. And we'll get to those things later. I was young once too. By the way… in case you're wondering… George is having a little talk with Roy about leaving him shorthanded at the store."

"Not about us eloping?"

"I'm sure he'll get to that too. For my part, I just want you to know that George and I have always thought highly of you… and we're both excited to have you as a daughter-in-law. Sure, we had hoped it would be under different circumstances… you know… with a huge West Texas wedding… though I don't think your aunt would have gone in for that. Truth be told, it's not our choice. So you've eloped… We accept your decision, and now want to help you and Roy get off your feet as best as possible in your new life together. I don't know what either of you are expecting out of marriage… but I'm here to tell you it's not going to be anything like that. Sure… it'll be fun and fulfilling… as anyone might expect in finding the love of their life. But you better start expecting it to be hard work too. It's not at all fifty-fifty, Marna – it's one hundred percent out of the both of you… or I'm sad to say that your marriage… or any marriage, for that matter… just won't last."

With many such admonishments, Ruby was applying a gentle sort of pressure that she was unaccustomed to receiving. Everything the woman said was true and apt, but none of it felt right in the receiving. Being married was supposed to be about freeing herself, not landing within a world full of new kinds of responsibilities. Of course, she took in everything Ruby said because it was her place to do so, but her eyes repeatedly shot toward the front door, hoping that Roy would soon emerge to rescue her from this scrutiny. Ruby rose before that happened, kissed her on the forehead… something Gwen would never have done… and then went inside to retrieve Roy.

She remained alone on the front porch, determined not to enter the Meitner house until Roy returned for her. She definitely wanted to be reunited with her new husband in the place where they had been separated. But more than that, from oversight or subtle intent, she had not yet been welcomed inside the house by Ruby. She bore the Meitner name, and by Ruby's eager admission was now a part of the family, but somehow she found herself feeling more alone than when she had said her forever-goodbye to the relief.

CHAPTER
12

CATV

From the very first week of living in the Meitner house, married life did not go as smoothly as she had hoped. When she and Roy returned from their honeymoon, they discovered that George and Ruby had moved Sybil out of her bedroom, hers being the next largest to the master. They spent considerable effort in fixing up this space for them, purchasing a bed and other pieces of furniture. She and Roy were exceedingly touched at all of the effort on their behalf. George and Ruby were going out of their way to show an acceptance of her. So she personally made sure to thank her new in-laws over and over for all that they were doing on her behalf, and even extended her sincere gratitude to Sybil for yielding up her room. Toward the rest of the Meitner family, Sybil displayed an unusual acceptance of the situation, seeing as she was heading off to college in a few months anyway. Everyone in the household took Sybil's cheerfulness as a sign of the girl's acceptance of the marriage.

She soon found out otherwise. The poison in her sister-in-law's manner was there for her alone. It set the tone for her first three months of marriage. Three months in which that recent high school grad had nothing better to do other than seek ways of sabotaging her efforts at fitting into the Meitner household. Everywhere she turned, there was Sybil lurking about with interference. Her bathroom habits were constantly criticized, her efforts at the family chores were double-checked, her participation in the kitchen was critiqued, and every little contribution to mealtime conversation got cut short with contradiction. None of the other Meitners seemed aware of the girl's hidden motives. Even Roy said to pay his sister no mind, seeing as that was just her way. She knew it went much deeper than that. None of it was owing to an understandable frustration at being displaced from a childhood bedroom… or having a sister-in-law show up on the scene in the very week of her high school graduation… or even in losing some measure of a brother's affection. Sybil's attitude was much more straightforward than any of those things. The girl simply did not like her. Never had.

For her, taking up residence in Sybil's old bedroom was not the blessing that George and Ruby had intended it to be. The southern and western exposures might allow a cross breeze, but the room was blazing hot on most afternoons, and nearly unbearable for sleeping at night. Unlike the master bedroom, there was no access to a second floor veranda on which to cool off. Worst of all, this space was directly over the family room where George was a habitual late-night TV viewer. Because she could hear him below laughing at the jokes of some talk show host, she constantly fretted over whether their love-making might likewise be detected through the floor boards. Then there were always those awkward dashes to the hallway bathroom afterward for cleanup.

Yet making Sybil's room her own was not all bad. If what was below and through the door seemed less than favorable, than what was above and outside was a pleasure. This room, as well as the master bedroom, resided on the front of the house where the two corner spires were located. As a result, both rooms had small alcoves opening up to where part of a third floor might have resided. The glass in this vaulted opening gave the space a bright, sky-like feel. Though the sun beat in unpleasantly during most of the day, she delighted in sitting there in the early morning with a cup of coffee while watching clouds float by and birds flitter about in the driveway's oaks.

To her, the Meitner house was a confusing contradiction. Outside, all was bright, welcoming, and as wide open as the West Texas landscape… whereas inside, the Meitners had opted for dark wood in their paneling, cabinetry and flooring. Both hallways, upper and lower, felt terribly closed in. The stairs, in particular, gave off an unfriendly feel. With walls to the right and left, and an angled ceiling above, this narrow stairwell felt cave-like every time she passed through. The Meitners used these walls and those along the second floor hallway as their portrait gallery. Most of the framed photos were of the current Meitners – George, Ruby, Roy and Sybil – though there were also others from generations past. She had paid little attention to these during her years of dating Roy, but now as his wife, felt it her duty to familiarize herself with the names and faces on both sides of the family – the Meitners and the Millers. All of this was difficult on many levels, the most obvious being that the only family she had ever known was Gwen… who was not inclined toward capturing moments in photography. Standing on the stairs to view these pictures was awkward, as the tight space made her feel a bit claustrophobic. That unease probably contributed to her imagining that the faces were scrutinizing her… something that those stone ones in the relief had never done. She often came away with the feeling of being a stranger intruding upon someone else's sanctum. In actuality, her real doubts lay closer to her feeling of insignificance to this family… and whether she would ever find a place on these walls as a true Meitner. Deep down, she was not even sure that she wanted to be memorialized here. These walls were frozen in time, unable to move beyond their past.

In contrast to the stairwell, the upper hallway was dedicated to collages honoring the lives of Roy and Sybil. She knew well the young faces in these frames, yet found that lingering too long before them now… with an unaccustomed last name… somehow summoned forth an indescribable feeling of regret. She never had a gallery like this dedicated to herself.

Aside from the downstairs hall closet – the place she clearly remembered having been trapped as a kid – the least appealing space in the house was the family room. Its main feature was its huge TV. Roy had once told her that his father was particularly proud of this combined TV and phonographic stereo system as it was, to his father's reckoning, the first color console sold in Lubbock by the Meitner Appliance Store. With the exception of the seldom-used fireplace, everything in the room faced toward this TV, which she thought not altogether healthy for family interactions. Even without it there, the space was too dark for her tastes, and very creepy owing to the deer and bear heads George had mounted on the walls. Too often, she found her attention being diverted from the TV to the small dots of reflected light coming from off those taxidermized eyes. She would spend time in this room at Roy's request, particularly since it was the usual after-dinner destination for the family, but she seldom went there of her own choosing.

There was only one room in this house that she considered most beautiful, though she only entered when invited. Her favorite spot was her mother-in-law's parlor, located below the master bedroom and accessible only through a paneled door off the main hallway. Ruby insisted that this room be kept exclusively for her own private use, though she invited her in for tea numerous times. Utilizing lighting from eastern and southern facing windows out onto the wrap-around porch, Ruby had fashion this sitting room to be her place of bright comfort. The furnishings were clearly antique – curved headers in gold leaf, clawed feet, and tightly buttoned upholstery. In the center was the tea table, around which were arranged a loveseat, a day couch and several armchairs. Beneath it all was an immense Persian rug. What amazed her most about this room was how Ruby had cleverly arranged the décor to make the space look much bigger than it actually was. Though its height was no different than the rest of the downstairs, she had used ceiling-to-floor drapes, ornate mirrors, delicate crown molding, vertically patterned wallpaper, inlaid shelves, and a glossy white ceiling to give off the feel of an expanse. Everything was both elegant... what with furniture bearing titles such as settee and secretary... and homey, as Ruby liked very much to have doily-covered surfaces supporting crystal lamps and bowls of dried flower petals. She loved this space... but knew it would never belong to her.

For her, it was important that she adapt quickly to the Meitner house, yet she still sought for a place where she could go to be herself... preferably away from Sybil. It took several weeks before she discovered the perfect site. Whether her sister-in-law was afraid of the dark or just things that went bump in it, she could be assured that stepping out onto any part of the wrap-around porch at night would bring instant relief from the girl's presence. It soon became her habit to spend the after-dinner hours in a folding chair just off the kitchen watching the night come on. Sometimes Roy joined her there... holding hands, cuddling, and talking over their day... but often he followed the rest of the family into the TV room. Those occasions of being alone were just as precious to her.

That rear portion of the porch happened to look out toward the north where the city lights of Lubbock did not tarnish the night sky. She often moved her chair out into the yard's stubble to escape whatever light might be coming from inside the house. Looking up into the expanse above her, she would locate the North Star and then find the neighboring constellations she knew to be detectable year-round in the Northern Hemisphere – the Dippers, Draco the Dragon, Cepheus the King, and his wife Cassiopeia. Then, she would follow in a line from the pointy part of the queen's five stars to where the daughter Andromeda lay. In no way would she ever have associated herself with the story of this mythological maiden... had she paid attention in Literature class long enough to hear it all in detail. She still learned enough to know that she would never have considered herself to be in need of a Perseus to rescue her from any sea monster... though the respective comparisons to Roy and Gwen amused her. The real reason she bothered to learn about these stars was because of a small dot of light within the constellation that bore that daughter's name. In Science class one morning, she pulled herself away from staring out the window at the flags on hearing her teacher say that the Andromeda Galaxy was the farthest thing from earth visible to the unaided eye, though only on the clearest and darkest of nights. Being in town had always made it impossible for her to see that distant light even with Gwen's binoculars, but now... living out in the blocks of farmland... the sky came alive for her. She spent night after night just off the Meitner back porch squinting up into the West Texas darkness until she found that small blob of light. As with many things in life, the hunt was more fun than the find. All too often her sad conclusion on locating that galaxy was not to rejoice in the accomplishment, but rather to bemoan that two and half million light years was not nearly far enough of a distance to be away from Lubbock.

On an evening in late June, she was on the back porch when Roy's father came out looking for her. Of the two, he was the in-law that she most gravitated toward... perhaps because Ruby reminded her too much of Gwen. George, on the other hand, was what she imagined her own father to have been like – caring, nurturing and gentle in how he imparted his wisdom.

"Mind if I join you?"

"Not at all."

He pulled up a chair and sat quietly beside her. Through the silence, she noted that his eyes were not up on the stars like hers, but instead staring out into the darkness of his own property. He eventually spoke, as she knew he would.

"What's it been, four weeks?"

"Just about. Pretty amazing times."

"You two have done really well with all of the changes. I just wanted to tell you personally how happy we are to have you as a daughter-in-law. You're good for Roy, and he's good for you."

"Thanks... a bunch."

"Marna... I know you want to get out on your own... test your wings and all that... but I really appreciate you being here while I sort out my legal problems. Just knowing that Roy's managing the store really takes a colossal burden off of me."

Since first hearing it from Roy, she had always wanted to ask George personally about those lawsuits, but had never felt it her place to do so. Since the family never openly discussed them, she found that this might be a perfect time to ask... though it would be kind to start with something simple.

"So... how did you come to start a cable business? Roy said it was years before the appliance store."

"That's true. I was a radio signalman during the war, and managed to learn a lot about all sorts of transmissions. When I got back here and was looking for something to do with myself... what with a young wife and a newborn that was conceived just prior to shipping out..."

He winked at her, and she instantly felt a tremor run through her over a subject that she and Roy had not once thought to discuss.

"...and I remembered reading about this guy in Oregon who had built a huge receive tower on the top of a hotel in order to capture signals from a TV station in Seattle. It was the only one in the Pacific Northwest at the time. He then set up his own CATV company... that stands for 'community antenna television.' Sounds complicated, but the guy simply ran cables along power poles and began charging for the service. So I thought... why not me? Lubbock didn't have a station at the time... nearest one was in Dallas. So I got a bunch of equipment through surplus and went about replicating what that guy had done. I then started selling cable TV service throughout Lubbock and the adjoining counties. It was Ruby who had the idea of selling TV sets. That's how the store got started."

"Wow... that's amazing. And it was profitable?"

"Most definitely. Those were really good years. Everyone wanted a TV, and everyone came to us to get broadcasts from Dallas. Even after Lubbock got its first station some years later, people were still looking to us for service... and to buy TVs. We made so much money that I was able to build this house for Ruby. She's always wanted to live far out of town. The store's still going strong... but things are starting to slack off with the cable company. Which brings me to you, Marna."

"Me?"

"Well, aside from the fact that you're now part of the family and should be included in the family businesses... if you'd like... I know you've been bussing tables for weeks in hopes of finding a better short-term job. Perhaps I can help you with that."

"Really?"

"I think so... if you're willing to work for your father-in-law. You see, the fella I had helping me run the cable company quit last week. I can't blame him... he got a better offer out of state. But I was thinking... seeing as you're looking to improve your situation... maybe you'd consider taking over for him while I focus on the lawsuits."

"I'm afraid I really don't know anything about cable TV. I'd probably..."

"You've got experience managing your aunt's shop, right?"

"Yes... but that's flowers."

"It's no different, Marna. I've got customers just like your aunt does... though mine are mostly ranchers, farmers and small town subscribers. There's billing and collections... handling customer service... scheduling installations and the like... shouldn't be anything for a bright person such as yourself. And I'm sure I can pay you much better than what you're currently earning."

"Then... I'd love to. When can I start?"

"Tomorrow... or as soon as you can free yourself from waitressing. I... ahh... might also need you to help me out a bit with the lawsuits. Nothing beyond what you feel comfortable doing. Just simple tasks to help lessen the legal fees."

"Sure. I'd be happy to. You know... Roy's told me a little bit about those, but not who's suing you and why."

"Well... not suing me *per se*. They're suing the West Texas Cable Corporation... for which I'm the only shareholder. My lawyer set it up that way fifteen years ago... long before the first rumblings of trouble started up. It protects the house and the store. Anyway... of the two suits, the more serious one is by the network affiliates in Dallas and Fort Worth whose signals we've been piping into West Texas via microwave relay stations. You'll learn how that works soon enough. Basically... they're claiming that we've been infringing on the copyright of their content by not paying for the signals. We're not the only cable company getting this treatment... it's happening all over the country. The FCC... that's the Federal Communications Commission... they're in the pocket of the networks. Even though TV signals are being sent out to anyone who can reach up into the sky and pull them down, the FCC's starting to say it's a whole different matter to retransmit those signals as a service. Doesn't make sense to me... No one out here would get decent reception without us. And we've invested huge amounts of capital into towers, relays and cabling... all so rural parts of West Texas could have TV. Why shouldn't we be compensated for that?"

"Yeah, I see your point. And the other suit?"

He went from staring out into the night to looking straight down into the dirt at his feet.

"That one's more... personal... and it's local... by people I've known well for nigh on three decades. It's a class action suit brought about by Lubbock County businesses who claim that our airing of content and commercials from the Dallas area infringes on their free trade rights."

"I don't follow you."

"There's no opportunity for local advertising on those signals. They claim that viewers are being led away to markets outside Lubbock as a result. I stand to lose a lot from that suit… even if I manage to fight it off. There's already some talk about boycotting the appliance store as a result. In fact, there was a huge article about the suit in the paper just two weeks back where a reporter listed all the businesses suing me. Forde's Flowers is one of them."

"My aunt's suing you?!"

"It would appear so."

"I can't believe this! That's just… just… it's just wrong! How could she get sucked into something like this?!"

"To tell you the truth, she was one of the originators."

"Mr. Meitner… I mean, Dad… as long as I've known your family, it seems she's always borne a grudge against you. Why?"

"Whoa… now that's a really long and complicated story… and not one I'd prefer getting into at the moment. I guess you could say it's got something to do with that hangar."

She followed his eyes off to the left where she knew the albatross of the property stood. That night, as on all nights, a single bulb mounted way up above the hangar door marked in dim yellow the oddest and most mysterious aspect of the Meitner family.

"Roy told me not to go anywhere near there, but won't say why. I asked Sybil… and she said it's because the place is… haunted."

"That's ridiculous! Sounds exactly like something she'd concoct for her own amusement."

She disagreed, but kept it to herself. In all her years of knowing Sybil, she had never seen the girl more sincere than when she had spoken about that hangar.

"She also said that there's been a plane in there for as long as she can remember. Is that true?"

"It's true. Care to see it?"

"Are you kidding?! I'd love to!"

Suddenly, all of the sad sort to him was gone. He slapped both thighs at once as a prelude to getting up… and then lightly patted her on the knee too. He was clearly excited… which made her even more so.

"Tell you what, let me go in the house for a flashlight, and then I'll give you the grand tour."

He was gone for just a moment, returning with one for her too. Then, stepping off the porch together, they became just two small points of light bobbing along together within the greater gap of darkness between the house and that solitary bulb suspended beneath the arc of the hangar. She held both flashlights as he fiddled with the clasp on the man door, then handed his back as he entered first.

"Let me cut on the main lighting before you step in."

He disappeared to the left, leaving her alone at the door. Panning her flashlight through, its diffuse beam lit up weakly a huge form directly before her, maybe twenty feet off. As wire-mesh covered fixtures in the ceiling came on, throwing the hangar into a bright white, the first thing she saw was the big three-bladed propeller, hanging in space well above her eye level. It took a few seconds for her to pull her eyes off of this to notice two other things. The plane was immense... much bigger than she had expected... and its wings were folded up nearly over its top, making it appear as if crippled.

"It's absolutely huge! But what's wrong with its wings?! They're... all bent up."

"That's the way they were made to be... for the limited confines of an aircraft carrier deck."

George came into her periphery, but her eyes remained fixed on the plane. It sat facing nearly directly at her, almost as if presenting itself to her alone. She did not understand why she suddenly felt this way, but this plane was beautiful to behold. Everything about it was amazing, from the tips of its wings up high to its wheels down on the ground. She just had to get closer, and found herself gliding right up to one of the metal plates above the wheels. They were the size of dinner platters and each bore the number forty seven. Stooping down a bit, she noticed a much smaller third wheel off in the back.

"It's not just a plane, Marna. It's much more than that. This is a *Corsair*." He said it with such unction, as if the mere pronunciation should signify something greater to her than the very impressive sight of it. "Such a remarkable aircraft... don't you think?"

Without knowing why, she found herself heartily agreeing with him. Why this thing – this hunk of metal – should suddenly seem so alive to her made no sense. It was covered in a layer of West Texas dust, but the fuselage's blue still shown through brightly in her eyes. There was not a shiny spot to it, yet the whole thing sparkled.

"It's incredible! Where'd it come from?!"

"That's another long story... but I'll try to make it brief. I was in the Marines during the war, you know. I'll never forget the first time I saw a Corsair. There was a whole mess of them on the deck of the *USS Hornet*. All those planes crammed in together with their wings tilted up just like this one... forgive me, but it reminded me of a wasp's nest... you know... because of the carrier's name. Anyway... I thought... that's the most amazing thing I've ever seen –

planes with wings that can fold up. And then I got to watch them fly almost every day. By the way, it was the Marines who made the Corsair famous... not the Navy. We used it all over the South Pacific to great effectiveness."

He ambled around one side of the plane, so naturally she followed, still very much filled with awe. She noticed him run a hand along the width of the wing's underside just above the joint where it bent upward... and almost in reverence, she did likewise in passing by behind him. Though hard to the touch, her finger tips slid easily along the smooth metal surface, over a riveted seam, and then on to the very edge of the wing. She had not had such a feeling of wonder since... well... not since the first time she laid eyes on Gwen's relief.

They came alongside the fuselage, and she noticed that a tarp was draped over the cockpit. George lovingly placed a hand on the metal just beneath this tarp's edge. It was several seconds before she realized with a twinge of disappointment that he had no intention of pulling off that covering so she could see beneath.

"As a signalman, I spent the war sitting in front of a radio... but that didn't keep me from visiting nearby airstrips and talking to pilots whenever I could find the time. They were the bravest men I knew. Many of them never came back. I lost a... a very good... a really good..."

He stammered to a stop midsentence and turned toward the rear of the plane.

"Sir?"

"Sorry... For a minute there, I got caught up in a younger version of myself. What was I saying?"

"You lost something."

"Not something... someone. The best friend I ever had. A person who changed my life forever. You see... it was he who introduced me to his sister... and I eventually married her."

"Ruby's brother?"

"Yeah. But that's another long story... and I seem to be full of them tonight. Let's just stick to the one about this airplane. The sad part that connects them is Brad... he was my age in school and a few years older than Ruby. Knew each other since we were kids. He was shot down over the Solomons. So... after the war ended... I went to a Marine airbase in California and bought this Corsair at surplus... as a tribute to him."

"You bought a plane?! They let you do that? That's...that's..."

"Ridiculous, I know. But the war was over and the military was selling off just about anything short of live munitions if it was deemed as obsolete. For years, I was so diligent about keeping up her maintenance... had a mechanic look her over regularly… and a fuel truck come by when needed… all just so I could start her up and taxi out of the hangar. Never to fly her, of course. My eyes are atrocious… and I get vertigo just looking out over the deck off our bedroom. But for a glorious hour or so… maybe once a month… I'd sit up there in that cockpit with the engine roaring away beneath me and pretend I was one of those brave souls like Brad Miller who flew the Corsair into battle over the Pacific."

He went silent, and she waited, knowing from the dreamy way in which he stared straight through the fuselage that he had once more gone somewhere else. But as this condition kept up far beyond the point of awkwardness, she gently placed a hand on his shoulder.

"Mr. Meitner…?"

"Yes… and it's Dad, remember?"

"So… Dad… you were saying about taking the plane out?"

"Oh, it doesn't work anymore. One day… she just wouldn't start. Hasn't started since. Now she just sits here… It's sad, but she'll never fly again."

George, choked with emotion, went off around the plane's rear, brushing dust off those smaller rear wing parts in a swipe of his hand. She gave him some space, staying where she was at as he jiggled the thing she assumed to be the rudder. Too overcome by the sadness in him, she looked up instead to the tail. It also bore the number forty seven. He was on the other side of the plane now, and in hearing his muffled voice calling for her, she hurried to catch up.

"Fastest thing in the Pacific theater. More kills than the Mustang. Matter of fact, it's got the highest kill-to-loss ratio of any aircraft in aviation history."

Such details were undoubtedly important in war, but she was not the least bit interested. She wanted him to speak about the inexplicable – how it was that she could feel so captivated by such a strange thing. Here before her was a marvel – an airplane! Though it might never fly again… it once had. It had been up there soaring free… and that was the very feeling she wanted most to explore.

"See those bends in the wings? Not the joints… just before them."

She turned about to look where he was pointing. At first, the way the wings were folded up made it difficult, but then she recognized what he meant.

"Is that… unusual?"

"You bet. Inverted gull wings… that's what they're called." Her mind immediately jumped to those beautiful birds in the relief. "You know… lots of work went into the design. The engineers chose the most powerful engine of the time… I won't bore you with its specifications. They next selected the widest propeller blade diameter for it… to translate the most engine power into moving air. Then… in order to ensure clearance of the prop tips from the deck, they had to put those bends in the wings… in order to boost up the nose. Turns out, it made it challenging to fly… not something your everyday Navy pilot could handle on an aircraft carrier. That's how the Marines got ahold of it. Did Brad ever love flying this plane! He would go on and on about it in his letters. Said for a pilot it was the most challenging and rewarding flying machine he ever flew. He said that being up in it was like being free from himself."

He turned away again, moving around to the front of the plane. Once more hurrying to catch up, a thought flashed into her mind of how wonderful it would be to command such a thing. To have it pick her up and take her away.

"Funny… don't you think? Imagine purchasing such a thing for only a few hundred dollars. Of course, I had to pay to have it trucked here… and stored until I could get this hangar built… and then I paid more to bring it up to operating condition. All of that took a lot of money. But Ruby understood… even if she didn't share my enthusiasm for planes. She knew that I was doing it to honor her brother."

He abruptly stopped with a look of appraisal on his face.

"Am I… boring you with all this plane talk? I mean… most women don't find such things to be of interest."

"I certainly do! Though I have to admit… it's rather odd having a plane in your backyard… especially one that can't fly."

"Oh, I don't own it to fly it. I own it to remember those pilots who did. One, in particular."

A unpleasant thought then hit her on seeing him reverently gaze up at the cockpit… almost as if paying homage to that fallen pilot.

"This… this isn't the same plane… is it? The one your friend died in?"

"No… That one crashed. Searchers recovered his body… but the plane was a smoldering wreck. I wouldn't have wanted that one anyway. I just wanted to own one of her sisters… to remember him by. I think this one was only ever used on training exercises. Never got into combat."

They were standing together back where they had started, with her having so many more questions than when they had stepped off the porch together. Yet one was on the forefront of her mind.

"So what's all this have to do with my aunt?"

"Ahh… nothing really."

"But you said that this hangar had something to do with Gwen's grudge against you."

"Did I say that? Not sure what I was thinking. Maybe it'll come to me. In the meantime… it's late. Wouldn't want to oversleep on your first day at the West Texas Cable Corporation, would you?"

Some hours later, as she and Roy lay in bed together, she related to him the things she had learned from his father that night. She was surprised… and considerably disappointed… to discover that he knew no more about the plane or the hangar than she did.

"Come on, Roy! The thing's been on the property for nearly all of your life! Surely you must know more than…,"

"Like I said – I never go anywhere near the thing! At least not since I was a kid. Marna… it creeps me out! Okay?! And it's not just Sybil spooking me. She won't admit it, but she's much more terrified of it than I am."

"Why? There's nothing to it but an old plane. It doesn't even work."

"I can't explain it… but every time I'm in there, it's seems like… now don't laugh at me… it feels like it's… whispering to me."

He shook himself with such a shudder that the bed actually moved. Despite his obvious sincerity, she was still having a difficult time biting back the giggles. Clearing her throat first, she put effort into voicing her question without any of the humor threatening to overwhelm her.

"What'd it whisper to you?"

"Now you're just making fun of me."

"No, I'm not. What'd it say?"

"Let's change the subject."

"Roy, I really want to know… in case I'm ever in there and…"

"It was only the wind moving through cracks."

Because his whole body had gone tense, she now seriously wanted to know. So she lifted her head off his chest to look him in the eye until he answered.

"Fine! If you must know, it sounded like… 'please'… three times in a row. Then everything went completely still. I gotta tell you… that first time… I bolted out of there like my life depended on it. I was only eight. I've heard it a few times since… so it's not my imagination. Funny thing… it's always sounded more like a woman's voice than a man's."

"Really?"

"Yeah… totally weird… and it's not just me. Sybil's heard it too. She was a little girl when she snuck in there one day to play with Dad's radio. There was a different kind of lock on the door then… and she got trapped inside for hours before Dad found her. She wouldn't talk for weeks afterward. Not a word. Took her near on a year to get over the shock. You know… Dad thinks we're both crazy… so I'm pretty sure he's never heard it… which is odd given how much time he spends in there."

"And your mother?"

"Mom says she's never heard anything… but I don't believe her. She won't discuss it, but I'm pretty sure she'd prefer the plane and hangar to be gone."

"But she tolerates it because of Dad?"

"Yep… He's in love with that plane. Sometimes I think it sort of… clouds his mind… which I find to be even more spooky than the plane itself. So… umm… did you… when you were in there… happen to… you know…?"

"Hear anything? No. Nothing."

"Okay. That's good. What say we… not talk about this anymore…"

They were still for a long time, with her thinking about whether or not she wanted to hear that voice, when she was startled by him speaking again.

"Are you actually considering working for Dad?"

"Definitely. The job sounds interesting and… Hey… you're not thinking it's a bad idea, are you?"

"No… if that's what you want to do."

"Roy… he says I'll be making more than I do as a waitress… and it'll help him get his lawsuits sorted out… which helps us in moving on. Right?"

"Yeah. I suppose so. Goodnight, Marna."

He kissed her on the forehead and rolled away.

"Roy?"

"Yes…"

"Are you bothered by me working for your dad?"

"No, it's not that. It's just… I'm worried about what these lawsuits might do to him. But you know… we should turn in. You have a busy day tomorrow."

He leaned back to kiss her again in the same spot as before, then went as dead weight on the mattress beside her, fast asleep. For a while, she lay there trying to imagine what working for her new father-in-law might be like… before concluding that it had to be considerably better than working for her aunt.

In the morning, the household was astir with excitement over her start at the cable company… with the exception of Sybil, of course. Ruby bustled about the kitchen in preparing an elaborate breakfast, George whistled all up and down the stairs, and Roy just kept trying to make out with her every time she held up an outfit for his opinion. Soon, mother-in-law and husband were at the front door sending her off with George into her first day of work in the family business. On the drive into town, she peppered him with questions about cable TV, hoping to get a leg up on her responsibilities. To most, he strayed toward the technical in his answers, which did not lessen her concern over doing the job correctly.

The West Texas Cable Corporation turned out to be a cramped three-room suite in a second floor corner of a downtown office building she had walked past countless times in her youth. From the lobby's placard, she noted that the cable company was just one of a dozen or so small businesses occupying space in this three story building. George led her up a flight of stairs to a hallway door bearing the company's name stenciled on its frosted glass. In coming through to a small reception area with its unoccupied desk, he commented briefly that a secretary had been let go earlier in the year due to a dip in revenues. Hopefully, she could take on some of those tasks along with the responsibilities of managing the company.

"You mean... *helping* to manage the company, right?!"

"Of course. I'll be with you every step of the way."

He continued his pre-employment briefing by ushering her into one of two inner offices. This space, no larger than the entry area, was cluttered with stacks of thickly bound books and paper-packed folders. The filing cabinets along one wall had half of the drawers pulled out to double as more surface area. Even the floor was cluttered with stacks of paper. In the center was a desk scattered over with a jumble of more paper.

"Forgive the mess. I've been occupied in helping my lawyer with our defense. What I want to show you is over here." He sidestepped her to a large wall map of West Texas decorated with countless little pins of various colors and shapes. "These large pushpins all around the county mark the locations of our receive towers. They take transmissions from Lubbock's broadcast stations... as well as the signals originating from Dallas... and then transfer them by cables to our customers."

"And all these smaller pins... they're your customer locations?"

"Exactly. Admittedly... the map needs updating. Some of these should come out... seeing as folks are getting better at picking up signals on their own. As you probably noticed, the pins are color-coded based on the tower from where the cabling originates. Here's the one on our property..." He pointed to a black pin northeast of Lubbock where she knew the Meitner house to be. "Haven't really used it for local signals in years. It's the first one that went up... that's why we built there. It's a bit outdated now. Over here's one of the microwave relay stations." He shifted his finger to another black pin on the eastern fringe of the map. "There's three of them, more or less in a line, bringing broadcasts in from the Dallas – Fort Worth area. That's essentially it... relay, receive and then retransmit via cable to the customer. Of course, there's a whole lot of scrambling and unscrambling that goes along with it, but it's all pretty standard stuff. The reason you need to know all this is in case there's a service issue. When that happens, you find the customer's location here, get the tower

ID, then contact our service crews. They're actually not 'ours'... We contract with the same folks who string phone lines. Let's go next door."

She followed him out, glancing back at the map on leaving. The way the paper was faded and frayed along its edges gave her the impression that it had not been updated in a very long time.

At least that's something I can easily fix.

"This'll be your office." This space seemed not to have been used in the recent past. The desk was nearly bare, the trash can was empty, and the file cabinets were neatly closed off. "You've got a phone with in-coming and out-going lines... and there's the company ledger on the corner of the desk. That's where I'd like you to start in. Get yourself acquainted with our current customers, what services they've signed up for, and whether their accounts are up-to-date. To be honest, I'm pretty sure we're several months behind on invoicing, so that'll be the next thing for you to work on. Let's see..." He picked up a rolodex and began flipping through its cards. "This has most of our customer contact information. Use it to make calls about overdue payments. I guess that sums it up for now. Well... have at it." He smiled, patted her on the shoulder, and then left the office.

She spent the entire morning trying to make sense of the ledger's entries, as well as compiling a list of delinquent accounts. After a brief lunch with Roy at a nearby diner, she took the remainder of that day to make collection calls. This sort of work was not foreign to her. In managing Gwen's shop, she had to occasionally prod customers regarding bounced checks or late payments. Adopting a polite and dispassionate tone often yielded the best results. After the first dozen calls, she found that complaints about the quality of service outstripped those who responded with immediate promises of payment. Gwen would never have allowed such a situation to linger in her books. She would have addressed any lapses in quality up front, but also not hesitated to pressure a customer into paying... even if it meant showing up on someone's front door step.

Which is probably why Forde's Flowers is thriving and the West Texas Cable Corporation seems on its last leg.

She made some progress on the accounts during her first week of working for the cable company, but was more successful at dealing with service issues pertaining to outages and poor signal quality. She personally arranged to meet the contractors who did the field work, ensured that these men were paid when the work was done, and made certain with follow-up calls that the problems were solved. She saw little of her father-in-law, either because he was cloistered in his lawyer's office or was on the phone with FCC representatives regarding the increased pressure they were applying to his cable operations.

By the third week, she was taking the company car out on collection runs throughout the counties about Lubbock. Brandished shotguns and angry dogs aside, she found that gentle persistence coupled with a willingness to hear customer complaints often yielded the best results. With the aid of her own map, she went out of the way to visit tower sites, though never bothered to gain access to their outbuildings. Her interest was purely in a fascination over how high into the sky these metal frameworks climbed. She would occasionally stand beneath one in wonderment that waves invisible to her eyes were coming in and then going out through cables to touch the lives of people who, by choice or heritage, had found themselves marooned in farmhouses far from neighbor and town. The reality that these signals were TV was of little account. She was more taken in by their immense presence and a feeling of their significance to the countryside. She sometimes even imagined herself as the tower, standing tall above the plainness of West Texas in a mission of connecting lives to the outside world. Such dreams only lasted until she was back into the car. Reality then bent her thoughts back toward the tedious task of navigating blocks of county roads in some of the flattest and most boring countryside imaginable.

At the end of August, the Meitners drove Sybil all the way to California for college, leaving the entire house to them for two weeks. Being alone with Roy brought the happiest time in her newlywed life. Though they both still worked each day, they had the liberty to eat when and what they liked, could make as much noise as they wished at night, and felt the freedom of traipsing about the house naked if they so pleased.

The eventual return of the Meitners brought back her awareness that this house was not her own, and that her preferences for living here did not apply. Once more, the nightly sounds of the TV in the family room below permeated through the floorboards. Once more, the kitchen and its operations were dictated by another woman. And once more, Roy became a son first, and a husband second. Ruby and George were as understanding as she could imagine any set of in-laws to be, but the house was still theirs. She did find a modicum of pleasure in being given leave to redecorate the hallway bathroom now that she and Roy no longer shared it with Sybil... and of course, the back porch remained her refuge. Mostly, she sought for comfort elsewhere... in embracing solitude during her service to a cable company that had her driving the lonely county roads of West Texas.

CHAPTER

13

THE CAPITULATION
OF MR. MEITNER

The civil suit of *The Lubbock County Coalition for Free Commerce versus The West Texas Cable Corporation* began in mid-October with jury selection. The point of contention forcing the suit rested squarely upon the coalition's insistence that the cable company compensate lost revenue to any area business that had advertised on local TV during the last ten years. This, George categorically refused to do… which essentially forced the suit. Sitting with him and his lawyer, she witnessed three intense weeks of negotiations with the other side prior to the trial. Admittedly, her role amounted to nothing more than a whole lot of paperwork shuttled between law offices. By the time the actual trial started, she had even less to do… other than to watch in the courtroom, and keep George's business afloat in the meantime. Just like Roy, she was in dread over what might happen should George lose the suit.

The day of opening statements, she sat with Roy and Ruby in the gallery directly behind the defendant's table. She fidgeted nervously waiting for the thing to get started, and then felt like she was holding her breath the whole time once it did. She listened attentively to all of the words that the opposing lawyer said about fair trade and equal access, but was more interested in watching the eyes of the jury. To her, that message seemed to resonate with them above that of George's lawyer's appeal for common sense. The actual testimony part of the trial started with the plaintiff's lawyers producing a stream of experts on media advertising and the extent of cable viewership in West Texas. One individual, a professor from the technical college, provided very convincing statistics on the impact of local advertising to area businesses, along with estimates for revenue losses incurred from not having access to cable. Several owners of Lubbock businesses were then called to provide their own accounts.

Throughout the morning, she had fought against the urge to look back into the gallery for a familiar face, but that moment finally came just before lunch when Gwen was summoned to speak on behalf of Forde's Flowers. Gwen took the stand looking very much as she had for all of her memory – slender and stern, with the austere attractiveness of a head held high and shoulders thrown back. As was the case for the other business owners, her aunt spoke with noticeable frustration over not having access to the Dallas broadcasts. When asked, Gwen gave an account of the number of commercial spots that Forde's Flowers had placed on local stations over the past ten years, as well as the benefit to the shop resulting from that advertising. With a tinge of silent reproach, she recalled that many of those ads had come about through her own creative input. As George's lawyer had no follow-up questions, Gwen left the courtroom without once looking her way.

For the remainder of the day, she sat in a private proceeding of her own, calling forth memories to testify against her aunt on the charge of disloyalty. She might now bear the same last name that her aunt hated so, but that was no grounds for rejecting a niece to whom so many promises had been made. Gwen had broken those promises, so it was Gwen who should be on trial here. Her grievances against her aunt were many, yet none more fresh than the hurt she was feeling because Gwen had purposefully avoided her.

Court adjourned for the day and everyone went home. All evening, George was all bubbly over how things had gone, not aware that she, Roy and Ruby did not quite share his optimism. More so, she struggled to sleep that night replaying the memory of having seen Gwen.

The next day in court came with George's lawyer calling forth his own economic experts, along with a stream of farmers and ranchers who provided testimony regarding the benefits of the cable service that they received from George's company. Arranging for these individuals to take time out of their own concerns for a trip into town had been one of her contributions to the trial. She had begged, pleaded and half-priced most of these men into the courtroom… and even chauffeured a few to ensure that they showed up. Her efforts were to no avail. The plaintiffs were ready with their own cadre of rural West Texans who freely asserted how many times they made the long trek into the Dallas – Fort Worth area to purchase a vehicle or go on a weekend shopping spree… all because of ads they had seen on cable TV.

In the end, the jury's decision to side with the coalition came as no surprise to anyone in the courtroom… with the exception of George. Compensatory damages in the many tens of thousands were awarded to the plaintiffs, with punitive measures of court costs and lawyer fees also falling on her father-in-law. At the end, the judge added a stipulation of his own – that all commercial activity airing on the Dallas broadcasts must be blocked before the cable company could continue doing business in Lubbock County. This, George bemoaned later, would require the hiring of an engineer and the acquisition of new equipment to scrub the feeds.

She knew that the Meitners had spent a significant amount in defending themselves against this suit, so it came as no surprise when Ruby insisted that no appeal be endeavored upon. It mattered not anyway. A week after the Lubbock County Municipal Court ruling, the FCC filed a lawsuit against the West Texas Cable Corporation on behalf of Dallas area broadcasters. This one effectively broke the will of George. For four grueling weeks leading up to Christmas, she drove him back and forth between Lubbock and Dallas to negotiate the terms of a settlement with the FCC in order to avoid another trial. She knew nothing about the law, federal communication standards, or fair trade policies. Even the appropriateness of what the West Texas Cable Corporation had been doing with the television signals of other broadcast networks was beyond her. She knew only what these negotiations were doing to George. Through all of the proposals and counterproposals, her eyes were constantly on him. There, she readily recognized the look of a person whose dream had been ripped away. She felt for him… for the hopelessness he must be experiencing in being trapped beneath the weight of a dispassionate federal agency. Their conversations during the trips to Dallas had always been filled with the hope of optimistic outcomes, but once in the meetings, George would turn stiff and non-responsive. His stupor was sometimes so deep that she had to tap his forearm or whisper in his ear to bring him back. The return trips then constituted the most depressing times in her memory, for George would slump down in the passenger seat and remain quiet the whole way.

The end result of the negotiations came in the days prior to Christmas. In order to avoid a trial, George had no choice but to give up. In return for a guarantee that no fines would be levied by the FCC and no repercussions would be pursued by Dallas area broadcasters, the West Texas Cable Corporation must agree without contest to cease all rebroadcasting activities on January first. Their last trip together to Dallas was for finalizing this settlement agreement. The meeting took all of fifteen minutes before they were back in the car to Lubbock. Though it had been heart-wrenching to watch George sign away his dreams, it was nothing compared to the anguish she witnessed on the return trip. He lay down in the backseat as she drove, trying hard to cover the sound of himself crying.

That miserable month of December was made all the more unpleasant by the return of Sybil to the Meitner household. Her first Christmas being married to Roy should have been something special on which to build a lifetime of memories. Instead, that holiday season was nothing but dreary. While Roy attended to late-night sell-a-thons and year-end clearance sales, she was kept busy with three activities – being Ruby's go-for in holiday preparations, putting on a one-woman cheer squad for George, and avoiding the sight of Sybil. By far, the latter was the highest priority. Somehow, that college freshman had gotten into her head the absurd notion that the outcome of the suits was on account of her poor performance as an employee of her father's company. The same was the case for how her brother was having to work at the appliance store because her father was not there to help. Snide comments to the effect went on all holiday season. But the worst encounter occurred on the front porch the very morning of Sybil's return flight to California. Just prior to being driven to the airport by her parents, the girl rudely grabbed her by an elbow and pulled her aside.

"I only have time to say this once, *Sister*, so you better get my full meaning. Don't you dare hurt him! He's vulnerable right now. So if I hear you've taken advantage of him in anyway, then so help me god, I swear I'll…"

"Who the hell do you think you are, Sybil?! For your information, I love Roy! I'd never…"

"I don't give a lick about Roy! You're welcomed to him as far as I'm concerned. I'm talking about Father – *my father*! You break his heart, and I'll live out my days with no other purpose than to break yours in return! Just so you understand me."

Without another word, Sybil tootled down the porch steps, cheerily calling after her parents as if she had been nothing more than a forgettable side trip on the way to the airport.

At the start of the year, having only worked at the West Texas Cable Corporation for six months, her role now became to oversee the company's complete liquidation. She travelled about the counties collecting on debts owed and seeing to it that whatever value remained in the company might somehow be recouped. Every tower was to be dismantled and sold off as scrap metal, the electronics in each receive-and-relay station would be auctioned off, and the underlying property put on the real estate market. She discovered sadly that not all of the company's assets could be recovered. Conversion boxes leased to customers were deemed by George as obsolete, and over two thousand miles of coaxial cable would be left in place for any scavenger with a ladder.

As she supervised the end of a company, she also witnessed a significant deterioration in the life of her father-in-law. The two of them had been comrades in arms throughout the lawsuits, but now he abandoned everything at the cable company to her, not even bothering to check in on her progress. Each morning, he stood at the front door in a bathrobe to wish her and Roy a good day as they headed into Lubbock to manage the two businesses he had founded… and each evening they returned to find him dressed as in the morning. By Ruby's account, all George did the entire day was putter about in the hangar, fiddling with his ham radio equipment. He went nowhere else despite her and his family's many promptings that he venture into town. It seemed clear to her that he was ashamed to show his face.

Most often it was on her to retrieve him from his hangar… for dinner, bed or whatever… as the other two Meitners had an aversion for the place. At such times, she personally tried to nudge him along toward something more positive in life than polishing a propeller blade, establishing a radio connection with someone in Alaska, or just staring off into space. Her efforts at relating the happenings at his cable company were largely ignored. He would not even watch TV with her. George had lost interest in everything except his hangar. She never really got concerned for him until one March evening when she found him play-acting on his ham radio. With all the vigor of a make-believe squadron commander, he was pretending to be leading his fellow fighter pilots into battle. The worst part – she was absolutely certain that he was oblivious to the fact that there was no one out there participating with him.

During those miserable months following the end of his company, she often overheard heated arguments coming through the wall shared with the master bedroom. Most often it was Ruby nagging at George about his lack of involvement in life, but sometime she picked up on a harsh word coming from him. She knew that she was drawn more to the man behind that voice than to the Gwen-ish sort of way that Ruby got when angry, but of late, she found herself agreeing more with her mother-in-law. It was high time that he stopped mourning over what he had lost, and started appreciating what he still had.

At the conclusion of her last day at the cable company, having emptied every filing cabinet and cleared out every drawer, she entered the Meitner kitchen with a box of George's personal items that he had left in the office. She was thinking of bringing these things out to the hangar as a means of stirring some dormant interest in him… but thought it best to check with Ruby first.

"Not just yet, Marna… he's been especially mopey today. I'll put those things in the cellar for now. Dinner's almost ready… mind going out there and bringing him in?"

"Yes, ma'am. Not at all."

The first sprinkles from an approaching downpour hit her shoulders and head as she dashed across the open space between the house and the hangar. With a crackle of thunder overhead, she made for the open man door on a run, leaping in just as huge drops began to pelt the ground. Skidding to a halt just shy of the plane's propeller, she took this first moment within the hangar to admire the Corsair… just as she always did… before turning to him. In the dim of the unlit hangar, she found him where she expected him to be – sitting before his ham radio mumbling into its microphone. He had not even noticed her popping in.

"Ruby says for me to fetch you for dinner."

"What's that?"

"Dinner's ready… it's time for you to come in."

"Oh… Might as well, what with this thunderstorm coming on. Let me shut down the equipment first."

As if on cue, the interior of the hangar suddenly lit up with a flash of light through the man door. Seconds later, the air resonated with a boom that only slowly diminish into low rumbles as an intense rain began to beat on the hangar's roof.

"Whoa! It's really coming down now, Dad. I think we may be trapped for a while."

He moved over beside her, both of them craning their heads through the man door for a look at the storm outside.

"Marna… what say we get the full feel of it?"

Without another word, he stood within the man door and pushed on its frame. The main door slid a few inches producing an open seam that ran some twenty feet upward. Working together, the two of them then pushed the immense door along its rails until it had opened into a large gap. As the wind swirled in, lightly sprinkling her with its spray, she laughed at the cool feel of it upon her face. Reaching over to place a hand on George's shoulder in a mutual appreciation of the moment, she instead found him stooped over on his knees.

"Dad... are you okay?"

"Just a tad winded. Forgot what it took to move that door. Remind me to get the bearings greased so it's easier next time. Well... what do you think? Is there any place on earth capable of producing a better thunderstorm than Texas?!"

He was right. One of the things that she had always enjoyed about growing up in Lubbock was when the sky got angry at the earth and pounded away at it with lightning, hail and rain. The deluge before her was so thick that the sight of the house... not much more than a hundred feet away... had become just a hazy outline within the gray. The rain was so intense that the sound of the drops hitting the concrete at her feet could be heard over the much greater drone taking place on the hangar's metal roof.

"I love it."

"Hey... someone has an anniversary coming up next week. Have you two figured out what we're doing to celebrate? Or is this going to be something special between just you two?"

"I'm not quite sure. We've talked over a few possibilities. To be honest... I'm not very good at celebrating dates. I know... kind of pathetic for a wife."

"Don't say that. You both have had such a tough go of it... all to help me. I really want to thank you for that... for standing beside me through those lawsuits. I don't think I'd have made it without you. You know, Marna... you're the only one who really understands me."

"How can you say that?! You're whole family loves you dearly."

"Loving someone is not the same as understanding them. I know you can't possibly love me as much as they do... and I'm not making a point of ranking one person's love over another's. It's just... you know what it's like to have an ambition gnawing away at your insides, busting to get out. That was me when I was your age... before the war. Back then, I had no idea what I wanted out of life, all I knew was that it had to be something really big. Anything less was a compromise. Then the war came along... and everyone put their dreams on hold for something more important. But for me... the feeling inside never went away. It just... sort of... bided its time. As soon as I was discharged, I knew exactly what I wanted to do with myself. I was determined to rule the airwaves with my cable TV plans."

"And you did that! You really did!"

"For a time..."

"It'll come back. You'll see. There'll be something new. Before you know it, you'll be back running the store like nothing's changed at all."

"No. The store's never been me. That was Ruby's idea. Besides... the store's Roy's now. I would never think of stepping between him and that. My dream,

Marna… it's gone. You won't say it, but I think you understand better than anyone else in the family. Not that they don't know what it's like to have dreams of their own." He tipped his head toward the house, and though it was mostly shrouded by the downpour, its outer beauty was still as crystal clear to her as on the first day she saw it. "That's Ruby's dream right there. That house is all she's ever wanted out of life. And Roy… he's already found his dream too."

The smile he sent her way was knowing… and so very uncomfortable in its receiving. Though Roy frequently said such things to her, she had always found a way of discounting them just enough so as not to be bothered. Somehow, she could not bring herself to have the same feeling regarding him. She loved him deeply… but obviously not enough. As George had just alluded to, sometimes love did not cover it all. She felt guilty admitting to herself that she wanted so much more out of life than Ruby's dream of a house or Roy's dream of having her. She was essentially lying to him… and fooling herself in the process. Anyway… she was pretty sure that Roy had set for himself too low of an aspiration to shoot for. So she spoke up quickly, hoping to deflect her uncomfortable feelings away.

"What about Sybil? What's her dream?"

"Between you and me… I don't think the girl places much stock in dreams. I get the impression that she thinks they're for… lesser beings."

After that, they watched the rain in silence… right up until George unexpectedly moved in close and wrapped an arm about her shoulders in a gentle hug… before stepping away just as quick.

"What was that for?"

"Oh… I don't know. I was just thinking… I'm proud of you, Marna. Proud to be your father-in-law."

Without considering it as anything other than natural, she nestled in close to him, making it clear that she would welcome his arm about her again. For several minutes, as the rain slackened into a drizzle, she felt for the first time in memory the wonderful warmth of being someone's little girl.

"Well… I guess we should head in now. Tell Ruby I'll be there as soon as I get the gear covered up."

Before she could convince herself not to, she quickly kissed him on the cheek… and then took off in an awkward side-stepping dash around the many puddles that had collected in the yard. Climbing onto the porch, she briefly looked back toward the hangar. There was George standing where she had left him. He gave her one of those casual salutes before turning away, leaving only the shadowy outline of the Corsair framed within the large rectangular mouth of the hangar's wide-open door.

At Ruby's request, she set the table, roused Roy from the TV room, and returned to help in any way she could.

"Where's Dad?"

"Still in his place, I suppose. You did tell him that dinner was ready, didn't you?"

"Yes, ma'am. I'm sure he just got caught up with his play things."

"That man'll be the death of me. Be a dear, Marna, and go roust him again."

When she stepped out a second time, the rain had completely ceased, although a blanket of dark purple still hung low in the sky. Turning toward the hangar, she noted that the huge door was exactly as before – wide open – but the approaching dusk now made it impossible to see within. Just as she moved off the porch, the western horizon suddenly lit up. Through a narrow gap, the setting sun cut beneath the distant cloud cover to blaze a bright line between earth and sky. Raising her hand to shield her eyes, she glimpsed through splayed fingers a slice of brilliant yellow… just before the sun dipped beneath the horizon, recasting everything into deeper hues. Somehow, she got a whimsical notion that God had peeled back the lid of the sky to peek in on how Texas was faring beneath the storm… and then sealed everything off for the night.

She found him sitting before his ham radio with headphones over his ears and his head slumped onto the table. The receiver was back on, sending out a faint hum to match its yellow glow. She called to him, but realized that he would not be able to hear owing to the headset. Tapping a finger to his shoulder, she was surprised when he did not immediately react.

I can't believe this – he's fallen asleep!

She shook him a little more vigorously… and still he did not respond. As fear began to rise within, she tugged him off the table top… only to have him fall back in the chair with his head drooped unnaturally to one side. The way his eyes were rolled upward, with his mouth lulled open in a crooked smile… it nearly made her faint.

What happened next was not altogether clear in her mind. She knew that she had shouted out his name while shaking him… to no avail… and then next found herself bursting into the kitchen screaming her head off. Somehow, she was back in the hangar again, but this time with Ruby and Roy. All three of them pulled George to the floor and began prodding him, breathing into his mouth, and begging him to come back. And then she was in Roy's arms, sobbing on his shoulder as the sounds reached her of Ruby doing likewise, her lying splayed across her husband's lifeless body.

At Roy's insistence, he ushered them through the muddy darkness to the front porch. There, they waited for the ambulance that would soon arrive to tell them what they already knew. George was pronounced dead on arrival at Lubbock County Hospital. They made the trip following in behind the ambulance… and then returned an hour later… both ways in complete silence.

No one in the Meitner house slept that night… and no one spoke either. Each of them was overcome by the shock. She sat on the family room couch wrapped up as a ball in Roy's arms. He was still… and she just cried. Ruby, having first called Sybil, went off to be alone somewhere else in the house, hiding herself there in her own grief.

A doctor would later inform them that George had died of an aortic aneurysm for which there could have been no warning or resuscitation. That news made little difference to anyone. For two days, she privately wrestled over how he had responded in opening the hangar door. The memory of him stooped over on his knees convicted her of some small measure of blame in his death… though she kept this to herself.

But the arrival home of Sybil from school for the funeral marked a wind of change for her in the Meitner house. With one look at that hangar door, still open in exactly the same position as before, Sybil pointed an accusatory finger at her and proclaimed to both her brother and mother that it was all her fault.

"He never has that door open. It's way too heavy to move. But you made him do it, didn't you?! Don't deny it! You asked a fifty six year old man to push that massive thing open just so you could watch the rain! How could you be so coldhearted!? He's dead all because of you!"

Though she vehemently denied it was her idea, she could not help but notice how Ruby's mouth fell open. To his credit, Roy came to her defense, but Sybil's words had already taken root in the widow's wounded mind. In the days leading up to the funeral, Ruby began casting dark stares toward her whenever they were in the same room together.

Who it was in the Meitner house that had arranged for the funeral, she would never know. She got herself dressed in black and was in the front seat of Roy's truck when told to be. She had no idea where they were going or what would happen once there… only that George was to be buried. Entering a brick building she knew to be a funeral home, she clung to Roy's arm, aware that he was doing his best to be brave for her and the other women in his life. But she feared that a personal storm was raging beneath his somberness.

They passed through a large, circular sort of room to a smaller one where the funeral service was to be held. Straight ahead of her was an open casket with the profile of the face she had grown so fond of. So she diverted her eyes down to the carpet and allowed Roy to guide her wherever she was to go. After walking down a chair-lined aisle, she lifted her head to find herself at the front row. Sybil and Ruby were already seated there. With a brief look back, she was surprised to find that the room was nearly empty. With a hundred or more seats, only the Meitners and a few of George's most loyal customers had shown up.

"Roy… where is everyone?"

"I don't know."

He took a seat beside his sister, with her falling into the one on the other side. Rather than look at the coffin, she kept her eyes down and to the left… away from where Ruby and Sybil were whispering through their tears. She heard one of them ask Roy to fetch something… a cup of water… and he was up instantly. She thought nothing of this until Sybil slid over beside her.

"Marna… you're not welcome here. The front row is only for family. You need to leave."

"But I am family. I'm…"

"No, you're not. You're a pretender."

This had to be nothing more than Sybil being her vicious self… but when she peered past to Ruby, she saw anger flash in the woman's eyes. Then came an unmistakable message mouthed out in silence – 'Get out!' It froze her in fear.

"Go now, Marna… before he gets back… and I'll just tell him you're not feeling well. Leave… or I swear, there'll be a scene right here!"

On the verge of falling apart, she rose quickly and hurried down an outer aisle. Through the doorway into the roundish entry area, she heard Roy's voice come from somewhere off to her left, so she staggered to the right down a wide hallway leading to the back… doing everything in her power to hold herself together. Straight ahead was a set of double doors out onto a carport… and a waiting hearse… so she took a side passage toward another exterior door, frantically pulling on its knob as the tears began to flow. Lunging through into a smallish garden area, she hardly noticed the latticework above forming a covered walkway out into the cemetery. She would not go that way, and sought refuge instead on a bench within a small recess. All about her, vines with the pinkish flowers of Queen Anne's wreath tickled at her head, neck and shoulders, compelling her to lean forward and bury her face in her hands. There, she cried deeply for George… but also for herself at having been so cruelly rejected. As the minutes dropped away with her tears, a pinprick of bitter thought began poking its way through her grief. Perhaps Sybil was right – she really did not belong with the Meitners.

A soft touch to her shoulder startled her to the presence of Roy.

"Are you okay?"

"No… I'm not."

"I know…" *No, you don't.* "…me neither. The service is over… I'm sorry you missed it. We're moving out to graveside. I'd… like you by my side… if you can manage it."

"I'm sorry, Roy… I'm falling apart here. I don't even know if I can stand. Please… forgive me… I need to stay here."

He nodded, but in so doing turned away, clearly disappointed with her choice. She really should follow him, but the memory of Sybil's words made the situation so very clear. So she would stay put.

After more sobbing, she became aware of car doors being closed. Without knowing why, she rose and followed these sounds to look out toward where the canopied walkway emerged into the sunshine. To her left, the hearse was pulling out from under the covered carport that she had seen at the back of the facility. It did a U-turn and moved away along a narrow lane, with only a single car falling in behind its slow procession out into the cemetery. It was not too long before both vehicles came to a stop. Though the distance was too far to discern faces, she easily made out the profiles of all three Meitners as they followed in behind the black-suited figures bearing George's coffin to its final resting place. For reasons she could not express to herself, the separation between her and those mourners somehow produced a calming influence in her. Not that she was over her grief. She could never see that happening. Instead… the feeling being unearthed in her was solely between them and her. They were Meitners… and she was still a Forde. Turning back to her bench, it suddenly hit her that today was her wedding anniversary.

Roy returned to work in the week following the funeral, but she kept to herself in the Meitner house doing everything she could to avoid contact with either Sybil or Ruby. She went so far as to eat her meals alone at odd hours of the day, and use the bathroom only when no one was around. Mostly, she stayed in her own room, sitting in the curved window seat beneath the spire. At times, the midday heat was nearly unbearable, but she still remained there. When Roy arrived home, he came up to see her, but soon left her be. For her part, she sought no reassurances from him as to the attitudes of his mother or sister. He would have said what any man would have – that she should not make too much out of their words simply because they were upset. Everything would eventually be back to normal. She knew that he did not understand them at all, for she saw the poison in their eyes… and knew it to be real.

The first time she left the house following the funeral was for something she had not anticipated – the reading of the will. She was not surprised that George had a will or that a lawyer might call the family together to make its contents known. It was that her presence had been requested. Clothing herself in the same black dress used for the funeral, she uncomfortably made the trip into town seated beside Roy in the family sedan, with Ruby and Sybil sharing the backseat together. All four of them entered the same law office that she had been in so many times before, waited in the same sitting room she had occupied with George as they plotted lawsuit strategies, and was ushered into the same inner office where she and he had expended so much fruitless effort chasing false hopes. The family lawyer delayed only long enough for them to all be seated.

"These things are best done quickly and with as little prelude as possible. You may not know this, but…"

"Before you start, I'd like to know what *she's* doing here!"

The voice was unmistakably that of Sybil, and the tone itself foretold of discontent if even a matchbox-sized bequeathal ended up coming her way.

"Miss Meitner, we'll get to that shortly. As I was saying, George had me make a few minor changes to his will in the aftermath of his cable company's liquidation."

She could not keep herself from glancing toward the others. Perhaps it was just her imagination… or her nerves… but all three seemed to sit more rigidly than before.

"This new will was notarized last month, and it replaces his previous one. I believe that George had intended to prepare some personal statements to go with this new version, but had not yet communicated those to me. Mrs. Meitner, have you by chance come across anything of the nature in his personal papers?"

She resisted the urge to look over again, but heard nothing coming from Ruby.

"That's unfortunate. Well… allow me to read what he did manage to prepare for this moment. Mind you, these personal statements reflect fully his wishes as specified in the will."

He cleared his throat before reading.

> *'To my loving wife and faithful partner in life, Ruby Louisa Meitner, I leave full ownership of the house and the lot we've shared together for so many years.'*

"Mrs. Meitner, you should know that with one exception, George has specified for the property to be…"

"What'd you just say? What exception?"

"I'll get to that in just one moment, Mrs. Meitner. It's important you understand that the property's completely paid off, and the appropriate papers have been filed with the county clerk indicating you as the sole owner. Now let's see… there's more.

> 'All investments, stock certificates, accounts, and any other form of financial asset held jointly or in private not otherwise designated shall be bequeathed to you in entirety.'

"Now to you, Mr. Meitner."

> 'To my son, Roy David Meitner, I leave full ownership of the Meitner Appliance Store.'

"As with the house, the property's paid off and the appropriate papers have been filed on your behalf. All assets in association with the store have been transferred over to you. All we'll need to do is update the business license."

He cleared his voice again before continuing.

> 'To my daughter, Sybil Lena Meitner, I leave a sum of fifty thousand dollars for use in completing your undergraduate education. This amount, or any portion remaining, is immediately transferable to you upon completion of your degree.'

"Miss Meitner, I understand that you are presently attending college in California. If you would be so good as to linger behind afterward, then you and I can go over the details of the trust. Finally… it would seem that George was able to prepare a personal note to go with this last bequeathal."

> 'To Marna Forde Meitner, my daughter-in-law…'

A very noticeable hiss came from her right, though she was far too gripped with anticipation to identify its source.

> "…I leave my hangar, with all of its contents, in hopes that she will one day find her place between earth and sky. To break free and fly high, yet fully dwell within the embrace of those waiting for her below.
>
> Marna, it is my earnest wish that you find balance in life, and not always be caught between one and the other.'

"Mrs. Meitner, I'm to inform you… actually, both Mrs. Meitners… that a small trust has been set up by George from which a proportionate amount of property tax will be paid each year to cover the hangar's presence on the lot. George also wished that the hangar be maintained and serviced with electricity for as long as Mrs. Meitner…" He looked up over his reading glasses at her. "…Mrs. Marna Meitner retains ownership. Similarly, he has instructed me to place a lean on the driveway ensuring your access to the hangar in the event that the rest of the property is ever sold."

She sat stunned, not so much thinking about what could be done with a defunct airplane and its derelict hangar, but that George had invested such care in both a personal note and a bequeathal to her.

With this, the lawyer indicated that the reading of the will was concluded, and that new deeds were to follow in due course. As they rose to leave, Ruby's hand shot out to detain Roy in his seat. The woman glanced up at her before leaning over to whisper into his ear. He shook his head and said he would be back for them. She waited only until they had left the law office to ask.

"What'd she say?"

"It's nothing. Put it out of your mind."

"She told you to stay with her… and make me take a taxi home alone… didn't she?"

"Marna, she's just upset."

"There's more to it than that… and you know it. She blames me."

"That's not true."

"And now Dad's made me the owner of his plane and hangar… the things she hates so much. Roy… she hates me too! I can see it in her eyes. You have to believe me, I didn't ask him to open that door… and I certainly had no idea about any of this. I've never asked him for anything. And I don't know what he meant by all that other stuff either." Which was something she longed very much to be true.

"Well… it's yours now… and if we're going to be completely upfront with each other… I agree with you about her feelings toward the hangar. Just the other day, I heard her tell Sybil that the only thing she really cared about now that Dad's gone was seeing that thing torn down. She might yet. On the other hand… you never know… maybe she'll let it go."

CHAPTER
14

THE MADNESS OF
MRS. MEITNER

Ruby did not let it go.

On the day following Sybil's departure from Lubbock to resume her summer studies in California, she found Ruby pounding away at the hangar door with a garden rake and cursing at the thing within. Fortunately, Roy had closed off the hangar after the funeral… but that did not stop Ruby from trying to knock the padlock off. She felt absolutely terrible for this grief-stricken woman… but equally stunned at how she was coming unglued. Though much afraid of being hit by the rake, she finally managed to pry the handle out of the woman's hands. Straightway, Ruby fell to her knees before the man door and began beating on it with both fists, begging through many tears that the whole thing be burned to the ground. She was beside herself over what to do. Roy was at work and Sybil was gone, so the burden obviously fell upon her to calm Ruby down… even though she was terribly unnerved by the fit. As a last resort, she promised Ruby that she would send the plane away… if the woman but get to her feet and enter the house first. Somehow, that worked.

After guiding Ruby inside, she got her to lie down on the day couch in her sitting room, made sure that she stayed put, and then hurriedly phoned Roy. To her great irritation, he said he was too busy to leave his store, and she should handle the situation herself. Phone the family doctor if she thought it necessary. She made that call, and was disappointed to hear that the doctor would not be free for several hours. Ruby had begun wailing again, so she went to sit with her, holding her hand, giving her a shoulder to cry on, and hoping very much that the doctor would show up soon. She had never been more torn in all her life. She felt terrible for Ruby, but also desperately wanted to get away from the woman before another fit came on. After much whimpering, Ruby finally fell asleep on the day couch.

The physician arrived in the late afternoon and examined Ruby in the privacy of the sitting room. He emerged to declare that the widow was suffering from a nervous breakdown, and then prescribed her with a new drug recently approved for treatment of high anxiety. She was to make sure that Ruby received the proper dosage of Valium, be kept comfortable, and in no way be agitated by anything remotely disturbing. So she left Ruby alone in her sitting room until Roy came home. Together, they then led Ruby up to the master bedroom. They easily got her climbing the stairs, but when they came to the part with the family photographs hanging on the walls, Ruby inexplicably went into hysterics that had them all on the verge of tumbling down the stairs. Only after they had her settled back in the parlor did she finally calm down enough for sleep.

Fortunately, Ruby was mostly back to herself the next day... but still requested that she be allowed to continue sleeping in her parlor rather than upstairs. So Roy moved a dresser in from the guest room, and they cleared out the hall closet. They then brought down in many arm loads much of Ruby's hanging-up clothes. Things gradually improved from there. She and Ruby actually had a good time going through her dresses one by one. Together, they rearranged the parlor in a way that made it easier for Ruby to stay there. They selected linens that went well with the décor and then figured out the best way to make up the day couch for sleeping at night. She next brought down all of Ruby's toiletries to the guest bath. She had been waiting for this moment... and offhand suggested in her most non-offensive tone whether it might be better for her to take up residence in the guest bedroom rather than the parlor.

"I... I don't feel good back there. It's too cold... and there's no sunshine. No... my parlor's perfect for... for... for being."

Ruby smiled sad and sweet, but she suspected that her mother-in-law's greater feeling was one of embarrassment. So she decided it best to let Ruby choose what Ruby wanted. And above all preferences, the woman was absolutely determined not to ever sleep again in the master bedroom. Fortunately, that afternoon of sorting and choosing through Ruby's things went a good distance toward covering over the mishap with the rake and the hangar.

Through the following months, there were many positive signs that Ruby was making progress at working through her grief. She entertained visitors on the front porch, watched TV with her and Roy on a near-nightly basis, and even cooked a few meals for the family. They got used to her sleeping downstairs, and though difficult at times on them all, they eventually grew familiar with having only three place settings at the dinner table. There, they went through the happenings of the day together. Everything was fine so long as the conversation never veered too near to the subject of George… particularly since Ruby had not yet shown signs of wanting to talk about him or his death. At least a measure of the old cheerfulness was popping up on Ruby's face from time to time. Above all positive signs, she felt most grateful that Ruby no longer showed an eagerness to see the hangar destroyed. Ruby did not openly speak about it or venture out onto those parts of the porch that offered a view of it, but that was understandable from how closely it was tied to the death of George. There even came a time in late summer when Ruby confidently proclaimed that she was ready for attending to all kitchen affairs on her own… and might even consider a move back upstairs.

This was the moment she had been waiting for. The corner that had been turned in Ruby that allowed things to get back to normal. They would all remain terribly sad over George… but life must go on. For her part, she was most anxious about finally getting out of the house to pursue work. She even secretly held out hope for leaving Lubbock soon… despite her fears that a widowed mother and full ownership of an appliance store might be causing Roy to waver on his promise. They had hardly had time to talk, what with everything that had happened since the lawsuits. Both of them were always far too tired at the end of the day for anything other than sleep.

So with a feeling of optimism, she ventured out on her first day in search of a job, starting by revisiting radio stations and combing through the newspaper want ads. For several days, she took her resumé around town without success. After her fourth discouraging morning of job hunting, she came home to find the hangar flanked with bulldozers and trucks. This was obviously some kind of a mistake, since Roy had not mentioned a thing about needing any such work done on the property. But she was barely out of the car when Ruby came charging down the porch stairs at her with such an intense look of anger on her face. The woman got toe-to-toe with her, hissing for her to not dare get in the way.

In a flash, she put it all together, with the hangar becoming a substitute for all of her unfulfilled ambitions. It was something worth fighting for, and Ruby was Gwen, crazed with deceit. So off she tore toward the workmen gathered about the hangar, shouting at them to cease whatever it was that they were preparing to do. Ruby was right behind her, ordering the foremen not to believe anything from this liar of a daughter-in-law. That really incensed her, especially with all of the sacrifices she had made on Ruby's behalf. So she got right into Ruby's face, making her claim of ownership so very clear for all to hear. But then Ruby threatened to have her thrown off the property. So she claimed Roy as her advocate… and Ruby claimed him as her son. That got her so hot that the foremen had to step between them. One of the workmen suggested that they call this Roy fellow and let him decide whether the Lubbock Demolition Company had a valid contract for tearing down this hangar. When the foreman agreed, Ruby suddenly cried out with a loud voice and went limp in the man's arms. Overcome with embarrassment at the scene, she implored the men to carry Ruby into the parlor and lay her out on the day couch. She then sent them and their trucks away before making calls to Roy and the family doctor.

In the course of an afternoon, all of the progress Ruby had made in the months since George's death was gone. She was right back to being her despondent self. On top of that, the destruction attempt on the hangar amounted to a constant argument with Roy that evening. She demanded that he figure out what was to be done about his mother, but he concluded that the whole thing was a misunderstanding. Somehow, she had given Ruby the impression way back when that it was okay to tear down the hangar. She would have none of that, and insisted that they focus instead on only one topic – who was going to bear the burden of being Ruby's caretaker. They should hire a maid… and get Ruby some serious psychiatric help. He categorically refused her suggestions, proclaiming to her face that Ruby's care was the responsibility of family alone. She rephrased her pleas, insisting that he see reason and consider the burden she was under. He countered with the burdens he was bearing at the store to support her and his mother. So she offered a compromise. She would trade the hangar for her freedom from Ruby. He could tear the thing down if he but agree to rescue her from this hell. All it would take was finding a place they could call their own. But he just callously asserted that to be ridiculous seeing as the house was already a place of their own. That was when she absolutely lost it. She had wanted to remain so even through this discussion, but the second she realized that he had no intention of putting her above his mother, she let loose with so many terrible words. She called him a liar and a fraud. That his father would be ashamed of him. And if he was even half a man, then he would know how to choose between wife and mother. She turned her back on him and left before he could say a word in reply.

After storming out, she took to the master bedroom in a huff... and only realized after calming down a bit that this was not the place where she wanted to be. But she stayed rather than risk showing him the slightest sign of weakness. Roy was right next door... so all he had to do was come over and apologize. She threw herself down on her in-law's bed and waited. It was dark outside when she finally realized that he was not coming. She was trapped in this room... and trapped in this situation. Tomorrow, he would surely head out to work early, leaving her in this house with that crazy woman... and there was absolutely nothing she could do about it.

They slept in separate rooms for the first time in their married life. Actually... she slept very little, if at all. She rose in the morning stiff from having been in a strange bed... and in her previous day's clothes. She could easily hear Ruby's voice through the floor calling out for her breakfast, but ignored her. Peering into their bedroom, she saw that Roy was not there. Glancing out the window, she noted that his truck was gone. He had already left for work. She changed... and would squeeze in a shower later once Ruby was finally down for a nap. Still frustrated and hurt, she descended the stairs to go about tending to Ruby... and being the responsible woman of the household. She had no gauntlet to throw down, no line in the sand to draw, and no real ultimatum to back herself up with. She knew that she would remain here caring for Ruby and caring for this house because... well... that was what she had to do. It was her job.

Once more, Ruby was insisting that her meals be brought to her on a tray, and absolutely refused to leave her sanctuary for anything other than using the guest bathroom. Her tray had to be left on a table in the hall, for Ruby would not allow her inside for any reason. Ruby even started dumping her laundry, dirty dishes, and trash out into the hall for her to deal with. Equally bad, the woman fought against any effort on her part to promote good personal hygiene. Her mother-in-law would not take a shower in the guest bath... or change her clothes... or allow the sheets on her day couch to be switched out. She only wanted to be left alone in her parlor. There, she would sit for hours on end staring off at nothing.

Ruby would no longer entertain visitors, take a phone call, or show interest in anything outside of her parlor. She slept there, dressed there, ate there, and made that room the entire extent of her being. Worse than all this, Ruby had inexplicably become twisted in her reckoning, for she frequently went off the handle with all sorts of wild accusations directed at her. It was she who had purchased the accursed plane. It was she who had erected that obscene hangar. It was she who had ruined a thriving cable company. And it was she who was responsible for the death of a beloved husband. At such times, not even Roy was able to dissuade his mother from her warped fury. Only Valium could take the edge off of it.

To all such things, Roy was there to defend his mother. If she complained about the amount of work Ruby was requiring of her, he would say that it was her job to bear. If she pointed out something harsh that the woman had said, he would counter that she had misunderstood… or that she had misinterpreted… or that she simply lacked the patience required in caring for someone who was grieving. She repeatedly tried to make him understand her frustrations, but found that her words were more frequently making him fly off the handle with a craziness nearly as bad as his mother's. Their fights would last into the night… so intense and hopeless that she often took pillow and blanket to the master bedroom. She knew that he was under pressure to manage his store without his father's help… but she desperately needed him to understand the pressure she was under. How neglected and unappreciated she felt all of the time. She was knocking herself out for Ruby, and getting nothing back in return. Of course she wanted them to be happy. Of course she wanted to do her part to support the family. Of course she wanted Ruby to get better. But surely there had to be places where they could put someone like her… if only he would consider it. But to him, this was Ruby's house, and no mother of his would ever be forced to leave it.

Weeks accumulated into months without the slightest sign of things improving. Every day was a battle with Ruby, and every night was an argument with him. Heading into the last week of November, she categorically refused to prepare a Thanksgiving dinner. That, she was confident, would finally show him how terrible things had become. To her immense frustration, he seemed not to notice. He was perfectly content to watch football all day while downing chips and salsa. So she stayed upstairs in the master bedroom's alcove reading a book, and crying herself through many angry tears. She did not see him on the next day… or the next… what with his store's all-day Friday sales event. They entered December sleeping in separate rooms as the only way of surviving. She was married… but had never felt more abandoned in all her adult life. And angrier too.

Sybil did not return to Texas after her exams, opting instead for an extended ski retreat in the Sierras with her college pals. She greeted this news with a mixture of relief and frustration. Though Sybil's sour temperament could do nothing other than pose additional harm to Ruby's imbalance, her absence also meant that she faced alone a Christmas season with the responsibilities of Ruby while Roy was consumed with holiday and year-end sales events. For the sake of peace, she threw herself into making the holidays a special time. Maybe it was guilt over the truly pathetic Thanksgiving or maybe it was hope, for somehow she thought that a festive Christmas might spark something positive in Ruby.

She got Roy to bring home a tree and set it up in the parlor rather than at its usual spot in the family room. To her surprise, Ruby welcomed this addition to her private space. Together, the three of them decorated it… and not once did Ruby show the slightest sign of weirdness. In fact… the parlor door remained opened for her. So she helped Ruby fill the space with Christmas cheer, setup a phonograph loaded with Ruby's favorite Christmas records, and worked hard to maintain a constant stream of baked goods flowing in from the kitchen. Her stringing lights, wrapping presents, and decking out the parlor made a real difference in Ruby. She was cheerful and talkative. Once more, Ruby spent time in other parts of the downstairs, even returning to having her meals at the table with Roy and her. Christmas morning was the best, for the three of them laughed and cried such happy tears through the unwrapping. The only difficult moment came when Ruby ventured into the kitchen to participate in preparation of the family's traditional meal. She could not recall what dishes she had made year after year, and got flustered doing the simplest of tasks. Fortunately, Roy was there to whisk her away into the parlor for some time alone with him.

To her relief, Ruby's good mood continued after Christmas. Everything was fine for the two of them together in the house while Roy was off doing his week-long end of the year sale. She casually chatted at Ruby about all sorts of things… her childhood life with Gwen, what their holidays had been like, and even a bit about what they remembered of Roy as a boy. In all these conversations, she was careful to steer their interactions clear of anything painful. Even New Year's Eve was perfect. The three of them toasted out 1967 and wished each other the best for the coming year. They watched the New Year's Day parades together in the morning… and then some football afterward. As Ruby retired to her parlor in the evening, she finally had Roy to herself. Without wanting to go much into it, she apologized to him for how she had allowed things to get the better of her… and he said he was sorry too. Though she really wanted many more words from him than this, she knew that his simple admission was sincere enough, so there really was no need to push it further. She slept with him that night just as when things between them had been so simple… back before George's death. They made love and then rested into each other's arms. Just as she was nodding off, a warmth came to her of believing that things were finally getting better.

On the third day of the new year, having persuaded Ruby to take an afternoon nap, she treated herself to a book in the window seat of their bedroom's nook. For a long while, she read peacefully in the winter sun, but soon fell asleep there due to her weariness. She was startled awake shortly before sunset by the phone.

"Meitner residence, Marna speaking.

"Marna, what the hell's going on?! I just got a call from your aunt – Mom's over at her flower shop talking nonsense.

"Roy, that's impossible. She's…"

"What'd you do, leave her there… because that's not even remotely funny!"

"I'd never do something like that! She's downstairs asleep in her parlor. Hang on – I'll prove it."

She dropped the receiver and ran downstairs to the sitting room. Pulling open its door, she was shocked not to find Ruby there. This threw her into a frantic search of the house, from cellar to the top floor. She even made a run around the porch, noting that their sedan was parked exactly where she had left it on the circle. After all, Ruby had not driven since George's death.

"Roy, she's nowhere to be found. The car's still here, so I can't see how in the world she could have gotten out of the house without me knowing it."

"It doesn't matter. I can't leave the store right now. I've got customers. You'll need to get over there and bring her home."

"You know I can't go there."

"Marna, just do it. Your aunt says Mom's acting real strange… going on about buying flowers for Dad's birthday. Gwen's doing everything she can to keep her in the store."

The ten minute drive into town seemed like a heartbeat in duration, as not one clear approach presented itself on how she was to get in and out without any kind of an interaction with Gwen. Catching herself before she happened to pull around the back of the shop, she parked in the customer lot instead, thankful that no other cars were there. The oddity of entering through the front door was completely lost on her at the sight of Ruby and Gwen together. She purposefully avoided Gwen to concentrate on Ruby, for the woman's clothes were a clash of nonsense. A knit dress pulled over pajama bottoms, and a flannel bathrobe as an overcoat.

"Ruby… I think you know this young woman."

After an uncomfortably long delay, she was relieved when Ruby's face slowly changed from confusion to recognition.

"Yes, of course. This here's my boy's gal. How are you doing, dear?"

"Just fine… ma'am. Umm… Mrs. Meitner… Roy called and said you might need a ride home. He's busy at the store, so we should…"

"Oh, don't bother, dear. My George'll be round any minute now. He's just checking in on how his cable company's fared this year, and then we're heading out to celebrate. Business has been so good that he's bought the family a brand new car."

She ventured a quick look toward Gwen, who silently mouthed out the word 'taxi.'

"Mrs. Meitner… Roy says George can't break free just yet. Maybe I can drive you home instead?"

"That's too bad… but I suppose a ride would be nice, dear. You know, you really should come round more often… maybe for tea. You too, Gwen. Do you good to share your grief with another."

She had no idea what Ruby was rambling on about, but quickly took her by the arm before anything else strange could be said. As she gently guided Ruby toward the shop door, Gwen suddenly interceded.

"Marna… these are for Ruby."

She looked back to see Gwen holding out a cluster of yellow roses.

"How much?"

"It's on the house."

She stared into those gray eyes with all of the intensity she could muster.

"We'll pay what we owe."

She left the shop toting the bundle of flowers in one hand and leading Ruby on with the other, all without risking a thanks to Gwen for her care. Her only thought was to end the encounter as soon as possible… and hope it to be the last time she ever saw her aunt. On gaining the outside, Ruby inexplicably came back to herself, wrenching her arm free and snatching away the flowers. She got into the backseat on her own without a word of thanks. The car trip back to the Meitner house started out in silence, which was fine by her. She was too angry and too humiliated to try coaxing words out of Ruby. The look on Gwen was reason enough.

'Little Marna ran off to get married… and fell flat on her face!'

Who gives a shit what you think, Gwen! You can just take your smug expression and shove it up your…

"Marna…?"

She was so startled that she almost swerved into the next lane. She knew the voice was Ruby's, but the soft tone did not blend well with her own bitter thoughts… or with how Ruby had entered the car, for that matter. She looked up into the rearview mirror. Ruby was seated in the very center of the backseat, staring down into the yellow blooms in her hands.

"Yes, ma'am?"

"Why am I holding these things?"

"We… umm… just purchased them from my aunt. From Forde's Flowers…"

She looked to the road quickly and then back to Ruby, who had not taken her eyes from off the flowers.

"I don't understand… I only ever bought these for… for… him. They were his favorite. But this can't be… because… because… he's… dead."

"I'm sorry, Mom."

She had no idea what else to say. Looking ahead once more, she came back to the mirror to find Ruby's eyes staring at her this time.

"Marna… I'm scared. Something's wrong with me. I… I can't remember things… simple things… like the name of these things I'm holding in my hands. I'm sure I know what they are… but I can't find the proper words… no matter how I try."

"They're yellow roses."

"That's it… yellow roses. I wonder how long I'll remember that?"

"Ruby, I'm…"

"Don't say it."

"Umm… don't say what?"

"That you're sorry for me. I appreciate it… I really do… but I don't want to hear it. I… I can't find myself well enough anymore to know where I should put such words. I don't know I'm me… or maybe I'm someone else. I feel… so alone."

The sincerity and the vulnerability… it had her near-on tears.

"You have Roy! And you have me! We're always here for you. I see you every day. We talk… and you tell me stories… and… well… we do things together. What say we have tea when we get home? Ruby… you'd like some tea… wouldn't you? Ruby…?"

Ruby's eyes were back down to the roses, and she would say no more.

Once home, she was quickly around to Ruby's car door, encouraging her into the house for a nap… or perhaps that nice cup of tea. But on gaining the porch just shy of the front door, Ruby abruptly stopped, turned about, and with a two fisted grip on the paper-wrapped stems, began thrashing the roses against the railing. No expression of anger accompanied this action, as Ruby simply went about it efficiently until all of the buds had been beaten to a pulp and every stem was broken. Dropping what remained of the bouquet to the porch floor, Ruby entered the house and closed herself off in the parlor.

That day, she gave up all hope of ever leaving Lubbock. On the best of days, Ruby treated her as a devoted servant. On the worst of days, the first sight of her in the morning would send the woman into a fit of rage. Yet all days had her totally exhausted, forsaking her ambition in exchange for watching over Ruby in the Meitner house. The more she tried to help Ruby through her grief, the worse Ruby got. So unpredictable was her mother-in-law's behavior at times that she could not tell whether it was actually designed to punish her for George's death, or whether Ruby was really going insane. The woman awoke at all hours of the night calling out for her breakfast, or put on pajamas with the house ablaze in the afternoon sun. Preferences for how she liked her parlor kept were always changing, and all respect for routine was lost. She would get summoned into the parlor by an insistent Ruby… and then Ruby would act like she forgotten why. The woman spent all day sitting in her parlor doing nothing, but always there was that intense anger lurking beneath the surface of her stupor.

Despite the calming influence of Valium, Ruby still found ways of tormenting her. One minute, she would casually address her as 'Miss Forde' while inquiring into the health of her aunt… and then in the next would curse her for stealing away her son. Ruby would go from vengeful sniping at the quality of lunch to graciously dismissing her with a casual wave of the hand. In between times were so many instances of bizarre behaviors. Like when she caught Ruby emptying the contents of the kitchen cabinets out onto the floor… or when the woman got ahold of her handbag and tried flushing it down the guest bathroom toilet… or when she found her at a parlor window swatting at the morning sun with a rolled up newspaper. Worst of all, it was absolutely heartbreaking to be awoken in the middle of the night by Ruby calling out at the top of her lungs for George.

The pressure of dealing with her mother-in-law's erratic behavior was beginning to take a toll on her own health. She was disturbed to discover that large amounts of her hair were collecting in the bathtub drain after a shower. She also found herself clinching her teeth at night, only to wake up with an unbearable pain in her jaw that would not go away… no matter how many aspirin she took. All day long, she felt as if on edge… nervous and jittery. Any opportunity to get out of the house was zealously sought after. On one particularly contentious Sunday morning when Ruby threw a fit about wanting French toast, she purposefully dropped a carton of eggs to the kitchen floor simply as an excuse for going to the store alone. Though it was real cold out that winter, she found that even five minutes spent on the back porch brought an hour worth of strength for managing Ruby. She even cooked up a desperate pretense of honoring George through the raising and lowering of the flag on the pole in the center of the circle… simply to be out of the house. At both morning and dusk, she fastidiously replicated the ceremonies she had learned in high school… yet always from the perspective of delaying her duties to Ruby. She kept up this ritual day after day until the flag, like Ruby's laundry and Ruby's meals, became just one more thing laying claim on her.

She felt altogether trapped as a result of George's death, though to blame him meant to blame herself. The image always came back to her of him bending over on his knees within the hangar's opened door. If only Roy had gotten them a place of their own from the beginning, then everything would have turned out better. And if only Ruby could just face the death of her husband and move on, then she and Roy could move on too. And if only Sybil had been born as a considerate daughter, then maybe she would not have to be one in her place. Never in her wildest nightmares would she have imagined herself being stuck as nurse maid to a lunatic mother-in-law. Working for Gwen had been a cakewalk compared to bathing Ruby, dressing Ruby, cleaning up after Ruby, and everyday raining down hollow threats upon Roy. That his store was failing could not possibly measure up to the sacrifices she was making on his behalf.

Let it fail.

Her heart whispered that she had heard such forecasts of doom before. Then, as now, it had all been to keep her as a servant to someone else's wishes. Yet her heart genuinely wanted to do a good job in looking after Ruby… and equally to do right by Roy as his wife. But being made to prepare Ruby's meals and then having to endure the insults about her cooking… none of that was why she had gotten married. She could no longer stand being addressed as 'missy' or 'hey you there,' or having Ruby go berserk whenever the woman caught a glimpse of the hangar. Worst of all, she hated repeatedly being accused by Ruby of bewitching her son and killing her husband.

She was at her breaking point. Only the approach of springtime weather suitable for escaping the house gave her any hope. So… on the first warm and clear morning to March, she served Ruby her breakfast in the parlor and retreated to her favorite rocking chair on the front porch with book in hand. Because the air was still cool, she pulled the hood of her sweatshirt over her head and stuffed the loose strands of her hair in where the breeze could not flap them about. Tucking her legs up under her… and putting off a nagging impulse to check in on Ruby one more time… she settled in to enjoy a rare bit of silence.

Near on noon, she put the book aside for the purpose of attending to the breakfast dishes and seeing what Ruby might want for lunch. On reaching the front door, she was surprised to find it locked. Not receiving a response from knocking and calling out, she moved around to the back and found the door off the kitchen to be locked too. From there, it took no great leap of reason on her part to figure out what was happening. Ruby's spiteful state of being was back. Coming around the porch to the windows off the parlor, she rapped on the glass and called out… to no avail. Since the curtains were drawn together and each window sash was bolted shut, she went about to the others of the ground floor, finding them to also be closed tight. With the car keys inside and no access to a telephone… other than the nearest farmhouse a half mile away… she began to fear for the first time that something terrible might have befallen Ruby in the course of her playing this cruel trick. She gave each door and each window one more try… and then went around the house in considering what it would take to reach the second floor. In desperation, she finally took a brick in hand and gently shattered a pane of glass in the rear door. Reaching her arm through to unbolt its lock, she was suddenly startled by a rather husky voice coming at her from behind.

"Hold it right there, buddy. Drop the brick."

With her arm still through the broken window, she awkwardly pivoted her head about to find a Lubbock County deputy standing on the porch.

"It's okay, officer. I'm locked out, so I had to…."

Without regard for a word she was saying, the man's hand slid down to his holstered firearm… freezing her midsentence.

"Mister, I won't say it again. Drop the brick and show me your hands."

She immediately did as she was told, hastily pulling her arm out through the broken glass. In so doing, a sharp edge grazed a ragged cut into her wrist. A trickle of blood had already formed as she extended both hands out to him.

"Sir, you're making a mistake. I live here! And I'm not a guy. My name's Marna Meitner. You can ask my mother-in-law. She's right inside… and she might be in trouble."

"Show me some ID."

"It's… it's not on me. It's inside. If you'll just let me get this door open, I'll…"

In turning about to once more reach an arm through the broken window, she suddenly found herself being jerked backwards by the shoulders. In a flash, he had both of her arms behind her back and was securing handcuffs in place. Despite her vehement protests, the only thing she accomplished while being walked around to the front of the house was in finally convincing him that she was a woman. When it became evident that he was leading her to his waiting patrol car, she began pleading in earnest that he call Roy. Instead, the officer bowed her into the backseat with a simple assurance that everything would be fine if she was who she claimed to be. He closed the cruiser door on her and proceeded up the porch steps.

Beside herself with anger… made all the more frustrating because of how one of the handcuffs was irritating her cut wrist… she screamed out in fury as the door was immediately opened to his knock. For just a second, she observed the indistinct outline of Ruby beckoning the officer inside.

I'm going to strangle that woman!

This is all Roy's fault. He's always taking her side. He's never believed me. Well, he damn well better believe me this time, because if he doesn't…

Just then, she picked up on the sound of a vehicle approaching on the driveway. Craning her head about to look through the cruiser's side window, she caught sight of Roy's truck entering the circle. It came to a stop directly behind where she sat. As he jumped out, she shouted his name… yet he passed right through the gap between the two vehicles on a run, bounded up the porch steps and was in the house without a single look her way.

For what seemed like forever, she waited… resting everything on who would emerge first from the house. The screen door swung open and out came the deputy. He made directly for her, helping her out of the backseat and taking off the cuffs… all the while apologizing for the necessity of following proper police procedures. She nodded an acknowledgement without expending an ounce of energy on him… for her sights were set on someone else. Up the front steps on the verge of exploding, she burst into the house and came to a stop just within the parlor's open doorframe. There was Roy, seated beside his mother on the loveseat. He was holding her hands and consoling her with many whispers. He had not yet noticed her standing there… but Ruby had. Slowly, a satisfied grin spread across the woman's face… just before she closed her eyes and leaned into her son's embrace.

CHAPTER
15

THE GRAVITY OF LAW

She had a colossal fight with him that afternoon over Ruby's stunt. He claimed that his mother swore she had heard glass shatter and an intruder enter the house. He said that Ruby had called out repeatedly for her, but received back no answer. Fearing for her life, she phoned the county sheriff to report the break-in. All of that, she asserted through precise logic, was nothing but horseshit owing to the fact that the deputy was already there by the time she had broken the window. She would get the truth out of Ruby, and insisted on questioning the woman herself. This, Roy categorically forbid, claiming that his mother was far too agitated from the ordeal. That left her with no choice but to throw out an ultimatum – he must choose whom to believe, his wife or his crazy mother. To this, Roy held firm to his statement that she was blowing the whole thing out of proportion. So she stuck her bandaged wrist into his face and demanded to know if the cut was out of proportion too. He backed off, yet refused to soften, offering only how unfortunate it was that she had acted so rashly. After all, none of this would have happened if she had been seeing to her responsibilities rather than lounging around on the front porch. That immediately sent her into a towering rage of unrestrained cursing and door slamming.

She spent the rest of the afternoon fuming over every detail to their argument, emerging from the master bedroom in the evening only after cooling off enough for another try. She found him in the family room sitting before the TV as if the whole horrible experience had never occurred. Despite her renewed efforts aimed at getting him to understand, the fight started all over again. She laid out her claims as to how supremely deranged Ruby had become and how he had broken promise after promise to leave Lubbock. He went on the counter-offensive, demanding to know what she had done to set off his mother... and did it have anything to do with how close she had gotten to his father during all those months of them working together? He was trying to push her to the edge, that much was clear, but she would push right back. Bellowing out her most caustic laugh, she polished it off by declaring how pathetically stupid such petty jealousy was. She would have switched places with him any day of the week. Sitting around doing nothing at the appliance store would have been a breeze compared to watching his father fall apart at the seams. His scowl showed that she had scored on that one... but then he responded by demanding that she explain again exactly how it was that the hangar door had come to be open on the day his father died. In total disbelief, she exploded with an accusation that he had obviously never believed her in the first place! She would not spare another word for him after that, retreating from the family room to spend yet another lonely night in the master bedroom.

She lay awake for hours crying over her situation. All of her sacrifices on their behalf as a couple were being distorted by him. Everything in her life had gone wrong! Her relationship with Gwen was over, George was dead, the CATV network was defunct, and her marriage was being torpedoed by a demented mother-in-law. All that remained to her was a beat-up hangar, a broken-down airplane, and a borrowed name. She had no skills, no education, no opportunities, and nothing to do day after day but fret over a cankerous fear that she had made the mistake of a lifetime in getting married.

From that night forward, the Meitner house became a symbol of her confinement. Its darken interiors were her prison, whereas all escape attempts to the bright outdoors were nothing but torture. Sitting on the porch just poisoned her mind, for every corner of that wrap-around taunted her with a view of the horizon. The world out there was so far beyond her reach. Weeks had turned into months, and those months became a year, yet still she waited just as when she was a newlywed. The reassuring lies she had once whispered to herself could no longer be endured. It was so very evident that he had no intention of ever leaving his mother or his store for her.

After having been treated like a criminal the day before, she awoke the next morning with the case for her heart decided... and she would not change.

There'll be no shadow of turning with me!

She had tried making compassion her way, but no longer. Morning by morning, she had pleaded with him to see her great need, yet he had not once extended a hand to provide. Summer to winter had been wasted, and now, in springtime, she would no longer do what was hardest.

The sun, moon and stars would fall from their courses above before he agreed to join me!

She did not need Nature or anyone else to bear witness for her. She would ask no pardon, endure no false peace, hold no shallow love dear. Instead, she would cheerfully be her own guide, for today she had the presence of mind to decide… to seek a bright future for tomorrow.

Ten thousand blessings'll be mine... but first, I've absolutely gotta break away!

She remained in the master bedroom until she was sure Roy had left the house for work, and then retrieved the phone book from the kitchen. Everything had to be done with the utmost secrecy. Without taking notes or dog-earring pages of interest, she rapidly combed through the yellow-pages. Though her personal opinion of the profession was not so favorable, she convinced herself of one thing in the sleepless hours of the night – she desperately needed a lawyer well-versed in the laws of divorce. She also needed a plan.

Ruby emerged from her parlor in midmorning and went about the downstairs demanding her breakfast. She just ignored the woman's commands. The door to the master bedroom was locked, so Ruby could call the sheriff again for all the good it would do her. Short of burning the house down, the woman was on her own.

Near on noon… after the ruckus of Ruby rampaging through the kitchen had died down… she emerged from the master bedroom to peak into the parlor. Her mother-in-law was asleep on the day couch. After stacking a pyramid of paper cups up against the parlor door as an early-warning alarm, she retreated to the kitchen with the phone book and began the tedious process of making inquiries into her ads of interest. After a half dozen unfruitful calls to the more substantial firms in Lubbock, she honed in on the one-person operations. She found one that offered a free initial consultation, then called to set an appointment for the following morning. She would tell Roy nothing, and just leave Ruby to herself in the house.

With another night of sleeping in separate beds, she left the master bedroom only after being convinced that Roy was gone. She could hear Ruby through the parlor door moaning to herself, but went out to the car without a single word to the woman. On the drive into Lubbock, her mind was fully on the case she was preparing for the lawyer.

The office of *Richard McBride at Law* was a backroom to a vacant warehouse located near the railyard. She knocked and then entered to rather sparse office furnishings. Against one wall was a row of metal file cabinets, each of such differing proportions as to suggest that they were all obtained second-hand. There was also a small metal desk, bracketed shelves with law books, and a plastic chair for her, as the perspective client, to sit in. All those things did not give her much confidence. At least there was a law diploma hanging on the wall... though the lawyer himself did not seem much older than her.

"Welcome, Mrs. Meitner... have a seat there. As I mentioned over the phone, this consultation is completely confidential... however, I do record my sessions for future reference." He pointed a thumb over his shoulder to a reel-to-reel that sat on a nearby table. "Do I have your permission to proceed?"

She nodded, having seen this sort of thing done routinely during nearly every encounter with a lawyer in her capacity as an employee of the West Texas Cable Corporation. He leaned back to start the tape and then positioned a microphone on the desk before her.

"Let's get started. I'll ask a few questions, and you answer to the best of your ability. First of all, Mrs. Marna Meitner, are you aware that this conversation is being recorded?"

"Yes."

"Excellent. Now as I understand it, you're inquiring about a petition of divorce, is that correct?"

She looked down at the microphone before her. Though it sat less than a foot away, she somehow felt it necessary to lean forward in providing her answer.

"Yes... that is correct."

"I take it that your husband has secured legal representation of his own?"

"No. I haven't brought up the subject with him just yet. I wanted to understand my rights before doing anything like that. But I'm pretty sure he won't grant me a divorce willingly."

"And why's that?"

"I suppose mostly because of the way he was raised."

"Hmm... So... how long have you been married?"

"Two years come end of May. Do you need to see the license?"

"Eventually... but only to verify from where it was issued. We'll get to that later. Are there any children from the marriage?"

"Hell no!" She instantly felt a flush of embarrassment at having responded so bluntly. "Sorry... I mean... no children."

"That simplifies things. Are there extensive jointly-owned holdings?"

"What do you mean by holdings?"

"Property... bank accounts... investments... that sort of thing."

"We have a car... and a truck."

"I see..."

He sprawled something on the notepad, though it was his deflated tone that most concerned her. So she jumped in with more in order to keep him engaged.

"He has a business. Meitner Appliances. The store's in his name... but I don't know if that matters. The family also once owned a cable TV network with a couple dozen receive stations scattered about..."

"You mean receiver stations?"

"What? No... they're called *receive* stations... because, well... they receive. Anyway... there was also a series of microwave relays between here and Dallas... but all that's been sold off. His father was the company's founder... but he passed away nearly a year ago."

"Any other properties or assets?"

"There's the house, but that's in his mother's name."

"Hmm."

He underlined something... but then she realized that he had actually crossed out a line. He then wrote a single word that she could not make out, but the way he circled it several times did not seem so favorable to her.

"I also own an airplane and an airplane hangar. It's not functional... and the hangar's not much to look at."

He raised his eyebrows at that, which gave her hope that he might now take her situation more seriously.

"So tell me in as few words as possible why it is that you're considering a divorce."

"Mostly because he just doesn't love me anymore... and I don't love him either. How could I!? He's completely abandoned me! You see... he makes me stay in that dreadful house with his mother. It's just me and her all day long... ever since George died. That's his father. And you need to understand something that's really important – his mother's crazy."

"George's mother's crazy?"

"No... my husband's. Ruby Meitner. She's my mother-in-law... George's wife. She called the police on me for nothing. For a joke. I can't live another day in the same house with her."

The man's mouth turned down in an unreadable frown. None of this was starting out the way she wanted it to. She needed to be more convincing so this lawyer would agree to help her. What she had provided thus far was somehow making her look more like an idiot than a neglected wife. She looked over at the reels rotating about with nothing being recorded. She should say something significant for that tape. Something with substance that clearly demonstrated her many grievances. But round and round the wheels spun, one feeding into the other, all with absolutely no regard for her pain.

"Mrs. Meitner, let me simplify things a bit. In order for you to obtain a writ of divorce in the state of Texas... whether your husband agrees to it or not... you'll need grounds. One of the most common grounds for divorce is infidelity. Has your husband been... unfaithful?"

"No. It's nothing like that. Roy wouldn't... I mean... he'd never. He's just not the type."

"Are you sure? Because the wife's usually the last to know."

"No... I'd know. He's faithful to me... just more faithful to his mother."

"Okay... then has he been abusive?"

"Well... he's never hit me or anything like that... but I certainly do feel abused."

"Because he's threatened you with bodily harm?"

"Ahh... no. It's nothing like that. It's more that he confines me in that house for..."

"So you'd say his abuse falls more in the category of gross negligence?"

"Yes! Well... sort of... but not exactly..."

"Is this house unsafe for any reason?"

"No. I mean... I do feel unsafe... what with his mother and all... but the house itself... it's not exactly unsafe. But I am trapped in it!"

"So he locks you in?"

"No. It's more like I can't breathe in there. The place absolutely makes me sick!"

"So it's adversely affecting your health?"

"You're getting this all wrong!" She took a deep, calming breath, and then fixed her eyes again on the rotating reels. "It's just that I want to get out and be a part of the world. I want to do something significant with my life. You know... make something of myself. I want to build a career. But he won't let me. You agree that's not fair?!"

She waited all of two seconds before concluding from the man's blank stare that she was not arguing her case nearly well enough. She needed to do much better than this.

"You see... I've been raised to believe that a woman deserves the same opportunities as a man. But that's not what he thinks! He thinks my place is *in the home* taking care of his mother. I can't handle that stress. That house is so huge... much more than a person needs to live in... and I have to do all of the cooking... the cleaning... the laundry... *and*... take care of his mother!"

With each chore, she drove the forefinger of one hand down upon the palm of the other, just so he would understand how difficult life had become.

"That's not why I married him. He promised me much more than that!"

The lawyer had long ago stopped writing, but now put the pencil down and eased back in his chair.

"Allow me to be frank with you, Mrs. Meitner. I don't know if I can be of much assistance."

"You have to! I have nowhere else to go. I'm telling you, his mother's insane! One moment everything's fine, and then the next she's screaming at me. And if I touch her... gentle like... you know, to help her along... she starts swatting at me like I was some kind of a bug! I've been living in that house with her for near on two years and she still treats me like a servant. When she does decide to recognize me, it's to browbeat me for not doing things just the way she wants. She's always complaining about what a terrible person I am. I don't understand it... she once was so nice to me... but now... I can't take it anymore!"

For the life of her, she wanted to break down into tears before this man simply so he would understand. Though her situation was desperate and her frustrations were real, she felt totally incapable of expressing any emotion other than anger. And anger was not convincing this man.

He picked up his pencil again... but not to write. Instead, he began twirling it about in an absentminded sort of way. That fidgeting, along with how the springs to his desk chair were squeaking as he rocked, told her he would not be taking her case.

"Mrs. Meitner, I wish I could help you, I really do... but there has to be more to it if you wish to convince a judge. He'll look at a young woman such as yourself and see..." He paused to place the pencil down before continuing. "Perhaps a psychiatric evaluation might be in order."

"Of me? How's that..."

"No. I was referring to your mother-in-law."

"Oh... there's no way Roy'd put his mother through that! And she'd have no part in it either. They're like this."

She held up her right hand for him to see two fingers tightly intertwined, but his eyes instead went to how the medical alert bracelet slid down her wrist.

"Mrs. Meitner, I'm not..."

"Will you please stop calling me that?! My name's Marna."

"Of course. As I was saying... Marna... I'm not in a position to arrange it, but

I'm sure there're ample counseling services available to young couples such as…"

"I don't want counseling! I want out!"

"Then there's really only one thing left for a person in your situation to do. In the absence of cause, a judge can only issue a writ of divorce if the two parties have been separated for at least three years."

"Separated?"

"Essentially. You must move out… but it's a bit more complicated than that. You also have to live independently. I've heard of cases where the wife's received…"

"I can do that!"

"Beg your pardon?"

"I can move out. Soon, as a matter of fact. I can be gone from that house and never look back. But you're sure about this?"

"Absolutely. Under Texas State law, you can obtain a no-cause divorce after three years of separation. There're some rumblings in the legislature about adopting 'no fault' divorce, just as is being considered in California, but it'll probably take years before Texas voters are willing to accept that."

Silence filled the small office as she waited for something more from him… something to assure her that this was the right decision.

"Marna… I'm not seeing any benefit in continuing this consultation. Take one of my cards, and if something more serious develops between you two, then feel free to give me a call. If you do decide to move out, please leave me a forwarding address. I'll need to document the date. In the meantime… take heart… three years can go by very quickly."

She left his office with a lightness not felt in over a year. There was likely more pain ahead for her… much more pain… but she now finally had a way out.

Leaving Lubbock had always been the first step toward achieving her dreams… but doing so in order to obtain a divorce was not something she had ever anticipated. She could tell herself that it was all because of his broken promises, but there was an unpleasant contradiction there. She was embarking upon a new chapter in her life by breaking promises of her own. Best not to think on that until all the promise-breaking was done. So, she would forge on with the first step in her evolving plan for escaping Lubbock. This, she undertook on the way home from the lawyer's office. Using her maiden name and paying in cash, she obtained a small box at the post office. This secret place would be her bastion… a fortress of confidence in herself. In a sense, its tiny little door was also her way out, for through it would eventually come the offer letter that ushered in her future. With her first real ray of hope in over a year, she opened and closed that door several times just to enjoy the full feel of its significance to her plan. She then placed the lawyer's card inside for safekeeping and closed the door with hope.

Heading out to the car, she was savoring an unfamiliar optimism when a series of thoughts came to her, each more unpleasant than the one before.

Ruby's definitely crazy.

I can't keep her from getting into my things.

She's dumped my purse out before.

She'll find the post office box key on my keychain.

Then Roy'll know...

She absolutely could not afford that to happen. Taking her nail file, she methodically opened up a small slit into the lining of her purse just beneath its zipper, and then slid the mailbox key inside. By tilting the purse just right, the small piece of brass could be made to slide toward this slit from where it could be retrieved with a finger. With the key hidden in place, she jostled the bag about, and even purposefully dumped the contents onto the passenger seat. Being reasonably convinced that the key could not be made to fall out of the slit on its own, she collected up her things and drove home.

In the days to follow, she allowed her relationship with Roy to stabilize into something of a truce. She returned to his bed, but without any desire for intimacy. Not once had he apologized for the way things had turned out. Not once had he taken steps toward dealing with his demented mother. Not once had he put his wife first. As far as she was concerned, their relationship was over. But because she was not yet ready to leave, she agreed to resume her caretaking responsibilities over Ruby... who remained just as hurtful as before. Her only demand was that she be given evenings to do as she pleased. Roy accepted this, not knowing that she was actually driving into Lubbock to check her mailbox.

Working on a public library typewriter the next evening, she fine-tuned a cover letter and resumé highlighting her experience as a shop clerk and a CATV accounts manager. Using the library's new Xerographic machine to make copies, she mailed out letters in response to every marginally suitable job advertisement she came across, all under the name of Marna Forde. She kept this up for weeks, with rejection letters discarded upon receipt and possibilities responded to by phone. Nothing of substance arose until she received a letter in early April from a Lubbock TV station inviting her to participate in its network's periodic open-interview process. She promptly called to set up a time.

This TV interview took place in the following week at the Lubbock network affiliate… and turned out to be a total bust! She and a dozen other applicants were told that no position actually existed at the time, but that the regional hub in Dallas would retain their information on file in the event that something opened up somewhere in its network of stations. She was so frustrated. Not just with the letdown but also because she had used up one of her best excuses with Roy in order to be there. Next time, she would have to think up something more elaborate than a checkup at her gynecologist's office.

She put the failed interview out of her mind in order to concentrate on other possibilities. Every morning, she secretly scoured the Lubbock paper for opportunities, and every night she visited her post office box and wrote more letters at the library.

One evening in late April, she entered the post office to check in the glass window of her box before heading over to the library. Most days, there was no need to open the door because it was easy to tell that the box was empty based on the trace amount of nightlight coming through from the mailroom. On this occasion, the small window was darkened. Dropping to one knee, she plied back the lining of her purse and fished out the mailbox key. Extracting a single letter from the box, a thrill ran through her because of its thickness. Flipping it about, she noted with surprise the name of the Dallas addressee, and then hastily tore open the seal. Her heart, already pounding away with excitement, went even faster as she pulled out a sizeable packet of papers. Flattening out the top sheet, she quickly began to read.

Dear Miss Marna Forde,

On behalf of our parent corporation, we wish to extend to you an exciting offer of entry level employment as a TV news production assistant at our network affiliate station, WYNG…

She barely stifled her scream of excitement, for this letter was her way out of Lubbock! She still found herself shaking the stack of pages up in the air with uncontrollable vigor in order to keep that scream from coming out. In the process, she accidently dropped both the envelope and her purse to the floor. Turning about, she slid down the wall of mailboxes to comfortably seat herself on the floor before continuing to read. Picking up from the start, she got to just about the same spot in the letter before halting once more.

…in Chicago, Illinois.

CHAPTER

16

EUSOCIETY AND THE LAST FLIGHT OF THE RED RINGED PAPER WASP

Chicago?!

How the hell am I supposed to get myself to Chicago?!

She read through the cover letter again, and then frantically searched through the accompanying pages for a clause that might make Dallas an option over Chicago. The remainder of the envelope's contents highlighted the particulars of the position and the station itself. The last page was a contract clearly stating that the offer was for employment at WYNG in Chicago. The deadline date for an answer was a mere ten days away. The offer letter also indicated that she would be responsible for all expenses entailed in getting there. The only assistance provided was the name and phone number of someone within the station's personnel department who could help with housing.

Rather than excitement, she felt a shiver of apprehension run through her.

I've… never actually been out on my own.

This was the moment she had been longing for… but for the life of her, she felt very much on the verge of tears. She gripped her knees tightly against the emotion, which made the pages slip from her lap to the post office floor. Scrambling to gather them up, she went at it with such absurd haste that she was somehow thrown into a spasm of sniffled hiccups. Pinching off her nose and locking her lips shut such that her cheeks bulged, she held her breath through several cycles until the fit had passed. Worn out from that ridiculous ordeal, she leaned back against the mailboxes to rest, closing her eyes in the process.

Surely she was tougher than this. Having lived with the Meitners for nearly two years, and endured Gwen for over five times as long, she definitely had what it took to be out on her own… even in a city as far away as Chicago.

So get a grip on yourself! Of course you're accepting this offer. It's your way out!

Her decision was made. So with the fingers of her right hand, she wiped away moisture from her left eye, and repeated the same with her left to the other. She then went about calming herself with several deep breaths before considering what to do next. For starters, she would sign the contract and mail it back right away. Tonight, in fact… once she got herself up off this post office floor and over to the drugstore for some stationary. She separated out the contract page and carefully folded the rest of the paperwork back into its envelope. Reaching over her shoulder, she slid the envelope back into her mailbox. With both hands to the floor, she pushed herself up… just as a second wave of emotion hit her.

Oh my… this is going to devastate him!

She fell back down in bringing her hands to her face, but in so doing ended up accidently getting dust from the floor in her eyes. The resulting sting of irritation became an immediate reminder of a childhood's worth of frustration over being forced to live in such a desolate place.

I hate it here! I can't wait to leave!

With new clarity of insight borne from old feelings, she picked herself up off the post office floor, locked her box, and slid the key back into its hiding place in her purse. By the time she reached the car, she was fully determined to leave Lubbock and enter Chicago as a new person.

After a week of secret planning, she had most everything worked out. Very much acting out the part of a caring daughter-in-law, she persuaded a neurological specialist in Lubbock to squeeze Ruby in for an appointment that afternoon. It would be tricky getting the woman out to the car without her flying into a rage, so she accomplished the feat with the aid of another despicable lie. She told Ruby that they were going to meet George at his office. She also found it helpful to dangle out a box of her mother-in-law's favorite Girl Scout cookies – thin mints. These, she tossed into the backseat… with Ruby promptly following the box inside. From there, barring a total meltdown in route, Ruby would be Roy's problem. He would be the one responsible for taking her. She finally got him to agree by offering to watch the store while he was gone. Her real objective was not so noble. She needed to make a series of long distance calls to Chicago, and could not risk placing these on their home phone. The store's would be safer, seeing as that account had a much greater volume of business-related calls.

After a quick check on Ruby in the backseat, she hustled up to the store's service entrance and pounded on the door, as per agreement with Roy. Then, waiting only long enough to ensure that the two of them had pulled away in the car, she rushed to the front of the store, locked the door, and hung the 'closed' sign in the window. At most, she had an hour in which to sort out her future living arrangements, as well as phone the station to verify that her acceptance letter had arrived. She accomplished the latter first using the reference number in the offer letter. The woman who answered confirmed receipt of her contract.

"Then we'll expect you here at nine in the morning, a week from this Friday. And Miss Forde... don't be late."

She spent the remainder of the time in a series of calls regarding housing. Starting first with the station's personnel director, she was given a list of affordable apartment dwellings. Based on those recommendations, she decided to focus on the outskirts of Chicago, even though it posed a long subway commute into the city. Having already gone through a guidebook in the library, she latched onto the Oak Park area as being ideal for a young woman living alone. After several phone calls, she settled on a modestly-equipped studio apartment on the third floor. The rent, two hundred and forty dollars, was outrageous by Lubbock standards, but an amount within her monthly budget. For twenty more, the manager said she could get something on the first floor, but she declined. Somehow, she liked the idea of living higher off the ground than she had ever done before. The landlord's only requirements were a security deposit and the first month's rent up front, all of which could be wired ahead. Lastly, she was given a move-in date and instructions on how to get there from Chicago's Union Station.

She quickly straightened up the office desk, hustled to the front of the store to put things in order there, and then waited by the displays of newly arrived washing machines for Roy's return. The drive back to the Meitner house with Ruby went better than she expected simply because Roy had gotten his mother a setting of pink carnations... from one of Gwen's competitors.

Risking much, she left Ruby at home alone again on the next day to run some errands. She purchased two suitcases and squeezed in time to pick out a new travel outfit. The cases would be temporarily stowed where Roy was sure not to find them – in the hangar – having already cut off the lock of its man door without him knowing. She next hurried to their bank. Throughout her short married life, she had kept her personal savings account a secret. After all, she had amassed these funds for the express purpose of leaving Lubbock. As a married woman, she had always intended to use this money for that purpose.

And since Roy never asked, she found it rather easy never to speak of it. Entering the bank, it suddenly occurred to her that the very existence of this private account, so critical to the success of her plan, suggested that she had never really expected her marriage to last. Facing this as fact, she stepped forward when a teller beckoned her, and then cleared out the account… everything that had been built up from years of arranging flowers for Gwen. She then had the teller wire the required amount to her new landlord in Chicago and convert the rest into traveler's checks. Coming out of the bank, she turned her face into the wind, allowing its drying influence to deal with the moisture in her eyes. She would cry no more.

From the first moment of deciding to leave Roy, she had furtively gone about sorting through her possessions in deciding what she did and did not want. Accepting the WYNG offer limited what could be carried away based on the two suitcases, as she could not possibly risk boxing anything up without Roy finding out. For certain, she would leave behind anything bearing a feel of Texas.

To accomplish the packing and the actual escape itself, she needed Ruby out of the house… and Roy to do it. With only a day remaining before needing to be off, she again resorted to deception. In separate conversations, she planted in the mother's ears a false expectation that her son would be taking her out to lunch, doing likewise with Roy.

"Take her someplace that she knows well. Maybe it'll jog that rust bucket of a memory. Do it tomorrow, Roy. That'll give me a chance to air out her parlor. It's a rat's nest in there!"

"Umm… are you sure you wouldn't like to join us?"

"Why in the world would I want to spend one more minute with her than I have to?! I'm surprised you'd even ask… you know… seeing as two's company and three's a crowd."

She noticed him wince, but he recovered too quickly. She needed to do better than this.

"It's not like you'd ever bother taking me out to dinner!"

"Marna… can we please not have an argument every time we discuss my mother?"

"I'm sick of her, Roy! It's all we talk about. Ruby this and Ruby that."

"But you're the one who brought up the subject!"

She held up her arms in mock surrender. Before he could say another word, she grabbed her pillow and headed to the master bedroom. She hated doing this… staging a pathetic argument just to make it easier on herself to leave. But it had to be done, seeing as it was important that she spend her last night in the Meitner house apart from him. She slept little in constantly running the plan through her mind. The night sounds of Roy next-door and Ruby below came to her from time to time, but she ignored them. Those two deserved each other.

Come morning, she went about her duties with a satisfied silence that it would be her last time. After tussling with Ruby over a mess she had made spilling her breakfast on the parlor floor, she finally managed to get the woman down for a nap. She then spent the next two hours cleaning the kitchen, as she was determined to put that part of the house in order before leaving it forever. She worked feverishly, suppressing a giddiness that she dare not embrace quite yet – that she would never have to see this place again.

Lunchtime arrived, as did Roy. She would not bother helping him get Ruby ready, as he would soon be doing that on his own. Besides, she barely had time to finish up on the kitchen floor. As the front door slammed shut, she stood stock still for long enough to note the start of an engine, and immediately ran for a parlor window to make sure his truck had actually turned onto the county road. Throwing herself into high gear, she dashed out to the hangar and retrieved her suitcases. With a twinge of regret, she said goodbye to the Corsair, knowing it to be the first thing that Roy vented his anger on. The whole structure would likely be torn down and hauled away, maybe even before her first day of work at WYNG.

She soon had her suitcases open on the bed and was hurriedly packing them with clothes, shoes, toiletries and other necessities of life. Knowing exactly what was to go, she made quick work of it. She had both filled cases positioned by the front door within fifteen minutes. She then took precious time in dressing herself for travel, determined to look her best on the day she left Lubbock forever. The skirt she had purchased for this purpose was of a solid gray with a hem at the knees and a high waistline. No need for a belt. Her blouse to match was a lemon drop yellow with a laurel leaf pattern running along its buttons. She had picked this one out because its sleeves could be fashionably slid up or down to match the temperature, though she also had a light sweater handy if need be. Her choice of footwear, she was sure to regret later… especially if she was on her feet for any length of time. She opted for her pair of creamy, shamrock-colored high heels because they pulled the color out of the laurel leaf. She then put some effort into her makeup, including extra hairspray in anticipation of many long hours of tedious travel. Finally looking herself over in the mirror, she was fully convinced that she gave off the appearance of a woman running toward something, rather than away from it.

For reason she could not articulate to herself, it was just as important where she wrote the note as was the wording she put into it. She had spoken to him so many times of her deep dissatisfaction with how things were turning out, but always that voice got overshadowed by the bleakness of tending to Ruby in the Meitner house. She moved her bags to the front porch and sat down there with pen and paper.

> *Roy,*
>
> *By the time you read this I'll have already left Lubbock. I've really tried to make us work, but it's clear that we want very different things in life. I now know it was a mistake to get married, and I think if you're honest with yourself, you'd agree. You should know that I've consulted with a lawyer. He's told me that by Texas law, I need to be separated from you for three years before I can get a divorce. That is my intention. No one knows where I'm going, not even my lawyer, and most definitely not Gwen, so don't bother asking around for me.*
>
> *Roy, I don't mean to hurt you. I know you've tried to be good to me because you are the most genuinely kind person I know. For that, I will always be grateful. I just hope that one day you'll meet someone who can love you the way you deserve to be loved. Please find a way to be happy without me.*
>
> *Goodbye,*
>
> *Marna*

She pulled off both rings and placed them in the very center of the note, then folded the bottom up and the top down. She slid this package of broken vows into an envelope already bearing the name 'Roy' on its front. Hesitating for just a second, she brought the flap to her mouth, telling herself to be careful that the rings were not tipped from the envelope. She knew that the real reason for delay was due to shame. Symbolically, she placed her lips upon the seal and closed off a dream. She then affixed the envelope to the front door where he could not possibly miss it.

Almost free.

Having already called for a taxi, she slung her satchel purse over a shoulder and hefted the two suitcases down the porch steps. Though the bags were heavy, she was determined to carry them all the way across the circle in order to wait on the opposite side. There, the house would be behind her and the long driveway ahead. Lugging her load along, she had to take many shuffled steps down the walk, over the gravel, and through the sparse grass of the circle's center. Stopping just shy of the far edge, she set the suitcases down parallel to each other, one on either side of her, and then caught her breath.

Standing there waiting with her nerves on edge, she picked up a mantra of sorts, to be repeated over and over in her head until the taxi finally arrived.

I'm doing right by leaving.

She was not very many recitations in when a sharp noise from behind interrupted her. It was singular in tone and not at all unfamiliar. The sound itself was not so irritating, but its rhythm clashed terribly with the cadence of the words she was repeating to herself. Keeping her feet firmly planted where they were, she pivoted herself about to vent one last morsel of annoyance upon the Meitner property.

Ping.

George had once bragged to her that even before the foundation was poured, the first concrete to touch this small part of Texas was used in erecting that thirty foot aluminum flagpole he had set before where Ruby's house was to be built. Today, the pole stood barren, just as it had in the months since she last tended to it. Her eyes quickly went up to the eagle truk on top, then slowly back down to where the wind was whipping the slack in the halyard up against the pole. She had not properly tied that off on the flag's final retreat.

Ping.

A better loop on the cleat would solve that, but to fix it now would require her to return toward the house. That, she would not do. She turned her back on the pole and stared down the long driveway to where the taxi was soon to appear.

I'm doing right...

Ping.

...by leaving. I'm doing right by...

Ping.

...leaving. I'm doing...

Ping.

She closed her eyes in frustration at the pole's interference.

It doesn't matter...

Ping.

...how I say...

Ping.

...goodbye. It just needs to be done, because I'm doing...

Ping. Ping.

...right by leaving.

Ping.

Fine! Then I'll take some of that along with me!

She gave up on repeating her phrase to instead embrace the pinging sound. She went about dissecting it into its parts, from impact to the dull echo at the end. The overall resonance, she knew, was only because of the pole being hollow.

So I'll be just as empty on the inside... and then maybe it won't hurt so bad.

A gust ruffled her hair, and she had to pull the loose strand behind an ear... feeling that she was always fighting against the wind.

Damn taxi! Hurry the hell up!

She told herself that she was getting what she deserved – her right to leave Lubbock. No... she was not running from something. She was running to something! That was most important to keep in mind... even though she believed none of it.

I refuse to...

Ping.

...feel guilty.

Her heart suddenly leapt with relief on seeing a cab slow on the county road to make its turn into the Meitner property. Keeping her eyes fixed on its progress, she reached down to lay hold on her suitcases.

Many societal structures are founded upon precepts in which the interests of the one must give way by necessity to those of the collective. As such, the individual is called upon to yield their all for the good of the all, with their sacrifice being balanced by the perpetuation of the society as a whole. Sometimes this is achieved peacefully and sometimes to brutal effect. Within the eusocial caste system of the *Hymenoptera* order, the queen commands all for the benefit of the colony. In the various families of ants and bees, control is established through subtle hormonal persuasions. But such is not the case for wasps. A colony's queen wasp achieves dominance through force and intimidation.

For the *polistes annularis*, better known as the red ringed paper wasp, the second generation daughters are subjugated into labor by the colony's far more aggressive foundress. These daughter wasps are made to labor all day in foraging for food, caring for the young, and tending to the queen. Yet upon emergence of the third generation females, the benefit to the hive of sustaining these daughters is quickly exceeded. The queen, in a mad rage, will often outright kill a daughter by stripping off her wings and pushing her from the hive. The more fortunate ones are able to flee, never to return again. These discarded daughters wander aimlessly, some falling victim to predators, but most often simply alighting one last time in some lonely place, and there, starving themselves to death.

On reaching down, she discovered by feel that the suitcase handles were not where she expected them to be. In having turned about to vent her scorn upon the flagpole, she must have inadvertently shifted herself relative to where the bags were, resulting in her undershooting the handles and hitting the cases themselves. No big deal. Taking her eyes off the driveway for just a second, she looked down to note the location of each handle. Her rather casual glance suddenly gave way to intense alarm, causing her to abruptly jerk her left hand up and reflexively pivot her whole body away from one of the suitcases. Off balance and unable to catch herself, she tumbled backward over the other suitcase. Flinging out both hands to brace herself against a fall, one came down in the circle's prickly grass and the other scraped through the driveway's gravel. Her hands hurt, as did her rear, yet her full attention was still upon the upright suitcase. Sitting on its handle, silhouetted against the nothingness of a West Texas horizon, was a wasp.

Though she had almost touched it… and then made a hullaballoo in falling over to get away from it… the wasp had not moved. It just sat there gripping the handle, not flexing a wing or any other part of its body. Without much thinking about it, she scrambled to her feet, pulled off a high heel, and began waving it about in the air over the wasp. The toe tip came within inches of it, but the wasp still refused to move. Glancing to her right down the driveway, she realized that the taxi was almost here, so she would not waste another second on this wasp. In her growing anger, she brought the sole of the shoe down decisively upon the insect, crushing it to death. She then used that same shoe as a broom to sweep the carcass into the grass. She had the shoe back on just as the taxi entered the circle.

The driver pulled alongside and rolled down his window.

"You the gal needin' a ride?"

"What the hell took you so long?! You're late! I'm going to miss my train!"

"Hold your horses. I'll make up the time."

He quickly got out, ushered her around to the passenger door, and then attended to her bags.

"What's the destination?"

"The train depot… and hurry it up! I need to be there in fifteen minutes. Can you do that?"

"No sweat, young lady."

The taxi continued its course about the circle, bringing her window around to the house. She was prepared for this, diverting her eyes down to her lap until she felt herself come all the way about. As the taxi accelerated out of the circle onto the drive, she shifted her sight ahead, concentrating on where that long stretch of gravel met the county road… hoping with all her might to cross that border before Roy's truck reappeared. Leaning forward slightly in the center of the taxi's backseat, she had the odd sensation of being a chambered bullet set for rifling… though the effect was lost on glancing up at the rearview mirror to where the driver's curious eyes were aimed back at her. She slumped into the seat as the taxi made the turn onto the county road. From there on, the ride should be easy. She could relax. She was home-free. She was not even nervous about making her train, for she had much more time than she let on to the driver. Really, she should be congratulating herself on a well-executed plan. But instead, her chest grew tighter, and she slouched down even further in the backseat.

I refuse to be ashamed of myself. What I'm doing… it's the right thing for me!

This theme had already failed her while waiting on the circle, so she needed something different to feel better about what she was doing. Something that made the break from Roy so much more justified. As the taxi progressed out of farmland and into the streets of Lubbock, she summoned forth a single argument in her defense.

If.

Instantly, she felt the power behind this smallest of words. Those two letters together brought her the full authority she needed for expelling the worst of those self-accusations.

If he hadn't tricked me into marrying him…

If he had turned out to be a better husband…

If he had kept his promises…

If he hadn't abandoned me to that god-awful woman…

If he had but listened…

'If' became her guardian and protector, pointing her forward into a new life untethered from the circumstances of her past. The word was a balm to sooth her wounded conscience and transform her mood to gladness. So she gave herself over to it, going beyond what was currently necessary.

What if he hadn't died…

What if she hadn't gone crazy…

What if his company had succeeded…

And what if she had truly cared about me… and not worked me so hard… and allowed me to attend college.

Something was not quite right with how she was using the word now, but the taxi had arrived at the depot. She paid the driver, tipping him modestly, and then delayed in the backseat as he made his way out to retrieve her luggage. In that momentary seclusion, she made one final gesture of completeness to her choices.

Looking back briefly as the trunk's hood came up to partially throw her into a protective shadow, she quickly unclasped the medical alert bracelet from her wrist and unceremoniously slid it down the backseat crack. There, it would join the other discarded trash and misplaced treasures of Lubbock. One day, someone might find it and ponder over its tragic significance, wondering who had lost it and what had become of them. But for her, this symbolic act of concealment would forever stand out as apt in her thinking. She stepped onto the pavement of the depot as a new woman, unbound from the weaknesses of her past.

She bought tickets, stowed her bags, and boarded the train bound for Fort Worth. Finding an empty bulkhead row and sliding across, she casually leaned against the window as she thought any experienced traveler might do. Focusing her attention outside onto a narrow seam in the platform's pavement, she concentrated all thought on the anticipation of movement. She was aware of the shuffled passage of other travelers along the aisle, and of her own seat wobbling as someone took up occupancy next to her. She still did not remove her eyes from off the platform. A voice over the speaker went through greetings, instructions and warnings, and by it she knew the time was near. She felt the vibration of the train engine, but her eyes were still on the platform. Soon, the train began to inch forward and that spot slowly slipped out of her field of view.

She was free at last.

The train was progressing along nicely now, pulling out of the railyard heading east. Her mind was elsewhere. She was mad about something, but could not quite work out what. Something small and insignificant. Not Roy... not Ruby... and definitely not Gwen. Those people already had their moment in her life, and each was worthy of every 'if' she could ascribe to them. She crossed her arms over her chest in mild frustration, noting the train's passage out of the city and into open countryside. The oddity of a bare wrist suddenly brought to mind that annoying thing.

What was up with that wasp?! It had wings! It could fly! But it just sat there... even after I tried shooing it away. Almost like it didn't want me to leave... which is ridiculous, of course.

Though she hated the creatures for the danger they posed to her, discovering one on the handle of her suitcase had messed with her jubilation over leaving the Meitner house. Killing it... that somehow made her feel even worse. Like she was the one with a stinger capable of delivering a lethal blow.

That's stupid. The thing gave me no choice! If only it had flown away... then I wouldn't have had to smash it.

Immediately, the feeling hit her of what was wrong with her usage of the word.

Don't say 'if only' or 'what if.' Just make it 'if'… plain and simple.

She would not soften the word to suit some other possible outcome, nor would she permit it to become diluted by casting her mind backward in time. Nothing would be allowed to tarnish this new start of hers. Not the wasp… or the clanging of the halyard… or any lapses in her usage of the word, admirable though those were in showing her earnest wish that everything had somehow worked out for everyone. The lulling rhythm of the train was all that mattered now, for it meant miles and miles of separation between her and Lubbock. She closed her eyes, not desiring to watch West Texas flow by out her window. She cared not for one last glimpse of cotton field or oil rig. She would fall asleep… and wake up in another world.

But the word was there with her when she detrained in Fort Worth, telling her that if she were rich, she could have flown to Chicago rather than have to endure the heat, humidity and hassle of changing trains in this crowded station. Halfway to her next platform, a passing porter offered to carry her bags, and all she could think about was how much easier it would have been if the man had come upon her just as she got off that train. She had an assigned seat with a window on the train to Chicago, but the seat faced backward. If someone had bothered to tell her, she would have known to request one that looked forward. That next train got underway, sliding out of the Fort Worth railyard northward. In a little over an hour, it came upon the Red River crossing. For one fleeting moment, she wondered if Roy had actually read her note. What if it had fallen off the door, or what if Ruby had gotten ahold of it first? Surely he would know by now, note or no note. He had to see that her clothes and toiletries were gone. Would he call Gwen? Would he even care?

It was darkening outside, with sunset not far off. She looked out her window at Oklahoma, deciding that it was far too much like Texas for her liking. So she went to the dining car, ate a sparse meal, and then returned to her seat. Her night would be spent there owing to the fact that she could not afford the cost of a sleeper compartment. She dozed lightly, made too many trips to the bathroom, and generally passed the time feeling sorry for herself.

By morning's light, the train had moved through most of Missouri, with St. Louis just ahead. Her attitude from the previous day had changed. She was now very excited about arriving in Chicago. 'If' became a thing of both wonder and concern to her.

If the city is easy to live in…

If my apartment and neighborhood are safe…

If the people are nice…

If I only could make some friends…
If the work could be challenging…
If there are opportunities for advancement…
And if everything could just turn out right…

Somewhere in the heart of Illinois, as the train moved through cornfields as prevalent as anything she had seen with cotton, she caught herself using the word way too much, as if 'if' were a place in itself.

'The land of If'… that's just plain ridiculous!

She knew there was no such destination in America… but still found herself fighting off a tremor of uncertainty over whether her decisions were leading her to just such a place.

END OF WASP 2

WASP 3

THE VENOM OF REGRET

CHAPTER

17

CHICAGO

The first thing hitting her on stepping from the train at Union Station was the humidity. Though only early May, the flush of heat to her face, neck and arms was like the worst of a West Texas summer. She could actually feel the frizz coming to her hair. Equally, she was worn out from twenty four hours of rattling on rails. Anxious to get somewhere cooler, she lugged her bags along the platform toward the station's exit with a mind for finding a taxi stand. Halfway through, she spotted a dime store. Though maps were not her thing, she purchased one out of the obvious need for getting to know the city's streets. Finally relaxed into the backseat of a cab, she spread the map in her lap and followed the driver's progression from the station to the Oak Park address she had given him. The whole way there, she kept swiveling her head about, trying to make sense of city blocks packed with pedestrians and vehicles. The way the tall buildings were situated in close on the streets gave her such a confining feel.

Onto a stretch of busy highway and then back off, the driver soon informed her that they had entered Oak Park. Looking ahead out the taxi's front window, she immediately fell in love with the place. This particular street was lined with so many trees, most of which were mammoths compared to Lubbock's finest. On both sides were multi-story houses packed in with narrow spaces between. Each was distinct from the next. Most had front steps that seemed to lift the structures right off the street level. 'Quaint' was the first word that came to mind, what with so many nice little porches and front yards. There was also a good number of people out for a stroll… something she would enjoy doing after getting herself settled in.

Her three-story apartment complex was located one block off Madison Street… which the driver said was one of Oak Park's major roads. This building was at the end of the neighborhood they had moved through, and also abutted the start of a commercial area. A busy thoroughfare was ahead… and a peaceful neighborhood with overhanging trees lay behind.

Perfect!

In the moment, she did not invest much effort into studying the building's architecture other than to note that the brickwork and double-hung windows seemed to be kept up well enough. As the driver unloaded her bags, her eyes went to the front entrance… to a small sign inside the glass door informing the passerby that there were no vacancies. Though she had already paid up front, a surge of concern hit her that perhaps this sign had been placed there as a message for her. Maybe the landlord had already rented out her room to another… or maybe there had never been a vacancy in the first place. In a panicked rush, she passed bills over to the taxi driver and quickly shuttled her bags through the entryway. Following arrows to the manager's door, she was greeted there by the man she had spoken with over the phone… and his middle-aged, t-shirted self was smiling back at her. She had never been more relieved in all her life.

"Got your room ready, Miss. This way, if you will… Allow me to carry those for you. That's not a fit thing for a pretty young lady such as yourself."

He led her up two flights of stairs, excitedly talking about how much she was going to enjoy living in Oak Park, and then transitioned into questions. Where was she from again? Did she have a good-paying job in the city? How would she be getting around? And was she single, seeing as he had a handsome young nephew in medical school?

"I'm married… but thanks anyway." She instantly reproached herself for having made such an admission, and resolved never to speak of it again to anyone in Chicago. "Actually… we're getting a divorce. He's in Texas and won't be coming here. It'll just be me. And don't worry… no boyfriends either."

Moving along an upper hallway, they came to a stop before apartment thirty three. The landlord nodded his indifference to her marital situation while extracting a key from a ring attached to his belt. He led her in and gave a brief tour of the essentials – a modestly furnished area that constituted a combined sitting, kitchen and dining area, off of which were connecting doors to a small bedroom and a bath. Very satisfied with this cursory tour, she promptly thanked the man right out the door. Falling back against the door's inner surface, she faced into her new home. On scanning over the space once more, she let out a scream, at the same time jumping up and down, then flung herself into a dive upon the couch's plaid upholstery.

All mine!

The landlord's wife came by later that afternoon with a handwritten list of recommended stores and eateries within walking distance of the apartment building. This woman was a tad long-winded, going on and on about a young woman's shopping needs. But the thing she immediately came to appreciate about her was the consideration. She had forgotten to pack linens, and the woman brought up a set of sheets, a blanket, and a towel for her to use until she could purchase some of her own.

Having changed into a set of breezy slacks and a short-sleeved blouse, she made her first foray into urban life. It was simply a two block walk to a corner grocer, but as she had grown up in wide-open Lubbock, Madison Street seemed more like Times Square in comparison. Inside the store, she ran across the same brands she was accustomed to from Lubbock, discovered that the cashier spoke the same language as she, and found that the same kind of dollars were accepted as payment. This was not such a foreign land after all. Though burdened with two arm loads, the walk back was lightened by her growing confidence. She was going to be fine after all.

Her first night in Chicago was surreal. The many strange street noises combined with an new bed in an unfamiliar apartment rendered a *Twilight Zone* sort of feel to her sleep. But with morning's light, she was up and ready for accomplishing things on her to-do list. She ate at a diner cattycorner to the grocery, purchased household items from a drugstore further down Madison Street, and then took her first ride into the downtown on the Transit Authority's L, just to get a feel for both the subway and where she would be exiting for work. In this first serious trek about the city, she marveled that for just thirty cents – the required fare – all of Chicago could be opened up to her. Once back to her apartment, she spent the remainder of the day arranging her things and amending her list of items needed.

On her second full day in Chicago, she set aside a strong tourist's desire in order to concentrate on her list. She mailed in a forwarding-address for her Lubbock post office box, arranged for phone service, and found out how to get an Illinois state driver's license and register to vote. Of all things, it was her hair that took center stage in preparations for her new life. She had no idea with what to replace it, but the bouffant definitely had to go! Yet finding the right sort of salon would be a challenge in itself. The phonebook she had borrowed from the landlord was jam-packed with options, but getting stuck in the wrong sort of place could spell disaster. After much internal debate, she did the only sensible thing at her disposal – she went downstairs to ask the landlord's wife. Though the woman's hair was far from stylish, she might still be able to provide recommendations. Within seconds of being asked, the woman's face lit up.

"Oh, have I got just the place for you! I don't go there myself… much too flashy for me. It's only for young things like yourself…"

The build-up went on for several minutes as the woman ventured into a side conversation on the kinds of salons she felt most comfortable with. Eventually, she pointed out the place in the phone book, and was even kind enough to take her out onto the street and set her off in the right direction. After a fifteen minute walk, she found the place one block off Madison Street. Even before entering, the posters of stylish-looking young women in the salon window, along with the glitzy displays of hair products, told her that this place had promise. She stepped into a narrow waiting area, fully aware that the actual salon portion was beyond the set of drapes from which came the unmistakable sound of hair driers. The receptionist, a young woman such as herself, pleasantly greeted her.

"Sure… we can fit you in, but you'll probably be waiting for an hour or so."

"That's fine with me. I'm not yet sure what I want in the way of a hairstyle. I just know it has to be something modern and really stylish… and fairly easy to keep up. I can't afford to spend hours and hours on it."

The receptionist sat her down with a stack of fashion magazines and hardback picture books. She carefully went through a dozen or so without finding anything that spoke directly to her. Sure… there were loads of wonderful styles, but nothing that jumped right off the page. Nearly an hour in and growing a bit disheartened, she came upon the perfect style. It was sleek and professional looking… and so very un-Texan. She popped right up to capture the receptionist's attention.

"What do you think about this one?"

"Oh, that's what's-her-name… ahh… Nancy Kwan… with Vidal Sassoon's angle cut. The style's a few years old… but still quite chic."

"Do you think it's possible with my hair?"

The woman tilted her head to the right and left in looking her over, so she obliged by rotating about in a circle.

"Well… you've got plenty of length… and you've not cut your bangs… so… I'd say yes. If you don't mind waiting maybe fifteen minutes longer… then Sandy'll know for certain. She's done that cut so many times."

Out of nervous energy, she switched seats to peruse even more fashion magazines, yet did not find anything that came close to the Sassoon cut. She was excited about its possibilities, but still debated with herself over the risk and the competency of this salon. Many customers came from behind the drapes, sometimes alone and sometimes in pairs, but always with satisfaction on their faces. Most were young like herself and reasonably fashionable in their dress. Their hair styles were really good too. So maybe this place would work out.

Of course… I can change my mind anytime I want.

To distract herself, she read some articles on Chicago's nightlife, went over the remaining items on her list, and tried to imagine what her first day at work might be like.

"Marna Forde?"

She did not straightaway register that the receptionist had called her name… and perhaps snatched up the magazine with the Sassoon cut a bit too eagerly in her scamper across the waiting area. The woman at the curtain, her soon-to-be stylist named Sandy, had a cut similar to what she wanted… though in a jet-black version. Resisting an urge to inquire as to who had styled her hair, she instead produced the picture and asked if the same thing could be done for her. Sandy took a moment to walk around her, picking at spots on the bouffant, before confidently proclaiming that she was sure it could be done perfectly. She was led behind the curtain, past rows of occupied salon stations, and up to a wall of sinks dedicated to the washing of hair.

It's not too late…

She sat where indicated, was covered by a cape, and then leaned back with her eyes closed as warm water ran through her hair.

Still not too late…

With a towel wrapped about her head, she was directed by Sandy to an empty salon chair. In Lubbock, the women to her left and right would immediately become her best friends for the next hour or so. They would complement, sympathize and encourage regarding each other's hair, but mostly gossip over recent town news and commiserate over life's woes. But since she did not yet know the beauty parlor customs of Chicago… and because she was altogether nervous about her first ever non-Texas hairstyle… she remained silent. As Sandy checked that the cape was still secure, she found herself gripping the armrests.

Decide fast… before it's too late!

Sandy, walking about her with scissors and comb in hand, began poking at limp strands, evidently deciding where to start in. She would select a particular wet clump, lift it away from the others to examine what was beneath, and then drop it back as if dissatisfied with its prospects. This only went on for a minute, though it felt like an eternity. All the while, Sandy smacked away at her gum and jabbered on about a black-beaded purse she had recently gotten on sale.

She's having second thoughts, I just know it! Now, Marna – get up!

Instead, she went stiff as a blade of the styling scissors sank beneath the surface of her brown hair. In terror, she clinched her jaw as Sandy did the first slice. With a snap that seemed guillotine-like, severed tuffs fell to her shoulder, slid down across her chest, and hung at the edge of the cloak… before finally tumbling unseen to the floor below.

No turning back now… I'm committed.

She closed her eyes and relaxed, allowing her mouth to take over. In short time, she was fully engaged in conversation with Sandy. The two of them intertwined their life stories to such an extent that an eavesdropper might have been hard pressed to sort out which tale was whose. Their biographies were as yet unfinished when Sandy slid a bonnet drier over her head. The windsock shaped covering expanded with a whizzing whirl just as the first rush of warm air struck her scalp. The critical moment of dread, dissatisfaction or delight was near. Sandy came back in a short time to lift off the drier, and then began the tedious process of fussing the hair into shape with comb, brush and spray bottle… occasionally reverting back to scissors for a snip here or there. Through it all, she tried to capture a peek of herself in the mirror, but Sandy seemed insistent on keeping the styling chair turned away. After forever, she finally got spun around in a half circle to face the mirror.

"All done. Have a look. Now aren't you the essence of chic?!"

Sandy swept off the cape as would a magician performing the finale to an act. Facing her in the glass was nothing close to the West Texas version of her old self. In place of the cutesy upturned curls about her shoulders, the tips of her hair now bent inward, angling from the back in a slight slant along her jawline… just like in the picture! Raising a hand, she glided her fingers down one side. The feel was so sleek and smooth… nothing like the unfortunate coarseness that comes with having to use so much hair spray on the bouffant. Tilting her head about to take in the sides, she was stunned to find that each hair lay ideally in place. Her new part was slightly off-center rather than down the middle, one side canopying over a cheek. It made her look so mysterious and sophisticated. Smarter too. With a handheld mirror, she followed the angle of the cut backward, and then fidgeted about for a good mirror-to-mirror view of the top and back… before proclaiming her complete satisfaction with the new look.

"Sandy… it's amazing… and absolutely perfect!"

For the next several minutes, she received instructions on how to wash and style, and what products would be best for maintaining the look. Sandy put her on schedule for a trim every two months. After paying for both the cut and the products, along with a well-earned tip, she left the salon as a new woman, ready to take on Chicago.

Her final act of preparation was done with the utmost care considering its impact on first impressions. With a severely depleted cash reserve, she nonetheless decided that it was important to purchase a new outfit to wear on her first day at WYNG, as nothing she had brought from Lubbock was worthy of this monumental moment in her life. After combing the greater Oak Park area for several hours, she finally came across a very professional-looking black skirt with tight charcoal pinstripes. She also purchased a thin belt with a sheen that provided a nice slimming effect at her waist. She then put considerable effort into picking out a pair of heels and blouse to match… the latter with sleeves that could be stylishly rolled up into tight cuffs for that 'hard at work' feel. Debating before a store mirror on whether to accessorize with a necklace, she finally decided to wait until she saw how the other women in the newsroom were dressed. As a final touch, she instead bought a silver watch band that nicely brought out the shine to the new blouse's buttons.

Having hardly slept the night before, she rose on her first day of work in a state of nervous excitement. Her utmost desire was to start out well at WYNG, so it was critical that she fit in. This was Chicago – the second largest metropolis in America. Here, she could cross through more than a half dozen ethnic communities in the same span of distance that it took her to get from the Meitner house to downtown Lubbock. The cosmopolitan area as a whole was nearly ten times the population of Lubbock County! So the last thing she could afford to do was come across as a small town Texan. In the days leading up to this one, she had made a casual study of the city's residents she happened to encounter, always with an eye toward learning how women her age behaved. From that effort, she came up with a short list of things to concentrate on.

Say 'you guys' and not 'y'all'… 'hello' and not 'howdy.'
Never drop a 'g.'
Don't smile too much… but don't frown either.
Talk fast, move fast, think fast.
Always act like you know what you're doing.

Above all, she felt that it was necessary to occupy with purpose whatever small amount of space the city allotted for her. That was what everyone seemed to be doing as they bustled about on their business. Whether it was on a subway car, a street corner, or any other public setting, she must adopt an air of someone very accustom to their fundamental rights as a citizen of the city. Beyond this… she had absolutely no clue as what to expect from living in Chicago.

CHAPTER
18

WYNG NEWS

Her start day at the station presented something of an oddity... until she learned that Fridays were typically the slowest news day of the week, and thus ideal for processing new employees. The station broadcasting WYNG's news programs was located on three floors of the Rollecastle building on West Washington Street, a few blocks from the L-train station she got off at. As instructed in the offer letter, she checked in first at the lobby. With her mind taken over with anticipation, she was not prepared when the building receptionist commented on her accent. So in the ride up the elevator, she reminded herself once again not to come across as Texan.

Because people don't think we're... I mean... they're... sophisticated.

Stepping off at the tenth floor, she was greeted first by the large lettering of 'WYNG News' embossed upon the opposite wall. Her eyes shot next to an adjacent floor-to-ceiling window affording a direct view across West Washington Street. Moving in close... almost to the point of resting her forehead against the glass... she was taken in by the immensity of the buildings all around her. Sure... she had marveled at these from street level on her previous visit downtown, as well as on this morning's walk from the L, but now she seemed part of them. Many stretched well above her level, making her crane her neck for a better view. The tops of several of those skyscrapers were lost in the upper limit of the window pane. Turning to the side, she peered down the narrow gap between the buildings along the eastern extreme of Washington Street… and then further on across a large park toward a narrow prospect of Lake Michigan's dull blue. Though blurred by the morning haze, she could just make out that distant horizon between lake and sky. Returning to the east-west thoroughfare, she followed it to the base of the building… and suddenly found herself staring straight down at the street below. She just had to shuffle backward at the feeling of dizziness.

"Pretty impressive, isn't it? Chicago's something else!"

She wheeled about to find a middle aged woman staring at her from within the opening to a wall of glass that separated an office area from the lobby. She quickly read the stenciling there.

Bertram T. Carswell
Executive Producer
WYNG News

"You Marna Forde?"

"Yes, ma'am."

"They called up to say you were coming. Welcome to WYNG news. Well… just don't stand there… get yourself in. The news waits for no man…" The lady stepped aside to wave her through, smiling in the process. "…or woman, as the case may be. Got your offer letter?"

The way her hand shot out, almost as if ready to snap her fingers, conveyed that this was more of an order than a question. Though a bit rounder and shorter than Gwen, this person still struck her as one accustomed to commanding the same kind of authority. Taking the letter from her, the woman moved about the desk to her seat before perusing it.

She allowed her eyes to stray down a hallway to her right as the letter was being read, but was brought back when the woman spoke without lifting her eyes from off the paper.

"Sales and PR offices are back there… as is Mr. Carswell's. He's not in today. Wouldn't matter anyway. He doesn't have time for PAs."

"Ahh… what's a PA?"

The woman thrust the sheet back across the desk toward her before answering.

"It's you, Sweetie. Check the first paragraph. You're being hired as a production assistant… 'PA' for short. You do realize that means you're essentially an intern and not a salaried employee at WYNG?"

"Oh… yes, ma'am. I knew that."

Dang! I definitely didn't know that!

A scary realization suddenly hit her – that she had just travelled over a thousand miles for a temporary position.

"It's only that I wasn't familiar with the acronym."

"Don't sweat it. You'll catch on quick enough... or decide to leave. Just do your job efficiently and you'll have nothing to worry about. By the way... I appreciate the show of respect, but you can drop the ma'am stuff. I'm Rosalind Barrett, Mr. Carswell's administrative secretary. Just call me 'Rose.' You know... there's really no need for pretense among us women. It's the men who get caught up in titles... instead of doing their jobs. Honestly, sometimes it feels like I have to run the whole damn place myself. But don't tell anyone I said that. Can't have my secret out, can I? Now let me show you around."

In moving before the desk, Rose unexpectedly stopped to scrutinize her outfit, scanning her from head to toe in a way that seem very much like what Gwen had done on so many date nights.

"Your attire is acceptable, but a word of caution – no heels. You'll be on your feet all day. Wear what your wearing now and you'll have corns for sure."

Not being able to help herself, she peered down at the pointy-toes of her new blackberry-tinted high heels. She had thought them rather stylish for one's first day of work. Lifting her eyes back up, she found Rose smiling at her in a knowing manner.

"I'll give it to you... they're super cute. I like shoes. First thing I noticed about you..."

Rose led her across the tenth floor lobby to another set of glass doors that she had not noticed before, them being tucked around the other side of the elevators.

"I'm going to leave the particulars of your job responsibilities to Billings."

She managed to catch the woman's eye with a questioning look as to that name.

"That's Albert Billings, your boss... the producer of the afternoon and evening newscasts. He just goes by Billings. You do know the difference between a producer and an executive producer, don't you?"

Pausing at the entrance to an immense open space within which was scattered a helter-skelter of desks... most being empty... she struggled not to show her ignorance.

"Well, umm... I'd say one does the higher level stuff, and the other... they... umm..."

"Billings puts on the news shows, and Mr. Carswell handles the overall business of the news. That means he's ultimately responsible for the programs making a profit. It's all about ratings, Sweetheart. The higher the ratings, the more advertising dollars the station gets. Mr. Carswell also does much more *higher level stuff* than that. He promotes the news programs, handles the operations, sees to all personnel issues, and ultimately answers to the station manager and the network. By the way, Billings also wears more than one hat. He's both the producer and the desk editor. Normally those jobs are done by two different people, but Billings is a machine. The news is his life. Now… I'm going to hand you off to someone else until he's free."

Rose waved toward a back corner where a few individuals were milling about… and then just took off in that direction, leaving her to catch up while gawking at everything she passed. They were heading toward where a black man was casually sitting on a desktop.

"Click, this here's Miss Marna Forde – a new PA. Miss Forde, this is Demetrius Clemons. He's our best photographer at the station."

"Damn straight. And it's *photojournalist*. Photographers do baby pictures."

"Tuh-may-toh, tuh-mah-toh. Listen, Click… mind babysitting the new kid 'til Billings gets out? I've got quarterlies to grind through."

"No sweat… but hey… it's only May?!"

"I'm talking about last quarter's. Corporate wants them redone. Goodie, goodie… more work for me."

Rose winked once at her and then headed back through the newsroom. On turning to Click, she was startled to find herself being eyed from head to toe… and not at all in the same way Rose had done minutes before.

"Damn, Mama! You're so fine!"

"I… I beg your pardon?"

"Relax… just saying hello. Where you from anyway… 'cause it sure as hell ain't Chicago."

"Lubbock… Texas."

"No shit?! I got an uncle in San Marcos. Know where that's at?"

"Yeah… but it's a long way from Lubbock. Listen, Mr. Clemont…"

"Clemons. Just call me Click. Nearly everybody does."

She nodded toward a nearby room… closed-off, yet with enough glasswork that she could easily see a group of people seated about a long table. The rise and fall of their voices suggested that a lively discussion was underway.

"What's going on in there?"

"That's the morning planning meeting. You'll learn about that soon enough. Just chill here with me 'til it lets out."

So she stood there awkwardly watching the movements within the meeting room… and trying not to think about whether Click was still looking at her. It had not been her habit, as a white woman, to spend much time conversing with black men. She neither wanted to offend or be offended as a result of that inexperience.

"So… Mrs. Barrett… she seems… like a sharp one. I assume it's 'Mrs.' because she was wearing rings."

"Looks like you recently wore one too…"

She was shocked to find him pointing down at her left hand, folded as it was over her right at waist level. She had completely neglected doing something about that tan line on her ring finger. Without considering the implication, she quickly shifted both hands behind her back… and then felt a flush of embarrassment as he smiled in recognition of the action.

"Not anymore. And I'd rather not talk about it, if you don't mind."

"No sweat, sister. It's all solid. Nobody 'round here messes with that shit anyhow. No first names either. Billings got no time for that. Rose's about the only one who gets the privilege."

After a few more seconds of standing in silence, she ventured a quick look at him… which perhaps he had been waiting for.

"You know… Miss Forde… it's nothing to be ashamed of. Sometimes things just don't work out right… and you gotta say goodbye."

"Thanks… but I… ahh… still don't want to talk about it."

Both of them turned as the meeting room door opened… and only a single person came out at first.

"That's Billings… your new boss. Best be on your toes now."

As the rest of the morning meeting spilled out into the newsroom behind this Billings, she instinctively smoothed out her skirt and came to attention beside Click. The man approaching them was past middle age, but still strode forth with all of the briskness of youth. He struck her right away as a nimble and wiry sort of person. Shorter than her, he still possessed an obvious stature that had nothing to do with height. With wrinkled shirt and pants, unkempt hair and a day-old beard, this Billings seemed to be the type who considered appearances as something beneath him… yet also someone you dare not evaluate based on such things. She quickly picked up on two other traits. His mouth seemed a bit out of proportion, as if one corner was accustomed to the presence of a cigarette dangling there. More than this, she noted the man's bird-like eyes darting about the newsroom… just before locking in on her. Coming to a stop directly before her, he paused first to take a sip of his coffee. She barely had time to make out the block lettering on the cup – 'I'M THE BOSS – GET OUTTA MY WAY' – before he spoke. Even though his eyes remained fixed on her, his words were directed at Click.

"Clemons – get off your ass and go with Ramirez to cover the Evanston situation."

"Come on, Boss… I'll be on the freeway forever. Send Clark instead. That's more his speed…"

"He's with Watkins on the Calumet sewage spill. Perhaps you'd rather do that?"

"Hell no. Evanston it is."

Out of the corner of her eye, she perceived Click hopping off the desk and making straight for a back hallway, but she stayed fixed on Billings.

"And who the hell are you… and what're you doing in my newsroom?"

Without hesitation, she stuck out her hand in as formal a manner as she knew how.

"I'm Marna Forde, your new production assistant. That's 'Forde' with an 'e' at the end."

He did not reach out to accept her hand, but she kept it there anyway… no matter how idiotic it made her seem. She knew he was appraising her, and she was determined to meet that scrutiny head on. Contrary to her previous admonition, she offered him a winning smile. Whether affected by it or not, he broke eye contact for the first time to shout over his shoulder toward the meeting room.

"Dixon! Get the hell over here."

Her eyes flickered that way… to a young woman who was the last to leave, her being laden down with a stack of paper cups. She looked back to Billings… and was surprised to see that his eyes were now on her outstretched hand. So she inched it forward… and after a slight hesitation, he took it… though quickly released the grip before the woman named Dixon appeared at his side.

"This is a new PA – Forde, *with an 'e' at the end.*" Though he sneered, she remained determined to smile her way through… even though she chided herself for having been so stupid about the spelling of her name. "Take an hour and show her around… but first get me that damn Nixon footage I asked for eons ago. If you don't mind, I'd like to have it sometime *before* the man gets elected president."

"Yes, sir. Of course, sir"

Her eyes went ever so briefly from Billings, who was still staring at her, to Dixon… and stayed there only long enough to note that this woman was miserable. She looked back at her new boss, refusing to turn away until he had dismissed her.

"Forde, you'll spend the next week being Dixon's second shadow. You'll go where she goes, but not be allowed to do a damn thing until I'm convinced there's value in you. Got it?"

"Yes, sir."

"Good. Now get the hell out of here." Yet it was he who immediately left, him dashing over to a horseshoe-shaped counter.

"That's the assignment desk. It's like his throne… and that's where you'll find him most of the time. Hold it a sec while I get rid of this trash." Dixon motioned to a nearby garbage can, where she dumped her load of coffee cups and turned back for a handshake of her own. "I'm Sophie… and I'm really glad to have you here. For one, it'll be nice not being the only female in the newsroom. This place is like high school chess club – all male, all smart, and all terribly homely… yet so very full of themselves. But most of all… I'm glad you're here because it means I'm no longer at the bottom of the totem pole."

"I'm Marna… and I'm not sure what to make of that. Are you saying…"

"Oh, it's nothing. There're generally four or five PA's here, and the newest one always gets the grunt work. Pouring coffee… cleaning up after meetings… stuff like that. Actually, we're all expected to do whatever we're told."

This Sophie, nearly a foot shorter and perhaps twenty pounds heavier, was not in the least bit attractive. When she smiled, there was an odd sort of hardness to her features. Even the young woman's voice was rather husky, as were her somewhat clunky mannerisms. Not at all smooth or ladylike. But when Sophie reached out a hand to touch her forearm, smiling more broadly in the process, everything that she had interpreted as hardness suddenly melted away. Here was a person with a softness on the inside… a person with whom she could be herself.

"So… where to begin…? You've already seen the assignment desk…" Sophie waved a hand over to where Billings and a flock of others were in a feeding frenzy over a stack of papers… grabbing them from each other and scribbling frantically. "Billings is still doling out assignments he didn't get to during the meeting."

"Who're all those people?"

"Mostly reporters… but some AEs too. That's 'assistant editors.' Let's see… sports, national, local, and special interest AEs are over there. You'll get to know those guys soon enough. There all from Chicago. You don't get to be an AE without an in-depth knowledge of the city simply because it's the AEs who send reporters out on location. Come on… I've got to get that footage for Billings before he cans me. I'll show you the archive first. Believe you me, you'll be spending plenty of time in there."

She took off after the hustling Sophie.

"So… what's it like here? I've only ever worked in small places… small offices and shops… and never with a lot of people… or this much activity. "

"It can get really insane, especially when a major story breaks. Everyone's running around like that chicken with its head lopped off. Then there're those times when the story's bigger than the news…"

"What do you mean by that?"

"For one thing, you'll soon come to understand that reporting the news is much more important than the news itself… and the personalities who deliver the news are way bigger than the reporting of it. Have that in mind, and you'll be forewarned whenever someone gets their nose bent out of joint. Still… every once in a while… something comes along to turn the whole world upside down. It's in those times that experiencing the news beats all. Doesn't happen that often, but when it does… everyone feels it. Like last month…"

She was trying to keep track of the doors, hallways and stairs that Sophie was using, but also wanted to show that she could maintain a conversation in the process.

"What happened last month?"

Sophie turned about in mild surprise.

"Reverend King?! Surely whites in the South were just as appalled by his…"

"West Texas isn't the South." She knew she had interrupted far too abruptly owing to her fear of coming across as a bigot. "Sorry… But yes… you're right… that was… horrible."

With all that had happened in her life over the last few months, she was ashamed to admit that the assassination of Martin Luther King Jr. had hardly made an impact on her.

The archive turned out to be a heavily air conditioned room laid out more or less like a library. There were bookshelves full of binders that Sophie indicated to be scripts from past shows. The majority of the large space was taken up by racks and racks of canisters, some new and some rust-covered.

"Give me a minute."

Sophie slid out a card catalog tray from a library-like cabinet and flipped for a while before pushing the drawer back in. Without pause, she took off through the racks.

"I'll explain how this works later… just got to get him what he needs first… then I'll take you on a tour."

Sophie pulled a can off a top rack and nearly collided with her on backtracking.

"Sorry… I'm just getting in the way."

"It's okay. Follow me out… we're heading over to video processing. You'll spend a lot of time in there too… mostly waiting on engineers."

They left the archive the way they had come, passing through a corner of the newsroom and turning into the hallway she had seen Click go down. In the hall's entrance, Sophie unexpectedly stopped.

"Lots of the key functions of the station are here. You'll get to know these places after a few days... or evenings if you've pulled the late night production. Let's see..."

She pointed first to the door on their immediate left.

"...there's the script room, then equipment storage and repair – that's mostly for the cameramen and engineers. Next is Billing's office. He doesn't spend much time in there, but if he ever calls you in... you're in deep shit. That door at the end leads out to a service elevator that takes you down to the dispatch bay. That's where the vans and drivers are. Billings really hates how much time it takes his reporters to ride the elevator down to the ground floor."

She sensed there was more to this statement, but let it lay in exchange for learning more about what her job would be like.

"And the one to the right of it?"

"That goes into the weather center... which connects directly to the studio. A word of advice – avoid Weatherman Morgan. He may seem like a cute, huggable grandfather type, but he's as horny as all get out. And he thinks he's the face of WYNG news. If Mr. Carswell doesn't give him exactly what he wants, he throws an unbelievable temper tantrum. Anyway... he's got his own meteorologist, as well as access to radar and local temperatures throughout the region. The weather does their own maps, artwork and stuff, even though the station has a pretty big graphics art team..." Sophie pointed upward, from which she gathered that those functions were on a floor above. "...but they're mostly used by other productions at the station. Next to the weather room is the receive room... that's where all of the wire service feeds come in. We're heading here... it's the edit bay."

They entered a space with walls lined by many reel-to-reel players, monitors, and other equipment Sophie said was for the purpose of doing film editing. At the far end was a sound booth for similar audio tasks. Sophie went to a machine and began threading her spool in.

"This is from the Nixon-Kennedy debates... The station's making a transition from film to video..." She picked up a cartridge to wave at her before pushing it into a slot. "...but most of the old footage is still on film. Billings wants a two minute excerpt in which Nixon was asked a question about China. He's got a remarkable memory."

"Nixon does?"

Sophie, in the process of mounting an empty reel on the player, turned back with a giggle.

"No, silly – Billings! He knew exactly what he was looking for. Even that it would be at about twenty five minutes into the debate. I just need to find the segment and transfer it from the film to video tape... then we're done."

She followed Sophie's every movement of fast-forwarding the reel.

"How'd you learn to do all this? I mean... is it part of the job?"

"We normally have engineers for this sort of thing... but they don't show up until later."

After what seemed like a purposeful delay, Sophie continued with noticeably less energy in her voice.

"I'm dating one of them... It's amazing what you can learn... you know... if you're willing to... lower your standards a bit."

Sophie soon began the transfer, and they watched with the volume turned off. It was so odd tracking this debate between the then-Vice President Nixon and the then-Senator Kennedy. Without the voices, it seemed that the camera was bouncing between the two and the moderator without any sane connection as to what was going on. After a minute or so, Sophie unexpectedly spoke up with a voice so soft that it was startling.

"Most men here... they're surprised to discover that a woman can do something like this. A transfer... I mean. Billings didn't believe me until I showed him. He... doesn't like women, you know."

"What?"

"Billings doesn't like women in his newsroom. Thinks it makes the place... soft."

"You're not serious?! I mean... you're amazing to be able to do this."

Sophie just shrugged her shoulders at the compliment.

"He's a bastard... that's for sure. I don't know of anybody in the newsroom who actually likes him... as a person, I mean. He has such unrealistic standards for everyone. And if you don't move as fast as he does, then he just writes you off. I'm not the only one who feels this way... but sometimes... I think he singles me out... you know... because he enjoys giving me a hard time. If it wasn't for the fact that I went out of my way to learn stuff like this..." She nodded her head toward the monitor. "...then I'm pretty sure he'd have fired me in my first month."

"So... how long *have* you been working here?"

Sophie did not right away respond, busying herself instead with rewinding the film now that the transfer was completed. She answered only after the reel was tucked neatly into its can.

"I'm finishing my fourth month... and I really don't think I can stand it here much longer. Sorry… we have to watch this again… just to make sure it came through properly."

She extracted the video cartridge from the machine and inserted it into a different slot. They sat without speaking as the same footage played over again. For her part, she was busy trying to figure out what kind of a place could cause such a capable young woman to consider leaving after so short of a time… and what that might mean for her personally. At the point in which Nixon commenced his answer to the China question, Sophie turned the volume down once more.

"It's nothing personal… but things should get a bit easier for me now that you're here."

"Because of the totem pole thing… or because I'm a woman too?"

"A bit of both. Don't get me wrong, he's murder on the guys too… but sometimes… I feel like I have to work double hard to win his approval. I know it must sound like I'm complaining… and I don't mean to alarm you on your first day… but you should know… Billings… he goes through PAs like no other station in the Midwest. He's got a terrible reputation for it. Just chews us up and spits us out. You were recruited from an affiliate in Texas, right?"

"Yes…"

"It's no wonder. I came here from Montana. You happen to be replacing a guy from Lexington. He got cursed out in front of the whole newsroom for spilling coffee on a script that Billings was working on. I was there when it happened… It just went on and on. I've never seen anyone treated so cruelly in all my life…"

Without warning, Sophie yanked the cartridge from its slot, sending the monitor blipping into a blank gray. Somehow, she found herself momentarily distracted by all those little random dots on the screen… until she realized that Sophie was already at the door. Because of that comment about moving fast, she ran to catch up… which was not so easy in her heels. Together, they made a detour on the way back to the archive, with Sophie depositing the cartridge on the assignment desk two feet from where Billings sat.

"About damn time…"

Sophie just kept walking, and did not speak again until they had reached the privacy of the archive. Hoisting the can up into its proper place, she glanced back with a most matter-of-fact expression on her face.

"I think he likes you…"

"What?!"

"Billings… I think he likes you."

"How can you say that?! I've only just gotten here. He doesn't even know if I can do this job properly. Besides, he was making fun of how I spelled my name. You saw that. So to say that he…"

"You're not afraid of him. I can see it in your eyes… which means so can he. I'm sure he'll try to intimidate you in the sadistic ways that only he's capable of… but I think he's already decided that it won't work. That's why I think he likes you."

She, with mouth ajar, was unable to say a word. Sophie just kept smiling in return.

"I'm not jealous, you know. Like I said… I'm glad you're here."

Still processing Sophie's odd conclusion, she followed her to the studio next, seeing as it was unoccupied. Coming inside, she found herself facing a set not unlike that of the TV news programs she had watched in Lubbock. There was a curved counter bearing 'WYNG News' on its front with the network's logo. The stage backdrop was a huge panorama of the city taken from somewhere out in Lake Michigan. Off to one side was a smaller set dedicated to the weather. Sophie nodded that way.

"That's pretty much the only thing Billings doesn't care about… unless it's the weather making the news."

Without thinking much about it, she stepped up onto the stage and turned her back on the set to face out toward the cameras. What she saw was mostly a hodgepodge of cables running every which way, some along the floor and some up into trusses supporting a bank of lights above. Beyond the cameras into the back recesses of the studio were doors that Sophie said led to wardrobe and makeup, along with the one they had come through from the newsroom.

For some reason, Sophie chose that moment to say that one world… the one the audience saw… was fashioned so as to be bathed in light, whereas the other was kept dark so as not to distract the anchors during the show. That, she offhand added, was the way of the news. Hidden motives and over-inflated egos that shined light upon the misdeeds and misfortunes of others. Lust for the story or lust for the stage – it was all the same to Sophie.

"It's… ahh… none of my business… but you… umm… don't seem to like the news very much… and yet here you are working at a news station."

"Ironic, isn't it. I thought I did… when I was growing up. But now… I'm not so sure. You know… I've never actually watched the show on TV. You can't view it from here anyway… even if you wanted to. Taggett… that's the floor director… he keeps a tight ship. He'll let in Billings… nobody in the newsroom dares say no to him… but he won't allow anyone else in during a show… not even Mr. Carswell. Personally, I find it more interesting to watch from a different sort of place. Follow me."

She trailed in behind Sophie as they moved around the set to a hidden door. They passed into a dimly lit hallway lined in glass on one side and a wall of framed photographs on the other. All of the pictures were of men posing at award ceremonies or some other public gathering. A wall-of-fame of sorts. Her eyes went to the left… to the glass barrier along the full length of this narrow hall. On the other side, running down in two tiers, were numerous consoles of electronics, sound boards and various other pieces of equipment, each having a captain's chair position before it. Both levels faced toward a wall jam-packed with TV monitors. Most were blank, but a few displayed programming currently airing on the networks or lower quality feeds from what looked to be various places about the station. The whole thing gave off a Houston Control sort of feel… though on a considerably lesser scale.

"Welcome to the master control room! We're in the observation deck. We just call it 'the cage' because if you're in here when the broadcast starts… you're trapped. See that 'on-air' box?" She pointed above the door they had just come through. "Once that's lit, the door to the studio is automatically locked. You'd have to leave through the door at the other end of the hall. That goes into Mr. Carswell's suite. Rose… have you met her?" She nodded without wanting to interrupt. "Well… she'll bite your head off if you walk through there for anything less than a fire."

About midway along the hall was a glass door through which Sophie led her down steps to the upper tier of the control room.

"This is where the pieces get put together into a show. The guys who work in here are true lovers of the dark. But don't let that mislead you… they're actually really nice. There's the newscast director… he's the guy who runs the show. Then there's his technical director… and several video and audio engineers. You'll get to know them real well. They start filtering in around noon and work straight through the late night show. Essentially, Marna, you have to view a news program as a script… like for a TV show or a movie… except this one has live components from both the studio and reporters in the field. Oh… and there's also video and audio clips interlaid in with those live feeds. Graphics too… you know… like 'Joe Blow at City Hall' showing up in a box on the screen while the reporter's talking. All of that… the news segments and the extras… it all has to be put together into a well-timed script, and then orchestrated by these guys. It takes the better part of the day to construct the script, get the bugs worked out… and the timing fine-tuned. We PAs spend the greater part of each afternoon running script fragments back and forth from reporters, editors and anchors to these guys…" She waved a hand about the control room. "…as they hammer out the final version. The engineers call each separate story… all of the video, audio and graphics… a 'package'… usually at about ninety seconds a piece."

She immediately jumped in on recognizing the overall implication for a news day.

"So for a thirty minute show, I gather that there can only be so many packages… and those have to be divvied up between news, sports, weather, and human interest stuff. Seems like there'd be lots of competition… you know… to be the one who gets their package put in… and at the best time."

Sophie did not immediately respond, staring back with something of an unreadable expression on her face.

"You're sharp. That's absolutely correct… Everyone fights tooth and nail to have their story included. I guess you can see why working in a newsroom can be stressful. And it's not just the reporters. An ad man only gets paid if their commercial's aired. Everyone's in it for themselves. Anyway… link all those packages together with face time from the anchors, the tease they give as lead-ins on each story… plus the commercial breaks… and you have a show. We PAs don't play a direct role in actually putting it together. It's just our responsibility to make sure everyone has what they need, when they need it… and that everyone's ultimately working off the same version for the show. I've never seen it happen, but I've heard stories about anchors and newscast directors working off of different script versions. You *do not* want that to happen to you! But don't worry… we've got systems in place to prevent that sort of thing. Of course, we PAs do other tasks too… like proof reading… retrieving footage from the archive… or running errands for Mr. Carswell's office. Once I was sent upstairs to the station manager's suite for his approval on a script fragment. It's a totally different world up there."

There came next an awkward silence through which she gathered that Sophie was giving her an opportunity to ask questions. She had plenty, but was more interested in getting the whole tour in first. So she gave the sort of a polite thank you one does to show that they were ready to move on.

"Okay… I'll take you to the assignment board next. That's where the reporters, editors and what-not have the stories they're supposed to be working on. PA's are designated on that board too. After that… we'll get to work. Tell you what… let's not go back through the studio. I think they might be setting up for the anchors to do their floaters. That's promos recorded for later use."

Sophie led her to a small flight of stairs off to the side that she said led into the editing room they had already been in. Realizing that the tour was almost over, she asked about what she had all along been expecting to see.

"So… where's the transmit room?"

"The what?"

"You know… the place where the signals get sent out through the antenna system. Where's that located?"

"On the building's roof, I suppose. I don't know of anyone who's ever been up there. Why would you be interested in that?"

"I use to manage a CATV network."

Sophie's eyes suddenly widened.

"Oh… it was nothing special. Just a bunch of receive towers scattered about Lubbock… that's where I'm from… and a microwave relay system for bringing programming in from the Dallas – Fort Worth area. My…" She caught herself just shy of saying father-in-law. "…boss essentially ran it into the ground fighting against FCC regulations. He eventually sold off the parts… and then shut the whole thing down. That's why I went looking for a new job."

"Wow."

"Like you said… it's important for a woman to pick up skills where she can."

As they made their way back to the newsroom, she had an embarrassingly uncomfortable feeling that Sophie might be wondering who she had lowered her standards with in order to obtain her skills. Of course, it was nothing like that… except… well… she *had* gotten married for the wrong…

Stop! I'm not going to think about any of that!

From then until well after lunch, she trailed behind Sophie as they ran pieces of script from reporter to editor to anchor and back to the same reporter. From time to time, they crossed paths with other PAs engaged in similar tasks. Sometimes there were lulls that afforded her an opportunity to chat with those guys. Just the usual kind of stuff… where was she from, how long had she been in Chicago, and was she seeing anyone in particular. Throughout these interactions, she was careful to keep her left hand well out of view so that others did not pick up on what Click had so easily done.

By the time the afternoon script review meeting came around, she had been on her feet for nearly three hours without a break. She had been in and out of the meeting room several times with Sophie to check the assignment board. Consequently, she knew the walls of this room to be covered in laminated maps ranging in detail from the downtown area to the entire world. In the center of the room was a long table, boardroom-like, with chairs crowded all around and a half dozen phones dispersed along its length. Sophie had already told her that the main objective of this afternoon meeting was for

Billings to give his final approval on the script, which had been a blank slate at the morning meeting. She also learned that the late-night editors typically sat in to piggyback off this script in developing their own.

Moving in ahead of Sophie, she found Billings already seated at the head of the table engaged in a conversation with one of his AEs. Very much looking forward to getting off her feet, she plopped down in a chair at the far end of the table, assuming it to be the lowliest of positions suitable for the likes of her – a PA. She fully expected Sophie to sit down beside her, and was in the process of pulling out a chair when the other side of the room went silent.

"Marna, don't!"

She heard Sophie's whisper and sensed her hands on the back of the chair, but her eyes were drawn down the length of the table. Billings was looking her way... but not actually at her. His gaze was slightly above and behind her. She quickly turned about to find Sophie pressed into a corner of the room with a hand over her mouth.

"Forde..." She swung back to Billings. "PAs do not sit in my meetings."

Lickety-split, she was up from the chair and back to the wall beside Sophie, who was whispering out an apology for having not mentioned the policy.

With the room now filling, the AE seated beside Billings piped up so all could hear.

"Miss Forde... as the newest PA, you should know that it's your job to get the coffee for everyone."

Having not yet seen anything in the station resembling a kitchen, she had no idea where the pot might be located, but nonetheless sprang off the wall in the direction of the door.

"No!"

Everything in the room came to a stop once more, with all eyes turned toward Billings.

"Forde... you stay put. Dixon... you get the coffee."

Sophie went ashen, with a good bit of that hardness coming to her face.

"I'll be happy to show her... but it's her...."

"Dixon... you'll be doing the job until I say so! Just so you know how I feel about childish pranks in my newsroom."

In a flash, she realized that from his perspective it must have appeared as if Sophie was pulling out a seat for her to sit in. She immediately jumped in on Sophie's defense, but Billings' tolerance for anything other than the news had already been exceeded. He raised his hand in a stop sign gesture... not unlike what Gwen would do... making it abundantly clear that he wanted silence.

After Sophie stepped out, Billings called the meeting to order and began working his way around the table in gathering progress reports on the script. While that went on, she was aware that the other PAs were inching away from her. From time-to-time, someone at the table would glance her way, perpetuating her feeling of having messed up. Long tense moments passed before Sophie returned with a tray of paper cups and a pot, silently moving about the room pouring out coffee. Once the task was done, Sophie took up a position on the wall away from her. She tried multiple times to capture her attention in order to offer a shrug or some other form of apology… but Sophie remained tight-jawed in staring down at the carpet.

There was nothing she could do about Sophie until the meeting was over, so she turned her attention to the discussion. Nearly everyone at the table was called upon, but not one PA ever spoke. From this, she came to realize that the news was a big-person business, and PAs were not included.

Billings was the first to leave at the end of the meeting. As the room began to empty behind him, she made her way around to where Sophie stood… but was brought up short on hearing her name being shouted back into the meeting room.

"Forde! Get the hell over here!"

"Yes, sir."

She grimaced toward Sophie, who stood stone-faced against the back wall, and then dashed out to join Billings in the newsroom.

"You're with me for the remainder of the day. Stick to me like glue, and do whatever the hell I tell you to… got it?"

"Yes, sir."

As he led her to the assignment desk, she glanced back into the already empty meeting room. Left behind, Sophie was collecting up the used coffee cups.

"Okay, kid… I'm only going to tell you these things once. First and foremost, the newsroom thrives on rigid routine, yet with flexibility for responding to any breaking story that might come along. Mess with the routine of my newsroom and you're fired. Two, efficiency is the name of the game. Time matters. Keep that watch of yours pegged to the station time." He pointed up to the nearest clock. "The world may have Greenwich, but your standard from here on out is WYNG time. I see you chit-chatting or wasting anyone's time… and you're fired. Third, this place is dynamic. The news is fast moving and in constant flux. I see you lulling about or looking bored… and you're fired. Finally, do what I say, when I say it, and better than I could possibly hope for…"

"I know… or I'm fired. I get it, sir."

"No, Forde. And don't ever interrupt me again… or you're fired."

For a fleeting moment, she was sure that he had smiled at her, but just as quick was back to his rigid way of being.

"I was going to say that you'd do fine… but I think you got the idea."

Billings did not let up on her all afternoon, giving her a steady stream of rapid-fire tasks, most of which got accomplished by means of what she had learned from Sophie. She would occasionally see her across the newsroom, but was always kept too busy to break away. In time, she began to wonder if that was Billings intent – to keep her from apologizing to Sophie… for being liked.

At the end of the day, she was so captivated in watching the evening production on a newsroom monitor that she completely forgot about Sophie… who was gone before the anchors had rapped their papers on the studio desktop to ceremoniously signify the end of the show. For some reason, someone was playing that ridiculous *Tra-la-la Boom-de-ay* song over the station's loudspeakers… which seemed altogether odd. Still… hearing that tune made her giggle. She was working at the perfect place!

Come Monday morning, she would learn that Sophie had quit WYNG news and gone back to Montana. Sadly, she knew that they would never see each other again.

CHAPTER
19

THE BATTLE OF THE BERTS

She spent the first hour of Saturday morning making a list of things still needing to be done in her small studio apartment. The bare walls required decorating, the windows needed curtains, and the floors could certainly use a few throw rugs.

Almost forgot... I need an ironing board and an iron. Oh... and a couple of pillows too! I can't keep sleeping on a balled-up t-shirt!

Her bustling about that day hardly masked over thoughts engaged in turning over and over the events of her first day at the station. She knew she was getting ahead of herself, but her mind was already constructing the makings of a career for herself in television news. The idea of taking random events... some bearing urgency and others very much hum-drum... fashioning each into a compelling story... connecting those stories up into a polished script... and then watching it all play out in thirty minutes... she could not wait to get back at it.

Work fast, work hard, and work smart... then there's no way Billings or anyone else at WYNG won't see my potential.

Getting on Billings' bad side, she was sure, would be very much like that of getting on Gwen's... so she would do all she could to avoid that. Of course, she felt terrible about how Sophie had been treated, and would do her best to smooth things over with her on Monday... starting with learning how to make coffee.

But really... Sophie should learn how to stick up for herself!

Everything but work got pushed out of her mind come eight o'clock

Monday morning when Billings entered the newsroom. She had arrived an hour earlier, still not confident of how reliable the L operated schedule-wise, and spent the interim quizzing the morning news producer about his show. She only had a moment to process the shock that Sophie had quit before Billings plopped her down with a thick binder containing 'quotables'... his word for anyone with expertise, authority or prominence relevant to a story.

"The spill on the Calumet's gotten worse over the weekend. Go to the tab labeled engineers and find me someone who knows something about water treatment. Watkins needs it in a half hour... or you're fired."

She was back at Billings' side in half that time.

"Sir...? Excuse me... here's the list. I called a dozen... but only got ahold of five. Based on what I learned, I think any of these three should work out. The first two are in their offices right now, but the third's in class... he's a professor at Northwestern. I think this guy here's the most promising. He's with the McHenry County..."

"You called all of these?! Already?! What in the hell did you say to them?"

"Only that I was Marna Forde from WYNG news, and that because they were recognized authorities in their field, would they be willing to speak with Watkins... I mean, Mr. Watkins... sometime this morning about the sewage spill on the Calumet River." She pointed back to the sheet. "See here... I wrote down the times each said they'd be available."

For a moment, Billings seemed less like a monarch sitting on the throne of his assignment desk, and more like a mute beggar holding out the sheet of paper like it was a tin cup. She noticed him swallow before speaking... which told her right off that she had done a good job.

"Put the binder back where it belongs and... go figure out how to make coffee."

She turned away, already scanning the newsroom for a fellow PA when he called her back.

"Forde!"

"Yes, sir."

"Fine work. Keep it up."

"Thank you, sir."

At minutes shy of ten, she had a tray of cups and a pot of coffee positioned on the meeting room table, herself standing in her proper place at the far wall. Her first morning planning meeting at WYNG turned out to be a delight. Being among serious-minded people attacking serious problems with an urgency of purpose was unlike anything she had ever experienced. Sitting about the table were most of the same individuals she had met on Friday afternoon – Billings, who impressively wore the hats of the show producer, the news director and the assignment desk editor, along with his army of assistant editors, assistant directors and a good many available reporters. In addition, Mr. Carswell sat in… something she learned that he did occasionally.

To her, Mr. Bertram T. Carswell stood out like a sore thumb… or more precisely, a stately adorned ring-finger in a room full of sore thumbs. Whereas everyone else in attendance wore beat-up denims, ratty polyesters, and even some nasty-looking tie-dyes, Mr. Carswell was in a three-piece of pinstriped gray with a richly purple paisley-patterned tie over a plain white shirt… all of which she chuckled to herself was quite a mouthful. Looked really good though! Later that day, she happen to overhear Billings jokingly refer to this as Mr. Carswell's birthday suit. She knew right off what he meant – that his boss had been born wearing an executive's attire. Mr. Carswell also stood out in this newsroom's menagerie of aggressive male tendencies for another reason – he was pure gentleman.

The first order of business in the meeting was to put together the run-down of what had come through on the wire services during the night, as well as what news stories were being aired by the morning networks. Sophie had told her that at most stations the news director owned the run-down, whereas the producer only got the content once it was being fashioned into a script. But since Billings owned every news story from cradle to grave, the run-down belonged to him too.

As his assistant news director progressed through the developments of the morning, Billings quickly went about affirming or dismissing the value of each story as a potential part of his script. Every person at the table was given an opportunity to offer comment, though Billings frequently interrupted to bark out questions or comments, especially when a tussle had developed over the significance of a story. Mr. Carswell also chimed in whenever there was something of interest to him. Twice, a phone call was made to a reporter out in the field, and once Billings sent a PA to the receive room for an update on the evolving situation on the Calumet.

Just as the final list of stories was agreed upon, Mr. Carswell took control of the meeting. No one seemed to think this unusual, so she gathered that it was part of the executive producer's job. For a few minutes, he gave a statesman-like address reminding everyone as to the demographics of WYNG's loyal viewers and what those groups expected from their news. Finally, each person had their assignments and the board was populated. Billings then dismissed the meeting, though not in the 'rise up and leave' sort of way that Sophie had said was his habit.

"All right, everyone… get to work."

With him remaining seated, there was a collective exchange of confusion owing to the awkwardness of deciding who would dare be the first one to leave ahead of him.

"Go on, clear the room!"

Everyone sprang up in a scramble of gathering notepads and papers. She made a mad dash about the table to do what she understood to be her job after the meeting – cleaning up.

"Forde… leave the mess… you can tend to it later."

She looked up to discover that of all the attendees, only Billings and Mr. Carswell remained. They were standing toe-to-toe with each other and not much more than a foot of space between them. She did not like the look of that, and hurried to obey… but only got halfway to the door before being stopped.

"On second thought… close the door and get over here."

She did as she was told, yet remained a respectfully safe distance away.

"Bertram, this is Miss Marna Forde, a new PA." He ever so slightly lifted his right hand in her direction, but did not remove his eyes from off of Mr. Carswell. "She's a Texan."

In contrast, Mr. Carswell came about to welcome her… even thank her for consenting to be employed at WYNG as if she were doing them a favor. As warm as his greeting was, Mr. Carswell immediately went back to his previously stern posture when Billings spoke again.

"I was telling Miss Forde this very morning about the program's key drivers… wasn't I, Forde?!"

"Yes, sir. You said…"

"See, Bertram… even the kid gets it! It's all about the news. That's the only thing that really matters. All that touchy-feely crap may play well in the heartland, but this is the big city. This is Chicago."

She drew a half step back, suddenly wishing nothing more than to be gone from this room. But then she noticed an ever-so slight downturn to the corner of Billings' mouth, thought better of her cowardice, and scooted forward to her previous spot… though ever so slightly closer to Billings than before. The same corner of his mouth softened into a sly smile, all of which she hoped so very much had gone unnoticed by Mr. Carswell.

"Miss Forde… you'll soon come to understand that the business of the news is that which enables the news to be told." Having turned to her boss's boss as he spoke, she recognized that his words were not being addressed to her. They clearly went out to Billings. "There is no such thing as a free press.

Though your paycheck may come from our network ownership, Miss Forde… as does everyone else's at the station…" His eyes narrowed on Billings. "…you should know that it is actually our advertisers who pay the bills. They keep this station going. They keep us alive. And they very much wish for us to respond to what the viewers are demanding, which is…"

Her head instantly went back to Billings as he interrupted.

"Hard-hitting news, Miss Forde. Breaking news. In-depth analysis into stories that matter. Chicago tunes into WYNG because we, unlike all those other stations, do not water down the news with childish bit pieces about dog shows… or canned food drives… or… stupid, idiotic, syrupy fluff concocted for enticing fat housewives into buying crap they don't need… all so our advertisers can feel better about their bottom line!"

Billings' smile deepened on scoring what he obviously considered to be a hit against his boss, but Mr. Carswell appeared not to notice.

"Statistics do not lie, Miss Forde – remember that. If the station's marketing data suggests that we can expect as much as an 8.5% increase in advertising revenue from the airing of an additional human interest story per show, then you can rest assured that WYNG's news programming will most certainly move in that direction."

In response, Billings gave off a deep, guttural groan… sort of like what she had sometimes heard from cotton farmers who got dragged by their wives into the flower shop on a Saturday afternoon.

"Don't make me sick!"

The air in the meeting room had turned stifling hot. Somehow, she had unknowingly stumbled into an ongoing turf war over the programming direction of WYNG news. Though these demigods probably only wanted her there so they could conduct their battle in as civil a manner as possible, her thought was on how best to avoid offending either… or both… and ultimately keep her job. Mr. Carswell was smiling at Billings' latest barb with an unscathed dignity that reminded her of all those times her aunt had adopted a similarly smug expression… right before lowering the boom on her.

"I'm sure Albert means well, Miss Forde. After all, he has been at this job for a very, very long time. Perhaps a bit set in his ways… but undoubtedly a quality newsman."

He turned to her with a sympathetic sort of smile and then left the room. Billings, however, stood right where he was at, not addressing her until Mr. Carswell had gotten a sizeable headstart into the newsroom.

"Why the hell are you still standing here?! Get back to work!"

She was out the door on a run.

Though that uncomfortable scene was not soon forgotten, she put it aside for the time being to get immersed into her assigned tasks… all of which kept her dashing about the newsroom. In that first morning on her own, she quickly discovered that the true value of a PA was not in their mind or in their hands, but in their feet. Though most staff had a desk phone, they seldom relied on those for internal calls. Messages carried by the feet of a PA… like the wings of a carrier pigeon… were often deemed more reliable during the heat of a deadline battle than waiting on a response over wires. Aside from being a gofer or a messenger, she soon found there was nothing like a PA for hunting down a reporter late in delivering a story. As annoying as that might prove to the reporter, she learned from her peers that the PA was actually their best friend, for they did the grunt work of making calls, fact finding, and even rounding off the ragged edges of stories. She got to do some of each that morning, as well as run messages back and forth from the receive room. All morning, she kept an eye on the light box hanging over the entry into the back hallway, for it was there to beckon for a PA runner.

There was absolutely no time to relax. She ate lunch on her feet, as an anchor got into a tiff over the wording of a story and insisted that she sort it out with the originating reporter. Just as Sophie told her a typical afternoon would be, she spent hours shuttling script segments back and forth between reporters, editors, anchors, and the master control room. The newsroom went through so much paper that day that bins and bins of it got collected at the end… all destined for the burner in the building's basement. Nearer to the afternoon meeting, she was moving cartridges of video and audio clips up and down the small flight of stairs between the edit bay and the master control room. Something or other always needed to be fixed… and just like Sophie said, there were not enough engineers to go around.

All in all, the most challenging aspect of the job was the noise. The flower shop had always been quiet… as had been George's cable company office… but this newsroom was constant chaos. To every conversation of hers, there was always the annoying subtext of someone's typewriter banging away or a phone ringing off its carriage. All that clatter made her feel as if she was losing touch with the doings in her head.

As on the previous Friday, she found the afternoon meeting to be the critical moment for finalizing the script. Unlike on her first day, Billings did not pull her aside after for special instruction. She discovered that his job was largely over by then. As she and the other PAs frantically scampered about with unfinished packages, she could hear Billings laughing it up with some AE at the assignment desk. That hour before air time was the most stressful. So many script mistakes had to be worked out between the writers, anchors and the master control room engineers… and all of those revisions required the frantic hustle of a PA.

Instead of planting herself before a newsroom monitor, she watched the Monday afternoon news show not as a spectator but as if this was her own child performing on stage… because unlike the show aired on Friday, this *was* her show. Standing in the cage atop the master control room, she could barely breathe as the director cued up the segment on the Calumet River sewage spill… and then she got teary eyed as the tape rolled through the segment of Watkins interviewing her McHenry County engineer about the environmental impact should the spill reach the Lake. Not until the director's final countdown to the end had finished off, with the word 'break' echoing through the master control room, did she actually relax. The broadcast went to commercial as her first show was over. Looking to a control room monitor, she noticed that the floor director and the anchors were kidding around after another job well done. She heard the click of the cage doors unlock, and glanced over to see that the light box above the studio door was unlit.

Suddenly, she was very tired and just had to collapse against the cage's back wall to rest for a moment. She had been standing for hours. Now at the end, all she wanted was a bite to eat, a hot bath, and hours alone with her feet up in which to replay the day. Just before dragging herself off the wall in order to head out for the long subway trip home, the sound of Cole Porter's *Too Darn Hot* filled the cage.

"You know… the man himself picked that one out."

Having been staring absentmindedly at a ceiling speaker, she was startled on finding one of the engineers standing beside her. She had noticed this particular individual working a panel of sliding knobs during the broadcast. He stood out in her mind then only because of his bushy black hair, with mustache and sideburns to match. She had not yet registered his outrageous outfit – wide-cuffed slacks striped in pink and green, along with a vibrant purple shirt buttoned up only halfway. There, against the unsettling sight of his chest hair, dangled a peace sign from a leather strap about his neck. She made eye contact with him… and found that his very round wire-rimmed glasses holding rose-color lenses gave off way too much of a psychedelic feel for her.

"Umm… the man?"

"Billings… can you dig?! Oh… allow me to introduce myself. I'm Angelo Terranova… the one and only sound master of the show!"

With this odd introduction, he also lowered his face and rolled his hand before him in several looping cycles, as if taking a theatrical bow.

"Terranova? That's…"

"Italian for 'new earth.' Really freaked on it as a kid… but now…" He turned up to the ceiling with an expression akin to ecstatic delight. "…it just blows my mind… know what I mean, Babe. You can call me Grass. Much better, you dig?"

She was not sure if this was a question… and was relieved over not having to labor the issue. He raised an imaginary reefer to his lips and took in a deep draw.

"And who might you be?"

"Oh… I'm… umm… Marna Forde… a new PA."

"Right on."

He stuck out a hand to her in an odd manner, it being with his palm facing upward. Though a strange way of going about shaking hands, she nonetheless obliged him by rolling hers over into his grip… until he suddenly yanked his hand away and re-presented it as before.

"Come on, Babe… gimme some skin."

Too late, she realized what he had intended, and quickly did her best to comply… doubting seriously whether her style of tapping his palm with her finger tips had met up to his standards. Still… he gave her a nod and another approving 'right on.'

"Listen, Babe, me and a bunch of the cool heads go out for drinks after the late show. What say you…"

"Oh… thanks… but I'm done for the day. I was just leaving."

"That's cool. That's cool. Stay loose, Babe. But before you split… I got this sweet deal to spill vibes after the gig… you know… mellow the mood. How's about you lay some titles on me… and I do you one?"

"Ahh…" She had absolutely no idea what he was talking about… until he pointed up to the speaker. She then realized that he meant the music. "Yeah. Sure. I can do that!"

She got away from him to the studio door as quick as she could, made a wide berth about the cameramen powering down their equipment, and then managed to make it through the newsroom without being stopped by anyone else. After what seemed like a long walk to the subway station… and a longer wait on the platform… she was finally on a train. So tired, she actually fell asleep in her seat, and woke just in time to squeeze through the closing doors at the Oak Park platform. Another long walk changed her evening plan. She got down a ham sandwich before crawling into bed at slightly after nine.

She slept all the way until the alarm clock roused her at five. She awoke with the kind of foot-sore that she knew would stay with her for the better part of the day. During that morning, and each day of her first week at WYNG, she repeatedly said the same thing over and over to herself.

I've never been so tired in all my life.

That afternoon, she managed to rattle off a few of her teenage favorites to that Grass fellow, not really expecting any of them to be used. Yet one of the things she had already come to appreciate about working at WYNG was the dynamic atmosphere of creative people such as this Grass, who personally came up with the idea of pumping music throughout the newsroom after a broadcast as a means of easing the tension. She learned from him that most times it was modern rock, jazz or soul, while occasionally he opted for show tunes, classical or folk. Most everyone felt that Grass's selections somehow perfectly polished off the day. "After all," he claimed on parting, "the music is the people."

Coming up on a month at WYNG, she had finally adapted to the daily routine such that her natural efficiencies were coming through in everything she did. The first order of business each morning was for Billings to be briefed on the previous night's happenings. This was typically done at the assignment desk by AE's who showed up before dawn to comb through wire service reports, the nightly police scanner recordings, and the station's hotline. Though it was not within the PA's duties, she made it her practice to arrive before these early morning briefings took place. She quickly came to see what kinds of stories attracted Billings' attention. He was a journalist first and foremost, which meant that he naturally gravitated toward anything impactful and away from anything 'fluffy.' For her part, she did not have to search much through the morning briefing material in order to find something capable of sparking his interest.

After all, this is Chicago.

Though she had become comfortable in her role as a PA to Billings, it was not as though she was immune to being chewed out by him. She made plenty of mistakes during those first few weeks… and like everyone else, found herself at the mercy of the man's fury. In one of her worst mess ups, she made a small wording change to a script, inserting a phrase about the 'distinctive trademark congeniality' shown by the mayor to a visiting UN delegation. The change made its way through the afternoon edits… which was more than affirming to her. Unfortunately, the anchor stumbled over the wording during the broadcast, resulting in her being soundly chewed out afterward in Billings' office.

"Of all the idiotic… imbecilic… Damn it, Forde – you weren't hired to be a friggin' wordmonger! If that bag of rocks we call an anchor can't get the words off the teleprompter correctly, than how the hell can you expect even the brightest bulb in Chicago to pick up on their meaning?! For the love of Pete, dumb it down next time!"

The good thing about Billings was that as long as she erred on the side of effort, he was usually quick to forgive. He was a professional... as was his boss... and she knew that both men loved the news. So, she came to see that the 'Battle of the Berts'... as Grass so keenly referred to it one Thursday following the afternoon show... was actually a staple of working at WYNG.

On that day, she had just finished watching the show from the cage above the master control room when the doors to either side of her simultaneously opened... and out came a 'Bert' from each end. Though Mr. Carswell took a moment to nod politely at her, Billings simply grunted for her to get lost. Instead of trying to squeeze past either man, she stepped through the glass door and down the center stairs to where the engineers sat. She had no real desire to watch the two go at it, so she turned down the aisle to where Grass sat. He looked up at her, back over his shoulder at the animated discussion taking place behind the glass, and then quickly scrambled about his station for a specific cartridge. Shoving it into a slot, the sound of Peter, Paul & Mary's version of *If I Had a Hammer* immediately filled the control room.

"I've been saving this one just for them."

She could not help herself – she turned around to watch the two men in their heated debate. Mr. Carswell, with arms folded across his chest, seemed hardly to get a word in edgewise, spending most of the unpleasant encounter vehemently shaking his head back and forth. In contrast, Billings... clearly yelling based on how his mouth and head were bobbing about... kept jabbing a finger at his boss's chest. She heard none of their argument owing to the glass barrier, but having to watch it overlaid with the Vietnam protest song really upset her. Without a word to Grass, she exited through the lower level door leading into the edit bay.

Making her way home, she was thinking about how the two men had gone at each other. Even with her limited experience at WYNG, she was fully aware that one Bert strove to make his viewers think, while the other depended upon them to feel. The inconsistencies between those approaches often put the two at odds with each other. She sensed that both men liked her, but she knew that the Battle of the Berts was not about her, even though their arguments affected her deeply. Of all the PAs, it seemed that she was the one most often in the vicinity at the start of one of their power struggles. Sure... it was tempting to imagine that they were contending for her opinion, but that was just a childish form of self-flattery. They were not asking her to choose. Still… witnessing them argue was as uncomfortable as watching one's parents fight. And though she had no childhood memory of such a thing, there was always the reminder of those terrible months with the Meitners just before George died… not to mention her own with Roy afterward. Those memories, as a wee voice in the back of her head, often whispered that she was a Meitner too… and fleeing to Chicago was such a pathetic way of hiding it.

Of course, the Berts were not the only persons at WYNG to engage in heated workplace disputes. It was not uncommon for arguments, some serious and some petty, to rise up between competing reporters, editors, anchors, and even PAs. She was fully aware that no one's career could be built on a foundation of altruistic cooperation. And neither should it be… despite the mentality of 'love and peace' that she was more frequently picking up from Grass during her trips to the master control room. Like most everyone else, she was determined to do whatever it took to advance her own career.

In sizing up the newsroom as a place she might want to make her life's work, she came to recognize its three common features, each of which could be seen on its many walls – the clocks, the 'on air' light boxes, and the TV monitors. Of these, the latter took the most getting used to. By necessity, the volume was always turned off unless a major story was breaking or their own news program was on. But having all that 'on-screen' motion happening in the periphery of her vision without accompanying voices was unnerving, especially with it being accentuated by a caffeine-induced jitter and the constant bustle of the newsroom. The screen flickering, along with its ever-present disembodied motion without sound, became the very atmosphere of the newsroom to her. It was a constant reminder to keep moving… because the news waited for no one.

But just as Sophie predicted, there came a day when an event happened that was bigger than its telling. It started for her when she awoke on the Wednesday morning of June fifth to discover that Bobby Kennedy had been shot in Los Angeles around midnight, having just concluded his victory speech from winning the California Primary. Sitting on the edge of her bed listening to the radio reports, she found herself unable to continue her routine of dressing, even though she really should be hustling into the station. Memories poured over her… and though she realized that Robert F. Kennedy was his own person, equally unique and full of potential, she could not help but convolve this tragic news with how she felt while sitting in a Skylark convertible on the dusty outskirts of a small West Texas town. Inexplicably, the younger Kennedy was now suffering the same fate as his beloved older brother.

Like most at the station, she arrived in an agitated state, fully expecting this to be a difficult news day. Though not especially rigid with regard to her politics, she nonetheless considered herself to be well-informed. Yet whether she did or did not vote for Kennedy in the fall had no bearing on the moment. Like so many others in the newsroom, she found herself caught up in his tragedy… and in the absurdity of a runaway world. Sure… to be effective in the news business, she knew that she needed to distance herself from the very thing obsessed over – the news. But this was different. Nothing guided anything anymore. Love and peace had become backwater words in the nation's chaotic tide of protest.

She spent much of the day in a constant state of heaviness made all the more difficult from hearing so many other 'where I was' accounts of that sad November day in 1963. Much of the afternoon news program was dedicated to the attempt on Kennedy's life. Everyone knew that his prospects of surviving multiple gunshots was not good. At the conclusion of the program, she was not surprised when Grass's voice came over the station's audio system to offer something extra. Through words completely devoid of 60s slang, he spoke slow and sincere.

"Before today's wrap-up music, a contribution from Marna Forde, I'd like to pause for a moment of silence on behalf of Bobby… and to pray for peace."

She had not expected this, and quickly scanned the exhausted faces all about her in the newsroom. Some made eye contact, perking up eyebrows at her as a prelude to discovering what possible contribution she could make on such a tumultuous day. Even she wondered, for all she really wanted was to go home. She knew that everyone in the newsroom, from the front office to the studio to the dispatch bay, had little energy remaining in which to reflect during Grass's silence.

Then, from out of nowhere, came the sweet, sorrowful sound of Skeeter Davis's melodic voice in *The End of the World*. The song had been one of those on her list to Grass, and somehow it perfectly capped off the feeling of sadness in her heart. Not a person in her sight was doing the usual thing of gathering up their belongings to catch a train or beat the wave of traffic out of the city. They, like her, were held motionless without a connection to anything other than a shared feeling of despair. Still… somewhere buried in the music's message came an unsung acknowledgement that tomorrow would be another day. That they would all get up with the sun and do what they must to go on living. As the last refrain faded from the overhead speakers, she wiped a tear from the corner of an eye and left the station for home.

Early the next morning, she rose to discover from the radio that Bobby Kennedy had died during the night.

———————————

Everyone in the newsroom had been hyped up all summer about the National Democratic Convention being held in Chicago. Heading into the tail end of August, the newsroom was on edge with anticipation over what the next week might hold. The country's uncertain politics, the renegade-like behavior of Mayor Daley, and the eminent threat of anti-war protests had turned the city into a proverbial powder keg ready to explode. On top of all that, the Party was still reeling in the aftermath of Kennedy's assassination, leading every prognosticator to conclude that the outcome of the convention was unpredictable.

For her personally, this was an incredible opportunity to see national news being made on her own doorstep. As a newswoman… a thing to which she was more frequently referring to herself… this could not have been a better time to live in Chicago. Everywhere and every day, there were stories bursting forth with importance. She and everyone else in the newsroom could sense it – history was about to be made. And she would be there to not only witness it, but more importantly to participate in the reporting of it.

But all of her excitement suddenly gave way to worry when riots broke out across the city on Sunday… only the second day of the convention. Along with the chaos in the streets, the events occurring on the Convention floor and within the mayor's office were requiring that the WYNG newsroom work around the clock. She and the other PAs fully accepted that they would be doing shifts from early morning until well after midnight. However, there were some things that she had not expected. While the senior reporters were covering events within the convention hall itself, the more junior ones were tasked with following the demonstrations outside. Two of these individuals and their cameraman were tear-gassed during a melee that broke out between protestors and the police in front of the Conrad Hilton Hotel. Another reporter received a concussion in Grant Park from a thrown bottle. Several then called in sick, as word got around the station that nobody wanted to take part in another 'Days of Rage' like when Chicago got torn apart after Martin Luther King Jr.'s assassination. Billings was beside himself with frustration in trying to find bodies capable of covering the news.

"Shit, shit, shit! Daley's about to hold a press conference, and how the hell is it that I've got nobody to cover it?! We've gotta have somebody – anybody – who can get their ass over to City Hall right away!"

She, in responding to the light box beckoning for a PA, decided to hang back from the receive room door in noticing that Billings was in a towering rage. Fortunately, most of it was being directed at the newsroom's dispatcher.

"I'm sorry, boss... but it's not my fault. There's no one left since you sent ..."

"You gotta be fucking kidding me?! What about Olsen?"

"He's outside the convention..."

"And Vickerman?"

"On the way to the hospital to get interviews from..."

"Shit! There's gotta be someone. Bertram'll toast my nuts if I miss out on this."

She was just about to clear her voice as a sign of her presence when Billings looked up from the microwave communication console.

"You! Forde! Get the hell over here. Ever done copy?"

"Ahh..."

"Never mind."

He turned back to the dispatcher. "Has Clemons left yet?"

She did not make out the man's response, but Billings replied back almost instantly.

"Well tell him to get his ass up here right away!" He came back to her then, holding up an index finger as a command.

"Don't you go anywhere!"

The next thing she knew, she was trailing Click into the dispatch elevator, trying to untangle the string for one of the station's standard press credentials well enough to fit it over her head.

"Listen up, Little Sister. You've only got the time it takes for this elevator to reach the ground floor to become a reporter, so you'll need to... Shit! This is hopeless! Never mind!" Without warning, Click got right up into her face. "Just follow my lead, got it?! Stay on my ass! We've gotta pass through a crowd of demonstrators... then persuade the fuzz to let us up the front steps... then persuade more fuzz to allow us into the building... and then make it through even more fuzz on the inside just to get to the press staging area. You understand what I'm saying?!"

Without waiting for her to respond, he began rifling through his camera bag... almost as if she was not there at all. She looked up to the elevator indicator as they passed the fifth floor. She had only four left in which to sort through her multitude of questions. But she barely got through her first one before Click cut her off.

"So what do you want me to do once we get there?"

"It's *if*! But all you've gotta worry about is sticking to me, got it?!"

He obviously knew something that she did not, but there was no time to ask. The elevator opened and Click bolted out of the dispatch bay so fast that she was hard-pressed to keep up with his sprint down West Washington Street… even with that camera bag slung about his shoulder. She was completely out of breath when they came to an abrupt stop a block short of City Hall. Ahead was a massive throng blocking their way. It was like… the pavement was bubbling up people right before her eyes… and churning them around in the process. And the noise… she could barely hear herself think. The whole lot of them was nothing more than a seething caldron of anger.… hundreds upon hundreds building into thousands as they watched.

No way we're getting through that!

She fully expected Click to throw his hands up and proclaim the effort as lost. He looked her way once… and then suddenly plunged into the rear of the mob! For the next several minutes, it was all she could do not to lose sight of him as he forcefully weaved a path through the demonstrators. This was another world! She was submerged within a protester's element and had no idea as to the rules.

If there're any rules…

She could just barely hear Click's voice some five feet away shouting what sounded like 'press coming through,' and occasionally the same 'down with the pigs' slogans that were being screamed into her ears. She got shoved repeatedly, stepped on several times, and once elbowed hard in the side of her head. The tensest time came when they finally reached the barricades, and she momentarily got swept away from Click as he was arguing with a wall of policemen. And then there he was, bowling over demonstrators to get at her. With a strong grip on her wrist, he dragged her forward through the barricade and into the vastly more open space at the base of the building's steps. It was loud here too, but more like a library compared to being within that mob. She barely had time to get out a word of thanks before Click was at it again with another group of police, waving his credentials all about like he owned the place. Not that the police were buying any of it… but they eventually let them pass.

Halfway up the steps, Click came to an abrupt stop and turned her way. He was not exactly shouting, but there was still lots of intensity to his words.

"Here's the deal… whether we make it to the press conference or not… we gotta have tape of you… the reporter… standing out here with this mob in the background. Footage of Daley can come from anywhere… a wire service or something… we can slap our station's call letters on it… claim it as our own. But what we really need is a reporter on the scene."

He suddenly stopped to look her over, and then pulled out a small mirror from his bag.

"Fix yourself up."

As she went about trying to smooth out her hair, she was startled to find a makeup brush thrust into her face.

"Hold still! Gotta take the sheen off those white-girl cheeks."

All about the streets behind them, a mob of anti-war demonstrators was screaming bloody murder while their targets – the police – stood by in riot gear… and here was Click applying blush to her cheeks as if the two of them were standing calmly in the studio of WYNG. He then went a couple steps up to survey her from the perspective of a camera.

"Take off those press credentials… and undo the top two buttons of your blouse. Go on… it's for the camera. And smile! Damn, Girl – Chicago could go a long way toward peace with a pretty face like that on the news every day!"

He came back down to her level, producing a piece of paper from his pocket.

"Billings wrote copy for you. There's maybe three ways for Daley to spin this. We've got each one covered. Do all three in turns… Start each with your intro…"

He pointed at the top of the page where Billings had typed out 'This is Marna Forde of WYNG news reporting from City Hall.'

"Let's do a practice first."

She read the line out loud as evenly as she could.

"Good… but put some more volume into it. And hold the microphone to the side… don't wanna block your face or chest. That's it! Now we need these lines to come across smooth as silk… you with me? Memorize what you can… adlib the rest. Billings says for you to beef up the Texas twang. Viewers'll love that. Now let's go at it."

For the next several minutes, as a mob of protesters raged in the background, she did as she was instructed, repeating the intro with the different lines in the way Click indicated. She was actually getting the hang of this… maybe even hoping to say a few things that Billings had not prescribed… when Click suddenly shifted his camera from her onto the crowd. Turning about in the same direction, she noticed an even larger mob of protesters approaching from Grant Park. These were not so peaceful looking as those already assembled. Even from a distance, she could tell that many of them were carrying sticks and clubs.

"We better get the hell outta here. Definitely don't wanna be caught on these steps."

"Aren't we going in?"

But one look at the wall of policemen now assembling at the doors told her that they were not getting inside. The new throng had reached the outer fringe of the already assembled demonstrators… battering directly into them. These new arrivals were not going to be stopped by barricades alone. She turned back to find Click quickly packing his bag.

"Same as before – stick close to me."

As was the sad case of a climber who rose to the challenge of Mount Everest's summit, only to succumb to the mountain on the way back down, it was painfully clear to her that they were not getting off the steps of City Hall as easily as they had reached them. The newly arrived protesters were already forcing the crowd forward. The section of barricades that they had come through was now bulging. So Click took off down the steps at an angle, evidently hoping to squeeze through at the far end. But by the time they got there, that section of police had crumbled. Even with all the noise, she still registered the thump and whirling whistle sounds… and then came the white smoke with the first painful tinge to her eyes. In a matter of seconds, she was essentially blind and hacking her lungs out. She felt a vise-like grip to her arm and heard the faint, far-away sound of him ordering her to keep moving. Bodies were crashing into her… and still he dragged her on through the scattering protesters. She open her watery eyes several times to the chaos all about, yet always there was that stinging pain. Once, she beheld in blurry terror as a policeman's club came down across Click's shoulders. But the acid in her face always compelled her to close her eyes again. Click still pulled her on. She managed to look again… just as a policeman's shield hit her broadside with such force that Click lost hold of her arm. She was spun about, pin-balling off other bodies with no idea where she was going. Someone collided with her, sending her into that slow-motion terror of losing her balance. But then she felt that wonderful pressure of Click's grip being restored to her arm. A yell came to her ear.

"Keep moving!"

Finally, they emerged from the tear gas fog, but not from the mass of fleeing humanity. More bruising collisions ensued. Twice she got punched in the side of the head and once squarely on her nose. Her free hand shot up to that throbbing pain… only to come away covered in blood spouting from both nostrils. Yet there was Click, still dragging her upstream through the crowd. Ahead was a clearing, and she sensed that he was making directly for it. She received one final blow… a glancing collision from a passing protestor who looked very much caveman-like to her tear-gassed eyes… and then they finally broke through to a relatively calm stretch of West Washington Street. Only then did Click let go of her. She did not have to be told – she followed in behind him as they slowly weaved their way back to the station. Only once they had reached the safety of the dispatch bay did she have an opportunity to thank him for saving her life. Catching up, she was completely stunned to find him crying… and not because of the tear gas.

"Click… are you okay?"

"That was too close… too much like before… when… when they shot him. It all came back… too close…"

He was shaking all over… so much so that the camera bag slipped off his shoulder to the pavement. She quickly made to wrap an arm about him, determined to help him into the elevator, when he winced terribly at her touch.

"Click! You're hurt bad! We gotta get you to a hospital!"

"I'll… be fine. Just… get my bag."

As she reached down for the camera bag, she met his eyes for the first time since leaving the steps at City Hall.

"Marna… there's… there's blood all over your face!"

"It's nothing. Let's just get you upstairs."

Neither she nor Click spoke all the way up the elevator… and not even to the shell-shocked engineer who took the camera bag from her. Before she knew it, Click was gone. He just disappeared right before her eyes into the newsroom. Someone had a hold on her… was steering her somewhere… but all she wanted was to stay with Click… just as he had stayed with her.

Her mind could only process part of what was going on around her. She was sitting in the center of the assignment desk… in the tall chair that only Billings ever occupied… and someone was whispering to her. It was Billings… and he was as white as a ghost in her sight. He put something to her lips… a burning came to her throat… and then everything was suddenly clear. She was leaning back, more-or-less looking up at the ceiling. Off to the side, a fellow PA was holding an open first aid kit as Billings went about personally attending to her wounds. He did not allow her to say anything about the riot until he was absolutely satisfied with his work… and that she also had promised to keep an ice pack on her nose.

The experience of weathering a Chicago riot immediately became a red badge of courage. For the next hour or so, she was repeatedly called upon to recount what she and Click had endured on the steps of City Hall. But the cherry on top was when one of the engineers came by to personally drag her into the edit room so she could see the final result of her work. The clip started with her on the steps and a mass of humanity serving as a backdrop. Without voicing it, she thought she looked quite good… despite the wind-blown feel to her hair. After her intro, she commenced telling the camera how Mayor Daley was fully behind the Chicago Police Department's use of justified force against the protestors. The clip jumped to the mayor saying something to that very effect, and then to her signing off on the steps. She felt a hand come to her shoulder… and then Billings speaking in her ear.

"That's work to be proud of, Forde."

Before she could reply with thanks, the edit room suddenly filled with the thunder of an unexpected voice.

"Albert! Are you completely out of your mind?!"

She turned to catch a glimpse of Mr. Carswell towering in the doorway… just as all of the engineers made a mad dash down the back stairs into the master control room. She had no thought to do likewise, and instead leaned around Billings to get a better look at the impressive stance of her executive producer. When their eyes met, Mr. Carswell turned from angry to completely crazed. Both of his hands went to his finely combed hair, gripping it such that many strands poked up between his fingers. She had not thought it possible, but he was suddenly all over Billings like a cat on a mouse, biting him over and over again with the harshest words she ever heard him utter.

"You damn fool! You self-centered… insensitive… depraved soul. Sending that young woman out into that mob just for your worthless story! She could have been killed! Wicked, that's what you are! Wicked and evil! Don't think for one minute you'll be weaseling your filthy self out of this! Look at her, Albert! Look hard! She's got bruises all over her face and… Albert, there's blood on her blouse! Her blood! It's all over her! I could gut you like a fish for this… and I may still! Get your lousy self to my office right now!"

To her great surprise, Billings inched his way around his boss and slunk out of the room… all without a single word in his defense. The fire in Mr. Carswell's eyes followed him the whole way out. For the first time since setting foot in WYNG, she was witnessing a complete reversal in the demeanors of the Berts. As Mr. Carswell turned back to her, she was bracing herself for a small measure of that displeasure. Instead, she received only the gentleness of his voice.

"Miss Forde… are you… okay? Do I need to take you to the hospital? Truly, you look terribly ill. Your nose… do you… think it's broken?"

"It's fine, sir. I'm fine. Just a bit beat up."

"Miss Forde… Marna… I've spoken with Demetrius about what happened to the two of you out there. In fact… I had Rose drive him to the hospital. I'm afraid he may have cracked ribs."

"Mr. Carswell, Click was absolutely amazing! I would never have gotten out of there without him! You should give him a raise."

She was surprised to see Mr. Carswell shoot her a quick smile… right before becoming serious once more.

"Swear to me you'll never attempt anything dangerous like that again… no matter what that fool-of-a-boss orders you to do. I'm serious – promise me!"

Only after she had nodded to him did he leave. She remained there for what seemed like hours, aware of nothing other than the slow creep of engineers coming back into the room. They all left her be. So she replayed the whole thing over and over, marveling at what she – Marna Forde of Lubbock, Texas – had just accomplished. But what brought her out of this daze was a voice of softness coming from the door, as strange in its source as was the anger from Mr. Carswell.

"Miss Forde… will you… please accompany me to my office?"

She followed Billings down the hall. Though they entered his place of power, he offered his desk chair to her, and then stood by meekly looking down at his own feet.

"I owe you an apology… I never should have sent you out there. It was wrong of me. It's completely within your rights as an employee of WYNG to file a grievance against me for…"

"Why in the world would I do that?!"

His eyes shot up to her with something resembling wonder.

"Mr. Billings, that was the most… terrifying experience of my life… and I wouldn't exchange a second of it for anything. I'd go back out there again… well… maybe not just yet… if you know what I mean. But to be out there… in that mob reporting the news… I loved it! It was like nothing I've ever done before. It was… exhilarating!"

"So… you're… ahh… probably wanting to become a reporter now?"

She looked him square in the face with a feeling coming to her that she had not thought possible prior to that moment. He was just a man… with only his life's work to stand as credit against a debt of harsh, lonely living. And she so admired him for it.

"No, sir. That's not for me. I'm not interested in becoming just another pretty face speaking someone else's words. I want to influence people with *my own* words. I want to be just like you."

Perhaps she was mistaken, but upon being dismissed from his office, she had the singular impression that her words were responsible for a wateriness coming to his eyes.

CHAPTER

20

A GRASS DANCE

The thing she really missed from her previous life was having someone to talk with… or more precisely, someone to talk to. Not that she considered herself to be a poor listener. She simply longed for someone with whom she could verbally process her thoughts… especially seeing as she seemed to make better sense of what was going on inside by dumping it out on a sympathetic ear. She had tried using the bathroom mirror, but always ended up feeling like an idiot standing there watching her own lips make the sound of her voice. Too often, she got distracted in dealing with something amiss with her appearance… especially in fretting over how long it was taking for the blemishes from the riot to heal. At such times, she instead pretended that someone was seated in her apartment, and would take off around the room in a running monologue… only to have it peter out without a set of engaged eyes fueling her transitions from topic to topic.

So many things had happened to her since coming to Chicago… not to mention everything that led up to her fleeing Lubbock. She desperately wanted someone to unload it all on… but only if that someone was safe. Perhaps this was why she sought out Grass as a suitable sounding block. He genuinely listened to her. Of course, he was plenty weird based on her West Texas way of seeing things… or perhaps just tried to be. She could tell that he liked her… and she liked him too… as a friend… so she took care not to give him the wrong impression.

Through the rest of the summer and into the fall, she developed a habit of seeking out Grass whenever there was time for a sit-down lunch. She usually found him in the edit room, as this was generally the first place he went on showing up for work. He would be sitting in the sound booth, fiddling with an audio segment for a promo or fine tuning a pre-recorded piece from one of the anchors. On those occasions when the warning light was on, she would wave to him through the glass and go find somewhere else to eat… but more often than not the light was out and he would beckon her inside.

For thirty minutes – the maximum time Billings allotted to PAs for lunch – she and Grass would casually chat about whatever was of interest in the moment. She might relate the details of some story she was helping with… or launch into a long-winded account of an interesting incident that took place in the newsroom… or just share a crazy notion about the future of TV news. On those instances when she gave him center stage, she found that his hippie way of saying things was mostly an act. Within the privacy of the sound booth, he spoke like any other person at the station, without the slightest trace of 'far out,' 'right on,' or 'cool, man' mixed in. To be sure, many of his perspectives remained steeped within the anti-establishment counterculture of the times, yet he still seasoned in just enough 'love,' 'peace' and 'freedom' to make her wonder what he truly believed. Mostly, she came to see that there was a good bit of the visionary to him. He was well-informed on politics, and especially the FCC's role in America. In having shared with him a portion of her experiences in Lubbock… well-cloaked as they were within the guise of a single woman… she found him to be more than sympathetic to the plight of small cable operators such as George Meitner. To Grass, the relationship between the FCC and the large media corporations was a puppet show in which the latter controlled the strings of the former. He said that in no place was that better revealed for the deception it was than in the evolving cable industry.

"Marna, there's not a single FCC ruling that hasn't been guided by the media. Not a one! Every regulation has been concocted for the sole purpose of protecting corporate control of markets. Take the FCC's *Second Report and Order* that came out in…"

Sometimes when Grass got going, it was difficult for her to keep up with the terms he flung out. Though she desperately wished to appear as well-informed as him, getting there often required swallowing her pride.

"Grass… I have no idea what that is."

He waved a hand dismissively in the space between them… likely to help her feel less stupid over how little she understood about the world.

"It's nothing. Just another propagandized finding. The details aren't as important as the fact that the FCC is secretly engaged in manipulating markets. Given your experience in Texas, you'll know exactly what I'm talking about. Basically... they put a stranglehold on the smaller CATV networks... just like the one you worked at in Lubbock... then they turn right around and grant the MSOs the right to..."

"What're MSOs?"

"Puuu-sha! It simply means 'Multiple System Operators.' Just a clever cloak for what they really are – the corporations! So... get this... the FCC puts the squeeze on the little guys, driving down their profitability, then turns a blind eye as the MSOs swoop in and take over their territories for a song... all with the aim of building up network control over media markets. And believe you me, the MSO's are big enough and powerful enough to find loopholes in any FCC regulation. Marna... that's why your boss went out of business."

They sat quietly for several minutes, and though she knew he was affording her the opportunity to think about his words, while at the same time eat a portion of her lunch, her thoughts were taken in a different direction.

My poor, dear father-in-law... I miss him so.

When Grass next spoke, she was surprised to find him adopting a more sympathetic tone... though not at all aligned with her sad feelings.

"Marna, things aren't all bad. Like we chant at sit-ins – the times, they are achangin'. There're voices in and out of Congress who are sensing how beautiful the future could be. I'm not saying anybody's going to be able to wipe out the FCC, but they'll have to respond to the people eventually... and the people can't be silenced! The 'Blue Sky' movement is just on the horizon. It won't be long before the government's forced to free the airwaves for the people. No more being held hostage by the corporate boob tube. Someday soon, anyone with a little bit of bread..." He sheepishly smiled his apology. "I mean... investment capital... will be able to produce their own programming, and then just walk right into any fat-cat's corporate media center..." He waved an arm about his head in a broad, sweeping motion that revealed his true feelings about his employer. "...and have full access to air that programming. Cable... or any other medium... belongs to anyone with a voice. You'll see... soon, cable will be granted the latitude to evolve based on the free speech rights of local voices... and not on corporate greed or governmental ineptitude... or some herd mentality of mass media appeal. Think of it, if you like, as a post-modern cultural expression of the visual arts... but without all the corruption that comes from technological commercialism. What I'm talking about is called 'Citizen's Access'... and it's our First Amendment right."

Despite the complexity to his words, such wonderful thoughts were tumbling through her head. Not of developing her own programming, but of her personally being given the opportunity to do something bigger with this new freedom. After all, it had not been that long ago when she, fresh out of her escape from Gwen's pathetic flower shop, had stood before one of George's towers and imagined what it would be like to sail through the airwaves with a message to the people. Suddenly aware that she was not remembering in private, she looked up to find Grass smiling at her.

"Nobody owns anybody, Marna."

These were the types of conversations that kept drawing her back to Grass in the edit room. Yet as stimulating as those were, she had to admit that there were others that made her terribly uncomfortable being near him. Just about every week, he would find some way of asking her out… or offering to share some weed with her after the show. Every time, she would graciously decline, seeing as she was absolutely determined not to get involved with anyone… especially him and his communal aspirations for a free-sex version of love. He had become a friend, yet she would remain vigilant at keeping that friendship safely within the walls of WYNG. Besides… technically speaking… she was still married.

"Grass, I'm really not looking for a relationship at this time in my life. I just want to focus on building a career."

"That's cool. That's cool. I can dig it."

With the calendar not far from turning over into 1969, she entered the station on a snowy Monday morning to discover something she had not considered as possible – she was now the senior PA at WYNG news. Over the weekend, the only one who had been there longer abandoned his dream of becoming a newsman and returned to his previous better-paying job at his father's deli in Springfield. Not that this new distinction brought her any greater level of prestige, but at least she finally began to embrace a notion that this was where she belonged. Of course, she readily acknowledged that it would take a lot more than people leaving and her moving up some imaginary PA totem pole in order for Chicago to actually feel like home. She had experienced her first stifling bout of homesickness in November. Though Gwen never put much stock in holiday celebrations… or Ruby, for that matter, after going insane… she had to endure a very dreary Thanksgiving in eating a pathetic turkey TV dinner all alone in her small apartment. Still… she was making it on her own… and even putting away a bit of her biweekly paycheck.

Now well into December, everyone's attention was turning to the station's Christmas party. This, she learned, was put on annually in epic fashion for the entire station – over a hundred employees in all. To be held in the building's ground floor ballroom, this party would have a host bar, a buffet dinner, and dancing deep into the night. She went out of the way several times to stick her head into the ballroom as the decorating progressed. She got to watch as lights were strung along the walls and across the ceiling, and then as four huge scotch pines were erected in each corner. The stage was festooned with holly in preparation for the party's traditional caroling competition in which the station's executives would serenade the staff. She could not wait to jeer at Ebenezer Billings as he, in his Scrooge-like voice, was compelled to bellow out *'Deck the halls with boughs of holly; fa la la la la, la la, la, la.'*

On the morning of the party, she excitedly dressed in the outfit she had purchased just for the occasion. Starting with a snow-white chiffon blouse that had really cute puffy sleeves and a neckline that fell in folds across her chest, she matched in a holly-berry miniskirt and jet-black tights. After some debate as to footwear… seeing as there would be dancing and she fully intended to cut loose… she settled on white go-go boots, as something with a solid heel would be best. To capture the final element of the season, she picked out a blazer of tulip-leaf green. As that undoubtedly would come off during the warmth of the party, she accessorized the outfit with a broad fabric belt of nearly the same color. Standing before the full-length mirror in her bedroom, she pivoted about to examine the collection, concluding that the outfit gave off the perfect balance between holiday spirit and chicness.

With the exception of a skeleton crew putting on the late show, everyone in the newsroom found it extremely difficult to be serious that day about anything other than the party. Even though they would be gorging themselves on a fully catered meal, many staff had brought samples of their own holiday cheer to share with coworkers. In moving about on her duties, she came across fruitcakes, decorative candies, and platters of Christmas cookies. With the afternoon show finally over and the start of the party an hour away, the entire newsroom was abuzz with much antsiness. For a first-timer such as herself, she was most anxious to hear stories about past parties. Currently lounging at a reporter's desk, she was listening to him wrap up an account of last year's event where Mr. Carswell had distributed WYNG-themed calendars while decked out in Santa gear. The reporter progressed into a warning about Grass's famous brownies when his phone rang. Rather than eavesdrop on the man's conversation with his wife regarding how their babysitter had unexpectedly backed out, she headed to the elevator, deciding to spend the next fifteen minutes roaming about the building's lobby before the ballroom doors finally opened.

Once the party got started, she and the other PAs staked out a large table on the edge of the dance floor. The Christmas music commenced with the Big Band tunes that the older crowd preferred, though she was assured that the music her generation thrived on would come later in the evening. For the next several hours, she joked and laughed so very freely. This was what she had been longing for… to be part of something bigger than herself. She was finally a member of a team, and could fully relax in celebrating with like-minded people dedicated to professional excellence in the news. She paced herself with the alcohol, even though its presence flowed freely at the table. With her being the only single female, she got lots of attention from everyone… even some being rather flirtatious. She could handle that. This was not her first rodeo.

To her surprise, Grass showed up a bit late, him bearing a plate of his homemade brownies. As he went around in a circle, offering but getting no takers, she did not notice until his circuit was nearly completed that it would end with her. He obviously had planned it that way. Pulling a chair up from another table, he squeezed himself in beside her, depositing his tray of brownies nearby. Before long, their conversation became like any other time of them sitting together in the sound booth. He asked about her most memorable childhood Christmases, relating his own in the process. Because of the warm feeling she had from being with him, she reached over and ate one of his brownies. Its rich and moist chocolatiness surprised her. Not at all what she had expected from the kitchen of a man… especially one who was an engineer. But then the station manager was on the PA system announcing that it was time for dinner. Through the prime rib and into the many elaborate desserts, she still found herself being drawn to the brownies… even though no one else at the table seemed to be. There was something distinctive about the taste, so she took another to explore it before asking… but then Mr. Carswell was dragging Billings onto the stage for the first of the planned entertainment… and she nearly passed out from laughing so hard! Another drink… and another brownie.

Together, she and Grass sat through all the comical performances, laughing and chatting as best friends. With the after-dinner speeches over, the DJ switched his repertoire toward the types of modern rock ideal for dancing. Without thinking much about it, she took hold of Grass and dragged him onto the dance floor. Once again, he surprised her. From the first song on, she found him to be an incredible dancer! He seemed to be creating his own footwork and body motions… complicated, yet always fluidly consistent with the beat. Powered by the music, the alcohol, the sugar-high of his brownies, and all of the rich food that evening, she cut loose and danced like only dance mattered.

A few others at her table stepped in for a song or two, but always she found herself back with Grass. They seemed, as dancers, to be made for each other.

Her head was spinning… or perhaps it was only something special prepared by the party organizers for just that moment. The lights all about the ceiling flashed and blurred as if racing in circles about the walls. The music, louder than ever, now seemed to be part of her. She was the source and everyone was dancing to the tune of her. She could feel Grass running his hands along her hips, but had absolutely no thought of rebuffing him. And why should she?! She was the dance floor itself. And just to show him how real that feeling was, she pushed him backward into a vacant chair, lightly kissed him on the lips, and took a step away. He made to get up, so she pushed him right back down again. The previous beat pouring from the overhead speakers slowly faded, and she waited, sensing something special to come.

After a moment of silence in which it seemed as if the entire party had turned their eyes to her, the next song started out with a drummer's beat and the Zombies' *Time of the Season* came on to fill her senses. With a slow seductive beginning, she performed for him, completely lost in the sight of how mesmerized he was with her every move. She felt her arms rippling up and down of their own accord to the rhythm, just as her body was swaying beneath her. She opened her lips to him, yet not to sing… only to mouth out inaudible words of invitation. Pivoting about with her eyes still locked on him, she shimmied to the beat, knowing that he was completely transfixed on her every move. How she knew to dance this way… to cause him to be as helpless as he appeared… it was totally beyond her. All she knew was that she wanted this feeling never to end. She had captured him.

By the time the song had come to an end, she was completely out of her mind.

She awoke to a pale light coming at her from an unaccustomed direction. It took several seconds of refocusing before she could identify it as the faint outline of the sun flickering through a gauze-like curtain that overhung an unfamiliar window. She closed her eyes, as the throbbing to her head made it certain that she was not seeing things properly. But with no other part of her body capable of moving, she feebly opened her eyes once again to the same dull sunshine. Except now, other oddities began piling up in her blurry account of this morning. The pillow her head was resting on had an uncomfortable coarseness to it. From under it poked her left elbow, it lying over a pale green sheet that she did not recognize as being part of her own inventory of linen. So she sought to prop herself up with her other arm… but was shocked to discover that she actually had three of them. One was bent under the pillow, one was lying like lead on the sheet before her eyes, and a third seemed to be dangling over her waist with a hand cupping her breast. For a fanciful moment, a pleasant memory flashed into her dizzied thinking of having once slept in the embrace of another. But then she came to see that this third arm was considerably more hairy than it ought to be. A groan was hummed out into the back of her head, and she… one hundred percent awake… realized herself to be completely naked and in close proximity to someone else.

No, no, no! This can't be happening!

Just as a spooked cat will react with an instantaneous upward jump, all four limbs jerking into action in order to put the greatest distance between itself and danger, so likewise she propelled herself out of this strange bed with feline-like reflexes. Shrieking at the top of her lungs, she yanked the sheet off to secure it about herself… only to find Grass sprawled out naked before her.

"Aaah! Put something on!"

Not waiting for him to comply, she threw the pillow her head had just been resting on directly at his midsection.

"I can't believe this! You vile… you disgusting… you pathetic… ANIMAL! How could you do this to me?!"

"Do this to you?! Babe, you…"

She did not wait for more of his words, overwhelming the room instead with her curses. Those could not possibly hurt him enough, so she grabbed the nearest thing at hand – a lamp with a gaudy-looking stained-glass shade – and pitched it directly at him. But in her agitated state, her aim overshot, with the lamp shattering in dramatic fashion against the opposite wall. She snatched up another item – an ashtray – and hurled it as hard as she could directly at his head. It hit him square between the eyes, jerking him backward in a tumble over the far edge. Now screaming with her full fury, she threw more things at him – a half empty liquor bottle, some book, and an alarm clock… until there was nothing left but the bedside table itself. As he meekly poked his head up and got off another pathetic 'Babe,' she heaved that entire tacky chrome-legged thing at him! He screamed and ducked down again… so she used the opportunity to re-secure the sheet about her. But she was far from done yet! Reaching to the bed frame, she made to flip the entire thing over on top of him… except it was bolted firmly to a fake-looking bamboo headboard. So she shifted her grip to the mattress and sent it propelling across the box spring directly into his face. Only as she turned about to rip the curtain rod off the wall and use it as a spear did she feel herself suddenly overwhelmed by the exhaustion. Worse, her head was pounding away with even more pain from her exertion. It was then that his girly screams gave way to words.

"Marna... please stop! You're wrecking my place!"

"I'll wreck more than that once I get my hands on you... you filthy piece of shit!"

"It's not my fault! You practically threw yourself at me! Just ask anyone at the party."

The party...?

It suddenly came back to her. The music, the alcohol, the brownies... and her dance. Without energy for another word, she fell back against the wall and slid to the floor in tears. Wrapping her arms over her head, she sought desperately for anything with the power of warding off her mounting shame. But the sobs just came on thick and fast, burning her heart with each breath. Nothing could take away this pain. She had messed up like never before. There was no correcting this mistake. So she just sat there and cried, completely overwhelmed by her own foolishness.

No! It had to be a lie! She was not that person! She would never...

Without warning, she felt a hand come to her shoulder and looked up to find Grass seated by her side. She could still spare some disgust, just for him.

"Don't touch me! Don't ever touch me again!"

He backed off... but not nearly far enough.

"Babe... there's... nothing to be ashamed of. We were beautiful together. We're still beautiful..."

"We're nothing together, understand me?! You wanna show me something beautiful?! Then go find my clothes!"

He made no effort to move.

"DO IT NOW, GRASS!"

As he scrambled to his feet, she turned inward, trying to rationalize how she had gotten herself into this terrible situation. Nothing came... other than the shocking realization that she had taken the ultimate step away from her marriage.

He was soon back with arms full of everything that she had so carefully selected the previous morning... all for the purpose of making a stunning impression at the party.

"Turn away. In fact... get out. Go... wherever... so I can get dressed."

"It's okay, Babe... I've already seen you naked..."

"I SAID GO!"

She had absolutely no thought of showering in his bathroom. The sticky feel of sex would have to follow her all the way home. But she went there only because of its privacy... and because she badly needed to relieve herself before leaving. She dressed quickly and then emerged from the wrecked bedroom into a smallish sort of kitchen-living area. He was sitting on a low couch, but she had a mind only for the way out. Fortunately, he did not speak… just lifted an arm in pointing to her left. Without a goodbye, she slid aside the door's security chain, turned its two deadbolts, and then slammed it behind her in stepping out. She only got halfway down a narrow hallway before realizing her situation. Reconciling herself to the necessity, she backtracked to pound on his door. He opened it immediately… almost as if expecting her to return.

"Where the hell am I?!"

"Let me get dressed and I'll walk you to the L."

"No. I can find it on my own. Just tell me where I am."

He gave her directions to the nearest station, and then moved to close the door. But she, surprising even herself, shoved a boot in the way. She needed to know something of what he could remember.

"Grass… everyone saw us leave together… didn't they?"

"Yes."

"I… don't remember any of it…"

Which was not entirely true. Already, she was actively suppressing the scattered snippets coming to her from the party. Her dancing seductively for him… Them sharing a taxi ride together in the cold, kissing and groping in the backseat… Her staggering along this very hallway with him clutching at her hips… and her giggling about it. She remembered the passionate kissing, interrupted only to drink some nauseous liquor he had poured out for them. It went down with a burn… and made things easier.

And then him… on top of her… in the darkness.

"Man… you were really stoned."

"Grass…" She did not know how to phrase it, and found herself staring down at his bare feet. Why should she notice that his toes contrasted so starkly with the bright blue of his shag?! "I mean… Angelo…"

"Don't worry, Marna. I won't say anything to anyone. You have my word. Contrary to what you might think… I care about you."

She could not thank him for this small kindness, as to do so required her to accept a portion of the blame she was already working hard to deny. She nodded and left. Two subway legs later, followed by a cold walk from the Oak Park platform, was all sufficient for her to accept that she could never, ever, go back to Lubbock again.

She did not leave the apartment all weekend, spending the majority of it balled up on her couch crying. The headache that had followed her all the way from Grass's place remained as her only companion. With shades drawn tight and phone disconnected from the wall, she sat alone in the dark, dwelling less upon what had happened that Friday and more on what she was soon to face at the station. New details of the party and its aftermath were still coming back to her, each invading her painfully hung-over thinking. Most damning was the sketchy memory of her making him watch as she pulled her blouse over her head and then stepped out of her skirt. Stripped of inhibition, the choice had been fully hers.

Her period came Monday morning… something she greeted with much relief. The hour of delay before heading out to work was only partly due to dealing with the situation. Her mounting dread over seeing her coworkers drew out every aspect of her efforts to leave. Her only hope was to sneak into the newsroom unnoticed… and remain invisible for the rest of her life.

It seemed that the L had never moved more efficiently, with hardly a wait at her platform or any station along the way. She soon found herself exiting at her downtown stop, breezing through a sparse crowd of subway commuters, and then climbing the stairs out into the bright exposure of a cold, crisp December morning. Nothing stood in the way of her arriving at the Rollecastle building. She entered the tenth floor newsroom, knowing that the morning meeting had already concluded. Every person seemed to anticipate her arrival with their knowing smiles and smirks… but a greater number of disapproving frowns. No one asked her why she was late, how her weekend went, or anything about what they had observed of her at the party. Still… she caught enough offhand comments about other happenings to know that she was certainly being discussed when not around.

The news day shaped up to be uneventful, though the rigor of the routine still won out. She, like everyone else, had to put conscious effort into preparing the script. As the hours went by, the number of sly smiles directed her way gradually diminished, but she still could not bring herself to relax. Soon, Billings would place in her hands the first bit of script that needed to be run to the master control room… and there she would come face-to-face with Grass. Fortunately, the moment came and went without incident, as he did not look up from his sound board to greet her. In making more of her usual trips back and forth there throughout the afternoon, she made absolutely no attempt to interact with him, hoping very much that the whole nightmare would soon be forgotten. Yet the entire station came to realize that a significant change had come over their sound engineer because of her. For the first time in her seven month experience of working at WYNG, Grass failed to cue up a post-broadcast song.

The absence of his music went on for the whole week, with everybody at the station giving her such nasty looks at the conclusion of each broadcast. She had to do something about that. So she put aside her anger for long enough to speak with him just this once. She would never spend another lunchtime with him. That, she had decided on Saturday morning well before reaching her Oak Park platform. But their friendship did need some kind of an official ending… and doing that might actually make her feel a little bit better about herself. So… she would take the high road… if such a thing were possible for someone like her… an adulteress. Pushing that unpleasant thought from her mind, she sought him out in the master control room after the evening show, and was relieved that he seemed to understand why she was there.

"We need to talk."

"Okay… let's go up there."

He motioned toward the cage, so she allowed him to climb the steps ahead of her, fully aware that the director and engineers were watching. She did not speak until the glass door was fully closed… and then only after making sure that there was plenty of distance between them.

"What you did to me… it was inexcusable."

"Marna… I thought…"

"I don't want to hear it."

"But you need to! I thought… that we were together at last. I've been crazy about you from the moment I laid eyes on you… right over there." Knowing full well the occasion of their first meeting, she did not turn about to where he was pointing. The disgust rising within compelled her not to. "Is there any way for us to get past this… and have things back to the way when…"

"No, Grass. There's absolutely no future for us together. What happened was a mistake… one that I'll never make again. I want you to fully understand something – I will never forgive you for getting me high. Never! From here on, you're just another stranger who happens to work at the same place I do. We will never speak again as friends. Do you understand me?"

"Marna… this is so unnecessary. You're still a lady worthy of my…"

"Just stop it!"

She immediately turned her back on him, wanting to get through the door to the studio as soon as possible. She got only as far as a hand to the knob before being brought up short.

"Who's Roy?"

She was hoping that she had not heard him correctly, and therefore only came about slowly to face him again.

"What'd you say to me?!"

"You called me Roy several times in the night. You kept telling me… I mean, this Roy… how sorry you were… and that you still loved me… loved him."

She stood there frozen in time, desperately trying to process how such words could have come even from her high-on-marijuana mind.

"I'm sorry, Grass. He's no one. Just my ex. It was only the pot speaking."

"I don't think so." She badly wanted to leave, but could not bring herself to move an inch. "Marna… what're you doing here?"

"What kind of a question is that?! I work here… just like everyone else!"

"That's not what I mean. What're you doing in Chicago? You don't belong here… and I think you know it. Maybe you should… consider going back to him."

"That's none of your business, Grass. And just so we're clear… I won't be intimidated by you into leaving."

Because I've got nowhere else to go.

Without another word, she left the cage… and the station… for another lonely train ride to an empty apartment on the west side of Chicago.

All that following week, she did her best to avoid being tasked with courier responsibilities to the master control room. She ate her lunch alone or with the other PAs, and watched the show on one of the newsroom monitors. She tried to act as if everything was normal, and hoped everyone else would too. Still… she picked up on small differences in how Billings and Mr. Carswell interacted with her. They never said a word to her about the party, remaining just as much the dedicated newsman and the dignified executive as she had always known them to be. Yet every once in a while, a hint of something else poked through. Less smiling than normal. Less banter. And always a downturned head as she parted from them. All of it was something that she only vaguely comprehended based on the accounts of her childhood friends. Looking at either of them, she had the distinct impression of an old man's sadness directed at a brokenhearted grandchild.

Sometime during the first few lonely days of the new year, she came to realized that all of her wonder at riding on Chicago's subway system was gone. Initially, she ascribed this lack of enthusiasm to a seasonal change. She, like everyone else, despised how the winter wind whipped at her during long waits on a platform. So her sour feelings were nothing more than the cold penetrating through a poorly insulated car… or the unfortunate consequence of riding to work in the dark and returning home the same way. But in her heart, she knew none of that to be the real reason behind her despair. Twice a day on the West-Northwest route, she dispiritedly rattled along with the rest of Chicago. She had absolutely no desire for securing a window seat, since watching the city fly by no longer stirred the imagination in her. Anywhere on the car was fine, as long as she could be left alone. When she did venture to look outside, what she saw was more than depressing. Shoebox houses packed together… one after another… each with spiked roofs desperately fending off the snow. The passing buildings were nothing more than an anonymous flow of brick, glass, mortar and wood. Wire upon wire between them did not connect – they bound and imprisoned. Workers lost to the ages had poured all of this concrete about her, placing pillar and pole with purpose… yet not for her. Railway switches with their converging and diverging tracks had meaning only in the mind of some anonymous engineer. Even the people inside the subway car with her were not real. At best, they were a collective testimony to a city's daily drudgery. So her eyes turned inward, avoiding the faces of her fellow travelers. For she had become like them, thinking only of herself. The 'if only' affairs of her heart had taken a full grip on her, and she was unaware of anything else. Not once did she offer anyone a hello, a pardon me, or a thank you. So very much unlike her Texas.

Day after day, the city of Chicago buried her. To never see the horizon, it being eclipsed by embankment and building… or blocked out entirely in tunnel and underpass… it became an indescribable burden on her. To continually exist in such a constricted state wore away at her. Chicago offered her no sky. Even the slivers she could see through snow-covered limbs or the narrow gaps between tall buildings were only gray colored. All of the blue had gone out of her life… and so had the wide-open feel of her homeland. To be sure, she knew that there was horizon to be had nearby. She could simply venture down to the lake. Along its shore, there were ample vistas offering an escape from the city… or so her coworkers claimed. But the thought of being so near to those waters disquieted her. The horizon across Lake Michigan was not hers, for it taunted at a different sort of view of reality… an unreachable one. That horizon teased her with a lie that she had never been able to fight off. For somewhere across that immense expanse of dark water to a far shore lay two graves… and a life she would never know.

In the third week of January, she entered the master control room to find a stranger occupying the sound board normally manned by Grass. She was mildly curious, but more so relieved that running back and forth to the control room would be considerably easier today. But the same stranger was in Grass's place on the following day. This continued for near on a week before she mustered up the nerve to ask the director.

"He's gone. Took a job in Cleveland. I'm sure going to miss him and his music."

The man suddenly looked at her with unease… right before abruptly steering the subject to the script fragment she had been tasked to bring him. On leaving the master control room and returning to the AE who had sent her there, it occurred to her that with Grass, it was now two – the number of faithful employees of WYNG news who had left because of her.

HIGH SKY AND LOW CEILING

She experienced an unexpected reprieve from the advances of the opposite sex in the aftermath of Grass's departure. This freedom came at a price, as she knew that rumors were still circulating about her. Grass had been very popular at the station… so it seemed that her male coworkers all believed that she had cruelly broken off a serious relationship with him over something trivial. Some shunned her outright, whereas others only awkwardly acknowledged her presence in their conversations. But as if overnight, her standing with them somehow changed. The single guys in the newsroom suddenly began asking her out in droves. Even the married men like weatherman Morgan were creeping her out with how frequently they kept popping up in her presence. As to this restored popularity, Rose unceremoniously offered her unsolicited opinion one afternoon in the ladies' room.

"What'd you expect, Marna… they're even more fascinated with you than before."

She need not ask Rose what was meant by 'before'… nor was she tempted in believing that any of this new attention was wholesome. Very unjustly, the newsroom had somehow come to the conclusion that she was easy.

Still terribly hurt because of Grass, as well as the unfair reputation she had received due to that horrible night with him, she purposed to remain fully on guard. She would not make another grass dance mistake. So, for the sake of her career, she chose to overlook those instances when a man laid a hand on her shoulder… or when his eyes concentrated on those regions of her person below neck level… or the not-so-veiled sexual innuendos she had to endure all of the time. She did this for herself… for her own advancement… and not because she felt tolerant toward their improper behaviors. But such concessions daily only weakened her self-worth… something she doubted seriously that any man ever had to deal with.

Like Gwen always said, it's a male-dominated world we're fighting against.

Billings had ordered her to go make coffee… so she obeyed. Standing here in the breakroom spooning out grounds into a percolator, she was fighting against a resentment toward him that had never before shown itself.

He doesn't ask any of the male PAs to do this for him… just me!

Of course, she knew that Billings liked her more than any of those PAs… but maybe that had nothing to do with her being good at her job. Maybe it was only because she happened to be an attractive young woman.

Sophie was right… we're always the ones at the bottom of the totem pole.

That bitter verdict was staring right back at her in the form of the one-eyed appliance sitting on the countertop. She was made to do this task nearly every day for the men of the newsroom, irrespective of her supposed place on the totem pole, all because Billings said that only a woman knew how to make good coffee.

She had already poured the water in… inserted the plug into the outlet… and was now waiting on the brewing. She had performed this task so many times… but now saw it differently. Making coffee was a symbol of servitude. Just as with her own frustrations, this pot had only slowly warmed up to its situation, yet finally was getting quite hot. The first bit of steam came to the window, fogging away all clarity. The bubbling soon began in earnest. With a violent churning, the drops began to splatter against the small window. But no matter how hard they hit, the barrier held firm. Nothing – not a single drop – ever made its way through that glass ceiling. There was no escaping the truth.

Women just aren't allowed to go very far in this business.

The only women working at WYNG were secretaries… or make-up artists… or lowly PAs like herself. Okay… sure… there were a couple female reporters and anchors… but somehow she did not think of them as professionals… at least not since those words of Click on the steps of City Hall. Those women were just pretty things for men to look at.

'If' became her motto. Something she repeated over and over until it was permanently on the forefront of her mind. She did nothing to fight off its influence. Instead, she outright wallowed in its bitterness.

If he says that one more time in front of me...
If he so much as touches me again...
If he insists on treating me like a little girl...
If only he could show me some respect...
If only he would just give me a chance...
If only I was a he... and if only he were a she... then he'd finally understand!

The identity of 'he' changed from day to day, but the feeling of 'if' stayed largely the same, feeding into her frustrations and beleaguering her thinking about herself. She knew the word was hollow. No amount of fretting could break her through that glass ceiling into a vast blue sky of opportunity. She needed to do things extraordinarily better than any man in order to receive even half the respect. She had to be creative... and resourceful... and shrewd. She might even have to take risks... such as coming across as a flirt in order to get the more coveted assignments. Above all, she had to remain in the forefront of Billings' admiration... even if it meant having to make coffee for him.

She had eclipsed a full year at WYNG, and therefore felt it necessary to begin searching for a way of turning her experience into something of a career. She considered herself clever enough... and good with words. She had the drive and the work ethic too. Yet one thing was lacking. Everywhere she looked, she was confronted with a singularly harsh reality that had nothing to do with her being a woman. If she ever hoped to make it in journalism, then she absolutely must have a degree. Nobody rose in the business without one. But that truth was too painful to bear. On her own at twenty four, with no money to her name, she could not possibly see how a college education would ever come her way.

So she headed into her second year at WYNG with no other option but to continue as she was. 'If' was now becoming more of a weaselly sort of word to her, used in connection with her searching for better opportunities. Contrary to her previous affirmation, becoming a reporter was beginning to look like her only way out of this PA purgatory. So with an ear to the WYNG grapevine, she remained ready to pounce on the first opening in the reporting core. That, at least, might get her a place at the meeting room table.

Perhaps the time was prime for her to make a change. The newsroom had been abuzz with gossip for weeks that the network was looking to modernize its flagship stations. The word was that WYNG, in particular, seemed ill-positioned for the future. Old ways had to be swept out the door, and modern ways must be ushered in. After all, it might only have been a week since Neil Armstrong and Buzz Aldrin made history for all of mankind, but everyone was already saying 'if we can put a man on the moon, then why can't we…?' It never mattered how that statement was ended, for the real message reflected a frustration over how things had been done in the past.

So… if they can put a man on the moon, then why can't I have a decent career without a college education?!

All of the summer rumors came to a head on the last day of July, as she arrived at work to find the entire WYNG newsroom thrown into a turmoil of intrigue. The network had abruptly pastured the current station manager the previous night, and was bringing in a replacement that very morning. This person was purportedly from a very influential Boston family with old money and a substantial financial interest in the station's parent company. More importantly, this man was a recent Harvard business graduate with both the youthful vigor and visionary skills necessary for leading WYNG into the space-age. This, they learned from Mr. Carswell during the morning meeting.

"And he'll be here any minute to introduce himself."

The room was suddenly astir with so much excited conversation. Not Billings though. She noticed that he just sat quietly in his chair, occasionally exchanging a whispered word with Mr. Carswell. She had been watching the two of them for a while when everything suddenly went quiet. Standing in the open doorway was a man who could not possibly be that much older than herself.

"All here, I see. Well done, Bertram."

As the young man scanned the table for an available seat, he seemed completely unphased that every eye was on him. Right off, she knew that made him out to be the type of person who was very comfortable with being watched. Since the only open spot was at the far end from Billings, and directly before where she stood, he moved to take this seat, smoothly stepping into the room with a very upright glide of a walk.

If she had once thought Mr. Carswell to be the epitome of business attire, this young man blew the room away. His suit was definitely of European tailoring – pencil straight pant legs, suit coat with sharp lines and tight edges, and the whole thing set in a robin eggshell blue that shouted out confidence. The suit fit him so snugly, also reinforcing a notion in her mind that it was expressing its gratitude in being worn by him. Whereas Billings had joked that Mr. Carswell had been born wearing a suit, the opposite was the case for this young man. This suit had clearly been born for him! Yet in an interesting and equally bold touch, she noticed that he had adorned his left lapel with a buttercup, very newly opened. Her inescapable conclusion was that this man made his own rules. She had just begun to admire the boldness behind his choice of a scarlet necktie when she sensed his eyes fall upon her. Quickly diverting her attention toward the far end of the table, she did not miss the look of disgust on Billings' face.

He's definitely thinking 'pretty boy.'

The young man took the open chair with an air that it had been saved expressly for him. He wiggled about in his comfort for a few seconds, leaning forward and then back again, but always with the knowledge that everyone was watching him. Or at least that was how it seemed from her vantage point of observing how all eyes were, in fact, still fixed on him. He cleared his throat in the silence of the room, again enhancing the overall anticipation over what would come next.

"Thank you for your attention. Allow me to introduce myself… my name is Clayton Fitzroy Azurean the third… but I would prefer very much being addressed as Mr. Azurean. I suppose most of you know by now that the station has a new manager." He paused here, and even from behind she could tell that he had lifted his hands from his lap in order to point all of his fingers back toward himself. "Perhaps you are wondering what has brought about this change in management, and what new priorities I bring from corporate in setting the station's future direction. I can assure you that in due time… after I've had an opportunity to see firsthand the strengths and needs of WYNG… that we will *together* be charting an exciting new course forward."

She looked over to the Berts. One, with a constant nodding of his head, was affirming the words of his new boss… whereas the other was having none of it. Still… both men seemed nervous, especially based on how they were leaning in close together. She returned to Mr. Azurean, who was now sitting back in his chair such that the only parts of him she could see were his finely combed hair and a bit of the collar to his suit.

"In order to accomplish this goal, it is of supreme importance that I first meet you, the employees of the station, and do my utmost to win your support. I will take no more of your valuable time today than this. I am aware that you have a news program to put on…"

All of a sudden, every face in the room burst forth into broad smiles… except that of Billings, of course. Whatever Mr. Azurean had done, the effect lasted for only a second before everyone was serious again.

"So… what say we go around once so I can hear your names?"

Without skipping a beat, Billings introduced himself and then progressed rapidly around the table in ticking off names. He had only gotten to the third individual when Mr. Azurean interrupted.

"What say we be a bit more… democratic. Let's have each person introduce themselves. Titles also… that is most important."

She saw Billings' jawline tighten… just before he started over with himself. But he barely got a syllable out on his role at WYNG before Mr. Azurean interrupted once more… this time, with such a display of mortification in his voice that it was so obviously artificial.

"Do forgive me… but maybe also where you hail from."

Billings had enough, and just waved for the next person to go instead. To each one, Mr. Azurean offered a polite acknowledgement before turning to the next. When it came time for the PAs… whom she doubted seriously Billings would have included… Mr. Azurean swiveled about to face the back wall. When it came her turn, she barely got out her first name before being interrupted.

"My… what an absolutely delightful accent!"

She was momentarily stunned in being singled out, but what really froze her was his smile. Starting with lips parting evenly to reveal perfect teeth, the smile's upward curl perked up his dimpled cheeks all the way to the corners of his eyes. Those sparkled as they took over… and the brow also got into it with a sort of 'hop'… as if surprised at being included in the pleasure coming to his face. The presentation did not stop there. Having taken in his eyes, hers were drawn back down the bridge of his nose to his lips again… which collapsed into a very modest arc. This last bit, as if giving off a feel of great modesty, was the thing that made her smile back.

"So much more interesting than all of this Midwestern plainness! A vernacular's vanilla, if you will."

He waved a hand about in the air behind his head. She followed its motion to the faces arrayed about the table. Not one of them was smiling now.

"So… where might you be from, Miss?"

"Lubbock, Texas, sir… but I was born in Michigan."

Why on earth she had added that last part was beyond her.

"Lubbock… that, if I'm not mistaken, is in West Texas?"

"Yes, sir."

Again, Mr. Azurean smiled deeply, and she must smile back. He continued on to the next PA. She could not help herself then in glancing toward Billings, whose brow was raised into a false surprise… just for her. She was sure to catch it from him later.

For the remainder of the meeting, Mr. Azurean stayed respectfully silent as Billings and his AE's went about discussing the pertinent stories of the day. Still… no one about the table could help from shooting furtive glances toward the new station manager as they spoke... almost if seeking his approval on their contribution about a massive gas leak... or a pile-up on the Northwest Tollway... or rumors of more bickering within the Mayor's office.

The meeting concluded with Billings bolting out of the room considerably faster than she had ever seen him do. Nearly everyone nodded first toward the new station manager before following their boss out. For her part, she was anxious to catch up with Billings in order to get his take... and his ribbing... on the new station manager, but had not reached the door before being called back.

"Hold it please, Miss... ahh... Marna. I say, Bertram, can you spare this young lady for the morning? I should very much like to have a tour of your newsroom."

She turned about to behold that winning smile again, but this time did not feel so inclined to return it.

"I'm sure she would be more than happy to give you a tour."

To her great unease, Mr. Azurean took hold of her hand with both of his in offering her a personalized greeting... and simply would not let go. Glancing out the glass barrier to the newsroom, she was embarrassed by the number of faces turned back toward her. So she pulled her hand away and quickly pivoted toward the assignment board as a distraction.

"So... Mr. Azurean... I'm sure you noticed how we keep track of who's doing what, but I'd like to point out..."

"Please, call me Clay. There's no need to be so formal when it's just the two of us."

The two of us?!

"But I thought you wanted...?"

"Yes, yes... for Mr. Carswell and his immediate reports. But under the circumstances, I think this tour would flow so much more smoothly if we dropped all pretense, don't you?"

"Umm... if you prefer, sir. So... umm... notice here that we have..."

"And let's not waste time on the routine things. Show me those things that you, Marna... ahh, pardon me... what did you say your last name was?"

"Forde... with... umm... an 'e' at the end."

He smiled in acknowledgement of her spelling, and just with Billings on her first day, she wanted to kick herself.

"So Miss Marna Forde... with an 'e' at the end... from Lubbock, Texas... what do you find to be most interesting about working here?"

She led him out toward the back hall to show him the receive room, but had already become convinced that the new station manager was more interested in receiving a tour of Miss Marna Forde from Lubbock, Texas, than he was in learning anything about WYNG news. All through the tour, he kept her busy with odd questions about her work day – what she did, whom she interacted with, and where she spent most of her time. After over an hour of this, she finally managed to steer him toward the executive producer's suite. There, she found Mr. Carswell standing in a fidgety sort of way within the glass door to Rose's office... obviously so very anxious to be back in the presence of his new boss.

"I do say, Marna... this has been the most delightful hour I've spent since arriving in Chicago. Please... allow me to return the favor. Perhaps you would enjoy a tour of the main station? I can assure you that the sets, control rooms, and equipment upstairs are all far more impressive than what you have down here."

Before she could respond, Mr. Azurean once more took hold of her right hand in both of his. She thought this to be exceedingly unprofessional... especially since both Mr. Carswell and Rose were watching. But what was she, a lowly PA, to do when her boss's boss's boss wanted to go overboard in showing his gratitude?!

"Umm... that would be... most kind of you, Mr. Azurean..." He cocked his head at her with a reproving sort of frown, and she immediately knew what he was after. Glancing toward the other two, she lowered her voice so as not to be heard. "I mean... Clay. Thank you, though... but I've already seen just about everything at the station... except the transmitter, of course. That's on the roof."

In no way had she intended this to be a suggestion, but he promptly latched onto it.

"Then I will personally see to it that you do."

Finally free of him, she made her way back into the newsroom. There, she found Billings waiting on her... and not at all in a mood to tease.

"That took forever, Forde."

"I know! I only just got shed of him."

"Well... what do you think?"

"He's definitely charming... and comfortable with himself. But... I don't know, sir..."

"You don't know what?!"

"Well... to me... he seems a bit... young... don't you think? I mean... to be in the position of managing a station. I'm not implying that he can't do the job. It's just..."

She hesitated in not knowing how to phrase a reservation about matters far above her.

"Spit it out, Forde!

"To tell you the truth, sir… I'm not at all convinced he's even interested in the job. He seems to have… other things on his mind."

"My thoughts exactly. He's up to something. Listen… Phillips needs you to confirm the rumors about Shirley Chisholm coming to Chicago next week… but before you do that…" He quickly glanced about the newsroom from his perch in the assignment desk. On being convinced of what it would take not to be overheard, he lowered his voice to a whisper. "…I want you to find out why the hell the network sent us this guy. By all accounts, he's got no experience for the job. Bertram's as clueless as everyone else at the station. I hate to ask you to do this… but if you could… you know… get close enough to him… maybe he'll let something slip. Don't do anything you don't feel…"

In a flash, he switched gears as another PA appeared at her side.

"Ferguson, what the hell took you so long?! Forget it… just give me the damn print out! Forde… stop lulling around like a moron and get back to work!"

How was she supposed to find out a station manager's intentions?! That job was so very far above her… both in scope and in terms of two floors to the building. Billings would just have to find out on his own. So she went about her duties, putting the weirdness of the morning out of her mind. The day passed largely as usual, with the newsroom having resumed its normal activities under the assumption that their new station manager had adequately satisfied his curiosity as to WYNG news. She took moments here and there to learn what others thought of the man, finding that the general consensus to be like hers.

An hour prior to the evening show, she was surprised when Rose made a rare appearance at the assignment desk to state before Billings… in equal measures of blandness and mock irritation… that Mr. Azurean had called down to request the immediate presence of one 'Miss Marna Forde' in the twelfth floor lobby. As she was so obviously standing at the far end of the horseshoe counter, very plain for Rose to see, the formal manner in which this message was delivered came across as very ridiculous. Billings, too disgusted to speak, simply waved a hand over his shoulder, giving her leave to follow in behind Rose.

"Well… it seems someone has made quite an impression on the new station manager."

The past year of working closely with Billings had rubbed off on her, so she was not at all surprised with herself in how she responded.

"Shut up."

Neither was Rose, who immediately started laughing.

"I guess I deserved that."

Rose followed her all the way to the lobby elevator… even summoned a car for her… and then stood by silently until it came. Just as the doors were closing, Rose stuck in a hand to restrain them.

"A word of caution before you ride up this elevator… Rich and powerful men are accustomed to getting what they want in life. You be careful up there."

She only had two floors worth of travel time to think over the implications of what Rose meant. Mr. Azurean was waiting for her in the lobby of the twelfth floor with another of his winning smiles. But he did not speak. He just stood there rocking back and forth on his heels with hands behind his back.

"Yes, sir… you wanted to see me?"

"I have it, Marna! I have it!"

He quickly produced a key chain from behind his back and started jingling it in her face with all of the enthusiasm of a sixteen year old who had just secured the family car for a date. She, however, had no idea of what he was referring to. Perhaps he sensed her confusion, as a bit of his smile wore off.

"The keys to the roof…" His eyes went upward, directing her thoughts that way too. "…for the transmitter room, of course! You did say you wanted to see it?!"

"Oh, yes! I'm sorry… I just wasn't expecting it… so soon."

"Well, you're still game, I presume? What say we explore together?"

Without waiting for her to respond, he motioned her back into the elevator, and they rode to the thirty fourth floor. After a few awkward moments of hunting for the stairwell door to the roof, they emerged into the wind and sunlight of an August afternoon. Aside from the heat, the first thing hitting her was the panorama of Lake Michigan stretched out in its deep purple, though the view was partly eclipsed by neighboring skyscrapers that dwarfed the Rollecastle building. She was so very high up. To stabilize her senses, she dropped her eyes to the gravel rooftop. There, stretching out from behind her was the shadow of the station's transmission tower. Turning about and looking up, her eyes followed the structure into the sky. Oddly aware that her dizziness was gone, she lifted a hand to shield her eyes from the sun… only to have Mr. Azurean grab it instead.

"This way, Marna! It's over here!"

He led her to a box-of-a-room situated in the center of the rooftop. Smiling at her with the mischievousness of a school boy intent on playing hooky, he fumbled about with the keys until he found the right one, and then wrestled the door open with a two-handed grip. He entered first, and she followed only after the lights had come on. Before her was equipment much more modern and orderly than any of her father-in-law's microwave facilities. George had tried so often to explain the roles that mixers, oscillators, amplifiers and boosters played in taking signals from wires and transmitting them through the air. To this day, she still chuckled to herself that all of that was 'over her head.'

In straining to recognize any of the components before her, she was only mildly aware of the door closing… or of Mr. Azurean approaching in behind her. She, intent on telling him about what she could recall from her past experiences, barely got out half a word before being spun about and pinned against the nearest rack of electronics. Her nose was immediately filled with the scent of his cologne, just as he impressed upon her a deep, passionate kiss. She could feel his hands gripping her ribs, holding her firmly against himself. Shocked to the core, she had her own hands on his chest preparing to shove him away… when something suddenly changed in her. Maybe it was because of who he was… or how handsome he carried himself… or how the kiss had begun to warm her. Whatever it was, she found her hands sliding of their own accord up to his shoulders. Wholeheartedly, she returned to him a measure of what she had not requested. How she had gotten here no longer mattered, for this very influential man had noticed her.

After several minutes of kissing, he was the one to break away… yet remained so close that she could look nowhere else but in his eyes. So very blue, they were.

"Miss Forde… Marna… I am not the type of man who hesitates when he sees what he wants. I can tell that you are intelligent, energetic, and oh so very attractive. Your down-home accent… it's nothing short of adorable. I want more of that… and I believe you are interested too. So… let us not dilly-dally about with the possibilities. Let us go with this feeling and see where it leads."

He seemed to be waiting for her to respond, and though she was preparing herself to speak… saying what, she did not yet know… he shook his head slightly to show that he was actually not yet finished.

"I shall arrange for a car to pick us up from the station after work, and you shall accompany me to dinner at…"

She needed to put a stop to this before it went any further. On the verge of declining, he again cut her off before she could speak.

"Please, Marna… allow me to finish just this once. I promise that if you do not enjoy my company tonight at dinner, then this shall be the one and only instance in which I openly express my interest in you."

She felt as one caught in a snare, with the trapper standing over her vowing to set her free if she but did tricks for him. He was so close… too close to permit clear thinking. Try as she might, she could not wrench herself away from his eyes… so blue… just like his name. Then… inexplicably… he released her and took a step back, smiling as he had done before. Somehow… that made up her mind.

"Yes... that would be nice."

By agreement originating from her desire for discretion, they met in the building's parking garage after work. Before having left the roof, she inquired about whether she should go home first to change into something more suitable for dinner at a fine restaurant, but he waved off her concern, saying that she was 'the essence of loveliness.' They entered his waiting car, and he gave his driver instructions. There then was a whole lot of uncomfortable talk on her part about being appreciative for this dinner date... and he just smiled right through all of her awkwardness. They were soon dropped off before the front door of *Le Petit Château.* Despite his assurances, she still felt so very under-dressed for the elegance of this French restaurant. Even the wait-staff were in formal attire... and here she sat at a candle-lit corner table wearing a boorishly-gray tweed business suit that she had thought so stylish that very morning.

When it came time, Clay did the ordering for them... speaking entirely in French. She hid how small that made her feel by commenting on how impressive his language skills were. He smiled back... and soon they were clinking glasses of red wine together. Only then did she consider what Billings had asked her to do, but her first sip brought a flush, so she decided that Billings' request could come later. She wanted to hear more about what Clay thought of her first. He complimented her hair, her eyes, the loveliness of her voice, and so much more. It was all coming too fast. She wanted him to slow down and make it last all the way through dinner. More sips of wine... and she was thinking about how handsome he was sitting there smiling at her... and how that kiss on the roof had done to her exactly what this wine was doing.

The waiter arrived to announce the first course.

"Young Portuguese hearts of romaine tossed lightly in a Viennese vinaigrette and sprinkled with shavings of Moroccan cashew."

Maybe it was the waiter's presence or just that a bit of her own mind had come back to her. What was she doing here?! This salad... so elegantly arranged... was very far above her standards. She nervously took up a fork... but found herself staring down at her plate. This place was not her... and equally, this man was not hers. How could she, in her heart, be treating this as a date?! It clearly was not. It felt off... and not because of some ridiculous geographic puzzle she was trying to figure out from the waiter who had served this dish.

"My dear, is there something amiss with your salad?"

"Oh... no, it's fine. More than fine... it's... amazing. Only... Clay... I'm a bit embarrassed to say... but I've never been in a restaurant as fancy as this before. To tell you the truth… I'm much more familiar with the kinds of places where the food gets served on a brown paper bag."

She caught a hint of perplexity coming to his face as he went back to his own salad.

Why in the world did you have to say that?!

Maybe it was for the better. If he saw the real her, then maybe she could put an end to this ridiculous charade before things got out of hand.

Just relax, Marna, and enjoy the food. You know that this date… if that's what it can be called… isn't heading anywhere.

She cleared her throat, pointing a fork down at her plate as he looked up.

"You know… in Texas, we call this sort of thing 'what food eats.'"

He stared back with a blank expression, oddly accentuated by the way a speared leaf was dangling from his fork. She had done it again… but this time it was absolutely fine. She was being herself.

But to her surprise, he burst out laughing, dropping his fork to the salad dish to commence a slow, genteel sort of clap… four fingertips lightly tapping the center of his palm. In contrast, his boisterous laugh resonated throughout the restaurant, with every head in the vicinity turning their way. He just kept it up until he was fully satisfied with his own enjoyment of the moment.

"Marna, you are such a delight! *What food eats!* My, my… you held me spellbound with that one."

"I'm… glad you think so."

To her further surprise, he turned about to take in the restaurant around them, clearly not dissuaded by any kind of embarrassment from the disruption of his own laughter. He seemed to be re-evaluating the place… perhaps as if through her eyes.

"Yes… I can see how this sort of establishment might fall short of your home state's exquisite barbeque standards. But let us make the most of it, shall we?"

They chatted their way through the salad, as she asked about what it was like to grow up in Boston and he asked about Lubbock. Though still far from at ease, the wine's influence fully reached her head shortly after the waiter had removed their salad plates. Its gentle buzz… it felt real good. Calmed her right down. Clay Azurean was likely rich… and certainly handsome too. She could sit across from him any day of the week. She again remembered that kiss… and wondered if it would be just as nice a second time around.

The waiter brought plates bearing a small amount of ground-up something presented on a thin gelatinous layer with a sprig on top. Pâté, according to Clay. She resisted the urge to tell him that a Texan would be upset about how much unused space was on this plate, and instead concentrated on replicating his mannerisms in sampling the dish. After all, she had already used up her allotment of homespun. Clay carefully carved out a small bit and followed it up with a sip of wine. Every movement of his was so elegant... so smooth and graceful. In august fashion, he proclaimed the appetizer a success and encouraged her to try hers. With one glass of wine down, she felt comfortable in deciding that she wanted this man to see a deeper side to her... a more sophisticated self than what an accent might convey. So she took a small forkful and brought it to her mouth with what she hoped was the same care he had displayed. It tasted salty.

More dishes came, and to each, she followed in behind his 'oohs' and 'aahs' with what she hoped was the same level of appreciation of a cuisine that was so very far above her palate's experience. They were into their entrées of duck à l'orange when he directed the conversation away from the food.

"Part of the reason I asked you to dinner tonight, Marna... a small one, if you will..." He smiled as before, adding on a little wink that gave her a moment of pause. "...is to request your assistance in a matter of great sensitivity. There are forces in motion that cannot be held back. After all, opportunity awaits at the doorstep only for those with the imaginativeness and force of will to seize it."

"I'm sorry... I'm... not following you. How can I be of help to you with any of that? I'm... just a PA."

"Why, Marna, you have the potential to be so much more than that. I knew it the very moment I set off with you on your tour. You spoke effortlessly and with such intelligence. Clearly you understand a great deal about the inner workings of broadcast news. You know, I absolutely believe that you have the insight necessary to be my eyes and ears in the WYNG newsroom."

Such compliments had her heart racing with pleasure... yet something was not quite right. She sat in silence for several seconds before finally understanding his meaning... and the wine gave her the boldness to be blunt.

"Are you saying you want me to spy for you?"

"No, no, my dear! That's far too boorish of a caricature for my true purposes. Allow me to begin again. We find ourselves on the threshold of a new era in communications... the satellite age. There has never been a time before in human history in which an event on one side of the globe can be viewed live in the safety of a home on the other. Even the moon is at our fingertips. There is a new dawn arising, and every network executive across the country senses it. In not too many months..." He leaned across the table... almost conspiratorially. "...and I have this on good authority... the FCC will open the heavens to the limitless utilization of satellites for telecommunication. Imagine what that will mean for business… for the news… even for the average person on the street. Perhaps you've heard of the term 'Blue Sky' in reference to the movement for freeing up the cable industry to local utilization?"

"Yes… I'm fairly familiar with the expression. Remember I mentioned this morning that I once worked at a CATV network before coming to Chicago?"

"Excellent! Yes! Now you know precisely where my thoughts lie."

She had no idea where he was going, but figured that interrupting him was a poor way of finding out.

"All that rubbish about local involvement and citizen's access… it all misses the greater point. We exist in a capital-driven society. Those who have the capital also have the responsibility… dare I say, the right… to use those resources in advancing the market for all. Cable's proven technological promise, when coupled with satellite technology… why, it will radically change the industry of broadcast TV! And that includes the news. You do realize that the newspaper and radio are practically dead media… They just don't know it yet. Soon, every American will be looking exclusively to satellite TV for news… for information and opinion about the things most important to their day-to-day lives. Imagine, if you will, being able to turn on your TV to discover, in real time, what's happening in… Hong Kong… or Cape Town… or Paris. And of course, it will work the other way around too. The world will be tuning in to Chicago. Just think of it – advertising with a global reach! And here's the most magnificent part – the FCC will be completely helpless! Unlike broadcast TV… which is a medium… they won't be able to regulate satellite TV because it'll be a market! Ironic, don't you think?! Marna… forget about 'Blue Sky.' The 'Open Skies' era is upon us!"

He paused to take a sip of wine. In that brief interim, her head spun about with all sorts of new possibilities. She knew that she, at the core of her being, was so very naïve about the things he was telling her. She was nothing more than a small fish who, for the moment, had come alongside a whale-of-a-person. But this man before her had set his designs on mastering the open sky… and she wanted that feeling more than anything else. Not to swim, but to soar. Within her was a desire to be much more than what she was. So to be present at the beginning of something new and important… that would be far more fulfilling than running bits of paper about a TV newsroom. This man… this handsome young man… so full of the finer things in life… was he offering her… so uncultured and inexperienced… an opportunity to participate in his dream?

"Which brings me back to my request. I am not asking you to spy… that sounds so vulgar, Marna. What I need from you… or anyone in the WYNG newsroom, for that matter… is cooperation. In order to see this grand vision of global news come to fruition, the industry must adopt new perspectives. The old ways of telling news stories within the confines of a half-hour block simply must go, because global events don't happen that way. The news will need to be more… nimble and adaptive… if you follow me. So… it is my ambition to reposition WYNG news… and the whole station, in fact… to seize that opportunity when the parent network comes calling. That's why I've been sent here, to revitalize the station from the ground up. And Marna, I want you… as well as other ambitious employees just like yourself… to help me lead that charge."

In the quiet pause, she became aware that her hands were wringing the napkin about in her lap, just as she was also leaning forward over the table, eager to catch his every word. Everything had changed in her. Beyond a doubt, she wanted what this man was offering. His grand vision… that was something worthy of becoming her vision too. Her opportunity for real significance in this world. This was more than just a chance to escape the smallness of herself. This was about becoming really big! Besides, he alone had seen her potential, and he alone cared enough to offer her a way of reaching it. That was truly rare!

Back in his car having just left the restaurant, the first words out of his mouth were not about the grand vision they had discussed during dinner, but in reference to their 'agreement' made in the rooftop transmitter room.

"Well… did you enjoy yourself tonight?"

"Immensely."

The word was hardly out of her mouth before his lips were upon hers. Not forcefully, but very much with a gentle persuasion as to his full intentions.

"Then it need not end here. Come with me… to my penthouse for a night cap. There, you and I shall toast to our new partnership."

He had a hold of her hand, gently stroking it with his.

"Clay… it's… really late… I should probably be getting home…"

"Come, come, Marna… where is your sense of adventure?"

"It's… umm…"

"Marna… I require no promises, but am prepared to make one to you. Come with me this night, and I will devote myself to helping you reach your dreams… together, you and me."

His words touched her. Sure, the wine probably contributed to her feelings, but it was much more than that. She had not been held close in a very long time, and she wanted that feeling back… badly. Especially tonight. And in her heart of hearts, she knew who she had become. So what did it matter to be that thing once more… or always and evermore. Considering such things was stupid anyway. She would go with this man to his penthouse, enjoy this moment with him, and hope for better as a result. He, being so much higher than her, was promising to open up vast new horizons of opportunity for her. He had recognized her true potential, and she would never find a man better than that.

Without further delay, she nodded her surrender.

She spent that night in the bed of Clay Azurean. Waking in the morning, she knew exactly where she was and how she had gotten there. Turning over beneath silken sheets, she watched him in his last few moments of sleep, deciding again that because he was handsome, rich, and interested in her, then perhaps through him she might come to discover something bigger of herself in this wide world. She was naked, though she noticed that he had covered his lower half during the night with a pair of royal-blue pajama pants. She poked him awake, seeking comfort in the embrace of a man she honestly could not call the love of her life. Not yet, at least. She once more engaged him in sex, and then they playfully went about showering together. Through the soap and steam, his affections for her had not lessened one degree. A woman just knows… this man was already devoted to her. Remarkable… one night together and he was already considering her his own.

As she set about dressing in the same clothes as the night before, Clay said he would fix that situation for her in the future… leaving her not quite sure as to his meaning. Regrettably, he could not spare time this morning himself since he had pressing business in New York that required immediate packing. Instead, he insisted that his driver take her home. They rode down together in his private elevator to the basement garage of the high rise, and there, he kissed her into his car. Within an hour of leaving his penthouse, she found herself safely deposited onto the sidewalk outside her apartment. During the ride, she had tried multiple times to subtly illicit some sort of judgment about her from the driver, but the man just faced forward the whole time, responding to her offhand comments with two-to-three word sentences. There was nothing in his demeanor or tone other than respectful indifference toward the woman who had so clearly spent the night with his boss.

She quickly changed and caught the subway back into town. It was not as if she could present a teacher's note excusing herself from arriving over two hours late for work. Surprisingly, neither Billings nor anyone else in the newsroom said a word to her about the offense. It was, more-or-less, business as usual. Yet all through that day, she faced a different sort of vibe coming from her colleagues at WYNG news. How they had found out, she could not say... and would never venture to ask... but somehow everybody knew that she had spent the night with Clay Azurean, the new station manager and the ultimate authority over everyone. She had become his lover, and that label made her radioactive.

Who cares?! He's amazing... and they're just jealous!

Being with him was all she could think about. Last night had been so wonderful! So eye opening! And the passion – she definitely wanted more of that! More of the smile. More of the arms about her. More of his inspiring words. She wanted everything to do with him! To bathe herself in the richness of him and make it her own. At last, she was on her way toward something incredible in life. How that would come about was unclear, but the mystery was the magic. Soon, his dreams would take shape, and then so would hers. Her paired with him... it was more than special. It was 'look out world, here comes Marna and Clay'! Oh, the things that they would accomplish together! The possibilities were endless! So handsome, so refined, and so... debonair! Only one day with him, and already she could feel the weight of her hicksville past molting off of her. The sense of liberation that gave her... that she was finally being recognized and taken seriously... that was worth every sideways leer she was receiving from her coworkers. Soon enough, they would come to see her for who she really was – a person of true significance.

She spent many more evenings with Clay in the weeks to come, and woke up each morning afterward in his bed. Day by day, the feeling grew in her that she was more to him than a lover. She was his girlfriend... just as he openly referred to her whenever they were together. Yet for her, she did not quite know what to call him. She was still waiting for that feeling – the one everyone knows when it hits them. She was just as crazy about him as on the first day, but could not yet feel that warm assurance of being in love. So what was she to make of herself in this?! She had only known him for such a short time, and yet their intimacy had jumped lightyears out ahead of her opportunities for building a true regard for him. She really needed to work on that. But what she did not need to work on was the feeling of significance he gave her. That was worth everything!

For now, Clay was somewhere between her lover and her boyfriend... much closer to the former than the latter. Surely with more time together, she would come to see him as a full-fledged boyfriend. She still considered him as being rich and influential, which made her feel real special. The visionary sorts of things that they had talked about on their first night were still present in their conversations, but added in now was a whole lot more of that romantic nonsense. She could come up with no better word for it than that. He wanted to coo about the stars in her eyes, and she just wanted to hear more about satellites. Odd… he did not seem to notice that there was less of the sweet sappiness coming from her than he was doling out himself. But as long as she was adoring him, commenting on his looks, charming personality, and how wonderful it was to be with him, then he was happy.

She was happy too, for she still considered him just as handsome as ever. His smile continued to draw her in. Yet as she spent more and more time with him, she was slowly coming to feel that something was lacking in that smile. An odd sort of deficiency that she could not quite put a finger on. Maybe a slight… insincerity… that somehow extinguished her feeling of warmth once the smile was taken away. No bother… he still treated her with such great respect, as he said was due to any girlfriend of his. He lavished her with many gifts… as well as the attentiveness of his presence. Whenever she was with him, she felt herself as within a glow… not so warm as very bright. He took her out to the finest restaurants and shows, and always seemed ecstatic in having her decked out on his arm. She did her best to earn that privilege by making him the center of the conversation. Actually… he was not the best of listeners… unless she was talking about him and his ideas. That was okay, as that was what she most wanted to hear from him.

But their time in bed… it never seemed to measure up to the passion they shared on that first night. It was still good, but his evolving approach to foreplay was beginning to annoy her. He expected to be flattered before, during and after… and not just with words of devotion. He wanted her utmost praise of his every move. Or maybe it was just that she was coming to see him as a less-than-considerate lover. For one, he would more-often-than-not get right down to the business of satisfying himself, and then leave her to coax out something similar from whatever remained of his desire. Sometimes, he even went out like a light after his own climax, leaving her wide awake in a state of incompleteness.

At such times, she would slip out of his bed to stand before the glass of his penthouse view and stare out at the city lights. Weather permitting, she would even cloak herself for a brief foray into the wind on the narrow deck outside. She would then fill her eyes with the wonder of the view below. The city always provided her with a sampling of its grandeur… yet never seemed to take her all the way into a confidence of knowing that she actually owned that view. Clay belonged in this penthouse, but not her. Odd… she had never really found herself requiring much from the starlight above Chicago. Generally speaking, the sky here was often shrouded in cloud and dampened by the city's substitutes below. Not like on those crystal clear nights in West Texas. There, nothing ever seem to interfere with her becoming part of the heavens. After getting her fill, she would return to Clay's bed, just as lonely as when she had left it.

She frequently told herself that she was not in love with Clay Azurean. Not really. But she was in love with how he made her feel about herself… and equally in love with what he represented. He promised her a high, blue sky, and the real opportunity of breaking through to it. With Clay, she had a bright future. And she was important to him too. As proof, she need only recall how often he sought out her opinion on the operations of the newsroom, as well as the overall efficiency of the staff at WYNG. He valued her every insight. He often said that she was everything a man could want in a woman – beauty, charm, intelligence, and such passion. In her, he said he recognized fully the drive needed for climbing all the way to the top with him. He knew plenty of important people who would come to see her the same way. And she wholeheartedly believed him. After all, he was one of those people, and he had chosen her. As proof to her hopes, he repeatedly promised that there was a place of significance for her in his plans for the station.

"Marna… I can't go into the details just yet… but it'll be earthshaking. You wait and see! I can easily see you in some kind of a leadership role… especially once my plans have taken shape… and everyone has become comfortable with you dating the station manager. After all, perception is as important as reality in the world of business."

She clung to his promises in considering him to be the most exciting thing that had ever happened to her. Truly, she felt a momentum building in their relationship that would sustain her through the waiting… because unfortunately, she could not always be with him. Most days, she was who she was – a lowly PA working at WYNG. She still had to do the tedious chores associated with shuttling paper around a newsroom. There were also plenty of evenings in which Clay was out of town. Though he made his penthouse available to her, she did not feel it right to be there without him. Instead, she slept alone in her apartment as before. Riding the subway on those days was such an irritation. She wanted Clay's life… wanted his influence to be hers… even if she was not quite sure about wanting him. She definitely enjoyed being with him, but did she actually enjoy him? She was not so sure sometimes. Really… he was not the same kind of person as her. He had been born into privilege. She aimed for that too, but could not quite wrap her head around the notion of getting there without having had endured the struggle of earning it. Actually, what she valued most was her own independence. That would always be the foundation upon which she built a life of importance.

But being made to ride the subway was to face again that which was base, dirty, loud, and so very pressed upon. Whatever vigor remained after a day on her feet always got rung out of her during the jostles of a clattered ride home. To be confined in a small space with the weary made her weary, which threatened to bring back the meaninglessness she had experienced prior to meeting Clay. The only remedy to this frustration, taken in doses daily by her and every other low wage worker of Chicago, was allowing herself to be lulled asleep by the L.

After a wild night out celebrating the month of them being together, she woke up feeling slightly hung over. She had far too much wine to drink at dinner, and would be paying for it with a headache that was sure to follow her into the morning meeting. Clay was already up and nearly dressed, so she needed to hurry herself along. Stepping into his walk-in closet, she would first pick out her outfit for the day and then squeeze in a quick shower. Still a bit disoriented, she was having a difficult time deciding while at the same time listening to him talk about his plans for the day.

"As it is… I'm afraid I won't have time for breakfast with you after all. As you know, this is a decisive week for WYNG. My marketing study is complete… as is the cost analysis. Didn't want to bore you with the details at dinner last night, but it's finally time for me to free up the necessary capital for initiating the first phase of my plan. And for that… I have you to thank, Darling!"

In spite of her many attempts, he had remained very much hush-hush about his plan. Hearing that she had already played some critical role surprised her. Sticking her head out of the closet, she found him sitting at the edge of the bed putting his shoes on.

"Me?! I haven't done anything."

"Darling, really… your insights have provided me…" He purposefully paused to do that thing where he pointed in at himself. "…the station manager, with everything I need to know about who's important in the newsroom… and who's not. As you know, today is the last of the month… and the last day of the quarter. Next quarter's budget absolutely must be finalized today for corporate. They're very excited about my progress, you know… told me as much in a communiqué from the chairmen himself. So you see, I simply must get in as soon as possible. I've so many changes to make. Big ones that I've been holding back on until the last minute. First things first – I'm doing away with that absurd Christmas party! What a miserable waste of time and money! Marna dear… there's so much fat to be cut! I won't burden you with the specifics… but very exciting times are ahead." He then sighed deeply… which she knew was his call for sympathy. "You know… there's bound to be some malcontents."

"You mean from the cancelled party?"

"Oh… yes, that too. I was referring more to the tedious business of issuing pink slips to…"

"Pink slips?! What're you talking about?!"

"My dear, surely you're aware of the deadwood in the newsroom! The entire station is full of it. So much pruning to do."

She was absolutely stunned… and could not be hearing him correctly. He was sitting there fiddling with the lace of his shoe, not at all aware that she had gone mute from the shock.

"Well just don't stand there with your mouth agape! I'm in such a terrible hurry to… Wait… Marna dear… certainly you're not thinking that I would include *you* in the downsizing! Why… I consider you to be my most trusted ancillary! You, my dear, are my comfort and my courage. Rest assured, I will always have a place for you at *my* station."

"I… I…"

"Darling, please don't stand there stammering! Hurry it up… you really should be dressed by now."

"Umm… why don't you go on ahead without me. I need to… ahh… shower first and then… you know… do my hair and stuff. And you know what – I just realized that I forgot some… umm… really important papers in my apartment. Things Billings needs today. I'll just… take the subway back there first."

None of that was true, but she must say something to get him gone. The full weight of what she had disclosed to him about the WYNG newsroom in their private moments together was suddenly crashing in upon her. This was a mess of colossal proportions, and she needed to do some quick thinking before deciding how best to act. Otherwise… many more people would soon be forced to leave their home at WYNG… all because of her.

"Nonsense, Darling! I shall arrange that a taxi be waiting for you below."

She was no longer paying attention to him. Quickly moving from the closet to the bathroom, her mind was in a tangle of panic.

How in the world am I going to explain this to Billings?! I've just destroyed the man's life!

She took a very quick shower without shampooing her hair, as there really was no time for that. She needed to get into the station as soon as possible and warn the Berts. With a towel wrapped about her, she went dashing out of the bathroom… only to be brought up short by the sight of him still sitting on the edge of the bed… exactly where she had left him. In his lap was her purse. With one hand, he was holding something small… her driver's license, by the look of it. He just kept staring at it with a supreme look of blankness on his face.

"Clay… what's the matter?"

Slowly, he brought up his other hand to point at the license… all without looking at her.

"I… I was retrieving your address for the doorman… but this… this can't be right. This license… it states quite clearly that your… your last name… it's… it's not Forde. Marna… according to this… you're… you're a married woman."

CHAPTER
22

THE EUROPEAN HORNET
AT SUMMER'S END

In a flash, everything changed forever between her and Clay Azurean. Straightway, she attempted a most sincere explanation for how she had fled Lubbock, but he wanted none of it. With a stone-cold stare of fury, he stuck a hand of insistence into her face as he made for the penthouse door. The only words she managed to elicit from him came as he stormed out.

"We shall speak of this later!"

In spite of how upset she felt, she fully recognized how important it was that she get to Billings as soon as possible. She dressed quickly, not bothering with make-up or fussing about with her hair. There was no taxi waiting at curbside, but the doorman hailed one for her. Within twenty minutes of leaving the penthouse, she was striding across the WYNG newsroom with Billings in her sights. She would not wait for him to finish up with the AE in charge of local news.

"Excuse me… I need to speak with you right away. In your office, please. It's regarding that thing you asked me to do a month ago."

They made their way down the back hall in silence, with her starting in only after the door was closed. She spoke the truth, accepting whatever came in the process. In a matter of a minute, Billings was on the phone demanding that Mr. Carswell drop everything and high-tail it over to his office.

"It's about you-know-who."

The moments of sitting there silently waiting with Billings were some of the most painful she had experience since leaving Lubbock. Fortunately, it was not too long before a knock came to the door and Mr. Carswell entered.

"Close the door, Bertram... and have a seat. I should offer you a stiff drink... because you're going to need it." Billings turned to her next. "Go on, Forde... tell him what you told me."

She had no idea how to phrase what she must say... even though she had just said it once already. Looking into Mr. Carswell's eyes, she fought off an impulse to cry, and purposed instead to be completely honest with these two men she had come to respect... and maybe even love.

"Sometime back, sir, when Mr. Azurean first arrived... I guess you could tell that he took a liking to me. Anyway... Mr. Billings asked me to get close to him in order to..."

"I sure as hell didn't tell you to hop in the sack with him!"

"Albert... please! Can't you see how difficult this is for her?! Allow her to continue without interruption. Besides, Miss Forde is an adult... with the right to make adult decisions..." Mr. Carswell unexpectedly turned a stern face her way. "...no matter the consequences."

Shaken by his implication, she nonetheless held nothing against either him or Billings. Her shame was only partly of a sexual nature. A far greater humiliation was rooted in what these two dear men would soon have to endure... all because she had been too stupid to recognize the true nature of Clay Azurean.

"I'm so sorry... to both of you. Truly sorry. I've been so... enamored with him... with everything about him... that it's taken me far too long to see him for what he really is – a fool. Sir... I just found out this morning that he's planning on slashing the newsroom's budget. In fact, he's fully intent on gutting the entire station."

Mr. Carswell slumped back into his seat with an ashen face. But Billings sprang up with another string of profanities... even though he had already done as much on first hearing her story... before turning back to her.

"Damn it, Forde! Will you get on with the rest?!"

"Yes, sir. Mr. Carswell, sir... I really don't know for certain what he's up to... but I have a guess. As you probably know, he's been making lots of business trips to New York. He's absolutely convinced that the FCC'll be allowing networks to piggyback off of communication satellites soon... so I think he's planning to convert WYNG into some kind of a... a surrogate of the parent station in Manhattan. He's not said as much... but I've read between the lines. He wants to pipe in programming via satellite… you know… instead of through broadcast. I think he's using WYNG as a test case for a twenty four hour news network… or something like that. One thing's for sure… WYNG won't exist anymore… at least not as its own independent station."

Billings picked up the cursing again, but Mr. Carswell lifted a hand to silence him.

"And you think he'll be starting in on this plan soon?"

"I don't know, technically speaking, what it'll take… but I think he's got his eye on using the newsroom's operations for capital. He's set to make some really significant reductions to the budget for next quarter. Said so this morning. Sirs… he intends for pink slips to go out later this week."

"My god, doesn't he realize where the station's revenue comes from?! If he cannibalizes the news programs… Wait, how's he going to justify that?! There's no way the network board'll…"

"He says he already has the board's approval. I don't know if that's true, but he's acting like it is."

The three of them sat in silence for several minutes, and though her personal situation bore no direct bearing on the desperation of these two men, she felt… for honesty's sake… that they both ought to know the full truth. Besides, she was sure to be on the list of those receiving termination notices. And knowing Clay, he would likely use her married name out of spite.

"Sirs… Mr. Carswell… Mr. Billings. I just feel terrible about this."

"Miss Forde… in no way are you responsible. If anything… as the executive producer… I should have seen this coming."

She glanced at Billings, whose scowl seemed to concur.

"I appreciate that, sir… but there's something else that you should know. It won't make a difference in any of this… but I've been keeping a secret. I'm… actually married."

She had lowered her face in confessing this, not wanting to see either man's reaction… but had to shoot right back up at Billings' instant outrage.

"To that moron Azurean?! Are you outta your frickin' mind?!"

"Oh, no, sir! Not to him! My husband's in Texas. We're essentially divorced… it's just not final yet. I know what you two must be thinking… that I'm such a horrible person…" Neither man budged an inch, so she lowered her head even further before continuing. "It's just… Clay… I mean… Mr. Azurean… he found out this morning. He's really angry… and I guess I can't blame him. But you should know… he's liable to act rashly… you know… out of hurt. I'll probably be the first to go when he…"

"Won't happen."

In disbelief, she lifted her head to Billings.

"Aside from the fact that you're the best damn PA this station's seen in years… he won't fire you. He can't."

"Albert's right. What's going to happen, Miss Forde, is… ahh… do you mind terribly if I keep referring to you that way? I've always liked the sound of it."

Incapable of stopping herself, she burst out crying right in front of them. Mr. Carswell's gentleness… and even Billings' ferocity… it was all out of concern for her… and she deserved none of it. As neither man seemed to know what to do with her in this state… other than Mr. Carswell producing a handkerchief… she fought her tears into a pathetic smile. Wiping her eyes, she was now determined to spare these dear men of the mess she had made out of her personal life.

"I'm sorry… I'm… better now."

"It's… quite alright. As I was saying… Mr. Azurean will avoid the hard decisions of who stays and who goes by simply cutting my budget. He'll force the three of us… that's myself, Albert, and Franklin, in his role as the morning news producer… to make the necessary staffing changes. I assume he'll be doing the same thing with the other executive producers at the station. We'll be the ones issuing pink slips. That's the way it's always done. So… if Albert says you stay… then you stay. But for now… if you don't mind… he and I have things to discuss in private."

"Forde… before you go… thanks. Don't think that Bertram and I don't realize the situation you're in. You could have kept quiet about this… let the chips fall where they may… but you chose to tell us as soon as you found out. That means something in my book. Now… send Phillips in here. He's going to have to run the morning meeting without me."

From that moment on, she purposed to keep her head down and concentrate only on work. All day, she had been bracing herself, yet heard nothing from Clay. No messages, no phone calls, no appearances in the newsroom. Nothing. She spent the evening by herself, moping about her apartment in a state of anxious despair. Her phone rang twice… but she did not answer for fear of it being Clay. She was not yet ready to face him… not until she had turned over and over every shovel full of words, feelings and happenings since the first time she laid eyes on the man. She had made so many stupid decisions over the last month. Most damning was the carelessness through which she had given her heart away to a man she barely knew… all because he was rich, handsome, and a visionary. She had not bothered to watch him first… to observe his character… and to see how faithfully he carried out his responsibilities. Of all that, she was most hard on herself for her own unfaithfulness… to Billings, to Mr. Carswell, to the employees at WYNG… and even to a man whose name she no longer carried.

After two miserable days of work expecting Clay to pop out at any second and confront her, she went home determined on a new course of action. She would put the station and its employees ahead of her own interests and go confront Clay… even if it meant getting fired in the process. She tried several times that morning to reach him by phone and in person at his office, but each time was turned away by his administrative secretary.

Before going home, she learned that Clay had called the executive producer of his news programs into his office on the twelfth floor and informed him that he would be charting a bold new course forward with regard to the news. Effective immediately, Mr. Carswell was to focus all of his attention on developing a detailed plan for a twenty four hour news stream comprised of feeds from all over the world… starting with those from their parent hub in Manhattan. The station manager confidently asserted that the satellite capabilities for implementing this change would be in place soon, so the programming switch from broadcast would occur coincident with the bringing up of a receive station on the roof of the building. In order to free up the capital needed for the signing of contracts, the acquisition of equipment and expertise, and the required permitting for rooftop construction activities, Mr. Carswell would have thirty five percent of his operating budget diverted away from the news. How the executive producer planned to implement the necessary changes was within his own purview, but the station manager stressed that the quality of the interim broadcasts and the level of the associated advertising revenues were not to be compromised. Mr. Azurean gave Mr. Carswell one week to submit a detailed plan for accomplishing the required restructuring of the WYNG news programs, which should include a list of staff reductions, programming changes, and other related overhead cuts. It was critically stressed that the executive producer was not to neglect the satellite news plans in the process of implementing the down-sizing activities.

All of this she heard from a very distraught Rose as they huddled together in the tenth floor ladies' room.

"I've never seen him more down in all of my time with him. He was near on crying when he came down from the twelfth floor. Not even Billings had ever done that to him. I don't know what to do… This is the end of WYNG news."

She immediately went back to the newsroom and volunteered to take all of the PA shifts over the weekend, simply so as to have something that kept her mind off her situation. All Saturday and Sunday, she did her job while largely keeping to herself. Each night, she went home late and each morning she woke up early. Not once did she hear a word from Clay. But come Monday morning, she was not in for more than ten minutes before receiving word from Rose that the station manager insisted on her immediate presence on the twelfth floor.

She had been in Clay's office so many times since that day he took her up to the rooftop transmitter. She knew it to be the essence of privilege – thick pile carpet, satin drapes, black leather arm chairs, a leather sofa, and an unusually plush leather executive chair behind his immense mahogany desk. His suite also had a conference room with more leather seating, a small bar, and a washroom. She always had the distinct impression that he was dissatisfied with this office, though its furnishings were of his own choosing. Maybe the view was not spectacular enough... or he thought his prestige warranted a corner of the building... or something on a much higher floor. On at least three separate occasions, he had tried to seduce her in that office, but never succeeded. Each time, she made it perfectly clear to him that the workplace must remain devoted to work. Today, on crossing the twelfth floor lobby heading to his office, she seriously doubted that she had to worry about such things.

When ushered in, Clay directed her to one of the armchairs facing him at his desk without speaking a word. For quite a while, he just stared at her while fidgeting with a letter opener... occasionally jabbing it into the blotter... just to unnerve her. She said nothing to any of it, purposing not to make his job any easier. When he finally spoke, it was without preamble.

"Don't think for one moment that I don't know what you've been up to, Marna. Don't think that I'm unaware of your betrayal. I know you've gone behind my back to those... dinosaurs. But don't expect me to let you off the hook by firing you. Oh, no! As far as I'm concerned... married or not... you still belong to me. I already told you what kind of a man I am. When I see something I want, I take it. So here's what you *can* expect. You'll stay at WYNG, but everyday you'll be called to my office and do my bidding. And you'll do exactly what I say without complaint... or so help me god, I'll make sure that you never find another job in this city... or any city... for as long as I live! But... in time... if you've been a good girl and done as I say... I might... just might... let you come back to me."

"Like hell I will! And you've got it all wrong! You'll die old and fat waiting for me to take you back!"

He smirked in return.

"Enjoy yourself for now, Miss Forde... or should I start referring to you openly as Mrs. Meitner? You know… maybe I'll mix it up. Either way… you'll need to improve that attitude of yours if you're going to be a production specialist working *under* me. Just think… every day I'll be looking at you exactly as I did on that very first day… when all I could think about was getting between your legs. It'll be such a treat for me!"

Trembling with rage, she clinched her jaw with such force as to cause herself pain. She could practically taste her own anger, and was fully intent on giving him back a full five-course meal of the same… in her own time.

"Will that be all… *Azurean*?!"

She was pleased to see him displeased at being brusquely addressed… though he recovered too quickly into that nauseatingly self-satisfied smile of his. That smile had once been so proficient at generating replicas of itself… but now, it was utterly revolting to her.

"Yes… but report immediately to the station's personnel office for your new assignment. They're expecting you. And then be back here at two sharp. You and I are going on a little field trip together."

At two o'clock, she was commanded to follow him from his office. He led her to the elevator in silence. She waited for him to enter first… and was irritated when he chose to stand in the very center. In moving around him to a back corner, she could not keep herself from flinching when he made a lunge in her direction… and then had to endure his childish chuckling all the way down to the building's garage level. There, Azurean escorted her to his waiting car. Speaking matter-of-factly to his driver, he informed the man that he would not be needed for this trip, since Clay would be doing the driving. As the man turned away, she resolved not to get into that car alone with Azurean… and perhaps he sensed it.

"James… one moment please. I would like you to know that I am taking Miss Forde on a short car trip. I won't be back until late afternoon, so I suggest you wait in the building's lobby or outside my office. If, for whatever reason, I do not return with a healthy and happy Miss Forde, please call the Chicago police and inform them that I, your employer, am responsible for her disappearance. I suggest that you have them drag Lake Michigan off Montrose beach. That's seems like a convenient place to dump her body."

"Yes, sir."

The man continued on his way, altogether bored. Azurean then turned to her with a most exasperated expression.

"Will that suffice in convincing you that I mean you no harm?"

"Where are we going?"

"It's a surprise."

"It doesn't matter. I'm not going anywhere with you."

"Marna… on my honor, I promise that no harm will come to your person. Neither will I impose myself upon you in any way. You have my word. Please… humor me… just this once. In fact, I believe you will find this trip very much to your advantage."

She should have the good sense to just turn around and leave… especially seeing as he had turned out to be such an ogre. But… she had caused him pain, so perhaps she owed him some small amount of consideration.

They drove out of the building and headed in a general northwesterly direction toward O'Hare Airport. She sat in silence, arms folded tightly across her chest as Chicago flowed by her window. All the while, he did not cease from lecturing her about her ingratitude and unfaithfulness toward him. How she was not as sharp as he had originally imagined her to be… particularly since she had lost sight of what everyone else clearly understood. His railing on her then transitioned into him talking exclusively about himself. He was special. No one was more special than him. Only he had the vision and force of will to embrace the future. Only he could make big things happen. Soon enough, everyone at WYNG would come to recognize his genius… and so would the corporate board. They would lift him up to where he belonged – at the very top. And then she would beg him to forgive her for the many ways she had wronged him… and so would his father.

His father?!

Never before had he ever spoken about his family.

After nearly forty minutes of riding uncomfortably through his monologue, she welcomed the change brought about by the car pulling into a mostly empty parking lot. The area was rimmed with several small, ratty-looking businesses of a diverse nature – a travel agency, a law office, a realtor, a hamburger joint, and others that she could not readily identify. Picking a space between the restaurant and the lawyer's office, he got out and went around to open her side, consenting to speak only after he had closed and locked the car door behind her.

"This is it."

"This is what?"

He did not reply with words, but instead extended an arm toward one of the entrances. It took her a few seconds to process the stenciling there.

Jackmann and Mauck, Attorneys at Law.

"Azurean… what're we doing here?"

"Well… you said you wanted a divorce from this guy in Texas… so here's your divorce. These guys may not look like much from the outside, but I've checked around – they're the best! They could get a divorce for the Pope… if he were to marry… and have it done with same-day service. Shall we?"

Again, he extended an arm toward the door.

"I'm not going in there. Take me back."

She would get her divorce in her own timing and on her own terms.

Before she knew what was happening, he lunged at her… just like in the elevator. But instead of faking it, he snatched her handbag out from under her arm.

"Give that back!"

"You want it… then you'll just have to follow it inside."

As he turned toward the door with that smug smile of his, she had reached her limit. With all her strength, she threw a punch aimed in the general direction of one of his kidneys… and was supremely pleased when the impact propelled him into the side of the building. When he turned back, there was a viciousness in his face that completely removed every sign of handsomeness from his features.

"You despicable bitch! And to think I was seriously considering asking you to marry me! I may have promised not to hurt you, but I never promised not to hurt this!"

After shoving it in her face, he threw the purse to the ground and began stomping on it, all the while cursing her for her betrayal. He concluded this tantrum by scooping up her heavily damaged purse and hurling it down into a nearby garbage can, sending a shower of wrappers, drink cups and food fragments bursting up into the air. For a silent moment, both she and he stood there seething at each other. That is… until her eyes were drawn to the swarm of disturbed insects emerging from the trash.

Vespa crabro is the only true hornet in North America, though it is not native in the least. Nicknamed 'the European,' this hornet's ancestors were brought to the continent some hundred and fifty years ago. Here, they sought a place to be at peace… a place to thrive on their own. Their contribution to the ecosystem was entirely beneficial, but they nonetheless faced constant hardship in their migration westward.

Her colony was only newly established in this part of Chicago, and thus far had experienced an especially difficult year. Intense competition and limited insect prey had forced her to hunt more broadly than she and her sisters would have liked. With summer at an end and autumn upon them, they were desperate for time. Her colony's population had abruptly declined due to an unexpected cold snap. Each day thereafter, fewer and fewer of her sisters returned from their searches. The surviving workers must now abandoned pursuit of their normal food sources for whatever might be available… which usually meant picking through mankind's trash. She had managed to locate this particular garbage can that morning, and then returned with a few of her sisters to gather what they could. Most of it had been picked over by her distant yellow jacket cousins. There were so many more of them, and they would not leave her be. Though their features somewhat resembled her distinctive brown-and-yellow stripes, as well as her colorfully reddish-yellow wings, she… unlike them… was adorned with very fine strands of hair. She was so much more stately than those wasps… and tougher too. The reverberating sound of her wings in flight was often enough to scare away many of her foes. But not these yellow jackets. Still, she would not be intimidated by them. She would fight for every opportunity to feed her colony. She would challenge whatever opposed her, and sting without hesitation if she must… especially if anything dared to distract from her most important work.

On edge, and in a panic with winter so near and so much at stake, she would risk much in making each additional trip from the nest. And always it was not enough. The need to provide food for the year's last brood drove her on. Soon, she would die within cold's grip, unsure of whether her labor had brought forth anything significant in the spring.

Azurean immediately began writhing and swatting about with the same vigor he had shown toward the destruction of her purse… except without all the cursing. Instead, he was blurting out frantic little yelps with each wild stroke of his arms. To her, he very much looked like a person drowning in the air.

"Clay, stop it! You'll only rile them up further! Just back away!"

She was already at the car… except the door would not open for her. Just like him! He had locked it in believing that she would have no choice but to enter the law office with him. She was about to call over for the keys when she suddenly found herself seized by the shoulders, spun about, and then shoved back in the direction of the trash can. Stinging things were darting all about her face, and in a terror of panic, she stumbled backward to the car… only to find Azurean already inside, jamming down the locking mechanism. She beat on the glass, begging him to let her in… for he knew not her peril. Yet the more earnest she became, the more he just sneered at her… even to the point of wagging a finger in her face.

One moment, she was in total fear for her life... and in the next, she stood stark still, staring through the glass. Slowly lifting a hand, she limply traced out the looping pattern he was not yet aware of. For inside of the car... on his side of the window... was a huge flying thing. Much bigger than a yellow jacket... and not one of those lumbering bumble bees either. It was more like a... a really angry hornet.

In a lightning flash of realization, Azurean went from smug curiosity at her pointing action to abject horror on being stung... repeatedly. His shrills of pain were so easily heard through the glass as he wildly fought off the creature. She, aware once more of the wasps all about her, did not wait for the conclusion to his combat. She immediately fled to the safety of the hamburger place. Once inside... and after being convinced that she had not been stung or brought any insects with her... she turned about to see Azurean starting up the car. Without looking back toward the restaurant, he pulled out of the parking lot, leaving her behind.

She approached a busboy about retrieving her beat up purse from the can, cautioning him to watch out for the stinging insects. After he returned with it... and as a reward to the establishment whose trash had so wonderfully served as the means of punishing her ex-lover... she purchased a cheeseburger, fries and chocolate milkshake. She then very much enjoyed a leisurely afternoon there reading a newspaper while replaying in her mind the stinging of Azurean... and hoping so very much that James, the driver, had called the police.

Only after the sun had set, and the fear of being stung had set with it, did she arranged for a taxi to take her to the nearest subway entrance. From there, she made her way home rather than return to explain her absence from work. Billings would not care. After all, she now reported directly to the station manager... and that man had just abandoned her.

She went to bed that night pondering on how it was that she, in the midst of a swarm emanating from the trash can, had not been stung, whereas Azurean... who had made it safely into the car... had been. Most likely the hornet had been on his clothing. Odd, she had not once thought about her life-threatening allergy in all the time since coming to Chicago. Lying there in the dark, she was thankful for that hornet. It had sacrificed itself in putting a proper end to one of the worst decisions in her life – giving herself to a fool. Her thoughts wandered back to Lubbock, to the people she had known, to the place she had grown up, and to a small bracelet slid into a taxi's backseat hiding place. Did she miss those people and that city? No answers came. What about the man she was married to? What had become of him? She wondered if Azurean had been telling the truth. Could those lawyers get her the divorce she had once wanted so badly?

Once wanted?! Surely nothing's changed?!

With only a moment of self-reflection, she shook off the question with an answer that could not be denied. If Roy knew what had become of her... if he was made aware that he possessed the ultimate of grounds... then he would most certainly beat a path directly to the doors of *Jackmann and Mauck, Attorneys at Law.*

CHAPTER
23

COLD, DARK AND DESTRUCTIVE

She was sure to pay dearly for defying her ex-lover... and for witnessing the humiliation inflicted upon him by a hornet. On the day following the ill-fated 'field trip,' Azurean put his new production specialist to work doing a constant stream of meaningless tasks. Duplicating decade-old paperwork, hand-delivering his messages all over WYNG, sitting around jotting down his every musing, and running errands for him around the downtown. He sent her out to pick up his dry cleaning, only to give her the wrong address. He ordered lunch from a corner deli, and then berated her for it not being what he wanted. Out she went again to correct the mistake, only to find him disinterested on her return... him having already eaten the first sandwich. Worst were all those periods of tense silence standing before his desk as he tried to figure out something else stupid for her to do. In all these things, she obeyed simply out of concern for herself. As unlikely as his blacklist threat seemed, she had absolutely no desire for testing his wherewithal for pulling it off.

Above all, he was most careful to send her out on some task whenever he needed to work on his 'grand vision' for the station. He even sternly instructed his administrative secretary and immediate staff in her presence not to share a single detail with her. At least she had the distinct pleasure of explaining to anyone who asked how it was that the station manager had so many puffy welts on his face.

From the moment he made her his personal assistant, she purposed to no longer address him in the manner he had chosen on his first day at WYNG. In his presence alone or before a multitude of employees, she called him only Azurean… right to his face. To her, he was more of a boy and less of a man worthy of her respect. His blue eyes and all of his wide-open blue skies talk had been as empty as the air… and she vowed never to forget it.

Such small life lessons did not go nearly far enough toward compensating her for how demeaning it was to be his personal slave. In no way would she resume a relationship with him, yet he persisted in openly referring to her as his girlfriend… or 'Marna, dearest'… or some other disgusting affectation that suited his fancy of the moment. He consistently went out of his way to exploit her proximity, taunting her with subtle touches. A finger brushed lightly along her shoulder blades… a puff of breath to flutter her hair… or moving in so close that she absolutely had to retreat. He frequently made inappropriate comments about her in the presence of others. About how his assistant was by far the most attractive woman in the building… or something on his opinion of her figure in a particular outfit… or how tragic it was that couples never stayed together for long these days. And always, she could sense his eyes moving up and down her body… remembering and wanting.

Not that she was entirely helpless in dealing with him… something she reminded herself every morning before heading into work.

He thinks my Texan is so charming. Well… in Texas… you mess with the bull and you get the horns.

On a near-daily basis, she brought to work some token of his past admiration. These, she desecrated in creative fashion… subtly enough that others only wondered, but far too blatantly for him to overlook. She poured the entire contents of an expensive perfume vial into the planter beside his desk, bathing the palm fronds in the process, and then watched in silent delight as he struggled all day to endure how the scent had overwhelmed his office. She spent a weekend shredding a bubblegum pink cardigan he had given as a belated birthday gift. She never liked the thing, but now… reduced to fuzz… it became her absolute favorite. All week, she scattered bits of the sweater over the back of his office chair or on his trench coat… any place where the clingy strands might end up attaching themselves to his clothing or hair. She then silently delighted in his comical frustration at having to constantly deal with those mysterious little fibers. Perhaps of all the ways she sought revenge during the weeks following the breakup, her favorite was nonchalantly loaning out his expensive gifts of jewelry to the station's secretarial staff… right before his very eyes. Of course, there were unfortunate times in which her zeal got the better of her. Like when she draped silk stockings over his desk lamp… and was mortified when Mr. Carswell had the unfortunate luck of being the first to notice. Or when she wrote 'I am a pig' in huge, backward letters on his office window with that flaming red lipstick he so adored. Rather than fire her on the spot… which a part of her was subconsciously shooting for… he cursed her out in front of the janitorial staff as they were made to clean up her mess.

All her childish ways of getting back at him slowly settled out of her system such that within a month of being made his personal production specialist, she hated him with a red-hot loathing… but hated herself even more. Her only ambition was to make it to five o'clock so she could get free of him. Day after day, she was forced to consider where she had gone so very wrong in having been attracted to this man. Azurean had once been like an oxygen high to her – deep and fast breaths leading to a dizzying of her senses. Back then, his smile had the ability to wiggle its way into the guarded chambers of her heart. But now… there was nothing but ugliness to all of his ways. He had spoken of lofty visions for the future while sipping fine wine… but as she watched him more closely, it was clear that he had no idea what it was like to do serious labor. He never took notes or did hard thinking about anything. Such work was for others to do on his behalf. He could throw a tantrum when circumstances did not go his way, or sit bored at his desk waiting for something amusing to present itself. No matter how she sliced it, the truth was inescapable. Azurean was a spoiled brat… and she had been the fool.

As time went on, Azurean slowly ceased from being the main thing beleaguering her. To be sure, she was still ashamed of herself for having fallen for him. Daily in being made to face this object of her poor judgment sitting there at his expensive mahogany desk, she more so faced her own unfaithfulness. Through Azurean's doing, everyone at the station eventually discovered that 'Marna Forde' was actually 'Marna Meitner.' Most of her colleagues did not seem to find much of interest in the story of a small town girl who ran away from her marriage to the big city… but that was of little comfort to her. She was drawn each new day to reconsider where she had gone so very wrong. Her thinking had been warped all the way back to Lubbock. Of all the Meitners, she had believed herself to be the one most wronged. But now… she thought differently. At twenty four years old, with a failed marriage and a history of two workplace lovers on the side, she was forced to accept that no one would ever take her seriously as a professional.

By the end of the year, she, being racked with guilt and shame, was seriously considering leaving Chicago… even though she had nowhere to go. Moving into the new year, regret became the bitter aftertaste to all of her resolutions.

If only I'd seen…

If only I'd known…

If only I hadn't done…

In a constant state of depression, she was now experiencing reoccurrences of the same dream on her tiring rides home on the subway. There was always motion in this dream, understandable owing to her dozing on a train. Instead of heading down a tunnel and along a track, she seemed to be hurrying toward a horizontal line that separated everything into light and dark… into a vibrant blue above and a deep greenish sort of gray below. She knew that line… had seen it many times before… but could not quite grasp its significance. In the dreams, this line never remained still, as it would bob up and down before her… or tilt side to side… or go into an out-of-control spiral. She would wake with a loud gasp, then have to endure the annoying stares of her fellow commuters for the rest of the journey home. This disturbing dream, coupled with her arriving home alone, going to bed alone, and rising in the morning to face another day alone, meant only that she was truly alone with no dream for the future.

'Someday' is a terribly painful word to find one's self disappointed with…

In a matter of months of initiating his plan, Azurean's efforts to cannibalize the programming at WYNG in order to fund his dream of a satellite-based news empire was crumbling beneath the weight of his naiveté and mismanagement. Coming into 1970, she learned that the FCC had decided to put off a ruling on the suitability of media corporations utilizing communication satellites. Without access to the raw material of global happenings in which to fill a twenty four hour news day, his plans for transitioning WYNG from a regional media center into part of a national hub were put on hold. In the meantime, the morning news show had been cancelled, with the station filling the time slot with yet another half hour of broadcast TV. That, of course, meant a smaller cut of the advertising revenues due to running someone else's ads.

But the poor public perception from a cancelled morning news program was nothing compared to that incurred with the afternoon and evening shows. From her position as an aide to Azurean, she was forced to witness the rapid dismantling of a well-tuned news machine. The first to go were the make-up and wardrobe functions of the studio. The current anchors were told that they would be responsible for such things, as well as stomaching pay cuts. So those recognized personalities of Chicago left in search of respect elsewhere, leading to the hiring of less-experienced anchors. These new faces were not readily accepted by the viewers. Mr. Carswell… whom she learned would have resigned had not Billings' pleaded with him to stick it out… had to let go many of his senior reporters, AEs and engineers. Click and the other seasoned cameramen immediately jumped ship to different Midwest stations. The obvious outcome was fewer live spots during the show, more recycling of national stories, and poorer quality video/audio editing. Rumors began to circulate that Azurean planned to close down the tenth-floor operations altogether and move everything upstairs. The news would have to make due with sharing the same facilities used by WYNG's sports and local programming shows, themselves already cut to the bone.

The worst blow came when the Nielsen Station Index rating for WYNG news slipped in the last quarter of 1969 from its solid position of contending for the number one spot to a distant last place. In particular, the afternoon news show, once the premier production for adult males, fell out of favor across the board. The response among advertisers was immediate. Contract renewals were down, as were the acquisitions of new clients. She stood uncomfortably through a quarterly station review on the last workday of January in which Azurean soundly chewed out his executive producers for their incompetence, also accusing them of purposefully sabotaging the station's future. She felt so terrible for Mr. Carswell that it was nearly unbearable to lay eyes on him from where she stood behind Azurean at the boardroom table. Yet when Azurean began laying out threats of future terminations if things did not turn around quickly, she could not help but grimace Mr. Carswell's way. She was surprised to find him sitting comfortably with a sly smile on his face. Not until the end of the day was she afforded an opportunity to search out Mr. Carswell in his office. She instead found Rose closing up for the weekend.

"The winds of change are blowing, Marna. Don't repeat this to anyone… but Mr. Carswell's finally heard directly from corporate. They're not happy with what's going on here. That's all he'd tell me… but it's enough. He's back to his pleasant self."

She spent the majority of the subway trip home trying to process this new information. Climbing the ramp from off the Oak Park platform, her legs… in autopilot… trudged the familiar five block route back to her apartment while the more sentient parts of her pondered over what Rose had said. To be sure, she was elated – absolutely thrilled – that the network leadership had finally awoken to the mess at WYNG.

It's their fault for sending us that spoiled brat anyway! They should be the ones to clean up his mess!

But what clean up might look like, she had no idea... especially for her. All she really wanted was a way out of Azurean's grip. If only she could get back to her previous position as a lowly PA. She missed it. Missed the thrill of working under deadline, building something new each day, and being part of a team. Most days lately, she spent her time standing before Azurean listening to him prattle on about his grand vision and why it was that all the little people could not possibly understand his...

She stopped stock-still on the corner just shy of her apartment's main entrance. A car idling at curbside was very familiar. She quickly shifted as near to the building's brickwork as the weeks of accumulated snow would allow. Illumination from the headlights of passing traffic revealed the silhouettes of two men in this car – a driver and a darkened figure slumped down in the back. She need not see that person in order to know who he was. Retreating along the sidewalk, she had a mind to slip around to the apartment's rear door, but then the driver raised a hand to point in her direction. Azurean was immediately out of the back seat and dashing across the icy pavement toward her.

"Marna! Marna! I'm so relieved to see you. Thought I might have missed you."

She had seen his face not much more than an hour ago when he lordly dismissed her from his presence... but that face was not this one. Even in the dull Oak Park lighting, she could tell that his smile was but a blank template. From his disheveled hairline... to his restlessly darting eyes... to his quivering lips, it was so very evident that Azurean had become terribly concerned about something in the interim.

"What're you doing here?! I thought I made it abundantly clear that you were never to..."

"Please, Marna! I'm desperate! I need your help. I need your..." He abruptly stopped to look off down the street in the direction of the Eisenhower Expressway... and then back around toward the busier part of Oak Park. His eyes fell upon his own driver, and his hand suddenly jerked up to clutch her wrist. "Please, let's go inside. We can't discuss this on the street."

She hesitated in consideration of her own safety, but also in the simple discomfort of having him around. She was especially concerned about what it would take to get rid of him once he got himself inside.

"Sure... but only for a minute. I... I have a date tonight and need to get ready. He'll be here any minute now."

The lie was not all that clever, but it would due in setting the stage for insisting that he keep his stay short. It might also gauge something of his true intentions. To her surprise, he did not respond as she expected.

"Yes, yes… that's nice. You should get out more often… Now please, can we step inside?"

He was not even looking at her, as his eyes had not ceased from scanning the streets. So she reluctantly led him inside, but stopped at the building's mailboxes.

"Okay, what is it? What's so important that you had to…"

"We can't talk here." His eyes were all over the hallway, on the doors of the ground floor and back out the way they had come. "Inside your apartment. Please, Marna. You have my word – just five minutes and I'm gone."

Now she was both curious and irritated at the same time over all of his childlike angst. Yet the longer she delayed, the more fidgety he got. So… up the stairs she went, him practically at her side. He hovered at her elbow as she unlocked the door, and then bolted pass to begin pacing the floor of her small living room. Not once did he bother to look about at his ex-lover's abode.

"You've heard something, Marna… I know. You're connected! People tell you things. Please… I need to know what's to become of me."

He was near on frantic, facing her for each of his short sentences, but then picking up all the pacing in between.

"I… don't know what you mean. I've not heard anything really… other than that corporate's…"

"Ah-ha! I knew it!" He raised a glove finger to the ceiling, showing real intensity for the first time. "I knew they couldn't leave me alone. Thank you, Marna."

He smiled firmly her way… but then resumed his previous pacing, muttering oddities about them being so controlling… that these things take time… and why is it that nobody understands him.

"Except you, of course. You're the only one who sees things the way I do."

Without warning, he suddenly got a wild look in his eyes… sort of like in that split second when a caged animal realizes it can run free.

"*You* could persuade them! That's it! Why didn't I see it before?! Marna, you're going to save me!"

She had absolutely no idea what he was talking about and instinctively knew not to ask… but still did anyway.

"Azurean, you're not making any sense. Just… calm down and tell me what you're talking about. Persuade who? Of what?"

He took a step away from her, which unfortunately did not bring her much relief. With clinched teeth and balled up fists, he grimaced toward the ceiling.

"The board, of course! Isn't it obvious! Keep up, Marna! I'll need you to be much sharper than this when you explain our vision to them."

Already back to pacing, he soon picked up that all-too-familiar tone of condescension.

"I certainly expect you to have grasped it by now… but you know… we should probably go over the details together tomorrow. They're sending representatives here… probably already here. Let me see… I'll introduce you… and then you explain our plans for satellites and the international network of news… why we need the rooftop receive station and…" He waved a dismissive hand her way. "Don't go into any of that Texas cable stuff. They're not interested in hearing nonsense about…"

"Azurean – stop!"

He went stark still, but with a slight quiver to his lips… almost like a small child that had been yelled at for no reason. In that moment, she realized that it would not be so easy to shed herself of him.

"I'm sorry… I really need to get ready for my date, so I'd like you to…"

"Forget about your date! You've time for all the dates in the world once we get this thing sorted out. Remember – you work for me! You do what I say! You and I… we're in this together! Whatever happens to me, happens to you!"

Now, more than ever, she was scared. He had moved in close, inching her backward to her apartment door, all the while thrusting that same gloved finger into her face. She was the caged animal now.

"Sure, Clay, sure! Whatever you say, Darling. How about we… get together first thing in the morning… in your office. I'll get the coffee… and maybe those Danishes you like so much. Then we'll… go over the whole thing… together."

For a terrible moment, she was not sure that he believed her. But then he slowly lowered his hand and eased a step away.

"I… would have preferred to get started immediately. There's so much to do. But as this is short notice… Yes, you may go on your date, but make it an early evening. I want you in the office by six. We'll begin right off by preparing an overview of the vision, and then we'll…"

"Don't you think you should start out by addressing the station's revenue shortfall?"

He was immediately back to his tense self, clutching the sides of his head with his gloved hands.

"I don't know! I don't know! I can't be expected to figure all this out by myself!"

"Clay… Clay! Calm yourself. Everything's going to be fine. Now you go home… get a good night sleep… and then you can start out fresh in the morning…"

With her hand resting on his back, she ever so gently steered him toward the door.

"And you'll be there? Say you'll be there with me, Marna! I so desperately need you!"

With many reassurances as to her devotion for him, she got the door open and stood aside with her head bowed as if he were the one commanding her. Still… he hesitated. So she did the thing that he was so well known for. She smiled wide… and to her relief, he returned the expression. But he was only barely into the doorway, so to nudge him forward the small distance needed, she actually pushed him out with a kiss to his cheek. To her immense relief, he blushed… tipped his head… and then strode off down the hall.

She waited just long enough to be convinced that his footsteps were taking him down the stairs before dead-bolting the door. She then ran through the apartment's darkness to the window in her bedroom and waited. She saw him step from the building, enter his car, and drive off into whatever make-believe world he was living in. Only after the tail lights had disappeared from view did she collapse onto her bed. Her mind was outracing her emotions, keeping her very far from tears. She must decide what to do next. Her first thought was to pack a bag and get out of Chicago for the weekend… but then that option was dismissed. She would not flee on account of that foolish man.

Maybe I should call Billings… but what could he do?!

Then it came to her. She would take the weekend off and do what she had always wanted to do – spend an entire Saturday perusing the downtown storefronts of this great city of Chicago. She would rise early, have a leisurely breakfast at the diner down the street, and then make her way by subway into the downtown. She would stay there all day and not return until very late, this time using the apartment's back entrance. She would repeat the whole thing again on Sunday once the stores were open, filling in the gaps of what she had missed on Saturday. Maybe even throw in a few museums. She would then boldly confront his wrath on Monday with the sort of courage that only a West Texas woman could muster.

Come Monday morning, it being the 2nd of February and that fabled day in which a distant member of the squirrel family decided the springtime fates of so many, she left her Oak Park apartment for work, determined to face whatever version of winter might remain for her in Chicago. After an especially cold and wind-blown walk from her subway stop, followed by a morbid elevator ride to the twelfth floor of the Rollecastle building with a half dozen Monday morning zombies like herself, she entered nervously into the outer area of the station manager's office suite. The person at the executive secretary's seat smiled at her in a very welcoming way.

"Oh! I... didn't expect to see you, Rose... What're you doing at Chanel's desk?"

Rose did not answer, but instead tipped her head toward the inner office, very noticeably fighting off the pressure of some hidden secret. So she eased herself inside... only to be shocked at the person seated behind Azurean's desk.

"Mr. Carswell... What're you doing here? Where's Mr. Azurean?"

"Miss Forde, you are now speaking with the new station manager of WYNG." He let out a laugh while directing her to a seat before him. "Actually, I'm only the interim... but I'm told it will be official within the week. A board representative... Mr. Azurean's father, in fact... came in over the weekend to remove him from the position. Seems our beloved station manager actually did not have approval from the board for any of the radical changes he's brought about. Seems he was sent here through his father's influence because this was deemed to be a role that no one could... how did Mr. Azurean Sr. put it... 'screw up.' Seems he and the board were mistaken. Turns out, his father... the board chairmen... has been having a difficult time finding a place where his son could succeed in life."

It was too good to be true... so he had to be joking. Then the washroom door opened and out stepped Billings drying his hands on a towel.

"About damn time you showed up for work, Forde. You've gotten soft. Well... now that you've had your little vacation up here on the twelfth floor, you think maybe it's time you got your ass in gear? Assuming, of course, that you're still interested in the mundane business of the news..."

"Oh, most definitely! I'd love to..."

She bolted right up from her seat... but Mr. Carswell interrupted.

"Not so fast. I'm still the executive producer of the news programs, and it's still my call. I'm sorry to say, Miss Forde... but I have a serious problem with having you return to WYNG news."

The blood fell from her face as she braced for the obvious. She was about to be fired.

"Well... not with you personally... but I still have a dilemma. You see... Mr. Azurean hired you into a fulltime position that he created himself..."

"Lucky you, Forde."

"Yes, Albert. Now if you don't mind... I'm trying to explain to Miss Forde that there's no comparable position in the newsroom for her... seeing as it's impossible for her to become a PA once she's been an employee. You should know that, Albert. Anyway... I'm afraid the best we can do under the circumstances is to take her on with the title of AE."

He turned to her with a smile… and she could barely breathe.

"I'm assuming that would not be such a severe burden to you, Miss Forde."

She was not hearing this correctly. To be an associate editor, at her age… and without an education… that was unheard of! Before she knew what she was doing, she sprang around the desk and threw her arms about Mr. Carswell, not caring how mortified he might be or that Billings was laughing his head off.

"Consider this as a thank you. Because of you, we managed to get some calls into corporate early on… and that helped us better prepare for the storm. Now rest assured… we won't be expecting you to perform at the level of an AE… that's far too much to ask… but you'll get to do some new things."

"Forde – you'll still be doing PA chores. Just so we're clear on that. And I've only got budget for two AEs… which means we can't pay you more than what you were earning as a PA. Hell, I'm practically a PA myself given how few bodies we got left. So don't let this so-called promotion go to your head."

"Sir, I'd do it for free just to have things back to the way they were!" And she meant it.

"It'll take a hell of lot of work to get this place back to the way it was before that idiot showed up. Forde… I'm assuming I can count on you to…"

"Yes, sir. Sorry to interrupt, sir. But whatever it is, you can count on me."

That day brought her immediate freedom from her twelfth floor prison. She would work at Billings' side… yet did not really feel the flood of relief she had expected. He gave her a place at the table with the men of the newsroom, but even before that morning meeting was over, she found herself looking longingly at those PAs with their backs to the far wall. Things had been simpler for her then. Aside from Billings… and perhaps Phillips, his most senior AE… she found herself being shunned by everyone else who had survived the layoffs. That whole day, her colleagues spoke with her only as was needed in doing their jobs. Not one of them gave her a welcome-back feel. She was not included in their idle chats or in their lunchtime plans, nor was she invited to participate in whatever after-work camaraderie was cooked up. The explanation was not that difficult to see. It came to her in every whispered conversation she happened to interrupt, and with every leer she received across the meeting room table. She had kept her job by sleeping with the station manager – the very man responsible for so many of their coworkers having been let go. Every single one of them… PAs included… resented her presence. She knew that they were talking behind her back… but she outwardly ignored them to do her part in restoring WYNG news.

Alone that night in her apartment, what she felt all day on the inside came pouring out in her frustrated tears. Youngest AE or not… her reputation was ruined. Worse, there was not one person in all of Chicago who would call her a friend. In a city teeming with over three million, she was completely alone.

She found relief only in constant work. She, like many of the remaining staff at WYNG, did triple duty in an effort to revitalize the station's stature in Chicago. Ten hour work days had always been the norm, but now it was near on fourteen… sometimes seven days a week. She did more live reporting, getting more camera time and more opportunities to compose her own words. She learned to do both video and audio editing, and even spent some time sitting in the dark of the master control room. Always, her thoughts were on the job of an editor, and learning about the business side of the station. How the sales staff generated advertising revenue, and how that revenue fueled the various functions of the newsroom. One built upon the other, as laying bricks on a foundation. Better sales allowed better programming, which coaxed in even better sales. Slowly, the mood of the station was turning around. Everyone could feel it – they were making it.

None of that changed how she felt about herself or how she was treated in the newsroom. Whether she was Billings' favorite or Azurean's favorite, it made no difference. Once, she had been accepted and appreciated, but now was only tolerated simply because she worked exceptionally hard at a job that no one thought she could do. So on she went, week after week, and month after month, burying her feelings of sadness deep inside in order to do her job at WYNG.

On a Saturday in early May, after an especially trying week at the station was made even more so difficult by a head cold, she returned very late to her Oak Park apartment far too exhausted for anything other than falling asleep. Billings had insisted that she take a day off to recharge, and even commanded her not to set foot into the station until Monday. She was ready to fight him on that… until he dangled out the possibility of her running her first production. He had called her into his office to say how impressed he was with her… a mere whelp of a newswoman… for going from PA to AE with so few hitches. She rose from her chair, went to open his office door wide, and then requested that he repeat the compliment… louder this time. That got a laugh out of him. He then laid out the plan for her. He would take Monday off… see his Cubs go up against the Braves in the afternoon… eat a decent meal for once… and have a relaxing evening away from the news. While he was out, Phillips would handle the afternoon show, and then shadow her in the evening, just in case she ran into any problems.

Waking Sunday morning with a misplaced sensation of being late for work, she recalibrated herself with a cup of coffee and then set about considering what to do on her day off. She had laundry… and grocery shopping… and definitely some spring cleaning… but then perhaps something leisurely like reading a book. She got the first load of dirty clothes going in the building's basement laundry mat and made a side trip to her mailbox on the way back upstairs. The thing was absolutely jam-packed with paper. She had not checked it in weeks. Taking the stack upstairs, she threw it all on her couch and set herself to sorting the useful from the junk. Halfway through, the sight of a manila-colored envelope instantly froze her. The upper left corner bore the name and address of the law firm she had consulted with before leaving Lubbock. Straightway, she recalled having forwarded her new address shortly after arriving here in accordance with the lawyer's wishes, but had not heard back from him since. For a moment, she considered it unwise to ruin her day off with what might be waiting inside... but inserted a ball point pen into a seam and ripped it open anyway.

Dear Mrs. Marna Meitner,

Greetings. In regard to your consultation with our law firm on March 26, 1968, we are pleased to inform you that the legislature of the state of Texas has passed a resolution permitting 'no fault' divorce. Governor Preston Smith is set to sign this bill into law next week, and there appears to be no opposition from the courts. As such, our previous recommendation that you remain separated from your husband for three years is no longer necessary. Assuming you remain in need, we encourage you to reply to our office at your earliest convenience as to how we might assist you in securing a prompt divorce from your current marriage.

Sincerely,

Richard McBride, Attorney at Law

She read the letter again, allowing its full meaning to sink in. She certainly should feel relieved. After all, disclosure of her secret to everyone at WYNG had been extremely embarrassing. And she did want a divorce. Then why did she feel so... empty. She looked to the letter again in wondering what to do.

I guess I could write back...

But the thought of putting ink to paper on the subject of her failed marriage was so unsettling... and definitely not something she wanted to do on her first day off in weeks.

Maybe I should just take it to Jackmann and Mauck.

She discarded that option too. Aside from the unpleasant thought of revisiting the place Azurean had dragged her off to, she also thought about all those wasps in that trash can. She could have been stung that day. No way should she go back there and tempt fate. For a moment, she considered instead having punched Azurean. Seeing him scream like a baby, that would always be one of her fondest memories of him. And what that hornet did to his face – priceless! But more so, she realized that she had somehow gotten a weird notion into her head – that the insect had prevented her from getting a divorce.

Which is stupid, of course!

Her marriage was over. Not officially, but close enough.

You know… I wonder what Roy's been doing all this time? Has he been trying to divorce me? Maybe with this new law in place, he'll be the one to act first. Maybe already has…

Somehow, that thought did not sit well with her. She should be the one to end it, not him. She stared back at the page again, thinking that she could ask this lawyer to find out if…

No… I can't ask my lawyer to ask my estranged husband what's on his mind. Jeez, Marna, how idiotic can you get?!

She stuffed the letter back into its envelope and pitched it onto the table, fully intending to come back to it…

Later.

Returning to the mail, she took on the bearing of someone who had just resolved a particularly difficult adult-like problem. After flipping through several more items, the stack once more surprised her. She stared down at another letter post-marked from Lubbock. The handwriting on this one was very familiar. There was also a yellow sticker placed on the envelope that showed it had been forwarded to here. The question of how Gwen had somehow discovered her old post office box address was revealed on the first page.

Dear Marna,

I recently ran into a fellow out of Amarillo who was planning a wedding in Lubbock for his daughter. He commented offhand on the spelling of the shops name, saying that he'd only ever known one other person with an 'e' on the end. I naturally asked who, and the man said it was you. Imagine my surprise. He recalled that you were one of the applicants for a job opening he had posted some time back. Your name stuck out to him because he thought highly enough of you to offer a part-time position, but you declined it for something else. Well, to make a long story short, I persuaded him to send me your mailing address – the post office box number I'm going to be putting on the envelope in a minute. I just hope the post office can forward this letter to you. Idiots! They refuse to tell me your whereabouts.

I heard long ago that your marriage with Roy had not worked out, and that you'd left Lubbock. I just want you to know that I've been searching for you ever since. But now that I've finally found an address, I've been debating with myself for weeks about what to write. That time of thinking is over, so here goes.

It's near on impossible to go through life without breaking a promise, but to do so with someone you love is unforgivable. I let you down, Marna. I broke my word to you, and I broke your heart in the process. I'm so sorry. I don't deserve it, but I'm writing to ask for your forgiveness. All your years you've heard nothing from me but sternness and pride. I'm sorry for that too. And while I'm at it, I want you to know that I also bear the guilt of you and Roy splitting up. I should have been there for you. But I just sat back and watched from afar as your marriage fell apart, savagely taking delight in the day I would say that I was right. Marna, I was so wrong, and I'll never forgive myself for it.

One last confession and then a request. When I took you on after your parents died, I purposed in my heart to never become a mother to you. I always kept you at 'aunt-reach' from me. To tell you the truth, I was scared. Scared of being hurt, and scared of hurting you. Turns out, that decision has done more hurt than I ever could have imagined. I'm so sorry, dear. Sorry for being so cold. Please, if you can find it in your heart to call me, or maybe write and let me know where you're at and if you're doing okay. I so want to be in your life again. Please know that I love you, Marna.

Your devoted aunt,

Gwen

She had expected this letter to bear some form of acknowledgement as to where things had gone wrong between them, but not that it would present a plea for forgiveness and an apology that went all the way back to the moment they first laid eyes on each other. Within a second of that remembrance, she could no longer hold her feelings back. In anguish, she screamed out curses to no one in reliving the despair of a childhood spent alone. She cried and beat her fists against the couch until only exhaustion was there to stop her. And even that was not enough. Curled up into a ball clutching a throw pillow to her chest, she crammed her face into the cushions and sobbed… and screamed… and sobbed even more over the recklessness of her own heart. It was not just Gwen, but Roy too… and George and Ruby. Even Grass and Azurean… along with all those poor souls who had lost their jobs at WYNG. Every single one of them brought shame crashing in upon her. Still more tears came to fully convict her. She had been angry with so many people, but now knew that it was all her fault.

I am the burner of bridges! I am the destroyer of lives! I am utterly terrible!

Having cried herself to sleep, it was fully dark outside when she was aroused by a knock at the door. The landlady was there with that basket of her laundry she had left in the washer.

"I dried it for you since... Dear... is something the matter? You look as if you've been crying..."

"Sorry... It's... just that I have a really bad head cold."

She quickly apologized for having neglected her clothes and begged the woman off in much too abrupt a manner considering the kindness shown to her. It could not be helped. Though already late in the evening, she had some serious thinking to do before morning. She went first to wash her face in the bathroom. The disheveled hair and redden eyes that greeted her in the mirror were likely the things that her landlady had observed. She stood there staring at herself, trying to find some of Gwen in that sad reflection before her. Nothing came.

I should call her... right now... but it's really late. She's probably already gone to bed.

She had rinsed her cheeks of tears, but more would come again if she call right now. Really... she was far too broken up on the inside to keep herself from falling apart again.

Gwen wouldn't like that. She never tolerated me crying. So since I'm an adult now, I need to face this as an adult would. I need to be steady... even show her how happy I am to reconnect with her after so long. I can't possibly do that tonight. Maybe tomorrow night. No... it'll have to be Tuesday. I've got the late-night show tomorrow.

So it was settled. She would call on Tuesday. But she still wanted to capture what she was feeling at this moment, so she would write a letter too... right now, while everything was still fresh.

Returning to the couch, she placed stationary in her lap and waited. It did not take long before the words came, and she collected them all up, decorating her feelings with her best flourishes across the fronts and backs of four sheets of paper. She knew there were likely many misspellings, run-on sentences, and other kinds of errors being recorded, but she would not allow herself to reread what she was pouring out for fear of changing something of her feelings. She addressed the envelope and folded the pages inside. With a lick along the seal and a stamp placed in the corner, she had the envelope tucked into her purse, ready to be mailed in the morning. It would arrive well after the call, but Gwen would understand.

She ate a bowl of cereal and then went to bed. She knew that her sleep would be restless, but she had not anticipated a reoccurrence of her subway dream. It started out with the usual boundary between light and dark, but that quickly got all tangled up, coming out more like a fur ball than a straight line. The dream then went psychedelic, with so many wild colors fading in and out of her mind's eye, and stars zooming all about. Azurean and Grass made brief appearances, but only as disembodied faces spinning by as they shouted out nonsense like 'yahoo' and 'wee-hee.' The dream ended in a most bizarre fashion. She was suddenly standing on the WYNG news set, with the floor director yelling out 'break, everyone – Marna has to pee again.' She awoke in confusion with only the clarity that she, in fact, needed to use the bathroom.

Rising Monday morning, she already felt exhausted from a fitful night… and her sinuses still ached from that stupid head cold. Dressing herself, her mind when to the two letters she had opened yesterday. This probably was going to be a difficult work day with those letters repeatedly popping into her head. Though tempted to bring both with her, she instead left them lying on her coffee table. Out the door and eventually onto the subway, her thoughts stayed on the fact that she had responded to one, but still had no idea how to do so to the other. Finally arriving into the newsroom, she dropped her letter to Gwen down the outgoing mail chute.

There! One down, one to go.

She steered her mind toward searching through the wire reports for something to distract herself with. Just before the morning meeting, a story came in over the wire regarding a battalion of airborne soldiers ambushed in the Se San Valley by the North Vietnamese Army. She and the other AE's briefly discussed how many had been killed and who was likely to be blamed for the debacle before deciding that the event did not carry enough news-worthiness for their viewers. Accounts of such battles had become commonplace at the network level. They turned their attention to the city's scheduled school board meeting that day. There were sure to be vehement debate over teacher pay, as union leadership had vowed to derail the meeting unless the mayor's office got involved. All agreed that this was worthy of sending a reporter and camera crew.

She and the other late night production staff sat through the afternoon meeting and watched the 5:30 news show. By and large, she knew that the majority of what she saw would be carried over into her late-night show, though she hoped to find something of her own with which to impress Billings.

The Boston Bruins had won their first Stanley Cup in nearly 30 years by beating the St. Louis Blues in four. She had already seen the remarkable clip of Bobby Orr flying through the air after scoring the decisive goal. She would keep that in her show. There was also the on-going SALT talks between the US and the USSR. She should also stick with the follow-up story on that west side fire, and one of the WYNG reporters had managed to get a quote about the union executive who had died in a plane crash over the weekend. There had been more demonstrations on the Northwestern campus regarding the war... but all of Chicago was getting so very tired of student-led protests. She reviewed the piece on the high schoolers getting their day to run city hall. Mr. Carswell would have said to rerun this story as it was sure to touch hearts, but she could hear Billings calling it 'cute'... and not at all in a good way. She decided to drop this one as it had gotten its due in the afternoon program. Besides, Mr. Carswell... as well as most parents of studious teenagers... would be in bed by eleven. She ate a quick take-out dinner while still combing through the bits of news that had come in since the afternoon.

Near on ten, her job in the newsroom was largely over, though she and the editing staff still had to hang around until the eleven o'clock show was over. She was relaxing in the meeting room with Phillips when the late night weatherman suddenly stuck his head in the door.

"Thought you should know... a major tornado just tore apart a Texas town. Several wire reports are coming in on it..."

He pulled his head out and shouted across the newsroom for the evening PA to get a move on with a printout from the receive room, and then grabbed the page from the young man without a thank you. That really ruffled her, but she let it go since this story was from her home state. The weatherman quickly scanned the page.

"Town called Lubbock."

She was immediately on her feet, dashing about the table to snatch the page away from him with much less delicacy than he had shown toward the PA. She did not care – this was her hometown. Her eyes flowed over the AP wire report to confirm the location, and then she began a more careful search for critical details.

May 11th

7:50. National Weather Service issues a severe thunderstorm warning...

She began jumping words, frantically hunting for the key one.

8:05. ...heavy rains... reports of golf-ball sized hail...

8:10. ...grapefruit-sized...

She finally found it.

8:15. ...tornado warning... ...strike reported in the eastern part of the city... ...minor damage.

She relaxed. This was just another much ado about nothing. But on looking up at the weatherman, she was surprised by the impatient expression on his face.

"We've really gotta hurry on this! The evening script's nearly finished. We'll have to make significant changes if we're going to fit this in."

He pointed back to the page, and she noticed that the print out went on.

9:35. Report of second tornado touching down on the campus of Texas Tech University... ...path of destruction cut through downtown area...

9:43. ...entire residential blocks leveled in Guadalupe neighborhood...

Oh lord! I went to grade school there...

9:46. ...city-wide power failure... ...extensive damage...

10:03. Lubbock Municipal Airport hit... ...communications with local National Weather Bureau station lost...

She looked at her watch – the report was only minutes old. She turned to Phillips, handing him the page in the process.

"Rework the lead-in and get the weather segment refocused. I'm sorry... but this is my hometown. I really need to make some calls."

She made directly for the assignment desk and began frantically dialing every number she could remember, only vaguely aware of staff dashing about in response to the script change. Everyone left her be. She called her aunt's house first, and then the shop, receiving the same 'no service' response for each. She tried numbers stuck in her head from old girlfriends and neighbors. Still no success. From directory assistance, she got the numbers for the network affiliate in Lubbock, the Lubbock police, and the Texas State Troopers. None of those calls went through either. She started the whole cycle over, yielding the same lack of success. After much debate, she reasoned that the Meitner house northeast of Lubbock might have been spared from the outage, but her courage in dialing was wasted. Still no service. She gave up and went to the receive room, hoping for something new to come in over the wire. Continuing to make phone calls, she only quit when WYNG's late news broadcast started at eleven. Reaching over to turn up a monitor's sound, her eyes and ears were fully on the anchor's opening story.

"Good evening, Chicago. A little over an hour ago, a powerful tornado tore through the downtown area of Lubbock, Texas."

A map immediately appeared to the right of the anchor's head, pinpointing the city. She had not expected this, and was suddenly overcome in feeling homesick... but more so just being worried sick.

"Eye witness accounts indicate that the tornado touched down multiple times in the heart of the city before cutting a wide swath of wreckage northeast

toward the airport. Power and other services have been knocked out. Reports are coming in from area hospitals indicating multiple fatalities from the storm, as well as casualties numbering in the many hundreds…"

She lowered her head to the console's tabletop and cried her way through the broadcast right up until the lead-in for weather. There was nothing new there… just a different twist applied to the pain in her heart. Back down her head went to the counter, there to stay until she was brought up by someone calling her name. Looking to the monitor, she noted that the news show had just finished, with the broadcast going to commercial.

"Marna? You still here?"

She sprang up and thrust her head out of the receive room, scanning about for the person calling her.

"In here. You heard something new on Lubbock?!"

"Ahh… no. But there's a call for you from someone there. It came in on the…"

"Never mind that – where is it? What line?"

She and the evening PA converged at the assignment desk, with him pointing at a phone's blinking light.

"There."

"Good. Thanks. Go help Phillips."

She knew that was a stupid thing to say, seeing as the program was over and Phillips was likely already on the way home. She nonetheless waited until the PA was out of earshot before snatching up the phone.

"Marna Forde here. Who is this?"

There was the static of a live line for several seconds before someone responded.

"Marna… can you hear me?"

"Roy… is that you?"

"Yes. I'm calling…"

"How'd you get this number?! Never mind that! What's going on in Lubbock. I've been worried sick. It's all over the news about the tornado wrecking the city, but I can't get through to…"

"Marna, stop! I don't have much time… others are waiting. I'm calling from a filling station in Idalou… It's the nearest place with service. It's… about your aunt…"

The line was suddenly filled with an unusual amount of static… so much so that she began shouting Roy's name while intermittently throttling one of the small plastic plungers on the phone's cradle. His voice came back in a matter of seconds.

"Marna? Are you still there?"

"I'm here, Roy… but speak up. I can barely hear you over the line noise."

"Marna… the tornado… it leveled the flower shop. It's gone. Completely destroyed. And Marna… I'm so terribly sorry. They found her… They found her body. Marna… she's… dead. Gwen's dead."

END OF WASP 3

WASP 4

ARCHITECT AND BUILDER

CHAPTER

24

BOEING 707

In a mere second – the time it took for a disconnected phone line to register in her thinking – every bit of the significance she had sought after through nearly every decision in her adult life had turned to nothing. Struck motionless at the assignment desk, she found herself constrained there by denial. Her hometown was obviously in great distress. Nothing could contend against that fact. The news was the news. But her own aunt Gwen being one of the dead... that simply could not be… even if her estranged husband claimed it as so. Surely it was total chaos there. People were confused. People were stunned. People were missing and unaccounted for. Likely, he had gotten bad information. It was only somebody that *looked* like Gwen… found by sheer coincidence in the rubble of the flower shop. He would call back soon to correct himself… so she should stay right here by this phone. Any second now, this thing would come to life. One of its little red lights would flash with assurance and its bell would wake her from this nightmare.

But Roy… he would never make such a call without being absolutely certain. I can tell from his voice… he had seen her with his own eyes. Aunt Gwen… she's… definitely dead.

The overhead lights to the newsroom suddenly went out, throwing her into a darkness offset only by a few scattered desk lamps left on. Everyone had gone home. She rose from the assignment desk and followed the beckon of an exit sign's neon glow out to the lobby elevators.

Tuesday, May 12th

She arrived back to her Oak Park apartment well after midnight. Immediately getting into bed, she slept little and was up before sunrise trying to figure out the fastest way to Lubbock. First, she called the newsroom for a run-down on the releases from overnight and left word for Billings that she would not be coming in. From the call, she learned that Lubbock's railyard was clogged with debris, but that was of little concern to her, as she was determined not to waste time sitting on a train. She would fly… no matter the cost. She also heard that the Lubbock airport had been closed by the FAA until every scrap of metal… every bolt, nail and screw… could be cleared off the runways. She spent the next half hour wrangling with a travel agent over the phone, finally settling on a round-trip ticket on American Airlines, arriving into Dallas Love Field at four in the afternoon. Getting from Dallas to Lubbock would be a different matter. Bus service directly into town was suspended owing to the fact that the station had been destroyed, and most of the city's inner streets were choked with wreckage. She would have to take the bus as near to Lubbock as it would go. Getting the rest of the way would be uncomfortable. In spite of her shock, she had managed last night to give Roy her apartment's phone number and requested that he call her first thing in the morning… by which time she hoped to have a plan sorted out for getting herself to Lubbock. That call from Roy came and went without much conversation. She did not seek an update on the city, and he provided none. He only offered to drive her from Dallas after her flight, but she informed him that she would take the bus instead… and would he very much mind picking her up in Slaton at eleven? She did not tell him that the twenty minute car trip from there was about all she could handle in being alone with him.

Minutes after hanging up that call, she had her suitcase completely packed. Out her apartment building and into a waiting cab, she made a quick stop at her bank and then was off to Midway Airport. She paid cash for her ticket at the airline counter, left her bag with the representative, and then moved in a daze past souvenir shops and eateries to her gate. There, she waited silently on the terminal's hard plastic seating, barely registering that this would be her first trip on a commercial airliner. In due course, her section was called forth for boarding, and she shuffled across a stretch of tarmac to the slow rhythm of those ahead of her climbing portable stairs into the plane. The polyester fabric of her seat was stained and badly worn along its front edge, but she did not care. Her thoughts were a thousand miles away. She had spent two years of her life in the place she was departing from and over two decades in the place she was heading to, yet she was leaving the known for the complete unknown.

She accepted a stethoscope-like headset from the stewardess, stuck its rubber tubing into the armrest's speaker holes, and put on the look of an experienced air traveler, hoping very much that other passengers would leave her be. She intentionally chose no music, instead allowing herself to become lost in the muffled drone of a muted headset. As the plane took off, banking through a slight arc in its climb over Chicago, she rested her head against the window and sought sleep… though nothing of the sort came. Instead, she found herself gazing out the window, as image after image of her aunt flew through her thoughts in a scatter… not unlike those passing clouds outside. Every wisp of them, in being disturbed by the plane's wing, disappeared to the rear in a tangle… just like her memories. The person she had known all her life was gone. Choices rejected and choices taken repeated themselves in her mind.

If only I'd called on Sunday to tell her how much I loved her… and that I regretted how things turned out… then maybe she might not have stayed late at the flower shop last night. Maybe she'd still be alive. But no… I had to be in control! I had to play it safe! Every decision I've ever made in my life has gone wrong!

The tray table latched into the seatback before her was rattling its agreement. Already, her legs were cramping in the shallow foot space below, and her hips ached from this uncomfortable seat. Even the storage bin above seemed to loom heavy in her mind. Nowhere she sought to put her arms felt right… not folded across her chest, not with hands wringing in her lap, and not with elbows on the armrests. She had only regrets to comfort herself with.

A tap to her shoulder startled her out of this fretful state. Pulling off her earphones, she turned to face the person seated beside her… and came to realize for the first time that this man was dressed in the uniform of the airline.

"You okay, Miss?"

"What? Oh… yes… I'm fine. I was just… Hey… are you a pilot?"

"Actually, a first officer… what you might call a co-pilot. I'm deadheading back here. Someone already got the jump seat."

"Pardon me?"

"I'm in transit… and there's no space for me in the cockpit. I… ahh… happened to notice that you were gripping your armrests. I just thought I'd let you know… everything's going to be fine. You can relax…"

Just then, a chime sounded… followed promptly by the voice of the captain announcing that the patch of rough air they were moving through would soon clear up. Everyone on board should remain belted in until then. Looking about, she noticed that the passengers across the aisle were sitting nervously in their seats, with one young woman giving off little gasps of panic every time the plane was jolted.

"There's nothing to worry about. They'll have everything under control soon. Just a little bit of the Dutch roll going on."

"The Dutch what?"

He held out a hand, palm down with fingers together, and began gyrating it about in a way that he obviously thought she would understand… tipping it side-to-side while changing the direction in which his fingers were pointing.

"It's when a plane's momentarily stuck in a cycle of yaws and rolls. Nothing to be concerned about… the 707 has stabilizing controls for dealing with the situation. It's just another one of those interesting things about flying."

She thanked the man and turned back to her window, hopefully communicating without words that she was not interested in conversing about air travel. True to his assertion, the plane settled down in a matter of minutes, allowing the cabin's occupants to relax. But not her. She had not really noticed what everyone else was troubling over… nor was she relieved when the conditions improved. There were no controls for the turbulence going on in her heart.

Time went on forever… and yet she suddenly found herself sitting in a taxi heading to the Dallas bus station. A ticket purchased… a bag stowed… a seat taken… all without her mind once moving from off her despair. Much of the six hour bus trip was spent in being jostled about between the grief of Gwen's death and the dread of seeing Roy again. Not that she was expecting anything harsh from him. He was, and always would be, a West Texas gentleman. Still… she could hardly make an appearance in Lubbock without venturing some form of apology toward him. His bitterness would likely show itself sooner or later. But she was determined to remain unaffected. Head-and-shoulders above every other bad decision she had made in life… with the possible exception of not calling Gwen when she had the chance… her elopement with Roy was the worst. Even her affairs with Grass and Azurean did not match up… though both of those relationships demonstrated her poor judgment when it came to men. So… she would be on her guard with Roy.

As the bus pulled off US84 in Slaton, her resolve was immediately put to the test. Roy was waiting at curbside. Out the window was the same face she had known since childhood…perhaps a bit more tanned than expected. What stood out most to her in the streetlights of Slaton was that he had allowed his sandy blond hair to grow out over his ears, across his forehead and down his neck. In this first look, she right off admitted to herself that he had a rugged handsomeness far exceeding those pretty boy looks of Azurean. Roy Meitner was a hunk. And then he smiled at her… and she wondered how it was that she had the balance to rise up on her feet. She could even sense it in her shaky steps down the aisle to the door. An anticipation grew in her during that hovered fraction of a second spent between bus and pavement, followed by a half hop-like prance and then a larger than normal stride… directly into his waiting arms. Even though this greeting was far from that of reunited lovers, she found that the feel of him was much better than the sight. There was no doubt as to the change in his upper body. Everything from forearms to shoulders, neck and back included, was so much firmer than what she had remembered from two years before. Only the droopiness to his eyes betrayed something of the weariness he must have experienced over the past twenty four hours.

"Marna, you look fantastic! And what you've done with your hair?! It's gorgeous!"

"Thanks. Funny… I was just about to say the same thing of you. The 70s suits you, Roy – never go back to the crew cut. And you're in such great shape! You've been working out?"

"Nah… just working. Let me get your bag. You must be bone-tired… and hungry too. Would you like a bite to eat before being dropped off?"

Despite the unexpected pleasure of seeing him, she instantly knew that it was time for separation.

"Thanks… but no. Just take me to Gwen's, if you don't mind. I've… got so much to deal with."

"Understood."

With her bag pointed out and him hoisting it into the back of his truck, she was brought up short when he cut in front to open the passenger-side door for her.

I forgot… Texas.

They moved out of Slaton along 84 toward a darkened horizon, as nearly the entire city of Lubbock seemed without power. That made the short drive all the more strange for her. She was seated not three feet from the man who was legally her husband… and heading into a blackness that was essentially her wounded hometown… yet none of it seemed real to her. To dispel this eerie awkwardness, she began rattling off questions that might be expected… anything pertaining to the subject of the tornado. To each, he responded without a hint of the strain that she was feeling on the inside. Whenever he glanced her way, it was always casual-like. No sign of concern at all. One hand managed the wheel while the rest of him slouched back comfortably in his seat. Roy seemed altogether at ease in her presence… which made her feel even more nervous.

On passing the last section of highway before veering onto Southeast Drive, the truck was suddenly plunged into darkness. With street lights out everywhere, she was at a loss for identifying the usual landmarks that served as indicators of an approach to her childhood home. She found herself shifted forward in her seat, scanning the full arc of glass in search of anything familiar.

"Not much damage done in this part of town… except for the hail. By and large, the neighborhoods to the south and west were spared."

"That's good."

She recognized that the truck had turned onto Gwen's street… and she had not yet asked about the state of the Meitner Appliance Store, it being only a half dozen blocks from the flower shop.

"What about the store?"

"We were one of the lucky ones. Most of the windows got busted out… and there's a good bit of water damage… but not much more than that. Roof needs re-tiling… but at least it's still intact."

As he came to a stop before Gwen's house, she was relieved that he did not turn the truck's engine off. Still… by the way he shifted about in the driver seat to face her, it was clear that he had things to say before she could get out. The dull yellow of the dashboard lighting cast half of his face into a mournful hue. With the other half dark and the downturned incline of his head, she picked up on a hint of something different in him. Maybe a survivor's guilt.

"It's inexplicable, Marna. Most of the buildings around us were severely damaged… some completely leveled… but not our place…" He reached down to his left, and a long stretch of her old street went into darkness as he lowered the truck's high-beams to normal. "You know… I'm thinking about doing something as a way of offering relief to the city. Maybe replacement appliances at prices substantially below wholesale… something like that. What do you think of the idea?"

"Sounds great… but why bother asking me? It's your store. Do what you think's best."

Roy stared back blankly at her.

"Good point."

The dome light came on as he made to get out of the truck.

Nice going, Marna! Real smooth!

She shot a hand over to grip his forearm.

"Roy... don't bother. I can get my bag. You've already done enough for me. I'm really grateful for you picking me up in Slaton... but I'm not going to impose on you any longer." She knew that more words than these were due to him. There were so many things that needed to be said... painful explanations going back more than two years. She had spent the entire bus ride struggling through their past together. All of that had to come out sooner or later. But first, she had to face a different sort of ordeal. She had to enter into Gwen's house. "Listen... I know we need to talk... I owe you that much... but please... not just yet. There's so much I need to deal with first. Everything... Gwen's death... coming back here... seeing you... none of it was on my mind when I woke up yesterday morning. Please... let me first sort through Gwen's affairs and... get past the funeral... then you and I can sit down together. Does that... sound reasonable?"

"Sure, Marna. Makes perfect sense. We'll talk when you're ready. In the meantime... is there anything I can do for you? Perhaps I could come by in the morning so you can see the shop."

"No. Not tomorrow. I'm... not ready for that yet."

He made another move to get out, and as her hand was still on his arm, she squeezed it firmly enough for him to understand.

"Stay. I can manage."

Which was true, though her real desire was to avoid an uncomfortable parting on Gwen's front porch. She relaxed as the truck's dome light went out... and then came back on as she opened her own door.

"Hang on, Marna. Before you go... there's a flashlight in there." He dipped his head toward the glove compartment. "You're welcome to it. Should come in handy 'til the power's back on."

"Thanks, Roy. That's... considerate of you."

Having removed the flashlight, she clicked it's button and shifted the beam out the car door on stepping down. A reflection came back from the vicinity of the driveway, and she noted an unfamiliar sedan parked there.

"Roy... there's a strange car here..."

She turned back to him as he peered around her through the open door.

"Oh... almost forgot." He slid forward a bit in the truck seat in order to scrounge in his pocket... and then stretched his hand across to her. "Here... Gwen's keys."

She did not at first register what he was implying. For the briefest of moments, a fanciful thought passed through her thinking – that if Roy had Gwen's keys... if Gwen's keys had survived... then Gwen must have also. But she quickly recognized the absurdity before he spoke again.

"It's another one of the odd things about the storm. Her car was parked behind the flower shop… I guess more-or-less where she usually left it. It's got lots of dents in the body from flying debris… but it's still in fine working condition."

"I don't understand, Roy… how'd you manage to get ahold of her keys?"

"They were in the ignition. Tell you the truth… I had a devil-of-a-time getting that car out of there this afternoon. Had to sneak past the National Guard… and then drive around bulldozers working the streets. I dropped it off here and got a ride from…"

"When'd she get rid of the Skylark?"

As he shrugged his shoulders, she realized that it was a silly thing to ask. Roy had no greater part in Gwen's life than she did.

Reaching back through the open passenger side, she took the keys from him and then closed the car door, instantly throwing him into the same pallid light as before. She hefted her suitcase out of the truck bed, rapped on the fender twice to let him know he could leave, and then brought the flashlight's beam onto the walkway before her. She heard the truck's gears shift, a slight rev to the engine, and then the sound of tires crunching off down the street. Moving to the front steps, she did not turn around to watch him leave, deciding that she needed to transition her thinking to Gwen.

She found the front door unlocked… something she had not anticipated after two years of living in Chicago. Entering the darken house, she instinctively went for the switch that she had, in times past, flipped to activate the sitting room's lights. When nothing happened, she felt a tremor of dread run through her, but then scowled at herself on remembering the city-wide power outage. Obviously, the house had not gone dead with its owner.

With the aid of Roy's flashlight, she passed through the sitting room and into the kitchen. Reaching into a bottom drawer, she pulled out a second flashlight, and then dropped it back on discovering the batteries to be dead. She instead drew out several candles, candle stands, and a half-used booklet of matches. Briefly noting the matchbook cover, a restaurant Gwen frequented, she ripped off three matches and dragged them as one across the charcoal pad. The burst of light startled her, particularly as it briefly lit up the kitchen with a bright orange glow. But almost immediately, all faded into shadow as the sulfurous ends burnt away. Starting with a lit taper, she went about the house placing others in strategic spots that provided her with an illuminated pathway in which to move about. She situated one on the kitchen table, another on a counter near the entry, one on the dining room table, and another on an end table across the sitting room. Pausing there to wrap a tissue about the base of the starter candle so as to prevent guttered wax from dripping on her fingers, she glanced back toward the kitchen's yellow glow.

Way too eerie.

With two candles remaining, she moved down the short hallway to place one on the bathroom vanity. Surveying the state of things, her eyes went from the towel draped over the curtain rod to the neat little heap of clothes lying on the floor at the base of the tub. The morning before, Gwen had stepped out of those pajamas and into her last ever shower. She did not like having that thought, so she kicked the pile into a corner before leaving the bathroom. One candle remained for three rooms – her old bedroom, Gwen's bedroom and the office, the doors of which were all closed.

Those places can stay dark for all I care.

She blew out the taper in her hand and returned to the front room. The little she had seen of Gwen's house thus far resembled what she remembered from that day four years ago when she last walked out the door. Purposing not to examine anything in more detail, she retrieved her suitcase from the entry way and toted it to the dining room table. Reentering the kitchen, she made a study of the icebox's contents using the flashlight, and was relieved to find everything still cool. She took out cold cuts, lettuce and a pitcher of what looked like sweet tea, then set about making herself a sandwich. Sitting at the kitchen table, she ate while staring into the fiery brand before her, trying not to think… or feel… or remember. In all this world, she longed for the small flame flickering beyond the rim of her plate to be all that mattered. Only it sensed her existence. It fluttered with each breath… and wavered whenever the air was disturbed by her raising the sandwich to her mouth. To be in such a state… just a dot of light devoid of all misery… was something she greatly craved. If only she could be like that small, fluid-like arrowhead of brightness. Holding her breath and sitting very still, she stared into the flame, allowing the likeness of its purity to be imprinted upon her retinas… hoping very much to have that as the only image following her into sleep.

She finished the last piece of crust, blew out the candle, and moved to place her plate and glass in the sink. Within, she found a small skillet, spatula and fork – the typical kitchen equipment that Gwen employed in making her favorite Tex-Mex omelet. She added her dishes on top and turned away, blowing out the remaining candle before leaving the kitchen.

Opening her suitcase, she rummaged about for night clothes, changed right there in the dining room, and then took up her bag of toiletries. Once more, she blew out another candle and headed for that dim light playing out from the bathroom into the hallway. In short order, she was finished with the bathroom, delaying there only to extract sheets and a blanket from its small closet. The familiar floral patterns of Gwen's linen teased at her mind, tempting her for memories.

Not yet.

She extinguished the bathroom candle and stepped out into the hall's darkness. Returning to the front room, she made up the couch as best as she could, shimmied herself between the sheets, and then drew close the only remaining sources of light – the last of Gwen's lit candles and Roy's flashlight. She looked between these, knowing that neither could be relied upon for long. Gwen was gone forever from her life… as would Roy soon be. She clicked off the flashlight and positioned it on the floor near the couch where it could be retrieved, and then blew out the candle. The living room was instantly thrown into the kind of darkness that she remembered only a West Texas night could produce – a dry and dusty sort of blackness, devoid of contrasts. Turning her back to it all, she pulled the sheet over her shoulder, balled a throw pillow under her head, and waited for morning's first light.

<u>Wednesday, May 13th</u>

Though waking in a predawn darkness, she easily recognized where she was. She had taken so many naps on this very couch in her youth. In the night, the slumbering skill for sleeping here had come back to her… sort of like the wobbly riding one experiences when having not sat on a bicycle for a long time. Actually… she had hardly slept at all from so many restless hours of pitching about. It had not helped that the power got restored in the middle of the night. With the sitting room lights having been switched on, she was launched fully awake in the sudden brightness, and then had a difficult time falling asleep again after turning everything off.

With the early morning sun finally piercing through the curtains at the front window, casting its muted beams across the easy chair where Gwen typically spent her evenings, she gave up trying to coax out one last hour of sleep. Tired and disheveled, she swung her legs off the couch and immediately registered the feel of the corded throw rug beneath her feet… something she had not noticed the night before. Leaning forward on the couch, she rubbed the dullness out of her eyes in order to focus on what her toes were feeling. This huge oval rug covered nearly all of the sitting room floor. The thing had always fascinated her as a child. In a single braided strand as wide as a finger, the weavers had looped the cord about itself in much the same way one might in rolling up a fabric measuring tape. Because of that, the strands changed colors as the cord whirled about itself from the center, blending through the spectrum and back again many times over before reaching the outer rim. She remembered often lying on her belly and tracing a path round and round through the colors… or moving to the edge with her face close to the weave, hunting for rainbows on the surface.

Sitting on the couch while staring down at that rug, she realized that she had an unpleasant task before her – one of deciding which of Gwen's things to keep and which to give away… or sell… or trash. Having to make a decision on every single item of Gwen's was sure to bring many more memories. All of a sudden, the rug did not seem so special after all.

I don't want it. I don't want any of it! Except the relief, of course. I've always cherished that.

Her eyes immediately rose up to the opposite wall, to the place that had always been the relief's home. In staring directly ahead, it was several seconds before she registered a difference.

It's gone!

In the place of the sculpture was… in her early morning reckoning… a tacky-looking piece of framed artwork comprised of globs of paint from a desert-colored palette smeared about in a rather modernish way of depicting a West Texas landscape. Looking to the other walls, she was surprised not to find the relief anywhere.

She sprang from the couch to make a quick search of the other rooms in the house. Not finding it in either the office or Gwen's room, she next entered her old bedroom… and was momentarily brought up short by its appearance. Once painted in a downy blue, the walls were now in a rather blandish white. All of the furniture she had grown up with was gone. Instead, the bare floor was scattered over with many boxes. Most seemed closed off and dust covered… except for the one nearest her. With a folding chair before it, Gwen had obviously begun emptying its contents into orderly stacks on the floor. She was really not interested in any of it. Noting that the relief was not in this room either, she returned to the sitting room and stood cross-armed before where it once hung.

I don't care if I ran away to Pluto, she had no right to sell it off without offering it to me first!

Disregarding the obvious – that Gwen could do with her own things as she pleased – she stared her consternation at the replacement, demanding it to account for the relief's absence. Realizing that her fingernails were cutting neat little grooves into her arms, she shifted both hands to her hips and continued to fight off the unpleasant thought that Gwen had gotten rid of the relief out of spite. Not having achieved any sort of satisfaction from this pouting, she stepped forward to grip opposite sides of the painting and lift it off the wall. The frame was wide and surprisingly heavy, making management of it more cumbersome than expected. Because of that… and the consequence of her growing anger… she callously released her hold on the painting short of the floor. The frame cracked loudly on contact. Ignoring whatever damage had been done to the painting, she studied the bare space on the wall before her. The heavy brackets that once supported the relief were obviously gone, though the outline of their presence had left a clear discoloration on the wall. It was easy to trace out where the relief had once hung. Try as she might, she could not fashion that rectangular spot into a re-creation of what had once so captivated her childhood hopes and dreams. Her eyes ventured down to the painting leaning against the wall, and instantly it became a target of her resentment toward Gwen.

Stepping forward, she took hold of the frame's upper rim with both hands to turn the painting around… but in awkwardly swinging the thing about, got the damaged corner snagged on the sitting room rug. Tugging at it, she nearly tore the lower portion of the frame off, while significantly snarling the rug in the process. Ignoring the harm done to both, she flung the painting against the wall and left for the bathroom, carrying along an awareness that she had just destroyed one piece of art for it not being another. On entering, her eyes fell upon the small pile of Gwen's cast off clothing that she had kicked aside last night. It instantly became a rebuked to her for the wreckage she had just done in the sitting room. She scooped it all up and hurled it down into the hamper.

There's no such thing as the ghost of someone's pajamas.

After a quick shower in the place where she had bathed for twelve years of her life, though now felt as an intruder, she went to the kitchen to make coffee and toast. More or less on autopilot, she then set herself toward sorting through the desk, file cabinets and closet in her aunt's home office, for this seemed to be a straightforward enough chore with little emotion to it. Without scrutinizing anything in great detail, she began sorting paper into piles. Designating one corner of the room for trash, she tossed there any catalogs, magazines, or brochures pertaining to flowers. In the center of the floor, she formed two separate stacks. One pile was for receipts, records, tax-related documents and other business paperwork. All of that would go to the accountant. The other was comprised of letters Gwen had received. To this pile, she added Gwen's address book. Given time and a proper state of mind, she hoped to personally write to as many of Gwen's friends as possible, telling them the sad news of her death. Then in one last pile, it being formed in the very center of Gwen's desk, she placed anything pertaining to property, bank and savings accounts, investments, or insurance policies.

Throughout the morning of sorting, she would occasionally lift the receiver off the desk phone to test for an active line. Having prepared herself a tuna salad sandwich for lunch, she came back to nudge the phone with an elbow, and was greeted with the sound of a dial tone.

Just get it done!

Even before taking a bite of lunch, she set herself toward making funeral arrangements for Gwen. Phone service was evidently still out for most of Lubbock, for she had to dial four numbers from the yellow pages before getting through to someone.

"Pritchett Funeral Home, sharing in Lubbock's sorrows for three generations, Marianne Pritchett speaking. How may I help you?"

She hesitated before responding. The voice, she did not recognize, but something about the name poked at her memory.

"Umm, yes… I'm calling regarding my aunt. She… recently passed away… and I need to arrange for her funeral."

"I'm so sorry for your loss."

"Thanks. I've… never had to do this before. So… to start off, I'm kind of hoping to have her service on Saturday."

"I'm so sorry… given the circumstances of the tornado and all, we're completely booked up for the weekend. Perhaps a time next week would…"

"She was killed in the tornado."

"Oh my! I'm terribly sorry! Of course! We've placed a priority on helping the families of those poor victims. I'm sure we can squeeze you in."

"Thanks. I really appreciate it."

"So, the best thing to do would be for me to make you an appointment to speak with our director. He'll sort everything out for you. Might I have the name of the deceased?"

"Gwen Forde. I'm her niece."

The line suddenly went quiet… then burst out into a loud shriek.

"Marna! This is Marianne! Marianne McCluskey from high school! Well… now it's Marianne Pritchett. But surely you remember me!? We had Social Studies together… and Mrs. Watkins for Home Ec… and French, and… wait, I never took French… maybe it was Latin. Oh, I don't know! But you… you were always the smart one. Of course, you were a year ahead of me. Hey – do you recall the time when we served together on the homecoming committee and…"

She could not register having ever known a McCluskey, and in no way could she put a face to the name… despite having evidently spent so much of their high school years together. With the woman showing signs of going on and on about their mutual experiences, she interrupted with a lie, hoping it would move things along.

"Sure… I absolutely do. So… I was thinking…"

But this Marianne just ignored her.

"*Of course* you heard that I got married. So sorry that you couldn't be there! You would have made such a scrumptious bridesmaid! But can you believe it's been two years?! Marna, it was such a beautiful wedding! You would have loved it! We had hundreds of lilies… And my dress! You should have seen my dress! I was absolutely stunning! I went all the way to Dallas for it. My mother insisted on something traditional… but I told CP that I wanted…"

CP? CP Pritchett! Oh shit! I completely forgot! His father runs a funeral parlor!

She was overcome with a desire to hang up and try her luck with a different establishment.

"…but how insensitive of me! Going on about my wedding when your own marriage hasn't worked out! No one ever imagines that a perfect couple like you and Roy would ever break up! Why, it was just yesterday that I was telling CP about…"

"Marianne… it sounds like you're terribly busy at the moment. Maybe I should call another funeral home."

"Nonsense, Marna! CP will definitely fit you in. You know he's been running the business ever since his father passed away… God rest his soul. His death was so traumatic. Anyway… and I have this right from the mayor's second cousin… the Summerset and Willabee homes won't reopen until next week. Tornado damage, you know. Not to worry – you have us! I'll just pencil you in to speak with CP at… eight tomorrow morning. He'll be so excited to see you…" The woman uncharacteristically lowered both her voice and the pace of her words. "…despite the tragic circumstances of your aunt's passing."

Marianne's conversational grip picked right back up in expressing her own disappointment over not being on hand tomorrow, seeing as she would be visiting her sister in San Angelo. It was several more minutes before she was able to divest herself from the call, hanging up with much uncertainty. It had been many years since she last saw CP. What would he be like… and would he willingly help her given their history together? She had to also put that issue into the bin of the things already bothering her.

One of which was the doorbell – someone was now ringing it. It was the neighbor from across the street, a woman she had not spoken with in years. As if it was obvious, the neighbor did not offer her name, so it was far too awkward to ask for it.

"Look here, dearie… I brought you a bunt cake. Orange glazing, just the way you liked it as a little girl."

"Oh… thanks."

"So terribly sorry to hear about Gwen. You must be all broken up on the inside. I was when I lost my dear Ralph. Cried for weeks and weeks. So if you should need anything, I'm just right across the street. Especially if you feel the need to unburden yourself about what's been going on in your life. Just know that I'm here for you."

"Umm… thanks. I'm fine for now… but I really need to get back to… urr… the thing I was doing."

She got the door closed just in time, for on handing over the bunt cake, the woman put a foot forward as if expecting to be welcomed inside.

She was only back in the office for thirty minutes or so before the doorbell rang again. Another neighbor, another home-cooked dish, more words of sympathy, and more curiosity about what she had been doing with herself since leaving Lubbock years ago. To her annoyance, this trend kept up through the afternoon. Every hour or so, a neighbor or a loyal flower shop patron stopped by for a visit, with her repeatedly being drawn forth from her seclusion in the office to answer the front door. To the more persistent ones, she just had to be blunt, as there was only so much time available for sorting out Gwen's affairs.

Sometime midafternoon, she came across a letter from a law firm in town dated nearly five years prior. The gist of it was nothing more than a few lines stating that an issue regarding easement along the alleyway behind the flower shop had been resolved. What caught her eye was that the lawyer – a Mr. Claude T. Peabody – had addressed her aunt as 'Dear Gwendolyn,' which suggested something of a long-term business relationship between the two. She dialed the number for 'Peabody & Peabody,' but received an outcome of no service. She went to the phone book and found a white pages listing for the lawyer's home, and was relieved when someone answered after two rings. Following a brief exchange of introductions and commiserations, Mr. Peabody agreed to handle all legal issues associated with settling Gwen's personal and business affairs. As far as he could recall, there was nothing in Gwen's will preventing her from acting on behalf of her aunt. Of course, it would take some time to retrieve that will, as the National Guard had not yet opened the downtown area in order for his law team to assess the damage done to their offices. Though he had a long list of clients requiring his assistance in making insurance claims and filing for disaster aid, he promised to make Gwen his personal priority.

She went back to sorting through the paperwork. By early evening, she had managed to clear out both sets of file cabinets and go through every nook of the desk. Just before taking a break for dinner, she came across a lock box hidden away in the back of a bottom drawer... the key to which was fortuitously attached to the cluster Roy had given her. Inside were the sorts of things people kept stowed away in a safe place – a passport issued in 1947 without any subsequent use, a thick stack of papers in a folder bound by a binder clip, a safety deposit box key, and a small black velvet-covered box. Initially intending to start in on the papers, she found herself reaching for the black box instead. Within was a diamond ring seated upright in the small slot of a white cushion. For a long time, she just stared at this ring, not once daring to touch it. The size and cut were of no remarkable distinction, looking very much like the one that Roy had once given her. Yet she knew simply by how Gwen had kept it hidden away that this ring was sacred. Closing the lid, she reverently carried the ring box into the sitting room and slid it into her purse. She immediately collapsed into Gwen's easy chair and began to cry. Of all the many secrets her aunt had never shared with her, seeing that ring was the worst. How they could have cried as one over whatever that ring had meant to her. That moment alone would have brought them so close together. But no... Gwen had remained closed off.

Sometime after having cleared her eyes of tears, she returned to the study. She next thumbed through the stack of papers taken from the folder. Within were deeds to the house and the flower shop, a copy of Gwen's will, several certificates of deposit in varying amounts between two and ten thousand dollars, receipts for the purchase of thirty five thousand dollars of long-term Treasury bonds, and documentation on the ownership of various stocks. Her one surprise was that there was no sign of anything in the pile resembling a life insurance policy. Seeing all of this made her tremble with such rage. Minutes ago she had been crying, but now... she was absolutely seething.

She put the papers back into the folder and dropped it beside her purse on the end table in the sitting room, all destined for the lawyer to sort out. Without pause, she headed out the front door into a pleasant West Texas evening... except nothing about it seemed pleasant to her. To be confronted again with proof that Gwen had been so very well-off... that she had ample funds for sending her niece to the college of her choosing… but had chosen to lie instead – there was absolutely no way she could stay in the woman's house for another second! Gwen's deception had been responsible for so much that had gone wrong in her life.

Beginning with a steady pace, she set off in a walk around the block while also fighting off resentments that went all the way back to her senior year in high school.

But… Gwen did apologize for those things. She was really broken up in that letter…

Well… what difference does that make now?! She's dead… and I'll never get the satisfaction of unburdening myself of this anger!

She went on with faster and longer strides, keeping up the loops about the block until weariness and the setting of the sun provided some small perspective to her frustrations. With no more energy for working out her bitterness, she returned inside to plop back down in the desk chair. The only thing remaining in the lock box was the safety deposit key. Twirling it about in her fingers as she calmed herself, she decided that this key should go to the lawyer too… along with so many other things in life that Gwen had kept from her.

Rather than continuing to fume, she started in on the closet, but was disappointed to find that its boxes contained nothing capable of providing new insight into the person of her aunt. It was all just a bunch of worthless catalogs, household knick-knacks, and seasonal decorations.

Near on midnight, she gave up on the office in favor of going to bed, still carrying along so many frustrations. One was especially perplexing to her, for in all of her searching, she had not yet uncovered a single clue as to the whereabouts of the relief. Given time tomorrow, she would start in on the boxes laid out in her old bedroom.

She changed, brushed her teeth, washed her face, and then stretched out on the couch as before. Having turned out the light, she immediately fell asleep.

CHAPTER
25

WHEN THE DEAD
UNBURY THE LIVING

<u>Thursday, May 14th</u>

Within thirty minutes of the all-clear signal sent out Monday night on the city's only functioning radio station, KFYO, an emergency operation center was established in the basement of City Hall. Lubbock then went to work. With the full authority of the city's newly elected dentist-turned-mayor, rescue teams comprised of various levels of law enforcement, along with citizen volunteers, began coordinated searches through the wreckage… mostly by aid of flashlight. Hospitals and fire stations within a hundred mile radius were already dispatching their rescue capabilities to Lubbock. Representatives from civil defense, public health, utilities, and various county agencies were also gathered in the EOC. By morning, the governor had declared the city a disaster area and dispatched over 400 National Guard troops for its protection. President Nixon would follow-up with a similar declaration the next day, activating a wide spectrum of national relief functions from the Army Corp of Engineers to the Federal Housing Administration.

Long before State or Federal aid could arrive, the city itself had already become fully engaged in its own recovery. The local Salvation Army and American Red Cross, along with area churches and civic groups, had begun organizing relief in the form of food, water, bedding and clothing to be delivered to make-shift shelters and field kitchens in such well-known locations as the Municipal Civics Center and the Texas Tech University Campus. Citizen support was being directed by radio and TV stations as they came back online, with the *Lubbock Avalanche* providing detailed information in each day's edition. Even amateur ham-radio enthusiasts pitched in to provide communication with the outside world.

The primary water pumping station was back functioning after eighteen hours, and though two of the three power plants had been severely damaged, electricity was restored to ninety percent of the city within days. Although phone lines to over thirty thousand customers had been knocked out, Southwestern Bell telephone engineers had over half of these back up within twenty four hours. The Army Corp of Engineers and the Texas State Highway Department, along with help from private owners of heavy machinery, had the majority of the city's streets and thoroughfares reopened in thirty six hours... though the wreckage of homes and businesses themselves would linger in place for many months.

The concentrated relief effort of the citizenry, and of local, state and federal agencies outlasted the devastation. The Lubbock recovery would become a model of effective disaster relief, garnering commendations from the President himself. From that very storm would precipitate the basis by which all tornados were to be categorized and understood – the so-called Fujita Scale. Meteorologists for decades to come would study the Lubbock tornado in order to improve predictive and early warning efforts. The whole nation held the city of Lubbock in high regard for what they had overcome.

These were the types of things that she would come to learn in the future while working on the news... but as she woke up on Thursday morning from a lousy night spent on Gwen's couch, she had absolutely no interest in what was going on in Lubbock. She simply could not spare a bit of herself for the city. Her own personal grief and anger had combined together to keep her completely detached. Of course she knew that extensive damage had been done to homes and businesses. Thousands had been injured and thousands more made homeless. She was also aware that a double blow of hardship would come in the following weeks as many of the city's bread-winners went without work. Yet there was something far worse on her mind. Twenty seven citizens of the great state of Texas had lost their lives because of that tornado, with Gwen Forde... her aunt... being one of them. She could not possibly think about contributing service... or gathering food... or offering any form of sympathy.

Sitting on the edge of the couch trying to rouse herself for the day ahead, she instead was replaying the opening story of WYNG's late show – her show.

She remembered distinctly how the WYNG anchor had first deepened his voice with all seriousness. So likely had countless other newscasters across the country in telling their audiences about Lubbock's tragedy… right before switching to an upbeat lead-in for sports. The end to Gwen's life had been nothing more than a digit conveying a particular day's happenings. 'Twenty six,' had Gwen survived, or 'twenty seven,' made little difference to the news… as long as the facts were presented both accurately and succinctly. Her aunt's death was already forgotten.

The news would never be the same for her.

Yet she also knew that the outrage of having her city and her loved one being reported on so callously was not the only thing ripping apart her insides. She was still bound up in the fury of a different kind of storm – one emanating from the choices of her own past. Gwen was dead, and there was now no making anything right by way of giving or receiving. That was her fault. A guilt worth being reported on by every newsroom in America. She wanted that letter back. She wanted that moment in time back to respond the way she should have – by picking up her apartment phone and calling Gwen when she had the chance. She knew it now – it had been her pride that had insisted on protecting itself. How could she ever forgive herself for that?!

And then there was still the matter of Roy to be considered. Really… she should put that one out of her mind for now and focus on the issue at hand… like getting herself going this morning. So she ate breakfast quickly, intent on leaving the house as soon as possible in order to avoid a repeat of the previous day's interruptions from her neighbors. After all, she did have a long list of things to occupy herself with. Taking her aunt's Chevy Nova… a car she considered super-dumpy… she made for the Pritchett Funeral Home, it being located in the northwest outside the Loop. The route there would afford her an opportunity to see something of the effect of the tornado on the city… and on the flower shop in particular. She was not looking forward to this, but somehow knew that seeing the damage done to the shop was a necessary prerequisite for putting Gwen to rest.

Hitting 4th Street from off of Avenue H and turning left, she was not prepared for the magnitude of the destruction. In an abrupt transition, she was suddenly presented with structures whose roofs had been peeled off or burst asunder as if from the inside out. Building after building she had walked past as a child was cleaved in two, half left standing and half crumpled up as if a mere wad of paper. Power poles were broken like matchsticks. A lumberyard she had always been impressed with was completely gone, with its inventory of wood scattered about like so many fallen pine needles. Only the massive Burrus grain elevator seemed untouched. Peering about it to the north, she was shocked to see what had become of the once vibrant Mexican-American neighborhood of Guadalupe. It was now a barren wasteland. Everywhere, bulldozers and tractors were making piles out of someone's broken dreams.

But the worst for her was reserved a block ahead. She came to an abrupt stop in front of where Gwen's flower shop should have been. Though a small portion of the back wall still stood, nothing else remained of the place where she had spent so many days, year after year, trimming stems and sweeping floors. What had become of the greater part of it in the storm was now a confused arrangement of broken timbers, roof fragments, and so much twisted metal. She did not get out of the car... did not even shift the transmission out of drive. The tears welling up compelled her to leave immediately. Pulling away from the curb, itself scattered about with much debris, she merged back into the uncharacteristically sparse traffic of 4th Street, concentrating hard on seeing nothing other than the passing of her lane's broken lines. She knew immediately that the flower shop would never be rebuilt.

She drove on to the northwest location of the Pritchett Funeral Home, it being situated on a large tract of land just outside the Loop. She had heard from Gwen that CP's grandfather purchased property in the rural outskirts of the city decades before planners had conceived of the idea for a beltway about Lubbock. It was CP's father who founded the business there by obtaining the necessary permits to convert the barren piece of farmland into a cemetery. With the Loop nearly completed now, Lubbock had expanded out to and surrounded the cemetery in the same way the Loop had encircled Lubbock. She remembered little of the funeral home from the last time she saw it. On that day, she had barely lifted her eyes from off the pavement as Roy escorted her inside for George's service. Now, she stood before the four immense white columns supporting a narrow façade that bore the black lettering of the establishment's name. Pausing there in the parking lot, she took in the gabled roof, the large wooden front doors, the black shuttered-framed windows, and brickwork wrapping around both sides to the rear. To her, the place rather gave off the feel of a church... or perhaps a bank.

She passed between the columns and across a narrow vestibule-like porch with its display of upcoming services. Through the front doors, she entered a large lobby-like area, completely devoid of seating. Nothing to the space seemed familiar to her... until she happened to peer down a rear hallway toward a carport. Back there was a side door out to a lattice-covered cloister.

Even without laying eyes on it, the feel instantly came back to her of being broken down in tears because Ruby and Sybil banished her from George's service. She shook off the memory, resolving not to convolve that dreadful experience with the present need. There were decisions to be made, with no emotional margin available for reflecting on the Meitners.

To her left were wide-open double doors leading into a showroom of sorts. Within, she could easily make out the displays of caskets, some closed off and some with lids propped open in full or split configurations. A sound of movement to the right drew her attention that way. CP was stepping from behind a black drape.

"Marna Meitner… or is it Forde? So good to see you again."

"Hello, CP… and Forde will do. I suppose your wife mentioned my aunt…"

"Yes… what a trying time for you. On behalf of my family, let me offer you our deepest condolences."

She thanked him warmly, yet wishing to get beyond the pleasantries to the chore at hand. There were so many other things requiring her attention.

"Please, step this way to a place where we can speak in private."

She followed him around the drape into what turned out to be his office. Someone had put effort into making this brightly paneled room feel homey. There were comfortable-looking couches, modest wall decorations, and a small consultation area before a very orderly desk. CP motioned her to a chair and sat down in an adjacent one. He repeated his sympathies again and then launched right into an overview of his parlor's services. Through it all, she strained to pay attention, but was repeatedly distracted by this older version of CP. Just as she remembered, his nose was narrow and pointy at its end, with a chin to match. The eyes had never been what she might call beady, though they always seemed to move about in a hawk-like fashion, searching for his next victim. Now, those eyes looked tired. Even his face seemed thinner than she recalled… and paler too… but without that spooky necromancer feel that she had often associated with undertakers. In fact, his suit was just as business-like as what Mr. Carswell might wear. If anything, CP seemed uncharacteristically somber. There was none of that devil-may-care feel to him.

"So you see, Marna, the best I can offer you… given the circumstances… is a graveside service late Saturday afternoon. Might even have to be in the early evening… let me check the schedule." He rose, went around his desk to an open appointment book, and then came back to her before speaking. "If you're determined to have the service on Saturday, then the only thing I can offer is an hour time slot starting at six."

"I was really hoping for something inside… with a private graveside burial afterward."

"Marna, I so wish I could provide that for you. Unfortunately, the parlor's rooms are completely booked from now until next Tuesday. Not to be crass, but we've been busier than ever before. You probably don't realize it… it's not the kind of thing a normal person would want to know… but on average, three point four deaths occur in Lubbock each day. Of those, we're typically called upon to provide services for one, maybe two individuals. As you know from the paper, twenty seven people lost their lives on Monday, one being your dear aunt. There was also a family of five… so tragic. What with other funeral homes being shut down because of the tornado… Marna… we're stretched thin beyond our ability to help grieving families lay their loved ones to rest. I'm sorry… it'll have to be a graveside service between six and seven on Saturday. Take it or leave it. To tell you the truth, I'm going to have a difficult enough time getting the driving lanes cleared out from the previous service so my guys can get in to set up for Gwen."

"Then I'll take it."

"Excellent. So… let's get started with the casket."

He rose and led her out of his office, across the funeral home's lobby, and into his showroom, all the while telling her about his latest models.

"CP, I just want a standard coffin. Nothing terribly elaborate. Gwen wouldn't have approved of anything beyond bare necessities."

"Okay… but you'll at least want something that looks nice. Consider this one over here." She followed him to a back corner of the room. "This is boned maple over a carbon steel liner. Very durable. You have several options as to the color and fabric for the lining. The wood finish gives off…"

"I'll take it. What's next?"

"The headstone. Allow me to show you our catalog from which…"

At least she was prepared for this. She quickly pulled a slip of paper from her purse and thrust it forward.

"This is what I think Gwen would have wanted. Just her name, birthdate and… the date of her death. And she wouldn't want a headstone. She'd have wanted one of those… those… stone thingies." The word had been on her mind earlier that morning when she prepared this note, but she could not produce it now. Instead, she held out her fingers and thumbs to form a rectangular box-like shape and acted out setting it down before him. "You know… it lies flat in the ground."

"You mean a flagstone?"

"That's it!"

"Marna, are you sure? I mean... your aunt was a prominent business-woman in Lubbock."

"That's what she would have wanted. I'm sure of it. Nothing fancy in life, nothing fancy in death. And don't make it out of something expensive."

"As you wish. We'll do a simple granite flagstone... but I insist it be weather-treated. I'll cover the cost of that myself. Now... I have a few more questions, and then I think I can prepare an estimate for you. If you would accompany me back to my office..."

They returned the way they had come. After resuming their previous seats, CP started to assure her as to the handling of Gwen's body. She waved him off, wanting to hear none of that.

"I definitely do *not* want an open casket! I... do have a formal gown of black satin in the car that I'd like her dressed in. I really want her to look nice." In fact, she wanted Gwen to look stunning in death... but would never have the courage to see it for herself. "Please... just make sure that she's there well before the service begins. I don't want her casket being brought up from a hearse while everyone's watching."

CP nodded.

"Now, as to the plot..."

"She really wouldn't care. Whatever's available would be fine."

He stared at her for several seconds before responding.

"Marna... remember that this service is as much for you as for your aunt."

She could not confess what she truly desired, which was returning to Chicago. Beyond a doubt, she would never revisit Gwen's grave.

"Then whatever'll work best for accommodating a bunch of people."

"Okay... I would have liked to walk you over the grounds... let you see the options... but as you wish. So... I will personally select a peaceful plot for her. Now... since your aunt was not much of a church goer... I mean no disrespect... it's fairly well-known in the community... would you be willing to have one of our partner clergy provide a brief eulogy? There'll be no charge for this."

"That would be very nice... but make sure it's nothing about Gwen or her beliefs. Actually... I'm planning to give a remembrance of my own." A memory suddenly hit her regarding Gwen's displeasure at having others comment on her choices in life. "But CP... I absolutely *do not* want anyone else to speak! No parting words from friends or any of that sort of thing."

He nodded his understanding.

"Just so you know... the weather forecast for the weekend is clear and warm. Might even be over eighty at the time of the service. You could have awnings for the attendees, but I'd advise against it… wind. Let's see… how many chairs should we set up?"

Though he seemed to be asking himself, she knew he wanted her best estimate.

"Maybe fifty…?"

Again, he stared back before speaking.

"Marna… this is Gwen Forde we're talking about. She's sold flowers to over half of Lubbock. You can certainly expect at least…"

"Oh my! I almost forgot about flowers! I want six large stands of yellow roses. Dozens and dozens per stand. I don't care how much it costs. Can you do that?"

"Certainly. That won't be a problem." He made a note on his pad. "Now, as to the number of chairs?"

"I don't know – you decide."

"We'll try to have two hundred set out by late afternoon. Hopefully more if we can spare them from another service."

She nodded without bothering to consider what that number actually meant. She was already looking forward to wrapping this up. So she asked for what amount he needed up front, and set about preparing a check.

"I'm sorry… I'm going to have to write you an out-of-town check. It's from my account in Chicago."

She was filling in blanks, not thinking about him. Only after tearing off the check and handing it over did she notice a heaviness to his cheeks and mouth.

"Don't worry… there's plenty in my account to cover this."

"It's… not that. Marna… what happen to you? What made you and Roy so unhappy together that…"

"I really don't want to talk about that, CP. It's not why I'm here."

She followed his eyes back down to the check, with his head nodding ever so slightly to her wishes. For the first time since being here… and perhaps only because of how he was leaning forward… she could just make out that faint scar where his forehead had collided with the runner board on his truck as Roy dragged him off of her. She wondered if he ever pondered before a mirror on that scar? She recalled that Roy had once said something about it. That the scar had ended his friendship with CP. She too had scars that ended a friendship with Roy… just not the kind that could be easily seen.

"Marna? Do you understand what I'm saying?"

She was startled back by CP's voice.

"I'm sorry. I was thinking about… something from long ago."

"Perfectly understandable… You're grieving. I was just reminding you to get her obituary over to the paper by this evening if you want her friends to see it in time for the service. Perhaps I should prepare it for you, seeing as you're not…"

"I can handle it, CP. I'll have her lawyer do it. I'll tell him – 'Graveside services at Pritchett Funeral Home, 6 PM on Saturday.' But I do have an odd request regarding the service… Would it be possible to have a bagpipe player? Gwen was really fond of the Irish bagpipes. I'd understand it if you couldn't… you know… given that…"

"I can arrange for it, Marna… but you'll need to pay him directly. Just get me whatever music you'd like, and I'll handle the rest."

"Thanks. Umm… one more thing, CP."

"Yes?"

She reached into her purse and removed the ring box.

"I'd… like this put into her casket before you close it off. Not on her finger, mind you. Just… put the box somewhere nearby. Maybe in her hand. Can you do that?"

The ring, she had already decided, would go into the ground with the woman who had kept it a secret. There, it would be buried with so many other mysteries regarding her aunt. She cupped the small box into his palm, noting only that his eyes went wide on recognizing its significance.

"I'll see to it personally."

They shook hands, and she promptly left the funeral home not thinking about Gwen… or CP… or Chicago… or anything about Lubbock. She pushed all of that out to focus on one thing – how Roy might have dealt with her rings on the day she walked out on him.

Next was the appointment with Gwen's lawyer. It was brief and rather unsatisfying. He had not, to her annoyance, made any progress toward sorting out Gwen's affairs. She handed over the items she had dug up in Gwen's office, including a copy of the will, and was disappointed to learn that he had not yet located the original. Neither had he contacted Gwen's accountant to get an overview of her estate. She was in the man's house for no more than ten minutes… just long enough to go over each item she had found. For now, all of that could wait, as it was much more important that he immediately prepare the obituary and get it to the *Lubbock Avalanche* in time for tomorrow's edition. This, she told him on first entering his house, twice while standing in his living room, and once again on stepping out his front door. Each time, he seemed not to take her seriously. His relaxed West Texas manner was absolutely driving her crazy. How could her aunt have felt comfortable with this man as her lawyer?!

"Before you go… I noticed that you're not using your married name like before…"

This was another reason for her not to like this guy. How was that any of his business?!

"I wasn't aware that we'd met previous."

"I'm sorry… I didn't mean to offend. I was actually referring to that court case some time back. I was one of the lawyers who deposed your father-in-law. Was pretty rough on him at the time, as I recall. Marna… I'm sorry about how things worked out for him."

"It wasn't your fault. You were just doing your job."

She turned down his front walk, not wanting another word to be spoken about George Meitner… the only man she had ever known as a father.

The remainder of her afternoon was spent in searching for a funeral dress. Unfortunately, a good many stores in Lubbock were closed due to the tornado. But the effort was not a total waste as a passerby outside one department store suggested that she make the two hour drive to Amarillo and shop there. A day trip would be the perfect thing for clearing her mind.

Back to Gwen's house after a stop at the grocery store, she treated herself to a dinner of fajitas. All the chopping and cooking felt like a mini vacation away from her concerns. She did a shortcut marinate process on strips of flank steak and then grilled them on Gwen's stove with onions and peppers. To these, she supplemented store-bought guacamole, sour cream, salsa and flour tortillas, and then sat down to a private little feast dwelling only on those things she enjoyed about Texas.

Because Friday had always been trash day, she spent the remainder of that Thursday evening collecting up the things from Gwen's office that she deemed unworthy of being kept. She hauled both of Gwen's metal garbage cans to curbside completely full, and to these she added a half dozen trash bags… all bulging. More undoubtedly would have come from the boxes in her old bedroom and other parts of the house… but those things would have to wait, seeing as it was late and the usual pickup time was early.

Standing in the twilight of Gwen's front porch, she looked out to the line of bags and cans constituting what she had collected from the house. At first, she was pleased with herself for all that she had accomplished thus far. But the feeling was short-lived as her eyes ventured up and down the street. Nearly every neighbor also had their trash cans out on the curb. Her mind jumped to the worst of the devastation she had seen that morning. Whole city blocks had been leveled. So many people's homes had been torn up and dumped out into the streets of North Lubbock like garbage. It would take so much more than a drive by from the municipal trash collectors to set things right for them. Except for chance… or fate… or the inapproachable ways to providence, the houses along this street might easily have ended up like those in the Guadalupe neighborhood. She knew that there was no real accomplishment to anything she had done regarding her aunt's death. Nothing at all.

She had a more difficult time falling asleep on the couch that night. The absence of the relief on the wall gnawed at her more than before. She flipped and flopped, laid bent and bow-legged, but nothing worked. After a couple heel jabs into the far armrest, she pitched onto her side facing the blank wall and stayed that way until she finally managed to fall asleep.

<u>Friday, May 15th</u>

She rose late and would likely not get herself out the door for Amarillo until noon. The day did start on a positive note, as Mr. Peabody had gotten Gwen's obituary to the *Avalanche* on time. Eating a bowl of cereal at the kitchen table, she carefully read through the column and a half account of Gwen's life. Though the obit indicated that Gwen was born in Lansing, no other particulars were provided on her life prior to arriving in Lubbock in 1945 at the age of twenty eight. From there, the article continued into her establishment of Forde's Flowers on 4th Street, then highlighted her involvement in a variety of floral societies, civic groups, and women's rights organizations. There were no references to any family member other than herself… and the idiot lawyer got her name wrong! She was quite clear how she wanted herself referred to, but he had not listened. Seeing herself put down in typeset as Meitner was so irritating… and it poked at her pride. She read the obituary several more times, each striving for a seriousness of mind that might be expected from a different vantage point – an aunt's, a niece's, a newswoman's, a floral customer's, and that of a casual reader. Each time on reaching the line bearing her own name, she could not escape having the same feeling. The greater Forde side of her rustled up immediate protest, but was unable to fully drown out how a teeny, tiny whisper of herself kept suggesting that 'Marna Meitner' still sounded good in her head.

This would not do. Right off, she called the newspaper to cancel Gwen's subscription. That obviously had to be done anyway, but felt really good in that moment. She folded up the paper, put her cereal bowl in the sink, and departed Gwen's house with new purpose for the day. As soon as Gwen was laid to rest, she would call her own lawyer about his 'no-fault divorce' letter.

After a quick stop at a bank to cash some traveler's checks, she was on the highway to Amarillo. Like Lubbock, she found that shopping in this West Texas town to be several rungs below Chicago. Still… the city did offer her enough department stores from which to find a funeral dress. The very first place had the perfect one in terms of fit and style… except its neckline exposed far too much of her upper chest. In no way could she risk coming across as bawdy. She moved on to another store, but rejected its best offerings for their atrocious lack of fashion sense. Beads and bobbles… and oddly cut hems and sleeves… all hardly suitable for one in mourning! After two more hours and two more stores, she finally came across the perfect thing – a solid black with modest neckline and hem just below the knees, yet equally shapely enough to suit her tastes. She accessorized the dress with a thin belt of a delicate leaf pattern that ran its length and then picked up a pair of sling back heels to match. She arrived back into Lubbock at six – the perfect time for touching base with Billings. She covered her circumstances with him, as well as the plan for resuming work on the following Thursday. Through it all, he was rather gruff… which she took as his way of saying that he missed her.

She ate part of a casserole brought over by a neighbor, and then stuck her head into her old bedroom. The job looked like too much work for a start late in the day, so she instead entered Gwen's bedroom with an earnestness to put that part of her aunt's life in order before the funeral. She stripped the bed of its linen, gathered up all of the dirty clothes in the hamper, and toted the entire wad to the little laundry room off the kitchen. Whatever became of these things, they should at least be washed first. Returning to the bedroom, she rummaged about in the drawers for anything of significance. Nothing she came upon revealed anything new about Gwen. To her aunt, a bedroom had always been the simplest of places in which to spend time. Its functions were best restricted to the dressing, undressing and resting of the human body. Yet this room brought back a presence of Gwen more than any other place in the house. It was in the smell – a rosewater sweetness that tickled at the fonder memories she had of her aunt. The two of them clothes shopping together… playfully competing for the bathroom mirror… spending evenings side-by-side on the couch talking about nothing in particular… those sorts of things. For no reason other than sentiment, she collected up the assortment of fragrances on Gwen's dresser and moved them in a pile beside her suitcase. She would take these scents back to Chicago as her most tangible memorial to Gwen.

She spent her last waking hour of Friday night rearranging the furniture in the sitting room. Shifting the coffee table up against the opposite wall, pinning the damaged landscape painting there in the process, she then rolled up the throw carpet and laid it on the table, completely obscuring the painting from view. Next, she rotated the couch around to face the opposite direction. The new arrangement was horrid as to room décor, but at least that stupid spot on the wall where the relief had hung would no longer be seen as she laid down for the night. The strategy worked, as she nodded off more quickly than before. Yet as with so many things in life that she thought to be behind her, the uneasiness of the relief's absence still flittered in and out of her sleep.

<u>Saturday, May 16th</u>

She awoke in such a dreary state that she purposed to remain in her pajamas right up until it was time for the funeral. She ate some oatmeal, and then once more poked her head into her old bedroom. One look at all of those dust-covered boxes was enough to convince her that she was in no mood for sorting through more of Gwen's things. Actually, she was really frustrated with how much still needed to be done... and irritated with CP for making her wait all day for the funeral. As important as it was, that funeral still constituted a logjam to her emotions. Getting past Gwen would allow her to get past Roy... and getting past Roy meant getting back to Chicago. Lubbock would be the final resting place for Marna Meitner. Reborn fully as Marna Forde, she would then get one more second chance at life.

As a first step toward all of that, she really needed to figure out what she was going to say at the funeral. Curling up on the couch with a notepad, she went about organizing her thoughts into words worthy of eulogizing her aunt. By midday, she had made little progress at the expense of so many pages crumpled up and tossed about the room. She went to the kitchen and spooned out some Jell-O brought over by a visitor. At three o'clock, with her bowl's Jell-O having turned to a mush of banana and strawberry pieces settled to the bottom of a reddish goo, she still had no idea what to say before Gwen was gone forever.

At quarter to four, she threw down the notepad on hearing the mailman fumble about with Gwen's box. This was a great time for a break. Knowing herself to be more eager than she should, she nonetheless bounded across the room to wait at the front door until the mail truck was gone. Still in her pajamas, she dashed out to curbside and extracted the bundle from the mailbox. After flipping past several nondescript pieces of mail, she froze just as she had done in Chicago a week before. In her hands was the letter that she had written to her aunt. In all the sorrow, anger and frustration of the last few days, she had completely forgotten about this thing. But like a chronologist knowing the date and place of a long-ago buried time capsule, that postman had unearthed her past.

Just great! I certainly didn't need to see this today! Thanks a lot Mr. Neither-snow-nor-rain-nor-heat-nor-gloom-of-night!'

A torrent of feelings was already coming over her – none of which she liked. This letter had been written by a different person. Yet her eyes could not leave it as she retraced her steps along Gwen's walkway, up Gwen's front steps, over Gwen's porch, and through the front door of the house that was Gwen's. She discarded the rest of the mail in a heap on the floor beside Gwen's favorite armchair and plopped down there. Continuing to stare at every detail of the envelope, she began begging it to provide some small measure of insight into what should be said at Gwen's funeral. Within this were surely truer feelings for her aunt than all of the rage she had been struggling with over the last few days. But did she have the right to break the seal?

Her eyes went to the stamp. Odd... she had not noticed on preparing the letter that it was of a white flower. Gwen certainly would have, because Gwen noticed everything. For no reason, it suddenly occurred to her that the last time she had seen her aunt was in the flower shop on the day her mother-in-law showed up there in a confused and demented state.

Unbelievable! I never even thanked her for watching over Ruby. All I could think about was getting out of there before she figured out that I didn't have my act together as a Meitner.

Looking again to the stamp, she remembered the bitter taste she had on licking it... sort of the way she was feeling right now. The flower was not so pretty after all... not with how those wavy lines were overlaid on it. The postmark may show that the post office was satisfied with the cost required for mailing this letter, but she was still paying the price. Her eyes followed those wavy lines away from the stamp to the large circle that conveyed the date and time that this letter passed through a Chicago post office. It was impossible to know what Gwen might have thought on seeing where the letter came from... only that it took a week to get here... and four years to be written.

Nearly four years to the day from when I told her I was moving out. That's... really not so long of a time... is it?

Her eyes strayed onward to the left... to the address she had put in the other corner. Surely Gwen would have been excited to see who this letter was from. She squeezed it between her fingers... just to confirm the feel of what she already knew.

Gwen would have noticed from the thickness that the letter had many pages to it. She certainly would have been excited about that.

Her eyes went back to the return address. She had identified herself as 'Marna Forde' since that was the person she considered herself to be. What would Gwen have made of that? Two weeks back, she would have laid down money on her aunt's approval… but now, she was not so sure. In her own letter, Gwen had earnestly regretted her prejudices against the marriage to Roy. But what would she have thought about the affairs with Grass and Azurean? That was too painful to imagine, so she diverted her eyes to the bold, confident way in which she had addressed the letter to her aunt. Sure… the number, street and city were very familiar. It had been home for twelve years. She knew it like the back of her hand. But the name above that address… how well did she really know that person? The answer came back even as her silent question to herself was finished.

Not very well. There's that ring…

Despite whatever pain and bitter disappointment had made Gwen keep that ring to herself, her aunt was still there for her to discover… had she really tried. But she had been just as content to remain as a niece as Gwen had been to stay as an aunt. Perhaps with more effort on her part, she could have finally broken through to Gwen's soft side… before she went and ruined their relationship by stealing a Buick Skylark to chase a train down some lonely back road of West Texas. That had been the beginning of her grand adventure for significance… one that would lead her to this unexpected stopover on the way to a wrecked and lonely life. For all her worth, she longed to cry… but only if it could be the sort that yielded a better feeling afterward. There was no guarantee of that… especially if she dared to read what her former self had written from a very different time and place. Actually… she did not want to remember… and certainly did not want to desecrate the privacy between Gwen and that person Gwen had sought out in love. That version of her did not really exist. The real her was the person who had not made that call… and instead sent this pathetic attempt at reconciliation. Whatever was written within, it should be taken to the grave unread.

She dropped the letter to the floor and went to dress herself for a funeral.

Arriving early enough, she drove the narrow, twisted lanes of the Pritchett Cemetery while wondering how she was going to hold herself together over the next hour. She had so much emotion welling up inside, and not all of it was good. She parked where a sign indicated for the family of Gwen Forde to do so, and then walked the short distance to the grave site CP had prepared. Row upon row of folding chairs had been set up, each in such a pure white that the collective caused a glare in the late afternoon sun. Her first thought was that such brightness had no place at a funeral… but as she placed a hand on the nearest chair, she was thankful for the white. The seat was not hot to the touch.

Walking down the center aisle formed by the two large sections of seating, she headed for the small podium positioned in front… and skipped a heartbeat on noticing the maple paneled coffin off to the side – the whole reason she was there. It was flanked by large stands of yellow roses, almost as if welcoming her on up. So she made for the coffin instead, without pausing to greet the few individuals who had already seated themselves. In laying a hand on its smooth wood as a tribute to the occupant, she came to notice a gaping hole on the other side. For some bizarre reason, she found herself leaning over the coffin to stare down into that hole, for it would soon be the final resting place for…

"Mrs. Meitner, I presume?"

She nearly jumped out of her skin, which led to her hand slipping on the polished wood surface so badly that she almost fell sprawled over the coffin.

"I'm so sorry to interrupt you from your thoughts."

She turned to face the man that CP had commissioned to act as the spiritual voice to the service. There was nothing particularly noteworthy about him… just a middle-aged man in a black suit. There was also another man, him outlandishly clothed in the traditional attire of a bagpiper. In short course, the three of them were rehearsing how the ceremony would go, all the while as she was aware of the sounds of attendees arriving. She purposely had her back turned on all those people, engaging herself in an unnaturally detailed discussion as to the timing so as not to be approached by anyone just yet. In due course, the clergy looked down to his watch, nodded to the musician, and then whispered to her that it was time to begin.

Turning to take a seat, she was absolutely astonished by the number of people who had assembled in the short time she had been facing away. Nearly every seat was occupied, with a throng of other individuals standing in the rear. Yet no one had dared to take a place in the front row. Though dozens stood, she had the entirety of some twenty-odd seats to herself. Not really expecting it, but pleased to discover it as so, she noticed that Roy had positioned himself in the second row on the aisle. As the bagpiper warmed up, she took the seat before him and leaned back to whisper.

"Please tell those people standing not to be silly – there're plenty of seats up front. Then… come sit beside me… I could certainly use the company."

She turned back to stare down into her lap as the bagpipes reached their full resonance.

She did not lift her head until Roy returned, him passing before her to take the adjacent seat. She was most thankful that he did not try to hold her hand. From the periphery of her vision, she sensed others coming forward to fill the front row. Only then did she feel at ease enough to watch the bagpiper... and hope that his music might speak to her about all that once was Gwen.

On looking up, she was surprised to discover that someone had erected an easel before where she sat. Positioned there was a poster bearing the smiling face of a woman that she did not know. This woman's image was so very young... certainly not much older than she was at that moment. Across the face cut an evenly proportioned smile, the corners of which seem to prop up each cheek with beautiful buoyancy, as the arc itself opened up over perfectly aligned teeth. But that smile was nothing compared to the eyes. Those were absolutely on fire with joy, burning a hole longingly into her own sight. There was no dream-soon-to-come-true feel in them. No hopefulness peering off into a future primed to burst forth with promise. This was the most here-and-now expression of elation she had ever witnessed in all her life. To be that happy was what every person lived for. If only those eyes were hers... or could at least find favor enough to look her way. But they teased, being shifted ever so slightly to one side at some long ago photographer's request.

Yet as beautiful as this face was to behold, it was not the thing that most surprised her. This young woman... her own aunt Gwen... was in a uniform! And not just any uniform. Even she, with limited knowledge about the military, easily recognized this as the finest of dress blues, suitable for only the most special of occasions. She tore her sight from Gwen's face to flow over every detail of that uniform, returning time after time to those wonderful eyes.

Atop Gwen's head sat a beret, cocked slightly to one side, it holding back her bunched-up blond hair, every strand of which so obviously was trying to burst out with pleasure. On the front of this beret was an eagle, crowned with stars, powerfully depicted with one claw gripping a bundle of arrows and the other an olive branch. Down her eyes drifted to shoulder loops, each fluffed up with so much pride in displaying their insignia pins. Down further she went to a set of wings pinned over the left breast pocket. She knew instinctively what those wings meant, but could not rationalize them being there. The buttons drew her eyes back up over a firmly knotted tie, boarded to the left and right by a crisply starched collar of white. More wings were positioned nearby on the jacket... almost as if they had slid from the corners of her mouth and fallen to the lapels. The smile and the wings... she knew that they were one in the same.

But with all of her wonder over this uniform, she was most confused by one thing. On each lapel was also position four block letters that spelled out the oddest of words.

WASP

She desperately wished for everything to stop... to beg off that horrid screeching so she could jump up to summon forth this amazing young woman in real life... or at least demand to have the person who had set up this portrait of perfection to explain themselves... before it was too late. She wanted to dispatch Roy as she had done before... make him scour the rows until he found the person fortunate enough to have known this beautiful young woman. They should immediately come to the front and share that knowledge with a niece who had only ever been fed morsels of this amazing visual feast.

The bagpiper finally gave way, though not to silence. The clergyman rose to speak. Surely words of comfort were coming from his mouth, as he had a Bible open upon his palm and was explaining the great ways to God's faithfulness. She could process none of it, for he was referring to Gwen as a dead person... not this beautiful young woman before her. Now he was praying... or so it seemed by the way his head went back, with eyes and arms lifted to the heavens. She could sense everyone about her doing the opposite... but she could not take her eyes off of Gwen.

The bagpipes were summoned forth once more – a mournful rendition of *Oft In The Stilly Night*. It was one of those songs that she could never quite understand why her aunt liked so much. For the first time since setting her eyes upon that poster, she tore them away because of something different... something terribly distressing. As the music went on, four young men in CP's employ began lowering the casket into its hole. She knew this was part of the plan. She had specifically requested that it go below before she took to the podium herself. But that was before she knew about this poster. Panic rose in her heart. It could not possibly be that they were burying the same woman as in the picture. Hardly realizing it, she reached over to grip Roy's arm. In her most earnest unspoken plea, she wanted him to stop this lunacy... right now... before it was too late. She wanted him to save that beautiful young woman about to be buried alive in the place of the older one. This Gwen before her... so full of life... could not possibly be dead.

"Mrs. Marna Meitner, Gwen's niece, will now deliver a remembrance."

She heard the words... they seemed to echo throughout the entire cemetery... but they addressed someone strangely distant. She could not risk taking her eyes away again from the young Gwen for fear that the next time she looked… the image would be gone. Only a whisper to her ear brought her back.

"Marna… he's calling for you."

She haltingly glanced at Roy, whose widened eyes and discreetly outstretched hand motioned her forward. She looked quickly toward the casket… and saw only the hole, with a mound of dirt on its opposite side, it covered with a dark, felt-like fabric. Gwen had already gone below.

She rose and walked forward with a power she knew not. On moving behind the podium, she came to discover that it was inadvertently positioned so that a speaker had to look almost directly into the westering sun… it being well past halfway down toward the horizon. Even though her eyes were already sore from crying, she knew she could not shield herself from more discomfort. Such a gesture would be terribly disrespectful to Gwen. Yet not too many words into her eulogy, she found the glare to be too much, forcing her to lower her head altogether while speaking. She could not face that horizon… for the thin line was making it so very clear that just as this sun would be buried beyond the edge of the earth, so must Gwen.

"Thank you for being here this evening. For those of you who know me as Marna, Gwen's niece, I would like to speak to you today as… someone different… perhaps as Gwen herself might. I could start out by saying something about how Gwen would have been touched to see so many of her friends set aside time within their own grief of all that Lubbock has gone through this week to remember her. She would also have wanted to remind you that her store does not close on Saturdays until seven, so there was still time for you to get those roses for your wife."

The smattering of laughter was accompanied by many smiles… neither of which would last for long.

"But Gwen's store is no more. Like many establishments downtown, hers was destroyed by the very agent of Nature that took her life."

She paused here to fight off the emotion. It was too soon to give in. Too soon to feel before these people the impact of her own coming words. Someone coughed… and she allowed that person's efforts at controlling themselves to be her own.

"As I said… I would like to stand before you as a different person… someone other than Marna, Gwen's niece. That person would tell you what most of you already know. Gwen was a special woman… but a complicated one. Fiercely independent… strong of body, mind and spirit… she could strike a casual acquaintance as overly reserved… and be just as likely to reserve strong words and strong feelings for anyone who dared to draw too near. She was…

in my childhood memory... just as a lawyer had once called her – 'a crafty old bitch.' That man came out on the losing end of Gwen Forde... which many can attest as being distinctively unpleasant. He, however, meant his words in a different way than I have come to understand Gwen. She was as tough as Texas... and I miss that. But Gwen was also so very soft."

She looked up into the sinking sun for the briefest of moments... just long enough for it to leave an imprint on her eyes.

"Gwen loved flowers. She dedicated her life to taking a thing so pure... so delicate... such simple forms of beauty... and arranging them with skill into something that spoke directly to others. As a young girl struggling to learn the difference between a daffodil and a day lily... flowers were not my thing... and I destroyed so many trying to be half as good with them as she was. She never gave up on me. 'Marna, I'll turn you into a florist yet.' She would... She would say..."

The emotions suddenly burst forth from deep within... from where she had tried so hard to bury them... in that place where no one else would see. The tears came on... and though she begged her audience to forgive her... to overlook her lack of control... her feelings still poured out all the more. No one stopped her. No one thought the worst of her. Men and women who had already cried for their city were now crying with her.

"I'm sorry... I'm so sorry. I... I told myself to hold it together... to just make it through this for her..."

She cleared her throat and wiped her eyes one more time... and then looked up again. Not into the sun's dull yellow but into the many faces before her. She needed to be steady for them... and for that young woman with such fiery eyes.

"One of the first things Gwen taught me were those parts that all flowers had in common. There's the... pedicel base on which the ovary sits. On top of that is the... stigma. Then there's the filaments supporting the stamen and anther... and everyone knows about the petals forming a corolla around the whole. To tell you the truth... I hated flowers. To me... they just meant work. But I remember this as vividly as if I was standing there today... and this is why I love flowers... because Gwen taught me that there were really only two important parts to any flower – the giver and the receiver. She said they were as much a part of the flower as anything a botanist could label."

"The flower connects two souls. She would say that if two people were struggling... wanting to get over their pride... or hurt... or anger... then the flower was there for them. Helping them find the means to kiss... or hug... or just hold hands. Gwen believed that the flower spoke words that could only be understood by the giver and the receiver. It spoke the language of love, joy, sympathy and shared sorrow. A single flower could loosen lips feebly offering an apology… or bring forth courage to the faintest of hearts wavering over how best to declare love. The flower, here today and gone tomorrow, is like a word. From one heart into another, it never really goes away. I am forever thankful for Gwen. For years of such flowers given to me by the only… mother… I would ever come to know."

Once more she glanced up into the setting sun, though she knew well that it was too far off to be of aid. She wiped away more tears… but unlike before, she was in perfect control. She knew where she needed to go, and finally had the will to get there.

"And yet… I'm sorry to say… I can not stand before you today without… without speaking the full truth. It's terribly sad… but some flowers never come into bloom. In the cold, cruel indifference of my pride… and the rending of my heart's savage wind… I left… so many words unspoken between us. I regret not having ever said 'I love you' to her… and for that, I will never forgive myself."

She could bear it no longer, and must turn from the podium to graveside… to that small pile left uncovered for ceremonial participation in the burying. Bending over, she took a handful of the West Texas dirt that her aunt had so often praised. Extending that clinched fist over the open pit, a shiny maple box lying placidly in its depth, she released all of the bitterness, the anger, and the self-importance she held in her heart… allowing those to fall along with the dust between her fingers.

"Gwen… I owe you so much. Much more than I can ever repay. You took in a frightened seven year old, lost in the trauma of death… cared for her… loved her… and turned that child into a woman. You loved me like a daughter… and for that I will hold dear every memory of you as would a daughter. I love you, Gwen. Goodbye."

She could say no more, retreating to her seat with an awareness of the bagpipes and their sorrowful provision of *Amazing Grace*. Voices rose all about her, offering in respectful tones the words to a hymn that she knew by heart, but could not possibly comprehend at that moment.

At the conclusion of the music and the service, she did not rise from her front row seat to mingle with mourners. Many came to her, paying their respects, offering sympathy, and sharing their happy or sad remembrances of Gwen. She listened attentively, but heard little. Some bent over her to offer uncomfortably positioned hugs or simply to shake her hand. A few of her old high school girlfriends and acquaintances… CP and Marianne included… ventured near enough for a kiss on the cheek and a tearful moment spent in the chair beside her.

Eventually, the space about cleared enough for her to stand up. With remarkable decisiveness, she strode forward the few paces it took to stand before the poster so close that no one could come between her and her aunt. There, she fixed herself once more upon the eyes. Above everything else, they told a silent story that she long to know… but never would.

"That aunt of yours really made those Santiago blues come alive… didn't she?!"

She was startled to find another person standing beside her. The woman was old, but not so old as to be readily classified as elderly.

'Seasoned' is what Gwen would have said.

"Yes… I wish I could have known her then…"

"Don't be fooled by that sweet smile! She was a firecracker even back then."

"You knew my aunt?! Are you…? Did you…?"

Her sheer excitement stopped up the words in her mouth. All she could do was point at the poster with expectation.

"You betcha! Bunk mates in the sixth class of '43. We were the gals of bay E8 – best damn pilots the war never saw."

"I don't understand… my aunt was in the military?! And a pilot?!"

"Well… no and yes at the same time. I took the liberty of having this blown up for her service. That photo was taken on the day we got our silver beauties. See those wings? To the military, we became pilots that day… not just trainees in a program. Actually… I was already a pilot before entering… a pretty good one… and so was your aunt. But learning to fly combat aircraft was a different thing altogether. We were good – real good! Should've been inducted right into the military… were, for all intents and purposes… but Congress got terrified of what it would look like to have women flying in the armed forces." She glanced about her for a moment, then leaned in, almost apologetically. "Bunch of shitless weenies. That's what Gwendolyn called them."

The woman suddenly got a most appalled look on her face, though not for the reason she initially assumed.

"Dear me… where're my manners?! I haven't introduced myself. Francis Willington, but you can call me Frankie. Knew you was Marna the moment I laid eyes on you. You carry yourself just like she did – standing tall with chin up… and not a hint of slump to you. You look like her too… in the mouth especially… though I don't suppose your hair does. I still remember when they cut off those beautiful blond locks of hers. Mine too. Second worse day I ever had as a WASP."

"And the worst?"

The woman cocked her head to one side, just prior to giving a slight shrug of the shoulders.

"Congress terminated the program in December of '44. Men were already coming back from the war... and they needed jobs."

So many questions were pouring through her mind, and the longer Frankie spoke the more frequently one got kicked aside for the next.

"I don't know what to say... My aunt was a pilot?! That can't be right! She hated planes. And what's that wasp pin mean anyway?"

She had spent nearly as much time staring at those four letters as she had into Gwen's eyes.

"Stands for '*Women Airforce Service Pilots.*' You're telling me you didn't know anything about your aunt flying? None of it?!"

All she could do was shake her head in disbelief.

"Oh, Honey... do we need to talk! Have I got some stories for you! Like the time when we were ferrying P-47s from Long Island to Newark. Your crazy fool of an aunt wanted to race right over the top of Manhattan at..."

Her story was suddenly brought up short by the shrill of a car horn, its sound accompanied by a young man frantically waving from the driver's side.

"Damn... That boy's just plain rude! My stepson... Promised him I'd make this quick. We've gotta drive back to Tulsa tonight. Listen – I don't know if we'll get a chance to speak again, but if you should find my address among Gwendolyn's things, write and I'll..." Another horn blast from her stepson made to interrupt, but Frankie pushed through. "...tell you more. Some girls never got over the insult of having the program terminated. Your aunt was one of those. She shut everyone out. I never knew what became of her other than rumors that she'd settled down here. Recently though, she'd been trying to reconnect with her old comrades. We've exchanged letters regularly for a couple years now. Maybe you'll find some of mine in her things."

Yet again, Frankie's stepson was leaning on his car horn, and this time with such vigor as to be an inescapable distraction to the few mourners still lingering about.

"He won't leave me... but if I don't go soon... he'll make the drive home miserable. Marna... I'm terribly sorry for your loss. Gwendolyn was special. Please write me, will you?"

"I promise. But before you go... can I have this poster?"

"Of course. You deserve more than that." Frankie partly turned toward her stepson, but hesitated in leaving. "Listen... it's... none of my business, I know...

but Gwendolyn… she wrote to me about your marriage not working out. I'm sorry to hear that. It hit her hard, Marna. Real hard. I don't suppose… is there anyway… you know… that you and your fella might somehow reconcile? It would have meant a lot to…"

"No, Frankie… that'll never happen."

"Pity. Take care, Marna. Goodbye."

Even as the woman turned away, she sought out Roy. There he was, standing just off the back row of chairs, chatting with one of the few remaining attendees. Their eyes met, and she instantly knew he had been waiting for her. She took hold of the poster by its top edge and made down the center aisle, meeting him midway. Her mind was already made up before either of them spoke. She would not hold him bound any longer. She had been cruel to this poor man, keeping him on a leash simply because it was inconvenient for her to fully face the mess she had made of their lives. She would set him free – today.

For his sake… and mine.

"Roy, thanks for sitting with me."

He nodded, then went into commenting on the turnout and how the things she said had struck a chord with him. She was not really paying much attention to his words. For one, she wanted the meaningless to give way to the imperative. It was time to shift the discussion to them. Yet the greater distraction was in the form of a swishing sound that had just picked up behind her. She sidestepped into one of the empty rows, noting briefly that CP's crew had begun folding up the chairs, starting in the back. She ignored them, as the more bothersome noise was coming from a man moving dirt in over Gwen. That man was soon joined by another… and then another. As the pace of the shoveling picked up, so did her urgency to get on with what was on her mind. They were moving dirt in as Roy was sending words out… and she had to interrupt both, before it was too late. Even though Gwen was dead, she had a mad impulse to issue the final verdict on her marriage before the last of the dirt covered her aunt.

"Roy, stop! I'm sorry… but we need to talk. I can't go another minute with the way things have been between us. I want a divorce… and I want it taken care of before I have to go back to Chicago next week."

Suddenly, all of the life went out of his face. If possible, he looked even more ashen than on that day three years ago when they buried George.

Fantastic, Marna! You couldn't possibly have handled that more cruelly than you just did!

He fell back a step… and then magically changed. He was still grim of face... no doubt about it... but with a slight nod of the head, he stepped forward again to speak with remarkable steadiness.

"If that's what you want, then I suggest we sit down together and work out the details before getting lawyers involved. How about if I come over tomorrow and we..."

"No! Not at Gwen's... please." Her eyes went over to the men with the shovels, not really believing that Gwen was there to voice disapproval over having *her* house take part in her niece's divorce. "Let's... meet at your place... tonight, as a matter of fact. I know we likely won't get much done, but even if we can talk for thirty minutes or so, I'll feel that we're making some progress. Please, Roy... I know this is difficult on you... it is for me too. Let's start with..."

"You know, that works for me."

She could tell by how quickly he spoke and how his front teeth finished off clinched together that he was angry. But he was holding it in as best as he could... especially considering how she had just sprung the topic on him.

"What's say you come over at..." He glanced down to his watch. "...quarter 'til eight. That'll give you time to go home and change... maybe even grab a bite to eat."

Without another word, he turned away from her, hands shoved into his pant pockets. She watched him make his way through a tombstone maze to where he had left his truck. Even though she had wanted to get this over with as soon as possible, she was now regretting the brashness with which she had given in to a misplaced urgency. Surely she could have waited until tomorrow.

With poster in hand, she made her way to Gwen's car, knowing full well what her aunt would have made of that interaction.

'You're a bull-in-a-flower-shop, Marna!'

Hardening her heart one last time, she purposed to no longer fashion internal arguments with vague terms about what was good for anyone. The matter was settled. She would be on a plane back to Chicago come Wednesday morning... divorce or no divorce. Whatever happened with anything remaining in Lubbock would be the sole concern of lawyers. She had a career to build... and all of the emotion regarding Gwen and guilt... and Roy and regret... all of it would be folded up neatly and buried within a pile of divorce papers. Fate be damned – she was moving on.

CHAPTER

26

PORCHED

Stowing the poster in the trunk simply so as not to have the sight of the young Gwendolyn there in the car to reprove her, she drove the narrow lanes of the Pritchett Cemetery having already made up her mind as to what should be done next. She would not go home to change. The same black dress she had picked out especially for her aunt's funeral would be what she wore on taking the first step toward laying her disastrous marriage to rest.

On hitting the Loop, she would not continue on 84 through the heart of Lubbock, not at all wanting to see more of the tornado's devastation. The North Loop would get her to the Meitner house more quickly, but much too soon based on the time Roy had set. So she went right, entering the Loop heading in the opposite direction, and then took her time in circumventing the city. On one hand, this would give her a final chance to say goodbye to Lubbock as a whole, but also allow her to kill at least thirty minutes with leisurely driving.

But the trip on Texas State Highway 289's loop about Lubbock was anything close to leisurely. Despite her mind being set on a divorce, she cried through most of the drive, once so badly that she had to pull off at a truck stop in order to clear her eyes and relax her grip on the steering wheel. Idling there, she faced a nagging realization that had been growing in her awareness the further she progressed about the Loop. Once again, she was handling a critical moment in her life with such Marna-esque rashness.

But I've been over and over this. It's what I want… and it's what he deserves.

She pulled back onto the Loop, stressing in her mind the latter point – that he should be set free from her. This, she wholeheartedly agreed to without once re-examining the painful reasons for why.

The whole rest of the way around the Loop, the West Texas horizon was before her in a sweeping panorama, interrupted only from time to time by occasional roadside features. But that flat line between earth and sky just mocked her, forcing her to pick up the theme.

Travel as far as you will and always it's the same thing. Marna… you're recklessly chasing that which never gets any closer. But what does it matter anyway… there's nothing left to chase.

Almost all the way around the Loop to the turnoff that would take her northeast in the direction of the Meitner house, she found herself fighting against the nonsense of her conflicting emotions. Grief, anxiety, frustration, foreboding and shame… none of it mattered. Besides, those feelings were not all that helpful toward putting an end to her marriage. At least not compared to anger. So… she would distance herself from everything else – Gwen's death, the tornado, and her future in Chicago – by using anger on herself. That way, she would be free to focus on one fact. Getting married to Roy Meitner had nearly ruined her life.

Pulling onto the farm-to-market road that would, in a mile or so, bring her to the turn off for the county road on which the Meitner place was situated, she concentrated on those terrible two years that had culminated in her escaping from Lubbock. The memories were still fresh and fully available for the summoning, but try as she might, the associated feelings of outrage kept falling far short of what was needed. Always lurking in the back of her mind was a hint of her own culpability, tainting the stern look she was preparing for that moment when Roy answered his front door. He might well have his own memories from which to be angry with her… and perhaps for better cause. So… she should use that expectation to her defense. Skip all of the preemptive talk and speak matter-of-factly to him. The marriage simply had not worked out. There would be no need for recalling who said what… or who had hidden motives… or which of them was most negligent in their responsibilities. She would open no portion of her mind to introspection and allow no warmth in her heart for old feelings. No part of the past actually mattered. This was 'no fault' divorce, with the goal of getting herself free.

These were the precepts by which she purposed to have a conversation with Roy on the subject of divorce. Since leaving the Loop, a part of her mind had shifted to a more practical problem. Turning onto the Meitner's county road, she reached a decision as to the setting of their discussion. No matter what, she would not go inside. She would start their business on the front porch and stay there throughout. Being within the dreariness of that house again might serve to rekindle some of her anger, but other memories came too close... went too far. Deep within, she also feared the effect it would have on her to bring the shame of Chicago into Roy's house... even if he were never to know anything about it. Besides... staying on the porch would avoid so much awkward reminiscing and provide an easy escape when it came time to leave.

Only three more miles down this dull county road, and she would see that line of trees leading up to that horrid house. Then it would only be a left turn onto the driveway, and so many memories would come back to her. She needed to be ready for that too.

Yet not halfway along that county road, she came upon two vehicles pulled off on her side. The one in front, she immediately recognized as Roy's truck, having been in it not four days prior. The other... a sedan... was unfamiliar to her. She momentarily lifted her foot off the accelerator on detecting a figure hunched over into the sedan's rear passenger-side wheel well.

Oh... Roy's changing someone's tire.

You know...Gwen always said there's no better place in the world to have a flat than in Lubbock.

Of course, her initial impulse was to pull over, but as he had not come up to look her way... and since she had purposed in her heart to remain distant from him... her foot came back down to hurry her car along. Coming abreast of the truck, she caught a glimpse of an elderly woman sitting inside. Their eyes momentarily met, and recognition came to her.

Old Mrs. Purvis.

She took in the scene one more time in her rearview mirror, reconciling to herself the likelihood of a long wait on the front porch before he finally finished his good deed.

Fine! It'll give me a chance to clear my head a bit... and maybe get used to being back at that house.

Now she was busy estimating how long it might take to change a tire, and had not really registered that she already made the turn onto the driveway. The house was just ahead, but her eyes locked onto the fact that the hangar was still standing. After two years, Roy had not gotten around to tearing it down.

I wonder if that plane's still in there?

She was tempted right off to go see, but thought it best to stick to the real reason why she was here. According to George's will, the thing in there was hers. So if Roy had left it be, then she would soon enough have to decide what to do with it.

She parked three quarters the way around the circle, remembering that Roy preferred to leave his truck directly before the house. More symbolically, she liked the idea that her own vehicle was pointing down the driveway, ready to leave. She stepped from the car and surveyed the house more closely. It seemed not to have changed either… though perhaps Roy had cleaned up the windows, for they seemed… more sparkly… then she recalled them to be. But the porch was exactly as on the day she had left… when she sat up there writing her goodbye note. She shrugged off the memory and moved up the steps. The front portion was partly in shadow, but the hangar-side was bright, as the sunset was still an hour or so off. She would not sit there… not with the hangar to tempt her. She also suspected that the front door might be unlocked, but had no thought for entering. She would go no further than this porch. The outside, she loved, but the inside, she hated. For a moment, she considered taking a stroll around the entire thing, but thought it best not to stir up too many memories. Besides, it would be really embarrassing to be caught on the back side when Roy came home.

She strode back and forth, leaned against a pillar for a good while, kicked some dead crickets under the railing, and even contemplated peeking through one of the parlor windows… all because she had grown bored waiting. She had already run through the course of the conversation several times, finding suitable ways around some of the difficult parts. There was nothing left to do but set the reel in place and press start.

Might as well have a seat then…

Of all the rocking chairs on the Meitner front porch, she made for the one with a tall back and seat shaped nicely to the human rear. This one had always been her favorite. So she rocked merrily for a while… and then ceased abruptly on recognizing that she was enjoying herself too much. With nothing better to do, she once more went over her strategy, checking off the key steps in a rehearsal that she hoped to be the last one.

Point one: I have no desire to get back together. I want a divorce. Non-negotiable.

Point two: I don't want anything of yours… and you can't have anything of mine. Again, non-negotiable.

Point three: I made mistakes and you made mistakes… but this is 'no fault,' so there'll be no need for any incrimination.

Point four: I love Chicago. You love Texas. Let's part as friends.

She had scampered down so many rabbit trails from these four points, weaving along his possible arguments and counterarguments. None of that was as alluring as before, because now she just wanted this done. Above all, she purposed not to be passive. She would not allow herself to engage in second guessing, and definitely would not get sidetracked by anything he said or did. She would say what she needed to say… and then allow him to say whatever was on his mind, though none of it would matter.

Just then, she caught sight of movement far off down the county road. In a matter of a minute, Roy's truck was progressing down the driveway. She stood up and casually moved to the top of the steps. She would greet him warmly there before conveying her eagerness to get on with the business at hand. After all, she still had so many things left to work out before returning to Chicago.

But all of her carefully scripted plans were thrown asunder even before a single one of his boots hit the porch steps. Roy was covered head to toe in mud… and the closer he got the more he reeked of swamp water. She could not help herself – she absolutely had to back away from him.

"Good lord… what happened to you?!"

"Sorry to keep you waiting. I got side-tracked changing a tire for Mrs. Purvis. You remember her… She's the one who usually won first prize at the fair for…"

"Yeah, I remember… but that doesn't explain why you're covered in… whatever it is! Roy… you stink to high heaven!"

"Sorry. I took the spare out of her trunk and leaned it up against the rear fender. Then like an idiot… when I was reaching in for the jack… I guess I shook the car too much. The spare rolled off down the embankment and into a drainage ditch. I had no choice but to go in after it. To make matters worse… I slipped and fell. Which is why I'm covered in it."

She should at least say something nice. Something about him having been a gentleman and how Mrs. Purvis must have been relieved when he stopped. But she could get no words out, for he stank far too much.

"Oh."

"Listen… I realize you've been waiting for a while… and you're probably anxious to get this discussion of us over with… but seeing as I'm a mess… would you mind so much hanging on while I get washed up first? Shouldn't take too long… maybe fifteen minutes or so."

"Of course not. You go right ahead. I'll just… wait over here." She motioned toward the rocking chair where she had sat before.

"I'd invite you in… but the house isn't fit for company. You'd probably prefer meeting out here anyway. I hope you don't…"

"Not at all. In fact, I do prefer it. It's really nice out… so take your time."

Roy turned toward the front door. Instead of sitting, she casually faced out toward the nothingness of Texas. She heard the banging of the screen door shut behind him… and then the front door doing likewise. Leaning against a pillar, she stared down the long driveway. All was quiet. She liked that. Nothing to distract. Her mind was set, their relationship was over, and she felt good.

It *was* nice out… but the air seemed overly still to her. Stagnant, even. Rather uncharacteristic of Lubbock in May. The leaves of the driveway's live oaks just hung there… as did the flowering laurel that rimmed the lower railing at her feet. Her eyes went to the flagpole, half expecting to see some kind of movement there. But the pole was barren. Probably had been ever since the day she left.

In all that quiet, she became aware of the residual heat to the day. It might be nice out, but CP was right – even though the sun was near to setting, it had to be in the eighties. She really needed some kind of movement… something to cool herself off. Returning to her previous seat, she began to rock. Picking up too much speed at first, she metered off into a slow and steady rhythm consistent with how relaxed she was feeling. Everything would go smoothly from here. He would get cleaned up, come out to the porch, and they would have an amicable chat about divorce. Then she would go her way, and he could go his. That conclusion made her feel real good. So she tilted her head back, noting the whitewashed slats of the porch ceiling, and closed her eyes. Soon, the gentle wood-on-wood creaking beneath her combined with a disorienting motion-without-sight sensation put her into a true state of calm. She no longer worried about anything.

Yet something odd was intruding upon her silence. It was just a faint little thing entering her hearing, but it instantly opened her eyes and made her bring the rocking chair to an abrupt halt. There was no doubt about it – somewhere nearby was a high frequency sound she knew all too well… and it was growing louder. Frantically, she began twisting around in a search of the airspace all about her. Nothing else mattered in the moment other than locating the source… and then putting as much distance as possible between herself and the wasp.

CHAPTER
27

MYSTERIES OF THE ORGAN PIPE MUD DAUBER

On first hearing the characteristic whizzing of wasp wings, total fear petrified her extremities. But once she had located the insect, the muscular responsiveness of her arms and legs kicked in. Catapulting herself out of the rocking chair, she bolted straight for the front door. Only after getting a hand to the latch did she hazard a quick look back at the wasp. It was still lulling about near the rocking chair. With her fingers poised to rip open the screen door, she watched as the wasp meandered off in the opposite direction. It was no longer so near, and yet too close for her to feel at ease with sitting back down again. Really… she did not want to go inside, but neither was she all that comfortable about being outside with that thing hanging around… irrespective of whether it seemed disinterested in her at the moment. So she stood there like an idiot watching the wasp make its chaotic looping patterns in the air about the porch. It was then that she noticed a rather ornate spider's web tucked into the corner space between pillar and crossbeam. From her angle, she could just make out that it was the kind comprised of many concentric circles constrained within a triangular framework of silk.

She brought her eyes back to the wasp… and was totally stunned to see it suddenly plunge directly into the midst of the web. She had never seen such a thing before – a wasp, for no apparent reason, purposefully sacrificing itself to a spider. Still on guard, her growing fascination made this oddity worth viewing. So she hurried closer, part out of curiosity and part out of savage delight at witnessing a spider ensnare a wasp. Sure enough, the insect was there twitching about in the center of the many sticky strands. The spider, having sensed motion to its web, was already straddling down from the upper corner to the site of its feast. As she watched, her fascination gave way to perplexity, which promptly gave way to denial. The wasp, which had appeared helpless right up until the spider was nearly upon it, suddenly sprang into action. In a flash, the two of them were in a tangle of wing and web. The strands all about their tussle where being torn up as if mere wisps of vapor. She could not believe what she was seeing. The wasp was all over the spider, clutching the balled-up thing in its grasp. Within a second of her realizing that the prey had actually been the predator, she jerked backward as the wasp launched itself from the web – right into her face.

To say that she screamed amounted to an understatement of so many decibels. She felt the thing bump off her forehead, got off a frantic swat or two at it, yet did not stick around for more. As fast as she could, she dashed to the screen door. Only after getting it open did she risk a panicked look back. To her relief, the wasp remained hovering in the vicinity of where she had witnessed its attack on the spider. In many circle-eight patterns, it seemed to be preoccupied with hovering near to the porch floor. She had just decided that it might be best to be inside when the wasp suddenly took off in her direction. She did not wait to discover its intentions. With a hand behind her searching for the front door knob, she yanked the screen closed before her, momentarily wedging herself between the two doors. She got the knob to turn just as the wasp collided with the mesh, sending her recoiling backward into the house. Regaining her balance, she saw the creature skid across the screen and out of view.

Very much relieved to be inside, she relaxed the tenseness in her muscles and breathed deeply, at the same time instinctively bringing a hand up to calm her still rapidly beating heart. It was then that she noticed an odd sort of dangly thing just at the upper edge of her vision, maybe an inch off her brow. With instant recognition, she began beating at her face and screaming out with new alarm. Even though she knew that the lifeless spider had fallen to the floor, she did not stop slapping at herself until she was absolutely certain there was nothing left. No more spiders, no more wasps, and no more dangling pieces of web. Only after brushing off every inch of her hair, face and neck, continuing on down to the full length of her dress, did she once again bring a hand up to calm her heart. With a few furtive looks through the screen door, she finally concluded that all was well. The wasp was gone, the dead spider was down there on the floor, and she was safe. Of course, no way would she risk venturing back outside. That would be real foolish, what with that wasp lurking about. She reached up to jiggle the screen door's latch… just to make sure that it was secure. Only then did she feel free to consider where the spider had fallen. There it lay at her feet, with its crumpled legs curled up just the way a dead spider's does… though she suspected that this one was only paralyzed by the wasp's sting. It was essentially dead. In the dismissive way such things deserve, she swept it aside with the toe of her high heel, satisfied that it would no longer pose a threat to her.

But as if by some strange enchantment, she instantly forgot all about the spider and the wasp, as her eyes had become fully transfixed upon the floor itself.

What's this?!

———

There are virtually no examples within the order of *Hymenoptera* in which the male wasp labors alongside its mate. Of course, in the *Vespidae* family branch, there are those drones that manage to coexist in the colony along with the queen and her female workers, but these serve no purpose outside of mating. Their presence is tolerated only up until the point at which they are no longer needed. When the last brood of eggs is laid, all males are banished from the hive.

There is an exception, though. In the *Crabronidae* family of wasps, both male and female *trypoxylon politum* remain together as one in the establishment of their nest. More commonly known as the organ pipe mud dauber, this docile wasp rarely stings… unless provoked. The wasp is shiny black all over except for what euphemistically might be called white socks on her rear legs. As with every other species of wasp, the female bears the responsibilities of nest preparation, egg laying, and hunting for prey, her preference being web-building spiders. She also hunts for water, fashioning many small globules of mud into long tube-like nests, usually constructed up under the eaves of buildings or such places that offer protection from the elements. Though interesting, the architecture of these structures is not the most unusual characteristic of the organ pipe mud dauber. For unlike nearly every other species of wasp, the male is involved. Though stingless and vulnerable to parasitic wasps seeking a convenient place to lay their eggs, the male organ pipe mud dauber will faithfully stand over their nest, defending it with his life while waiting patiently for the return of his mate.

———

Beneath her feet was not the rough wood slats she had been accustom to from her years of familiarity with the Meitner house. She stood instead within the bounds of a large marble slab, an edge of which fit neatly up against the front door's threshold. Shifting her eyes, she discovered that this piece gave way on the right and left to others, each possessing their own unique grains and hues. The narrow spaces between the slabs were not grouted, as she would have expected from typical tile work. Instead, a thin piece of some polished metal had been neatly wedged down into the gap. To her surprise, this metal provided an amazingly distinctive highlight to the stone.

Without much thinking about it, she placed a hand against the opened front door to steady herself as she bent down for a closer look at the marble… and completely lost her balance when the door swung open much further than she expected it to. Falling right around onto her rump, she was totally stunned to discover that the entire length of wall on one side was gone. The narrow hall leading past the stairs into the kitchen was instead a wide-opened space that expanded into where the dark TV room used to be. Everything was bathed in light. Upward, her eyes went to where the low first floor ceiling used to be. Up past where that barrier should have been to a second floor bedroom that no longer existed. Up along walls that had once held her in. Up past its boundaries to regions that she had never laid eyes on before… and then all around her. She sat in awe, for the family room, the upper bedroom and the hallway of the Meitner house had been transformed into one huge space. Its very ceiling vaulted all the way up to the rafters of the house's roof!

Unbelievable!

She made to get up, but her eyes were once more drawn to the marble flooring. It ran off in a continuous pattern toward the kitchen where that wood-slat flooring used to be, but also laterally into the new wide-open space around her. Still stunned by the stonework, she ran a finger along a metal-filled groove.

Wow! Perfectly smooth!

She allowed that finger to trace the strip for as far as she could reach… and then once again looked upward. As if lifted by the airiness of this new family room, she rose from off the floor and glided into the center of this marble-floored miracle, rotating about as if in another world. Somehow, Roy had completely removed their old bedroom above the cramped family room and created a space that naturally combined the rock of earth below with the airiness of sky above. The space was completely empty, as he had not yet set himself to fill it with new furniture… but this just better allowed her to take in the marvel of it. The old windows on the western side of the family room were gone, as were those of their old bedroom above. In their place, he had installed huge expanses of glasswork that went from just shy of the marble tiling to near where the second floor ceiling should have been. Outside, she could tell that he had also done something with the porch roof. Sections of glass had been installed there so as not to obscure the view from inside. The afternoon sun was sure to beat through, but oh… the sunsets that could be seen from this room!

In between these two huge windows was more stonework, similar to the floor's but rougher and in many different hues… creamy tans to blue-grays to deep rich blacks. This rock continued up to the same height as the windows, but below to a stone hearth that seemed wider than in her memory. Her eyes went upward again, noticing for the first time the blades of two ceiling fans spread out like opened flower petals over large, ornate glass spheres. Following the angle of the new ceiling upward, she saw it crest at where the roof of the house likely was, and then slope back down into the recesses of the upper hall. Amazing! Roy had ripped out the previous staircase and replaced it with something that seemed much broader. Even more stirring to her, it was completely open to the space where she stood, being guarded only by a spindled railing. The same was the case for a banister that ran along the upper hallway. The whole thing gave off to her the feel of a limitless expanse.

So captivated by all this wonder, she only then became aware of the distant sound of running water. Roy was using the hallway bathroom for his shower. Somehow, that observation seemed completely unimportant compared to taking in more of this amazingly remodeled house.

Her eyes came back down to a set of French doors leading into Ruby's parlor. There was something odd about that wall, but since she really had no interest for going that way, she instead drifted as on a cloud to her left. She was much more curious about the closed-off pocket doors leading toward the back of the house. Through these, she discovered that Ruby's kitchen had been completely gutted, with every counter and cabinet removed. The breakfast area in back was scattered with sawhorses, wood, and many tools. Roy was evidently using this space as a staging area for his remodeling. Through the rear windows, she could just make out piles of lumber and sheetrock – things that she would have noticed had she taken that walk around the porch. In the very back reaches of the downstairs were the door to the cellar and the short hall leading to the guestroom. Those places were in shadow. So she moved instead over the rough floorboards, now stripped of a vinyl that she could only vaguely recall, and through plastic sheeting into the dining room. Unlike the unfinished kitchen, Roy appeared to be nearly done with this room. She took note of the absence of furniture on the new flooring of some lightly colored wood, but was immediately drawn to a large wooden crate lying on a tarp. The lid had been pried off, making it easy on her curiosity. But with only one peek inside, she threw off the lid in a rush, disregarding how papers on top were being scattered across the floor. Within was the relief, wrapped in plastic and nestled within a sea of Styrofoam peanuts. And just to convince herself of it, she fell to her knees and began sweeping the packing material back and forth with her hands until she was absolutely certain.

This makes no sense! What's Roy doing with my relief?!

She quickly gathered up the scattered papers, which amounted to three stationary-sized sheets and two envelopes. One envelope bore Roy's name. The other was older looking and thickly packed with papers. She disregarded both in favor of focusing on the stationary, for it possessed the big, broad strokes of her aunt's handwriting. After hastily sorting the pages into a sensible order, she started in on reading.

> *Dear Roy,*
>
> *Well… here it is. Thanks for finally agreeing to take the thing off my hands. I tell you, I can't stand the sight of it anymore! Reminds me too much of her, and how terribly I miss her. I don't mean to dump that burden on you. I know you have ones of your own, having borne her absence so much more painfully than I have. Still, here's hoping that when you look at this you'll see more than the memory of her. I give it to you gladly, yet fully aware that your owning it may cost you more than it's worth. On that note, enclosed is the original bill of sale.*

She tilted her head slightly in order to make sure that water was still running in the plumbing above, then picked up where she had left off.

> *Like I mentioned before, I came by it fairly cheaply. Never had it appraised or even bothered to figure out where it had come from. Just loved the sight of it from the get go. Anyway, I recently had the thing looked at by an expert up from Austin. Nearly knocked my socks off when I heard back on its value. Imagine – I've had a small fortune hanging on my wall all these years! Might want to beef up your insurance policy.*
>
> *Now, I couldn't care less about the thing. Glad to be rid of it. It depresses me. I found a fine piece of art in Fort Worth that I think will cover its spot on the wall nicely. Looking forward to showing it off next time you come over.*
>
> *I know I've said this nine ways to Sunday, and I know you've told me it's not my fault, but I still feel responsible for how things turned out*

between you two. You were so good for her, Roy. But I've still not given up hope. Sooner or later, she's going to make her way back to Lubbock. Maybe that's the real reason I'm giving you this relief. I can't explain it, but she's irresistibly drawn to it. One day you'll see, she'll show up on your doorstep just begging for a look at it.

I also give it to you as something of a thank you for everything you've done for me over the past two years. Getting to know you has been really special for me. I appreciate you so very much. I could say you've been like the son-in-law I never had. But don't you dare go calling me Mom, or the two of us are going to have a real problem. I suppose you're also getting tired of hearing me say it, so I'll just put it in writing for one last time – thank you for forgiving me.

Love,

Gwen

PS. Try to keep the crate covered until I can get over there next week. I think between the two of us, we should be able to pick out a good place and get the thing hung properly. It might not look it, but it weighs over sixty pounds!

PPS. Make sure those idiot delivery boys didn't crack the thing in two. I swear I'll strangle them if they have!

Her arms fell limply to her sides, pages still in each hand, as she stared blankly at the crate's lid. This was too much to process. Gwen giving Roy the relief, and Gwen and Roy together as friends. Her head was spinning.

She thanked him for everything he's done! Even shared her love with him! What in the world's going on?!

She looked at the first page again – there was no date of writing. Her confusion was now turning into envy. This relief was hers! She should be the one feasting on its exquisite details! Her hands went back into the Styrofoam, pushing it all about to not only see but to sense again the relief's delicate contours. But the feel of it was not the same. Gwen had given this relief to Roy... and it was now his. She must walk away from both of them. None of it mattered. Not the remodeled house... or the relief lying before her... or the surprise friendship between two people she had thought hated each other.

She dropped the pages to the floor and turned away from the relief, accepting the reality that she would never see it again. Moving as in a fog, she knew only that she must head back out to the porch where she belonged. Back out with that wasp to wait through the remainder of Roy's shower. After all, she was nothing but an intruder in this wonderful house.

Passing from the dining room directly into Ruby's private sitting room in making for the front door, she suddenly realized that there should not be an opening here. The two had never been connected before. More so than that surprise, she stood stunned at the look of Ruby's special room, as it had been completely gutted! And shock upon shocks, Roy had opened the space beneath the stairwell directly into the parlor! That miserable closet… the one she hated so much from the very first moment she unwittingly hid in it as a child… that terrible place where she had been forced to move all of Ruby's clothes after George died… it was completely gone! She had not even noticed the absence of a hallway door, so captivated she was by the wide-open family room. Though the woodworking was far from finished, she could tell that Roy was fashioning this space into a nook. The feel of it came to her instantly. Here would be a place where a person could be alone to hide in comfort and coziness. There would be a cushioned bench long enough to nap on, with built-in bookshelves at each end. He would mount lamps on the wall and then fill the space with pillows. It would be exactly as she had once told him such a space should be used.

On that day when I was babbling on and on… just so I wouldn't have to think about my parents.

But Roy had taken her seriously. He had kept that in his memory… and purposefully transformed his mother's cherished sitting room into something just for his estranged wife.

I can't believe it! He's… he's done all of this… for me!

He still loves me!

But the surprise of this wonderment did not last. That longing deep within her heart suddenly got choked on an arid awareness. Though he had retained her in his dreams, she had completely removed him from hers. She had rubbed him out of her life while he was laboring alone to transform this house into something that she could call her home. How was he to accept her back now… now that she had come to love him too late?!

The ache in her chest soon took over so strongly that she was bent over gasping in half-breaths at the pain of it. Her hands came up, clutching as a single fist against where her heart lay convicted.

I've so ruined my chances with him!

She was sobbing now, vainly covering her mouth so as not to offend this house that he had labored over for her. She deserved none of it. She must leave, right now before she offend it any further.

But coming to a stone-still halt, she clearly heard the sound of a valve turning… and a trickle of water slowly diminishing to stillness. Without thinking her decision through… for there was no time to do so… she threw open the French doors and slingshot herself around the edge toward the stairs. On reaching the bottom step, she already had one hand on a strap, ripping off its high heel… and then the other… discarding both behind her. Up the stairs she flew, taking two at a time as noiselessly as possible… feeling, though not really registering, the very fine layer of grit that covered a more-or-less cleared pathway up the middle of these sawdust-covered steps. At the top, she awkwardly pirouetted in the wrong direction simply out of ingrained habit, and nearly toppled over a section of banister that had once been the doorway into their old bedroom. Pushing herself off, she knew immediately where to go – through the door into the house's master bedroom. And though what she beheld there in a snapshot should have drawn her up short, there was no time.

Her hands were at the back of her neck, frantically struggling to unclasp the eyehook at her collar. Drawing the zipper down only as far as was needed, she yanked upward at the black funeral dress from grips at waist level, not caring how indelicately it was being inverted over her head. Quickly taking up the most obvious seat, at the foot of his low-lying bed, she pitched the dress out of sight and directed all effort toward preparing herself. Clothed only in a peach-colored bra and pantie set – the last remnant of clean undergarments brought from Chicago – she consciously slowed her breath and then smoothed out her hair. Those things accomplished, she inched forward a bit on the edge of the bed, placing knees together and pivoting toward the door. Shifting her shoulders back, she took care to adopt a posture that would best show off her figure. Then… she waited, not entertaining any of the craziness to what she was doing. She would offer herself to him… her husband… in hope.

Amidst many furtive looks out the door and down the upper hallway to where she knew Roy would soon appear, she began to take in this room that had once been George and Ruby's. Somehow… the dimensions were all wrong… or at least her memory protested them to be so. It was wider than it ought to be in one direction and narrower in another. The old furniture was obviously gone… she knew even Roy hated that ugly four-post bed of theirs… and in its place beneath her was this simple queen-size mattress atop a flat bed frame extending back to a low headboard. Clearly masculine in its sturdiness, yet with clean lines that spoke of a modern style. The whole was covered over in a taupe bedspread. She shifted a foot backward to confirm what she suspected.

Open beneath.

Still keenly alert to the hallway bathroom door, it suddenly occurred to her that he had not chosen to use the master bath. Her eyes darted there… to the wall that had seemed closer in. With two doors where there should only be one, she noted that both were covered over with plastic sheeting. Roy was obviously working on whatever lay behind. For a moment, she was tempted to rise for a peek… but then a rattle from down the hallway froze her on the edge of the bed. In an instant, she was gripped with a horrible, terrible thought. Irrational, yet overpowering with its possibilities, for it rained down icy shame upon her reckless nakedness.

What if… what if none of this was actually done for me?! What if there's another woman in his life?!

Every muscle from jaw to toes tensed with apprehension of discovering it as so. But she could do nothing about it, as no movement on her part was possible. For Roy had stepped out in the hall, wrapped about by a blue towel from waist to mid-calf level. He was so very tanned… and there was that upper body with all that firmness she had fleetingly noticed on getting off the bus. His shape… it was so captivating! That, and the cute way his tossed about damp hair lay across his forehead. He had not yet sensed her, but moved directly to the new banister overlooking the stairs and the renovated living room below. Frozen in silence, she watched him crane his head over that railing, stooping down in order to shout toward the front door.

"I'll be down in a minute, Marna!"

On registering her own name, she relaxed her grip on the comforter, flattening out the fingers of both hands, and dared to risk herself on what she had seen. With as much love as she could offer, she loosened her lips toward the hall.

"Roy… I'm in here."

There was no doubt in her mind that the direction from which her voice came amounted to one of the supreme shocks of his life. He did not so much flinch as jolt, nearly losing a grip on his towel in order to catch himself from falling over the banister. Yet it was his little yelp that most lightened her heart.

"What're you doing up here? I thought…"

He did not complete the sentence, perhaps in becoming aware of how she was clothed and where she was seated. Without offering a word, she cast her eyes downward to the floor. She would wait in hope sitting exactly like this. She could sense him entering the room and fumbling about in some drawer, but she did not lift her eyes from off the floor. Against all of her fears, she found him kneeling in the exact spot where she was looking. But as he made to speak, she jumped in ahead of him, fully aware that he was holding something out to her.

"Roy… I'm so sorry. Sorry for all the pain I've put you through. I've been so stupid… so full of myself, that I couldn't see clear to how much you love me… and how much I love you too. If… it's possible… if you have it in you… I'd… like to come back to you. I want to be forgiven and… have a second chance at us. Is that possible, Roy?"

She lifted her eyes to his… and he was smiling!

"You know… I've dreamt of this moment so many times that I can't say what's been real in my life and what's been fantasy. This seems real… I've saved these for you." Without delay, he took hold of her left hand and slid into place the rings that she had so callously abandoned two years before. "Do you remember what I told you when I proposed…"

At first, the feel of those rings was beyond wonderful… but within seconds of having them on her finger, their metallic embrace became viselike, burning in pulses of pain up through her wrist, arm, shoulder and neck. And then her lips parted against her will, bringing forth voice to squelch this newfound happiness. She had not intended for any such thing to be spoken, yet still the truth of Chicago came bursting forth.

"Roy… I… can't accept these back. Not yet, at least."

She could no longer bear to look into his eyes… only at her own hand as she pulled it from his gentle grip. Slowly, she drew both rings off her finger and extended them back to him.

"Since I left you, I've… been with others."

Not taking back the rings, he leaned away from her.

"Others?"

"Roy… I've… I've made so many mistakes. So many stupid, terrible mistakes. I have no excuse for how I've lived…"

She could sense him drifting even farther away, but more than ever needed him close so he might come to understand how terribly sorry she was.

"What do you mean by others?"

"Other… lovers."

He instantly shot to his feet. Though she lunged out for him with her free hand, she completely missed him. He was backed up to the wall, and by the hardness coming to his face, she knew for certain that he would no longer have anything to do with her.

"Wait, Roy, please let me explain…"

"You – want me – to listen – while you explain other lovers?! What possible explanation do you think I'd want to hear?!"

Her eyes darted down to his hands. They clutched at the towel about his waist as if his life depended on remaining covered. No longer was he looking her way. He instead faced up toward the ceiling, shouting as if to the house itself.

"What a complete ass I've been! What an incredible fool to think that she'd kept a place in her heart for me! Here I was being like a hopeless school boy imagining that she'd remained just as faithful to me as I was to…"

He abruptly brought his face back down to look fire into her eyes.

"Get out!"

"No… please, Roy… I'm really…"

"NOT – ANOTHER – WORD!"

He took a hand from the towel to swing that arm toward the bedroom door.

"Go on – get out!"

Backed all the way against the newly painted wall, his outstretched hand then went to cover his face. His next words came soft and slow, but they were more painful to her heart than all of his shouting.

"Please, Marna… just leave. Go… and never come back again."

She closed her hand about the rings, groped behind the bed for her dress, and then obeyed without another word or glance his way. Scooping up her high heels on the way down the stairs, she heard the master bedroom door slam shut behind her. Toes on bare feet attempted to grip the wood of the stairs… and then the marble work… but neither texture allowed her to take hold. Nothing of this newly fashioned house was reaching out to embrace her into one last second chance with it. She was aware only of her own smallness in passing through its vast open space. Without a look at what ten minutes before had so filled her with wonder, she paused at the front door only to pull the black dress of mourning over her head, not bothering to zip it up after. Out on the front porch, she scooped up her purse from the table where she had left it… awkwardly rifling within for her car keys. Uncontrollable tears were on the way… and she must get off this porch and away from this house before disgracing either with her presence.

Down the steps, she tread out onto the yard's already brittle Texas buffalo grass, and then across the sharp gravel to her car door. Both surfaces cut new kinds of pain into her. Fumbling with the keys, she accidently dropped her high heels on the gravel, yet did not bother to retrieve them until she was seated within Gwen's car. Laying the keys in her lap, she reached out to drag those shiny shoes that she once thought so cute across the rocks into the car, and then hurled them down into the passenger side foot well. Closing the car door, she sat in excruciating silence. The blood of her shame was pounding through every inch of her, making her tremble with an awareness that her heart was broken forever. And yet she just sat there with the most ridiculous of distractions desperately trying to take up space in her mind.

Why can't I pick up the keys from my lap?

Lifting her right hand to her face, she slowly opened its clinch fist to reveal the rings she had unknowingly retained all the way from Roy's bedside. Due to her grip, they had cut deep impressions into her palm. The circular marks, in a morbidly dull shade of blood red, seemed so much more real to her than the rings… and more symbolic of her broken promises. Those scars bore for her an appalling purity far beyond that of precious metal or gemstone. She closed her hand again… more gently this time… and spoke in desperation to the tokens within… though she hoped so much more that her message went out to the house that she had never really given a chance to find a place in her heart.

Please… Please help me… Help me find a way back to him… and I promise with all my being, I'll never ever leave him again!

She straightway burst out into a fit of weeping… one that would not stop, accompanying her all the way back on her solitary drive into Lubbock.

CHAPTER
28

INWARDLY DRIVEN

Having neglected to turn on the porch light prior to departing for the funeral, she returned in complete darkness to the place where she grew up. Still barefoot, she climbed the front steps and collapsed against the nearest pillar, not yet ready to enter the house. A stranglehold of regret forbid her from doing so. Instead, she pressed her knuckles into her eyes and slid down the pillar, wanting to conceal herself behind the holly-rimmed railing. Elbows on her knees, she once again began to cry. She was alone, her aunt was dead, her marriage was doomed, and though Chicago waited, going back there now meant nothing to her. Just as in the car on the Meitner circle, her tears gave way to such overpowering sobs that she could not keep herself from teetering over into a ball on the porch. She would remain that way forever, mourning over how much she loved Roy and what little regard he now had for her.

After who knows how long, she finally felt calm enough to wipe her wet cheeks with her finger tips… only to end up spreading dust from the porch into her eyes. The discomfort immediately reminded her of having once done this on the floor of the Lubbock post office. Her younger self had so easily done away with love. That person had tricked and deceived her way right out of Lubbock… and into this miserable state instead.

If only I'd stayed there and never responded to the WYNG offer letter.

Her crying might be stilled for now, but she absolutely could not yet enter Gwen's house. Not with the echo of Roy's words still in her ears. She opened her watery eyes to dispel those painful memories, craving to see anything other than recollections of herself. Everything about her was already cast into the deep gray of twilight. With her head lying on the porch floor, she concentrated all effort toward finding something capable of distracting herself from her wretchedness. Owing to the proximity of the floorboards, vision in one eye was blurred. All she saw through it was grayness. The other eye picked up on the fuzzy outline of a groove between two boards. Bringing that eye's vision into better focus, she was able to follow how that crack led off away from her. Once, she had thought about escaping her childhood concerns by taking off down a row sort of like that crack. For a moment, she could almost see herself as a miniscule creature down there in that groove, forever following it onward. These images, of solid grayness in one eye and an open row in the other, superimposed themselves in her optical reckoning. Up close, she could vaguely make out a line leading away from her, but off across the porch, all was rendered into a charcoal black oblivion. There was absolutely no hope for her in the future.

She abruptly rose, dusted off her dress, and entered her aunt's house with no extraordinary effort. Moving through the rooms, she flicked on every switch and lit every lamp. It was necessary... even imperative... that she dispel all gloom from sight. Returning to the sitting room, she took to her aunt's favorite armchair, only to stare out at nothing. The day, unbidden, was rolling through her mind, though not linearly in smooth transitions. Herky-jerky, her thoughts jumped back and forth from the moments before the funeral, to the funeral itself, and to the time at the Meitner house. Always she came to settle upon the same image – of Roy telling her to leave and never come back again. In the stillness of Gwen's house, she knew for certain that he meant it... and it would take a miracle for him to un-mean it.

An unseen weight of shame forced her to slump down in the chair, and though she bravely tried pulling herself up, she soon was pitching about in a futile pursuit of comfort. During a sideways convulsion on an armrest, her finger tips brushed up against something lying on the floor. Eager for any kind of distraction, she leaned over to notice the day's mail down there. Atop the stack was the letter that she had written a week ago. Staring at it, she reluctantly accepted the sour verdict that the young woman who had penned this letter was a fool. She had known of an aunt's brokenhearted longing to hear from a niece, but could only produce this pitiful rag in response. She had no desire for opening the letter this afternoon, but now was in great need of finding her Chicago-self as more pathetic than how she currently felt. She snatched up the envelope and ripped it open.

Dear Aunt Gwen,

I can't fully express to you how glad I am to have received your letter. I'm ashamed to admit that up until today, I had no thought of ever contacting you again. But sadness has brought back sense to me. I also did you wrong, Gwen. I broke your heart and turned my back on you. For that, I deserve all of my own tears, and a good measure of yours too. Tears do not come easy to me. I guess you could say that we Forde women are tough. We don't cry much. But on reading your letter, I wept like I'd never done before. I wept over my wrongs to you. I hurt you. I shut you out, Gwen. I shut you out of my life, and swore it was my right to do so. You took me in, and was better to me than a mother because you did the duty of both parents – a caring touch and a stern voice. Both were there when I needed them most. I wish now I had heeded that voice, and allowed myself to be softened by that touch.

I'm terribly sorry for the wreckage I left behind when I fled Lubbock, but I do need to be up front with you, Gwen. I have no desire of ever moving back. I love it here in Chicago. More on this below. But that doesn't mean I don't want to be in your life. I want to visit, and have you visit me here. Can we start over, me and you, my beloved aunt? Can you forgive me enough to start over with me, if only as friends?

Please don't punish yourself over my failed marriage. I have no idea what the future holds, but can safely say that there's no chance of me ever getting back together with Roy.

She could read no more. It mattered not. She knew that the letter just went on to recount the happenings of her time in Chicago… minus the painful parts. There were likely more expressions of love toward Gwen, but those now seemed so hollow… so untested by the aunt abandoned and unproven by the niece who did the leaving. Based on all she had learned this day about Gwen's past, she now felt her letter to be so miserly… so very lacking in showing the love and appreciation due to her aunt.

She folded the pages along the original creases and thrust them back into the torn-up envelope… to be buried within and never read again. She rose, staggered into the kitchen, and dropped the letter into the trash.

Not really understanding why it mattered, she set herself to rotating the couch back to its original orientation facing the blank wall. Without going through the usual preparations for bed, she roamed about the house extinguishing all of the lighting and then returned to the sitting room. Throwing herself down on the couch, she would lie there in her funeral dress, just as Gwen was doing so that night in hers, until perchance darkness might fall upon her too.

But that spot on the wall refused to grant her sleep. Wide awake staring at it, she was gripped by how the rectangular outline taunted her into accepting that the relief was gone forever. In a meager defense, she tried to recreate in her imagination the full wonder she had experienced on first seeing the stonework, and how that same fascination continued on and on throughout her childhood. But nothing of the sort came. That spot just mocked her, swearing that it would forever preserve this wall as blank because of her mistakes. It would go on day by day making that sad wall bear its burden of a heavy roof. Roof and more walls would encompass her, keeping whatever joy was outside from getting in and confining what sorrow was within from ever escaping out. Tossing about on the couch, she told herself that such was now the feel of her life. She was destined to construct walls all about her heart in an effort to shut out the sadness. But the sadness came from within. She might go on adorning the outside of her walls with beauty and fashion, but all such efforts would be futile. Her insides would forever remain bleak. Without Roy, life had no meaning.

Think about something else. Try again to imagine every detail of that amazing relief.

She lay there in the dark, once again straining to picture it on the wall where it once hung… but only the sculpture's faces returned from memory. She now saw them as clear as day – their rage, hatred and lust for dominance, along with their fear, misery, enslavement and defeat. Yet worst of all, she felt each one's empty longing. She fought to push those faces out of her mind and instead behold the wonder of flight… but nothing of the birds ever came.

There's got to be something beyond that relief's false promise of breaking away.

Now wide awake, she forced her mind's eye to see through the wall to its other side.

Well… there's the porch. I've sat there so many times. Once I was out there for hours with Gwen arguing over… over Roy.

She shoved that memory away and moved on.

Over the railing is the narrow stretch of yard between this house and the one next door. That use to be the Jones's… I think.

She had been sent over there a few times in her childhood to borrow an egg or a cup of sugar, but had never really gotten to know them.

They seemed happy enough...

Next door to them was... that guy with the crooked nose.

She skipped past him, not much caring to recall the names of strangers. There would be more houses before she reached the next major street... and then more on the other side. Onward her mind took her across the avenues partitioning off the various neighborhoods of South Lubbock. She crossed the Santa Fe rail lines, and then flew over warehouses, granaries, and so many small businesses. Her mind led her over the Loop into farmland... and along rows of cotton... onward into the West Texas flatness. Before her now loomed only a lonely horizon, hollow sky above and hard earth below. She was racing toward it, trying desperately to lay a hand on that barely discernable line separating dark gray from deep purple nothingness. Ever the same was before her no matter how fast she sped. It could not be grasped... could not be touched... could not be reached... and always it grew into a singular darkness.

She jerked up from shallow sleep and her half-dream, one that started in distraction and ended in shadowy reality. It was still as dark out as before, and likely no time at all had passed since she dozed off. But that dream would not permit her to reenter sleep. She was so very tired, and yet wide awake. Surely more hours were destined to be spent in flailing about, trying hard not to think about how badly she had messed things up with Roy.

Staring through the wall had not helped her reach meaningful sleep. It had only resulted in a stupid dream and a crick in her neck. She needed to try something else. Faint moonlight was now casting its flickering impressions across the wall, making it even more difficult not to see the spot. The rectangular pattern marking where the relief had once hung was so much clearer. Tightly closing her eyes, she strained to see only blackness, but her mind's eye still produced that ghostly outline of where the relief once hung.

This is so ridiculous! I'm never going to get any sleep until I deal with that spot on the wall. Just cover it up again with the stupid painting!

She had almost resolved on this course of action... was even debating with herself whether to turn on the room lights... when the recollection came to her of how she had mistreated that painting. She had broken its frame so badly that the thing would probably fall off the wall in the middle of the night.

Well then... put something else over it!

Anything capable of hiding that spot would do, so long as she could shut her eyes knowing that it was not there staring back at her. If only she was strong enough of mind to put it out of her thoughts or imagine it as blocked.

She would do it herself, if only she could be in two places at once. She would gladly stand there in body, shielding her heart from the implication of the relief's absence. And just to make the whim real, she started imagining it as so. She could almost feel herself climbing up, hooking herself to the wall, and then hanging there like a scarecrowish version of herself. She would put on such a terrifying gawk to frighten away her sorrows.

In a flash, a startlingly new realization came to her. She was the relief. She was one of those sad faces forever constrained within its misery to watch time and the lives of others flow by. Aware of all the world's joy outside of where she hung, yet herself cut firmly into the stone of her pitiable state. All those teenage aspirations of hers for breaking away now amounted to nothing more than a sad view of this room. Roy or no Roy, all of Gwen's furniture would soon be carted off and the room emptied. The whole house would be made vacant for others to come appraise relative to their own aspirations for the future. Eventually, some stranger would claim this space as their own, sweeping it clean of all past dreams and decorating it with those of their own. And still she would hang there, covering that ugly spot on the wall, forced to witness how easily life went on without the absurdity of herself. Her spot could never be removed or covered up, nor could it be reframed or overlooked. The real truth of the relief was staring her in the face. She, not yet twenty five years of age, had made a complete mess of her life.

<u>Sunday, May 17th</u>

She awoke in a shambles, having garnered maybe three fragmented hours of sleep amidst all of her tossing about in the night. She went first to the bathroom to peel off the black dress, discarding it on the bathmat in exactly the same spot where Gwen had left her pajamas. For no other reason than that it felt good and was an activity to which she could claim some success, she stood in the shower until she had drained the hot water heater down to a cold shutter. After, she did not brush her teeth or bother with her hair, for to do so meant beholding herself in the mirror. She dressed in the dining room, not in the least bit concerned about privacy. She was dwelling only on an unfulfilled longing for Roy.

For the first time since arriving at Gwen's house, she felt that sorting through the boxes in her old bedroom seemed the only suitable thing for her to do. To be sure, going through each one was part of her responsibility to Gwen. No different than the effort she had already invested into the office. But that was not the reason she sought refuge in her old bedroom. Taking a glass of orange juice and an untoasted bagel, she closed off the rest of the world and submersed herself within the life of Gwen Forde.

Where in the world all these boxes had come from, she had no idea. There was not enough space for storing them in the house… and certainly not at the shop… so they must have been somewhere else. Most of them were sealed shut, clearly from long ago given their overall dusty appearance. They spread from just inside the door to all corners of the room, with only that one lying open. It seemed clear that Gwen had recently decided to revisit the contents.

But only got a short way in before…

She would not finish the thought. Instead, she sat right down on the hardwood floor by the opened box and began going through the three stacks that Gwen had made in sorting through its contents. The easiest of these to recognized was also the least interesting to her, but she started in on the pile of newspaper clippings as a first step toward understanding a woman she hardly knew. All of them were highly faded and likely from long ago. In briefly thumbing through the pile, she noted that most were small bits cut from interior sections, whereas others were full front pages from various Detroit newspapers – the *Times*, the *News* and the *Free Press*. The dates were all in the late 30s to early 40s. Most of the articles had to do with the war. In more closely examining them, she began to see a pattern emerging. Virtually every clipping had something to do with flying. There were numerous articles about specific planes and their manufacturers, about the details of aerial combat over Europe and the Pacific, and about the exploits of pilots. She cared not for any of that. She lingered more on Gwen's clippings pertaining to local airshows at the time. In particular, she read in detail anything to do with the father-daughter biplane performances of Horace and Gwen Forde. Those articles, though extremely faded and terribly frayed along their edges, were precious to her, so she laid them with care upon the seat of the folding chair.

She next found an advertisement dated in late 1939 offering Army-sponsored 'Civilian Pilot Training' classes at Michigan State University. Faintly underlined sections could still be seen. *'For only $40…' and '…open to men and women, eighteen years and older.'* She found another advertisement seeking women pilots, but something had been spilled on this such that she could make out little of it. Nearer to the bottom of the newspaper pile was a small cutting without date or byline. It may even have been a segment taken from a larger article. From the feel of it, she gathered that the war was already in full bore because the Army and Navy were struggling to find qualified pilots who could fly their many newly constructed warplanes from factories to ports of embarkation. Gwen had circled the last paragraph several times. The U.S. Army was exploring the possibility of utilizing female pilots with pre-existing flight experience in purely non-combat capacities. Training programs were being set up in Delaware and Texas from which the Army would evaluate the suitability of women as ferrying pilots. She also put this fragment of paper on the chair, for it was clearly the start of something big in Gwen's life.

The remaining snippets were largely more of the same – articles and letters-to-the-editor from women readers supporting the potential roles of female pilots in the war effort. None of this was of interest, so she put them all aside. She was finally beginning to see how Gwen Forde, the teenage pilot, might have become Gwen Forde, the WASP… though there were still so many holes in her aunt's life story. Most of all, she had a growing craving that she feared would be left unfulfilled. The clippings told her nothing about what she cared most to know – how her aunt had felt and what she had experienced personally.

Turning to the next pile, which was smaller than that of the clippings, she picked up the top sheet of paper. It was an official record of some kind, even more weathered than that of any of the newspaper articles she had read. Its meaning was unfortunately hidden within so much smeared out typewriter ink. She could make out only the words 'Michigan State University' across the top, and assumed this to be related to classes Gwen had taken. Another document was equally blurry, but it did seem to bear the official seal of the U.S. Army. Other certificates in the pile were easier to read. Gwen's private pilot's license, dated in 1933 when she was not yet sixteen, a 1935 Lansing High School diploma, and an award for the best young stunt pilot at the 1937 Michigan State Fair. Next was a faded telegram, dated on January seventh of 1943, informing Gwen that she had been accepted into the Women's Flying Training Detachment, and was directed to report on April twenty fifth at Avenger Field in Sweetwater, Texas. She reread again the telegram trying to imagine herself as Gwen. Surely her aunt would have been thrilled to be finally on the way to something truly grand in life… but likely also a bit scared.

She then noticed that there was only one thing left in the pile – a framed certificate of Gwen graduating from that program on September fourth of that same year.

I bet that's when Frankie's poster of her smiling so big was taken!

She sat for several minutes staring at these two items – the extremely yellowed piece of telegraph paper and the glass-encased certificate. Less than a year's time separated them… yet the gap seemed unfathomably huge to her… with only Sweetwater connecting the two. That small town was a mere two hours from Lubbock. She had passed through it many times… the most recent being on her bus trip the previous Tuesday night. She also remembered having gone by the place in chauffeuring George back and forth to Dallas. In fact, Gwen had personally driven her past there countless times, but never said a word about the significance that the place might hold for her.

Instead of starting in on the last of Gwen's three piles, she came to her knees beside the box and began rummaging around for more clues in what remained inside. The bottom few inches held mostly more newspaper clippings. Nothing of great value toward uncovering the mystery of Gwen Forde the pilot.

She turned to the last pile, a tall stack of bound notebooks of varying sizes. Taking the top one, she opened it at random. It was a ledger of sorts, written in the same hand, yet with different types of ink from different types of pens.

You know… I think this is a logbook of flights.

She flipped back to the front and went page by page. There were well-defined columns for such things as the type of aircraft flown, its identification number, codes for the 'to' and 'from' airports, and various technical remarks… none of which she understood. In fact, most of the details aside from dates and times made little sense to her. She flipped back to the front again to note the initial entries. They were in April of 1944. Without much thinking about her method, she quickly rifled through the entire pile… setting aside a few that were clearly journals and not logbooks… until she found the oldest one. This had to be Gwen's first logbook. Starting with the first flight on June sixteenth of 1932, the initial entries were in a bold print… likely of a man's hand. These gave way in a month's time to more delicate, girl-like cursive. She browsed the pages of this one very slowly with a strong longing to have known her teenage-pilot-of-an-aunt. In flying all over the Midwest with her father, Gwen had filled up this logbook before she even graduated from high school.

A rather sad thought unexpectedly hit her. Repeating the previous sorting process, she now hunted for the newest-looking logbook. It was not that difficult to find. She simply sought out the one that was not full. Flipping to the last entry, dated in March of 1945 for a flight in Lubbock, she immediately realized that this was the last time Gwen had ever flown a plane.

As tears welled up in her eyes, she quickly set aside the logbooks and took up one of the journals. Unlike the ledger-like format of the flight books, the entries in this were free-flowing. Finally, this was what she had been looking for – something of Gwen's thoughts and feelings about flying. Each entry started with the specifics – dates, places, aircraft and that sort of detail – but immediately thereafter got into a description of her flight. Starting in on one at random, she was soon disappointed to find that Gwen's use of cryptic aviation jargon, acronyms and abbreviations made the reading difficult. Moving along, she found that all of them were like this. In particular, Gwen was very technical in describing how an aircraft met up to its performance specifications. She soon stopped reading altogether and began instead to thumb through while enjoying the sight of the younger Gwen's handwriting.

Somewhere within the back portion of this journal, a particular word flashed by in her viewing… but got lost in a flurry of pages. She raced back through the same section several times, but was unsuccessful in locating where she thought she had seen this word. Resolved in frustration to conduct a more thorough search, she opened to the middle and went page-by-page. Her diligence was finally rewarded. The page in question had been used to record a flight occurring in January of 1944. She read the entire entry for that flight several times over, focusing on one small section.

> *"Ferrying Jugs to Newark with Mags, Frankie, Stitches and Potts. Came upon F3A Corsair at 033' off our 9. Test flight out of Brewster. Potts says those got bugs. Still… what a beaut! Matched airspeed and heading to Sound. Must write Brad about comparison with F4U. Same P&W double wasp as P47. Would love to get mitts on that. Damn Navy jackasses."*

The fact that she had seen a Corsair before, it being the old relic in George Meitner's hangar, was the very reason why she had been determined to find this particular page. The surprise at her aunt having known about a Corsair now struck her as a bit silly, especially given that Gwen had obviously been a pilot familiar with military aircraft. Yet the entry, as a whole, was not why she had reread it several times. Frankie likely was the woman she had met just yesterday, but as to the other individuals Gwen had been flying with, she could not care less. She was equally unconcerned with what Gwen had meant by Jugs… or Brewster… or what a double wasp was… or who in the Navy were jackasses. She closed the journal on a finger in order to ponder on two thoughts – both questions. Did Gwen know that there was a Corsair in the Meitner's hangar… and who was this Brad?

She spent the rest of the morning and on into the afternoon carefully reading through the journals in the stack… some dating back to Gwen's teenage years. She never found another reference to either a Corsair or Brad. In closing off the last one, a terrible suspicion was already beginning to grip her… and she wanted nothing to do with its possibilities. Loading everything back in… including the items on the chair… she moved that box against a wall to signify that its contents should never be opened up to her again.

The sadness over Gwen's unfulfilled life in flight, compounded by the mystery of this Brad… suddenly overwhelmed her with an unintended association. At that very moment, Roy was likely mourning over the first time he had ever laid eyes on her. Every expression on his face from the previous day came back to her in a rush, and their collective force compressed her into a ball on the very floor where she had spent so much of her childhood playing alone. And though she repeatedly beat a fist against that smooth wood grain, mixing her fury with tears, it was all directed at herself. She knew that he too had closed off a box of remembrance, never to be opened again.

Sometime after shadows had crept in through the bedroom window, she rose from off the floor. Neck to knees, her muscles ached from having fallen asleep on a hard surface. She left that room, purposing in her heart to never enter it again.

Monday, May 18th

She slept better that night, though not at all because she was over Roy. Sometimes, it was simply not possible for the human body to avoid sleep. This was to be the day that she reconnected with the lawyer to begin wrapping up the details of Gwen's estate. While such matters had been prominent in her thinking on Thursday when all that mattered was getting back to Chicago, her mind was elsewhere this morning.

Despite the previous day's resolution, she was right back into her old bedroom. Using a pair of scissors from the kitchen, she cut open the seam on the next box to find it jam-packed with envelopes. By the look of them, she concluded that most were personal letters written to Gwen. The majority had been thrown pell-mell into the box, though one corner was occupied by a stack neatly tied off with ribbon. She picked these up first… and then dropped them back in as if they were the plague itself. After many seconds of just staring at the bundle, she finally called up the courage to once more lift out these letters, more delicately than before. She had absolutely no intention of opening any of them, or even severing the ribbon that held the entirety together as a block of paper, because the top letter in the pile was addressed to Gwen in Sweetwater by a masculine hand. The upper left corner of that letter revealed the sender to be a Brad… more specifically, a Lt. Bradrick Miller. His return address, an FPO in Honolulu, Hawaii, told her everything that she dared to know. She wished now so very much that these love letters had gone into the earth with her aunt, for in squandering her own chance at love with Roy, she knew that she did not deserve to read any of them. She did not even merit touching the stack.

Gingerly, almost reverently, she laid the bundle aside, suspecting that the truth of them would come forth from another envelope in this box.

Without taking much note of the sender, she began sorting the letters into piles on the floor based on Gwen's mailing address. These fell into what turned out to be four groups, one each for Lansing, Sweetwater, a New York City APO address... which seemed to be how Gwen got her mail while on Long Island... and Lubbock. The latter, by far, was the most significant in size. With this simple task completed, she experienced another twinge of conscience. A part of her held that the very act of sorting indicated her willingness to read any of the mail before her. After all, Gwen was dead, and it was a niece's job to make sense out of what remained. But a stronger part... one that kept glancing over at the letters from Lt. Miller... argued that Gwen had made none of this known in life, so none of it should be broached upon in death. After continuing this debate of indecision for some time, she finally settled on a sensible compromise. Any letter sent by one of Gwen's parents, Horace and Elizabeth Forde... which so happened to be her grandparents... could be read without seriously infringing upon her aunt's right to privacy. And since she was just as interested in learning about those senders as she was of the recipient, she went with relish into the earliest of these – the two dozen or so letters sent to Gwen in Sweetwater.

Without having to take note of the envelope's sender, she soon became familiar with the block lettering of her grandfather and the flourished curves of her grandmother. Both were equally expressive in their writing to Gwen, though the former showed more excitement over the planes his daughter was learning to fly, whereas the latter tended more toward fretting. In following these letters through Gwen's training and then onto her time of ferrying planes from Long Island as a WASP, it became clear to her that both of her grandparents were so very proud of their daughter. Though neither ever mentioned her own parents... which struck her as rather odd... both would make occasional references to Brad. In these, she gathered that he was a pilot in the Marines, and much more significantly, Gwen's fiancée. Both grandparents seemed very much pleased with the match, and often commented about the upcoming wedding or the couple's post-war plans.

Not until opening a particularly lengthy letter from her grandmother, sent to Gwen in late March of 1944, did she discover the thing she most dreaded. She got only as far as the start of the second sentence in which her grandmother had asked when Brad's body would be shipped back from the Solomon Islands... and then the whole terrible truth of Gwen and the Meitners came crashing over her like a storm, wrenching her insides apart.

Without reading another word, she fled her old bedroom for the privacy of the sitting room couch where she could cry… far, far away from those letters.

After forcing herself to eat something… a stale slice of poppy seed cake… she finally felt calm enough to reenter her old bedroom. Without reading any more of Gwen's correspondences, she loaded them all back in and moved that box to the wall beside the previous one. She wanted to get the letters out of her mind, and thus selected a new box at random. It and the next four were all packed with an assortment of items from Gwen's time as a pilot – maps with special meaning to only her, flight manuals, flight apparel (goggles, leather jackets, gloves, and some extremely stiff uniforms), and photographs of her with her comrades posing before various planes. One box had lots of unused postcards and souvenirs from places her aunt had evidently visited – little replicas of the Statue of Liberty, the Eiffel Tower, and London's Big Ben. Most of these things were of little interest to her, so she promptly closed the box and shifted it to one side.

There were only a half dozen boxes left, and these all bore signs of having been shipped from Lansing to Lubbock. All were sealed with so much packing tape that it took a good bit of hacking with the scissors to get the first one open. Lifting the folds, she suddenly came to a breathless halt. At first, she stared down at the contents in disbelief. Then, reaching in to convince herself, she drew out a small giraffe. Its neck was slightly bent from having been shoved in among so many other stuffed animals, but it was just as colorful as the real thing. She began rifling through the entire box, extracting plaything after plaything. Some were as familiar as if it had only been yesterday when she last cuddled it, whereas others were completely foreign to her.

I don't understand… Gwen said that all of this had been lost in the mail.

All of a sudden, her bitterness toward an aunt who had refused to be a mother came screaming back. For some warped reason, Gwen had lied about these boxes. Worse, Gwen had actually stolen a childhood from her by hiding them away. The rage in her grew red hot… but then faded away as quickly as it had arisen. She was left with only a much stronger feeling of sadness. She dropped the handful of toys she was holding back into the box, just as she had done with the dirt that fell between her fingers into Gwen's grave.

The other boxes had more of the same – more things from her childhood. Books, toys, and much clothing… all things that she had been made to believe were lost. She dwelt on none of them for long, for all of it was just summoning forth more tears. Near to the bottom in the very last box, she found a black-and-white photograph in a wooden frame. In it was a little girl, perhaps no older than five, standing in what looked to be a lightly colored dress with a cute little jacket over top. To this girl's left and right were a man and a woman, both holding one of the girl's hands. They too were dressed in fine clothes – him in a suit and her in a dress to match that of the little girl's. All three were doing their best to smile for the photographer, though the sun's glare was clearly making it difficult on them all. She stared at this picture for several minutes before dropping it back into the box.

I have no memory of this. No memory of them... and no memory of me.

She rose and turned out the light on leaving her old bedroom, closing her lost childhood off behind her in the process.

She was awoken in the dim light to the sound of a shrill ring. Jerking up into a sitting position, she half expected to find herself in her Oak Park apartment responding to an early morning alarm. Instead, the nature of the ring convinced her of where she actually was. Rolling from off Gwen's couch, she hurried into the kitchen, glancing up at a small wall clock as she picked up the receiver.

Ugh... eight forty!

She had been napping for nearly three hours, and would likely have a difficult time falling asleep again.

"Forde residence, Marna speaking."

"Is Gwen available?"

She had not been prepared for this. In all the time since returning to Lubbock, she had received several calls on Gwen's phone, but always from individuals who knew what had become of Gwen.

"This is Gwen's niece. I'm... sorry to say... but Gwen passed away." She hesitated for just a second before continuing. "She was killed in the tornado."

"Oh my! I'm so sorry... I had no idea... or I certainly wouldn't have called. This is just horrible! Please accept my sincere sympathies to you and... everyone else in your family."

"Thank you. So... is there something I can help you with?"

"Oh no! I was just hoping that Gwen could... but I really shouldn't trouble you."

"It's quite alright... seeing as I'm Gwen's niece. I'm in town to help sort through her affairs. By the way... with whom am I speaking?"

"Forgive me... I'm Gloria, an attendant at Havens Home here in Lubbock. I know it's late... but I've been trying to track down Roy Meitner all..."

"Roy Meitner?!" She was suddenly wide awake and fully attentive. "Why're you calling for him here?"

"It's all I could think to do. I've tried everywhere else. It took forever to reach someone at his store... but they haven't the foggiest idea where he's at. His home phone just rings and rings. I thought perhaps your aunt might know… seeing as she's listed as a point of contact."

"I'm sorry… I'm not following you. Point of contact for what?"

"For his mother, of course. That's why I'm calling because she's…"

"For Ruby? Ruby's still around?"

Unbelievable! Not once did I think to ask him about his mother! I'm such an incredible clod! I just… assumed that she was out of the picture.

"Why… certainly. Listen… if you happen to run into Roy, please have him call."

"Certainly. Sorry, I've gotta go. Goodbye."

She did not wait for a response from the woman before hanging up. Dashing to her suitcase, she quickly changed into a clean blouse and slacks, then ran to the bathroom to brush her hair and teeth, along with applying a bit of makeup, and was out the front door within five minutes of ending that call.

CHAPTER

29

ON THE ROAD TO
SECOND CHANCES

She disliked the gravel grinding beneath her tires. It might warn him of a car approaching on his driveway… though he would know soon enough anyway. What bothered her more was that the sound brought back the unpleasant memory of her anxiously listening for the arrival of his truck at the end of the day.

Just so I could have him take Ruby off my hands.

It seemed especially dark out. Much thicker than what she recalled from a West Texas evening at the Meitner house. She concentrated on the arc of light being thrown forward by her headlights, trying not to think about how Roy would react to her return. The entire house was ghostly still. Not a single light seemed to be on. Coming to the end of the long drive, her headlights lit up the reflectors on a truck parked there. Roy was definitely home. She swung Gwen's car into the Meitner circle, with its beams panning across the porch before collapsing into focused spots on the truck's tailgate. She lifted her wristwatch into the backwash of light.

Not yet nine thirty. He should still be awake.

Out of the car and standing before the house, she was instantly thankful for the darkness. Glad that the moon, stars, and porch bulbs did not light up the place where she had sat rehearsing her stupid spiel about divorce… just before that wasp showed up. The magical way in which the creature had intervened, forcing her inside to behold the wonder of what Roy had created for her, that was just another reason why she refused to accept any version of the future that had her separated from him. She might have spent a good part of the drive over contending against the memory of her humiliation two days before, and would likely receive more of the same, but was resolved to endure it all. She could not anticipate what he might say or do, but she was determined to say and do whatever it took to save their marriage. For as if overnight, she had come to love him so dearly.

Climbing the steps and crossing the porch, she made no special effort at being quiet. Certainly Roy already knew that someone was here. She would knock, but had a plan for getting inside if he chose not to answer. Just prior to setting a knuckle to the door, she paused to listen. From somewhere inside came the irregular rhythm of a dull thumping. She rapped three times and waited. The thumping ceased for a moment, but then picked back up.

"Roy?! It's me… Marna."

The thumping halted once more, and again she waited. When the noise did not resume, she called out even louder.

"Roy?! I know you hear me! Open this door!"

She immediately recognized the uselessness to her shouting. He was clearly not going to answer the door. She drew back the screen and tried the knob anyway, not surprised to find it locked. Without pause, she stepped down the porch stairs to a specific loose brick in the foundation. Behind this she found what she had hoped would still be there – a spare key. She had hidden this away on the day after her mother-in-law locked her out. The thought flashed into her mind that if it had not been for Ruby's trick, she might not be getting into this house tonight.

The key fit, as she trusted that it would, and she stepped through to the marble tiling. Even before she could get a word out, the smell of the place had her pinching off her nose. Two days prior, the inside of this house had possessed the pleasant aroma of freshly cut wood. Now… it was the stench of something terribly rancid. She had an immediate association to that alleyway she usually scurried past on the way to her Oak Park grocery. That narrow service access bordered two popular drinking holes. She right off recognized the reek of day-old alcohol. Then another smell memory came to her from a month back… of doing a live spot in front of a massive heap of rubbish during the city-wide trash collectors' strike.

"Roy… where are you?"

In response, the thumping returned, sharper and more vigorous than before. She followed it through the parlor doors, around past the stairwell nook, and into the dining room. The source of the sound was sitting with his back to an inner wall. She did not need to see him clearly in order to smell him clearly. He was the essence of a drunk. Now nearer to him, she picked up on his body odor… and something even more unpleasant.

Ugh – urine.

As to the thumping sound, she noticed that he held something in his right hand… a small sledge hammer, by the look of it. He just sat there lifting it up a few inches and allowing it to fall back down… over and over. She could even feel the vibration of its impact through the floor. Without a word of warning to him, she reached around the opening and flicked on the light. He immediately cursed her for the brightness that sent him cowering. Likely, he could no longer make her out clearly, but she could vividly see what had become of him since she left this house. She stood over a wreck of a man consumed by a two day long binge. His hair was going every which way, and it, along with all the rest of him, was covered in sawdust. The worst was the front of his t-shirt. From collar to lap, he had a brown stain from repeatedly dribbling on himself. Her eyes went to the bottle of a caramel-colored liquid in his left hand. Its contents were partially consumed, with the rest sloshing about with his effort to shield his eyes from the dining room lights. All around him on the floor was a scattering of empty beer cans and whiskey bottles. Though Lubbock was a dry county, there were still plenty of ways to get ahold of alcohol.

"Roy… what're you doing?"

He stopped cursing in order to focus on her. Slowly, a sour sneer took shape on his face.

"Hez, lookee eres houze! Lookee waz cum… crawlin' back. A wive! Say howdy, houze… to da long lozt wive."

He more-or-less shouted these slurred words toward the ceiling, lifting his head that way to make his point clear, but then he came back down to face her… her knees, actually.

"Houze sazs it don't 'member no wive. Houze sazs fur… pur-tend wive to go 'way."

He took a drink and resumed with his hammering, perhaps more vigorously than before. In the light, she could now make out what he was doing to the floor. The array of dents and gashes to the wood were extensive, each blow generating iridescent-like wood fibers that had previously been concealed beneath a beautifully stained surface. He was clearly enjoying himself now that she was there to witness the damage.

"What're you planning on doing with that thing?"

"Gonna buz 'er up."

"Bust what up?"

Instead of words, he made to use the sledge hammer as a pointer, extending it in the air across his legs. Perhaps he misjudged its weight, for the thing slipped from his fingers and bounced head-first off his thigh. With a yelp, he dove for the tool… perhaps thinking that she might swoop down ahead of him. After a shiver, he raised the hammer more deliberately and pointed it toward the crate holding the relief.

"Iz gonna buz 'er up!" He took another pull on his bottle, with a good part getting spilled down the front of his shirt. "In da powdur… eree damn bit uv id."

"Why would you do that, Roy? Why would you destroy something so beautiful as…"

He straightway went back to jeering at the ceiling.

"Houze! Lookee whosid's talkin' 'bout… destoyin' bee-u-dee-full stuv." Back down to her with another leer. "Iz alwaz thoud we waz… beudaful. But noooo… ya hadda go an' buz uz up. So houze sazs fur me to buz 'er up. Put 'er… outta 'er misry."

She had never felt more sad and more disgusted together in all her life. She wanted to console him… comfort him… reassure him… anything to open up his heart to a second chance. But his drunken looks were as filthy as his clothes. Equally, she was not very comfortable with that sledgehammer in his hand.

To her surprise, his voice got softer, with less of a drunken slur to it.

"Go 'way… Marna. Not… wel-come here. Don't… wanna ya… watchin' thiz. Don't… wanna ya seein' me…"

"I'm worried about you, Roy. I love you."

Again, he went back to his shouting self.

"Je' 'ear dat house – shez luz uz! Shez… worrin' 'bout uz!"

With a mocking laugh, he threw his head back… only to send it crashing into the dining room wall. She was immediately on her knees beside him… but he lifted a hand to hold her at bay. Another drink… and more liquid spilled down the front of him. The way the bristles on his chin retained a translucent wetness from that drink, and how his eyes seemed so swollen with past tears… she found herself overwhelmed with the despair she had brought upon him.

"Please, Roy… let me help you."

"Ya're hi-lar-ee-us… ya know dat, Marna?! Don't ya sazz zo, houze?!" He cocked an ear upward in a very theatrical manner. "Houze saz… ya're hilareus. Saz for ya to go back to Shit-cog-o… wherze ya belong."

"You know I belong here with you."

The words came out so naturally, as if they had been poised on her lips for two years, biding their time there. Since seeing what he had made of this house… and reading her own letter to Gwen… she had decided to never again be fooled into believing that the shallow things in life were important. She had made up her mind on him.

"Bull-shet, Marna!"

She was not surprised by his response. In fact, she was not particularly surprised by anything she had seen since returning to the Meitner house. It was all on her – all of it – and she was determined to push pass through to whatever may lay beyond.

Roy went into a fit of coughing that made him spill some of his drink onto the floor. After several shuttered breaths, he beckoned her closer with an unsteady wave of his bottle-filled hand.

"Houze saz… izz saz… cain't neber trust… won't neber igan…"

"Roy… I'd like to tell the house something."

"Ell no! It'd no wanna 'ear no… fake wive!"

"I'm going to try anyway. I have to!"

She ignored his further protests over what the house did or did not want to hear, as well as the kind of woman it would listen to. She simply shook him off until he finally went silent. Very near to him, she lifted her face toward the ceiling, just as he had done.

"House… I'm so sorry that I've hurt you. I'm so sorry that I've hurt your Roy. I've been such a terrible… unfaithful wife, and I know I don't deserve to live here with you… or him. Please… if you can forgive me… and let me try a second time… I promise to never leave you again. And I promise never ever to leave him either. I will love you both forever. I promise."

She brought her tear-filled eyes back down to him… and was startled by his response.

"Gotta take a leak."

Without acknowledging her words, he slowly leaned forward into a staggered crawl across the dining room floor.

"Where're you going?"

On all fours, he just lifted his head with a nod in the general direction of straight ahead. She then noticed that a far corner was stained from his previous visits. In no way would she allow him to embarrass himself like that again. Squatting over his back, she wrapped both arms about his chest and lifted him to his knees.

"Come on, Roy… I'm taking you to bed."

He did not resist her, but also did not provide much in the way of assistance in getting himself into an unsteady standing position.

"Iz… 'on't 'eel zo good…"

From there, it was a massive chore to keep him moving through the parlor and around toward the staircase. All the way, she offered little encouragements of 'just a bit more,' 'you can do it,' and 'lean on me.' She helped him place a foot on the first step… and was relieved when he managed the next on his own. And then another… and another. She had him halfway up when he abruptly stopped, teetering about in his effort to come face-to-face with her.

"Whooz yooz?"

"Who am I?! I'm… Marna. Marna Meitner…. your wife."

"Iz noze yooz?"

His foot slipped, and both she and he crumbled sideways into the railing. For a second, he became dead weight, and it took all of her strength to keep them both from toppling down the stairs. She finally got him back under control.

"I'm… sorry, Roy. I've… been away."

"But yooz… yooz's nod again. Neber again…"

His plea was so earnest… so tender. Like that of a child's. It brought her new strength.

"No, Roy… I'm never leaving you again. I promise. I'm back for good."

Slowly, his opposite hand came up to rest upon her shoulder. For a moment, the drunken blankness in his face gave way to a broad smile… right as his eyes bulged, his lips locked, and both cheeks ballooned. Before she could react, he threw up on her… from the neckline of her pale blue blouse all the way down to the white pumps on her feet.

Covered in his gook and fighting off a host of new smells, she essentially had to haul him up the remaining steps, into the hallway bathroom, and over the lip of the bathtub. She was soaked through to the skin with his vomit, and repeatedly had to fight off the feeling of doing likewise. But he… he seemed happier now, and he was considerably easier to deal with in being confined to the tub. She stripped him of shirt, boots, socks and jeans amidst his many drunken objections, yet she was pretty sure that he had no idea of what was happening to him. With only his boxers left on, she watched him slump down into the tub as if he were settling in for a nap. She did not allow him to stay that way for long, as he sprung up with the curses of a soaked sailor the second she turned the shower head on him. He struggled to climb out, but she kept a hand on his head, pushing him down and telling him to take it like a man. Finally, the water heated him up enough that he settled in. From there, she let the soap and a whole lot of scrubbing with a bath cloth take over. He still protested, but it was more like a six year old being firmly bathed by his mother than a drunk being brusquely dealt with by an estranged wife. Boy or drunk, he was the man she longed to be near.

Through the process of bathing him, she felt herself becoming clean too. Not outwardly. Her blouse and slacks remained just as disgusting as when he threw up on her, even with the huge amount of water being splashed, sprayed and sloshed on her during all this heavy-handed bathing. Yet inwardly, she felt a part of her heart was being cleansed. He still went on fighting with her, but more playfully. If he slapped her hand away, she was confident of being able to bring it right back. Starting with his hair, she worked downward, bypassing the private regions of his boxers. In short course, he stopped refusing her touch… even began playfully patting her arm as she scrubbed. He allowed her to clean him, and in turn, he smiled at her, laughed with her, and accepted her affection. She could sense it. Even in his drunken state, he was offering her a path forward toward a second chance with him, and that made her heart swell with hope. Maybe he was forgiving her, and a longing for that forgiveness went further in cleansing her than anything that she was accomplishing on him with soap and water.

The sit-down shower brought Roy enough vigor to claim that he was capable of doing the rest on his own. ("Iz can do it myself, Marna.") So she stepped out into the hall while he grunted and groaned himself dry. He finally emerged from the bathroom as a much wobblier version of the handsome man she had beheld two days before on that exact same spot, except now wrapped about in a beach towel. He was still drunk, but when she smiled to him, he smiled back, and that was all that mattered to her. She led him down the hallway to the darkened master bedroom… to the very place where she had sat waiting for him. There, she dropped him into the bed and turned to leave.

"Marna…"

"Yes?"

"Thank you."

"You're welcome. I'll be downstairs if you need me. Otherwise… see you in the morning."

She closed his door and set herself to work.

It would be a waste to shower, do what she needed to do, and then have to shower all over again. She would clean the house first, and then tend to her own condition later. Starting with the bathroom, she collected up all of Roy's filthy clothing into a towel-wrapped bundle and wiped the place down. There was no telling where the remnants of her old wardrobe might be… assuming Roy had not pitched it all in the trash on the day she left. She briefly stuck her head into the other two upstairs bedrooms. One had been gutted and was in the process of being rewired. The other was the one that she knew to have been his bedroom right up until the time that they got married. The single bed was piled high with his clothes, and his old dresser had drawers pulled open. He seemed to be using this room until the master bedroom was fully ready. She found a pair of clean boxers for him, but decided not to use anything of his for herself just yet. She tossed the clean underwear into the hall bathroom, available there for his next visit.

Making her way down the stairs, she carefully side-stepped the vomit and headed for the cellar door at the back of the kitchen. Flicking on the light, she descended its narrow stairway beneath the house with a degree of apprehension. This space had always been dark and closed in. Nothing of her memory about it had changed. At the bottom, she glanced back up the stairs and smiled to herself… for she had always feared that Ruby might one day lock her in.

She threw Roy's dirty clothes in the washer and turned to the shelves. Right there in front of her were three boxes labeled 'Marna's clothes.' Her feeling of hope immediately increased on seeing that he had not only saved her things, but had positioned the boxes where they could easily be seen whenever he came downstairs. She pulled a box down and opened it to a wave of naphthalene vapor. Within, she found all that she needed – a pair of cutoffs, an old Masked Rider t-shirt, and some underwear. She stripped down to nothing and placed her clothes into the washer with Roy's, adding in several indiscriminate fistfuls from the box, and then started the load. Her shoes were a different matter. She rinsed off the vomit as best as she could and left them on the cellar floor to be dealt with later. From the utility sink area, she gathered up bucket, mop, scrub brush, rags and cleaners.

No rubber gloves…?

Her hands would just have to weather the chore. Her first target was the stairs.

Get it before it dries.

For the next several hours, she scrubbed every spot in the house soiled by Roy's drunkenness. Most of the work was pretty straightforward – picking up bottles and cans, wiping up vomit and spilt alcohol, and generally straightening up. Of all the tasks, cleaning the urine out of the dining room corner that Roy had selected as his in-house out-house brought the most unexpected effect upon her. Face down on her hands and knees scouring the floorboards with a brush, she found herself remembering having done the same thing with so many of Ruby's messes. She loved Roy, so doing this for him was no great burden.

But if I'd taken the time to love Ruby too, maybe... just maybe... things wouldn't have turned out the way they did.

Straightway, she decided then and there that she would pick up where her aunt had left off. She would do even better than be a point of contact for Ruby. She would become the Forde woman who showed Ruby Meitner real love, and she would transform herself into the daughter-in-law that Roy's mother deserved.

First thing once he's able, we'll visit her... together.

She worked harder now, moving up the walls and into the seams about the baseboard, determined to have all signs of the past wiped clean so they could start anew.

<u>Tuesday, May 19th</u>

It was well after midnight when she finally got herself showered and dressed in pajamas brought up from the drier. She then returned to the cellar to start a new load, and to search for something to sleep on. The guest bedroom was unavailable, as Roy had packed it with furniture and things from the kitchen. She found an air mattress and a sleeping bag that would do. She set up this makeshift bed on the floor of the family room partly because she could quickly respond if Roy needed her, but mostly because she had already come to love this room. With the upstairs hallway lights left on, a soft glow spilled through the banister's railing, casting complex shadows across the family room's walls and floor. For a good long time, she lay on the mattress tracing out their patterns and imagining how she might decorate this space. She even ventured so far as to picture herself lounging in Roy's arms on a couch as a fire softly crackled in that fireplace. How all that would take shape, she could not say, but she was beginning to see herself building something significant out of this second chance with him. Giving up a career as a Chicago newswoman was really not such a big sacrifice if it meant a lifetime spent together with him.

After all... I can do whatever I want!

Laying there in the semi-dark, she was marveling at this new vision of herself with Roy when she heard a loud thump from above. Up the stairs in a flash, she reached the master bedroom door just as Roy emerged crawling out on hands and knees... completely naked.

"Are you okay?"

He waved her off and continued his crawl into the bathroom. In short course, she heard the toilet flush, and then Roy emerge wearing the boxers she had tossed in there. Without a word of forewarning, he threw his arms about her in a tight hug. She was overwhelmed by his show of affection, and wished very much that she could have gotten her arms unpinned in order to return the embrace. But as nice as the hug was, what he whispered was far better.

"Thank you, Marna… for coming back. By the way… the house says 'welcome home.' It's missed you. Now… if you don't mind… I'm going back to bed. I feel terrible."

He released her, clumsily kissing her on the cheek in the process, and then staggered back to his bed. She stood there in the hall listening for several minutes just to make sure that he was okay, and then she took the stairs back down to the main level, very much content to resume her watch through the night.

CHAPTER
30

RENASCENCE

She rested no more soundly on the air mattress than she had on Gwen's couch. Rather than worrying about a spot on the wall, she was now concerned for Roy... and her relationship with him. At least when stirred from sleep, she got to re-experience the wonder of this renovated family room. For one long period, she lay on her stomach listening to the night sounds and tracing a finger along the grains of marble in the slab before her, wondering what it would take to make this house her own.

Having had no notion the previous day that she would be spending the night at the Meitner house, she had nothing nice to change into. With first light, she returned to the cellar to move the wet things from the washer to the drier. The blouse and slacks were clean, but she would not put them on in adhering to a basic fashion principle that no woman should wear the same outfit two days in a row. She opted instead for more mothball-laced clothes. Changing into a pair of sweats and a pink tank top, she dragged box after box of her old things off the shelves and began raking their contents into the washer. After adding laundry soap and adjusting the setting to normal, she returned upstairs to explore the dismantled kitchen area. With a bit of searching, she found a can of coffee, a percolator and some cups in the guest bedroom. What she had not noticed the previous day was that the kitchen sink had been removed, so she set about making coffee in the guest bath.

With cup in hand, she spent a good part of the morning sitting on the floor of the dining room re-familiarizing herself with the relief and perusing again Gwen's letter to Roy. Both continued to generate utter amazement in her. After a long time switching back and forth between the letter and the crate, she took up the envelope with the relief's original bill of sale in it. For whatever reason, she did not consider looking at this to be a breach of another's privacy. Not anything like delving into someone's old love letters. This was about the relief, her oldest of friends.

In another shock from a week filled with shocks, she discovered for the first time that the piece of art she had only ever referred to as 'the relief' was actually one of a pair that Gwen had obtained from an art dealer in Kingston Upon Thames, somewhere outside London. Purchased during the war while she was in Britain for some reason, Gwen had managed to safely ship both reliefs back to Long Island, and then eventually to Lubbock. The name ascribed to the one she knew well was actually '*Fino al Cielo*,' which the letter indicated could be translated as '*To the Sky.*' Its mate, currently on loan to some Dallas Museum based on a note that Gwen had paper-clipped to a photograph, was called '*Sulla Terra*,' or '*On Earth.*' She pulled the note away to reveal the same smiling Gwen as in the poster, except she was dressed in a flight suit of some kind. Her aunt stood between the two reliefs – sky on her right and earth on her left. Despite the photo's poor quality, she could just make out that 'Earth' also possessed a wide band of characters compressed together. Each and every one seemed terrified as they huddled together teetering on the edge of a precipice. At the bottom of that relief was a narrow band of stone depicting flames shooting up from caverns beneath.

Creepy! No wonder Gwen never kept this one around!

The appraiser, having apparently driven to Dallas to authenticate the sister relief, stated that the value of the pair was likely in excess of a hundred thousand dollars. Gwen paper-clipped another note to Roy on the appraisal.

'Expect to hear from the museum regularly. They have designs on the pair of them!'

It was not like she had discovered herself to be a twin separated from a sister at birth, but she still felt that way. The situation with the two reliefs made her question how sure she knew herself and all that was going on around her. Roaming about in a house that was not hers contributed to her feeling of uncertainty. In replaying her interactions on the previous night with a drunken

Roy, she realized that she was getting *way* ahead of herself. He had welcomed her home on behalf of his house, but not himself. Besides, allowing her back did not necessarily mean that he trusted her. He had not yet learned about all of the terrible things she had done. So it was stupid for her to be fantasizing over plans for decorating rooms, or outfitting the kitchen, or being back with him in his bed. When he finally came to his sober senses, Roy might just as likely throw her out of the house again.

To distract herself from these fears, she took her first trip out to the hangar, but was annoyed to discover its doors padlocked. Because of the brightness of the morning sun, she found that peering through the small square of glass set in the man door revealed nothing. All within was opaque. After an unsuccessful search in the torn-up house for the key, she settled on using a flashlight to peer through the glass. By contorting its beam about, she was finally able to make out the faint outline of the Corsair, sitting mournfully where George had parked it over twenty years before. According to his will, that plane belong to her. It might as well have been a submarine for all the good it would do her. Having a plane and a hangar on the Meitner property did not ensure Roy's faith in her. Still… she longed to see her Corsair up close again, and through it, remember George… and Gwen… and the Brad she would never know.

Sometime around noon, Roy managed to drag himself out of bed… blurry eyed and terribly hung over. The first thing he said to her was that she stank of household cleaners and would she mind backing away from him so he did not upchuck on her. She did not have the heart to tell him that he already had. He nonetheless managed to get out brief instructions for her to call about Ruby and to check up on the repairs at his store, and then crept back into the master bedroom's dark. He came again an hour later complaining of a migraine so bad that it had him sitting around his bedroom with his face in a bucket. She managed to get a bit of chicken broth down his throat and sent him back to bed with aspirin tablets and a glass of water as his only companions. His headache had somewhat lessened when he arose shortly before seven, but he was still suffering from nausea. He ate some saltines and drank part of a coke while sitting with her on the balcony off the master bedroom. He did not remember much about his drunken spree, which she gathered concerned him more than his head. He managed to ask about Ruby's well-being and what his assistant had said regarding the happenings at the store. She told him what she had learned – that both were doing fine. They also talked briefly about Gwen's death and the funeral. She did not ask him about the relief or the renovated house, but did comment on the locked hangar. The key, he said, was lost… and that was all he cared to discuss of the matter. Neither one of them brought up Chicago, though she was pretty sure it was on his mind also. He showered and returned to bed well before nine.

Wednesday, May 20th

By eight in the morning, she really should already be checked in at the Lubbock airport for a flight set to depart for Dallas in thirty minutes. From there, she was to make a connection for Chicago's O'Hare. Instead, she had a cup of coffee in each hand and was humming to herself as she climbed barefoot the sawdust-covered stairs of the Meitner house. She should be packed and dressed for travel, but currently had on only a t-shirt and some old gym shorts. Pausing momentarily at the master bedroom door in order to balance one cup atop the other, she knocked twice and then briskly entered without waiting for a response.

"Time to get up, lazybones. You and I have things to do."

Roy was curled into a ball near the foot of the bed, evidently having spent a second hangover-ridden night. He muttered out an objection from beneath the sheets ("don't want to") which she ignored. Setting both cups down on the dresser, she stood before the closed drapes of the room's eastwardly facing balcony and waited for the precise moment in which he poked his head out. She then flung the drapes open wide to bathe the room in the sunlight of a bright West Texas morning, taking pleasure in the scream as he scurried back beneath the covers. Giggling loud enough so it was impossible for him not to hear, she patted the sheet at his head and heard him moan in response.

"Come join me on the balcony for a cup of coffee. I'm buying."

Retrieving both mugs, she seated herself outside in a deckchair. After several minutes and several sips on her coffee, Roy staggered out dressed only in his boxers. To her great surprise, he leaned over and kissed her on the top of the head before taking his coffee.

"How're you feeling?"

"Not much better… I still have a headache… and this… this unsettled feeling inside." She assumed his meaning to be about the state of his heart, which took some of the glow off her hopes for the morning, but then she noticed that he was clutching his stomach. "Best not drink too much of this until I get something solid into me."

"That fits in just fine with my plan. I know you should probably be overseeing the repairs at the store, but I'd like you to let them know you won't be coming in today."

He raised an eyebrow her way… and she felt a tingle on the inside. She

453

had forgotten all about how he could lift either one independent of the other in communicating different things. To send off a question or act like he had all of the answers… to appear mischievous, coy or curious… or just be super cute!

"If you must know… I'm taking you out for breakfast, and then we're both going over to the nursing home to visit Ruby."

"And after that?"

"Then I thought you and I could… talk… about us. I have so much to tell you… and so much more to beg your forgiveness for. But I don't want to get into any of that just yet. Go ahead and change. I'll be downstairs."

She waited for him on the small platform of finished flooring a step up from the marble tiling. Once again, she was filled with the splendor of this spacious family room and a longing to fill it with things that they might pick out together. He soon came down the stairs and around to stand on the tile before her. He had on jeans and a collared V-neck shirt… sort of a teal color. The fit of it revealed a bit of that muscleman look she first beheld on stepping off the bus in Slaton. Somehow, he was even more handsome with his three-days of scruffiness. As to her own outfit, she was still in the gym shorts and t-shirt, accessorized now with a pair of flip-flops she had found in the cellar.

"That's what you're wearing?"

"It's about all I've got that doesn't still smell like moth balls. Everything needs another wash. Actually… I was kind of hoping to swing by Gwen's before breakfast so I could change. By the way, thanks for saving my clothes…"

"You're welcome."

"I'm… sure that wasn't easy."

He shrugged his shoulders without a word, but the pained look on his face showed that something else was going on.

"You've still got that headache…?"

"Yeah… pretty bad. I'm telling you – I'm never doing that again! I've taken something… but it's not kicked in yet. Let's just get going."

"Mind if I ask you something first? Did you do this… all of this… for me?"

He leaned over awkwardly to provide his answer in the form of a kiss on her forehead, then extended a hand as an offer to help her up.

"I'll tell you about it later… just not now. My head's killing me. You're driving."

She moved out the front door as light as a feather, for Roy… despite a headache… had not given up her hand. He was with her across the porch, down the steps, and all the way around to the driver's side of Gwen's car, opening the door for her. Again, she felt a hope springing up within that they would make it through the difficult conversations ahead. She would be able to lay her soul bare before him, now confident that he still loved her. She got the car started, but did not wait to clear the circle before taking the first step toward repairing the damage she had done.

"Roy... I want you back. It's all I want... and I'm willing to do whatever it takes to restore us... our marriage and our friendship. But for now... I'm only seeking the chance to make things right. I don't deserve it... I know that so painfully clear... and you don't owe it to me."

With hands at the top of the steering wheel, elbows bent down toward her lap, she pulled herself forward for a better view of his face. With each look over, she sought for some hint of what might be going on inside him. But he just faced forward, looking straight out the windshield.

"Roy... I know I need to regain your trust. That's why I want to start over... and go only as fast as you want."

She was at the turnoff for the farm-to-market road leading into the city, yet he had not responded.

Maybe he's not believing me...

But then he spoke haltingly with a rasp in his voice.

"I'm sorry... I need to close my eyes. You can talk if you want... I just can't say anything... my head hurts too much."

She scolded herself for being so insensitive, purposing to remain quiet for him. But as she passed the Loop on Idalou, the urge to tell him more of her heart had grown beyond what she could contain.

"I want you to know something... I'm staying in Lubbock. I'm never going back to Chicago. I'm absolutely committed to making our relationship work."

"What about... your job... at that TV station... and all your stuff? What're you planning on doing about that?"

"I don't know, Roy. We'll figure it out later."

"*We'll* figure it out?!"

She ventured the smallest of smiles in his direction, so very glad that he had picked up on her meaning. Of course... achieving a true 'we' rather than 'me' language of love would take a lot more than clever talk, especially since her old way of thinking already had a twenty four year headstart. She was sure to make more mistakes, but was equally determined not to make the same ones all over again.

"Here's what I propose... I'm going to move into Gwen's house and then find a job in town. That way we can start over from the beginning. You know... like when we were first dating and everything was..."

"I want you all the way back, Marna. Not halfway… and not in itty-bitty steps. Yeah… I know we've got stuff to work through, and… yeah… I know it's not going to be easy. But we're going to get there faster… and in the right way… if we're together working it out. So… if you're willing… I'm ready for you to come back. In fact… I want you back. You know I still love you. Always have."

She barely got the car into Gwen's driveway before falling apart. Throwing her arms about his neck, she let loose and cried… for how long she did not know. All she could think about was an overwhelming feeling of being free. Free to start over with him.

She finally pulled herself together to wipe away her tears and thank him for being so wonderful. Into the house as if in a dream, she moved with him hand in hand. She broke away only long enough to change clothes in the bathroom, and then gather up all of her toiletries and dirty laundry. Everything was stuffed into her suitcase, which Roy closed and lifted off the dining room table. She paused at the front door's threshold before locking up. Her eyes panned over the sitting room's state of dishevel and then came to rest on the spot where the relief had once hung. She immediately realized that owing to Gwen's dislike of Roy, she never had the opportunity of sharing with him all that the relief meant to her. The best kind of longing then flowed over her. She could not wait to see it mounted on a wall of the Meitner house and then stand arm in arm with him before it. The image of the relief's two birds flamed into her mind. Together, she and he would break away into a clear blue sky. The feel of it became so real that her heart was shaking every inch of her with anticipation. A gentle touch to her shoulder startled her out of one dream-come-true into another.

"It's okay, Marna. We'll be back over here plenty. This won't be the last time."

She had not registered that tears were gliding down her cheeks until he reached a hand up to wipe them away.

"Oh, Roy… it's… it's just that I can't wait to be back together with you."

"You silly girl! We're already back together."

She would never know how she managed to get out to the car, get the thing started, and pull out onto the street. All the way as she drove, she had one hand on the wheel and the other holding his, squeezing it every once in a while just so he would squeeze back… and let her know this was not just some dream of hers. Probably not the safest way to operate a motor vehicle, but she did not care. Roy directed her to a diner off 87 not far from Ruby's nursing home. She could tell that his headache had lessened, as he was smiling so big… and being such a gentlemen. Into a booth together, it felt so surreal sitting beside him as they ordered from the same menu. Here was the man she had grown up with, dated, married, abandoned, and then returned to. Throughout the wait for their breakfasts, she was bubbling with excitement over the opportunity of rediscovering this person seated beside her. It was a magical expectation that could not be ruined by anything… other than herself. Despite her pleasure at being with him, she knew the thing went the other way too. What kind of a person would he discover her to be? But really, she absolutely could not worry now about the ways in which she had changed. She just wanted to enjoy him. So she needed to start up some kind of a conversation that directed her thinking away from herself.

"So… what's up with Sybil?"

The smile on his face fell. She had chosen poorly.

"I haven't heard much from her since Dad died. As you might recall… she and Mom were never that close. Not in the typical mother-daughter kind of way."

"They certainly seemed united as to the cause of Dad's death."

"Marna… you need to understand something… that was Mom's illness kicking in. She really loved you. Oh… and for the record… I don't blame you in the least for Dad's death. I hope you believe me about that."

"I do. Sorry…"

"No need to apologize. We both misunderstood what was going on with Mom. And it came on so fast. Anyway… what was I saying?"

"About Sybil…"

"Oh yeah… I've tried to keep her up-to-date on Mom's condition… but she's really not interested. She's only been back once since you left… to argue over Mom's affairs. Frankly… I think she just wanted to know about the house. She took off once I was awarded power of attorney. I've written her several times… but she never writes back. You know she's already gotten her degree. Graduated on the Friday before the tornado. Wasn't interested in having me see her walk."

"Roy, let's not talk about Sybil. Just forget that I brought her up. Tell me instead about Ruby. Her condition… it's serious, isn't it?"

"Yeah… it's serious. Remember that neurologist you made her an appointment with?"

She did, but did not want to. She had used that as a ploy in her overall plan for escaping Lubbock. So she tipped her head as nonchalantly as possible, hoping that he would just move on.

"That guy diagnosed her with early onset Alzheimer's. It's a brutal disease, Marna. She's gone from difficult to nearly nonresponsive in just two years. She hardly eats or drinks anything… just sits around staring off into space. You'll see… it's heart wrenching. The doctors don't understand why… but they think that Dad's sudden death sort of… triggered it. There's a new medication they'll be…"

At that moment, an older couple appeared at their table. She right off recognized them as long-time customers of the appliance store. Roy perked right up, shaking their hands and making sure that they both acknowledged her as being back in town for Gwen's funeral. They knew of Gwen, so all four of them talked on somberly for a few minutes about the tornado and Gwen's tragic death. Maybe it was her imagination, but through the conversation, the couple seemed to prefer making eye contact with Roy over her. The talk soon shifted to how the appliance store was recovering, and the two were all smiles toward Roy… and nothing toward her. She had the distinct impression that they knew all about her and Roy's marital struggles… and by not looking at her, they seemed to be laying the blame squarely on the party who had fled town.

The couple finally left, allowing them to get back to their breakfast… but the taste of it was no longer the same. Her mind was stuck on the feeling of being shunned… and it was not her imagination. Ever since entering the diner, Roy had nodded toward this person or that, some she was familiar with, but none had made meaningful eye contact with her. Just inquisitive little glances. Try as she might not to, a bit of that unpleasant radioactive feel had crept over her.

I wonder how long it'll take for people to accept me back?

In being a Texas gentleman, Roy insisted that he pay for the tab… which reminded her that she also had things to confess regarding money. The two of them then exited for Gwen's car… but she was surprised when he delayed in opening her door.

"That's the nursing home over there…" He pointed across the highway to a complex she had seen a time or two. "… but before we head over, mind agreeing to something for me?"

"Anything."

"Mind staying in the car while I go in by myself? I've got no idea what state she'll be in… seeing as I haven't visited her since the day before the funeral. I do try to go nearly every day. So… if she's doing okay, then I'll come out and get you. But… if not… let's just say, I don't want you to get your hopes up. She's likely not to recognize you anyway… especially with your hair done different from before. By the way… I like it… a whole lot. You look nice. Real nice!"

"Thanks, Roy. I'll do whatever you thinks best."

"I just don't want you to take it personally. She doesn't say much about anything anymore. Although a couple months back, she did mention you… I mean, 'that nice girl with the flowers.' That's about all she's said about you in a long time."

"Hey! That gives me an idea! Preston Floral's nearby – what's say we make a stop there first?"

In short course, she was in and out of Gwen's major competitor in Lubbock with a dozen yellow roses. She then anxiously sat outside Ruby's nursing home as Roy went in by himself. After only a short wait, Roy came out of the same side entrance and held the door open. Out came a nurse pushing a wheelchair. She could not keep herself from gasping – Ruby was a wisp of the woman she had last seen. Frail and stooped over, Ruby stared vacantly down at the quilt that covered her lap.

She was immediately out of the car and dashing across the sidewalk to present her gift of yellow roses. She hugged Ruby, caressed her hand, kissed her cheek, and spoke genuine words of affection… but Ruby registered none of it. All the while, Roy stood by silently as the nurse offered many allowances on behalf of her charge.

"I'm sorry, you just caught her on a bad day…"

"Of course Ruby remembers you!"

"Not to worry – she'll be back to her old self soon enough."

"I thought we'd get some fresh air, but I'm thinking the sun's too bright for her…"

She hugged Ruby one last time, handed the vase over to the nurse, and retreated to the car with a sinking awareness that she had not been here as a supportive wife to help Roy through a terribly difficult time in his life.

I just made everything worse by leaving! Poor Ruby… If only I'd have seen that it was her sickness… and not me.

The passenger side door opened and in came Roy.
"Sorry that didn't work out, but there'll be plenty of other opportunities. One thing I've learned from her disease… it's important not to take one bad day into the next. Now… if you don't mind a side trip… I'd like to stop by the store, just to see how the repairs are progressing."

She drove him downtown, but chose to wait in the car. He was only in there for a short time anyway, and returned pleased that the insurance company had already approved his claim to replace the boarded up windows, fix the roof, restore the water damage, and cover the cost of the ruined merchandise. Taking the long way around the downtown area so as not to see any more of the tornado's effect, she drove them back to the Meitner house… arriving just before noon. Roy was opening his side to leave the car when she quickly tapped him on the forearm.

"If you're up to it, I'd like to continue our talk about us now… before going inside. Roy…I absolutely do not want anything I have to tell you being said anywhere near this wonderful house." She had thought this through during the many lonely hours of his recovery. She needed a spot that neither of them cared much for. A secluded place where an association with her stain might only rarely creep back into his memory of them as a couple. "I was wondering if we could grab lawn chairs and head over there?"

She watched him follow her outstretched arm toward the hangar.

"You want to talk in there?!"

"Actually… I was thinking of beside it. That faces north, right? We'll be in the shade while we talk, but more importantly, we won't be able to see any part of this house. It'll just be dirt and sky."

He nodded, and they both moved from the car about the house's wrap-around porch to the kitchen side. There, he opened a large bin that George had fashioned long ago as a storage place for lawn furniture and outdoor equipment. They each took a vinyl-laced folding chair and continued in silence to the far side of the hangar. She had only been back here a few times, knowing it to be a place where George like to pile long sections of unused aerial antenna. All of that had been sold off as scrap years ago, leaving the place bare. She set up her chair and was about to sit down when Roy placed a hand on her shoulder.

"Before you say anything, Marna, I just want you to know… I love you… and I forgive you."

Without forewarning, he wrapped his arms about her and squeezed. From thighs to shoulders, he held her tightly against himself… and then kissed her in the way she had always felt a woman was made to be kissed – him leaning over her just enough to arch her back. She closed her eyes into that embrace and imagined that no words from her would be necessary. That this moment… in this oddest of settings… would go on and on… and be more than sufficient for covering over all of her sins. But when he broke off without once looking into her eyes, she realized that the kiss and the embrace had been mostly for preparing himself.

"I know you're about to tell me things that'll be difficult for you to say… they'll be difficult for me to hear. I'm not going to promise that I'll take it well… only that I'm not going to walk away until we're both satisfied."

He stepped back and motioned to her chair. They then sat in silence facing out across the barren northern section of the Meitner tract. Beyond the property line were cotton fields, fully in bloom… and then farther off – the horizon. She put her eyes on that line, aware only of a yellowish-white speckled mass of green below, and above… a hazy blue dotted about with dull white puffs from many flat-bottomed clouds. In deciding where to start, she was mindful of this scenery, but mostly thinking about what an amazing man this was. He had given her the courage and confidence to speak, despite knowing that nearly every word of hers was destined to bring him pain. He was already looking beyond that pain… and so too could she.

With her speaking and him listening. She began at the point of her secret consultation with a divorce lawyer and then progressed toward her desperate decision to flee Lubbock for Chicago. She told him about how easy it had been to convince herself that she had been wronged, and how those wrongs justified her in pursuing a course destined to hurt him. She made no effort to describe any of the exciting aspects of living and working in Chicago. There would be ample time for such meaningless conversation after he had heard the worst… and still forgave her. So she got right to the point of her unfaithfulness. From her humiliating night with Grass to the much more demoralizing affair with Azurean, she painted an accurate picture of her wanton lack of judgment. In pursuit of her own significance, she had gotten high on both men, albeit in very different ways, before being brought so very low by the recklessness with which she had thrown herself at them.

She did not spare Roy's feelings in any of this. In being tricked by Grass, she revealed how her passions had deceived her regarding her own vulnerability. In giving herself to Azurean, she laid bare for him not only how her low opinion of herself had driven her decisions, but also how the craving she had for a greater role in this world essentially blinded her. How exposure to Azurean's ways had warped and weakened her perception of loyalty to the Berts, and how it was only through their understanding and forgiveness that she was able to continue at WYNG in cleaning up the mess she had made.

For the most part, she spoke in even tones with only brief interruptions from her tears… or occasional embellishments of her words with apologies. In fact, she rarely glanced over at Roy to assess the effect of her account… mostly out of fear that she would interrupt herself with more crying. He did ask questions, most often that she repeat some aspect so he could better understand. Through it all, he only touched her twice… and both times it was with a hand shot over to clinch her knee. Once was when she described having awoken in Grass's bed, and the other was when she had returned Azurean's kiss in the transmitter room atop WYNG. In both instances, Roy's grip was firm, but far short of painful. For her, there were many more times in which she wanted him to show some stronger emotion… to shout out in fury, irrespective of how it might shake her up. She wanted the confidence that he had heard the absolute worst… and still cared. But he stayed uncharacteristically calm through it all.

Yet midway through her account of Azurean and the hornet, she was completely shocked when he erupted from his chair and hurled it into the side of the hangar. Pacing in silence back and forth before her, he was sort of like a caged lion looking for a way to get through the bars at her. This outburst made no sense. He had been so even through her confessions about sleeping with those men, yet now… he was actually growling at her. And then he came to a stop with his hands on his hips, towering over her with so much anger that it made her cower beneath his words.

"Damn it to hell, Marna! How could you have been so abysmally stupid as to get in a car with that idiot… especially after everything you'd learned about him! I'm so pissed off at you right now! You're sure as hell smarter than that!"

"I'm… I'm sorry, Roy! Truly, I'm so…"

"Of all the dumb ass things to do! He could have done you harm! You know it! Have you no regard whatsoever for what you mean to those who truly care about you?! We've been worried sick! Not knowing from one day to the next what's become of you! Here you were walking the streets of Chicago alone at night… and you, my wife, taking up with strange men!"

He ceased his pacing to direct a series of violent kicks into the metal siding of the hangar. Then, he just stood there completely still. Seeing him that way… unable to move because of her… it was the first time that she felt the full weight of fear he must have endured during her absence. All she could do was cry in shame. She was aware that he turned about to pick up his chair… but just threw it right back down again when he could not get the thing unfolded. So she dashed over to help him set it up, for he was clearly beside himself with anger. Motioning with an arm that he should sit, she was thinking about the other things she still needed to say. But without warning, he grabbed her arm and craned it about into her face.

"And how do you explain this?!"

She tugged against his grip, herself getting angry for the first time at being mistreated after having just done something nice for him.

"What're you talking about? It's just my wrist! Now let go!"

"Really!? Just your wrist, huh?! Where's your medical alert bracelet?! Why aren't you wearing it?! You just told me a story about almost getting stung… and look…" He paused to shake her arm for emphasis. "…you're not even wearing the very thing that could save your life! What'd you do with it?"

"I… uhh… took it off… and… threw it away."

"Whatever for?!"

"I… didn't want anyone to know."

She knew her answer was not nearly good enough. She had been so foolish with her own life. He knew that too, for he tossed her arm back in disgust and collapsed into his chair. Ashamed of herself and ashamed of how she was making him feel, she looked to do something… anything… that might get him to see how much she regretted having hurt him. But looking at how he was beating the thumb side of his clinched fists against his forehead, she knew better than to try. He would not welcome being touched. Leaning forward with his face between his legs, he just looked straight down into the dirt.

"Roy, I'm so sorry I…"

"You've said your peace… now it's my turn. I'm so mad at you, Marna… but ten times madder at myself. It's all my fault. It was my job to protect you… and all I did was drive you away."

No way she was going to allow him to place such a burden upon himself. Had he not heard a word she said?! It was all her fault! Coming right before him, she fell to her knees and yanked up his head in order to force her way in close between his legs. She would get right into his face to make him understand.

"Roy… you're being stupid! You can't possibly hold yourself responsible for my poor judgment! I'm the one who ran out on you! I'm the one who wasn't grown-up enough to see past the struggles we were having! I'm the one who…"

"No, Marna, I'm the one! I'm the one who allowed his father's absurd obsessions to sidetrack our marriage. I'm the one who gave into his mother's bullying. I'm the one who refused to hear his wife's pleas for help. How stupid can a man be! I was raised better than that!"

He tried to push her away, but she would have none of that. So she took hold of his collar and shook sense into him.

"Not – your – fault!"

"Stop it!"

Terribly easily, he took her by the wrists and peeled her grip away… only to collapse with his face into her neck. He was so obviously crying, but she could also hear him muttering that he had failed her… and driven her away. She believed none of it, but held him near… hating herself for having reduced this proud man to tears.

In time, he lifted his head off her shoulder… and she edged backward a bit in order to give him space for collecting himself.

"I'm sorry. I'm making such an ass of myself.

"Roy… don't! I'm the one…"

"Will you cut it out?! We've been over this! I got what I deserved… even though it took such a long time for me to see it. Marna… I didn't believe your note for one minute. I was so sure you'd be crawling back any day. Man… was I ever wrong."

"Roy, I should've…"

"I'm not finished yet. You need to hear what I went through in order to understand why it's not your fault. You see… it didn't take me long to realize that Mom's behavior had nothing to do with you. I mean… I've always known her to be stubborn… kind of in a good way… but I had no idea how terribly sick she was. I can't believe I put you through that. Marna… she was a devil to manage… and you'd been doing it for a year. I went crazy after a week. I had to let so many things slip around the house and at the store… you know… while trying to get Mom under control. That's when I realized how stupid I'd been in not getting help… and that's when Gwen showed up on my doorstep. Right off, she convinced me that it was necessary to get Ruby into a place where they could offer her around the clock care… see to her needs and her medications… stuff like that. I don't know how she knew what I was going through. She just said 'a little birdie' told her. I'd always thought that was you, except… you never came back."

"I'm sorry, Roy. So sorry that I was such a coward for…"

"Shush! Like I said… you had your time, now it's my turn. Besides… what you did in leaving Lubbock… that was brave. Incredibly foolish and downright crazy… but real brave. You know… the thing that nearly sent me insane was learning that Gwen had no idea where you were. I was sure she would know… regardless of what your note said. That's when I went out of my mind with fear. But she just kept telling me that you were a Forde and that I shouldn't worry. You'd know how to take care of yourself. That really didn't help. Still… I'd have given up all hope without her. She… ahh… also told me what a complete jackass I'd been for moving in with my parents after we eloped. '*A woman needs a place of her own.*' I can still hear her scolding me on the front porch."

"Yeah… she was good at that. But… I'm thankful, Roy… very thankful that you two had each other. I only wish I'd…"

"Seriously! Will you stop it! I'm not saying that everything's worked out for the better, but you're leaving was the thing that woke me up… got me off my ass. It's what's responsible for me deciding to fix the house up… for you. Gwen helped out a bit… getting me to visualize the space differently… but it was mostly just me thinking about you. About the things you liked and didn't like."

While talking, he casually reached a hand up to shift a strand of her hair behind an ear. What he had to say mattered, but that simple gesture of intimacy communicated so much more than his words. He could not possibly know it, but he had just set her heart racing off in a completely different direction.

"Those first few months of you being gone were miserable. I've never cried like that before. I was so lonely without you… but also so angry and… full of shame. It seemed like everyone in town knew about you leaving. I couldn't go anywhere without someone asking me about you. That's when I closed myself off in my private misery… hoping somehow to survive. I went to the store earlier than was needed each morning, and buried myself in the emptiness of selling people stuff they may or may not need. Then I'd come home to an empty house. The only purpose I had in life was checking the mailbox. Every day that divorce papers didn't come was another opportunity to do something of value… you know… working on the house. I went to bed exhausted nearly every night. Tell you what, it was the only way I could sleep without thinking about you. I'll say this – ripping up wallboard was damn… ahh… what's that word… you know… when you do things to relieve stress?"

"Cathartic?"

"That's the one. It was damn cathartic to be swinging a sledge hammer into a wall, or ripping up something with a crowbar. You know… I actually enjoyed getting rid of my parents' stuff. Made me feel… good on the inside. Like whether or not you ever came back, I was at least making a step forward in life. I just kept telling myself not to give up hope."

To her absolute delight, he placed both hands upon her cheeks, gently cupping her chin within his palms. The feel of his touch was so tender, enhancing a tingle that had already taken over all of her.

"Do you remember the first time I ever saw you?"

"It was in the flower shop?"

"Yeah. Know what I was thinking?"

"You were just a boy…"

"I'm still just a boy at heart. That doesn't matter. I was thinking…"

"I know – that I was the girl for you."

"No. Not even close. I thought… I wanted to be the boy for you. I was so in awe of you, Marna… from the very moment I laid eyes on you. I've been striving for that ever since… to be the man you'd want."

"You are, Roy! Really! You are!"

He shook his head sadly, yet still holding her cheeks.

"No. I've never stopped being enamored with you long enough to truly win you over to me. I mean *really* win over all of you. All of your hopes and dreams… and make those things a part of me too. All I ever thought about was how lucky I was to be with you. I'll never make that mistake again. I'll never take for granted what it means to win you over. You'll see! Every day, I'll win your heart to me… I promise! I'll start by…"

"Roy?"

"Yes?"

"Can we please go inside now? I mean – *right now*!"

She had patiently remained on her knees before him, but could wait no longer. Grabbing his hands in hers, she sprang up and tugged him from off the chair. And just so he fully understood her intentions, she threw herself upon him, jumping up and wrapping her legs around his waist such that he was pitched back against the hangar. She was totally crazy for him… and did her best to show it by sucking his face off with her lips. In a matter of seconds, they were dashing around the hangar, hand in hand, making for the front porch as fast as they could run. There, they paused to catch their breath, but did so much more laughing and kissing that it took several minutes before she could master herself enough to speak.

"I want you to go inside… and take a shower."

"I don't need a shower."

"Just do it! Exactly like the other day… and I'll be waiting for you when you get out. And Roy… make it a quick shower!"

He tried to start up with the kissing again, but she swatted his rear into the house. She made for her suitcase in the back seat of the car. Out of her mind with excitement, she started hurling the contents all about the interior until she found exactly what she was looking for. Bounding onto the porch, through the front door, and up the stairs, she picked up on the sound of running water as she flung herself into Roy's bedroom… soon to be *their* bedroom together. Tossing off her clothes, she dressed in the same peach-colored undergarments she had worn before… with just enough time to relax into a pose on the end of the bed. This time when he stepped out in a towel and called her name, he was already on the way down the hall toward her. Feet away from lunging upon her, she thrust out a fist to indicate that he should first take what was within. He dropped to a knee with understanding as she released her rings into his palm. Then, as if a veil had been lifted from off her eyes, she came to realize that his wedding band was still on his ring finger. Likely always had been.

"Remember when I proposed to you? I said…"

"Let me, Roy! Let me be the one to say it to you!"

His lips quivered, but he nodded his agreement.

"Roy Meitner, love of my life, I make three promises to you, never to be broken. I promise to never leave you – ever! I promise to always be faithful. And I promise to forever be in love with you."

Then, with some small difficulty owing to the fact that they were both trembling, he slid the rings back onto her finger. From there, she had no mind for thinking – only feeling. He stripped her bare and was all over her, and neither of them held back in being instantly overwhelmed with making a love that was both pure and powerful. To her delight, he just lay there on top of her afterward, neither of them moving other than to kiss over and over. That eventually evolved into a whole lot of playful poking and tickling, as each vied to be the most adamant one in expressing how much they had missed the other. Soon, they were just expressing their love for each other, her nestled up against his chest… and then with the two of them on their sides facing each other across a shared pillow. After not too long, she pulled him on top of her again. They went at it slower this time, and more patiently in pacing themselves through the afternoon heat. Once again, they lay unashamedly bare before each other, neither feeling in the least degree embarrassed at how the other's eyes scanned the full length of them together.

Wrapped in sheet and towel, they left the bed at dinnertime to briefly raid the refrigerator of whatever easy-to-eat things might be had, and to make private side trips to the hallway bathroom. But in short course, they were back at each other again as the setting sun cast its waning rays from the new family room windows through their open door and across the foot of their bed. As dusk took hold, they laid together with the sheet pulled up to their chins, whispering simply because it felt most intimate.

For what reason she could not say, but with the light now faded, she inexplicably burst out crying at a sudden awareness of how much pain he had endured due to her absence. As he held her close, a question came to her that she had not intended, and definitely did not mean as a test. She simply wanted to know how he had made it on his own without her.

"Roy… were there ever any… others?"

"You mean other women? No. I mean… sure… there were a few in town who showed interest in me… and I occasionally toyed with the idea… but only as a distraction from thinking about you! I was never really tempted to do anything. I thought only of you. Besides… Gwen would have killed me if I'd taken up with another woman."

He shuddered, which she naturally assumed was from the prospect of facing Gwen's fury.

"It doesn't mean I didn't… you know… struggle with urges."

"Urges? You mean masturbation?"

"Damn, Marna! Still as blunt as ever! You know, there're some things just not meant to be said by a guy… even to his wife."

"I don't think so. You can tell me anything."

"Well… yeah… sure… but let me do it in my own way. So… to answer your indelicate question – 'yes.' I was alone… and I was heartbroken… and I was depressed. So… I struggled."

She tugged at him, intending to roll him from off his back and onto his side facing her.

"Cut it out. I'm not proud of myself."

It was important he understand that such a thing… or anything… could never be allowed to come between them. Throwing her left leg over his thighs, she hooked her heel behind his knee and yanked at him with many outlandish grunts, while also pulling at his opposite shoulder. Perhaps only because he allowed it, she was eventually able to shift him over onto his side. She spoke only after getting him settled in facing her.

"I like your urges. They go so very well with mine."

She knew, by the way he smiled, that she had won him over.

"Yes… I noticed."

"So… let's not be ashamed to tell each other… difficult things. I certainly have my own share. I'll be needing your help to become a better person."

They lay in silence for a long while before he spoke.

"You… umm… do realize that renovating this house wasn't done just to deal with… sexual tension."

"I know."

"I did it as an expression of… my hopefulness… and to remove the memories of our terrible fights together. Marna… our old bedroom is completely gone. That's how I want all those terrible things said between us to be."

To her surprise, he suddenly moved nose tip to nose tip with her.

"Hey! You wanna see something really cool? You're gonna love this. It's not quite finished yet… but close enough for a christening. Up for a shower?"

Without waiting for her to understand what he was talking about, he had her by the hand and was dragging her off the bed to stand before one of the sheets of plastic that covered a gap in the bedroom wall.

"Oops… almost forgot. Wait here."

He was back quickly with two towels.

"Now close your eyes. I need to get a light on and clear a path."

She did as instructed, and then felt him leading her by the wrist around the plastic. She was greeted by the smell of plaster and cut ceramic, as well as the feel of an unfinished surface beneath her feet. He took a second to position her in the way he wanted before telling her to open her eyes.

"Ta-da! Just for you! Because I know how much you hate taking a shower while standing in a bathtub."

She instantly understood why the master bedroom wall had been moved. She was standing in a bathroom that was deeper than in her memory. While much of it still seemed unfinished, before her was a large walk-in shower.

"Wow! It's amazing!"

"The tile and fixtures are in… but I haven't gotten around to grouting it yet. I think it'll be fine for an inaugural shower. After you…"

He swung open the glass door and reached in to turn on the valve. She shivered at the first draft of air laden with mist, pausing only long enough to ensure that the water was hot before stepping into a slate gray wonderland. All about her running up three walls was tiling in a toggled pattern, interrupted only by an inlaid shelf that ran the width of the shower. Within were soap trays and ample space for whatever bathing products a woman might need. To her right was a marble-topped bench, perfect for relaxing in the shower's stream. Roy stepped in behind her, and with the door now closed off, the space became wonderfully warm and steamy. He held her near and did a little half turn so that the water fell upon her back and shoulders.

"Well… what do you think?"

"I love it! I could spend all day in here."

"Look up."

He shuffled her out of the spray so she could tilt her head back without getting splashed. Between canned lights was a wide-open skylight revealing the night beyond.

"I'm probably going to regret this… seeing as those things are such a bear to keep clean… but I figured you'd enjoy a view of the sky while showering. At least I can reach the outside from the balcony."

"Roy… this is absolutely perfect!"

She had never felt more loved in all her life. This was a place for her to wash away all the cares with which the world might soil her. Of course, what with the hot stream and their naked bodies, it was not too long before he began exploring her again. She let him fool around as he wished… a bit clumsily at first. The actual experience, their first in that shower, probably meant much more to him. Yet for her, it was just being near to him in the wet and knowing that he was enjoying her. That was pleasure itself.

With their shower completed and both of them wrapped in towels, he kept her there for one more surprise. Pointing to a pocket door she had not yet noticed, he slid it open to reveal a walk-in closet that obviously connected to the bedroom through where the other sheet of plastic was. Though not yet finished, he had managed to install shelves, rods and even a fold down ironing board.

"What do you think?"

"It's huge! This is amazing! I can't wait to get my things in here. But Roy… where're you planning on keeping *your* things?"

"Very funny. I'll have you know that I had to move waterlines and knock out the hallway linen closet just to create enough space. You'd think that'd merit me some consideration."

Speaking most matter-of-factly, she replied with her best look of uncertainty.

"I don't know… perhaps… I could spare half a rod. You do realize that a woman of fashion needs plenty of space."

She kissed him on the cheek and turned away, all in that hit-and-run sort of way meant to leave him wondering whether she was being serious.

I've so missed messing with him.

He chose a night shirt for her from his own things. Clothed for the first time in hours, they stripped and remade the bed together. Then, with crackers, cheese and glasses of ice tea, they sat out on the balcony huddled together under a blanket watching a nearly full moon rise in the night sky. She had really not thought much about it until they reentered the room together, but it occurred to her then that she would be sharing a bed with this wonderful man for the rest of her life. She would be sharing her entire life with him. The thought brought her much more warmth than the shower had. She was ready. More than ready. And to prove that to herself, she used his toothbrush as her own.

She curled up beside him again, this time to sleep. All night, she felt the cool West Texas air flow through their bedroom's open windows. She woke several times due to an unfamiliarity with the bed and pillow. Sometimes she lay listening to the house settle after a hot day, or watch him softly breathing in his sleep. So many bizarre things had happened to her over the last ten days… some tragic, some odd and some wonderful. Collectively, they had brought her back to him. From that first moment of hearing his voice in the WYNG newsroom, she had…

She sprang upright in the bed from a perplexity she had not considered before now. Try as she might, there was no accounting for this puzzle. She must wake him right away to solve it. Even though she had not slept with him in over two years, she started shaking him like it was something quite normal for a newly-returned wife to do.

"Roy! Wake up! Wake up!"

"Whurtt…"

This would not do. She needed him to be fully awake. Since the bedroom as yet did not have end tables with lamps, she found his shoulder in the dark and sank her nails in far enough for her insistence to be clearly registered.

"Ouch! That hurts!"

"WAKE UP!"

"Marna, what the…?! Not again, please… I'm way too worn out for more…"

"Never mind that! Are you listening to me?! Are you awake?!"

"Yes… what's the matter?"

She paused just to make sure he was totally alert, and then framed her question.

"Something just occurred to me. How'd you know that you could reach me at WYNG… you know… when you called about the tornado? No one in Lubbock knew where I was working. Not even Gwen. Nobody, Roy! I was very careful about that. But you knew. How?"

Even in the darkness, she could tell that he had closed his eyes. Two small sparkles of some reflected light disappeared from off his face. For a moment, she thought that he had gone back to sleep, but then he opened his eyes again and sat up against the headboard.

"I was hoping you wouldn't ask about that…"

"Whatever for?"

"Because I figured it out from the phone bill."

"What phone bill?"

"Remember the day you had me take Mom out for that doctor appointment? It was in the week you… took off. You made some long distance calls from the store. Sometime after… I don't know when, maybe a couple of months later… I was looking over the monthly bill… you know… just the usual… making sure everything was in order. That's when I came across this string of strange numbers. They were all close together in time, but one was much too long for one of my typical calls. So I gave the area code to directory assistance… and the operator told me they were all from the Chicago area. I call the first on the list. It was for WYNG news. Oh… by the way, thanks a lot! Those calls cost the store something like forty bucks!"

She could not believe what she was hearing, and in her shock, she searched out his hand to hold.

"It's no biggie, Marna… I was only kidding."

"Are you saying you knew all along that I was in Chicago at WYNG?"

He inhaled rather deeply and then let out a slow stream of air.

"Yes… I knew. When I called that number, some woman… I forget her name."

"Rose?"

"That's her. I immediately thought of *The Yellow Rose of Texas*. Anyway… I asked her if there was anyone working there by the name of Marna Meitner… and she said there wasn't. I was just about to hang up when the woman came back to say that there was a Marna Forde. That's when I knew you wanted to be left alone. So I made up a story about you being older… like Gwen's age… just to throw her off. I never called back again… until that night. Like I said, I knew you wanted to be alone. So… I left you alone."

He stopped there, but she wished him to go on. He could say anything that he wanted to. That he did some private research into WYNG… or that he sometimes looked at a map and thought of her… or that he had been tempted to take a vacation to Chicago so he could accidently run into her. Anything at all other than leaving the story with her wanting to be left alone. But it was clear that he had nothing more to say. So she burst out crying all over again for the pain she had caused him. Balling up in his arms, she repeatedly begged him to forgive her. Over and over, he gave her many assurances… until she finally somehow fell asleep.

<u>Thursday, May 21st</u>

As the sun's glimmer appeared on the eastern horizon, slowly brightening their bedroom, she enthusiastically awoke to greet her first morning wholeheartedly as Marna Meitner. Never again would she be tempted by her old ways of thinking. She was Roy's wife, and proud to be so. She would walk a straight path forward in life with him, fully convinced that a new day had dawned for them both.

END OF WASP 4

WASP 5

GIANTS

CHAPTER
31

REMODELING

She was being such a nuisance, but did not care. So what if the gate agent had to shoo her out the door?! And so what if she was the last one to leave?! She wanted to be with him for as long as she could. Practically walking backward the whole way across the tarmac, she was absolutely determined to keep her eyes on where he stood in the observation deck. At the top of the stairs, she gave Roy one last wave goodbye before boarding the plane, and then hurried down the aisle to find her assigned seat.

Just great! I'm on the wrong side!

She still did her best to bob about for a view of him through the opposite windows… even though she was making a spectacle of herself in the process. Unfortunately, she was not able to catch another glimpse of him before needing to fasten her seatbelt. She finally gave up trying as the plane taxied out to the runway. With the takeoff, she thought back over the previous week of being reunited with him.

I'm so happy! Truly happy!

Then why am I risking it all by going back to Chicago?!

She had been over and over her concerns with Roy, reluctantly agreeing with him in the end that serving out her two weeks notice was the right thing to do… even if it did not feel right. Her previous life in Chicago was no longer important… and she wanted no part of being exposed to it again. Having to be separated from him was such a terrible price to pay for being responsible.

Crossing her arms in frustration, she looked out her window as West Texas flowed by beneath the plane. Okay… she had to go back. She already told Billings and Mr. Carswell that she would. Those calls had been more difficult than she had expected. Both men were surprised in their own way. Billings was clearly disappointed in her as he snarled out a 'you gotta do what you gotta do,' but Mr. Carswell, being more statesman-like, expressed his concern over whether she had fully thought through her decision. She certainly had… and would make both men understand once she got back there.

She spent the entire leg from Lubbock to Dallas rehashing her feelings, putting those on hold only during a short layover that had her fighting through an airport crowd to her next gate. Back into a window seat for the flight to Chicago, she started in where she had left off.

Okay… I get it! Giving two weeks notice means that you actually have to show up for those two weeks.

She knew that WYNG was still terribly understaffed, and the other AEs were doing double duty in her absence. In the end, that was a problem beyond her. More importantly, she needed to say goodbye to the people who had made such a difference in her life. Then there was her apartment. She needed to ship her things back to Lubbock and find someone to take over the lease.

So what's really bugging you?!

She was in love, and wanted nothing other than to be with the one she loved. The best of both worlds would have been if he could have come with her… though that was absolutely impossible. He had his mother and his store to take care of… the very things that had once propelled her into making the worst decision of her life. In fact, she really admired him all the more because of his faithfulness to those responsibilities. Of course, that did not keep her from imagining the pleasure of having him all to herself for two weeks in Chicago. There was such a long list of wonders in the city that she could show him during the day, and then have their nights together nestled in her Oak Park apartment. But the fantasy always seemed to fade away with the thought of showing him off at WYNG. Even though he knew everything scandalous that had happened to her, she could not bear exposing him to the shame of what those people knew about her. Her second chance with Roy was too precious. Everything she had once pursued in life had been turned on its head and shaken down into something so simple.

Home.

It was not just returning to Lubbock… or taking up residence in a house that she now felt very comfortable living in… or being with the man she loved dearly. Something else had been added in that she could not quite put a finger on. Something that had finally settled into its proper place in her thinking. Somehow, she knew that she had finally set herself on the path toward becoming the person she was meant to be.

She did not bother trying to explain any of this to Roy. She just let her own happiness speak to him. Still… she was a bit surprised that he was not more concerned about her going back to Chicago. Surely he was aware of the mess that she had made of herself there. She had told him enough times! Ambition… significance… achievement… she was absolutely certain that those things lay dormant within her, waiting for the first sign of her renewed love to falter. But Roy… he just kept dismissing her worries with a sweet little 'I trust you.' She was touched… but he really should know better!

I certainly don't trust me!

She felt the airliner accelerate down the runway for its takeoff from Dallas. The sensation of being forced back into her seat oddly accentuated her chief fear – a tendency she had recklessly demonstrated over and over during the past four years. Whether Forde or Meitner, she was always on the verge of making another terribly thought-through decision in life. Her vulnerability in fully acknowledging this to Roy was admirable… but that changed nothing. Neither could her love for him be relied upon. What if she got back to Chicago and discovered that she actually missed the city? What if seeing the Berts again rekindled the old fire? What if the joys of preparing the news and doing something significant pushed the love of him right out of her heart? Such a thing might be inconceivable at the moment, but in the blink of an eye she could flip. It happened before!

No! I refuse to believe that! My going back to Chicago is actually taking a step forward with him.

Roy had her heart, and with Roy it would stay. None of those old tendencies would reappear – she was sure of it. More likely, she would embarrass herself explaining to the Berts how it was that she had chosen to radically change the direction of her life. No one at WYNG could possibly comprehend what she had experienced during the last two weeks. No one could understand her desire for being with Roy over all other things in life. Over the news and over having a career of her own. Likely, they would think that she had been messed up in her head all along. She was just as they pegged her to be – a confused girl not yet ready to be a professional woman. Worse, they would think she was going from one man to another in her insecurities. From her husband to

Grass to Azurean and then back to her husband. Well… she would get right up into their faces to show them that Roy was nothing like those other two. She was confident that she had chosen something far better for herself. The Berts would surely understand this. Of everyone at WYNG, they knew her the best, and cared for her the most. They would not think the worst of her for pursuing her happiness over the news.

The little chime sounded to inform everyone that the airliner had reached its cruising altitude. It was now safe to move about the cabin. But she stayed put. Once more, she had reached that point in the progression of her thoughts for which there was no answer.

I'm letting them down… again. They'll show their excitement… that's the kind of men that they are… but they'll be hiding their disappointment in me.

Try as she might, it was impossible to brush aside her feeling of guilt. The station and the news – those things were their lives… and she was turning her back on them. To make matters worse, the station was still struggling and would likely continue to do so for some time before it could climb out of the pit that lunatic Azurean had dug for them. In spite of all her faults and the part she had unwittingly played in bringing WYNG down, they still needed her. And here she was betraying them to pursue a love so dear.

Isn't that a contradiction? If I love someone, shouldn't the proof of that love be my willingness to sacrifice it? Wasn't that love itself?

No… that's stupid. Besides, it's simply not possible for everything to always work out for everyone. If that were the case, then Gwen would still be alive… and so would George… and so would my parents.

She could not have both Chicago and Lubbock, even though those places might lay claim on her. But she did have the right to choose what was best for her. With a quick look at a cloudless sky out her window, she put aside the past four years in once again embracing her heart's choice. Smiling to herself, she pressed the little button on her armrest and leaned back in her seat. Closing her eyes, she slept peacefully for the remainder of the flight into Chicago, irrespective of whatever turbulence might be going on with the plane.

Arriving at O'Hare late in the evening, she waited for what seemed like forever for her bag to come off the conveyor belt, and then rode the subway through a couple of exchanges to the Oak Park platform. She had obviously done this many times before, but now felt as if she were visiting a foreign land. Worse… even though she had daily tread the same route from the platform to her apartment, it had not occurred to her until now that she would be lugging her suitcase for blocks. Nearly exhausted from the walk and then having to haul her case up two flights of stairs, she changed into pajamas and collapsed on her bed's month old linens.

Come morning, the order of business she had prepared in her mind for the first day of her last two weeks at WYNG was rather simple.

Touch base with Billings.

That was about as far as she could get in her thinking. What she said to everyone else, and how she went about the many details of ending a job and clearing out an apartment, would all come once she had gotten past the man.

She arrived to the station early and strode through the newsroom, making directly for Billings. But before she could get to within a comfortable distance for speaking, his voice bellowed out at her with his usual brashness… and a twist.

"Meitner, get the hell over here! About damn time you showed up. Get with Jenkins on the latest bank heist. He'll brief you. Third one since you've been gone. Come time for the morning meeting, I expect to know everything the cops know and more, got it?!"

"Yes, sir. On it!"

He smiled, tipping his head in the process, and then went back to the printout he had been reading.

She worked the entire day just as on so many others, except this one with rings on her finger, a different last name, and a changed attitude in her heart. Maybe others sensed these things, though she could not be sure as the demands of the news day gave little time for anything other than chit-chat about her situation. She was offered many genuine expressions of sympathy for the loss of her aunt, as well as concern for her hometown. A few greeted warmly the news of her being reunited with an estranged husband, though most offered their congratulations without any interest in the details. That was fine with her. These were all busy people with lives of their own. Only Mr. Carswell took time out of his day to hear her story over lunch.

Unlike her previous practice at WYNG news, she did not remain to watch the completed show. As soon as her responsibilities were over, she made a beeline for the subway, for the thing she had looked forward to all day was getting back to her apartment so she could call Roy.

With her last day at WYNG completed, Rose arranged for a goodbye cake, a card and a gift – a t-shirt with the words '*Chicago's WYNGin' it*' printed across the front. Many funny stories about her were exchanged over the cake, as well as many sincere wishes for her future happiness. She accepted them all with a gratitude tinged by sadness. She was leaving a place that had taken in an inexperienced and naïve young woman doing her best to hide her insecurities, and turned out a professional capable of facing life wherever she might belong. She would forever be thankful for her years at WYNG.

As the gathering broke up, Billings uncharacteristically put an arm about her shoulders and leaned in to whisper.

"Before you leave, Bertram and I have something for you in my office. Can you spare a minute?"

She followed the two men down the familiar hallway off the newsroom to the office where she had been lectured, chewed out, cursed, congratulated, and even consoled. Without a word, Billings pulled out a bottle and three glasses from a bottom drawer. After pouring out a bit of liquor in each, he held up his glass.

"To the best damn PA this newsroom has ever seen."

Before either man could clink their glasses against hers, she added what was most on her heart.

"And to two dear gentlemen who helped this girl grow up into a newswoman!"

'Damn straight' and 'hear, hear' led into each person taking a sip. She allowed hers to burn into her heart the debt of gratitude she had for these two men. Billings then pulled another item from his drawer – a video cartridge with 'Forde' written across it.

"I know it's not your name anymore, but I'll always remember you that way. Here, Marna, we want you to have this. It's the clip of your story from the steps of City Hall during those riots two years back. We want you to watch this whenever you're afraid about something… about your future or about missing this place. Watch it and remember just how tough you are… that even a crazed Chicago mob couldn't hold you back. Watch it… and think of us."

She was overwhelmed, both by his words and by the fact that the handwriting on the cartridge was his. From it, she knew for certain that he had dug the footage out of the archive himself and performed the transfer… just for her. Without thinking, she threw an arm about each man and drew them in close, shutting her eyes off against the tears welling up within. Only Mr. Carswell's mumbled voice made her release them.

"Umm… to tell you the truth, Marna… I don't feel all that comfortable being held this close to Albert."

She allowed them both to chuckle themselves into silence before saying her most heartfelt goodbye.

"I have such wonderful memories of you two together 'discussing' the news. Thanks, to both of you. Thanks for all you've done for me. You know… I'm not even twenty five yet… much too young to think that I can know anything for certain in life. But I do know this one thing. The greatest journey a person can embark upon is to find the place where they belong. For two years, this is where I belonged." She turned to Mr. Carswell first. "Sir... I think it's fair to say that everyone at WYNG knows you belong in that suit leading the station with patience and confidence. And you, Mr. Billings, your suit is to be encircled about by the assignment desk with a team striving with all their might to love the news if even half as much as you do. I've learned so much from you two. I wish I could stay... truly, I do... but I don't belong here anymore. Maybe I've known it all along. The wonder of this place just drew me in... and gave me a temporary home... until I could grow up. And now, my real home is calling me back. I have to go, sirs. I have to go back."

They stood in silence for a long time before Mr. Carswell extended a hand to her. She took it... and was immediately surprised to find him gently enclosing hers in both of his.

"Goodbye, Marna. I sincerely hope that the Miss Forde we've come to love never goes away... but even more so that she finds her place within the Mrs. Meitner you long to be."

Billings was unable to speak, hugging her for much longer than expected before turning his teary eyes toward the newsroom.

"He's going to miss you terribly. You were almost like a daughter to him."

"I know..."

The anticipation of being back with Roy occupied her thoughts as she bustled about her apartment in preparation for leaving. She got the place cleaned up and handed the key back to her landlord, thanking him for two wonderful years of living there. Catching a cab to the airport, she checked in and then waited at her gate. Eventually, she boarded the return flight home. Only after getting herself comfortably seated did she realize that she could be frank with herself about the last two years of her life. Professionally speaking, she had been all about a day's news and *the* news. One intertwined stories in a way that was memorable for a day, whereas the other was a noble calling that gave her voice an opportunity of being heard. All of that changed after Gwen's death. Most everyone at WYNG had already forgotten about a tornado that tore through a West Texas town, but she could not. That day's news altered her life forever.

To her, the daily news was now as perishable as a flower... with the telling of it being no different than floral design. Sitting before a video editing machine or standing at a cutting table... both were labor spent on something that was not meant to last beyond the viewing. Arranging a script or arranging a bouquet… it was all the same. She might be good at one and pitiful at the other, but neither would ever be part of her life again.

As her plane taxied out onto an O'Hare runway, she decided that the real 'her' lay out there somewhere waiting to be discovered. Her ambition was still strong, as was her drive for significance, but she would no longer allow either to sit in the pilot's seat of her life. In running off to Chicago in the first place, she had allowed the wrong things to chart a course for her. Now, those things were just pieces of luggage on a journey with her. To where, she did not yet know… only that it would be her and Roy travelling together.

Back from Chicago, she reentered life as Roy's wife with a single word as a theme on her mind – remodeling. Those two weeks away from him were just a segue between an old life and a new one. Yet for her, focusing only on the present was true work, as her mindset had always been about the future. So she began remodeling her life in parallel with two other on-going restoration efforts. The city of Lubbock was already well into its recovery. Many business owners, including Roy, had banded together with city and county governments to promote the restoration of the downtown, for it had been the hardest hit. She was stunned to learn that the estimated storm debris requiring disposal essentially amounted to a seventeen story building if everything got piled within the dimensions of a standard football field, end zones included. Neighborhoods had to be rebuilt, and funds had to be raised for the construction of a new civic center, a downtown public library, and many other municipal projects.

Similarly, their own house was in the middle of a significant makeover. In returning from Chicago, she purposed not to seek any kind of employment, but to instead stay home and focus on remodeling. With a can-do attitude, she took over spackle and paint from Roy. What a great opportunity to reconnect with this house and with her husband! From him, she learned the ways of the hammer, saw, trowel, putty knife, tape measure, and brush. Starting first where the need was greatest, she concentrated on the master bath and kitchen. Day by day, she occupied herself with the tasks that Roy set out for her. He had started the process in hope, and she picked it up in love. Together, they would transform the Meitner home into a place that they could call their own.

What she had once seen through the eyes of a distracted mind, she now re-examined from the perspective of a loving wife. In every part of the house, she purposed that light should flood in… from new fixtures, from the outside, and from the sincerity of an open heart. Texas itself was a wide-open world of their own making, so she invited it into every room by the means of as much glass as Roy was willing to install. From the walls, she scraped away the reminders of her past anger and resentment, spreading out instead delicately plastered textures begging to be caressed. These, she decorated in the softest of shades – creams, sages, and sky blues. She removed old doors and opened spaces one into another. She chose ceramics with as much texture as that of the rock-veined colors of the family room, and all of her linoleums just had to have wispy patterns that mirrored the sky. Every floor would be made to be felt by feet and toes in ways that had hands and fingers jealous to be down there too.

Outside, she removed the railing between the pillars all around the porch, then cut back every shrub and bush. She removed anything that might get in the way of having the wide-open feel of Texas extend right up to her feet. She considered the wrap-around to be the gateway into her house, so she had Roy open up the eastern wall of the parlor and put in glass doors. Now, the joy of the morning flowed naturally into both the upstairs and the downstairs. Just as importantly, she decorated the southern-facing side so as to welcome the visitor right off the circle and up to their front door with the brightness of the noon-day sun. She put in flower beds, hung wind chimes and streamers, and painted the rocking chairs in brightest of whites. Then, since the sun set low and hot in the western sky, she put up retractable shades under the eaves to protect her kitchen and family room from the worst of a West Texas summer. Lastly, out toward the silent north's barren fields of their quarter mile track, she and Roy would huddle in close together in new lawn furniture, greeting the starlight of a night's delicious call to sleep. Every trip around her porch was like a new day, and in each, she was thankful for a fresh start. All would be made new.

One nail at a time.

While laboring each day with her hands, she also exerted great effort toward remodeling her thinking. She put her head down and got to work on her attitudes, deriving daily inspiration from Lubbock being her town and the Meitner house being her house. Vividly aware of the ways she had messed up in the past, she went about peeling back the surface on those mindsets. As in any do-it-yourself project, she found that addressing one faulty perspective often uncovered others that she had known nothing about.

The first wall in her mind got knocked down while she was still in Chicago. Knee-deep in boxes while packing up her apartment on a Sunday, she received an unexpected phone call from Roy... and his first words stunned her.

"Happy fourth anniversary, Darling!"

"Same to you too! But to tell you the truth, Roy… I'd completely forgotten. It's today, isn't it?"

The laughter coming back over the line made her smile, yet it did not really make her feel any better.

"Marna, don't sweat it. We've been living apart for so long. It's only natural that…"

"But you remembered! You've probably been thinking about it for… I don't know… ever since I left for my two weeks notice."

"Well… yeah… but you're busy with…"

"So I should have too."

They went on talking about how they would celebrate once she returned, but in the back of her mind, she kept on reprimanding herself. Just because Gwen raised her with an indifference toward the commemoration of dates was hardly an excuse for her, as a wife, to do likewise. So she swore then and there never again to forget another May thirty first… or his birthday… or any holiday opportunity for them to spend special time together. Each event would become a celebration of them, for her life was no longer about herself. Of course, she knew that changing her pronoun way of thinking required more than carefully selected words. No more separate bank accounts, no more private plans, and no more 'ifs' to fall back on when things did not go her way. She was absolutely determined to never again allow any version of herself to eclipse them as a couple.

This resolution got tested right away on returning from Chicago in the form of the relief. She wanted it hung in the family room where she could see it every day, whereas he wanted it in a formal place – the dining room. Previously, she had held tightly to this relief as hers, but now she yielded the choice of its location to him. Once they got it mounted on a dining room wall, they stood close in together as she explained to him all that its artistry meant to her. Her aspirations to break away, like the birds, she gave over to him, just as she had fully given over her heart… for they were one in the same. From now on, the relief was theirs… which to her meant that they would be holding each other's dreams together.

Wearing again a medical alert bracelet became very different from in her youth. When Roy presented her with a replacement, she received it as a precious gift from him… one that she could actually be giving right back in the form of his peace of mind. Getting used to wearing the thing again was not without its annoyances, but she reframed those into a reminder. In going without one for so long, she had actually wasted all the previous years of getting used to its presence. She would waste no more years. Interestingly, she found that the bracelet had another benefit, as Roy enjoyed playing with it whenever they were close. She would allow him to get distracted in spinning it about on her wrist, sliding it along her arm, or sticking a finger under it… and then tease him.

"Roy… you're doing it again. Maybe I should get you some jewelry of your own. How about a nice set of ear rings? I have several that you could choose from…"

In a totally different area, she had to put considerable thought into checking whether she was being true to her husband. Not in terms of fidelity. That issue was firmly resolved in her heart. He was the only man for her. She worried more about the intangibles… moving at his pace rather than hers, not overwhelming him with her intensity, and caring about the things he cared about. His opinion mattered to her. Now back in Texas, she embraced being Texan in her heart like she had never done before. That same kind of pride went into how she carried the Meitner name. Never would she do anything to embarrass him. He was her husband, so she began a habit of calling him that as a way of reminding herself. She wanted him to have confidence in her as his wife… especially given all of the terrible ways she had done her best to undermine that role in the past. She was adamant about date nights, holding hands in public, and showing lots of affection. Each night, she made him play spoons with her, no matter how tired he was. This, she did mostly because she enjoyed being cradled by him, but also because she knew how important it was given their past that they end the day close to each other. She showed no subtlety in this nightly practice, pushing him to the brink of falling out of bed until he agreed to turn her way.

"Submit, Husband, and you won't get hurt!"

Her most unexpected remodeling project came from her visits to Ruby. Sad to say, she found the nursing home to be creepy… sort of like a mortuary for living people. The place was just so gloomy, what with all those elderly imprisoned by their failing bodies. To be confronted with the hopelessness of old age tarnished the joy she had in being back with Roy. But she pushed passed those feelings by watching closely how he interacted with his mother. He was always cheerful and kind. So she endeavored to mimic him, reminding herself not to express any impatience for leaving.

Stay as long as he wants to. Stay even longer. Stay as if there was no other place on earth but here.

It was still difficult on her. Too often, she came away from a visit confronted with the harsh reality that she had not achieved anything of significance. She would sit at Ruby's side without receiving back any acknowledgement of her presence – no nod of the head, no flash of recognition in the eyes, and not a single word spoken. Ruby just sat there as a small speck of humanity, so far from the person she had once been. In finally departing the place with Roy, she would only silently acknowledge having accomplished a task. But on those occasions when she visited Ruby alone, the first thing she did on leaving was crank up the car radio as loud as she could stand it, just to get herself some intense contrast from the place.

When it happened, she could not really say, only that somewhere in her second month back, she caught herself actually wanting to go see Ruby. The unpleasant things about being there – how bad it smelled, how bleak the setting was, and how every face she beheld reminded her of death – those things had not changed. She simply got better at looking past them. She might confess that being there was her duty, and that it took a burden off of her husband so he could manage his store, but that was not the real reason she wanted to see Ruby. Somehow, she had come to love the woman and remember fondly the person she once was. She was glad to spend the twenty minutes it took to get there, and the twenty minutes back, simply for the opportunity to sit just as long holding Ruby's hand. In this small way, she honored the dear woman who had given her a husband and accepted her as a daughter.

Then there was the issue of Gwen. No matter how she busied herself in her renewed life, her aunt still remained on the threshold of her thoughts, and always with an unresolved guilt over having not been the niece she should have been. Her missed opportunities with Gwen were just as evident to her as were her failings at being a supportive wife. Gwen was family. Imagining how terrified her aunt must have been in those moments leading up to her death… it was the worst sort of torment to bear. She could perhaps make amends to Ruby by holding her hand through the desolation of the woman's sickness, but no one had been there to hold Gwen's hand when a tornado tore off the roof of the flower shop and sucked her out into its torrential fury.

Her being there would not have saved Gwen's life. They both would have been killed. But at least her aunt would not have died alone. Instead, Gwen's death had given her a second chance at happiness. There was no way she could ever repay Gwen for that sacrifice.

While she was in Chicago, Roy had arranged for an estate sale of everything in Gwen's house, removing only the boxes from her old bedroom beforehand. She was thankful that he handled it all, for she had no heart to be there herself. He even put the house on the market, and it sold in under a week owing to the large number of homeless families in the city. With a lawyer's help, he also oversaw the city's annexation of the flower shop's lot. So about the only remaining task for her on returning from Chicago was to write letters to Gwen's floral acquaintances and WASP colleagues. In these, she thanked those who had offered condolences and informed others who might not have yet heard. Only with Frankie did she enter into a lasting correspondence, being eager to tell her about getting back with Roy and to hear of any wartime stories about Gwen. For now, she did not have the heart to ask about Bradrick Miller, and was not disappointed that Frankie never ventured in that direction.

She also had the matter of Gwen's safety deposit box to resolve, which was something that she wished to handle personally. Having arranged for the lawyer to obtain a court order permitting her to claim its contents, she came to Gwen's bank with key in hand, presented the necessary documentation to a manager, and was escorted into the vault for the metal box. The manager then led her into a small room where she could be alone with the box that she hoped was filled with answers to her many questions about Gwen. Inside was a folder containing the stock certificates that the lawyer expected to be there, but the only other items were a small photo album and a black felt bundle tied off with a ribbon.

With considerable anticipation, she went first to the album. Unfortunately, inside were only a couple dozen photographs, mostly of her aunt's days as a WASP. In these, Gwen was often in fatigues with a gaggle of other pilots all about her. In each, she soaked in Gwen's expressions of confidence and pleasure, trying to imagine why that particular photo had been deemed special. Then came several of Gwen in the arms of a young man, him sometimes in a uniform and sometimes in street clothes. From the flat backdrops, she guessed that several might have been taken somewhere in West Texas. Gwen's smile in these was unlike any with her comrades. More vibrant in hanging to the arm of her man. It was the same kind of smile as in Frankie's poster. So strong was its intensity that it actually embarrassed her… as if she had been caught prying into Gwen's happiness. She took her eyes off that smile to study the face of Bradrick Miller, for he held a strong family resemblance to Roy. Same sandy blond hair, same body frame, and same sweet smile. What had Gwen thought about those similarities? Had seeing Roy caused her pain? She was not sure how she felt about knowing the answers to these questions, seeing as Brad had died in the war… and she considered her Roy to be his own unique person. The final photo of Brad was in a portrait like that of Gwen's WASP poster. He was so handsome in his dress uniform and obviously proud about his own set of wings.

The very last photograph in the album was considerably older than the others based on the overall grainy quality of the print. It was of a foursome that she could confidently identify as being her grandparents, her own father as a toddler, and a grade-school-aged Gwen. Seeing these four faces only caused her sadness over how little she had experienced of their lives. She closed the photo album, set it atop the documents, and turned to the felt bundle.

Gradually pulling on both ends of the ribbon so that the knot's loops collapsed at the same time, she gave a final little tug at the end. The bundle unfurled flat upon the tabletop as a flower might in opening from its bud. Being layered toward the middle, she unfolded a section of the felt toward her and then another away to reveal an amazing array of sparkles. These were of many translucent glassy facets interspersed among creamy white stones hanging from what looked to be a single chain. With great care, she gently filtered her fingertips through to locate the ends, and then gradually extended out the intricate silver of a necklace. Carefully lifting it by the ends, she felt its significant weight, and all the more so slowly stretched out the chain. Suspended in space before her was crystal and pearl encrusted in many aligned pendants hanging from the chain, those nearest the ends being shorter than those in the center, with a triangular shape to the whole.

After a sheepish look at the curtained barrier of the room behind her, she lay the necklace back down on its felt, crossed her arms over to take hold of opposite ends, and then in a delicately fluid-like motion, lifted it while switching her hands to their proper sides. Carefully bringing the necklace to her chest, she allowed its tiered pendants to array themselves naturally from her collar bone downward before fastening the clasp behind her neck. The weight of it gave her such a feel of substance that she doubted seriously whether this necklace could be worn without a constant awareness of its elegance. So she closed her eyes for a moment and concentrated on that feel, imagining that she could somehow distinguish between the softly rounded touch of each pearl from those of the edgier crystals.

In a flash, she began rummaging about in her handbag for a compact. Finally locating and opening it, she began examining herself from every conceivable angle – with the small mirror set on the tabletop, held at arm's length, and then up real close.

I've never seen anything so beautiful in all my life!

Wearing this heirloom was not at all like the sacrilege it would have been to touch the engagement ring she had found within the strong box in Gwen's office. One was clearly private, fit for no other place than to rest forever beside its intended. But this necklace, it begged to be worn, if for no other reason than the observer's enjoyment at knowing that it had once belonged to Gwen Forde.

Besides, this was no ordinary piece of jewelry. It was meant for something special.

All of a sudden, there was no doubt about it in her mind. This necklace had been intended for Gwen's wedding day. She was overwhelmed with that realization. This beautiful work of art must be rescued from the sad waste it had become in sitting forsaken within this box. Something must be done to correct the injustice! Somehow, there must be a way for the niece of Gwendolyn Forde to adorn herself for the nephew of Bradrick Miller, and thus fulfill the purpose of this necklace.

With nothing of significance in mind, and a small measure of heartache from her own grief, she reluctantly removed the necklace, laid it carefully upon the felt, and wrapped it as before. Re-tying the scarlet thread with tenderness, she placed the bundle back into the safety deposit box, resolving to keep the account active in her own name.

CHAPTER

32

FAIRCHILD PT-26

Early on that summer, Roy had suggested that she consider passing her resumé about the Lubbock TV stations to see what interest she might generate. That, she could do, and likely find some form of newsroom employment given her experience and a favorable recommendation from WYNG. She told him instead that she was not yet ready to pursue work… and definitely not in the news business. Her old life was over, and something new lay ahead. For now, her heart took pleasure in laboring room-by-room in the steady transformation of their house into a home. As he was spending near-on sixty hours a week at the appliance store, the majority of the renovation work had fallen to her. That was both good, as it afforded her the solitude necessary for becoming reacquainted with the house… but also bad, in that having too much time on her hands with spackle and sandpaper left her mind free to wander into a future that she was not yet ready to face.

How long should she remain focused on remodeling? When should she explore some new line of work, or should she consider getting an education? Maybe her priorities should be turned toward starting a family? No… not that… at least not yet. Still… it came down in her mind to the issue of finding that ideal formula allowing a woman to have it all – be wife, professional… and one day, mother… all at the same time. Until she figured all that out, the person she was meant to be would just have to wait.

She told herself repeatedly during this summer of renovation not to needlessly generate anxiety about the future when she was already so obviously happy with the present. At least she had come to recognize her tendency for making herself unhappy simply because she had no idea of what to do with such happiness. Instead, she was determined that each new day should at least be used to reinforce in her heart a thankfulness for him. It was almost like being a newlywed all over again, though with a more mature mindset protecting them both.

Aside from the certainty of being done with the news, about the only thing she really felt strongly for was the hangar. That subject, unfortunately, amounted to their first quarrel as a newly reunited couple. Not one week into being back from Chicago, she took bolt cutters to the padlock on the man door. Standing just within, she felt the anticipated torrent of memories come rushing over her... most notably of George seeking asylum day after day within this place. She had returned to the hangar partly to re-experience those feelings. Gwen would always come alive for her when she stood before the relief, so she hoped that this place would do likewise for the memory of a dear father-in-law. The Corsair fulfilled that aim.

I can't believe George actually gave me this plane!

On seeing the it for the first time in over two years, the plane struck her just as the relief often did. Both seemed so oddly delicate, yet timelessly resilient. There it sat in the middle of the hangar just as it had the first time she laid eyes on it. After looking it over from within the man door, she moved to the breaker box for the switch that controlled the main lighting. In so doing, she passed the bench still bearing George's radio gear. The electronics had a thick layer of dust on them from having never been covered after his death... which probably had ruined them. Her eyes went to the empty space beneath the bench. With a measure of guilt, she reluctantly recalled having retrieved her two hidden suitcases from under there on the day she fled Lubbock.

With the hanger now lit, she moved to the plane and was just about to pull the canvas off the cockpit when Roy's voice came to her from just outside the man door.

"Marna!"

"Roy... I'm in here."

"Marna!"

"Roy... I'm just looking at the..."

"I know you can hear me, so stop pretending that you can't!"

This is ridiculous! If he'd just step inside, then we wouldn't have to be shouting back and forth like two morons!

Leaving the plane, she came to the man door without purposing to step out. There he was off to the side with hands on his hips.

"I've been calling you over and over…"

"And I've been answering! Why didn't you just come inside, then you wouldn't have to…"

"You know full well that I hate this place… and I don't especially like the idea of my wife being in there alone either. Why'd you cut the lock off?! Wasn't it obvious that I wanted it kept closed!"

"What's the use of owning it if I can't go in?! And if that's the way you feel about it, why didn't you just tear the damn thing down when you had the chance?!"

"Believe you me, I would have! Many times! Except I… I couldn't."

He just stood there stymied while she grew irritated waiting on him to continue.

"You going to tell me why… or do I have to guess?!"

"For your information… I felt that removing it was like… admitting you'd never be coming back. I couldn't bear that."

Her annoyance with him instantly disappeared. She stepped out and threw herself at him in a big hug, even though he stayed more-or-less rigid in the process.

"I'm sorry… I shouldn't have been so short with you. Thanks for not getting rid of my plane."

"You're welcome. Besides… Dad gave it to you… and I would be dishonoring him to tear it down. But now that you're back, we can finally get rid of that plane."

"Roy… I want to keep it."

"What?! You're joking!"

"No… I don't know why, but I love that plane. It reminds me of Dad."

He was on the verge of pointing out the obvious, so she cut across his words.

"I know! That's where it happened! And I know how you feel about this place… but please… let me figure this out on my own. That plane's got to be worth something to somebody. Maybe I can… I don't know… clean it up a bit and… see if there's anyone interested in buying it. Roy… let me keep it long enough to do that. If I can't find someone to take it off our hands… then I'll just give it away. Then we'll have the hangar torn down… if that's what you really want… and that'll be the end of it."

Her first and only purposeful lie to him since coming back was one that she would willingly repeat, for she had no intention whatsoever of getting rid of the plane or the hangar. In the weeks to follow, this burden turned out to be not so grievous for her to bear, for Roy seemed content to allow her back into the hangar. From then on, she was careful to only spend time in there when he was at work. She would enjoy looking in on her plane… but keep her visits brief. One way she decided to protect herself was in never pulling the canvas from off the cockpit, for she feared that doing so might lead her down a path of obsession like the one that trapped George… inconceivably silly though it seemed.

In late June, with Roy preoccupied with the store's upcoming Fourth-of-July sale, she secretly arranged for an aviation mechanic to look at the Corsair. Apart from the man's astonishment that such a thing had been hidden away for nearly twenty five years, he concluded that the plane's engine was likely shot, as the prop simply could not be budged. So it would be best if she did not throw good money at bad. The plane would never fly again. She told him not to bother with the cockpit or the engine, and just do some obvious maintenance to ward off any further deterioration… lubricate accessible bearings, joints, and the like. She paid in cash, and then closed up the hangar, content that the expense be kept a secret. If need be, she was ready to tell Roy that the effort had been a prelude to selling the plane.

Though she had no idea why she felt this way, the last thing she actually cared about was knowing the monetary value of the Corsair. She had declined the mechanic's offer to have an appraiser swing by to authenticate it, not needing anyone to legitimize how much the plane meant to her. Its worth could never be assessed in dollars. Just knowing it was hers and that it was waiting there for her in the hangar… that was value beyond description. The plane was like a promise to her. Out there somewhere in the world was the thing that she had been made for, and though that purpose was currently locked away, hidden from view just as this plane was in its hangar, she would hold on to both the plane and the hope that one day her purpose would be revealed.

In misleading Roy about her true intentions regarding the Corsair, a part of her heart had to be set aside for the management of the lie. Her motive was to prevent him from getting hurt again… which required her being on the lookout for any sign that he might be catching on. Soon, that which was unhealthy became that which was noble to bear. Such vigilance, she told herself, was simply another aspect of her responsibility to him as a loving wife. Besides… she had never actually promised to do anything with the plane. Not really. So if she slipped up and he found out, she would simply state that she had changed her mind. She told herself that this was such a small thing to be concerned about, as what she did with her things was her own business. The plane would stay put, and that was the end of it.

Through the ensuing month right up to her August twelfth birthday, she remained especially attune to Roy's mood. At times, he seemed to be watching her almost as much as she was watching him. He was always peeking in on whatever she was doing with concerns over how she was feeling at being back in Lubbock. She supposed this attentiveness to be nothing more than his care for her and some small fear that she had unknowingly planted in his mind regarding her restlessness. Each time, she responded with the simple truth. She was still sad about her aunt, but had never been more happy in all of her life.

After a week of enduring his many 'what do you want to do on your special day' questions, she gave in to her earlier admonition to herself and agreed to celebrate a birthday that had seldom been observed since before junior high.

After all, Gwen's idea of a birthday treat was giving me the day off.

They went to a popular pizzeria where she giggled over him sticking candles in pepperoni slivers and chanting out the *Happy Birthday* song amidst the clamor of a packed restaurant. He was so precious, and she loved every moment of it… even when he made her wear a plastic princess crown he had picked up at some toy store.

"That's not your present, by the way."

"I should hope not."

He handed over a cream-colored envelope with that boyish smile she loved so much, him quivering with a mixture of pleasure and eagerness. She delayed long enough to enjoy the 'For my wonderful wife' sprawled across the front before tearing open the flap. Within was a simple store-bought card depicting a bright blue sky with cartoon puffs of white floating by. Below were the words:

For your 8th birthday
here's wishing that you…

Roy had crossed out the number eight and written in her age – twenty five.

"Really?! This is the best you could do for the woman you *claim* to love?"

She acted as if affronted, and was amused by how dramatically he drew a hand over his mortally wounded heart.

"Such pain, Marna. Best withhold judgment until you see what's inside."

As she flipped open the card, a slip of folded paper fell into her lap. Though she retrieved it, her attention was on the card's interior. The same skyscape as on the front was repeated on the inside, except in the midst of it was now a comical presentation of a biplane being piloted by an oversized puppy dog, it being donned in goggles and a fur-collared flight jacket. Below this was the card's concluding message.

Fly high!

In his own hand, Roy had added his love along with birthday wishes. Nothing else was there for her to read.

"Okay… nice card… for a kid."

"Look at the slip of paper."

At first glance, it appeared to be a coupon of some kind… but then she froze on reading Roy's handwriting across the top.

Good for one private pilot's license.

She took in the name of the 'Carlyle Flight School' at the bottom… along with its address at the Lubbock airport… before coming up to face him.

"You're not serious?!"

"Of course I am. You're going to have a blast, just you wait and see."

She looked down once more and noticed that the slip of paper was actually a receipt.

"Five hundred dollars?! Husband… are you out of your mind?! We can't afford this."

"Of course we can. Besides, it's an investment in you! But, umm… that's just the first installment. It's gonna cost more than double that before you're done. You know… I'd kind of like you to consider this as being a present from both me and Gwen… seeing as it's coming from her inheritance to you."

"Roy… this is crazy!"

"Hey… I understand if you're scared."

"Who said anything about being scared?! It's just… I should be spending my time fixing up the house or… or whatever. You know, doing something with more permanence to it. It's not like I'm going to make a career out of flying."

"I'm not suggesting that you try. I'm only thinking that you need something to do other than visit Ruby and remodel all day. Since you're not ready for work, then… why not!? You'll be great! And I know you'll love it. You're going to have to, because it's nonrefundable… and they're expecting you tomorrow morning."

For the remainder of the evening, she carried the receipt about with her to reexperience the surprise… and have it available to wave in his face while asking if he had lost his mind. To each of her sarcastically phrased protests, all thrown out to see if there was the slightest of cracks in his assurances, she found that he responded with nothing but excitement for her. At bedtime, with her nestling against him in the dark, her objections began to shift away from self-doubt and toward a craving to know what he actually thought. Did she have it in her to fly, and did he have any reservations about her doing something so dangerous? After all, flight was a realm generally restricted to men.

496

"Marna, you're being ridiculous. I have complete faith in you. Besides, I've seen the way you look at that plane. You're totally fascinated by it."

"Roy?"

"Yes."

"I… have a confession to make. Please don't be angry with me. I've… never had any intention of getting rid of the Corsair."

"I know that. You're not so difficult to read, Marna Meitner."

"You've known all along?

"Of course. You might not want to admit it, but you and your aunt are a lot alike. I could always tell what was on her mind just by looking at her."

"But, Roy… I… umm… did something without asking you. I paid a man fifty five dollars to service the plane… just to make sure that it wouldn't rust up anymore."

"That, I didn't know."

"I'm sorry. I was… afraid of you saying no."

"What happen to us being completely honest with each other?"

She came up over him to look fully into his eyes, unable to hold back the tears in begging him to forgive her. He did, but she was just as relieved that he kept on stroking her hair until she had managed to stop crying. He fell asleep effortlessly, but she lay beside him for a long time struggling with herself. Yet again, her thinking had become turned around inside her head. It was stupid of her to believe that she had made any kind of progress in life… and stupid to think that she could learn how to fly.

But Gwen had…

Yeah… because Gwen was Gwen!

Despite having grown up with a florist, she had rewritten in her mind everything that she once knew about her aunt. Of course Gwen was a pilot! Of course she had learn to fly at an early age! Of course she could handle fighter planes such as the Corsair with no problem! Gwen displayed a force of will in everything she did.

But I'm just Marna… scared sick of heights. I can't even climb a ladder without getting dizzy. What kind of a pilot would I make if I froze up at the controls simply because I glanced out the window. I nearly passed out on the roof of the Rollecastle building.

That thought instantly brought the unwelcomed memory of being kissed by Azurean in WYNG's transmitter room. She looked over to where Roy lay facing away from her. All of a sudden, it seem terribly important to her that she learn how to fly, if only for him. She rolled onto her side and nuzzled up against his back, wrapping an arm about his chest and burying her face into his neck. He moaned out an appreciation in his sleep, and she imagined it as being his wholehearted acceptance of her... or perhaps the purr of a plane's engine in flight.

In the morning, she was waiting for him to join her at the bathroom vanity to continue the conversation she had started in the shower. Normally a very confident person when it came to new challenges, she felt that flying was unlike anything she had ever attempted. It was... serious. If she happened to ruin a flower arrangement, served the wrong meal to a restaurant patron, messed up someone's cable bill, or even threw Billings into a towering rage over a script error, there was always a way of putting things right. But make a mistake piloting an airplane... that was an entirely different matter.

He was taking his sweet time in the shower, bellowing out some terrible country music song he had heard on the radio. The steam continued to billow out into the bathroom. With blow drier in one hand and a comb in another, she stared into the fog-covered mirror. She really wanted him standing beside her here at the vanity so she could finally get the truth out of him before it was too late.

Come on... you've been in there long enough.

She replayed again his reassuring words from last night, but they still were not doing it for her. In a few hours, she would be showing up for her first flight lesson. She was fairly confident that she could learn how to fly a plane, but that would not make her a pilot any more than cutting stems had made her a florist. She knew that the thing most at stake was a heart that had dreamed for years to one day be like those birds in the relief. So the real question was whether she had it in her to break away into flight... just as those birds had.

Finally, the valve turned, the water stopped, and out stepped Roy, working a towel into his hair.

"You're *absolutely* sure about this? I mean, it's something that not everyone can..."

"How many times do I have to tell you?! I wasn't fooling last night, and I'm not fooling this morning either."

"But Roy..."

"*But Roy* nothing. You know... you're more like Gwen than you care to admit. Once you get something into your head, then..."

"How can you say that?! We're not at all alike!"

"Really?! Well I know better. You know she'd stop by every Sunday for a visit and we'd sit on the front porch talking for hours. Most times it was about how I was doing, but sometimes she told me stories from her time as a pilot.

Man… your aunt was fearless! That's you too."

She buying none of that... especially in her having been deprived of those stories all her life.

"Well… one person's fearlessness is another's foolishness."

He gave no response, which was just as well by her since she had been speaking more to herself than to him. She peeled the damp towel from her hair with one hand and began wiping the mist off the mirror with the other. Starting out small, she expanded her circle beyond what was necessary for viewing her own reflection, as she wanted to keep track of him too. There he was… smearing shaving cream on his face without a clue as to how anxious she was feeling on the inside. He took up his razor, and smooth as silk, started making casual strokes to his neck, swishing the razor in the sink's hot water after each pass. She was studying him, but thinking more about all those missed opportunities with Gwen.

"Marna… don't go there."

"What?"

"You know full well what I mean. She'd not want you living with regret. I'm not trying to make you feel bad about the things she never shared with you. I just want you to understand that what was in her – the love of flying – might very well be in you too. Hey… remember that time on my eleventh birthday when Dad arranged for…"

"It was your twelfth."

"No... pretty sure it was my eleventh."

"It was your twelfth, because I was only ten."

"You sure?"

"Definitely. I was in fifth grade and you were in sixth. Remember, you're a year and a half older than me."

"Alright. Whatever. Remember that pilot?"

She put down the blow drier without having yet started it up. Resting her hands on the vanity, she leaned in closer to the mirror for a better look at his reflection. On his shaving cream covered face was that 'I know something you don't know' smile of his. And then the name on the birthday card receipt came back to her.

"You're not saying I'll be learning from the same guy?"

"Yep. Butch Carlyle."

Still staring at his reflection, she strained to remember what that man had looked like. All she saw in memory was the boyhood likeness of her husband. Some of that was still present in the grown-up version… shaving cream aside. As her eyes were drawn to the narrow streaks of white left over from the path of his razor, it occurred to her that the two of them had come a long way together since then. Suddenly, she wanted very much to wrap him up in a hug, except he might cut himself… or get shaving cream on her.

"I met with him when I signed you up. He said he remembered you."

"Get out! There's no way!"

"Marna… I'm telling you… he remembered. He's the one who said you were a natural."

"You heard that?! And you remembered it?!"

"When're you ever going to accept that I've been in love with your every move since the first time I laid eyes on you crammed under that counter at Forde's Flowers?!"

Though the bathroom had been steamy for a long time, she now felt especially warm.

"Okay, okay… I get it! You're crazy about me… and I'm crazy about you too. Now tell me what he told you… and everything that you can remember from back then."

He went on making a show out of the final strokes with his blade, whereas she could tell that he was actually teasing her because of how that eyebrow of his kept twitching so much.

"Well?! I'm waiting!"

"Let's see… I recall that I was standing behind you, listening to every word that he said about you. He swore that he'd never taken up a kid like you before. Remember that I went up first… and sat in the same seat as you did. I couldn't take my eyes off the ground the whole time. Sure… I saw the gauges and the knobs… there were all plenty cool… but I really didn't care about how the plane worked. The only thing I wanted was to see Lubbock from the air. But that wasn't you. Butch said that you weren't in the least bit interested in what was happening on the ground."

"Doy! Because I was scared to death!"

"Believe what you like, but Butch told me a different story. He said you kept peppering him with questions about how to fly. He also said that you were really into the plane… like you were part of it. That's why he called you a natural. So, 'Natural'… you gonna take flight lessons or not?"

She turned back to her part of the mirror without responding, and instead began to blow dry her hair. The drone of the small fan combined with how her hair flapped about brought a silly image to mind – of her flying in a genuine biplane. Her birthday card's message came into her imagination too.

Me, flying high!

Her hair was dry, but she kept the blow drier tossing the strands about.

One day soon, she could be sitting in an open cockpit soaring through a cloudless sky. In a quick glance to her right, she realized that he had been watching her the whole time.

"Cut it out."

She gave him a backhanded slap to his bare chest, sufficiently sharp enough to wipe that gloat off his face. But that was not nearly enough for her, so she started poking at him with her blow drier… until he finally got with it and pulled her into a hug. She loved it… but broke away on noticing that he still had plenty of shaving cream left on his face.

"Seriously, Husband! I want to know the truth! Do you really think I can do this?"

He gave her another one of those raised eye brow looks, along with a puckering at the corners of his mouth, dotted as they were with small bits of foam.

"Okay. Then I'll do it! I'll go over there today and… become a pilot."

She dressed in her sharpest pair of blue jeans and a sleeveless button-up top… white with an Oxford collar. Slip on a tan belt with some flats to match and she was ready to go.

Super cool looking!

Bounding down the staircase, she had it in her mind that this first flight lesson might actually be some kind of a validation as to a theme in her life. No – that was not the right word. An indication. That was it. An indication of how true her childhood fascinations with the sky had been. She was departing a half hour sooner than was necessary, but was so anxious to be there already. Hurtling the lower portion of the porch stairs, she cut across the lawn for her car. Off the circle, down the drive and out onto the county road, she was imagining what Billings might say about all of her hustle to become a student in flight school.

He'd have thought I was crazy!

But then his parting words came to her.

No. He'd have said that I could accomplish anything I put my mind to. I really miss him.

A typical trip to the airport could not possibly be taking this long! Every traffic light went against her, and the slowest of Lubbock's slow just had to be occupying the lanes ahead of her. Finally, she was at the airport… but it seemed like forever before she found the address among all the access roads rimming the airfield. The Carlyle Flight School was situated along a smaller section of runway off one of the two main strips that serviced Lubbock's commercial airliners and cargo carriers. His place was a large sheet metal building in opal green with a huge picture of a biplane painted on the front. That immediately made her think of Roy's birthday card. Hurrying up to the door, she stepped into a smallish-sized sitting room with two worn-out couches rimming a coffee table piled with magazines. In a corner, a TV silently aired a morning news program with no one there to watch it. She moved to a counter behind which was a small office space. From somewhere back there came the low static of a poorly tuned radio. She put a finger to the bell on the counter and waited. Turning about, she realized that the walls around her were decorated with dozens of cloth fragments haphazardly stapled to the wood paneling. Each appeared to have been raggedly cut from some larger garment, and all possessed a handwritten message of some kind. Many also had drawings of a plane. Stepping up to the nearest one, she noted that its writing included a person's name, the date, and a string of letters and numbers, with 'CFI Carlyle' sprawled at the very bottom.

"That'll be you one day soon."

She swiveled about with a start to find an older gentleman standing just behind her. He was something like what she remembered him to be, except with a lot more gray beneath his ball cap.

"Hi. You must be Mr. Carlyle. I'm Marna Meitner. I think you're expecting me."

"Yes – welcome! I see you've noticed the shirt tails. It's sort of a tradition between student and instructor to commemorate the first solo. You won't be needing your shirt tail anymore since there won't be anyone there pulling on it from behind. You'll soon see what I mean. So… are you ready to get at it?"

"Most definitely."

"Then your first lesson as a student pilot will be your most valuable one, Mrs. Meitner – you've got paperwork to do."

"Eww – that makes me sound so middle-aged! Please… Marna will do fine."

"You can call me Butch. Hold it a sec."

He leaned over the counter into the small office and returned with a clipboard.

"The top sheet's your application. Your husband's already filled it out, but I need you to sign it. The next pages are the required legalese… a contract stating what you're responsible for… along with disclaimers and the like. You can have a seat over there while you…"

She knew that he was motioning her toward one of the couches, but went right to the signing and dating of the last page.

"Not gonna read it?"

"Nah... I wouldn't understand any of it even if I did."

"Yeah... I know what you mean. Lawyers..."

He took the clipboard from her and flipped it over the counter, then grabbed a duffel bag that was waiting there.

"Need to use the facilities before we get started?"

"I'm fine."

"Good. Follow me."

He led her to a door on the other side of the lounge. She was expecting this to be a classroom where she would be given a lecture on flight, but on passing through, she found herself within the interior of an immense hangar... much larger than the one she owned. Butch was ahead of her, cutting across a corner toward its open bay doors, but she could not help but stop on finding herself in a genuine place of aviation. Spread out across the hangar's concrete were several planes, some being serviced and some just sitting there waiting to be flown. She knew none of their names by sight but instantly craved that ability of recognizing a model and manufacturer based on the shape, size, configuration, and engine type... just like some people can do with cars and trucks. Her eyes fell upon one plane in particular, it being positioned at the back wall. Unable to prevent herself, she veered in that direction for a closer look. The propeller blades were badly bent out of shape, the wings were warped, and the tail section looked as if some giant had squashed it. At any other time in life, she would have been repulsed by such a wreck, but in starting out on an adventure in flight, she somehow found herself engrossed in this plane's tragic state.

"You probably don't recognize it, but that's the Cessna you went up in as a kid."

"It's terrible! Was it in a crash?"

"Oh, nothing like that. It was outside when the tornado hit. Probably got flapped around on its tie-downs like some toy plane tethered to a stick. I'm afraid that one's beyond hope. Still waiting on the insurance check. Got three others being repaired. You know, all toll, there were over a hundred aircraft damaged that night. Only one of mine survived without a scratch. Had it inside for maintenance at the time. Come on... I'll show you what you'll be training on."

Moving outside, the eastern sky was alit by the morning sun, momentarily stunning her with its brightness.

Gotta get me some of those cool fighter pilot shades!

Shielding her eyes, she noted off in the distance a portion of the main runway, beyond which was the familiar West Texas horizon. It occurred to her then that she had been here once before as a little girl in a sailor suit. Hurrying alongside Butch, she thought it funny if her ten year old self could see her now – a woman determined to fly.

He was making a beeline for a nearby plane, yellow all over except for black on its tail and above its engine.

"This here's a Fairchild PT-26, nicknamed the Cornell. I don't much care for that name, so I just call it the Fairchild. It's got a metal-framed body, except for the wings and tail. They're mostly made of wood."

As he put a hand to the wingtip, so did she.

"Feels like fabric."

"Yep. Covered in canvas. Some call these 'rag wings,' but don't let that mislead you. She's a tough old bird. The PT-26 is just like the PT-19. That model was extensively used as a trainer during the war. Your aunt probably got started out on it."

"You knew my aunt?"

He paused just long enough for her to gather that he regretted having brought up Gwen.

"Yeah. We crossed paths about town every once in a while. She was an amazing woman. I'm sorry for your loss."

"Thanks. I do miss her. So… what were you saying about her training on this plane?"

"That was the PT-19. The PT-26 is different in that it was outfitted with a canopy for the Canadian Air Force… because it gets really cold up there. I bought this one from a fella in Vancouver a while back with a mind for using it here whenever the dust gets bad. Most times we'll fly with it open." He dropped his bag to the ground and bent down to point beneath the plane. "Fixed landing gear makes it easier on the student. What's going to be more challenging for you is that it's a tailwheel… or 'taildragger' as some call it."

"Why's that matter?"

"Mostly because of the difficulties associated with controlling its orientation on landing."

She stared at the plane's back wheel trying to figure out how that might matter. Surely the thing was on a swivel… but it did look sort of flimsy compared to the front wheels. Maybe that was what he meant.

"So… when you say 'its orientation,' are you referring to the back wheel itself… or the whole plane?"

"Good catch… I meant the plane. You have to think of any aircraft as a set of axes… you know… x, y and z… with the origin being at the plane's center of gravity. As a pilot, you've got to control your craft against rotations about all three. So, for the x… that's along the fuselage… we call that rotation a roll. That's mostly controlled by your ailerons. Your y's along the wing span. That's the pitch… and for that we have the elevators in back. Then there's the z… vertical through the plane. That motion's a yaw… for which there's the rudder. A taildragger's particularly susceptible to yaws on landing because of such influences as cross winds and the P-factor… but that's a bit beyond you right now."

She really disliked it when Billings or someone else at WYNG said such a thing to her. She always wanted them to elaborate, even if she got more confused as a result.

"No… I really want to know. What's a P-factor?"

"Well… basically… when you perform a normal landing in a taildragger… all three wheels hit at once. In that condition, the nose is up… just like how it's sitting on the ramp right now. Because of that… look at the angle of the prop to the deck."

He pointed up and down along the propeller, and she could easily see a difference.

"It's tilted… the top's back and the bottom's forward. That's what you mean?"

"Exactly. That slight orientation difference results in uneven stresses at the top versus the bottom… causing a yaw at low speeds. Like on landing. Don't worry… I'll teach you how to compensate for that… and how to know when to do a two point landing versus a normal landing."

By the way he was now smiling at her, she could tell what was coming next.

"I like you're inquisitiveness… but let's not bite off more than we can chew."

"Okay…"

"As it turns out… the challenge of a tailwheel landing is exactly why I would have preferred to start you on a tricycle like the Cessna…" He motioned back over his shoulder toward the hangar. "…but seeing as its out of commission, we'll make do with this. But nothing you won't be able to handle with the proper training. Oh… and another thing… this is a tandem trainer, so you won't have the benefit of being seated beside me like in the Cessna. I actually think that's good. The sooner you get accustomed to the feel of being out on your own, the better you'll be as a pilot."

He moved about the left wing and climbed up along what she recognized to be a foot path running beside the plane's body.

"Come on up… just like I did."

In this, he did not offer her any assistance, and she was more than pleased to show herself as capable as any man. Still… she took care to place hand and foot exactly where he had. On getting up, her eyes first went to the interior of the cockpit… but then she was startled when he rather abruptly slapped her on the back.

"Just don't stand there – climb in!"

"Really?"

"Of course. It's time to begin your education."

Being nearer to the rear seat and thinking it the one designated for a student, she was searching for suitable grips when Butch took hold of her shoulders and shifted her toward the front.

"You're up here. Throughout your lessons, Marna, you'll be what's called the PIC or 'pilot in command.' You'll be seated in front where you'll best be able to carry out the operation of the plane."

"You're sure about this?"

"Of course. Now throw a leg over and get settled in… and don't fuss about stepping on the seat. That's what it's there for."

This was altogether a different matter than climbing onto the wing. Though her execution at getting over the canopy railing was without the sort of panache an experienced pilot might show, she was altogether relieved on settling herself in without having fallen over the other side. Before her now was a visual feast of aviation significance. Once again, she was a little girl taken in by the wonder of an instrument panel.

"Comfortable?"

She nodded, not having the wherewithal to speak with all those gauges before her.

"You can make adjustments to the seat with a lever on your right."

Again, she nodded, as the control for a seat was the least interesting thing in this cockpit. Leery of touching anything, she pointed from gauge to gauge with her questions, ignoring how he chuckled over her eagerness. They worked their way through the eight main instrument indicators and progressed to the controls – throttle, rudder pedals, starter, flaps, and so on. When he started in on the operation of the ailerons, she knew without being told to take hold of the stick. Gripping it in the place worn smooth by so many other pilots, its feel seemed perfectly fit for her.

"Hop out, and we'll go through the preflight checklist."

"You're not actually thinking about taking me up now… are you?"

"No, Marna – *you're* taking me up." He pointed a finger upward, and she followed his direction into the sky. "Your classroom's up there. I'll do the takeoff and landing, but you'll do as much of the actual flying as I think you can handle."

"But..."

"Relax! You'll be fine! I won't be asking you to do anything difficult. Besides... it's a perfect day for flying. High ceiling and not a bit of runway crosswind."

She scampered out of the cockpit and down to the ramp without giving much thought as to how it was done, being taken in by the unexpected prospect of getting up into the air. Following him in a clockwise circuit about the plane starting at the left wing, he showed her what to look for on a 'walkaround.' At each step along the way, he had her doing the actual inspecting, checking for freedom of motion in the ailerons, ensuring that the flap hinges were secure, and that the wings had no obvious damage to them above or below. After making her get back into the cockpit to verify that the starter was off... something that he told her he had already done, but wanted her to understand the importance of double-checking... he then had her climb out and turn the two-bladed propeller through a half dozen rotations. This, he said, was done in order to inspect each blade's structural integrity, and also clear the engine cylinders of excess oil and exhaust. He had her check the tire and oleo strut pressures, make sure that the fuel gauge was registering, and that the fuel and oil levels were topped off. She made certain that the engine cowling was secure, and that all of the intakes were clear of debris. To the rear, he made her wiggle the elevators and rudder about as she had done with the ailerons. They both then came around in a wide loop for one last big picture inspection before removing the tie downs and wheel chocks.

"You'll do that every time you fly, both before and after. Stay true to your checklist and inspection procedures, and you'll solve most problems before they can occur."

Standing over his duffel bag, he removed two sets of headgear and an extra pair of sunglasses.

"You can use my spares today, but you'll want to get your own. They're pricey, so take good care of them. Get yourself a sturdy flight bag. Now... what say we start her up?"

Before she knew what was happening, he had her strapped into the front seat and was showing her how to connect up her headset. That done, he gave her a thumps-up and disappeared behind her. She sensed the cockpit rock as he climbed in, and then felt a pat to her shoulder. Awkwardly turning about, she noticed him pointing to a small mirror affixed to the canopy's windshield. She straightway realized that this was in order for her to see her instructor.

"Marna, do you copy?"

His voice came into her ears with a trace of a ringing echo, almost as if he were shouting at her from down a very long hallway. She quickly flipped the microphone down to her lips.

"Yes… or should I say 'roger'?"

"Roger that for any kind of an acknowledgement… some prefer 'wilco' for compliance to an instruction. But I'm not picky. Let's crank her up."

He went through a step-by-step procedure for starting the Fairchild. She carried out each instruction with care, while also trying to cram the information into her head. It was all rather overwhelming.

Pull back on the stick.

Adjust the fuel mixture.

Prime the fuel pump.

Set the magnetos and the master switch.

Shout out for clearance about the prop.

"CLEAR!"

Her own voice sounded unearthly in her ears muffled by a headset.

Then… activate the starter.

The blades immediately began to turn, haltingly at first as the engine coughed its way into life, and then with smooth revolutions to match its pleasant rumble. She, as much as any female she knew, possessed an assortment of perfumes to match her mood, yet her first whiffs of spent fuel and hot oil immediately became a fragrance that she associated with the thrill of flight. The engine's roar shook her, so she closed her eyes for just a second to concentrate on its vibrations. His voice then came into her headset again.

"Good job! Now I'll take it from here. Keep your feet off the rudder pedals while we taxi. We'll be stopping on the ramp just shy of the runway to do our preflight checklist."

"Roger that."

She listened carefully as he called on the radio for ground clearance, providing the controller with the plane's call letters and a request for taxiing instructions. The ground controller's response was succinct and business-like. She felt the engine rev as Butch nudged the plane forward.

"A rudder steers a plane on the ground… sort of like it does with a ship at sea. But once we're in the air, its functions are different. We'll cover that later…"

He took the plane on a gradual left turn and proceeded along in a little zigzagged pattern in front of other hangars and parked planes. Her view was surprisingly good given that a great big engine was blocking her sight straight ahead. Yet she still felt like she was missing too much. Everything was happening so fast… and they were only taxiing.

In short course, he brought the plane to a stop at the end of the taxiway. There, he patiently ran through with her each item from a checklist on the laminated card in her side pocket. With the brakes set, he had her confirm that the flaps were up, and then that the ailerons, rudder and elevators were responsive. He next had her rev the engine to near full throttle, and make sure the magnetos were functioning properly. She set the fuel mixture, and then confirmed that the engine temperature and oil pressures were acceptable. One last check to the harnesses, and Butch called up for tower permission to move out onto the runway. Just as he finished inching the plane into position, his voice came to her in the headset.

"Put your right hand on the stick and left to the throttle. You're taking off."

"But you said…"

"No dickering… we've got clearance. Just hold the stick even and slowly advance the throttle…"

Nearly petrified, she sucked in breath through clinched teeth and moved the throttle as he instructed. The plane lurched forward down the runway.

"Keep it up. Call out your speed…"

"We're at 20 miles per hour… 25… 30… 35…"

Everything in her tensed up as the plane's incline shifted.

"Tail coming up."

"Roger that… 45… 55… 60…"

"Wheels up."

She quickly glanced out the open canopy to her right. Where before had been a bit of the plane's shadow cast on the runway was now nothing but sunlight reflecting off the asphalt some ten feet below. Looking up to the nose, she saw in a flash that the plane's orientation was shifted relative to what remained of the runway before her.

"Yawing to the left."

"What do I do?!"

"A tad right rudder'll fix it."

What's a tad?!

Her foot nonetheless responded despite her mind's confusion. With a gentle push to the right pedal, she was rewarded with the plane's immediate realignment.

"Ease up on the rudder at 85. The wings'll take over then."

She did as he instructed, relieved that the yaw did not return. As they climbed over the North Loop, she felt a pat to her left shoulder and looked to the mirror. Butch was giving her another thumbs-up signal.

"Congratulations, Marna – you've just performed your first takeoff."

She smiled at him, and then in total astonishment brought her eyes back down to the cockpit controls.

Wow! I can't believe it! I just took off in a plane!

Already, she was eager for the next challenge. Butch's voice came back to her then.

"Release the stick and throttle… I'll take us out a bit so we can have space to work. Keep a lookout for other aircraft."

"Roger that."

She felt the plane bank to the left and looked down each wing at the aileron positions before searching the instrument panel for responses in the turn indicator and artificial horizon. Both held steady positions through the plane's bank to the east.

"Butch… why'd it do that… the yaw on takeoff?"

"It's caused by a number of things… propeller torque… slipstream corkscrewing on the tail's left side… gyroscopic precession. We'll get into all that later.."

Canopy open and wind tossing her hair about, she could not be more happy. She did not need to look up at a mirror to know that she was smiling from ear to ear. As the plane cleared the city, Butch set her to work acquiring a feel for how the ailerons responded to her touch. She made multiple banking turns in both directions, keeping her airspeed where he told her to and being careful not to pull back on the stick. As in her childhood memory, the horizon on the instrument panel and the one just off nose tip were her guides through these turns.

It was difficult for her to say how she felt. She was likely both nervous and excited at the same time, but could not spare any of herself from the exercises to know for certain. Mostly, time had no meaning for her within this joy of flying. But Butch too soon took control of the plane, instructing her to pay close attention to his approach into the Lubbock airport. He radioed a request for clearance to land, and then maneuvered the plane into place. She had no idea what he was doing other than decreasing the airspeed along a line heading into the designated runway. The feel of it was so smooth and easy, like gliding on a breeze. All three wheels touched at the same time with hardly a jolt. If only she could do that herself, it would be like having all of her dreams come true.

They did the post-flight checklist and walkaround together, him pointing out the things she should pay attention to before stepping away from the plane. As he spoke, she noticed him glance up a couple times to the top of her head.

The next time he looked away, she did a little post-flight check on herself. Sure enough, her hair was all fussed up. She quickly smoothed out the fluffs, casual as can be, before he turned back.

Note to self – put 'wear hat to protect your hair' on the preflight checklist.

Heading back inside, she was thinking about whether there was anything else to her appearance that needed checking when Butch motioned her down a short hall and into the office space behind the counter.

"Before you go, Marna, I've got a couple of things for you… all part of the package. The first is homework."

After rummaging in a stack of papers, he produced a manual of no great thickness. On the cover was a picture of the plane she had just been up in, minus the canopy.

"This here's the pilot's handbook for the Fairchild. I'm going to have you start in on the first few sections. Make notes of anything that you don't understand, and we'll discuss it when you come in on Monday."

"Why not tomorrow?"

"I don't normally instruct on Fridays. Which reminds me… As to schedule, I'm planning on going at your pace…"

"So you'll be in tomorrow after all?"

That got a smile out of him.

"I think four sessions a week is ideal. Here's the last thing… a sort of gift for taking flight lessons with us." He held out a black hardback with nothing on its cover revealing the contents. "This'll be your first flight logbook. As your instructor, I have the privilege of making your first entry."

He opened it to the initial page, so much like one of Gwen's. As he went about making notes – the date, aircraft and its ID, their location, and time flown – the tears began to well up in her eyes at the significance of this moment. She had not expected this singular honor, for this logbook proved that she was as much a student pilot as any person who had sat in a cockpit and tasted the sweetness of their first flight. As he went on to pen in his remarks, she discreetly slid a finger up to wipe the corner of each eye.

He noticed.

"Yeah… I felt the same way after my first flight. This is a moment that you'll treasure forever. Congratulations, Marna. It doesn't seem possible, but it only gets better from here."

He extended a hand, and she shook it with every bit of the enthusiasm welling up inside.

CHAPTER
33

THE EARTH, A BOWL;
THE SKY, A DOME

The wonder she was feeling in her heart would not stay put. She had flown a plane all by herself! Well… sort of, but that hardly mattered. She had been the one at the controls, and made it do exactly what she wanted it to do. She felt like part of it in the process. The rush of the air, the sound of the engine, the shaking and swaying about… all of it belong to her! She could not wait to get back up there again. Really, she must tell someone right away, or she would burst from all of this excitement. Maybe drop in on Roy at the appliance store for a few minutes… though she probably would not be able to keep it short. She had so much to recount. Best not to impose on him while he was busy at work. Besides… she would have him all to herself in the evening.

Who then?

For the first time since returning to Lubbock, she was disappointed with herself for having not put effort into reconnecting with her old girlfriends. In her defense, not enough time had separated her from Gwen's death… or from having run away to Chicago without a word to anyone. Roy was the only person with whom she had explained herself, and she simply did not have the heart to relive the shame just yet. So in concluding one of the most extraordinary experiences in her life, she was left with no one to share it with. Clutching both the logbook and the Fairchild manual to her chest, she crossed the Carlyle Flight School parking lot reconciled to head home.

Taking the Loop rather than slogging her way through town on 87, she travelled the fifteen miles from the airport to the nursing home as if flying it in the Fairchild… because basically that was where she still was. She arrived as the residents were being served their lunch. There was a tray with a bowl of split pea soup and a cup of fruit cocktail before Ruby. Taking over from the attendant, she did her best to intersperse the most vivid descriptions of flying during lunch. Ruby opened her mouth at the tap of the spoon to her lips, but did not speak. She went on about how scared she had been when Butch told her to do the takeoff… and relieved when the plane stopped its yawing… and how impressed she was with herself that she did it all so well. Butch was the perfect person to learn from. Kind, firm and very knowledgeable about planes. And she had done bank after bank on her own! She, Marna Meitner, had operated a flying machine! Unbelievable!

With the lunch tray taken away, she had her logbook out for Ruby to see… and was absolutely stunned when Ruby actually shifted her eyes for a second to look at it! So she explained to her each detail of the entry… and that she would be the one doing the writing soon enough… and that she had her sights set on filling up the entire book! On she went, pouring out her feelings of pride and pleasure over having become something that Gwen once was – a student of aviation.

An attendant came by with Ruby's medication, so she decided it was probably time to leave. She kissed Ruby on the forehead and promised to be by on the weekend. She departed from the nursing home with her heart lightened and her eyes drawn up to the sky.

On the way back, she made a detour to a bookstore and purchased a hardback journal with a rather plain-looking cover. Once home, she took to her stairwell nook to capture her observations and feelings from her first-ever flight. She did not really expect to be doing this type of thing as a habit, having never kept a diary or a journal in all her life. She much more enjoyed looking forward than jotting down things that would end up being part of the past. But for this one time, she wanted to know that feeling Gwen had in recording her own impressions of flying. Starting with Roy's birthday card, she wrote her way through to the point of receiving her first logbook, and then concluded with the line that had been on her mind the whole time.

Now I know a little bit of what it feels like to be one of those birds in the relief.

In the end, she was somewhat disappointed with the writing experience.

It had been a whole lot of work for something that she might never read again. Instead, she derived much more pleasure in dumping on Roy once he got home. She would rather record all of her experiences on him anyway. So from dinner to bedtime, she kept his ears full of her excited words. He was so patient, smiling with that 'I told you so' crimp of his lips when she thanked him for the most incredible birthday gift ever.

In her sleep that night, she dreamt of slowly closing in on a long, diamond-sparkled runway lined in bright white, felt her wheels touchdown with the softest of landings, gentle as a kiss, and then got bathed in a symphonic crescendo of an engine's roar, it praising her for a feat well done.

Waiting all weekend to get back at it was pure torture. Most of it, she took out on Roy by constantly reliving every detail of her first lesson. Come Monday morning, she was finally back at the Carlyle Flight School for the second one. But the first thing Butch did was sit her down on a couch.

"So, Marna… let's you and me have a little chat."

He was obviously having second thoughts about her suitability as a student pilot. While she had spent the weekend looking forward to her next flight, perhaps he had not. She would deal with his skepticism by jumping right in with how much she had learned from the first two sections of the Fairchild's handbook. If that failed to impress him, she was prepared to go even further, for she had read the entire thing… though understood little of it.

"Hold it, Marna. We'll get to the homework during the post-flight briefing. I've got something different in mind before we head out."

"Oh… fantastic! That means we're flying together. I'm mean… of course we are. It's not like you were going to… put me off… as a student."

He smile back way too knowingly.

"No… you're stuck with me. I was going to say that we'll be working on mastering flight controls this week, but I wanted to talk with you first about the psychology of a pilot."

She simply could not help herself in her embarrassment and just had to add on more.

"Guess that's why we're on a couch…"

"No… but this is just as serious. By psychology, I mean how you have to be wired in your thinking. The thing you need to understand about flying is that it's contrary to everything you're used to doing. You've grown up as a creature of the earth and know well it's ways. From your first baby step onward, you've been conditioned by gravity. It's constant influence has been hammered into your thinking all your life. You know that to be low is safe and to be high is dangerous. But creatures of the air don't think that way."

"I know. They're not in the least bit afraid of heights."

"It's got nothing to do with that. They fly because they instinctively understand the air in the same way that fish understand the water. They move through it. Not us here on the ground. We tend to think about how things support our weight. You know from experience what's solid enough and what's not. This couch is a great example. You plopped down without a second thought because you were confident it would hold you up. So… here's a question for you. Why is it that a bird has the confidence to fly?"

"Umm… I guess because it knows how to use its wings… you know… to generate lift."

"That's part of it. Birds know how to *operate* their wings up there… but also to use their legs down here. I'm trying to get at something fundamentally different. Down here, everything we do is based upon being *on* the earth, whereas up there, it's about being *in* the sky. It's a totally different mindset requiring different ways of thinking. Consider motion. Anyone who's ever driven a car knows that the faster you go, the more dangerous things can be. Sure… collisions can happen in the sky too, but they're actually quite rare. Down here, it means nothing to sit still… no big deal… because you're being supported *on* something. But up there, if you're not moving… better yet… if air's not moving over your wings, then you're sure to fall out of the sky. You have to understand how it is that air supports a plane. Do you see what I'm getting at?"

"I think so. You're basically saying that I need to retrain my thinking. That as a pilot… airspeed and altitude are my best friends."

"Exactly! Couldn't have put it better myself. Here's another example of where you have to retrain your thinking. As a typical driver, you probably want to cruise along without having to hear anything from your vehicle. Silence is golden when you're out on the road. The slightest squeak can be an irritation or cause for concern. The opposite is the case up there. The rattles, vibrations, engine hums, and whistling of air… an experienced pilot appreciates them all. You'll be able to sense exactly what's going on with your aircraft simply based on the sounds it makes. And you'll come to depend upon those sounds. Same thing holds for the feel of it. You'll know when a stall's coming on simply by how floppy the stick gets. Then there's steering… completely different up there. Like I was telling you the other day, the rudder on a plane isn't anything like the helm on a ship. It's more like a weather vane keeping the aircraft aligned in the relative wind that's generated by your engine. Ever seen a bird with a tail rudder?"

"Of course not. That'd be ridiculous."

"Then that's got to tell you something about its relative importance on a plane. The rudder doesn't steer – that's what the ailerons are for. Those things by the tail aren't little wings, they're there to stabilize the plane... hence the name 'horizontal stabilizers.' And the adjustable sections on them might be called elevators, but they don't elevate the plane any more than flaps flap. They're only meant to control the elevation of the tail. You'll learn it's the throttle that makes the plane go up and down. What I'm trying to tell you, Marna, is that a significant part of your job as a student is to develop your flight instincts. When you're in the sky, there'll be a side of you that remembers what it's like to be on the ground. That little voice'll be telling you to respond in ways that might seem right for down here... but they'll get you in trouble up there. Might even get you killed."

Butch, grim of face, had her complete attention. The way he kept emphasizing the distinction between sky and earth – by the changing direction in which he was pointing – it somehow brought to mind images of the beleaguered humanity bound on the ground of her stone relief. Even the relief's birds flying above now seemed a cautionary depiction to her... that she should not carelessly venture into a realm that was not her own.

"So... what if... I'm unable to readjust my... perspective? Does that mean I don't have what it takes to be a pilot?"

"What we're going to be doing over the next couple of weeks is developing those flight instincts by getting you to understand not only what it takes to operate a flying machine, but also what it means to fly. Those really are two very different things. So let's start out with the simple stuff – operating an aircraft. What would you say is the number one cause of most aviation accidents?"

She was pretty sure that he did not mean this as a trick question. There was not a hint of clever amusement in his voice.

"I'd say... it's because something breaks. An engine goes out or there's some kind of mechanical failure."

"Those things do happen occasionally... and you'll be trained on how best to respond... but that's not it. Try again."

"Okay... umm... let me think. Something... weather-related. Like strong winds or fog... or heavy rain."

"Nope. Wrong again. An experienced pilot knows not to be in those situations in the first place... though they can crop up unexpectedly. No... nine times out of ten it's because the pilot lost control of the plane. Most times it's due to inexperience, but often times it's not. A pilot gets distracted... or overconfident... or even fearful, and then reverts back to a ground way of thinking. That's why it's critically important for you to be serious about your training. But you also have to understand yourself… your own tendencies. If a person's stupid on the ground, then it's even more likely that they'll be stupid in the air too."

Those words instantly cut through her, for she knew all too well of her tendencies for being stupid on the ground.

"Marna… I don't think you're stupid, but I'm going to be drilling you as if you were. So let's get personal… The five bad tendencies of a bad pilot in a bad situation are as follows."

Her eyes were drawn to his fist, suspended in the air in order to count them off for her. With each trait, a finger came up, and she flushed with the recognition of herself.

"One – rebellion. Rejecting authority and being a law unto one's self. Not doing what's required because some rule or procedure seems too idiotic. This is most often seen in a neglect of checklists and tower instructions. By the way… a plane's not some bus or trolley car that you can pack willy-nilly with passengers. A pilot must respect its tolerances and specifications."

"Two – passivity. Attention to detail matters. When an issue shows up… even a small one… the pilot has to take it seriously. Believe it or not, I once had a student who froze up whenever the stall warning came on. He wasn't afraid… he simply could not bring himself to act on it. After a couple times of that, I brought the plane in myself… and that was the end of him as a student."

"Three – arrogance. This happens way too often with new pilots who get filled with bravado simply because they know how to operate an aircraft. Makes them think they can show-off or flat-hat. Oh, they see the risks! They just think they can handle whatever the skies might throw their way. In fact, they're actually drawn to the thrill of taking risks. Marna… daredevils do not survive for long in aviation."

"Four – impulsivity. Acting without thinking and acting against training. Believing that to do anything quickly is better than being patient enough to reason out the situation… or seek guidance from another pilot or a controller. This tendency is especially dangerous for the pilot who doesn't instinctively understand the difference between earth and sky."

"And five – invulnerability. No pilot should ever consider themselves above failure… that accidents only happen to idiots, chumps and unlucky saps. Too often, these pilots feel safe when they should actually be scared out of their wits. But for some reason, they're completely blind to the dangers all about them."

He drop the five traits back into his lap, and she knew what was coming next.

"All of these behaviors end up causing accidents. So, Marna… which one is you?"

She wished that she needed time to think before answering… which in itself revealed her greatest weakness.

"Oh, I'm definitely the impulsive one! Though… I guess I've got a little bit of them all. But impulsiveness is my worst. I get so worked up on the inside that I… you know… just sort of… act without thinking. I always end up regretting it later."

"Take heart… that's what your training's there for. Stay true to it, and you'll be best prepared for dealing with yourself."

In the days to follow, Butch took her through a series of lessons to develop her flight skills, as well as sharpen those instincts required for becoming a creature of the sky. She quickly picked up on how to operate the main flight controls of stick, throttle and rudder, being pleased to find herself coordinated of hand, eye and foot… something she had not expected from years of being a floral designer, store manager, or newswoman. Soon, she was doing all of the takeoffs, even in stiff crosswinds that required careful control of the rudder. Butch then progressed her into glides and something he called mushing, which she discovered was essentially holding the plane's speed just shy of the wings giving up air. For several days, he made her 'mush' at a crawl over the West Texas farmland until he was convinced that she could manage the plane on her own.

"Marna, any idiot of a pilot can handle a craft at its cruising speed. Only a true pilot can hold her calm on the verge of a stall."

Her first trying moment as a student came when she began stall recovery training. She knew that a stall was essentially when a wing lost its ability to generate lift. Despite Butch's demonstrations, she found that being the one responsible for bringing the plane under control from a stall was terrifying. Her gut reaction was to turn upward by pulling back on the stick, but that only made the problem worse. She had to instinctively respond in the exact opposite way. To climb out of a stall, she needed to head down into it and use gravity for regaining air flow over her wings. Because her ailerons were nonresponsive, she also had to learn how to use the rudder. Once she got all this down, stall recovery became her favorite activity. Irrespective of how a stall was brought on, she loved that confident feeling she got from facing downward into her fear.

Three weeks into her flying lessons, Butch shifted her toward learning how to land the plane. He had routinely talked her through their daily landings, so she knew the five stages to keep in mind – the approach, the glide in, the flare, the touchdown, and the de-acceleration to taxi speed. Of these, the glide was initially something of a contradiction to her way of thinking. If she wanted to increase the glide angle such that the plane came down more steeply, then she had to point the plane's nose up a bit. Conversely, if she wanted to come down more gradually, then she had to point the nose down a bit. This finally made sense when she came to accept that the concepts of up and down were far less important than understanding how the orientation of her plane influenced the angle at which the air hit her wings.

She picked up on the other aspects of landing from the beginning, especially that the controlled flare of her wings using the flaps had a lot to do with mushing. But she was still struggling with adopting a proper approach vector, so Butch dedicated a special session to just that. Heading out to the Fairchild for that lesson, he stopped her on the ramp well short of the airplane.

"Before we do the walkaround, I want you to tell me what a landing is. Just put it in your own words. None of those aviation terms we've been using."

"Alright… umm… well, every flight has to go from up there to down here… and from fast to slow… to a full stop on the ground… all in a controlled manner. I think that's the important thing… controlling a plane while it gradually loses its ability to fly. I assume that's why you had me doing all of that mushing… right?"

"Correct. You've done well at including the flaps and rudder with two skills you're good at – gliding and mushing. But we still need to work on your approach. You're not quite lining yourself up right, and everything depends on that being done properly. Now bear with me for a moment… I have an analogy that most students don't care for. In my thinking, every flight is like a lifetime. The takeoff is being born, the flying part – heading to a destination and managing all the maneuvers along the way – that's like day-to-day living. So then the end of the flight… the landing… it's sort of like… facing death. After all, no flight can go on forever… the plane's gotta land no matter how much you're enjoying piloting it. Most students are down-right afraid of the landing just like they're afraid of…"

"Not me!"

"I'm not saying that you are… but allow me to continue. Just as most folks don't plan well for the end of their lives, most student pilots don't tend to plan well for their landings. You have to set yourself up well ahead of the runway. As I've mentioned before, all sorts of things come into play on the approach – retrimming, adjusting the fuel mixture, the visibility, the weather conditions, cross winds, familiarity with your surroundings... and even the possibility that someone's gotten out ahead of you when they shouldn't have. You have to be mindful of all those things, but it's most important to have your vector set properly."

At twenty five years of age with her whole life before her, nothing of what he was saying analogy-wise should be affecting her. But she had spent so much time over the past months thinking about how Gwen had died. She also had the memory of holding George in her arms minutes after his death, and could still vaguely recall having been so near to her own parents. Then there was Ruby, who was not doing well. She did not need some stupid illustration from an instructor to be reminded that some flights do not end well.

She was startled by a hand to her shoulder.

"Marna? You okay? Hey... I'm sorry. That was insensitive of me."

"What?! Oh... think nothing of it. I was just trying to... you know... visualize in my mind what you were saying. So... umm... perspective in landing... what's that mean?"

He was still eying her with more sympathy than she cared for, so she smiled and turned casually toward the Fairchild as if he should already be back to teaching.

"Well... for you, as a student... it's all about learning how to assume the proper approach angle and speed based on the conditions. This is where the pilot's perspective of the horizon comes into play. Assuming you continue on to IFR..."

"What's that?"

"Instrument Flight Rules. Just as the name implies, you're rated to fly by instruments under most meteorological conditions. But it doesn't matter for what I'm trying to tell you. In either case... by the actual one you see out your cockpit window or by the artificial one on your instrument panel... the horizon is the pilot's reference point for landing."

He backed a few steps away from the plane, so she followed.

"Let's have a little demonstration of what I'm saying. Here on the ground, we see the earth as flat... especially in West Texas... and the sky as concave... sort of like a great big blue dome overhead. Now... I want you to pick out a cloud... any cloud'll do. Just don't point it out to me. I'm going to figure out which one based solely on what you tell me."

It was one of those wispy mornings in late summer. The sky was scattered about with so many raggedy swirls chaotically being reshaped by mid-altitude winds not apparent from the ground. She turned about in a full circle before settling on one morphing out of a duck-like appearance.

"Okay, I got it. It's just north of east… not quite halfway up."

"Give it to me in degrees. Remember your high school geometry."

"I'd say it's about thirty degrees up from the horizon."

In an instant, she knew exactly what he was trying to teach her… and by the smile on his face, he knew that she understood.

"See what you did? Even without thinking about it, you used the horizon as your reference point. You could've said something like… 'it's just to the left of the one that looks like Mickey Mouse.' But you didn't because clouds move and change shape… and what you think you see up there is not what someone else sees. So you instinctively used the very thing that's always there in the same place. No matter where you are in this world, the horizon's there as an immense circle about you, orienting you with the aid of a compass and simple geometric perspective. Let's do the walkaround… and then we'll continue this conversation up there. You'll soon see what all this has to do with landing."

She turned back toward the Fairchild with her flight bag slung over a shoulder when he unexpectedly stuck out an arm.

"Hold it a sec. Forgot one thing."

He stooped down to point at the Fairchild's silhouette, so she stooped down beside him too.

"What angle would you say the plane's making right now relative to the ramp?"

"I don't know… a bit less than fifteen degrees?"

"Pretty good guess. It's actually very close to twelve. When you set the plane down on the runway for a three-point landing, that's the ideal angle you're flaring out at. We'll get back to that in a minute."

He had her do the walkaround and preflight checklist as usual. She then did the takeoff and climbed to a suitable cruising altitude before he picked up the horizon lesson from where he had left off.

"So… look out the cockpit. Tell me what you see."

"Sky… clouds… things on the ground."

"What's the sky look like to you?"

"I don't know… just blue with lots of gray and white puffs all about."

"Does it have the same feel as when we were down there?"

Then it hit her. Being immersed in it, the sky did not seem so dome-like anymore. It was just the thing that they, as fish of the air, were swimming in.

"It's… sort of flat. Very thick… but flat. That's so odd."

"You ain't seen nothing yet. Pick out a distinctive landmark on the ground… something I can see from my seat. Then tell me where it is… just like you did down on the ramp with that cloud."

Now he was asking too much. West Texas possessed such boring terrain. After searching about, she finally located what might be the small town of Abernathy on the highway to Amarillo. She banked the plane slightly so as to give him a better view of it.

"At your eight… about thirty degrees down from… Hey! That's incredible! I get it! The horizon's my reference point in both directions – up into the sky and down to the earth! That's so cool!"

She was so excited that she could not keep herself from bouncing about in her seat, even though snuggly strapped in. But she stopped on becoming aware of his laughter in her headset.

"Excellent, Marna. I'll make a pilot out of you yet. Now bring her around on a heading back to the airport. We're going to do a couple fly-bys… and use the horizon to practice you're approach. I'll do the first one… then I'll have you takeover."

As she swept the plane through a near one eighty bank, she began picking out landmarks at random – a particularly large crop circle, a bend in a county road, and a cluster of buildings marking yet another isolated West Texas farm. For each, she estimated to herself the declination angle from the horizon. In doing this over and over, she was gradually struck by a rather odd sensation. In moving her eyes up to the horizon and then back down to something on the ground, she had the weird impression that the earth was not so flat after all… and not like it was curved as the surface of a globe. It was probably just an optical illusion, but to her, it seemed as if the distant terrain slanted *upward* to the horizon… almost as if the ground below her was an immense greenish-brown depression, arching upward to the rim of the world.

So weird! Down there – flat earth and a dome of a sky. Up here – flat sky and… the earth's like a great big bowl! Only the horizon's unchanged!

She had to put the earth-bowl quirk out of her mind as Butch was telling her to observe how he was lining up the plane for an approach to the airport. Since he had planted the seed in her mind, she could not help but notice that his approach angle to the runway never altered relative to the horizon. Everything else about them… the city itself and the features they were passing over… it all changed in perspective to the horizon dead ahead. But not the runway. It stayed the same. Steadily, the plane moved closer to it at that set angle.

Butch had her call for a fly-by, and then made her circle around to repeat what he had just done. Her descent angle was not as steady as his, but she was pleased with herself on pulling up into another fly-by. She was finally getting it. He had her repeat the same thing three more times before telling her to land the plane. Only after they were on the ground with the post-flight walkaround completed did he stop to point out the angle of how the plane sat on the ramp.

"As it turns out, that's the angle for the ideal approach vector. That wasn't engineered into the design at random. That's how the maker of the wings wanted a three-point landing to be done. And that's more-or-less the angle you've been mushing at. It's close to the stall angle of the wing. Tilt the nose up a bit and the wing stalls. Tilt the nose down a bit and you're at the ideal cruising position. Down even farther and you start to climb. Getting a feel for the wing's orientation relative to the air flow – that's what's called the angle of attack… and it's the core of flying. Flight's not about zooming around in the air. It's all about being in such control of yourself that you can effortlessly hang right on the verge, comfortable with the plane tipping over in either direction. To soar or to stall."

I absolutely adore flying! I want to be doing it for the rest of my life! I so want to be a creature of the sky! I want to be just like the birds in the relief, free to glide upon my own wind. I don't want to be a creature of the earth anymore. Not like those pitiful faces. I'll leave the earth below and break away into the wide open sky!

I just wish I felt better…

Standing over the egg that she had just cracked into a skillet, she was overcome by the sight of the yellow blob, slipping around there in a transparent glop slowly sizzling into white. The setting was on low, but she could clearly pick up on the smell of burnt egg. Roy would just have to make his own breakfast.

She slid the pan to the back and turned off the eye. Nothing had settled her unease… and nothing she tried was settling her insides either. Not antacids, not making herself rest, and definitely not more pep talks from Roy. This was so unlike her. Why was she so worked up about this solo? Her training had her ready, but her nerves had not. She hated having to cancel that lesson yesterday for a doctor's appointment, but Roy had insisted. They only did some tests… blood work and the like… but in the end, the doctor just recommended blander foods and more antacids. What a waste of time!

Learning to fly was supposed to be thrilling… not this plague of anxieties she had been experiencing over the last few days. Ever since Butch mentioned that the solo was the most critical obstacle a student would face on the way to becoming a pilot, she could not keep herself from fretting. She was absolutely terrified of screwing it up.

There Roy sat munching on his toast while recommending that she eat a slice herself. The sight of that dried-up sliver of brown roof tiling coated over with yellow grease just nauseated her.

"No thanks! Food makes me gag. I can't even take a sip of coffee without it churning up my stomach. Roy... I'm so worried! What if I mess up? It'll be absolutely humiliating after all that talk about me being a natural!"

"Marna... you're getting yourself worked up for nothing. I'm sure you'll do just fine."

"That's easy for you to say. You're not the one going up in a plane all by yourself."

"You know... maybe I should come over after all. You probably could use the encouragement..."

"Please don't! I'll be even more nervous knowing that you're on the ramp with Butch watching me flub up."

"That's not going to happen and you know it. Listen... I should get going. Just promise that you'll call me as soon as you're done. I wanna rush over for that... that shirt cutting thing."

He made to kiss her on the lips, but she dipped her chin so that it came to her forehead instead. This was so unlike her. She had always been ready to conquer the world. Confident about everything! But right now, at the most critical moment for any student pilot, all she wanted to do was curl up in a ball with her face in a bucket. That, more than anything, warned her that she might not be as ready to solo as she had hoped to be.

She heard Roy call out goodbye... and then the front door closing... but she stayed put at the kitchen table. Perhaps reviewing her notes will distract her mind from her stomach. After fifteen minutes of unsuccessfully working at it, she was interrupted by the kitchen phone.

"Hello. Marna Meitner speaking."

"Mrs. Meitner. This is Alice from Dr. Crammer's office. How're you feeling today?"

"Still really queasy. I don't get it. I'm taking those antacids Dr. Crammer recommended, but they're not making a dent in my indigestion."

"Well... that's why I'm calling. I have your test results. Are you sitting down?" *Oh no! It's an ulcer – I'm sure of it!* "They came back positive. Congratulations, Mrs. Meitner – your pregnant!"

"Say what?!"

"That's why you've been experiencing so much nausea. You're going to have a baby! Isn't that exciting?! Now... doctor wants to see you in three weeks for a follow-up. How does the fifteenth look?"

In a daze, she made a note on the calendar at that date and concluded the call. But her eyes remained locked on what she had just written. The crooked numbers of her own handwriting made no sense. Just chicken sprawled hieroglyphs.

I'm pregnant? This can't be. They've made a mistake.

Yet her body told her otherwise. She knew it to be true as if she had run the test herself. She was pregnant. The next thing that came to her lay much heavier upon her insides than whatever was going on with her gut. She should be excited, as the nurse proclaimed. She was going to be a mother. But right now, all she felt was denial… and anger.

For the rest of the morning… right up until the point in which she was at the airport with Butch getting a pre-flight briefing… she struggled with thoughts over how things were about to change. She had discovered the joy of flight, only to face giving it up too soon. She pushed that conclusion out of her mind to concentrate on getting ready for her solo. Butch wanted her to do the takeoff into pattern work. After three laps and a landing to each, then she would be done with her first solo. Through his last minute instructions, she tried hard to give him her full attention, but instead found herself fighting off uncertainties about her future.

"Remember – right rudder on takeoff. And don't forget to re-trim the tabs. I'm a hundred and ninety, so without me, that'll shift the CG toward the front. Now once you're up, pay close attention to all radio calls… even if they're not about you. Keep your spacing from other aircraft. For your landings, don't forget to use power to adjust your descent rate and remember your feet! Make sure to work that rudder to keep your sight picture aligned along the runway. If for any reason you don't feel comfortable on a landing, then just ask for a go-round, got it?"

"Got it."

"Ground and the tower already know it's your first solo, but still make sure they're aware of any touch-and-gos, okay?"

"Okay."

Heading out to the ramp alone, her stomach was doing barrel rolls all the way up her throat. At least she now knew that her nausea had nothing to do with nervousness about flying. She was ready for this… even if her stomach was not. She went through the walkaround, checking off the steps to herself. Yet part of her was repeatedly straying elsewhere.

I can't believe I'm going to have a baby on my hands. How am I going to tell Roy? I wonder how long I'll be able to keep flying? Am I even ready for this?

The questions went on competing with aileron, strut, and pitot tube. Checking the fuel level, she got a whiff of avgas and nearly lost her cookies. Out of nowhere came a hand to her shoulder, startling her into a small taste of bile.

"Marna?"

"Butch! You scared the life out of me! I thought you were going to hang back."

"Sorry. Are you… feeling okay? You look a bit off-color."

"I'm fine… just nervous."

"There's nothing to worry about. Concentrate on your training and you'll do well. Three go-rounds and then I'll meet you here on the ramp, okay?"

He patted her on the back again and moved out in front of the plane. She climbed in, did the usual pre-flight checks, and then looked up past the nose. He was still there, anticipating her call for clearance. She then gave him a thumbs-up that all was well.

But it's not…

She waited for him to move off the ramp before starting the engine.

"Ground… this is Fairchild seven–three–four–golf–x-ray on ramp requesting taxi clearance for closed traffic."

She waited through the crackle for a response from the ground controller.

"Fairchild seven–three–four–golf–x-ray… base seven thousand… winds two one five at five… gusts one zero. Proceed to hold at runway one seven left via hotel."

"Roger that. Proceeding to hold at runway one seven left via hotel."

With slight left rudder pressure, she slowly eased the throttle forward and the plane crept out onto the taxiway. Without understanding why, she suddenly realized that the queasy feeling inside had left her… or maybe it was being masked by adrenaline. On reaching the hold position, she went through her checklist before turning to her radio again.

"Tower… Fairchild seven–three–four–golf–x-ray holding at one seven left… ready for takeoff."

The response came back immediately… much sooner than she had been prepared for.

"Fairchild seven–three–four–golf–x-ray… you're a go for takeoff on one seven left. Make for left closed traffic."

"Roger. Taking-off for left closed traffic on one seven left."

For the next fifteen minutes or so, she took the Fairchild through three counterclockwise square five mile patterns out toward the east. Each was finished with a tower-approved landing and another takeoff. She handled all of this as if Butch was seated behind her… except perhaps that her grip on the stick was especially firm. On completion of the third lap, she requested and received clearance for the final landing. Wheels touched down, and she right off called for taxiing instructions. What she received back was congratulations from ground control for a solo done well. Very touched that someone out there had thought of her, she relaxed for the first time in weeks. She had done it. She proceeded back as instructed, shut down the engine, and went into her post-flight routine… aware that Butch was waving excitedly at her from the hangar. She waved back and returned to her list.

Break set… check.
Flaps up… check.
Ignition off… check.
Fuel mixture to full lean… check.
Oil dilution… check.
Lights off… check.
Master switch off… check.
Engage control lock.

As soon as the last item was completed, her insides once more became balled-up. The queasiness was back.

Uhh… I feel sick. How could this happen?! We were being so careful.

And then the memory came to her of them reclining together in a lawn chair chaise just off the back porch one evening a week or so before her birthday. She had been fretting over something stupid… something about not knowing what to do with herself. He was being so sweet… assuring her that there was nothing in this world she could not handle… and he would always be there to help her. And there he was beside her looking so sexy in his tight white t-shirt.

Okay… it's my fault. I'm the one who attacked him. It just sort of… happened.

All their careful planning ruined in one impulsive moment of passion. She dropped her chin to her chest in resignation… and then realized what she was wearing – her sky blue satin top.

Shit! I forgot to change before takeoff!

She had left Roy's t-shirt in her flight bag. Now she would be destroying one of her favorite blouses by cutting its back off and stapling it to the wall of the Carlyle Flight School.

Just great!

She detached the harness straps and climbed out of the Fairchild, sliding the canopy back into place. She had just hopped off the wing when Butch ambushed her, shaking her hand with such vigor that she once more was aware of her stomach. Somehow, his enthusiasm woke her up to a feeling of pride at her accomplishment… both of them. She had soloed… and she was going to have a baby!

How stupid of me?! This is such fantastic news! I can't wait to tell Roy!

Butch offered to take over the post-flight walkaround, but she reminded him that it was her job to do. She hugged him instead… and sent him sheepishly retreating back to the hangar. In finishing up, she decided to get through the shirt tail ceremony first before sharing her news with Roy. Into the breakroom, she received more congratulations from Butch as well as from the other instructors and students lounging about. While making her call to Roy, she overheard Butch telling someone that she was the school's first female to solo.

And the first pregnant one too. Weird… I remember being here as a little girl and thinking that flight was only for boys.

Soon, Roy was there hugging her and beaming with so much pride. Everyone was laughing and whooping it up as the back of her blouse got lopped off by Butch. Her eyes were on Roy… who rushed over to cover her up with the t-shirt she should have been wearing… and then to the look on Butch's face. He was on the verge of cardiac embarrassment at having unexpectedly uncovered a bra strap running across her back. He quickly handed over the shard of her blouse and turned away. She then stapled it to the wall and briefly scanned the neighboring displays for pointers before stepping up to hers with a black marker.

Marna Meitner

Solo

Sept. 4, 1970

Fairchild PT-29

N734GX

CFI Butch Carlyle

Opting for a front-on view, the cartoon airplane she drew beneath came out close enough to what she was shooting for.

"Hey, Marna… that's really terrible artwork! Your wings are bent… and you should certainly know by now that the Fairchild's got a two–bladed prop!"

She ignored Butch's critique, as her eyes were on Roy. She could not say what it was that she saw on his face. He just smiled and turned away too soon, for surely he had recognized that she drew a Corsair. Grabbing him by an elbow, she spun him about for a kiss in front of everyone… and then made him pose for a Polaroid with her before the shirt tail. The gathering broke up, and as there were still things needing her attention before leaving, she took hold of his arm once more and whispered into his ear.

"I'm walking you out… I have a surprise for you."

She waited until they were beside his truck before putting her arms about

528

his shoulders and pulling him in close. Putting on her most sincere smile, she kissed him gently on the lips before speaking.

"I got a call this morning from the doctor's office…" She paused to build his anticipation, but did not delay too long so as to cause him worry. "You're going to be a father."

"You're… pregnant?"

He stood there in her arms for several seconds as the words sunk in… and then he suddenly swooped her into the air, twirling her about as if she was a propeller blade. After a few go-rounds, he set her down gingerly with such an alarmed look on his face.

"Calm down, Papa. You didn't hurt it. The thing's probably not yet as big as a pea in a pod. But I do feel like throwing up… so no more spinning.

"This is… this is fantastic! This is really great! Oh, I'm so proud of you! I can't believe this – I'm going to be a dad! Let's celebrate! No, let's put that on hold until tomorrow – you need your rest. Do you… ahh… think it's safe to go on flying?"

"Listen… I need to get back inside for my post-flight debrief with Butch before he has to takeoff with another student. I'm sure he'll know the regs regarding pregnant pilots… so don't worry."

He kissed her goodbye, and then before climbing into his truck, sweetly patted her where a baby would soon be showing.

As it turned out, Butch Carlyle knew as much about FAA guidelines on pregnant pilots as she did… which was nothing. His ignorance did not prevent him from showing her the same kind of excitement that Roy had. He shook her hand over and over… and then made her sit on the softest of the breakroom couches as they discussed what it would take to finish out her private pilot's license. All the while, he kept offering reassurances as to her unborn child.

"Don't worry… we'll keep things simple… and safe. Learning to fly's great, Marna… but it's hardly comparable to the thrill of starting a family."

Maybe it was a coincidence, but her nausea got especially bad at that moment. She might have a fragment of her accomplishment stapled to the wall for future students to see, but that was not what Butch was most excited about. She too was happy about the new life growing in her… even though it was sure to keep her below the horizon, confined within this bowl of an earth.

CHAPTER
34

COTTON FIELDS FOREVER

That evening, Roy sat her down in the nook while he took on the responsibilities of dinner. Throughout the meal, he peppered her with questions about how she was feeling, what the doctor's office had said about the due date, and what to expect from her first checkup. She gave answers to each while fiddling with bits of the flank steak he had prepared. The feel of it in her mouth was altogether like salted tree bark. After doing the dishes, he made a show out of following her about the house, clearing a pathway for her by rushing ahead to scoot away a chair or pick up some fallen item. Not the least bit interested in TV, he instead led her by the arm out to the front porch and got right down to the business of them deciding which room should be converted into a nursery. With that topic exhausted, he turned to the issue of Gwen's old car, which he insisted was not suitable for an expecting mother. He would begin a search for something with a better safety record. Sitting side-by-side in rocking chairs, he took a sunset's worth of the evening to throw out baby names, switching back-and-forth between boy and girl with ease.

Through it all, she waited for him to say something about her solo, being determined not to bring up the subject. She told herself repeatedly that this was not a test. She simply wanted to know for certain that he was thrilled about *all* of the things that she was thrilled about. But as the remaining hours of the evening waned away and she found herself before the bathroom mirror preparing for bed, she could not hold off her frustrations any longer.

"Roy, you've not said a word about my solo. Aren't you even excited for me?"

"Of course I am. It's a major accomplishment. I'm proud of you."

She waited, but nothing more came.

"That's it... you're proud of me?! You do realize that the solo's only the first step toward me becoming the pilot I want to be. It's not a license. There's still loads more required of me. I haven't even filed my first flight plan yet... much less built up the hours I need. I've got cross countries to do... and a night flight... all before my FAA exam. And that's just for the private pilot's license. After that, there's an instrument rating... and then a commercial license... and multiengine..."

"Hold it a sec. You're not seriously considering doing all of that, are you? I mean... I know you've talked about nothing other than flying for the past month, but now... you're going to have a baby. Marna... you're going to be a mother! Moms don't do risky stuff like that. They stay home and take care of their kids while their..."

He suddenly clamped his mouth shut and turned away.

"Go on. While their what do what?"

"You know... while their husbands... provide."

Very close to outrage, a different sort of thing came over her first... from where, she could not say.

"Husband, are you with me or not?"

She waited, trying to make out something from his blank stare. She finally picked up on the first trace of a softening in his jawline.

"I could ask the same of you... but I already know the answer. I'm sorry, Marna... I'm not doubting you. It's just... Tell me straight up... are you absolutely sure that this is what you want... to continue with flying while balancing being mother and wife?"

"Yes... absolutely! And daughter-in-law too. It's what I want to do more than anything I've ever wanted... all of it. And I want you to have the things you want too. I want the store to succeed, and for you to have a family you can be proud of. Believe me... I'm just as committed to all of that because I'm committed to us."

"Then, Marna... I don't know how we'll manage it... but I'm with you."

She went to bed that night feeling better about becoming mother and pilot. How those two together would be done, she could not say, but Roy was holding her close... and that was all that mattered.

She performed another solo the next day, concentrating on refining her landings. Owing to high winds and intermittent rains, she saw fewer opportunities for flight during the next week. Which was all well enough as the churning in her stomach was keeping her up at night and greeting her first thing in the morning. She was in an all-round irritable mood, angry at the weather, angry at herself for her slow progress, and angry at everyone around her who could carry on life unhampered by nausea. It was equally irritating how both Roy and Butch fawned all over her every move.

Gah! What's it going to be like when I'm actually showing?!

The weather improved in the next week… and seemingly in sync with clear skies and gentle winds came a change in how she felt. Her nausea lessened and then disappeared altogether. In its place came a ravenous hunger to consume anything not nailed down. The next stage of her training would require longer periods in the air away from a snack machine, so she made sure her flight bag was packed each morning. Instead of Alka-Seltzer and Pepto packets, she loaded it with as much food as she could discretely carry with her on a flight.

Her first cross country would be with Butch, and then she would repeat the same trip solo two days later. After a minor revision, she filed her first flight plan, it being to the Ector County airport in Odessa. The two of them took off in the early morning. The entire flight was spent in knowing exactly what she was doing, having Butch there more as a mentor than an instructor.

She landed in Odessa smooth enough, and with the post-flight walkaround done, made directly for the pilot's lounge of the fixed-based operator where the Fairchild was being refueled… to use the bathroom and to raid the vending machines. Then, with Butch at her side, she enjoyed the unexpected pleasure of chumming it up at that FBO's dispatch counter with two other pilots, both older gentlemen with military flight experience. She was delighted that they treated her as an equal in the conversation, and even gave her some advice on how to make a career out of aviation. In finally heading back onto the ramp with their plane ready, she was bubbling over from the comradery of being with fellow pilots.

"I know we Texans are friendly… but those guys were especially nice."

"I think you'll find that most pilots are fairly affable… except for the corporate types. Bigheads."

He gave her an odd look before turning away.

"What?"

"It's nothing. Just… you're also sure to run into some who don't take kindly to the idea of women pilots… present company excluded."

"I've figured that out already, seeing as you took me on as a student. But honestly, Butch, don't sweat it. It's no different than what I've experienced in working at a TV station. I'm pretty used to it by now. Some simply don't accept that a woman can do whatever a man can."

They did the walkaround and took off. Because she was still in a jovial mood, she sought for some of that lighthearted pilot camaraderie she had experienced in the FBO. But every topic she could think of involved her, the student, speaking to him, the instructor. She noticed an oddity below and quickly latched onto it.

"Butch… crazy looking A-frame at my two. Can you make it out over the wing? Orange and white stripes on its roof. Second one I've spotted since takeoff."

"Probably a Whataburger."

"What-a-what?"

"*What-a-burger*. A hamburger chain."

She took the plane through a gradual bank to the north before picking up the subject again.

"Any good?"

"Is what any good?"

"The whataburgers, of course."

"Heck if I know. Never had one."

Her headset went silent for a moment before his voice came back with a chuckle.

"You hungry again?"

"Maybe."

They both had a good laugh, though she reflexively slid her left arm down… just to make sure that her flight bag with its stash of snacks was within reach.

"A guy named Dobson started it back in the 50's. I think the first one was in Corpus Christi. Quite the thing down there. Not sure Lubbock's got one yet. Interesting thing about Dobson… he was a pilot. Absolutely crazy about planes."

"Who's not?"

She added a smile in the mirror for him.

"Roger that. You know… I read somewhere that the stripes were so he could spot his restaurants from the air. Sad thing is… the guy died a few years back when his Cessna went down on takeoff."

Butch went quiet, only coming back after she had cleared Midland's airspace.

"Don't know why I told you that."

Hearing that some hamburger tycoon had died in an aviation accident no more affected her flying than if she, as a driver, had learned that the man had been killed in an automobile crash.

"Doesn't bother me. Just makes me want to be a better pilot."

"Roger that."

Unfortunately, Butch spoke from there on only of things that an instructor might. The carefree pilot-to-pilot feel of the FBO was gone, and she was pretty certain that this change in him had to do with her being pregnant.

After he finished with a reminder about her heading, she flipped up her headset's microphone. Reaching down to her flight bag, she began munching on popcorn... one piece at a time. In not too many months, she would be giving birth. It was probably time for her to start thinking about her obligation to this new life. Unbidden, her thoughts went to her parents having died in a car crash. That event had left her as an orphan. She knew that they had not abandoned her, but sometimes it felt like that. She could not bear the thought that her own child might one day end up that way too. If she continued with flying, was there a possibility that she might follow in the same tragic path as this pilot named Dobson? It could happen. An accident could leave her child motherless. The stick felt harder in her hand, and each gauge on the instrument panel became a warning. She needed to take her responsibilities as mother and pilot very seriously.

On completing the cross country and tying down the plane as part of the post-flight walkaround, she glanced up to notice that Butch was lingering at the hangar door. He seemed to be waiting for her.

"Did I miss something?"

"No, you're fine. I just wanted to speak with you privately before going inside. Are you in a hurry to get the post-flight briefing done?"

"Not particularly."

"Good. I was hoping I could... apologize for something."

"If it's about Dobson's crash, then don't bother. I'm tougher than..."

"It's not that. It's something that I should have mentioned when you first started with me. You know how I said that some pilots don't take kindly to women flying? Well... that used to be me. Not recently. I've grown up as I've grown older. But I think you know what I'm talking about."

Actually, she had no idea what he was referring to and told him so.

"You're aunt... she never mentioned me? Never said anything about what happened between the two of us?"

All kinds of things were suddenly ping-ponging in her head, and all of them pertained to an aunt who had closed off her life.

"No... she never mentioned you."

"That's odd. Maybe we should go in after all."

She followed him to his private office where they sometimes did their post-flight debriefs. They sat, and he began fidgeting with the strap on his flight bag before finally bringing himself to speak.

"I'm not sure how to put this… but I took a job away from your aunt, and she never forgave me for it. Did you know that?"

"No. Never heard anything about it from her."

"You have to understand, Marna… the war was coming to a close and lots of men were being discharged back stateside. Jobs were scarce, especially for pilots. And that's all I knew how to do. I wasn't able to find anything for months after returning to Houston… and then I received a call from George… you're father-in-law. I'd come to know him during the war. We were both Texans, so we kept up with each other. He let me know about a position flying civilian cargo out of the airbase here. Said he was good friends with the owner and could guarantee the job to me if I wanted it. So… I snatched it up. Here's the thing… I took that position away from a woman."

"My aunt?"

"Marna… I felt terrible about it… less so when it happened, seeing as I had a wife and child to support. But I'll never forget walking into a flower shop one day with my Sally… and there was your aunt. I tried to apologize to her… but it was too late. One of the most embarrassing moments I've ever had before my wife. She was… real disappointed with me."

For the first time, Butch looked up from the strap of his flight bag to meet her eyes.

"You might not know this, but your aunt and George's brother-in-law were engaged."

"Yeah, I know… but let's not talk about that, okay?"

"Sure. Are you disappointed with me too?"

"No. Just sad… and not because of you and my aunt."

"I understand. You know… I was tickled pink when George Meitner's son came in to sign his wife up for flying lessons. But then I got the shock of my life when he wrote down your full name on the application. I knew right off that you were Gwen's niece. You… ahh… probably don't remember the first time we met."

"I do… but only vaguely. I was just ten. It was at Roy's birthday party."

She had been thinking about that day on and off ever since taking up flying, but not once had her thoughts progressed toward her aunt's reaction after that party. Maybe Butch was the reason why Gwen had lost it. As with so many things over the past few months, her ability to capture the real Gwen Forde had become jumbled up in her childhood memories.

"Well… I remember you like it was yesterday. Marna… I've done loads of discovery flights, but I never met a kid like you. Somehow, I just knew you'd make for a great pilot one day. Since you only mentioned your first name, I asked George about your last after the party was over. That's when I discovered who you were."

She had nothing to say other than to express her appreciation for him giving her lessons, and then shift the conversation toward the post-flight briefing. She had gone her whole life without knowing much about Gwen's past, whereas what she had learned over the last few months only left her confused and conflicted. On leaving the Carlyle Flight School, she had a strong yearning to rush home. On a shelf in the cellar were boxes from her old house. One box in particular had letters that might shed light on the mystery of Gwen Forde. Just as with her aunt, she too had experienced the marvel of flight… and just as with her aunt, circumstances might be forcing her to give it up. Perhaps those letters provided a hint of what was in store for her.

But having a baby… that's a really big thing! That should be more than sufficient for dealing with my disappointment about not flying. You know… I wonder if Gwen felt that way about starting a flower shop.

From her very first days in Lubbock onward, Gwen had always seemed sad to her. Likely, her aunt's feelings for flying had been much stronger than her own.

She quickly went through the math in her head.

I was born a few days before the end of the war, so when I showed up, it had only been eight years since she quit flying. That's really not that long of a time. Eight years ago, I was a junior in high school itching to get out of Lubbock… and already resenting Gwen for how hard she worked me.

Partly because of that unpleasant feeling and partly because she just remembered that Gwen had lost a fiancé at about the same time, she headed for the Loop rather than for home. She would visit Ruby as she normally did… and not because her mother-in-law could provide insight into her own brother's engagement to Gwen. She would sooner see herself rooting about in a darken cellar for a bunch of musty old letters before she would be so cruel as to dredge up that sad subject… irrespective of whether the woman's mind was capable of revealing its secrets. No… she simply longed to hold Ruby's hand, and perhaps cry in her place over the loss of a brother so long ago.

She arrived at the nursing home, came in through a side door, and entered the familiar room. The nursing staff had Ruby in her easy chair by the window where the autumn's rays could warm her. She pulled a chair alongside and took her mother-in-law's hand. As usual, it was cold, bony, and lifeless in response to being touched.

"Hello, Ruby. I hope you're feeling good today."

Her eyes ventured over to a partially-eaten meal in a tray on the over-bed table.

"You had cornbread for dinner! I bet that was good. I remember how you used to love making that."

She gently ran her other hand along Ruby's arm.

"I see someone with fashion sense dressed you this morning. I love this blouse. It brings out the color in your cheeks. Hey… what do you think of this blazer I picked up the other day? I know… a bit flashy for flying, but I simply had to show it off. You won't believe the deal I got on it – fifty percent off!"

She paused in her heart's ache for Ruby. As mother and daughter, they could have had so much fun shopping together.

"Ruby… I want to tell you about my flight today. It was absolutely incredible! We flew to Odessa… me and Mr. Carlyle… and I'm going to get to do the same thing all by myself on Thursday. Don't worry – I'm being careful! I wouldn't do anything to endanger your grandchild. I just can't wait for you to meet her… or him. It won't be much longer now… just five months. You can hold off that long… can't you?"

Without knowing how it had gotten there, she found that her hand had shifted to her own midsection. Bringing it back to Ruby's arm, she gave her a little squeeze before continuing.

"I want to promise you something. I'm going to do my best to be a good mother to this child. You know how I love flying… I've droned on and on to you about it so many times… but I'm going to love being a mother too. And your Roy's going to be the best dad that ever was! If you can believe it, even better than your George… who you know was a fantastic father… especially to me."

How terrible it must have been for you on the day he died! Much worse than when you learned about your big brother.

Not wanting to remove either of her hands from Ruby, she lifted a shoulder to wipe each eye in turn before nodding out the window toward the sky.

"Like I was saying… I want to tell you about something I saw while flying today. You know we've hardly had a speck of sunshine all week, but the sky finally broke up a bit so I could get some time in. I have to stay out of the clouds… you know that. I'm not anywhere close to having an instrument rating. Anyway… I'm flying along with this sheet of gray above me, and then all of a sudden, these rays come bursting through gaps in the clouds to shine right down upon the ground. They were like… huge celestial spotlights. Ruby, I'm sure you've seen this before. They were so crystal clear… the rays, I mean…

streaking through the sky like pillars of light. It seemed as if the heavens were being held up on shiny stilts. But even more cool was how the ground got all polka-dotted wherever the beams fell. It was so amazing that I had to throttle back on my airspeed just to take it all in. And you know it's gotta be something special if I decide to go slow!"

She rubbed her mother-in-law's hand playfully for a few seconds before continuing, wishing very much that Ruby could respond back.

"So these spots… they weren't holding still in one place. They were moving along the surface… mostly because of winds gusting at… but that's not important. What's really amazing is how those spots kept… morphing in shape. Sort of like an amoeba does. I was watching one when it hit me that those rays weren't actually rays at all. They were like… portals. Not falling from the sky but going upward. To me, they were illuminating a pathway into the sky. I know – real twilight zone kind of stuff. I must admit, it was kind of creepy at one point when a gap in the clouds closed up and its spot suddenly went out. Sort of like the sky had taken a huge mouthful out of the earth and was chewing it up. But then another opened nearby to replace it. You know… I felt like those sunbeams were speaking directly to me. From all of that dull purple above came a hint of something… like a promise. 'Soon, Marna… soon all of your dreams will come true.' I… kind of like that I can tell you silly things like that."

She paused to look into her mother-in-law's eyes. Not a hint of recognition was there. No belief or disbelief. Either way, she would have preferred that it mattered to Ruby… although clearly it did not. But even she was unsure about her own dreams.

"Ruby… I'm sorry… I've never really apologized to you for the terrible things I did. I hope you can forgive me. And I just want you to know that I don't hold anything against you. I know that your sickness confused and scared you. I… also hope you know that I love you."

She sat quietly after that, softly caressing Ruby's hand and looking out into the sky.

Back home and with dinner completed, she and Roy went to the rocking chairs on the front porch. She had spent the last hour telling him about her conversation with Butch, but still felt that there were so many things left for her to work through. She would not go to those letters in the cellar for answers. She would try Roy first.

"I don't have the slightest idea how Gwen got started in on flowers after she stopped flying. Did she ever say anything to you about that?"

"Not that I can recall."

"And you never asked?"

"I had other things on my mind."

"Seriously, Husband… that's the kind of thing a wife would want to know!"

He made to retort, so she quickly waved him off in knowing where he was going. She absolutely did not want the subject sidetracked to Chicago.

"What I can't figure out is how they met."

"How who met?"

She could not believe how dense he was being. The who pieces to the puzzle had been sorted out months ago with her account of Gwen's letters. Then again… he probably never really understood the significance of the Corsair to his father.

Men…

"I'm talking about Gwen and Brad… Bradrick Miller… you're uncle… Ruby's brother!"

"Oh… You know I never met him. He died in the war. Shot down, I think. Somewhere in the Pacific. Mom never talked much about him."

This is ridiculous! He's being so painfully slow!

"Roy… why do you think your father bought an airplane he couldn't fly and built a hangar for it miles away from the nearest airfield?"

"I don't know. Because he was crazy?"

"And why do you think your mother let him do it?"

"Honestly… I don't know. She always said that Dad had…"

"It was on account of your uncle."

He sat blank-faced in the growing dusk for several seconds… and then his expression went ghostly white as he jabbed a thumb back over his shoulder toward the hangar.

"That's not the same plane, is it?!"

"Of course not! Don't be ridiculous. It's the same type, but not the one. Don't you get it?! Your dad and your uncle were best friends before the war. Almost like brothers. He told me as much the very first time I laid eyes on that plane. Did you know that Brad introduced your father to your mother?"

"I… I think so."

"This Uncle Brad of yours somehow met Gwen. Like I said, I haven't figure that part out yet. Maybe it had something to do with a mutual love of planes or… Sweetwater."

"Sweetwater?! What's that got to do with anything?"

"Please, Roy, try to keep up! But you know… the timing still doesn't make sense. I'd have thought that your uncle was already in the Pacific. Oh…

I can't believe there's something I've forgotten to tell you, Roy! They were engaged to be married!"

"Who was engaged to be married?"

"Ugh! Aren't you listening?! Your uncle and my aunt were engaged to be married. I found the ring among her things… as well as some letters to the effect. What do you make of that?"

"So you're saying that Gwen came to Lubbock after the war because of my dead uncle?"

"I don't know! Maybe she met him here or maybe she wanted to be close to Ruby… or maybe it was just because of the memory of him. I don't understand any of it! I guess I could read more of Gwen's letters… but I really don't want to. Not yet, anyway. All I really know is that your father and Gwen had a falling out over flying… like I told you during dinner. And that's probably why your mother put so much effort into trying to remain friends with her over the years."

"And the plane? What's that got to do with your aunt?"

"I have no idea other than your uncle died in a Corsair… and maybe that Gwen's always wanted to fly one."

"How do you know that?"

"Something I read in one of her journals. But there's got to be more to it than that. All I know is… I can't ever get rid of that plane until I finally understand it all."

She spent the majority of the next day studying for the flight exam that Butch would be scheduling for her soon. Repeatedly, she resisted the urge to rummage about in the cellar for Gwen's old letters by reminding herself that passing this exam was critical to getting her license. She could not afford distractions. She had her own story to write and was determined that a good part of it would be with her up in the air.

Come Thursday morning, she was back at the Carlyle Fight School for the solo version of the cross country she had accomplished with Butch two days before. After a briefing with Butch and the usual preparations for flight, she was soon in the Fairchild gaining speed down the airport's east-west runway. Climbing over the northern part of the city, she veered the plane southward, remaining attentive to the restrictions about Reese Air Force Base. With that airspace cleared, she made directly for Odessa. Butch had repeatedly warned her that flying in West Texas required vigilance to one's course owing to the scarcity of landmarks on the flat terrain. So she took up a southern heading by keeping 87 off to her nine.

She soon found herself doing something that she did not normally undertake during flights about Lubbock – studying the West Texas farmland. The most obvious features below were the square tracts possessing central pivot irrigation systems. In full or partial circles, those generated a tessellated pattern that struck her as odd… yet not something unfamiliar from her previous flights about Lubbock. These grids of farmland were mostly defined by the county roads crisscrossing this part of the state. She had driven many of these in her work for George's cable company, and knew that the blocks were laid out irregularly owing to how the network of roads got disrupted by towns and highways. She noticed in particular that many half circles were formed because those roads forced farmers to make do with oddly laid-out cultivation. Yet something else was contributing to the overall feel of disorder.

As with a thing hidden in plain sight, it took her several minutes to put her finger on the source. Most of the irrigation systems ran in full circles, but not all of them were of the same size and not all had vegetation of the same color. For reasons she could only guess at, some circles were green in partial arcs… half way or sometimes only in a small wedge. The remainder of such circles were in a dull brown from not being irrigated. The spectrum of lushness, along with the haphazard presence of partial circles, gave off that feel of randomness to the countryside.

Periodically, she came up to her instrument panel in verifying her flight conditions, but always went back down to reconsidered the landscape. She knew that the overall pattern was a collective reflection of the vitality to West Texas agriculture. What was green was doing well, and what was brown was otherwise. The barren circles and arcs were nothing more than economization – a thoughtful assessment on the part of some farmer as to how much should be cultivated and how much should be left farrow.

You know… it's not possible for every circle to reach its full potential since there's just not enough water in West Texas. I guess unforeseen circumstances can also come into play.

Maybe there was a financial shortfall limiting the amount that could be planted, maybe a critical piece of equipment had failed, or maybe a farmer had experienced a debilitating injury that kept him out of the field.

Suddenly, what she saw in the farmland below came to her in a wholly different and unexpected manner. Each square tract of land was the bounds of a farmer's influence – the extent to which his existence contributed to the patchwork of West Texas. Within the boundaries of those squares was the circle of his life. Some lived big and bold, and some barely had space to squeeze their lesser presence in between more prosperous neighbors. Yet irrespective of how large each was laid out, not enough of them ended up being the kind of green that signified a truly fruitful life. Too few of them went full circle to completion, ending up being abruptly terminated with brownness at one quarter, half or three quarters the way around. She ignored the fully green circles to hone in on those incomplete ones, as she searched for some obvious reason why these had not been allowed to finish out the arc of their lives into fullness.

Like Gwen, George and Ruby… and my parents.

All of the space needed was there for a full life, yet why these circles should come up short was beyond her. Even some of the fully green ones were not green enough… as if, for them alone, not enough water had been brought up from the earth or fallen down from the sky. Blessed or cursed, it made no sense to her. She would be hard pressed to find a circle that did not touch another, yet the condition of each circle down there was independent of its neighbors. Each one was painted alone upon this bowl of an earth. From her sky, she could make out where each fell short of fullness. See even better than they could see themselves. But if she were down there, she knew that her own circle would seem so very flat. She had absolutely no idea how far her own life went or how green it would be. Not one of those circles knew. Not one could see the bounds of their own existence well enough to make sense out of their significance to the overall picture on the earth.

She brought her eyes back up to the instruments of her cockpit, to the only things that she had some control over, wishing very much that she had mountains or forests to fly over. Anything that might hide the reality of herself. She was thankful that her life touched that of Roy's… and of the baby she was carrying. But from horizon to horizon, she knew that she was so very alone in this world.

She made the landing and turn-around without a problem. Back on the return leg, the oil rigs of the Odessa-Midland area soon gave way to crop circles, so she kept her eyes on the instrument panel as much as possible. It was midafternoon when she landed back in Lubbock. For the next half hour, she paid close attention to Butch's debrief and a discussion of her upcoming night flights. They would do one together on Tuesday and then he would schedule her night solo for two days later. With near on forty hours of flying under her belt, she would be in an ideal position for taking the written examination. From there, Butch promised a few more weeks of refining and reviewing, building up her flight time to over fifty hours in the process. She would then be ready for the FAA's designated flight examiner.

She left the airport still thinking about crop circles. No way could she allow this ridiculous analogy of a person's life to creep back into her mind while flying. She needed to address that weakness head on as a part of her training by putting all such depressing notions into their proper perspective. For that, she had in mind a little field trip. Something that she expected would substitute the vague imagery of unfulfilled dreams with a concrete, textural bit of reality.

A quarter mile from the airport was an intersection to a county road that she normally passed through. Today, she took a left along the stretch that rimmed a portion of the airfield. A couple hundred yards down this road, she pulled off beside the crop circle that she often flew over in climbing out of a takeoff. Though round in shape, this field was cultivated in linear furrows, as was commonly done for crops watered with central pivot irrigation. It being late September, the cotton plants were dotted in white with the year's second crop. She got out of her car and chose a specific row, walking down it until she was convinced that the road could no longer be seen. She then sat down in the dirt facing back toward the airfield. After a short time, the first of what she had been waiting for came lumbering off the runway – a twin engine Piper. She tracked it's progression directly overhead, concentrating on the look of the aircraft from beneath and its changing pitch while passing over. From those sensations of sight and sound, she went about constructing a new impression of a crop circle. Whatever her circle in life might look like at the moment, or end up being at the end, she would dwell only on the here and now of flying. She would make this mindset permanent… even if getting there took hours of sitting in the dirt of a cotton field.

Between planes, she found herself studying the cotton as a way of not thinking about the circumstances of her own life. On both sides of her were many bolls that decorated stems at eye level. As a child, she remembered being fascinated with the organization of a cotton field… particularly from a moving car. The crop itself held no interest for her, as agriculture was not her thing. Instead, she had always been taken in by the optical illusion of row upon row melding into a single image that mystically undulated upon the terrain. The effect had always been enchanting to her… which probably explained her childhood yearning for taking off down that one magical row that would lead her off into her dreams. She never actually got to try in real life, as Gwen was always too busy with her morning circuit of greenhouses to stop the car for such foolishness.

She had not remained a child, but her dreams of significance had stayed childlike. She eventually seized her chance for getting out of Lubbock, only to find the fantasy of escape to be so very lacking. No matter which row she might have selected as her way out, she brought her weaknesses along on that wistful journey. Now as the adult, she had claimed the driver's seat for herself… but passing these rows no longer felt the same. It was all just cotton.

She reached up to cradle the nearest boll and began examining its four segments of white fiber about the seed packet in the center.

Gwen always said that the flower was there for the fruit.

Of course, her aunt had been more interested in the former than the latter, but her point was nonetheless clear. The flower had many meanings, but it ultimately existed for one reason. All of its fragrance, color and amazing complexity was there for the purpose of bringing about the fruit.

Another plane passed overhead, so she waited for its sound to diminish before taking a long, undistracted breath of the air. The smell was that of green things in growth… a staple of living in farmland. To be honest, neither the cotton's flower or fruit ever made much of an impression upon her. The buds, themselves, had some interesting color, going from white to a fuchsia just before the bloom shriveled up and fell off. Those changes signified its successful pollination. The flower was only there for a few days, but the fruit of the flower – the fibrous residue of the boll – could last for decades in providing both warmth, cover and fashion. Beautiful in sight and scent, the flower was for the moment as well as the future. Gwen often said that not enough people paid attention to the cotton flower. The farmer certainly did. Every spring and in the midsummer crop, he looked longingly for the bloom, as by it would come the boll and the seed.

And all those terrible things that sting… they're the ones responsible for the flower's transformation into fruit.

She rose from the row and walked back to the car, no longer caring to think about crop circles.

———————

"Okay… before you takeoff, do you have any concerns about what you'll be doing?"

"Nope. I've got it down. Do the same three-point route we practiced and trust my instruments."

"Good. Got that flashlight in your bag?"

"Yep… and spare batteries too. I'm gonna be fine, Butch. We've already done this together, so I know exactly what to expect."

"I realize that, but it'll be totally different when you're up there alone. Night flights can be eerie, to say the least. Perspectives change, and the horizon can be difficult to pick up on. Fortunately you'll have clear skies tonight… as opposed to the cloud cover we had on Tuesday. That reminds me… when you get out to your first marker, I want you to try something… different. But only if you feel up to it."

"Sure. What is it?"

"So… get the flashlight into your lap first. Then I'd like you to turn off the instrument panel's lighting… but just for a few seconds, okay? Do it right before you turn west. That's when the city lights'll be behind you."

"Any particular reason why?"

"You'll see soon enough. Now get going."

She stepped out of the hangar into the evening's semi-dark about the ramp, did the walkaround with the aid of her flashlight, taking it slow as Butch had instructed. Soon, she was taxiing to the ground-designated runway for takeoff with her mind on the task at hand. She had already done several night takeoffs and landings, as well as the same sixty mile triangular route in the dark with Butch sitting behind her. So she felt totally prepared for this solo.

Just follow your training.

She was well along a northeast heading from Lubbock, more-or-less on a line toward the small town of Floydada, and set to veer westward when she remembered Butch's odd request. Pulling the flashlight into her lap and testing it, she reached up with her left hand and toggled off the instrument panel light switch. The cockpit was thrown into darkness, with only the plane's exterior lighting still on. She flicked the flashlight on once more to reassure herself that she could make out the gauges with only its beam, and then turned it off again. Venturing quick looks out both sides of the plane, she saw nothing below other than small pinpricks of light marking the sites of isolated farms and villages. The horizons to the left and right were barely discernable lines between faint starlight above and a pitch black nothingness below.

She was just asking herself why in the world Butch had made a point of this exercise when her eyes ventured forward… and then upward through the open canopy. Spanning an arc from behind her almost straight ahead down to near the northeastern horizon was a brilliant band of starlight. Except that it was not so much a band or strip stretched across the dome of the sky as it was a continuous thing of wonder displayed there just for her, totally without reference to anything upon the earth. The extreme of where that band met the horizon was easier on her neck to behold, but her eyes stayed directly overhead. She thought she had known the pleasure of seeing the Milky Way before on cloudless nights from her back porch. What she saw now was so much sharper and nearer... or so it seemed. In fact, she was convinced that to run her fingers through those luminous fibers required only to stretch out a hand. Better yet, she could nudge her plane upward just a bit and enter into the middle of that brilliant cloud of starlight. Then... she would not just be viewing it, but becoming a part of it. She would be gliding through a starry realm.

Amazing! The night sky seems... swathed in iridescent cotton. So many stars... the beautiful fruit of the heavens!

A jolt of turbulence brought back her pilot's sense. After a few more longing glances upward, she flicked back on the cockpit lights, recalibrated her eyes within the glow of each indicator, and then prepared herself for the bank westward. For the remainder of her flight, she would glance upward to the stars from time to time, but the sight was not quite as before. Not with all that interference coming from Lubbock's lights off to the south. She finished out the circuit by landing uneventfully back at the airport, only fifty minutes from when she had started, yet forever changed by what she had experienced. To fly through a West Texas night was to be free of her earthly self at last.

CHAPTER

35

MOTHERHOOD

She stood a long time before the bathroom mirror scrutinizing her figure. At twenty five weeks, there was absolutely no way of denying the baby bump. Of all her concerns regarding the check ride, her biggest was that of being found out. If only she could hide the fact that she was showing... without actually looking like she was trying to hide it. Into the closet, she began an agonizing search for something that might conceal her plumpness. Now that none of the jeans fit, her options were limited to sweatpants, overalls, and baggy jumpers. No way was she going to face her designated pilot examiner wearing any of that. Even her most fashionable maternity clothes shouted 'baby on board.' She definitely needed to come off cooler than that. After much indecision, she settled on a wrap that matched a set of burgundy slacks with an especially springy elastic waistband... and hoped that her belly got covered by her bulky flight jacket.

I guess for once I'm happy that I've not been able to find a women's flight jacket. I should be bigger than this. Ha! I mean... above being nervous. But really... I absolutely can not have the DPE find out.

Under normal circumstances, she would be heading into this morning absolutely pumped up. She knew her stuff and had no problem being tested on it. In fact, she relished the opportunity to show off what she could do. She had successfully weathered two years of male scrutiny at WYNG news, so she could certainly handle whatever man the FAA threw at her. But being pregnant... that changed everything. Butch's assurance that she need not disclose anything did not really help, for she still feared that the examiner would hold her condition against her if he found out. So above all, she must keep the pregnancy a secret.

Arriving at the airfield, she discovered that the FAA's designated pilot examiner assigned to her check ride… a Mr. Eikenberry… was not particularly fond of the concept of a female pilot. With flat-top crewcut, starched shirt of bright white, and large plastic horn-rimmed glasses, this man made clear his point of view not seconds after being introduced by Butch. In his opinion, a woman's place in the sky should be limited to serving drinks from a tray. Neither did he care much for those feminists ramrodding their *Equal Rights Amendment* through Congress. She bit her lip through it all, purposing not to give him cause for failing her.

Butch then excused himself, at which point Eikenberry got right down to the business of giving her the ground exam. To her relief, he started into the questions without a hint of bias. He asked most matter-of-factly, and she answered as succinctly as possible… him frequently nodding his head to show his approval. After an hour or so of being quizzed on her knowledge of aviation principles, procedures, regulations, and meteorology, he shifted the exam to the flight portion. She conducted the walkaround, him occasionally interjecting questions. Finally content with her rigor, he motioned her to climb up into the Fairchild. This was the moment that she felt most nervous about, for getting in and out had become difficult of late. On top of that, the plane's rather stiff seat was murder on her tail bone. Lumbering up and in, she hid her discomfort as best she could. She headed right into the preflight checklist with him, started the engine, and contacted ground for approval to taxi. He allowed her to do the takeoff in silence, but was right back at her with more questions once they were up. After thirty minutes of executing various maneuvers, he seemed satisfied enough with her performance to have her make the approach for landing. Everything went off without the slightest hitch. Halfway through the post-flight walkaround, she became aware that he had moved off toward the hangar. There, she noticed him shaking hands with Butch… and Butch was smiling! She had passed.

Mr. Eikenberry waited for her to come over, and then congratulated her for having done well… and also for expecting. Totally stunned… and probably turning so many shades of red… she thanked the man before quickly changing the subject to when her license might come in the mail.

If having completed her first solo amounted to a mountain-top experience, passing her private pilot's exam left her underwhelmed. Butch, having another student requiring his attention, left her alone in the breakroom. So she gathered her things and headed out to the parking lot. On entering her car, she told herself that very few women had accomplished what she just did… even if no one was there patting her on the back in agreement. In leaving the airfield, she told herself that she had it in her to go much further… to do things in aviation that even fewer women had attempted… to make a career out of it… even though no one was there to add their voice of support to this dream. Out onto the farm-to-market road heading home, she ventured a look into the sky… and wondered when she would next get up there. Not just to dabble in the occasional flight, but to truly live it. Pulling off the county road into her drive, she saw ahead the familiar sight of the Meitner house… her house. For a fleeting moment, she felt again a bit of that old bitterness toward this as a place of confinement conscripting her to the care of another… a newborn rather than a crazy mother-in-law. But no matter what came from giving birth, she would not go back to living that way. She would fully embrace her new life. So she sat in her car on the circle, refusing to get out until she had properly adjusted her attitude. She would gladly give up her flight bag in exchange for a diaper bag, because becoming a mother was a blessing… even if she had to work hard at making it so.

Then a thing happened that she was not expecting, even though it had been anticipated for weeks. She felt her baby kick for the first time. Just a fleeting moment of pressure on her insides. Gentle, yet unmistakable. Instantly, she knew that a connection had been made between her and her baby so much stronger than the obvious nature of her condition. Within her was a unique life of her own making. A part of her and a part of Roy. That was a marvel both believable and fairyland-like at the same time. So she remained still in her seat for a long while concentrating on every little sensation to her body, but the kick did not come again. Growing cramped beneath the steering wheel, she left the car and entered the house, intent on immediately calling Roy.

She felt the baby several more times that afternoon. For each, she stopped whatever she was doing to greet the life within her. To her great joy, Roy also sensed it that evening. With his hand resting on her stomach, she watched a smile come to his face. Seeing that smile… savoring that it was from the father of her child… it was the first time that she actually felt part of a family.

Her girlfriends treated her to an aviation themed baby shower in the week following the private pilot's exam. The whole thing was so touching, what with games like 'guess the baby item in the flight bag' and 'best parachute made out of diaper and string.' Everyone had such fun referring to her baby as 'the plane in Marna's hangar'… or pay the price of sucking on their pacifier until someone else messed up. She was given so many adorable gifts – an ultra-soft blanket with charming little cartoon planes all over it, a baby mobile of puffy white clouds, a cute infant flight suit… goggles included… and one of those 'Little People' toy airplanes. Sitting there celebrating with these women, most of whom were already mothers, she experienced a belonging more tangible than anything she had enjoyed as newswoman or pilot. She did not have to earn their esteem, as they were genuinely excited for her. They understood the step she was taking in life better than she did, yet all treated her as if she was already one of them. That was an acceptance she had not felt in many years.

She gave up flying, but still made occasional trips to the airfield in the months following her private pilot's exam in order to stay connected with her friends at the flight school. She also kept up her visits to Ruby. Maybe not daily, but at least a couple times a week. She made a habit out of holding Ruby's hand over the baby… even if Ruby never acknowledged its kick. But as her baby steadily grew within her, so did Ruby begin to deteriorate. There came a time in her last month of pregnancy that Ruby could no longer swallow without gagging. The poor woman was already so weak, but those coughing spells stole so much of her strength. Ruby became bedridden. Eleven heartbreaking days followed in which she and Roy witnessed Ruby's condition steadily worsened to the point where the poor woman was barely hanging on to life. The nursing home called in the middle of the twelfth night with the sad news that Ruby had passed away.

For reasons that she did not venture to ask, Roy decided that his mother's service would be kept private. He only wanted immediate family present. Sybil, over the phone, promised to be there.

On the day of the service, they waited at graveside for a half hour before concluding that Sybil was actually not showing up after all. So it would just be her and Roy, along with the pastor from Ruby's old church. That man's message was brief – a few words about the hope of Heaven before Ruby's casket was lowered into the plot beside her husband's. As the pastor spoke, she could not keep her eyes from moving between George's four year old headstone and the new one that was Ruby's. She was utterly gripped by the injustice of it all. Inexplicably, Roy had been deprived of both parents before the birth of his first child.

The casket had disappeared from sight when the pastor gestured for her and Roy to offer their parting words. Because she knew that he was not yet ready, she hurried to go first.

"Thank you, Ruby. Thank you for accepting me as a daughter… and as a wife to your Roy. I promise I'll do my best to take good care of him. I know how precious he was to you. I just… wish you could've been here to see your grandchild. I'm really sad that you won't be. I'll… always treasure all those times of you listening to me go on and on about flying. It meant so much to me. I'm going to miss you, Ruby. I already do."

She could say no more. Looking to Roy, him standing so near to her, she was startled by his expression. It seemed all over the place – on the verge of tears, angry, confused and embarrassed. He was so obviously fighting to control his emotions… likely as a childhood worth of memories rushed through his thinking. So she went on clinging to his arm, gently squeezing it as her sign of support. It was only then that he cleared his throat. Low and gruff, he spoke directly toward the hole in the earth.

"I love you, Mom. Always will."

He nodded to the pastor that he was done. To her surprise, Roy wanted to remain there as the men began to shovel. So she stood with him, watching the clods burst on the wood surface and slide off in a shower of dirt to either side. Only once the casket was covered with a complete layer did he abruptly spin her about in the direction of their car.

With Roy's arm around her, they walked in silence, her cradling their baby within. The setting suddenly came to her with such clarity, and so starkly dissimilar to the reason for why they were there. The three of them… they were moving as if in a bubble. The sad reality of this place… its finality and its despair… could not possibly break through to her. She was floating above this scatter of graves where absolutely nothing could touch her. All about were the names of strangers chiseled upon memorials to death, but the heaviness to all that stone… it was no weight to her. Tombs were of the below, and she belonged above. She was going to have a baby, and that made her untouchable. Strangely, this conclusion also somehow made her feel proud of herself… as if she had accomplished some great feat in lifting her heart off this dull brown earth into a clear blue…

"Would you like to visit Gwen's grave before we leave?"

As easily as it had formed, her bubble burst.

"No… that… wouldn't be right."

They drove home in silence, him gripping the steering wheel with such obvious hardness to his grief, and her stuck within remembering.

———————

Of all places for her water to break, it just had to happen while she was standing on the ramp waiting for the arrival of Butch's new Cessna. The irony was not lost on her. One minute she was watching his plane taxiing in from being delivered, and the next she was thrown into a panic by the first stage of her own delivery. Before she knew what was happening, Butch had her sprawled out on a breakroom couch just as the first serious contractions came on. People were hovering about her with such indecision... until someone finally had the wits to call for Roy. Butch was so kind to stay at her side until he came, gripping her hand whenever the spasms became too much. Between times... to stem her fear and embarrassment... she kept up a silent recitation of the five bad tendencies of a bad pilot in a bad situation... except with a birthing baby slant.

Rebelliousness. I swear I'll do exactly as the doctor says!

Passivity. Don't be ridiculous! I'm like... so far beyond that! I want this thing landed!

Arrogance. I... I thought I could handle anything thrown my way. Was I ever wrong!

Impulsivity. I'm absolutely not touching that one! It's why I'm pregnant in the first place!

Invulnerability. That one's so not happening either! This baby's killing me!

Ow-ow-owww! It hurts, it hurts, it hurts! Hurry the hell up, Roy!

The car trip to the hospital felt like the bumpiest ride she had ever taken... and just as scary with the thought that her baby might pop out at any second. Yet once there, a nurse casually informed her that the contractions were not nearly regular enough. She still had a long way to go. After four hours of nervous discomfort ending with a whole lot of tormented pushing, Travis Lane Meitner was born to her on that blustery afternoon in April. Though completely worn out and terribly sore, beholding her baby for the first time... cradling him in her arms... it was joy inexplicable. She was in complete awe of his every feature. Wispy blond hair... blinking blue eyes... tiny crinkled nose... little puckered lips... itty-bitty fingers balled up into fists. So sweet and so dependent upon her. She had brought this new life into the world, and the skies were the limit for them together.

Giving birth was like nothing she had ever experienced. Flying came close... but that was all about power and speed. In holding newborn Travis close to her, she wanted forever to be near him. To nestle him against her chest and let time pass by. It was the ultimate in tenderness. She would forever be connected to this child... to go on kissing his cheeks... his forehead... his little hands. Everything about her baby was special, and every feeling he brought her was something new to this world. Only she understood this wonder. Only she could comprehend the miracle of this baby. Her baby! But seeing the pride and pleasure in Roy's eyes... that was almost as good. Watching him hold his son for the first time... him taking such care to be solid while also straining to be gentle... that was a sight for her to always cherish. And then to have him smile at her with such admiration and thankfulness... it was the warmest thing she had ever felt.

Out of the hospital and back home, it was no time at all before she came to see motherhood in a way not unlike that of her first solo. Roy was a new parent too, but she was largely flying by herself when it came to meeting her baby's needs. She was learning as the days flew by, yet always felt that she was up to the task. There were so many thrills, but also a feeling of needing to be constantly attentive to every little detail of his care. That vigilance kept her hyped up so much of the time as she bounced from a longing to hold and cuddle him, to a nervousness that something was going wrong, to an excitement over every little thing he did... and all those precious moments in between of getting to know him as her baby.

She also found that caring for a newborn sometimes required her to go on autopilot. Functioning on little sleep, she responded whenever he did... especially at the slightest sign of fussiness. Travis was such an alert baby, responding to just about everything around him. That made him an absolute bear to put down... and he never seemed to stay that way for long. She knew all about the constant feeding, changing, and cleaning up from the stories of her girlfriends, but experiencing it firsthand was a whole different matter. She often had nothing left at the end of the day, and considered herself supremely lucky if she was able to squeeze in a shower.

She accepted that her life had changed forever. It was now up to her to take care of another. This new responsibility left her in no state for contemplating all that had happened to her. Only a year ago, she was on her own with a budding career as a newswoman. Now, she had a family to look after. She lost her aunt and fell in love with her husband. She found a home... solid ground to stand on... but also found herself settled into the last place on earth that she had ever expected to be. She discovered the thrill of flight... and lost it too soon. She had a baby... and was just too tired for anything else. She was Marna Meitner, mother and wife... but sometimes was losing track of herself. She felt pressed down all of the time... compacted and spent. Her emotions seemed always on the verge of a breakdown, and the good things about being a mother barely stayed out ahead of all the weariness. She was no longer her own. Her body belong to her baby, and she existed solely for him. She had not really prepared herself well enough for feeling this way. But given time and more energy, she would surely come to embrace fully this new life of hers.

Fortunately, things got considerably easier once Travis started sleeping through the night. With more rest, she began to feel a breath of herself coming back. She could plan her day, and accomplish small things around the house that had nothing to do with caring for an infant. Then as Travis began to crawl… and sit up on his own… she grew more excited about taking him out to explore the world together. Parks, malls, playgrounds, pet stores, and even the airport… any place where she could show him new things. Her baby soaked it all up with such fascination. It was clear that even at one year of age, her son possessed such a sharp mind. Through her, he was destined to become someone special.

As her care of Travis became more routine, she started thinking that she had it in her to go further. She would prove to herself that this new life of motherhood was her true life to live. With this ambition, she began to remold her previous yearnings for a career into thoughts of a second child. A boy and a girl, that would be pure symmetry. Two children, a house and a loving husband – surely that was the substance of an accomplished woman. So with Travis at a little over a year old, she became pregnant once again. Nine months later, she gave birth to a second boy – Chad Jonathan Meitner. If she was disappointed at not having a daughter, it was a thing so small and insignificant as to show up only fleetingly in her thoughts. She was the mother of two boys, and proud of it.

But having two in diapers immediately changed her perspective on what it meant to be tired. While Travis had become a rather dependable two year old, Chad proved to be a terror from the moment he gained the ability to crawl. He was always making a mess out of whatever he got his little hands on. Worse, he was constantly beating on things – toys, furniture, his older brother, his father… and her. Never would she have imagined it possible that a nine month old could so easily bruise an adult, but that was Chad. He was a beast of a baby to manage. Oddly though, it was his older brother who displayed the greatest knack for controlling him. From infancy on, Chad was fascinated with every antic that Travis put on for him. At barely three, it was Travis who first got words out of Chad. It was Travis who taught him to walk. Travis who played with him, wrestled with him, and egged him on to do so many crazy stunts. Like the time she caught him encouraging his one year old brother to climb the stairs. The two of them together gave her a heart attack on nearly a daily basis. But without Travis watching over Chad, she would never have had time for cooking… or cleaning… or breathing.

She still held out hope for a daughter and tried once more. Two years after Chad, she gave birth to her third boy – Wade Bartholomew Meitner. Unlike his older brothers, Wade was frail from birth on. His infancy seemed filled with colic, ear infections, fevers, terrible bouts of teething, respiratory difficulties, and a constant running nose. She weekly found herself at the doctor's office trying to manage her two hooligans while Wade wailed in her arms. How she made it through his first year was a complete mystery to her, but shortly after Wade turned one… and following a week of contentious debate with Roy… she made an appointment with her gynecologist and had her tubes tied off for good.

She might have drawn the line at three, but that did not mean that caring for those three proved too much for her. She was in complete control. No matter the difficulty, she, as a doer, never folded under pressure. She whipped her three preschool boys into shape, teaching them respect for their elders, appreciation for family, and the importance of household responsibilities. She took pride in her work as a homemaker, and was constantly looking for new ways to be efficient. As a chore, laundry could never be conquered as a whole, for it perpetually went on and on. But if she viewed it in parts, then there was always a small feeling of achievement to be had. Collecting, washing, drying, folding, ironing, sorting, and putting away the final product each became a thing in itself, somewhat numbing the insanity of clothing the four males in her life. It was often inglorious labor, but she measured her unheralded successes by the basket load, and never allowed the small setbacks of stains, rips, shrinkage, or mismatched socks to undermine her feeling of accomplishment. Her mind remained fixed upon the management of her household, and she never allowed the day-to-day drudgeries to blur her belief that she was building something significant with this family.

Her life was her boys and her husband, and she was content. Yet whenever she found the opportunity, her eyes still went upward in admiration of the sky and the memory of having once been up there. She made a habit of pointing out passing planes to her children, taking time to explain the ways of aviation in terms suitable for the imagination of a preschooler. Her boys thought planes were cool enough, but their interests were generally on the below – with their toys fit for dirt. That was fine, for she knew that young boys could not be kept engaged for long… especially on stories from a mother's past. Accepting that was a bit disappointing, but also understandable. What small boy was really capable of viewing his mother as a pilot?! Mothers were supposed to hug a lot, bake cookies, put Band-Aids on boo-boos, and cheer from the sideline at every little crazy thing a boy could do. Her boys were simply too young to share in her dreams. So… when she spoke enthusiastically to them about planes, she was really speaking to herself, striving to keep kindled her own childlike fascination with flight.

Who knows… maybe she would one day get back up there. But when? Wade would soon be out of diapers, so she more frequently caught herself doing the math in her head. Twenty five when she gave up flying… twenty nine when Wade was born… thirty one now… and thirty five before she could get all three fulltime into school. That would be ten years. Ten years spent on the ground. Perhaps it was foolish of her to have ever dreamed about making a career out of flying… and foolish to think that she would ever be anything other than mother.

CHAPTER

36

A FLAG'S POLE

"Good morning. How'd you sleep?"

"Pretty good. You?"

"Not bad. The boys up?"

"Yep… and already glued to the TV set."

"Figures. Probably'd be there all morning if we let 'em."

"Speaking of which… I put your list on the kitchen table. Don't forget it on the way out. I'm thinking you should start out by getting…"

"Hold it, Marna… I need to change plans."

She glanced at him by way of the mirror and realized that he was shaving. He never shaved on a Saturday morning… unless he had to.

"You're going in, aren't you?"

"Have to. There's a…"

"Roy, we discussed this last night. You agreed to take the boys off my hands so I could have a day to myself."

"Sorry… I forgot about the truck coming in at nine…" He glanced at his wrist… to the watch that she now realized he had put on coming out of the shower… an obvious sign that he was in a hurry. "…which only gives me an hour to get the warehouse floor cleared… and then we've got to reorganized the showroom. Might take all day. You'll have to manage the boys on your own."

"I do that all the time… which is the point of me getting a day off. Why's it so important for you to be there anyway? And how come what's-his-face can't manage things on a Saturday by himself?! That's what you're paying him for."

"Clyde's a good enough salesman, but he's not ready for a shipment of this size. Not on his own. Everything's got to be inspected and inventoried… and then we've gotta…"

"Yeah, yeah, I know! But I haven't had a break in months! Can't you put the truck off until Monday?"

"They deliver when they deliver. Besides, you know I've been really psyched up about this shipment. We're getting the 78 models weeks ahead of those guys over at…"

"I don't care. You promised me!"

"Listen… I'm really sorry about this… but it can't be helped. I'll make it up to you next weekend."

He went back to shaving with an air of the whole matter having been neatly resolved… which was not at all how she felt. She could go on making a fuss, but that would accomplish nothing. He had made up his mind. So rather than stand there as he shaved, she turned into the closet… especially since this might actually be her only moment to herself all day. Shuffling hangers back and forth with no clear thought for dressing, her mind was on her disappointment. Something always seemed to come up, leaving her as the one holding the short straw.

Truth was, she had not actually made any concrete plans for her day off. She might have gone out shopping on her own… or taken to the nook with a novel… or had a good long nap… but most likely she would have cleaned the cellar. Its mess had been annoying her for months. Or perhaps she would have ventured out to dust up the hangar. It would have been nice to spend some time out there admiring her Corsair… taking that tarp off for the first time… and maybe investing some thought into what she would actually do with the plane. Roy still wanted to sell it, but she could not bring herself to do that.

Oh well… best roust the boys from their cartoons and see about breakfast.

She dressed for a busy day and stepped out into the upper hall. The noise from downstairs immediately filled her ears. She very much liked the openness of her family room… except for when the TV was on. She peered over the banister to where her boys were sitting before the tube. Three little Roys all in a row, each still in their pajamas. Chad was leaning on his older brother, pushing at him as his way of showing his pleasure. Travis had always been tough enough to take that abuse without getting upset. Not Wade. With his blanket clutched in his arms, her baby boy sat off a bit from the older two so as not to get clobbered by their horseplay.

There was something special about childhood, so she went on watching them for a while, envying the pleasure that the three derived from seeing the tricks a roadrunner could play on a coyote. She and Roy... they really had done a good job raising these boys... even if Chad had ants in his pants. The heebie-jeebies of boys notwithstanding, all three were respectful and well-behaved. Sharp too! They would make for good students once they were in school. Each enjoyed learning, and each loved being read to. She was very proud of them... and proud of herself too.

But even from up here, it was pretty obvious that all three had become scraggly of late. They badly needed haircuts. She could do that herself... had many times before... even though it was such an ordeal. Especially with Chad. That boy simply would not sit still for her. For some reason, he would for his father... though Roy never bothered cutting their hair himself. When he saw to the chore, he took them to the barber and made an event out of it. All four would come back so happy... like it was some grand adventure that only boys could understand. Well... she was capable of doing that too. She could turn a trip to the barber into something special... then perhaps they would be settled enough for some clothes shopping afterward. Travis needed new jeans for school... and Chad's sneakers were on the verge of falling apart... again. And little Wade... it was always so much fun looking at toddler outfits for him. Maybe she could even squeeze in a bit of bargain hunting for herself... if things had not gotten ugly. Of course, there was the food court to bribe them with... assuming she had any energy left for it.

Let's see... what else was on that list? Umm... I remember groceries... dry cleaning... school supplies... oh... and a new mop. Probably need gas in the car too. All that'll keep me out the entire morning.

She descended the stairs with a smile on her face, fully resolved to start out this Saturday of chores with a positive attitude.

———

Pulling into the nearest available slot, she paused to gather herself for the task ahead. She had never done this before, and doubted seriously that her years of experience with beauty parlors could prepare her for a trip to the barbershop with three boys.

"Alright you two... remember to behave."

She received back the required response from each, but knew too well from experience that she would still have to maintain an eagle-eye on them both. How two young boys could get into such trouble was beyond her. She slung Wade's diaper bag over a shoulder and unharnessed him from his car seat. Hoisting him into her arms, she caught a whiff of something unpleasant.

Just great! I'll have to change it in the barbershop.

Herding the older ones before her through the door, she quickly sized up the two barbers currently working on their customers and opted for addressing the older one.

"Mind if I use your bathroom?"

She noticed the man appraising the fidgety Wade in her arms before pointing his comb toward the door in back.

"Travis… Chad… have a seat until I get back. Stay put, you understand me?"

She did not wait to hear their acknowledgements, being much more concerned about how the state of Wade's diaper was affecting the atmosphere of the barbershop.

This was far from the first time she had changed a diaper on the floor of a cramped washroom, but such experience never made the job more pleasant. She unfurled the changing mat on the cleanness stretch of tiling she could find and got to work, bemoaning to herself that Wade had not yet shown the slightest interest in being potty trained. She soon had him into a new diaper, with the old one closed up in an air-tight bag. Re-entering the barbershop, she was immensely relieved to find that the other two had remained where told. As a reward, she handed each a quarter's worth of nickels and sent them to a rack of gumball machines in the front of the shop. The two customers being worked on both smiled sympathetically at her, pausing their conversation to say how well-behaved her boys had been. She, as much as any mother, enjoyed drawing out compliments about her children, but at the moment was not quite recovered from the frazzled experience of changing that diaper. She thanked the men without elaboration… and shortly they went back to chatting at their barbers. With Wade perched in her lap, him content to watch the activity of his older brothers, she could finally relax. The wait should not be too long, as there was no one in line ahead of them.

"What's that you was saying about your nephew?"

"Just got himself a job back east. Real good pay, I hear."

"Which one's he?"

"Lila's boy. The one who graduated from Tech."

"That little squirt?! Always with his nose in a book?"

"Same one. Smart as a whip."

"He the engineer?"

"Electrical… or aerospace. I forget which."

"Sounds complicated."

"That, it is. He works with satellites."

"Helping the government spy on citizens, huh?"

"No… They're for *telecommunications!*"

Instantly, her attention shifted over from the mild tussle her boys were putting up over whose coin should go into which machine to the conversation of the four men.

"Your nephew involved in the launching… 'cause I'd sure like to see one of those."

"Nah… His job's got more to do with *bouncing* signals off those satellites."

"What kinda signals?"

"Television, I 'spect. He's explained it, but I don't rightly understand how the whole thing works. All I know is that TV goes up to a satellite… comes down to a local station… and then to your house on a cable. Pictures as clear as the summer sky. No more fussing with rabbit ears."

"Imagine that."

"Any of you heard tell about this fella in Atlanta who's set up a *superstation*? Beaming his shows all over the country. Your nephew doing something like that?"

"Exactly. He's into…"

"If this here's the same fella you're referring to… I heard he's getting ready to start up a cable news station. News from all over the world, twenty-four hours a day."

"I'll take twenty-four hour football instead."

She was aware of them all laughing, but took no interest in the humor. Her mind had gone back many years. Seated in a fancy restaurant, she was sharing an elaborate dinner with a young man she wished now not to remember. His words nonetheless rang clear above the barbershop talk.

'Twenty four hour news. A new era. The satellite age. The open skies.'

Wow – that guy Azurean was actually right!

The wonder of that evening suddenly flowed over her. Of how enthralled she had felt on finding someone taking note of her. Someone influential enough to make her dreams of significance come true. Someone to transform her youthful potential into something grand. Her opportunity to make something of herself in this wide world.

But it had all been lies. His intentions had never been pure. He had only wanted her for himself… as a confidant and lover. She had been so naïve… so foolish in her rush to believe his empty words. Her mind came back to the now, for of late she had been fending off a similar feeling… of fearing that she was valued only for what she could provide as mother and wife.

"Tell you what, I'm getting me one."

"What? A satellite?"

"Don't be absurd! I'm talking about cable TV."

The barbers finished with the two men at nearly the same time, and up into the swivel chairs went Travis and Chad. Each one was wrapped about with a cape as she was called forth to give instructions as to how their hair should be cut. With Wade in her arms, she then sat back down in the same seat as before to keep watch on her boys with the attentiveness of a shepherdess over her flock. But her mind was actually elsewhere.

Someone out there was accomplishing what Azurean had only been able to envision. Someone was building a satellite news empire that spanned the globe. That person had dreamed big… and had the will to see that dream happen. Not her. She had become the mother of three… wiping noses and butts. Yet for a very short time, she had imagined herself to be part of something grand. With Azurean, she was going to conquer the skies. Even though it all turned out to be a farce, she could still well remember the richness to her feeling of importance during that time. Given the chance to see far off into the future, she had dreamed a dream of accomplishment.

Haircuts done, she soon had all three boys loaded back into the station wagon and went about checking off the other errands from her list. All morning, she kept mulling over the barbershop conversation with something of a personal implication slowly ripening in her mind. What that was, she could not really say, but refused to give up on it until she finally knew.

Once back home, she fed the boys lunch, got Wade down for his afternoon nap, and sent the other two out into the yard. She put away her purchases, got a load of laundry churning in the washer, and straightened up the kitchen before moving out onto the porch to watch the boys play. With an ear out for Wade, she went on wrestling with that uneasy feeling left over from the morning. Azurean's dream had come true. Not for himself… for he deserved none of it. He had used her… lied to her… humiliated her. He had made her feel like a fool for believing in herself. But surely she was over that hurt by now?! She had come a long way since then. She was a totally different person. So why relive the outrage and shame? No… something else was bothering her.

Her duties as mother soon took over once again. Wade was calling from his crib… the older boys needed to be cleaned up… Roy would be home soon… and dinner had to be prepared. Then there were the baths… and the goodnight rituals… and a couple of hours with Roy in front of the TV.

Later that night, she found herself standing before the bathroom mirror staring into her blue-gray eyes. She was still young, but could feel herself changing. The kid in her was gone... and so was the dreamer. She was all the way an adult, with so many adult-sized responsibilities. The bags under her eyes were proof enough. In those, her face displayed a kind of weariness she had not known before having children. Her skin might still be clear, but it was definitely paler. Not at all healthy looking. Her body had changed too. She did not stand quite as square as before... slumped over too much... with extra pounds that simply would not go away. Had not Roy even confessed the other day that her face looked more full ever since she had become a mother?! He said he meant it as a compliment, quickly following it up with a claim that she was more lovely than ever. Staring into the glass, she concluded instead that he must have meant her face was more mature... which was a kind way of saying that she was growing older. Come to think of it, her high school girlfriends had sometimes teased about her haughty, runway-model appearance. Maybe Roy had actually meant that motherhood had softened those features.

How could having three boys soften any woman's look?!

No... she was convinced of something different. Her face had actually become more stern than ever... worn and edgy. That matched exactly how she felt on the inside.

Lying awake in bed with Roy having fallen asleep long before, she replayed the barbershop conversation in her mind, striving to dismiss its deeper inference. But the more she picked at the memory in an effort to pry it loose, the farther it settled into her thinking. Someone out there had acted on Azurean's cable news dreams, and that somehow offended her. Not the accomplishment itself, but the notion that a life of importance was passing her by. She had wasted so much time dabbling in different things... flowers, cable TV, the news, and flight... but left her mark on none of it. She was newly turned thirty two, with nothing to show for herself other than a husband, three kids, a house, and an expired pilot's license. Not that she cared about cable TV or the news... and definitely not about that horrible man. It was more that she had once tasted something special... a real opportunity to become so much more than what she was... but that moment was gone.

That old longing for significance came rushing back, wedging itself into the gap between what she owed others and what she yearned to have for herself. This was no small thing. No tiny seed of self-reflection that had somehow worked its way down into a small crevice of her self-worth. This was a giant ripping away at her insides. Strong and terrible it had suddenly become. Her chest was tight with it... for its weight bore down upon her, compacting her estimation of herself. The pressure of it swelled her throat and raced her heart. She had it in herself to be so much more than mother and wife... and only by a determined will would she be able to seize her chance before it was too late. It was now or never.

She simply must fly again.

She loved her boys and her husband... deeply... but could finally admit to herself that her love for them was not enough. Yes... she wanted to be with them always... but she also longed to be up there logging hours and hours of flight. Yet also doing something much more significant than building up a number. She wanted to conquer the pull of earth. To break free and experience again the grandeur of the sky. She wanted to be an aviator... just like her aunt... a master of flight. But she also wanted not to be like her aunt. Not to give up on flying simply because circumstances had not worked out her way. Not to bend at the offense of others. Not to be tainted by those who did not have it in themselves to understand. Not to become hardened and closed off by disappointment. No... she would not give in. That was not her way. Even when things got difficult, she had always been a person of action.

Actually, why not have both her family and her dreams?! She could do it. She could find a way to soar up there and still come back down to her responsibilities.

But how?

She eventually fell into an unsatisfying sleep with no answer to her question and no clear course forward.

In the weeks following the trip to the barber, she gradually felt a burden of loneliness grow upon her. No one she knew would appreciate her longing for building something special out of her limited experience in flight. Her friends, most of whom were mothers themselves, could not fathom how flying was anything more than a whim. How could they, for none of them had tasted the sky! They only occupied themselves with the typical things that Texas made women out to be – feminine, attractive and submissive. As to her own family, the boys were simply too young to see her as anything other than mother, whereas Roy... it was so unfair of her to burden him with this hidden ache in her. He had burdens of his own at the store.

Too much that had once been important to her was forgotten. Motherhood had boiled down her life into the dregs of caring for others. Noble work for some... but not for her. She had dreamed higher aspirations born from countless hours of standing before her relief. She had so often sworn to herself that she would never become like one of those faces... but that was her now. Weighed down and beleaguered. She had neither the time nor resiliency for reliving what the birds had once meant to her. The same for the hangar. She had not stood before the wonder inside there for… it must be years now. That plane was as her ambitions – closed off and forgotten.

Fall arrived, and with it came a shift in the wind, flowing from the north both cold and persistent. More so than in the windier springtime, this autumn's gusts were especially annoying to her, for they required closer attention to anything unattended. Toys in the yard… a window left open… things being loosely carried. On nearly a daily basis, she found herself chasing after some item that had gotten swept from the car as its doors were opened – newspapers, mail, the kid's things, and so much trash. No one in her family or about town seemed the least bit concerned that the season had turned especially tumultuous. It was just Lubbock being Lubbock. School had restarted with such optimism, cooler temperatures were at hand, and the talk was of football. All about the city, things were alive with motion. Trees danced, wires swung like never before, and every flag waved out a colorful salute of rippled glee. The wind filled everything with such gaiety… but not her. Whenever she went outdoors, the air tore at her, tangling up her hair and fussing with her clothes. She constantly felt unsteady, as if any second she could get whirled about, tumbled over, and swept away. Even while indoors, she still found herself unnaturally attune to how her house rattled and shook with unease. That was her too. The outside world beat against her, leaving her terribly anxious and unsettled within. She never realized before now just how weary of heart she had become. Day after day, she did nothing but be mother and wife. Though if asked, she would certainly claim to be content, for what else could she say?!

But no one ever asked.

She bore each day that burden of being wanted. Never to have a free moment to herself. She had to be there for them… always. To comfort, to care, to affirm… and to answer their endless number of questions. The airwaves were always abuzz with their voices. She loved her boys… but they wore on her. Always calling for her. Making her dash from one disaster to the next. Grabbing her, pulling her, punching her. Demanding that she attend to their every need. Three hellions that required constant picking up after. She was nothing more than their servant.

But that was not how they viewed their dad. He was play and she was work. She was the crib and he was the playground. So unfair! What did she know about play anyway?! Digging in the dirt for the sake of digging! And all that make-believe nonsense about army men, dinosaurs, and anything to do with a ball. She had no interest in any of it. She was all about accomplishing things. But none of them were old enough to appreciate that. Whereas Roy…

he and the boys could sit for hours on end watching cartoons… laughing their heads off as three morons… stooges… slapped, poked and pummeled each other. It made no sense!

If only she could get the boys alone with her one at a time. That was when her nurturing side best shown through. She loved hearing all about their childhood dreams for growing up, and she had it in her to guide them toward whatever they hoped to be. But young boys were not much interested in mother talk… and mayhem always flowed whenever any two of them got together. Somehow, Roy could handle that. He was the fun one… and she was the heavy. The odd woman out. The bad parent in the household.

But she was also the person in the family that everyone depended upon. It was on her to carried the entire weight of them all. She daily delivered Travis to first grade and Chad to preschool… there again to pick them up on time afterward. All day she clung to little Wade while doing the chores expected of her… so that everything would be in perfect order when Roy came home. And then… later in the night when the mood was sure to hit him… she must make herself alluring in exactly the way he liked her to be.

That was her job, so she had to be strong for them. Solid and immovable. Out there in the world, the wind of life was a constant pull on them, so she must hold on tight for their sake. She had to be bedrock for them. It was on her to lift them into the sky, for she gave them a place to fly without fear of coming loose. So much depended on her. She must be firm and unbending no matter the stress. To look good… shiny… a woman of steel. Standing tall and firm against it all. Unmovable… with everything tied down tight. For them she flew the flag of love and acceptance… duty and faithfulness. Always there for them. Mother… sweetheart… homemaker.

But on the inside, she felt hollow. Stuck in one place. Stuck in a role. Anchored down into the concrete of family, she pointed up for them, but she herself was going nowhere. Not to unfurl her own worth. Not to exhibit proudly her own dreams. She bore others upward with no glory for herself. No proud wave. Wide openness all around, but always she must have her eyes down on where she stood. Never to look up. Everyday made to resent those she lifted up into the sky.

Would it not have been far better had she never flown?!

THE CICADA KILLER'S KILLER OPPORTUNITY

Better leave the diaper bag in the car. This is already going to be one of the most awkward things I've ever done.

There was really no way around it. If she wanted to explore what it would take, then she would have to bring her two year old along. Shifting Wade to her left hip, she allowed the bag to slide off her shoulder into the backseat. Pushing through the entrance into the familiar lobby, her eyes swept the vacant room before moving to its walls. Without too much searching, she located hers. Stepping up for a closer look, she put Wade down while still maintaining a firm hold on his hand. It was a marvel that the ink had not faded in the seven plus years since she stapled it there. That day seemed like a lifetime ago... accomplished by a totally different person than her. She felt the pull of Wade on her arm... could distinctly hear him asking for something or other... but purposely chose to ignore him. It was only right that she be given half a second to admire her shirt tail – the only legacy she had left from her few months of flying. Such wistful dreams she had back then... drawing a cartoon of her Corsair and imagining herself one day flying it. Looking to her left and right, up and down, there was so many other monuments on that same stretch of wall to ones like her who had soloed for the first time. Hers, it now seemed, was rather insignificant.

She heard a noise and turned about to find Butch coming from the back hall.

"Marna… so good to see you again."

"Butch! You too. It's been a long time."

"Five years, I think. Not since you last dropped by to show off your baby… which can't possibly be this strapping young lad!"

"That was Travis, our oldest… he's now in first grade. This here's our youngest. Wade… say hello to Mr. Carlyle."

To her mild embarrassment, Wade slunk around back of her, clutching her leg at knee level. Rarely did he exhibit for strangers… not like his outgoing older brothers. While doing his best to hide himself, she still noticed how his eyes shifted between Butch and the lobby's TV.

"He's our shy one. Mind if we sit over there and talk?"

She picked a spot on the couch closest to the TV, and was not surprised when Wade climbed right up into her lap. That was fine in a normal setting, but no way did she want to carry on this conversation looking and feeling very much like a mother. She slid him off onto the couch beside her, pointing out the flashy lights to the game show currently airing, and then turned back to Butch. To her relief, she felt Wade lean into her back and knew that he was content for now in watching TV.

"Thanks for seeing me on short notice. I really appreciate it."

"The pleasure's all mine. Anything for a former student… especially one who was as capable as you. Now… you mentioned over the phone something about getting back into flying?"

"It's what I've been wanting to do for a long time. You see… I came across this magazine article a few years back about the first woman to become a commercial airline pilot. Then more recently, I heard about how the Navy's started training women as pilots. So… I was thinking… why not me?"

"You're not wanting to go into the Navy?!"

She had rehearsed this opening over and over, yet somehow it was coming out wrong.

"Heavens no! Sorry… I'm only talking about restarting my training."

"Ha! You really had me going there for a second. Well… what'd you have in mind?"

"Mostly picking up where I left off. I'm sort of motivated by what those women have accomplished. So I'd like to know what further training's available, how much it'll cost, how long it'll take… and most of all, what options it'll open up for me in the future."

"Umm… that's… quite a mouthful. So… if I'm reading you right… you're meaning to do something like… get a job flying?"

"Not just a job, Butch. I want a career."

"You don't say…"

His surprise was in every syllable. This was not going well. If she was having trouble sounding credible to her old instructor… the man who had once called her a natural… then how was she going to convince anyone else. Roy, especially.

"Butch… I detect a note of skepticism."

"Sorry. It's not my intent to discourage you, Marna. But a career in aviation… that's not very practical for a person in your position… for a whole bunch of reasons."

"Such as?"

"Well… first off… you're going up against a swarm of Vietnam vets with similar aspirations. Some of those are already pilots with thousands of flying hours… and those that aren't have the GI Bill to help them get there. My business has never been better. Then there's the fact that you're starting out… kind of late. Most of those guys are still in their twenties. The same goes for kids coming out of college looking to get into aviation. So you've got a lot of competition. Then there's the obvious…"

By the way he paused, she knew what was coming next.

"That I'm a woman?"

"Well… to be frank… yes. But it's more than that. Marna… you're the mother of small children. That's not exactly something in your favor, if you know what I mean."

She was afraid it would come down to this. As he spoke, his eyes had several times darted over to Wade. She knew he was thinking about her duty to this child, and how that would affect her employability. It was hardly fair, though she had already come to accept it as a valid point. She had heard so much about the job hunting frustrations of girlfriends with small children. Landing a job in aviation would be ten times more challenging. The training alone was going to put such stress on her family. But she had finally come to accept that being a pilot was who she longed to be. It was in her blood. Somehow, she had always known it… even going back as far as the second grade.

"I don't want to worry about any of that just yet. I'll manage it one step at a time. For now… just tell me what'll it take to get a good job as a pilot."

"Well… to start off… there's an instrument flight rating. There're some jobs that don't require it, but those won't pay much… and are generally spotty. We can get into the details later, but to get your instrument rating, you'll need near-on a hundred hours of flight time under various conditions.

That's obviously going to take longer than the private. The cost'll be higher too. So you're looking at… maybe five thousand or so… and most likely next summer before you're done with that first step."

"And after that?"

"A commercial license'll take longer… and double the cost. You'll probably want to add on a multiengine rating and an ATP… that's an airline transport pilot certificate… along with a variety of other endorsements if you're planning on flying passengers. And then you've got to find ways of building your hours. Right now, you have… what… fifty?"

"Fifty three."

"You'll need twenty times that amount just to be taken seriously. All your training's only going to get you to… say… two fifty… three hundred tops. Marna… nobody lands a commercial airline position these days without seven… eight hundred hours… and that's just for a regional carrier. I certainly wouldn't want to work for one of them. Those jobs are murder."

"Sounds a bit like you're discouraging me from trying."

"I'm not… I just want you to be realistic. It's a long road, Marna."

He paused again… almost as if half expecting her to get up and leave. She had no such intention, and widened her eyes while adding a cock to her head, all in an obvious show of her anticipation that he continue.

"Listen… I'd be more than delighted to help you get your instrument rating… you know that… but that's as far as I should take you. You could get your commercial with me… but I'd advise against it. I think you'd be better off logging hours on a multi-engine aircraft… which unfortunately I don't have one of. For that… I recommend that you enroll at a certified flight school… what the FAA designates as Part 141 in its regulations. Airlines look much more favorably on those. But there's only one in the county… the Lone Star… and it's real expensive."

"Mommy… I hungee!"

She was startled by Wade pulling on her elbow.

"In a minute, Sweetie… I'm almost finished here."

She came back to Butch… and caught the last remnant of a frown, quickly and awkwardly turned into a smile. She knew that look… and would certainly be seeing more of it in the future. And not just from him. Sooner or later, her girlfriends were sure to express their doubtful concern over her decision to resume flying… as would Roy.

"You were saying…"

"Only that it's your call."

"Butch... I'm absolutely determined to do this. So when can we start?"

Juggling Wade in one arm while working her keys with the other hand, her mind was on Butch's last words. She had completely forgotten about what it would take to recertify her private pilot's license. That would require a medical and an FAA check ride, which meant that she would have to put extra time and money into refreshing her rusty skills... all before she could think about starting on the instrument rating.

"Mommy... I real hungee."

"Well then, what's say you and me go to that McDonald's place you like so much?"

Situating him into his car seat, she concluded that lunch out was the least she could do for him. He would soon go into daycare, for the occasional babysitter could not possibly give her the time needed for training. How was she to explain that in terms this precious little boy might understand? He would see only the separation... all so his mommy could do something called flying. Sure... some mothers had to put their kids in daycare in order to work, but she had never encountered one who did it so they could chase a dream. Well... that was not her either! She would be doing it to further her education. After all, she had never gone to college... and flight school was practically college. But getting to that point meant getting through Roy... which was not exactly how she wished to view the conversation she was planning for that evening.

She picked up the older two from school and then started preparations for a meal of corn bread and chili, just the way he liked it. She put the house in order and had all three boys out on the front porch to greet him when he came home. Everything was perfect from dinner through until the boys were put to bed. Then, she waited for him to get through his favorite evening TV shows before asking for time to talk. Trying to be as nonchalant as possible, she invited him out onto the front porch, hoping that the evening's cool temperature and gentle breeze would make the upcoming discussion a bit easier. Allowing a short amount of silent rocking to transpire, she eased herself in.

"The boys are doing well."

"I noticed. You've done a real good job with them."

"Thanks... Travis has really taken to elementary school. Mrs. Lipscomb says he's about as sharp as any student in her memory. He's already doing well in math... and is nearly reading at a second grade level."

"Hmm... must get it from you."

"Chad's also settled in nicely at preschool. You know... having him in a double session has really worked out. It certainly gets him worn out by the end of the day. And Wade… he's enjoying having me to himself. But I've been thinking, Roy… he could probably benefit from having some time away… you know… in a structured environment with other kids. Might help him over some of his shyness. What do you think?"

"Sounds reasonable."

"And that would give me some time to do other things."

"Like shopping without having a two year old pulling stuff off the shelf when you're not looking!"

"Yeah… but that's not exactly what I was thinking. Roy… I'd like to start flying again."

"Really? I kinda thought you were going to say more time for hanging out with your girlfriends. But okay… if that's what you'd like to do."

"Umm… I should probably clarify something. I meant restarting my flight training."

"Your training? I'm not sure I follow you."

"Well… if you recall… early on… I'd envisioned going beyond my private pilot's license. But when I became pregnant with Travis… I put those plans on hold.

"For something far greater."

"I don't disagree… but allow me to finish. You know me. I'm a driven person. Driven to accomplish things that…"

"Hey – being a homemaker's no small thing. Raising three boys and managing a household… that's a big job. You should be proud of yourself for how well you're doing."

"I am. It's just… well… when I was introduced to flying… I didn't really expect to enjoy it so much… but I did. In fact, I've fallen in love with it. And I'm really good at it too. You said so yourself."

"You're also good at being a mother."

"Roy… please don't get me wrong… I love being a mom. It's just… I've always wanted to grow a career."

"Being a homemaker's a career… even if people don't think it is."

"I realize that… I'm not downplaying the importance of stay-at-home moms. It's just… I don't know how to express it any other way. I want to get out there and do something with my life… and I want that to involve flying. Roy… when I'm up there… it's like… the whole world feels right. Like I feel right… know what I mean?"

"I think you're trying to tell me that you're not happy with the way things are. You know… if this is about you not getting time to yourself… then I fully agree. You deserve a break from the boys. What's say we set aside every other Saturday for you to...."

"Roy... you're not understanding me. It's got nothing to do with time off. Becoming a pilot is what I was meant to be."

He had been looking out toward the darkness throughout the conversation, glancing over at her every once in a while. But now, he turned to fully face her.

"I have no idea what that means. What exactly are we talking about here?"

"I want a career in aviation."

"Again... I have no idea what that means."

For a moment, the shadows falling across his face made it seem as if he was intentionally goading her... but then it occurred to her that he really might not understand what a career in aviation looked like.

"Flying's the type of thing where the more you do, the more options there are that open up for you. Right now, I'm sort of like a... a freshman in college. I have so much more training to do before I can get a real job. So here's what I'm thinking... I'm going to get back on with Butch Carlyle and pick up where I left off. But he can only take me so far... so then I'll have to enroll in an aviation school. I'll get the certifications I need from them... work on gaining experience... and then hopefully have enough hours built up so I can get a job once the boys are all in school."

"A job like flying for an airline?"

"That's one possibility."

To her disappointment, he rolled his eyes and turned away.

"Jeez, Marna... this is so ridiculous! You're not being very realistic."

"I think I am. And even if I'm not, I still think it's only fair that I be given the chance to try."

"Fine. Let's assume for argument's sake that you could actually get there. That kind of a job... we'll never see you. You'll be off... who knows where! You do realize that the boys still need you. And I can't manage the store if I'm having to pick up the slack around the house. Things have been difficult enough as it is. That new Sears in the South Plains Mall is killing sales... and now Penney's has brought in TVs! Same models as me! There's no way I can compete with their margins! On top of that, the downtown's shrinking. Ever since the tornado, the city's been growing south and west. You know that. People aren't coming in like they used to, so I have to work even harder than ever to promote the store. How am I supposed to do that if I have to go pick up the kids from school because you're off flying somewhere?!"

"There's always daycare."

"My kids aren't going into daycare! That's not fair to them… and it sends the wrong message to my customers. I run a *family* store."

"Yeah… well… the message I'm getting is that I have no say in the matter! So why's it that you can have your dream but I can't have mine?!"

"It doesn't matter anyway. We don't have the money for it. Not with what you're private whatever-you-call it ended up costing."

"I still have Gwen's money."

"That's for the boys' college fund."

"No – it's for *my* college fund! For the education that Gwen never gave me."

"I can't believe this! I've got work in the morning. I'm going to bed."

Without warning, he vaulted up from his rocking chair and made for the inside. As the front door closed behind him without a slam, she relaxed in realizing that his anger simply meant that he had been caught off-guard. So… she allotted for him an untolled number of rocks in her chair until the delay felt right, and then followed him inside. She found him standing before the bathroom mirror brushing his teeth.

"Roy… what're you most worried about, the store, the kids, money… or you and me?"

"I think I'm concerned about them all.

"Well… so am I. Your concerns are mine too. I just want you to know… I'm not going to do anything that affects your ability to manage the store. But frankly… I don't think the success of the store depends on what I do with my time. As for the kids… Wade's old enough to be away from me for a few hours a day. Like I said, he could actually benefit from daycare. He's way too clingy. As for the other two… they're in school six hours a day. That's plenty of time for me to get some training in. So I think I can manage things without it much affecting them. As for money… I understand that some has to be spent. Flying's not cheap. But I think it's only fair that I be given the freedom to use some of my aunt's money on something I feel strongly about. That leaves you and me…"

She watched him finish up with his teeth, making a show out of demonstrating that his mouth was not yet available for speaking.

"Roy… I love you. I hope you know that."

"Of course…"

"You do realize that I had not planned on getting pregnant. But when I did, I gave parenting my all. I have no desire for changing that. But I did put my dream on hold… and I'd like the opportunity to pick it back up again. I know it's going to put stress on the family. It's going to be especially hard on me. But this is something that I have to do. And I have to do it now… or I'll regret it for the rest of my life."

She said all that she could say. Now it was his turn. He seemed aware of that fact by how deliberate he was being in rinsing off his toothbrush and drying his hands before turning her way. To her surprise, he wrapped her about in a hug. It was not a happy one, as his arms did not so much embrace her as just hold. Still… even if his body had not softened, she could tell by his somewhat forced smile that he had.

"Life with you, Marna… it's a constant adventure. Okay… start flying again."

She already had the bag packed last night, but doublechecked it again before leaving. Every conceivable thing needed was there. Since the paperwork had already been filled out, submitted and accepted, she left the house reasonably optimistic about how this first time out would go. There might be some hiccups, but that was to be expected. She would keep the time short. Just a few hours as a trial run. From then on, she was fairly confident that everything would work out.

But the transition did not go nearly as well as she had hoped. The moment she placed Wade into the arms of a woman at Shining Star Daycare, he burst out wailing like she had never seen him do before. Tears flowed nonstop as his screams echoed throughout the facility. Far worse, seeing those little arms thrashing about, pleading for her… that absolutely broke her heart. Nothing she said could soothe him. No assurances, no promises, no bribes. She was also painfully aware that everyone there… the workers, mothers peacefully dropping off their charges, and even the other children… had paused in shock at his display… yet more so at her. She was the author of this terrible scene. Her child might be the one completely out of control, but it was all of her own doing. She was betraying him… breaking *his* little heart… all for the love of flying.

The daycare provider eventually told her to leave, promising that they could handle the situation. It was only a little separation anxiety. Nothing they were unfamiliar with. He would calm down once she was finally gone. Those words registered sourly in her hearing, but she complied, handing over Wade's diaper bag and backing away from him with many assurances that she would return soon. Then came the moment when she turned away from her child and left the center. Out the door, she could still hear Wade screaming inside. She lowered her head to the pavement, wiped away her own tears, and made for the car.

Unfortunately, Wade showed very little progress at adjusting to daycare in the ensuing weeks. Always it was the same no matter what tricks she played. Bringing a familiar toy of his, getting down on the floor to engage him in play, slipping out the moment he was distracted, or that cold-turkey exchange

– nothing seemed to help him adapt. And nothing she told herself ever dampened that dreadful feeling of abandoning him. Even the joy of picking him up… seeing his face light up with excitement at her return… that was such poor redemption for having left him in the care of another.

Each day, the sidewalk from the door of the daycare center to its parking lot seemed miles long. That short stretch of concrete became her grueling walk of shame. Every time, no matter how Wade had responded to being dropped off, she felt the same guilt come flooding over her. Almost as bad, she simply could not keep herself from believing that the childcare workers were talking behind her back about what a terrible mother she was. They were certainly judging her for the decisions she was making… which caused her to question even more why she was doing what she was doing. She was putting her dreams above her son's well-being. None of her mind games ever convinced her otherwise. She could tell herself that the socialization was doing him good… toughening him up and getting him used to being separated from her. But she knew all such words to be lies told for covering her shame. So what if she had done her research before selecting this as the best place in Lubbock?! So what if she had gotten recommendations and then taken time to watch the providers at work?! So what if she had spent an afternoon there with Wade in hopes of getting him acclimated?! None of that forethought excused her. Every night she tried to convince herself that she was doing the right thing, but every morning's tears told her otherwise. Dropping Wade off at daycare was an ordeal to which her heart would never become hardened.

She nonetheless was determined to fly, heartache or not. Butch right off put her in a Cessna… the very one she had witnessed being delivered on the day she went into labor with Travis. Flying that front wheeler was a breeze compared to the Fairchild. Such easy takeoffs and easy landings. Best of all, she had Butch seated beside her rather than behind. Her time spent in the air with him was delightful, as they talked aviation together like old friends.

She easily passed her FAA check ride for recertification of her private pilot's license. So her optimism was high as she started her first day of instrument training. The fun immediately wore off as the initial stage became an unexpected drudgery. For weeks, Butch had her doing patterned laps around the airfield with a visor-like hood over her face until she had mastered navigation by instruments, for that was a prelude to accomplishing instrument approaches and landings. She knew that the hood was there to make her depend upon the ways of the gyro, the compass and the altimeter, rather than sight out the windows, but the work was so tedious and boring, and deprived her of some joy in flying. Yet the real irony of the hood was not lost on her, for it conveyed something about her future as a pilot. She could only see a short distance off, with everything else shrouded in uncertainty.

She had Wade in daycare three days a week, which permitted her to squeeze in six or so hours of actual flying. But what with the weather and Wade's tendency for getting sick, it took near-on three months to amass the twenty hours under the hood that Butch required before she could transition to the next stage – instrument pilot-in-command training. With the laps having become routine, she was now flying greater distances away from the airport. Her first cross country required that Roy pick the boys up from school and daycare, something he consented to do… even though she could tell that he was not happy about it. She did that cross country to Killeen perfectly, but at the price of him being testy with her for days afterward. Not once had he expressed any interest in hearing about her flight.

She continued on with her training while juggling her household chores, the boys, and doing her best to keep her husband happy. Too frequently, she found him with an undertone of irritation over how she was fulfilling her responsibilities. How she kept the house… how she paid the bills… the way she got the boys ready in the morning… and anything that was compromised because of her flying. He snapped at her whenever meals were not up to his liking, and she called out his attitude just as frequently. So what if the quality was not to her past standards?! That was no reason for making the dinner table so frosty! Let him do the cooking for a change! Oh sure, he might be quick with an apology, but too often it was with a grandiose manner that pointed out where he thought the true offense lie. Other times, she could tell from his silence that he was struggling with his expectations. But why should it be so unreasonable for a father to pick his children up from school?! And why should he resent being asked to help out?!

Despite Roy's bad attitude, she still strove to keep everything normal before the boys, even though she suspected that Travis sensed things were not right between his parents. That made her feel even more guilty about her choices. At least Chad was as he had always been – all boy and totally clueless to anything other than food and play. But little Wade… she had this terrible feeling that he was no longer as devoted to her as he had been before daycare. He had finally come to be excited about going to Shining Star each morning. That was what she had hoped for… so why did she get so upset over the thought of some other woman having fun with her little boy?!

She was becoming terribly anxious about her progress, especially with all of the tension in the household. Summer was coming, school would be letting out soon, and there was no way they could afford to have all three boys in daycare. She must complete her instrument rating before then… or see her progress wasted. So whenever she was not flying, her thoughts constantly bent toward getting back up there again. But when she got up there, she could not keep her mind from straying back down to the things below. How her boys were managing without her, those things that were still needing to be done around the house, what other women were saying about her, and how her relationship with Roy had gotten rocky. She had sacrificed so much… and put her family through such stress… all so she could fly. There was no balance to be had between this resentment and guilt. No contentment to be found, whether up or down. How unfair that her heart should be torn between the two… and how unfair that no one seemed to understand.

The months of April and May were absolute torture. She had Wade in daycare each school day and called in every babysitting favor she could scrounge up for Saturdays, just to get her instrument training completed by June. But finish she did. With the check ride accomplished and an endorsement signed into her log book, she reluctantly bid farewell to Butch as a flight instructor, being far too exhausted to expend emotion on anything approximating a bittersweet goodbye. For the next three months, she would have all three boys on her hands, with no possibility of flying.

She muscled her way through the summer, sometimes being a stay-at-home mother who tried to savor every moment with her children, and sometimes wanting to be shed of them so she could read everything she could get her hands on regarding a career as a commercial pilot. Fortunately, her relationship with Roy improved, most likely from the natural consequence of her not flying… which did not seem quite right to her. Still… her thoughts were always on the calendar with an eye on that glorious day in late August when Travis would enter second grade, Chad to kindergarten, and Wade back into daycare.

She had it all figured out. With Butch's recommendation, she got enrolled at the Lone Star Flight School located off the airport's main north-south runway. She knew a bit about this place by pilot word-of-mouth, but learned much more in making a visit there herself. They gave her a tour of facilities that were more elaborate than Butch's operation, and then she got about thirty minutes with its owner, Dwight Eisenhower… same as the president. He sort of looked like the man too – a kindly face with a softness of speech, yet an overall air of having spent so many decades flying that she simply must respect him as a general of the sky. Right off, he assured her that she would be treated as any other student at Lone Star… which made her think that the opposite might be true. As for Butch Carlyle's suggestion that she get her CPL on a twin engine, Mr. Eisenhower was in full agreement. She could start her eight week commercial ground school course in the fall. If she passed that, then she would be allowed to get her multi-engine rating and begin logging hours on a twin engine.

"Looks like you're all set, young lady… but allow me to make one thing absolutely clear before you go. Carlyle runs his Part 61 operation with a looseness that we frown upon here at Lone Star. We're a totally by-the-book outfit, which means strict adherence to FAA regulations, no fudging from the course curricula, and absolutely zero tolerance for throttle jockeys or that macho, macho man mentality. Understand me?"

"Yes, sir. Of course, sir."

"Stay true to your training, young lady… and you'll do just fine here at Lone Star."

"Yes, sir. Let me assure you, sir – my aim is to become a professional."

She left his office with a strong sense that taking lessons at Lone Star was going to be totally different from flying with Butch. Suddenly, something arose within her to defend him. To go back in and set the general straight as to her former instructor's competence. She would not allow Butch to be insulted or her own training to be discredited. But she kept on walking. In that moment, she somehow came to accept that learning from Butch had been her childhood in flight, and now it was time for her to grow up.

She finally had the kinks worked out in her daily schedule. Wade was comfortable being back in daycare, and the older two were settled nicely into their school routines. Even Roy seemed resigned to her flying, though he was not exactly bubbling over with excitement. So she was all set for her first day of ground school. Having not been a student for nearly fifteen years, she had no clear idea of what to expect on arriving at Lone Star. With a flight bag hanging off her shoulder, she entered as the first one into the designated classroom, and took a seat in the front row to wait. Between where she sat and the chalkboard was a table piled with notebooks, each rather thick-looking. Those must be the course material… which might be worth taking a quick peek at. She was on the verge of getting up when the next student arrived – a young man who could not be that long out of high school. She introduced herself to 'Tyler,' and immediately got into a conversation with him about their respective flight backgrounds when the next student arrived. One by one, others gradually filtered into the small room… all males and all younger looking than her. A few seemed surprised at her presence… as if it was so very odd that a grown woman should be seeking her commercial.

The instructor soon arrived to take his place at the podium. Even before he opened his mouth, the camel suit coat and plain black tie, both over a cream-colored button-up tucked neatly into blue jeans, told her that he was all business... Texas style. Somewhere in his fifties, this man had such a strong military air about him – a firm jawline and eyes that seemed accustomed to doing most of the talking... which was odd since he so smoothly got down to the job of teaching.

"Welcome. This is multi-engine ground for a commercial rating. I'm Max Bender, and I'll be your instructor for this course as well as the CFI for the practical. I preferred to be called Max, and I'll be calling you by your first name. My job's to prepare you with the aeronautical knowledge required for becoming commercial pilots. As time is short, we'll skip the formalities. You can introduce yourselves to each other on your own. Everyone show me your logbook and a 1978 edition of FAR."

She quickly held up her logbook and then her copy of the Federal Aviation Regulations... perhaps a bit too enthusiastically. Still... she was silently pleased to discover that her copy was considerably more worn than those of the others about her. Hers was also the only one with color-coded tabs. She had put those in herself.

"Good. As you should expect, we'll be using FAR from day one... but let's start with the course syllabus first."

From the pile on the table, he handed out a binder to each of the eight students in the class, and then had them turn past the lengthy background on the school's philosophy to the first page of content. She noted the heading 'Course Prerequisites' across the top. Skimming down the list, she was pleased to see that her experience put her in decent shape.

"Each of you should obviously have a valid private license and a current class three medical. You'll be updating the latter to a class two. You should also have an instrument rating and at least a hundred hours of powered flight time. Anyone out of compliance?"

She discretely looked about to the fact that no one raised a hand.

"Excellent. Now this course is geared for multi-engine operation... so I can assume that a good number of you have set your sights on an airline position. As it is, you'll need other endorsements to help you toward that goal. We'll be discussing those in the weeks to come. For now... turn to the next page."

In bulleted format, he went through the twenty some odd areas of focus to be covered during the class. He entertained questions along the way, so she casually asked about the level of math required, and was privately pleased to find that her high school education was sufficient. He finished up the list by moving to a paragraph at the bottom of the page.

"As you see, there'll be a course exam at the end. That's the FAA's test… not ours. You need a seventy percent or better as part of your license. While that score might be acceptable for the FAA, it's not for me. I'll consider it as an insult to my teaching if any student in this class registers less than ninety. I assure you that I will *personally* hold any such individual responsible for rectifying their deficiencies. Plainly put… no one moves on to the flight portion of the class until I'm satisfied… so I suggest that you take each topic seriously. Let's get into the first – basic aerodynamics of the twin engine craft. Turn to page twelve."

It did not take her too many days at Lone Star to conclude that she had never been more brain-tired in all her life. From the first lecture onward, Max talked nonstop for ninety straight minutes and every word had to be feverishly jotted down. He did that for the three days of her first week before she realized that the amount of information he covered was only a fraction of what she was required to know for the exam. That meant loads of studying on her own. She was at the kitchen table every night doing her homework alongside Travis. He colored, did phonetics, writing and new math, whereas she had near-on five hundred pages of FAA regulations to become familiar with.

Emergency response operations… Accident, damage and system malfunction reporting… Inspection guidelines… Airworthiness… Pilot qualifications, training and certifications… Operating as the pilot-in-command… Flight plans and alternatives… Navigation and dead reckoning… Terrain and airport maps… Traffic patterns… Airspace classifications and restrictions… Radio communications and emergency calls… Aircraft performance parameters and limitations… Weight and center-of-gravity calculations… Flying by VFR and IFR… High-altitude flight… Meteorology, radar and weather reports… Takeoff, landing and ground procedures… Banks, stalls, ascents and descents… Fuel consumption rates and ranges… Preflight and postflight inspection procedures… Risk assessment… Basic emergency medical responsiveness… Human behavioral factors… And so many codes, acronyms and designations! All of that and more had to be crammed into her head. She studied weekends and nights, sometimes well after Roy had gone to bed.

No one in the class complained about the work load, for the seriousness of Max's lectures warned against it. He frequently made a point of saying that a private pilot primarily had themselves to worry about, but a commercial pilot held the lives of many in their hands… so everyone in his class was damn-well expected to work their ass off in knowing their stuff. She had not expected such rigor from being a student at a 'genuine' flight school, but there were other things she was even less prepared for. At Butch's place, everybody knew everybody… which meant that everybody knew her. She had always gotten individual attention whenever she wanted it. Best of all, Butch had been a mentor to her. She could confide in him about anything, and was always sure to get the best of him in return. Not so at Lone Star. Max was plenty strict… sort of like Billings… except that he showed absolutely no favoritism among his students. She knew from day one that she had no hope of getting special treatment from him, as he was only available to answer her questions during class and in office hours. She was just one of fifty students enrolled at the school, and not even the only female. Nobody there had time for relationship building or shooting the breeze… much less helping a thirty two year old mother of three feel like she belonged.

Eight weeks of lectures and one week of frantic study led up to the exam day in the first week of December. Three hours were allotted for the one hundred bubbles needing to be penciled into her scan sheet, and then she had an equally nerve-wrecking week of waiting for the result. Contrary to her feeling of impending doom, she passed with a ninety seven. She was absolutely beside herself with elation… even if Max still called her into his office for the purpose of making her explain how she had missed three questions.

Through one of her best Christmas holidays in memory and then into the new year, her mind was always on the anticipation of flying again. For her first flight lesson, she met Max in the Lone Star hangar for an overview of what she would be training on – the Piper Seminole. They walked up to the plane nose-on while he was already speaking.

"This here's a brand new craft… I spent a couple weeks getting trained on her in Florida… and then put in twenty hours here to get the full feel of her. That's important for a CFI. We'll still be taking it slow. She's obviously a twin engine. Two 180 horsepower Lycoming O-360's. Notice the prop blades. What do you see?"

She compared the two sets for several seconds, fully aware that Max was evaluating her observation skills, when it finally hit her.

"Oh… wow! They're oriented differently from each other."

"That's right. The two engines spin in opposite directions. No critical engine. Gives the craft a symmetric slipstream. You'll see – much better handling. If you remember your aerodynamics, having the engines in close to the main thrust line also provides stability. Thirty eight foot wingspan… twenty seven foot length… hundred and ten gallon capacity, two of which are unusable… range at a little under seven hundred nautical miles… all in all, a very fine aircraft. We'll get to the rest of the performance specs later, but let's first do a walkaround. Here's your personal copy of the checklist. Get to know it well."

He handed over a laminated sheet, covered front and back with preflight preparations for the Seminole. She did not tell him that she already had a copy in her flight bag. As soon as the ground course was completed, she made a point of picking up both the checklist and the pilot's handbook for the Seminole.

Max took her through the entire list before starting in on a detailed walkaround in which he made her do the checks herself... just as Butch always had. They eventually came full circle to where they had been standing previously. There, he paused at the plane's nose as if debating what to do next.

"Before we climb in... remember in class what I mentioned about the fallacy of the twin engine?"

Mentioned?! He spent something like a whole lecture on it!

"Yes, sir. Two engines may provide greater performance, but it doesn't necessarily mean greater safety."

"Go on."

"It's pretty obvious that an engine contributes a disproportionate amount of weight to a small craft. So a dead engine ends up being a huge amount of dead weight... which causes the entire craft to effectively exceed the maximum power capacity of the remaining functional engine. Makes it nearly impossible to reach the Vmc of the..."

"And what's that?"

"Umm... the minimum control velocity... right?"

"Just making sure you're not slinging terms around without knowing their meaning. Continue."

"Well... ahh... remember when you passed out those performance curves for the Seminole in class? I was looking those over last night... A fifty percent loss of power to one engine results in something like an eighty to ninety percent overall performance loss to the aircraft."

"And what's that mean to the pilot?"

"You mentioned that many twin engine accidents come about as a result of the pilot losing control following partial or full power failure to one engine... you know... due to asymmetric thrust. The first thing that happens in that situation is an immediate yaw toward the failed engine. The pilot's instinct is to apply opposite rudder... but that only generates sideways lift to the functioning wing... which pushes the tail away from the good engine.

"And the result..."

"The failed wing dips... and you get a rollover."

"So what did I say was the thing to do?"

"Maintain airspeed with a nose-first descent... while... cutting back on the power to the functioning engine. Regain control of the aircraft... and then... slowly power-up the good engine."

"And if all this happens on takeoff?"

"Better to go belly down on no engines than to wingtip-it on one."

"Glad to know you were paying attention. Now this may not sound exciting, but you'll be putting in hours and hours of training into dealing with asymmetric thrust situations. Two engines may make you feel like a professional, but trusting in them too much can get you killed. Learning how to fly on low power... that's the mark of a truly proficient pilot. As I said in class, you'll find that it's all about achieving balance."

They moved to the cockpit door, he had her climb in first, and he followed. They then spent the rest of the lesson in going over the instruments, with her feverishly making notes in her handbook along the way. At the conclusion of this first lesson, she left feeling very excited about flying the Seminole. But stepping into her car, the issue of balance immediately came to mind. There on the passenger seat was her list of to-do items needing to be accomplished today. Dropping off the dry cleaning, getting some chicken wire for Travis's volcano project, stopping by the grocery store for milk and other badly needed items, and picking up the boys from school. They would want after-school snacks, and she would want some individual time with each of them... finding out what was going on in school... and just letting them know that she cared. But she still had last night's dishes to deal with before starting in on dinner. She should get on that as soon as possible. Roy would be home before she knew it... and she really wanted the house straightened up first. Then there was all of those Christmas decorations that still needed to be taken down, put in their boxes, and moved back down to the cellar. She would have to squeeze that in this weekend between loads of laundry and reviewing her notes on the Seminole's engine performance specs.

Ugh – I totally forgot about the boys' bathroom. It's absolutely revolting! It's gotta be cleaned before I do anything else this weekend.

Above the horizon or below the horizon, she was running herself ragged trying to maintain balance between flying and all of her responsibilities.

———————

She was finally getting the hang of the Seminole... and after only a few lessons. This twin was clearly more powerful than the Fairchild or the Cessna. Two engines roaring away just for her was so much better than one! Yet the takeoffs and landings were as smooth as silk… and already Max had her doing those on her own. Now on her fourth time out, Max said he would start her on the next phase of her training. Banking out to the east, she was heading for open space in which to conduct her first low power maneuvers. For the next forty minutes, he would throttle back on the power to an engine and show her how best to respond under normal cruising conditions. Once she got that down, he said he would progress her to climbs, banks and descents. Finally, he would take her through the difficult situations of takeoffs and landings, and when the aircraft was experiencing severe crosswinds or other adverse conditions.

The first time he cut back the power to an engine was alarming. The Seminole's functioning engine immediately raced out ahead of the other, shuttering the plane into a yaw. As she quickly sought to decrease the throttle on the full-power engine, she felt the low-power wing begin to dip as the plane made to roll over. Using the rudder, she brought the plane into a controlled dive that restored air flow over both wings, then she gradually increased the power to the 'good' engine while maintaining overall control of the aircraft. They did the same thing over and over for the next several weeks, varying the engine and the degree of power loss at different cruising speeds. With his guidance, she was finally beginning to condition her instincts into responding according to proper procedure.

Today, they started in on performing low power banks. She was listening to Max's instructions, but could not completely clear her mind of the argument that she and Roy had last night. She felt it rather considerate of herself to inform him that she soon would be doing cross countries that might require him to pick the kids up from school, but it all backfired. He immediately lost his cool at her. They went to bed angry with each other and woke up just as…

"Sharpen up the next one. That bank wasn't your best."

For Pete's sake, Marna! Have your mind on what you're doing!

"Roger that."

"Wouldn't you agree that a pilot should always strive for the absolute best in whatever maneuver they're doing?"

"I don't know. Something's got to be said for just staying within acceptable margins."

"Well put. Just testing you."

"What's that mean?"

"Most pilots… there're all about topping their best. That's too much pressure. Distracting too."

"Most pilots are men."

"And your point?"

Okay… you've stuck your foot in it. Might as well go all the way in.

"Mind if I be frank?"

"Go for it."

"We mothers don't have time for such nonsense. Rather than your absolute best… sometimes you just have to focus on doing much better than the minimum. That's how you survive the day."

He was silent in response. Shoulder-to-shoulder in the cockpit, she could not keep from noticing that he was staring straight ahead with pursed lips at her mother-of-a-pilot comment.

"You know… that's incredibly wise. I think I'll use that in the future. Now… let's work on that same bank again."

She did as he requested, with a tiny bit of herself wondering if that was the first time anyone had ever called her wise. Training with Max… it was actually much better than she had initially expected. He was really not all that different from Butch. The two men had their own demeanors, but both were such great sources of aviation knowledge, and both were an encouragement to her in their own way.

"You realize that part of becoming a proficient pilot is being able to carry on a conversation while you're flying."

"Umm… roger that… I guess."

"Come on. You have to be able to communicate with someone else… in the cockpit or over the radio… without being distracted from what you're doing. So… let's start a serious conversation while you execute those low-power banks. You just carry on… left, right… left, right… and we'll talk. I actually do have something on my mind to discuss with you. From what I understand, you're considering going after an airline pilot position one day. Is that correct?"

This opening to the 'conversation exercise' caught her off guard… but not so much that she messed up the one eighty she was currently performing. Still… after nearly two months of flying with him, he had not once taken the time to get personal with her… much less ask about her career aspirations.

"I think so. Hope so. But to be honest… all I'm looking for is the opportunity to build a career out of flying. I don't exactly know what that'll look like yet."

"Guess it's time that you did. By the way, that's part of my job… helping young whelps reach their professional goals. What good's a flight school if its students don't end up getting jobs. You realize becoming an airline pilot is a long haul?"

"So I've been told. Do you… umm… think I have it in me to do the job?"

She sensed him shift in his seat to look fully at her. Even with those aviation glasses of his, she could still picture the intensity in his eyes... so much like what she could remember of her aunt. Gwen's stare always made her nervous... but something else too. Weird… Before this moment, it had never really occurred to her how much she missed being looked at that way. It sort of… got her juices flowing.

"Of course. If that's what you want, I'm sure you can get there. It's difficult to stand in the way of a determined person."

"I've heard that one too…"

"Then let me give you a word of advice." He paused, almost as if for effect in making her brace herself for whatever was coming. "If that's what you want… then you'll need nerves of steel."

He paused again, but this time obviously in waiting for her to seek clarification.

"You mean… in order to become the right kind of a pilot?"

"That, I'm fairly confident you can handle. It only took me a couple times up with you to tell that you're a pure tactician when it comes to flying. Every 'i' dotted and every 't' crossed. Yet somehow… you also come across as one who flies by feel. You know how to do your maneuvers well, but are not compelled to make each one better than the last. You're very relaxed… even with me breathing down your neck. No… I'm actually referring to something that the average pilot never has to face… the male one's, at least. I think you know what I'm getting at. It's not right… but that's the way of the world."

She finished the current bank, leveled off, and hoped that this was the end of the advice. Unfortunately, he continued on.

"So when you find yourself up against it… and you will… take my advice. Don't lash out, don't burst into tears, and don't crumble under the scorn. Keep it all in. You have to. For yourself… and for those who're putting their lives in your hands as their pilot. But also… you need to be thinking about those women who'll be following in your footsteps. The impression you give off is the one they'll be labeled with. So have nerves of steel, Marna… as if nothing could touch you."

She was overwhelmed, and not just because of the compliments or the blunt nature of his advice. After only a short time together, he already knew her… maybe even better than Butch did. Yet try as she might to acknowledge his insight into her, she had no words of appreciation, denial, or hope for better ways in the future. She knew he was absolutely right. Her time at WYNG had taught her that much. So she would respond to his advice in exactly the same manner as he was recommending."

"Roger. I'll do that."

She finished out the flight and attended to every detail of a thorough walkaround. They set a time for the next lesson… her first cross country with him… and then she left for home. In crossing the ramp, she took the long way around the hangar for the parking lot rather than pass through the flight school, as was her normal habit. Carried along was a burden that she had not borne prior to taking off that morning. The entire weight of the skies seemed laid upon her shoulders, with all of the solidness to the earth beneath her feet being a measly feather holding her up.

Nerves of steel… How in the world am I to accomplish that?! How do I stay soft as a woman and still become the kind of tough that a man expects from a pilot?!

In the following months, she went on making steady progress in her training, but always at the expense of harmony in her household. No matter how she tried reasoning with Roy, he remained frustrated with her over how much time and money went into her flying. She was pretty sure that if things had been flipped around, he would have gone about getting trained without batting an eye, at the same time expecting her to take care of the kids while running an appliance store. It simply was not fair. She was expending so much energy managing his expectations and keeping their disagreements from spilling over into family life. None of that was working, as she was sure that all three boys knew 'Mommy's flying' was at the heart of the arguments between their parents.

It was not the way she wanted to be thinking, but more often she found herself wondering what life would be like if she could dedicate herself fully to only one thing. Imagine what she could accomplish if she was given the luxury of just flying! To rise excited in the morning and make that short drive out to the airfield with only planes on her mind. She would arrive in such a stress-free mood, with a flight bag dangling on her shoulder and a set of aviation shades slipped over the zipper of her leather jacket. She would have the freedom to chat it up with other pilots before becoming serious about that morning's flight. To be totally undistracted while planning, checking and double-checking. She would then start her engine and run down that long, straight stretch into the sky without a care in the world.

Unfortunately, that was not the way things were… and likely never would be. Something always seemed to pop up. Whenever one of the boys got sick or needed a parent on hand, it was on her to drop everything in response. It was so frustrating. And she still had such a long way to go with her training, being thirty hours short of the minimum needed for a commercial. There were more cross countries, a night flight, and a bit of high altitude flying, all before she could think about finishing up. After that, she would still need to build up her hours. As yet, she had no plan for addressing that problem. There was no doubt in her mind that Roy would go on resenting her flying... and she had absolutely no plan for addressing that problem either.

The only way to handle the situation was moment by moment... one flight at a time. Get the requirements in... get past the check ride... and stop spending money on flight training. That, at least, should make Roy happy.

In that case, she really should have her mind on this current cross country flight and not on whatever was going on with Roy. Hopefully, she could make this a quick turnaround, seeing as she needed to be back home before dark. Taxiing up to the FBO designated by Lone Star for refueling at Love Field, she was wondering whether this place would give her the same snappy service as when Max was with her a few weeks back. The dispatcher had dropped everything to make sure that he was happy. Max had that effect on people. Everyone simply respected the very sight of him.

She decided that it would be better to get the Seminole refueled first, then she could tidy up the cockpit before heading home. Climbing out, she was immediately greeted by the mugginess of a June afternoon in Dallas. All about the airfield, the pine forest rippled in the heat rising from off the tarmac. She was damp with sweat long before she got the plane tied down. Worse, the humidity completely took the life right out of the shag hairstyle she had been working so hard to maintain. Every strand seem to wilt against her cheeks, forehead, and neck.

Crossing the ramp in a hurry, she made a beeline for the pathway that led through an opening in a low hedge up to the pilot's door of the FBO... and the air conditioning within. Cutting the corner from the ramp through sandy turf, she gained the sidewalk just shy of the break in the hedge... and came to an immediate halt. To her left and right, the bushes were alive with the seething sounds of many insects. Though the FBO door lay some ten yards ahead through a picnic-like area defined by the hedge, there was no way she would risk it. Some of those bugs were likely harmful to her.

Backtracking to the fringe of the ramp, she took the long way around the building so as to enter through the front. Keeping to asphalt and concrete, she came to a carport drive-thru where she suspected that the bigwig corporate types got picked up by limos after their flights. Through a lobby-like area decorated so as to promote the reputation of the place, she made her way to the dispatch counter and waited for the man there to notice her.

"Can I help you?"

"I just came in on the Seminole..." She pointed over the man's shoulder through the tinted glass that rimmed the back wall of the FBO. He did not turn about to where she was pointing, from which she gathered that he already knew of her arrival. "Could you please arrange for it to be fueled? I'm with Lone Star out of Lubbock." She pulled a card from her back pocket and handed it over. "Here's the account number and the grade of avgas the Seminole needs."

"Sure thing. You've been her before, right?"

"Definitely."

"Then you're familiar with the place. Anything you need, just let me know."

She thanked him, got the latest weather forecast, and then made her way to the ladies' room. After a bag of chips and a coke from the snack machines in the pilot's lounge, she looked out the window to notice that there was no fuel truck anywhere near her plane. Scanning the outside, she found it parked some hundred feet off. She probably should have told them that she was in a hurry. Marshaling a diplomatic demeanor, she strolled back to the dispatch counter.

"So… I ahh… noticed that you haven't had a chance to get at my plane yet. Is there a problem?"

"Oh… sorry. We had to bump you. There's a corporate jet coming in. They've got priority over flight schools."

She looked out the windows, both to the ramp and the taxiway leading from the runway she had just landed on. There was no jet anywhere in sight.

"You sure? I don't see anything out there."

"They're on approach."

"So… umm… how long do you think that'll take? You see… there's that front of thunderstorms coming through from the southwest…" She pointed to the screen that maintained a constant stream of the National Weather Service forecast for the area. As before, he did not turn about to look. "I was really hoping to get out ahead of it."

"Can't say… but I'll let you know on the loudspeaker as soon as you're up."

She looked again to the long range radar. There was maybe an hour at most before things got messy. After that… she would be stuck in Dallas for who knows how long. This was so ridiculous. They could have had her plane refueled by now. On the verge of arguing her case further, she instead decided that it would do no good. The corporate types always won out.

Nerves of steel, Marna.

"Mind if I use your phone?"

"Dispatch phones are only for flight-related calls. You can use the payphone in the lounge for anything personal."

"This is to my school back in Lubbock."

He nodded his approval, and she called Lone Star to appraise them of her situation. The dispatcher there was aware of the weather approaching the Dallas area and reminded her that she was not yet instrument approved for commercial. She should stay put until the weather cleared. She hung up and returned to the pilot's lounge. Plopping herself down on a stretch of couch, she set about pouting. Something was bothering her. Something more than the annoyance of being bumped by the dispatcher. Irritating, yes… but not a thing that she was unaccustomed to from her years of flying. Planes did not fix or fuel themselves. No… something else was bugging her. Not the prospect of unfavorable flying conditions or her VFR restriction. The weather was what it was. Waiting on a front to clear was pretty standard stuff. No experienced pilot would take off on a flight plan that led them willy-nilly into the teeth of a storm. She looked out the window again… still no corporate jet in sight. Her fuel truck was sitting exactly where it had been ten minutes before. In frustration, she got up to peruse the vending machines once more… when her eyes fell upon the payphone.

Might as well get it over with. He needs to know.

After getting a pile of quarters from the dispatcher, she was back standing before the payphone. She had not intended that such a call would be necessary, all along expecting a quick turnaround. Holding the first quarter poised in the slot, she took a deep breath… and let it drop. Dialing with determination, she resolved to make this as matter-of-fact a conversation as any wife might have in informing her husband that she might get stuck in Dallas. A recorded voice requested seventy five more cents for a three minute call, so she complied.

"Meitner residence, Travis Meitner speaking."

"Travis… it's Mommy."

"Hey, Mommy. Where are you?"

"In Dallas. You ready for tonight?"

"Yes, ma'am. I think so. I've got my poem memorized and… but the dang robe keeps scraping at my neck!"

"I'm sorry, Honey. Maybe you could have your father adjust the collar for you."

"He doesn't know that kind of stuff! I need you to fix it. When're you coming home?"

"Hopefully soon. Listen… this is a long distance call. Could you please hurry and get your father for me?"

She heard him place the receiver down on the counter… and it was picked back up again after only a few seconds.

"Minner res-dunce… Wade Minner speakin'."

"Wade! It's Mommy! Sweetheart, you did that so well!"

"Mommy! Mommy! Daddy's teachin' me the phone!" There was the slightest of pauses before his voice came back sadly sweet. "Mommy... when you comin' home?"

"As soon as I can, Wade. You know how I miss you. But... ahh... could you pretty please put Daddy on for me?"

"Mommy?"

"Yes, Darling?"

"Chad called me a poop... and then he hit me. Real hard!"

"I'm so sorry, Darling. You should tell him how that makes you feel. Now could you..."

There was a sudden clunk... loud and plastic-like... and she realized that Wade had dropped the receiver to the floor. Off in the background of the call, she detected the indiscernible voices of her children arguing. She glanced about the empty lounge before concluding that she could risk raising her voice.

"Wade?! Anyone?! Please pick up!"

There was nothing for several seconds other than that distant collection of voices. Then all of a sudden, there was a loud clutter of sound, sort of like someone was juggling the receiver, and everything went blank. The next thing she heard was a dial tone.

I can't believe this! They hung up on me!

She scooped up another quarter and redialed, shoving in the next three while swearing feebly to herself that she would not allow the same thing to happen again.

"Meitner residence, Chad Meitner speakin.'"

"Chad... this is Mommy. Could you please put..."

"DADDY! MOMMY'S BACK ON THE PHONE!"

His voice bellowed so loudly that she had to yank the receiver away from her ear.

"Mommy, guess what..."

"Chad, I'm sorry... I really don't have time for..."

"I got stung by a bee."

Her mind immediately jumped in a panic across the three hundred some miles separating her from her child.

"Are you okay?! Is it..."

"I squashed it."

"What?"

"I squashed the bee for you. I saw him on the porch... and I squashed him so he couldn't get you. But he stung me."

"Chad, when did this happen? Tell me quickly!"

"Here's Daddy…"

She heard the phone changing hands… and could not believe how long it was taking.

"Marna?"

"Roy, what happened with Chad?! Is he okay? How's his breathing? Has the spot swelled up any?"

"Take it easy. There's absolutely no sign of a reaction. He shed a few tears… but he's completely over it now. Actually… he's quite proud of himself. Thinks he was defending you from…"

"Maybe you should take him to the hospital just in case."

"Marna… trust me… he's fine. I have everything under control. Now… when're you getting in? You do realize that Travis has his graduation tonight."

The whole purpose of the call came back to her. She was doing more than checking in. She was delivering bad news.

"Roy… there's a possibility that I might get held up in Dallas."

"What's going on?"

"They're not fueling my plane for another… I don't know… forty minutes or so. They put someone else out ahead of me. And there's this front coming through. I'm afraid that by the time they do get to me, I'll probably have to wait for the weather to pass."

"Great! I just knew this was going to happen!"

"You knew that thunderstorms would be moving into the Dallas area?"

"Don't be cute! You know what I'm talking about. Travis is going to be crushed if you're not here."

"Roy… stop! It's not my fault! And you're making me feel even worse than I already do! Don't you think that I'd want to be…"

"All I know is that when you took up this flying thing, you promised that it wouldn't get in the way of family life!"

"No… that was the plan. There's a huge difference between a promise and a plan! I can't possibly promise that the weather'll always be in my favor. You know that my plan was to work hard at managing my flying so it wouldn't inconvenience the family!"

"As usual, you're using words to cloud the issue."

"And exactly what's that supposed to mean?! What issue are we talking about?!"

"That you'd rather be off flying than at home with your kids."

Suddenly seething, she could not believe he would say such a thing.

"Really?! Spoken by the man who works nearly sixty hours a week at his store! But how's this for a promise, Roy – I'm sure as hell not flying through a storm simply so you can avoid the discomfort of having to manage the boys on your own for an evening!"

"Ha, ha! Real funny. And it's more than just an evening. It's his second grade graduation ceremony. The one where he'll be honored for writing the best poem in..."

"I know all about the poem, Roy! I'm the one who helped him write it!"

The phone clicked... and for a moment, she thought he had hung up on her. But then that recorded voice came on to declare that she must insert another dollar for the next three minutes. She was dropping in quarters when Roy's voice came back.

"Marna... are you still there?!"

"Yes! Of course! Don't you think I want to get home?! He's my son too! I'm just as proud of him as you are! But I'm stuck here and there's nothing I can do about it!"

"Well... obviously I don't want you flying through a storm. I just want you to be more considerate with your schedule."

"I'm trying, Roy... but you know this was the only time I could get for the..."

"Listen... I gotta go... the boys are fighting over something. Call me back when you can. Fly safe."

He hung up for real this time, leaving her beside herself with frustration. Of course she wanted to be there for her son's graduation! She would never willingly miss out on an opportunity with one of her boys. He might... for some late-night sale-a-thon... but not her. She had gone to countless school events on her own... so why not him?! No... the real issue here was his pride!

She had another quarter up to the slot... but held onto this one firmly before deciding to return the payphone's receiver to its carriage. She should save her quarters for when she finally got clearance to leave.

Why does everything have to be so difficult?!

Looking out of the lounge windows into the sky, she spotted the forming thunderclouds... but also perceived that there were still patches of blue up there. Maybe she would get lucky. Coming back down to the ramp, she observed the arrival of the long-awaited corporate plane – a Learjet 24, by the look of it. A truck with jet fuel was creeping out to meet it. She continued to watch as the FBO's ramp rat stepped from the cab. The jet's door came down... and out climbed a crew member... and then two passengers, one old and one young... both in suits. These were followed by another crew member. The former was pulling bags from a cargo hatch while the other stood by chatting with the passengers. The bags were out… the plane was buttoned up… and still all four men just stood there in a cluster. She looked back to the fuel truck… that guy was just leaning against the front grill waiting for them to clear the area before he got to work. After what seemed like forever, the four finally came wheeling their luggage toward the FBO. Her eyes were suddenly drawn to the far off signs of lightning going on within the darkened sky above the horizon, and she realized that she was not getting out of Dallas anytime soon.

Oh shit! I left my flight bag in the Seminole. Better hightail it out there before it's too late!

Still very irritated from the call and the whole situation, she decided to wait until the four men had gotten inside before heading out to the ramp, seeing as she was in no mood for being social. Tracking the group making its way down the walk toward the back hedge, she was surprised when all four men suddenly bolted through the patio area to the back door. They came bursting inside laughing their heads off.

It can't be that it's raining already.

She looked back out toward the jet. The ramp rat was casually unrolling the fuel line from his truck, showing no sign that rain was falling.

This is going to take forever!

With the four men having finally reached the dispatch counter, she slipped past them to the back door. Stepping outside, she was immediately greeted by the same heat as before… except something else was there too. The FBO door had hardly closed shut behind her when she realized where she was. Six paces into the courtyard, she found herself standing in the midst of the angriest… noisiest… and most every-which-way swarm of insects she had ever seen. Some were rifling by like bullets and some were doing drunken circles in the air, while whole clusters of others were clumped together into such big wads of wings, legs and bodies, rolling around on the ground at her feet. To make matters far worse, these things were absolutely huge! The size of her thumb or greater… and every single one of them was a wasp!

———

Sphecius speciosus – the 'beautiful wasp' – that was her name! A far better one than cicada killer! Of course she was beautiful! Reddish brown with such lovely yellow stripes. Fearsome and massive too! Nearly fifty millimeters in length. There was no wasp in the world as formidable looking as her! And so strong – she could do a full power lift even while clutching one of her largest of prey. Yet as impressive and showy as she was in appearance, she much more preferred to go unnoticed. To be on her own where she could skim through the air in glorious flight. To hunt alone… build her nest alone… and seek a peaceful existence all on her own.

But they simply would not let her be. Somehow, they knew exactly where to find her… in the only stretch of sandy soil anywhere near her favorite hunting ground of those pines. She came here to build her burrow… but they came for her. Dozens of them were suddenly all over her, each one wanting her to be their own. Crawling all over her… clinging to her… fighting with each other to have her as their own. Even after one had managed to attach himself, still the others fought to dislodge him and take his place. Writhing about in their anger, they bashed and tore at each other, completely neglecting that she was trapped in the center of it all. The only thing they cared about was their orgy of need. Oh… and the screams they made! A horrific drone of a buzz that was driving her insane. There was absolutely no way she could fly with them hanging all over her. With no other choice, she gave herself to them… until they had gotten all that they wanted. She let them satisfy themselves, for only then could she finally break free and fly far, far away from them all.

———————

Filled with horror, she stumbled back to the FBO door… but not before one of those terrible creatures bounced off her thigh and another flew by her face so close that she could feel the draft of its wings. Frantically struggling to get the knob turned, she could almost feel the entirety of them crawling all over her. In utter panic, she finally forced open the door, jerked herself through, and then slammed it shut behind her. Very swiftly, she went about brushing off every inch of her, just in case one had attached itself to her clothing. Now reasonably convinced that she was safe and had not been stung, she glanced back out the glass door to the appalling sight of a large cluster of those wasps tumbling around – exactly where she had been standing! It was an absolute brawl. A mêlée of little monsters! As one detached itself from the cluster, in came another to replace it. Totally repulsed by the chaos of it all, she still could not tear her eyes away. Whatever they were doing all balled-up was beyond her reason, but how horrifying it would be to find herself trapped within the center of that nightmare!

Odd… her mind jumped to a time recently when she had been peacefully sitting in the nook and all four of her boys suddenly ambushed her with tickles. It started out cute, but quickly turned into a wrestling match… with her at the very center. Her fingers absentmindedly came up to massage out the memory of the fat lip that one of them had given her. Looking back out at the wasps, she had the distinct impression that there was a single female in the center of each ball of turbulence. The males all about were still shaping and reshaping their angry selves in trying to get at her. If that were the case, then she could sympathize... even though it was disgusting to do so. The cluster that she had been watching heaved itself into the grass, leaving the pathway clear all the way to the hedge. But no way was she going back out there again. Just the thought of it made her skin crawl. Like before, she would go the long way around the FBO.

With one last shiver, she made for the main entrance with her mind still stuck on the ghastly sight of all those wasps. But not looking where she was going, she emerged through the building's front doors directly into the midst of the party of men who had come off that corporate jet. Supremely embarrassed with herself, she was quick to doll out apologies.

"Excuse me – I'm so sorry! Forgive me for..."

"Marna?! Marna Forde?"

Stunned to be known, she looked into the eyes of the elderly gentleman who had used her maiden name.

"Mr. Carswell?! I can't believe it! Is that really you?!"

"Yes, my dear... come to invade your state!"

Before she knew what she was doing, she wrapped him about in a huge hug, not caring whether she was embarrassing him in front of his colleagues. It was just too wonderful not to!

"Sorry... It's so good to see you again!"

"No apology needed – I heartily agree. But look at you... you haven't changed a bit. Oh, you have a different hairstyle, but you're still as lovely as ever!"

"Thanks! You're too kind... and just as diplomatic! But how about you... still in that three piece suit... just like I always remembered you!"

She did not need to say that he looked much older, with more gray and a bit stooped over. But it had been nearly ten years. A span of time that had likely put some lines on her face and pounds on her rear.

"How are you?! And what brings you to Dallas? Certainly not WYNG news!"

"Oh, I haven't worked there in years. But I expect our good friend Albert is still there toiling away at his assignment desk. I took a position in New York with the network's satellite telecast division... and then I was transferred to a leadership role in their subsidiary, NASCorp. That's why I'm here in Dallas. We're scouting out sites for the manufacturing of satellite dishes. NASCorp's also likely to move their corporate headquarters down here... for tax reasons.

Anyway… I'll be around all week. What's say we get together and catch up?"

"I'd love to… but I can't. I'll be leaving for Lubbock as soon as they get my plane refueled."

"You're plane?! Don't tell me you're a pilot?!"

"Oh, yeah! I should have mentioned that."

"Unbelievable! But not really… I always figured you could do whatever you set your mind to. So how'd that come about?"

"Well… my aunt who raised me was a pilot… so I guess it's kind of in my blood. Anyway… my husband signed me up for training shortly after returning from Chicago. I put it on hold for a while to have kids, but am now back at…"

"You have kids?! That's fantastic! How many?"

"Three boys… eight, six and four. Oh darn! I left my purse in my flight bag or I could show you some pictures. They're a handful… but each one's special."

"Wow! Marna Forde… pilot and mother of three. Or I should say Marna…"

"Meitner."

"Still happily married?"

"Yep! Hopefully I can get back home to them tonight. There's a front coming through."

She noticed him look over his shoulder at the other three members of his party. They had politely shifted off to the side so that she and Mr. Carswell could talk.

"Let me introduce you to my colleagues. Gentlemen… this is Marna Meitner, one of my favorite people in all of the world. We used to work together during my days at WYNG in Chicago."

"Don't listen to him. He was my boss's boss."

"Of no matter. Marna… this is Peter Denning, manufacturing engineer at NASCorp…" She shook the hand of a pleasantly-groomed man whose business suit looked nothing like what an engineer would wear. "…and by their uniforms, you can probably tell that these are two NASCorp pilots… Ty Westervold… and his second, Quinton LaBaer. Gents… Marna here's a pilot too."

She was still glowing from Mr. Carswell's warm introduction when she noticed the eyebrows on both men go up. Preparing herself for the worst, she instead received warm smiles and warm handshakes.

"Was that your Seminole on the ramp?"

"Yes… but it's not mine. It belongs to my flight school. I'm finishing up my commercial."

"That's great. So… what's she like?"

"Runs like a dream… and super powerful! Two one eighty horsepower four-cylinder Lycoming O360's. Gets up to twenty seven hundred rpm. Counter-rotating props…"

"I've read about that… no critical engine."

"Yep… that makes low-power situations in either engine a lot easier to deal with. Thrust lines in close too. The flaps are mechanical… but I don't mind. All-in-all… she's easy. Easy to fly, easy to land, and probably the easiest light twin to trim. You know… it *could* use better cabin ventilation. But hey… this is Texas. Everything's hot here."

To her relief, both pilots laughed… and both kept smiling at her through it all. Out of the corner of her eye, it seemed to her that Mr. Carswell was puffed up a bit. She was making him proud.

"There's nothing like a twin engine prop to keep a pilot on the edge of their seat. You stay sharp. Keep that greasy side down!"

"Oh, definitely! My CFI would have my scalp if I didn't."

She was about to ask them what it was like to be a corporate pilot when a limousine pulled up to the curb. The pilots and the other man expressed their pleasure at meeting her, and then moved into position to have their bags loaded up by the driver. But Mr. Carswell stayed at her side.

"It's so good seeing you. Brings back such fond memories. I'm really sorry we don't have more time to talk. I've got a meeting across town before we can get checked into our hotel. Marna… here's my business card. Please call me when you get a chance. If this deal works out, I'll be moving to Dallas… and looking for a pilot. These guys here… they're based in New York. I don't know where you are with your training… or what your plans are… or anything to do with pilot qualifications for that matter… but it wouldn't hurt to have you apply. If you're anything as good as you were at WYNG… I'd fly with you any day."

"Wow! Thanks, Mr. Carswell!"

"Please… Bertram."

"Okay… but that'll take a lot more training than anything I've been through as a pilot!"

As they both laughed, she glanced over at the limo. The three men were already seated inside, and the driver was standing at the back with his hand on the open trunk lid, obviously impatient to get going. But since Mr. Carswell showed no sign of moving yet, she could risk an awkward question.

"So… umm… this satellite thing you're doing… it doesn't involve that guy Azurean, does it?"

She wanted to use the phrase 'that idiot Azurean,' just to make sure that Mr. Carswell fully comprehended how she felt about the man. For a second, he looked at her with a perplexed expression… and then burst out laughing.

"Oh, my… I forgot all about that dabster! No… I haven't heard anything of him since he left Chicago with his tail between his legs. Not to worry – he's nowhere in the picture."

"I'm really relieved… for you… but satellites… does that mean he was right… his vision of a twenty-four hour news station and all?"

"The vision was right… but it wasn't his. Turns out… he sat in on a single network board meeting with his father, heard the concept being discussed, and then took it to Chicago as his own."

"You're kidding?!"

"Sad but true. He had absolutely no idea what he was doing. Anyway… we *have* entered the satellite era… and now I'm working on behalf of the network for their subsidiary that manufactures and distributes dishes. Market projections look pretty good… if we can get this facility up and running in two years. Well… I best be going. Keep that card handy, Marna. I expect to be hearing from you soon."

He gave her another hug before entering his limo. She stood there watching them pull away… until the car was completely out of sight. Only then did she looked down to the card he had given her. A feeling indescribable swelled up within her, so strong that she simply must cradle that card to her chest. Only as the hopefulness of its significance slowly ebbed away, being replaced by a firmer sort of determination, did she carefully slide the card into a front pocket of her jeans and continue on to the Seminole. Stepping from under the sheltered overhang, the sky suddenly lit up… just as the first huge drops of rain fell upon her head.

END OF WASP 5

WASP 6

THE ONE WHO STINGS

CHAPTER
38

BEECHCRAFT BONANZA

She had always believed that in starting any great endeavor, there came a moment when things got decided. For her, the long hours of waiting for a stormfront to clear the Dallas area were more than sufficient for solidifying her mind. When she finally received clearance to leave, the heavy rains had washed the wasps away, cooled off the temperature, and put her back into a determined mood. It was time to embrace her future. She would not wait for things to happen – she would make them happen.

Still… she thought it wise to delay a full week before phoning Mr. Carswell, part out of curtesy to how busy he must be and part because he said he would not be back into his office until then. When she did reach him, they had such a wonderful talk together. She filled him in on her life, and he told her more about what he was doing with NASCorp. She eventually got to the point of the call – to find out if he was serious about one day needing a pilot. He was… though again, he knew nothing about how the parent corporation made such hires. For that, he put her in contact with the corporate head of aviation, a Mr. Randolph Tugbuddy. That man was cordial with her over the phone, but equally blunt. She neither had the required training or the minimum experience for employment as a pilot by the North American Satellite Corporation. But if, having reached a thousand hours with all her certifications in place, Mr. Carswell still wished for her to be interviewed, then he would gladly see that it happened. She hung up with her heart lightened. She now had a specific goal to shoot for, and that made all the difference in the world.

The first order of business was to finish her training. So she put her head down and concentrated on getting her two hundred and fifty hours in. Then came the check ride… which she passed on the Seminole with flying colors. Max promptly called her into his office to congratulate her on receiving her CPL, but also had a proposal.

"I've been doing some thinking about your problem…"

"Which problem's that? I have so many."

"Cute. I'm talking about flight time. I think I have just the solution for you. The best way to build your hours… outside of the military… is to become a flight instructor. You know that. So… would you consider staying on for your CFI rating? If you do, I can almost guarantee you a job afterward. Eisenhower's real impressed with you… as am I. And who knows… maybe you'll like it so much, you'll want to stick around for your CF-double-I."

He was paying her such a huge compliment, so it was important right off that she show her appreciation. She knew plenty of pilots who would love to be working at Lone Star.

"Thank you, sir. I really appreciate the offer… and the advice. I really do. But I think I'm ready to be out on my own."

She did not add that Roy would strangle her if she accepted. Gwen's money was almost gone, and the store was not doing so well. No way could they afford for her to take more flight lessons. If anything, she should be out earning a wage, not studying for more tests.

"But you could keep an ear out for me instead. I have one or two small possibilities already… little jobs that Butch Carlyle's pointed out to me. I'd still appreciate hearing about any opportunities that you might come across. Anything to help me build my hours."

"I'll certainly do that. Good luck to you, Marna."

Her first ever paying gig as a pilot did come about through Butch's connections. She was taken on as a temp by a small charter company whose pilot had turned his ankle playing volleyball at a family picnic. The job was fairly straightforward. For three weeks in May while her kids were in school, she flew a Cessna out and about West Texas on a variety of errands… most times shuttling passengers to some remote airfield and back again. Not the glamourous work she dreamed of, but it put nearly twenty hours in her logbook. To her surprise, the charter owner… a Mr. Gifford Curtis… commented that several of his clients had enjoyed having a woman fly them around. She gladly took the compliment… and the three hundred dollars… into a summer of watching over her kids. Flying now mostly on weekends or whenever she could scrounge up a babysitter, she did more odd jobs for Mr. Curtis. As a sign of his appreciation, he personally arranged for her to be the one flying banners over the South Plains Fair in the third week of September. On the fair's closing day, she took special pride in doing this job, because somewhere down there, her husband and sons were looking up into the sky at her plane.

With her kids back in school, more small jobs soon came her way from the fall into winter. Ferrying oil surveyors, doing pipeline and powerline patrols, some range riding, assorted charter work, and more dragging of banners… this time over Padre Island during spring break. She even did a stint of crop dusting, but gave that up after a few weeks seeing as she was getting tired of the nasty smell to her skin and hair.

Her first truly great break came in the early spring with a phone call from Max. A buddy of his in Austin with the Department of Agriculture needed a pilot familiar with the Texas panhandle. Since he remembered her having said that she had thoroughly driven all over the counties surrounding Lubbock in her work with a cable company, he right off recommended her.

"They've chartered a craft from us for the summer. I've got two guys that could split the time, but the client wants a single pilot for the whole contract. You up for it?"

"Are you kidding?! You bet!"

"I thought you might be. But you should know… it's with our Bonanza."

"The V-tail?"

"Yep. As you might expect, they're paying for an experienced pilot… and the V-tail takes some getting used to. You know it's rudder and yoke are interlinked."

"Yeah… ruddervators… I've read about those."

"The Bonanza can be quite tricky on landings and take-offs in a crosswind. Also somewhat susceptible to weight imbalances, so how you load it can be critical."

"Hey – I'm up for the challenge! But how much will it cost me to get a couple days in with it on my own?"

"Glad you asked. Eisenhower's agreed to give you ten hours at cost, which includes two hours of my time to show you the ropes… absolutely free."

"Wow! He must really like me."

"Marna… everybody likes you. So… I've got you penciled in for next Monday at nine. We'll first take her up together and then you can get the balance of the time in on your own. The ag team's coming in on Thursday to brief you and outfit the plane with a camera."

"A camera?! What in the world will I be doing?!"

"No idea. All I know is you'll be flying real slow. See you in a week."

She hung up in amazement that of all people, she had been given this opportunity.

Everybody likes me... I don't know about that! But it's going to be really cool flying a Bonanza!

She hardly got far down her mental track of relishing this new challenge when a completely different thought derailed her excitement.

Good lord – what am I going to do with the boys all summer?!

For a moment, a tart of a notion hit her. She could make it Roy's problem. After all, she had been saddled with the care of the boys for the last... oh... every single moment of their lives! Let him take on the responsibility for once and see how much he liked the juggling! But that was stupid. He'd probably throw a couple of boxes of Fruit Loops at them and lock the doors of the house on the way out. Since it was actually her job, then she would do it right... even if she only had a couple of weeks to get everything arranged before school let out. So she took to the phone in a flurry.

After a long, heated conversation with Roy and several frenzied days of cobbling together possibilities, she finally managed to fill a good bit of the calendar with summer camps, church VBSs, trades of evenings for afternoons with girlfriends, the occasional babysitter on-demand, and of course, daycare. She did not bother going over all of it with Roy. Everything would be posted on the refrigerator door if he cared to know. She also decided not to spring too much of it on her boys. Just ease them into a summer without their mother. Besides, what did a nine year old really need to know about her plans?! Travis would take the news as the brave young man he was... and the other two would be totally clueless when the inevitability of daycare finally came.

She spent two delightful hours with Max learning the ways of the Bonanza. She found the plane to be challenging at first... what with there being no traditional rudder on the V-tail. But then she remembered from long ago the words of Butch... that birds carried on quite well without one. As for being with Max, post-CPL style, she was surprised to find him looser... more of a fatherly colleague than an instructor. He even went out of his way to downplay the Bonanza as a 'doctor killer.' She already knew that nickname came about because of accidents involving so many extremely accomplished men with an underestimation of what it took to fly a plane.

"By all means take her seriously, just don't put too much stock in the lore. It's not a perfect plane… and that Buddy Holly crash was really an unfair knock against its reputation."

He did not need to bring that up. Anybody who grew up in Lubbock knew well that Buddy Holly had died in a Beechcraft Bonanza accident that also took the lives of the Big Bopper, Ritchie Valens and their pilot. She was thirteen when it happened. Could still remember the day – February 3, 1959. She and her girlfriends cried for weeks.

That'll be the day… when he died.

"Whatcha thinking?"

"That I'm not that pilot… and this here's not that plane. I know better than to jam-pack my aircraft and then take off in bad weather."

"Roger that."

With the two hours up, she landed, set Max down on the ramp, got the plane refueled, and was right back up again. Now on her own, she went about exploring the Bonanza's characteristics more deliberately. She could easily see how this V35B variant might lull an inexperienced pilot into an awe of its performance. A two hundred and eighty five horsepower engine… hundred and seventy knot cruising speed… rate of climb nearly as good as the Seminole's. But there were oddities to watch out for. First off… she hated that the switch for the landing gear was positioned close to the flaps. She would have to watch out for that. Also, the wings were incredibly easy to stall… and the tail… it had this strange feel of wag to it. This Bonanza was clearly a strict, fly-by-the-numbers sort of craft that was sure to keep her on her toes.

She got her ten hours in on the day before the ag team arrived from Austin. Showing up early to the pilot's conference room at Lone Star, she chatted up Max about what he knew of these guys. The head of the team – a Dr. Colt Abernathy – was not just a 'good buddy' of his, but his wife's first cousin. She was asking for more details from him when in came three men… one old and two young… all three dressed as if they might have come off any street in Lubbock. Max and the older one immediately went for each other as friends might do, leaving the other two to awkwardly size her up as their pilot. She was about to introduce herself when Dr. Abernathy turned her way.

"And this must be our pilot…"

"Hi… I'm Marna Meitner."

"Yes… Max speaks quite highly of you."

She shot a quick glance at Max, and gathered from his smile that more private talk than this had transpired about her.

"It goes both ways. I'm thankful to have had him as an instructor."

"No doubt. Now… let me introduce you to my team…" He turned to the other two, each stepping up to shake her hand. "This is Brixton Mathers… he goes by 'Brick'… and this is Theo Piccard." Neither said anything to her other than hello. With the introductions done, both young men looked to Dr. Abernathy, who glanced down at his watch before addressing her again.

"I'm sorry… time's short. I've got a return flight to catch in three hours… so we better get at it. Correct me if I'm mistaken, Max, but I believe we've got this room reserved for the summer."

"That's right. So I'll leave you to it."

Max turned from the room without another word… and still she did not know what was expected of her as the pilot. Dr. Abernathy motioned to Brick… who she already noticed was leaning on the end of a fairly hefty tube. Brick immediately lifted that tube up onto the conference table and began busily pulling out maps sections with the help of Theo."

"While they're doing that… let me give you an overview of the project. I assume you're familiar with the Ogallala aquifer?"

"Yes, sir. It starts somewhere up north… Nebraska, I think… and stretches down to us."

"Correct. That aquifer's heavily relied upon for irrigation… and nearly done in. Because we get the tail end of it, Texas farmers, rural community leaders, conservationists… and we at the Department of Agriculture… are all concerned about the level to which it's being oversubscribed. To the point… the region needs alternatives to the central pivot. So in order to better understand the problem, we were funded to do an extensive aerial survey on irrigation usage."

"I assume that's where I come in."

"Right. We'll be employing a camera system proven effective in many of our other projects. It'll be mounted under the Lone Star plane we've contracted for. We'll have you fly a grid pattern over this portion of the state."

He slid a map of Texas in front of her, and with a finger made a huge circle that encompassed much more than the panhandle.

"Our most recent data's five years old… patched together from a variety of different flyovers." He threw a thumb back over his shoulder to where Brick and Theo were busy hanging large map sections to the wall with masking tape. "No one since has conducted a comprehensive snapshot of the region during a single growing season. So… what we're after is determining the percentage of farmland being cultivated, how much is currently setup for central pivot irrigation, and how much of that is actually being irrigated this year. From the latter, we're especially interested in gauging the vitality... the shade of green, for lack of a better term... in order to estimate how much aquifer water is being used. With knowledge of the crop and the seasonal weather conditions... adding on a reasonable percentage for overspray, evaporation and soil retention... it's not too difficult to set a bounds on the amount of water being applied to any given irrigation circle. That's all fairly well understood. What we don't have is the current survey. You with me so far?"

"Yes, sir... of course. You need a plane and a pilot to get you that survey."

"Correct... and please call me Colt."

"Cool. So I can assume that we'll be using aerial videography rather than photography... seeing as there's so much terrain to cover. You know, a reporter can capture a lot more information on a reel than on a roll of conventional film. Not with the same resolution... but hey, there's always trade-offs." Surprised that he did not immediately respond, she ventured a quick explanation. "I used to work at a TV news station."

"Very good..."

He glanced over at the other two... and they smiled back at him.

"I see this is going to work out..."

"I'll certainly do my best that it does. So... I suppose someone's figured out the TAS tolerances, as well as the optimum GS and AGL for capturing the desired granularity with this camera of yours?"

"Ah..."

"Sorry... that's 'true airspeed,' 'ground speed' and 'above ground level' altitude. We pilots use way too many acronyms."

"I've noticed. I'd say mostly... except West Texas has considerably less humidity than the rest of the state, so you may be able to fly a bit higher and still get good images. But what we need to work on first off is your grid pattern. The region's huge... so it'll take some time to cover it all."

"We should also stay mindful of airspace restrictions. There aren't a great many, but several to be taken seriously. Hey... out of curiosity... are you wanting to follow the progression over the course of the summer with multiple passes?"

"We're hoping to for certain areas... if we can manage it. We'll point those out as we go. The more important thing is to get the initial pass done right. So we'll be doing some trial runs first in order to get you trained on the camera system."

"Umm... I don't understand. Won't someone be monitoring that while I fly?"

She looked to the other two... assuming it to be one of them. They paused their map hanging to face Colt.

"No… it'll just be you up there by yourself. Theo and Brick will be taking turns here in Lubbock processing the film into print and analyzing the results. Don't worry… we'll make it easy for you by setting up a live video feed to a monitor that'll be in the seat beside you."

She looked from one to the other again… and decided that she could probably handle the extra task. Clearly, other pilots had.

"Sure. I have to climb in and out over that seat… but I'll work around it somehow. I assume you know that the Bonanza's electrical system is twenty four volts?"

"We got the specs from Max. The equipment's already here. In fact… I understand his people are installing it as we speak."

They then got down to the business of hammering out the details of her grid pattern. The northern border was about a hundred and seventy statute miles in length. Broken into five mile wide swaths… which was an extreme field of view for his wide-angle camera if she flew at about two thousand feet… that made for over forty trips there and back, each leg being more than two hundred miles in distance. Colt was also interested in a region stretching as far south as Denver City and Lamesa… which was why he had chosen Lubbock over Amarillo as his base. As she took notes, the four of them discussed the grid pattern using the wall maps. She was really getting into this planning… factoring in prevailing winds, fuel economy and ways of not covering the same ground twice… when Colt abruptly indicated that he had a plane to catch. It was only then that she casually glanced down at her own watch to notice that the hours had slipped by without her registering the time.

"Oh shit… excuse the French… but I've gotta go too! I'm late for picking up my kids from school. Ahh… by the way… just so you know… that won't be a problem in the future."

In quickly gathering up her things, she found that all three men were looking at her rather blankly… almost as if she had been expressing a concern over the phase of the moon. Colt, perhaps in being the oldest, smiled sympathetically.

"Not a problem. You can come up with your own schedule. I have a feeling you'll be producing film much faster than we can analyze it."

"That's a huge relief. So… umm… who'll I be working with first off?"

She found out that Brick would be there early in the morning, and that they all would have a conference call first thing. She then quickly bowed herself out. Dashing across the Lone Star parking lot, she had so many things bubbling up in her mind. Grid patterns, crop circles, altitude-speed-course variations, and the wonder of having the Bonanza all to herself. If what Colt was planning actually came about, then she would be flying all summer and into the fall. The hours that got put into her logbook would be incredible. But what would Roy think about that… and how would her kids adjust? Really, she should not have to worry about any of that just yet. She should stick with the good thoughts. About how this was the most exciting thing that had happened to her professionally since that first day at WYNG. But she had been on her own then, with nothing splitting her attention. She just got up every morning and went to work. No… this situation needed careful managing or it would likely fall apart before she even got started. She still had so many holes in the summer calendar to fill… and only a week left to figure it all out.

Her flying during the last week of school had gone well, but now with the summer break starting, it was time for the alternatives. So she broke the news to them the night before… and was absolutely stunned when Travis put up holy-hell about being put into daycare the next morning. Of course, whatever he did, his seven year old brother just had to follow suit. The two of them whined and complained all evening… until she was so glad to be closing off the bedroom door on them.

Come morning, Travis was right back at her, pleading to be left at home on his own. He even volunteered to watch over Chad. He just kept bombarding her with promises that they would stay inside the whole time, not answer the door if a stranger came by, not make a mess, and not cook a single thing. She knew better. If she left those two unsupervised for even a day, she would come home to a smoldering wreck burned down to its cinder blocks. But no matter how firm she became, the two boys refused to soften. So she naturally looked across the breakfast table for Roy's support, him with his face buried in the newspaper.

"Husband… you tell them."

Without looking up, he mumbled out his best effort at involvement.

"Do as your mother says… and don't yell in the house."

That might be enough to quiet the boys, but a far cry from settling their sour attitudes. They just sat there jabbing at the breakfast she had made for them, every once in a while looking up to shoot nasty glares her way. So… it was going to be solely on her to bully them into their first day of daycare.

"Shiny Star… what a shitty name!"

She looked in shock at Travis, and then to Roy… who did nothing.

"Watch your tongue, young man… or you're liable to be losing it!"

"Yes, ma'am…"

"And for your information, Shining Star's a fine place. You're little brother's been going there for years."

"Yeah, Travis, I like it a lot!"

"Shut up, squirt!"

"What's that you said to your brother?"

"Nuttin."

"Best be nothing. Now get yourself ready to go. You too, Chad. We're leaving in five minutes."

"But Mom… it's so unfair! I won't know anybody!"

"You'll make friends quick enough. Plenty of kids your age there."

"Yeah… but none of 'em are my friends!"

Thankfully, Travis said no more, slinking from the table to brush his teeth with Chad following behind. She made them say goodbye to their father… him still sitting at the breakfast table… and then herded all three into the car. The drive to Shining Star was uncharacteristically quiet. She got them checked in, and then tried to put on a chipper attitude in hugging each boy goodbye. Coming in close to Travis, she was shocked by the rage in his eyes, and instantly knew that this nine year old would not soon forget her offense.

Finally free to head for the airfield, her thoughts should be shifting to today's flights, but they remained in a tangle of frustration over Travis's lousy attitude, Roy's detached indifference, and the guilt competing with her joy of flying. It was all wrong! How was it that a man, with the roles of father, husband and job-holder, could keep everything so neatly confined in its own box… each with such thick walls that prevented one concern from spilling over into another? If things got bad for him at home, then so what?! Just get to work and everything would turn out fine! She had no idea how to achieve that kind of thinking… except maybe that it involved a whole lot of cold-heartedness. Actually… she was pretty sure that Roy never thought of himself as having roles. He just did whatever was right before him!

Wouldn't that be nice! I'm tired of getting all-knotted up over whether I'm being a good mother or a good wife! I'm so tired of second-guessing myself… and I'm like super-decisive compared to most women! But even more than that, I'm so sick and tired of being judged by those women for my choices. This has got to stop!

If only my life was more like an instrument panel. Everything laid our clear and simple! Each role so well-defined. The altimeter doesn't have to worry about what the manifold pressure's doing! That's not it's job. And it doesn't get all… emotional… simply because the lazy airspeed indicator just sits there at the breakfast table doing nothing but sucking in air through its stupid pitot tube!

I wish there was only one gauge in life. Just give me that one gauge… and I'll be happy!

All day, she struggled with concerns over what her older two boys were doing at daycare. Were they adjusting? Were they having any fun at all? Or would she be greeted by anger when she picked them up? Maybe she should finish out this flight and dash over there to see how things were going? Might not take too long. Just pop in and out… and maybe bring them a treat from a convenience store. A little piece offering.

She had just decided that taking a break between flights was something a concerned mother should do when she received the go-ahead from the LBB air traffic controller. She enriched her fuel for descent and retrimmed as needed before entering the approach funnel in sequence. Having decreased her airspeed through her glide path to landing, she went to extend her flaps with an odd sensation that something was not quite right. Just on commencing the flare, she suddenly realized that she had not lowered her gear. In a split second of panic, she quickly throttled up, brought her flaps back into their normal position, and radioed for a fly-by instead. Still very much shaken, she circled the airfield and came back around for a second try at the landing.

In all her time flying, she had never made such a bonehead mistake. She could blame it on the Bonanza's landing gear controls, but it was hardly the plane's fault. She was the one who had become distracted. What good was it to be thinking of her kids while bellying her aircraft into a runway?! She pulled the Bonanza onto the ramp outside Lone Star and made directly for the ladies' room. Only there could she be free enough to calm herself down over the magnitude of what might have just happened.

Her next several hours of flying were especially tense. To anyone else, knowledge of her mistake would have been no big deal. They would have said that she responded appropriately in avoiding an accident. Not so with her. The mishap was a rebuke to her divided mind.

Either fly… or don't fly.

But fly she did. Following her carefully laid out grid pattern, she covered a significant portion of the Panhandle in the weeks to come. It was the West Texas Cable Corporation all over again. Instead of carrying a ledger, she had a camera bolted into a recess in the bottom of her plane and was recording crop circle after crop circle. The feeling was still the same. It was so blazing hot out. Even with a slight breeze pulled into the cabin, she still sweat like a pig. But worse, she had never felt more alone in all her life. Hour after hour, she flew a straight course with absolutely no one with whom to talk. There was plenty of chatter on her radio, but none of it was for her. She had only thoughts about her choices to keep her company.

It was odd that her feeling of loneliness now brought back that strange optical effect in which the Texas farmland seemed to possess an upward curve at the horizon. As when she was training on the Fairchild, the earth appeared as a wide and shallow bowl beneath her. Somehow, that felt more true to her than just an artifact of light and perspective. Down in that bowl of the earth was everything that she cared about. Everything that she had willingly left behind to go floating upon this dome of the sky. Was that wrong for her to do? She found no answer in herself. So to this bowl of an earth, she sent out a silent plea on behalf of her family… that they might be kept safe while she was up here flying.

But maybe it was foolish of her to be entrusting so much to an illusion. She drew her eyes back to her instrument panel, feeling it irresponsible of her to neglect the task at hand by making such a whimsical wish. Double-checking her heading, airspeed and altitude, she concluded that all was well. She needed to maintain this course for another fifteen minutes or so, and that should put her at the border. She would then make a one eighty, re-acquire her new heading, and start in on the return trip. She glanced to the monitor in the seat beside her. Everything seemed fine. The camera was doing its job of recording. By its perspective, the earth below had absolutely no curvature to it. Just flat terrain. That was the way she needed to see things too. Be detached and remote controlled.

Another grid sector done and another two hours in her logbook. She made the low bank over Oklahoma's own panhandle and was in the process of climbing back to the proper altitude when she caught sight of something below. A train… creeping along on some errand of its own. Yet what struck her about the scene was the blur of the Bonanza's shadow as it momentarily crossed over the tracks some distance behind the train.

Maybe she could risk a distraction. Descending to well under a thousand feet in an effort to sharpen up her shadow, she leveled off and decreased her airspeed to slightly above the stall point. Using the monitor in the seat beside her, she put the shadow of her plane on the tracks, and did her best to creep up on the train from behind. Of course, all of this would end up on the tape, and she would have to explain herself to Theo… or Brick… or Colt. But that was okay. Pilots sometimes got away with doing strange things.

In spite of the monitor's flicker giving the ground a disjointed feel, she still managed to bring the shadow of her plane over the caboose. Up the length of the train she went, keeping herself perfectly centered. Her shadow eventually passed over the engine and out onto barren track. There was no reason to go any further with this game. She turned about for Texas, to pick up where she had left off from her grid. In regaining the appropriate altitude and airspeed, her shadow gradually widened and lost definition. Soon, all signs of her presence in the sky were completely gone from the face of the earth. This had been such a ridiculous thing for her to do… imagining herself covering that train with her wings. Even at her slowest speed, she still moved much faster than it ever could. Sooner or later, she was destined to fly out ahead of it. She would go her way… just as it must also go its own. In all likelihood, no one on that train had even noticed her. They were down there, she was up here, and the shadow of her wings was far too vague to leave any kind of an impression on anyone.

She felt a flutter to the Bonanza's tail, retrimmed the ruddervators a touch, checked her fuel consumption, and cast her mind forward to her job. Ahead to the south was a silvery sky, pure and distinct in how its light got dispersed through the clouds. She wiped the lenses of her aviator glasses on her shirt tail and decided to be at ease. This plane was a gift. Her chance to break free.

Five hours a day, five days a week for nearly four months, she flew a tight grid pattern over the forty some odd Texas counties that derived irrigation from the Ogallala aquifer. Unfortunately, the job went away with the harvest and would not return in the spring. Colt had all that he needed for his study. But in the process, she added nearly four hundred hours to her logbook. She had finally eclipsed seven hundred hours of total flight time. The summer had done her good in other ways too. She lost weight, sensed a firmness returning to her arms and legs, and had gained a rich color to her skin from all of her time spent in the sun. She felt younger and more energetic. Hungrier too… and ready for her next big challenge in flight. With Travis having entered fourth grade, Chad into second, and Wade into kindergarten, she now had more free time to roam about the FBOs and pilot hangouts of the Lubbock airport looking for opportunities. A month into the new school year, she happened upon Max outside the breakroom at Lone Star.

"Hey, Marna… I was hoping to run into you today. Come in here… I want to show you something."

She backtracked with him into the breakroom as he led her up to the large bulletin board that Lone Star used for posting ads. She had just been over every scrap of paper thumb-tacked to its cork.

"See here… Ranger Airlines is accepting applications. You interested?"

"Of course… except I don't think they're going to be interested in me. I've only got a little over seven hundred hours."

"You're *exactly* the type of person they're looking for. Remember that exposé I showed you last winter on the number of female pilots in the airline industry?"

"Yeah… sure. It was something like… fifty."

"Among over thirty three thousand positions."

She had the same feelings come over her that she had from reading that article. The same ones that her aunt likely would have had too. Outrage, frustration and a reluctant acceptance of the way things were.

"What's your point, Max?"

"I have it on good authority that Ranger's really looking to hire its first female pilot. They're not coming out and saying it… in case they don't find who they're looking for… but that's what this advertisement's all about. On top of that… they're aiming for that person to be a Texan."

"Really?! And you think I might have a shot?"

"You'll never know until you apply. As a matter of fact… I've been trying to call you all morning. If you decide to put your name in, then I'll be more than happy to help you prepare. You know those airline interviews can be grueling."

"Wow, Max… I… don't know what to say… other than… okay. I'll talk it over with Roy and get back with you."

That night, she brought the subject up with Roy as they were preparing for bed. In the most noncommittal way she could phrase it, she expressed her desire to apply without really expecting to receive an invitation to interview. After all, there were thousands of applicants per position and she did not exactly own the best resumé for getting her through the extensive screening process. She did not tell him the scoop that Max had obtained about women having an inside track. Best not to overplay the opportunity until it actually revealed itself as such.

To her disappointment, Roy seemed not at all interested. His mind was somewhere else… off in a place he had refused for months to share with her. She knew he was under pressure at the store, but his grumpiness probably also involved her. Most likely all of her excitement about flying… or something that she had let slip around the house. She put aside the question of the application to ask if anything was bothering him, but he just said that it was nothing for her to worry about. That was it. They went to bed lying back to back, her planning out her resumé, worrying about the kids, and wondering what was on his mind.

After a week of struggling over how much of her non-aviation background to highlight, she sent in her application to Ranger Airlines, waited another week before calling to make sure it had been received, and then put the whole thing to simmer on a backburner of her mind. Returning to her circuit of pilot hangouts about the airport, she was pleasantly surprised to discover that Butch had been contacted by someone from Ranger about her. The same she learned later that afternoon was the case for Max. Her application was actually being followed up on.

As the days went by, it became more and more difficult for her to hold back her antsiness. She stayed at home just to be near the phone. But since it was impossible for her to sit still, she dedicated herself to catching up on her household cleaning. The stove... the oven... the refrigerator... the kitchen floor... more floors about the downstairs... the woodwork... up into the kids' bath... and then into their own bathroom. Every time the phone rang, she practically jumped out of her skin in a mad rush to reach it. And every time it was someone other than Ranger Airline, she would return to her chores just a bit more deflated than before. After a week at home without news, she finally decided to continue beating the bushes for local jobs. The phone rang just as she was heading out the door.

"Meitner residence... Marna speaking."

"Mrs. Marna Meitner... of Lubbock, Texas?"

"Yes... How can I help you?"

"My name is Agnes Lancaster from Ranger Airlines." Her heartrate immediately jumped through the roof. "I'm calling in regard to your application for a non-rated second officer position with us. Is this a good time to talk?"

"Oh yes! Definitely!"

"We've reviewed your application... contacted your references... and would like to interview you for a position."

"That's... that's fantastic! Thank you so much."

"You're most welcome... but it's only the first step. The overall process is quite rigorous. You will enter a pool of over three dozen candidates to be interviewed by a panel of seasoned pilots. Only those deemed as possessing the highest level of knowledge and proficiency will be selected for the next stage... the so-called psychological evaluation. A decision on whether or not to extend an offer follows suit."

"I understand. Should I be prepared to answer any technical questions regarding your fleet and its operations?"

"Heavens no! Not for an unrated hire. The panel will be mostly evaluating candidates based on their existing experience and the likelihood of them adapting well to our training program. Nothing more than that is expected during the flight proficiency portion of the interview. So... with your permission... I'm going to include your name on the list of those to be interviewed on… Monday next." *So soon?!* "You'll need to come in the night before, as your panel review might be early depending on your slot. Be prepared to stay two more nights. One for the second stage of interviews, if you get that far, and another in case you need to be called back in for additional evaluation. We'll be putting you up in the Monarch at our expense… that's in downtown Dallas. All of the information will be coming to you in the mail. Any questions?"

"Umm… no. I think I've got it. Thanks again."

"Best of luck."

She had all of five minutes to float on a cloud before the magnitude of the situation sent her careening into the parlor to haul from the nook's shelves every aviation manual and textbook over to the dining room table. She had heard from multiple sources about how brutal these panel evaluations could be. In fact, one of Max's former students told her about being raked over the coals during an interview with Continental. He had a month to prepare… and she only had ten days.

She studied straight through until it was time to pick up the kids from school, made them a snack of peanut butter on crackers, and then set them loose in the house to do whatever they willed. Lost in her copy of FAR, she was startled to find Roy standing in the opening between the dining room and the parlor. It was six o'clock, and she had not given one thought to his arrival home.

"What're you doing?"

"Roy… I'm so excited! I got a call from Ranger Airline today. They're going to interview me for a position."

He was staring at the table without a hint of a smile on his face.

"So… what's with all the books?"

"You won't believe the interview process! Candidates get grilled by a panel of pilots… and then they have to go through a stringent psychological evaluation before…"

"What I don't believe is that dinner's not ready… and by the looks of things, won't be anytime soon."

"Ahh… sorry. I got carried away. Maybe you could…"

"So this is the way things are going to be, huh?! You… shirking your responsibilities for some whim of a…"

"Stop! I don't have time for this! Handle dinner on your own for a change! Go warm up a box of fish sticks or something! I've got hundreds of pages of federal regulations to review… not to mention every performance detail of every aircraft I've ever flown! Now just leave me be!"

She was mildly relieved when he stalked out through the parlor.

Yes – this is how it's going to be!

She put her head back down and continued reviewing her notes, ignoring as best she could the hubbub going on at the kitchen table. The TV soon came on in the family room, so she closed off the parlor doors and kept at it. With it having long ago grown dark outside, the three boys came dressed in their pajamas to say goodnight. Sometime thereafter, Roy came in.

"Are you going to be up all night? It's already eleven."

"Just go to bed without me."

She sensed him turn away. The lights in the parlor went out… and then those in the family room. She was alone without a single word of encouragement from him.

Why's he have to be like that?!

After more than a week of studying her brains out while doing the minimum required in maintaining a household, she felt that she was about as ready as the short notice would allow her to be. Stepping to the curb, she quickly ran through her list of things needed for this trip.

Wallet… tickets… notes… logbook… license… make-up… interview letter with instructions… suitcase… that about covers it. Oh… where the heck's my mini-Dictaphone?! Phew… got it!

The only way she had found of ridding her speech of those interview-killing 'ums' and 'ahs' was to listen to herself. Looking up from her purse, she notice Roy coming around from the car trunk with her suitcase. He had an agitated sort of grimace on his face… likely because the boys were dancing all about her in the crowd with their goodbyes. She kissed each one several times before Roy shooed them back into the car.

"I'm so sorry, boys… I'm running really late... or I'd have you all come inside with me as I board the plane."

"Here's your bag."

He put her suitcase on the pavement at her feet and just stood there. There was no warmth coming from him in this send-off. No voice of encouragement. No sweet words about how much he was going to miss her. Nothing. In all the time since she found out about her interview, he had not once shown any true excitement for her.

Best not make an issue of it yet… especially since this is such a long shot.

"Remember to check the note I left for you on the refrigerator about the drop off and pick up times for the boys."

"You already told me that once."

"Sorry. Listen… I know the last week's been difficult on you. I really went overboard in preparing for this interview. I just want to do really well."

"Sure."

"Roy… please don't be upset with me for…"

"You better get going or you'll miss your flight."

He kissed her on the lips… fast and decisive… before heading back around the car. To dispel her utter disbelief, she went about waving furiously at the boys, all three of whom had their faces pressed against the glass while flapping their hands at her. But not Roy. Already into the driver's side, he started up the car and pulled away from the departure curb without looking back at her… standing there waving at him like an idiot.

I can't believe this! One of the biggest opportunities in my life… and he's got to be such a jerk about it! What the hell's wrong with him anyway?!

She shook off the hurt and entered the terminal, trying to reset her mind for the interview. By no coincidence, she boarded a Ranger Airline flight from Lubbock into Dallas Love Field. Sixteen rows back in the cabin, she spent the majority of the short flight craning her head about for a view into the cockpit, imagining what it would be like to pilot a huge craft like this 737. It could be her! If this interview went well, she could be one of those seated up there!

Trying to act casual during deplaning, she took one last peek into the cockpit on passing by.

So cool! But don't get out ahead of yourself!

She caught a cab to the Monarch Hotel, got checked in, made a quick call to Roy at the appliance store, and then threw herself into a review of her notes. There were so many questions that she was likely to be asked… procedures and regulations pertaining to commercial aviation… typical aircraft operational situations… flight training… and anything to do with her past experience. There were also sure to be some of those odd scenarios that a pilot only came across once or twice in a lifetime of flying. Max had dropped some real doozies on her… like what should she do if she caught a whiff of alcohol on her captain's breath!

After a sparse room service meal, she revisited her notes on good interviewing practices, worked again on removing a few unprofessional tendencies to her posture, and then listened to a bit of her recorded voice while ironing clothes for the two interviews. By far, this was the thing she felt most unsure of. She could answer just about any question on FAA regulations, but if her outfit screamed the wrong message, that would be all they heard. So she spent hours in her closet wrangling over options spanning the spectrum from butch to beauty… and finally came up with these two. For the panel of pilots, she would stylishly edge toward the masculine side of things. Her tan blazer with its good-sized lapels and sharp shoulders over top of her creamy goldenrod blouse. Perfect! Add on a nice wide black belt over the buttoned up blazer… a pair of black slacks with inch cuffs… and some modest heels. That should show them that she meant business! But for the corporate interviewer… the so-called psych assessment… she would soften things up a bit. Let him know that she was proud to be both feminine and a pilot. For that, she brought her silk blouse of midnight blue with its absolutely gorgeous pearl buttons, and paired it with her creamy beige pencil skirt. That should do nicely. With heels and hose, she was sure to come off as both sophisticated and stylish… with a touch of elegance added on.

Good grief! Being a girl is soooo exhausting!

She spent a few more hours on her notes before calling home to say goodnight, and then turned in. She slept poorly, waking periodically through the night to vent her frustrations out on the strange bed and pillow. Truth was, her mind simply would not calm down from all her hyped-up studying. Fortunately, she had time for a decent room service breakfast… and a gallon of coffee… before her interview slot. She ate and sipped while taking another run through her notes. After showering, she dressed and spent some time fussing with her hair before the mirror. Finally, she was ready to go. She took the elevator down to the mezzanine level, went to the assigned meeting room she had already scouted out the night before, and got checked in by the woman stationed behind a table decked out with Ranger Airline pamphlets.

"Have a seat here in the corridor. They'll call you when it's your turn."

She positioned herself directly across from the door, straining to hear anything from within… yet without looking like she was trying to do so. It was perfectly quiet inside. The door opened after a few minutes and out stepped a young woman with a frazzled sort of frown. They made brief eye contact, and then the woman took off down the hall.

That one's not happy. At least she's got a sharp-looking suit jacket. Goes really well with her…

"Mrs. Marna Meitner?"

She was startled by the man standing at the door, him dressed in a military uniform that she had no hope of identifying.

"That's me."

"You're up."

Nerves of steel, Marna.

The room was huge, but the only furniture was a single chair placed before a table where sat three men, the one who had led her from the door and two others. They gave her a moment to get settled in before addressing her.

"Welcome... I'm retired Navy Commander Stinson, and this here's Captain Hillsboro..." He motioned to the man on his left, who nodded her way. "...and this is Captain Summerland. Both gentleman have twenty years in as airline pilots. The three of us have been contracted by Ranger Airline for these interviews. As time is short, let's begin. Mrs. Meitner... please provide us with precise definitions for the seven airspace classifications in the United States, as well as how those differ from ICAO designations."

This was an easy one. A softball pitch to get things rolling. She answered succinctly, knowing that the next question would likely be about special use airspaces. That one came and went without a problem. Questions then flowed freely from the three men, some that could be answered with a word or two, and some that required her to elaborate. The rhythm of ask-and-answer became a thing in itself so that she soon lost track of time. More classifications and designations... but also a whole lot of specifications, regulations, restrictions, limitations, operations, qualifications, certifications, communications, and inspections added on. Her head was awash with 'tions.' But there came a moment when all three men went silent, each looking back-and-forth to the others with an odd sort of hesitancy that went beyond the courtesy of determining whose turn it was next.

"Mrs. Meitner... nicely done. You're excused. If you will, please remain in your hotel room until six o'clock. You should be hearing from our panel by then as to whether or not you will be included in the next day's stage of interviews."

Though Commander Stinson motioned her toward the door, she could not help herself. She sprang right up to the table and shook the hands of all three men. On leaving the meeting room, she gave the next woman in line a huge smile and carried on down the hall as light as a feather. Unless terribly mistaken, she was pretty sure that she had just aced this part of the interview.

Now she had hours of sitting around in her hotel room waiting for the call, not knowing if she should be cramming or packing. Best to use the time going over that list of impossible scenarios Max had laid out for her. She got out her mini-recorder... found the tape of him speaking... and spent a couple hours listening before concluding that she had enough. After a late lunch, she perused her book on pilot psychology and then reviewed the material sent to her by the Ranger Airline recruiter. It was four o'clock when her room phone rang. Before picking it up, she decided then-and-there that if she failed to make the cut, she would not give up. There would be other airline opportunities in the future.

"Hello..."

"Mrs. Meitner... this is Agnes Lancaster... from Ranger Airlines. We spoke some time back."

"Oh yes... How're you?"

"Quite well, thank you. Listen... I'm sorry... we've had a bit of a snafu with the hotel over rooms. Everything's gotten shoved back into the late afternoon. Not to worry. We'll cover you for another night and then get you on a flight back home the next morning. Now... as to your time slot... I've got you down for... four thirty tomorrow in the Sandstone Room. Please remember to bring your logbook and your license."

"Excuse me... but are you saying that I've made it through the first round... successfully?"

"Of course... or I wouldn't be the one calling you. I'd offer you congratulations... but you're not there yet. You should know that we're seriously looking at two other candidates... and there's only one position. Our head of pilot hiring... Mr. Hepple... will be making the final decision. He'll be the one conducting your interview tomorrow."

She hung up with such a feeling of lightness coming over her. Regardless of what might happen tomorrow, she had beaten out three dozen other women... not to mention all of those others who were not even invited here in the first place. That was a feeling of significance worth hanging on to.

She waited through an hour of excitement management before becoming reasonably convinced that Roy was home with the kids, and then made the call.

"Roy! You won't believe it, but I did it! I got through the first round of interviews!"

"Congratulations. What's that mean?"

"I passed the flight portion... so they've asked me to stay on for the psychological evaluation. That's tomorrow. They said I'm one of three... out of three dozen interviewed!"

"So you'll be gone another night?"

"Umm... yes... probably two... if all goes well."

"If all goes well...? I thought you'd be home by tonight."

"Ahh... only if I didn't make it. But you knew that before I left."

"Yeah, well... knowing it... and being faced with it are two entirely different things."

Terribly crestfallen, she tried to rally some small measure of pleasure from him over her accomplishment.

"Aren't you excited for me?"

"Yeah… sure. It's just… now I need to find someone to pick the kids up tomorrow. I got this guy coming in from… Never mind. "

"A guy coming in from where?"

"It doesn't matter. Listen… I need to make some calls. Let me know when you can about your return flight… okay? And good luck on the next stage."

She was about to run through possibilities from her list of girlfriends when he hung up. A sinking feeling took over. It was hopeless. She could not possibly make him happy… in the process of trying to make herself happy.

She had a better night's sleep the second go-round on this hotel bed, ate another hearty breakfast, and then once again dove into her notes. Working all the way through into the afternoon, she only started getting ready a couple hours before the interview time. After a long shower and some extra work put into her hair, she got dressed in her skirt and blouse. Scanning herself over in the mirror, she thought the outfit gave her a look of enthusiasm and energy… even though on the inside, her heart still hurt from last night's call with Roy.

Just remember to smile. You're actually really excited, so show it!

She was just about to step away from the mirror when something caught her eye. The medical alert bracelet. That had mostly been obscured on her wrist yesterday by the cuffs of her suit jacket. But not now. Having the sleeves of this blouse rolled up with such a casual flair allowed the bracelet to stand out rather starkly. She unfolded the sleeve on her right arm, but the bracelet still showed. Because that thing raised more questions than she felt comfortable answering in a psych eval, she undid the clasp, tossed the bracelet on the dresser, and then rolled back up her sleeve.

Perfect! You're going to knock that interviewer dead!

Grabbing her logbook and purse, she got down to the Sandstone Room just in time. Stepping into a small conference space with her confidence high, she was brought up short on finding two other women there. Both were seated about the room's meeting table, and both immediately scanned her up and down. As for her, it only took a split second to realize how they were dressed relative to her.

Oh shit! Power suits! They look so professional! And here I am like something that fell out of a fashion magazine!

She had erred big time with this outfit! On top of that, neither woman seemed as young as her… which would obviously be another stroke against her.

But then an oddity hit her. Why were these two women… obviously the other candidates… here in her time slot? Or at least she assumed this was her time slot.

She was about to introduce herself to them when a man stepped through an adjoining door. He was dressed in a gray suit, white shirt and black tie… very much what she might expect from a typical manager. He was not as tall as her… but not so short either. With a very round face and eyes to match, it was the bald patch on the crown of his head amidst salt-and-pepper hair that dated him to be some twenty years older than her.

"All here… Let's cover some common ground before beginning. I assume everyone has their logbook?"

How she kept herself from waving hers in the air like a school girl, she would never know. Just in time, she nodded instead, aware that the other two women were doing likewise.

"My name is Mr. Vincent Hepple, and I am the chief hiring agent responsible for the selection of pilots at Ranger Airline. As you probably are aware, our company is a bit behind the times in that we do not yet have a woman on the flight deck. Hopefully, one of you will help us change that perception. Now… this is the part of the interview process where we evaluate candidates for their soft skills and their psychological compatibility with being an airline pilot. It's not at all an easy job… as I'm sure you're all aware. Exceedingly stressful and demanding at times, but also rewarding. In turns, I will be asking each of you to step into the adjoining room. To the others… I request only that you sit here quietly. You may review your notes… but please refrain from conversation until it's your turn. So… where to begin… I have a Marna Meitner."

He looked up from his clipboard, for some reason honing in on the woman across from her.

"That's me."

His eyes came around to her and then back down to his clipboard.

"And a Charlotte O'Brien?"

The woman he previously looked to raised her hand.

"And that leaves you as Rebecca Wingate?"

"Please call me Becky."

"So… let's start with… you, Charlotte."

He rose from the table… as did this Charlotte… and both went into the adjoining room. She made eye contact with Becky, smiled at her, and received back a similar expression. But neither of them spoke.

I should have brought notes or something. But really, this makes no sense. Why have us sit out here doing nothing?! Or maybe… it's all part of the evaluation.

As discretely as she could, she scanned the walls all about her. No two-way mirror or obvious sign of a hidden camera.

This is ridiculous.

Having nothing better to do, she started thumbing through her logbook, from time to time glancing over at Becky. That woman was reading an aviation magazine… and seemed as uncomfortable with the situation as she personally was feeling. Twenty minutes went by… then thirty. She relaxed her pace through the logbook, trying to remember a detail or two about some random flight. Well past forty minutes and having gotten nearly all the way through, the adjoining door reopened a crack.

"You're both still here!"

With his head stuck through, Mr. Hepple chuckled to himself, then stepped back inside and opened the door all the way. She could now see that the adjoining space was a sort of antechamber to the Sandstone Room. Out came Charlotte, with him and his clipboard following behind.

"Please have a seat. I'm going to ask you to remain until the end so I can speak to all three of you together again. Now let's see… I'll have Rebecca next. Excuse me… Becky."

Becky followed him in. Once the door was closed, she glanced to Charlotte. The woman did not speak, but the way her eyes shot to the ceiling and back down again, it was clear that the woman did not think much of the evaluation or being asked to remain afterward.

She returned to her logbook, starting at the front again and moving more slowly than before. She got to her first solo… and then on to her last flight before giving birth to Travis. What followed was a seven year gap before the next entry in her logbook. Seven years without a flight.

An unbidden, bitter sort of memory came popping up – of how unappreciated she had felt during that time. Somehow, that feeling had not really gone away when she picked up her training again. Through that time of flying a Cessna for her instrument rating and then a Seminole for her commercial, her handwriting in the logbook remained forced and hurried. Returning to the air had not made her happy. She shoved that stupid conclusion out of her mind and jumped forward to her time in the Bonanza. Now things were different. For each entry, she had invested effort into writing clearly, as well as providing more descriptive notes in the remarks section. Flying that plane had made all the difference to her. A lonely summer, yes… but one with the truest purpose she could remember since working at WYNG. In that plane, doing that job of surveying, she had finally found herself. She had become a professional... and she would endure anything to have that feeling again.

The door abruptly opened and out came Becky, no more or less affected by her experience with Mr. Hepple than was Charlotte.

"Marna... you're next."

She stepped into the smaller space, it having only a narrow table and two chairs. As a courtesy to him as her examiner, she shook his hand as he took the seat across from her. His fingers felt fatter than they looked... and unnervingly clammy. Of course... this small space was unusually warm... so she was now actually thankful for having not worn a suitcoat. Up close for the first time, she noticed some age spots about his forehead and blackish pores on his nose, but pushed all thoughts of blemishes away as he began to speak.

"Before we begin... I feel it necessary to point out that of the three candidates, you have the fewest flight hours and no experience to speak of with passengers." The words struck her all the more painfully due to the blankness of his expression. Before he had even asked a single question, she felt that her hope had ebbed away. But then his face suddenly broke into a wide, toothy grin. "In your favor, you did exceptionally well on the pilot evaluation, and there are some interesting aspects of your application lending support to you."

"Really?! Such as what... if you don't mind me asking?"

"For one... you were highly successful at..." He looked down to his clipboard and then gave her another one of those toothy smiles. "...W-Y-N-G news. Funny, don't you think... 'wing' news?"

This interview was starting out so differently than what Max had prepared her for. When she did not know how to respond, he cleared his throat and went on.

"Anyway... according to one of your references... a Mr. Albert Billings... that was a heavily male-dominated environment, and you held your own. Even rose to become an associate editor."

"That's correct."

"You then entered into aviation a bit later than most pilots do... but have done quite well for yourself. Nothing but glowing recommendations."

"Thank you."

"But on the negative side... you've never been matriculated."

"Excuse me?"

"That simply means that you've never been enrolled in college... so you don't have the benefit of an aviation degree.

"Oh..."

"And your high school transcripts… not exactly stellar, if I might add."

"Well… I didn't really get serious about my…"

"Tut-tut… Let's not dwell on bookish matters. I'm sure there's much more to you than meets the eye. A regular autodidact, if you will. Shall we proceed?"

He gave her another smile… but this one hit her as being less sincere. Her interview was not going well.

"Give me your thoughts on what most qualifies you to be a commercial airline pilot? Please answer with all probity."

Probity?! What the heck's that supposed to mean?! Sounds like… he wants me to be brief.

"I'd say… above all… it's about professionalism."

She left it there… but his eyes only looked back blankly at hers… eventually straying downward in what she could not help but interpret as disappointment.

"I mean… it's more than just following regulations and proper procedures. It's having a pride and dedication that holds the job to the highest standards of excellence."

He seemed more pleased with that, and began giving her a string of 'what if' questions that were much more in line with what Max had prepared her for. Occasionally, he employed other words that she had never heard of… paralogize, froideur, oscitant, and equipoised… leaving her to guess their meaning from the context. Still… she managed well enough through his scenarios, and was beginning to feel reasonably good about her overall performance.

"One last question before we wrap matters up… to what extent are you the type of person whose willing to exceed the limits in order to get where you want to go?"

That was rather oddly phrased… but surely the intent of the question had something to do with following well-accepted industry practices.

"As a pilot, I'm trained to know the limitations of my aircraft, the flying conditions, and my own…"

"Excuse me… allow me to rephrase. How badly do you want this position?"

"Umm… ahh… I'm not sure I understand your meaning?"

"As I've already pointed out… you're the least qualified of the remaining candidates, both in terms of experience and flying hours. But you do have assets beyond such metrics. I am simply inquiring as to what measures you're willing to exert in overcoming your… deficiencies."

"Well… I'm certainly open to more training… and more time building my hours on the types of aircraft that…"

He smiled that smile again, except this time he was wagging his head in a disappointed, fatherly-like manner. Sort of like his meaning was so painfully obvious, and he found her youthful ignorance to be heartwarmingly naïve.

"I'm going to go out on a limb here, and say that I think you can do this job... especially with the right kind of mentor helping you along the way."

"Mentor?"

"Someone whose support will be invaluable in bringing you up to speed. Someone experienced with the ins and outs of commercial aviation who will get you the best routes at Ranger. Someone who recognizes that your potential goes far beyond your... attributes as an attractive young woman. Someone... like me."

She was dumbstruck, and at a loss as to how she should reply, until the obvious hit her.

Oh... I get it! This is another test!

"Wow! Thank you so much, sir. I'm... exceedingly flattered. Umm... just out of curiosity... is this an offer that you've extended to the other candidates as well?"

His smile went away as his eyes ventured over her shoulder toward the meeting room.

"Them? No. They might possess the technical experience, but not the bearing... the charm... or the physical attributes needed for becoming the first female pilot at Ranger. You know... you could be that young woman... with my help."

This was making no sense... or at least she was hoping it made no sense. Perhaps it was the awkwardness she was feeling on the inside, but she now imagined there to be a sort of hunger behind that smile of his. One that she had not picked up on during all those times of his eyes studying her.

"I'm... not sure what you have in mind."

He glanced down to his watch and then came back up again with that nasty smile.

"Unfortunately... we only have these rooms for another few minutes. Not nearly long enough to walk you through an employment contract. However, I am available later tonight... if you're agreeable. Say... nine o'clock in room three sixty two?"

"Ahh... that sounds like a hotel room."

"Of course. It's mine. But even if we had the time now, it would be rather... inappropriate... don't you think. What with the other candidates sitting right outside that door."

"Umm... I suppose so... but... I... ahh..."

His demeanor got bland again.

"My offer is simple. If you would like a position with Ranger Airline, then come by room three sixty two tonight at nine o'clock. Again… that's room three six two. If you do not show up… I will understand. The position will go to one of the women seated outside. Now… if you will accompany me back into the meeting room, I have a few final instructions to provide you three about reimbursement."

She kept her face down through his brief explanation of Ranger's decision timeline and on how they should send in their receipts, then was the first to the door as soon as he was done. Moving down the hall ahead of the other two women, she was doing her best to gain an elevator without having to share it. But all three of them piled up together in the mezzanine's lobby. She held her eyes down… as her mind raced.

This can't be! He can't actually be asking me to do what I think he's asking me to do?!

It was all she could do not to burst out into a rage.

Stunned and confused, she moped about her hotel room all the way into the evening trying desperately to talk herself out of what she had already decided to do. Really, she should call that Agnes woman at Ranger and report the guy. But what could she say that would make a difference?! 'The man invited me up to his hotel room.' That sounded lame even in her own ears. Instead, she contemplated calling Max for advice… but already knew his response. 'Just come back to Lubbock and try again later.' Easy for him to say. This was her chance of a lifetime! A real airline position! Something that she could build a successful career off of. And all it took on her part was a little compromise.

This whole situation was torture! No way was she calling Roy. She could not handle the stress of hearing his voice, and would surely crumble. In fact… she had to entirely push him out of her mind. Take him and her commitments completely out of the picture. They just fogged up the resolved she needed for making it through this night. Nothing mattered but her getting this offer. Not her self-respect, not her comfort, not any notion of right or wrong. She had made up her mind. She would obviously never be able to face Roy if he discovered the extent to which she was willing to tarnish herself. That was something she could not endure. So he simply must never find out.

Actually… she was doing this as much for him and the family as for herself. The store was failing, and he was too blind to see it. She had to act… or it was his father all over again. Soon, it would be on her to provide for the family… and dig them out of whatever debt that was sure to come with where things were heading. She had to do this… for them.

But having the courage to follow thru… that was an entirely different matter! Compromising the heart of her integrity for the sake of getting a job – it was so unfair! Men never had to deal with such situations. They were the cause! Worse… to subject herself to that disgusting man! The thought made her shiver all over.

But it's so stupid to be stewing over this! If you don't go to his room, then you don't get the job. You've already made your decision, so… just swallow your pride and do it! It'll all be over soon enough… and you'll walk away with an offer letter in your hand. That's all that matters.

She left the safety of her room an hour before the time… accepting fully that she might be slinking back in shame sometime later in the night. She went down to the lobby, first to rummage about in the hotel's small convenience store and then to the bar for a glass of courage… anything that might cloud her indecision. She ordered a strong drink of something that the bartender recommended, and turned resolutely to face the many bottles of liquor lining the mirror before her, concentrating everything on a curious little reflection there. It took several minutes for her to work out that the thing was from the flag flapping about on its pole out the window behind her. Instead, the country's emblem of freedom seemed more like a little flame of fire, flickering red at its tips and darkest of blue in its heart. The look of it matched the alcohol's burning sensation in her throat… and oddly, a cold chill creeping up to dull her mind. An omen… and a blessing to get her through this terrible night. Once again, she was shaking all over.

The bartender interrupted her.

"You want another?"

"No thanks."

"Is… something bothering you?"

"No… I'm fine. Hey… on second thought… do you think it's okay if a person does something… wrong… for the right reasons?"

"Depends… What're we talking about here? Breaking the law… or breaking something else?"

She looked down to her watch in response. It was time to go.

"Never mind. Keep the change."

She threw a ten dollar bill on the bar and turned for the lobby elevator.

Standing before the door of room three sixty two, she considered one last time the magnitude of what she was doing. But the moment for thinking was over. So she rummaged through her purse past wallet and perfume for that item she would be needing. She held that thing in her fingers for a few seconds, repulsed that she should be needing to use it on him… and then moved it to her purse's outer pocket for easy access. That decided, she knocked once. It barely took him any time to answer... and for a terrible second she thought that he might have been spying on her indecision through the peephole.

"My dear... I can't tell you how pleased I am that you've come."

"Yeah... I'm here."

His hair was slicked back with something greasy, and on his face was that revolting smile. To her further disgust, he was wearing some kind of a bathrobe... royal blue with a scarlet fringe. In the vee formed at its fold, she made out a hint of chest hair... and immediately feared that he might have nothing else on beneath. But as he was motioning her inside, she slid by quickly... silently gagging on a nearly overpowering scent of musk that had her holding her breath until she reached the room. The first thing she laid eyes on was the bed... king sized with both its sheet and comforter folded back neat and crisp. At the headboard, a line of pillows had all the signs of having been fluffed up. The rest of the room was fairly orderly... only his briefcase occupying the desk chair and on the desk itself, a small tub of ice and a single bottle within, it being tilted slightly askew. To the left and right were two empty champagne glasses.

"I took the liberty of ordering something special."

"Ahh... thanks." She resisted the urge to add a comment about how much she would be needing it. "But Mr. Hepple..."

"Please... call me Vincent... or Vince, if you prefer. More familiar, don't you think?"

"Yes... umm... you do realize that I'm happily married?"

"And that matters how?"

"Ahh... well... I just thought you'd..."

"My dear, you're a remarkably beautiful woman! That's all that matters! By the way... I am so pleased that you didn't change your clothes. You know... during the entire interview... I simply could not keep my eyes from off of you. That skirt... and that blouse... they conform so nicely to your figure."

It was then that he made his first move... to simply touch her or to get something more, it did not matter. She quickly backed away.

"Hold it please! Not until we've had a chance to talk."

"Certainly. Would you care for a drink first?" He motioned toward the champagne.

"No thanks... not just yet. I'd... like to discuss the pilot's position first."

"Naturally."

He moved to the foot of the bed and sat... patting a spot on the sheet for her to join him. She ignored the gesture and continued on.

"I don't really know how to phrase this… without sounding… crass… but I… I just feel I need some sort of… assurance from you. That if what I'm agreeing to happens… you know… sleeping with you and all… then you'll… you know… actually follow thru."

"You're worried about me not extending an offer of employment to you? I thought I was quite clear on that. I agree to be your mentor at Ranger, and you agree to be my… how shall I put it… favored consort."

"For only this night?"

"For only this night. But perhaps in the future, there might be some… other service I might render to you."

He patted the bed again… and again, she ignored him.

"I don't want to talk about that. I just want to concentrate on the now."

He showed his first sign of frustration in that his smile lessened.

"I think I've covered this. But if it helps you get into the mood… I always carry with me blank copies of our employment agreement." He pointed over to his briefcase… not at all with the same subtlety in which he had been patting the bed. "You stay with me tonight… and I promise to put my signature to a copy with your name on it afterward. Then, you're an employee of Ranger Airlines… no matter what happens in the morning."

"Okay…"

So it was finally time for her to commit. When he patted the bed a third time… more insistently than before… she consented to sit there, keeping her purse in her lap. He seemed not to notice that it was there. As he touched her for the first time… piggy fingers placed upon her shoulder… she could not keep from cringing. Again… he seemed not to notice.

"The moment I first laid eyes on you… I knew it… there was something special developing between us. A connection. Tell me you felt it too."

As his hand slid down to press firmly against the small of her back, she swallowed the agonizing revulsion rising up in her throat. A wisp of his breath came to her cheek, just as she felt his fingertips slide around to hook about her waist. She smelled again the overpowering reek of his musk, and absolutely must turn away at the sight of him licking his lips. Praying that it would all be over soon, she closed her eyes in doing everything she could to hold herself together… even though her heart was rattling away with fear. She felt his other hand come to rest upon her knee, putting her on the verge of a breakdown, when the thing that she had been desperately waiting for finally happened – a knock to the door.

About damn time!

She opened her eyes to see his as wide as saucers… for he had obviously not anticipated someone else's arrival.

"Are you expecting room service?"

"No… of course not. I already have our champagne."

The knock came again… louder and with more beats."

"I guess you'd better answer it."

"This… this will only take a minute. Please don't move an inch!"

He stood right up… but seemed to waver in his desire not to leave her. So she smiled sweetly and tipped her head in the direction of the door. So off he went… with it only being a few seconds before she heard his voice again.

"What the hell?!"

She rose to find him peering through the peephole.

"Who is it?"

"It's them! The others! What in the world are they doing here?!"

"Oh… I invited them."

Without another word, she moved around him to open the door, immediately returning to her place on the bed. Into the room came Charlotte… and then Becky… and then an extremely confused and embarrassed Mr. Hepple. She was ready for him. This was the moment she had been nervously planning for all evening… ever since confiding in those two after the interview. From the front flap of her purse, she pulled out her mini-Dictaphone… thrust it forward so that he might see the little wheels spinning away behind its transparent plastic cover… and then slipped the recorder back safely inside.

"Mr. Hepple… Vince… I don't appreciate being propositioned by the person who's supposed to be evaluating me fairly in a job interview. So here's how it's going to be. You do exactly as I insist or this tape goes to Agnes Lancaster… along with letters from the three of us."

After that, the whole thing went by in a blur. The next thing she knew… she was moving down the hotel hallway with a signed copy of an employment contract, Charlotte and Becky following her with ones of their own.

"I can't believe that actually worked. Marna – you were amazing!"

"Hey! What the hell took you two so long?! When I said give me five minutes and then knock… I really meant five minutes! Gack! The creep actually laid hands on me! Another second and I was bolting outta there!"

"Ahh… sorry. It's all my fault. We got off at the wrong floor."

"So… what're we going to do about him?"

"Bah! I really don't think he's going to say anything! I'm sure he's back there now spinning the decision in a way that'll look good for him."

"I'm glad someone can! I'm still shaking all over! And I really don't like resorting to trickery. It doesn't sit well with me. I like to earn what I get."

"Marna… you did what you had to do… so don't punish yourself. He's the one who should be ashamed of himself."

"I absolutely agree. Besides… you said he wasn't going to hire you over us. Not that I'm crowing. Only one of us would have gotten the position. But now… it's all three. Just think of it – we'll be training together! That's so cool!"

They had stopped before the elevator. Without warning, Becky threw both arms around her… then Charlotte followed suit.

"Thanks, y'all."

She got off the elevator first… waved to the two still within… and continued on to her room, a signed contract to be an airline pilot warmly tucked into her purse. Only on entering and closing the door behind her did the enormity of the evening come rushing over her. Every horrible moment of the role she had played sent her crashing into a fit of tears that lasted all night.

CHAPTER

39

CRYSTAL AND PEARL

She decided long before checking out of her hotel room that it was high time for showing Roy some appreciation. When they got married, she was absolutely certain that he had never envisioned her as flying… much less becoming a pilot for a regional airline. So much more disruption to family life was sure to come. Who knows what schedule Ranger would put her on, or how many nights a week she would be away from home. On top of that, he might never openly speak of his fears, but she knew that her safety and well-being were always on his mind. So she really needed to figure out something incredibly special to do for him.

After a cab to the airport and all the rigmarole of getting checked into her flight, she was once again into an airliner for the return trip to Lubbock. This time, she had no interest in the happenings of the cockpit, for she was toying with an idea… a very elaborate and expensive idea… for letting Roy know just how much she loved him. It would take months of careful planning… not at all the sane enterprise for a person starting out on a stressful career… but she was determined to make it happen. She owed him… and he deserved it. But how best to brooch the subject with him? Just as the wheels touched down in Lubbock, she got that first part of her plan worked out.

He had insisted on picking her up at the airport, even though it meant leaving his store to do so. Before he could get a word of greeting out, she threw herself upon him with the most passionate of kisses that a woman could offer her man while standing in a throng of arriving travelers.

"I missed you."

"I missed you too. Congratulations again on the job offer."

"Thanks… but that's got nothing to do with why I kissed you."

"Really?"

She took hold of his hand and turned him about toward baggage claim, content to let the wonder linger for a moment in exchange for just being with him. Leaning into his shoulder, she walked as close to him as the bustle about her allowed. Only after getting her bag did she reveal a bit of what was on her mind.

"I'm taking you out on a date tonight. No kids. Just you and me. It's my little way of saying thanks. I'll handle the sitter and everything. And then afterwards…"

"Yes?"

"You'll see."

She gave him a quick peck on the cheek, just so there was no doubt as to her intentions.

She had the sitter show up before he arrived home from work, which gave her ample time for getting ready. She took a shower and then did her hair just the way he liked it – smooth and straight. By the time he came in through the front door, she was in jeans and a blouse of white cotton under a black denim jacket, with cowboy boots and hat to finish it off.

"Wow! You look amazing!"

"And that's only what you can see. Now hurry along and get yourself ready."

How men did it, she would never know. He was back downstairs in fifteen minutes dressed in jeans, boots, hat and a denim shirt… with a huge smile on his face. They said goodbye to the kids and the sitter… and finally she had him all to herself. For the next four hours, it was nothing but fun. BBQ… live music… line dancing… and so much laughter! Just the two of them! It was like being newlyweds all over again.

Back home, she did everything she could to keep herself from throwing the babysitter right out the front door. Quickly assuring herself that all three boys were fast asleep, she took hold of Roy by the shirt sleeve and dragged him into their bedroom. Out on to the deck, she had a bedding of cushions and blankets already set up. With only the soft glow of a couple candles flickering in the breeze, she placed his fingers on the buttons of her blouse.

"Undress me… right out here."

He got as far as she expected – down to the bra, thong, garter and hose

– before throwing off his own clothes and pouncing on her. They made love there on the deck outside the bedroom, the stars as the only witnesses to their fierceness for each other. Them having satisfied themselves, she was delighted that he showed no sign of wanting to leave for the indoors. Curled up in his arms, they cuddled under the blankets against the cool October air.

"Roy?"

"Hmmm?"

"I want to get married again."

"What?!"

"To you, of course."

"I should hope so!"

"And I want it to be on our fifteenth anniversary. I've looked it up – that's a Sunday. And I want it to be right here at our house… with all of our friends watching. I never gave you that, Roy… the chance to see me come down the aisle in a white dress. It was… selfish of me."

"No… there were other reasons."

"It doesn't matter. I want to do it anyway. As a matter of fact, I've already started planning it in my head."

"Really?! Then why here?"

"Well… you prepared this house for me… you know… when you were hoping for me to come back from Chicago. So I want to honor that. I want to prepare this house for our next fifteen years together… and beyond."

"That's… pretty amazing, Marna."

"We'll have catering… and decorations… and dancing. The whole works!"

"And how're we paying for this?"

"We still have some money left from Gwen's estate. I think there's enough to cover what I'm planning."

"I don't know… Sounds expensive."

"Please, Roy… I think this is really important for us. At least it's important for me. Not having had a traditional wedding… I feel… kind of incomplete. Not that there's anything lacking in our marriage. It's just… I want us to have made vows to each other in front of friends. I want all the toasts… and the cake cutting… and the music throughout the night. Roy… I want to dance with you… you in a tux and me in a gown. I want all of those memories so badly. I can't say what the future holds… but I desperately want you to know that I'll be holding on to you no matter what comes our way."

"Wow! How could I say no to that?!"

"I'm glad you feel that way… because the second honeymoon's yours to plan."

She felt his breath on her neck, a kiss come to that tickly spot just beneath her ear, and then his arm cradling her body into an even tighter embrace.

"Anything for you."

The next thing she knew, sunlight was pouring over the railing, the kids were pounding away at the bedroom door, and they were both making a mad dash for clothing… him, fully naked, and her, dressed only in her lingerie.

The next month had her divided between starting out well as a second officer for Ranger Airlines, being the best wife and mother she could be, and thinking about what she wanted in the way of a wedding. For reasons that were totally beyond her ability to comprehend, those three things somehow coexisted in perfect harmony. Back in the summer, she had thought her life to be falling apart due to the many competing concerns on her mind. But now… she was totally excited about the future. Ranger had her four days on and three days off, which put her at home more often than she had expected. In every way possible, she worked hard at making this transition toward her working fulltime to be easy on her husband and the boys. With a festive holiday season bringing her into the new year, she started in earnest on her wedding plans… beginning with the dress.

She might not have wanted to count those two years in Chicago, but it was pointless not to. The upcoming thirty first of May would be their fifteenth anniversary… synonymous with crystal. So whatever she settled on for a dress, it just had to shout out crystal. That was how she wanted to be for him… pure and clear. Equally important, she wanted the dress to balance perfectly with her aunt's necklace of crystal and pearl. She had not revisited that special heirloom in years, it being tucked away in a safety deposit box. So the first step in deciding on a dress was to become reacquainted with that treasure. On her next day off, she drove to the bank and brought home the necklace, being careful that Roy and none of her boys saw it… for the bride's tradition of secrecy still held true for her. She spent several hours alone that day getting the feel of it around her neck, both by weight and by appearance. The tricky thing would be to have this necklace accentuate the dress, as well as the other way around. They had to complement each other… be in perfect harmony… without one appearing to outdo the other.

It only took a weekend of making the rounds about Lubbock's bridal shops before she concluded that those places were totally useless to her. Everything she ran across was so full of lace and frills. The 80's, it would seem, was going to be a decade of the big and the boofy, with mile-long trains that were sure to overwhelm any church chancel or stage.

Jeez! Leave some room for the groom!

Really… she should have gotten her dress back in the 60's when the style was sleek and smart, for what she really wanted was something with an elegant balance of crystal and pearl. With only four and a half months until the day, she realized that what she really needed was a dedicated seamstress. But how to find such a person willing to work on short notice?

She spent a day in Dallas bringing her necklace from shop to shop until she finally found the right person. Even before skimming through the woman's portfolio book, she knew that Harmony Davis was the seamstress for her. The woman was absolutely gaga for her necklace, and immediately started drawing out concepts on a sketch board.

"Honey… you got the perfect figure… ain't no reason to let folds and whatnot get in the way… know what I'm saying? Let *your* shape be the shape of the dress. So what I'm thinking…"

Harmony let her pencil do the talking… and what came out was a modest A-line… a natural waist exactly where a waist should be… and… sleeveless, with thin straps supporting a neckline like a vee… but with a bit of a scoop. That would leave room for the necklace.

"Whatcha think?"

"I love it. Maybe little wider at the skirt… and straps a bit more over the shoulders… you know… less close up to the neck. I really want the neckline to stand off from the necklace… and sort of mirror its profile. Oh… and I definitely want a fitted bodice… but without a whole lot of boning. And no lace or frills over it. Just smooth fabric. I don't want anything to distract from me and my necklace. I'm… also hoping for a fabric that has a… crystal-like sparkle of its own. Know what I mean?"

"Uh-huh… I getcha. What's say we sketch the back next. You thinking full, partial or open?"

"I don't know. I'd like for you to tinker with that a bit. Oh! But I definitely want pearl buttons over a small bit of lace at the seam. That's a must! I want him to feel those pearls when he wraps his arms about me."

"That's so sweet! I like the way you think. Now… how's about the train?"

"Absolutely no train! I want a sweep… or a court… but nothing more. I want everyone's eyes to be up on me and my necklace!"

After another hour together talking over details of the design and fabric possibilities, Harmony measured her, and then photographed her from every angle with the necklace on.

"I hate to ask you this, Sugar… but could you see it in you to leave that necklace with me? Not to worry… I'll take good care of it. I've a safe here in the shop."

Though it hurt a bit, she handed over the felt bundle, knowing that Harmony needed it for getting the initial design right.

She left Dallas a bit nervous about her necklace, but very much breathing easier about the dress. Harmony clearly had what it took to do the job.

Between now and the screening of the first dress concept in a month, her mind bent toward planning the ceremony itself. Right off, she decided against having a preacher up there with them. They were already married, so there was no need for any 'now I pronounce you man and wife' stuff. No bridesmaids or groomsmen either. She absolutely did not want anybody stealing the limelight from her and Roy. It would be just the two of them… and their boys… so that meant tuxes for four. She also needed invitations… a caterer… cakes… flowers… tables and chairs… settings… a band… a dance floor… lights… decorations… a photographer… and who knows what else more?!

What in the world have I gotten myself into?!

Planning all of that would take so much time and lots of choices, but her biggest challenge was the simple logistic of bringing bride to groom. She could see the exchange of vows perfectly, with both of them at the top of the porch steps and their guests seated in a semicircle array out in the yard below. But where was she to come from in order to give him the opportunity of seeing her approach in her dress? Not from inside the house and not from around the porch. What about constructing a bridal pavilion out in the yard somewhere, and her coming down the front walk toward him?

Ugh! That'll never work! I'll have to climb the steps in my dress! Besides… I'm not changing in some tent!

She was determined to crack this nut on her own without hiring a wedding coordinator. If she, as a highly trained pilot, former newswoman and floral designer, was unable to figure it all out, then who was to say that anyone could?! After a week of batting around the possibilities, the perfect solution came to her. It might be a bit unorthodox, but it would definitely give him an absolutely perfect view of her in the dress. That was what she wanted more than anything else.

Harmony had the initial concept ready for her in the second week of February. She fell in love with it the moment she laid eyes on it. A pure white silk was closely overlaid with a very thin transparent sheer that gave the fabric a liquid-like glimmer… just like crystal. The way it shimmered as she twisted about brought tears to her eyes. This was the one! Sure, the fit and length were not quite right yet, but that was hardly important at this point.

Standing on a stool before a mirror as Harmony primped at the fabric, she felt very much like Roy's queen, preparing herself for her coronation.

The neckline needed some alteration, for it was a bit too scooped. Along that neckline, Harmony had woven in a few tiny white pearls into different trial looped settings. Of these, she liked the smallest the best, as it seemed to naturally lead her eye from the fabric across her chest to her necklace. Turning about, she tried to imagine what the same pattern of pearls would look like flowing along the edges of an open back down to the buttoned seam of the dress. It would be perfect!

"I really love this one. It's so subtle and delicate. You see it… but it doesn't overwhelm you. Do you think you can have it go all along the entire neckline and down the back too? Maybe at a… half inch or so spacing?"

"I can certainly do that. Sorry… still working on the lace and buttons. Those should be done next time you come. I'm thinking they'll extend down to a silver belt of some kind… same finish as the necklace… maybe with bits of crystal in it. Still huntin' for that. You know… a belt'll allow the dress to shape itself nicely at your waist before gliding over your hips. By the way, I need you to decide on your undergarments so I can get the bodice right.

"Oh… I haven't thought about that yet."

"No rush. Now stand still… I need to do more measurin' and take some photos. Not satisfied with that neckline yet. Oh… but you can take that necklace back witcha. I don't need it no more."

She left Dallas excited that everything was coming together. In fact, the only mildly uncomfortable moment she had thus far in the planning had come about regarding the guest list. Of Roy's buddies, long-time customers, business associates, employees, former employees, community connections, and friends of the family, along with her aviation circle, her girlfriends, the kids' sitters, and people she had known going back to her days at Forde's Flowers, there was only one person that they could not agree upon – Sybil. Roy, rightly so, felt it important to invite his only living relative, whereas she would rather fall into a pile of manure than have that woman around on her special day. Thankfully, the issue was settled when Roy surreptitiously discovered from one of Sybil's remaining friends in Lubbock that the woman would be in Europe from spring into summer. She breathed easily in sending out that invite, knowing that she was going to have a Sybil-free wedding.

In all, she sent out a hundred and fifty invitations. She had the caterer and the menu settled upon, and engaged a band with its own portable dance floor to be positioned off to the side of the circle. Her dress was coming along nicely, with the final fitting set for three weeks before the ceremony. She had the tuxes picked out, had ordered the bride's and groom's cakes, and had a bartender ready to go. She engaged a rental company to set up tables and chairs the day before, along with removing everything on the following morning. She had another company providing the linens and place settings. She arranged for several outdoor pavilions to be erected, and lights to be strung from the top of the flagpole to spots along the eve of the porch and the nearest of the driveway's live oaks. On those lines, she also arranged for many little chandeliers of crystal to be hung. She had a guy to lay out a red carpet running from the porch, down the steps, and out to the flagpole in the circle. One of her girlfriend's was a professional photographer, so she had that one covered too. She even managed to get the parents of her kids' best friends to whisk the three away for a week of sleepovers, starting with the night of the ceremony.

The last thing really needing her attention was the party favors. She had an idea in mind for these from the very moment of considering this wedding. In tiny white boxes to be wrapped off with silver ribbon, she personally nestled into a bed of cotton small pieces of quartz and little white beads, along with a fortune cookie sized note that wished each guest a love as pure as crystal and pearl. She even had a special plan for giving these out – something that she and Roy would have an absolute blast doing as the very last thing before bidding their guests goodnight.

On the morning of the day, she stood on her porch directing the preparations, feeling very much like an air traffic controller in her tower. The weather report had a slight chance of showers in the evening, but fortunately to arrive an hour or so after their scheduled vows. The guest bedroom and bath were set up as her bridal boudoir, and come afternoon, she banished all males from the rear of the house. Roy and the boys were only permitted inside to use an upstairs bathroom, and would dress themselves in one of the outside pavilions. With the help of her girlfriends, she got her hair and nails done, and make-up applied. That took hours in which they all sat together in the kitchen sharing memories of their own special moments and laughing it up over their funniest wedding stories.

It eventually came time for the dress. She held her breath as she carefully stepped into it and her girlfriends pulled it up around her. Daring herself to look, she turned about to the mirror… and could not keep herself from gasping. It covered her perfectly! Just like it was part of her. The final step was a frill of silver and pearl nestled into her hair… and then it was time for

Gwen's necklace. As that went around her neck, she could not keep herself from crying… even though it was messing up her makeup. The necklace went perfectly with the dress. Crystal and pearl… a gift from her to Roy. If only Gwen could have been here to see it.

But then the music she had selected for the arrival of the guests started up… and her girlfriends were bustling all about in making the finishing touches… and then they were hustling her into position. They left her there, making their way outside by the back. Now all alone, she could finally take a measure of herself. Anxious… yes, but there was something much more significant going on in her heart. The weight of the necklace and the weight of the dress, both of them clinging to her, made her feel precious… and valuable. Someone worthy of being claimed.

She was suddenly startled when the wedding processional began… and with a little peek out a family room window, she beheld so many seats filled with faces looking up expectantly to the front door. She had one last moment of nervous jitters… all of which she put away with a deep breath.

It's time! Marna… this is what you've been longing for!

She had been married for fifteen years, but at that moment, felt very much the bride. She moved through the opened front door to the music, with all of their guests suddenly coming to their feet. Gliding upon their cheers, she stepped to the edge of the porch, and waited there amidst the camera flashes and so many faces filled with awe. She was searching for only one. Down the carpeted center aisle and out to the very back near the flagpole, she found there her young man poised to claim her as his own. In brisk steps, Roy came down the aisle with eyes locked fully upon her. In those eyes, she caught a glistening of his anxiousness to reach her. Briskly ascending the steps to her side, he took hold of her hands in his… but delayed in doing what they had planned. He just stood there… soaking in this gift of herself that she had prepared for him. The music had stilled, with the only sound being giggles from below to remind him of their guests.

"I'm… I'm sorry… she's just… she's so beautiful!"

Someone from the bride's side… likely one of her aviation buds… gave out a whoop, and then the whole lot of them on both sides were cheering and clapping for her. It went on and on… and now she was the one crying. So Roy gave her the time to wipe away her tears before continuing.

"For myself, Marna and our children, thank you. I can't tell you how much we appreciate you being here to celebrate this moment with us. Thank you from the bottom of our hearts."

Out from the crowd came a call for him to 'hurry up and kiss the bride,' with even more laughter and clapping to follow.

"In due time, I guarantee it! But first… Marna and I will be sharing our vows. We'll be speaking these together… to each other at the same time. So please bear with us as we prepare."

He turned to her and whispered so only she could hear.

"You ready?"

"Definitely."

"By the way… you are absolutely stunning! And this dress… it's amazing! Never have I seen you more beautiful."

"Thanks… You're pretty darn handsome yourself!"

"Okay… here goes."

Then in voices clear enough for all to hear, she and Roy repeated the words they had practiced together. The very words that she wanted to make true for the rest of her life.

"To you… the love of my life… and you alone… do I make these promises… never to be broken. I promise… never to leave you. I promise… always to be true. And I promise… forever to love you. Will you be married to me?"

In a flash, she was in his arms, and all she could think about was kissing this wonderful man. But then the whooping started again… and their boys were up the steps, dancing all about them. People were clapping and cheering… the music was restarted… and Roy was shouting out that everyone should make for the buffet line. As the boys dashed down the stairs, she had him all to herself for just a moment.

"Thank you, Roy. This means so much to me."

"No… thank you. But you do realize… it's just begun!"

He helped her down the stairs, to be greeted there by so many of their guests come to offer their well wishes. The laughter and fun took over… and she was lost in a whirlwind of joy. She ate little in an effort to protect her dress, but made up for it in drinking… and dancing… and doing a whole lot more laughing through the ridiculous toasts and cake-cutting shenanigans. She had so much champagne that the bubbles kept her in a constant state of giggles. Somewhere in the evening was a sprinkling of rain, with everyone dashing for cover under porch or pavilion… but then it was gone as quickly as it came… and everybody laughed so hard at the feel of it. She drank more… and danced more… until everything about her was a whirl. The next thing she knew, Roy was helping her up the front porch steps. Turning to face their guests below, he shouted out for all to hear.

"For those of you still left… please proceed around to the side of the house. Marna and I have a little surprise for you."

She was so dizzy that Roy had to help her up the staircase and onto the balcony of their bedroom. Fortunately, he had the clear thinking to switch on the bubble-makers she had set up that morning. As soon as those got going, she and Roy started tossing the little boxes of party favors over the railing to those jumping up and down below. She was giggling so… Roy was laughing… and everyone was cheering. When the boxes were finally all gone, she and he waved goodnight to them, and reentered their bedroom. Standing there alone in the soft glow of a single candle, he turned to her with a look of concern.

"Does it… bother you… knowing that all those people are out there while we're up here?"

"No way! That's how I planned it. I want them to know… but please don't make me talk anymore. My head's spinning so! Hurry up and undress me!"

She could feel his fingers fumbling with the pearl buttons in back and knew that he was trying to be gentle… but it was taking too long! Outside, the band was playing and the partying was still going on… but inside, he was moving so carefully in helping her step out of the dress. He left her for only a moment to hang it up… and thankfully was back before she had toppled over. He then unclothed her fully, leaving on only the necklace at her request. They made blurry-headed love to all that party noise… and it was perfect!

She spent that first night of their sixteenth year of marriage in their own bed… without boys in the house. She awoke to that wonderfully warm feeling of disarray that only comes from a tipsy night spent in passion. Outside, the yard about their house was as fussed up in the aftermath of the party as was her head… but she had guys coming soon to clean the place up. She and Roy would be long gone before then. As for her head… hopefully that was something coffee and aspirin could handle.

Being already packed, all she cared about before leaving was putting her necklace away safely on the top shelf of their closet. Out to the car, they both then discovered that it had been done up with streamers, cans on strings, and so many painted-on messages of 'just married.' They took it all in with such delight, and then headed off driving west with the rising sun at their backs. Along the way, cars and trucks they passed honked out their congratulations. That kept her laughing through her headache. After a few hours, the mountains of New Mexico loomed ahead. He kept on driving, still refusing to disclose their destination. They passed through the wide basin of the Rio Grande at Albuquerque, and still he continued on over more mountains and westward across the Arizona border. There were times that she wished to stop for a sight along the way… a painted desert or a petrified forest… but he said there would be time on the way back. He wanted to get where they were going before sunset. Just past Flagstaff, they bore northward. Her guessing and pleading then gave way to a hint of knowing, though he still kept his mouth shut. He just drove on with that smug little smile of his, refusing to give her the satisfaction of having figured it out. That was okay… even though she could not keep herself from wiggling in her seat with anticipation. Once, he caught her looking to the western horizon, and must have known what she was thinking.

"Don't worry… we'll make it before sunset."

They came into the touristy town of Tusayan. Again, he must have read her thoughts from how she was eying the motor inns that lined the wide thoroughfare.

"In case you're wondering… we're not staying here."

"I wasn't…" Though clearly she was hoping not to.

Onward, they came upon an immense archway of a gate where he paid a visitor's fee and took maps and brochures in exchange. There were many more winding highway miles through scrubby-looking trees that kept blocking her view. Every turn seemed to tease her with a 'not quite yet' sort of insistence. They took to following the signs toward the main visitor center, but Roy soon veered off to a place he had chosen for her first look. He had her close her eyes at this point… which was terribly unfair. The car stopped and he came around to her side, reminding her to keep her eyes shut. He led her over a curb and across a short stretch of sidewalk… had her put her hand to a metal rail… and then said she could open her eyes.

The first thing she saw was immediately downward on the other side of the railing. They were standing on the brink of an immense precipice that went hundreds of feet below in cascades to a narrow pine-forested plateau… which gave way to more cliffs, each falling in many levels downward. Far off at the bottom, she caught a glimpse of a muddy river snaking its way around a bend. Lifting her eyes… she suddenly could not keep herself from weeping with joy. The setting sun had cut beneath a cloud layer to light up the majestic hues of the Grand Canyon… just for her. Clinging to Roy's arm… for a wave of that fear of heights had hit her… she cried on through her laughter and amazement at the beauty of this inconceivable expanse before her. So different from her wedding of crystal and pearl the day before, yet just as precious to her.

They spent that first night in the Grand Canyon Lodge… it, a wonder of its own on a much smaller scale. They took the whole next day to roam back and forth along the South Rim, fighting through waves of dazzled tourists just like themselves. Though constantly among a hoard of others, she still felt the delight of being only with him.

The following day, they drove eastward, giving her a chance to see how the canyon slowly diminished in scale. They took in both the upper and lower slots of Antelope Canyon, whose rich pinks, subtle reds, and shadowy grays were equally stunning to her. They then progressed back westward to the North Rim. Not quite as close-in to the bottom, this side still possessed views equally majestic as that of the southern. They spent the remainder of the week in a tiny little cabin situated within a cluster of others, each having no more than a minute walk to the greatest view on earth. The North Rim was like no place she had ever been. It made her feel so small… in a good way… but also very big from sucking in all of its grandeur. Away from the rim, the tall pines seemed to go up as high as the canyon went deep. All about her, huge cones fell like pennies from heaven. Even the chatter of birds and squirrels up above were a constant reminder that she was in a wonderland unlike anything in West Texas. But mostly she took pleasure in long walks with Roy, or those silent moments of sitting together on the edge of some rocky outcrop, staring down into the canyon. She had absolutely no troubles in the world, and was immensely thankful to be alone with him.

Too soon, the time came for leaving. They drove eastward all day, enjoying the moments they had remaining together. Arriving back after dark, they made the circuit of picking up each boy, and then headed home. Tomorrow would come... and with it, a return to her lonely life as a pilot.

CHAPTER
40

SELLING DISHES
DOOR-TO-DOOR

For whatever reason, Ranger Airline did not 'arrange' for its first three female pilots to train together. She did run into Becky and Charlotte at employee orientation, and afterward was able to share a private dinner with them. The talk was mostly about the future, as all three of them were excited about becoming 737 pilots. In starting out, they each knew that their actual opportunities for flying this craft would be limited, as second officers seldom got their hands on a yoke. Personally, she was most eager to discuss the prospects of a career path to first officer, and maybe one day far off in the future, to captain. Despite her lingering revulsion, she eventually brought the conversation around to the subject of the interview… and whether or not they should do anything about that creep. Personally, she would love to see him canned, but agreed with the others that it would be foolish to try. Even with how the tape clearly exposed him as soliciting sex from her, the disclosure would tarnish her career as much as his. They therefore all agreed to never speak of it again.

She spent two weeks in Houston getting certified on the 737, with time in both a simulator and a cockpit. For the most part, she felt that flying this massive plane was a breeze compared to operating any of the props she had flown, but had the good sense to keep that opinion to herself. A jet engine might sound complicated, but they were more straightforward than a piston engine. Simpler to start and simpler to operate. On top of that, the 737 cockpit was more spacious than any plane she had ever sat in.

On completion of her training, she requested the early morning Lubbock-to-Dallas and late-night Dallas-to-Lubbock routes as bookends to her work day… and was totally stunned to actually get her wish. To her utmost delight, she started out her employment at Ranger in early November with a daily routine that had her sleeping in her own bed, arriving at the Lubbock airport before five, and then getting back home by ten. In between, Ranger filled her time with flights between Dallas and some other regional city. Later on, she would come to learn that this preferred treatment was highly unusual for a new hire, but since Ranger very much wanted the investment in its first female pilots to pay off, she was granted her choice of routes.

Even with a somewhat cushy schedule, it did not take long for her to experience firsthand why flying for a regional carrier was so grueling. She came home totally exhausted at the end of each work day, with energy only for kissing her sleeping kids and husband before crashing into bed. But with four days on and three on-call, she did manage to find time for recuperation. The pay was peanuts… only twenty three thousand a year… but the experience was golden.

At first, she had not been keen about being the third member of a flight crew seeing as her engineer's station was not close enough to the action. But the hours of sitting in a cockpit talking shop with two veteran pilots… men not that much different from Max or Butch… was an absolute delight. To her surprise, the captains and first officers she served under generally treated her with respect. Same for the ground crews. Sure… there were plenty of awkward moments in which propriety and sexuality tended to muddy up her interactions with these men. After all, a cockpit was a cramped place where people could not help but bump into each other. But because this was serious work… and her colleagues were professionals… uncomfortable situations were usually brushed aside.

Mostly, she simply loved doing her job. Though fully trained on the 737, she only seldom got to fly one… which constantly had her telling herself to cool her jets, so to speak. Her responsibilities were mainly to monitor its various system functions, manage fuel consumption, and do any needed in-flight calculations. It was also on her to oversee the loading of baggage and in-flight services, relay any changes in weather or flight details to her captain, coordinate with the first officer on walkarounds, do cockpit system checks, and verify the final number of passengers on board. By far, the latter was the most unpredictable. On the plus side, flying in and out of Lubbock often had her greeting travelers that she knew. On the minus side, flying in and out of Lubbock often had her greeting travelers that she knew. Some of the more difficult ones took her to be a sort of glorified flight attendant, whereas others readily expressed their astonishment that a former shop keeper would be flying their plane.

"Trust me... I'm much better at this than I ever was at arranging flowers. Can't you tell from my pilot's uniform?!"

Actually... having to wear a uniform every day turned out to be a blessing in disguise. Her boys were totally impressed with it, and Roy, for some odd reason, thought her sexy... which made absolutely no sense. The tie and the cut of the thing was so dreadfully masculine! But the real benefit came in the wee hours of each morning as she stood in her closet getting ready to dress. Gone was the agonizing indecision over choices. Gone was the worry over not having enough seasonal variety to her wardrobe. And gone was the stress of matching, accessorizing, or finding anything without a run, stain or tear to it. This uniform was hideous to be sure, but in wearing it day after day, she had never felt more free of morning stress in all her life.

Of course, there were plenty of other stresses from being a regional pilot that totally overshadowed any benefit from wearing a uniform. Tight turnarounds, weathered-in flights, instruments going tech, delays upon delays, and getting shuffled about like some pathetic chess piece – it was all so very different from the leisurely flying of a single engine craft out of the Lubbock airport. But somehow, just knowing that it was never a pilot's call whether to fly or not took away so much pressure. Sure... the passengers might not see it that way, as they often blamed the flight crew whenever there was a problem. They never realized that procedures, regulations, controllers, and dispatchers made all of the hard decisions for pilots.

Getting stuck away from home was terrible. The ice storms of January marooned her in Dallas several times. Being at the mercy of the weather might be a part of flying, but having to bunk out overnight at some Ranger Airline crash pad was real annoying. The constant radio chatter around Dallas was another thing that took some adjustment. But like in her early days of dealing with the noise in the WYNG newsroom, she eventually came to filter out anything not pertaining to her aircraft. Navigating the chaotic airspace about Dallas became more of a challenge than a hassle. Through it all, she was building her skills, gaining experience, and improving her professionalism.

Of all the surprises that came with working for a regional carrier, she never would have predicted the absolute worst part of her job. As second officer, it was primarily on her to interact with the flight attendants and gate personnel... most of whom were women. Going all the way back to her years in high school, she had never encountered a group of females more resentful of her status in life. There were some that she considered quite nice, especially in expressing an interest in how she had become a pilot, but far too many displayed a sort of viciousness in their interactions with her. They snapped at her instructions as if she was demanding way too much in simply asking them to do their jobs, or they just turned a cold shoulder as if she was not there at all. She knew they would never treat a male of the flight crew that way. Max had probably not meant it so, but having nerves of steel was never more necessary than when she had to interact with a grumpy flight attendant. From time to time, she tried to engage these women with 'female talk'... especially with regards to the planning of her fifteenth anniversary celebration. It never really worked. She was never accepted as one of them.

She could easily tolerate those stressful interactions for the joy of flying. The power and the speed of a climb from takeoff... the effortless glide... the graceful touchdown – no way would she ever give any of that up. The shine of calling herself an airline pilot might have worn off, but the thrill never did. Even having to do walkarounds in the muggy heat of a Texas afternoon could not dampen the feeling of awe she got from standing beneath the immense wings of a 737... no matter how blazing hot it was outside. Some pilots might complain about the dizzying pace of route schedules that had crews strung out and drawn back like yoyos, but she considered that a small price to pay for getting to fly a passenger jet. Even her post-honeymoon blues did not seriously tarnish her enthusiasm for getting back at the job. She simply loved flying too much. And for once in her aviation life, she was no longer stunned to consider herself a pilot. That actually was who she was.

But everything changed for her at Ranger in the span of a day. On August third, thirteen thousand air traffic controllers went on strike... right at the height of the year's busiest travel season. Thousands of flights across the country were delayed or cancelled, including many involving Ranger Airlines. Two days later, President Reagan instructed the FAA to fire the lot of them for breaking the oaths of their employment contracts. The FAA then had to bring in anybody with a pulse capable of directing a plane. It was absolute chaos in the skies! Butch had once told her to assume that every controller was out to kill her, that way she would always doublecheck their instructions. But with this strike and all these inexperienced scabs, she found his words to be totally accurate. Some rookie ATC screwed up and got her aircraft stranded in Little Rock. She and the other members of her crew spent the night there nervously fretting over rumors of reduced pay and layoffs. Nothing had improved after a week, at which point Ranger had nearly half of its operations in limbo. She received her call in the afternoon of August twelfth – the very day she turned thirty six. In a heartbeat, her life as an airline pilot was over.

To have a career ripped away… to have a dream doused in the cold reality of how the big world worked… she never would have made it through the humiliation and disappointment of that moment had it not been for Roy. On hearing the sad news from her, he dropped whatever he was doing at the appliance store and came rushing home… despite her lip quivering insistence that she was fine. They both knew that she was not. She was crying in the stairwell nook when he got home.

"Hey… don't. You're braver than this. You just need a hug."

That was far from the case, but she would take the hug anyway. Lying in his arms, she went through the whole thing all over again with him – from the strike all the way through to hanging up the phone after being let go. He listened attentively, even though he had already heard the entire story from her over the phone. Yet it was different for her this time, for he held her close and whispered sweetly whenever her tears came back.

"You shouldn't feel ashamed. It's only a setback. In time, you'll…."

"Oh, Roy! That's just it! I have no idea how I'm supposed to be feeling! When I'm here with you and the boys… I'm happy. So I should be glad that I lost my job. But there's a part of me that feels… dead. Roy… I'm afraid that I'll never get back up there again."

"Shh… that's no way to talk. You know this isn't the end. As a matter of fact… I don't want you to give up."

"What…?"

"Yes, I miss you when you're off flying… I know the boys miss you too. But… something's… sort of changed in me since our anniversary. Marna, I believe in you."

"What're you saying?"

"I don't know… maybe just that I want you to reach your fullness in life. And if that means you flying… then that's what I want you to do. You know… I thought about this on the drive over from the store… I'd like you to call that guy who offered you a job."

"What guy?! Nobody offered me a job!"

"That guy you knew from Chicago. The one from whatever corporation."

"Mr. Carswell?"

"That's the guy. You said he wanted you as his pilot. So… give him a call. Consider it my birthday present to you… even though I already got you one."

"But Roy…"

"Marna, if flying's that important to you, then it's that important to me too. Give him a call. What could it hurt?! Do it now… before you change your mind."

To her surprise, he suddenly lifted her right out of the nook in his arms… which was no small task regardless of how dainty a burden any woman might want to consider herself. As he set her down on her feet, the smile on his face made her laugh through her tears. He was kissing her… and then just hugging her. She could not believe that this man loved her so.

"Okay… I'll do it."

For the next three days as she resumed her role as a fulltime mother to a ten, eight and six year old, she also played phone tag with Mr. Carswell's office. Through the uncertainty of not reaching him, she often struggled with thoughts about how useless all this effort was. There were commercial pilots out of work all over the country… many of whom were probably already flooding aviation offices of places like NASCorp with calls in search of opportunities. What made her any more special than them?! She was deep into this line of thinking on Saturday evening when the kitchen phone rang.

"Travis… answer that for me, would you please. My hands are covered in soap suds."

Out of the corner of her eye, she was aware of him picking up the receiver… heard him give a greeting… and then there was a pause.

"Mom… it's for you. Some guy about a car."

A car?! That's weird! Probably a wrong number.

She wiped her hands on a dish towel and took the phone.

"Marna here…"

"Marna… so sorry I've been difficult to get ahold of."

"Mr. Carswell! It's so good to hear your voice. What's it been… over two years?"

They batted pleasantries around for several minutes, all the while as she tried to figure out the best way to inquire about a job.

"So… I was wondering…"

"The answer is yes. I still need a pilot… and I'd be happy if that person was you."

"Really?! You're not just…"

"As a matter of fact, our facility in Dallas starts production next month. I'll be moving down there fulltime. Marna… I have so many leads to follow up on and such a limited staff… but that's really not your problem. Please… I'd like you to pass your updated resumé on to the same individual I mentioned before."

"Mr. Tugbuddy, right? I've actually tried calling him..."

"Well... with my recommendation, I'm sure he'll get back with you. Call me after you've spoken with him, and I'll tell you more about what I'm needing in a pilot. Okay?"

He made to say goodbye, but she just had to keep him on the phone for one more question.

"Mr. Carswell, I can't tell you how special it would be to fly for you... but... mind if I ask you one more thing before you go?"

"Not at all."

"You're... sort of sounding like it's a done deal. You're really not implying that, are you? I mean... you don't even know anything about me as a pilot."

"Are you saying that you're not qualified?"

"Oh, no! I'm definitely qualified! I have *loads* of experience! I can fly just about anything you would want me to. It's just... I'm sort of curious why you'd..."

"Marna... I know a whole lot about you as a person. If you get through the interview process, I have no doubt that you'll be a pilot I can put my trust in."

"Wow! Thanks."

"Besides... you're a Texan who knows Texas... and I'm a New Yorker who doesn't. Any help you can give me in adapting to being down there would be much appreciated."

Come Monday, she had her first ever chance to use a fax machine. From the main office of Lone Star, she sent her resumé to the number Mr. Carswell had given her. Just as she was leaving the office, Mr. Eisenhower's secretary beckoned her back in.

"Marna you have a call from the NASCorp's aviation division in New York. They're requesting a time for you to have a phone conversation with a Mr. Tugbuddy."

"Umm... tell them anytime would be fine."

She waited as the secretary relayed the message.

"Here's the phone. They said for you to hold."

Totally dazed, she took the receiver just as the line clicked... and there was Mr. Tugbuddy.

"Marna Meitner... good to hear from you again. Bertram alerted me to your call. I've just scanned over your resumé. My, you've been busy over the last few years!"

"Definitely... up until the air traffic controller debacle this month. But we pilots have to roll with the punches. So... Mr. Carswell expressed an interest in me interviewing with NASCorp… and I'd really like to. Do you think that might be possible?"

"I can definitely arrange it. As you probably know, most corporate pilot positions aren't advertised. We get candidates strictly through personal recommendations. As it turns out… I happen to know a good friend of your Mr. Eisenhower there at Lone Star…" Her eyes went to the secretary still staring at her, and wondered if the woman was overhearing any of this. "…and the word is that you're worth looking at. So… how's about you coming up to Newark for an interview?"

She really should check with Roy first. But seeing as this was his idea… and she was really excited in the moment… she setup a date and hoped it would work out with him.

"Thank you, Mr. Tugbuddy… I can't tell you how much I'm looking forward to meeting you and learning more about NASCorp."

"Please… call me Randolph."

Against her will, her mind unexpectedly jumped back a year to that terrible situation with Ranger. Being asked by a company official to address him in an informal manner really should not be a big deal. A shiver still went down her spine as she wondered if it would always be like this… her doubting the sincerity of influential men in whose hands she might find herself. She shook off the concern and went on.

"Certainly… Randolph. See you in a few weeks."

This was all happening so fast. One day she was being let go by Ranger Airlines… and three weeks later, she was stepping off a flight in New Jersey to interview for a position that she really knew nothing about. Okay… everybody knew that NASCorp was part of a multimedia conglomerate with its fingers in just about everything from cable TV to the manufacturing and sale of satellite dishes. Its Fortune 500 parent corporation owned hundreds of stations across the country, yet was just now establishing a foothold in Texas. She had picked up on all of this from magazines in the library. What she did not know firsthand was what flying for a corporation would look like… even though Max had given her an earful as to the 'serendipitous' ways to corporate aviation. The one thing that she did know… the thing that seemed most appealing to Roy… was that the pay, benefits and working conditions rated considerably better than those of the airline industry.

Coming out of baggage claim, she met a black-suited man holding a 'Meitner' sign, and decided that this trip might not be so stressful after all. When he settled her into the back of a rather plush limousine with soft leather seats and a wet bar, she concluded that this was a pretty good deal. When he pointed out the controls for the stereo system and then closed off the partition to give her privacy, she imagined how neat it would be to make a fulltime job out of interviewing.

For this trip, she was especially careful about her choice of an outfit – a strictly conservative business suit with no frills. No way she was making the same mistake twice! But Mr. Tugbuddy... Randolph... he was all gentleman from the get-go. Dressed just as formally as Mr. Carswell always was, he shook her hand once... and never came close to touching her again. He opened doors for her... gave her a private tour of the corporate aviation offices... even pulled out her seat in the conference room they met in... but the whole time, he treated her like a professional. He asked the same kinds of situational and proficiency questions expected during any flight interview, but the way he asked them – it was totally different! She knew she was being tested, but theirs felt more like a conversation about shared knowledge. The next thing she knew, she was being shuttled over to one of NASCorp's hangers to meet some of its pilots and take a short out-and-back on a Gulfstream III. Again, she knew that this time in the second seat was actually an interview, but she could not be having more fun... or be more excited about the possibilities.

She had dinner that night with Mr. Tugbuddy and Mr. Carswell... Randolph and Bertram... and though it started out awkwardly given the age and gender differences, she found herself at ease long before the entrees arrived.

This might actually work out.

"So... now we get to the difficult part of the job, Marna. I'm sorry, but there's no other way around it. In order for you to have a position with us, you'll need to be living in the Dallas area. Preferably within a short distance of our facility at Love Field."

"Oh... I... hadn't really thought about that... though it makes perfect sense."

"We can offer you a generous relocation package... or even reduced rates at our corporate guest house... but you'll need to be in Dallas on the days you're flying with us."

"I understand. Umm... I'm afraid that's something I'll need to discuss with my husband. I'd certainly love to work for you... your planes are amazing... and everyone I've met is incredible... but... family does come first."

"Tell you what... take a week and talk it over with your husband, then get back with me."

That night in the hotel... and for the whole flight home... she was absolutely convinced that working for NASCorp was a bad idea, irrespective of it being a chance-of-a-lifetime opportunity. No way was she going to be separated from her family, and no way would she even remotely consider moving them to Dallas. She came home ready to put the whole thing out of her mind, talking it over with Roy being but a formality before declining. Sitting with him on their deck as the boys played in the yard below, she went through the whole interview with him, concluding with her decision to call Mr. Tugbuddy and decline. Then she waited… ten seconds… twenty… a minute before he finally spoke.

"I'm not so sure that's a good idea."

"What? You think I should write instead?"

"No… I mean declining."

"I don't understand… You're not actually thinking that I should accept the offer?! Roy… didn't you hear me?! They'll have me living in Dallas! I'll be there for a week at a time. That'll never…"

"Marna… the store's failing. I seriously doubt it'll last another year. It's been forever since we turned a profit."

"But I thought everything was doing better. Not great, but… you know… well enough."

"I'm sorry… I've been meaning to tell you for the longest time… but when you started with Ranger… I just couldn't burden you with the store's problems."

"They're my problems too!"

"Yes… but you already had your share with becoming an airline pilot. And then you got so excited about planning our anniversary… and our second honeymoon was absolutely incredible… I just couldn't spring this on you. But things have… gotten real bad since the start of summer."

"How bad? Don't hold back on me, Roy."

"Well… for one… I've not taken home a paycheck in months. I'm sorry… but we've been living off the dreg's of Gwen's money and what you were able to bring home from Ranger. We obviously can't go on like that. In fact… I had to let Benny go last week. Now it's only me at the store. Marna… I have such a backlog of merchandise that can't be sold… not even at cost. I've run sale after sale… and played every trick I could think of… but people just aren't coming in like they used to. The downtown's dying."

"Roy… I'm so sorry. You must be devastated! I know how much the store means to you… and how much it meant to your father."

"It's rough… I won't deny it… but I'm not going the way of my father. I'm not going to lose it like he did… just because the family business fails."

She was completely at a loss for words, but still managed to babble out whatever nonsense came into her mind as a means of denying the situation. Surely she could apply herself to finding new ways for the store to succeed.

She could scour Southwest Lubbock for better commercial properties. She could find a job that would keep her nearby to help out. Why... she could even think about selling her reliefs... or maybe even the plane... though doing either would break her heart.

"It won't come to that... for your sake. I just need to find ways of surviving for as long as I can. In the meantime... I think you should take the job. Otherwise... I don't know how we'll make ends meet. Marna... I'm afraid I can't keep the store afloat... not without risking selling off something that's precious to you or taking out a second mortgage on the house."

Suddenly, everything became clear to her. This family... and this house... they came first. So if taking the job with NASCorp was the difference... if it took pressure off of him... then she would do it... even if it meant putting pressure on herself in the process.

They broke the news to the boys later that night. Because the store was not doing well, their mother would be taking a job in Dallas that had her away from them for a week at a time. Chad and Wade seemed clueless to the news, but ten year old Travis... she could see it in his eyes. He was wrestling over a connection between his father's store failing and his mother moving to Dallas for the purpose of flying planes.

Though she and Roy were in agreement, she still waited out the full week before calling Mr. Tugbuddy in hopes that something unforeseen might arise to save the day. She got off the phone with him promising to have a signed contract in the mail right away. On a week and off a week would not be so bad. But it did mean a separation from her family... one that frightened an undefined part of her somewhere near to the heart.

Nerves of steel, Marna.

They put her up in a NASCorp guest room near their corporate offices in Dallas. The area was rather industrial-looking, and the room was nothing particularly special. A small kitchenette on one side with a sliding door out onto a narrow, stuccoed-wall enclosed patio, a bathroom and closet on the other side, and a bed, dresser, and desk in the middle. It was more like a hotel room than an apartment. But the cost was exceedingly cheap – a mere fifty dollars a week. She would decorate it as best she could for a feel of home.

She started training immediately on a Gulfstream III and was certified within days to function as the second seat to one of six captains that NASCorp would be rotating into the area. Her very first flight was to bring Mr. Carswell and his wife from Newark to Dallas as part of their relocation. She had not met Lorraine in her years of working at WYNG, but certainly had a blast during the down times of the flight in straying back into the cabin for visits with this rather regal-looking lady. Only after Lorraine made a passing reference to the dark time of Azurean's reign did she decide it best to stay up in the cockpit. She did not want her first flight with NASCorp to be tarnished by memories of that horrible man.

In many ways, her responsibilities as a corporate pilot were not unlike those of working with Ranger. She did the walkarounds and the system checks, got flight instructions from the NASCorp dispatcher, and had briefings with her captain as to the weather, the flight plan, the notices to airmen, the maintenance log, and the passenger list. But it was also on her to ready the cabin. This was where things got different from Ranger. As first officer, she was both pilot and flight attendant. She might be one of two up front flying the aircraft... doing landings and takeoffs... but it was her who attended to the passengers. Before they arrived, she cleaned all of the cabin surfaces and its bathroom. She double-checked the safety equipment and then restocked the cupboards with snacks, drinks, ice, newspapers, magazines, and comfort items for sleep. She oversaw the loading of luggage and any other baggage required for that trip. She and her captain were then standing by to personally greet each passenger with worry-free smiles, making sure that they were comfortable and appraised of any changes to the flight plan. Through it all, she maintained the bearing of a professional, as she was an ambassador of NASCorp wherever she flew.

She would not deny it – the life of a corporate pilot was exciting! She visited so many far-flung places across the country, landing in airports that she never knew existed. As a flight student, she had always considered an FBO to be not much more than a service station for planes. Some were done up fancier than others, but all had the same essential ingredients – a dispatcher, a pilot's lounge to hang out in, fueling services, and an aircraft maintenance facility. Now, she was seeing things differently, and in large part because of the deluxe treatment she was receiving as a corporate pilot. She never had to beg or cajole for fuel, service or maintenance... and when she did have to suck up to some dispatcher, she usually got exactly what she wanted. They mostly flew in and out of smaller airports, thus avoiding the ATC chaos of the larger hubs. The FBOs at these places took pride in having an identity of their own. She especially appreciated seeing how they decorated up their foyers and breakrooms with a local flair. More so, she enjoyed meeting interesting pilots and seeing their planes. In a way, she even tried to be as interesting herself, often embellishing her conversations with a rich Texas accent... just for fun. Most of all, she was respected. She could engage any pilot as an equal without feeling intimidated by the so-called 'thousand hour men's club'... for working at Ranger had made her a full-fledged member. Hers was a blessed profession. She might spend most of her time crammed into the tight space of a corporate jet's cockpit... but oh, the views out her office windows were stunning!

Most often, she flew Mr. Carswell and his team as they made sales pitches to TV stations all over the country. The majority of these were NASCorp affiliates that the parent network was trying to usher into the satellite age, whereas others were sales calls to private businesses, municipalities, or public sector service organizations – any place with an interest in becoming a satellite receive center. Most trips were there-and-back, but many were overnighters in which her passengers had several days of meetings. Sometimes she flew other NASCorp executives around, often between Dallas and New York, but also to corporate offices elsewhere in the country. Her first time into Chicago, she took a cab ride by her old Oak Park apartment for a look-see. It was more-or-less as she remembered it to be... maybe a bit smaller and plainer-looking than she would have preferred. For a moment, she contemplated popping in on Billings, but decided against it. He would be pleased to see her, as she would be to see him, but going back to WYNG... it simply did not feel right. So she went shopping along West Madison Street instead. The memories of having once lived in Chicago were there, rich and full, and she had a blast re-experiencing every one of them.

As the months went by and the calendar turned over into 1982, she finally felt that she was getting the full hang of this corporate aviation thing. Her adaptability, positive mindset and pilot professionalism were showing through in everything she did. If someone got snippety at her... a captain, an NASCorp dispatcher, or one of her passengers... she would never lose her temper or show emotion. She always kept in the forefront of her mind all of Gwen's emphasis on customer service, Billings' demand for excellence, and Max's nerves of steel. Within the cockpit itself, she was especially mindful of melding Butch's 'feel the flight' with Max's strict fly-by-the-book mentality. She was good at it... good at flying and good at appeasing the temperamental ways of the executive. Beyond a doubt, this was the career for her.

Most travel days were long, starting with getting up before dawn to prepare for the flight, and sometimes getting to bed late in seeing to the plane's servicing before night. When not actually flying, she often had a whole lot of downtime for resting while the passengers conducted their business. Sometimes she would visit a museum, do some shopping, or go sightseeing. She often ate meals with whatever captain she was flying with, but was careful not to spend too much free time hanging out with him. Not having a comrade with whom to share her experiences sometimes lent a sort of loneliness to her adventures. Staying in a different hotel each night... being shuttled about by vans, taxis and limos... constantly packing and unpacking... living by the watch... one trip melding into the next – all of it took some getting used to. But far worse was the constant feeling of missing out on her kids. Of course, she was with them every other week, but that was small consolation for all those times of gripping a hotel phone while Travis, Chad or Wade spoke enthusiastically about something going on in their young lives. Most of all, she missed Roy... terribly.

As she became more comfortable with the job, she also began to feel some side effects to this new career in flight. In down times on the road, her thoughts sometimes slipped into a longing for a life left behind. More so, she found herself dealing with a dread that her family was getting along just fine without her. So when she was back home for a week, there was almost a panicked rush to make up for lost time. She wanted to have the boys all to herself... but they just wanted things to go on as normal. At least the weekly reunions with Roy were always special for her. They did the full spectrum of being together on their date nights... from sweetly holding hands to outright going for it in the front seat of his truck. But mostly, they enjoyed talking about whatever was on their minds. In living apart from him, she still began to sense some changes to her preferences while at home. For one, the bathroom had always been a place they had to themselves, but now... what with all her time alone... she no longer quite felt the same way. She sometimes liked to shower by herself, attend to her bathroom rituals without being distracted, and dress herself without him watching. Living in two different places, she had to own two sets of everything... a Dallas wardrobe of clothes and a Lubbock wardrobe of clothes. That meant that there were things that he never got to see her wear. For some reason, that really did not bother her. Even being out about town with him or the kids had changed... and not because of them. Somehow, all the time she was spending in big cities and interesting places was rekindling a bit of that old dissatisfaction she once had for Lubbock.

There were other challenges to being a corporate pilot. Many of her trips had a haphazardness to them. One day to the east, then to the west, and then next to the north. Additional legs were constantly being added at the last minute, requiring her and her captain to maintain a spirit of adaptability. In the end, they went wherever the NASCorp dispatchers sent them, as that was their job. Time to kill became time alone in some far-flung FBO or cheap hotel. There was little consistency. No routine and no carefree, typical day. The extent of her life was her travel bag. Even in summers, she still had to pack for the potential for cool nights at some northerly destination… which was especially difficult on her as a warm weather girl. She got good about bringing along things to entertain herself with on long flights – books, cassette tapes of music, doing some exercises to prevent cramps, or just going back to chat with one of the passengers while her captain flew. Mostly, she wondered about what was going on back home at that exact moment. Were the kids doing well in school, did they miss her, and what hardships was Roy going through as a single parent?

Somehow, flying a jet made all those feelings of loneliness so much worse. At twenty five thousand feet up, she was above all but the highest of strata. There, the clouds were less majestic than those lower down. More ripped and torn. Up there, she had no bowl of an earth to see. Hardly any earth at all to behold out her cockpit windows when cruising upon a cloud layer. Nothing to remind her of those she had left below. By any practical sense of being, she existed in outer space.

CHAPTER

41

OF A LIFE SPENT
ON THE RAMP

The store somehow made it through 1981 with a reasonably profitable holiday season. Coming into the new year with high hopes, all of the steam that Roy had built up was lost when the nation's recession got worse. The floor fell out of the business altogether with dreadful sales in each quarter of 1982. By the start of 1983, the fate of the store was sealed. After two months of wrangling with creditors, Roy finally decided to closed the doors for good. Every asset was liquidated to pay off the debt, leaving only the building to their name. That, he tried to sell or rent out, with no success. The Meitner Appliance Store became just another abandoned landmark within the diminished downtown.

She cried the day they ripped off the sign from the front of the building, for she had never known Lubbock without it. At least Forde's Flowers had been completely removed, with the site replaced by a greatly expanded Fourth Street. But having his vacant and boarded-up store left as a constant reminder… that was a far greater insult than what the tornado had done. She knew this was humiliating for Roy, even though he put on a brave face for her and the family. His father had a similar experience and chose to hide himself in his hangar. Not Roy. The store had not been closed for a week before he went out to find himself another job. By sad happenstance, he landed a part time retail position with one of the very department stores that had put him out of business. "I know my appliances," he kept saying to her and the kids over and over, trying to bolster the family's pride. She doubted that even seven year old Wade bought it.

The month of April had always been special to the family, what with the birthdays of all three boys and then Roy's on May first. But this year, everyone was so gloomy in spite of the parties, presents and cakes. Roy had become quiet of late. Sometimes she found him staring off in the distance, even though she and he had been in a lively conversation not minutes before. The toll on him must be unbearable, so much so that she worried more about him than the kids on those weeks she was away. Yet she was careful not to offend his pride by making her concerns known. She would remain strong for him and for the boys… even though it was heartbreaking to see the shadow of his father in him. Losing his business was a mark of shame that she feared he would never recover from.

Unlike Roy who kept it in, her boys let it out, either by being angry or sullen. More frequently, she was finding out on her weeks back home about Travis acting up in class, or Chad getting into fights, or Wade pulling up into the cocoon of himself. She knew that seeing their father switching roles to the-stay-at-home parent must confuse them, and too often they took out on her that which they did not understand. Part of her wanted to treat their bad attitudes as a phase, and not apply pressure on Roy to better manage them. But when they sassed her, lashed out with inexplicable anger, or flat out refused to obey, then she had to act severely in response. No child could be allowed to disrespect his mother. Yet every week she came back from Dallas, it seemed that the three had grown just a bit further away from her.

Finally with school out for the summer, she hoped that things might calm down. After seven unusually exhausting days of crisscrossing the country, she headed home in the second week of June with grand plans for taking the whole family to Dallas at the start of her next week away. Six Flags had added a new rollercoaster and some 'Pac Man' themed rides, all of which she was sure the boys would love. She also hoped that getting Roy out of Lubbock would do him some good.

Having come in late the night before to crash in bed beside him, she had the supreme joy of waking to the sun pouring through the glass doors out to the deck… along with his bright smile holding out a cup of coffee for her.

"Wake up, weary world traveler! Here… just for you."

"Thanks… do I ever need this!"

She took her first sip while appraising him standing at her bedside. He seemed happy enough. A bit worn, but far from the reclusive failure that his father had been. Maybe the worst was finally behind him.

"If you can call airports in Cleveland, Raleigh and Moline as seeing the world."

"Well… you're home now, so enjoy it. Sorry… but I've got to go. Double shift at Sears. You have the boys all day today, right?"

"Of course. And then tonight, I have you?"

He smile wider this time, warming her heart more than the coffee had.

"Not if you can't survive the day. Hurry up and get yourself downstairs before they destroy the place. Caught Chad carving on the breakfast table the other day."

"Hey… before you go. You do know that I'm making a special dinner for tonight? To match a special time with you later."

"Counting on it!

He came back to her bedside for another kiss before leaving. She followed the sound of him bounding down the stairs, his shout-out to the boys, and then the front door closing behind him. She heard his truck start up, and then decided she should do likewise with her day.

The hours could not have gone by more perfectly. She had time alone with each boy and caught up on how sixth, fourth and second grade had ended. After a lunch with all four of them at the table, she sent them outside while making chocolate chip cookies for them. With a plate fresh out of the oven and glasses of milk, they sat on the front porch together talking about Six Flags, summer days of goofing off, and any little thing that a boy's heart might care to share with his mother. She left them after that in order to get some time lounging around in her nook before setting herself to preparing dinner. This one would be a family favorite – roasted chicken and a gravy that everyone just loved ladling all over everything. She planned for that to be mashed potatoes, nice and buttery, with sweet peas and homemade biscuits. All throughout her preparations, her boys were in and out of the kitchen looking for handouts… which was something that she had always considered to be one of the supreme delights of cooking for her family. The three seemed elated with the day, and maybe they too were turning a corner from the difficulties of the spring.

With dinner not yet ready, she heard Roy's tires on the gravel drive and ran to meet him at the front door with a kiss and a bottle of beer. She then plopped him down to watch the news as she finished with things in the kitchen. Fifteen minutes later, she had everything ready, and called to him in the family room before sticking her head out the back door. There, she found Travis and Chad on the porch snickering in a huddle.

"Dinner's ready… get yourselves washed up. Where's Wade?"

Neither boy responded, as their faces went flat in looking to each other. Really… she had no time for this nonsense. The house might be on a quarter mile tract, but her youngest hardly ever left the porch. And her dinner was getting cold!

"Travis, just don't stand there… go find your brother."

To her surprise, he said nothing and did nothing.

"Well, son – comply!"

"Yes, ma'am. I… I was just thinking to…"

But it was the way Chad gave off a humorous grunt that really told her something was amiss.

"Hold it a second, you two… What's going on?"

Before either could answer, their expressions went blank at the exact moment Roy came out of the kitchen.

"Why's everybody standing around?! I'm starving!"

"Roy… something's going on here."

She nodded toward the two, thinking that their sheepish behaviors should be plain enough for him to see. Travis chose that moment to show some life.

"It's nothing, Mom! Really! Absolutely nothing! Everything's fine. I'll just… umm… go get Wade… all by myself. Y'all go ahead and start dinner."

"No, sir! You're clearly hiding something, young man. Now where's your brother?"

The two boys looked to each other again, with Chad breaking down first.

"It's not my fault! He made me do it!"

"Did not!"

"Did too!"

"Do what?!"

"Lock… Wade in the… you know what."

Travis limply lifted an arm to point back at the hangar… almost as if hoping that she and Roy would not understand. To her surprise, Roy pushed forward to seize each boy by the collar and fling them into the house.

"Get to your room right now! Both of you!"

By the sudden intensity to Roy's anger, she was absolutely sure that the boys obeyed, but she did not stay to guarantee it. She was already dashing from the porch to rescue Wade. Of all the mean things the older two had done to their misunderstood brother, this was the worst. In the short run there, all sorts of visions came over her. Of him beating on the door with his little hands as tears streamed down his face. Of him fearing that he would be locked in the dark forever. And of how a similar, long ago childhood experience of her own had left her devastated.

Roy, being faster than her, passed her on the way, both of them already calling out for Wade. She arrived in time to see that one of the boys had wedged a stick into the man door's clasp, making it impossible to open from the inside. Roy yanked out the stick and lunged inside without pause. It was too dark to see much of anything other than a hazy outline of the Corsair straight ahead in the weak light coming in from the open man door. But she clearly heard a soft whimpering off to the right. Following the faint line of light that managed to creep in under the base of the wide hangar door, she could just make out the huddled form of Wade curled up in a far corner. As swift as was her desire for reaching her boy first, Roy's was swifter. He scooped up Wade in his arms and pushed back past her through the man door before she could get so much as a word out. Once into the sun's brightness, Wade burst out wailing… and still she could not keep up with how fast Roy was moving with him in his arms. He stopped only after reaching the porch, and together they sat on the edge with their sweet boy nestled between them. As Roy rubbed his back, she stroked his hair and kissed his forehead, both of them finally soothing his tears enough for him to speak. In many disjointed half-sentences, he fought through his sniffles to recount how Travis and Chad had tricked him into entering the hangar… to visit the magic fairy within that would grant his every wish.

"I'm so sorry, Sweetheart… that was so cruel of them. You know there's no magical fairy in there. Just an old plane."

"No, Mommy… I heard her. She's there. She whispered to me."

Her eyes immediately came up to Roy's. All of the sympathy he had shown before was gone. His jaw and brow were now as hard as a rock.

"I'm… sure you're mistaken, Sweetheart. It was only the wind whistling through…"

"Wade – what'd the voice say?"

"Roy, please don't…"

"Shush, Woman! I'm speaking with my son! Wade, you answer me now!"

Wade just shook his head… right before burying his face into her chest.

This was so wrong – the way he was treating her and the way he was treating his son! Surely such questions could be saved for later.

"Roy – really?! Don't you think…"

To her shock, he yanked Wade out of her arms, spun the boy about to face him, and then spoke just as sternly as before.

"I asked you a question! What'd that voice say?"

Wade was no longer the whimpering little boy, for he was wide-eyed with the fear of his father.

"It was… it was like… 'too late.' Over and over. Too late. That's all, Daddy! I promise! She only said too late."

Roy released Wade, so she pulled him back into her arms, for he was crying as hard as before.

"Roy! Was that really necessary?! Look what you've…"

But the fiery look in his eyes stifled the rest of her sentence.

"Take him into the house!"

"Roy… I'm sure it was only the wind."

"Now!"

She straightway complied, for he was shaking with a rage that she feared might once again be directed at Wade. With her little boy sheltered under her arm, she led him around the front of the house, briefly glancing back only on reaching the corner. Roy was still sitting there on the edge of the porch, staring out at the hangar.

"Wade, Sweetheart… how would you like to watch some TV while I speak with Daddy?"

She got him situated with a cartoon show on cable and immediately left him. Back out the front and around to the side, she was surprised not to find Roy there. Looking next to the hangar… and then around the yard, she located him coming from the toolshed at the back of the house. He was striding with determination toward the hangar, gripping a long-handled sledgehammer in his hands. She might have yelled something, but the greater part of her was in a panic to reach the man door ahead of him. That, she somehow managed… though he easily pushed her aside. Catching him by the shirt tail, she held on tight and used what breath she had to plead with him.

"No, Roy! Please… please don't!"

How she had gotten there, she could not say, but she found herself on her knees before him, tears streaming down her cheeks as she held him at bay with both hands gripping at his chest. He just towered above her, his sledgehammer ready to strike the first blow. Despite the panic and fear, she somehow became aware of an odd little tap to the back of her head… and knew it to be from the tip of a Corsair propeller blade.

"I said get outta my way!"

"Please don't do this, Roy. I beg you! I'll do anything! Anything! Just don't hurt it!"

"*Hurt* it?! I'm going to destroy it!"

"No, please! I'll… I'll sell it!"

"I don't care anymore! Now get the hell out of my way!"

"I'll give it away! As soon as possible! Just please… please don't hit it!"

After a long, tense minute, she finally sensed a change in him. He was no longer pushing against her resistance. Slowly, the sledgehammer slid from his shoulder to the hangar floor.

"I want this damn thing gone! Do you understand me?!"

Without another word, he left her there on her knees… him disappearing out through the man door into the sunlight.

More of her tears came. Not the desperate kind, but those that flowed from despair. Groping about for something to grip, she found herself clutching the handle of the fallen sledgehammer. Sobbing in that semi-dark, every terrible decision she had ever made seemed to come back in waves of shame. Chicago… Gwen… Ranger… and now NASCorp. On, she wept… because it made no sense not to. In her heart, she knew that she would never give up this plane, no matter what promises were made. She would put off the decision… mislead and deceive… lie, if need be… but she would not be parted from it… even if it was destined forever to sit here in the dark. She simply was unable to. So what did that make her out to be?! One who would always allow a thing to come between her and him? It would have made more sense if he had taken this sledgehammer to her… to her foolish dreams, rather than to this old plane.

Deciding that was a terrible thing to think, she released the wooden handle and turned about on her rear to look up into the propeller blades. Now sitting before the plane, she suddenly felt very small… as if whatever bigness she might make of herself could never possibly exceed that of this broken down relic of an aircraft. She sucked in a deep breath and held it, listening with all her might. Nothing.

"Why won't you speak to me?"

The plane just sat there, absolutely still.

So stupid of her to entertain such a childish notion. It was just a plane… just a thing… no more significant than herself. Over she tipped into a ball, beating the hangar's concrete floor with her fist until a new kind of pain might distract her from a far greater one. No matter how she tried, her dreams would always be there in her heart, forever tarnishing her love of others.

It was dark out when she finally left the hangar… to match the dark within her. Entering in through the kitchen, she noticed right off that two of the five settings at the table had been used. The other three – hers, Travis's and Chad's – were untouched. The remains of the dinner she had prepared with such enthusiasm sat in the center. She passed into the darkened quiet of the family room. Up the stairs, she paused for a moment on the landing. From down the hall, she made out a sniffle from one of the older boys. Travis, by the sound of him. Roy had evidently visited them with punishment. She stepped across the hall to the door of the master bedroom and entered into its dark. Roy was already in bed.

"Are we going to talk about this?"

"No."

"I think we should."

There was a long pause before he answered.

"Think what you will. You always do. As for me... I don't think what happened was the fault of the boys."

"Really?! Then whose fault would it be?"

"Yours... and mine too. I... just don't want Wade ending up like Sybil."

"What're you talking about?!"

"Never mind. I've said enough. I'm going to bed. Good night."

He offered no more... and she was too upset to risk any other words on him. She closed the door and backtracked down the stairs to put away what remained of dinner.

For the first time in their marriage, she spent the night in her stairwell nook. She slept very little in mulling over Roy's comment about Wade and Sybil. Mostly, she dreaded the coming of morning. But the sun rose, and with it came all four of her boys down the stairs. She was stiff from not sleeping well, but they seemed even stiffer than her. Nobody said much. Roy ate the breakfast she made for him and then hastily left the house to 'run some errands.' She heard his truck recede down the driveway, and decided this was probably the ideal moment.

"Wade... you're excused from the table. Why don't you go watch some TV. You two stay put."

She waited until she heard the sound of cartoons coming from the family room before speaking again.

"I want to know what you both were thinking... locking your brother in that hangar. Travis... you first."

"Yes, ma'am. I... umm... I'm sorry. Dad already made us apologize to Wade... right after he whipped us with his belt."

"Yeah... so hard that..."

She held a finger out to Chad, and he immediately clamped his mouth shut.

"Go on, Travis... why'd you do it?"

"Mom! He was bugging us... and whining about not being included... or something stupid like that."

"Yeah... he's a total pain in the..."

Again, she held up a finger to Chad… and again he bowed his head in silence.

"So you two thought it would toughen him up to play a trick on him?"

"Yes, ma'am… I mean… no, ma'am. I mean… well… it was actually an experiment."

"To see how fast you could make him cry?!"

"He cries at everything!"

"Young man… this is the third time you've talked out of turn. I suggest you keep quiet. You're already in enough trouble as it is. Continue, Travis."

"I… I just wanted to know if he could… you know… hear it too. The voice… the thing inside there. I wanted to… make sure we weren't the only ones."

Trying to keep her expression even, she fought against the tremor that was running the length of her.

"So… you've heard it… this voice?"

Travis lowered his head in nodding. She wanted to know so much more from him… but also wanted none of what he might say, or what it would cost her to know.

"Okay, Chad… you're turn."

"Yes, ma'am. Ahh… what's the question?"

"Why'd you lock your little brother in the hangar?"

"I don't know… I just thought it would be fun."

"And the voice?"

His eyes strayed over to his older brother and then back to her.

"I don't know nothing about no voice."

"So you've never heard anything inside that hangar?"

"Yes, ma'am… I mean… no, ma'am. It's… just a really creepy place… with that big old plane staring at me. Dad says to stay away… so… I stay away… mostly."

"I see… Well, neither of you will have to worry about that hangar for a very long time. You're both restricted to the house for the rest of the summer."

"But, Mom! Dad's already…"

"That was his punishment… this is mine. And no TV until I say so… you understand me? Now get up to your room and stay there until I tell you it's okay to come down."

Both nodded meekly and crept from the table.

Travis… Wade… Roy… Sybil… and probably Ruby too… they all seemed to have heard a strange whisper from within that hangar. She had never heard so much as a peep. Neither had George… or apparently Chad… though she doubted he was being truthful with her. It made no sense. The feel then came to her of Roy standing over her with a sledgehammer. The violence he had intended for her plane… with the anger that he still bore into this day toward her… that would not go away anytime soon. She rose to put the breakfast dishes into the sink and went to find Wade… to hug him… to console him… to do something… anything… that might wipe away the memory of last night.

Later that morning, Roy affixed a hefty padlock to the man door, and for good measure, bolted on a crossbar of steel that spanned to the hangar's frame. It was now impossible to open either the man door or the hangar's main door. He said nothing to her about any of this activity… even though it was quite evident that she was watching from the porch.

The rest of the week home remained tense. She tried repeatedly to engage him on the subject of the hangar and what had happened to Wade… but he just brushed her off each time.

"There's no need to discuss it. The thing's locked up for good now."

She returned alone to Dallas on the next weekend, having abandoned her plans for a family getaway. That whole week of flying, her mind was on him… on what great disappointment and shame he must be dealing with in his heart to account for how he had behaved. She spoke with him over the phone each night, as was their practice. Their conversations were pleasant enough, but she never felt close to him. In the back of her mind, she knew that he had vented his anger over his failed store upon her hangar and plane, but likely a good part was directed at her too. Her absence was being felt. This decision to work for NASCorp… it had been theirs together, and even more so his than hers. But maybe it was time to rethink their priorities.

When she came home next, she found that several odd things had happened around the house in the interim. For one, Roy had planted a line of arborvitaes along the western side of the porch. Though only three feet high at present, he said that they would eventually grow tall enough to shade much of the house from the afternoon sun. She was sure that his true motives lay elsewhere, for he had also moved their many rocking chairs from the western to the eastern side of the porch. From there, it was impossible to see the sunset… or the hangar. But worse than these changes, Roy had purchased some kind of a video game thing that hooked up to the TV. Atari something or other. He said he had picked it up cheap at some garage sale… as if that mattered. The entire week she was home, the three boys and him did nothing but shoot down invading spaceships, run that little Pac-Man guy around to its irritating music, and completely ignore her.

Moving through the summer, she began to sense that Roy was finally over the hangar incident. In fact, he greeted her homecomings with obvious excitement, which brought renewed joy to her heart. She felt him grow close to her again… whereas her boys had become totally obsessed with playing video games. She swallowed her weekly disappointments at not getting much time with them by focusing on Roy instead. Yet as school restarted in the fall, she slowly began to realize that the distance between her and her sons had little to do with those video games. In her frequent calls from Dallas or wherever on the road, she repeatedly tried engaging Travis about his new experiences in seventh grade, Chad in fifth, and Wade in third. They seldom shared details willingly, and most always got off the line too soon. Matters were hardly better during her weeks at home. They repeatedly showed no interest in being with her. Roy was of little help in resolving her feelings of separation from them, saying rather definitively not to make too much out of the ways to boys.

"Geez, Marna… I don't think I spoke word one to my mother for nearly the whole three years I was in junior high."

"I'm not buying that. You and your mother were always close. Something else is going on, and I want to know what it is."

"Listen… it's really nothing. They're just boys… dealing with… stuff."

"What sort of stuff?"

"Mostly stupid stuff. Nothing serious."

"Roy… I can tell you're not being upfront with me. I want to know what's going on."

He sat for a while staring out into the night from his porch rocking chair, obviously considering how best to fess up to whatever he was holding back from her.

"We're actually doing really good lately, wouldn't you say?"

"Of course. I had thought so… at least from my perspective."

"Mine too. It's just… they hear things."

"Meaning what?"

"Nothing. Just the typical things kids tease each other with at school."

Getting information out of him was worse than dealing with a passive-aggressive dispatcher.

"Roy, would you please come out with it? Your dancing around's only making me feel more nervous."

"Okay – fine. There's a notion that's been building for several years among their friends that you and I… that we're… separated. Sort of like before… except that you come home every now and again for the sake of… appearances."

The impact of his words shook her to the core, dislodging into her mind instance after instance she had downplayed. How she had lost track of her girlfriends ever since starting up with NASCorp. How mothers seemed to be stand-offish toward her on those times she picked her boys up from school. How her boys never wanted to be seen with her around town or at school events. And how people must be misinterpreting the failure of the appliance store. This was absolutely unbelievable! After all that effort invested into their fifteenth anniversary celebration as her way of showing everyone how much she loved Roy… to have it all forgotten after only a few years… that made her want to scream! Or bash some heads together! But she was the one who had created this problem by willy-nilly immersing herself within a man's world without staying connected to women in Lubbock. Her mind had been so preoccupied with guarding her limited time at home that she had not given one thought to what others about town might be thinking. She had created a stigma and done nothing to help her family deal with it.

"Roy… I want to sit all three boys down tonight and have a talk with them. I want to clear this up once and for all."

"I… really don't think that's such a good idea. Marna… they all understand our situation. They know that the store's failure had nothing to do with you flying. I've told them enough times. They also know that there's nothing wrong between us. But whether they believe it or not has no bearing on what they hear from their friends. Trust me – you're talking to them'll just get them more mad. They really need to work this out on their own."

"Then we're going out for dinner tomorrow night as a family. I want to show people that the rumors aren't true. Let's go to that spaghetti place. The one that's always packed. And then I want to walk around the mall together. And maybe take in a movie."

Their night out as a family started on an off-note with all three boys complaining about her choice of a 'little kids' restaurant. She did not care about that, as it was far more important to be seen. The dinner went off well enough, as they saw a few couples there they knew. She smiled big and bright for each, and tried so very hard to look like a normal family. Once at the mall, she cut the boys loose to do as they pleased, and just walked about holding Roy's hand. They came across more people they recognized. For each encounter, she made a show out of hanging all over him. She chatted only about the doings of her wonderful family, not once mentioning Dallas or flying. It felt good… but whether it did any good was hard to say. The whole evening, she could not keep herself from reading between the lines of a conversation, or interpreting something hidden behind a sideways glance. She just knew it – each person they ran into was thinking that things were not well in the Meitner household. Almost as if she, as the wife, was more of a mark of shame on Roy than was the loss of his business.

They eventually rounded up the boys and left the mall. On the way back, she compiled in her mind a list of girlfriends to reconnect with over the next few days while at home. She would do her darndest to spend time with at least one of them whenever she was back in town. But more important than that, she must show her sons how much she loved and appreciated them.

She began with Travis. Getting quality time alone with him at home had always been difficult. Wherever he went, Chad always followed. So she took her oldest out for dinner, just the two of them. They had a pleasant enough time talking about the kinds of things that she supposed a twelve year old most cared about – his friends, classes, and favorite sports teams. Nothing really substantial… but it was a start.

She was plenty drawn to him as her son, but also as a unique person. Travis had always been the child most like her – an achiever, driven to succeed in whatever he did, and always in command of the moment. He was a boy any parent could be proud of. Yet she had sensed for years that the connection between them was lacking from his side… perhaps in there not being a thing he could latch onto about his mother that might strengthen their relationship. Since school had always been a thing that he enjoyed, she arranged with his seventh grade Texas State history teacher to be a guest speaker. Because he took the news with mild disinterest, she was fairly confident that he was inwardly excited about showing off his mother. So she put considerable effort into preparing a talk about the WASPs of Sweetwater, highlighting Gwen's role in ferrying planes… with a bit about herself as a corporate pilot thrown in. She thought the whole thing went off exceptionally well given the interest from the class. Travis sat calmly through her presentation, not smiling but not abhorring every minute of it either. As the class period ended, the teacher thanked her… and then casually turned to ask Travis if he ever thought about becoming a pilot like his mother.

"No, ma'am. I'm not really interested in anything she does."

His words immediately took the pleasure right out of her. She knew she should have kept her mouth shut, but just could not prevent herself from rescuing the moment.

"That's okay, Travis. Nothing wrong with that. You've got your own interests… right?"

He stared at her for a penetratingly long moment before answering.

"Yes, ma'am. Just ask Dad… he knows."

Travis immediately joined the rest of his classmates turning into the busy hallway, leaving her standing there feeling like the uninvolved mother that she was. From that moment on in their relationship, she knew for certain that he resented her for flying.

Throughout his teenage years, she remained determined to connect with Travis on whatever level he might allow. Helping with his homework... Being on hand as a volunteer parent when he got involved in high school drama... Or just trying to get him to talk about the things on his mind. Somehow... all of her hopes for growing close to Travis collapsed on the day she took him out for some practice driving. Perhaps it had been because of a latent CFI tendency ingrained in her from years of flight lessons... or maybe just her bent toward following proper procedures. Whatever the cause, the outing turned out to be a disaster. She simply could not keep herself from correcting him at every turn... literally... which she also mistakenly referred to as 'banks' several times. She so wanted to help him be a better driver... whereas he just wanted to drive. He eventually pulled over and insisted that they switch places. Whether he meant it to be heard or not, she caught his muttered words as he stepped from the car.

"Just can't be a normal mother!"

Those words cut her like a knife, exposing his childhood's worth of grievances against her as wounds that she feared would never heal.

Connecting with Chad was even more difficult. He was not such a complicated boy, being both aggressive and compliant at the same time. He thrived on physical contact... of the bruising kind. From the time he was old enough and sturdy enough, he thought of school only as a venue for wearing a helmet, jersey and cleats. But he also had other appetites than sports, namely fun, food, and eventually... girls. That was where she thought she could best reach him. Chad always had a school boy crush on some girl, which in high school evolved into his first real girlfriend. That girl's name never sat well with her from the first time that Roy mentioned it. The 'Tiffany' part was fine. She had been enamored with the movie when it came out in the early 60s, and likely so had Tiffany's mom. As a matter of fact, the name had been on her own short list, and she might have settled on it had she given birth to a girl. But pairing Tiffany with the last name 'Brackenfest'... what in the world had the girl's parents been thinking?!

Through Chad's many crushes, she had tried numerous times to reach into his heart for insights into why he liked certain girls. Too often, he came across as dumb as a box of rocks to her questions, which she suspected was a front... particularly seeing as he was quite smart. He was holding back on her, and perhaps that made sense. How many boys confided in their mothers about girls? Probably not many… but even fewer would act ashamed of their mothers before those girls.

That happened on the night she was to meet this Tiffany Brackenfest for the first time. She arrived late into Lubbock by no fault of her own. Heading directly to the high school's football stadium, she fortunately arrived before the game was over. Moving through nearly empty stands, she found Roy four rows up waiting for her.

"I was beginning to worry."

"Crappy weather over Dallas. How's the game going?"

He pointed up to the scoreboard. The numbers were in Lubbock's favor, but the few minutes remaining on the clock were not in hers.

"I'm sorry… I've missed it all."

"They'll be other opportunities. He had a pretty good game. Five tackles and some assists. He's out now. See… that's him there at the end of the bench."

She followed to where Roy was pointing – to the boundary between where the football player's area ended and the cheerleaders' space picked up.

"Is that the girl… the one he's talking with?"

A smile came to Roy's face.

"The one and only Tiffany."

"Have I missed out on meeting her?"

"Nope. He's bringing her up into the stands at the end of the game. So you're just in time."

They did not have to wait long. With the final horn came all that handshaking and noise making… and then Chad was clomping up the bleacher steps in his cleats with a petite little blonde following in behind, her in a short cheerleader skirt with ribbons tied up into her hair.

"Dad… this is Tiffany… my girlfriend."

The girl came right down the bleacher row to shake Roy's hand.

"Very pleased to meet you sir."

"You too, young lady."

"And that… that's my mom."

Rather than offering a handshake, Tiffany's face burst out into a huge smile.

"Ooh – the jet pilot! I've heard sooo much about you! My mom's says you're…

"Not now, Tiff."

"No… I'd really love to hear what her mother says. Go on Tiffany."

It was not her imagination – Chad took a step downward in the bleachers. She had somehow embarrassed him.

"She says you're a new breed of woman!"

"I'm… a breed… of woman?"

"That's what she says! Oh, I'm absolutely certain she means it as a compliment!"

Chad took another step down.

"So…. Mrs. Meitner… tell me something really cool about jets!"

"Tiff… don't get her started."

"But I really wanna hear! Please, Mrs. Meitner!"

"Certainly, Tiffany. Umm… did you know that there are three main ways to start a jet engine?"

"Ahh… no… I didn't."

"It's all about compressed air. First, there's the onboard APU…"

"Jeez, Mom… enough with the acronyms."

"…that's the auxiliary power unit. Then there's the…"

"We gotta go."

Chad lunged forward to grab Tiffany by the wrist and drag her back down the bleacher steps.

"Bye, Mr. and Mrs.. Meitner. Really nice to meet you…"

She watched them move out onto the field with what remained of the team still down there.

"That didn't go so well. I don't think Chad appreciates having a 'jet pilot' for a mother."

"Personally… I thought the whole thing was hilarious."

"You're not helping, Roy."

"Sorry. You know… I kind of think the girl was expecting something more… romantic."

"Yeah…"

As they rose to leave, she resisted the urge to say what was really on her mind – that Chad had not seemed proud to introduce her as his mother. She and Chad… they had never been able to resonate on anything. Not sports, not fun, and not girls. They were like oil and water… earth and sky.

She would never claim to have favorites among her sons, but Wade had always been special to her. Maybe that was because he most resembled Roy in appearance… though he did not have Roy's cheerful, easy-going personality. Wade was sensitive, reflective and often times sullen… just like his Aunt Sybil. Yet at all times, the boy was lost amidst the big personalities of his older brothers. He was a black box where everything went in and nothing came out… except for his music. Even at an early age, he had always shown himself to be the most talented member of the family. She got him into piano lessons at the age of six, and by the time he was a teenager, Wade was already playing a half dozen instruments with proficiency.

One of her greatest frustrations was how many of his concerts, recitals and competitions she had missed because of flying. But more than that, what really concerned her about him was that the more he played, the less he did in life. He was all about his music. No scholastics, no sports, no girlfriends, and no clubs. It was just him and his circle of musical friends. Because of his sensitive nature… and later because of his many instruments… she had always wanted him to have a room to himself… which perhaps contributed to him being a loner in the household. So to her, it had always been important to draw him out of his shell.

She naturally tried building a bond with him through music. Not that she had any personal experience with it. She had never played an instrument in all her life. Gwen would not spare time or money for such things. Not that she was in the least bit jealous of Wade because of her own childhood, for she truly enjoyed his love of music. That was why she had always been keen on taking him to piano lessons. Discretely sitting in the other room, she would do her best to listen as he and his teacher went at the keys.

There was one time that still sticks in her mind when she overheard his instructor talking about the chords and the melody… the bass and the treble… the left hand and the right working together for the mutual purpose of creating beautiful music. For some reason, those words really reached her, for she had been trying for years to bring into harmony those parts of her that were earth and sky. Middle C was the anchor point on the piano… whereas she could find no such place on the keyboard of her life. That fine line of the horizon always seemed far too fuzzy for her.

She had been most eager to share with him these thoughts on Middle C after that lesson, but he just shrugged his shoulders in response. That had always been his strongest form of rejection of her. She could poke and prod, but he just shrugged on. He had been that way toward her from his early childhood. In the depths of her heart, she feared that he would always hold daycare against her. His music could draw her in, but she could never tweedle him with anything about herself.

In fact, none of her boys had ever shown interest in her flying. None of them had been up in a plane with her, in spite of her many invitations to take them. None of them were interested in the things that she was interested in. Not airplanes and certainly not her relief hanging on the dining room wall. She had tried countless times to engage them with its intricacies. Travis thought it creepy, and Chad was bored with it… which she was silently relieved about because she had always been afraid that he might break it. But Wade… her most artistic and insightful child… he would not go anywhere near it. Whenever they ate in the dining room, he sat as far away from the relief as possible. So she had never bothered taking any of them to the Dallas museum to see the sister relief. Not even Roy was interested in going back there a second time.

Year in and year out, she was Dallas and she was Lubbock. When she was in one place, she always worried about the other. Being torn between the two became something so familiar that it was life itself… almost the way she had always known things to be. She had her 'Sky' in Lubbock and her 'Earth' in Dallas… though sometimes thought it should be the other way around. At least she now got to see both reliefs on a regular basis. In time, she came to appreciate the artistry of Earth just as much as she did of Sky, though its message of frightened faces and flames never spoke to her. The thing she really did like was that the museum kept a placard beside Earth indicating that the relief was on loan from 'Gwen Forde, of Lubbock.' That was how she wanted it to stay. Gwen deserved the credit… even if none of her grandnephews had ever shown interest in hearing about the great-aunt who had raised their mother.

She woke up one morning in her tiny Dallas apartment to the awareness of having turned forty. In the blink of an eye, she no longer considered herself as being young, even though her skin was still smooth, her hair was still thickly brown, and her figure *mostly* resembled the one that used to draw so many second looks. She simply accepted that her time of youth was over. There might be a whole lot more prettier women out there, but her Roy was still enamored with her… and that was all that mattered. Oh… and that she could still dress the socks off most women with her excellent taste in clothes.

She had been doing this job of corporate piloting for… what… five years now, and still had a desire for more. The pay was real good, the benefits were great, and they were finally putting money away for the kids' college fund. Then it was seven years with NASCorp… and then ten… and unlike so many corporate pilots in the industry, she had survived. Mr. Carswell retired and a new breed of executive had come to take over the corporate offices in Dallas. The company's interest in satellite dishes had waned, and was being replace by something that her new passengers often referred to as a 'digital cellular network.' That meant nothing to her… other than that her job with NASCorp was as solid as ever. She got more say as to her schedule and more vacation time, all of which meant that she was able to get home for the really big events in life – holidays, birthdays, and their anniversary. Her living halftime in two places was a routine that she and her family had long ago grown accustomed to. One day had blended into the next… and Travis was graduating from high school with her tearfully cheering from the stands. Two years later it was Chad… and then Wade.

Before she knew it, she and Roy were empty-nesters… which right off meant a few significant changes. The first thing hitting her when Wade moved out of the house for a dorm on the Tech campus was that her hangar could now be reopened. So on the next opportunity back in Lubbock, she took bolt cutters and a crow bar to the man door of the hangar. The place had been closed off to her for over ten years, but no more. After much grunting and groaning, she finally managed to pry open the door. The plane was as she remembered it to be, though considerably dustier than before. But to her dismay, the previous night's rain had left many large puddles scattered about in various places… some much too near to her Corsair. She would engage a roofer as soon as possible to patch those leaks, and maybe have them shore up the rest of the structure while there were at it. Fortunately, a good many of the overhead lights still worked, but she should find someone with a cherry picker to replace those burnt-out bulbs. She was just about ready to take a walkaround her plane when Roy's voice came to her from the man door.

"What're you doing in there?"

"Taking a peek at my plane."

"You know… I had wanted this place closed off."

"Not any more. Now with Wade gone off to Tech, I'd like to be able to enjoy my…"

"I don't see that Wade had anything to do with it."

Without another word, he turned about for the house. She wanted to stay with her plane longer, but felt it was more important to head this issue off at the pass. She turned out the lights, closed up the hangar, and left for the house. She found him sitting at the kitchen table, evidently waiting for her return.

"Roy… I just want this to be clear between us. I love you… but that's my hangar… and I want it open."

"Obviously."

"So that's what I'm going to do."

"That's fine with me. Just leave me out of it."

He rose from the table, kissed her on the forehead… and that was that. She knew instantly that the subject would never come up again. Finally, she was free to visit her plane anytime she wanted to.

Despite the momentary tension over the hangar, she and Roy becoming empty nesters turned out to be such a blessing to their relationship. For the longest time leading up to this point, her greatest fear was of Roy being all alone in that huge house for a week at a time. He might have his jobs in retail to keep him busy during the day, but nights before a TV would be terribly lonely. Then a completely different thing came to them. Not every week away, but for a good many of them, she was able to take Roy with her to Dallas. Together in the small guest apartment she had hung onto for years, Roy was now sleeping with her there in the same bed. It was magical. The two of them, both closing in on their fifties, acting like young newlyweds who could only afford to live in a shoebox. She got to show him her favorite hangouts in Dallas, spend night after night eating at restaurants the likes of which Lubbock had never seen, and then make love to him in that tiny little apartment. Nearly as good, she got permission from NASCorp aviation to bring him on select flights about the country. The pride on his face as he watched her do her job in the cockpit, that was worth a lifetime of aviation training to her. And then she had him all to herself in some far-flung city on a minivacation. It was the absolute best. Her burden of loneliness was finally lessening… as was some of her guilt from over a decade of living apart from him.

By far, her most proud moment in her aviation career came when Randolph Tugbuddy called with the news that she would be promoted to Captain. She would be the first woman in NASCorp's fleet to have that honor. Because of that distinction, Randolph arranged for a division-wide event in recognition of her accomplishment. She flew Roy to New York with her for the ceremony in which he was given a spouse's privilege of pinning the four stripes on her shoulders. He beamed all the way through, from her introduction to the ovation she received from the assembly. From then on, she would have command of her own aircraft. But that was nothing compared to knowing that she had Roy's utmost admiration.

Everything was finally looking up for them.

CHAPTER

42

THE THREE DILS

Menopause hit her like a stiff crosswind on takeoff. For nearly an entire year leading up to her turning fifty, she had to deal with periodic bouts of fatigue, hot flashes, headaches, and soreness to her breasts. Then in a flash, it was over. Right about that same time, she received from her doctor a relatively new thing that he said would remove a great part of the anxiety associated with her life-threatening allergy. This epinephrine pen thing, he said, had been on the medical market for a few years, but he had delayed in recommending it until he was certain that the bugs had been worked out of the delivery system. The only requirement for her to have full insurance coverage was a positive allergy test. The doctor pricked her on her back with a needle containing the venom equivalent of one thousandth of a bee sting… and the spot immediately swelled up to the size of a golf ball. She went home that day with her first prescription for an EpiPen, and a sore back that kept her from flying for a week.

Age had brought so much unanticipated prospective. She was no longer ashamed of wearing a medical alert bracelet or carrying an EpiPen about in her purse. Having a life-threatening allergy was peanuts compared to what some of her friends and coworkers were dealing with. Arthritic joints, severe digestive problems, chronic headaches, and terrible cancer scares… compared to those things, she lived a relatively worry-free life. She had the confidence of years, and a growing feeling of pride over what she and Roy had accomplished together as a couple. Her time of youth might be over, but she still felt that the best was yet to come. Time together with Roy and time to watch her sons become men – those were the things she looked forward to most.

In raising their boys, she and Roy had always focused on turning out individuals who would have a positive influence on the world. She expected each to build a career for themselves, and eventually start a family of their own. As to sharing things with her about their relationships, she knew that they were more drawn to their father than to her. So she used Roy to learn about their girlfriends. Same with their heartbreaks. She counseled and consoled whenever they were open to receiving something from her, but found it more impactful to artfully communicate her advice through Roy. She still remained attentive from a distance to their choices for companionship. But for the most part, she considered their dating to be their business, as was their ultimate choice of a life partner. Having been there herself, she still remembered well carrying the burden of her aunt's disapproval. Ultimately, she knew that her sons would love whomever they chose to love. She still strove to show her interest without appearing as if she was interfering. Acceptance was the key. Just as Ruby had accepted her, she would accept any daughter-in-law as a daughter of her own. With time and effort on her part, she was confident of being able to build a meaningful relationship with whatever kind of girl became part of her family.

The rigors of flying for NASCorp did not provide her with many opportunities for being around her sons' high school girlfriends. She kept up as best as she could, meeting them… having them over for dinner… and learning about their families. She never got the impression that any of her sons' high school relationships were all that serious… which was fine with her seeing as she had little reserves for spending time with teenage girls. In turn, each of her sons went off to college – Travis to UT and then Chad following in his older brother's footsteps two years later. Travis graduated on time and got accepted into law school at Duke, whereas Chad stretched out his four year engineering degree into a fifth. Wade's love for music took him to Tech's well-respected music department… though he unexpectedly dropped out two years later to join a band in Austin. She first learned about that from Roy while stuck in Cheyenne by a freak snow storm. He seemed not to take his son's decision nearly as seriously as he did the weather. Not so for her. A mother can have two children on course, but if one veers off… then everything has gone wrong. Wade had left Lubbock before she could get back home from that trip, leaving her feeling sort of like she was the one who had moved away from him.

For the first time in her life as a mother, all three of her sons were on their own.

Travis was the first to become engaged. A year into law school, he came home one break to introduce a girlfriend turned fiancée. Amanda Fleming was an altogether perfect young woman. With a finance degree from UNC, she was at Duke getting her MBA when the two met. Finding themselves seated side-by-side at a basketball game, it was love at first sight.

By all measures of importance, she was absolutely elated with Travis's choice for a life partner. Amanda was the perfect refinement of the Southern graces… so much so that it was absolutely impossible to think of her as ever having been a girl. Amanda was a young woman, and a very promising one at that. She was articulate and highly educated, but also exceedingly driven to succeed. Amanda was everything that she would have wanted to be had she been allowed to attend college. So she could not help but approve of Amanda, even though everything about the young woman made her jealous. It did not help that Roy was over-the-top excited with the prospect of having this young woman as his future daughter-in-law. And who could blame him?! Amanda was flat-out gorgeous with that sweet smile of hers, a clear and creamy complexion, and all that richly flowing amber hair. Toward him, she was both respectful and playful… if not a bit too affectionate. Amanda always put forth a pleasantly clever sense of humor for him… one that frequently had her leaning on him through their mutual laughter. Roy just soaked it all up. But toward her, Amanda seemed distant and unusually formal… as if the young woman had not yet decided whether to accept her as a friend. She definitely was not imagining the prickly vibe she got whenever the two of them were together in a private conversation. Try as she might not to, her mind too often spun that feeling into a doubt over whether she was meeting up to her future daughter-in-law's standards. She was not being judged, but still felt that way. For having not gone beyond high school… for having not been a stay-at-home mother… for doing something so unladylike as to fly planes… for living so much of the week apart from a husband… and for who knows what else. Amanda was always polite toward her, never once vocalizing a single negative word. But the difference between the smiles she gave Roy and the tight-lipped reserved toward her spoke volumes. She was not fooled by the show of manners either, for a tiger of a person dwelt beneath this young woman's pleasant demeanor. So she put extra effort into upping her vocabulary whenever conversing with

Amanda, and only discussed those subjects worthy of the newswoman she had once been. Anything at all not to come across as a stupid mother-in-law-to-be.

Travis and Amanda's wedding in Raleigh was one of the most thought-through and well-organized events she had ever attended. Conducted at a quaint little country church in the cool of a clear April afternoon, everything was done perfectly. Amanda's parents and all of her siblings... her entire extended family... were just like her, so very well put together. They treated her and Roy with such honor for having produced the fine young man that was to marry their Amanda. The entire experience was pleasant through and through. Amanda knew exactly what she wanted and went about arranging every detail with a cool, calm ease. When they arrived in North Carolina, nothing was required of them other than to preside over the rehearsal dinner that had been worked out long ago over the phone.

The morning of the ceremony, she bustled about with the other women doing last minute tasks, but did not lay eyes on the bride until she emerged into the sanctuary on her father's arm. Amanda's dress was the height of elegance – a modest trumpet of an ivory silk with a heart shaped neckline and a touch of off-the-shoulder lace. The bride needed no veil with how an intricate array of silver leaf jewelry had been woven through her braided bun such that the delicateness of her neckline was fully on display. Even the train was perfect – just long enough so as to require the attentive help of a bridesmaid. The entire ceremony through to the reception was beautiful... one of the best weddings she had ever attended. Through it all, she hung off Roy's arm trying very hard to seem half as graceful as the bride.

Travis and Amanda graduated from Duke together, and both found jobs with the same computer chip manufacturer in Dallas, him as a lawyer and her in project management. She thought this to be such a fortuitous outcome, as it would give her a firsthand opportunity to bond with her new daughter-in-law. In the beginning, they got together for lunch or coffee on nearly a monthly basis, but as Amanda's job became more demanding and her own schedule of flying never let up, the occasions dwindled down to holidays, birthdays, and a few dinners over. Amanda seemed content with the situation. Eventually, she came to accept that she and Amanda were two very different women, with little in common other than Travis.

Stacey McMaster was like no female creature she had ever come across in all of her adult years. She was first introduced to this girl as Chad's date at the celebration dinner they gave Travis upon his graduation from UT. From the get-go, she found this coed to be an overwhelming torrent of expression… one readily capable of producing an opinion on any issue or nonissue known to womankind. If she had once thought herself to be a talker, Stacey blew the doors off the concept and turned her mute long before the salads arrived. The girl spoke whatever was on her mind without thought-filter applied. Her favorite topics, it would seem, were how she had set herself on attending UT before solid food graced her infant lips, and how omega-delta-something-or-other was the only sorority worthy of her association, it being a part of her own mother's legacy at UT. She did manage once to squeeze in a question about how the two had met, and then had to endure a drawn-out account of the fraternity-sorority doings at UT before Stacey finally got around to saying that it was at a mixer.

"And we've been a couple ever since!"

The surest bet she could have ever made in this world would have been that Stacey was an only child… a fact she happened to learn before the waiter brought their entrees. It seemed that this girl grew up in the suburbs of Houston with money as her best friend. Blessed by a highly successful real estate agent as a mother and the owner of an engineering firm for a father, Stacey had the financial resources to sample every good thing in life. She was the quintessential East Texas princess, with a BMW at sixteen, a walk-in closet of designer clothes that turned over with each season, and her own college condo overlooking the Colorado River in the trendiest section of Austin's downtown. With Chad as her boyfriend, she had everything in the world that she needed… which included a captive audience for her boodles of conversation.

Unfortunately, an unhappy estimation of Chad's girlfriend got cemented in her mind long before the check arrived. This girl was a silver-blond nightmare… a spoiled priss very much accustom to having her way… the worst sort of Texas teenager bestowed with the privilege of college… and the absolute love of her son's life. How Chad had come to be a trophy to this girl was beyond her understanding. Outwardly, her second son was big, bulky and a bit of a nerd, whereas this Stacey was so very petite, delicate and accustom to being pampered. That, of course, was only appearances. Stacey had the will to dominate, and her least clever of sons was the girl's captive. Maybe that was the making of an ideal relationship, as throughout that dinner, he did whatever his girlfriend told him to do. To her credit, Stacey did have excellent taste in clothing. So… if Chad's relationship with this girl happened to develop further, then perhaps fashion might be a thing that they could build a friendship upon. But in reality, she suspected that shopping with Stacey would be anything but fun, for the girl had hardly allowed her to get a word in edgewise during dinner.

On the drive back to Lubbock, she talked over Chad's choice of a girlfriend with Roy. For some reason, he considered Stacey to be perfectly fine. Vixen or viper, he saw none of it. The girl was just a cute little sweetheart enamored with his son.

"Come on, Marna… give the girl a break! She's just perky."

"Totally overwhelming, you mean!"

Years later, she learned that Roy loaned Chad ten thousand dollars to purchase the most god-awful engagement ring she ever laid eyes on. A grossly huge two and a half carat diamond encircled in its setting by a whole host of littler ones there to worship it. The size of the thing seemed as a bottle cap fastened to Stacey's tiny finger. But that ring was ultimate power to the girl, for it gave her complete control over Chad. As to Stacey's own opinion of the ring that Roy had given her, it was 'lovely enough'… which was code for it being rather plain. In such ways, Stacey made clear her advantage over her future mother-in-law whenever they spent time together. Unlike Amanda… who never uttered a word about her having not attended college… Stacey right off recommended that she restart her education with some night courses, seeing as being back on a college campus might prove too much for someone as old as her.

Chad and Stacey's wedding week was a flamboyant and completely out of control series of events. Whenever things did not go precisely as she had expected… which was often… Stacey was either in tears or a towering rage. The days had been chaotically scripted with so many moving parts. Everyone was going every which way to multiple bachelor/bachelorette parties, a chartered cruise down the Colorado, an exceptionally long rehearsal dinner, a stuffy Saturday morning brunch, an elaborate photo session before the ceremony, and a Sunday morning breakfast for the exhausted out-of-towners. The wedding and reception were held at an exclusive Hill Country resort that was nothing short of extravagant. A half dozen bridesmaids and groomsmen, three flower girls, and two ring bearers made the lead up to the bride an excruciatingly long ordeal. Finally, out came Stacey on her father's arm, frills molting off of her every side and a glacial-sized train following in behind. The ceremony had so many solos to be sung, with pastors from both her home and UT churches speaking. The vows were too short and the recessional parade took forever. As to the reception, it was difficult for her to say which centerpiece was the most outrageous – the side of beef turning on its spindle over an open firepit or the Cadillac-sized ice sculpture that very much resembled the fountain horses on the UT campus. The live music was far too loud for conversation, and the free flowing alcohol turned the many boorishly crude toasts into such an uncomfortable situation… especially in her having to hear about some of Chad's less than savory exploits in college. She found the whole event to be overwhelming, particularly as she felt lost in a throng of people she had never met. For good reasons or bad, Stacey had conscripted a relative to be their personal escort for the reception. Everywhere they went throughout the evening, there was Great Aunt Maureen explaining the McMaster family tree, and presenting them to a state senator or some million-acre land baron. Poor Roy… he was repeatedly introduced as the retired owner of an appliance store, whereas she at least had the conversational benefit of being known as a corporate pilot. He seemed not to be bothered, for the entire affair was a party to him. She, on the other hand, had never felt more useless in all her life.

From the wedding onward, she sensed a reluctant sort of inclusiveness coming from her newest daughter-in-law. Sort of like she was some old sorority alumni back on campus to marvel at how well the current generation of sisters was managing things. Roy became 'Dad,' but to Stacey, she would always be 'Marna'… just as she was informed not minutes into the reception. Chad took a job two hours away in Midland working for the engineering firm of Stacey's father, which ensured that she would see way too much of her new daughter-in-law.

Inconceivable as it might have seemed beforehand, Wade's new girlfriend was destined to become her least favorite daughter-in-law. Valerie Plotchney had absolutely no ambition in life, being content just to exist day to day doing whatever. Of course, there was no mystery as to why Wade was attracted to this girl. Valerie was the epitome of cuteness with how her clear blue eyes were perfectly set within a heart-shaped face, it being framed by her buoyantly brown hair. The girl was absolutely adorable. The only shortcoming to her otherwise perfect figure was the unfortunate flaw that she slumped her shoulders too much, giving off the impression that the girl had little backbone. That, unfortunately, was fairly accurate. Most of the time, Valerie's vacant stare matched her timid nature, for seldom did she put two words together without first looking away. To make matters far worse, she had the IQ of a turnip. How this girl had managed to graduate from high school was beyond reason, as the only thing she seemed suited for in life was waiting on tables. But Valerie was perfectly happy to galumph along in life, content with whatever was put before her. Her one redeeming talent was that she had the singing voice of an angel… which seldom got used for earning money owing to stage fright. That happened to be how Wade and she first met… him sitting in on an informal gig where she sang. Yet Valerie did seem adept at soothing Wade's moody artistic side… though she showed no inclination whatsoever for pushing him toward finding a decent job.

More so than the other two, Roy was especially protective of Valerie, and did not want to hear a single word of criticism about the girl. Her best guess was that Valerie somehow reminded him of his grade school sister... though the two were really nothing alike. His only frustration was that Wade and Valerie were living together outside of marriage. That, of course, went away the moment Wade announced that they were finally engaged. As for her part, whether it was because she was a pilot or because of some weird perspective picked up from Wade, she sensed that Valerie was afraid of her... which unfortunately made spending quality time with the girl nearly impossible.

Having already lived together, Wade and Valerie decided on a private ceremony. Though the girl had a huge family, she did not want any of them in attendance... and Wade was insistent that no one ask her why. So it would only be his brothers, their wives, she, and Roy. Wade's only other request... a very earnest one... was that Valerie be allowed to wear the crystal wedding dress. This was a gut wrenchingly difficult decision for her to make, seeing as that dress was so special. But since Valerie had no means for affording one of her own... and since Wade was nearly in tears when professing to Valerie how beautiful his mother had been on that night... she reluctantly passed the dress over to the girl. He had only been six at the time of that ceremony, and in constant daycare as she built up her hours flying. The memory of all those times of abandoning him into the arms of another made it impossible for her to say no. The dress would surely require alterations in being fit to Valerie, but perhaps seeing her youngest son's bride adorned as she had been might just be the thing to bond her to this new daughter-in-law.

Three weeks later, they drove to Austin where the ceremony was to be conducted in a small music hall just off Sixth Street. As the processional music started up, she rose with Roy and the others to follow the bride's entrance and short walk up to her groom... except Valerie was not wearing the crystal dress. She was instead in a rather simple-looking nightgown-like garment of satin white. Her immediate thought was that they had not been able to get the dress altered properly, and that Valerie must be heartbroken to wear something so plain. To the girl's credit, she still glowed very much like the ecstatic bride. Not until the ceremony was over and the congratulations had been handed out did she delicately ventured to ask. After a kiss and a hug to the bride, she stepped back to offer words that she hoped would be both complimentary and conciliatory at the same time.

"Valerie... your dress... it's so lovely... but I'm so disappointed that you weren't able to wear mine. I was really looking forward to seeing you in it."

"Thanks… umm… did… umm… Wade not tell you?"

"Tell me what?"

Valerie took her new husband by the elbow and pulled him around in front of her… right before sliding off toward the other women.

"Now, Mom… everything's going to be fine… so don't panic."

"Just tell me, Wade… has something happened to my dress?"

"Well… to be honest… we don't know."

"What's that supposed to mean?!"

"It's like this… Valerie had a little fender-bender on I35 last week… you know… on that section with the upper and lower decks. Hellacious to drive even without traffic! Anyway… she sort of… pulled out and got rear-ended. She's obviously okay… thank God… but the back of her car… it kind of… got smashed in."

"And what's this got to do with my dress?"

"Oh… well… umm… it was… sort of in the trunk when it happened."

"Are you telling me that it's ruined?!"

"Ahh… no. It's just that… we can't find it."

"WHAT THE HELL?! "

"Chill, Mom! It's not our fault!"

"How's this even possible?!

"The tow truck guy took the car to the body shop… but the mechanic wanted too much… so we decided not to do anything. But when we got it back… someone had pried open the trunk… and your dress was gone."

"I can't believe this! I absolutely can not believe this!"

"Mom, we're doing everything we can to find it! I've already been over to the body shop, and I'm planning on talking with the tow truck driver again on Monday. We'll find your dress. I promise. You know… Valerie feels absolutely terrible about this."

"Wade, she should! That dress is really special to me! And I trusted you both with it!"

"Please don't get upset! This is my wedding day, after all! And you're not even thinking about Valerie. She was scared out of her mind… not to mention that she had to pick out a new dress in less than a week. She's been through a lot. So… if you don't mind… I want to go be with her."

As he turned away, she found herself being drawn backward into a corner. She desperately wanted Roy to be at her side… but he was off kidding it up with his sons. Wade included, for he had gone there instead of to his bride. She looked diagonally across the room to the opposite side where her three daughters-in-law had collected into a tight circle. She could not hear them over the music still playing, but it was evident that Amanda and Stacey were expressing their admiration over Valerie's dress. The bride, with a beaming smile, was soaking it all in. No way would she go over there to join them... not as Roy was doing with the three boys. She would definitely lose her cool at Valerie. It did not matter anyway. She likely would not be welcomed by them. Tolerated, yes... but not accepted.

From that day on, she found herself thinking of her son's wives not as daughters-in-law, but as the three DILs. Sure, she could blame it all on an aviator's propensity for using acronyms, but that was far from the truth of it. She was close to none of them. Amanda made her feel inferior, Stacey just plain irritated her, and Valerie... she was totally disgusted with anybody who could treat another woman's wedding dress like a rag left in the trunk of a car. She spent the whole drive back to Lubbock pouring out her tears of frustration to Roy. Losing her dress was like losing a part of them as a couple.

She only had one day at home with him before having to return to work, yet spent so much of it standing before her relief, as it seemed the only thing capable of comforting her. Surprisingly, she found herself perceiving the DILs within the context of that stonework. Amanda... she was the rock itself, beautifully carved yet so very hard and distant. Just as with the relief, being in Amanda's presence required so much self-examination... with the all-too-often unsettling conclusion of finding herself lacking. In contrast, Stacey and Valerie... they were the faces. One was domineering and the other was cowering, yet neither toward each other. Those attributes were reserved exclusively for their mother-in-law. Somehow, this assessment of the three DILs seemed to match how each had first responded to seeing the relief. Amanda stood studying it with detached interest before walking away without the stone having gained one tiny foothold in her thinking. Stacey just wanted to know how much it was worth. As for Valerie... she was absolutely terrified of it... so much so that she only reluctantly entered the dining room during their visits. Oddly, not one of them was interested in being shown her plane.

Yet most revealing to her was that each of her sons had settled on their mate without ever once having sought their mother's opinion.

43

THE HARM TO A HARMLESS MASON WASP

Roy spent three days visiting Wade and Valerie in Austin the week after they were married, helping them get settled into a new apartment. She knew that he was really there to personally hunt for her dress. He went from the tow truck company to the body shop and back again without success. Just as Wade had professed, not one person at either establishment fessed up to having taken her dress. All of this she learned over the phone during a quick turnaround in Kansas City. By the time Roy finished explaining to her the pains through which he had questioned everyone involved, she was not altogether convinced that Valerie ever had the dress in the trunk of her car in the first place. In all likelihood, the airhead had left it in the fitting room of some bridal shop in Austin.

She had another week of shuttling executives between Dallas and New York, with side trips to Orlando and Portland before she could get back home again. That Monday through Friday of flying had done nothing to dull her seething anger at Valerie for having lost her dress. It would likely take years. That dress had been priceless to her. She had poured her heart into its design so that it matched her aunt's necklace.

Thank God I didn't loan that out to the DIL too!

It may have been near on twenty years since she last wore it, but the feel of the dress had come rushing back to her the very moment she took it out of storage. Everything that she hoped to be as a wife for Roy – pure, precious and sparkling – had gone into the making of that dress… and now it was gone. Worse – she had spent those twenty years fighting against a feeling that the sparkle was also vanishing from her marriage, what with all of her nights away and so many miles travelled. Her dress was not lost – it had left her because she was not so clear, not so pure, and not so precious anymore. She feared that so much time spent living in strange places had also made her a stranger to her husband.

Unfortunately, she only had a weekend off before needing to be in Dallas. Back home on Friday, she went to bed that night wishing very much that she had not spent the last hour flipping through the photo album to reminisce over her crystal dress. Her intention had been reasonable enough. She hoped that seeing pictures of herself beside Roy at their fifteenth would somehow redirect her disappointment… soften it a bit… and put her in a more intimate mood for making love to him. It turned out to be a stupid plan, as beholding her dress totally backfired. She once again relived the anger and sadness of her loss… which made concentrating on being with him so very difficult.

Come Saturday morning, she had a sizeable list of things needing to be accomplished – laundry, shopping for a new travel bag, having her hair done, and perhaps some effort put into cleaning the cellar. She got most of that done, but neglected to spend much time with Roy in the process. He was acting sheepishly toward her anyway… so obviously tip-toeing around her bad mood. That just made her feel even worse.

She wasted Friday night being sour, all day Saturday moping about on her errands, and now… Sunday afternoon… still could not get Valerie's gross negligence off her mind. She swore all kinds of things to herself. That she would never trust the DIL again, never send another check to an out-of-work Wade, and never compromise on something that was special to her. Her beautiful dress was gone forever… and she had allowed that unfortunate fact to wreck her entire weekend with Roy. After tonight, she would not see him again for another week, as he had decided to stick around Lubbock rather than go with her to Dallas.

This whole debacle over her wedding dress was making her look at life differently. Maybe it was finally time to retire from NASCorp? She was not young anymore… and being a corporate pilot took a sort of panache for which she no longer had much interest. For her, the value of a thing had always been found in the accomplishing of it… and she certainly had accomplished much. She was blessed with such an amazing career in flight. The first woman pilot for Ranger Airlines, the first female captain for NASCorp, and well over ten thousand total hours in the cockpit. She had flown the 737, but also Gulf Streams, Dassaults and Learjets… not to mention all those wonderful props from her youth. Taken up on a whim, flying had turned into the endeavor of a lifetime. But maybe it was time to land for good. Get a part time job on the ground in Lubbock… find someone who can help them do a bit of financial planning… talk to that new lawyer of theirs about an updated will… and go flying just for the heck of it. Above all those things, she would make the most of her years with Roy, because he was the one thing in life that had always brought her joy.

So then how's about you stop being such a grump and think about making him something special for dinner tonight! It's not like you'd ever be able to fit into that dress again anyway!

She entered the kitchen with her mind set on preparing him a special meal, and was surprised to find him sitting at the kitchen table rather than off in the family room watching football.

"Hey. I was just about to start in on dinner."

"Before you do… I'd like to discuss something… difficult."

"If this is about my bad mood all weekend… I'm really sorry. I'm still super ticked off at Valerie about my dress… and I've probably been taking it out on you."

"Thanks… but it's not that. I fully understand how you feel. I'm thinking about something totally different. Would you… mind giving me a hand with something while we talk?"

"Sure… What is it?"

"I want to open up the main hangar door."

So out of the blue, she just had to sit herself down at the kitchen table to process his words. A small spark of excitement then found its way into her thinking – that perhaps he had finally changed his perspective on her plane now that the last of their kids was married off. Perhaps he was ready to embrace it as something she could enjoy whenever she was home.

"That would be awesome! I can't tell you how much I'd like having it open so I could…"

"Actually… there's something I haven't told you. Now don't be upset… I have a guy coming in the morning to look at the hangar… and I want the door open so he can get a better feel for the inside."

"Whatever for?"

"It's like this… I heard about this friend of a friend whose hunting for a… a suitable place to conduct his auctioneering business. You know… selling of repossessed farm equipment… bankruptcies… estate sales… stuff like that. He's looking for a new space as he's tired of paying the outrageous fees over at…"

"You're not thinking of using my hangar… and without asking me first?"

"It's not *your* hangar any more than this house is *my* house…"

"That's not the same thing."

"…and I happen to be asking you right now."

"No, you're not asking me – you're telling me. You know I'll be heading back to work early in the morning. So actually… you're not giving me much of a say in the matter."

"Please, Marna… just listen to what I have to say. It'll all make sense. That hangar's the ideal size for him… big enough for the biggest of equipment he auctions off with plenty of room left over for the people bidding. We've got lots of space for parking… and we're not far from town. It's exactly what he's looking for. Marna… this is a great opportunity for us to earn some extra money. I'm telling you – the guy's willing to pay for storing his auction items here… not to mention conducting the auctions on the weekends. And we don't have to do a thing. He'll handle all of the details."

"And you're proposing that his throng use one of our bathrooms?!"

"He'll have porta potties. That's all pretty standard. And they'll be back around where we can't see them. Oh… and on top of the rent, he's going to give us a small cut from the concession trucks that he normally has around for his auctions. It'll be perfect."

"Well then, what about my plane?! I guess you're expecting it to be parked out in the yard as some kind of an attraction! A play thing for the kiddies?!!"

"No… I'm actually suggesting that it be the first item to go on auction."

Suddenly, what had been an irritating conversation turned far worse. She could feel the rage rising up in her throat… just like when she learned that Valerie had lost her dress.

"How dare you…"

"Listen, Marna… just think about it from a different perspective. You've had that plane sitting around in that hangar for over thirty years. Thirty years, Marna! And I've been incredibly patient with you. I've tolerated it because…"

"You've tolerated it?! Wow! I had no idea that the thing's been posing you such an inconvenience! Been tripping over it lately, have you, Roy?!"

"Obviously not. I'm just thinking that it's high time we considered using the space for something of value. You hardly ever look at the thing anymore, so why not…"

"I'll tell you why I *hardly* ever look at it anymore – because it's been locked up most of the time! Besides, I don't get the pleasure of being here! But go ahead, take away something that's special to me! You've never liked that plane anyway, and you've never bothered to consider what it means to me! And why should you?! You're absolutely terrified of it!"

By his scowl, she knew that she had gone too far… but honestly did not care. He talked about having to tolerate something… well, she was the one who had to tolerate being away from home week in and week out. She sacrificed so he could enjoy his early retirement… and now here he was proposing to start up some ridiculous boondoggle that required her to give up one of the few treasures in her life.

"I'm not afraid of it – I just don't like it. And you don't need to rub it in my face either. You know… you more than once promised to get rid of that plane!"

She had heard enough. Jumping up from the kitchen table, she made for the back door, pausing there just long enough to get in the last word.

"Do whatever the hell you like! I don't live here anyway, so what difference does it make?!"

She slammed the door especially hard on the way out, taking a distinct pleasure out of the shock she hoped it might send his way. But she would not linger there on the porch, for he could surely see her through the window. She was definitely not in the mood to have him come outside with more of his selfish whining… at least not until she had an opportunity to arrange words that he could not possibly argue with. Yet what should she do with all this anger? Not go toward the hangar. That would be exactly what he wanted for getting the door open.

Just… go around to the other side… as far away from him as possible!

After a quick look toward the hangar, long enough to note the deep purple clouds looming up around it, she set off toward the parlor-side of the porch.

I can't believe he'd spring something like this on me the night before I have to leave! I just lost one of the most precious things in my life… and now he has the audacity to go behind my back about the hangar. Unreal! No way in hell I'm giving up that plane!

She plopped down on the edge of the porch to stare out toward the east. Beyond that darkened horizon was Dallas and her job as a corporate pilot. She had planes there too. Not hers, but ones that she could actually fly. Maybe it was stupid to get so worked up over that piece of junk, but somehow she could not keep herself from doing so. The thought of that Corsair took her into the sky in a way that no Learjet ever could. But it was all so hopeless! She had followed her dreams… and they had taken her nowhere. She had spent so much time separated from him that he no longer cared about the things she cared about… and maybe it was the same with her.

In desperation, she looked about for something to take her frustrations out on until she could calm down enough to go reason with him. About the porch pillar to her right were those potted black-eyed Susans she had bought a couple weeks ago to spice up the place. The fact that they were still blooming was proof that Roy had been faithful to water them. That just annoyed her even more, as it suggested the problem in this situation might reside somewhere else than with him. She snatched up the nearest pot and shoved it between her knees. Taking a distinct pleasure from each snapping sound, she went about plucking off the deadheads and hurling them out into the yard.

But really, it was all so insensitive of him! And unfair too! What right had he to auction off her plane?!

I make the sacrifices! I endure the hardships! I bring home the money! You'd think all of that would earn me some consideration! All I ask is that I get to have my off week for rest. And if that means keeping my hangar and my plane... then I've earned it! You'd think he'd be happy to give me that pleasure!

Finishing with one pot, she set it aside to take up another. That guy at the nursery had said that the black-eyed Susan symbolized love's determined persistence... or something idiotic like that!

Some old fart of an English poem about a sailor dodging cannonballs to get back to his true love! Absolutely ridiculous! They'll say anything to sell flowers... and of course, I was stupid enough to buy them!

At that very moment came a high-pitched screeching sound, so painfully loud and long that it actually made her shutter. Only as it ground to a halt did she realized that he had just opened the hangar door all by himself. Nothing she had said even registered with him. He was going to show off her hangar in spite of her earnest plea to the contrary.

Fine! I'll – just – go – back – to – Dallas – where I belong!

She knew that she was ripping the heads off of perfectly good blooms, but did not care. She had a right to vent her hurt on something... and these flowers would just have to pay the price of being so near. Having torn off the color from the plant in this second pot, she unceremoniously dropped it over the side and picked up the last one. Staring into the depth of one prominent bloom, she concentrated on the center's deep color, blocking the bright yellow from her mind. To her, the black of the flower's name was more of a reddish brown. Not nearly dark enough for her mood.

It was not her fault that she had ended up in a job so far away from home. She had no choice. His store was failing... and they were without a source of income. They had three boys to raise. They were depending on her. She took the job because she had to... and with his full blessing. More than that – it was his idea! So he, as much as she, had compromised their marriage for the expediency of a paycheck. Her being able to pursue a career in flight had nothing to do with…

Her eyes were suddenly drawn down to a movement on the flower she was reaching for. Something was crawling across its center. Immediately recognizing the source, she sought to shove the pot away. But the wasp had already lifted from off the flower, completed a tight circle of flight about her hand, and alit upon her wrist. As quick as she could, she brought her other hand over to swat the insect away… but too late. In slow motion horror, she watched the creature flex its lower extremity and thrust downward with its terrifying part into her skin, finishing the violent act by writhing about the connection between it and her. She instantly felt a twinge of pain… and screamed.

The world of the wasp is a female-dominated one, with the male having little place in it. The female is larger, stronger, has more powerful wings, and lives much longer. Only she builds and hunts, for only she has the will to dominate… and the stinger to make it happen. The female wasp is both mother and warrior… leader, nurturer, worker and pioneer.

Such is not the case for the male. He is a rather passive creature, sucking nectar for most of his adult life while doing nothing much useful beyond carrying bits of pollen from place to place by sheer happenstance.

Call it a quirk of Nature, but there is a wasp species in which the male is capable of delivering a sting… albeit without the slightest trace of venom involved. Perhaps long eons ago, the male ancestors of the four-toothed mason wasp might actually have possessed a true stinger, and some cruel plot of evolutionary intent bred the poison right out of them. Yet within his genes is still the latent desire to be fully all that is a wasp… for the male *monobia quadridens* can be quite aggressive. When provoked, he will set about mimicking the female's pattern of attack, thrusting the hardened tip of his abdomen into a foe. But unlike her, he is completely harmless. At best, he causes a pin-prick of damage with virtually no pain. Yet he goes on masquerading himself as her… both of them being solid black all over except for white shoulder pads and a white band about the abdomen. He, however, also bears a mark of shame – an added small blotch upon his forehead labeling him as one without true sting.

There is, however, a more distinctive characteristic of this male wasp. Though he may endeavor to imitate his mate, his real skill is found in lovemaking. Unlike the males of many other species who attach themselves for but a minute or two, the male mason wasp remains connected to his mate for a half hour or more – a bond of intimacy unlike so many in the wasp world. Though fertilization has already occurred, he persists in clinging to his mate.

But the female desires only to be done with him and move on to her greater purpose in the world… accepting that his role in her life should come to an end.

Having not been stung since she was a small child, she suddenly felt the panic of a lifetime's worth of fear condensed down into a single intake of air… and then she sprang into action. She had rehearsed this moment over and over, and knew exactly what to do. Reflexes obeyed without hesitation. Tearing around the porch, she made for the EpiPen in her purse, it lying somewhere within the kitchen. She shouted out once toward the hangar for Roy, but did not linger in a second attempt when he had not answered. She knew from the countless warnings of medical experts over the years that there was absolutely no time for delay.

Flinging open the back door, she threw herself into a crazed search through the clutter on the kitchen counters, sweeping some items to the floor and pushing others to the splashboard. Finding her purse lying beneath a dish towel, she did not bother to hunt within. She dumped the entire contents out onto the counter and began frantically sifting through the debris as the progression of steps scorched through her mind.

Find the EpiPen… administer the shot… call 911… all before the venom stops my heart!

Yet somewhere within a deep place to her thinking, a few small inconsistencies were vying for a piece of her attention amidst the weightier matter being wrangled over. For one… that sting was fairly lame. Not anything like the searing pain she had expected… though there really was no time for a closer examination of the wound. That could come later. After all, it was clearly a sting. She saw the wasp jab its rear into her wrist and felt pain.

And another thing… where were those early symptoms of anaphylactic shock?! Her heart rate should be slowing down, and she should be gasping for breath from her throat closing up. She was clearly winded… but struggling for breath?! Not in the least! Surely nothing more than what was expected from dashing around the porch and tearing the kitchen apart in a frenzied search for her purse. If anything, her heart was going ninety-to-nothing, and in breathing so fast, she was near to passing out from hyperventilation. But all this thinking was stupid, for what did she really know about being stung?! Best to be on the safe side and focus on finding the pen.

Where the hell… Oh! Got it!

She had read the instructions a hundred times… almost to the point of knowing them by heart… yet all of that had been while she was calm and capable of clear thinking.

Where's Roy when I need him?!

She had hoped that he would do the actual injecting, her not being fond of needles. But she really could not risk going off to look for him. Any second now, her throat could collapse and her heart seize up.

'1. Pull off the safety cap.' Why the hell does it have to have a safety cap?!

She struggled to get the little blue plastic thing off, with it unexpectedly squirting out of her hand to spin across the kitchen floor. She ignored it and quickly moved on to the next step.

'2. Swing orange tip into the outer edge of thigh. Make sure of the click. Hold for ten seconds as the drug is delivered.'

Without further delay, she jabbed the pen into her leg halfway up from her knee… right through her jeans, as she knew she should. Her doctor had said not to bother stripping down. It was that serious. She heard the click… or thought she did… and was pretty sure that the needle had pierced her skin. But was anything actually going in? Had not her doctor said that the amount injected was quite small? Just six tear drops worth…

What if that wasn't the click? Or what if it didn't click enough?! I could be standing here dying and… Wait… it's tingling. Oh shit – I forgot to count! One… two… three… four… but what if it's not supposed to be in there for too long?!

Contorting her head around, she struggled to read the label's next step from where she clumsily held the pen protruding into her leg.

'3. To reset…' Good night! I don't want to reset! I want it to work!

Then, as if on cue, she felt the first significant sign of the epinephrine kicking in. A jitteriness was rising within her chest. Convinced that the time was well past ten seconds, she yanked the pen away from her leg and dropped it to the floor, lunging for the kitchen phone before the venom… or the drug… could take hold of her faculties.

"911 – what is your emergency?"

"Marna Meitner here – I have a life threatening allergy to bee stings! And I've just been stung!"

"Have you…"

"I've… I've already given myself a… a shot from my… EpiPen. I can… I can feel it. It's… it's taking hold! Ohh… my head! I think… I think I might…"

"Ma'am – lean over and put your head below your heart. I've got your caller ID info and am dispatching an ambu…"

She dropped the phone and fell to her knees as everything suddenly went black.

She awoke to a buzzing sound in her ear, and immediately thought that the wasp had come back for more. But it was just the dial tone of the phone, dangling from its tangled up cord a short distance from her face. That she had already called 911 was something that only slowly registered in her scattered thinking. Much more than that, she knew for certain that she had been stung… and somehow managed to inject herself… but that was about all she was sure of.

If this had been a more self-reflective moment, she might confess to a belief that such an event would never have actually happened to her. All of her vigilance over the years had relegated the concept of being stung to that of a childhood scary tale… a rumored horror akin to witches, goblins and trolls. She had come close on several occasions, but like the bravado of an overconfident pilot, she had never actually crashed. Lying flat on her face sprawled across the kitchen floor, she had certainly crashed this time. The side of her head was throbbing from where it had hit the floor. Worse, her heart raced and the rest of her shook out of control.

I need Roy!

That was the absolute height of her logic. So she drew up to hands and knees, pausing there to ensure that she did not pass out again. Using drawer handles, she pulled herself up into a standing position and leaned for a moment over the countertop. After clearing her head as to her bearings, she managed to make her legs work more-or-less as they should and staggered through the kitchen door to the porch. Walking a rickety line, she made for the hangar, confident that Roy would know what to do next. He would have to… for her brain's wiring had gone all wrong. The ground between here and there, it had become grossly uneven… up a hill and down another… with her slipping side to side as if everything had been greased. She was even seeing things – flashes of light and many small vertical streaks cutting downward across her vision. All about her was a gray haze, with a mysterious moisture pelting at her face. Halting some distance from the edge of the wide-open hangar door, she wiped her eyes to make sense of what she was seeing.

Boots in feet… toes pointing up… jeans… to the knees?

Her dizzied mind was in a muddle of confusion, for she seemed to be seeing things sideways. But no… that was definitely Roy's boots lying on the ground. So she lurched forward to take hold of the hangar door in order to pull herself about its corner. There was the rest of him, spread out flat on his back. Her first thought was that he too had been stung… and injected himself… and passed out just as she had. But that was stupid.

"Roy! Get up – I've been stung!"

And still he lay there...

"Roy! Did you hear me?!"

His eyes, wide open, were not seeing and not moving. There was absolutely no expression on his face. Neither fright, nor frown, nor grimace of pain. Just blankness.

Then a new kind of panic kicked in, heaping itself upon the mass she was already experiencing. No longer caring about the wasp or the EpiPen, she immediately threw herself down to shake him. When he refused to respond, she slid her fingers up and down his wrist, searching for the pulse spot... not at all convinced that she was able to find it in her disoriented state. She brought her fingers to his neck instead. But on neither side could she pick up anything suggestive of his heart's beat. Quickly to his mouth with her ear... there, she neither heard nor felt any sensation of breath. She shook him again with both hands upon his chest, and then from grips at his shoulders.

"Wake up, Roy! Please wake up!"

CPR! Do CPR!

She had been fully trained on this... but at the moment had absolutely no idea how to administer the technique properly. She nonetheless set about making vigorous pulses to the center of his chest with the heels of her overlaid hands, hoping that the sincerity of her effort might count enough for the restarting of his heart. Moving to his lips, she gave him all of the breath her lungs could muster, then immediately resumed working at his heart. She pounded... and breathed... and pounded some more... all the while begging God to spare him and take her instead. She paused her desperate efforts only once – to search again for a pulse – and then continued at it until her arms gave out and she fell exhausted across his body. Lingering there for only a moment, she rose right back up with an absolute refusal to concede. Quickly straddling him, she brought much more of her weight down upon his chest... and still he did not respond. The epinephrine had her own heart racing... yet not a beat of it would transfer over for his rescue. Nothing was working. None of her pounding or breathing. So she took hold of his shirt collar with both hands and shook him much more vigorously than before... halting only once to look into the depths of his vacant eyes... and then went right back at him, the whole while begging with every promise she could conjure. And then... in stroke after stroke... she just beat him all about his shoulders and chest with her fists, screaming out curse word after curse word... hoping that one might somehow startle him alive.

"Damn you, you bastard – come back this instant! Do you hear me, you son of a bitch?! Don't you fuckin' leave me! Don't you dare! Don't leave me. Don't… Please, Roy… come back."

Completely spent and with every part of her on fire from the EpiPen… she collapsed over her husband and cried, spilling her tears out onto his impassive face. Tears… and saliva… and mucus… defiling the man she loved. She stopped calling to him… stopped saying anything at all. She just lay there and wept.

The far-off sound of an approaching siren instantly brought her up. She could not allow him to be found like this… polluted by her. Using the hem of her blouse, she hurriedly wiped his face, straightened his shirt, and combed her fingers through his hair… all the while whispering her parting words of love.

CHAPTER

44

BECOMING RUBY

She staggered across the vacant stretch of muddy stubble leading up to the house, screaming for the ambulance to pull off the circle and make directly for the hangar. She fell once… twice… a third time before collapsing into the arms of a man clothed in black.

"Got you! You the one…"

Barely able to speak, she rasped out only the essential words.

"Not… me… him!"

"Aren't you the woman who…"

"Him!"

Frantic out of her mind, she flung both arms back toward the hangar.

"Is… someone over there in need of help?"

Nodding vigorously, she felt a sliver of hope run through her as he looked Roy's way.

"Lyell… over here. I think she's the one who called 911. Get her stabilized… I'm going to check out that hangar. I think someone else might be in trouble."

She was passed to another man, with the first trotting off through the rain, medical box in hand. She made to follow in behind, but the partner had a strong hold on her… saying things that she could not make out. She found herself being twisted about and drawn toward the ambulance. She must get back to Roy, yet could not break free from this second man's grip. Every bit of her was convulsing from the drug, making it so difficult to stand on her own. Worse, her heart beat with such a continuous stream of fury that she had no strength for enduring anything else... and certainly not for resisting the pull of this man.

All around, things swam in the reflected backwash of the ambulance's gyrating lights... and then everything suddenly went bright white. Somehow, that man had gotten her through the back doors and had her lying down. A plastic covering came over her face... stealing the volume she needed for screaming out her urgency. Bellowing through the mask, she called for Roy over and over... and each time the pounding in her head got worse. Hot with a flush of fear, she felt sweat pouring across her face to sting her eyes. She must get back to him... so she fought against this thing muffling her voice... fought against the arms restraining her... and fought against the terrible lie threatening to overwhelm her. Roy needed her.

Roy...

And then... everything sort of went hazy. Not black, as she could still make out shapes and movement. It all seemed... just a... cream-colored mess. Warbled voices... two of them... very near... then far... then near again... were saying such horrible things. No pulse... no heart rate... no breath... nothing they could do. And then she heard only one voice with its weirdly warped mouth looming directly over her, it uttering such complete rubbish... telling her to take it easy... they were bringing her in. But she needed to get out. She needed to get back to Roy.

She found herself being pitched rather abruptly to one side... with the man's face going every which way in her blurred vision. Another jostle... and then a crunching from somewhere beneath her. To that sound came the man's slurred words competing with the pounding of blood in her ears.

"Hang... on... lady... you're... going to be... fine."

"Roy..."

"Relax..."

"Roy..."

She must not close her eyes... but keeping them open was making her insides twirl into knots. None of this was real. She must still be passed out on the kitchen floor, dying from the one wasp that had finally gotten to her. She could hear its smooth, low hum filling the place where she lay... telling her that death was not so bad after all. It felt like... being rocked in a cradle. Back and forth... back and forth. Even... steady... calm.

Sleep, Marna... sleep.

She awoke with a jolt... and someone leaning over her. It was that man... the same one as before… telling her that they were there… so she could relax. How in the world could she do that with his heavy hand pressing down on her shoulder?!

"Roy…"

"Take it easy, lady. Don't fight! We'll wheel you in… and then you can talk with an ER nurse."

She felt herself being pulled feet-first downward at a tilt… felt all of herself unexpectedly bounce… and then both men, one on either side, were shuttling her headlong through much jostling. A door frame passed above… and she slid beneath bright lights, flowing by one after the other from head to toe… each burning a hole in her eyes.

"Where's… Roy?"

"What's she saying?"

"I think she's calling for her husband."

"Shit. Umm… he'll be just fine, lady. It's more important right now that you take it easy."

She felt a gentle pat to her shoulder… and this time, the man did not prevent her from pulling the mask away from her face.

"Is he… okay?"

"Don't worry. There's a county sheriff with him now. He'll watch over until we can send someone back for him."

"Should… be there."

She released the mask, for the pull of its elastic band had become too much for her.

Having come to a stop before a counter, one of the men spoke words she could not make out… and a woman in green appeared before her face. All three wheeled her on. Without a hint of warning, she felt a board-like thing slide beneath her… and she was promptly spilt from it onto an adjacent bed. For a second, she caught sight of the two men pushing their stretcher back the way they had come… and then a curtained barrier closed her off. Someone was fiddling with her… had a hold of her wrist while talking gibberish.

"I understand that you have a life threatening allergy to bee stings… and that you've been stung."

With her head crammed up with so much confusion and her ears still pounding out the rhythm of her heart, she strained to focus on the woman speaking. It was a nurse… reading the print on the medical alert bracelet.

"The EMTs indicate that you self-administered epinephrine through an EpiPen. Did you give yourself the full dose?"

"I… I don't know. I think so."

"Into your thigh?"

"Yes..."

"Which one?"

She strained to think why it mattered.

"Ahh... right. The right one."

"I'll need to take a look at that. Where were you stung?"

"Other... hand."

The woman reached across to make a brief inspection of her left wrist... dropping it as a rather disapproving sort of look came to her face.

"Doesn't seem so bad... I'll put something on it anyway. I'm going to take your vitals... and then check on that injection wound."

"Where's... my husband?"

"I'm sure he'll be along in no time. Just you relax."

Why's everyone telling me to relax?!

"I'll be starting an IV... just fluids for hydration."

She felt the twinge of a needle to the back of her wrist... oddly more painful than the sting of that wasp.

"Try to hold still."

She soon lost track of what the nurse was doing... but eventually found her standing before the curtain.

"An ER doctor should be in to see you as soon as possible. You need anything... just push that button."

The nurse backed out, giving off a lazy sort of smile before closing the curtain. She could hear sounds coming from the other side... muffled voices... things clanking against other things... fingers on a keyboard... but was unable to concentrate on any of it.

What's going on?! Roy should be here by now. He was just at my side in the hangar when I got stung.

No... I was stung somewhere else. On the porch... and then... I went to find Roy.

God, my head's killing me! And my chest... it feels like it's about to burst! Where the hell's that doctor?!

Wait... I went inside first... to get my EpiPen. Then I... jabbed myself with it... right before calling for an ambulance... and they... they told me to lie down. But I didn't... I... fell down. No... I got back up... went to find Roy... in the hangar.

Such a terrible sight then flashed into her mind. Roy's feet sticking into view from behind the hangar door. Her memory jumped the gap to bring her straddling directly over him. And just like in that moment, she wept beneath her breathing mask... for she remembered it all. Her begging and pleading...

and him not moving. He was not beside her in this emergency room because he never again would be.

Sometime later… it could have been minutes or hours… an ER doctor appeared through the curtain… not at all in the smiling way that the nurse had left. She disregarded his first words, for they were meaninglessly about her.

"How are you feeling?"

She pulled off the oxygen mask, and the doctor did not object.

"Tell me about my husband."

With a rather dull expression coming to his face, he took his time in considering her request.

"I'm terribly sorry, Mrs. Meitner… there was nothing that could be done."

"I don't understand…"

"I was just going over the EMT's report… but we should probably talk about that later… once you're feeling better."

"I want to know now."

"As you wish… It appears that he had a massive heart attack."

"That's not possible. His heart's perfectly fine. He… can't be…"

"I'm afraid so. Please accept my deepest sympathies. But right now… my primary responsibility is you."

Without much in the way of explanation, he set about the business of moving a stethoscope around her back and upper chest. She did her best at breathing deeply when told to, though her lungs simply would not take in the quantities of air required… not without sending her into a fit of coughing. He finally gave up in favor of making other readings.

"I'm going to have to keep you here a bit longer… for observation. Your blood pressure's way too high. Do you have someone who can sit with you… and then take you home when it's time?"

"My son… in Midland."

"That's two hours away… but I suppose it'll take that long for the effects to wear off. You'd better call him now."

"I… don't have my cell phone."

"No problem. I'll send a nurse in to get the number."

"Doctor… before you go… can I see my husband?"

He paused at the curtain, giving her what so obviously was his medical appraisal of her state of being.

"Perhaps later…"

He slipped through the curtain before she realized that his answer had actually been no.

She gave Chad's number to a nurse, requesting that nothing be said about his father... only that he was needed at the hospital because his mother had been stung. She knew that he would immediately try the house, her cell, and Roy's... but get no answer from any of those calls.

Alone again, she lay in the alcove staring up at the lights, trying not to think. Seeking for a distraction, she concentrated on making a list of her pains.

The bump to my head from where I fell... a twisted knee from running... this stupid IV needle stuck in my wrist... and... my heart.

She closed her eyes and began to cry, disregarding whatever medical personnel were coming and going. Time went on in her disbelief. Maybe she had fallen asleep, for suddenly in burst Chad and Stacey with so many questions she could not answer. They were aware that she had been stung... but somehow also knew what had happened to Roy. Both were displeased that they had not been phoned immediately.

"I'm sorry... the ambulance... it took me away."

"And you just left him there!?"

She tried to explain about the wasp... and the EpiPen... followed by the 911 call... and her passing out on the kitchen floor... and then finding Roy... but her thinking still spun about so badly that nothing was coming out right. The only thing they seemed convinced of was that she had fallen several times, as both made a point of commenting on the muddy state of her clothing.

They left her for a time, how long she could not say, but returned when the ER doctor gave his approval for her to leave. Despite her fervent requests, no one would take her to Roy. It was not altogether clear whose decision that was – the doctor's, or Chad's and Stacey's. They shuttled her by wheelchair to the ER entrance, loaded her into Chad's car, and then drove her in silence back home. The two of them put her to bed, and then disappeared somewhere else in the house.

She could not possibly sleep... and the rain beating on the side of her house certainly was not helping. Its drone just kept up her confusion. Yet sometime deeper into the night when the rain had stopped and all was quiet, she got up for the bathroom... but instinctively was drawn to her bedroom door instead. Opening it just a crack, she made out the hushed voices of many people downstairs. All of her sons and their wives were there. She closed the door, used the bathroom, and fell to silently crying upon her bed.

In the morning, with a sky so clear and blue as if to avow that nothing ill had transpired in the night, she rose with the side effects of her first-ever epinephrine shot gone... but also fully aware that so was her husband. All six of the young ones were in the kitchen. For the next several hours, she cried on each of their shoulders. They talked through what had happened, and she cried even more. By midday, she had nothing left for them and returned to cry alone in her bedroom. When she awoke again late in the evening, only Travis was left in the house.

"Everyone's gone for the night, Mom... but I'll be crashing in the guest bedroom. I thought... because you're probably not up to it... that maybe I'll get a headstart tomorrow on making arrangements for Dad. I promise I won't settle on anything before discussing it with you."

"I appreciate that... and I think you're right... I'm not up for it. I trust you to handle things."

In the days to follow, her boys and their wives were over to the house more or less continuously. For whatever reason, none of them chose to stay there, and she ventured no word of invitation, as they must have situated themselves elsewhere in town. Throughout the hours of their visits, they showed a pattern of taking care of her in turns. One or two of them would attend to her while the others huddled off beyond earshot. She did not mind their secretiveness, for she knew that they too were in shock. So she simply went where she was led and did as she was told... whether it be to sit, stand, walk or lie down. Mostly, they tried to get her to eat, for they said she had not had anything for days. She could not seem to remember, and it certainly did not matter anyway. She had absolutely no appetite for food.

The night before the funeral, each couple came in separately to console her before bed. They meant well, but their voices of sympathy registered as nothing more than a continuous stream of meaningless words. Running water flowing on and on, never ceasing. She knew it was just another storm front coming through. More rain hitting... beating... pounding away at her heart... mocking her pain with its steady sprinkle. It would not stop tapping at the windows... trickling along the gutters... and drowning this precious house of his. But it was not rain, after all. It was tears. Her tears and the house's tears. From now on, it would be just her and this house... forever alone.

Sometime in the night well after everyone had left, she found herself sitting at the foot of her bed with absolutely no idea how she had gotten there... nor did she have a muscle capable of moving herself on. Outside was still that gentle rain, but within her raged a storm of blame. Despite having decades in which to act, she had never gotten rid of that plane. Instead, she whined... and complained... and pleaded... and lied her way around his many requests... always finding a means of putting him off. All these years, he bore her selfishness… and that patience wore away at him… weakening his heart… leading to his death. All because of her. Now… she had no hope… no purpose… and no making anything right. She deserved this sorrowful state. It should last forever as her punishment.

These self-incriminations just brought back more memories fresh and strong. Times she had disappointed him… angered him… betrayed and abandoned him. She could not possibly have loved him as much as she claimed. Not after all of the terrible things she had done. And how easy it had been for her to spend weeks on end… years… flying all over God-knows-where just to sell something that no one used anymore. She had wasted so much precious time in their marriage being consumed with an ambition that now could not restore to her a single second of his life.

During the morning of the funeral, her sons left her mostly in the care of the DILs. Taken to her room, they undressed her and then dressed her in clothes of bereavement. Somehow, she found her way into the backseat of a car… and then into the lobby of the Pritchett Family Funeral Home. There, she did her best to bear her grief with regal austerity, suitable for the likes of any West Texas widow. For the sake of all those other mourners, she put on a grim face of courage in order to both receive and distribute sympathy. When it came time, she walked that lonely center aisle to a front row seat commanding the closest of views to the pallid shell of the love of her life, him lying not three feet away in the mouth of an open casket. Even then, she sucked in her sorrow, bearing it as a burden of composure for the ones he had loved… to be released in full only after she was finally alone.

Just as the minister was taking his place before the altar, into the corner of her vision came a person she had least expected to be there. Having reached the front row, Sybil Meitner took the turn in her direction, slid into an empty seat beside her, and leaned over to whisper. Whatever came out of her sister-in-law's mouth, she heard only words from long ago.

"Marna… you're not welcome here. The front row is only for family. You need to leave."

"But I am family. I'm…"

"No, you're not. You're a pretender."

This worm… this filth… this backbiting horror… could not be allowed to defile the sanctity of Roy's service! For that terrible creature had no right to sit beside his widow with the pompous pretense of a sympathetic sister-in-law!

Straightway, she was on her feet pounding away at this wicked person with both fists, shrieking out curses that flowed so effortlessly from the depths of her despair. Someone too soon got a hold on her from behind, pinning her arms at her sides. So she kicked out wildly at Sybil's shins, taking vicious pleasure in knowing that she made contact. Stronger bodies were now pulling her backward along an outer aisle toward the lobby, but she still hurled out insult after insult at Sybil. With a hundred or more eyes on her, she commanded them all to drag that abomination from Roy's presence instead. Her anger did not lessen as she felt herself being hauled into the lobby. From there, she somehow got seated in an office… CP Pritchett's office. She had been in here only days before… calmly planning the service she had just been forcibly removed from.

"Here, Marna… drink this."

"What is it?! I don't want anything! I demand to see Roy!"

"After you've calmed down. Now drink. You know… you made quite a scene in there."

She reluctantly put the cup to her lips and took a sip. It burned all the way down… but somehow cleared her mind to the realization that she had just ruined her husband's memorial service.

"CP… what's… what's happening to me?! I'm falling apart…"

"You're grieving… that's what's happening to you. You've just lost the most important person in your life."

"Is he… really dead?"

CP did not answer… and neither did she need him to. She just collapsed into his arms and sobbed. After a time, he moved her to one of his couches, promising to be back soon. While he was gone, she collected enough of herself to realize that no one was coming for her. Not one of her sons, their wives, or any of her friends. She lay weeping alone on an undertaker's couch.

After how long, she could not say… perhaps hours and hours of crying… she heard someone call her name. Wiping her face as discretely as possible, she sat up to find CP's head peering about the door frame.

"May I come in?"

"Of course… it's your office."

"I just wanted you to know… the service is over."

"What?!"

"I'm sorry… it's the way your boys wanted it to be. But I've taken the liberty of arranging for you to have a private moment at graveside. Your family's already had theirs… so I've sent them all away. It'll just be you and Roy. Whenever you're ready… just say the word."

"Thank you, CP… that was… most kind… and I know I don't deserve it. But I think… I'm ready now. If it's okay with you… I'd like to walk out there on my own."

"Certainly. You know the plot… I'll meet you there, and then… drive you home."

He disappeared back the way he had come.

Trying not to think about the scene she had made… or what it would be like to give an account to her children or friends… she straightened her dress and wiped her eyes one more time. Taking in a deep breath as much to put on a dignified front as to calm herself, she stepped from CP's office into a completely empty foyer. Being careful not to look into the room that had been used for Roy's service, she made for the back hallway and took a side door through an alcoved area rimmed with flowering vines… vaguely aware that she had once sat there crying over a much smaller loss in her life.

The sun was considerably lower in the sky than she had expected… near to setting… as she made her way around tombstones marking the sites of other people's heartbreaks from the distant past. She had no eyes for those sad endings or for the hopelessness with which someone else… also long gone… had invested effort into a stone epitaph. She made directly for the final resting place of the only man she had ever loved. His casket had not yet gone below… and without pause to consider the site or setting, she threw herself upon it and cried. The hard, cold surface did not give her comfort… would not allow her to feel him one last time. That polished wooden barrier absolutely forbid all consolation. So she must go on weeping… for herself and for the loss of the love of a lifetime.

When she opened her eyes next, she found it to be dark out… and CP was gently gripping her shoulder.

"Marna… it's time. We need to lay him to rest."

She knew that CP had to do more than his share of lifting, for she had little strength left. She was also aware of him steadying her on her feet before moving off as she collected herself. About her were the hazy outlines of grimly hunched-over men… ghostly forms waiting to do their duty.

"Would you like to say anything in parting?"

"I want to leave… right now. I don't want to be here when he goes below."

Without another word, she turned away… vaguely aware of CP hurrying alongside to escort her into his waiting car. Against her will, she strained to hear what might be going on behind her… and was immensely thankful at not being able to pick up a single sound.

How she got from the cemetery to her home, she would never know. She simply stepped from CP's arm into his car… and in the next second stepped out the same way. He led her up the porch steps, contending with her over whether she should enter the darken house on her own. He finally gave up at her insistence that she could go it alone. At the door, she waited for his car to clear the property before entering. Just inside, she stood for a long time scanning over the family room that her husband had loved so much. Not expecting it, she caught a glimpse out its window of the wide open hangar door, and immediately made for the stairs. But halfway up, she changed her mind and took to the parlor instead.

For a long while, she sat in her darkened nook, crying herself into silence. Having finally reached a temporary calm, she tried to imagine what Roy might be doing right then… if he was here. It was early Saturday evening, so he would surely have just finished up an afternoon of yard work. Perhaps he had gathered up fallen branches from the driveway's live oaks, finished up that brick edging about the circle, or trimmed the bushes along the side of the porch. He would have come in the back door all in a sweat and hungry as could be. Of course, he would have made to hug her… and she would have sent him scurrying out of the kitchen to deal with his grime… after a kiss to his lips and a swat on his rear. She would have waited to hear his shower start, and then set herself to cooking… humming over how happy a person could be. She imagined herself slicing… chopping… stirring… all the while keeping an ear out for his shower to end. Soon, he would be all cleaned up and ready to eat.

From her nook, she strained to listen. In the stillness of the house, she could almost hear the faint dripping of water somewhere above. Her wounded reckoning turned that imagined sound into a trickle making its way through some pipe. The noise of it soon became that of a steady stream, gushing along merrily. A voice seemed interspersed within the spray… laughing… singing… making joy out of the water. And then she heard it as plain as day – the abrupt screech of a valve being turned and a flow of water diminishing.

Without thinking what she was doing… for thinking only brought pain… she sprang from the nook, threw open the parlor's French doors, and slingshot herself around the edge toward the stairs. On reaching the bottom step, she already had one hand on a strap, ripping off its high heel… and then the other… discarding both behind her. Up the stairs she flew, taking two at a time as noiselessly as possible… feeling… though not really registering… the texture of the carpeted pathway running up the middle of these well-worn steps. At the top, she awkwardly paused to catch her breath while leaning on the banister that overlooked the family room. Pushing herself off, she knew exactly where to go – through the door into the master bedroom – and though what she failed to behold in there should have drawn her up short, there was no time.

Her hands were at the back of her neck, frantically struggling to unclasp the eyehook at her collar. Drawing the zipper down only as far as was needed, she yanked upward at the black funeral dress from grips at waist level, not caring how indelicately it was being inverted over her head. Taking up the most obvious seat at the foot of their low-lying bed, she pitched the dress out of sight and directed all effort toward preparing herself. Clothed in some undergarments that did not seem nearly as pretty as he deserved, she nonetheless consciously slowed her breath and smoothed out her hair. She then inched forward a bit on the edge of the bed, placing knees together and pivoting toward the door. Shifting her shoulders back, she took care to adopt a posture that would best show off her figure. Then, she waited… not entertaining any of the craziness of what she was doing. Any minute now, he would step from the hallway bathroom wrapped only in a towel, go to the banister railing, and call out her name.

"Roy… I'm in here."

Nothing.

Why was he delaying? She was ready… ready to embrace him as her lover. Soon, he would be there for her, and they would forever be together.

"Roy…?"

Still nothing. Her eyes went to the pair of doors leading off their bedroom, one for the walk-in closet and the other to the master bath. Both spaces were dark inside. Those, she now realized, were *their* spaces… so that would certainly be where Roy came from following a shower. After all, they had not used the hallway bathroom in many years. Not since going back to when they first remodeled this house together.

In a flash, reality came crashing in upon her. Collapsing back on the bed, she pulled the comforter over, wrapping herself within her sorrow and wept. All the while, the rich, earthy smell of West Texas flowed through the bedroom's open windows. She woke several times during the night, searching through the sounds of the house for any sign of Roy. Their bed… it seemed so large… so empty… and she found herself moving pillows into a line up under the sheet, rebuilding the fantasy that he lay there beside her. In the faint light, she watched for any soft movement… any sign of breath. Nothing.

Nothing would ever bring him back to her.

Having cried through much of the night, she rose in equal parts exhausted and ashamed of herself. Moving into the bathroom, she immediately recalled that most mornings with him had started out this way. Stepping within the shower, she thought of the many times that they had been in here together.

In the flow of hot water, they had discussed, debated, argued, sympathized, cuddled and teased… and even made love. Through steam and soap, this small space had always been their sanctuary away from work, kids, and the cares of the world. She looked up to the skylight. Mold was taking hold on its edges… with dirt and some windblown leaves having collected on the outside. Roy would deal with all that… if he was here.

She turned off the water and stepped out to wrap a robe about herself. The mist-covered mirror instantly brought back more memories – of the two of them standing side-by-side going about their morning preparations. Very reluctantly, she reached up to wipe away the condensation, not really expecting to see his reflection… as in times past… yet still remembering it as so. She watched the blotched droplets form at the extremes of where her finger tips had caressed the glass. They haltingly gained weight from smaller drops nearby… and then in a rush slid down the mirror through the part she had just wiped off, each tumbling along in broken streaks that cut across the image of her own face. Always downward… like tears.

The ache was too much.

From that day onward, she kept to the downstairs of the house. The upper rooms would remain closed off and uninhabited. From her closet, she brought down only those few items of clothing comprised entirely of black. She slept in the parlor's stairwell nook, and dressed or undressed herself only in the guest bath. For hours each day, her realm of existence extended no farther than the boundaries of her nook… for to see more of the house was to see Roy in it… and she would never see him again.

Throughout the weeks following the funeral, she ventured out only in the dark of night… and only to make quick stops at a grocery store or gas station. Visits from her sons and the DILs were fairly steady in those weeks, but gradually became less frequent as the months went by. Initially, they took it upon themselves to bustle about… cleaning or whatever… and she endured their presence simply because it seemed the fastest way to get them to leave. Their expressions of dismay at how the place was falling into disarray steadily grew more adamant with time. Always, they kept up their prodding that she should get out into the light of day… and maybe go with them to visit Roy's grave. Each time, she persistently refused. Roy was not there. He was in this house – in every room and every corner. So why would she leave him to go stand above barren earth?! Besides, the pain of that place would be far too much for her.

From time to time, she also had to deal with friends stopping by for a visit, though seldom did she spare much energy for them. Just like her sons, some tried valiantly to cheer her out of her gloom, talk through her sadness, or nudge her on toward something new. She never paid much attention to any of their efforts, knowing that they would take their sympathy, advice and scrutiny right out the front door with them, leaving her alone with her grief.

The death of a husband, she was repeatedly told, did strange things to a wife. She had personally witnessed Ruby come unglued over George's death… and treated her abominably as a result. She now knew better. She understood firsthand what Ruby had gone through. She and Ruby… they were one and the same. Their grief was so much more than half a bed unoccupied or a vacant place at the kitchen table. She was living the life of a half person… less than a fraction of a being. Roy had been so much more than a partner to her. He was her… and she was him… and neither could ever be whole without the other… so what hope was there in continuing?! She, the wife who lived on, nevertheless had died with her husband… and nothing would ever be the same.

Through Thanksgiving and into Christmas, her children did their best to encourage a festive spirit in her, but she repeatedly declined their invitations to visit. In turn, she made it clear that her house would not be decorated nor made available for the season. Holiday cheer only made the magnitude of her loss more clear. Instead, she pulled herself up into the cocoon of her nook and repeatedly languished through the only photo album she had managed to populate over the years. But seeing pictures of Roy only caused her more pain. She tried submersing herself within some novel, hoping to somehow distract her pain. But the falseness of those stories never really took hold…. never really moved her out of her sorrow. She vaguely recalled in some previous life having had no patience for those who dwelt in the past. Now, the future seemed such an inconceivable thing to her. Memories were her only reality… and so many of those were reconstructed within her heart's devastation.

In living alone, she came to feel the presence of the house like never before. Its creaks and groans spoke to her… though not exactly as a substitute for Roy. The house was its own person, feeling the absence of its friend. She often found herself talking to the house's sounds, telling them her heart's sadness. It always responded back with many pained echoes of stillness. This house fully shared her loss, for only it understood.

Each day, she came to know the passing of time only by the changes to sunlight. If she had slept at all during a night, then to wake in the morning meant to face the glare coming through the glass of the parlor doors leading out to the eastern side of the porch. She hated that light most of all, for it callously shone its optimistic cheer. It cared not for her despair, gleefully flickering its youthful limbs across the room to where she lay. When those beams could find no companionship in her, they slid around the house's corner to search for better prospects out front. Through the parlor's southern-facing windows this sun soon peered, allowing its winter rays to dip beneath the porch eaves before starting in earnest its climb into the sky. She had no memory of that blue… though she personally had risen into it many times. Slanting across the room, the light went this way at first… and then that way… eventually throwing the long shadow of the barren flagpole across the floor. Those terrible streaks… they kept searching out the parlor for her as they crept in to light up her room. So she pulled herself deeper into her nook and waited. Soon, they would find this space of hers lacking and disappear. But not for good. Later… there was never a 'when' to it, just later… they would make one more intrusion into her parlor… unless perchance some cloud on the western horizon arose to defend her. But most often, she found those rays coming back to briefly extend from some family room window through the parlor's French doors. They just took pleasure at taunting her… telling her that the time was short, and all that was bright and lovely would soon be gone. Then, mercifully, they blinked out… and all of the gloom within her came seeping forth to gray over her hiding place. Only then did she know for certain the time… for it was night – when all hope went cold and cruel memory returned brighter than day.

This terrible parade went on and on for time immortal, as her one true love lay alone in the ground's decay.

She stopped bathing, stopped changing clothes, and stopped attending to her teeth and hair. She completely gave up on doing the sorts of things that a normal person cared about. No matter how many times it rang, she absolutely refused to answer the phone. The mail just piled up in the box until the postman came to grumble at her front door. If a room's light happened to be left on or off, she exerted no effort to change its condition in going from night to day and back again. She slept as much as she could, for only in sleep did she find a hint of relief. She nonetheless awoke at odd hours… in bright light or in full dark… and then sat waiting for the soft persuasion of sleep to return and wipe clean her waking tears.

Mostly, she obsessed over the wasp that had not killed her. That creature doubly cheated her, for it had not taken her life or spared his. If only she had not injected herself, then she would have departed with him. Who knows, maybe she would have had the strength to make it out to the hangar and die in his arms. Both of them, gone together forever. That would have been so much better than this hell of being left alone without him.

On a morning sometime well after the daylight hours had grown longer, she sensed a hint of something in the air. A new season had come with all of its false hope. But its renewed warmth did mean one thing very significant to her – insects were returning to Lubbock. That knowledge brought her springing up in her nook with a reckless idea – her first true moment of sanity since losing Roy. Why had she not thought of it before now?! Through that horrible autumn, the solution to her problem had been right there, but she had failed to see it. There had been no need to endure such a cold, cruel winter.

Well… she would not go through another day without Roy. Vaulting from her stairwell nook, she went first to the set of glass encased doors leading out onto the porch. Swinging these wide to their fullest extent… and placing a chair before each to keep it open… she next moved to a window. Unbolting its clasp, she threw up the lower sash… only to be affronted on finding the opening barred by a screen. Off to the kitchen… to the drawer bearing the sharpest of knives… she was right back to that same parlor window. In this first one, she did not restrain herself from slashing and hacking with vicious intent, as she unexpectedly experienced a temporary release from her sorrow. But in subsequent ones, she went about the job most methodically. Pushing the blade into a bottom corner, she pulled it up along the edge, across the top, and then carefully down the other side… leaving the fragmented flap to dangle out at its base. Next, she swung open the front door wide, blocking it with a chair, and then disfigured the screen door. Then to the back, she did the exact same in the kitchen. From there, she went to every remaining window in the downstairs, opening them up, destroying their screens, and pulling down any curtains, blinds or shades that might get in the way. Up the stairs, she repeated the same treatment on its windows, barring open every hallway door. Only on entering the master bedroom did she pause, as she had not been in there for months. The memories she beheld instantly froze her in place with new pain… but also gave her a stronger resolve to complete her task. With callous disregard for the care that she had once invested into the decoration of this room, she ripped down the curtains of the alcove, tore away the blinds, and cut up the screens. She flung open the doors out to the deck and… for reasons she did not stop to consider… pushed the mattress over to act as a doorstop.

With the house now wide open to the dusty winds of West Texas, she returned to wait in her stairwell nook. Soon they would come for her, and it would only take one. A special one destined just for her. This one would not fail her, for she had no answer to its sting. She had never renewed the EpiPen, so nothing could steal her relief from this unbearable grief. If need be, she would roam through the house to find one that had gotten in… provoke it… make it fight back… and finish the job the other had failed to do. She would gladly give herself to any stinging thing… if it but promised to take away this terrible pain.

After three days, her house had collected a mass of flies, gnats, mosquitos and moths… but not one wasp or bee.

Unfortunately, Chad showed up for a visit on the fourth day, and berated her so unfairly for the state of the house and what she had done to its screens. He closed up everything and was soon gone. Leaning forward in her nook, she followed the progression of his truck out onto the county road. Once convinced that he was not coming back, she immediately went through the house to undo everything he had done. But he came back on the next day, bringing Stacey with him. Together, they went through the house to again hamper her plans. This time, they threatened to nail the windows shut if she continued with her 'lunacy.' Fortunately, they were gone within the hour, and she once more reversed the damage they had done. She would do that every day, if that was what it would take. Just one small sting… just one brief moment of pain… and then she would be free of this misery… and see him again. She could not face such a long, slow life without him. If only they would come…

O Death, where is your sting?! Where has your precious poison gone?!

For weeks, the mournful currents rushed through the house… his house… witnessing her grief, but passing on without regard. Not one breeze brought the mercy she so desperately sought, as there did not seem to be a single wasp in all of Lubbock.

She clearly heard the knock to the door frame, but refused to rise from her nook. It likely was just one of her sons come to make another fuss over the state of her house. Another knock… and then an unfamiliar voice offering a tentative hello. Obviously not one of her sons. They would have stomped right in. Had to be someone else… a visitor.

Just ignore them and they'll go away.

More knocking… along with her name… and an even louder call of greeting. Clearer now, the person had entered inside… a man, by the sound of him.

Great! Strangers waltz their way in, but I can't get a single bee or wasp to save my life!

"Marna… are you in here?"

Through the parlor's French doors stuck the head of CP. She could not say whether he was the last person on earth she cared to see, for she cared to see no one… other than Roy.

"Oh, there you are. The… ahh… front door was open… so I hope you don't mind me stepping inside?"

Such a stupid question… She was so tired of stupid questions. There he stood, gaping at her like she was the strange one. Only she knew for certain that life had no meaning. Yet maybe she and he were not so different after all. He buried dead things… and she wanted to be dead. So she glanced up to him expectantly… but his eyes were roving around the parlor with a look of dismay.

Just leave, CP.

"Did you know… your house is… full of flies."

"I hadn't noticed."

"Would you like me to… close off the doors and windows for you?"

"No."

"That screen there… it looks like it's gotten… ripped. You know… I could have someone come by and fix it for you?"

"That won't be necessary."

She absolutely refused to look at him again, but still clearly heard him sniff a few times.

"I suppose you're just airing the place out. Does seem a bit… stuffy. Maybe something's gone bad in the kitchen."

"I don't smell anything."

He got quiet… and so much time went by that she was beginning to think he had finally left… but then his voice came out of the nothingness to disturb her sorrow again.

"So… how are you doing?"

She hated that question above all, and categorically refused to ever answer it.

"The… umm…. reason I stop by… this is a bit awkward. It… ahh… has to do with your sons. Strictly speaking, I shouldn't be telling you this… or more accurately, Marianne shouldn't have told me, so I wouldn't have to tell you… and our daughter shouldn't have told her. But I guess that's neither here nor there. You know she's got a job clerking at the courthouse downtown? Lana, not Marianne. Anyway… the other day… Lana happened to run into one of your sons. The one she went to school with. I don't remember his name. Your oldest, I think. Anyway… he came in with a lawyer to file a… a motion seeking… umm… an evaluation of your… state of mind. Marna… Lana thinks he thinks you're a…"

He paused again… so she looked up this time, hoping it would help him to finish.

"…a danger to yourself."

His eyes shot about the parlor… following any of the dozen or so flying insects circling about the room. Unfortunately, none of them were the stinging kind. She had not seen one of those lovely creatures in many months. So unfair that it had turned cold outside again… to match the terrible cold inside of her.

"Of course, I told her that was ludicrous. Right?!"

She said nothing to agree or disagree, wanting him so badly to leave.

"I mean… you're getting better every day. Soon, you'll be back to your perky self. You just need more… time."

"Yeah… time."

"Hey! Did you know there's going to be an airshow in town this weekend? You should go! You like airplanes, don't you?!"

Airplanes? I don't remember airplanes…

"Marianne and I happen to have Lana's daughter for the weekend. She and her husband are heading out on a little getaway…"

I used to have a husband…

"…and we're taking her to the airshow. Melissa really loves planes! Wants to be a pilot when she grows up. Hey! Perhaps you'd care to come with us! You know… reminisce a bit about flying… and give the girl the inside scoop on what it's like to be a pilot. I bet you've got some real amazing stories that you could…"

"Thanks, CP… but no thanks."

"Are you sure? We'd love to have you… and it wouldn't be any problem to swing by and pick you up."

"Don't bother."

"You know… it would do you good to get out a bit…"

I'm never leaving this house. I'm going to die in this house.

"Tell you what… just give us a ring if you change your mind. As a matter of fact… if you need anything… absolutely anything at all… just call. We'd be happy to rush right over. We… care about you, Marna."

And still he stood there.

"Well… umm… I'll just… see myself out. Bye for now…"

She did not lift her eyes from off the opposite wall of the nook in order to follow him out of the parlor. She heard his footsteps recede… heard him move down the porch steps. His car started and pulled away. But on and on the feeling went. Vaporous in substance, yet crushingly heavy in effect. Ever nearer, but never there.

"Roy…"

She immediately started crying again.

That very evening, all three of her sons and their wives showed up at once. They were extremely pleasant… greeting her in pairs… asking if she had been out of the house lately… and offering to make her something to eat. But she knew what the other couples were really doing in the meantime – going around the house to close the windows. When all of them had collected back in the parlor, they seemed to take care not to come off as confrontational… even though they had arrayed themselves in an arc before her nook. The inherently submissive ones… Chad and Valerie… were backed off just a bit with eyes moving along the line to see what the others would do. The more assertive ones… Travis and Stacey… stood the closest, ready to vie for control over whatever the group was here to say. The other two… Wade and Amanda… were their usual contemplative selves in scanning about to make a study of her, the nook, and the rest of the parlor. None of them mentioned that the windows and doors were wide open when they arrived… and only the women flinched whenever a moth or fly happened to dart their way.

"Mom… the six of us would like to have a… a serious conversation with you about how you're doing."

"I'm doing fine."

"Mom… come on! Look at this place!"

"Looks normal to me."

"We… umm… were hoping you'd be willing to spend some time with us this weekend."

"Assuming you can pull yourself away from this nook."

"You know, Mom… I've tried calling you several times this week."

"We've all tried calling you."

"I wanted to tell you that Amanda and I are moving to the Bay area…"

"That's in California."

"Stacey… she knows it's in California. She's not stupid."

Stacey muttered a 'could've fooled me' at such a volume that it was easily heard… and just as easily denied.

"I thought we agreed that I'd be the one doing the talking."

"Whatever."

"Mom… you know it's not going to be very often that the seven of us'll be able to get together like this. So I was thinking… there's this airshow coming to town. It starts tomorrow and runs all weekend. We were hoping you'd come with us to…"

"Marna – we've got it all figured out! All of the food, a grill, chairs… everything! It'll be just like tailgating at a Longhorns game! We'll have such fun! And all that's lacking is you!"

"Mom… you really do need to get out of this house."

Her eyes went from one to the other along the line, wondering if CP was right. Were they trying to have her declared as unfit? And was this all a trick to get her out of the house so they could gather up her things… change the locks on the doors… and steal from her the only thing she had left in life – her memories.

"I appreciate the offer… but I'm going to decline. You six go and make a day of it."

Without fail, 'I told you so' looks flowed up and down the line. The younger two couples said their goodnights and peeled off for the family room, leaving Travis and Amanda to linger behind. She noticed him give his wife a little nod, and Amanda immediately turned toward the kitchen.

"Mom… I'm concerned about your sleep. By your own admission, you're up at all hours of the night."

Amanda was promptly back at his side with a glass of water. She handed it over to him and then also left for the family room.

"I'd like to give you a mild sleeping aid… nothing too strong. It should help you not have any bad dreams."

He held out two small red pills in one hand and the glass of water in the other. She looked between the two… and then into his eyes. There, she picked up on an expectancy that went beyond a simple hope that she might comply. She took both pills and the glass… doing as he requested. Without delay, he took the glass from her hand and placed it on the shelf beside her, kissed her on the forehead, and turned out the nook lights. Closing the French doors from within the parlor, he moved out through the dining room. She heard those doors close off too… and then knew for certain.

Spitting the pills from her mouth, she took up the glass and dumped it over the side of the nook… not in the least bit concerned about what the water might be doing to the wood flooring or whatever else was down there. She quickly placed the open end of the glass against the power outlet on the wall, adjusted her ear to its bottom, and then waited. She heard several odd noises, but nothing resembling a voice. Just when she was considering giving up on this foolishness, a voice came through clear enough for her to pick up on every word… though an echoed resonance made it difficult to know for certain who was speaking.

"Think she's asleep?"

"Probably… I gave her some Sudafed. That always knocks her out."

That's gotta be Travis!

She heard more movement… steps across the marble floor… and then a slight vibration at the parlor door. The same voice came back after a few seconds.

"I don't hear anything… but we should keep our voices low."

"Travis, did you finally get ahold of someone in her personnel department?"

"Yeah… She's still not returning their calls. They wouldn't tell me much… but it seems that they've changed her status to a long-term furlough without pay."

"What's that mean?"

"Duh! It means she's been canned from her job! You know she's going to be expecting us to support her from now on!"

"It doesn't mean that at all, Stacey... though I'm afraid it might if she doesn't respond soon."

"Travis… Stacey's right. I'm worried about what happens if she loses her job. She's showing absolutely no signs of snapping out of this… this sorry-ass depression of hers. Being sad about Dad's one thing… but this… this is totally overboard!"

"That's what I've been saying all along! But none of y'all are listening to me! She's wearing the same clothes day after day! I don't know what she's eating… if anything at all. The kitchen doesn't look like it's been used in weeks."

"That's because Valerie straightened it up while you were…"

"*My point is*… she needs looking after… and not by us! You know Chad and I have done the lion's share of driving here to check up on her. We can't keep this up! You know… we're seriously thinking about starting a family!"

"Really?! That's so exciting! What're you hoping for, a boy or a…"

"Y'all – we need to focus! We've got to figure out what to do about Mom!"

"Personally… I think she should be moved into a rest home or something like that. A place where…"

"That's stupid, Stacey. She's only fifty five."

"Acts more like seventy five!"

"Can we please be serious?! We've got important things to discuss. Now… I agree… she'd do better in a different environment… but that's not why we're…"

"Being cooped up in this old house would drive me crazy!"

"I don't think anyone's saying she's crazy."

"I think…"

"I certainly am! Did any of y'all smell her?! I swear she's not taken a bath in a month! That can't be healthy."

"Stacey… hygiene's the least of her problems."

"You certainly don't have to tell me that! I'm the one who's had to deal with all the doors and windows being left open. You do realize what she's trying to do?!"

"Obviously… that's why we're…"

"It's a sad cry for help, that's what I say! I think she's losing it. She just sits there day after day like a zombie. Y'all… we agreed to give her a month into the new year to snap out of this funk. But she's just not improving! If anything, she's getting worse! Like I said, we should've acted months ago!"

"Come on, Stacey…. some of this behavior's to be expected. She's grieving."

"No – she's trying to kill herself!"

"I think…"

"Just take a stroll about this house. Every single screen's been cut up. Good lord – nobody in their right mind does that! What if the place got robbed?! You know that thing on the dining room wall's worth a ton of money!"

"Everything's insured… okay?! Can we just stay on topic?! We need to agree on what's to be done. Chad… you've been quiet. What're your thoughts?"

"Chad and I are in perfect agreement."

"I'd like to hear it from him… if you don't mind."

"I don't know… I guess Stacey's right. Mom's losing it. I mean… we're all sad about Dad passing… but she… she's not dealing with it. I think she needs… counseling or something. All those years of neglecting us have finally come back to warp her…"

"Good God, I don't want to get into this! It's so old! My childhood wasn't ruined because she decided to spend it flying the hell all over the place!"

"I think…"

"But you can't deny she's got guilt over Dad dying! Guilt makes a person do strange things. What if she…"

"Wait, y'all – Valerie's been trying to say something. What is it, Sweetheart?"

"I think… she's just sad."

There followed an unnaturally long pause before someone else piped up… Stacey, by the sound of her.

"Super helpful, Valerie. For *my* part… I think getting her to move out of this house would be the best thing for her. It's way too big. She's no spring chicken, you know! She could fall down those stairs and no one would be around to help her. What she needs is a fresh start… you know… to get away from her sad memories. Maybe some kind of a… retirement community closer in to town where she can make some new friends… and have more supervision. You know she's not safe on her own. Lord knows I've suggested it enough times, but will she listen to me?! No! So we have to find a way of persuading her."

"What're you saying?"

"That we take the burden of making these decisions away from her. That's why I'm in favor of… whatever it is that Travis's trying to do. Except I don't agree that you should be the only one with decision-making privileges. We're all responsible for her care, so we should all have an equal voice in her affairs."

"It's not at all like that, Stacey."

"Hey... I don't get it, Travis. If Dad and Mom gave you that power thingy over their stuff, then why can't you just... step in and take over?"

"What you're talking about is a durable power of attorney. They didn't give me that kind of authority. Theirs is what's called a springing power of attorney... which means that it springs into effect if both of them become incapacitated."

"She's certainly incapacitated, don't you think?!"

"It doesn't matter what I think. We'll have to convince a judge that she's incapable of managing her own affairs, and then get the court to grant me limited guardianship over her..."

"We've certainly got enough proof of her craziness! Look at this place! Look at the windows! Why can't we just sit a judge down and explain it all to him?! I'm sure I could convince him to see things my way."

"It's much more complicated than that, Stacey. First we've got to petition for an examination by a physician... that's what I was doing on Wednesday. Then that doctor'll provide the court with what's called a 'certification of medical examination.' It's the basis for declaring someone incapacitated. Then a judge'll..."

"It's got to be more than medical, right?! I mean... what about all the psychological stuff? The problem's in her head – she's trying to kill herself! That's not going to show up by taking her temperature! Besides... she's not paid a bill in six months. Y'all, if it weren't for me and Chad, there'd be no electricity in this house!"

"Stacey, there's a big difference between someone being incapable of handling their financial affairs... and someone who's unwilling. Honestly... I think it's unlikely that any doctor will declare her as unfit."

"Then why're we doing this?!"

"To wake her up. To snap her out of the state she's in. I'm hoping that a doctor'll recommend antidepressants or something like that."

"That's crazy, Travis. She's at real risk of getting herself stung again. You know that! We can't wait around for some kind of treatment to kick in. We have to act now!"

"So, Travis... what happens if a doctor says that she's not right mentally?"

"Then a judge'll look over the evaluation and decide whether to have a hearing. If she doesn't have the wits to bring in a lawyer, then one'll be appointed for her... what's called an ad litem attorney. Someone to represent her as the prospective ward. Then we go from there."

"Shouldn't we… tell her?"

"Absolutely not. I understand how you're feeling, Valerie… but that wouldn't be a good idea. As a matter of fact… after tonight… none of us should have contact with her until a judge rules on whether she's to be examined, understand? We'll just have to hope she doesn't get herself stung in the meantime."

As her wrist was cramping up, she quietly shifted the glass away in order to shake out the stiffness. In so doing, she ended up missing a bit of the conversation, but quickly gathered that they were now talking about the memorial service.

"…never handled death well. You know that."

"Aunt Sybil said that Mom did the same thing at her father's service. Dad had to remove her because she was making a scene."

"Aunt Sybil's never liked Mom."

"I know that… but it doesn't mean she's wrong.

"You know… Sybil did mention something very interesting. I was telling her all about what happened in the ER that day… and how dealing with Marna's bee sting had made everything so… complicated… and Sybil said she doubted seriously that Marna was stung at all. She said Marna probably panicked when your dad went into palpitations… and injected herself."

"That's ridiculous."

"Come to think of it… didn't that ER nurse say there were no signs of her having been stung? Mom just had a… a little pin prick on her wrist."

"See! That's what I'm saying!"

"You know what… she always said that we'd know if she'd been stung because the spot'd swell up like a grapefruit."

"So you think she was faking it?"

"I don't know."

"But you can't deny that there's something seriously wrong with her! We've all heard her muttering to this house. Not in the silly way that Dad used to do. She's absolutely serious! She thinks the house is alive. It's… freaky."

"I don't care if she thinks the house is alive or not. I'm just tired of her making Dad's death to be all about herself. She's not the only one who's lost someone important to them!"

"Okay – let's not lose sight of why we're here. We need to be in agreement that interceding on behalf of Mom is the best thing to do."

She heard only silence… but from Travis's next words, it seemed that they were all in.

"Good. I'll go on handling the legal process, but I'd like someone else to deal with Sybil. She's pestering me to be included."

"I think Sybil's been more than supportive…"

"Get off it! She's only gunning for a piece of the house."

"Everyone just relax. I'm confident that Aunt Sybil won't be able to worm her way into this. I just don't want her bugging me while we're trying to persuade Mom to move out of here. But… I could use some advice on a… a different matter."

It got oddly silent, as the other five seemed to be waiting for Travis to continue.

"I was contacted by a reporter last week who wanted to do a story on Dad's death. Not just on him, but on the coincidence that he and his father both died in the same place from exactly the same condition… thirty three years apart."

Her glass was suddenly filled with Chad's voice, so loud that she also heard it with her other ear.

"Tell him to fuck off!"

Another voice… Amanda's… quickly jumped in.

"There's no call for such language!"

"Shh, y'all – you're gonna wake her!"

"For your information… I did not. I thought it best to put him off… at least until I could speak with all y'all. Frankly… I don't like talking about that hangar. The thing still gives me the creeps. But I'll tell you this… if ever I did exert POA responsibilities over Mom's affairs, one of the first things I'd do is have a collector over here for a look at that plane. Dad's been trying to do it for years. You'd be surprised… World War II relics like that are fetching a pretty penny these days. That's why I'm keen on going to that airshow this weekend. I'm hoping to find someone there who'll give me an idea of how much it's worth."

She fell away from the receptacle, suddenly having no appetite for eavesdropping. The plane… the relief… and the house… they would be the first targets of her children. How did she feel about that? It should… anger her. The things she cared about in life… they were the things that her sons were now bent on profiting from.

But I don't actually care.

Whatever they were planning… aboveboard and honest with her, or hidden in deceit… it really did not matter. For the millionth time since that dreadful day, she blamed herself for not getting rid of that plane. She should have known that she was burdening him with its presence. If only she had helped him open the hangar door… and if only she had made him get his heart checked… then he would still be alive today. After all, his father had a weak heart… only stands to reason that the son might also. Though Roy never seemed like he had a problem… or maybe she never bothered to consider it. So consumed with herself… with all the stupid, trivial little things going on in her head. She failed to take care of the one thing in life that she truly cared about. It was all her fault.

She rolled onto her side away from the nook wall and buried her face into a pillow. Only then did she become aware of the sound of the many flies buzzing about in the dark… each searching the room for some source of light. Somewhere deep in her memory, there seemed to be a time in which flies, mosquitos and stinging things had tormented her. She could not say that such fears now moved her. Even the sad urge to dwell on the ways in which she had proved herself to be a terrible wife and mother seemed oddly distant. The only thing that mattered was dying.

The conference in the family room broke up, with the couples filtering out of the house to their respective cars. Someone stuck a head into the parlor and whispered her name, but she remained perfectly still until they too were gone.

Finally, she was alone with her grief… the only place she deserved to be.

END OF WASP 6

WASP 7

FULLNESS

CHAPTER

45

THE FAITHFULNESS
OF FLIGHT

First thing on waking up, she went through the house to reopen the doors and windows her family had closed off the night before. That hint of spring was finally back, with the morning air already growing warm, so surely it would only take a short while before the first stinging thing came flying her way.

With the house once more wide open, she returned to her nook, watching and listening. But those idiotic birds along the driveway's live oaks were making it difficult, what with all that racket from their twittering! She wanted them all to die. Have their little hearts stop beating so they fell out of their branches to the ground. Nothing had the right to greet this day with such love of life. Nothing deserved to be happy… not when she could never be again. At least they should have the curtesy to fly off and torment someone else. She absolutely must have complete stillness in order to pick up on that splendid little sound of buzzing wings.

Then… everything suddenly did get still… terribly still… without the least breath of movement to the air within the parlor. Straining to listen, she could not make out a tweet, chirp or flutter from any of the birds outside. One moment, they were chattering away, and then in the next… it was as if every single one of them had frozen mid-note.

What if… What if death had actually come to them?! What if it had finally shown up for her!? Not dark and dreary like she had envisioned it so many times, but light and cheerful… with the sun's rays dancing all over her parlor. That would be perfect… though it really did not matter. Bright or dark, she was ready. More than ready to embrace an end of her own. She waited… one… two… three seconds for the sound of the wings that would come save her from this horrible despair.

Instead… she picked up on something rather odd. A smallish sort of noise coming to her as a faint whistle. Just a little hiss in the air. Not at all nearby, for it seemed to originate from some far off place. So chilling, this growing sound prickled at the tiny hairs on the back of her neck. It just kept intensifying… like how the rending of paper can be made louder by tearing it faster and faster. Before she knew what was happening, its magnitude had become like that of a million crisp sheets being wadded up all at once. The entire parlor vibrated with its presence. Then, in a colossal crescendo, a resounding boom tore through every timber of the house, shaking her insides so severely that she must cover her ears or burst, for this was a sound felt as much as heard. Its roar then echoed into a scorching rumble, much louder than any thunder. Only gradually did it wear down. Sort of like the same way as the sizzle from a hot skillet does as a dancing droplet evaporates away. As the last remnant disappeared, she found herself held rigid in place with a strange sense of longing. She knew all of those sounds from the beginning to the end. Knew that she had heard them many times before. Maybe even relished in them during some long ago stage of her life. But now… they seemed so… strangely fresh and different.

As one who has awoken from a dream, straining to listen in the dark for some small fragment of its meaning, she suddenly sat bolt upright. There it was again – that faint whistle! Without delay, she sprang from the stairwell nook, dashed out of the parlor, and flung herself off the porch onto that small stretch of grass bordering the eastern side of the house. The sun, full in her face, was making it challenging… but she had once been very good at this. Better than most pilots she knew. It came from a lifetime of searching the air for little buzzing things. With only a few seconds of hunting, she located that small dot ripping its way across the northern horizon, coming back around for another pass over the city. The same jet, having announced its arrival into Lubbock, was looping back for more. This time, she would be ready for it. Ready to fully embrace the boom it would deliver. As the plane passed over a second time, shaking her as resoundingly as before, a dormant part of her seemed to kick in. Though it moved at supersonic speed, she still managed to pick up on the jet's bifurcated V-tail… and what appeared to be diamond-like intakes… and knew instantly what it was.

Unbelievable! An F/A-18 Super Hornet… here!

If she had stopped to think… which was difficult given how the second boom was still echoing in her ears… she would have realized that this particular craft was a common attraction at airshows. And since Lubbock was hosting such an event this weekend, the Hornet's abrupt arrival had surely been anticipated by many in town. She would realize this in a bit, but at that moment, the plane was a special gift to only her… for it had awoken her eyes to up.

Hoping that the Hornet was coming around for a third fly-by, she raced about the house trying to track where it went and from where it might pop back up. She soon spotted it making directly over the city, more or less on a west-to-east heading some fifteen degrees up from the horizon. The third boom had her jumping up and down like a little girl, waving her arms about all crazy-like at a pilot who so obviously could not see her. Two more times it cut across the city… and then sadly, it disappeared… no doubt on a subsonic heading into the Lubbock airport. With her lungs strained from her running about, she had to stoop over on her knees to catch her breath… and only then realized that tears were streaming from her eyes.

Still very much filled with a sense of awe, a natural disappointment nonetheless crept over her. This jet had made its last fly-by… and once again she was left with remembering her loss. Turning back up the short stretch of driveway she had unknowingly run down, she aimed herself back to the house and her lonely nook… when another sound came to her. From the east, she picked up on a second dot in the sky… and soon a different plane tore directly overhead. Not as deep or as resonant as the Hornet's, this swept-wing MIG nonetheless brought all the fullness of its own characteristic boom. As with the Hornet, the MIG made several fly-bys over Lubbock, once again causing her to scamper in circles around the yard in order to keep up with it. Being nearly exhausted from all her running and whooping, a tinge of reason finally came to her. These two impressive jets must be the forerunners of the parade that traditionally preceded an airshow… so more aircraft were sure to follow.

Within this realization, she welcomed her first true moment of joyful anticipation in many months. In a dash, she was back into the house crashing all about to locate items she had not thought about in a half year or more. A sweater… sunglasses… a bottle of water…

Where the hell are my binoculars?! Oh… in the drawer beneath the nook.

Throwing a light blanket over a shoulder and snatching up an aviation encyclopedia from off the shelf, she hurried to the back door just as something new came cutting across the sky. Grabbing a kitchen chair… for there was no time to fuss with lawn furniture… she popped out just in time to see a dot disappear over the roof of the hangar, it heading in the general direction of the airport. Chiding herself for having missed out on some mysterious moment of aviation delight, she trudged across the empty space between the house and the hangar, purposing not to allow another plane to pass her by without seeing it. With the briefest acknowledgement of where she stood… near to the place where her beloved had died… she positioned her chair up against the hangar door, pulled on the sweater, and sat down to wait with binoculars in hand.

I wish he was here with me…

But just then, the next dot appeared on the eastern horizon, heading directly for her. Pressing the binoculars to her face, she searched about for the plane… and realized it was actually several of them. Four T-6 Texans, flying in a diamond formation. She had once sat in the cockpit of one of those, and recalled that it's owner explained how the tips to its prop going supersonic gave the plane its distinctive reverberating sound in flight. She followed these all the way over the top of her and out of sight above the hangar's upper lip… and then immediately brought the binoculars back down to the eastern horizon. More aircraft soon came flowing over, sometimes in a continuous wave and sometimes with such large gaps between them that she found herself sitting on the edge of her chair with much anticipation.

That's a… Thunderbolt… no… a Mustang.

Cool – a Sabre!

Here comes a… B25 Mitchell.

I've no idea what… Oh, wait… it's a Messerschmitt.

That's definitely the twin booms of a P38.

A Spitfire… make that two.

A Hellcat! Wow! I haven't seen one of those in years.

Unbelievable – that's a C130!

A plane so massive, she knew it could cover the entire space between the house and the hangar… and still have wingspan leftover.

Next came a craft with tanks at its wing tips. She should know this one, but somehow could not bring it to mind. Rifling through the encyclopedia, she soon found it to be the T33 Shooting Star – the 'Ace Maker.' While studying the picture of this plane in her book, skimming through details of its design and historical use, she happened to glance up to the next arrival… and lost her breath at the sight. There was no mistaking that distinctive inverted gull wing design.

Oh my… it's a Corsair!

For this plane only did she spring up from her chair and dash about the hangar in order to follow its flight all the way into the airport. When the Corsair had banked into its descent and was lost from sight, she walked back slowly, fingertips gently running along the full length of the hangar's side. She would certainly love to get a better look at that one in person, for inside this structure sat its sister craft. Maybe she should consider going to the airshow after all. Seeing a functioning Corsair and talking with its pilot would certainly be worth the awkward likelihood of running into her family, CP, or who-knows-who from town. Maybe… if she was careful to wear only black… she could pull it off without showing the slightest hint of disrespect toward Roy. Returning to her seat while pondering over the notion as more planes flew over, she finally decided against going. She was just not yet comfortable being around people. All of her moping about in the stairwell nook was proof enough that she remained very much a wounded soul.

As morning progressed into afternoon, the flow of military style planes gave way to slower civilian ones – stunt performers, biplanes and other single engine craft. Even a few helicopters passed over, though those never held much interest for her… no matter how fervently the rotorheads she knew insisted that it was the only way to fly. Many of the smaller planes seemed to venture low over her property. Not until a Waco dipped a wing… as if in salute… did it occur to her that they were checking out the oddity of a hangar isolated without a runway in the middle of West Texas cotton fields. Realizing this somehow made her feel proud.

All day, she sat before the hangar luxuriating herself with the long-forgotten sights of flight… with every roar, scorch, chug and sputter that went along with it. In the stillness of the intervals between aircraft, her thoughts always went back to Roy, and how much she would have enjoyed him being here. She had taken him to airshows before, so that was hardly the point. Re-experiencing this love of flight just seemed to make the loss of his love so much more real… in a good way… if that were possible. For the first time since his death, it occurred to her that he would have wanted her to go on with life… which nonetheless made her pain no easier, because *she* only wanted it to have gone on *with* him. That desire would never change. But a new thing was creeping into her thoughts… although she would not have considered it as 'new,' and not at all as a light dawning or a hint of life beyond the pain. In fact, she thought of this growing feeling as very much part-and-parcel with the sadness she had become accustomed to. She wanted him to always be proud of her… even if he was not here to show it.

In following a plane's path overhead, more often than not she would look up to find it move out of sight over the roof… and in repeatedly becoming aware of the hangar behind her, she more often thought of the Corsair within. Her Corsair. It was not really the plane's fault that Roy had died. That plane was just a thing sitting in there forlorn and forgotten. An association then grew in resonance with her own grief… almost to an extent that she felt a personal burden to do something about it. During the following intervals of aircraft-free sky, her eyes ventured toward the man door… padlocked off by one of her sons. It would be no problem to cut that off. She had done it before. But was this now a sacred place she should not dare to desecrate by entering? A tomb, of sorts?

Immediately following the air parade, she went through the house to close its doors and windows. She then emptied the refrigerator of all its nasty contents, wiped down its surfaces, and hauled out the trash. She showered in the guest bath, changed into clean clothes, and set a load of laundry churning in the washer. First thing tomorrow, she would deal with the insects that had collected inside her house.

Rather than sleep in her nook that night, she took blanket and pillow to the family room couch, for it provided her a view of the hangar. Being dark, she noticed for the first time that the bulb above the hangar door was out. Maybe it had been that way for months. Without that light, the hangar cast a faint shadow before its face due to the westering moon. The whole feel of the night gave the structure a ghostly stillness. Not scary though… just sad. Almost as if the building had enjoyed her presence all day, but with sundown had come to accept that she would never be back again. That was far from true… which happened to be why she had chosen to spend the night on this couch. Not so the hangar could see her and be reassured, but that she would be assured of a vaguely familiar feeling somehow made new within her heart.

For a long time, she lay there looking between the hangar and the setting of the half-moon off to the hangar's left. It had been a long time since she had taken in such beauty. In fact… she could not remember when it was that they last sat out on the back porch staring up into the stars. Perhaps it was only that previous summer. Yet all the times throughout all the years suddenly came melding together within her memory. In her mind's eye, she saw herself sitting side by side with him, leaning in close and holding hands. They were not young or old… not married or single… they simply were… as the night's sky played out its slow drama just for them.

Her tears came… along with a hollow longing to be held… and that very familiar shell-of-her-former-self feel. Yet something was different. She missed him… terribly… but also fondly. He certainly would have enjoyed watching her dash all about the property like a wild woman trying to catch up with those jets… and then teased her mercilessly for it. But only he understood what 'up' meant to her. He had always been so kind, sympathetic, and bizarrely in tune with her every mood. He just somehow knew what she was struggling with… even before she did. So handsome… strong… gentle… and faithful. What an incredibly faithful man! To her… to his family… to everyone he knew. He was an amazing person… and she was so fortunate to have been called his wife.

For the first time in months, she fell asleep to a warm thought.

With a long list growing longer by the minute, one neglected thing after another kept popping into her mind as she sat at the kitchen table with coffee cup in hand. Groceries and cleaning supplies… stamps for mailing off those overdue bills… gas in the truck… some large plastic storage bins, garment bags and mothballs… and a bunch of phone calls to be made. All of that would have to wait, for her first trip out of the house this Saturday morning was for the hardware store. She had been the one to destroy the screens, so she was going to be the one to fixed them… even if she had no idea how to go about it. She would also pick up a can of WD-40, a set of bolt cutters, some plastic sheeting, and enough bug bombs for every room in the house.

She spent a few minutes before a mirror getting her hair somewhat acceptable before heading out the door. Pulling the truck out onto the county road, she heard the airshow planes tearing through the Lubbock skies, but resisted the urge to look up. She was determined to make this a day in which her eyes were concentrated on 'down.'

In and out of the hardware store, fortunately without running into anyone she knew, she was soon back home again. The first thing she did was cover the relief with a sheet of plastic, taping it down well along all four sides. Next, she stripped the nook bare of all its blankets, doing the same with the linen in the other rooms of the house. Every item of clothing she possessed, along with every towel and cloth, was hauled down to the cellar for washing. In gathering up some of Roy's clothes… his hanging up things and every item from his side of the closet… she had in the forefront of her mind to spare it all from the bug bombs, though she knew a much greater decision loomed ahead regarding his belongings. She then went about the house shrouding each piece of furniture with plastic sheeting. In going room by room, she removed the damaged screens, shut the windows, set off a fogger, and then closed that space. Throughout this process, she found herself repeatedly apologizing to the house for what she had to do in order to set things right. She was responsible for all of the dust and every single bug that had gotten inside over the last few weeks. Somehow, she viewed the mess as being made by a different person than her. She was still a brokenhearted widow, but no longer one who was confined to her nook waiting to be stung while her house went neglected. Equally, she was determined not to dwell on that past. In fact, she viewed that time of grief as being due her, and she would not have changed a second of it.

With the damaged screens she had collected set out on the porch and the house sealed up to a poisonous mist wafting through every room, she had four hours in which to be outside while the foggers did their thing. None of the time would be wasted. Taking the new bolt cutters, she went to the hangar and clipped off the padlock that one of her sons had affixed to the man door. With flashlight in hand, she made directly for the breaker box to turn on the lights. Less than half of them lit up, casting the Corsair into a rather mournful gray. This would not do. Though in no way finished grieving for her husband, she was determined that from now on her sadness should not darken the light of day. The main hangar door must be reopened... and stay that way.

As best she could, she lubricated the bottom runner wheels all along the massive door with WD-40. For a moment, she considered getting out a ladder in order to work on the upper bearings... but a vision of herself falling off put an end to that stupid idea. Instead, she tried shooting some of the spray upward, if perchance to get a bit where it could do some good. She only ended up making a mess all over the inside of the hangar door. So it was finally time to try moving it.

If opening this thing doesn't kill me, then I know I'm meant to go on.

After much pulling at the seam with her finger tips... to no avail... she recalled that her father-in-law had once showed her how to get the thing rolling. Stepping within the open man door, she pushed on its frame... and was surprised when the huge hangar door budged a few inches... just wide enough so she could get her fingers into the resulting gap. After much pulling, she managed to widen the space enough to fit her body within, and then used the opposite side of the frame to exert leverage. Lowering her head and throwing her weight into it, the door reluctantly jolted forward. Straining to keep the massive thing moving, she concentrated on the screeching of the bearings, wondering if it had been the last sound he ever heard.

Despite a few rough hitches, she finally managed to get the door slid all the way open, and then stopped to catch her breath. The chore had not been that difficult... not unlike that of moving some heavy piece of furniture... yet she immediately found herself completely drained. She was standing in the very spot where Roy had fallen. Straightway, she collapsed to her knees on the hangar floor and began to cry… not wanting to remember, but accepting that she must.

In time, her breathing calmed and her eyes got done with being wiped. She reached out to caress the concrete where he had lain. This was not the site of a pitiable human tragedy. Roy deserved better than that. This was hallowed ground. More tears came, but different from those she had shed on reliving that terrible moment. She was just as brokenhearted, but underlying that feeling was a hint of some indescribable courage pushing its way to the forefront. 'Until death do us part' could never alter the love she had for him. She might go on crying like this for the rest of her life, but it was her privilege to do so.

Looking up, she beheld the Corsair towering above her, its propeller lit up by the morning sunshine pouring through the hangar's opening. She had never seen it like this before. So bold and beautiful, yet so sad. There it sat, facing out toward a sky that it would never soar into again. That was exactly how she felt – never to love again.

She rose from the concrete and moved around the plane's left side. Standing within arm's reach of the fuselage, she hesitated to touch it… though not because she was afraid. She had never bought into her family's ridiculous notions that this plane was haunted. It was something different. All those years, she had resisted venturing a look into the cockpit out of respect for George… and a reverence toward his reasons for owning this plane.

She stopped herself.

That's not right. It's high time that I learned to be honest with myself.

She allowed that little bit of shame to come crashing in and then ebb away. Truth was… she had kept this plane hidden away both in the hangar and in the back of her mind for the same reason. The Corsair was her private treasure… something that she had always refused to share with the rest of the world. She had always tried to keep the depths of her devotion toward it as a secret, walking that fine line between owning the plane and having it own her. That was why she had never tried to sit in its cockpit… and that was why she could never give it away. The Corsair and the relief… they both represented her craving for something grander from life. Something she could never quite reach. Most of all, she had always feared that Roy would come to know that having him and the boys was never enough for her. So she worked hard at keeping the many responsibilities of life wedged into her day-to-day thinking. That way, there would be less danger of her obsessions spilling out and doing damage… like before. She had been confronted many times with the need to give this plane away, but had always found the means of putting it off.

Not anymore.

She had been consumed with her mourning over the past six months, yet now somehow found a way of imagining that this plane had dwelt in such a state from the very first day her father-in-law had confined it to this hangar. Finally reaching out, she caressed its smooth metal side in the same way she had done to the concrete floor where Roy had fallen. Her eyes went up to the heavy canvas tarp draped over the cockpit. How strange that in the thirty-some-odd years of owning this plane, she had never once removed that covering. There had been many times that she had thought to try, but life had always found a way to distract.

Without pause, she reached up and dragged off the canvas in one pull... not expecting it to come off nearly as easily as it did, nor there to result in such a huge cloud of dust that sent her into a fit of coughing. On finally clearing her throat and eyes, the first thing she beheld was the plane's bubble canopy, it being slid back to reveal a wide open cockpit.

Dang! How do I get way the heck up there?! I mean... pilots of the day were in and out of this thing all the time... but I don't see any footholds on this side.

She recalled that George had talked about starting up this plane and moving it out of the hangar all by himself. In retrospect, not having asked him was a pretty significant oversight on her part as a pilot.

Wait... Duh! I didn't start flying until years after his death.

A bit embarrassed by her poor memory, she refocused on figuring it out herself. She did not bother looking about for a ladder, knowing that this plane was designed for operation on an aircraft carrier's deck where no sailor would bother with such a thing. She moved to the other side of the plane. Owing to the burnt-out bulbs above, the light was weaker here. So it took her a few minutes to recognize the faint stenciling on the right wing designating where a pilot was permitted to stand. This was the way up. After a bit more hunting, she located two small, door-like panels, one in the flap and one at chin level on the fuselage. She immediately recognized what these were for, though neither budged when prodded. Into and out of the house for a screwdriver, she was promptly back at the plates, delicately prying with one hand while coaxing with the other. The little door on the fuselage sprang open to reveal a recessed area big enough for anyone's foot. With more persistence, she managed to get the one on the flap to open also. Then moving back a few steps, she took a moment to imagine how a pilot might utilize these footholds to get up into the cockpit.

It's gotta be that the right goes into the flap hole first... then I step up with the left to the one on the fuselage... using that hand grip up there... and then I move the right to the step pad on the wing. From there... I guess I just have to haul my sorry ass in. Man... this's going to be murder my back!

Already feeling a bit sore from having run around the yard during the air parade, she thought it wise to stretch first. Without putting too much effort into it, for her anticipation was steadily growing, she briefly worked her thighs, hamstrings, calves and hip flexors, ending with a few pulls on her shoulders and triceps. Wedging the flashlight into her back pocket, she sprang up onto the plane's two footholds with unexpected ease... and then awkwardly froze there in clinging to the handhold. The cockpit opening was much narrower than she had expected. With its sill now at waist level, there was absolutely no way she could get a leg over. She would have to somehow step up onto the sill itself. Dropping the flashlight over the edge onto the seat, she leaned back to her right and awkwardly swung her left leg up, wedging her foot into the corner formed by the sill and the canopy's edge. With finger grips about the windshield, she more-or-less tugged herself up into a crouching position on the sill. After a momentary pause to get her balance, she stepped into the Corsair for the first time.

Such a huge plane... yet this cockpit was amazingly cozy. Comfortable too. She felt neither cramped nor lost within its space. Putting her feet to the rudder pedals, she was surprised to find that they moved... yet jerkily and not at all with the smoothness required for safe operation. She then tried to shift about to see if the rudder was responding, but could not get a decent view of it in the hangar's dark. Hesitating for a second, she took hold of the stick instead, and felt the pleasure of having it in her hand. It shifted about fairly easily, despite having not been used for a long time. Looking up to the ailerons looming above in the wing sections to the left and right of her, she made a mental note to get ahold of a copy of the pilot's handbook for the Corsair. She would certainly enjoy reading that. Probably needed to anyway if she wanted to understand this plane. Turning her eyes to the cockpit instruments, she realized that she should have brought along a rag. No matter... She started cleaning the dust layer off each gauge using her fingertips, intermittently wiping those on her jeans. She went about this task slowly... methodically... savoring the features of each gauge as they were unveiled to her.

Attitude indicator... my horizon.

Compass...

Turn and slip indicator...

Altimeter...

For several, she tapped the glass as a means of seeing if a dial could be nudged or gyro made to wiggle… but more so to enjoy the forgotten wonder of being in a cockpit. The only obvious damage she found was a thin crack running across the glass to the cylinder head temperature gauge.

I'm sure that can be replaced.

She then pivoted the flashlight to her immediate right and left. Some of the things she discovered there were readily recognizable – controls for the throttle, fuel-to-air mixture, flaps, landing gear and trim knobs – but many others were a complete mystery.

Aside from being very dusty… and a bit worn… the state of this cockpit did not seem any worse than that of other older planes she had sat in. Certainly no different than the Fairchild she had trained on. This Corsair, long forgotten, was actually in decent shape.

The feeling instantly came over her. The one deep inside that she knew would spring forth if only she was able to sit in this cockpit. For this was the very reason she had climbed up in the first place.

"You know… it's not too late for you. You could still fly again… if you wanted to. Tell you what… I'm personally going to make that happen for you… no matter what it costs. You have my word."

CHAPTER

46

CORSAIR

Through a shriek and sputtered cough, she was born into a resonant roar. The heart of her pulsed as cool air surged into her fires, and then flowed out hot from the power within. In perfect harmony with that heart of hers spun fast a three-bladed wind – her wind – now dancing before her as a vibrant disc of reflected light. From nose to tail, she felt the rush of this wind shake every strut of her, quivering an exhilaration that fluttered up to the very tips of her. Her wind tugged her forward, matching a growing craving within to unleash herself into speed. But something was pinning her in place. Though she strained against those hidden anchors, she was unable to move. Too soon, the heart of her went out and her wind stop spinning. But the rest of her… she was still very much alive with certainty, and keenly aware of being destined for something far greater than idleness.

About her to the right and left… before and behind… were others just like herself. Sisters arrayed in many lines. They too were alive, and they too sat anxiously. For a period of light and dark, she silently dwelt with these sisters of hers, waiting to discover her true meaning. Into a second light… and then one by one, her sisters were moved away. Once again, that heart of hers was made to pound with power, and her turn came. The most amazing of wonders then occurred. Her folded arms swung down wide… just like wings. She was unblocked and moved alone across to a much wider space. Before a long, straight strip, she became the focus of it all. Far off, she beheld a faint boundary between bright blue above and dull green below, and knew instinctively that it was in her to chase after that line. Her wind suddenly pulled her forward with a thrill of speed. Faster, she tore along that long stretch until something within her limbs gave leave. With a shutter, she felt the air lift up the very arms of her… and she broke completely free from the grip of earth. Into the sky, she knew only her own wind, the power of her heart, and the smooth, soft nothingness of flight. This was what she had been made for. To break away… to bank… to roll… to dive… to soar faster and higher… above, upon a carpet of white. Soon, every part of her was flexing with the pleasure of herself… as the heart of her burned on.

Such a cruel thing to be asked… to be called back to that hard place below. But she touched down with such grace… such ease and beauty. So proud… so happy… so in awe of herself, she went to join her sisters. They, like her, had also tasted first flight, and the anticipation of more ran through them all.

She and her sisters waited through another time of bright and dark … until finally she was back up into that blue again… but not alone. She was with her sisters this time… and not just to lap about this gray place as before. All of them climbed high as one, and together they turned toward that bright yellow face in the blue. On she went, just her sisters and her, sometimes leading, sometimes nestling within, and sometimes trailing behind in the wonder of them all. A great long time they flew, crossing green contours, tiny bands of blue, and many great clusters of light. She and her sisters came down only for the food of flight – her liquid power – and then were right back up again. On and on they went, over wide flatness and then amidst immense white-covered thorns that rudely thrust themselves up into her domain. She and her sisters outlasted those rocks-of-the-below, and as the spikes diminished, a new thing came. An endless mystery of a different kind of blue… deeper and much more foreboding. Its meaning, they all instinctively knew.

They alit to rest for a time… to be prepared… for each was aware that they would cross that deep blue. All about her and her sisters was much activity – a grim determination that they anxiously greeted. One by one, her sisters were outfitted with something new… something serious. A thing capable of bringing death.

When it came her turn… they said there was a problem with her. Some hidden defect within the recesses to her arms that had not been detected before. This mark of shame, they said, deprived her of the ability to sting. She was moved to the side as they went on with her sisters. For many periods of light and dark, she watched from afar as wave after wave of ones just like her came and went… and always she waited, longing to taste again the sweetness of sky… to push the limits of flight.

They eventually came for her, for surely now she was to rejoin her sisters. Out onto that long stretch she moved, and then into flight once more. But she was turned away from the vastness of that deep blue, back toward the dull brown direction she had come. She was kept low… and landed too soon. For countless more periods of light and dark, she longed for so much more. But they only flew her over barrenness, with an unseen barrier above separating her from the heights. An invisible domed cage… just for her. Nothing she was allowed to do was real. Just games. For always it was the same thing – never high, never fast, just short laps out across a wasteland and then back again. Over and over, never to fulfill her purpose. And on and on they talked about her sisters, fighting and dying across that deep blue.

Then came a time when she flew no more, though not because a single thing was amiss with her. They said she simply was no longer needed. They folded her arms and left her in a desolate corner of the field, to be forgotten beneath those cruel orbs above – the bright fiery one that taunted her with its heat, and the sad, silvery one that mourned over her darkened heart. Other ones not quite like her kind went on flying above, some never to return and some made to do those senseless laps that she had once hated so. What she would not give for just one more opportunity to be up there doing those laps about this place… for they said that she would never fly again.

She slept, awaking from time to time in crying out her black tears, but then always to sleep more. After how long, she could not say, a thing with wheels startled her awake. It was nothing like her. Just one of those unfortunate ones destined to creep along on the below. But she envied it and all of its kind, for they could move. Beside her, a long-armed thing lifted her up and placed her upon the creeping one's back. They strapped her down… and then hauled her away. She was moving with arms extended now… but it was not the same. Not at all from the power of her own heart. She was kept close to the ground and made to go so terribly slow. Not nearly fast enough to bring back a dream.

After many more cycles of light and dark, she was set before a place for her kind… one that was said to have been built just for her! Finally, after so long of a time, the food of flight was brought to her. Once again, she felt the power of her youth come alive in her heart. Soon, she would be back up there! But this new home of hers was cruel, for it was not at all a place of flight. Her arms were folded, her heart was put out, and she was dragged backward into that lonely place of darkness. From time to time, someone would awaken her, start her heart, and allow her to creep back out beneath that yellow orb within its blue. But always it was the same. Her heart was warmed without flight, and then she was hauled back into the dark. She was a captive. A performing beast made to roar without teeth. Over and over, she begged them, yet not one gave ear to her pleas. So old. So tired. She gave up trying… gave up hoping… and waited silently upon the slow work of decay.

———

If it were not for a full bladder threatening to bust the button right off her jeans, she would have stayed in the Corsair's cockpit all day. She had gotten in easy enough, yet not until that moment did she give any thought as to how one was supposed to climb out. There was nothing at all obvious about it… other than the fact that she should do her best not to break her neck in the process. Jumping down was completely out of the question, so she went about replicating a backward version of how she had gotten in. Lumbering up into a sitting position on the cockpit sill, legs dangling over the side, she awkwardly pivoted about in a half circle to rest with her waistline straddling the sill… and then realized that it was pressing right into her bladder. Desperately clinging to grips on the cockpit windshield and canopy, she slid down a bit further and frantically groped about with her toes until her right came in contact with the fuselage foothold. Quickly shifting her left foot there, she got her fingers into the handgrip and gingerly lowered her right foot onto the wing's stepping pad.

Okay… that was far less pilot-like than I hoped for, but at least I'm down in one piece.

Stepping off the wing to the hangar floor, she did not miss how the entire plane creaked on being liberated of her weight. Well… she had grunts and groans of her own to contribute, for neither of them were that young anymore.

Even with half of the day remaining, she must leave the hangar because of the many other things requiring her attention. For one, the time prescribed for the bug bombs had expired. So she quickly ventured inside to the guest bath, relieved that the foggers in that part of the house were done. Unfortunately, the whole place smelled like fertilizer, so she needed to get busy airing out the house. Her immediate task now was the screens. She set up a workplace on a western stretch of the porch, even though it was full in the sun and already quite warm. She went to work there with a mindset of occasionally looking up at the Corsair, a hundred feet off. It had sat in the same spot for as long as she could remember, but she nonetheless wanted to keep an eye on it, not unlike the way she had done as a mother watching over one of her toddlers at play. Following the directions of the man at the hardware store, she managed to get six screens rebuilt, none of which were as taut as the originals. She took the handful into the house, and then realized she had forgotten to label which screen went to which window. After a ridiculously long trial-and-error matching process, she finally got the six installed. Now she could air out the house without the possibility of more insects getting inside.

For the rest of the day, she swept, vacuumed, wiped and washed, pausing whenever she could before a westerly-facing window in order to get a glimpse of the Corsair. Just as frequently, she came up with some excuse for needing to go into the kitchen.

Gotta get some fresh water in this bucket.

I don't much like this sponge.

I need something to drink.

I should probably go check on the laundry.

Each time, she peeked out the back door and found that her Corsair was right there, perfectly framed within the wide open hangar... almost as if expecting her.

By evening, she had managed to install the remainder of the screens, along with getting the master bedroom, its bath, and a good part of the downstairs wiped down. She ate a light dinner at the kitchen table while staring out at the Corsair, trying to figure out if it were really possible for such a plane to fly again. Of course, age was not the issue. In all her years of flying, she had run across plenty of WWII era planes still capable of flight. The real problem, she knew, was money and parts... and whether she could find the right sort of person capable of doing the job. Someone who would understand what this plane meant to her... and maybe esteem it at least half as much as she did.

With the sky past dusk, she conceded that it was time to turn out the hangar lights for the night. Rather than taking a flashlight with her, she brought along a single taper and a big bag of tea candles she had come across while cleaning. Without lighting any of the candles just yet, she flipped off the breaker first, which immediately threw the hangar into a darkness offset only by the house's porch lights and a half-moon peeking through the clouds. Crossing before the open hangar door, she went about setting up the three dozen tea candles on the concrete floor just inside where the wind could not reach them. Having lit the taper's wick, she carefully transferred the flame to each of the tea candles until the entire spot where Roy had fallen shone forth with a bright, velvety yellow glow. Standing back a bit, she took in this memorial to him. It was such a far cry from what he deserved.

I miss you…

Wiping her eyes, she took another step away to better survey the scene… and was startled on bumping into something behind her. It was a Corsair propeller blade.

"Oh… hello there. Did *you* miss me?"

With the lit taper in one hand, she ran her other along the stretch of blade she could reach. Just as she had done with Roy's memorial, she moved back a few paces from the plane to better take in how her small light played upon the whole propeller, the nose and the bent wings. In most places, the plane absorbed the light shone upon it, whereas a few spots managed to send back a dull reflection of the candlelight. The effect was not spooky in the least. More like pleasantly warm… as if the plane was gratefully acknowledging her care in putting it to bed for the night. She moved back another step toward the threshold of the hangar door… where a stiff cross breeze from outside unexpectedly blew out her taper. The remaining light now was from the solemn glow of the tea candles off to her right, each gently fluttering in some swirl of air making its way around the hangar door. The plane seemed more somber now. Sad, just like her. After another look to Roy's memorial, she headed back to the house, not venturing to turn around until she was on the porch. Only faintly apparent through the open hangar door, the Corsair seemed more like a dimly burning wick, and she, still very much a bruised reed, nevertheless vowed that its little flame would not be extinguished.

After six months of sleeping in the nook, she was determined not to spend another night there. Having turned out the lights below, she climbed the stairs slowly, concentrating on the grip of her hand on the railing and the feel of each step beneath her feet. She had been in and out of the master bedroom several times that day… the most recent being to wipe up a splatter of plaster dust she had caused from yanking the curtain rods off the wall. But this time was different. This time, she was declaring a resolve for moving on in life. With a steady pace, she crossed the landing into the master bedroom and closed the door behind her. She remade the bed with clean linen, dressed herself in pajamas, brushed her teeth and washed her face, all the while doing her utmost to suppress memories of him. Those, she could entertain tomorrow… and the next day… and every one after that… but it was important that she get through this first night. She went to her side of the bed, turned off the lamp, and lay down facing away from where Roy had always slept. Instead, she purposefully stared out toward the balcony. She needed to keep her mind clear until sleep naturally did that job for her. Yet against her best efforts, a distinct image came to overpower her. She clearly saw him out there in a tux and her in a beautiful gown of crystal. Both of them were laughing as they threw party favors off the balcony to their guests below.

That memory flowed through with her tears, and soon others came in to replace it.

Cups of coffee out there in the morning.

Watching the boys play in the yard.

Spilling out my frustrations to him at the end of a bad week.

Snuggling together as we tried to spot where the rising moon was going to poke itself up above the horizon.

She allowed the whole lot of them to come over her and do as they willed. Those memories were no different than any of the other pieces of him scattered throughout this house. Each would forever keep her crying.

She rose before the sun to make coffee, looking out toward her Corsair during the brewing. The plane sat just as before – waiting. She returned upstairs with cup in hand to watch the sunrise from her balcony. On this fine March morning, she tenaciously bent her mind away from remembering, for she had a notepad in her lap and was reviewing her list of things to be done. Some items could already be scratched off, but even more got added as she thought through what it would take for the house to recover from her six months of neglect. Looking down at the pen in her hand, another thing came to mind.

Ugh! Got to get these nails done. They're atrocious! Better make a hair appointment too.

Having drained her cup and refilled her list, she left the balcony to start in on the most difficult task first. She had decided just before falling asleep last night that remembering the past and dwelling in it were two very different things. So she went to Roy's bedside table and dresser, quickly emptying their contents into a large storage bin. She did the same thing with his things in the bathroom, and whatever remained of his in the closet. She took that container down to the cellar, there to join those items of his clothing she had already brought down before setting off the bug bombs. She then went throughout the house to collect up more of him… anything that might cause her to regress back into that pathetic state of before.

For the remainder of that Sunday morning, she went about washing and neatly folding his things into the plastic storage bins she had bought just for this purpose. Someday, she would go through these things again, cherishing some items and giving others away. But for now, she would treat each as a treasure worthy of safekeeping. With great care, she layered some items into the bins with only a moment's pause, whereas others were lingered upon in considering their significance to his life.

This is that flannel shirt he liked wearing around the house on Saturdays.
Oh... that handsome blazer he wore on our date nights!
His work boots... I always seemed to be tripping over these.
What a ridiculous Christmas tie!

All of these and more she sealed away, trying to convince herself that not one of them was being buried in the cellar.

By midafternoon, she had a dozen filled containers stacked on the floor, each labeled as bearing Roy's things. She turned next to the packed shelves lining the interior walls of the cellar. She had no mind for sifting through that junk, only wanting to find space needed for getting Roy's things stowed safely away. Walking along the line of shelves, she shifted some things about and took down others that clearly could be parted with. In particular, she found several boxes bearing things that her sons had left at the house. Stacking these at the base of the cellar stairs, she purposed to haul them up to the family room... to be claimed by her boys or thrown away. She also came across an unlabeled bin similar in appearance to those of Roy's. Inside was a helter-skelter of papers and envelopes that she immediately recognized as being what remained of her aunt's things. She had saved this for who-knows-why, having long ago given away most of Gwen's stuff. Well... this should go upstairs too, for it was far less important than her husband's things.

After twenty minutes of rearranging, she managed to clear off enough shelf space. With Roy's possessions safely stored away, she stepped back to consider how his name was being displayed on the various containers along the shelving's rows. It was not as if she was sealing him off forever... to be forgotten like the things her boys had abandoned at the house. Every time she came downstairs, all she needed to do was face these shelves and there would be Roy's name displayed on bin after bin. She could pull one down whenever she wanted, and keep the memory of him fresh.

She toted her sons' boxes, along with Gwen's, upstairs to the family room, and then paused to consider what should be done next. She had those bills to pay so they could go into the mail in the morning... and there was still so many things in the house that should be cleaned. She also needed to do some more thinking about her plan for the Corsair. Above all else, coming across her boys' possessions in the cellar had pushed her children to the top of the list. Going from one to the other, she made call after call to the cell phones of her sons and their wives, not once getting through. To be fair, having calls to

Stacey, Valerie, or any of her boys go unanswered was not uncommon, but all of them at once – that was different. Most of all, it was highly unusual for Amanda not to pick up. In each case, she left a voicemail asking the person to call her back when they could. Resisting a notion that they all were screening her calls, she resolved to try again tomorrow.

After paying bills, she spent the remainder of Sunday night scouring the internet for information on the Corsair... particularly anyone who owned or had restored one. She was shocked to find that so few were still in operating condition, which diminished her hopefulness for her own. She nevertheless wrote down the name of an owner in the Dallas area whose plane made frequent appearances at airshows. That was likely the same one that she had seen pass over her house. Come morning, this would be one of her first phone calls.

Her second night back in her bedroom when much better than the first, likely because she went to sleep bone-tired. On pins and needles, she sat at her kitchen table with her second cup of morning coffee waiting for the clock hands to move past nine, a respectable hour for anyone to be in on the first day of a work week. She immediately called Bright Star Aviation in Dallas. After three more attempts spaced an appropriate ten minutes apart, she finally reconciled herself to leaving a voicemail. She gave her name and cell number, ending with her claim to being the owner of a Corsair that she would like restored... and could someone there please point her in the right direction for seeing that happen. For the remainder of the morning, she kept her cell phone nearby and put off her other calls for fear of not being available when someone from Bright Star responded. Not until after lunch did her expectations wane enough for her to attend to other matters. She called each of her sons again, along with the DILs, and left more voice messages... these being a bit more insistent than those before. She had just finished making an appointment to renew her EpiPen, and was about to start in on the arduous process of sorting out her situation at NASCorp, when her cell rang with a number that she did not recognize.

"This is Marna Meitner."

"Hello... this is Bernard Stevens from Bright Star Aviation. You called this morning about a Corsair?"

"That's right. Thanks so much for returning my call. I'm really hoping you can help me. What I'm interested in is exploring what it would take to have my plane restored to an airworthy condition. It's World War II circa... but I don't know the actual model. I think it's in pretty decent shape. I've had it in a hangar for..."

"Excuse me, did you say restored? I'm sorry... but I was under the impression that you were interested in having it appraised for sale."

"No. Not at all. I only mentioned restoration in my message."

"Don't you live in Lubbock?"

"Yes. How'd you know that?"

"My pilot spoke with a fella by the name of Meitner at the airshow there on Saturday. Hold it a sec… It was a Travis Meitner."

"Umm… that's my son."

"Well… he was inquiring about what the plane might be worth. I was just about to call him to set up an appointment when I saw your voicemail."

"Mr. Stevens…"

"Call me Benny…"

"Of course… Benny… my son is mistaken. I'm the owner of the plane, so I can assure you that it's not for sale. I'm only interested in whether or not it can be restored."

"Okay… that changes things a bit. I'm still interested in taking a look at it, but I'm not promising anything. Restoration of World War II era planes is a long and very expensive process. But… it's not every day you come across a fully intact Corsair. So… when can I send someone your way?"

"Whenever you'd like. Should I cover the cost?"

"For the opportunity to see another Corsair… definitely not a problem. Tell you what, Mrs. Meitner… with most of my show planes out at the moment, my senior mechanic doesn't have much to do. Would it be possible for him to visit tomorrow… say… sometime around noon?"

"That would be fantastic! And you can call me Marna."

"Thanks, Marna. There is one other thing. From what I understand, your son was shopping your plane around at the Lubbock airshow. I know for a fact that he spoke with several pilots other than my own. So… if what you're saying is true… that you're the sole owner… then I'm willing to send someone all the way to Lubbock, but only if I can have your word that Bright Star is afforded a fair opportunity at bidding on the restoration of your plane."

"Absolutely… and I'll be completely upfront with you, Benny… as I'm sure you will be with me. Right now, you're the only one I've spoken to… so you'll definitely get the first crack at it. Would you… like me to email you a picture of the plane? It's truly beautiful!"

"To be honest, Marna… I've already got a picture of it from your son."

"I see. Benny… I'm sorry to put you in this situation, but I'd appreciate it if you didn't contact my son. If he happens to call you, then please tell him that you and I have spoken… and that should be the end of it."

"Will do."

Hanging up, she realized that it had been a very long time since she last experienced this level of anger. Travis had absolutely no right to be off peddling her plane to the highest bidder. He had not even shown the decency of broaching the subject with her first.

So why should I bother reaching out to him with an apology for my six months of… despondency?! He should be the one calling me!

She took her notepad and drew a straight line through the entry about Bright Star, and then totally blackened out the wording of the reminder to call her sons again.

True to Benny's word, there was a man at her door come noon the next day. He was a rather husky-looking fellow with a ball cap on his head bearing the name of his aviation company encircling a multifaceted star. Through his slow introduction of himself, she did not miss that his eyes darted along the porch in the direction of the hangar, which he no doubt had seen on driving in.

"Mrs. Meitner… I'm Earl Cummings… from Bright Star Aviation. You spoke with my boss, Benny Stevens. I hope you were expecting me?"

"Yes… of course. Please to meet you, Earl. You're right on time. Can I offer you anything before we head over to the hangar? Perhaps a glass of ice tea?"

"Thanks… but no. Already stopped for lunch on the way over. I'd… sure like to get at your plane… seeing as I've got a long drive back once I'm done."

"Certainly. This way."

She led him around the house to the Corsair, stopping just shy of the hangar's threshold. She had been telling him how it came to be here, but was not convinced of him listening. His eyes were glued to the plane, so she gave him leave to enter the hangar. He delayed only in asking for permission to take photographs. He set off on a walkaround, and she stayed where she was in granting him the benefit of not having her tail along. Actually… it was rather fun watching him from afar as he snapped photo after photo. From time to time, he would look back at her with astonishment… and then go right back to fiddling with the plane. He peered into the wing joint, and then ran a hand upward along the outboard flap before stooping down to examine the inboard section. Seemingly satisfied with the flaps, he moved alongside the fuselage, tapping at its metal sheeting several times. Around the tail, he wiggled the elevators and rudder before disappearing from her view. She next caught sight of him climbing up for a look into the cockpit. He did not get in, but leaned over so far that she was afraid he might fall headlong over the sill. He was soon back down to move around the right wing, and then spent a very long time stooped under the plane, peering up into the recesses of the landing gear cavities and the engine's cowing ports. Occasionally, she heard him whistle, hum or mumble to himself. He flexed the one blade within reach but did not attempt to rotate the prop itself. After jumping up a couple times for a peek into the nose ring, he came back to her and just stood there silently looking at the plane.

"Well, what do you think?"

"Ma'am… all I can say is… it's remarkable. She's absolutely incredible. You know… most warbirds we restore come to us in rusted up pieces from a wreck that's been sitting in some jungle for decades… or as a museum exhibit that's been assembled from the parts of several other planes. But to have a whole bird like this… well… like I said… it's remarkable. How'd you say this plane came to be here?"

"I inherited it from my father-in-law. He purchased it from surplus shortly after the war ended. I don't think it ever saw combat."

"No… I'd say not. It's got spots under the wings for rocket launching rails… Doesn't seem like any were ever mounted. My best guess is… this one here was used for training. By the way, it's a F4U-1D. That's the model. I suppose you know what the 'F' stands for?"

"Fighter. Actually… I'm a pilot. I've been flying since my twenties. Single and multiengine. Jets too."

"Really?! Good for you."
The way he said it… more impressed than surprised… tipped the scales for her. She liked this man.

"I envy you pilots…"

"There's nothing to it. I might be able to fly a plane… but I don't have the slightest idea how to fix it when it's broken. So… what's the rest of the model number mean?"

"The '4U' designates Vought as the manufacture… and the '1D' is the variant. You can tell this one by its three-bladed prop… and the absence of horizontal supports in the bubble canopy. I'd say this was likely built in '43."

"So, I guess the real question is… can it be restored to flight?"

"I'd prefer not to give an opinion on that just yet. But generally speaking… if you've got the money, just about anything's possible these days. It used to be that the only way to restore a plane like this was to cannibalize two or three others. Fortunately, times have changed. The computer age and CAD programs allow companies like ours to generate our own parts. By the way… we've got a complete set of the Chance Vought blueprints for nearly all of the F4U models. Copies, mind you… but good enough to make many of our own parts. What we can't machine ourselves, we get made by other shops. The hardest thing's the jigs."

"What's a jig?"

"That's the framework for holding parts while you're working on them. Sort of like scaffolding. There aren't drawings for those. We gotta make those up as we go."

"Earl… getting back to my question… if you're not comfortable saying anything about its airworthiness, how would you rate it's overall condition?"

"Darn good! Amazing, actually. Everything looks great in the cockpit. Landing gear assemblies seem pretty decent too. No corrosion to either the exhaust or intake manifolds. Same with the insides of the speed ring. Can't say anything about the engine, of course. A plane this old… it's likely got cracked cylinder heads… or worse. You said your father-in-law picked it up at surplus… know where?"

"Some airbase in California. I think it was in the desert."

"And it's been here ever since?"

"That's right."

"That explains it. Two dry climates. You know… the Navy didn't design the Corsair to last. They built it to beat the Japanese. Worrying about what happened after was the farthest thing from their minds. That's why this plane's made with lots of corrodible metals that don't stand the test of time… especially in a place like the South Pacific. Not unless it's been kept in ideal conditions. Which brings me to my next point – mind if I ask you a personal question?"

"Go ahead."

"How's it you've been able to keep this plane hidden away? I know of a dozen brokers… my boss included… who'd swoop down here in a second if they knew. You wouldn't believe how many collectors and museums there're who'd be interested in buying this bird. Just the engine itself would attract a huge amount of attention."

A terrible fear got thrust into her mind, so she studied his eyes for a shred of its possibility.

"You should know… this plane has a special significance to me. I'd just as soon see the whole thing burned to the ground before I allowed someone to hack it up for parts."

"Hold it, ma'am – that's not what I meant. What you're describing… that would be a crime. There're so few of these planes still flying… out of twelve thousand or so built. Pretty soon… even the operational ones'll face extinction… unless someone does something about it. So… my perspective's the same as my boss's. These planes played an important role in history. They should be preserved as such."

"I'm glad to hear that. I just hope you can appreciate my interests too. I want to see this plane restored because it's... beautiful... and it deserves to fly again. So I won't be entrusting it to anyone who doesn't feel the same way."

"I understand, ma'am. Truly, I do. Let me be just as up-front with you. Benny'll most likely make you an offer on this plane as is... but there's no disrespecting your wishes in it. Something as unusual as this..." He paused with a wide sweep of an open hand toward the Corsair. "...it's too important not to. But I'll give him my report... and express your wishes. In the end, I'm sure he'll be just as happy to contract with you for the restoration... assuming you can bear the cost. If we can get her airworthy... which I can't guarantee... then... her value goes way up. Somewhere over two mill."

"Two *million* dollars?!"

"Yeah... but it might cost you half that much to restore it. At minimum, the engine'll need to be rebuilt. That'll require plenty of careful machining. Won't be cheap. Then there's the hydraulics and cabling... not to mention every bit of the electrical system that'll have to be... "

"Pardon me a sec... That Corsair that flew in the airshow here last week... did you have a role in its restoration?"

"Certainly did... and I've spent plenty of time working on her since. Why do you ask?"

"Just curious. I'm looking for someone with capable hands."

"That, I have. I've been working on aircraft since my teens. You know... if Benny and you was to reach an agreement, then you'd be more than welcome to visit during the restoration."

"Really?!"

"It's your plane. And I agree with you – it's beautiful."

She took his card and shook his hand with a goodbye. From the front porch, she watched his truck all the way down her gravel driveway and out onto the county road... until the dust his tires kicked up had faded away in the breeze. She then swiveled about to face the hangar and her Corsair staring back from within. If that plane could really talk... beyond the ridiculous moaning her late husband and the boys often attributed to it... what would it say? It would most certainly be excited over the possibilities... but also scared.

Just like me.

CHAPTER

47

LOST LOVE'S LETTERS

So what are my assets?!

She obviously had the house and the hangar… along with the underlying property. Worst case scenario, she could take out a second mortgage, though she doubted it would cover the full cost of the plane's restoration… especially if what that guy Earl said was true. But that question was academic anyway, for Roy would not have approved. She also still owned the boarded-up Meitner Appliance Store, as they had never been able to sell off that property. Most of their savings had gone to the boys' college funds. All she had left was of the rainy day sort. Not nearly enough to cover a sliver of what was needed for the Corsair. Her IRA from working at NASCorp was pretty substantial… but she could not touch that for years without paying a huge tax penalty. Besides, that was all she had to live off of in her old age… even if she went back to work. The only other things of significant value that she owned were the two reliefs – the one here in the house and its sister in the Dallas museum. That the two had been separated for decades, she no more blamed Gwen than she did George for confining the Corsair to a lonely hangar.

She rose from her writing desk and moved through the parlor opening into the dining room. There on that short stretch of wall shared with the parlor hung her relief… which Roy had sometimes joked was actually his, seeing as Gwen had given it to him. Its stonework was just as beautiful as the first time she laid eyes on it, yet so much more meaningful than she had ever expected. She had lived the lives of those faces, but had also broken free… just like the two birds. Standing there, she found herself asking the birds what they thought of her plan for the Corsair and the cost it might mean to them. For some reason, she felt that they would understand. But the faces… they were as immutable as ever. No matter her mood, they always stared out of their rock in exactly the same way. All of them together reminded her of the full spectrum of her life's sorrows and ills. Each stone expression was so terribly familiar, yet she had never bothered to name a single one of them. Never even had the inkling to do so. She had always preferred to call them 'the faces,' even though the artist had obviously sculpted bodies to go with them. She had felt so many different emotions over the years in standing before this relief… most of which could be echoed in those faces. They all seemed near to the touch, yet so far away. Now… she wished that she had been more personal with them, for she went from one to the other not knowing how to ask.

In truth, she was ashamed of herself for needing to come before this beautiful sculpture with her crude request… more so since she had spent her life privately indulging in its presence. She, like Gwen, had kept this relief separated from its sister, depriving every museum-goer of the full story. All those people out there only ever had Earth, for she had jealously kept Sky to herself. Surely the reliefs belonged together… and surely Gwen would understand. So maybe now was the moment for her to right two wrongs. To truly set those beautiful birds free… and to bring back flight to the Corsair.

She went back into the parlor and found on her cell the contact information for a person she had not spoken to in a long time.

"Yardley and Associates, how may I direct your call?"

"This is Marna Meitner, a client of Cliff's. I was wondering if I might be able to have a moment of his time?"

"Let me see if he's available."

She waited through several minutes of hold music before the line became active again.

"Marna! So good to hear from you! I hope you're holding up okay."

"Better… of late."

"You know… I didn't get a chance to speak with you at your husband's funeral, so please allow me to express my deepest sympathies to you now on his passing. Roy was a good man, and I'm honored to have known him.

"Thank you, Cliff. That's… very kind of you to say. I… ahh… recall seeing you there, but as you probably remember… I didn't handle the memorial service very well. His death hit me as a terrible shock."

"Perfectly understandable. Think nothing of it. Unfortunately, Marna, I only have a few minutes to speak... so how can I help you?"

"Then I'll make this brief. I should have contacted you after Roy's death... you know... to discuss things pertaining to his will... but I really didn't have the wherewithal for it."

"There's no cause for worry. We've already handled everything for you. I knew you were... indisposed. Fortunately, Texas is a community property state, and since we previously put your name on all of the deeds, everything transferred over. We didn't have to go through probate."

"I'm really glad to hear that... because I definitely wouldn't have been able to deal with anything. But I guess I should start on the process of revising my own will..."

"Certainly. I'll get something scheduled for you."

"Thanks. There's... one other thing. I was wondering... do you think you could put me in contact with a reputable agent of antiquities... and then be ready to write me a contract? I want to sell my reliefs."

Two silent days went by following the mechanic's visit and the call to her lawyer. She heard nothing from either one of them, nor from her sons or the DILs. She had gotten the house more-or-less back into shape, in the process proving to herself that she was not. So maybe she should consider joining a gym... especially since better upper and lower body strength would be critical toward accomplishing her goal. After several hours on the phone, she managed to finalize her retirement from NASCorp. Her old life, with all of its joys and complexities, was over.

For the first time since the airshow, she hazarded a return to her stairwell nook. In being cleaned up, the space felt markedly different from the months she had spent hoboing there. She was still hesitant that an unpleasant version of herself might pop up again, but was pleased to find that she could sit there without too much self-reflection. Actually, her mind was bent toward her sons, as she oscillated between being irritated with them over the Corsair and irritated with herself for having put on a six month exhibition that caused them concern. She was in the process of thinking through the possibilities... good and bad... of just driving down to Midland for an unannounced visit with Chad and Stacey when her cell phone rang. Excited by the caller ID, she quickly answered.

"Hello."

"Marna – this is Cliff. Sorry to be calling so late, but we need to talk. Is this a good time?"

"Certainly. Did you find me a..."

"Nothing yet, but that's not why I'm calling. Best be seated if you're not already. It's about your sons."

"Don't tell me… They want to have me declared incompetent."

"How… how'd you know that?"

"I have a friend with an ear in the courthouse. He told me last week what they were trying to do. I'm sorry… I really meant to bring it up the other day, but forgot because we didn't have time to talk. Has something happened?"

"Actually, incompetent's not the proper term… it's 'incapacitated.' And I also have an ear in the courthouse… as any good lawyer should. I just heard that your sons have requested a court-ordered medical examination of you. Their petition will come before a judge tomorrow. I don't know what's going on in your family, Marna… but we should squash this thing before it reaches a judge. After that, it's on record… no matter which way it's decided."

"Cliff… my boys and their wives… they've been through a lot over the past six months… both with their dad dying and me not taking it well. I really want to believe that they mean me no harm. So… I'd like to find a way not to have a fight over this."

"My thoughts exactly. With your permission, I'll be submitting a relief first thing tomorrow morning requesting…"

"What'd you say? Submit a what?"

"A relief. It's a written motion that a judge take certain actions in a case… which in your case, really isn't a case at all. But that doesn't matter. I'm going to request an immediate conference prior to a ruling. The judge really should meet you first, and see that there's absolutely no reason why you should be subjected to a medical examination."

"Do you think my boys will know you've done this?"

"I don't know who's representing them, but that person'll most definitely be notified of my relief."

"So that means they'll know too?"

"Most likely."

"Then, Cliff… by all means… go ahead. They've not been returning my calls."

"Umm… it's actually probably best that you not speak with them. Not until this gets resolved. I haven't laid eyes on their petition yet, so I really can't…"

"Cliff, it's okay. I'll follow your advice. Please let me know what you can about your… relief thing… and mine too."

She went to bed angry… but equally anxious about the morning to come. Meeting a judge did not sound like much fun.

Turning onto the county road for the drive into town, she was still wrangling over second thoughts to her second thoughts… even though the issue had been settled on long ago. But just as when she lingered in her closet, she found that continuing to fuss over her choice of clothing was a great distraction from thinking about where she was heading. In truth, she had already settled on an outfit for this meeting long before stepping out of the shower… but acknowledging as much exposed her to thinking about more painful things. So… she had put on a debate over a variety of bright spring dresses, each with bold floral prints that would surely show her off as very feminine and full of life… even though she had absolutely no intention of wearing any of them. Those dresses might convey beauty and delicacy, but also a sort of 'PTA mom stepping out of church' feel. Much too weak… and she knew from experience that men of power tended to exploit weakness. She next spent an inordinate amount of time in matching blouse and slacks combinations that might display her stylishness… even though inwardly she felt no greater flair than that of jeans and a t-shirt. She then went back into the bathroom to do her hair… stepping once more into her closet with a determination to finally face the day. She absolutely would not dress herself below the professional level of anyone there… which required her to wear a suit jacket, skirt, hose, and heels. But not a power suit. That would be overkill. She had in mind a light gray blazer with a floral blouse to match. Soft, elegant and colorful… but sharp enough to communicate a down-to-business mindset. At least that was the impression she was shooting for.

Pulling into the courthouse parking lot, she was now reconsidering the power suit.

Because this is so stupid!

She scanned up and down the lanes, less for an empty spot and more for the sight of a familiar vehicle. She came across nothing that might reveal whether any of her sons were here. Per agreement, she met Yardley just inside security.

"Morning, Marna. How're you doing?"

"I'll be fine once we get this over with."

"There's really nothing to worry about. We'll play it just as I mentioned over the phone. You speak only to me or the judge… and I'll do the rest, got it?"

"Of course."

She made to move on toward the stairs, but he stuck out a hand to delay her.

"Hold it a sec. Your sons are already up there with their counsel.

"All three of them?"

"So it would seem. I… umm… thought it best if we stay down here until the judge's ready. I've arranged to get a text message from his clerk once they've been admitted to chambers… that way you won't have the unpleasantness of waiting in the same room with them. Shouldn't take long…"

He gestured toward a bare stretch of wall, and they both went to lean on it. "Any questions?"

"Nope… I think you've covered it all."

He nodded and went to working away on his cell phone. She, however, was far too nervous for anything other than standing there blank-faced, staring vacantly at the security line packed with others like herself – people who somehow found themselves at the mercy of a judiciary they did not understand. How was she supposed to feel? Her three sons – the most substantial product of her love for Roy – all thought that she had lost her mind. Well, maybe she had… but it was hers to lose!

Without expecting it, she felt Yardley tap her on the shoulder to say it was time. She followed in beside him, not at all tracking where they were going. Her thoughts were on Roy… and what he might make of this mess. He would most definitely be angry at his sons… and embarrassed that they were dragging his wife into the silliness of this courthouse meeting. But would he also be ashamed of her? Would he feel that she had somehow sullied the Meitner name with her reclusiveness?

No. He would have known how much I loved him.

Through a very solid-looking wood door, she and Yardley were ushered into a modest sized space that was nothing like the expanses to the judicial chambers she had seen in TV dramas. A balding man was seated dead-ahead behind his very orderly desk. She was about to do as Yardley was doing in shaking hands with that judge and another man standing there when she caught sight of her sons arrayed in a line somewhat behind the opened door. Travis had a folder clinched in his hands, but the other two stood with arms behind their backs… exactly the way Roy did whenever he was nervous. Turning to greet them, all three suddenly faced resolutely toward the judge, not budging an eyelash for her arrival. No way was she going to tolerate being ignored, and was just about to step right up into their faces when Yardley more-or-less yanked her off to the side. He gave her a stern look before turning to the judge… but that man just raised a hand to each lawyer, holding them at bay.

"Before either of you say a word, I intend to deal with this fairly quickly. Mrs. Meitner…?"

Still engrossed in glaring at her boys, she had not at all anticipated being called upon. To her further surprise, Yardley stepped aside to give her a clear path for replying to the judge.

"Umm… yes, Your Honor?"

"I'm going to ask you a few questions… and you just answer with what comes off the top of your head, understand?"

"Yes, sir."

"Did you brush your teeth this morning?"

"Uhh… yes, sir."

"And I assume you dressed yourself?"

"Of course…"

"Can you tell me who the President of the United States is?"

"George Bush."

"Good. Now I'm going to give you three words that I'd like you to remember – apple, table and tree. So… what city and state do you live in?"

"Lubbock… Texas."

"Do you happen to know what the date is?"

"Umm… Wednesday… March fourteenth… two thousand and one."

"What were those three words again?"

"Apple… ahh… table and tree."

"And how is your overall health?"

"Fairly good, sir."

"Any problems getting around… climbing stairs… driving a car… that sort of thing?"

"No, sir."

"No debilitating or life threatening conditions?"

"No, sir."

"But from what I understand… aren't you severely allergic to bee stings?"

"Oh… sorry, Your Honor… I forgot about that."

"And are you trying to use that condition to do yourself harm?"

"No, Your Honor." Somehow, she managed to stifle herself before adding on 'not anymore.'

The judge turned to the two lawyers, glaring back and forth between them.

"I see no compelling reason to grant this petition."

He let it hang there for a few seconds, perhaps to see if either dared to say a word in response. Her sons' lawyer just dipped his head.

"Close the door on your way out. I've got far better things to do with my time."

Very much surprised to find the whole thing over, she still hesitated to move in not being sure of herself. In contrast, her sons were already out the door. So she quickly nodded her appreciation toward the judge and hurried to catch up with them… only to have her lawyer once more take hold of her arm.

"Marna… best give it some time. What's say we go get a cup of coffee?"

Down the long hallway, she noticed that her boys had gained the stairs to the bottom floor without once looking back her way. As the tops of their heads disappeared from view, she knew that Yardley was right. It would take days… maybe weeks… before any of them would be willing to speak with her again.

"Cliff… thank you. I really appreciate what you've done for me. And I'm pretty anxious to hear your thoughts on an art dealer. But for now… I think I'd like to be by myself."

Once home, she gave the boys time to calm down and then called them, youngest to oldest. When that failed, she dialed their wives, but without success. She waited until the afternoon was old before trying again… finally getting through to Amanda. She found her to be courteous, but quite insistent that Travis was not available to speak with his mother.

"I'm sorry, Mom… he's just got back from Lubbock. To be honest, he has a lot on his plate right now."

"I understand… what with your move to California and all… but I was only looking for a few minutes to clear the air with him."

"I don't think he wants to talk about that now. Your abrupt turn around… it completely caught him off guard."

"But I've been trying to reach him all week! I've left message after message on his…"

"I know, Mom! I'm not a lawyer. All I know is that he said we weren't supposed to speak with you until that petition was resolved. I'm sorry, but you should know… he's really upset at you. We all are."

"Explain to me why."

"Well… for starters… you're frustrated with us about not returning your calls over the last week, but we've gone months without you answering ours. We've been so worried about you… so much so that we've all taken time off of work to check up on you. And when we drove all the way to Lubbock, what did we find?! Your house was a total wreck… and so were you, Mom. We tried everything we could to reach you… but we only really got scared when you started cutting up your window screens. Please try seeing it from our perspective. We were desperate… and felt it warranted us doing something drastic."

"You tried to have me declared as incapacitated. That's pretty drastic!"

"From our point of view… you were. Mom… we were trying to keep you from doing harm to yourself. Can't you see that?!"

"Yes… of course. And that's why I've been calling… and that's why I've left messages saying how sorry I am for what I've put you all through."

"But when you showed up perfectly normal to that meeting with the judge… you made Travis look like a fool. And there's nothing worse for a lawyer than to be made a fool of in front of a judge."

"I certainly didn't mean to do that. And I'm not trying to justify my behavior since… since Roy passed. Amanda… you have no idea what it's like to lose a husband so unexpectedly… and I hope you never do. It's devastating! I'm not back to normal. In fact… I'll never be normal again."

"I'm sorry, Mom. I don't mean to be callous with your loss. I'm just trying to get you to understand why he's angry with you."

"And I don't have a right to be angry at him?! He's been trying to shop my plane around without my permission."

"Mom… I really don't want to get into that. I'll just respond by saying that's not the way he sees it."

"The way he sees it is all wrong. It's been wrong for a long time. Amanda… he's held a grudge against me ever since I took up flying."

"That's not true. He's always treated you and Dad exactly the same."

"You think so?! Then allow me to tell you a little story to show you otherwise. It's about your husband and his brothers when they were young."

"Mom… I really don't have time for this. We've got so much to do before the movers come next week."

"It's really important that you understand… so I'll make it brief. One Christmas, Roy and I gave the boys a backyard swing set. The kind with swings, slide, monkey bars, and a million pieces for holding it together. Because he was busy with year-end sales at the appliance store, Roy promised to put it up in the new year… but Travis and his brothers couldn't wait. They tried erecting the thing by themselves. It was a complete disaster. They lost parts and broke others. In the end, it was impossible for Roy to fix it… so he left the mess in the yard as a lesson to them. And there it sat for months… an albatross of scattered tubes, bars and chains… until Roy finally hauled the whole mess off to the dump. Here's the thing, Amanda… years later when we were all together reminiscing about past holidays, Roy and I were stunned at how the three remembered that swing set incident. All three of them got angry at me, and swore up and down that it was my fault. That I made them put the thing together by themselves just to get them out of the house."

"I'm not sure I see your point."

"Amanda… we remember things the way we're disposed to. Your husband

and his brothers… they have deep-seated resentments toward me… toward the choices I've made in life. I'm not saying I'm perfect. I've made plenty of mistakes. But Roy and I… we were always a team. When a decision was made, it was made by us together."

"I don't think anyone's doubting that…"

"Really?! Then you have no idea what it's like to be a wife, a professional, and a mother all at the same time. I have loads of doubts! I've spent my whole life doubting my decisions. I know I've fallen short as a mother. But I've always cared deeply about my children. Hopefully, one day you'll be a mother too… and then you'll understand what I'm trying to say."

"Mom… Travis cares about you too. He was just trying to do the right thing by you… even if you don't realize it."

"See?! That's exactly what I'm trying to say."

"What?! No… it's… it's not at all the same thing, Mom."

"Listen, Amanda… you're the only one who's still speaking with me right now. So please… tell the others that I'm sorry… and that I still want to be in their lives. All six of you. Can you do that for me?"

"Sure… but there's still the matter of the airplane."

"I thought you didn't want to get into that."

"I don't… but it's another area where you made Travis look bad. He called that aviation company… you know… the one you're looking into for doing the restoration of your airplane."

"You know about that?"

"They told him… and they were quite rude about it. They said he'd misled them as to the true ownership of that airplane. I can say for a certainty that's not what happened because I was at his side throughout that airshow. All he did was ask about how much it might be worth."

"But it wasn't his to ask. And what I do with my own things is my business!"

"Not if it suggests something's not quite right with you. And certainly not if it means you burn through your life savings on a whim… and end up becoming a financial burden to your children."

"Amanda… I think we should stop here. It's been nice talking with you. Please tell Travis that I called. Goodbye."

She hung up completely beside herself with frustration over not knowing how to reach her children. They all thought she was crazy. She could try to reason with them… drive all the way to Midland, Dallas and Austin to talk with each couple… but somehow the gulf between them had grown far greater than all those miles combined. So she spent the remainder of the evening crying the sort of tears that came more from trying to figure out how things had gotten so bad… and fretting over how much time to give her sons before reaching out to them again.

Somehow, the hours were made all the more miserable from an awareness that she would soon be parted from her Corsair. Not minutes after hanging up with Amanda, Benny called to ask if Bright Star could look the plane over in greater detail at their facility before agreeing to restore it. With her permission and an understanding that they would bear the expense of the move, they hoped to come the very next day and truck her plane to Dallas. After a couple of weeks of looking it over, Benny promised that his company would then be ready to provide her with a decision. She was excited, but also scared… and already anticipating something of the coming emptiness to a hangar she had only recently found to be a refuge.

First thing in the morning, a crew of men arrived in trucks. They hauled the Corsair out of the hangar and then explained to her that the wings had to come off for transit. This, Benny had already warned her about. Though he swore that these could easily be remounted, it was still excruciatingly painful to endure the shearing sounds of saws cutting through the hinge bolts. After long hours, the wing sections were detached at their joints and hoisted by crane onto a flatbed. The fuselage came next… and she watched nervously as its wounded form, cradled within many straps, got lifted onto the same flatbed by the crane. Everything was tied down, with a large tarp secured over the canopy. Despite the starkness of its grotesquely wingless form, the plane did not look so sad to her now. On that flatbed, it seemed almost ready to take off. She could feel it – her plane was going to be restored!

Through it all, she took plenty of pictures of the plane from the front, back, below, and above from a second story window of the house. When it was finally time, she had the driver detail the entire route, assuring her that the plane had the proper clearances for all underpasses, powerlines and road signage. She then watched somberly from the front porch as her plane moved down the long driveway and out onto the county road, eventually disappearing from sight. After thirty years of not knowing what was to become of this plane, it was suddenly gone in the blink of an eye. So she stayed there on the front porch rocking away in the coolness of this March afternoon, trying to imagine what Roy might have said at that moment had he been seated beside her. He would surely offer some encouraging word to lift her spirits, and would most definitely have reassured her that the men knew what they were doing. That was the way of a man… to trust other men with the things that were dear to a woman. She shook off the thought, venturing instead to consider whether George might have been proud of her. Certainly he would have been glad to see the plane restored… but Ruby would be immensely relieved to finally have the thing off her property.

She spent the afternoon into the evening sitting before the relief, taking in its every feature. It was not as if someone was scheduled to haul it off on a flatbed truck in the morning… though she still felt like it was true. So much had happened to her in the last few weeks. An air parade snapped her out of her despair. A courthouse meeting led to a falling out with her sons. Her Corsair was taken away… with her pursuing the sale of this wonderful relief for that plane's sake. It was absolutely impossible for her to sort out those things from each other, for the feeling of one flowed into another. She was sad, embarrassed and hopeful, all at the same time, and no more capable of separating those feelings than she was of fixing the Corsair. But even if that plane was unable to fly again, she was absolutely determined never to confine it again within her hangar. Somewhere out there in the world, the Corsair still had a purpose to fulfill.

So… what's to become of me?

Such a question was never to be. She, the person so full of aspirations, had nothing left. No work, no family, no husband. Just a house and a hangar, both vacant for the first time in her life. She could walk through the extremes of each, but all their spaces were now just cavernous shells. That was her too. All alone with no purpose, no dreams, and no one left to share her life with. Empty earth and empty sky.

It grew dark out, and by happenstance, the only place in the house with a light on was the family room. So she, like a witless insect, found herself drawn in that direction. Plopping down on the couch, she stared out the window over the top of the arborvitaes that Roy had planted long ago. Despite his original intent, he had always kept that hedge trimmed low so she could see her hangar. That was the way he was. Of course, he had also wanted the hanger emptied. And now it was. She had no idea what to do with that emptiness. Surely not tear it down, but not fill it up with something either. Definitely not her husband's notion of using it for some outlandish auctioneering business. The last thing she wanted was strange people roaming around. With no sensible thing coming to mind, she allowed her eyes to drift back inside… to the boxes she had brought up from the cellar. Managing a weak smirk, she entertained a wild notion of using those to re-forge a connection with her sons.

'Come get your boxes, boys.' Yeah… that'll never work!

Off to one side, she noticed a plastic bin that she had set apart from the boxes. It took her several seconds to realize what this was. With her feelings taken up by the Corsair, Roy, her sons, the relief, and an uncertainty regarding her own future, everything suddenly condensed down into an association from long ago. She was instantly up from the couch to drag over the bin of Gwen's things that she had found in the cellar, absolutely determined to go through it item-by-item. Whatever she found might not dispel her gloom, but it might at least act as a temporary distraction.

Prying off the lid, the first thing to hit her was a dry sort of tingle to her nose… something she had not picked up on when she briefly opened this container in the cellar.

Really old paper.

The smell instantly reminded her of being in a library… a place that nobody visited anymore, even though it still had many hidden secrets.

Sort of like what I hope's in here.

Without venturing to touch anything just yet, she scanned over the topmost layer of paper, looking for the right place to start in. It was all just a jumble of envelopes and newspaper clippings… yet tucked away in the very center was a video cartridge displaying her name. Her maiden name. Beneath in smaller print was a date – August 28th, 1968.

Hey! I know what this is! It's that footage what's-his-name… Billings… cut for me on my last day at the TV station. I think this was taken during those riots at City Hall. Unbelievable! I wonder how in the world it got in here?!

She pulled out the cartridge to marvel at the feel of it when her eyes fell upon something that was beneath it – a simple strand of looped ribbon poking up from the depths of the box. In faded blue, the curl to it inexplicably drew her in much more than the video cartridge had, for it was so odd to see an item of soft delicacy amongst Gwen's things. Her aunt, skilled in the fineries of floral design, had not been a typical female. At least not as far as she could recall. For some reason, it then hit her that Gwen had died at about the same age Roy had. This was the deciding factor for her. She would go for that ribbon before anything else in this box. Putting aside the cartridge, she slid a finger beneath the loop and lifted out the thing hidden beneath. In a series of starts and stops came forth a tall stack of ribbon-bound letters. In wonder, she held this marvel before her face with that finger, twisting it about to take in its sides.

Oh my! I remember these!

She quickly placed the stack on the coffee table and scooted up to the edge of the couch so she could face directly over the top. Nothing else in the box mattered now. For here before her printed in block letters was the name of the man Gwen had been engaged to marry. Her own husband's uncle! Over her came a sadness wholly unrelated to her own loss, yet sympathetically strengthened by it.

Lost love's letters.

On the verge of tears, nothing else in all this world seemed as important to her as reading these letters. Not daring to cut the ribbon, she carefully worked the bow with her fingers until its knot finally came loose. The whole stack – maybe a hundred or more letters – stood of its own accord on the table before her. Sifting through the first dozen, she confirmed what she had already suspected. Gwen had organized her letters in chronological order, for that was the way she would have done it too. And that was the way she intended to work through the sad tale of Gwen and Brad. With only one side of the correspondence available to her, she knew that she would not get the full story. She would nonetheless put herself in Gwen's place and try to feel what her aunt must have felt – from the beginning joys until the bitter end. The niece would become the aunt… the nephew, his uncle… until Gwen's loss became fully intertwined with her own. Then maybe she might have some gaps in Gwen's life filled in… and perhaps also come to better understand her own feelings of loss.

In taking up the top envelope, she noticed that Gwen had neatly slit a seam along the right side with a letter opener. She had seen her aunt do that so many times. She quickly looked to the stack. One side was frayed and the others were crisp. Gwen had done the same to each. After a moment of studying the envelope, it being addressed from Brad in Hawaii to Gwen in Sweetwater, she drew out a single sheet, written front and back. Its sprawl was somewhat difficult to make out, being of compacted cursive with little space between the words. She took in the date – July 12th, 1943 – and filed its significance away for later consideration, as Brad's salutation captured her eye.

'My Sweet Pea Gwendolyn.'

Wow – how tender! They must already be dating. You know… I think there's a flower by that name.

She put the notion aside in order to read on.

I've only just arrived back on base and imagine my surprise. There's a letter waiting for me from you! I must say, you're a tricky girl. I see you mailed it while we were still together in Sweetwater. So many surprises. That's what I love about you! Seeing your handwriting makes me really miss you. But your smile continues to light up my thoughts. The memory of holding you in my arms, that's something I don't think I can find the words to write about. To think that when I opted to become a liaison at Avenger Field I'd be meeting the gal for me! I wonder if I should put that in my final report? Probably not. My CO would send me to Alaska next. That wouldn't be so bad if you were there with me. I do get a say in what comes next, like I told you. I guess that's one of the benefits of having already spent a year being chased by Zeros. Hopefully we can talk about that next month. I've put in my request for leave, so you can count on me being back there for your graduation. I can't wait to see you again!

I know it sounds daffy, but these Hawaiian Islands seem dull compared to West Texas. I miss you. Only you could make this place a paradise. Honestly, you're the only thing I can think about. I still have this vision of you waving goodbye to me at the airfield. You make a zoot suit look so fine! I also had a letter waiting here for me from my sister. Haven't opened it yet. I wanted to write you first. You were such a peach to use your weekend pass for a trip to meet her in Lubbock. Ruby's terribly lonely with her husband off at war, but she does get to see him here in Hawaii on R&R later this summer. Wish you could be here too. I'll say this much, Ruby's crazy about you. I guess it runs in the family. She's amazed at how courageous you are, but doesn't know the half of it like I do. You're clever too, and beautiful through and through. Just holding your hand makes me all warm inside.

I guess I better sign off for now seeing as this is my last sheet of stationary and I've nearly filled it up. I'm heading right over to the MCX to mail this and buy more.

Fly safe, my flower.

Your devoted Brad

Her first thought was that Roy had probably been conceived during that R&R reunion between George and Ruby. But her smile faded on considering the overall letter. For some reason, it had fallen short of her expectations. His words were sweet and sincere… even touching in places… but not enough. Perhaps such a critique was unfair for the first letter, so she took up the next, written by him a day later. This one was several sheets longer, but filled with much of the same – many silly expressions of his admiration for her aunt sprinkled amidst paragraphs about the day-to-day happenings at his base. She went on to the next… and the next… right up until the letter indicating that he was a day away from leaving for Gwen's graduation as a WASP.

In this first batch of letters, she felt that his affection toward her aunt had been put down in a rather clumsy manner, with simple words and run-on sentences. In other places, he did not seem to go nearly far enough toward expressing the richness of a deep love. He was far too cautious, with only hints here and there about his hopes for them together. These letters… they were too youthful. Just puppy love.

If I'd have been putting my own love down in ink, then I'd definitely have said…

She was suddenly filled with an indescribable pain. Try as she might, she was unable to summon forth a memory of her own feelings from those early years with Roy. They had been high school sweethearts, doing the same kinds of hand-holding and making out that Brad was awkwardly alluding to… but somehow, the wonder of her having been in love then would not come to her. At least not until he had accepted her back from those miserable years in Chicago. It was only then that she had fallen crazy in love with him. But they were already married by then… and she soon got distracted with flying… and became pregnant. She never really had that wonderfully awkward period of young love with him. Always, her ambitions had gotten in the way of her feelings for him. She had completely wasted her youth.

She took up the small pile of letters she had been through and read them again. This time, the simplicity of Brad's love for Gwen seemed so beautifully depicted and rare to behold. Her unfamiliarity with such sincere expressions… it became a rebuke to her. So much so that she felt embarrassed to be prying into these private feelings of a Bradrick Miller toward a Gwen Forde she never knew. Deciding that she was not worthy to go any further, she sorted the letters back into their proper order and made to place them on the pile. It was then that she noticed the next letter had been addressed to an APO in New York. Gwen had moved on from Sweetwater. Curiosity got the better of her, so she quickly took up the next envelope. The pages of its enclosed stationary had lots of creases and considerable wear along the edges – all signs that they had been revisited many times over.

Dear Sweet Pea Gwendolyn,

I miss you. It's only been a day since we were parted but to me it seems like years. I know you think it's funny that I go on and on expressing my gratitude to you for accepting my proposal, but you have to understand how nervous I was. If you had said no, I don't know what I'd have done. Joy to my heart, you said yes, and we will one day soon be man and wife. How I look forward to that day, as I know you do too! Until then, I really should start addressing my letters to you as my 'Sweet Fiancée Gwendolyn,' though you will always be my Sweet Pea.

"Wow! They're engaged!"

She felt an instant thrill of excitement to discover the details. Evidently Brad had gone to Gwen's graduation to propose. So she read on with growing anticipation for a reenactment of the proposal. Instead, what followed was paragraph after paragraph of his hopes for them together as husband and wife, with not a word written about how and where he had popped the question. Neither was there the slightest hint as to Gwen's joy or surprise. She went into the next letter and found it to be more of the same – his plans for them in settling down after the war, dotted as his letters were with the happenings of the day. There was nothing at all regarding the proposal. Back to the engagement letter, she read it more slowly a second time, looking for any small detail that she might have missed. Nothing.

Ugh! So typical of a man!

But memory came back to rebuke her once more. Roy had proposed to her in the most deep, most sincere, most loving way in that train yard… and she had essentially blown him off. She went back to the next of Brad's letters with a small hollowness inside. He continued to express his excitement about having Gwen as his wife, along with comments on planes that she must have written to him about. There was more news of the happenings in Hawaii, and in closing, his longings to be with her.

Then came a letter whose pages had obviously been wadded up and then smoothed out again. Brad had decided to go for redeployment in the South Pacific over taking a cushy training assignment in California. In a long apology consisting of many pages, he laid out his reasons to her. There were so few experienced pilots like him to lend air support for the Marines slugging it out with the Japanese in the Solomons. That he would finally get to fly the Corsair in battle as a member of a newly formed squadron. That he could see his best friend George Meitner more regularly. And ultimately, that it was his duty. By the looks of these crumpled pages, it was clear to her what Gwen had thought of his decision. More letters from Brad repeated his reasons as he vowed to be careful. He repeatedly promised to come home safe, for nothing would be allowed to separate him from her.

The next letter switched tone. He still offered many earnest expressions of his love for her, but in shorter sentences and paragraphs. There were also fewer descriptions of his daily life, for he was back in the South Pacific flying combat missions with the Marines. He never wrote of his battles or how the war was going, only that he loved her… and that he loved flying the Corsair. It reminded him of her – beautiful, graceful in flight, mysterious in its ways, terribly formidable when necessary, but always a joy to fly. He was so proud of it and so proud of Gwen. Proud of her wings and proud to call her his own. He wrote to her as both pilot to pilot and man to woman, yet always as one in love with another.

With midnight coming on, a feeling of dread was growing in her, for the pile of letters had steadily gotten smaller. Amidst all the descriptions of flying and life in an island jungle, there were also references to their upcoming wedding. They obviously had decided on a huge West Texas affair, rather than be married in her hometown of Lansing, but the reason why was not clear. She sensed in his writing that there was something not quite right with Gwen. In some letters, he danced around with offhand references to an unkind thing her aunt had expressed in a letter of her own, whereas in others he went head-on at her bitterness. There was no sense being angry at the Marines… angry at his friend George Meitner… or angry at him. Declining to be rotated stateside was not a sign of wavering in his love for her. He knew she was going nuts, but he too was edgy about her flying. In another letter, he took pains to calm her down regarding the Army's refusal to induct the WASPs into the military, and then in another about Congress taking up the issue of whether to cancel the program altogether. He tried to get her to look beyond… into the future of them together. He had already arranged for his sister to purchase a piece of property along 4th Street on their behalf as a couple, with the ownership papers coming soon to Gwen for her signature. After the war, they would settle down in Lubbock and start that little hardware store he had always dreamed about. Then they could go flying together whenever they wished. But first… she really must settle that beef with her brother, for he and her parents were the only family Gwen had left.

She sprang to the edge of the couch, gripping this letter in both fists. Brad was writing about something that she had not at all expected. She went on more carefully now, sometimes having to read between the lines. It seemed to her that her own father and mother had been against America getting involved in another European war. They had years before signed some such affirmation in association with the Episcopal Church expressing their conscientious objection. Brad wrote that he could understand the embarrassment that Gwen's brother had brought to the family, as well as the lingering outrage she felt over being called a 'war monger' by him. That term had obviously not gone over well with the parents, who were very proud of their pilot-of-a-daughter. But Brad also wrote that it was time for her to mend those fences, for the war would soon be over. Surely she would want her entire family in Lubbock for their wedding.

She had no idea what to make of all this, having no memory at all of her father or mother. She also had no siblings from which to gauge the kind of grudge Gwen seemed to be holding against a brother. Surely if she had been in Gwen's place, she would have reached out to William and Betsy, for the bedrock of family was more important than anything.

With only two letters left in the pile, she took up the next, being careful not to allow her eyes to fall upon the last one before its time. She would read this second-to-the-last letter slowly, doing her best to pretend that it was just a normal correspondence connecting up all of the previous letters with a dream that never came true. Relieved at finding this particular letter to be more-or-less routine, she gladly reread again the brief recap of his squadron's week of boredom in waiting for their next mission, a description of rain so heavy that it blurred his sight of everything beyond ten feet away, and how he happened upon some exotic flower in the jungle bordering his base. All of this was decorated with his many expressions of love to her aunt. There was not a single word of tension in the whole thing.

She put the letter back into its envelope and braced herself for the last one. But the letter at the very bottom of the pile was not from Brad, for the handwriting on the envelope was clearly that of a woman's. She looked to the addressee. The writer had left off her name, providing only a street address in Lansing. The date stamped on the face was March 31st, 1944. She opened the envelope and went first to the bottom of the enclosed letter. There, penned so elegantly, was a signature of 'Betsy'... Betsy Forde... her own mother.

Dear Gwen,

We just heard the terrible news about your fiancée. How your heart must be breaking! There is no way for us to comprehend what you are going through, but please accept our deepest sympathies for your loss.

Gwen, it has been too long since you and I have spoken. In terrible times such as this, one needs their family. Please allow me to come to you. Please allow me to be a comfort to you. I promise it will only be a short visit. I only wish to offer words of consolation in hopes that one might be capable of helping you through another day of grief. If you would prefer, I shall sit quietly beside you, somber and still, if only for the opportunity to share your tears.

I know William feels the same way. He tells me that he has already written to you, so I will add my voice to his apology. Horrible things were said long ago between us all, and now William and I wish nothing more than to wipe clean the slate and start anew. That is my most earnest hope. Please, let us make amends, Gwen. Life is too precious – as I know you know deeper than most. We cannot take away your pain, but we can do our best never to add to it again.

Why was this letter here? Was it on purpose or by accident? Did Gwen ever respond? This silly breech between them over a war that had cost so many so much, was it ever healed? She could not remember her childhood well enough to know for certain… only that she had been raised by Gwen after her parents died. Perhaps there had been reconciliation between them. Perhaps they had grown so close that her parents naturally entrusted their daughter to Gwen. She wanted to believe this… but somehow knew deep inside that it was not true.

Even though it was already late in the night, she tore through the remaining contents of the box, searching for anything that might suggest at a resolution between her parents and her aunt. Ripping open letters that were obviously from her grandparents to Gwen, she carelessly pitched them aside one after the other when they disappointed her. Not one made mention of her father. Deeper into the box she dove, until all that was left within amounted to old newspaper clippings. She nonetheless dumped these out onto the coffee table and began sifting through them, desperate for the slightest of clues. It was all just nonsense about flying.

There had to be another box, for she vaguely recalled that there were many moved from Gwen's house. She immediately hurdled down the cellar stairs and began rifling through the shelves, shuffling aside Roy's things as if they were an afterthought to some puzzle already solved long ago. She hauled down box after box, knowing that she had already been through these things only a week prior. She still hoped that her grieving mind had missed something. But she did not find a single scrap of Gwen remaining on the shelves. Knowing it to be senseless, she nonetheless poked into every corner of the cellar, and then back upstairs to sift through the guest bedroom closet… and even those spaces previously inhabited by her boys. Nothing.

She would never know.

Lost in a new kind of despair, she returned to the family room couch and began cleaning up the mess she had made of Gwen's things. Restacking Brad's love letters, she re-tied the ribbon as before. While repacking the container, she strained to put a face on her mother… to add something soft and sincere that could bring to life more than the woman's words. Try as she might, not a single fragment of memory came to match the kindness of that letter. So she gave up on remembering her mother, and instead tried to recall the faces from those photographs that had once lined the old staircase. Somewhere in there was a fragment of what Brad Miller looked like. Again, nothing came other than some vague assurance from somewhere long ago that Roy had resembled his uncle. Funny that she had never asked him what had become of all those pictures when he remodeled the house. They were most definitely not in the cellar. Maybe never had been.

So much in her life had been lost… and so much more taken away. Yet if her parents had not died as they did, then she never would have met Roy. And if her aunt had not died when she did, then she would most likely have stayed in Chicago and never been reunited with him. Never come to love this house. Never flown a plane. And never had her three boys. Three boys she somehow found herself estranged from. It was so unfair that she should lose a husband so cruelly, and then have her sons turn on her as a result. But it was also not fair that they should lose a father and a mother. In no way would she allow that to happen. She would not perpetuate a senseless feud like that of Gwen with her father. Neither would she pass on a sad mystery to her future grandchildren. She would do now what she could to reconcile. She would fix the plane and fix her relationships… for oddly, they somehow went hand in hand.

CHAPTER

48

THE MEITNER ACADEMY
OF AVIATION

She wrote letters to her sons and their wives the next day, apologizing to each for her behavior at Roy's memorial service, for her months of despondency, and for her foolishness with the house's windows and doors. She took pains to thank each individual for their efforts on her behalf, and promised to do better at staying in touch. She followed these letters up with phone calls, all of which fortunately got answered. Each couple was cordial with her, yet nothing beyond a formal air that communicated things still were not right between them. She nonetheless made requests to visit them, seeing as they all had been to Lubbock so many times over the past six months. None took her up on the offer, but for differing reasons. Travis and Amanda, because it would take some time before they were settled in at San Jose; Chad and Stacey, because they their nights and weekends were already booked up; and Wade and Valerie, because their Austin apartment complex was being fumigated. Whether true or not, their excuses carried no warmth with them. She would have to be patient and allow time to soften their hardness toward her.

She had just gotten off a rather frustrating call with Wade, one in which he dully responded to her questions in one or two word answers, when her cell rang.

"Marna... we're ready with our conclusions regarding your Corsair. Which do you want first, the good news or the bad news?"

"The bad, of course."

783

"The drive shaft's got a crack in it."

"Oh no! That sounds terrible! Can it be repaired?"

"I'm afraid not. Some things broken can't be fixed."

Though gripped with disappointment, her mind inadvertently jumped back to the sinking feeling leftover from her conversation with Wade.

"So you're saying it's hopeless?"

"We've been debating for a week about the machining of a replacement. It'll be real expensive and time consuming. I'm sure you're not up for hearing about…"

"Stop toying with me, Benny! Can you restore my plane or not?!"

"Well… now for the good news. Marna… if you can cover the cost, then we've decided to do the job. Your plane will fly again."

She could not keep herself from screaming with joy… right into her phone's mouthpiece.

"Woe! My ears!"

"Sorry… I'm just so excited! When can we get started?"

"That's why I'm calling. We need to go over the work plan so you understand what you're getting yourself into. Then we'll settle on a timeline and a payment schedule. I'll get all that into a contract for you to look over. You know… it might be a good idea if you came here, that way we can go over the plane together as we discuss what needs to be done. Do you think you could…"

"Name the day, Benny, and I'll be there."

Her drive to Dallas was nothing. The miles flew by effortlessly, matching her growing anticipation. Having arisen before sunrise, she pulled into the parking lot of Bright Star Aviation at the Mesquite Airport on time for her meeting with Benny. Briefly scanning the single strip for any activity, she was only mildly disappointed at seeing none. She did pick up on a faint hint of avgas in the air. Most people would not appreciate the smell, but to her, it was better than the aroma of cookies baking. Smiling to herself, she hurried from her car into the front entrance. Two men were waiting to shake her hand – Earl, the mechanic who came to Lubbock, and Benny Stevens, an older, thinner and faster-speaking version of Earl.

"Marna… welcome to Bright Star. Have any trouble finding us?"

"Nope. It was pretty straightforward."

"Great. Before we begin, is there anything I can get you? Coffee? A coke? Or maybe you'd like to freshen up?"

"I'd really like to see my baby first."

She smiled with every bit of her excitement, and was pleased when they did likewise.

"I thought so. I'll have Earl walk you around the plane, and then the three of us can sit down to lunch… our treat… and start in on the plan. If we have time after, I'll take you across the way to our machine shop and show you some of the projects we're working on."

Benny parted from her, and Earl motioned her down a paneled hallway lined with framed photographs of various aircraft. She ignored them… at least mostly… as the greater part of her aviation appreciation was being reserved for seeing *her* plane. Through an end door, he led her into a hangar suitable for a single craft. All about the periphery were racks of hardware and other things that she had no real mind for looking at, as in the center of the space was her Corsair. Its wings were still off and nowhere to be seen… but that was not the thing that made her insides drop. The engine's cowling had been stripped away to expose the inner works. With a scaffolded platform built snuggly all about, the Corsair looked like some derelict building facing a long and painfully involved restoration process.

"Oh my!"

"Sorry… I should have prepared you. To the non-mechanic, the planes we work on always seem worse off than they really are. Yours is actually in pretty good shape. Shall we?"

He motioned her ahead to climb a ramp that paralleled the plane. The incline, running from the tail up toward the nose, was close enough so that she could run her fingers along the fuselage as she climbed. That simple act of touching her plane… making a connection between it and her hopes for it… somehow helped lessen her fears. From then on, the time seemed to have no meaning as Earl went about detailing the condition of her Corsair. Every step along the way, his optimistic can-do manner bolstered her spirits. He spoke matter-of-factly about rebuilding the engine, recalibrating the cockpit controls, restringing the cables and wiring, and refurbishing the hydraulics. It all seemed rather routine to him. So maybe she was seeing it too. Her plane was actually going to fly again.

With box lunches laid out on a table, she took a seat with Earl and Benny. This particular pilot's breakroom was like any other she had been in during her thirty years of flying – vending machines, a popcorn maker, a coffee pot by a sink, walls packed with flight memorabilia, and couches between end tables piled with aviation magazines. She registered it all with a quick, long-ago sort of familiarity, and then turned her full attention to Benny as he laid out his plan for her Corsair. She ate little, being much more interested in catching every detail of the work to be done. Barring any major surprises,

Earl expected her plane to be finished in less than eighteen months. They would schedule monthly visits for her along the way in which she could shadow Earl and his mechanics. Lastly, he handed over the contract of service between her and Bright Star.

"Best that you look it over before signing it. Just send it back as soon as you can, and we'll get started then. As we discussed, we'll need the first payment up front to get things going, but it'll be pay as the work gets done after that. Also… you should know that there's a clause in there regarding what happens if you default on your payments. Basically, we retain the plane as collateral."

"I see."

"I hope you understand. That's to protect us. We've had it happen before."

"I'm sorry to hear that, Benny… but it won't be a problem with me. As long as you're up front regarding these estimates, I can handle the full cost. But there's one thing that I'll want included with this contract. I feel so strongly about it that I'm having my lawyer write up a separate agreement for you to sign."

"Ahh… and what's that?"

"The first time the plane's tested, I expect to be the one flying it."

Working her way through the insanity of Dallas traffic, she was unable to spare a moment's thought for her time at Bright Star. Not until she had gotten out of the I20 congestion on the other side of Fort Worth could she giggle to herself over how Benny had practically freaked out when she insisted on being the first to fly the Corsair. She had been ready for that. Promptly revealing her plan for renewing her tailwheel certification, she then vowed to follow whatever training program his pilot deemed as appropriate. With eighteen months to get ready, she was confident in her ultimate ability to fly the plane. In fact, she had already been through both the Navy's flight manual and the pilot's handbook for the Corsair, as well as scoured the web and purchased every Corsair book she could get her hands on. All of that material gave her a fairly good notion of the rigors involved in flying the plane. After laying out her case, which included appealing to the nostalgic side of an aviation enthusiast, he eventually conceded… but only after obtaining her assurance that she would willingly backout if they concluded she was not ready for the plane's first test flight.

Near on dusk, she pulled off the interstate at Sweetwater and made for the fringe of Avenger Field. Sitting on the hood of her car, she stared out at the expanse before her, trying to imagine what it might have once looked like. She had seen plenty of black and white pictures of the place from back then… such a shame that the airfield was not at all the same. The barracks and training facilities had been torn down long ago, and even the current runways were laid out differently.

The women too were gone, along with their dreams and sacrifices.

Gwen flew planes here. She took off and landed on nearly a daily basis for four months of her life. Somewhere out there, she met Brad Miller for the first time… fell in love with him… and consented to be his bride. If she were alive today, she would be in her eighties. Not too old to remember… and not too old to dream.

With the sun having disappeared below the horizon off to her left, she wiped her eyes and slid from the hood of the car to complete the trip home.

After personally screening a dozen art dealers who specialized in sculptures, Yardley narrowed down the field to three he considered best suited for the job based on recommendations he had garnered from various museums. One individual in particular showed a strong interest in the reliefs, and took it upon himself to fly from New York for a closer examination of the Dallas one. This dealer then promptly called Yardley to say that he was on his way to Lubbock for a look at the sister relief.

All this, she learned on being awoken from a Sunday afternoon nap. With less than an hour of warning to get her house and herself in presentable order, she quickly straightened up things before running upstairs to change. She was just finishing with her hair when the front door bell rang. The man standing on her porch was rather short, yet well-dressed in suit and tie… in spite of the day's heat. To her, he very much looked like someone whose life had been spent in books, what with his steady eyes behind perfectly round lenses and a runway of a bald patch from his forehead all the way to the back. Most revealing was that he had his card out to her before a word had come from his mouth.

"Mrs. Meitner, I presume."

"Yes. Please call me Marna. And you must be…"

"Dr. Isaac Rosenblum. I believe your representative informed you of my arrival. Please excuse the short notice. I thought it best to examine both reliefs before my return. May I enter?"

"Oh, yes… of course. Come in. Can I get you something to drink? Sweet tea, perhaps?"

"That would be nice… with mint, if you have it."

"Coming right up. Let me take you to the relief first."

She walked him through the parlor and motioned toward the wall where her relief hung. Standing three feet off, Dr. Rosenblum did not display any kind of appreciation for what he was studying. Only his eyes moved, as they darted over every feature of the stonework. When she returned with his ice tea, he had a magnifying glass in his hand… and it suddenly occurred to her chagrin that she had never once considered using one herself. He spoke only haltingly to her… as if sparing a word from his lens might somehow compromise the findings.

"Clearly of a Renaissance theme… Fashioned much later… Likely the late 1700s… Not Neoclassical… Prevailing style of the times… Nothing like this piece… Different in every way… Works with such graceful expressions of motion… Arms and legs extended… That sort of thing. Lots of air… Many with mythological themes… Such as Monnot's *Andromeda and the Sea Monster.* A personal favorite of mine. It's in the Met."

"That's the Metropolitan Museum of Art in New York… right?"

"Yes. Have you been?"

"Once or twice over the years. But I don't remember the Andromeda statue."

He seemed to give her admission no thought, once more being occupied with the relief. She noticed then the notebook in his hand. Placing his glass of tea on the dining room table, she slyly peered over his shoulder. Within were many hand-drawn reproductions of her relief in Dallas. For several minutes, he went about making a comparison of this relief with his notes, murmuring occasionally in confirmation of some silent point of comparison between the two. Then rather abruptly, he snapped shut his notebook and stepped back to her, taking a sip of his tea before speaking.

"I'll have to verify the age, of course… scrape off a miniscule amount from the side for laboratory analysis… as I've already done with the sister in Dallas. My best guess… both together were likely uncommissioned works… which is hardly a fair descriptor. Any serious sculpture always starts out with meticulous models in clay or wax. The artist never begins with stone. Like a diva that has sung her aria countless times before ever taking to the stage, the sculptor will repeatedly practice the theme and style, varying size and perspective, before progressing to something permanent. By then, the concept has been perfected in the sculptor's mind and heart."

He turned to her before continuing.

"I am in agreement with the curators in Dallas. These two reliefs appear to be a throwback in style… likely an exercise by the student of some master. With input from my colleagues, I might be able to identify that master by comparing techniques. If you would allow me to do some additional research, I hope to provide you with an origin… as well as the pathway from there to your wall. That sort of information greatly increases the value of a piece… which makes it considerably easier to broker a sale. Otherwise…"

He dipped his head while shrugging his shoulders… gestures that she interpreted as an obvious reticence.

"And you're sure knowing all that's important?"

"Let me put it to you this way… when a museum's curator goes before a board of trustees regarding an acquisition, the quality of the piece is only one factor discussed. How that piece compliments their existing exhibits… and plays a part in communicating the overall message of the collection… those things are critical toward reaching a favorable decision. Same more-or-less goes for a private collector. Right now, your relief in Dallas has no history to go with it… which is fine with their board, seeing as it's on loan from you. If we can provide a tangible story… which does not necessarily require identification of the sculptor… then we greatly increase the attractiveness of the two reliefs. Sometimes having the artist unknown brings a certain air of romance."

"I see… Hey… did Cliff Yardley pass on to you the appraisal my aunt got some thirty years ago?"

"Yes. I have that and a copy of the article regarding her purchase from the previous owner. If those individuals are still available, I hope to track them down… but it'll take time."

"So, what're you thinking… I mean about how much time it'll take?"

"Well… from past experience… I'd say six months minimum. More likely a year."

By the way she was able to hold his eyes, it seemed that he was being upfront with her. A year would be far too long of a time for keeping up with her payments on the Corsair.

"Okay… but I'd rather not be parted from this relief in the meantime."

"Oh, I don't need to bring it with me. That wouldn't assist in the sale… nor would it be safe. If I were to engage a prospective buyer, I would be bringing them here… with your permission, of course. Now… if you don't mind, I'd like to make some detailed drawings and take a few photographs, just as I did with its sister in Dallas. That should suffice for now. By the way, I don't need to see the back. They tell me there are no distinguishing markings on the one in Dallas other than its name – *Sulla Terra*. That is a fact revealing in its own right. There's an obvious Italian connection here. So that's where I'll start my investigation. Now, should you decide to engage my services, then I'll…"

"Dr. Rosenblum… let's make it official."

Aware that she was being very Texan, she stuck out a hand to him. To her surprise, he blushed before receiving it. His grip was tight. Not at all soft like she had been expecting.

"So… once I identify a suitable buyer, I want you to understand that you need not be parted with this relief until you're ready."

"What're you saying... that I can still have it on my wall even after it's been sold?"

"I've brokered many deals where the art remained in the owner's possession for a prescribed period of time as part of the terms of the contract."

"Really?! That would be fantastic! Though it doesn't seem quite right. Who pays for something without receiving it?"

"Suppose you had the *Mona Lisa* to sell. I can guarantee you there's not a museum in the world that wouldn't come to terms with your wishes to keep it on your wall until the day you died."

"Yeah... but this isn't the *Mona Lisa*."

"Doesn't have to be. As long as it's story is compelling enough... and the buyer is suitably motivated."

"By you, of course."

He smiled without an ounce of sheepishness.

"That is correct. A ten percent sales commission can be a significant motivator... even for a lover of art such as myself."

Having debated the issue with herself while he took pictures, she finally decided to be upfront with him. Once he was ready to go, she ushered him around to the hangar side of the porch to explain her situation. Repeatedly gesturing toward the empty hangar as proof, she revealed her intention of exchanging one piece of history for the restoration of another. No doubt he thought her crazy to be valuing a fifty eight year old hunk of metal over two exquisite pieces of two hundred year old art. But he did seem to understand her passion for setting both free. With that, he promised his best effort at expediting the sale, starting with a pitch to the Dallas museum that already had half of her earth-and-sky story.

After he drove off, she returned to her parlor to do some serious thinking. Outside of a quick sale, she needed a backup plan for making her Corsair payments until the reliefs were sold. Having already liquidated her investments to cover the first installment, she was now seriously reconsidering a second mortgage on the house. That was a move of desperation opposed to by a slew of memories... including one of her sitting on the back porch looking up at the stars.

Andromeda and the sea monster... what a blast from the past! I completely forgot that I used to sit out there hunting for that little blob of light. Funny how things change... Back then, I had so wanted to get out of Lubbock... but now... I can't think of any place on earth I'd rather be. This is home.

Except... I miss Roy.

She went to bed that night in an uneasy state of mind. It was not so much the house, the relief or the plane, as it was the absence of Roy in her life. She could certainly use his wisdom in making this decision. Her day-to-day without him may have gotten easier in time, but living without him never would. Accepting the fact that she lived alone, ate her meals alone, slept and woke alone, and did everything else that life required all alone… was not easy. The odd quiddity to the word was that she had no one with whom to share its sad meaning.

She now faced the need for mastering those tasks that had once belonged to him. She was doing both the bills and the taxes… and with April upon her, she was having a devil of a time collecting up the necessary paperwork for her accountant to complete the latest return. With a new EpiPen in her back pocket, she had even undertaken the yard work and some minor repairs around the house. Whenever she struggled with a job that had previously been his, she found herself remembering him with appreciation for all of his diligence. He had maintained the upkeep of this house with pride and attentiveness. But since he was no longer here to show her how things were done, she had to develop her own methods. This often led her to a bittersweet outcome – the satisfaction of discovering that she could do a new task on her own, coupled with the disappointment of having missed out on the simple pleasure of learning how it was done from him.

Living without Roy brought a shaky uncertainty about the future that required her going moment by moment. Whatever sadness a night might bring, a spring sunrise had a surprising way of stabilizing her. No matter how she felt on going to bed, there was the sun creeping above the eastern horizon to reset her mood. She was coming to depend upon the faithfulness of each day's new light. So whenever the urge came on her to retreat into her nook, she need only step out onto her porch and track the day from the east around the front of her house to the west. The early morning brightness always brought on a clear midday blue, which in turn yielded to a sunset of so many spectacular reds, yellows and oranges, all crammed into a layer between the horizon and a deep purple above. And if a melancholy tinge still persisted in her heart with the coming of evening, she would move around back and allow those twinkles in a sea of black to remind her that all darkness must eventually give way to another day.

Soon, she would be back to flying, having signed herself up with the guy who had taken over Butch's operation when he retired. Come summer, she would throw herself into refreshing her training with the ultimate of taildraggers – the Piper Cub. She had never been up in this small plane, but was confident that her experience with the Fairchild would make it easy. But getting to the summer meant getting through May, which was something she feared would pose the biggest challenge to her since the airshow. That month began with Roy's birthday and ended with their anniversary… both to be commemorated for the first time without him. She was sure that would make all of the days in between so very stormy.

To her disappointment, it rained that month like no other May in memory. Without being able to see a sunrise or sunset, she was left with so many sad clouds hanging over her thoughts. Sitting in her nook as the rain beat against her house, she repeatedly fought through the memory of having lost him. She only made it through those days by being proactive. Each morning, she got out of the house for a time… shopping, coffee with a friend, working out at the gym, or just going on a drive. Anything to avert a tendency for moping about. In considering some symbol that she might latch onto in keeping herself turned in the right direction, she decided to fly the flag again. Yet feeling unsure of her consistency for daily attending to the raising and lowering of it, she engaged an electrician who ran conduit out to the circle and set up sensor-activated spotlights aimed upward at the flag. Now it could be flown continuously. Its ripple became a comfort to her. Just a soft reminder that she should not think of herself as being completely alone. Similarly, the reflections from the spotlights at night could easily be seen through her bedroom windows, making the dark a bit easier to endure. Sometimes, she sat on her front porch just to admire how her flag flew proudly on the tall pole. That was something she could emulate. To be as bright and as resilient as those two together. As one, they flickered and flexed in Lubbock's relentless wind, but never failed.

She did one other highly unusual thing to survive the month of May. From time to time since the airshow, her thoughts had ventured back to CP. Both the warning he had given her and the effort he had made to draw her out were worthy of some sign of appreciation. In calling to offer him her thanks, she ended up accepting an invitation from Marianne for dinner that evening. She went there feeling slightly apprehensive since they were married and she was widowed. Yet chatting it up with them in the kitchen as Marianne finished preparing dinner, she felt surprisingly at ease because both were so obviously steering the conversation away from anything Roy-related. They just let her ramble on about the Corsair and her reliefs. Then into dinner, she suddenly found herself speaking openly for the first time about Roy's death. Somehow, Marianne's chicken cacciatore kept her from crying while she spilt out words about how her despair had clouded her mind. She knew that CP was aware of her trying to get herself stung, but he said not a word about it. With dessert came a fortunate shift in the conversation, as she more eagerly shared her plans to fly the Corsair. It was only then that she remembered their granddaughter's interest in planes.

"You know… looking back… I think I would have enjoyed hanging out with you two at that airshow. It would have been fun. I'm sorry I wasn't… in a proper state of mind to talk with Melissa about being a pilot."

The two immediately looked at each other with such knowing smiles that she could not help but think they were waiting for this moment.

"What?"

"Marna… do you think you might still be willing to do that?"

"Sure. Why not?! Next time Lana has her over, just give me a call and I'll…"

"We were actually thinking about something… slightly different."

She instantly saw that look in CP's eyes, somewhat mellowed by age, yet nonetheless clear enough for her to know that he was up to something. Turning to Marianne, she nodded back to her husband.

"You know… this guy was the sneakiest… trickiest… pain-in-the-ass in school. How is it that you came to marry such a troublemaker?"

"Purely humanitarian, Marna. I knew well the boy you're talking about… and there's still a good bit of that imp in him. Always popping out of some hidey-hole to scare the life out of me! But he did change. I guess it all started when his father passed and he had to…"

"Ehh… let's not get into that."

She noticed him shoot a hand over to his wife's… yet not to grip it with an insistence that she stop. Instead, what she saw was something like a gentle plea.

"You know, Marna… I was pretty cruel to you as a kid. I'm… really sorry… especially for the time when I… took you out to…"

She knew what was coming and cut across his words for the sake of all three of them. Yet out of the corner of her eye, she was surprised that Marianne did not seem at all confused about what was going on.

"Forget it, CP. If you have to apologize for everything bad you did as a kid, then we'll be here all night and deep into the morning."

"Good point. Thanks… a lot. It's always been a… an embarrassment to me. So… let me get back to my request. Melissa's finishing up second grade at Westside Elementary, and her class has career day next week."

"Second graders have career days?!"

"It's more like parent show-and-tell. Turns out… neither Nick or Lana can make it, so they asked me. But I know that Melissa's never been comfortable hearing about what her grandpa does for a living. You know… Dead things, Mikey. Dead things."

"Huh?!"

"Oh… sorry. That's just a line from a kid's movie that Melissa's crazy about. She's made me watch it over and over. I really don't get what she sees in it. Anyway… I was wondering… would you be interested in standing in for me?"

"To talk about dead things?"

"Ha, ha… real funny. You know what I'm asking. Would you be up for talking to her class about being a pilot? It'll only take a few minutes… five tops. After all, they're only second graders. And it doesn't have to be polished or anything like that. Just a bit of your experiences. You know… you may not think of it this way, Marna… but you… and women like you… really have forged new ground for those to follow. What you've accomplished has helped open up aviation for girls like Melissa. That's worth sharing."

"I… I guess so. I mean… I've never thought of it that way. I just loved flying."

Quick as she could, she ran through her life in flight, seeking for any kind of validation to CP's kind words. She had flown all kinds of planes… props to jets… met so many interesting pilots… been to countless airfields… with a few near-death experiences thrown in. Try as she might, all she could get excited about was the now. In fact, the only plane she could picture clearly in her mind was the Corsair. Whatever she had accomplished in life, it was nothing compared to seeing that plane fly again. As CP and Marianne just sat there waiting, both holding their dessert forks suspended above their cheesecake, she gave in to her impulsive side.

"Sure… why not?! What the heck… I'll do it."

By agreement, she met Marianne at the front doors of Westside Elementary, and with her was another woman… younger, yet clearly resembling Marianne.

"Yay, Marna! You made it! You remember Lana, don't you… she's our oldest."

"Yes. Hello, Lana… but I thought CP said you couldn't make it?"

"That's Dad for you. Truth is… I've spent so much time volunteering in Melissa's class that the kids already know me. Oh… I see you've brought your laptop."

"Yes. Melissa's teacher… I forgot her name…"

"Mrs. Ingersoll."

"Yeah… she said I could give a little slideshow of the planes I've flown. I've also got some audio clips so the kids can get a feel for the sounds of flight."

From there, they walked together to the classroom, and she was introduced along with the other adults lined along a chalkboard. She waited as an agronomist, a construction worker, a software programmer, and the owner of a bowling alley all went ahead of her. When it came her turn, she somehow found herself speaking as one from a long line of aviators going back to her aunt and grandfather. As she highlighted her experiences, the room's projector flashed images of the planes she had flown… ending with the Corsair and her plans to add this one to her list. In all, she spoke for only a few minutes, but spent much more time answering questions from this class of second graders. Their raw enthusiasm and uninhibited curiosity was so refreshing.

On leaving the class at the end, the teacher asked if she would be willing to speak again if the opportunity presented itself. Not really expecting anything of the request, she expressed her willingness and then left for her car. Pulling from the school's parking lot, her mind was already on other things. Getting restarted on her flying… whether the bank would approve her loan request… and what was happening at that very moment with her Corsair.

Flying a Piper Cub was nothing like a Learjet, but not at all in the bicycle-to-Ferrari comparison her instructor had joked about when he signed the tailwheel endorsement into her logbook. To her, being up in that single engine prop was like living childhood all over again. So if that was what he meant, then perhaps she agreed after all. The complexity of flight she got to re-experience with this plane's simplicity, along with its engine noises and getting pitched about by every little air current, it all somehow felt like play… which was something that she had never been very good at. That was partly why she went on booking time in this plane even though her recertification was done. Of course, it was more than just the fun, as she wanted to keep her skills fresh until Benny was prepared for her to train on a T-6 Texan. Now that would be true fun! Once she had proven herself capable of flying that iconic military trainer, then he would finally be convinced that she could handle the Corsair's first test flight.

Gliding along in the Cub on a westerly heading, she set about taking a more-or-less leisurely circuit around Lubbock County. Amidst the blocks of farmland below her were a few scattered crop circles, not nearly as prevalent in the region as she recalled them to have once been. It was probably a good sign. Less water being used. But their absence still made her sad. It was as if so many bright green faces to the landscape had blinked out of her memory into a brownish haze. Shifting her eyes up to that portion of the sky not blocked by the Cub's overhead wings, she found that the clouds were just as beautiful as they had always been. Checkered board below and white fluffs with flat bottoms above… and here she slid peacefully between the two. There was nowhere she needed to be and nothing she needed to accomplish. She could go on like this forever. Just her… the plane… and that horizon teasing her onward.

I've so missed this!

With a bag on the passenger seat beside her and a hotel reservation in her back pocket, she set out for her first overnight trip in nearly a year, eager to spend two full days thinking about nothing other than her airplane. Actually… this visit to Dallas had two purposes. Spending time with Earl and his mechanics, and meeting with Dr. Rosenblum to discuss her reliefs. Weaving herself off the Loop onto Southeast Drive with 84 just a mile or so ahead, she chuckled over her inability to call her art dealer by his first name. Through much clever bargaining, Dr. Rosenblum had negotiated the sale of both reliefs to the same Dallas Museum. She was more than delighted that the trustees had outright bought *Sulla Terra* for a generous amount, with a promissory note for the future purchase of *Fino al Cielo* to be carried out at an already-agreed-upon price. She could still visit Earth anytime she wanted, and Sky would stay put on her dining room wall until she was ready to be parted with it. On top of all that, she now had the funds needed for completion of the Corsair… all without having to take out a loan on her house. For the first time in a very long while, she actually felt as if she did not have a care in the world… other than that her sons were still being jerks. Not a one of them wanted her to visit.

Just be patient, Marna. They'll eventually come around.

She practically had a heart attack on stepping within the Bright Star hangar to behold what had become of her plane. With the engine completely removed and the cockpit stripped bare… it was as if they had cut the plane's head off and gutted it like a fish. Benny must have seen the horror on her face, for he was quickly at her side.

"Don't worry, Marna! Things are going really well. Your plane's actually in pretty good shape. Like I told you on the phone, we'll be doing most of the machining here, but the pieces'll be reassembled over at Love Field. I'm going to hand you off to Earl in a minute so he can go over the details, but there's something I want to show you first. Let's have some fun."

He led her back the way they had come… down the photograph-lined hallway and then through a door into a darken room. With him cutting on the lights, she found herself standing before a rather large, open-faced box, it having a seat within. She immediately recognized what this was from having once been trained on one. It was no big deal to her, but Benny was bopping about beside her with such excitement as he turned its power on.

"You're not going to believe this! It just came in last week! I got it on loan from the University of Connecticut! Know what it is?"

"Ahh… aside from the obvious… it's a flight simulator. So what?!"

"Marna… this is a one-of-a-kind!"

Then she noticed the stick… and realized that modern simulators all had yokes. Her eyes quickly panned over the computerized display of gauges.

"You're not serious?! Is this what I think it is?! A Corsair simulator?! No way! Is it realistic?"

"That's what you're going to find out."

"Meaning what?"

"Did you know that the Connecticut legislature has declared the Corsair to be the state's official plane?"

"Benny… don't go through the back door on me. Out with it."

"Sorry… I've been keeping this a secret from you. I've been working over the years with university faculty there who're funded by grants to preserve the state's wartime history. I assume you know that a good number of Corsairs were constructed there?"

"Sure. I've read all about that. But what's that got to do with me and this simulator?"

"Well… as one of the few owners in the country of an operational Corsair, they came to me some time back about using my plane in conjunction with their studies. When I told them about you… about you're wanting to fly your restored plane… they practically jumped at the possibility of taking part in your training. It's an incredible opportunity for them… and you too. Assuming you don't mind being a guinea pig."

"They want to study me?!"

"Not so much you as how well their simulator prepares you. Is that a problem?"

"Well… no… I guess not. If it helps me learn how to fly my own plane."

"I was hoping you'd say that… because they want to get started as soon as you're ready."

But Benny simply would not allow her to touch it just yet, saying that it had not been calibrated for use. She would not get that opportunity until her next visit. So she went back to hang out with Earl and his guys as they fished cable through her plane.

On her next visit to Bright Star, they had the pilot's seat back in and were working on the electrical wiring. She was enjoying watching them… until Benny came to drag her into the simulator room. Via phone, she met the graduate students working on the project and got her first chance to sit in the simulator. Initially, she was a bit disappointed to discover that its capabilities were limited to the throttle, aileron, elevator and rudder functions, but soon found it to be much better than that. The grad students had designed in a computer interface that allowed them to program in realistic tension responses mimicking what she might expect from a variety of landing and takeoff conditions. She was sure it was not the same as the real thing, but having the stick in her hand and her feet on the rudder pedals got her really excited for being in her own plane again.

Now if only they could have built in the engine sounds!

For the most part, their study of her responses was done remotely through an internet interface. Over time, she got to know the graduate students by their voices. The two, both Asians whose names she could never pronounce properly, daily walked her through landings, takeoffs, and a variety of maneuvers. It felt so odd not having a visual connection to either of them. Not at all how she had been raised as a pilot.

Somehow, being trained remotely accentuated a struggle she was having with her sons. Not one of them cared to have her come for a visit. Not even Chad, who was only two hours from Lubbock. The three couples were still so frosty toward her. She nonetheless continued her efforts at calling them every weekend, for she was determined to push through their bad attitudes. If she could not regain their devotion, then she would at least try buying it back. The calendar gave her ten opportunities to do this – their six birthdays, three anniversaries, and next Christmas. Starting with Wade and Valerie's upcoming first anniversary, she opened her checkbook and her imagination to the things that she knew were special to them. She gave her youngest son and his wife an all-expense paid weekend at the Grand Ol' Opry in Nashville. For the first time in memory, Valerie actually put more than two sentences together at one time over the phone in expressing her gratitude for the gift.

She interrupted her pattern of training only once that summer – to commemorate the anniversary of Roy's passing. She purposely did not visit his gravesite for fear of being overwhelmed by the memories of despair she had experienced there. Instead, she made a week out of going to the fun places in town that they had frequented together, just to remember being with him. She walked the rail lines, returned to the school grounds they had both attended, and made stops at their favorite haunts about town. Some of those places had so changed that she was disappointed to find the association with Roy as rather weak, whereas others threw her back in time to such sweet moments with him. Her only truly poor choice had been to re-enter the closed up appliance store. She had expected to encounter ghosts from the past, but also many fond memories. Instead, she left rather disgusted with the place. The back of the store had graffiti all over it, and the lock on the rear door took forever to open.

Inside, she found the emptied-out interior to be so dusty and dank. Not at all the ship-shape enterprise that her husband had run during his day. She left without exploring either the main showroom or warehouse.

She kept up her training through the fall, but also took time out to promote aviation to school children. The third grade teacher of CP's granddaughter had heard about her life as a pilot and asked if she would serve as a volunteer chaperone for a field trip to Lubbock's glider museum. This led to more opportunities for visiting classrooms and speaking about women in aviation. She made the circuit of Lubbock's elementary and middle schools that academic year, giving over and over the same presentation that spanned from her aunt's experiences as a WASP through to her own as a corporate pilot. From both girl and boy, the youthful inquisitiveness she encountered was a constant fuel to her still grieving heart. Not one child ever expressed anything other than awe that she, a fifty six year old woman, had set herself toward flying the Corsair. So neither should she.

The new calendar year brought the first test firing of her plane's rebuilt engine. They had already spun the new shaft several times without issue, so Earl was satisfied enough to remount the prop and repeat with battery power. With no noticeable hitch or wobble to the blades, he called her to say it was time for the true test. She arrived at Bright Star in the first week of February to find that her Corsair's engine had been bolted within a huge metal frame connected to something that resembled a flatbed train car… except there were no wheels or rails to it. In a control room of sorts constructed behind the engine, more-or-less where a pilot would sit, they had set up a panel consisting of a simple starter, a fuel-to-air control, a throttle, and various engine gauges. She watched excitedly as one of Earl's guys primed the fuel pump, and then Earl turned to her.

"We'll get the shaft spinning on the battery, then I'll give you the sign. Just hit that button."

"I get to be the one starting it?!"

"Of course. It's your plane."

Suddenly filled with an eagerness that eclipsed her previous fear over something going wrong, she held a determined finger over the red button as Earl engaged the prop. The blades responded into a slow clockwise creep. Then he nodded… and she jabbed the button. Immediately, the engine coughed out smoke from its exhaust manifold, encompassing the small control booth in a black cloud. But as if waking from a dark sleep, the cloud was dispersed as the blades rapidly spun. The rumble became louder and louder as Earl steadily gave the engine throttle… right up to the point where the whole platform was fervidly vibrating. As he went about making his various system checks, she allowed her ears to be filled with the delight of the engine's sound, at the same time keeping her eyes glued to the spinning disk before her. It was the most marvelous expression of power she had ever experienced. The test firing went on until the ideal oil temperature was reached for each of Earl's benchmark rmp levels… and then all too soon, her Corsair's engine was shut down. Earl said he would know for sure after a detailed inspection, but his initial read was encouraging. Smooth rotation, stable pressures and temperatures, and excellent sound.

I can't believe it! My plane's actually going to fly!

The months following the firing of the Corsair's engine went by in a blur. She upped the frequency of her Bright Star visits to a weekly event, as she was eager to witness the progress of her plane's reconstruction. She took loads of pictures, and began assembling these into a photo album for a time-lapse chronology of her plane's rebirth. Her weeks soon became a juggling act of those visits to Dallas, and requests that she speak in Lubbock-area classrooms, scouting groups and women's organizations about her exploits in aviation. On occasion while in Dallas, she also took time out to visit Earth. Somehow, she felt she owed this relief a measure of the affection she had once shown it while living there.

Moving into the second summer of the Corsair's rebuild, she was given two weeks of training on a T6 Texan. Actually, she spent twice as long learning about the plane's operation beforehand, and then paid a considerable sum for the experience of flying it. Overall, she found the Texan to be a regular beast… though nothing she was incapable of mastering. Benny then proclaimed that she was ready to start ground training on the Corsair. For this, she was introduced to his F4U-4 for the first time, it being housed in a hangar at Love Field. With a more powerful engine and a longer span to its four bladed prop, his plane was clearly more advanced than her F4U-1D. As he walked her about his Corsair, she had to fight off a strong temptation to be jealous. Calling to mind instead all that her plane meant to her, she took that silly emotion and turned it into thankfulness. A week of hands-on education into the systems of his plane would be indispensable toward preparing her for hers.

During that week of training with Skip Lancaster, one of Benny's pilots, she had an unexpected question put to her. Skip was discussing the optimal oil pressures for the range of rpm settings for ideal cruising, making contrasts between the Double Wasp engines of the two planes, when he offhand inquired as to what she was ultimately planning on doing with her Corsair.

"Honestly… I haven't really thought that far ahead. Preparing myself to fly it has taken up all of my thoughts. I'm not planning on keeping it… but I haven't considered selling it either. Which I guess I'm up for… to the right sort of buyer. Why do you ask? Do you have someone who's interested?"

"Actually, I think I have just the person you're looking for."

"And that would be you?"

"Only in my dreams! I definitely don't have that kind of cash. But I do know a guy right here in Dallas who'd pay just about whatever you might ask. Of course, I'd have the added benefit of being able to fly it for him in airshows."

"That would be amazing!"

But in truth, the suggestion made her sad. She had put so much effort into seeing her plane restored, and in learning how to fly it, that she had not invested an ounce of thought into what it would be like afterward. Losing the Corsair would obviously not be as painful as losing Roy… but the inevitability of being parted from it somehow brought back that feeling. A hopelessness that was impossible for her to see beyond. She told herself not to be so stupid. Flying the Corsair would be a dream come true. But some dreams did have their dark awakenings.

She felt ready to fly her rebuilt plane, had the confidence of her training, and the support of so many people who had prepared her for this moment. Everything she needed to know had already been planned out – the course headings, the climb to a cruising altitude, engine rpm for the desired airspeeds, and the management of every system on the plane. So on the night before leaving to Dallas for the Corsair's test flight, she was as ready as she would ever be. She even knew exactly what she was going to wear. But none of those assurances were strong enough to keep her from being scared to death of messing it all up. Somehow, a face from long ago came back to her. Billings' words on her last day at WYNG rang crystal clear in her mind.

"We want you to watch this whenever you're afraid about something. Watch it and remember just how tough you are… that even a crazed Chicago mob couldn't hold you back."

She immediately went to her computer in search of the video file of her younger self. Shortly after finding the cartridge among Gwen's things, she had arranged for it to be digitized at a Lubbock TV station. They emailed the file back to her, but she had not yet found the courage to watch it. Every time she had gone to it, something about being faced with a younger, more beautiful version of herself made her put off the viewing for later. Now, after it had sat untouched on her computer for a year, she was finally ready.

The video quality was a bit grainy, but crystal clear in bringing back the memory of that day. The first few seconds were of a riot gathering behind barricades at the bottom of some steps, but then the camera panned from off the mob and onto her. She immediately lost her breath at the sight of herself. So young… so beautiful… and so full of confidence in the face of a storm not thirty feet off in the background. Then her own voice came chiming through the computer's speaker… so sweetly Texan and yet so very authoritative.

"This is Marna Forde of WYNG news reporting from City Hall."

Her younger self went on with such boldness to proclaim that Mayor Daley would use whatever force was necessary to protect his city.

She watched the clip over and over, each time honing in on a different attribute of herself. The way her lips moved as she spoke… The steadiness with which she held that microphone… The determination in her eyes as she made her message known… The clear, smooth complexion of her face, neck and chest… The airy, wind-blown look of her short hair… without a hint of gray to it. Even that casual way in which she glanced back at the mob halfway through her spiel was inspiring. All of the ambition came back to her, along with the optimism and clarity of her young dreams. So full of life… and yet so very inexperienced in it. What would that younger self say if she were told that in thirty years she would be flying that same Corsair airplane that she left behind on fleeing Lubbock for Chicago?

It probably wouldn't even of registered with me… seeing as I was about to be beat up and teargassed.

But what would the reaction be of that younger self to hear that she was now wavering at the challenge? More than a challenge. The fulfillment of a dream!

I could never face myself again knowing that.

The last time through, she noticed the absence of a medical alert bracelet on the hand holding the microphone, and realized that this younger version of herself would soon go through so much hell of her own making. Though it was preposterous, she nonetheless found herself warning that sweet young woman on the screen about the heartaches coming her way. But she would survive… because of a miracle and the forgiveness of the man she had abandoned.

No way am I screwing up like that again. I'm flying this plane, no matter what!

Arriving at Bright Star's hangar at Love Field, she found several television vans parked in its lot. She barely got into the door before being swarmed by reporters and camera crews. They all right off peppered her with questions about how it was that a woman at her stage in life, a recent widow too, had decided to restore a World War II relic for the purpose of flying it only once. And there was Benny standing in the background with a huge smile on his face. She ignored him… for now… and concentrated on the reporters. Recently reminded that she had spent time on the other side of a microphone, she understood that these professionals had a story to complete on deadline. So she answered as enthusiastically as she could, smiling the whole while for their cameras. Fortunately, it was soon time for her to get her preflight briefing from Skip. She broke away from the reporters to make a slight detour pass Benny.

"I don't know how… but I'll get even with you for this. Now I'm twice as nervous as when I showed up."

"Hey… who could blame a guy?! You're a gold mine of free publicity. Just… don't crash the plane."

"Thanks for the vote of confidence. See you on the ramp."

Of course, the reporters were waiting for her beside the Corsair when she was done with her briefing, and each one wanted to take more pictures with her standing before the plane. At least Skip was there to shoo them away, saying that they would have to wait until after she returned. She did the walkaround, thankful that Skip stayed at her side so she was not tempted to look over at the reporters. Having been in and out of the Corsair's cockpit so many times over the last few months in conducting engine and system checks, she had gotten quite good at maneuvering her way onto and off of the sill… almost to the point where she no longer had to think about what she was doing. But this time was different. Everyone on the ramp was watching her. Maybe even filming her.

Relieved to have climbed in without incident, she got strapped down and tucked her hair in around her helmet so as not to get in her way. A smiling wave toward the camera crews, and then she started in on her prestart checklist.

Engine controls first…

She scanned over the gauges to the right side of the instrument panel, making sure that everything was well.

Flight controls next…

She checked that the break was set before working the stick and the rudder, verifying free movement in each.

Ignition switch to off… Mixture control to idle cut-off… Boost the fuel pump… Confirm suction… Check for hydraulic pressure… Open the cowling flaps…

She put the battery in the on position and then called out for clearance in order to send the prop through a few slow rotations for purging the cylinders of exhaust. Adjusting the fuel-to-air ratio for a rich setting, she engaged the starter and heard the engine turn over as the blades lurched into action, picking up speed to the point of spinning wildly. As the cloud of black smoke around the cockpit got dissipated to the rear by the Corsair's wind, she paused to take in that wonderful roar. The sound was perfect… and eager. Through several cycles, she brought the engine rpm level up and down, watching the various pressure and temperature gauges for their appropriate responses. Everything was behaving just as it had on her previous engine checks. She then lowered the wings and raised the flaps.

With the warm-up finally accomplished, she called ground control, and promptly received back an acknowledgement of her intentions. As the controller wished her luck, the last words of encouragement that Skip said in the briefing came back to her.

"Marna… you're an experienced pilot who's more than capable of flying this bird. So… you and her go have some fun."

We can do this!

She slid the canopy closed and began to move off the ramp. With the Corsair having a rather long nose and a cockpit set back from the wings, it took her a week or so before she got good at using the rudder and brake for taxiing about. Now, she felt it no big deal to zigzag herself out to the holding position. Once there, she ran through her preflight checklist, cycling the engine rpm up and down as before. With the last item checked off, she reminded herself to trust in her training.

This is the moment we've been hoping for.

She called up for tower approval.

"This is Corsair niner-three-niner-november holding at one three left, requesting clearance for takeoff."

The seconds ticked by, amassing into near a full minute without a reply, which just enhanced her fidgetiness to get going. Everyone up there certainly knew that she, newly turned fifty seven, was about to take off in a renown warbird on the maiden flight of its restored state. What were they all thinking?

To take cover because I must be crazy!

"Corsair niner-three-niner-november… you're cleared for takeoff on one three left. The skies are yours."

Opening up the throttle, she felt the power of the Corsair tear her down the runway. She gave it a bit of right rudder on sensing the wheels lose their grip on the earth. She was up. Retracting the landing gear, she banked into a ninety degree heading before checking her engine pressure and temperature. All was good. Steadily climbing to twenty three hundred feet, she bent her concentration toward clearing the Dallas airspace. Adjusting the rpm level to give herself a pleasant one seventy knot airspeed, she breathed easy for the first time. She had done it. She was flying a Corsair. Her Corsair! The very same plane she had lovingly ran her fingertips along some thirty five years before.

If asked back then what it would be like to fly this plane, she would probably have said something akin to riding a dragon. How utterly wrong she would have been! This beautiful bird – it flew like a dream! The ailerons and rudder… they were so smooth… so responsive… so light and airy to the touch. She had even been expecting that 'whistling death' sound from which the Japanese had fearfully referred to this plane. She obviously heard how the air was flowing through the engine's cooling system, but to her, the voice of the Corsair was life… even though its engine really did roar with dragon power!

The plane's blood was her blood. Its sinews flexed as her own. Every move of it was her living through it. Wonders of wonders, she swam through a sea of pure blue! To break away… to bank… to roll… to dive… to soar faster and higher… above, upon a carpet of white… and to feel again that heart of hers burn on with delight! She and this plane… together they could forever chase after that thin line, for she wanted never to come back down again.

But it was time to adjust the fuel mixture, do the retrimming, decrease her airspeed down to seventy knots, extend her landing gear, get her flaps set, and then… land. Too soon, she felt the gentle jolt of all three wheels making contact at once. Quickly checking her watch, she was surprised to find that the flight's duration had only been thirty five minutes.

Funny… it seemed like time stood still.

"Well… congratulations, old girl. We did it!"

She had hardly gotten herself down to the ramp before being swarmed by reporters. Still in a complete daze of euphoria, she bubbled out every answer in trying to reconstruct an experience for them that she would surely be reliving for many years. When they had gotten enough of her, Benny had the wherewithal to escort the mob off the ramp. She was finally alone with her plane.

"Don't pay any attention to them. You're not a forgotten rabbit pulled out of a hangar-sized hat. You're also not some… relic. A fragment of history left over to be studied. You're a mighty warbird, through and through… and I'm so terribly proud of you."

She ran her hand along the fuselage beneath the pilot's toehold, releasing words to this plane that were meant solely for her own hearing.

"The moment's come to say goodbye. You've meant so much to me… and I'll never forget you. But you could be so much more in the hands of someone who would fly you more often than I ever could. Someone who's actually got the skills to take you to the fullness of all you can be. More than anything, I want people to marvel at you while you fly, so I'll… be leaving you with him. I promise he'll take good care of you. Thank you… you beautiful airplane.

Thank you for bringing meaning to my life."

She felt the tears coming and quickly turned away, not understanding why it was so important that she not cry before this plane.

That night, she watched the TV news from her motel room in Dallas, and then read in the morning paper a brief article with a photo on her exploits with the Corsair. Returning to Lubbock, she found herself to be something of a local hero, for a time at least… until those she ran across had gotten tired of congratulating her. If they ever saw it, none of her sons made mention of her accomplishment with the Corsair.

To fill her time and the hole in her heart from the Corsair being gone, she took up in earnest the promotion of aviation to children. She joined several national and local organizations dedicated to that mission, volunteered as a pilot to take kids up on discovery flights, and continued speaking at schools whenever the opportunity presented itself. She had no expectations that her efforts would actually lead to very many kids becoming pilots, for her main goal was simply to have them look up… and maybe think about those brave souls who dedicated themselves to becoming pilots. She mostly had young girls on her mind, though it was equally important to her that boys admire what women like her aunt had accomplished. After all, the WASPs were not just female pilots. They were true aviators.

Yet in the space of a week, her concept of herself was drastically altered by two phone calls delivering fantastic news. Amanda and Stacey were both expecting. She was so excited for them… excited for her sons and excited for herself. She would soon be a grandmother! So many wonderful changes were coming for her boys. Parenthood would certainly be a milestone that stretched them, bringing new perspectives… and maybe also a deeper appreciation for their only remaining parent.

So… what kind of a grandmother will I be?

Right off, she knew that she would not be the get-down-on-the-floor type. The balls, blocks, army men and toy cars that her own kids had played with never really resonated with her. Even the dolls and stuffed animals that she knew most girls enjoyed had never much occupied her thinking as a child. She obviously knew that play was important in the development of a child's mind, and would certainly do that with her grandchildren. Yet play would not be the thing that defined her relationship with them.

She also could not see herself as being the kitchen table type. Not that she gravitated away from listening to all the sweetly silly ways in which kids explained the world as they saw it. That would be more than fun to experience as a grandmother. She had so many fond memories of her family talking around the kitchen table, but the kitchen itself… that had always been a place where she took pride in her work. Not that she was devoid of an appreciation for the fun that good food brought to a family. The thing was… she could do homework with the kids at the table, but she simply did not have it in her to be baking cookies all day.

She was not so sure about being a babysitting grandmother either, especially while they were still babies. Of course, she was excited at the prospect of holding her new grandbabies, but probably would be equally happy to pass them back to their mothers once they got fussy. Somehow, she suspected that the aura of sitting in a rocking chair ogling a sleeping infant in her arms would wear off pretty quickly… leaving her feeling trapped. Surely that was not the way of a grandmother?! She should be more than content to settle herself down in any spot and hold her grandchild for hours on end. The parents should have to beg for their child back. But she knew that was not her.

Neither would she be the type who gladly chauffeured her grandchildren all over town to the ridiculous kinds of activities that this generation of parents were filling their offspring's lives with. Sports, gymnastics, music lessons, and an endless string of extracurricular nonsense – that was for moms and dads to endure. Not her! Neither would she be up for driving her grandkids over to so-and-so's house just for hanging out. She had a mind for being more strategic in her outings. She could easily envision trips to the mall, a park, a museum, or the airfield. That was more like her… to have the child alone in a setting where she could impart something of her own dreams. So when her grandchildren got older… pass all those diaper changing and potty training nightmares… then that was when her truest attributes of being a grandmother would come shining through. She would be at her absolute best holding the child's hand while they explored the world together.

Both of her grandchildren were born in February of the new year. Amanda had a boy – Duncan, and Stacey had a girl – Merriweather. She made several trips to see her grandchildren during the first month of their lives, delivering gifts, sharing in the joys, and displaying her pride in each couple. She was glad to be with them, but took care to make her visits brief, as she well-remembered the stresses of being a new mother.

Despite the joys of becoming a grandmother, she was still sadden at not having Roy there to share the moments with. That terrible day might have happened well over two years ago, but it felt like only yesterday that she had lost him. He would have made such a fantastic grandfather… and also helped her to be a better grandmother in the process. Irrational as it might seem, she was coming to think of herself as a second class grandparent. Both new mothers had living fathers, as well as strong relationships with their own mothers. It was only natural that they leaned in that direction for advice and assistance. Despite her best efforts, neither Travis or Chad showed much in the way of a connection to her, leaving her feeling like a poor example of a matriarch bearing the Meitner name.

She did not get the thrill of seeing her grandchildren that often... even with Chad and Stacey being only two hours away. Most days had her home alone. With the Corsair sold for a sizable amount, she was financially set for life... which was good, seeing as she no longer had an appetite for work. About the only thing of excitement she had in her life was promoting aviation to kids. In fact, she was scheduled to speak with a class of eighth graders tomorrow morning... but was having a difficult time getting pumped up for it. She could still go to the airfield and chat it up with pilots, but a middle aged woman pushing sixty was hardly much of an attraction. Or... she could go all the way to Dallas for a visit to the Corsair... though she could no longer call it her own. Same was true for the reliefs. She had sold the one in Dallas and finalized the contract for the sale of the other. Though that one still hung on her dining room wall, she no longer considered it as her own. It belonged to a world waiting to take it away from her.

Funny... not owning the relief anymore had changed how she viewed the faces. They had always tormented her with their fear and anger, making her gravitate more toward the raptured delight of the birds above. She had finally broken away like those birds... or at least considered herself to have up until when Roy died. Still... she had flown free, but now had her eyes turned downward. Those faces below in the relief tore at her heart like never before. Down there were those whose dreams had not yet been fulfilled. Maybe they had never actually discovered what their dreams were... or even knew how to dream. This new perspective completely changed how she viewed the birds. They were not blissfully unaware of the faces. They were actually trying to capture the attention of those faces. In diving down, there were trying to show the way up! Trying with all of their might to have the faces look away from their hardships and petty disputes.

That was what she wanted to do too... to inspire others who had not yet broken through to their dreams. To not give up... even when other faces about them failed to understand. So in speaking before kids about flying, she was not really promoting aviation. She was talking about an altogether different kind of flight. Getting them to look up… to take their eyes off what was below, and all those terrible things that caused pain. That was actually what she was trying to do in visiting classrooms. Except… she knew they would only find a way up in life by first changing how it was that they looked down. She took these thoughts of up and down into sleep that night, sensing that they would be important tomorrow.

In the morning, she readied herself for the talk that day with her mind still on up and down. She had done this particular presentation many times before. There was nothing special about it. Just planes and her stories of them. But because of her new insights into the relief, a different kind of clarity had entered into her thinking about this opportunity given to her. All the way on her drive to the middle school… and even while being ushered into the classroom… she was pondering on how she would have gone about inspiring her teenage self. Just like her then, these eighth graders sitting before her were on the cusp of forming their lifelong dreams. And just like her, many were likely already experiencing the hardships of life… or soon would be. Loss of a family member, disappointments, mistakes, embarrassments, doubts, and so many sad realizations. She had been there, and knew fully what they were facing.

"Class… this is Mrs. Marna Meitner. As you may recall, Mrs. Meitner is the intrepid pilot who flew a fighter plane over Dallas last summer. She has graciously consented to share with you some of her experiences from her lifetime of flying. Please give her your full attention."

The teacher nodded to her, so she started right in on her prepared presentation.

"Good afternoon class. Thank you for giving me this opportunity to speak with you about aviation."

For the next several minutes, she narrated a slideshow of the planes she had flown, highlighting the many joys and challenges of being a pilot. This class, like so many others, showed genuine interest in her exploits… especially her having flown the Corsair. Everything went as it always did. She entertained, and they enjoyed. But in concluding, she attempted something that she had never done before.

"As a wrap-up… I'd like to say that it's okay if planes aren't your thing. As a matter of fact, I'd like you to take a second to think about what you're personally drawn to, because flying is really about your dreams."

She paused here, making sure that she had their attention.

"Fulfilling your dreams is never easy. Sometimes… you're absolutely convinced that you know what you want and can't keep your mind off of it. But everything you try... everything that seems to make sense for reaching what you desire... it all backfires. You make bad choices in trying to get where you want to go... and then find yourself in a hole too deep to dig out of. I know... I've been there many times. I've lost faith in myself and in others because of those bad choices. I want to encourage you to do something different next time that happens to you. I'll try to illustrate this with a fundamental concept of aviation that we call 'the angle of attack.' I know... it sounds like something out of a computer game. But it's nothing at all like that. In aviation terms, it's the attitude of the plane relative to its direction of flight. Simply put, the attitude of your plane is where you point your nose. Yet your plane hardly ever moves where your nose points. Its direction actually depends on the angle in which the relative wind is hitting the wing. You know... the wing is a funny thing. You've probably all seen movies or shows where some pilot's desperately pulling back on the yoke to keep their plane from crashing into the ground. Well... that's mostly nonsense. It's not how a plane actually works. It's completely counterintuitive. Point your plane's nose up and the angle of the wind hitting your wings actually makes your plane drop. Whereas if you point the nose down, the wind hitting your wings causes lift... which makes your plane rise."

"There's a life lesson here for us all. Just as planes create their own wind... with propeller blades or a jet engine... so you also create your own wind in life. Sure... there're other winds to deal with. Crosswinds, tailwinds and headwinds. But they're nothing compared to your own wind. Your wind is the power to your life. But be aware... if you point that nose of yours up into the sky and neglect all that's down below, then that wind of yours won't do you any good. It may not seem that way at first... you're looking up just like all those other planes who turned their noses up at the world... but your wings are sure to stall and your plane will fall out of the sky if you allow the wind of your life to hit your wings the wrong way."

"So... if you wish to truly rise in life... to soar into your dreams... then point your nose down... to your responsibilities and the things below that will make you a better pilot. Let the wind of your life hit your wings the right way, and it will surely lift you. Look to the little things down below... your chores, your homework, your family members, and being a good friend to others. Attend to those things faithfully and you will definitely soar. That's a promise."

When she finished, the class was stone quiet. Looking to the faces before her, she had absolutely no idea whether her words had influenced any of them.

So she just kept standing there at the front of the classroom staring at the children… or maybe this was the next class in line for her to visit. It was difficult to say which. But the teacher was motioning her to say more. She therefore bore her soul to them, putting into words her lifelong craving to break away from the mundane and soar upon wings into the heights above. Only there would she truly find meaning to her life. She spread out her arms wide to these teenagers, offering to share with them this grand vision of hers.

But this class did not greet her words well. She was far too old for them to take seriously. Airplanes, they scoffed, were stupid and boring. On and on, they rained down their abuse, calling her such terrible things – weirdo, witch and hag. They were up on their feet, backing her against the blackboard with insults aimed at ridiculing her wasted life. She was a fool to have dreamed, and a failure for not having achieved. What could someone so pathetic possibly know about breaking away?!

Then in horror, she watched as the children before her became clothed in gray tunics. Without reason, they suddenly turned upon each other, some dominating with vicious strokes and others cowering beneath the blows. But not a sound came to her ears from any of them to match the freakish mouth motions of their curses and pleas. She heard only her screams for them to stop! And then… they did. Inexplicably, they froze solid with their contorted faces and unnaturally postured limbs. Slowly, the line of them collapsed inward from both ends, melding the stone children into one body that bore all of their arms, legs and eyes in a horribly facetted array. This grotesque ensemble sprouted wings, but could not fly. Instead, the creature crumpled in upon itself, writhing around on the ground. Out of the midst of its agony came the face of a young girl, longingly looking upward into the sky.

She screamed herself awake. Sitting up in the dark of her bedroom, she finally managed to pant herself into a calm. Whenever she had a disturbing dream in times past, there had always been a husband to comfort her. But now, she was completely alone to work her way through this terrifying nightmare. Elements of it were coming back to her. A classroom of children like the one that she had spoken with today… they all became as the stone faces in her relief! And then a dying wasp that looked like a girl! Whatever did it all mean?!

She lay back down clutching a pillow to her chest, struggling to get back asleep. She had no desire to relive that dream, yet still found herself fretting over its troubling imagery. After tossing about for so long that she was on the verge of wrenching her neck into a headache, she rose from bed, pulling the comforter along with her. Out onto the balcony, she wrapped herself about in as warm a manner as possible and collapsed into a deck chair. Toward the east, she saw a thin line of pale blue at the horizon, suggesting a sunrise… but maybe one not so imminent since the remainder of the sky was still black. She nevertheless decided to wait there for morning to fully bloom… and then start her day as if nothing odd had happened during the night.

Within the dark were still many twinkles to the cloudless sky above, but she settled upon watching one particularly bright star, calling upon it to be her sign of the coming sunrise. At first, the pinpoint remained clear to her, and easily reacquired if her eyes happened to stray elsewhere. But slowly, it began to fade within the growing light all about. At the same time, the softer night sounds were giving way to those of waking birds. Now, she must concentrate fully on that star in order not to lose it. Just as a sliver of sun announced itself, her morning star was gone.

Sunrise and sunset – the horizon showed both the beginning and ending of her days. This spring morning, fresh with a flush of heat already coming to her face, was not hers. She still felt as bright as that morning star had been, but also knew that her time was fading. In the blink of an eye, her life would be gone.

But not just yet.

CHAPTER

49

A TRUE TEXAN

"You want to do what?!"

"You heard me plain enough, Cliff. Please don't make me repeat myself just to see if I waver."

"I'm not. It's just… Wow! I get it – nobody likes living alone. But this… this is crazy! I mean… someone at your age… no offense… but it's not exactly the kind of thing that a woman heading into her sixties should be doing. Know what I mean?!"

"Duly noted. And for your information, I'm only fifty seven… I don't think that's so old. And I'm fully aware of the other things you might be thinking. That I'll get in over my head or end up being taken advantage of."

"No comment."

"Well… I'll admit to those possibilities, but I'm still fully decided. I've been over and over this… and done lots of research. I've gotten on with this amazing agency that has a support network of seasoned veterans for first-timers like myself. They walked me through the application, got my background check done, and they were there with me during the CPS interview and home assessment. I've finished my training. I know how to fill out the paperwork. And I'm prepared for most emergencies. On top of all that, the agency's really helped me see what I'm getting into. Cliff… I have absolutely no illusions that this'll be easy. In fact… I know it won't. So my expectations are definitely in check. I'll do my job… and if I can do some good in the process, all the more better. So you see, the ball's already rolling."

"Then what're you looking for me to do?"

"Honestly… I'd like you to be there as both my legal representative and someone who knows me well. Also… I'm figuring that with a lawyer at my side, I'm less likely to freak out when I actually meet the girl."

The prospect of living alone into her latter years was only a small part of her thinking. She could still fill her days with volunteering, but that did not mean she was filling up her life in the process. The calendar and the heart were two very different things. With the Corsair fading into the past, she was gradually coming to realize a much stronger unfulfilled longing hidden deep inside her. Her thoughts more frequently were going back to her childhood… to both the most solid and most shapeless of memories from having been raised by an aunt. Above everything else, she found herself inexplicably drawn to that defining moment of having lost her parents. For her, this was almost like being one of those fish that somehow could retrace a long and torturous watercourse from the ocean upstream to the spawning site of their youth. She had only been a foster child for a short while… just a summer… yet that time of fear and uncertainty came back to her more clearly than ever before. The faces in that disturbing dream she had some months ago… they were being reinforced daily by those she saw in her relief. Both, she now understood as belonging to those of her fellow foster children whose names she could no longer remember. Anger, sadness and fear were the only labels she was able to put on them.

In considering taking on a foster child, she was not looking for a second chance at parenting. She and Roy had successfully reared three boys. Each still had their issues, but all three also had everything that they needed for raising families of their own. Neither was she longing for what it might have been like to raise a daughter… only that if she was going to embark upon this most farfetched of endeavors, then it might as well be with a girl. Most of all, she felt that she still had so much to give… and something to experience in the process. So finding out what it was like to be on the other side of where she had been as a child… that was a bookend worth giving some of the last years of her life to.

She had already related most of these thoughts to Yardley over a cup of coffee, but found herself doing it all over again as they sat in the front seat of his parked car. Not that she needed his understanding in order for him to be there, only that he had become more than a lawyer to her. He was a good friend. One who knew a lot more about what was important to her than did many of her longstanding friends. Having his support, along with all those legal braincells filling up his head, might actually give her the confidence to do the outlandish thing she was about to do.

"Are you thinking that I'm being impulsive? I mean… it's a trait that's gotten me into more trouble than I'd care to admit. But it's also brought some good things too."

"Okay… I'll bite. What's the difference between good impulsiveness and bad impulsiveness?"

"I'm not really sure… I guess whenever I jump into something without regard for others, that's almost always turned out bad. But when I have a chance to do something worthwhile… I mean… really, really good… why should I second guess myself?"

"Well… since you told me to bill you for this time, then I'll give you my professional opinion."

"Which is what?"

"There're far easier ways to do a good deed than taking on a foster child."

"No doubt I'll be agreeing with you in a few months. You've got kids, right?"

"Two… both teenagers."

"And you know I have three. So believe me, I'm not looking for a warm-and-fuzzy."

"Point taken."

"Cliff… for most of my life, I've been totally obsessed with finding significance in this world."

"That's not uncommon."

"No… I don't suppose it is. But some have it worse than others… and some allow that drive to get out of hand. That's me. I think my boys know I have this weakness… and they've always felt neglected as a result. So… I want a chance to be better."

"I understand… but that's no excuse for doing something so risky."

"It's not an excuse… just an explanation. You know… I've had so many people close to me experience untimely deaths. My parents… my aunt… my in-laws… and more recently… Roy. I guess I've conditioned myself into believing that a person's fullness can be measured in years… and what they were able to accomplish. You know… how green their life was. That kind of thing. Know what I mean?"

"Certainly."

"But I don't think of life that way anymore… and not because I'm living alone with time on my hands. Nearer the end than the beginning… that sort of thing. I don't know if this'll make any sense to you, but when I sold off my airplane and my reliefs, it finally occurred to me that I had been holding on to those because of the feeling of significance they gave me. Whenever things went wrong in my life, I clung to their symbolism as a sort of down payment on my dreams. Only when I finally gave them up did I see the opportunities I had for helping others."

"But don't you still have one of those reliefs on your wall?"

"I do… but I really don't consider it as belonging to me anymore. And it's definitely not there for my personal enjoyment. I have it for a bit longer just to remind me of something."

"Which is what… if you don't mind me asking?"

"Of the reason why we're sitting in this parking lot outside of a juvenile detention center staring through a chain linked fence waiting for a bunch of… Hold it a sec… Here they come. Now watch carefully."

She had already shared with him about her previous visits to this parking lot over the last two weeks, and how she studied those young girls who came out into the fenced-off patio to eat their lunch. Though it had only taken her a few days to find the one she was interested in, she spent another week in confirming it to herself. She would not bother packaging up her way of knowing in any sort of sophisticated wrapping. She just knew, even though the foster care workshops she attended cautioned her against getting caught up in believing that there was one special girl out there whose tragic life story could be turned around by her. No child had ever entered foster care being grateful or expectant. She certainly had not. She mostly remembered being angry, scared, distrustful, and terribly heartbroken. But she had come up with a very simple means of screening a prospective foster child… and one girl in particular had consistently met her criteria.

"You do realize that these girls come from troubled backgrounds?"

"Are you worried about me getting murdered in my sleep?"

"No. Just overcome with their problems… and maybe robbed blind in the process."

"That's very considerate of you, Cliff. Now pay attention."

As on those previous times when she sat alone in her own car, she watched through Yardley's windshield as a group of grade school age girls filed out to the picnic tables in the enclosure before her. Each girl carried a cafeteria style tray in their hands, and each was in an orange jumpsuit… which to her felt unnecessarily stark for children so young. There had always been a mixture of ethnicities, though she had not focused on such distinctions. Her eyes were taking in their behaviors… and the one thing that would tell her for certain. At a hundred feet off, she was not nearly close enough to clearly make out faces, but even with the razor wire capped chain link separating her, she was consistently able to pick out the same girl.

The four tables gradually filled up, with the children going at their lunches as any typical grade schooler might. Some talked in groups, some in pairs, and some sat alone.

"Watch that table at the end on the right."

"What am I looking for?"

"You'll see soon enough… though it might take a few minutes. Mind rolling down the windows so I can listen?"

"I doubt you'll be able to hear anything from here."

"I'm not listening for them."

He shot her an inquisitive look and then brought the windows halfway down. Since she had already recognized her girl, she was putting more effort into listening. With a glance at Yardley, she chuckled to herself at his expression. He was leaning forward with real intensity on his face. Clearly, he wanted to show himself as observant enough to spot any anomaly in the girls… but there was also that slight scowl betraying his skepticism. That was fine with her. She just needed him to see what she had seen.

Come on…

Then she heard it – that low rumble of a plane climbing out of its takeoff from the airport. Her eyes locked upon that one girl… and just as on every previous occasion, she was the only one of the dozen or so to lift her head from her tray in a search of the sky. On the day it first happened, her heart practically came out of her chest with excitement, for she instantly recognized this girl as someone who had eyes for up.

"Do you see her?"

"No… Where? Which one?"

"The one who's shielding her eyes from the sun. She's looking for the plane."

"That's how you're choosing a foster child?! Because she's looking up at an airplane?! Marna… that's insane!"

She did not begrudge him of his astonishment, for surely he saw nothing beyond a scraggly-looking waif whose dirty blond hair kept getting in her eyes as she searched the sky. But she saw something different – a young girl with a longing that even she was probably not aware of having. A desire to be up there with that plane.

As on previous times, the girl found the aircraft and then followed it out of sight before returning to her meal. She had seen the girl do this every day while secretly watching, and that was good enough for her. This was a girl that she had something in common with… and maybe could even help.

"I'm calling the director. Can we head to the front?"

Whatever Yardley was thinking, she was sure he would get to it soon enough. In the meantime, he started his car and pulled around to a visitor's spot. They then made their way into the detention center's lobby and waited. Through wire-reinforced glass doors, she had a view down a wide hallway to another set of doors, these being of solid metal. In a matter of minutes, a man and a woman came through those heading for the lobby. She had already met the woman, but not the man. With a buzz and a loud metallic clank, the glass doors unlocked for them to pass through into the same hallway. A guard then stepped out from a control room and blandly went about sweeping a wand over them, lastly peering into her purse. The approaching man and woman reached them well before the security screening was completed.

"Forgive the intrusion. Standard policy. You must be Marna Meitner. I'm Ronald Pierson, the director here…" He hesitated for a second to eye Yardley before continuing. "…and this is Margarette Perez, the girl's CPS caseworker."

"Oh… this is my lawyer and friend, Cliff Yardley. I've asked him to sit in on our meeting."

Everyone shook everyone's hand, and then the director led them through a door opposite the guardroom. She found the space to be set up rather interestingly, as it was half conference room for adults and half playroom for the children being discussed. They all sat about the table as Miss Perez started in by opening her folder.

"First off, Mrs. Meitner… everything in your application's in order. You're already approved as a foster parent. I know we've covered this, but I thought I'd revisit a few things for the benefit of Director Pierson."

"Of course."

"As I mentioned to you over the phone, it's not uncommon for a prospective foster parent such as yourself to specify a certain child, but perhaps you could take a minute to give us your thoughts on why you want to be a foster parent and why this particular child."

"Glad to. As I pointed out in my application, I was a foster child myself for a short time after my parents were killed in a car accident. I ended up being raised by an aunt I'd never met before. So I'd guess you could say that I have a soft spot in my heart for orphans. Now… as to this specific girl, I thought I might…"

"Excuse me, Mrs. Meitner… if I may. It just occurred to me that it might be good if I were to point out a few details on the girl's status for the benefit of your lawyer before you started in on explaining your choice."

She naturally nodded her approval, and Miss Perez turned to Yardley. She noticed that his eyebrows perked up in anticipation of hearing things that he perhaps already suspected.

"Her mother is currently incarcerated in the state penitentiary on her third strike. As part of her sentencing, she's fully yielded her rights to the child. Unfortunately… no one's come forth to claim her… and by her mother's account, the father's unknown. So… the girl's not in permanent managing conservatorship… which obviously means that she's eligible for adoption. I understand that this is something Mrs. Meitner is considering for the future."

By the way Yardley's head swung about in her direction, she realized that she had neglected to mention this little detail to him.

"That's correct… though I've… umm… not yet had a chance to share with my lawyer the particulars regarding how… Miss Novik… came to be here. Perhaps you could fill him in for me?"

"Certainly."

She kept her eyes away from Yardley, for she sensed that he was still glaring her way. Instead, she watched Miss Perez run a finger down a sheet in the girl's file.

"Let's see… Her mother was convicted earlier this year on multiple drug charges. The girl returned to foster care at that point… but ended up running away. It's not that uncommon. I can't go into specifics, other than to say that she was apprehended while shoplifting from a convenience store some days later. She was properly adjudicated… and has been here for… two months. Regrettably, this was not her first offense. It seems that her mother had used her as a decoy in the robbery of a clothing store in Fort Worth. Normally, we wouldn't be putting such a child back into the foster care system just yet, but given that Mrs. Meitner has come forward specifically requesting her… and the girl's latest offense was under unusual circumstances… then we're considering an exception in her case."

Yardley jumped in with what likely had been on his mind ever since the moment they first arrived.

"How many times has this girl been in and out of detention centers?"

"I'm not permitted to say, but she has been in foster care several times over the years while her mother was serving time."

He immediately turned to the director instead. "Would you consider this girl to be a troublemaker?"

"Not particularly. She's one of the quiet ones. We've not had a need for putting her in disciplinary seclusion… or to have her take part in any of our corrective programs. Anger management… conflict resolution… that sort of thing. She has had a good bit of counselling, but I think Miss Perez would prefer if I didn't go into any of that. I hope you understand. So, no… she's not a troublemaker… but that doesn't mean she's incapable of causing trouble."

"Now, Mrs. Meitner…"

"Yes?"

"Getting back to the question of why her…"

"Oh… yes. Umm… I should start off by making it clear that I have no prior knowledge of her or her family. So this isn't a friend-of-a-friend sort of a thing. My choice is actually somewhat arbitrary. There's a bit more to it than that… but I'd prefer meeting the girl first before explaining why I'm interested in her specifically. Would that be okay?"

The caseworker and the director briefly exchanged glances, with the latter shrugging his shoulders in a dismissive sort of way.

"Certainly. We've already told her that there's a prospective foster parent interested in being her caretaker… and she's expressed a willingness to meet you. Allow me to go get her…"

With the director having departed the room, Miss Perez unexpectedly became stern.

"You are aware that the child has a say in this?"

"Of course."

"Given her adjudication, we can have her stay put in this center rather than reenter foster care."

"Yes, you mentioned that when you came over…"

"And as her caseworker, I have full authority to decide on her behalf. I can easily return her back here if I feel that things aren't working out for her."

"I understand. Really… I do."

"And do you also realize that this meeting is a trial run? I'll be looking for any sign of…"

Without forewarning, the meeting room door swung inward, and there was the director standing in the hallway all by himself. After a brief pause in which he frowned off down the hall, he gave a quick thumb jerk meant as a command… and into the door frame stepped the little girl she had been watching for two weeks. From a distance, Vierny Novik seemed to possess a rather compact build, but up close, she now realized that most of the look was due to the starchy form of the orange jumpsuit. The arms and neck of this girl were more stick-like, which immediately gave off the distinct impression of her being under-nourished. The same could be said of her face. She might have a graceful-looking jawline, but that supported sunken cheeks. The child's overall demeanor was that of a sedentary dullness very much out of keeping with a happy and healthy seven year old. But this girl's dark eyes were so very active, already roving about the room even before she stepped in. Quickly going from person to person, the girl latched onto her as the prospective foster parent, scanning her up and down without a hint as to what was thought. She then did similarly with Yardley and the CPS caseworker, before more-or-less slumping her way inside and stopping well beyond arm's reach of anyone at the table. Margarette rose first, and then so did she, extending her hand to the girl on being introduced. She was surprised at finding Vierny's grip to be soft and delicate… like that of a child's… and then realized she had been expecting something harsher based on the jumpsuit.

"Vierny… this is the woman I was telling you about… Mrs. Meitner."

"Hi."

"Hello, Vierny. Such a beautiful name! I'm so pleased to meet you. I suppose you know why I'm here.

"You're a foster parent. I've had those before. I know how this works."

"Well… I was once a foster child too… so I understand a bit of what you've experienced. Would you… be willing to sit over there and talk, just you and me?"

She motioned to the side of the room with the toys. Vierny looked first to the director… who nodded his head… and then moved that way without a word. She waited for the girl to pick a spot and then pulled over a child-sized plastic chair, scootching it up close enough to speak privately without infringing upon the girl's personal space. Not uttering a word, Vierny took up a barbie doll and began making it trot around its dollhouse. The way she went about it… forcefully with staccato-like hops… told her that the child was not really into this sort of play. Actually, the girl's eyes had stayed on the adults seated around the table… the director, in particular.

"I would very much like to invite you to see my house, that way you could get to know me better and decide if it was a place where you might want to live. Miss Perez can drive you over tomorrow and the three of us can have lunch together. Would you be interested in doing that?"

"Sure. Why not…"

"That's great, Vierny. But… you should know… when a child's speaks to an adult… it's more polite to say ma'am or sir."

With an intensity that was not wholly unexpected, the girl's eyes came around to lock onto hers. They were not as dark as she had first presumed, being more of a chocolaty brown than black. She held those eyes in silence, smiling in the most reassuring way as the girl made her first choice in the relationship.

"Yes, ma'am… I'll come to your house. Do you have any kids?"

"No… not any that are still living there. I have three sons… but they're all grown up and out on their own. I do have a rather large house… and plenty of space for playing."

Whether this made any kind of an impression at all was hard to say, for the girl just nodded and went back to making the doll stomp about the dollhouse. For a fleeting moment, she caught a glimpse of a scar under the girl's chin, the remnant of some accident… or worse.

"Do you have any questions that you'd like to ask me?"

Vierny first wagged her head as a response and then followed it up with words.

"No, ma'am… no questions. They don't like questions around here."

"Well… I love questions. You can ask me as many as you want… and I'll always answer truthfully."

Again those eyes… this time fleetingly with so much obvious doubt displayed in them.

"So… what about tomorrow? Would that be okay with you?"

"I have class tomorrow. We're not supposed to miss class."

"But it's the start of summer break…"

"Not for us. We don't get summer."

"I see… So… if Miss Perez can arrange for you to have permission, would you be up for a visit tomorrow."

"Sure. I mean… yes, ma'am."

"Excellent… let's go tell her."

Then came the moment that she had been waiting for. Something that would tell her what kind of a situation this girl had been in. A little test much more significant than asking her to say ma'am. As they turned toward the adults, she gently placed a hand upon the girl's shoulder… and felt an immediate flinch… subtle, yet quite clear. Her heart instantly went out to this girl, whose own heart was so obviously in pain.

She spent the morning bustling about the house, even though everything was quite orderly. She was cleaning things that were already clean simply as a means of curbing her excitement. The caseworker would be arriving with Vierny any minute now. At the ready, she had a lunch consisting of three kinds of sandwiches, a pot of soup simmering on the stove, a big bowl of potato chips, a saucer of apple slices, glasses of sweet tea, and a plate of homemade snickerdoodles. With this first meal, she was determined to show the girl that food was something to be lavished upon her. She was just going over the kitchen table's setting for three when she heard tires crunching on the gravel drive. Throwing a few dirty dishes into the sink and divesting herself of the apron, she dashed to the front door… calming herself there for a moment before stepping outside to greet them.

Vierny, popping out of Margarette Perez's car, was not in a jumpsuit. Whether wearing her own clothes or not, the shirt and pants were clearly a few sizes too big. But the girl did not at all seem self-conscious about her appearance, for her eyes were roving all over the front of the house, moving from window to window in her appraisal of the place. On registering her standing on the front porch, Vierny abruptly extended an arm off toward the hangar.

"Hey… isn't that an airplane hangar? Do you have an airplane? Can I see it?"

"It is. But I'm sorry… there's no longer a plane in there. It's a long story… so I'll have to save it for some other time. Did I not mention to you that I'm a pilot?"

The girl looked back vacantly as if still processing the question.

"Umm… no, ma'am… you didn't. Seriously?"

"Like I said before… I wouldn't lie to you. I even have pictures to prove it."

By then, Margarette had come around her car, and both of them climbed the stairs together. It was not the first time that the CPS caseworker had been here, but the young woman obviously had decided to pretend that it was.

"What a lovely house you have, Mrs. Meitner. Thank you so much for inviting us."

"You're welcome. So… I was thinking of giving you both a quick tour, and then maybe the three of us could sit down for a nice lunch."

"Sounds delightful."

"Vierny… getting back to your question about the hangar… we can take a walk over there after lunch if you'd like, but how about if I show you around the house first? Feel free to ask any question you like."

The girl nodded and started right in.

"So… you live here all alone? It seems really big for one old lady."

"Well… it'll still be big for one old lady and a sassy squirt of a little girl too." She smiled as playfully as she could, and was relieved when the girl smiled back. "This porch wraps all the way around. It's my favorite part of the house. There's always a spot to match my mood. But what say we go inside first so you can take a look about?"

Stepping within, Vierny's mouth immediately opened into a wordless expression of surprise as her eyes went up and all around. The wide open family room was apparently hitting her with the same airy feeling of wonder as it had on that day so long ago when she first beheld it herself.

"Through this opening here is my parlor…"

"That… just for you?"

"Not really. Feel free to go in."

After a pause of hesitancy, Vierny moved to the opening of the French doors, but did not venture in.

"I like it… especially that little place off to the side."

"I call that my stairwell nook."

"That your special place?"

"No. You'd be welcome to sit there too. There're plenty of special places in this house. Come on… I'll show you the upstairs next."

She motioned toward the stairs, falling in behind with Margarette as the girl took off ahead. As they moved up, she noticed Vierny looking out through the family room windows toward the hangar. At the top, the girl stopped in the hallway and looked to each of the rooms. She had left the doors open so as to give the impression that there were no secrets behind any of them.

"This is my bedroom. It has its own bathroom and a deck outside. Care to see it?"

"No thanks. I mean… no, ma'am. What're these other rooms?"

"A bathroom that you'd have to yourself and your pick of one of two other bedrooms."

She expected the girl to investigate, but Vierny remained right where she was at.

"You're welcome to look into any…"

With a quick glance at Margarette, Vierny turned about and headed back down the stairs.

Ugh. This could be a tough nut to crack!

Waiting for them at the bottom, the girl's eyes were already back out the family room windows at the hangar.

"Let's head in here next. It's obviously the kitchen."

Stepping within, Vierny once more came to a standstill, showing absolutely no intention of moving any further. Her eyes did pan in an arc from the counters to the back door, and then all the way around to the entrance of the dining room.

"That's the table where we'll be having lunch… and around the corner there are stairs to the cellar… as well as a small guest bedroom and bath. Tell you what… feel free to explore while Miss Perez and I finish getting things ready."

After a moment of indecision, Vierny shrugged her shoulders and moved into the dining room.

This is nuts! What do I really know about being a foster parent?!

That this was the right girl for her, she had no doubt, but there was obviously much hidden within. Pain, distrust and shame… things that only time and lots of love would ever make a dent in.

Steering the conversation clear of the subject of Vierny, she chatted with Margarette about how the young woman had gotten into CPS as they set about making the finishing touches on the table. They had everything ready when it occurred to her that Vierny was still in the dining room… or perhaps had ventured through into the parlor's nook. With Margarette excusing herself to use the guest bath, she went to retrieve the girl.

"Vierny… lunch is ready."

She found her standing before the relief.

"Oh… there you are. I see you've found my relief. Pretty amazing, isn't it?!"

With eyes locked on the sculpture, Vierny spoke without turning about.

"I want to go now. Tell what's-her-name I'll be in the car."

"But you only just got here…"

Whether listening or not, Vierny was already moving through the parlor as she spoke. No other sounds in the house could compete as she heard the opening and closing of the front door.

Somehow, she had scared the girl away.

She managed to put away the lunch before falling apart into tears. She then spent the afternoon in her nook with nothing to keep her company other than questions lacing themselves through the holes in her heart. Had she tried too hard? Or not hard enough? Should she have pursued the girl out on to the porch, promising her that she would get rid of the relief? What had that stonework done to her anyway? Had the faces brought back things that were best left buried? It was so stupid to have allowed her into the dining room without being there too. Explaining to Margarette that her charge had inexplicably bolted from the house… that was far easier to endure than those anxious moments of watching from the parlor window as the woman tried persuading the child to come back inside. But Vierny just sat there in the front seat shaking her head vehemently. Humiliation and sadness… those were the feelings welling up in her as the caseworker started up her car and left. Vierny did not once look back at the house.

Tomorrow… she would call the caseworker and apologize again. She would withdraw her name as a potential foster parent and give up this foolish presumption that she could make a difference in a child's life. That she could have helped that girl be someone – what a ridiculously naïve thing to believe! The agency had warned against that, but she had not listened.

Tomorrow… she would arrange for the relief's transfer to the Dallas museum. She had kept it for far too long. There had to be people out there for whom that relief could do some good… unlike her.

Tomorrow… she would go to the cemetery and visit Roy's grave for the first time. He was not really there… that much she knew… but that hidden coffin was all that remained for her. She would empty out new tears there… and if she could still walk afterward, then she would go find Gwen's final resting place… and maybe George and Ruby's too. For only the dead understood her pain.

Tomorrow… she would start life again from zero… and try to figure out where she might still belong in this world.

After having put on a brave face through the process of making breakfast for one, she took up her cell phone along with a cup of coffee. Moving to the front porch, newly alit by the rising sun and yet still with that lingering coolness from the night, she sat in her favorite rocking chair to gather herself into a dignified frame of mind. Going to her contacts, she scrolled through to the one for Margarette Perez. Closing her eyes and taking in a deep breath of the morning air, she resolved to make this call as business-like as possible. She was almost ready when the phone happened to vibrate in her hand.

Oh! It's Margarette… calling to tell me what I already know.

"Hello…"

"Marna… how are you doing this morning?"

"Fine… I guess… but not really."

"Listen… I feel absolutely terrible about yesterday. I should have come back inside before leaving… you know… to explain what was going on. But Vierny… she was on the verge of tears, and wouldn't tell me a thing. So I thought it best just to leave. You know… I had to spent a good part of the afternoon trying to calm her down."

"Margarette… I should be the one apologizing. I don't know what I did to set her off, but it was obviously something terrible. Like I told you, one minute she was fine, and then in the next… she just wanted to leave. I promise I didn't touch her or say anything mean to her."

"It's okay, Marna. That's the way it is with foster children. Two steps forward and one back… sometimes two or three back."

"I understand. So… would you do something for me? Would you please tell Vierny that I'm sorry for having upset her? It was the last thing I wanted to do. Please tell her that I wish her nothing but the best."

"Maybe you should tell her yourself."

"Excuse me?"

"That's why I'm calling. She's agreed to be placed in your home as a foster child."

After picking her jaw up off the floor… and then biting her lip so as not to scream out with the excitement coming over her… she settled on a time for meeting Margarette at the detention center. Since there was no way she could sit still for the next two hours, she ran around like a chicken with its head cut off trying to do something constructive in preparing her house for a child. The place was actually ready, so she instead got herself dressed and then paced about the parlor until it was finally time to leave.

It required the remainder of the morning to fill out the paperwork allowing Vierny to be discharged into her care. She would have her for a day and a night before Margarette came by to check up on how the transition was going. Despite an admonition for restraint, she simply could not keep herself from lavishing all sorts of bubbly excitement on the girl once they brought her out. Vierny took it all in coolly. They were soon out the door together. In crossing the detention center parking lot, she noticed Vierny's eyes scan the sky.

"We should have nice weather for the rest of the day… don't you think?"

"Umm… I guess so… ma'am. Which car's yours?"

"The white Explorer straight ahead. Climb in. First things first – I'm going to get a good lunch into you… and then maybe we'll go do some shopping together."

She spent the drive engaging Vierny in the kinds of small talk that an unfamiliar adult and child might exchange while confined in a small space together for the first time. What the girl liked to eat, her favorite things to do, and sights they were passing along the road. Through it all, she tried to keep her own excitement at a moderate level while going over the spectrum of new clothes Vierny needed, what sorts of linens she might like, and the room decoration possibilities for a child her age. For the most part, Vierny sat quietly with her face straight ahead. So she instead found herself searching back into her own childhood, trying to remember how she had felt under similar circumstances. Surely she had been afraid and distrustful. Yet the only thing coming back to her were scattered impressions from that first time she made an early morning circuit of greenhouses with Gwen. Lubbock had seemed so wide open… and her aunt had been closed.

"Remember I mentioned that you could ask me any question you wanted to?"

"Yes…"

"Do try to say ma'am when you respond."

"Yes... ma'am."

"Well, you must have something on your mind."

"What's that thing on your wrist?"

"Oh... That's just my medical alert bracelet. I'm allergic to bee stings. Are you allergic to anything?"

"No. I mean... no, ma'am. But I don't much like the food at the detention center. It makes my stomach feel... gurglely."

"That's definitely something I can fix. Do you have any other questions?"

"What should I call you?"

"How about 'Mrs. Meitner'... or perhaps... 'Mrs. M,' for short?"

"I like that. So what happened to your husband?"

She had not expected that question, but answered it seeing as she had just promised to be open with this child.

"He... died of a heart attack... almost three years ago. It was... the worst day of my life."

To her surprise, she found Vierny looking at her for the first time since getting into the car.

"Has it been... lonely... being without him?"

"I miss him terribly. He was such a good man. Kind through and through. You know... I think he would have liked you... a whole lot."

"How do you know that?"

"Just a hunch. He and I... we knew each other since childhood. We were best friends. I'm pretty sure he would have said that you reminded him of me when I was your age."

"Is that why you picked me?"

"No... and yes at the same time. You're your own person, Vierny. You don't have to live for me or anyone else. But I think you and I do have some things in common."

"Like being a foster child?"

"That... and a bit more. I like planes... and I think you do too."

Vierny turned her face away without agreeing or disagreeing.

Careful. Don't move in too close too soon.

She left the girl to her own thoughts and concentrated instead on driving. She was just about to the turnoff for the county road leading to the house when Vierny spoke again.

"Why do you live way out here? Was your husband a farmer?"

"No. We just liked being away from the city. Out here, you see the whole sky... from horizon to horizon. Such amazing sunrises and sunsets... along with every cloud and every star that's up there. But actually… we're not that far from town. Less than ten minutes away."

Vierny gave her a nod and looked straight ahead as the car turned into the driveway. It was not the girl's first time here, but she tried to pretend as if it was, just so she could read something of Vierny's first impressions of the house. Venturing a peek, she was pleased to see that the girl had come up in the seat, eyes scanning along the line of live oaks down the long stretch of gravel to the place that had been her own home for the better part of forty years. She knew how she had felt that first time of laying eyes on this wonderful house… and was hoping that Vierny might be feeling the same way.

"Your house… it's… really big."

"Yep."

"And… sort of… beautiful."

"I'm glad you think so. You know… this house can be your home for as long as you want it to be."

The girl said nothing in response… at least not until the car had come to a stop on the circle. With a hand held near to her chest, she gestured weakly toward the hangar

"Can we… maybe go over there first?"

"Certainly… and I'll tell you the story about the plane that was once in there… if you're interested."

The girl nodded back, yet with an ever so slight smile coming to her face. As they walked to the hangar, she started in on how her father-in-law had bought the Corsair after the war to remember a friend. She had inherited it from him when he died, and there it sat in the hangar for years and years before she finally decided to have it restored when her husband passed away. She paused the story at this point because they had reached the threshold of the hangar. Since Vierny had stopped there, so did she.

"Feel free to go in. As a matter of fact… you can play in here anytime you like."

"I don't think a kid should play here."

"Really? Why's that?"

"It's a hangar! That's a serious place for planes. It wouldn't be right."

"I see your point. Well then… maybe we'll make it a place to imagine instead. How's that sound?"

With eyes still sweeping back and forth, Vierny gave off a tight-lipped smile of a nod… all of which suggested that the girl was already imagining.

"Let's pick out which room'll be yours, eat some lunch, and then we'll head over to the mall."

The shopping experience began awkwardly with Vierny moving hesitantly through the first store. Really… she should have started the girl out with something less personal than clothes. So she bought them pretzels and they sat by a fountain to talk through bed and bath linen. There, she got her first glimpse of what this girl might be like if she was happy, for Vierny swung her legs back and forth merrily while taking in the sights of shoppers passing by. They next progressed to selecting room decorations, which required a bit more interaction from Vierny. Another trip to the food court for milk shakes, where she had the girl giggling as they vied to be the one making the longest slurping noise. After that, Vierny was more than ready to pick out her own clothes and pajamas, and even showed genuine excitement when told that she need not choose between three pairs of shoes that she liked. By the time they got home with a dozen shopping bags, Vierny was actually smiling. So she left the girl to put her new things away and went to see about dinner. They ate chips and BBQ sandwiches while chatting about the things they had purchased. That is, whenever Vierny could manage a free moment of not having her mouth filled with pulled pork.

The first tense moment in the arrangement came just as they had finished cleaning up the dishes.

"So where's your TV?"

"I don't have one. I gave it away when my husband…"

"I don't understand. Who doesn't have a TV?!"

"Someone who chooses not to."

"That's not fair! No one told me you didn't have one!"

"It wasn't a…"

"I'm not living here unless you get a TV!"

"Vierny… you'd better have a seat… because we need to talk."

With arms crossed and a scowl capable of ruining any pretty face, the girl fell back into her kitchen chair while doggedly looking away.

"First off… it's not my job to provide you with a TV. My job is to feed you well, clothe you well, protect you as best as I can, and give you a place where you can live in safety. Your job is to respect me… which means doing things my way… because this is my house and I'm the one in charge. I might also add that it's your job to respect this house… which includes the things in it and the things I choose *not* to be in it. So while you're living here, you'll be expected to keep your life orderly… which means more than just cleaning your room. You're expected to contribute. Lastly… it's your job to be honest with me… just as it's my job to be honest with you. So for your information… I won't tolerate sass any more than I'll tolerate lies. Do you understand me?"

Vierny spoke without taking her eyes from off the tabletop.

"Fine! Whatever!"

"Really? Is that a respectful way for a child to answer?"

"How should I know?!"

She refused to move an inch in continuing to stare at the girl, not having the slightest inclination for reacting to the impertinent question. For her part, Vierny kept her face turned away. A minute went by... and then two... before the girl finally relaxed her arms to her lap.

"No... it's not."

"Try again."

"No, ma'am... it's... not a respectful way to answer. It's just I've watched TV nearly every day of my life! It's the only way I could stand the... noise."

"What noise?"

"I don't want to talk about it."

"Okay... that's your choice. Just know that whenever you do, I'll be here for you. Now... there's one other requirement I'm going to place upon you as a condition for living in this house. Stand up."

Instead, Vierny very noticeably cringed away in her seat.

"I'm not going to hurt you... I promise. Please... just stand up."

She waited until the girl had come to her feet, and without putting her through more suspense, quickly pulled her into a hug. At first, Vierny remained tense in the embrace, but eventually relaxed enough so that her arms fell limp at her sides. Only then did she move the girl away, taking care to keep both hands rested gently upon her shoulders.

"This is my special rule. Whenever there's a disagreement between the two of us... my fault or your fault, it doesn't matter... once we've resolved things, then we'll end the matter with a hug. No exceptions! Also... every morning when you rise and every night before bed, regardless of how you feel, we're going to hug. I'm not budging on this, Vierny. Understand me?"

"Yes, ma'am."

"Good. That way, you'll always know for certain where you stand with me. Now grab that plate of cookies and follow me out."

Without explaining what she intended, she led Vierny through the kitchen door onto the back porch. The sun was minutes from setting, so she moved along the western side to a spot where the hangar did not obscure their view. Motioning toward the rocking chairs, she allowed the girl to choose first... and Vierny opted for her favorite. Pulling up a different one, she took the plate of cookies from the girl, holding it for her to select one, and then set it on a nearby table.

"Been meaning to get some cushions for these chairs… you know… the kind with tie-downs. Maybe you could help me pick those out."

Vierny, with a mouth full of cookie, nodded agreeably. With eyes out toward the hangar, she swallowed, but hesitated before taking another bite.

"This is… kind of boring."

There was absolutely no judgment in the girl's voice. Only something akin to a child's unfulfilled expectation for fun.

"It's supposed to be boring. That's how you free up your mind for imagination."

She left the girl to nibble at her cookie and turned her own eyes toward the sunset. Such a familiar sight… so many witnessed in the past right here on this porch. They always settled over her heart in the same way… so beautiful, so peaceful, so majestic… and so sad. Just as the dull yellow orb touched the horizon, she became aware that Vierny's chair had stopped rocking. Together in silence, they followed the sun until it disappeared, being replaced by dusk's softer spectrum. With the porch lights off, it soon became so dark that they blended into the night's features. It was time for bed, but she hesitated in considering the proper wording for this first time. Yet Vierny spoke before she could.

"You know… they let us watch TV every night."

"Really?"

"I liked it because it's the only time when everyone's being nice. Kids are busy watching… so nobody's mean to anybody. It's the best time. But then… the TV… it just… goes out. All by itself. They don't even wait for the show to finish. You hear the bell… and the TV goes blank."

"What happens after that?"

Vierny delayed in responding… almost to the point that she was certain the girl had chosen not to answer.

"They give us ten minutes before lights out. Some of the kids don't like that. They get… mean."

"I'm sorry…"

"You're supposed to be allowed out of bed to go to the bathroom… but they won't let you."

"The guards?"

"No… not them. The… mean kids."

"That must have been real… frustrating."

"Yeah… Can we… do this again? Watch the sun go all the way down until it's dark out?"

"Anytime you want."

Having bathed herself and brushed her teeth, Vierny was in a pair of new pajamas – bright blue all over. Standing together at her bedside, she gave her a hug that was not resisted, yet not quite fully accepted either. As the girl got into bed, she gestured toward a nightlight she had set up on the dresser.

"I'm going to leave the light on in the hall, but thought you might appreciate this one being on too… just until you get used to being here."

"Thanks."

"Certainly."

Before she knew what she was doing, she leaned over and kissed the girl on her forehead. Feeling a bit embarrassed by her own boldness, she made to turn away… except Vierny shot out a hand to delay her.

"Before you go… could you… umm… would you… mind sitting here and telling me a story? Not kid stuff. Just… something serious about flying."

"Of course… I'd love to. Let's see…" She searched through her memory of all the planes and all the times… then settled on the perfect thing. "The very first time I was ever up in a plane… I was just about your age… but I remember it like it was yesterday…"

By the time she got to the part of the story where Gwen arrived at this house to pick her up following Roy's birthday party, Vierny was fast asleep.

In the morning, she arose to find Vierny's bed empty. Resisting an impulse to yell her head off, she hurried downstairs to search the house.

"Vierny?"

"I'm in here."

She followed the voice around through the kitchen into the dining room. There was Vierny, sitting in a chair pulled up in front of the relief. To her surprise, Vierny rose to give her a quick hug and then was right back down looking at the relief as before.

"I've been trying to figure this thing out ever since I got up. What's it mean?"

"You tell me. What do you see?"

With her eyes fixed on the sculpture, Vierny took her time in answering.

"Down there…" She pointed a finger along the line of stone characters. "…I see… sadness. Both kinds… the broken heart kind… and the… mean… cruel kind. It makes me not want to look at them. But I can't help it. They remind me of…" The girl lowered her hand, seemingly with no intention of finishing her sentence. As she looked closer, she noticed that Vierny was biting her lip.

"What do they remind you of?"

"My life… at the detention center and… before."

Then Vierny's eyes strayed to where the birds flew.

"But up there's a different kind of sadness. The sweet kind. You know…

how a person wants to feel… but can't get there. Those birds… they seem so… happy. They make me wanna… I don't know… break out from below to be a part of their world. I… I can't explain it any better than that."

"You don't have to. That's exactly how I felt the very first time I laid eyes on it. I was just about your age. And I still get the same feeling every time I look at it. By the way… this is called *Fino al Cielo*… which means 'To the Sky.'"

Vierny gave a little tight-lipped nod, coolly delivered, as if its name was so very obvious to even her.

"I don't know why… but I like it. A lot! Where'd you get it?"

"From a woman who spent most of her life down there with those faces… but eventually did break away."

Moving into the longer summer days, she concentrated on caring for Vierny as would a mother, even though she knew that winning the girl's trust would take a whole lot more than cookies, hugs and bedtime stories. There were so many moments in which a darker side to the girl came through – a distrust of the world that no amount of pampering seemed capable of shaking. She had been instructed many times by Margarette not to press the girl about her past… something that those in her foster parent support network also cautioned her against. Vierny would share only if and when Vierny was ready to. Whatever those hidden burdens were, they never seemed to go away. Too often, the good things she had to offer the girl were received with a skeptic's pause, and seldom were words given back to reveal what was going on deep inside. So she went on doing her best to bury the girl under a mountain of kindnesses, and endure her own heartache in the process. Several times during the first few weeks, Vierny awoke screaming from some nightmare in which she was being chased by a man, sometimes through the dark and sometimes along a crowded street where nobody would stop to help her. Because of the stupid restrictions, she knew that she was not permitted to have Vierny into her own bed, and neither could she sleep with Vierny in hers. So the best she could do to comfort the girl was sit at her bedside holding her hand. Sometimes they talked deep into the night about anything that might distract the girl from her bad dream… planes or something from her own childhood. But the thing that always seemed to do the trick in calming her back to sleep was promising over and over to always be there for her.

That, unfortunately, was not a promise she was confident of keeping. In the back of her mind, she feared that any day now the caseworker would take this girl away from her. That might happen for any number of reasons – because she had neglected to fill out some obscure piece of paperwork or had broken some forgotten rule. To keep any of that from happening, she maintained a checklist of dos and don'ts, not unlike that of a pre- or post-flight rundown. She kept the doors locked at all times, had medications securely stored away, never left hazardous cleaning products out in the open, and always maintained an orderly household. She was careful to report every bump, bruise or cut that Vierny got... and then followed those calls up with an accident report detailing how the injury had occurred and what she had done in response. She never took pictures of Vierny so as not to risk inadvertently posting one of those online, and she always got the necessary permission before taking the girl for a medical checkup, a dentist appointment, or even to have her hair cut. But most of all, she was always prepared for the caseworker's periodic visits.

Her first month as a foster parent was tense, but also special. Just having someone else about the house was a delight in itself. They did virtually everything together, including cooking, eating, and cleaning up. They shopped, had picnics in the park, movie theater nights, and even a ridiculous attempt at bowling. As to play, she discovered that Vierny's previous experiences had been limited to coloring, so they spent a whole Saturday morning pillaging the toy aisles of several large retail stores. In each, Vierny gravitated toward arts and crafts over dolls and whatnot, yet admitted to having never played a board game in all her life. So, along with kits dedicated to beads, clays, building blocks, glitters, paints, and yarns, she purchased some of the games that she knew her boys had once enjoyed – Monopoly, Clue, Trouble, Sorry!, MouseTrap, and Chutes and Ladders. Lastly, in the spirit of her aunt's insistence that girls be treated no differently than boys, she went crazy in buying a dozen model airplane kits. Assembling those soon became Vierny's favorite activity for them together. When their evenings were not spent on games or projects, they mostly sat on the porch talking, or lounging around in the stairwell nook as she read books to the girl. In everything they did together, she kept the time unstructured and carefree. Whatever fun things Vierny wanted to do, that was what she wanted to do too.

She also had serious things on her mind for Vierny that summer. With permission from Margarette, she got Vierny into swim lessons at the fitness club, and was delighted in sitting at poolside as her girl took to the water like a fish. As the fall approached, so did the need for getting Vierny ready for school. Though Margarette had been rather sketchy as to her previous schooling, it was not difficult to see that the girl would be behind other second graders as to the basics. Her reading skills were sluggish, and she was not at all clear on the concepts behind simple addition or subtraction. With approval from

Margarette, she registered Vierny at a learning center. Together, they spent an hour each day at the kitchen table working on her lessons. That time was so delightful, for Vierny loved to learn. By enrollment time, the girl's hard work had qualified her for the second grade.

Having the wonder of school shopping over, they entered the last week in August with Vierny turning gloomy. It was not difficult to understand why. Though she had only once entered a school year without knowing anyone… that also being in second grade… she still could clearly recall the full terror of it. By Margarette's account, Vierny already had that experience multiple times in first grade as her mother skipped about Texas doing who knows what. All of the excitement she mustered did little to abate the girl's fears.

Sitting together out front of the school on the first day of second grade, she was not surprised when Vierny showed hesitation in leaving the car.

"Mrs. M… I'm going… but… I don't want you walking in with me."

"That's understandable. You want to do it on your own. But I'd be happy to… if that's what you're worried about."

"Don't! I mean… thanks… but please don't."

"Okay. Is there… something bothering you… other than that it's the first day of school?"

Vierny turned her face away and spoke so softly that she could barely hear her.

"If you go in with me… everyone'll know you're not my mother… and I won't know what to say if… if someone asks me about… her."

Throughout the entire summer, Vierny had not once mentioned her mother.

"What do you want to say?"

Vierny looked back with a longing in her eyes that was heartbreaking to behold.

"I want to say that you're my mother."

"Well… feel free to do that. Tell them that you live with your foster mother."

"But what if someone finds out that my real mother's in jail?"

"Then you hold your head high. *You* are not your mother! You are your own special person! Besides… none of them can possibly understand what you've been through."

That was not nearly good enough for putting a smile on her face.

"Listen… I got teased terribly for being an orphan. One thing I learned early on – the bad kids will be bad. You can't change that. But you don't have to associate with them… and you don't have to tolerate their nonsense either. If their behaviors get out of hand, then feel free to tell your teacher. That's what she's there for. Most of all… don't worry. You'll make friends… I just know it. You're a beautiful girl with lots to offer. So very kind, brave… and really fun to be with. So you just be yourself. Your classmates'll be lucky to have you as a friend. And if anyone does dare to be mean to you, then they'll have me to answer to!"

She leaned across and hugged her, finishing with a firm kiss on her forehead. This time, Vierny smiled big and strong.

"Now you go get 'em, girl! And I'll be right here waiting for you when school's out. I promise."

Not until she had waved Vierny all the way into the school and pulled away from the curb did she realize just how tired she was. Hyped up from three months of constant attentiveness, she drove home and collapsed in her nook. On waking after a long nap, her thoughts immediately went to Vierny. The girl was halfway through her first day of second grade. Probably had a cafeteria tray before her at that very moment… just like when she first laid eyes on her. Was she sitting with classmates… or alone, like in all those times at the detention center?

I sure hope she's made a friend. She's had such a hard life.

So strange… A year ago, I was sitting in the cockpit of a renown warbird… and now I'm sitting in a stairwell nook fretting over a seven year old that I only met… Hey… I wonder when it is that she turns eight?

She hopped from the nook over to her writing desk and shuffled through her folder of papers on Vierny.

Oh my! September fourth! That's like… a week from Saturday! What kind of a mother would I be if I'd missed my own daughter's birthday?!

That she was only a foster mother was an unimportant detail to her rabid thinking, for she immediately recognized a personal significance to the date. Thirty three years ago on that day, she had soloed for the first time… and also found out that she was pregnant with her first child. These two coincidences combined to throw her mind into an instant flurry of planning, for she was determined to make this the best birthday Vierny ever had.

The girl entered the car smiling and then would not stop talking about her first day at school. The things she learned, her impressions of her teacher, and the friendliness of the kids she met… every word of which lightened a mother's heart. Not until they were seated at the ice cream parlor she had selected as a treat, with Vierny concentrating on her banana split, did she get her chance to steer the conversation.

"So… someone's birthday is coming up."

She expected at least a smile, but only got back a shrug of the shoulders.

"Come on… it's your special day! I've been thinking… what would you say to inviting a few of these new friends over for…"

"No!"

"No?"

"I mean… no, ma'am."

"I appreciate the respect… but that's actually not what I was referring to. Are you saying you'd rather not have a party?"

"Can it be… just the two of us? I'd like that much better."

Though she should want Vierny to have a stupendous event with a dozen new friends there to revel in the girl's birthday, hearing that it would be only them was far better.

"If that's what you'd prefer. But I do have some tricks up my sleeve. In fact… I've already started planning. But don't bother asking for details, because it's going to be a surprise. Hopefully one you'll never forget."

Come that Saturday, she had a private party for two set up in the dining room. She strung streamers, dangled balloons from the chandelier, had two colorful birthday hats, a small cake with the girl's name surrounded by eight candles, and a present of Vierny's first ever bicycle. That was something the two of them had talked about for weeks, seeing as the girl did not yet know how to ride. But none of that was the big surprise. It took her a week to persuade Margarette, and she only succeeded by bringing in a pile of documentation. So when the cake and ice cream were finally done, she had Vierny head out to the car.

"Where're we going?"

"I'm taking you up in an airplane. I've reserved one for just the two of us."

"You're not serious?!"

As they drove to the airport and she went about the process of renting a Cessna Skylane for an hour, Vierny remained silent. But the girl's wide eyes and big smile through it all showed that it was the good kind of quiet. Holding hands on the short walk out to the plane, Vierny's eyes were all over the ramp, taking in every detail that she could cram into her eager mind. And still the girl did not speak unless spoken to. Even after getting her comfortably strapped into the second seat, all Vierny could do was nod her head with an eagerness primed for busting out of her smile.

"Now… I'm going to run through the preflight checklist before I start her up. Let's get your headset adjusted first. How's that feel?"

Again, more smiling and head nodding.

She's so happy… she can barely stand it!

"Com check. Vierny Novik… do you read me?"

"Roger, Mrs. M." There was a brief pause before the girl came back. "I've been wanting to say that for a long time." And then Vierny burst out into a fit of giggles that kept popping up throughout the preflight checklist.

"Sorry… I'll be serious now."

"You don't have to be. You just have to be a kid."

Vierny went silent again, but smiled even more broadly than before. As the engine started, the girl gave a little squeak of excitement into her headset's microphone. Through the take off and clearance out to the east, Vierny's eyes were all over the place – on every instrument, out the windows to both the ground and the outside parts of the plane, and on her pilot… always with that big smile. Going into a brief explanation of the controls, she was not surprised that Vierny asked no questions, for it seemed obvious that the girl was doing everything she could to prevent her mouth from stealing one ounce of the wonderment that her eyes were desperately soaking up.

With the plane having reached a suitable altitude and air speed, she was finally ready for the moment she had been waiting for.

"Vierny… what say you take the yoke and do some flying?"

"Seriously?!"

"Go on… I'm right here. Nothing bad'll happen."

She then guided Vierny through a series of gradual banks to the left and right, instructing her at every step along the way as to how the plane was behaving. Again, Vierny said little, though her head kept up the nodding. After about five minutes or so, she picked up on a tenseness in the girl's forearms and decided to relieve her of the yoke's burden.

"What'd you think of that?"

"Totally awesome!"

"Tell me… can you see the horizon out over the nose?"

The girl lifted her chin and straighten her back.

"Yes, ma'am."

"That's the pilot's reference point… where sky meets earth. Got one in here too." She tapped the gyro. "Now watch this…"

For the next several minutes, she went about varying the pitch and roll of the plane so Vierny could make comparisons between the two horizons.

"This is sooo cool!"

"I thought you'd like that."

"I like *everything*!"

With the time allotted for their flight nearly over, she brought the plane about for an approach into the airport. Vierny was silent for the landing, giving off only a little yelp of anticipated pleasure as the wheels touched down. But from the moment the engine was cut off, the girl's mouth completely took over in motoring through a constant run-on of questions and exclamations about this or that aspect of their flying experience. It was Vierny's turn to talk, so she soaked in every one of the girl's words. Holding hands on the walk across the ramp, Vierny remained twisted about in order to keep her eyes on the plane as she jabbered on.

"I can't believe it – that was the most incredible thing I've ever done in my entire life! Hey – what're those things at the end called again? 'A-ler-ons'… right? Did you see how those moved for me?! I can't believe it – I flew that plane! I want to do that again. Can we please do that again? Not right away… I know it costs loads of money… but soon? How much does it cost anyway? What if I got a job, do you think I could pay for flying? Never mind… I'll just become a pilot like you… and then they'll have to pay *me* to fly. Ha! Isn't that funny?! I'd do it for nothing. So how old do you have to be to learn… and how old were you? Do you suppose they'll teach a kid like me? I mean… I know I'm not ready… I'm sure there's loads to learn… but I bet I can. The whole thing… taking off… flying… and landing. Ohh… but my favorite part was all the shaking! Sometimes I couldn't tell if it was me or the plane! And the noise! I *really* love that too! Kind of… muffly in my headset… but still really cool! I don't know why, but plane sounds are the absolute best! Don't you think so?! Especially the time when it went 'chug, chug, chug.' Wait… that's not it. It was more like a… 'tha–chunking' kind of thing. And then the plane just dropped out of the sky! I thought I was going to die! Not really! I was just so excited! You know… for a second… I actually felt like a bird… flying all by myself! I was up there just *floooating* on the wind. That's the best feeling ever, know what I mean, Mrs. M?"

"Yes, Vierny… I know exactly what you mean."

Their summer together had shown her that she was in love with everything about this girl. How sensitive she was in the face of the hardships she had been through, how quick she was at picking up on new things, and how both the girl's smiles and tears could melt her heart. The hugging rule had gone right out the door, for Vierny was now hugging her throughout the day. The tender side to her had finally won out. Best of all, though she still addressed her as Mrs. M, a very obvious devotion had crept into the girl's voice… one that seemed on the verge of calling her something entirely different. She could sense it – Vierny was finally accepting this as her home.

Yet she did not overlook that there was still much to learn about the girl's ways. How best to protect her from her own weaknesses, what mistakes to allow her to make, and when to get into her face with correction. They had their battles… particularly over how late Vierny could stay up on school nights and whether the girl had the God-given right to lock her bedroom door whenever the whim hit her. Always, she tried to handle such conflicts with perspective. Particularly in the heat of an argument, she endeavored to put herself in the girl's place and imagine the worst of what she had been through. Being repeatedly rejected by a mother who so obviously did not love her would have warped any child's perspective on life. So she did not resent Vierny on those times when the girl tested the limits of either discipline or love. What abandoned child would not?! This girl must struggle with all sorts of self-doubt and self-loathing… along with a terrible suspicion of anyone who claimed to care.

But even if she were to fully gain Vierny's trust, she knew from experience that raising a young girl would be no piece of cake… irrespective of puberty's mood swings. If this eight year old version of an occasionally sassy, pugnacious and sullen girl was any indication, then the teenage years would likely be even more challenging. Somehow, she had absolutely no fear of such things, for she had already come to love this girl as her own. More than anything, she wished to wipe away the years of sadness and fill the child's life with joy.

As her desire for adopting Vierny steadily grew, so did her indecision over how best to go about doing it. There was an abundance of advice out there regarding approaches for incorporating either a foster or an adopted child into a family. Yet none of it seemed to fit her particular circumstances of three grown sons with wives, all six of whom thought she was crazy. Not one of them understood why she had taken on a foster child. Worse, none of them had expressed the slightest interest in meeting Vierny. They always had their excuses. Wade and Valerie were out of work… again… and changing apartments, so the only time they had free was that required for getting a check in the mail. With infant children of their own, the older two couples were completely preoccupied with being first-time parents. In particular, Chad and Stacey expressed their wishes that she not drive down to Midland for a visit if she was planning on bringing Vierny along.

"Marna… Merriweather's only seven months… which is not nearly old enough to be around strangers… especially strange children."

"But don't you put her in daycare?"

"Of course. The very best in Midland! But that's totally different. She's with *professionals* there."

So she gave up trying during those summer months to concentrate instead on getting Vierny comfortable in her new home. But with September coming to a close and Vierny having settled in nicely at school, her longing to make the girl her daughter had become overwhelming.

Chicken or the egg... which is best? Do I first introduce her to the boys... let her get a feel for what they're like... and then bring up the subject of adoption? Or... do I bring up adoption first with her, and then let the chips fall where they may as to how the boys and the DILs responded?

She wrestled with these questions for several weeks before finally deferring to the opinion of Vierny's caseworker. Margarette was quite clear. Though Vierny, being under twelve, did not have the explicit right to deny an adoption, every foster child should be given the benefit of knowing as much as possible about the family prior to adoption. Only then could the child feel as if they were part of the decision.

So... she forced a Sunday afternoon visit upon Chad and Stacey. The greetings were done well enough... even though neither showed Vierny much warmth. Still... they were past that awkward moment and into the exchange of pleasantries within the entryway to their house when Vierny reached over with obvious tenderness to tickle little Merriweather under the chin. To her shock, Stacey yanked her child away with such blatant revulsion.

"Don't you dare touch her!"

"I was just..."

"I said don't touch her! Marna – will you please control your foster child?!"

She was too stunned to know what to say... and all the more when her own son piped in with harsh words of his own.

"Geez, Mom... this should already be obvious to you. If you insist on visiting, then you keep that girl away from our Merriweather... understand?!"

Before the tears could come, she took hold of Vierny's hand and pulled her out the front door.

"I'm so sorry, Sweetheart. You didn't deserve that."

"I... I was only trying to play with her."

"I know... It wasn't your fault. Like I said on the way over, Chad and Stacey... they're difficult people. They always have to be cruel. It makes me so mad! But I'll tell you this – I'm not allowing them to treat you like that. So if you don't mind... I'd like you to wait in the car while I go have a word with them. It'll only take a minute... and then we're leaving."

She gave Vierny a quick hug and kiss on the forehead before gently sending her off toward the car. After a deep breath to get her wits about her, she stepped back inside.

"Chad... Stacey... Vierny and I are leaving... but first... we need to talk."

"I suppose you're expecting an apology or something lame like that! You should be the one apologizing to us! You knew full well that we didn't approve of you taking on that... that delinquent as a..."

"She's not a delinquent… and I won't allow you to treat her as one! So here's how it's going to be. I'm planning on adopting her, so you'll…"

"Mom, you've got to be kidding me?!"

"No… and don't ever interrupt me again! So it's as simple as this – if you two can't accept her as a sister… then you can't accept me as a mother either."

"I can't believe this! You're actually giving us an ultimatum! This is so like you! You just… do whatever the hell you want with no regard for anyone else! You don't care if it embarrasses us! And why should you?! Because of you, I don't have a father to be a granddad to my child!"

"You just hold it right there!"

"And now you're expecting us to accept this little criminal as an aunt to our Merriweather?! We shouldn't be made to…"

"I'm not making you do anything! Your predisposed bent's already decided everything for you!"

"What the hell's that supposed to mean?"

"Chad… I'm sorry… but if you can't figure that out on your own, then me explaining it to you certainly won't make a difference."

She took one last look of longing at her granddaughter nestled in Stacey's arms, fearing that it might be a very long time before she saw her again.

"Goodbye."

She left their house without another word. In the front seat was Vierny, obviously doing her best to quickly wipe her eyes. She stepped into the car and immediately pulled the girl into a tight embrace, with Vierny instantly returning to her tears.

"Forgive me… it was really foolish of me to put you through that. I was just trying to give you a chance to meet my family before asking you to become part of it. But it's all backfired… and I wouldn't blame you if…"

Vierny abruptly pulled away.

"What'd you say?"

"I was going to ask you if… perhaps you'd be open to being adopted by me. But after meeting those two, I wouldn't blame you if you…"

"Yes, ma'am."

"…had second thoughts about… Come again?"

"I want to be adopted by you. I've wanted it since… I don't know… ever since the first time you hugged me. My mother never touched me… except to grab me… or hit me. So when you did… I sort of… started pretending that maybe you could… you know… care about me… sort of like… a real mother would."

"Vierny… that's exactly who I want to be for you. But first… there's something really, really important that you need to understand. We can't choose our family members. I can't choose who my sons are any more than you can choose who your mother is. We have to love who we're given. But that's not the way it is with being adopted. I've chosen you, Vierny… and I love you so much. You need to know that this feeling of mine wasn't forced upon me. I pursued you wholeheartedly. It might not seem like that at times, but it's true. So whenever you're feeling less of a daughter because some numbskull like one of my sons or their wives goes out of their way to remind you that your adopted… then you just remember this – I chose you! Do you… understand what I'm trying to say? I want you to be my daughter."

"Yes, ma'am. I mean… yes, Mom. I understand."

They did so much more crying together… right there in Chad and Stacey's driveway. But it was all of the good kind. The trip back to Lubbock was some of the sweetest time she had yet with this soon-to-be daughter of hers, as they laughed and giggled for nearly two hours straight.

It took over a month for the approval to come down from a judge, but on November ninth, Vierny Novik finally became Vierny Novik Meitner. As far as she was concerned, this day would be commemorated as Vierny's second birthday, having almost as much meaning to her as the girl's first. As they sat on the front porch late that afternoon watching a very faint crescent moon win its race to set before the sun, they were actually more waiting upon a delivery man. That was Vierny's idea… which she found amusing to no end. To be so pure that the pinnacle of rewards for the signing of adoption papers could best be expressed by a pepperoni pizza with extra mushrooms! Actually, she… as the girl's new mother… was secretly working on the details of something much more special in the way of a celebration.

Watching Vierny rock, she wondered what was going on in the girl's mind. They had only known each other for less than six months, and here Vierny was swinging herself back and forth in the rocking chair with such trust in the security of this new home and this new name.

She's such a marvel! I wonder if…

"What is it, Mom?"

She was startled to discover that Vierny had stopped rocking and was staring over the arm of the chair at her.

"Sorry… I was just enjoying watching you. I won't do it anymore."

"That's okay. I don't mind."

The girl went back to rocking as if they had been discussing the weather.

"So… what's it like knowing that this'll be your home until you're all grown up?"

"I don't know... Pretty cool I guess. It's as good as any of the places I've ever lived."

As Vierny gave her a sneaky sort of smile, she noticed in wonder for the first time that the girl could do that same thing that her late husband had been so good at... make one eyebrow shoot up on its own. So cute, it made her heart skip a beat! Of course, she knew she was being messed with, but was also absolutely loving every second of it.

"That's nice to hear. But all joking aside... you know you can talk to me about anything."

"I know."

"And you won't mind me asking you things either? You know... like about the places you used to live."

"No... but there's not that much to say. I've slept in the back of a van... in a bunch of apartments... some foster homes... and in that detention center. None of them were nice. Your house is the absolute best!"

"I'm glad you like it... but you do realize that it's *your* house too?"

"I do... but I sort of feel like I'm in one of those fairytales... you know... where your wishes come true... and you get to live in a big castle... but you still can't believe it. Like you're not sure what's real and what's a dream. Know what I mean?"

"Definitely. And I guess this house sort of does look like a castle... what with the spires on the front... and the porch being like a moat."

"Mom... I was actually thinking that's my castle over there."

Her daughter nodded toward the hangar, and then turned back with a smile so big that it made her face flush.

"Ahh... the regal realm of Princess Vierny. I've noticed you spending more time playing in... I'm mean... *imagining* in there. So... speaking of that hangar... I've got a really big surprise for you."

Vierny instantly came to a stop, this time leaning really far over the arm of the rocking chair to gape in her direction.

"You're getting me a plane!"

"Dream on. It's not *that* big of a surprise! But it does have to do with a plane."

"Uww, uww... you're signing me up for flying lessons!"

"Umm... no. We'll... have to revisit that subject when you're sixteen."

"Seriously?! That's like forever from now! Then what is it?"

"We're going on our first overnight trip together this weekend. I'm taking you to see the plane that was once in there."

"Are you serious?!"

"Absolutely! I do have a few more surprises than just the plane, but I'll be keeping those a secret for the time being."

Stories of flying had always been one of those subjects that Vierny returned to time and again before bed… and of course, she did her best to encourage her daughter's interest in the Corsair. Vierny already knew much about the plane's history, as well as repeatedly expressed her interest in one day seeing it. That was the inspiration behind this trip… to make the dreams of Vierny's bedtime stories come true.

The two of them could now go anywhere they wanted and do whatever they wished, all without having to get approval. So they woke early on Saturday morning and set out on a leisurely drive, conversing when they felt like it and looking out at the scenery when they did not. But seeing the Dallas skyline had such a somber effect on Vierny, for she said she could still remember having been homeless here with "You-know-who." So she went a little faster on the interstate than was necessary, just to spare her of the sight.

Arriving at the Mesquite airfield, she took pride in introducing Vierny as her daughter to Benny, Earl and the other employees of Bright Star. Earl then took them on a tour of the restoration projects currently being worked on. She felt so much pleasure in seeing her daughter's fascination as Earl explained the various components of a Tigercat's dissembled Double Wasp engine. Then the moment she had been waiting for finally came, as Earl led them into a separate hangar. Though she had not seen her Corsair in over a year, she actually had eyes only for her daughter standing in awe of the plane.

"Mom… this was yours?!"

"Yep."

"And you flew it all by yourself?!"

"Yep again."

Vierny turned back to the Corsair, eyes moving from prop to tail and back again, sighing as she spoke to herself.

"I have the coolest mom ever!"

She stepped back to wipe her eyes, and then started taking pictures as Earl led the girl in a tour around the plane. Vierny ran her fingertips along the fuselage, wiggled the elevators, peeked up into the engine cowlings, and flexed the only blade tip she could reach. All that brought her the memory of having done the same thing when her father-in-law led her around this plane so many years ago.

With their circuit completed, Vierny came to her side and sought out a hand to hold.

"Mom… it's so amazing! I wish I could have seen you in it?"

"You know what, I forgot… I have a video of myself flying it."

"No joke?"

"Completely serious. We'll watch it when we get home. But right now… I have to admit… I'm rather disappointed in you."

Vierny's face instantly fell, as she knew it would.

"Did I… do something wrong?"

She nodded toward Earl, who immediately went off on his own, and then she looked back down to Vierny's mortified expression.

"Honestly… I'd have thought any daughter of mine would've asked ten times by now to sit in that cockpit! But I guess if you're not interested…"

"No! I am! I am!"

At that moment, Earl returned pushing along a stair ladder on wheels. He positioned it at the cockpit and motioned for Vierny to climb up. But she hesitated before putting a foot to the first step.

"Do you think… maybe there's enough room for both me and my mom?"

Those were words to melt a mother's heart. So she climbed the stairs first, got herself situated in the Corsair's cockpit, and then reached out her arms to receive her daughter. With Vierny balanced on a thigh, she lost track of time within the joy of explaining one miracle to the eager mind of another. The delight on her daughter's face and the closeness of them together in the Corsair's cockpit… those were things she would never forget.

After Earl took many pictures of them, they finally climbed out of the cockpit to pose together before the plane's prop. And then sadly, it was time to leave. They thanked Earl and then walked hand in hand to the car. To her delight, Vierny did not once look back at the plane, being much more content to move along nestled up under her arm.

They ate dinner that night at a Japanese steakhouse, where she took nearly as many pictures of Vierny cracking up over the chef's juggling act as she did of the girl before the Corsair. They slept together nose-to-nose in their hotel room's king-sized bed, whispering themselves to sleep.

In the morning, as they lazily made their way through the hotel's complimentary breakfast, she revealed her two other surprises for the day. For the first, she took Vierny to the Dallas museum that housed *Sulla Terra*. Together, they stood before this sister relief and shared their thoughts on its meaning. They both concluded that one was just as artistically done as the other, but Sky was so much better than Earth. Yet they did not stay there for long, as she sensed that this relief disturbed Vierny. Quickly moving past the museum's other exhibits, they left to accomplish one final gift to Vierny for becoming her daughter. For the next four hours, the rides and rollercoasters of Six Flags Over Texas completely purged the girl's mind of the second relief.

On the way back to Lubbock, she veered off the interstate at Sweetwater. Without turning off the engine, she pulled to the shoulder and pointed out the airfield that she had told Vierny so many stories about. It was there that her aunt Gwen and other women like her had forged new ground as aviators. Those women had dreamed big, and sacrificed much to reach those dreams.

"And you know… so can you, Vierny… in whatever you choose to do."

They left Avenger Field as the sun set, taking a backroad to US84. It was then that Vierny unexpectedly opened up, by choice or by some inducement of the dark. Sometimes in a hush of whispers, Vierny told of having been beaten by a woman who more often than not was strung out on drugs. How the girl was afraid to fall asleep on those nights when one of her mother's boyfriends was staying in the apartment. How she got bounced in and out of foster homes whenever her mother ran afoul of the law. How she found that looking up into the sky became her only way of escaping the misery of her life. And how she learned to take care of herself… because no one else would.

The rest of the way to Lubbock, she drove with one hand on the wheel and the other holding her daughter's. Somewhere along the way, she became aware that her girl had fallen asleep. With some exertion, she managed to carry Vierny into the house without waking her, and laid her to sleep in the stairwell nook. Spreading a blanket over her, she ran her fingers through the girl's hair, shifting strands from off her forehead before gently kissing her there.

Such a gift…

"Goodnight, my beautiful daughter. Sweet dreams."

CHAPTER

50

THE TARANTULA
HAWK'S TALE

Scoot around a little more… nice and easy. Careful – don't make it so obvious! Okay, now… lean over and bring a hand to your forehead… casual-like.

Perfect! I can finally see her without…

"Mom… are you watching me again?"

"What?! Of course not! What a notion?! Why would a mother be watching her daughter?! I've never heard of such a thing! That's just… Alright… I admit it. I was watching you. But you were being so cute with your…"

"You're weird."

Lately, that was her word – weird. Good things were weird, bad things were weird, and weird things were weird. Everything was weird.

Oh! Here comes that smile I love so much! Such a pretty face!

"You're still looking at me…"

"Sorry… Go back to your homework. I won't interrupt again."

Vierny rolled her eyes – a clear indication that she was buying none of it. But then she gave back another one of those cute smiles… every single one capable of blessing a mother's socks off. Living with Vierny was the most wonderful thing that had ever happened to her. Every day was a delight.

But I guess I should get serious about finishing this thing.

Shifting back to a posture more suitable for writing, she gave one more quick glance toward Vierny lounging there in the nook and then returned to her half-completed letter. To her defense, she had *mostly* been studying her daughter for the purpose of describing how the fifteen year old was blossoming into a lovely young woman… though Travis and Amanda probably would not care much about that. The subject of an adopted sister was still something of an annoyance to them… even after seven years. At least they had not flat out rejected Vierny. Not like the other two couples had. It was unbelievable that Wade and Valerie were still afraid of the girl, whereas Chad and Stacey…

Such total assholes!

Unable to stop herself, she leaned away from the writing desk to throw down her pen. Out of the corner of her eye, she picked up on Vierny looking over.

"You okay?"

"Absolutely. Just taking a break."

In going back to her homework, Vierny did that cute little eyebrow twitch to show her skepticism. The girl obviously knew that her mother was wrestling with something unpleasant. Which was an understatement, to say the least! The month since the incident had not diminished one degree of her anger toward Chad and Stacey. Truth be told, the two had always treated Vierny like a total stranger, so she should have known better than persisting in a fruitless effort aimed at altering their lousy attitudes. But in her never-say-die determination to break through the couple's wall of prejudice, she just had to drive down there with Vierny on Christmas Eve under the guise of delivering presents. That was the straw that broke the camel's back. She still could hear how Merriweather proclaimed quite authoritatively that she need not respond to Vierny.

"Cause Mommy says you ain't really an aunt. Not like Aunt Valree or Aunt Manda. They're real aunts. You ain't even part of the family."

In promptly correcting the second grader's misconception, she probably came across a tad too stern on behalf of her daughter, for Chad and Stacey immediately jumped in to their child's defense. That unfortunately started a heated argument during the Christmas Eve dinner. She ended the visit short of dessert… which was just as well, seeing as the couple had not troubled themselves to get Vierny a present. So she was absolutely determined to make that her last attempt at reaching Chad and Stacey.

She picked up the pen and returned to the letter meant for Travis and Amanda.

Just fill up the rest of the page and be done with it.

On she went, valiantly trying to chip away at the older couple's aloof reserve with her periodic attempts at correspondences and phone calls. Somehow, she was still counting on Travis with his law degree, and Amanda with her MBA, to have the educational benefit of perspective in moderating their biases against an adopted sister. She nevertheless remained careful not to patronize them in her letters by focusing too much on how Vierny was scholastically a model ninth grader. So in this particular one, she had a mind inclined toward highlighting something of the girl's imagination.

Like that time in fourth grade when she spray-painted that huge runway on the hangar floor. Man, was she ever cute! Putting wings on her bike and constructing a cardboard box hangar big enough for it. She even piled up more boxes into a tower and decorated it like the real thing. She flew around that hangar for months and months pretending that she was a plane!

Ugh... but I can't use any of that. I keep forgetting... Travis doesn't like to be reminded of that hangar.

In fact, there was nothing about the girl's fascination with airplanes that had ever resonated with any of her boys or their wives. So it would be totally useless for her to describe how Vierny had dangled model planes from her bedroom ceiling and hung aviation posters all over her walls.

Write about something else.

As with other letters over the past six months, she was trying to wheedle out an invitation for her and Vierny to visit them in the upcoming summer. Except for pictures posted online by Amanda, she had not yet laid eyes on her two year old grandson Dillon.

It's so unfair! They've made plenty of trips to Amanda's family in North Carolina, but not once to Lubbock!

She shook off the bitter thought and returned to her letter. Maybe she should focus instead on depicting Vierny as a normal teenage girl. That should appeal to Amanda's feminine qualities... and certainly be nonthreatening to Travis.

I could write about that sleepover. Vierny and her girlfriends had such a blast. They kept me up all night with their giggle-screaming!

No... best not risk that. It might make her look flighty... and a bit rebellious. I don't think Amanda's ever gotten over her having been in a detention center.

Maybe she should just stick with insights into parenting. Something like... the importance of getting to know one's child.

That might work... I could write about the time I figured out how to deal with Vierny's grumpiness. Just feed the girl some meat, and she immediately snaps back to her sweet self.

Better not chance that either. It'll make her look like she's... weird. Besides, Amanda's never valued this mother-in-law's advice... particularly when it comes to the subject of raising children. Best just stick with the boring stuff –

that book I'm reading, the classes Vierny's taking, and how I hope those crocuses I planted last fall actually come up.

Reconciled to finish this letter blandly, she made to use her pen… except her right hand was shaking… just like her left had been doing for many months. Glancing up to make sure that Vierny had not noticed, she discreetly went about flexing her fingers.

It made no sense. She was using one of those hand exercisers to strengthen her grip… and was pretty faithful to her New Year's resolution of giving up caffeine. So far, nothing had helped.

Probably just arthritis. Getting old really sucks!

After working her fingers for a while, she was finally able to overcome that annoying trembling sensation. But as it was near-on time for bed… and she was in no mood for completing the letter… she gladly set aside her frustrations in exchange for the prospect of sitting for a few minutes with Vierny in the nook.

"I think I'll finish this tomorrow. Mind if I join you… assuming I'm not interrupting anything?"

"No, ma'am. That'd be great. Let me clear a space for you."

As Vierny went about gathering her school books, she hopped up from her writing desk… only to have the damnedest thing happen. From thigh level down, her left leg went stiff, causing her to lose balance. She only narrowly averted a fall by getting a hand over to the wall.

"What're you doing?"

"I… I don't know. My leg… it sort of… fell asleep."

"Weird."

"Vierny… I can't move it at all! Could you… would you help me please?"

Without delay, the girl was at her side shuffling her backward to the writing desk.

"Mom… what's going on?"

"I have no idea."

"You know… I've noticed that your shaking's getting worse."

"What shaking?"

"Come on, Mom… I can feel it every time we hold hands. I know you're trying to hide it from me."

"It's nothing. Just too much coffee. Besides… it comes and goes."

"So you've had this happen before?"

"Well… no. Not this. But see… the feeling's already returned to my leg."

Doing her best to act as if everything was normal, she managed to bend her knee back and forth several times until the worried expression on Vierny's face had softened.

"Okay... but maybe you should... get it checked out or something. Just in case it's serious."

"Sure... I'll see to it as soon as I can."

"No, Mom. If you say that, then I know it means you're not going to. What was it you were telling me the other day... that thing about the five bad qualities of a bad pilot in a bad situation? Isn't this the passivity thing? You know... ignoring a problem when it shows up?"

"Unbelievable! I just had to have a really smart daughter. Okay... fine! I'll make an appointment if you promise not to worry."

It was one of those things she occasionally forgot was necessary in being a mother. She needed to be in tune with her child's concerns. Unaddressed, those led to fretting... and fretting stole happiness. Resolving not to give her daughter any cause for worry, she made an appointment in the morning with her general practitioner, seeing as it was well past time for a checkup anyway.

Unfortunately, her doctor provided her with no great insight, and instead gave her a referral. In two weeks, she found herself sitting in the waiting room of Lubbock's finest neurologist, having grown quite worried during those days. The leg freezing thing had happened two more times. She was absolutely no fan of doctors or their waiting rooms, as both were a reminder that she could not always be in control. But this situation was different. She had grown very anxious to find out what was going wrong with her leg.

In short course, she was called forth by a nurse to an examination room. After all the folderol of blood pressure, temperature and heart rate readings, she was finally introduced to Dr. Steven Kilpatrick, neurosurgeon and newcomer to Texas... or so he oddly made a point of saying on greeting her.

"I've read over the notes your GP provided... so let's have a talk about these symptoms of yours. Can you describe for me what's been going on?"

"Sure. Umm... I guess it started with my hands. They sort of... shake. Not all of the time... But when they do, it gets really difficult to hold little things... you know... a pen or a makeup brush."

"How long's this been going on?"

"I'd say... about a year."

"Did it start off with both hands or just one?"

"It was only the left at first. I could get by with that. But now the right's acting up too."

"I see… Let's get to these incidences of your leg freezing. The first time it happened, what were you doing?"

"I'd just risen from a chair and my leg… it simply wouldn't work. I've never had anything like that happen before. It was so weird. I mean… no one has to tell their body what to do. It just does it. But no matter what I tried, I couldn't get it to move."

"Show me where."

She held her hand at thigh level.

"From here… all the way down."

"Would you say that the sensation was similar to or different from the feeling of having a limb fall asleep?"

"Pretty different. My leg didn't have that pins-and-needles sort of feel. It just… wouldn't move."

"And this was definitely only in the left?

"That's correct. I could still move my right."

"Hmm…"

He turned away to a computer screen… staying there for longer than she felt it necessary.

"Doctor…?"

"Sorry… I was looking into your family's medical history… but you put down 'not applicable' in your paperwork. Were you adopted?"

"Sort of… I was raised by my aunt. My parents died when I was very young."

"That must have been difficult…"

She shrugged off the statement, having no real desire for discussing something that had happened so long ago… especially since her chief concern was the now.

"According to your file… I see that you'll be turning… sixty six in August."

"That's correct."

"Okay… let's return to your symptoms. Have you had any instances where you've felt like your arms or your legs were fidgeting or pulsating uncontrollably? It doesn't have to be severe… even something slight."

"Umm… yes. It sometimes happens at night while I'm lying in bed. My left does these… I don't know what you'd call them… little wobbly motions. I have to hold it still in order to make it stop. I kind of thought it was just tired legs."

"Could be. Has a similar thing shown up in your arms or shoulders?"

"Maybe a little… but definitely nothing like in my leg."

"What about general stiffness to your muscles and joints?"

"Oh, I've got plenty of that! Try keeping up with a fifteen year old without being sore at the end of the day!"

"So you'd say that you lead an especially active lifestyle?"

"I… I use to. But not so much lately. I sort of… get tired easily."

"Understandable… So how about your speech? Any noticeable difficulties annunciating or making yourself understood?"

"I don't think so. Not that I'm aware of."

"Any problems swallowing?"

"No."

"How about your sense of smell?"

"Umm… maybe it's a bit off. My daughter usually picks up on things long before I do. I kind of thought… maybe it's just hay fever. Lubbock's wicked on that."

"So you've been experiencing congestion or sinus pressure?"

"Well… no… not really. So I guess it's not hay fever then."

He smiled, but not in a reassuring sort of way.

"What say we skip the questions for now. I've got a few simple neurological tests for gauging your responsiveness, dexterity and mobility. Then we'll talk more."

For the next ten minutes or so, the doctor poked, prodded and tweaked her hands, legs, arms and back. He then made her walk about the room, stand as still as possible on each foot, and do a variety of other simple movements. Throughout, the competitive side of her took on each task with a determination to excel… but all too often, she found that the doctor's little sighs took the pleasure of success right out of her. He finally had her return to the examination table and pulled up a stool before her.

"There're a few abnormalities in your gait. You don't swing your arms much… and you're stooped over a bit as you walk."

"I never noticed that."

"You also exhibit a stiffness in your overall range of motion. Along with the tremors and this muscular rigidity that's arisen over the past month… and that these symptoms manifested themselves initially on one side… I'm concerned that it's consistent with a neurological condition of some kind."

"Condition?! That sounds serious."

She fully expected him to wave off the poor choice of words… but there he sat nodding with an 'I'm sorry for your loss' sort of look coming to his face.

This can't be! He's definitely blowing this whole thing out of proportion!

"There're several possibilities to consider, and the best way to narrow it down is to see how you respond to medication."

"Then you're not really sure about this?"

"All I can say is that your symptoms are suggestive… and by your account, they seem to be progressing. We should take them seriously."

"So what're you thinking?"

"Let's not get ahead of ourselves."

"But I'd still like to know what you're thinking… especially if it's something serious."

"I'd prefer to wait until I know for certain… but I understand. Mrs. Meitner… in my opinion… you show many of the early warning signs of Parkinson's."

The word hit her like a ton of bricks.

"Pa… Parkinson's? Are you sure?"

"Like I said… we'll know better once we see how you respond to medication. It could be something entirely different."

"But if it is Parkinson's?"

"Then… you can rest assured that the medical field's come a long way in treating that disease."

"So you're saying there's a cure?"

"Umm… actually not. I won't mislead you, Mrs. Meitner. If that's my final diagnosis… then you're likely to have a difficult road ahead of you. That particular disease never goes into remission. It only gets more challenging with time. But the road is long… meaning that the disease is not life threatening. Today, a Parkinson's patient can expect to live just as long as anyone else their age."

That assurance was hardly a comfort to her. She had heard enough about that disease… and wanted no part of it.

"Ahh… one other thing before I send the nurse in to check you out. I noticed from your file and that medical alert bracelet on your wrist that you're allergic to bee venom."

"That's correct…"

"I suppose you have a prescription for an EpiPen?"

"I do. Do you need to see it? I've got it here in my purse."

"No. Just wanted to point out that epinephrine can exacerbate many neurological conditions such as Parkinson's. The same is the case with most anesthesia. We'll need to be looped in on all of your medical and dental treatments. I'm sorry… but life might soon be getting more complicated. But then again… we shouldn't be getting out ahead of ourselves. Let's see how you respond to medication."

She left the neurologist's office with a prescription and a follow-up appointment for three weeks off. The next twenty days were a battle in which she inwardly hoped that the medication – a low dosage of levodopa – would not work. Facing the unknown was far better than facing the unpleasant certainty of something like Parkinson's. But from the very first dose on, she found that the drug worked like a charm. Her hands stilled and her leg remained fully functional. She did not need the follow-up appointment to confirm to her the terrible truth.

From the moment Dr. Kilpatrick offered his official diagnosis, she felt all hope of a bright future slip away. She might have heard him offer reassurances. That his Parkinson's patients maintained active and productive lifestyles… That she could manage her symptoms with proper medication… That her day-to-day would only marginally be affected... All of that entered an ear and went out the other side without displacing one concern she had picked up from her online research. So she pressed him, making him run through the stages of the disease in reference to his treatment plan. Only then did he confirm what she already feared. Levodopa might be working now, but it would eventually lose its effectiveness. Same for the other dopamine derivatives they might explore. There would even come a day when medication caused more problems than it solved. Long before then, she would lose the ability to drive a car, and then the danger of falling would necessitate even more drastic changes to her lifestyle. Simple tasks… brushing her teeth or buttoning a blouse… would take forever to accomplish, and she would certainly need someone's help. Her face would freeze, her speech would soften, and her sleep cycle would be completely altered. In the face of these terrible inevitabilities, he only offered one assurance in return – that he and his team would be there with her every step of the way.

Being diagnosed with Parkinson's was a bitter pill to swallow. She walked from the neurologist's office to her car in total shock, wondering how many years she had left for being out on her own. The simple ability of putting one foot in front of the other… that was a thing she had always taken for granted. Somewhere down the line… hopefully many years off… she would find herself unable to walk without assistance. It could even come sooner, if she ended up being one of those unfortunate of the unfortunates whose condition inexplicably accelerated. If she was to gamble the moment away… ignore the disease for the time being by sticking her head deep into the sand of a medicated denial… where would she be when things got real ugly? For today, her symptoms could be masked, but what about tomorrow? No way could she allow this disease to creep up on her. She needed to act decisively while she still could… because sooner or later, a wheelchair loomed in her future.

She entered her car with a pilot's confidence for mastering this disease… but only got as far as buckling her seatbelt before collapsing into tears.

How am I ever going to tell Vierny?! I can't just spring something like this on her. Not after all she's been through! She deserves to be happy for once in her life!

What if… What if this makes her think that I only adopted her to take care of me in my old age? I can't allow her to believe such a…

Oh my god! What if someone at CPS finds out?! Is it possible?! Can they annul an adoption?! I certainly wouldn't put it past them! Vierny absolutely can not go back into the system! It'll destroy her! And I'll die before I allow that to happen!

From that moment on, she purposed to keep her condition a secret for as long as she could. She would wholeheartedly dive into whatever treatment or medication Dr. Kilpatrick recommended, but she would not confide in anyone. Not her friends, and certainly not in her sons or the DILs. No one but Vierny need know.

Even though I have absolutely no idea how I'm going to tell her.

Of course, the best way was to come right out with it, especially since the girl already knew about the day's appointment. With two hours before needing to pick her up from school, she decided not to go home. That would mean sitting in the nook and giving way to the tears. Neither would she go anywhere in town and risk running into someone she knew. She would stay hidden within her own little world of fretting and spend the hours in meaningless driving. Around and around the Loop she went, trying to dull her worries over how to deliver the bad news. Starting in on her third circuit… or maybe it was the fourth… she happen to catch sight of an airplane's contrail fading from the sky, and instantly knew what she should do.

Trying to smile as wide as she normally did when picking up her daughter, she waited for the girl's seatbelt to latch before asking about the school day. She then used Vierny's account of a funny incident in algebra class to cover her own unease… and also to cover as much distance as possible before the oddity of their route registered with the girl. They got to the turnoff for the airport, making it to a service road where she intended to stop, when Vierny finally realized where they were.

"What're we doing, Mom? This isn't the way home."

"I know, Sweetheart. Hold it a sec while I park… and then I'll explain."

Pulling the car off the road so they faced a chain link fence bordering one extreme of a runway, she shut down the engine and began searching for the right words to start off this terrible conversation. As a momentary distraction, she tracked the path of a plane taking off into a climb directly over their car. Out of the corner of her eye, she noticed that Vierny was not following the plane.

"It's not good… is it, Mom?"

"No, Precious. It's not good at all."

"Then tell me everything. Don't leave anything out. I'm not a kid anymore."

So she started out as matter-of-factly as she could about Parkinson's, but soon had them both taken over with tears. Everything she put into her mind while driving the Loop was supposed to be communicated with courage and confidence for Vierny's sake. But it all came out haltingly… and so very wet due to the many interruptions necessary for wiping her eyes and blowing her nose. Nevertheless, she held back nothing and gave Vierny every opportunity to ask questions. The worse part – she was terribly disappointed with herself for the number of times she had to answer with 'I don't know.'

"I'm so sorry, Sweetheart. I can't believe I've done this to you."

"Done this to me?! What're you talking about?! You've not done anything to me!"

"That's because you don't realize what's coming."

"I don't have to know what's coming. All I need to know is that I love you. No disease is ever going to change that."

"I know… and I love you too… but you don't deserve this." Vierny made to object again, so she cut her off by shifting the subject where she wanted it to go. "We need to talk about plans… or I'm going to sit in this car crying all afternoon. There're things that should be done in order to get out ahead of this disease. I've already started a list, so we'll…"

"Of course you have, Mom. That's the incredible thing about you. You're always thinking ahead."

She could not keep herself from falling apart again. Reaching over, she pulled Vierny into a tight embrace, and thanked her over and over. Eventually, she calmed herself enough to start the car. With one more look out at the runway, she reminded herself of why she had chosen this place to break the bad news. No matter what difficulties lay ahead, she was determined that her dreams for Vierny would always come first.

As Dr. Kilpatrick expected, levodopa continued to give her relief from the symptoms. The next six weeks went by as life should, though she wasted none of the time. Every day, she put effort into determining what changes were needed to her lifestyle and the layout of the house. She also considered her financial situation, deciding to make one very important inclusion into the circle of those who knew about her condition.

Sitting opposite from Yardley at his conference room table, she handed across the sheet of paper she had labored over on the previous night while Vierny was asleep. As she watched his eyes progress along her list of instructions, his brow got tighter and tighter. When finished, he set the page on the table and leaned back in his chair. To his face came that all-knowing lawyerly smugness that she both admired and found to be irritating at the same time.

"Well... all I can say is... you've never failed to astonish me. Oh... and that your sons are going to be really pissed at you."

"Maybe... likely... but I'm only determined to pass on to them that which was passed on to their father. That's the house and the lot... minus the value of the hangar, if that's possible... along with the property of the old appliance store. That should be worth something, seeing as the downtown's finally making a comeback. As to those things that were passed on to me... the hangar, the plane and the reliefs... those I intend for my daughter. Everything that I received from the sale of the one relief in Dallas had to go into the restoration of the Corsair. But as you can see from what I've written there, the plane went for a very sizeable amount. I want all of that designated exclusively for Vierny. We have enough to live on from my IRA and social security. I have all of the investment paperwork ready once you need it. After I finalize the sale of the second relief, I want that going to her too. Whatever else remains of my estate... my possessions and other savings... those can be split four ways. Oh... except for a crystal necklace and my rings... those go to Vierny. I guess I should probably include anything in the house that has to do with aviation."

"Just make me a list of the items and I'll see to it that they're incorporated into the will. If you like, prepare any personal statements to go with your wishes."

"I'll get on it right away, but Cliff..." She paused to make sure that she had his full attention. "...I want this airtight. I don't want the least chance of it being contested... especially if something tragic should happen to me. I want Vierny taken care of. More than that – I want her protected. You do realize that my eldest is a lawyer... and a pretty clever one at that. You remember that he's tried something before. He'll do it again. I'm sure of it."

"Then I think it best that you not wait. I'm going to recommend that we immediately establish a trust for your daughter, and then put into it everything you intend for her. Then it's essentially untouchable."

"Really?!"

"Absolutely. We'll need to engage a trust company and set up a fund for its management. In the meantime, you should do some thinking about the timeline and if there are any conditions by which your daughter is to receive disbursements from this trust. We can go over the options later, but have in mind her education, potential health needs, purchase of a car or house… that sort of thing.”

“And can we keep it all a secret?”

“We can certainly try… but trusts have to be filed with the state… and your eldest’s likely still has connections here. The details shouldn’t get out… but perhaps the fact that you’ve filed might. You should probably be prepared for personal backlash anyway.”

“Understood.”

“So let me start the process rolling with what you’ve given me thus far… then we can go over the first draft in a couple of weeks. Now… you’re sure about this… the disease, I mean?”

“Unfortunately… yes. And I want that kept quiet too! Nobody in your office needs to know.”

“Of course not.” The saddest expression then came creeping over his face. “Marna… I really feel for you. It’s not fair. You deserve a break.”

“Thanks, Cliff… but I’m actually alright. The first week or so after the diagnosis was more than difficult. But I’ve got my daughter’s support… and yours too. I’ll get by… break or no break.”

“Yeah… about that… I’m thinking that you should… be getting yourself ready. Know what I mean?”

“No… I don’t.”

“Marna… you’ll be needing a medical directive and a power of attorney. Because if what I’ve heard about this disease is true… you’re eventually going to need someone’s help in managing your affairs.”

“I… really hadn’t thought about that.”

She left Cliff’s office having a great many things settled, yet with a new concern added on.

Two and a half years! I absolutely have to contain this disease until Vierny’s old enough to act as my power of attorney. She’s the only one I can trust.

She had not even gotten the girl into driver’s training yet, and here she was contemplating strapping her with the legal responsibilities of managing a mother’s health and finances. Right off, she asked Yardley if he could act on her behalf, even though she already knew what his answer would be. As her lawyer, he was ethically constrained from doing such a thing. So that meant it was either Travis, or she somehow had to find a way of holding off this disease until her daughter turned eighteen.

She continued wrestling with the issue while making a mad dash through a store. Back into her car with her trunk loaded down with groceries, she needed to get home, put everything away, and then head back out to pick up Vierny from school.

Really! There's no way I should be burdening her with the responsibilities of managing my life. She's got her own future to think of! I'll… just have to find someone else. Of course… I could always ask Sybil…

Despite the serious circumstances, she could not help but burst out laughing at the thought.

Hilarious! She'd have me living on the street in a week!

Why her sister-in-law had popped into her mind was odd, seeing as she had not laid eyes on the woman since beating the crap out of her at Roy's memorial service. That was over ten years ago.

That's all I need… having her show up in my life again!

Actually, what I need is a miracle.

In making the turn off the farm-to-market road, her hands inexplicably lost their grip on the wheel. Unable to compensate in time, her car overshot the turn and veered onto the grassy shoulder. In a panic, she fought to steer with the heels of both hands, at the same time breaking… except her right foot simply would not move from off of the accelerator. Knowing for certain that there was nothing preventing her car from heading over the embankment, she instinctively brought both arms up to cover her face. An eternity went by in which she may or may not have screamed… but eventually she became aware that her forward motion had ceased without a collision. Looking up, she was relieved to find that her car had come to a stop in a mostly-dry drainage ditch. Yet in spite of the fact that she was no longer moving, she could still hear the engine revving like crazy. Her foot had remained pressed down on the accelerator. Sliding her hands beneath her thigh, she lifted with both arms. The engine immediately settled down. But she could not, as her heart was still racing.

First things first, she needed to calm down enough to call Dr. Kilpatrick. She went about flexing her fingers until they finally showed the dexterity needed for shutting down the engine. She made the call on her cell… only to reach that annoying automated phone system she hated so much. She left a message when prompted to, explaining what had happened and requesting that her next appointment be moved up to as soon as possible. Then she set her hands to working out the numbness in her leg. After some feeling had been restored, she restarted the car and shifted it into reverse. Gradually applying pressure to the accelerator, the wheels just spun in place. Into drive… into low gear… back into reverse… the outcome was the same. Her car was going nowhere. Hesitantly opening the door, she looked down into a few inches of muddy water that extended far beyond her reach. No way was she stepping out into that muck! So she made a call for a tow truck… contending with the dispatcher over how long it would take. Next, she debated with herself whether to text Vierny about the possibility of being late to pick her up… and decided not to until it was truly necessary. From there, she had nothing to do other than to stew in her own sweat, just as her groceries were baking in the trunk beneath the afternoon sun.

None of this should be happening. Her medicine was supposed to control the leg freezing… it had for the last two months. Maybe she had missed a dose? It could be… She had been rather preoccupied with her will. So she really needed to get one of those plastic pill boxes… the kind with the little bins for each day of the week. But what if she had not missed a dose? What if her medication was simply not working anymore?!

Don't jump to conclusions!

But jump or no jump, she could not risk having another freezing incident happen while she was behind the wheel… especially if Vierny was in the car with her. She knew this day would come sooner or later… but having to face it profoundly sooner than later was something she had not been prepared for. She could go on beating her steering wheel in frustration, but that changed nothing. She was stuck in the ditch-end of her life. No more freedom. No more independence. No more liberation through speed's thrill. No going or doing. No being herself. From now on, she would be dependent upon another, for she must accept the fact that her driving days were nearly over.

After a half hour of wallowing in her despair, the tow truck finally arrived to rescue her. The driver – a quintessential bubba – did not seem at all concerned about wading around in the drainage ditch as he hooked up her car. She was pulled out in no time, and after generously tipping him for his effort, she was back on her way. Pulling into her driveway, she was already coming to see the whole mishap as nothing. Could have happened to anybody. Besides, it was likely just a matter of getting her medication adjusted. No need to burden Vierny. And if she were especially quick about putting the groceries away, she could even get back out on the road being only a few minutes late. No big deal. The whole ditch episode would soon be forgotten.

Stepping from her car on the circle, she beheld a muddy mess that ran from fender to fender due to her wheels spinning uncontrollably in the mud… and absolutely could not keep herself from breaking down into tears.

She had always planned on enrolling Vierny in driver's education during the upcoming summer, but her mind was now changed. She got her enrolled that very day. Within a week, Vierny had met the requirements for obtaining a learner's permit. They then began driving together in earnest. After fulfilling the State's stipulated thirty two hours of training, followed by a week of intense driving, Vierny passed her Texas State driver's examination on the first try. With paperwork provided by Dr. Kilpatrick's office, Vierny was granted a hardship license four months before her sixteenth birthday. From then on, her daughter did all of the driving for the both of them.

In the aftermath of the accident, her doctor upped her dosage of levodopa and told her to get herself prepared for the worst. So with her full foresight bent toward accepting an unpleasant future, she entered the summer intent on adapting her house for the inevitable. With good weather at hand, she arranged for a construction company to extend the gravel drive around to the rear of the house, pour a concrete slab at its end, and build a wheelchair ramp from there to the rear section of the porch. Next, she engaged another company to conduct modifications on the guest bathroom for handicapped accessibility. She also hired a handyman to put up railing in strategic sites about the downstairs, and also level the sill at the base of the rear door so anything on wheels could easily move through. Her summer time became filled with fixtures, cabinets, and finishings that had to be picked out, plans that needed to be revised, and a host of renovation surprises that must be worked around. She had heard all kinds of stories about the nightmares of dealing with contractors, but instead found that having them as a daily distraction was a welcomed reprieve from thinking about her disease.

Now that the projects were finished, she was left with facing the ultimate purpose behind them. For Vierny's sake, she needed to get herself fully prepared. With her handwriting already showing signs of the disease, she decided that it was time to craft something personal for her daughter's future. Having entered the first week of Vierny's sophomore year, with her sixteenth birthday only days away, she took up pen and paper for a bittersweet task. First, she wrote the note to her daughter, and then the one to Yardley. Intending to use only one envelope, she put on its face the address of her attorney.

Cliff,

I hope you can make this out. My hand's gotten really shaky lately. As I mentioned over the phone, I'd like you to deliver the enclosed letter to my daughter once she enters college. That time may be years off, but I'm unlikely to have the wherewithal for writing then. I've composed this letter now so she'll have a little something from me to open on that day.

Thank you for your work on my will and the trust. Both look solid. With any luck, I'll be able to cope with this disease until Vierny turns eighteen, and then we can put a power of attorney into action.

Thanks also for your support. You're such a good friend!

Sincerely,

Marna

Struggling with the pages, she had to fold and refold Vierny's letter so many times before finally getting it down to a size that would fit into the envelope. Out of concern that the many creases might obscure her message, she reread the letter one last time.

Dear Sweetheart,

My intention is that this finds you as you're starting out on your first day of college. So many wonderful things are soon to come your way. New friends, new experiences and new knowledge. I need not tell you to cherish them all, for I know you will. I'm sure to have already told you all sorts of things about studying hard and also taking time to enjoy college, so I'll skip that for now. I just want you to know how proud I am of you. I'm absolutely confident that you'll excel in whatever you attempt because I know you're smart, resilient and determined. You have such a bright future ahead of you. Nothing can stand in your way! Unfortunately, seeing as my condition is steadily worsening, it's unlikely that I will be standing there with you on your first day, which is why I've arranged for this letter to be delivered then. Whatever is going on with me, know that I long to be there with you sharing in your excitement. I'm so fortunate to be your mother. What a gift you have given me! You are the bravest, kindest, most beautiful girl in the world! You'll do such amazing things, I just know it!

Because I do know you, Vierny, I know that you are likely to struggle with homesickness. It's okay to miss me. I certainly will be missing you too. We've had so many special moments together. Let those warm your heart whenever you feel cold.

By the way, I happen to be writing this letter a few days before you turn sixteen. I still have so many memories to build with you. So when you read these words, you'll already know the amazing surprises I prepared for your birthday. You deserve each and every one. You are so precious to me!

In closing, I want you to know that where your heart is, there mine will be also. I love you, Vierny, with all my being, and I believe fully in you. My deepest desire is for your dreams to come true, just as mine have in you.

She slid both notes safely into the envelope, sealed it, and then handed this letter within a letter over to Vierny, who promised to drop it into a mailbox on her way to school... thus unknowingly sending herself the last letter that her mother would likely ever write.

She sang the song with her croaky voice, yet her sixteen year old daughter did not seemed to care. Vierny smiled big through the whole thing, and then blew out the candles that she had just lit for herself. They each ate a piece of cake, and then it was time for presents.

"So... I have two for you. The first is something that I've kept hidden away for years... right up until the time when I was diagnosed. Here you are, Sweetheart. Go ahead and unwrap it."

Pushing aside the remnants of the birthday cake, she slid over the velvet-wrapped bundle, and then sat back in her chair to watch. With care, Vierny untied the ribbon and unrolled the fabric... pausing once to look at her before slowly lifting off the last fold. The girl's eyes instantly lit up as the crystal necklace was revealed to her.

"Mom! It's... it's amazing! I've... never seen anything so beautiful!"

"You like it?"

Vierny answered first with her hug... and then words.

"Like it?! I love it! It's so incredibly elegant!"

"I know... Look at the care with which each pearl and each piece of crystal is held in its silver. Just the weight of it always made me think it was valuable. I should probably get it appraised."

"Where ever did it come from?!"

"Oh, I've had it for ages. Actually... I have no idea where it came from... or even how old it is. I got it from my aunt. I've only worn it a few times... like when we were married. Actually... that's not quite right. Roy and I... we eloped first, and then later we..."

"You eloped?! Seriously, Mom?! How absolutely scandalous of you!"

"It was nothing like that... so you can wipe that little smirk off your face! Couples eloped all the time back in my day. We just... wanted to get it done. You know... without having to go through the whole shebang. But later... for our fifteenth... we had such a grand affair right here at the house. A formal wedding with over a hundred guests before whom we renewed our vows out there on the front porch. We had a huge party afterward... fully catered...

and then a second honeymoon. My dress, Vierny… it was so amazing! It shimmered like crystal. I wish you could have seen it… but it's gone now."

"What's happened to it?"

"Uhh… that's a sore subject. Let's just say… I loaned it out and it was never returned. Anyway… I wore this necklace at that ceremony… and now I want you to have it."

"Wow… thanks! A whole lot! But you're sure?"

"Definitely… from mother to daughter… the way it's meant to be. But I'd kind of like it to be returned to the safety deposit box… until you're really ready to wear it. I just wanted you to see it first. Put it on."

With silent pleasure bursting forth all over her face, Vierny took the ends of the necklace up under her hair and around her neck, fiddled with the clasp for a few seconds, and then brought her arms back down to her side.

"How's it look?"

Crystal and pearl resting gently upon the creamy smooth skin of her daughter's chest… the sight completely took her breath away!

"It's… it's… so lovely! You're so lovely! Go see for yourself."

With Vierny scurrying off in pursuit of the nearest mirror, she gave in to the tears. As if by a crystalline touch of magic, her little girl was transformed before her eyes into a woman. Beautiful, delicate, graceful, and so very kind. If only she could make it to the day that her daughter next wore this necklace…

As the second part of her surprise, she informed Vierny that she was enrolled to start flying lessons in the following week. With crystal and pearl still about her neck, Vierny threw her arms up into the air and screamed with such excitement… and then brought them down for another good, long hug. Both of them cried themselves into so many questions asked and answered about what it meant to be in flight training. The whole time, she could not keep her eyes from moving back and forth between the sparkle of the necklace and the sparkle in her daughter's eyes. Vierny was happier than she had ever seen her to be.

On that first day, she sent her girl off by herself, just as Roy had done for her, knowing that the experience would be so much more meaningful that way. The smile on Vierny's face when she returned home from the airport was worth every minute of the wait. For weeks afterward, listening to Vierny ecstatically talk about the things she was learning became the highlight of each day.

But as the coolness of an early fall came on, she found herself turning cold. She so wanted to be out there watching her daughter learn how to fly… but she no longer felt comfortable in being out of the house. Why had she, a person who lived to move, been so cruelly straddled with the ugly prospect of debilitation?

She could not blame her parents, as she had read that the link between Parkinson's and hereditary was weak. Only ten percent or so had a family history of the disease. But since her parents had died young... as had her aunt... there was really no way of knowing. She recalled that something read offered a possible connection to pesticides... and her mind jumped to a childhood of Gwen's daily circuits about Lubbock's greenhouses and nurseries. Or maybe it was as simply as breathing the Lubbock air for the last sixty plus years.

Oh, shit! I forgot... I crop-dusted! It's... my fault.

Whether it made sense or not, she was suddenly overwhelmed with the magnitude of her choices in life. Collapsing into a ball within her nook, she began to cry the tears of her despair, for her pursuit of flight at all cost had come full circle. It was now time to pay. Life was so unfair. Given the gift of a daughter, she now found herself shackled by a disease that would not allow her to watch that daughter's dreams come true. Her fear of wasps had always been a fear of death, but this fear was far worse. This was the fear of losing herself... and losing a connection to her precious daughter. She had been stung... not to death, but to a slow paralysis... just like some wasp's helpless victim.

Entering October, her doctor's assessment of her condition was not good. Her balance and reflexes had significantly worsened to the point that he dolefully concluded she had moved into stage three of the disease – the turning point toward things much worse. The risk of falling now became his primary concern. As he questioned her about her daily habits, she reluctantly found herself relating to him several scary moments of nearly falling... and twice in tripping on a stair. He then advised her that it was time to make the change.

From that appointment on, she took up occupancy of the guest bedroom. Rather than having such rich memories of her bedroom, closet and bath to dwell on, this room gave her nothing, for she had not slept in it once during her four decades of living within this house. To her, the guest bedroom had always been located in the darkest and coldest corner of the house. She found its night noises to be especially unsettling. Instead of the flag gently fluttering on its pole or the rustling of the driveway's live oaks, she now had to deal with the wind whipping around the back porch and the clunking of the furnace in the cellar below. Even the room's floorboards had an unnatural creak to them. The wide-open feel of the master bedroom's spire was replaced with the crampness of a low ceiling. With only one window, it facing out toward the north, she no longer had the joy of seeing the sun peek through her curtains in the morning... or the moon rising into the night sky. Now with the daylight hours shrinking, she more often than not found herself sleeping to well past the time when Vierny left for school, depriving her of a joy far greater than that of watching a sunrise.

After a week-long debate, she finally persuaded Vierny to claim the master bedroom as her own. From then on, the upstairs became Vierny's domain. Watching her daughter bound up and down the stairs was gut-wrenching, for the regions up there became a place of exclusion to her. The way her late husband had fashioned the upper hallway to be wide open had once been a delight, but now served as a terrible reminder. A part of her life with Vierny had been ripped away. For in a reversal of roles, her daughter now came to her in the guest bedroom for their goodnights.

Having only been diagnosed eight months before, she entered November forced to accept that her disease had progressed years ahead of where it should be. Anything she tried to do with her hands became an instant frustration. Brushing her hair or teeth... dressing herself... doing the simplest of household chores... it all took so much longer than before, and never came out as smoothly. She could still get around the downstairs, but had to go at it slower and with care. In nearly every way, she found herself confronted with how challenging her life had become.

But despite her limitations, she could still spend quality time with Vierny every day. They ate their meals together, sat for hours side-by-side in the nook, and even took drives about town... though she seldom got out of the car for anything other than a doctor appointment. The one exception she made was in the week prior to Thanksgiving, as she wanted to watch from the ramp as Vierny soloed for the first time. It might have only been a few patterned laps about the airfield in a Piper Cherokee, but Vierny's accomplishment was more significant to her than anything she had done during her own aviation career. When the wheels touched down and the taxi was over, the first thing Vierny did was dash across the ramp to share a tear-filled hug and kiss with her. The essence of unassailable joy then came when Vierny gave her the privilege of cutting out the back of her shirt. Though she struggled with the scissors, making the task an ordeal to complete, her daughter patiently giggled through it all. Vierny then drew a picture of her plane on that fragment of cloth and stapled her prize to the flight school wall. It was her proudest moment as a mother.

She set her alarm to rise early on Thanksgiving Day morning. With her first dose of medicine kicking in, she felt reasonably sharp enough for getting a headstart on some of the meal preparations. She also had the exhilaration of pride from her daughter's accomplishment still powering her on. Vierny was poised for such an incredible future... but the girl really needed a break.

Vierny was juggling far too much. Her school work, flight training, all of the driving, the majority of the household chores, and taking care of her mother... all that left no time for relaxing. They had talked about this being Vierny's first Thanksgiving meal to prepare... but now she was having second thoughts on the matter. Let the girl sleep in. At least she could get things out on the kitchen counter so Vierny would have an easier go of it... starting with what was needed for the stuffing. Working from memory, she gathered spices from the rack... bouillon, wild rice, pecans, and bread crumbs from the cupboard... measuring spoons and cups from the drawer... and the mixer from the cabinet.

Not thinking anything of it, she went up on her toes to reach for a large mixing bowl on an upper shelf. With the oddest sensation coming to her of the cabinet backing away, she felt the room tilt in a direction that it was not meant to go. Her split-second of confusion instantly gave way to panic as she flailed out for a grip on the cabinet door. But over she went, screaming all the way until her hip, shoulder and head made contact with something hard. Pain instantly shot throughout her body. After several fretful seconds of shock, she found herself coiled up on the kitchen floor. Once the ache to her hip had ebbed away into something dull, she risked stretching out that leg. With a few tentative motions, she was immensely relieved not to feel the level of pain that might be expected from a fracture. Slowly, she shifted to her hands and knees, but went no further toward standing. Instead, she crawled across the floor to a kitchen chair and hoisted herself up. Only then did she have the wherewithal for breathing easy, and then checking herself over. There was a bump swelling beneath her hair, a soreness to her shoulder, and no doubt a colossal bruise taking shape on her hip. Fortunately, no other part of her seemed damaged. Looking across the kitchen to where she had fallen, everything she had collected still sat on the countertop. Those things would just have to wait for Vierny because she was absolutely not moving from this chair until then. Her good intentions had almost ended in disaster.

For the rest of that Thanksgiving day, she went nowhere within the house without Vierny at her side. Perched at the kitchen table, she guided Vierny solo through the preparation of their traditional meal, doing her best to smile and laugh through it all. But inwardly, she was very much embarrassed, both from the fall itself and from having confessed it to Vierny. Worse, she was far too shaken to risk one last moment of joy that would have come from standing shoulder-to-shoulder with her daughter as they cooked.

Still smarting from the lingering effects of her fall on Thanksgiving Day, she significantly downsized her holiday expectations on moving into December.

Vierny took on all of the decorating for the both of them. Their gifts to each other were picked out before a computer screen, and then delivered to the house by a large brown van. For Vierny, it was a laptop. For her, it was a plasma TV… the first one in the house since her husband passed away. Vierny set this screen up in the family room against the wall shared with the kitchen, and then arranged for a satellite cable provider to connect it to the rest of the world. Three days later, a man showed up to hang a two foot dish on the western side of the porch, it being oriented up toward a realm that she had once ruled. The irony was not lost on her. What she had flown executives all over the country to peddle could now be delivered to her house by a guy in an installation van.

The TV became her daily companion from New Year's Day on. Movies, sitcoms, the news, talk shows, documentaries or soaps… it did not matter. She watched because that was the only safe thing for her to do. Besides, turning pages in a book had become too difficult, as had talking on the phone. But more often than not, she fell asleep while watching. Facing frequent periods of wakefulness at night, she had Vierny purchase a smaller set for her bedroom. She was now before a TV at all hours of the day.

Into her second year of Parkinson's, she still had not yet grown accustomed to the cruel habits of her medications. On the prescribed cycle, she took her pills and in short time felt the burst of liberation they gave her. She could just about do anything she had done before… move about the downstairs without a walker, cook a simple meal in the kitchen, or engage in conversation over the phone. It was almost like being her old self again. But within a few hours, the benefits gradually lessened and the symptoms reappeared. Soon, the medication's influence had altogether left her, and she was right back to the worst of her crippled self… hanging on until it was time to take the next pill. Daily, she relived this vicious cycle over and over – euphoria, denial, frustrated limitation, and the terrible acceptance of a bleak future. She went outside only when it was necessary, and then only with Vierny there to steady her on a walker. She felt completely trapped by her condition, and sometimes even jealous of Vierny's youth and vigor. As her daughter's social life outside of the home expanded to parties, dates and nights out with her friends, so her own sphere of life collapsed. She entertained no visitors, being too embarrassed to be seen in her condition or heard slurring her words. Her circle of associations had become limited to the cleaning ladies who came into the house for a few hours each week to lighten the burden on her daughter.

Having completed her flight training at the beginning of spring, Vierny passed her check ride and earned a private pilot's license. They celebrated together at home, and then Vierny went out with her friends. In the stillness of just her and her house, she sat in the nook thinking about how rapidly her life had degraded. Soon, she would require a wheelchair for getting around. Her mind was also showing the effects of the disease, for whole mornings would disappear into afternoons without her having the slightest inkling of the passage of time. That, more than anything else, told her that the moment had finally come. With deliberate care, she moved by walker into the dining room and sat before her relief. She did not speak to it, as in times past, for she no longer had a voice of strong confidence. Neither did she look it over from face to face… or up at the birds. In fact, she fell asleep right there until Vierny came home. The whole time, she was making the relief come to terms with what had become of her, for only then would it accept what she must do.

She made the calls in the morning and set the date. From there, one day went into the next, with her steadily becoming more and more dependent. From walker to wheelchair, she only felt comfortable in moving when someone was doing it with her. She had eyes for only Vierny, TV, and her relief.

On a warm morning in early summer, Vierny came off the phone to voice the words that her heart had been dreading to hear for months.

"They're coming tomorrow, Mom. I'm so sorry. I know how terrible this is for you."

The two of them passed the hours of waiting by sitting before the relief together. Vierny spoke of all that its artistry meant to her, while she listened and remembered.

A man she had not seen in over ten years appeared on her doorstep. Isaac Rosenblum was perhaps a bit grayer at the temples, but altogether as much the scholarly art dealer as when she first laid eyes on him that day he drove to Lubbock for a look at her relief. Then, she had stood above a rather short and balding man. But now… he towered over her wheelchair as a god. Just like one of those mythological sculptures he loved so much. She hated being seen by him like this… and not just because of the wheelchair. Of late, her face had become frozen with a mask-like blankness. She could no longer smile or laugh… or even grimace at some painful thought. Even her blinking was done so terribly slow. It was torture to behold herself in a mirror, and by the shocked expression on Isaac's face, she knew that he too felt the same way. To him, she was nothing more than one of those stone faces in her relief.

Pulling herself together, she rasped out an introduction of her daughter, whom Isaac greeted warmly. Then to her great surprise, he came down on a knee in his tailored suit to take her hand.

"I'm so sorry, Marna. Sorry for what you've had to endure with this terrible disease."

She could say nothing in return, and let the tears collecting in the corners of her eyes be a sign of appreciation for his kindness. After a moment, he leaned in closer to whisper so only she could hear.

"I've… so appreciated your letters over the years. They always brightened my day. You're such a dear woman. Thank you for allowing me to represent you. It's been an honor."

He straightened up and turned toward Vierny with obvious emotion in his voice.

"Young lady… please take care of this fine woman."

"Always! It's my pleasure to do so. And thank you for coming all this way. It means a lot to her knowing that you'll be overseeing the transfer."

"The pleasure is all mine! So… I understand that you two are planning to make a trip to Dallas to see both reliefs together…"

"We hope to… if… things work out."

Isaac turned back to her.

"Excellent. I'm sorry I won't be there to share that moment with you, Marna… but I have prepared a little surprise for you there. I hope you enjoy it."

He smiled once more, and then went into the dining room to oversee the packing of her relief. Soon, two men emerged from the parlor carrying a wooden crate. Out the front door they went. After only a short while, she caught a glimpse through the family room window of them sliding it into the back of their delivery truck. Isaac said goodbye one last time… and then her relief was gone.

She hardly slept that night as visions of the faces flashed through her mind. In the morning, she was keenly aware that two symbols of her life had left her forever. A Dallas tycoon had her Corsair, and a museum had both of her reliefs. Nothing was left to her except a simple hope… the fruit of a very different, much more meaningful dream planted as a seed within a trust reserved for her daughter. Yardley had made absolutely sure of that. Vierny was aware only that her college education had been secured by that trust. She had absolutely no idea what else was reserved for only her. Of all those bearing her and Roy's name into the future, only this child could be entrusted not to have two and a half million ruin the rest of her life.

Vierny had never driven more than an hour at a time, so she knew that this would put the girl's fortitude to the test. But she simply must see the two reliefs hanging side by side… before this cursed disease forever bound her in one place. Rising early on Saturday, Vierny drove her all the way to Dallas for the last time. The trip there was tedious, and endurable only because her daughter worked so hard to keep up her anticipation. They were met at the entrance to the museum, and given an escort directly to her reliefs. There they hung, side by side for the first time in over sixty years. Earth to her left and Sky to her right. The two were mounted at a normal person's eye level, but in her wheelchair, she could not quite make out the birds as well as she wished… whereas the stone flames in Earth were right before her eyes. In holding Vierny's hand, she squeezed it to get the girl's attention.

"Bbback me up… please. Too… close."

"Certainly, Mom. How's this?"

Vierny drew her wheelchair back a short way, and then moved from behind to the wall placard beside Sky.

"Hey, Mom… get a load of what's written here. This must be the surprise that your art dealer was talking about. Let me read it to you. It says… 'Fashioned in white marble, these companion works of an unknown 18th century Florentine sculptor were likely an exercise in Renaissance low relief. They symbolize two great failings of humanity. *Fino al Cielo* – 'To the Sky' – depicts a disregard for lofty endeavors, whereas *Sulla Terra* – 'On Earth' – warns of the inevitability of death."

Though Vierny had finished reading, she was still leaning in close.

"Mom… there's more. You won't believe what's written below in fine print! 'These works came by way of the faithful patronage of Gwen Forde and her niece, Marna Forde Meitner, both of Lubbock, Texas.' That's so cool! They've got your name here!"

Her thoughts, though, were on the birds.

The museum's got it wrong. Goodbye my faithful friends. I owe you so much.

As a parting gesture, someone from the museum took pictures of them before the reliefs. Vierny was so kind to first fluff her hair and straighten her blouse, though no amount of coaxing on the part of the photographer could compel her face to eke out even the weakest of smiles.

On the way back from Dallas, she found her thoughts straying from the birds to 'the inevitability of death'… it being much nearer to her crippled state. By the time she was through the humiliation of her sweet daughter struggling to get her into the non-handicap stall of a convenience store bathroom in Abilene, she was determined never again to leave the safety of her home.

She was up all that night from having dozed so much in the car. Truth was, she hardly slept for very long these days. Finally into the early morning, she somehow managed to get herself in and out of the bathroom… and then into the kitchen… where it took her forever to setup the coffeemaker. She also made an absolute mess in spilling a good portion of it. With a travel mug wedged between her legs and her pill box in her lap, she wheeled herself into the parlor. There, she watched the sunrise through the glass doors out onto the porch. It was beautiful, but the sight only brought her pain.

Sometime well after the sun was up, Vierny appeared in pajamas at her side.

"I see you've managed on your own."

"I spilt coffee."

Vierny leaned over to bring an ear near to her mouth.

"Sorry, Mom… I was yawning. What's that again?"

She knew that was not the case, so she put more effort into annunciating the words this second time.

"I… spilt… cof-fee."

"Not a problem. How about if I go make you some breakfast…"

She watched Vierny move out through the dining room, noting also that the girl briefly cast her eyes toward where the relief once hung. The sadness of its absence would be a topic that both of them avoided. If it were not for Vierny, that bare spot on the wall would be impossible for her to endure. Her daughter, now busying herself in the kitchen with a skillet on the stove, had to be tired. She had driven all the way to and back from Dallas, not to mention hefting a wheelchair in and out of the trunk a half dozen times. Vierny needed a break, but would never come right out and…

The kitchen phone rang, with her daughter sweetly answering it. After a pause, Vierny's voice picked up, this time with considerable agitation to it. She was telling somebody to calm down… and then defiantly refused something that was being insisted upon. Over and over, she repeated the same phrase into the phone – "No, I won't." She finally hung up. It was quiet in the kitchen for a long while before Vierny came creeping into the parlor.

"Mom… that call… I'm sure you heard me yelling… it was from Chad. It seems… Wade saw a picture in the Austin paper this morning of you and me before the reliefs."

"The paper…?"

"Yes… I know. I didn't realize it either. Mom… Chad's furious. He says we should have told him… That it wasn't right to keep the wheelchair a secret. He insisted on speaking with you… but I refused. He can't possibly understand how difficult it is for you to talk on the phone. But he… umm…. says he's coming. Right now. He'll be here in two hours. Mom… he said that the article said that you had Parkinson's. I'm sorry… now they all know."

"You… did… fine. This day… would hap-pen… soon-er… or later. Call… Y-ard-lee."

"Mom… it's Sunday. I won't be able to get ahold of him until tomorrow. There's nothing he can do anyway. But don't worry about Chad… I can handle him."

She liked the look of determination on her daughter's face, but doubted that anybody could manage her largest son… especially when he got angry.

Vierny went on with preparing breakfast. They ate French toast silently at the kitchen table. Vierny then helped her get in and out of the bathroom, and then aided in dressing her. From there, they sat together in the parlor waiting for the sound of tires on the gravel drive. She must have nodded off, for when she opened her eyes next, the lighting in the room was different and Vierny no longer had a look of concern on her face.

"Hi… I let you sleep. It's been three hours. I don't think he's really coming."

Following a somewhat relaxing afternoon of Vierny reading to her, and then a simple dinner of chicken tenders, the phone rang again as Vierny was cleaning up. Her daughter listened for a minute before putting her hand over the mouthpiece.

"Mom… it's Travis. He's asking to talk with you. I'm going to put it on speaker."

Vierny pushed a button and then held the phone between them.

"Travis… Mom's listening now. Go ahead."

"Mom… I was hoping to speak with you in private."

"No… I… want…Vierny… too."

"What'd you say? I can't hear you. Hold the phone closer to your…"

"Travis, she can't."

"Just tell her to hold the phone up to her mouth."

"Travis… you don't understand. Her voice's too weak because she's really tired right now. I'll repeat what she says."

"Okay… fine. Is it true… what Wade says… that Mom's got Parkinson's?"

"Yes… I'm afraid it is."

"Why didn't you tell us?! This is obviously not something that she can handle on her own."

"She's not on her own. She's got me."

"I know that… and I'm thankful. It's just… this is a serious disease with many long term consequences."

"We're taking it very seriously. She's getting the best medical care. We've got an in-home service that helps out… and we've already made the downstairs wheelchair-compatible for her."

"What about medications? Is she on something?"

"She's been on a regiment for over a year now, so we've…"

"A year! Are you telling me that you've known about this for over a year and not told any of us?!"

"Travis… I've lived in this house for nine years. You know how many times any of you've visited during that time?! A big fat zero!" Vierny looked down at her… smiled with a little wink… and then went right back to being stern with Travis. "Funny… by an odd coincidence, that's exactly the number of times that you've invited us to visit you in California. You do realize that Mom's never laid eyes on Dillon… her own grandson!"

"Yeah… well… we've been really…"

"You never call or write… and you show absolutely no interest in what's going on with her. So don't tell me that you're all broken up to hear about her disease."

"Verny, you're missing the point."

"It's *Vierny*… as in do you *hear* me… because here's the real point. You're not involved in her life, so why would you want to be involved in her disease?!"

"Okay… let's start over. *Vierny*… there are many difficult decisions to be made here. One's that require a responsible adult's attention. And you're how old?"

"Almost seventeen…"

"Which puts you as a minor… and incapable of acting on Mom's behalf as far as Texas State law is concerned."

"We're getting along just fine."

"You only *think* you're getting along. But you're not an adult capable of making that decision. Now put Mom on the phone."

She waited until Vierny had the mouthpiece held steady before her mouth.

"I… don't want… you… involved."

"I can't hear you, Mom… you need to speak up."

"She says she doesn't need you're involvement."

"You see! This is exactly what I'm talking about! She can't make her wishes known, and she's only got a minor speaking on her behalf."

"No… she has her lawyer, Cliff Yardley."

"Yardley? I know that name…"

"Well then go talk to him."

"No. I want to talk with my mother!"

Mustering what strength she still possessed, she gave all her voice into a shout at the phone.

"TRAVIS MEITNER!"

"Umm… yes, Mom?"

"STOP PLAYING GAMES WITH ME!"

"I'm sorry, Mom. I'm just… concerned for you."

"Tell him… to… call… broth-ers."

"She'd like you to call Chad and Wade. Tell them that she's okay." Vierny peered at her with something of a question, so she nodded for her to go on. "She's happy for any of you to visit… anytime you'd like. Then you could see for yourself how well she's doing. Just let us know a time… okay?"

"Umm… sure… but probably not until the new year. We've got to…"

She had heard enough. Falling back in her wheelchair, she waved off the phone.

"Travis, I'm sorry to interrupt, but we need to go. We were just finishing up with dinner. Goodbye."

"Oh… okay. Goodbye."

She felt really tired and needed to rest. With another little wave of her fingers… plenty for Vierny to understand… she motioned for the girl to come nearer. Forehead to forehead, she closed her eyes at the feel of Vierny's presence. Squeezing the girl's hand first, she then motioned toward the back room. So patient… Vierny got her ready for bed… kissed her on the same spot where their heads had previously touched… and then closed her door.

Ever since her relief went to Dallas, she had the distinct impression of being watched during every moment of the day. She knew from the beginning what it was. Those faces… they were after her! Somehow, they had peeled themselves off of the stone and followed her home. Now, they were scattered all about her house. They tried to hide, but she could see them out of the corner of her eye sneaking about. Some dashed past her wheelchair while she was watching TV. One climbed onto the kitchen counter and hid behind the toaster. Another was up there on the ceiling fan… just going round and round with the blades. They mostly liked to crawl beneath things… cushions, piles of magazines, or any item of clothing left lying around. Then they would sort of… wiggle there. Just enough for her to know that she dared not touch that thing. No matter how much she tried rasping a shout at them, they never said a word in return, for they very much enjoyed tormenting her with their silence. Always, they hung just out of reach, waiting to do her harm. But at night… they all came together beneath her bed to whisper cruel things at her. That she belong to them and they would soon take her away to Dallas, for she had become a stone face just like them. So she had Vierny put up nightlights throughout the house, and kept her bedroom's lamps lit at all times. Yet the faces still lurked in every darkened corner. Her doctor said it was all just a trick of the disease in her mind, but she knew better. The relief was angry at her for betraying it.

The only time she felt secure was with Vierny nearby. Her daughter's happiness was far too much for them to bear. Sitting together at night in the parlor was the best. She in her new power lift easy chair and Vierny in the nook, they would talk about whatever they wanted to. Well… Vierny talked and she mumbled… but she could still nod or shake her head. She loved to hear her chatter away about the things going on in her life… especially anything concerning her aspirations for majoring in aviation science and one day becoming a pilot. Listening to Vierny… soaking up her every word and smile… that was the only thing that kept those faces away.

Okay… Dr. Kilpatrick could keep the faces away too, for they never had the courage to show up at his office. He was so good to her in how gently he touched her arms and legs. He always listened attentively to whatever Vierny had to say. Sad that none of the pills he ordered for her could prevent her body from wobbling. She altogether stopped taking them because they upset her system too much. No way could she risk that, for it had become such an ordeal to get in and out of the bathroom on her own. Vierny had to help in the morning and evening… and those nice ladies were here throughout the school day. They always smiled big for her. They were decent enough cooks, yet not as good as Vierny. Her daughter always knew what she liked to eat, how things should be kept around the house, and how to sooth her many frustrations. The ladies were pretty good too… but none of them could figure out that stupid TV remote! Why so many tiny buttons?! It was impossible to hit the right one… or even know which was the right one. If she dared touch the thing, the channel got switched to some god-awful home remodeling show, a disgusting documentary about animals eating other animals, or a brainless shop-at-home network. Worse, that remote thing sometimes got the TV stuck in a flickered nonsense… or turned it off altogether. She had to rely on Vierny to set the channel for her before leaving for school… and there it would sit until she came back home. That was okay, because she mostly slept during the day. Oh, she could still do so many interesting things, but only in her mind. Like flying… Her memories of being up in the sky came back to her over and over… but sometimes her daughter had to repeat a story, just to refresh her mind as to some forgotten detail. Vierny was such a sweet girl, always held her hand as they talked. Her precious Vierny was growing into such a beautiful young woman. Why… it seemed just the other day that she was a quiet little girl making…

What the heck's gone wrong with the stupid TV this time?! Unbelievable – it shut itself off! I definitely didn't touch that thing!

In looking up from her wheelchair, she noticed that Vierny was holding the remote in her hand.

"Mom… Mr. Yardley just called to say that he's on his way."

"Wah?"

"You know… your lawyer. He's got the final version of the paperwork ready for us now that I'm eighteen. By the way… they'll all be here soon."

Eighteen…? That can't be right! She just turned seventeen! I certainly would have remembered her turning eighteen!

She did her best to object, but every word in her mouth just came out as a muffled grunt. It was clear that Vierny would not be turning the TV back on. In fact… Vierny was shifting her wheelchair away from the TV so she faced the front door. Something weird was going on, for Vierny just sat on the couch looking at the front door too. The expression on her face… it was sad. Not her normal lovely self. So she would wait there with her daughter… for what, she did not know.

Then the doorbell rang. In a parade of shock, she followed as a stream of horrified faces entered her family room to look directly at her. She knew those faces. Wade, her son… so very long since she had last seen him. And then that ditzy wife of his. Next came Chad and Travis… and her friend Yardley… with a woman she was not sure to have ever laid eyes on. Each one of them greeted her, but none stayed at her side for long. They sat on couches and chairs… just staring at her. What were they doing here?! She had not noticed that Vierny had left her, but the girl was back with a tray of drinks, going from person to person. Lastly, Vierny brought a straw to her lips…

Ahh… sweet tea! My favorite!

The drink gave her strength to ask… but only so Vierny could hear.

"Why… 'em?"

"Mom… I'm sorry… you've forgotten again. Today's the day we've been talking about for months. The day you've decided for yourself."

"Da… decided?"

Try as she might, she could not connect what was before her eyes with anything in this world. But neither did she have the energy to try. She waved a hand of submission toward her daughter, who turned to address the entire family room.

"We need to keep this brief. This isn't the best time of day for her."

"Of course… To the point then."

Her friend Yardley looked about at each face… skipping over hers. He then pulled something from his briefcase… a stack of papers… and spread them out on the coffee table.

"I've drafted the document exactly as the four of you've settled upon. Travis… you will have primary oversight of her finances. Vierny… you will have full authority to act on her behalf in all medical matters. The two of you will coordinate together in these responsibilities. Chad and Wade… you've agreed to sign as seconds to act in the place of the other two if need be. Valerie… I understand that you have consented to be a witness. Thank you. I've brought along my assistant Samantha to be the other. She's also a notary… which Texas allows to function as a witness in such matters. Now… I suggest that you each take turns signing where specified."

In a flurry of confusion, she watched as her sons and Vierny moved to the coffee table. Each took a pen to Yardley's papers. When everyone was finished, he turned to her.

"Marna… this is that day you've been hoping to reach. All of your children are old enough to act on your behalf. I just need your signature to make it official."

A twinkling of what was happening then hit her. Something about these people and signed papers was poking at the back of her mind. But before the terrible thought could fully crystallize, into her ear came the calming whisper of her daughter's voice.

"It's okay, Mom… we've talked about this. Trust me – I'll never let you down."

Vierny left her side for a moment, returning with papers from the table. She felt a heavy book of some kind being placed in her lap with those papers on top. Vierny gently slid a pen into her hand and shifted its tip over a blank line. Then Yardley's voice came to her again.

"Marna… if you consent to have your children act as your power of attorney, please make your mark where your daughter's indicating."

She looked up into Vierny's face… to that sweetly sad smile of hers… and then down to the page. To make her daughter proud, she scribbled out her name as best as she could.

The papers then went to the other women… to Valerie and that stranger. There was so much more talking after that… with each of her boys and Valerie drawing near to kiss her cheek. Yardley was there too… patting her on the shoulder… telling her how brave she was… and not to worry. One by one, they all left her with only Vierny.

"They'll be by to see you in the morning… before they have to leave.

Would you… like to watch some more TV… or perhaps head off to bed?"

"Bed. I want… bed."

She rarely had dreams these days, for seldom did she sleep more than an hour or two at a time. Yet that night, she had a crystal clear vision for the first time in many months. She found herself locked within a hangar… except it was no ordinary hangar meant for an airplane. It did have a very large door, yet the space within felt terribly cramped. The pressure of the walls made it so very clear that she was trapped inside. She was on wheels… or had wheels… it was hard to say which. Either way, she could not roll. She was completely incapable of moving at all. One after another, people she knew would pull open the hangar door and stare at her… and then close her off again. Her sons, the DILs, old friends, and even her late husband. Some regarded her coolly, while others were horrified to find her sitting there. To each, she begged to be set free from this confinement, but her voice came out only as a whisper. Time and again, the hangar door slammed shut in her face, throwing her into total darkness. But then… to her great surprise… she found her daughter standing behind her, humming sweetly as she pushed the wheelchair out into the sun. But the worst part of having that disturbing dream was that she had no voice for sharing it with anyone once she woke up.

Time passed sluggishly, for Vierny had to tell her the days, the weeks, the months and the seasons. Fall to winter and into spring, she was aware of no significance to one versus the other. She woke only to an expectation of eating, watching TV, and seeing Vierny's smile come gliding her way. But at least she still had her house, so rich in memories.

She saw other faces too. A doctor's, a nurse's, and those whose hands helped her get dressed each morning. They took her to the bathroom… bathed her… pushed her into the kitchen… the parlor… the family room. She ate, watched TV, and slept. Everything else was a fog. Except for when Vierny sat with her recounting the happenings of her day. Then her mind was perfectly clear. Sometimes she found herself being taken about the porch by her daughter in order to enjoy the outdoors. On rarer occasions, she got wheeled down the ramp to Vierny's car for an outing to a doctor's office. But most days, she only saw her daughter for a moment in the morning and a moment at night… and then a lifetime of loneliness in between. But being with Vierny again… that was worth it all. Such a beautiful young woman with a bright future ahead of her. Top of her class and in demand by every college she applied to. The girl would surely hold true to her dreams, for she would only attend a school with the best of aviation programs. The sky was the limit for her Vierny.

Despite her many periods of confusion, she still had moments of clear thinking in which she easily picked up on her daughter's frustrations. Someone was always pressuring Vierny over the phone to do things that she disagreed with. Sometimes her daughter's voice got so loud that she could make out her saying the name of Travis, Chad, or Stacey. Vierny never spoke those names in a good way. Sometimes she could tell that the arguments had to do with her... her house... a trust... or money being spent on the ladies that helped her each day. She had no memory of life without those women. Most times it was a familiar face, but sometimes it was someone new. She could never remember their names... only their faces. And of course, Vierny was always there with her beautiful smile.

On a bright spring morning... or so said Vierny as she was wheeled down the ramp to the car... she discovered that they were going on an outing together. Yet it did not seem to be one that her daughter was pleased about taking. None of Vierny's typical warmth was coming along with them. After a long and silent drive, she found herself moving through automatic doors... the kind that her wheelchair could open all by itself. Vierny pushed her into the lobby of a large place and then up to a table. Her daughter then pulled alongside a chair and sat... again, without smiling.

"Wherr der oin on, Ernee?"

Whatever's going on, Vierny?

"We're meeting Travis here. He's flown into town for the week."

"Ey?"

"I've tried to stop him, Mom... but I can't. He's put the house on the market... and there are already several interested buyers. I'm sorry, but he's... arranged for you to live here instead."

Vierny instantly changed, throwing herself into enthusiastic high gear in proclaiming the good things she could expect from a move to this nursing home. Around the clock professional care... More opportunities to socialize... A safer environment... But Vierny's words flowed by without any real joy to them... and her own thinking crept along far too slowly.

Leave my house...?

Then Travis and a strange woman appeared at the table. They both greeted her warmly... but then the three of them were hurriedly talking to each other, and again she could not keep up. Papers were passed back and forth between the woman and Travis... with him signing each... while Vierny's hand gripped hers beneath the table top. When the signing was done, this mystery woman welcomed her... saying that her room would be ready in the morning... and then shook the hands of both Vierny and Travis before leaving. Travis paused only to kiss her on the cheek before he left too. Only Vierny remained with her.

"I'm sorry, Mom… I've failed you."

"Wher?"

"We best get going. There's lots to be done."

They spent the remainder of the day going through her possessions… her sitting in her wheelchair and Vierny holding up items for her opinion. Clothing, pictures, comfort items and the like… she was too tired for it all. So she closed her eyes and allowed Vierny to decide.

Her last night in her house did not register as such until it was morning. Even through breakfast and the arrival of Chad and Travis, she really was not aware of the things going on around her. Her mind was in a haze of thinking… and not thinking. She somehow found herself parked in her wheelchair within the family room, watching as the three went about loading up Chad's minivan and Travis's rental with things meant for a room at a nursing home. They were going at it rather amicably, carrying boxes from the back of the house out onto the front porch. She tried not to dwell on anything, even though a strange sadness had already come over her. Somehow, watching Travis and Chad muscle her power lift chair out the front door convinced her of the truth – they were moving her out of her house. From then on, she made herself study the three faces rather than what they were doing. Two were showing great determination in completing a much anticipated task, whereas a third was nothing short of heartbroken. Vierny only smiled on those few times when she glanced over at her.

Travis, having gotten his rental car filled first, announced that he was going on ahead. She surveyed him as he paused in the entryway to take one last look about the family room, and then he left the house without a word to her. Somehow, having Travis gone made Chad all the more insistent that things be sped up. He started snatching baskets of clothing from Vierny's hands before she could step out the front door, immediately dispatching her to the backroom for more. She could hear him bounding down the porch stairs… and right back up on a run to intercept the next load. Not once did he look her way.

With everything destined for her new place finally outside, Chad sent Vierny about the house for one more walkaround to make sure that nothing had been forgotten. As the girl disappeared into the parlor, she felt him take hold of the wheelchair and abruptly swing her around toward the back door. She muttered an earnest plea to be taken once more about the downstairs, but his determination to get her out to Vierny's car trumped all. He hurried her through the kitchen and out onto the porch. Speeding too fast down the ramp, she felt herself sliding forward in the wheelchair.

Then out of nowhere came Vierny, jumping from the porch onto the ramp to block the way down.

"What're you doing?!"

"Wheeling her out to your car… obviously! It's time to…"

"That's not the way you do it! She'll fall out! You have to go down backward… and slowly!"

After a long, tense moment, she felt her son's hold on the wheelchair slacken.

"Whatever…"

The whole time, her eyes were only on her daughter. With a hand gripping an armrest and another gently placed against her shoulder, Vierny gradually eased the wheelchair down the remainder of the ramp. The entire way, the girl just smiled at her… so loving and so kind.

Once at the bottom, she was surprised when Vierny spun her around and began to push her back up the ramp. Now it was Chad who stepped in the way.

"What're *you* doing?!"

"I'm taking her around the house for one last…"

"We don't have time for this. I want to get her into the new place as quickly as possible, and then hit the road. I've already wasted too much…"

"Just leave! I've got it from here."

"I'm supposed to lock up."

"I think I can manage… seeing as I've lived in this house for the last ten years of my life."

Chad muttered something that she could not make out as he had to step off the ramp because Vierny was pushing through.

"Actually… it is my house! And I'll still be living here even after I graduate next week."

"Just make it quick, will you?! Travis is probably already waiting at the nursing home."

"Then I suggest you get going. *We'll* be there when we're there."

Completely disregarding Chad, Vierny continued to push her up the ramp and into the kitchen for one last trip about her beautiful house. The whole while, her daughter kept whispering sweetly into her ear. In each room, Vierny paused to remind her of the things they had done there together. School projects at the kitchen table… Meals cooked over the stove… Dinners in the dining room… Shared moments before the relief… Lounging together in the stairwell nook… Decorating the family room for Christmas… These made up the most wonderful years of their lives. Time stood still for her in the worst sort of way, for everywhere Vierny wheeled her were memories that she could not possibly hold onto. Voices… smiles… laughter… and tears… they were all slipping away from her. A lifetime gone in one slow circuit about the downstairs.

Vierny then brought her wheelchair about at the base of the stairs.

"Sorry I can't take you up there, Mom… but what's say we look together for a minute."

They remained in silence for what seemed like forever, as her girl gave her an opportunity to remember. She had so many special times on this lovely staircase spanning the forty years since the very first time she bounded up them. Each was special, and each brought her pain. But then Vierny's voice softly sounded in her ears.

"I'll never forget when I first climbed these stairs. I was so excited that this house might become my home… but I was also scared it might not. I'll never forget that first bedtime story from you… or any of the others. Mom… I want you to know that I cherish every single one. Hearing about your adventures and all those planes you flew… it was the best part of my childhood. I so wanted to be like you. Hey… remember that time you caught me trying to slide down these stairs on a piece of cardboard? You almost had a heart attack! What a crazy little girl I was! Could have broken my neck!"

Vierny came around to kneel before her… and suddenly the upstairs did not seem so remarkable any more. Taking in this beautiful face… this incredible young woman… was so much more special to her.

"I know you're going to miss living here. So am I… We had such wonderful times together. Thank you for taking me in… for giving me a chance to live in this incredible house with you. You saved me, Mom… You saved my life. I just want you to know that I'll never forget it. I love you so much, Mom. I always will."

The only part of her that still worked was her eyes, so both poured forth their tears. The two of them just cried on each other… like never before.

Vierny eventually made herself break away.

"We better get going… before Chad and Travis have a cow. There's… umm… still something I'd like to do."

Without explaining, Vierny backtracked her through the parlor and out its doors. She could hear the girl fumbling with her keys.

"I thought it'd be nice to take you on one last trip about the porch as I lock up…"

Then very slowly, Vierny pushed her the long way about the wrap-around to the ramp in the rear. East… to south… to west… to north. Morning became noonday, through afternoon into the evening of her life… and then sadly, night fell… just as Vierny carefully backed her down the ramp.

After the usual struggles of getting her into the car… and Vierny having to wrestle the wheelchair into the trunk… she braced herself for a rigidity far worse than anything to do with her disease. She was leaving her wonderful home forever.

"Mom… what say we take one last look into the hangar before we leave."

Without elaboration, Vierny started up and pulled across the stretch of stubble to idle the car within the open hangar door.

"I want you to do something for me. It has to do with the very first time you ever showed me this hangar. I stood right here and brazenly informed you that a hangar was not a place for play. How ridiculous of me! I spent so many hours in here playing… No kid in the world had it as good as me – a huge airplane hangar as her very own playground! But do you remember what you said to me back then? You said that this could be a place for imagination… and I definitely did a lot of that. Well… now I want you to do some imagining. I want you to close your eyes and remember all of the wonderful things that went on in here. Let them all come wash over you. And when you're ready… I want you to open your eyes and imagine that you're back there… and always will be. Can you… do that for me?"

So she closed her eyes… and with very little effort, beheld them all… the good and the bad. Her father-in-law standing with a hand reverently placed upon the Corsair. Him slumped over his ham radio. Her mother-in-law cursing the plane in her despair. Her husband braving his silly fears to rescue Wade when his brothers had locked him in. Him standing before the plane with a sledgehammer as she begged him not to swing… and then him lying spread out on the concrete. She saw herself sitting in that cockpit, making all sorts of silly promises to the Corsair… ones that she somehow managed to keep. She remembered them taking her plane away, leaving this place empty. But then a little girl came and filled it back up with her dreams.

When she reopened her eyes… she saw none of it. Everything was gone. The hangar lay barren before her. Doing her best, she mumbled out words that her daughter deserved to hear.

"Ernee… Iz zeez id. Iz zeez id ull."

"I knew you would, Mom."

With a smile on her face… one that she did not have a heart to ruin… Vierny looked over her shoulder in backing the car out of the hangar. On a creep, Vierny then took her one last time around the circle… and she watched her lovely front porch flow by for the final time. Having accomplished a full loop, she expected the car to pull directly onto the driveway, but instead it proceeded on around the circle a bit too far.

"I'm going to do a thing I think you'll like. Just look straight ahead, Mom. Keep your eyes straight ahead."

Once again, Vierny pivoted about in the driver's seat as she adjusted the gearshift. Slowly, her daughter began to back the car down the long driveway. Out the front windshield, she beheld a view not unlike that one she first had as a child… except in reverse. Slowly, her beautiful house shrank before her eyes… with the hangar suddenly blinking out of sight behind the foliage of the driveway's live oaks. She was so desperate to drag along those sweet memories, but the house just kept getting smaller and smaller… until it was nothing more than a sad little face poised upon the horizon, peering at her from far down a long groove of green trees that cut into the sky.

Goodbye, my love.

Vierny brought the car to a stop at the entrance of the driveway, herself turning about to take a look that was not yet her last… for she must come back to this place alone. Without a word, she then backed the car into the county road, shifted the gears to drive… and her house was gone forever.

They sat in silence for a long time until Vierny suddenly spoke up with a noticeable strain in her voice.

"Mom… I've… been wanting to talk with you about something… really important… but having Travis and Chad around… it's been impossible. I've… umm… been doing some thinking about college…"

"Nurg… bluz."

No… please.

"Just hear me out. I know we've been over and over this… and I do want to honor your wishes… but you've got to realize that I'm eighteen now. I can make my own decisions. I'm not going all the way to Florida for school when you clearly need me here in Lubbock. And it's not like I'm giving up on college. I can easily get into Tech… all I have to do is apply. Lots of my friends are going there. Probably missed the deadline for the fall semester… but that's not a problem. I'll get a job until the spring semester starts. I'm sure I can find a place to live near the nursing home… and then I can drive into campus whenever I need to. Just think of it – I'll be able to see you every day and still go to college. It'll be perfect!"

"Bluz thunt thu nas. Nuth ur ee."

Please don't do this! Not for me!

"Now don't say anything else just yet until I'm finished. I get it… okay?! Tech doesn't have an aviation program. So what?! I mean… I can get a degree in just about anything I want… and then pick up flying later. You know… after things have calmed down and you're better. And I already know what you're going to say. 'You need to follow your dreams, Vierny. Get out there and spread your wings.' Well… I think it's more important that I stay here with you. I've got all the time in the world for… *wing-spreading*. What's the big deal about aviation anyway?! It's really just a hobby for me. I think I'd rather take some business courses… see what they're like. You know… maybe major in… marketing. Or I could do the science thing. You know I liked chemistry. So here's my revised plan. I'm getting you situated in your new place… and then on Monday, I'm calling my admission advisor at Embry-Riddle to decline. I'll just tell him… 'thanks for everything, but I've made other plans.' Then… I'll call what's-his-face over at the trust place and tell him that I'm going to Tech instead. See if Mr. Yardley can delay the sale of the house until I can find an apartment near you. You know they don't care where I live or go to school. They just put money into my account whenever they're supposed to. And you've already made sure there'll be plenty to take care of me for years and years."

Her daughter left it at that, with her having no voice capable of contradicting. Neither had she the power to lift a finger of protest in expressing how very much opposed she was to this new course of action. Not a muscle in her face could be contorted enough to show even a miniscule amount of the displeasure she was feeling on the inside. That Vierny would sacrifice those aviation dreams to take care of her – a cripple – might go to the girl's credit, but it was all wrong. This was exactly what she had worked so hard to avoid in meticulously arranging her affairs so as to protect her daughter's future. But being trapped in this shell of herself, she had absolutely no ability to communicate either her outrage or despair. No way of stopping this foolishness. This mistake of a lifetime. No torture was worse than this! To witness day after day her precious Vierny exchanging such a bright future for the burden of being chained to a wreck of a woman. No way would she tolerate that! But her meager voice of objection just got drowned out by the soft hum of the car moving along the Loop. She would have to wait for the next opportunity when they were alone together… and hope to have the strength necessary for changing the girl's mind.

When they arrived at the nursing home, Vierny popped out of the driver's seat with such haste that she could tell the girl was avoiding the possibility of being confronted. As was usually the case, they both had to concentrate fully on her getting out of the car and into the wheelchair… and then Vierny immediately took off in pushing her along the sidewalk to a back entrance of the facility. Turning a corner, the girl abruptly halted... for Chad's minivan was backed right up to the wheelchair ramp, making it absolutely impossible to get inside. Unnoticed at first, both of them then saw Travis leaning against the front of the van, working away at his cell phone. With very noticeable irritation, Vierny came around the wheelchair to assess the situation.

"Where's Chad?"

Travis lazily looked up.

"Ahh... I don't know. He was here a second ago. Probably carrying in a load. No... wait... He said something about using the bathroom."

"His van's blocking the entrance! Can you go find him and..."

"Go find him yourself... or is that something beneath Miss Millionaire?!"

"I need to stay here with Mom... and I really wish you wouldn't call me that."

"Whatever. But for your information, I'm expecting to hear from an important client... and there's lousy reception inside. I'll stay out here while you go find him."

After a moment of hesitation in which Vierny peered back the way they had come... and then up at the sun's prospect of burning her mother... she leaned over to whisper.

"I'll be right back, Mom. Don't you go anywhere."

She got one of those heart-melting smiles from her before getting kissed on the forehead.

"Travis... please keep an eye on her, will you?"

"Yeah... of course."

Vierny squeezed about the van and headed into the facility. Just as she entered, the phone in Travis's hand rang. He looked briefly her way, and then moved around to the other side of the van before answering his call. She could hear his muffled voice, dully speaking to his important client.

With nothing better to do... and a body incapable of much anyway... she scanned about that portion of the grounds she was able to see. Parts of it were pretty enough. Flower beds ran along the facility, with a narrow of border of well-tended grass between those and the sidewalk. To her other side, things were very different. Beyond the low-lying brick wall that Vierny had left the wheelchair parked against was nothing but West Texas stubble stretching over a vacant lot. The ground was scattered about with all sorts of debris – fast food wrappers, crushed beer cans, a rusted hub cap, and so much other nondescript trash. One side of the low wall was her new home... and the other was how she felt – discarded.

Suddenly coming into the corner of her vision was a rather odd sight.

A little creature was making directly toward her along the top of the wall…
but backward, as it appeared to be dragging a rather larger something-or-
other along with it.

———————

She only did that which she was made to do, so being known as the one
to possess the most potent of stings was so terribly unfair. There was so
much more to her than death, for always her mind was on new life. Some
call her the tarantula hawk, for her winged hunt was like that of the
bird's. That name, she did not merit, as by nature she considered herself
to be most docile and not easily provoked. When she hunted for herself,
it was always to sip the nectar of her favorite flower – the milkweed.
Only for her children did she kill.

So by sight and by scent, she patiently roved low over the ground in search
of the spider. With her first conquest, she took for herself that creature's
burrow and laid a single egg upon its paralyzed form. She closed off that
egg within a chamber of its own, and then hollowed out others within
the same burrow for more of her children. A home that was not hers was
turned into a tomb… that in hope it might also become a nursery.

This particular burrow was more than adequate for her great need, being
in a secluded field of brush and sandy soil. But its previous occupant…
that spider was far too small. Suitable for only a son. Of course, she could
choose which egg to lay, with the largest and the best of her prey always
reserved for a daughter. That was the way of her world. But now she must
leave to hunt far and wide for such a spider… battle and subdue it… and
then drag it back to this place.

With amber wings and a body of midnight blue, she… *as pepsis grossa…*
is of formidable size. But even at fifty millimeters in length, she is not
nearly strong enough to carry back her huge prey. So over a great distance
she must pull along this spider, so much more massive than herself… and
always backward as the weight of it was otherwise impossible to manage.
That she must abandon flight… become bound on earth to this paralyzed
burden in her long, blind march… was such a small price to pay. Never
did she waver in not seeing where she went, for she somehow knew based
on where she had been. Always backward into the unknown… for a
daughter's sake. She must fulfill her purpose… lay her egg and close off the
burrow… knowing that she would not live to see the fruit of her sacrifice.
For she was destined to die long before her daughter appeared.

———————

Surely this was a wasp... dragging backward its prey of a paralyzed spider along the top of the wall! Her immediate gut response was to cringe away, for this was her life-long foe. Yet as the wasp drew nearer, she realized that the thing would likely pass her by without noticing, for it was fully preoccupied with its burden. Not once had it turned about to see where it was going. Always backward it went pulling its load.

In a flash, she came to see herself in both the spider and the wasp. In her own paralyzed state, she sat completely helpless within this wheelchair... no better off than that spider. But she was the wasp too... dragging her dead dreams backward into this hellhole of a nursing home. Yet she knew the likeness to be far worse. All her life, she had never really known where she was going... always with her back turned on her responsibilities, blindly trusting in her dreams. Those dreams were now such a pitifully poor guide for her soul. Maybe her boys were right, for they had always doubted her. Not once had they ever shared their own dreams with her... not like they had with their father. Neither had they bothered to know hers. In her heart, she knew that not one of them had ever really cared.

But Vierny... she's different! She'll live a better life because of me. I've certainly left my mark on her... and she on me. If only for her, I'd go back and do it all over again... exactly the same way... with every one of my failures and mistakes. I wouldn't change one painful thing if that's what it would take to give her a chance at fulfilling her own dreams.

On pure impulse, she reacted without a care for herself... neither to end her own suffering nor to relieve others of theirs. No impending sorrow or grief registered with her... nor did a surety of the embitterment to coming guilt and blame. She thought only of her daughter... to ensure for that heart of hers the best possible future. Vierny would certainly burn with many tears... but only for a short while. In time, she would come to be thankful... and love her mother all the more. After all, was it not a far greater crime for a mother to commit if she spared her loved one from a moment of sadness, only to willingly inflict such a burden as herself for decades to come?! Even if she were destined to reach a hundred, she could never allow such a thing to be! Fully, she believed that there would be so much more for her precious child if she gladly gave herself over to the worst of pain. For only then would her daughter be free.

The wasp was nearly alongside her now. So in conquering a lifetime of fear in a split second, she lurched forward in her wheelchair with surprising ease to cup the creature beneath her right hand. She felt the thing writhe about in a struggle to escape, with its angry buzz of protest reaching her ears. So she called forth what strength and balance she still had to clamp down even tighter with her feeble fingers.

Do it! Do it now!

As a sharp cross of light flashed into her eyes from the sun's glare off her bracelet, she felt the sting's bitter spear sear into the center of her palm. Far beyond what she had expected, the pain's excruciating intensity sent her reeling backward into her wheelchair. No longer had she a mind for the wasp or its prey, as all of her hand was on fire from the sting. But within seconds, the venom's first spasm had reached her chest. She felt her heart slow and her throat tighten. An urgent plea arose within her to call out for relief, but there was no voice to this scream… just a mouth gaped wide open without sound. Screams nonetheless rocketed through her mind, for the pain to her hand was no longer of chief concern. Her entire body was in the throes of convulsions. But that cruel disease of hers would not allow her hands to stagger to her throat, as she gasped out vainly to open the constriction within. Her tongue swelled to fill her mouth, stealing even more breath, as her lungs seared with many desperate rasps for air. Her throat closed and her heart's beat faded.

Within this terrible agony, Marna Forde Meitner threw back her head… beholding a wisp of white winging its way upon a dome of blue… and died.

THE END…

to a most faithful life.

ACKNOWLEDGEMENTS

Pam, thank you for venturing into Marna's mind with me. Her voice is so much richer as a result! Thanks also for your insights into what it means to juggle the roles of wife, mother, and professional. But many, many more thanks for your patience and endless support in writing this gargantuan novel.

Bond, I don't know how you manage to fly both planes and helicopters. The magnitude of what you have to know is unreal. Many thanks to both you and Bryan for your patience in answering my many ridiculous aviation questions. Thanks also for screening the technical details.

Bryce and Britt, thanks for taking burdens off of me while I wrote.

Thanks to Janos and Antonella Szanyi, along with their cohort of Italian friends, for helping me name Marna's two reliefs.

Thanks to Clif Dyer at Sundance Aviation for granting permission to use the call sign 'seven–three–four–golf–x-ray' for the plane that Marna soloed in, as that was the call sign on their plane that my daughter first soloed in.

I wish to express special thanks to those individuals who consented to be interviewed by me for background material into this novel: Pam Henderson (the above and so much more), Bond and Bryan Durham (your wealths of aviation knowledge), McCall Parrish Hubenak (stories of you and your mother as pilots), Mark Seekins (for what it was like growing up in Texas as a northerner), Bruce Kay (for insights into the Chicago of the 60s), Gary Potts (on Texas Aviation), Sarah and Dave Barr (on caring for someone with Parkinson's), Katie Banks and her father Cary Banks (in being long-time residents of Lubbock).

Many apologies to the citizens of Lubbock and Chicago if I have in any way misrepresented your fine cities.

For those who hold dear the hymn *Great is Thy Faithfulness*, which entered the public domain this year, please forgive what I had Marna's despair do to it in chapter fifteen.

The title of chapter four is a shout-out to VegiTales.

The Meitner name was chosen in honor of Lise Meitner, the German physicist who many believe was denied a share in two different Nobel prizes… simply for being a woman.

Thanks to the countless number of individuals whose YouTube videos helped me understand the operations of floral shops, TV news stations, airports, and planes.

Wikapedia, where would I be without you?

BOOKS AND RESOURCES DRAWN FROM IN PREPARING THIS NOVEL

"Corsair: The F4U in World War II and Korea," by Barrett Tillman.

"Developing the Gull-Winged F4U Corsair and Taking It to Sea," by Ralph Harvey.

"Vought F4U-4 Corsair Pilot's Flight Operating Instructions," United States Navy technical manual, reprinted by PeriscopeFilm.com.

"Vought F4U Corsair," volumes 1 and 2 by Tomasz Szlagorand Leszek A. Wieliczko, and volume 4 by Barrett Tillman.

"F4U Corsair In Action," by Jim Sullivan.

"WASPs: Women Airforce Service Pilots of World War II," by Vera S. Williams.

"WASP of the Ferry Command: Women Pilots, Uncommon Deeds," by Sarah Byrn Rickman.

"Wings, WASP, & Warriors," by Travis Monday.

"Girls of Avenger," by Alyce Stevens Rohrer.

"Yankee Doodle Gals: Women Pilots of World War II," by Amy Nathan.

"PT-19, PT-23 and PT-26 Airplanes Pilot's Flight Operating Instruction," United States Army Air Force technical manual, reprinted by PeriscopeFilm.com.

"Stick and Rudder: An Explanation of the Art of Flying," by Wolfgang Langewiesche.

"Sixties Fashion: From Less is More to Youthquake," by Jonathan Walford.

"The Sting of the Wild," by Justin O. Schmidt.

"Behavior and Social Evolution of Wasps: The Communal Aggregation Hypothesis," by Yosiaki Itô.

"Wasps: An Account of the Biology and Natural History of Solitary and Social Wasps," by J. Philip Spradbery.

"Bees, Wasps and Ants," by Eric Grissell.

"Lise Meitner: A Life in Physics," by Ruth Lewin Sime.

"The Rise of Cable Programming in the United States: Revolution or Evolution," by Megan Mullen.

"Television Operations: A Handbook of Technical Operations for TV Broadcast, On Air, Cable, Mobile and Internet," by Frederick M. Baumgartner and Nicholas A. Grbac.

"First Ladies of the Flight Deck," by Stuart Nixon, Airline Pilot Magazine, May 1978.

The National WASP WWII Museum at Avenger Field in Sweetwater, Texas. (https://waspmuseum.org)

Texas State Historical Association. (https://www.tshaonline.org/home/)

Chicago Transit Authority (CTA) archives. (http://www.chicago-l.org/index.html)

MedicAlert Foundation. (https://www.medicalert.org/about)

Footage of the 1970 Lubbock tornado by Dub Rogers, found in the Texas Archive of the Moving Image. (https://www.texasarchive.org/library/index.php/Dub_Rogers_-_KLBK_Archival_Footage,_no._30_-_Lubbock_Tornado,_1970)

City of Lubbock's webpage dedicated to the 1970 tornado. (http://www.lubbocktornado1970.com/default.aspx)

The iNaturalist listing of Bees and Wasps of Texas. (https://www.inaturalist.org/projects/bees-and-wasps-of-texas)

The Federal Aviation Administration website on aircraft. (https://www.faa.gov/aircraft/)

Flying Magazine's Top 100 Aircraft. (https://www.flyingmag.com/photo-gallery/photos/top-100-airplanes/?pnid=31514)

Warbird Alley's Fairchild PT-26 Pilot Report, by Boots McCormick. (http://www.warbirdalley.com/articles/pt26pr.htm)

Vulture's Row Aviation, Cameron Park, CA. (http://www.vulturesrowaviation.com/vra/Welcome.html)

The Connecticut Corsair Project in conjunction with the University of Connecticut, which in fact has constructed a Corsair simulator. (www.connecticutcorsair.com)

Classic Jets Fighter Museum, Parafield Airport, Adelaide, South Australia. (http://www.classicjets.com)

National Naval Aviation Museum, Pensacola, FA. (https://www.navalaviationmuseum.org)

Upbring's guidelines for being a foster parent in Texas. (https://www.upbring.org/14310/how-to-become-foster-parents-in-texas-9-steps/)

Texas Department of Family and Protective Services on foster care. (https://www.dfps.state.tx.us/Child_Protection/Foster_Care/)

"What's It Like To Be A Female Pilot? Captain Danielle Stoney Reveals All," Forbes article by Jenny Southan. (https://www.forbes. com/sites/jennysouthan/2018/04/03/whats-it-like-to-be-a-female-pilot-captain-danielle-stoney-reveals-all/#1a2a2e7c227d)

InsectIdentification's site on the wasps of Texas. (https://
www.insectidentification.org/insects-by-type-and-region.
asp?thisState=Texas&thisType=Bee,%20Ant,%20Wasp%20and%
20Similar)

Recover-from-grief's description of the seven stages of grief.
(http://www.recover-from-grief.com/7-stages-of-grief.html)

"How to Declare Someone Incompetent to Manage Affairs in Texas,"
by Teo Spengler. (http://legalbeagle.com/8682824-
declare-incompetent-manage-affairs-texas.html)

"5 Stages of Parkinson's Disease," by Wendy Henderson. (https://
parkinsonsnewstoday.com/2017/08/23/five-stages-of-parkinsons-disease/)

The DVD "F4U Corsair: The Young Pilots Amazing True Stories," by
Roaring Glory Warbirds Productions, featuring Steve Hinton as pilot.

AUTHOR'S CONTEMPLATION

(Spoiler alert)

First off – thank you for trudging through the marathon of *Marna*. In this novel, I was drawn toward exploring faithfulness in the context of a person's life, from their earliest childhood recollections to the day they died. Throughout the story, I have tried to weave in symbolism that I hope helps to illustrate my thoughts on the novel's theme. Prominent examples include the earth, the sky and the horizon; the flag and the pole; the hangar and the house; a furrowed row of cotton in a crop circle; the flower's giver and its receiver; an airplane and a stone sculpture; and a life threatening allergy that guides Marna with unseen purpose to the fulfillment of her dreams.

The seven wasps (okay, one was actually a hornet) that make up the seven parts of this novel were selected because each possesses an interesting characteristic relevant to what Marna is experiencing at the time. These seven encounters, in a sense, are symbolic of a providential influence. Throughout her life, the fear of wasps represents her fear of being found unfaithful. In repeatedly being torn between her dreams and her responsibilities, she is often stung by her choices. But the wasp signifies something deeper than a thing capable of delivering a sting. Much maligned because of that sting, the wasp also represents an admirable trait that is hardwired into its nature. To the extent that one might refer to an insect as a sentient being, the female wasp believes fully in her aim in life. She is relentless in her pursuit of the next generation. She builds, hunts, nurtures, protects and makes the hard decisions necessary for ensuring that fullness is realized in her offspring. In this sense, she is a remarkably faithful creature.

Marna's life may seem like a palindrome that begins and ends with her being stung, but hopefully she is not thought of that way. Yes, the parentless little girl who sat on her bed in the middle of the night dreaming about becoming a pilot does end up being the person who gives up her life for the sake of one just like her. But she is more than those bookends. In many ways, Marna is as faithful as the wasps she fears. She is determined, single-minded, hardworking and amazingly resilient… all noteworthy facets to faithfulness. But in her heart, she does not always believe in what she is being so faithful at doing. For example, in doggedly carrying out the job of a florist, she sees her work as an obligation that restricts her from pursuing her dreams. In this and other settings, she struggles to know where her loyalties end and her aspirations pick up. For her, the sky is a place where her spirit can break away, just like the birds in her relief, whereas the earth is all about servitude. Same with the flag and the pole. One epitomizes liberation and the other is anchored deep into the ground. Similarly, her obsessions with the Corsair and the relief illustrate her conflicted spirit over things of the above and things of the below. She battles resentments when she can not pursue her dreams, and then regrets when her dreams cause her to fall short in her responsibilities. Being a goer and a doer, she seldom sees herself clearly in the moment. Whether she be niece, girlfriend, wife, daughter-in-law, employee, mother or mother-in-law, she strives to carry out her role to the best of her abilities, but does not always have confidence in what she is doing. Same with her dreams. She knows the feelings she wants out of life, but doubts herself in getting there.

It takes Marna a lifetime to realize that faithfulness is not an obligation. It is not something prescribed by contract, code, command or proper conduct. To say that faith is foundational to faithfulness seems obvious based on diction, but in real life, faithfulness easily gets tangled up in duty, dedication, diligence and dependability. These things are only byproducts of faithfulness, for it seeks no merit of achievement or significance, only an outcome guided by hope and hard work. Faithfulness presses on to a fullness that blesses both the giver and the receiver.

Obviously not all faith leads to fullness... just as being 'full' is not enough. Because of the many losses she experiences, Marna comes to view fullness as the crop circles she often flies over. A full life goes full circle in a perfection of green, whereas half circles and brown wedges betray a life that has not reached fullness. This thinking repeatedly plays into her drive for significance. Only nearer to the end of her life does she see that fullness is measured in the moment and not in the lifetime. That sort of faith makes a person willing to sacrifice everything in the blink of an eye, just as Marna does. In that split second, she sees differently her life of regrets, mistakes and troubles, and proclaims that she would do it all over again exactly the same way if only it led her to that moment of deciding. In this, hers is the ultimate of faith in another's fullness.

Faithfulness is faith. It is the substance of things hope for, the evidence of things unseen. Faithful living does not always see the impossible made possible, yet it clearly sees fullness as the ultimate desire. In this sense, the opposite of faithfulness is not unfaithfulness, just as a diligent person with many accomplishments in their life can be plagued with regrets and resentments. The opposite of faithfulness is disbelief... or belief in the wrong thing, such as Marna's pursuit of significance at all costs.

So what to believe in? What things merit a faith set upon fullness?

In *Marna*, I have endeavored to explore the frustration that I think many experience – the tension between what is owed and what is desired. Obligations versus aspirations. Too often these conflict with each other. In repeatedly experiencing this struggle, Marna would never refer to herself as a faith-filled person, even though her father-in-law had once said it was believing in both, not either. But as a pilot, she begins to see something different in herself. The sky can not be depended upon without the earth, nor the earth without the sky. Instead, the pilot must rely upon the horizon as their reference point for both sky and earth. No pilot takes off in an aircraft without a full belief in the horizon out their window or the one on their instrument panel.

God is like the horizon. We can depend upon Him as the ultimate of reference points to guide in the conflict between dreams and responsibilities. He, like the horizon, never fails. Seemingly unreachable but always there, He is new every morning. Great is His faith in fullness.

Faithfulness… against such things there is no law.